RICHARD PARKER;

OR,

THE MUTINY AT THE NORE.

A ROMANCE.

BY THE AUTHOR OF

"GALLANT TOM," "JACK JUNK," "THE DEATH SHIP," "THE SMUGGLER KING," "MY POLL AND MY PARTNER JOE," &c., &c.

PREFACE.

On the completion of a work which has been crowned with such great success as that which has attended the present romance, there is nothing left for the Author to do than to express his most unqualified thanks for the encouragement and patronage he has received during the many months that his little offspring has been before the public ; and a most pleasant duty, indeed, is this to perform.

From time immemorial the writers of Romance have considered themselves licensed to tax their imagination to the utmost limits, even to the exaggeration of matters of fact, in some instances, in order to endeavour to amuse and instruct their readers, and to point to a certain moral. Of this license the author of these pages has availed himself ; and that he has done so to the satisfaction of the public, the immense number of patrons his work has obtained, affords him the flattering and gratifying assurance. In conclusion, therefore, it behoves him once more to return his warmest thanks to that generous public by whom he has been so frequently similarly honoured.

Sept. 25th. 1851.

RICHARD PARKER;

OR,

THE MUTINY AT THE NORE.

A ROMANCE OF INTENSE INTEREST.

BY THE AUTHOR OF " ELA, THE OUTCAST ;" "ANGELINA ;" " THE GIPSY BOY ;"
" GALLANT TOM ;" JACK JUNK ;" ETC.

RICHARD PARKER REFUSES TO OBEY THE COMMANDS OF CAPTAIN ARLINGTON.

CHAPTER I.

THE LOVERS.—A MAIDEN'S DEVOTED-NESS.—THE PREDICTION.

THE resplendent monarch of the day was just retiring to rest in a flood of purple and gold, tinging the summit of the distant hills, and the surface of the Western Ocean with its departing beams. Nature was sinking to that calm repose, which soothes the troubled breast, and brings a respite to the weary labourer, after the toils and anxieties of the day. The flowers had closed for the night; the feathered tr bes had ceased their daily mellifluous warblings; the bleatings of the sheep in the downy pastures no longer were heard, and all was hushed in silence.

At this hour might have been seen strolling along a romantic walk which led immediately to the sea beach, and which was over-shadowed on either side by stately poplars, a youthful couple, male and female, of the most interesting description, deeply immersed in conversation, but which seemed to excite in their bosoms mingled feelings of pleasure, hope, and pain.

The one was a young man of graceful and muscular proportions, handsome and intelligent features, but still with a certain melancholy expression in his fine dark eyes, that ill accorded with the happy smile that played around his lips, and imparted such animation to his countenance. The other was a female of the first order of simple yet surpassing loveliness, against whom to raise one impure thought would have been a monstrous libel on the Supreme. It would be a waste of time to attempt to d scribe the personal charms of that fair maiden further, and it may be sufficient to add that all the perfections of her mind were in the strictest unison with her outward attractions. A pause of some two are three minutes occurred in their conversation, when the young man, who had one of his arms affectionately encircling her slender waist, said—

"Oh, Mary, my own Mary!—for you are mine in soul, in heart, in hope—though cruel fate has thrown a barrier between us, can you—do you doubt the sincerity, the intensity of the love I bear you? From the earliest period of childhood we have been companions; assimilating ideas, encouraging the same principles, joining in the same innocent sports, looking forward to the same bright prospect of happiness which only souls cemented like ours can imagine. Oh, those were indeed halcyon days! But time has wrought a woful change in our prospects, though not in our hearts; like yon retiring orb of day, have our hopes declined, and the dark night of despair is rapidly succeeding. Mary—my dearest Mary! though

Heaven knows the insupportable misery it will cause me to do so, since fate so wills it, I absolve you from your fond vows, and may the just God who reigns above us make you tenfold more happy than the humble Ric ard Parker would have tried to render you!"

"Richard—dear Richard!" replied the lovely girl, turning very pale, and tears starting to her eyes, "what rash, what cruel words are those you have just now given utterance to? Do you doubt the sincerity of that love I have so often acknowleded to you, and which is registered in Heaven?"

"No, Mary," replied her lover, "I should be a wretch, totally unworthy of the sentiments you express towards me, could I for an instant seek to impugn their purity and truth. But fortune frowns upon me!—the patrimony left me by my late father is almost exhausted, God can bear me witness through no improvidence of my own;—you are the daughter of a wealthy man—he disapproves of our love, and —"

"Richard," interrupted the damsel, hastily, and a gentle expression of reproach for an instant passed over her lovely features, "can you believe me sordid?—Think you that the mere idea of the dross of gold can mingle with my passions? Heaven forbid that they should ever receive such contaminating alloy! Oh, what is the value of wealth, if unaccompanied by happiness? Richard, a cloud seems to have absorbed your reason; alas! woe is me!—how dreadful is the misconception you now seem to form of my feelings. Richard, we have been companions from childhood, as you just now observed; we have indulged in a golden vision of happiness from our earliest days; and now would you banish that blissful vision, and supersede it by the stern and dark reality of despair? I have solemnly vowed in all the innocence and sincerity of my heart that there is no other man on earth that can ever engage my affections but you, and I now swear —"

"Oh, hold, my fond Mary," interposed the young man, deep y affected by the earnestness and fervour of her manner, "do not give utterance to any rash vow, which stern fate may compel you to b eak. I must, unless a great and unexpected change comes over my fortunes, shortly become a beggar; I see no other prospect before me but the toils and perils of a seaman's life, to which, I must confess, I have always had a predilection, and I should consider myself little better than an unprincipled scoundrel, could I for a moment think of plunging you into the same state of poverty to which it is not at all unlikely I may be reduced. Captain Arlington is wealthy; he professes to love you, he has made overtures for your hand; your father approves of his suit, and has commanded you to look upon him as your future husband, and, therefore, all the hopes we have entertained are at once annihilated."

"Captain Arlington!" ejaculated Mary, with an expression of disgust; "you know, you must be sure that I view him with feelings of the utmost abhorrence, and that I would sooner encounter any fate, however dreadful, rather than become his wife. Oh, the very thought is horrible and revolting!"

"But, Mr. Mason, your father, I know, my dear Mary, is inflexible," returned her lover, " and should you persist in rejecting the man of his choice, he would discard you, and, though great as the sacrifice would be to my own feelings, never can I endeavour to persuade you to——"

"Richard," interrupted the maiden, with the greatest energy; "have you forgotten all those solemn and affectionate vows we have so long plighted together, beneath this our loved and trysting tree?"

"Mary, what mean you?"

" Does your heart beat with the same warm pulsations as it formerly did towards me?" eagerly demanded the damsel.

"By all my most sacred hopes, my beloved Mary," replied Richard Parker, "if it were possible, the passion I now bear towards you is more ardent than ever. My whole soul is yours, devoted only to your service and happiness; it is my greatest felicity to acknowledge myself your slave, and to own that I have no will but your own. Still am I prepared to sacrifice my own hopes—to become the most wretched being, as I must be, that ever crawled the surface of the earth, rather than that you

should become an alien to your father's bosom."

"And hear me, Richard," said Mary, solemnly. "Much as I love my father, ready as I am to obey his will in all things that reason and nature demand, should he persist in enforcing me to become the wife of a man I despise, though I by so doing incur his heaviest malediction, and his eternal hatred, I will not hesitate for an instant to abandon him, and throw myself upon the mercy of the Supreme Judge of all our actions and the world."

"Mary, dear Mary!" said her bewildered and astonished lover, "know you what it is you say?"

"Yes," replied our heroine, firmly and calmly. "I know full well; it is no rabid wandering of the mind—it is the life-spring of all my hopes of happiness in this world, that prompts my words. Richard, I speak in all sincerity, and I know your noble nature will not permit you to judge me wrongfully by what I say. I love you with all the purity and fervour that virtue can dictate; I believe your heart beats in unison with mine own; why then should our hopes, our wishes, be blighted by those who entertain harsh and sordid views? Heaven alone has the control of human hearts. Richard, do you consider me worthy to become your wife?"

"Oh, my beloved, my adored Mary," cried the young man rapturously, and straining her still more fondly to his bosom. "Why ask me such a question?"

"Then, by Heaven I again most solemnly swear," replied the maiden, "that, let whatever may be the consequences that ensue, even though it be the curse of the author of my being, though the direst poverty and misery should pursue me, I will be yours and yours only!"

Richard Parker clasped the beauteous damsel with the most passionate ardour to his bosom; they mingled their sobs together, and for a few minutes neither of them were able to give utterance to a syllable.

"Oh, Mary!" at length ejaculated our hero, "best, most devoted of girls, how can I ever repay you for this generous confidence?—how sufficiently convince you of the love I bear towards you? Yes, you say truly that Heaven alone has the control of human hearts, and to its Almighty will I submit! You have proffered to become the partner of my fortunes, whatever they may be, and most gratefully do I accept the offer; and if I fail in my duty—if I ever abuse the confidence you repose in me, may the curse of God pursue me to destruction! Again, I say, I yield myself your slave, and will be guided alone by what you shall dictate."

"My love—my *husband*!" said Mary, looking up in his face with an inexpressible feeling of affection, and at the same time throwing her fair arms round his neck.

"My fond one!—my devoted one!—my *wife*!" replied her lover, in the same tones of ardent feeling, and again they were both of them so overpowered by the violence of their emotions, that for a short time speech was denied them.

"Then," said Mary, partially recovering herself, "then, beneath this, our trysting tree, we both solemnly swear that, come ill—come weal—we devote ourselves to each other, and that, if fate should ordain that we should never come together as man and wife, neither of us will ever give our hand to another."

They both knelt down beneath the umbrageous foliage of the tree, on the trunk of which were inscribed their names; and Richard Parker, holding one of the delicate hands of Mary in his, and with his other hand raised solemnly towards Heaven, said,—

"I swear! and as I fulfil or break my oath, may Heaven judge me!"

Mary solemnly responded to the vow, and after they had for some time remained upon their knees, they arose, and again embracing, were too much overcome by the feelings that were passing in their bosoms to articulate a syllable.

"It is a solemn compact we have entered into, Mary," at last said her lover, "and it is imperative upon us that we should act with the strictest prudence and propriety. Your father seems determined that you shall now become the wife of Captain Arlington, although when fortune smiled upon me more favourably than she does at present, he had no objection to my paying my addresses to you, although I was never your equal in point of worldly riches. I would yet win him, if possible, to favour our love, instead of using any clandestine means to thwart him in his wishes."

"What, then, would you have me do, dear Richard?" demanded our heroine, eagerly.

"I would have you, Mary," replied her lover—"for you know that your father has latterly forbidden me his house—I would have you make one more appeal to his feelings, and if that should fail——"

"Let the consequences be whatever they may," added Mary, determinedly, "I will abandon the home I have so long cherished, and become the wife of the only man who does, or ever can possess my heart. Though the most abject poverty be my lot, it will be Heaven's bliss to that which I must experience in being united to one whom I so utterly detest as Captain Arlington. Oh, Richard, even in the humblest cottage, and enduring the greatest privations, my heart assures me that I can be happy and contented with you. You shall never hear a single murmur escape my lips, and——"

"Dear, confiding girl!" interrupted her lover, unable any longer to control his feelings, "what can I say? How can I convince you of the manner in which I appreciate the sentiments you feel towards me? If ever I abuse your confidence, may the curse of God pursue me! But hope again re-animates my breast, from your sweet example, and I feel certain, that however the clouds of adversity may for a time darken over us, we shall ultimately be happy—that we shall have no cares to disturb our minds."

"Sweet hope!" ejaculated the lovely damsel, while tears of joy trembled in her eyes; "may we both, my dear Richard, continue to indulge in it. Oh, I picture to myself the bliss that we shall experience, even though humble may be our circumstances in life; what need have we to covet wealth, when we shall posses the boundless riches of the heart's warmest affection?"

"You say true, my Mary," replied her lover, "and such a prospect as that which your glowing imagination has depictured, I would not resign to become the monarch of the mightiest kingdom in the universe."

Again they embraced, and gave free indulgence to the feelings which throbbed in both their bosoms.

"Poor things, poor deluded mortals! how vainly do ye flatter yourselves with hopes that are never destined to be realised!"

These words proceeded from a solemn voice near them, but the tones of which they had both of them often heard before. They started, and looking up, beheld the individual whom they expected it was, standing before them, and gazing at them with an expression of pity.

It was an old woman of cadaverous aspect, and emaciated form, who was known in the village where the lovers resided by the name of Mad Moll, from her eccentric, though harmless habits; and her appearance at that particular moment not a little disconcerted them. But Richard Parker quickly recovered himself, and assuming a jocose air, he said—

"Why, how now, mother, what wind has blown you hither? Have your wits again forsook their natural tenement; and come you here to amuse us with some of your eccentricities?"

"This is no time for joking, Richard Parker," returned Mad Moll, "when the thoughts of yourself and the fair maiden who is leaning so affectionately on your arm, are fixed on such serious subjects. I know they deem me mad; laugh at me, despise me, call me old witch, impostor, fortune-teller; be it so—I heed not a straw what any one says of me, thinks of me; Mad Moll has been known to speak the truth to the cost of those who at the time derided her. It is that which brings her here now; and though you, like other sceptics, may scorn my words, and mock at my predictions, depend upon it they will come true."

In spite of all her efforts to the contrary, Mary could not help feeling alarmed at the observations of the singular old woman; she trembled violently, and clung still closer to her lover, who himself felt somewhat uneasy and discomfited at the seriousness of the tone in which Mad Moll spoke, and for a moment or two he was unable to make any answer to her.

"My good woman," he at length said, "I have no wish to offend you, I assure you; but at the same time I must tell you, that if you think to play upon my credulity, you will find yourself much mistaken. What is your business with us? Tell us at once, and leave us, for we wish to be alone."

"Alone?" repeated the old woman, with a half sarcastic smile; "yes, full well I know that, Richard Parker: it would not be well for the proud and haughty father of Mary, or the designing villain, Captain Arlington, to know that you were together. You affect to despise what Mad Moll, as the idiots term me, says; but still I will crave your attention while I give utterance to a few predictions, as to that which is destined to befall you."

"Be quick then, old woman," said our hero, whose curiosity was somewhat excited, "for I have no time to spare, and my patience is nearly exhausted."

"I will not detain you long, Richard Parker," said the old woman quietly. "Yourself and Mary Mason love each other sincerely."

"Why," replied Richard, laughing, "I should have thought that it required no prophet to tell us that."

"Laugh not, young man," returned Mad Moll, solemnly, "for that I have to say, is much more serious, and of deeper importance to you, than you now seem to imagine. Alas! alas! 'tis a pity that two fond hearts should be doomed to such terrible sufferings."

Mary stared at her aghast as she gave utterance to these words, and trembled more violently than before, and Richard could not help feeling somewhat uncomfortable, although he was not at all disposed to superstition, and felt far more inclined to join in the general belief of all those who knew her, that the old woman was mad.

"What mean you?" he demanded. "Be more explicit."

"Mary's father opposes your love," said the old woman.

"He does," coincided our hero; "what then?"

"Captain Arlington is paying his addresses to her, and his suit is sanctioned by Mr. Mason."

"True; but will Captain Arlington

ever possess her hand?" asked Richard, eagerly.

"He will not," answered Mad Moll; "but, mark me, he will be the means, when you least expect it, of bringing you to misery and disgrace. Oh, maiden, you will for a short time be a happy wife, but soon a heart-broken widow!"

"Gracious Heaven!" exclaimed the terrified damsel, "what could put such fearful thoughts into your head?"

"I speak the truth, Mary," answered the old woman, and the expression of her countenance became more solemn and sorrowful; "he whose arm now encircles your slender waist so affectionately, to whom your heart is so fondly attached, and who returns your love with equal fervour and sincerity, is destined to die a violent, an ignominious death!"

Mary Mason uttered a scream of horror, when she heard those words, and sank almost fainting in the arms of her lover.

"Mad woman!" exclaimed the excited Richard Parker, "know you what you say?"

"Alas, too well," replied the old woman, with a sorrowful look; "would that I had no occasion to utter the awful prediction. I repeat, that you are doomed to die a violent and ignominious death; *death by the halter!*"

Richard Parker started and turned ghastly pale; his tongue refused its office, and ere he could recover himself, Mad Moll, fixing upon him and Mary a look of the deepest regret and compassion, hurried from the spot, and was soon hidden from the sight in the shadows of the evening which had now descended upon the earth.

It was several minutes ere the lovers could recover themselves sufficiently from the surprise and the shock which the observations of the old woman had caused them, to speak; but when they did so, Mary said, while tears of anguish trembled in her eyes:

"Oh, Richard, dear Richard, what horrible words are those to which we have been listening? My blood freezes in my veins when I think of them, and the most fearful forebodings take possession of my mind."

"Heed them not, my beloved Mary," replied our hero, assuming as much composure as he could, though, as may be

imagined, ridiculous as the whole circumstance might appear to be, his mind felt ill at ease; "heed them not, my sweet one, for they are totally unworthy of a serious thought; they are but the preposterous ravings of a mad woman, and should in no way trouble us. Come, come, we have tarried beyond our time, and your father, if he misses you from the house, may suspect the cause of your absence, and devise measures to prevent our future interviews; we will meet again to-morrow evening, if possible, at the same place, and I hope that we shall then have to congratulate each other on a change in our prospects for the better."

Mary did indeed try hard to banish from her mind the impression which the observations of the old woman had made upon it, but she succeeded only indifferently, and without making any remark, she suffered her lover to conduct her from the spot, and to lead her by a way where they were the least likely to be observed by any one towards her residence, and having arrived in sight of which, after many affectionate adieus and fond embraces, they separated.

CHAPTER II.

MARY'S FRUITLESS APPEAL TO HER FATHER.—THE ELOPEMENT OF HER WITH RICHARD PARKER, AND THE SECRET MARRIAGE.

At one end of a rural village in the vicinity of Exeter, stood the stately mansion of Mr. Mason, the father of the heroine of our tale. It was a fine building in the Elizabethan style of architecture, and had been in the possession of the family of the Masons from the period of the reign of that sovereign.

Mr. Mason was a widower, and had been so for several years, and Mary was his only child. His principal faults were pride and irascibility of temper, which often led him beyond the bounds of reason, and caused him to do that which he afterwards bitterly regretted. Independent of those failings, he had ever been a kind and indulgent parent, and well did Mary repay the affection he bestowed upon her. The early part of her life passed happily away·

she was highly esteemed by all who had the honour to be acquainted with her, and little cause had she to anticipate the fearful troubles it was her hard lot at no distant period to experience.

The father of Richard Parker, the hero of our tale, was a respectable farmer, in the neighbourhood of Mr. Mason's mansion, and being a man of considerable attainments, they were on terms of the greatest intimacy together, and thus it was that Richard and Mary became companions from the earliest period of childhood, and that affection sprang up between them which nothing could ever afterwards destroy, and Mr. Mason encouraged their passion, for, as the father of our hero was a man of considerable property, he did not consider his son an unworthy match for his (Mr. Mason's) daughter. Time, however, wrought a wonderful change in his ideas. The father of Richard Parker died suddenly; misfortunes lighted upon his son; his patrimony became gradually diminished, through the failure of crops and other casualties, and he was reduced to a state of comparative poverty. Then it was that Mr. Mason began to look coldly upon our hero, and it was soon too painfully evident to the youthful lovers that a fatal change had come over his mind in the sentiments he had formerly entertained towards Richard, which they could not fail to attribute to the unfortunate alteration that had taken place in the circumstances of Richard, though it was through no misconduct of his own.

We need not seek to describe the many pangs which this caused them, and the despair which now began to settle upon their hearts; and when they could find an opportunity of being alone, which was not so often as they had hitherto been accustomed to, they gave free vent to their sorrows, and deeply lamented the sad and unexpected change which had so suddenly came over their fortunes; but still they solemnly vowed that let the consequences be whatever they might to each other, nothing whatever should banish from their bosoms the ardent passion that had been implanted in them from the earliest days of childhood, and which Heaven had hitherto seemed to sanction.

It was in vain that Richard Parker exerted all the energies of his body and mind to retrieve his broken fortunes; his circumstances every day became worse, and a spell seemed to rest upon him. It was just at this time, too, that accident introduced Captain Arlington to the house of Mr. Mason, and then the visits of Richard were peremptorily prohibited, and Mary was commanded to forget him in any other character but that of the companion of her youth, and to raise her thoughts to more ambitious views, as he could never for a moment think of encouraging the addresses of one who was so far beneath her in position of society.

This was a terrible shock to the feelings of the lovers, though they had long expected it, and their hopes were now almost entirely annihilated, especially when Captain Arlington made the most bold and unmistakable advances towards Mary, and which were evidently approved of and encouraged by her father. Still, however, they contrived at intervals to meet by stealth, and at such times they gave vent to the feelings of anguish that inhabited their bosoms, at the sudden change which had so suddenly come over their prospects, and in vain endeavoured to devise some means by which they might escape the fate with which they were threatened.

Captain Arlington was a man of plausible manners and insinuating address, but, at the same time, it needed no deep penetration to discover that the villain lurked within his breast, and that there were few things which he would hesitate to do, in order that he might obtain the gratification of his desires. From the very first moment of his introduction to her, Mary had felt a most unconquerable aversion to him; the most painful misgivings took possession of her mind, and she felt truly wretched whenever she was in his society. This was increased when her father informed her that Arlington had made proposals for her hand, and that he had given his consent, without consulting her feelings, to his paying his addresses to her. In vain she supplicated him with tears in her eyes, and with a bursting heart, to take compassion on her, and to abandon such harsh and cruel designs which were so revolting to her feelings; he was perfectly invulnerable, and commanded her, on pain of his everlasting displeasure, to receive the addresses of Captain Arlington with favour, for that it was his determination that he and no other should become her future husband; and thus were all the ideal scenes of happiness she had indulged in, in an union with Richard Parker, destroyed at one fell swoop, and she could anticipate nothing but the greatest misery to herself, and he to whom she was so fondly devoted, and whom she was convinced loved her with all the fervour that man could possibly bestow upon woman. But still she was firmly resolved at all hazards to resist the harsh determinations of her father to the very last, and that she would never, unless she was forced to it, become the wife of any other man than Richard Parker. Thus matters stood when the secret interview took place between the lovers which we have related in the previous chapter.

Mary, after leaving Richard, regained her own apartment without being observed by any one, or her absence being known to her father or Captain Arlington, who, fortunately, happened to be from home at the time; and the agitation and excitement of her mind were almost insupportable. The singular meeting with the old woman, too, and the fearful predictions to which she had given utterance, also created the greatest alarm in her breast; but still she was determined to conquer her emotions as well as she could, and to seek the interview which she had promised her lover with her father in the morning, and to make a final appeal to his feelings, though she entertained but little or no hopes that it would be crowned with success.

The meeting took place, and a most exciting one it was. With what simple but touching eloquence did the poor girl appeal to the heart of her stern parent! But it was all to no purpose; he heard her with the utmost impatience, and when she had concluded, he gave vent to his feelings in the most cruel and passionate observations; rejected all her arguments, and threatened her with his heaviest malediction if she any longer persisted in seeking to oppose his will. Mary retired from his presence with a bursting heart, and when she had reached her own apartment, she threw herself on a seat, and gave free indulgence to the violence of the grief and despair which filled her breast. At length she arose, and while her pale features assumed an expression of firmness and determination, she exclaimed—

"'Tis done—'tis decided!—my resolution is formed. Cruel father, it is you who by your stern decree urge me to this desperate course, and the consequences that may follow will rest upon your own head. Richard, dear Richard! in spite of everything, though the greatest misery may be my future portion, though the most abject poverty may overtake me, I am yours, yours for ever!"

* * * *

A few mornings after this, the servant maid on going to the chamber of her young mistress in order to assist her to dress, was surprised to find the room deserted by her, and it was evident from the appearance of the bed that she had not slept in it on the previous night; her boxes were also standing open, and every article of wearing apparel was removed from them. She immediately made Mr. Mason acquainted with the fact, and the utmost consternation prevailed, the rage of Mr. Mason and Captain Arlington exceeding all bounds. Search was made for her in every part of the mansion and the neighbourhood, but without the least success, and it at last became too evident that the poor girl had eloped, which was confirmed when it was found that Richard Parker had quitted his home abruptly, and no one could give the least information as to whither he had gone. The following day set the matter at rest; a letter arrived in the hand-writing of Mary, in which she confessed that she had become the wife of the man of her heart, and most earnestly and pathetically craved the forgiveness of her father for a step to which she had been driven by the strength of her despair and the unconquerable power of her affections.

To attempt to pourtray the rage of Mr. Mason on the receipt of this letter would be a fruitless task, but at length he invoked a terrible curse upon the head of his hapless daughter, and discarded her from his heart for ever. In a few days afterwards, Captain Arlington quitted the mansion, and filled with the utmost rage and disappointment, he vowed to have a terrible revenge if ever the opportunity should present itself.

CHAPTER III.

THE MUTINEERS.—THE COURT OF DELEGATES.—THE SCENE ON BOARD OF H.M.S. LONDON.

SOME years have now elapsed since the events we have recorded in the foregoing chapters had occurred, and the scene of action is changed. It was at a period which forms one of the most striking and important epochs in the history of this country, and on which the principal incidents of our narrative are founded. The mutiny at the Nore, in 1797, must be familiar to most of our readers, and we will therefore not dilate upon the subject further at present, but proceed at once with the startling and romantic events of our tale, and for that purpose we must request the reader to accompany us in imagination to a street in Portsmouth, along which two rather eccentric-looking characters were walking, and apparently bent on some important mission. The one was Timothy Bubble, a lawyer, and an arrant knave, and the other was a simple, good-natured fellow, ycleped Dicky Chicken, who acted in the capacity of a servant, and who carried under his arm a bundle of pretty moderate size.

"Bring the bundle along, Dicky," said Mr. Bubble, who seemed to be in no little state of excitement.

"Oh, sir," replied Dicky, "but who knows that it mayn't go right, after all ?"

"Who knows ?" returned the lawyer, impatiently. "I say it can't go right. I, Timothy Bubble, late a lawyer, then head clerk in His Majesty's dock-yard here at Portsmouth, now retired on my property in the Isle of Sheppy.—Dicky, Dicky, I have a head."

"But do you know, sir——"

"Know!" interrupted Bubble; "I know the law, though I never succeeded. Had I had my deserts, I should have been at the bar long ago."

"That you ought," said Dicky, quietly.

"What satisfaction it would have given me," continued Bubble, "to plead against these rascals, these mutineers."

"Belay there a bit," exclaimed a rough weather-beaten tar, advancing towards them.

"Ah, Master Jack Adams," said Bubble, "surely you haven't a good word for the rebellious varlets ;—wouldn't you hang every one of them ?"

"No, I wouldn't," answered Adams; "it's all mighty well for fellows like you and your lubberly boy, there, to talk about hanging and rebellion, and all such stuff; but we'll just suppose, now, that all the hands in that fleet were strung up like dried haddocks aboard a Dutch lugger, where the devil would you get such another navy ? Would you turn to at the capstan? or should we wait till your young ones came up to stand at the wheel or go into the chains ? You're a hippopotamus !"

"Better words, Mr. Adams—better words !" said Bubble; "one would have thought that your frequent visits ashore would have polished you a bit."

"Polished !" replied Adam; "they've spoiled me !"

"Spoiled you ?"

"Yes," returned Adams; "for I knew a time when, instead of listening to you, I should have knocked you down."

"Very well—very well !" said Bubble, swallowing the retort as well as he could; "but when you know that every man in the fleet is a rascal who ——"

"Avast !" interrupted Adams, passionately, "or, I'll knock in your head-rails. I know that every sailor (though there may be something to complain of, and they've gone on the wrong track to remedy it), has done old England service; I know that many a brave heart there has watched, fought, bled, for his country; has spent years upon the salt sea in storms and peril; has had the waves beating over him, and the shots flying about him, whilst you, and such as you, have been scratching your sixpences together, taking your grog with your curtains drawn, the doors listed, your feet upon your fender, and your wife and children around you."

"Tut—tut !" said Bubble; "we bear our part ;—we pay taxes.'

"Taxes !—Master Bubble, there's a mighty difference between taxes and duty on board of a man of-war !"

"I don't see it," said Bubble.

"Don't you?—look, now. We'll say your lad, Chicken, there, is (what he'll never have the luck to be). a sailor, and you are (what you ever will be), a gurnet-headed land-lubber. Well, the ship's cleared for action;—now, Dick is a fine, strong, healthy fellow—the first broadside has poured in;—where's Dick?—sprawling or crippled for life upon the deck! Now, what are you doing all this time? Why, sleeping your twelve hours a-night, and taking your soft tommy and butter in the morning. What's Dick's luck?—Why, he's lying in the cock-pit, with the surgeon and his mates, with their short sleeves tucked up, clattering their knives and saws; and there the poor fellow lies with a docked limb, thinking of his old mother or his young wife at home; thinking, mayhap, upon the babes, amidst groans and sobs, and prayers for water. This may be every sailor's lot in that fleet, and these are the men you'd hang! —You be d——d!"

'Oh," returned Timothy Bubble, "as for death and wounds, and such matters, that's all glory, and what I admire."

"Yes," retorted Adams, sarcastically, "you may admire glory clapped into a picture frame, and hung over your mantel-piece; but how would you like it in the waist of a fourteen gun-brig?"

"Still," remarked Bubble, "you ought not to excuse these mutineers; why, the whole fleet's in a state of rebellion; there's the court of delegates, as they call themselves here, and Heaven knows what other court at Plymouth, under arms."

"That's true, sir," said Dicky; "all the sailors are officers themselves now, and have run ropes from the yards of all the ships, to hang up those that may offend them. They think no more of the Admiral's flag, a cocked hat, and a pair of epaulettes, than I think of the Grand Turk. Now, what I'd do——"

"I tell you what you do," interrupted Adams; "go and fish for littlebats, or shoot sea-gulls with skillygoree: don't you talk of British seamen. What have you got hugging up there?"

"Ah! that's it," said Bubble, with an air of much importance. "If I'm not knighted for that piece of service, why,

there's no reward for loyalty. You don't know what I have taken to-day."

"No. Physic?"

"Physic! Treason, disaffection, rebellion!"

"Much good may they do you," returned Adams, ironically.

"Here it is," said Bubble, taking a bill from his bundle, and preparing to read. "Perhaps you haven't seen this yet? I'll read it. 'British sailors! now is the time! Britons, strike home! Look at your officers; consider their pay, and then look what is yours; your grog is stopped, and no short-allowance money; wages are not paid for seven years, and who benefits but the purser? Now is the time; be men, and redress yourselves! Rule Britannia! and three cheers for Richard Parker!' There! what do you think of that? Here is a whole bundle of them; and this I, Dicky here, and two constables, manfully took from a rascal in the High-street."

"Well," said Adams, "you took the cargo, and what did you do with the craft?"

"Zounds!" exclaimed Bubble, "you don't suppose we could take both? The fellow fought like a devil. I lost a knee-buckle in the fray. Arn't you surprised? You haven't seen any of these?"

"Haven't I," answered Adams, scornfully. "I lighted my pipe with two yesterday. What are you going to do with them? Sell 'em to the cheese-monger?"

"Take them to the Admiralty," replied Bubble. "If my exertions save the British Navy, why, rewards must come —they'll make a lord of me, at least."

"Oh, a lord—a duke!" said Adams.

"No—no, a lord!"

"A duke!" repeated Adams, with a laugh. "The Duke of Puddle Dock!"

"Come along, Dicky," said Bubble, "bring the bundle; there's enough there to make your master's fortune, and leave something for his servants. Adams, if I should get any interest with the Lords of the Admiralty, I'll add two-pence a day to your pension for wounds. Come, Dicky, mind the parcel. His Majesty shall find at least he has one faithful servant, and I—I was royal from my cradle; for I came into the world on the king's birth-day, only three minutes and three quarters after my gracious sovereign. Good-bye, Adams: you shall have a triffle for tobacco yet. Mind the bundle, Dicky ; mind the bundle."

Thus saying, the sapient Mr. Bubble and his man took their departure.

" That fellow now," said Jack Adams, when they were gone, " would make a fortune on the Goodwin Sands. Ah ! these are bad times. But all's one : it's a stiff gale which never shifts. Here comes Molly Brown, my sweetheart. That girl is as full of talk as a seventy-four is full of port-holes."

"Oh, my dear Adams," said Molly, as she made her appearance, " I've been looking for you. What will become of us ?"

" What may happen to the best of us," replied Adams, carelessly. " I shall be hanged !"

" Hanged !" repeated Molly, with a look of alarm.

"Ay," returned Adams. " Hallo ! what, shipped a sea ? That's the worst of you women : you believe everything that is told you."

" My dear Adams, why will you frighten me ?" said his sweetheart. " Hanged !"

" Why, if I am not hanged to-day, I may be to-morrow," returned the sailor. " It's as well to prepare you for it. What can you expect ?"

" Why," said Molly, " you are no more to blame than any of the rest. To be sure, you're head man in the court, and, I'm told, talk better than any lawyer."

" Ah," returned Adams, " that doesn't say much in my favour."

" Well, but our marriage, Adams ?"

" How can you be so unreasonable ?" demanded the latter. " Here am I, Jack Adams, captain of the maintop of the Queen, your sweetheart, to be sure, but at the head of the mutineers ; and now, whilst all the fleet's in a blaze, you are talking of marriage !"

" Well, you know you promised," said Molly.

" I know that ; Jack Adams stands to his word as he does to his gun. Let me again see the admiral's flag flying, all the crew returned to their duty, and, unless they run Jack up at the fore-yard arm, we'll be spliced. Though, I say,

my girl, you had better have Timothy Bubble ; he's a warm widower."

" Have him !" ejaculated Molly.

" Why," replied Adams, " you know he wants to have you ; he's rich ; full of gold as of——"

" Wickedness !" rejoined Molly ; " No, it's a hard thing to say, but I really do believe that I'd sooner not be married at all."

" Hush !" said Adams, with a smile, " you don't know what you mean ; however, you have my word, and when I see all that square again——"

" What then ?"

" Then, hey for the fiddles and the white ribbands," answered Adams, as he threw his arm around her waist and led her away.

In the ward-room of the Queen, the mutineers who composed what they called the court of delegates were sitting in deep consultation, and a singular court it was.

" No, no, my lads," observed one of the men who was called Jack Morris ; " if we flinch back now, we know what awaits us ; the fore-yardarm, keel hauling, and the cat-o'-nine-tails through the fleet."

" Right !" coincided another member of the court, named Allen ; " take my word for it, unless we pull together, we shall have the yellow flag at every yard-arm in the navy."

" But after all, my lads," said Morris, " let us prove that we are worthy of what we ask ; let us prove it by our moderation, and never let us doubt, if we are only true to ourselves, that the Lords of the Admiralty must harken to us."

" Captain Lock is come aboard, and wants to speak to the court," said a sailor, who at that moment entered. He was ordered by Morris to show the captain in, and departed accordingly.

" I warrant me, the captain," observed Morris, " he that used to swear a bit over us, hasn't learnt manners through our turning him ashore."

He was interrupted by the entrance of Captain Lock.

' So, gentlemen," began the latter, ironically.

" Avast, captain !" said Morris ; " no half-laughs ! We can do our business better, I take it, for pattering clearly."

"What do you want?" demanded Captain Lock.

"Want!" returned Morris. "Have you come aboard to ask that? The Lords of the Admiralty know what we want. But lest it should have slipped their memory, and you are about to pay 'em a visit, we'll tell you again what we want. We want more pay, better provisions, and less flogging, captain."

"Insolent ruffians!" cried the enraged captain; "your boldness ——"

"Boldness!" interrupted Morris; "ay, it was our boldness that saved old England through many a rough gale;—it was our boldness that kept the French from our shores, and the merchantmen safe in the ports;—it was our boldness that saved everything that was British, and now we'll see if our boldness can't save ourselves!"

"Return to your duties!" commanded Captain Lock, with a frown.

"We are at them now," answered Morris.

"Yes, captain," remarked Allen; "nor shall we leave them till —"

"Rascal! another word!" interrupted the captain, passionately, "and —"

"Captain Lock," interrupted Morris, "if you would be safe, be quiet; you are not now upon the quarter-deck; you are with your equals."

"Equals!"

"Ay, with men standing up for their rights! We think nomore of your epaulettes now than of so much moonshine."

"Am I not your captain?"

"That's as it may be," answered Morris.

"The Lords of the Admiralty offer you pardon," said Captain Lock.

"Nothing else?" demanded Morris.

"They will forget all that's past."

"Yes," remarked Morris, "that's what we complain of—now, we'd have them overhaul their memory a bit!"

"What would you have them remember?" asked the captain.

"That we have fought and bled for old England; that we are men, and men determined to have our rights!"

"And is this your answer to their lordships?"

"It is," answered Allen.

"Indeed!" sneered the captain. "I would that the Admiralty were of my opinion."

"Indeed, captain!" said Morris. "Mayhap you'll tell us what you'd do?"

"String you all up for a set of rebellious ——"

"Leave the ship," commanded Morris.

"Villains!" exclaimed the infuriated captain.

"Ah!" cried the sailors in a breath, and rushing simultaneously upon him, they seized him; at the same moment he drew his sword, and struggled violently with Allen, whom he succeeded in throwing down; but Allen drew a pistol from his belt and presented it at him, just as Jack Adams entered hastily, carrying in his hand a white flag.

"Avast a bit!" cried Adams; "what, captain?"

"How now, Adams?" demanded Morris; "what's the meaning of all this?"

"The meaning?" replied Adams; "why, here am I, Jack Adams, come on board to tell you all's right, and how do I find you?"

"Adams," said Morris, "isn't this the court of delegates?"

"That! for the court of delegates," answered Adams, snapping his fingers contemptuously; "it isn't worth a bucket of spray."

"Am I not president?" demanded Morris.

"No," returned Adams, "for the Admiralty has settled it all!—You are not going to leave us, captain?"

"Yes, my fine fellow," replied Captain Lock; "had all my ship's company been such as you, I should have been proud of commanding them; as it is, I blush to have ever been their captain."

With these words, Captain Lock departed, and Adams, turning to the sailors, observed—

"I say, my hearties, haven't you got yourselves into a fine hank now? Here am I come aboard to tell you all's right, and——"

"How do you mean all's right?" interrupted Morris.

"Admiral Pole, in the quarter-deck of the George, has pledged his word to you, that the Lords-Admirals have accepted your petition, and that every demand shall be complied with."

"I won't believe a word of that there story," said Allen; "if it were true,

Mr. President, why did not Admiral Pole come here himself with the news? For my part, I think he has been gammoning Adams."

"Gammoning!" repeated Adams; "I tell you, Mr. President, it was Admiral Gardener delivered the message to Admiral Pole; and that's what the ship's company of the George know; and as for his gammoning me, I've the conceit to think so highly of myself, that I believe I'd be gammoned by neither Admiral Pole nor Tom Allen."

"Glory, Adams, my hearty—glory!" said one of the sailors.

"Order, gentlemen," said Morris. "What say you? Shall we take Adams' message for truth or not? You see, Tom Allen of the Mars is of opinion that he has been gammoned."

"Mr. President," said Adams, "don't you put the truth or falsehood of this upon my shoulders. It isn't Jack Adams' message; it's Admiral Gardener's message—I believe it to be true—I believe——"

He was interrupted by the firing of a gun, and a sailor hastily entered.

"The red flag's hoisted on board the George," he said.

"The red flag?" repeated Allen.

"It can't be," said Adams.

"There's at least twenty boats full of officers making for the shore," said the sailor.

"That doesn't look like a settlement," observed Morris. "What have you to say now?"

"Say?" answered Adams; "why, that there's some blunder in the business. But give me a boat's crew, and I'll go ashore to the admiral."

"Be it so," said Morris.

"And," continued Adams, "if Jack Adams don't bring you off goods news, why, scratch him off as A. B., and make a lubberly boy of him. Gammoned, indeed!"

"Well, Jack," said Morris, "I hope you may not find yourself deceived, but if you do, we shall know how to act."

"Of course you will," answered Adams. "But do not fear; I am very much deceived indeed if I am disappointed in my expectations."

"Away, then, my hearty," said Morris, "and we shall await most anxiously your return."

"Ay, my lads," said Jack Adams, "and as I before observed, depend upon it, it will be with good news."

Adams now departed, and the members of the court of delegates, as they thought fit to designate themselves, remained in profound deliberation until his return.

Mr. Timothy Bubble having disposed for a short time of his important bundle and his slavey, Dicky Chicken, took a deliberative ramble from his own domicile, and while thus occupied, he accidentally encountered her upon whom one principal portion of his thoughts were centred—to wit, the fair Molly Brown, and to whom, as the opportunity presented itself, he pressed his suit with more than ordinary energy. But, alas! for the little man, Molly was totally invulnerable; her heart had been taken possession of by the hardy seaman, Jack Adams, and it was a useless task for Mr. Bubble now to lay siege to the fortress of her affections, even supposing that, at any other time, the charms of his person, and his intrinsic qualities might have made any impression on her.

"Now, Mrs. Molly," said Bubble, persuasively, after a brief pause, "will you hear me?"

"I can't help it," returned Molly.

"Depend upon it," observed Timothy Bubble, "you'll not have such another chance. You are not aware, perhaps, that I am to be promoted?"

"Promoted!" repeated Molly, with a sarcastic look; "why, what can they possibly make of you?"

"That," replied Mr. Bubble, raising himself to his full height, and a little beyond it, by the aid of the tips of his toes, and looking as dignified as he possibly could; "why—why, I leave that entirely to His Majesty's discretion. It isn't for me to say whether I'll be a lord or a knight; but you know, Mrs. Molly, that whichever it is, I shall be able to make you a lady."

"A lady?" said the simple Molly. "No!"

"She begins to smell," thought Bubble. "A lady, Molly!" he said, aloud. "Now, what coloured silk should you like to be married in; blue or white, or —— ?"

"Neither," interrupted Molly, with

an arch smile. "Black: it would do remarkably well for the other ceremony."

"The other ceremony!" said Bubble, with a vacant stare.

"Certainly," replied Molly, with the most provoking irony; "for, you know, if you were to be so unconscionable as to marry me, you couldn't be wicked enough to live a long time afterwards."

"Not live!" ejaculated the sapient Timothy; "why, you wouldn't marry me with such a prospect?"

"Do you think I'd marry you with any other?" asked Molly.

"But consider," said Bubble; "husbands are not very plentiful!"

At this juncture, Jack Adams and several sailors arrived at the spot, and observing his sweetheart and Timothy Bubble engaged in such earnest conversation, he said,—

"Eh! why, there's my Molly, and that land-shark! Let us retire aside here, messmates, and watch their proceedings."

They did so, accordingly; and Molly observed, in answer to what Mr. Bubble had said to her,—

"You see, Mr. Bubble, I'm the more fortunate; for I've chosen one already. There's my Adams!"

"Adams!" repeated her companion; "don't deceive yourself, my dear!—he'll prove but the shadow of a husband!"

"The shadow!"

"He hasn't eight-and-forty hours to live!"

"Not to live!"

"Not to live!" replied Mr. Bubble, positively. "So, you'd better have me, a rich, well experienced widower! I shouldn't wonder if his death-warrant isn't made out now."

"What for?" demanded Molly, eagerly.

"What for?" repeated Bubble. "Here has he been principal rebel, and spokesman of the whole fleet, and now you ask, 'What for?'"

"Oh, but that's all forgotten," rejoined Molly. "The Lords of the Admiralty have promised to redress all grievances, and to publish a general pardon."

"All smoke," said Bubble, taking a newspaper from his pocket; "that's just to gull 'em, to pacify 'em a bit, till there's rope enough to hang 'em all. Don't be alarmed; but Jack Adams, your dear Jack, as you call him, will

hang higher than any of 'em. Look here," he continued, reading from the newspaper, "'House of Parliament,'—I'll put on my spectacles."

"Mayhap, I can read it," said Adams, suddenly starting forward, and snatching the paper from his hand.

"Adams!" exclaimed Bubble, starting, and gazing at him with no small degree of astonishment and confusion.

"Yes, Adams," returned the hardy seaman; "why, Molly, and are you to be frightened by a lubber like that?"

"But that paper, Jack?" said one of the sailors, anxiously.

"Ah!" exclaimed another, "we've been tricked, and if there's been foul play——"

"Avast, shipmate—avast!" interrupted Adams. "You don't believe what he says, do you?"

"But the paper—the paper!" said the sailor who had first spoken, impatiently.

"I' faith," said Adams to himself, aside, and looking at the paper; "but they mustn't know it, either; there's none of 'em can read."

"The paper—the paper!" demanded the sailors, in a breath.

"Well," replied Adams, "I'll read it to you. This is the part you mean, isn't it?" he added, speaking to Bubble.

"Y—e—es," stammered out Bubble, and trembling most violently. "Oh, would that I were out of their clutches!" he added to himself.

"Well, let me see," said Adams, reading. "'We understand that the Lords of the Admiralty have determined to grant the petition of the fleet at Spithead, Plymouth, and the Nore.'"

"Hurrah!" shouted the sailors, tumultuously.

"Pray, Mr. Adams," said Bubble, simply, "where did you go to school?"

"Where did I go to school?" replied Adams. "Why, in the maintop of the Royal Billy."

"In the maintop, Jack?" said the sailors, with looks of astonishment.

"Yes," answered Adams. "You see, I was always fond of larning when a child. Well, Tom Cipper, he was once what they call a usher in a Yorkshire school, he was captain of the top, and there he used to give me my edication, making me spell the names of the merchantmen as they passed by us. I learnt my letters through a telescope."

"I should think so," returned Bubble, drily, "and through the wrong end, I should suppose."

'Why what do you mean?" demanded Jack Adams.

"Why," answered Bubble, "I mean to say, that if you've read that paper correctly, I know nothing of a telescope."

"I say, Jack," remarked one of the sailors, "no half-laughs, you know; we are no scholars."

At this moment Allen joined them.

"How, now?" he said; "didn't I say that the Lords of the Admiralty were deceiving us? Why, look here," he added, producing a newspaper, "here's the whole account on't from London."

This announcement caused the greatest excitement amongst the sailors.

"Why," said one of them, "Jack Adams says that it's all in our favour."

"Yes, you know," returned Bubble, ironically, "but then, you know, he didn't read through a telescope."

"Our favour!" exclaimed Allen; "yes, till they get us all under hatches."

"Why, then," said the sailor who had before spoken, "all I have to say is this, Jack Adams has thrown out false signals, and is a disgrace to——"

"Avast!" interrupted Adams, indignantly; "a round turn there, messmate! Jack Adams a disgrace! And are you, a lubberly boy, to talk to Jack Adams, that was rated able seaman before you had strength to crack a biscuit?"

"Then why deceive us? Why gammon us, acause you had the luck o' edication?" demanded the sailor.

"All for your good," replied Aadms.

"Good!" repeated Allen; "why, Jack you don't flinch from the cause?"

"No," returned Adams; "and I think I but prove my love to the cause, by keeping a set of mad fellows from running headlong into halters. Can't you wait?"

"Wait?" said Allen; "what's the use of waiting? Arn't we treated as dogs? Come, my lads, let Jack Adams do as he pleases, I'm for the London. Who jumps into the boat with me?"

The sailors all agreed.

"And as for waiting," added Allen, "let 'em wait—But it's no matter; heave ahead, shipmates!"

Thus saying, Allen, followed by the sailors, departed, and left Jack Adams, Bubble, and Molly Brown to themselves.

"Now," said Adams, turning to Bubble, and fixing upon him a look of the most superlative contempt, "I dare say you think yourself as great as the Port Admiral, for what you have done?"

"Done, Mr. Adams?" returned Bubble.

"Mr. Adams! None of your gammon. I've a great mind to give you an upholsterer's jacket."

"And what's that?" asked Bubble, in a tremulous voice.

"Why, tar and feather you," replied Adams. "Push off your boat. Damme, you're like a mermaid, you never appear but a storm follows."

"Mr. Ad——Good morning, sir. There's one comfort," he added to himself, aside, "I shall see him hanged, and that to a loyal subject, and a good Christian, is an unspeakable satisfaction."

He then made his exit abruptly, without venturing another look towards Adams or Molly Brown.

"Why, Molly," said her sweetheart, "you look as white as a washed hammock."

"Oh, Adams!" sighed the damsel, trembling, "if, after all, anything should happen to you!"

"Happen to me!" repeated Adams; "why, what can happen? All along I've done my duty; I've——"

The report of a gun for a moment interrupted him.

"Eh!" he said; "there's some mischief afloat. I must be off, or there'll be bloodshed. Farewell! As soon as the admiral's flag is flying at the main, then, hey for the white favours!"

They parted, and Jack Adams made his way towards the London, while Molly with a heavy heart, slowly retraced her steps towards home.

All was excitement on the quarter-deck of the London, on which Admiral Colpoys, Captain Griffiths, and Lieutenant Sims, of the Marines, were assembled in deep consultation. The Marines were under guard, and everything showed that some important event was expected to be on the eve of taking place.

"See, my lord," remarked Captain

Griffiths, addressing himself to Admiral Colpoys, "the red flag is still flying aboard the Queen; depend upon it, the day will end fatally."

"Let it end as it will," said Admiral Colpoys, firmly. "I am determined to do my duty. Lieutenant Sims, are your men under loaded arms?"

"No, my lord," replied Lieutenant Sims.

"See that they be prepared," ordered the admiral; "see that——"

He was interrupted by the voice of a sailor alongside, shouting—

"London, a-hoy!"

"My lord," said Captain Griffiths, "here are men from the Queen, desirous of entering the ship."

"Not a man of them," said Admiral Colpoys, sternly; but the words had scarcely passed his lips, when Morris, Allen, Senator, and several more of the mutineers, rushed in at the gangway.

"So, my lord," said Morris, "we are told not to come aboard? Now, here we are, you see; you must allow us to settle our business quietly aboard your ship."

"No—no, my lad," answered the admiral, "for really I see no end to this business of yours; the more you get, the more, seemingly, you would have; it is high time that such turbulent conduct should be put an end to. Return, therefore, to your respective duties, and bless your stars, and be content with what his Majesty has at present granted you."

"Pray, what has he granted us," demanded Allen, "more than your lordship is doing now—giving us a very pretty treat of your jawing tackle? Bah! to the devil, I say, with all such grants!"

"You are indeed a well-finished scoundrel," said Admiral Colpoys, frowning; "and were it not that you stand where you do, and I might injure a better fellow, I'd order a ball to be sent through your head immediately. Away with you! It is such knaves as you, you villain, famous alike for your turbulence and cowardice, that bring honest, simple men into tumult and disgrace."

"Away with me, my lord?" said Allen, scornfully and firmly. "I'll away when I have done my duty: and though I may be turbulent in your eyes,

I can flatly give you the lie as to cowardice. Here stands Tom Allen, of the Mars, whose ears have heard the whistle of ten shots to one more than ever your lordship did; here he stands, I say, open before you; fire upon him, if you dare."

"We must really go into the wardroom to hold a counsel," said Morris, with the utmost coolness imaginable.

"I tell you, my lad," answered Admiral Colpoys, endeavouring to conquer his rage as well as he could; "I tell you, my lad, I repeat, that I cannot agree to it. If your business is so very importunate, in heaven's name take yourselves off, and meet wherever else you please; but on board this vessel, while I command her, you shan't."

"Bah!" ejaculated Senator, impatiently, "never mind the old fellow, Morris; he's got his jawing tackle aboard, so, come along, Jack."

They now advanced towards the cabin, when the admiral exclaimed,—

"Marines, make ready! I advise you once again, my lads, before you go further, to keep to your boats; for, by mine honour, I declare that if you attempt to proceed, it shall be at your own ——"

"If he dares to fire upon us," said Senator, over the ship's side, "he may look out for squalls! Come aboard, my boys!"

Several of the mutineers now rushed desperately and determinedly on board. Lieutenant Sims, who was greatly excited, struck Senator with the flat part of his sword, but he had no sooner done so than the former drew a pistol from his belt, and discharging the contents at him, he fell. The Marines were now about to fire at the mutineers, when the crew of the London joined them to a man, and the victory was immediately decided in their favour, and the flag of the admiral was struck. At that critical juncture, Jack Adams entered hastily at the gangway, holding in his hand several papers.

"Hold!" he exclaimed, "the day is ours! Lord Howe has arrived! The Admiralty consents to our claim! Here is the paper!"

The sailors uttered a simultaneous shout on hearing this declaration; quick as thought, the admiral's flag was again hoisted, and all was joy and exultation on board the London.

CHAPTER IV.

THE FORTUNES OF RICHARD AND MARY PARKER.—THE GATHERING STORM.— THE PRESS-GANG.

It now becomes necessary, for the better development of our plot, to revert to the earlier period of our narrative, and to relate what befell Richard Parker and our beauteous heroine immediately after their marriage.

It was past ten o'clock at night, and the mansion of Mr. Mason was hushed in the most profound silence, when Mary prepared herself to put the designs she had formed into execution after a desperate struggle with her feelings. But she was left no other alternative, albeit her heart felt the greatest repugnance at doing anything in a clandestine way; her father was inexorable, and the bare idea of her being compelled to become the wife of Captain Arlington chilled her blood with a sensation fast approaching to horror. She was determined that it should not be, let the consequences be whatever they might to herself; and, consequently, now that she had made her last appeal to her father and had heard his determination, she knew full well that there was nothing left for her but to put her plans into effect without delay.

She had contrived to make her lover acquainted with the result of her interview with her father, and resigned herself entirely to his will; at the same time solemnly assuring him that if he refused to accept her for his bride, her fate was sealed, and that she would never live to become the wife of any other man. The reader may readily guess what was the decision of our hero, so doatingly, so passionately fond of her as he was. He consented to a secret marriage, and made his preparations accordingly, though it was with a sad heart and many dismal forebodings that he did so, for his honourable nature revolted at the idea of doing anything in a clandestine manner, and the broken state of his fortunes filled him with many misgivings as to the future.

Mary had made the plea of indisposition to retire early to her chamber on the evening of her intended elopement, and not the least suspicion was excited in the mind of her father, or it is certain that he would have taken the necessary steps to prevent it; but for some time she was so violently agitated by the contending feelings that struggled in her breast, that she could not collect herself sufficiently to make the necessary little preparations for her journey. She listened with the most breathless attention and anxiety to catch the least sound that might be stirring in the house, and she seemed as if she were on the eve of committing some dreadful crime. But at length she heard her father close his chamber-door, and she knew well that he had retired for the night. All was perfectly still in the house, and the moment for action had consequently arrived.

It was a beautiful night, and the tranquillity which reigned around was every way calculated to calm her feelings, but still it failed to do so, and she gazed at the bright moon, which flooded her chamber with its silvery beams, with a feeling almost amounting to apathy.

"God forgive me!" she fervently ejaculated, "if I am about to act wrong. Dear Richard, for your sake, I sacrifice everything—a father's love, a once happy home, fortune, all; I cannot live without you, and I feel assured that so sincere and ardent is the love that you have ever professed towards me, so honourable are the feelings that hold their dominion in your breast, that you will never abuse the confidence I place in you."

She gently opened the door of her chamber, and again listened breathlessly, her heart palpitating violently against her side; but all remained hushed as before, and once more invoking the protection of Heaven, the lovely Mary Mason took up the small bundle which contained the few articles of value she had in her possession, and emerging from the room, made her way towards the back of the house, and with noiseless steps descended the stairs, until she arrived at the door which opened upon the country, and the key of which she had possessed herself of. When she had got a few paces from the house, she looked towards it, and the emotions that struggled in her breast almost overpowered her.

"Farewell to you, dear sacred house, in which I have passed so many years of happiness!" she ejaculated, whilst convulsive sobs almost choked her utterance. "I quit you for awhile; but shall I ever again be allowed to revisit you? Shall I ever more be permitted to cross your threshold? Alas! alas! I fear not! Bless you, my father. May every health and happiness attend you, and may you not estrange from your heart that poor girl, whom your cruel determination has driven into this act of disobedience!"

For a moment she passed her fair hand across her brow, and the tears streamed fast between her taper fingers; but making a powerful effort, she partially recovered herself, and hurried on her way. Her lover had appointed to meet her at a certain place, and towards that spot she now made her way, deeply wrapped in thought. She had not, however, proceeded far when she beheld the dark shadow of a human form upon the ground, and looking up, she was surprised and alarmed to see Mad Moll standing before her, and whose attenuated form and cadaverous countenance were fully revealed in the mellow light of the moon.

Mary felt a strange shuddering sensation, almost amounting to horror, steal over her as she contemplated this singular being, and remembered what had occurred at their last meeting, and the extraordinary observations to which she had given utterance; but the old woman seemed to eye her with an expression of melancholy and pity, and slowly advanced towards her, until she stood within a few paces of her.

"Be not alarmed, maiden," she said; "a poor, feeble, old wretch like me could not harm you, if even I were so inclined. 'Tis, however, an unseasonable hour for one so young, so lovely, and so innocent to be rambling from home."

"Oh, what brings you here?" said our heroine, in a faint voice.

"Accident, nothing more. damsel, depend upon it," answered the old woman.

"Oh, for Heaven's sake do not detain me, nor mention to any one that you have seen me," supplicated Mary; "it will do you no good to do so, and me—But here is money for you, and in God's name do not any further obstruct me, for my happiness, my hopes, nay, my very life depend upon——"

"Put by your money, young lady," interrupted Mad Moll, with a look of offended pride that ill accorded with her miserable appearance; "I need it not. Your lover awaits you at the place of appointment."

"Ah!" exclaimed Mary, gazing at her with the most unspeakable astonishment, "how know you that?"

"How do I know it?" repeated the old woman, with a faint smile. "Oh, maiden, there are more things in this chequered world of ours than your mind can yet fathom. I tell you that Richard Parker awaits you at the place of assignation, anxious to embrace his future bride. He loves you, and is worthy of you; but alas—alas! how terrible are the misfortunes that Fate has decreed shall befall you both. Remember the predictions I gave utterance to when last we met; they will be realised."

"Woman!" cried Mary, in accents of the most indescribable emotion; "know you what you say?"

"Yes, girl," replied the old woman, calmly; "Mad Moll, as she is called, never gives utterance to anything that she has not previously well considered; the storm, though distant, is even now gathering. Heaven help you when its fury bursts upon you. Farewell—to your lover, to your chosen husband, I will no longer detain you; but once more I enjoin you not to forget the words of prophecy I have spoken to you."

With these words, the old woman waived her hand, and turning round, hastily retreated from the spot, before our heroine could sufficiently recover from her astonishment and alarm to give utterance to a single syllable. The adventure was altogether so remarkable, that she was lost in amazement and confusion, and for a few minutes was unable to move from the spot, while her heart beat violently against her side, and she was, in all other respects, most violently agitated. At length she was sufficiently recovered to proceed on her way, though she found it utterly impossible to banish from her mind the impression which the extraordinary remarks of the mysterious old woman had made on it. In a few minutes more she beheld the approaching form of her lover, and who, seeing her at the same instant, rushed towards her, and clasped her fondly in his arms. We will pass hastily over the scene which followed ; they were both of them for a time rendered totally incapable of uttering a word ; but the expression of their countenances fully revealed the feelings that animat d their breasts.

"Beloved Mary," at last ejaculated our hero, "and are you, indeed, mine ?"

"Yours, and yours only," said the lovely girl, "as I have often so solemnly vowed to be."

"Sweet girl," returned her enraptured lover, "how great is the sacrifice you have made for me ; how can I ever sufficiently evince my gratitude for your love and constancy ! But Mary, how is this ? How ghastly pale you look, and you tremble violently also ; do you repent of the course you have adopted and——"

"Ah, no—no—no, dear Richard !" eagerly interrupted Mary ; "do not, I implore you, for a moment, entertain such a thought, for indeed you render me an injustice by doing so ; let whatever may be the consequences to myself, I have acted according to the dictates of my heart, and I shall, I am confident, never regret the step I have taken, but——"

"But what, my own Mary ?" anxiously demanded Richard ; "there must be something to cause this violent agitation ; has anything particularly occurred to disturb you ?"

"Yes, Richard," replied the damsel, looking fearfully behind her, as though she were apprehensive that some one was watching them ; "and yet, perhaps, I should deem myself weak and foolish to——"

"Do not keep me in suspense, dear Mary," said her lover ; "you should now have no secrets from me ; whatever affects you, must likewise concern me ; tell me then, what is it that has thus affected you ?"

"Richard," replied our heroine, "I had not proceeded far from the mansion when I again encountered that mysterious woman whom we saw the other day."

"Ah !" exclaimed Richard ; "is she then a spy upon our actions ?"

"No, dear Richard," answered Mary,

"I do not believe that, though she is well acquainted with our intentions."

"Impossible !" said Richard ; "how can she have acquired that knowledge ?"

"I know not," replied the damsel ; "but so it is. But more than all, Richard, and it is that which has caused the agitation you have seen me evince, she repeated those strange and fearful predictions, to which she gave utterance when we encountered her together."

"Pshaw, Mary," said her lover, after a brief pause ; "heed them not ; they are totally unworthy of a serious thought. The very idea of their ever being realized is perfectly preposterous. But, come, my love, every moment that we tarry here is fraught with danger. The time, too, is getting late ; let us at once proceed to the residence of my cousin, Amy Parker, where you are to sleep to-night, and who is to be your bridemaid in the morning. We must depart at an early hour in the morning, before your father shall have discovered your flight."

"Alas ! dear Richard," sighed Mary, "how hard is it to think we should be driven to such a course. How terrible will be the rage and excitement of my father when he finds that I have abandoned him."

"It will soon pass away, depend upon it," said Richard, "for he has himself alone to blame for what has happened. Fear not, a reconciliation will soon be effected, and in a short time all that happiness we have long so fondly anticipated will be ours."

"God grant that it may," ejaculated Mary, fervently ; "but with you, dear Richard, though surrounded by poverty, how can I be otherwise than happy ?"

"Bless you, my sweet girl," said her lover, again embracing her with the utmost fondness ; "and if ever I abuse the generous confidence you repose in me, may every curse attend me."

Mary made no reply, but her looks expressed more, much more than words could even have done ; and suffering her lover to take her arm, they walked hastily towards the residence of Amy Parker. Here they passed a short time in conversation, and then with many affectionate farewells, they separated till the morning, Richard having arranged to be there by daylight, and to bring with him a vehicle he had hired for the purpose, and which was to convey them to a town some few miles off, where the marriage ceremony was to take place.

We need not inform the reader that Mary slept little that night, and she awaited the arrival of that eventful morning which was to decide her fate, with a palpitating heart. It came at last, and punctual to the time he had appointed, Richard came. Mary and her bridemaid, the amiable Amy Parker, were already dressed and awaiting him, and after a scene of the most interesting description, they stepped into the coach, and were soon rapidly on their way to the town in which the church was situated. The ceremony was completed, Mary Mason became the wife of the man to whom she had been so fondly and firmly devoted from the days of her earliest childhood, and the harsh and unjust designs of her father and Captain Arlington were thus completely frustrated.

After the marriage, Richard Parker took his young and beauteous bride to temporary lodgings, which he had hired for the purpose, and it was then that Mary, when she could sufficiently tranquillise her feelings for the task, wrote an affectionate letter to her father, in which she informed him of what had happened, and earnestly and pathetically supplicated his forgiveness and blessing. The next day she received an answer, an answer which was all that her worst fears had anticipated; her father bitterly reproached her for the act of disobedience she had committed, discarded her from his breast for ever, and told her that from that moment she and her husband were strangers to him, and that he would not on any account whatever hold any further correspondence with them.

As may well be imagined, Mary was for some time completely inconsolable after receiving this cruel shock; but the affectionate attentions of her husband at length revived her, and she was enabled to resign herself to her fate with more fortitude than could have been at all anticipated under the circumstances.

Richard was compelled to dispose of his farm at a great sacrifice; and taking up his residence at a village close to the town in which they had been united, he obtained employment as an agricultural labourer; but humble as were their circumstances, and limited their means, Richard Parker and his wife were supremely happy in each other's love, and indulged in the fond hope that something would yet occur to brighten their prospects, cheerless though they were at present; but, alas! how little did they then anticipate the cruel sufferings that were in store for them! In due course of time, Mary Parker presented her delighted husband with a lovely boy, and the happiness of them both increased tenfold.

It was on a beautiful summer evening, about two years after their union, that Richard Parker having returned from his daily toil, was seated with his young bride and her tender offspring, in the parlour of his comfortable but humble cottage, engaged in the most affectionate conversation. They never were more happy than they felt at that moment.

"Dear Mary," said her husband, "what cause have we to regret our humble station, while our hearts remain unchanged towards each other?—We have that our humble wishes covet, and I do not yet despair that something will yet occur to place us in a far different position in society."

"For your sake, my husband," replied Mary, "and that of our dear and innocent offspring, I ardently hope that it may. But I am quite content to remain as I am, while I know that I possess that which is far more valuable to me than all the gifts of fortune—your faithful heart. But should anything occur to separate us?"

"Dear Mary," said our hero, "how could you suffer such a sad thought to enter your mind? What can ever occur to separate us but death?—which God grant may not be for many, many years yet. Come, Mary, you must banish all such melancholy ideas from your breast, for——"

He was interrupted by a knock at the door.

"Some of our neighbours called to see us, and to pass an hour or two away with us, I dare say," said Richard, going towards the door.

He opened it, and in an instant the room was filled with armed men, whose appearance showed plainly enough what they were. It was the press-gang, and Richard Parker saw at once that his fate was sealed. Mary uttered a cry of terror, and then clung frantically to her husband.

"What means this intrusion?" he firmly demanded; "what brings you here?"

"Oh, our business is soon told, shipmate," answered one of the men, who appeared to be the leader of the gang. "You see, his most gracious Majesty wants a few able seamen at present, and you are just the very man cut out for the service. It is no use offering any resistance; there is no compulsion, only you must. So, come, my lad, I must get you to accompany me on board the Sandwich, Captain Arlington."

Again Mary uttered a cry of horror, especially on hearing the name of the man whom they had so much reason to dread; and she clung to her unfortunate husband more frantically than before.

"Captain Arlington!" repeated Richard. "Ah! it is he, then, who has been the cause of this to gratify his revenge? The villain!"

"You had better not let him hear you call him so," said the man, "for he is to be your future officer."

"Oh, spare him—spare him!" shrieked the distracted Mary; "do not, I implore you, tear the husband from his wife and tender offspring! What is to become of us if he is separated from us?"

"Why, as for that matter, Missis," replied the man, "you will be better off than ever you was in your life, I'll take it; your husband will get lots of prize money, and you will receive his half-pay while he is away. Come, it is no use standing palavering here; we must to our duty."

"Forbear, I earnestly beg of you!" said our hero; "for the sake of my wife and child!'

"Oh, we must have nothing to do with those matters, shipmate," returned the fellow. "So, come along; it is of no use being obstropolus!"

"You shall not take him from me!" cried Mary, still clinging more frantically to the form of her husband. "Oh, Richard—dear Richard, speak to them—remonstrate with them; they will not—can not, surely, remain invulnerable!"

"My poor wife," ejaculated Richard, in a voice half choked with emotion, "it is useless to appeal to these men; I cannot resist my fate, and must, therefore, endeavour to meet it with manly fortitude! Farewell, beloved, best of wives! My prayers shall constantly ascend to Heaven for your welfare and that of my innocent boy; and I trust that ere long we shall meet again, no more to be parted from each other!"

Mary tried to speak as her distracted husband pressed his farewell kisses on her lips, but her emotions overpowered her, and with another cry of horror and despair, she became insensible. A female neighbour, who had been alarmed by her screams, at that moment entered the cottage, and expressed the utmost consternation at the scene which presented itself, not being at first able to understand it. It would be impossible to describe the agony of Richard Parker at that moment; again and again he kissed her pale cheeks, and those of his infant boy; but the men became impatient, and rudely seizing him, in spite of his struggles, forced him from the cottage.

It would be a task we fear our pen could not accomplish, to describe the scene of anguish which took place at their parting the following day, on board the Sandwich. Mary was conveyed in an insensible state on shore, and for several days she was almost unconscious of what was passing around her.

CHAPTER V.

THE AFFECTING MEETING OF RICHARD PARKER AND HIS WIFE.—THE TALE OF WRONGS.

Mr. TIMOTHY BUBBLE's farm-house was situated in the Isle of Grain, and it is to the exterior of that establishment we must now direct the attention of the reader. Dicky Chicken, and Dame Grouse, the housekeeper of Mr. Bubble, were engaged in conversation. This was just seven years after the events related in the preceding chapter had taken place.

"I tell you, Dame Grouse," observed Dicky Chicken, "I tell you again, you've done wrong."

"That may be," replied the dame, "but compassion, Dicky."

"Compassion!" repeated the latter; "our master never knew what compassion was, and now he's too old to scrape new acquaintances. There, while I have been with him to Portsmouth, you, left to take care of the farm-house in the Isle of Grain (and a precious island it is; very like a lark's turf afloat in a washing tub), you, as I say, left here to war with the rats and spiders, must turn the place into a lodging-house, and let my sleeping-room to a genteel young woman with a flaxen-headed little boy."

"Ah! Dicky!" said the dame, "but such a young woman! I lived servant with her father, eight or nine years ago. Ah, who then would have thought that the beautiful Mary Mason——Ah! this love!"

"Oh, it's the devil, dame," said Dicky. "But what has love done to Mary Mason?"

"Why, it made her marry imprudently," replied Dame Grouse.

"Was her husband poor?"

"Very poor; but so amiable."

"I see," remarked Dicky; "not a farthing in his pocket, but plenty of gold in his heart; a man who talks guineas, though he can't give change for any. Fathers think such youths make very bad sons-in-law."

"But a better man than Richard Parker does not live," said the dame; "though, to be sure, he's only a common sailor aboard the Sandwich here at the Nore."

"A common sailor!" repeated Dicky. "And did your young mistress marry a common sailor?"

"No, he wasn't in the navy then—he was a genteel, high-spirited young man, brought up in the same village as Mary, and when they married, her father deserted her: and then fresh troubles came."

"I see," said Dicky, with a wink; "the little flaxen-headed boy."

"And then poor Richard Parker was pressed, and went to sea; his wife has come many a long mile to meet him—she has lodged here this month."

"And Mr. Parker comes and takes tea with you here on Sundays, I suppose?"

"It is but seldom he can come ashore," answered the dame; "for, as ill-luck would have it, he who is now his captain, was his very rival in love, and persecutes him beyond all bearing. Would you believe it?—his wife doesn't know it—poor thing, 'twould break her heart—he was accused wrongfully of theft; for the criminal afterwards confessed——"

"Well?"

"And by the malice of the captain," continued Dame Grouse, "he was tried and they do say—hush! here comes my poor young lady."

"Well, truly," said Dicky, "she's a meek and pretty creature—Dame, shake me down a truss of straw anywhere; she's welcome to my bed, board, and lodging."

Mary Parker now came from the house. She was still lovely, but the paleness and melancholy expression of her countenance showed plainly the many troubles it had been her lot to encounter.

"Good dame, I—A stranger with you?" said our heroine, starting in some confusion on beholding Dicky Chicken.

"No stranger, Mrs. Parker," returned Dicky; "I'm just a remnant, a selvage belonging to the house—a thing that takes wages. Is there anything I can do for you?"

"I thank you," replied Mary, "this kindness——"

"Kindness!" repeated Dicky; "not at all! Bless you, when first I looked at you, I saw a little angel peeping out of your eyes, that said—'Dicky Chicken, do what you can for this lady.' You may laugh; I heard it, and I will do what I can for you."

"Again I thank your zeal," said Mary, "and——"

"Zeal!" interrupted Dicky; "nonsense! Now, what shall I do? Shall I snare a rabbit for your dinner—kill a chicken? I'll tell master that it died; or, if you like a relish, I'll catch some shrimps for your tea! I'm like Robinson Crusoe's rusty fire-lock, not very showy, but on an island like this, extremely useful."

"Don't talk so, Dicky, don't talk," said the dame.

"Bless me," said Dicky; "why, there's a boat landed! I'm off! Dame, come and show me the improvements about the island."

"Improvements!" repeated Dame Grouse.

"Yes," answered Dicky, who had taken her under his arm; "when I left it, there were three cabbages on the whole place : considering we have had fine weather for this last month, there may be another sprout by this time."

"Yes, Dicky," said the dame; "don't sneer at the land you live upon."

"The land!" said Dicky; "call this Isle of Grain land! Why, it lies upon the top of the water, barren and bleak, like a great fish. I never go to sleep but I fear that the island may be taken for a sleeping whale, and I have a harpoon driven right through my body."

Dicky and the dame now departed, and left our heroine to herself.

"He comes," said Mary, with a sigh, and looking anxiously towards the boat; "at every succeeding interview, I fancy I perceive a deeper gloom upon his brow; a more settled sorrow at his heart. Oh! Providence! but let me not complain; a brighter day may yet arrive."

At that moment, Richard Parker arrived, and clasping her fondly to his bosom, exclaimed—

"Mary! my own loved Mary!"

"Oh, Richard!" said our heroine, tears of joy trembling in her eyes, "this meeting repays me for all the hours so anxiously passed in silence, and in solitude. Why is this? Why do you turn your eyes from mine?"

"I—I cannot look upon you!" faltered out her husband, with much emotion.

"Not look upon me?" repeated Mary, with the most inexpressible astonishment.

"When I remember," continued Richard, "that you were wooed by fortune, had every comfort strewed about your footsteps; when I remember this, and see you torn by my hands from every hope of life—thrown a poor outcast on the unfeeling world—humiliated, broken-hearted, beggared—can you wonder if I blush to meet your eye? Can you marvel, if, like a felon, I shrink beneath your gaze, ashamed to meet the victim I have made?"

"Oh, Richard!" ejaculated his wife, "talk not so; do you think reproach can spring from love like mine? Think you I can regret the loss of wealth, and of those summer friends that clung while fortune shone? Oh, no! I am rich! rich in your love, and our darling boy."

"My poor William!" said Parker.

"Oh, away with such reproaches," cried Mary; "you have manly courage, Richard; but add to it a woman's strength."

"A woman's strength, Mary?"

"Ay, the power of sufferance; you, in the wild storm or wilder battle, hang above the heaving billow, or rush upon the sword; this, this is lion-hearted daring! But think you the sailor's wife has not a deeper courage, to listen to the roaring sea; to hear the minute-gun, to read of shipwreck and of battle, yet, with terror for her daily partner, to hush the whispering fear, and with a deep tranquillity of soul, confide in Him who feeds the sparrow, and sustains the flower? Mere courage is the instinct of brutes—'tis patience, the sweet child of reason, stamps and dignifies the man."

"My dear Mary!" said her husband; "yes, you'll love me still?"

"Love you! Though poverty and wrong had made you unjust to me—forgetful of yourself; though shame had scourged you——How now, Richard! husband!"

"'Tis nothing!" he replied, with a shudder.

"Nay," cried our heroine, in accents of the greatest anxiety, "your colour goes; the veins swell within your brow, and your lip works;—what—what have I said!"

"Nothing—nothing, my poor wench!"

"Oh, it is not so; I have awakened some horrid thoughts that still convulse and shake you—Tell me, in mercy—"

"Mary," said our hero, after a violent struggle with his feelings, "I will tell you. You spoke of shame! To a heart rightly endowed for its fellows, it is a kind of shame to see in silence wrong and outrage done to others."

"True—true; but —"

"I—I am a sailor on board a king's ship," continued her husband; "my mind may be as noble, my heart as stout as are the minds and hearts of those who stand upon the quarter-deck, and are my masters—No matter, 'tis my fate, and I should obey them."

"For Heaven's sake," said Mary, with a look of alarm, "let not the violence of your temper betray you to acts of mutiny;—have you not seen —"

"Seen!" repeated Richard; "I have served the king seven years; in that time I have seen enough to turn the softest heart to stone; to make me look with eyes of lead upon the blackest violence; to make me laugh at 'virtue,' 'feelings,' as words of a long-forgotten tongue. Seen! I have seen old men, husbands, and fathers, men with venerable gray hairs, tied up, exposed, and lashed like basest beasts: scourged, whilst every stroke of the blood-bringing cat may have cut upon a scar received in honourable fight. I have seen this; and what's the culprit's fault?—He may have trod too much on this side, or on that; have answered in a tone too high or too low his beardless persecutor;— no matter, the crime is mutinous, and the mariner must bleed for it!"

"Oh, Richard!" exclaimed his wife, with a shudder of horror, "and have you looked on scenes like these?"

"Looked!" said her husband. "Listen!—then judge you whether the gloom upon my face is but the cast of a sickly fancy, or the shadow from a deep and settled wrong. It tears my soul to shock thy delicate spirit; yet thou must know all, that in what I henceforth may do, thy mind may justify me. Dost thou hear me, Mary?"

"I'll strive to do so, Richard," replied his devoted wife, in an agitated tone.

"'Tis now some years," commenced Richard, after a brief pause, during which time he had had a violent struggle with his feelings; "'tis now some four years since I had a friend, a sailor, on board a king's vessel; his fate was somewhat like to mine, for chance had given him an unsuccessful rival in love to be his captain and his destroyer. I knew the victim, knew him! But to my tale. The sailor was preferred—rare preferment for one of cultivated mind— to wait upon the steward, and do his lofty bidding. Time wore on. At length a watch was stolen; suspicion lighted on my friend; he was charged with—my heart swells, and my brain swims round

—charged with the robbery; before the assembled crew, despite his protestations and his honest scorn, he was branded with the name of thief!"

"Oh, heavens!" exclaimed the agitated Mary.

"Stripped and bound for brutal punishment," continued Richard Parker, every muscle of his fine manly countenance convulsed with the powerful emotion of the feelings that struggled at his breast; "picture the horror, the agony of my friend, bleeding beneath the gloating eye of his late rival in a woman's love; picture his torment and despair to feel, while the stripes fell like molten lead upon his back, that keener anguish, his rival's triumph! Imagine what were his thoughts, what the yearnings of his swelling heart, towards his young wife, his precious child at home."

"Oh, horrible!" gasped forth Mary.

"A short time after he sought to escape," resumed Richard, after another brief pause; "he trusted the secret of his flight to another, and was betrayed. What followed then? He was tried for desertion, and was condemned to death."

"Gracious powers! and did they?—"

"Oh, no, the judges were merciful."

"Heaven bless them!" ejaculated Mary, fervently.

"Stay your benediction," said Richard; "they were merciful! they did not hang the man—it would have been harsh, they thought; the more so, as he who had stolen the watch, touched by compunction, had confessed the theft, clearing the deserter of the crime he had been scourged for. Still, discipline demanded punishment; they did not hang the man, and thereby bury in his grave the remembrance of his shame; no, they mercifully sent him through the fleet!"

"The fleet?"

"Listen! then wonder that men with hearts of throbbing flesh within them, can look upon, much less inflict such tortures. They sent him to receive five hundred lashes, so many at the side of every vessel, whilst the thronging crew hung upon the yards and rigging, to hear the wretch's cries, and look upon his opening wounds. What was the result? Why, the wretch they had tied up, a suffering, persecuted man, they loosen'd a raging tiger! From that moment revenge took possession of my soul. I lived, and only breathed, contented to look on the day's blessed light that I might have revenge!"

"You, husband! you!" cried Mary, with a look of the most inexpressible horror and astonishment.

"Yes, Mary Parker," replied her husband. "I am that wronged, that striped, heart-broken, degraded man!"

"Oh, Richard!" sobbed Mary, convulsively, and throwing herself upon his neck; "Heaven have mercy on them!"

"Amen!" said our hero, solemnly. "Mercy is Heaven's attribute—revenge is man's. Ay, look upon me, Mary; do you not blush to call me husband?"

"Oh, talk not so!"

"You must, for I feel degraded, a thing of scorn and restless desperation; but the time is almost ripe, and vengeance——"

"Think not of it!" said Mary, with a look of alarm.

"Think not of it?" repeated Richard. "I only live upon the hope of coming retribution. Think not of it! Would you still embrace a striped, a branded felon?"

"That stain is wiped away!" said his affectionate wife.

"No, but it shall be, and in blood!"

"In mercy, Richard——"

"Hear me swear!"

At that moment their lovely boy rushed from the house and run up to his father exclaiming in a voice of innocent joy—

"Oh, father! dear father!"

"Ah!" ejaculated Richard Parker, solemnly, and kneeling as he spoke, "be this the subject of my oath. May this sweet child, the fountain of my hopes, become my bitterest source of misery—may all my joys in him be turned to mourning and disquiet,—may he be a reed to my old age, a laughter and a jest to my gray hairs,—may he mock my dying agonies, and spit upon my grave, if, for a day, an hour, I cease to seek for a most deep, a most bloody revenge!"

"Hollo! house ahoy!" at that moment came from a voice not far off.

"A stranger's voice!" said Richard; "we are disturb. Farewell, my love! I must aboard; to-morrow you shall learn news of me. I have promised my ship-mates to bring William with me. He shall return when I do."

"Promise, then, to be more calm," said Mary; "let patience, Richard, counsel you."

"Farewell!" said Richard, once more embracing her. "Now," he added aside, "now my child shall see his father's wronger at his feet. Arlington, I come to triumph!"

Thus saying, Richard Parker and his son hurried away, and poor Mary, with a heavy heart, and her brain distracted with horror at the dreadful recital she had heard, re-entered the house.

CHAPTER VI.

THE REVOLT ON BOARD THE SANDWICH. RICHARD PARKER'S REVENGE.

RICHARD PARKER and his wife had no sooner separated, than Dicky Chicken made his appearance, followed by Jack Adams and Molly.

"This way, this way, sir," said Dicky; "I must carry it off, somehow; for if it gets to Bubble's ears that we have lodgers——"

"Heave ahead, Molly," said Adams: "I do think by the cut of his canvas it was he. I say," he added, looking at Dicky, "haven't we been in convoy before? Why, you're the very pinnace that old Bubble used to tow along. What, have you parted company?"

"Yes," answered Dicky; "I—I—the fact is, our tempers didn't agree."

"Well," observed Adams, "I should have thought you'd have sailed capitally together."

"Why?" asked Dicky.

"Why? Because he's all shark, and you're all flying-fish."

"Likely," returned Dicky: "but you see, my wings were too much for his jaws. Bless me! I beg your pardon, Miss Molly Brown; how do you do?"

"Molly Brown!" repeated Molly, tossing her head; "Mrs. Mary Adams if you please."

"Oh, changed your name?"

"Yes," replied Adams, "Molly hoists the pendant now—king's ship, you see. I always said, that when I managed to settle the mutiny at Spithead, I'd be married."

"Ah!" observed Dicky; "as soon as you got out of one, get into a greater."

"Come, Mr. Dicky," said Molly, "none of your impertinence; marriage is not to be joked at in that manner."

"A joke!" repeated Dicky; "I'm too timid to joke upon such a subject. No, thank Heaven, I treat marriage with all the respect becoming a stranger."

"Now, clap on your stopper, and set your rum afloat," said Adams.

"Rum!" repeated Dicky; "Timothy Bubble have rum in his house! Rum, did you say?"

"Did I say rum? Damme! do you think I'm talking Japanese? Rum, I said, 'R U double M—rum,' isn't that English?"

"Yes; that's English rum," replied Dicky; "but the fact is, we don't keep it, and all the Jamaica's out; we should have some nice gin, but the smugglers haven't been here some time; but I tell you what we have, delicious! What do you think of a pint, or a pint and a half—for stomachs vary—of nice, fresh skim milk?"

"What—milk!"

"With a lump of sugar at the bottom," said Dicky, "a little nutmeg at the top, and a silver spoon in the middle of it?"

"Milk!" said Adams; "why, I haven't tasted milk since I was seven month's old!"

"You should have some, now, then," returned Dicky; "it would make you again think of home and of innocent childhood."

"I tell you what, Master Dicky," remarked Adams, "unless you want my fist to run foul of your figure-head, you'll bring me a pint of real West-Ingay rum: and—and—what'll you have, Molly?"

"We have no peppermint; the anniseed is out; and we sent to Sheerness for cloves this morning," said Dicky Chicken.

"Well, then, Molly," observed Adams, "you must have some rum, too. So, do you hear? bring a pint of rum for me, and half a pint for the lady."

"You'd better let me recommend our milk," said Dicky.

"Milk!" repeated Adams; "do you want to poison us? Rum, I say."

"Well, then, to tell you the truth, there isn't a drop of spirits in the whole island."

"No! Why, when was this place made?"

"It never was made," answered Dicky; "it rose up to the top of the sea by accident."

"And if there is no rum upon it," said Adams, "the sooner it sinks to the bottom the better. Well, Molly, I'll go off to the Sandwich, and —"

"What! do you belong to the Sandwich?" asked Dicky.

"Yes," replied Adams; "you see, I and two or three of my shipmates that belonged to the Queen, have been drafted aboard other ships here at the Nore; just, you see, in case the crews should be obstropolus. Jack Adams and his loyal shipmates might set them a good example."

"Well," observed Dick, "it strikes me you'll have enough to do, for Mr. Parker was here just now."

"Parker! Damme! I said it was he. I sailed with him once; a finer fellow never put his foot on rattlin. What ship does he belong to now?"

"Why, the Sandwich."

"Here's luck!" said Adams; "goodby Molly. I'll go aboard, get fresh liberty, and bring Dick Parker with me, and we'll have a night of it."

"What, here, Mr. Adams?" said Dicky.

"Here?" replied Jack Adams. "But stop! as this is a nice quiet place for a married man, I think it shall be here. So, look you—there's money for you; paddle over to Sheerness, bring back a hogshed of rum; a chest or two of lemons, half-a-dozen loaves of sugar, and —I suppose you have water? Not that we shall want much of it."

"Beautiful water," returned Dicky, "and for all tastes, hard and soft."

"Then look alive," said Adams; "and there, Molly," he added, kissing her, "let that comfort you till I come back."

He then hurried away.

"What a considerate husband," said Dicky. "Oh, Mrs. Molly, little did I think——"

"Now, don't you stand talking here," interrupted Molly; "but go upon your errand."

"That's unkind," said Dicky; "I wished to have a little serious gossip with you. I suppose you have got Mr.

Adams's will and power ; because if any unlucky shot, and you know shots do fly upon the sea——"

"Yes, and upon land, too," added Molly, slapping his face ; " take that."

" Well I——" said Dicky, rubbing his cheeks ; "but your petticoats protect you. Now, if the lady within——"

"A lady ! who is she ?"

" Quite a lady, Mrs. Molly Adams," replied her companion ; "none of your slappers."

" Now, there's a good creature," said the curious Molly, " do tell me."

" It's Mrs. Parker, Mrs. Adams."

" Why didn't you tell me that before, Mr. Chicken ?" demanded Molly. " How lucky ! I shall have company till Adams returns. I'll run and introduce myself directly."

She hastily made her exit accordingly.

" Now," remarked Dicky, when she was gone, " here am I within call, left with three women. I begin to feel alarmed, and—Oh, dear, if Timothy Bubble, Esq., should return to his country villa, and find it turned into a house of accommodation for newly married English sailors—But I'll trust to fortune, and so, with gold in my pocket, I'll jump into the boat, and return like a West India trader, full of rum, sugar, and lemons."

With these words, he took his departure.

Jack Adams, Richard Parker, his child, and several sailors, were assembled on the quarter-deck of the Sandwich, and the two former were engaged in deep conversation.

" Well, well," said Adams, addressing himself to our hero, " I know, mate, we have had enough to complain of ; but patience : 'tis better to take the bight out of the cable than to cut it."

" Patience !" repeated Richard Parker ; " we have had patience, endured every kind of scorn, chastisement, and ruffianly contempt : endured it, until at length the spirit of man is roused, and walks abroad, and cries for vengeance !"

" I tell you, you are wrong, Dick," said Adams : " you'll have all set right by the Admiralty : you'll have your rights."

" Not till we have shown ourselves determined for them," replied Parker.

" Are we not hourly goaded, spurned. treated like dogs ? Even this very morning, ten of the crew, as bold and honest tars as ever braved a storm, or met a foe, have been placed in irons, are now below, with marines standing with loaded muskets over them. And what have these men committed ? Why, the captain did not like their looks : he thought he saw mutiny gleaming in their eye, and swelling in their lip. Act as you will, Adams, I am resolved."

" But consider a bit, Dick ; your life——"

" My life !" repeated our hero : " Heaven is my witness, I have kept it but for this hour ; let me but see that ruffian at my feet, let me but see that villain Arlington——"

He was interrupted by the entrance of Captain Arlington, attended by several officers from the cabin.

" How now ?" said Arlington, sternly. " Go forward, sir ; what, sulky again ? Boatswain's mate, turn the hands up for punishment."

There was a low murmuring among the crew.

" Why am I not obeyed ?" demanded the captain, passionately. " Oh, is it so ?"

The sailors now came forward, and crowded about our hero, who stood surveying his bitter enemy with a look of contempt.

" Now, Richard Parker," said one of the sailors, " do you speak."

" Mutiny !" exclaimed Captain Arlington. " I see it. Sir," he added, addressing himself to the captain of marines ; " march your men aft."

The captain obeyed, and the marines arranged themselves at the back.

" Now, you set of disaffected rascals," said Captain Arlington : " what would you ?"

" Richard Parker—Richard Parker !" shouted the sailors.

" I answer not that man," said Arlington, with a terrible frown.

" Parker, sir," remarked one of the crew, " is our leader ; he knows what we want :—'tis him you must speak to."

" Must ! Well, Richard Parker, I will answer you. You are leader of these wretched men ; you shall not, if I can help it, lose the reward of such honourable distinction. What do you want ?"

"Captain Arlington," replied Richard, firmly, "you bear His Majesty's commission; to you are entrusted the comforts—nay, the very lives of men who never failed to risk those lives in defence of the British flag: how have you used that commission?"

"How?" exclaimed the captain; "do you dare to question?"

"Softly, sir," returned Richard. "You see, we have dared thus much; what we may dare still further is yet to be shown."

"Insolent!"

"Fair words, sir! We have risen against the tyrant; what heed, we then, of the bully? Men, husbands, fathers, have been entrusted to your command—how have you used them?—Like beasts; their torture has been your hourly pastime; now we have resolved to wipe away the stain; we have sworn to justify the name and nature of man, violated in our persons. We will have justice!"

Captain Arlington stamped his foot, and bit his lips with rage, and at the same time he could not help feeling a sensation of dread stealing over him; while the sailors shouted aloud in admiration of the observations of Richard Parker.

"You hear that shout?" he said; "nay, I see your cheek is pale."

"Villain!" said Captain Arlington, "another word, and I'll place a bullet in your brain!"

"For Heaven's sake," said the lieutenant, aside, "be calm; the men are desperate."

"Desperate!" repeated the captain. "Well," he added, turning to the sailors, "what do you want?"

"First," replied our hero, "the release of those men placed in irons this morning; next, your solemn pledge, before these gentlemen, of better treatment towards your crew; next ——"

"I will not release the men," interrupted Captain Arlington, resolutely.

"You hear?" said Parker, to the crew.

"And as to your treatment," continued the captain, "you have nothing to complain of; I have ever been considerate, merciful ——"

"Merciful!" repeated our hero. "Oh, yes, where shall we see your mercies, Captain Arlington? Shall we see them in the worn ankles of your fettered sailors? Shall we read them in their scarred and lacerated backs? Mercies! By Heavens! an eye of stone would melt, to look upon your mercies."

"I know your personal malice," returned Arlington. "I know your drift—the watch—Yet I acted but according to my duty. Even when I punished, I did not wrong you."

"Not wrong me!" said Richard, turning to the sailors; "not—You, my shipmates, friends, beheld me branded as a thief; saw me tied up, scourged, beheld that creature look laughingly on my writhing and dishonoured frame; you saw this; saw me cleared, acquitted—what was my consolation? More stripes—deeper infamy; and yet he says he has not wronged me; says so, and the lie blisters not his tongue, but there he stands, white, cold, and as bloodless as the marble!"

"Ruffian!" exclaimed Captain Arlington, furiously.

"Three cheers for Parker!" shouted the crew.

"Men, go down below!" commanded the captain; "let every blue jacket who remains true to his king and country, walk to this side of the deck."

After a pause, Jack Adams alone walked over to the captain, and the sailors expressed their disapprobation and indignation by loud hisses.

"My lads," said Adams, "I have fought too long for my king and country to go the course you are steering now. If you have wrongs, as mayhap you have, write to the Admiralty."

"We know our course, then," said Richard Parker, firmly. "Now, my lads, three cheers, and to the work!"

The sailors parted, and then discovered the forecastle guns pointed aft, at the mouth of one of which the boy William was seated on a keg, his hand in the gun, and his head resting against it. He was fast asleep. The men ran up from below, matches were brought; our hero lighted one, and was about to fire the cannon at the end of which his child was seated, when Jack Adams rushed before the mouth of the gun, at the same time exclaiming—

"For the love of Heaven, Parker!"

"Stand back!" replied the latter, "or I fire!"

"Not upon one man, Parker," said Adams, "and he, too, unarmed—what, fire upon Jack Adams? I'm not worth powder and shot, and your friend, too!"

"We have no friends on that side of the deck," answered our hero.

"For the love of Heaven! as you love your peace of mind,—by all that's dear, do not fire!"

"Keep off!"

"If I do, I'm d—d!" cried Adams, springing forward, and snatching up the child in his arms, Parker and the crew recoiling with horror. "Would you blow off the head of your own child?"

"My boy! my boy!" ejaculated our hero, in accents of the deepest emotion. "Adams, may He in Heaven bless you for this."

"Present!" commanded Captain Arlington, suddenly seizing the boy, and placing him between two marines. "Retire! or, the first new act of disobedience, your child dies!"

"Monster!" cried Richard Parker.

"Are you ready, marines?" said Arlington.

"Stay, you, Davis!" said our hero, addressing himself to one of the marines, tucking up his sleeve, and pointing to his arm; "see you this scar? I saved your life: will you murder my child?"

This appeal was electrifying; the two marines shouldered their arms, and their example was followed by the others. Adams caught up the child in his arms, the marines retreated over to Adams and his party, the officers threw down their swords, and the villain Arlington crouched at the feet of the man he had so deeply injured, while Richard Parker stood over him in triumph.

CHAPTER VII.

THE PERILOUS SITUATION OF RICHARD PARKER — THE AFFECTING INTERVIEW BETWEEN HIM AND HIS WIFE. HIS NARROW ESCAPE.

THE sensation which the events we have just related excited in all parts of the kingdom, was immense; but the agony and alarm of poor Mary Parker at the fearful situation in which her unfortunate husband had placed himself was almost indescribable.

Mr. Timothy Bubble had returned to his house in the Isle of Grain, and in the course of one of his rambles he accidentally encountered Molly Adams; from her he learnt the particulars of her marriage, much to his own chagrin and disappointment.

"And so, you are spending the honeymoon here?" he said. "Well, Molly Brown—I mean Mrs. Adams—as what is done is past remedy, and you have chosen Jack Adams, in preference to Timothy Bubble, Esq., late clerk, now landholder here in the Isle of Grain, why, there's no help for it."

"Certainly, Mr. Bubble," replied Molly: "that's a very sensible remark."

"So, as love is quite out of the question," observed Bubble, "what do you think of friendship?"

"Oh, I can have no objection to friendship."

"Very true;—so, when Mr. Adams goes to sea—and the fleet will be off in a day or two —"

"No, indeed!" interrupted Molly; "not till Admiral Parker ——"

"Admiral Parker!" repeated Bubble; "here's rapid promotion!—but there's yet a higher destiny for him. Molly, his Admiralship isn't worth a biscuit—I heard it all at Sheerness. Bless you, all the crews have come to terms; the government has acceded to everything—and at this very moment there's marines in all directions to apprehend the *Admiral.*"

"Mercy on me!" ejaculated the thoughtless Molly, "I must run and give him notice."

"Notice!" said the astonished Mr. Bubble. "What! you don't know where he is?"

"Yes, he is—But may I trust you? Will you betray the generous and unfortunate?"

"Look at my face, Molly," returned the crafty Timothy; "did you ever see more honesty crowded into one set of features?"

"Well, then," said Molly, "he and his wife are now at the same inn that we are."

"Inn!" repeated Mr. Bubble; "inn! here!—What! at the Isle of Grain? Well, I've just returned from Portsmouth, after an absence of six weeks; and when I started from here, the devil an inn was there in the whole island."

"Oh, but there is now," said Molly, "and your late man, Dicky Chicken, is waiter there."

"Why, it isn't the thatched house at the corner of the field?"

"Yes, but it is."

"The rascal!" said Timothy, aside; "he's been turning my mansion into a tavern, and taking in all customers that offered.—Oh, and Dicky is waiter there?"

"Yes; and see, here he comes."

Dicky Chicken now made his appearance with a basket on his shoulder.

"Well," he said, "I've brought the fowls, the quarter of lamb, and the green peas; and, ecod!—we'll make a dinner of it. Let me see—there's the Parkers, the Adamses, Dame Grouse, Dicky Chicken, and—and ——"

"The Bubbles," added Timothy.

"Master!" cried Dicky, starting, and letting the basket fall.

"Surely you'll let your old master take a snack?" said Bubble. "How much is your ordinary at the—the—what's the sign of your house?"

"The—the—the devil!"

"Indeed! an odd sign to paint."

"Oh, we have no need to paint it now," returned Dicky.

"Why?" demanded Bubble.

"The original is just come to hand," said Timothy, going.

"Stop!" said Bubble; "don't leave me here; for as the island is so much altered during my absence, it may be difficult to find out my way—I suppose your house is not very full?"

"Why, really, I've just met with more company than I know what to do with."

"Never mind," said Mr. Bubble, "you can put me anywhere."

"Yes, anywhere will do for Mr. Bubble," said Molly.

"Oh, yes," remarked Timothy, "in the attic."

"Or the cellar," said Molly.

"Or the hayloft."

"Or the horse-pond," muttered Dicky, aside.

"Here's a condition I'm in!"

"Now, lead the way, Dicky," said his master; "Mrs. Adams and I will follow."

"What will become of me?" aids poor Dicky, aside. "This way, sir;—I've no other chance than to turn sailor and run for it."

"We follow," said Bubble; "and when Mr. Parker's disposed of," he added, to himself, "I'll lay you by the heels, depend on it. Am I far from the house?"

"Not so far as I could wish," thought Dicky.

"Bless me!" said Bubble, "the paths are very dirty."

"All your paths generally are," muttered Dicky.

"But I suppose I shall soon get to my journey's end?" remarked old Bubble.

"Not so soon," again muttered Dicky Chicken to himself; "for there isn't a gibbet in the whole island."

"And I'll reward you, Dicky, be assured," said Mr. Bubble, ironically.

"As for the reward, sir," returned Dicky, as his master and Mrs. Adams took their departure, "the pleasure of doing good ——"

"Yes—yes," said Bubble, as he retired, "I know all about that."

"Do you?" observed Dicky, when he was gone. "It's very recently, I take it. My only refuge is a blue jacket, and in half an hour ends my profession of landlord and waiter. Oh! that he might stick his foot into a clay-pit, and wait till I came to deliver him!"

And what were the feelings of poor Mary Parker during this dreadful period? —Who can attempt to describe her anxiety for the critical position of her husband, hunted down as he now was like some wild beast?—That he had wrongs, great and manifold to complain of, after the fearful recital she had heard from him, she could not but admit; and how deeply did it wring her heart when she reflected upon the ignominious and unmerited degradation he had received. But still she lamented that the impetuosity of his temper had led him to adopt the desperate course he had, the more especially as she heard that the principal portion of those men upon whose fidelity he had relied had deserted him. The predictions of Mad Molly flashed upon her memory in the most vivid colours. They were in part fulfilled; and in the anticipation of the future, the devoted wife was truly wretched.

They were seated in one of the rooms of Timothy Bubble's house, engaged in deep and earnest conversation, and the tears were fast streaming down our heroine's cheeks.

"Your fears wrong the brave men whose cause I have championed," said Richard. "What! when I have ventured all, when I have stood forward as a mark for peril, think you they would fall from me now?"

"No, Richard, no," replied his wife, whose face was ghastly pale, and the convulsive heaving of her bosom plainly showed the deep agony she was suffering. "And yet, 'tis a desperate stake for which you play."

"Desperate evil," returned our hero, his fortitude and self-possession never for an instant forsaking him, "requires a desperate remedy; but even say I am offered up a sacrifice——"

"Oh, talk not so," sobbed Mary, "think of your child; think of me, Richard!"

"Nay," said her husband, "it is a noble practice of the mind to fortify itself for the worst, that, when the blow is dealt, it finds us armed for the buffet. But let giddy fortune change as she will, let her make me her meanest toy, her most wretched plaything, still, still I am revenged!"

"Oh! and what is vengeance, if——"

"What is vengeance?" interrupted Richard Parker, his features animated with the power of his feelings. "By my soul, when I saw that villain prostrate, when I beheld the tyrannical, black-hearted Arlington writhing like a crushed worm at my foot; when I beheld his terror in his ashy cheek, saw him crouch like a serpent-cur beneath my glance—by Heaven! in that fleet exulting moment, I lived a joyous year of life! Death, come when it may, has lost half its anguish, for I die revenged!"

"Death, Parker!" said Mary, with a shudder of horror; "what mean you? Why speak you thus familiarly of death?"

"It must come one day, Mary."

"Oh, yes," returned his wife, "but when it finds you, may it find you ripe in years; may it find you circled by your children's children, rich in their love, honoured by the respect of all men—may you sink from life as into a gentle sleep, and when all is hushed, may one grave tenant you and Mary!"

"Amen! amen!" said Richard, with the deepest emotion.

"Nay," said his wife, hastily, and with the strongest anxiety depicted in her countenance; "you are moved with some terrible fears—a tear trembles in your eye—Parker, by our early days of love—when life——"

"Life! oh, Mary, once, how beautifully rose the world before me!—with what a deep and fervent love I looked upon all my fellows—with what a rich creative fancy I pictured all around me with objects tender and beautiful; the world was, in reality, all that I have pictured since of Paradise. Your smile gave a brighter sunshine to the earth; your voice gave a deeper music to my ears! Poverty marked me with her felon brand; my heart's sanctuary was violated, for I was torn from you, from my babe, torn, degraded, and now—"

"Oh," interrupted his wife, "do not sadden the aspect of the present by remembrances of the past."

"Nay," returned Richard; "such recollection has a sweet and bitter feeling: wretched is the man, who, looking back on thirty years, exclaims—'There is no hour I fain would live again!'"

At this moment, Jack Adams rushed into the room, hastily.

"Adams!" said Parker, somewhat surprised.

"Ay, shipmate," replied the former, "even Jack Adams. Avast a bit, Dick," he added, as our hero was about to leave the room, "you and I have been old friends."

"I forgot that the moment you crossed the quarter deck of the Sandwich," replied Richard.

"Well, then," returned the warm-hearted seaman, "I mean to say that you shouldn't have made such clear decks of your memory; and yet, Master Richard, it's as well I did make that Jack, for, had I gone on your side, I couldn't have well seen your child's head in——"

"Adams, forgive me," interrupted our hero, and at the same moment cordially grasping his hand; "bless you, Adams! It should seem I were fated to remember only injuries"

"I say," said Adams to him aside, "get your wife to part convoy."

"Mary," said her husband, "leave me."

"Leave you?" repeated our heroine.

"Ay, you heard me."

"Husband," sobbed Mary, in accents of the deepest anguish; "this is my first act of disobedience,—but I—I will not leave you; there is,—I see it—oh! too well—there is some danger!"

"No, no danger in the least," answered Adams, "only a little squall. It will soon blow over."

"Proceed, Adams," said our hero; "you'll find her a true sailor's wife. What threatens?"

"Why," answered Adams, "the Admiralty has given all that was asked."

"Then, I am rewarded," exclaimed Richard.

"Yes," faltered out Adams, "only, you see—you see——"

"Come, out with it."

"There's a bit of an afteraccount about the ringleaders," said Adams.

"As I suspected," returned our hero, coolly. "Well?"

"They've agreed," again faltered out Adams, "that—that—you see, they—da—n it! it's all coiled up in my throat, and I can't get it out. Thus it is, Dick: the Admiralty, as a price for giving what is asked, demand that you shall be given up to them."

"Oh, husband! husband!" ejaculated the terrified Mary, "that it should ever come to this!"

"Hush, Mary, hush!" said her husband.

"The marines are out after you, with Captain Arlington, so much does he want to take you, at their head," observed Jack Adams, in a whisper.

"Ha!" exclaimed Richard Parker. "I'm glad of that. If I die——"

"Die!" interrupted Adams; "pretty fellow you are here, with a wife and child, and talk of dying! Now, I'll tell you what you shall do. I've taken a lot of prize-money—get a fellow lying in a creek here, with a lugger; you, and your wife, with your boy, bless their hearts, both on 'em! you jump into it; land on the Essex coast; then—here's a plan for you—when you go there, get quite inland, change your name, mount a smock-frock, take a little cottage,

keep a cow and some pigs; and then, with your wife and your dear babies, live till you are as old as Monkey Island."

"Oh, Richard," said his wife, anxiously, "let us haste."

"And have you such friendship towards a mutineer?" asked Parker.

"When you were aboard the Sandwich, and carrying the day, I treated you as a mutineer," answered Adams; "now you are here, and in distress, why, now, I only see my friend. But, come, we've no time to patter. Here, Dick," he added, giving our hero a purse; "and take a sailor's good wishes with it. If you and I meet again, we'll have a stiff can together; if not, I shall sometimes, in the middle watch, think of Dick Parker; and you, mayhap, at your cottage-fire of a night, when the wind blows, may drink a cup of your home-brewed to the health of Jack Adams."

"Now then, Richard," said his wife, eagerly, and bringing William, their son, forward.

"Come along," said Adams, "I'll show you the way; and whilst I pilot a friend in trouble, an innocent woman, and a helpless child, it must be a cruel quicksand that—Ha! Parker, stand to your guns—the red jackets!"

He had scarcely given utterance to the words, when Captain Arlington and several marines entered the room.

"Here is the culprit!" said Arlington, pointing to Richard Parker; "seize him!"

"Mercy—mercy! Captain Arlington!" shrieked Mary.

"Madam," returned Arlington, "once you knew not the word. Advance!" he added, addressing himself to the marines. They moved towards Parker, who drew his cutlass, and in a determined voice, said—

"The first man that stretches forth his hand, I'll cleave to the earth."

The marines recoiled.

"Cowards!" cried Captain Arlington, passionately, "draw, and secure him!"

Still the marines hesitated, daunted by the determined demeanour of our hero, and moved to pity by the melancholy situation of his wife and child; and, with a fearful oath, he rushed upon

Parker and struggled violently with him; but it was only brief; our hero drew a pistol from his belt, and discharging the contents at his head, he sank a corpse at the feet of the appalled Mary.

The marines were petrified to the spot with astonishment and horror, and were unable to act. Richard Parker, with remarkable presence of mind, took advantage of their confusion, and taking

THE ATTEMPT TO CAPTURE RICHARD PARKER.

the arm of his wife, who held their boy, he led her from the room, without any obstruction, and they were soon hurrying on their way towards the place to which Jack Adams had so earnestly directed them.

CHAPTER VIII.

TIMOTHY BUBBLE AND DICKY CHICKEN. —THE FLIGHT OF RICHARD PARKER AND HIS WIFE.—THE STORM.

IT may well be imagined the sensation which the death of Captain Arlington, and the escape of Richard Parker and his wife and child caused. Persons were sent in pursuit of them in all directions, and large rewards were offered for their apprehension, but without success; not the least clue could be discoverd as to the place of their retreat.

It may, perhaps, be unnecessary to inform the reader that it was the officious Mr. Bubble who had given the information to Captain Arlington, which brought him and the marines to his house; but he had never bargained for such a result, and he was in a considerable state of excitement when he heard of it.

"Bless my soul!" he said, running from his house, "here's an event! What a rascal! But he'll be hanged if he's taken, and that can't be long first. Mr. Richard Parker will swing for it; there's comfort still."

At this moment Dicky Chicken arrived at the spot.

"What, you're here, are you?" he said, addressing himself to his late master. "Well, you have made a fine morning's work of it."

"Done my duty, Chicken," replied Bubble; "done my duty, I tell you; I shall sleep the sounder for it."

"Sounder!" said Dicky; "and don't you expect the ghost of the murdered captain to put his head throught the curtains, and call upon you all the long night?"

"The ghost—murdered!" said Bubble, alarmed; "why, Chicken, what do you mean?"

"Don't you know that Parker has shot the captain?" asked Dicky.

"Oh, the traitor!" replied Bubble, with pretended astonishment. "You know I didn't see the business: I've a horror of steel and gunpowder. I heard the report of fire-arms, and then I ran."

"Why, what could you expect?" demanded Dicky. "What business had you to tell the marines where he was? They were passing your house, and if you hadn't called to them, like an old raven as you are——"

"A what?"

"A raven! I've said it! Nay, a vulture, a wild cat, a——"

"And do you know who I am?" interrupted Mr. Bubble.

"Yes," answed Dicky; "haven't I just told you?"

"Do you know that I've the power of hanging you?" said Bubble; "haven't you turned my house into a nest for mutineers?"

"Mr. Bubble!"

"Well, sirrah?"

"That for you!" said Dick, snapping his fingers contemptuously at him; "that for you, Mr. Bubble."

"Why," said the enraged Timothy; "you—I'll lay you by the heels, you—Here! hilloa!"

"Take my advice now—don't raise your voice."

"And why not, sir?" demanded Bubble.

"Because," answered Dicky, "if any of the sailors (and there are a few of them about the island) should happen to hear you, they'd crack your skull as soon as they'd crack a biscuit."

"Here's a reward for doing my duty! But I discard you."

"Discard!" repeated Dicky; "you don't suppose I'd live in your house after the blood that's been shed there?"

"Blood! Phoo! phoo! what of that?"

"What!" said Dicky; "only fancy, now, on a bleak winter's night, the wind howling outside, the rain coming hissing down the chimney, you sitting alone, for nobody will come near you——"

"Now, don't—don't!" said Bubble, shuddering.

"You sitting alone, thinking of all the knaveries of your wicked life; then by degrees, you are afraid to look about you: then you try to whistle, but it won't do; go to your money-chest, but for once the gold in it doesn't make your eyes sparkle, or your fingers clutch together; then you draw up to the fireside——"

"Chicken—Chicken!"

"The fire burns black, and the candle runs in the socket; the death-watch is ticking in the wall, the cat looking up at you with her green and yellow eyes; Bob, the mastiff, howling in the yard, and the sea-gulls shrieking at the window——"

"Now, don't!—d—don't!"

"And there you sit, cold as a rock," continued Dicky; "and the sweat stands upon your face like water on feathers, and you hear your heart beat, and you breathe as if by stealth——"

"Chicken, I say, Chicken!"

"And then if they should take poor Richard Parker and hang him, his ghost rises before you, and the captain's, all over blood, and poor Mary Parker, in her grave-clothes, and then they rush and whirl about you, and laugh, and point, and mock at you; you try to shout, but your voice dies in your throat —your veins swell like whip-cord in your forehead—your brain is turned to ice; terror shakes your soul from out of your body, and when daylight comes, the neighbours find you black and stiffened in your chair; then——"

"Hold—hold!" gasped forth the terrified Mr. Bubble, seizing Dicky convulsively; "I—I have been to blame."

"I believe you have," said Chicken. "Blame? why——"

"You buccaneer!" shouted Jack Adams, rushing forward, and seizing Bubble; "if I haven't as good a mind to send your life on liberty——"

Bubble, who was greatly terrified, sunk on his knees.

"Don't, Adams, don't hurt him," said Dicky; "you see he's on his knees."

"Knees!" repeated Jack Adams: "what! and is such a grampus as this to have one of the finest men that ever handled rope boused up to the yard-arm? and to think it's all made square again if he falls upon his marrow-bones? Why, I should think no more of putting a bullet into you than I should of throwing grains into a porpoise."

"But they haven't taken Mr. Parker, have they?" said Dicky.

"They haven't," answered Adams; "but no thanks to this lubber."

"Let me go—let me go!" said the terrified Timothy Bubble. "I'm an old man!"

"An old man!" repeated Jack Adams. "The more shame for you; those who have but little time to do duty in this world, should take care to do such things as will best count for them in the voyage to come."

"True, true," stammered out Bubble; "only let me go for this time, and I——"

"Scud, then, you piratical rascal!"

said Jack Adams; "and as for your rhino, if you have any, I'll tell you what to do with it."

"What?"

"When you die—and a black heart like yours can't thump much longer— leave it to Greenwich Hospital."

"Why—why, Master Adams?" asked Bubble.

"Why," answered Adams, "'cause it's the only return you can make to the service for having robbed it of so brave a fellow as Richard Parker."

"I'll think of it," said Bubble.

"Yes, think of it!—But shove off your boat."

"I'm going, Mr. Adams."

"Off, I say," said Adams, shouldering him.

"I'm gone, Mr. Adams," said Bubble, abruptly making his exit.

"Poor Dick Parker!" said Adams.

"Should they take him, will there be no hope?" asked Chicken.

"Oh, no," replied Adams; "they will be sure to make quick work of it; they are certain to find him guilty, and, poor fellow, they'll hang him off hand."

"Lor, bless me! Will they, though?"

"Ah, that they will," said Adams; "however, I hope they'll not take him."

"And so do I, I'm sure, most sincerely," said Dicky Chicken.

"Farewell, shipmate," observed Adams; "I must aboard."

"Stop!" said Dicky; "as for living with old Bubble, I'd sooner live with Beelzebub; so, I've been thinking that I'll even turn sailor."

"Well said," returned Adams. "The Sandwich wants hands; come with me, and we'll have you on the books. Poor Dick!—poor Dick! but d—n whimpering. Let's put a stout heart on the matter, and face misfortune boldly—he may escape after all—poor Dick!—poor Dick!"

Thus saying, Adams departed, accompanied by Dicky Chicken.

It would be a difficult task to attempt to describe the anguish of Mary Parker's mind after the appalling event which we have related in the previous chapter; but her fears for the safety of her husband overpowered every other feeling, and for some time she suffered him to lead her with hurried steps towards the place to which Jack Adams had directed them in silence; but at length, exhausted, she was compelled to pause to take breath, and had it not been for the support of her husband, she must have fallen to the earth. Parker, however, was firm, and his boy bore it with more fortitude than could have been expected.

"Oh, Richard," at length sobbed his wife, "what a horrible event is this! Would to Heaven that you had not taken the life of Arlington."

"Ay," said Parker, "my hands are stained with human blood; and I am convinced that you must henceforward look upon me with repugnance and horror. Leave me, Mary—abandon me to that fate which I feel must shortly overtake me."

"Leave you, Richard?" said Mary.

"Yes," replied her husband; "for why should one so pure and innocent as yourself, follow the fortunes of a wretch like me? I am a doomed man, an ignominious death is before me, and—"

"Oh, hold, dear Richard," said our heroine. "You drive my brain to madness by giving utterance to such terrible words as these. And think you so meanly of my love as to imagine I could abandon you in the midst of your troubles? No, no, my husband, I am still your affectionate, your devoted wife; whatever your sorrows, I will share them with you; whatever your fate, that fate shall also be mine."

"Alas, Mary!" said her husband, "you know not what you say; my fate is sealed—that fate is death, and——"

"Oh, no—no—no!" interrupted Mary, with a look of horror; "that can never be. Providence it its infinite mercy will not permit it; you will escape, and in some distant part of the country, we may live unknown and unpersecuted; and happily in the tranquillity of the future, learn to forget the bitter sorrows of the past."

"Oh, Mary, beloved wife!" said Richard Parker, "I feel how fallacious are such hopes. It is not possible that I can long remain concealed, so vigilant will be the search that will be made for me; but were it not for you, and our poor boy here, I could meet death without a murmur, since I have gratified my revenge in the blood of the villain Arlington."

"For Heaven's sake do not give utterance to such frightful words as these, Richard. Would to God that you had never encountered the guilty man, Arlington."

"It was what I longed for, prayed for," returned Richard; "and had not the gratification been allowed me, I should have been miserable; but oh, Mary, it wrings my heart to think what will become of you and my poor boy when I am taken from you."

"You will not be taken from me, Richard," said his wife. "I feel convinced that the Almighty will look down with pity and mercy upon us, and will not allow such a calamity to take place."

"It would be cruel to encourage you to entertain such hopes which can never be realised," said her husband. "My fate may be retarded, but cannot be avoided. Do not flatter yourself with any such thoughts, but endeavour to prepare yourself to meet with fortitude the awful trial which inevitably awaits you. Whither can I fly?—where shelter myself from the hands of justice?"

"Oh, Richard," said Mary, "we have not a moment to lose; let us hasten to the lugger Adams spoke of, and if we can only reach the Essex coast in safety, disguised, we may effectually avoid discovery."

Richard Parker shook his head despairingly, as he replied,—

"Alas, Mary, I feel too well convinced that that is impossible! Oh, what a wretch have I been!"

"A wretch, Richard? Oh, why thus cruelly, thus unjustly reproach yourself?"

"It is just, my poor wife! I am a degraded, guilty wretch, and doubly so for having brought you to misery and shame! Oh, when I think of your days of innocence and happiness, of which I deprived you, it drives me mad! Mary, it was a fatal hour when first we met."

"Why so, dear Richard?" demanded his wife.

"Because," answered Richard Parker, "had we never seen each other, you might still have been wealthy—happy—instead of being the wife of a branded felon—a—a murderer!"

"A murderer!" gasped forth Mary, with a shudder of horror.

"Yes," returned her husband; "is it not so?—Would it not be madness for me to deny it?—Are not my hands, I say again, polluted with human blood?—and what can I expect but a murderer's fate?"

"Oh, God! Richard!" exclaimed Mary, "those fearful words! For the love of Heaven cease to talk thus, or you will drive me to distraction! Come—come! let us on our way, for every moment that we tarry here is fraught with the most terrible danger!"

"Flight is useless," said Richard, "for our pursuers will be sure to overtake us, and —"

"Ah!" interrupted Mary, with a faint shriek of terror, and suddenly looking round, "by Heaven we have delayed too long! Oh, Richard, why did you not take my advice in the first instance? See—see! the marines are approaching us! My God, we are lost!"

"Be firm, Mary," said her husband, embracing her tenderly; "they dare not harm you or our child; as for myself, I am perfectly resigned to the fate which inevitably awaits me. Let them come and seize their prey, I will not shrink from my destiny, since Providence so wills it; Richard Parker has often faced death in its most awful shapes, and they shall find that he is still prepared to meet it like a man. But this brief moment to bid you and our innocent offspring farewell, and then ——"

"Oh, let us fly!" again interrupted the distracted and devoted wife; "they have not yet observed us—we may still escape. Quick! quick!"

"Nay, my beloved Mary," returned our hero; "it is only retarding the fate that is certain to overtake me. Be firm—be firm, and resigned; pardon me, best of women and of wives, for the misery into which I have brought you; my boy—my William, endeavour to prove yourself a better man than your unfortunate father; be faithful to your king and country—be faithful to your fellow-men, and look back upon the memory of the author of your being with reverence. Mary—William, it is but a brief parting; to the protection of the Almighty God, who knows the honesty, the integrity, the nobility, and generosity of my motives, I commit you! Now let the bloodhounds pounce upon their prey as soon as they will; I have zealously and sincerely endeavoured to do my duty toward my fellow creatures. I have resisted cold-hearted oppression to the very death; I have been avenged, and, thank Heaven, I can die resigned, and with confidence in the mercy that will be extended to me hereafter."

"For the love of God, Richard!" ejaculated his wife, "do not thus abandon yourself to a fate which you may still avoid."

"How avoid it, Mary?" demanded our hero, looking towards the marines, whom he could see in the distance; "I would fain do so, though life is no longer precious to me, for your sake and that of our child."

"Father! dear father!" said the poor boy; "you will not leave me and poor mother thus? Oh! what would become of us in the world without you? Father! see, they come!—Mother! beloved mother, talk to him, and——"

"Husband!" cried Mary, looking frantically and appealingly in his face, "can you resist the supplications of this innocent child? They have not, I repeat, yet observed us; this shelving rock conceals us from their view. It is madness to hesitate, when the means of escape are offered to us."

"Escape!" repeated Richard Parker; "they are immediately upon our track, and it is impossible that we can escape them. Whither can we fly? Where conceal ourselves?"

"See, Richard," replied his wife, hastily, and at the same time pointing to a shed just off the road-side: "there we have the means of concealment, and, if Fortune deserts us not, they will pass by without having the curiosity to search for us there. Come, come, dear Richard; there is not an instant to lose."

Parker made use of no further observation, but followed his devoted wife and child into the shed or outhouse to which she had directed his attention, and they had scarcely done so when they heard the heavy tread of the marines, as they advanced toward the spot.

The moon had just risen, and shone brilliantly, and through the various chinks and cracks in the planks of which the frail building was constructed, the unfortunate fugitives had a full opportunity of observing all that passed outside. Mary's heart palpitated violently against her side, with the anxiety of her feelings, and the terror that held all her faculties, as though it were, spell-bound; while the boy, William, clung to his father's knees, and felt all the terrible anxiety and anguish that his parents did, though he could not express his emotions so explicitly.

"See!" said our hero, looking through one of the chinks; "they come; they are approaching in the immediate direction of the place of our concealment. They have observed us. Mary, farewell! It is useless to attempt to avoid a fate which, as I before observed, is inevitable. Bless you, bless you!—Bless you, my poor boy—I——"

"Hush — hush!" interrupted Mary Parker, in a stifled voice, "they are here;—they may not think of searching this place. There is yet hope! God, look down in mercy upon us!"

As she spoke, the marines arrived outside the shed, and there paused.

"Well," observed the leader of them, "I begin to think this is a fruitless errand of ours. The panic which the murder of Captain Arlington caused in us all, gave Parker sufficient time and opportunity to escape; and, if I must acknowledge the real sentiments of my mind, I would much rather that any one had the chance of apprehending him than myself, if it be only out of consideration for his beauteous wife and innocent child!"

"Pardon me, captain," said one of the men, "but I think we ought not to abandon the pursuit so readily. Duty is duty; and we must not flinch from it. Richard Parker is a mutineer and a murderer; and justice demands that the laws of the land should be vindicated! I could almost swear that I saw some persons lingering near this spot. Had we not better examine this shed?"

"Well, Martin," returned the captain, "perhaps you are right, though I do not expect that we shall make any discovery, notwithstanding. This to me seems not to be a very likely place where any one would attempt to conceal themselves. However, we will e'en inspect it."

"My God!" gasped forth our heroine, when she heard these words, "what will become of us? We are lost!—Ah, quick, Richard, child!—This straw!"

There was a large heap of straw in one corner of the hovel, and poor Mary drew her husband and child hastily towards it, and prostrating themselves, they, with the quickness of thought, concealed themselves beneath it, just as the captain of the marines, at the head of his men, entered the place.

"Bring forward the lantern," said the captain, addressing himself to one of his followers. The man obeyed, and the captain and the others surveyed the place minutely.

"Well, Martin," said the captain, "what think you of it now? We have nothing here to discover, I imagine, unless it be a colony of rats. Come—come, we are only wasting our time by remaining here. My opinion is that Parker and his wife are concealed somewhere on the island, in the house of a friend; but we have not yet got on the right scent, and what is more, though I am a loyal man, I do not care if we never do. Follow me, lads."

The captain led the way, and the marines followed him according to his commands, and the heavy tramping of their feet gradually receded in the distance. The unfortunate fugitives came from the place of their concealment, and sinking on their knees, fervently clasping their hands together, Mary exclaimed—

"Great and merciful God, I thank Thee for this deliverance! We are saved, husband! we are saved!"

"For the moment only," said Richard. "Oh, Mary! it would be cruel in me to flatter you with any such delusive hopes. The hand of Fate is upon us, and we cannot avoid its decrees."

"Oh, talk not so!" ejaculated his affectionate wife, looking in his face with an expression of countenance that moved his very soul with the most powerful and indescribable emotion; "we shall be saved, dear Richard, I feel convinced that we shall, if you do not thus give yourself up to despair. It is evident that our pursuers entertain not the least suspicion as to the course we have adopted; they believe us to be concealed in the house of some one on the island. Come, then, for we have not a moment to lose; let us hasten on our way towards the place which Adams has indicated to us, and before many hours have elapsed, we shall be far beyond the reach of detection."

"My dear Mary," said our hero, "for your sake, I will exert myself, though, alas! I know full well it is all to no purpose. My hours are numbered, and——"

"Oh, horrible! Richard—husband!" gasped forth Mary. "Why give way to this awful state of despair? Our enemies are not upon our track; the kind-hearted Adams, I am certain, would not deceive us; he has liberally supplied us with pecuniary means—the world is before us; let us but reach the creek, we no doubt shall find the vessel waiting for us, and, I say again, in a few hours we shall be far beyond the reach of danger. The excitement which these unfortunate events have excited, will, in time, pass away, and in some secluded part of the country we may in future live unknown and unmolested."

"Alas!" said Richard Parker, "what madness would it be to encourage such hopes. Think you that my enemies will fail to pursue me to the last extremity? —to destruction—to death?"

"To death!" repeated our heroine, with a shudder of horror. "Oh, Richard!"

"Ay, it is even so," replied her husband. "Mary, it would be cruel, it would be bitter mockery in me to seek to deceive you with false hopes in this our last awful trial! For the present moment I may escape from them. But am I not a murderer? Though it was a villain of the blackest dye whom I slew, and from whom I had received such injuries as man has seldom endured, yet it is useless, it would be idle to call my offence by any other or milder name, and therefore, what hope of mercy is there for me? And why should a poor degraded, broken-hearted wretch like myself wish to live? My sun of hope and happiness is set for ever, and the grave alone presents itself as the resting-place from my earthly misery."

"Richard—dear Richard! do you still love me?" sobbed our heroine, throwing her fair arms around his neck.

"Do I still love you?" replied her husband, straining her to his bosom, while the tears, despite of all his efforts to the contrary, trembled upon his manly cheeks.—"Oh! why ask me such a question? Do I love you, Mary?—Oh, what a heartless, insensible villain I must be, did I not, if possible, love you even ten times more for this generous devotedness! 'Tis that feeling which wrings my heart in this terrible hour of trial more than all the horrors of the doom that is in store for me. My God!—my God! what a wretch have I been to bring you into the difficulty in which you are now placed. But for me, you might now have been happy, surrounded by every means of luxury and enjoyment; it is I who have deprived you of all this—it is I who have made you a felon's wife—brought down upon your head a father's curse, and made you a wretched outcast upon the world. It is fit that I should pay the penalty of my guilt, and I would not murmur at it, could I by my death make atonement for the wrongs I have done you; could I be assured that when my cold remains are mingled with their native dust, you could blot from your memory the name of such an unhappy being as Richard Parker, and become the happy wife of one more worthy of you, but who could never love you more than I have done."

"Richard, your words frenzy me! Each cruel word that you have uttered has pierced my heart with the murderous keenness of the dagger's point. Oh! how have I deserved this? What has there been in my conduct to cause these doubts? But your brain is distracted—you know not what you say. Come, come, let us away, I implore you; why do we tarry here, when every moment is so fraught with danger? The darkness of the night will shield us from detection, and should we any longer delay, the man whom Mr. Adams has employed to assist us in our escape will imagine that we are not coming, and depart from the place where we are to meet him. If you love me, if you love our child, if you would not drive us to misery and despair, you will no longer hesitate. Come, husband, come."

"I yield, Mary," replied our hero: "and may God in His infinite mercy protect us!"

Once more they knelt down and fervently offered up their supplications to the Supreme, and then becoming somewhat more firm and calm, Richard took the arm of his wife, and laying hold of the hand of William, they emerged from the place in which they had concealed themselves, and entered upon the open country.

They looked anxiously and fearfully around them as far as their eyes could penetrate through the darkness of the night (for the moon was now obscured by ponderous clouds, which portended a coming storm), but perceiving no human being, fresh courage re-animated their bosoms, and they proceeded on their way towards the creek to which Jack Adams had directed them, and which was little more than a quarter of a mile distant. Neither of them ventured to give utterance to a word as they went on their way, and, notwithstanding all their efforts to the contrary, they could not subdue the fears and misgivings which took possession of their breasts. Suddenly, however, the moon having once more peeped out fitfully from behind a cloud, they imagined they beheld the dim shadow of a human form before them, and advancing towards them, and they started back alarmed, Mary clinging with distracted eagerness to her husband, and watching the approaching form, which every instant became more distinct, with a delirious eye.

" It is too late," said Richard Parker; " we are discovered, and there is no chance to escape. But at present there seems to be only one of them, and since it has arrived at this crisis, I will at least sell my life and liberty dearly."

As he spoke, he drew a pistol from his belt and cocked it.

" Richard, dear Richard," cried his distracted wife, " what, oh, what would you do?"

" Mary," replied her husband, " this is no time to hesitate ; Heaven pardon me for what I am driven by desperation to do, and for all the sins I have committed ; to its care I commit you and our child. Be firm, my beloved wife, for this is indeed an hour of dreadful trial. See, the form approaches nearer. It is evident that it beholds us, and—"

" Hold—hold !" said our heroine, grasping his arm, and shuddering with horror, " would you thus coolly and deliberately shed the blood of one who

perhaps means us no harm? You must be mad, Richard, or you would never allow such terrible thoughts to enter your mind."

" Mad—mad !" repeated her husband, wildly ; " yes, I am mad ! Mary, do not attempt to withhold my hand, for I am determined."

" Nay, then," replied his wife, resolutely releasing her hold, and starting before him, holding the child in her arms ; " so am I ! The contents of the pistol you hold in your hand, Richard Parker, ere they reach their destined object, must first pass through the bodies of your wife and child !"

" Mary !" gasped forth her husband, in a hollow voice, starting back aghast, and dropping the pistol.

" Ay, husband !" returned his wife, " I am determined ; by the Almighty God who made me, I mean what I say. But forbear your murderous designs ; the danger is not so great as you apprehend—the person who approaches us, for aught we know to the contrary, may be a friend ; besides, it is but a single individual, and—Ah ! by Heaven, it is her ! 'Tis that mysterious woman who uttered those fearful predictions which have in part been so fatally realised. What can bring her here, at such a time as this ?"

Richard Parker started with astonishment, and almost incredulity, when he recognised in the moonbeams the person of Mad Moll, whom he had not seen for years before, and who now stood immediately before them, and gazed upon them with an earnest and sorrowful expression.

" Old woman !" demanded our hero, when he had partly recovered himself ; " what brings you here at this moment, and what is your business with me ?"

" Alas !" replied Mad Moll ; " it is a sad task I have to perform ; but I must speak the facts that are struggling in my breast ; Mad Moll, as the fools calls me, is no enemy of yours, and, oh ! how willingly would she, were it in her power, save you from the terrible fate which is impending over you ; but she cannot, she cannot. You remember what I prognosticated years since, and which at the time you affected to despise ; but have they not in part been fulfilled ? Have not misery, shame, and degradation (unmerited, oh, most unmerited, I admit) been your lot? And the whole will be realised! Yes, Richard Parker, you may for the present escape; but it is written in the book of fate that you shall die a felon's death!"

"Oh, God! oh God!" groaned the terrified Mary Parker; "fearful woman, recall those awful words; have you no compassion for our wretched situation?"

"Oh, yes, Mary Parker," returned

MAD MOLL FORETELLS FUTURE TROUBLES TO RICHARD PARKER.

the old woman, "there is no one who more deeply commiserates your misfortunes than I do. But I cannot conceal the dreadful truth, even though it break your heart to hear it. Your husband is doomed to die an ignominious death; you are destined to become a sorrowing widow; the last portentous cloud is about to burst, and may Heaven in its mercy give you strength to support the dreadful shock!"

"Horrible!" gasped forth our heroine,

staring at her wildly. "Is there no hope?"

"Alas! none!" answered Moll; "his fate is sealed! I say again, there is no escaping from it!"

"Harbinger of evil!" cried Richard, who was wound up to a pitch of the most insupportable excitement, "I will hear no more! I will not heed your idle predictions! Begone! and do not any longer obstruct my way!"

"You do not heed my predictions, Richard Parker?" returned the old woman; "but you must—you do! Your blanched cheek, your quivering lip, and your frenzied eye convince me that you do. They will be fulfilled; I tell you again they will, and that, too, at no distant day! Unfortunate man!—hapless devoted woman! how sincerely do I pity you; how willingly would I save you, if I could; but that is not in the power of mortal being! Farewell! Perchance we may never meet again in this world. Richard Parker, remember the words of the old sybil!—do not despise them; but on the contrary, as you value your soul's welfare, and the happiness of your wife and child, prepare yourself for the awful change which you must shortly undergo!"

Thus saying, the singular old woman turned abruptly away; and before our astonished hero and his wife could attempt to make any reply, she had got a considerable distance away from them, and was soon hidden in the darkness from their sight.

It was several moments ere Richard Parker and his wife could at all recover themselves from the state of astonishment and alarm into which this unexpected meeting had thrown them, and Mary, throwing herself into her husband's arms, gave vent to the poignant agony of her feelings by weeping upon his bosom.

"Oh, God!" she sobbed at last, "to what horrible words have I been compelled to listen! Richard, dear—but unfortunate Richard, and will the remorseless vengeance of the law pursue you to destruction? Is there no hope, not one ray of comfort for my distracted breast?"

"Alas, none! my poor Mary," replied her husband; "the woman, I feel too well assured, has spoken the truth, and that there are no means of escaping from the awful and ignominious fate which is impending o'er my head. But why should I seek to escape from it? Why endeavour to prolong that wretched existence which has now become so hateful to me? Oh, Mary, I feel a weight like lead pressing upon my heart; my brain is on fire; let us return to whence we came; I feel that it is completely useless for me to attempt to avoid my fate. Be firm, Mary, and Heaven, no doubt, will watch over you and my child when I shall be no more."

"Oh, Richard!" groaned his horror-stricken wife; "your words drive me to madness. They shall not part us, and if the Almighty decrees that death should be your portion, we will at least die together. But, no! I cannot, will not believe that such is written in the book of fate. Heed not the wild predictions of this extraordinary woman; who shall presume to penetrate into the dark and hidden secrets of futurity? Oh, it is blasphemy, and is unworthy a serious thought. Exert all your energies, I implore you, and let us fly from the terrible dangers by which we are at present surrounded. There is mercy in Heaven, and in that let us put our trust. Why do we tarry here? The hour is getting late, and if we any longer delay, we may lose the only chance that is now allowed us. Oh, for God's sake arouse yourself, and do not hesitate for another instant, if you would not see me perish at your feet."

Richard Parker was much moved by the eloquent appeal of his devoted wife, and the feelings which struggled in his manly breast, were almost too powerful for utterance.

"Oh, Mary," he said, at length, "that ever I should have been the means, though Heaven knows not wilfully, of laying desolate all the prospects of one of Nature's most beautiful creations, and thus —— I cannot, dare not think, or my brain would go distracted under the terrible reflection. Leave, me, Mary, for the present leave me, with our child, our innocent boy; here is gold, which the kindness of that inestimable friend, Adams, has so generously supplied us with. Take what you will of it, it will enable you to find friends and shelter, till this storm has blown over, if it is ever destined so to do; and then, if Providence should interpose to save my life, (which, for your dear sakes, I devoutly hope it may), I will rejoin you. Leave me—you have already endured too much—you must not now share the dreadful perils to which I am exposed."

"Leave you, Richard!" returned our heroine, with a look of horror and gentle reproach. "Oh, what has become of your early love, the fond confidence you reposed in me, if you can believe me capable of such a thought! Leave you! By Heaven! I should consider myself the most despicable thing in existence, I should hate, abhor myself, if such a monstrous, such an unnatural idea could for an instant find a place in my mind. Leave you, husband? and now in the midst of your despair; surrounded as you are by the breakers of evil fortune —when you want some friendly and affectionate voice to cheer you on to meet the overwhelming tempest, and to stimulate you to hope and energy— leave you alone to your misery—leave you with the reflection that you are a wandering, wretched outcast, with an ignominious death momentarily staring you in your face—and that I, unpitying, abandoned you to your fate!—Horrible! horrible! Richard—Richard! if you ever loved me—if you ever believed that I had devoted my woman's heart of hearts to you—you will no longer urge so frightful, so revolting a proposition. But should you do so, it will be of no avail! Whatever your course, that shall be mine; whatever you misery, that will I also be a partaker of; come weal, come woe, death alone shall separate us, and then I trust that the Almighty giver of all good, will suffer our souls to be re-united in Heaven?"

Overpowered by her emotions, so eloquently expressed in those observations, the faithful, heroic, and affectionate wife, once more sunk sobbing on her husband's bosom, and for a minute or two, Richard Parker was unable to speak.

"Oh, pardon me, best of women, and of wives!" he said at length, "if I have been driven by the distraction of my feelings to give utterance to anything which may sound harsh and ungenerous. God knows, I spoke but from the purest of motives. Could I doubt your sincerity, your fidelity, your unexampled devotedness of heart, I must indeed be a villain of the blackest dye; but——"

"Nay—nay, dear, but unfortunate husband," interrupted Mary, eagerly, "say no more, I beseech you. Time presses—oh! how fearfully it presses! Every succeeding instant that we tarry, is fraught with tenfold danger. Do not hesitate, nor waste words, at present, in reply to what I have said. I know full well your heart, your feelings. Come— come, let us, for the love of Heaven, be gone! See, the moon is overcast with black and threatening clouds—a storm is rapidly approaching—the time waxes late, and the man whom Mr. Adams has so kindly employed to convey us to a place of safety, by this delay may imagine that something fatal has happened, and may retire from the place where it is appointed we shall meet him; and, oh, God! what would then become of us? I shudder with horror at the bare thought! No more, no more, dear Richard, till we are safe, and then——"

"Do, dear father," said the fair and intelligent boy, clasping his little hands together, and looking up with an expression of the most moving supplication in his face; "do as poor mother begs of you, or it will break her heart and mine too."

"My boy! my noble boy!" exclaimed our hero, with a burst of the most passionate feeling, and clasping him to his bosom; "is it possible I can resist this? No—no, I will yet make a desperate struggle with the fate which is impending o'er me, for your dear sakes —all that I now value upon the earth. Come, come, let us hasten."

As he gave utterance to these words, he kissed and embraced his wife and child, and then enclosing the arm of the former in his own, they moved hurriedly away from the spot, in silence, their hearts being too full to suffer them to speak.

The moon was now totally obscured, and all was involved in the most intense and impenetrable darkness, which added to the terror of their feelings. The voice of the thunder was also heard murmuring in the distance, and large drops of rain began to descend, giving ample warning of the storm which was so rapidly approaching. Our hero and his wife had but little knowledge of the way, and the darkness which prevailed served to increase their perplexity ; but still they hurried on, as fast as their trembling limbs would permit them, trusting that Providence would guide them aright.

In this manner they had pursued their way for some distance, when the murmurings of the ocean smote their ears, and inspired them with fresh hope. The rain had now began to descend in torrents, and everything gave taken of a fearful night.

"Courage, my beloved Mary!" said her husband. "That sound convinces me that we are near the place of our destination."

He had scarcely given utterance to the words when the form of a man abruptly crossed their path, and they started back in astonishment and alarm, Richard at the same time drawing a pistol from his belt, and preparing to defend himself and his wife and child.

"Who are you?—speak!" he demanded, in a determined voice; "and for what purpose do you thus abruptly intercept our path ?"

"Why," answered the stranger, "in the first place, I am a man, and as honest a one, too, I believe, as the world will allow me to be."

"This is not the time for equivocation," said our hero ; "will you answer me candidly, and tell me who you are ?"

"First," returned the man, "allow me to tell you who you are. If I mistake not, you are Richard Parker, and those who accompany you are your wife and child."

"Ah!" cried Parker, clasping his wife round the waist with one arm, while he levelled his pistol at the head of the stranger. "Discovered!—nay, then—"

"Be not alarmed, for you have nothing to fear," interrupted the latter. " Ben Binnacle was never yet the man to injure his fellow man, much less to betray the confidence which an old friend has reposed in him."

"Ben Binnacle!" repeated Richard.

"Ay, shipmate!" answered Ben, "the old friend of Jack Adams;—I am the man you seek!"

"Oh, thank Heaven!" ejaculated Mary.

"You are so long beyond the time at which I expected to see you," observed Ben Binnacle, "than I began to fear that something had happened to intercept your flight, and so I started forth with the idea of being able to ascertain the facts. It is lucky that I have met you. But, come, do not let us stand palavering here, for the storm begins to rage rather fiercely ; and I fancy it will not much agree with the constitutions of your wife and son, Mr. Parker, whatever it may do with yours. Besides, every moment there is fresh danger afloat, and we do not know how soon the land-sharks might be down upon us. Everything is in readiness; I have given my word to Jack, and damme, if I break it, if it costs me my life! If fortune favours us, we shall soon reach the Essex coast, where I must leave you, with every good wish for your future safety."

Richard Parker grasped his hand vehemently.

"It is that of an honest man I clutch, I feel convinced," he observed.

"Ay, shipmate," returned Ben Binnacle, "you may say that, and not be far out, neither. But, come, we will patter more upon this subject when we are safe on board and under weigh. We have not many yards to go, and, as I said before, all is in readiness."

"Oh, my friend," said our hero, "how shall I ever be able to reward you for ——"

"Reward be da——I beg your pardon, Mrs. Parker," interrupted the honest, plain-spoken man ; "what reward do you suppose that old Ben Binnacle requires for performing no more than what is merely his duty? Why, it is not the first time that I have risked my life to save that of a fellow creature's, and I hope it is not the last that I shall have an opportunity of so doing. But, come, come, I say."

Richard Parker and his wife did not offar to make any further observation, but followed the footsteps of their conductor, now for the first time feeling somewhat elated with hope.

The storm now raged most violently, and it was lucky for the fugitives that, as Ben Binnacle had informed them, they had not far to go, or they must soon have been drenched to the skin. In a very few minutes they arrived at the mouth of the creek, where they beheld a boat, containing two men, in waiting, and, as well as the darkness would permit them, the lugger at a short distance off.

Ben Binnacle handed Mary and William first into the boat, and then himself and our hero following, it was immediately pushed off, and a few minutes more beheld them safe on board the vessel which was to convey them from the scene of danger. The feelings of our heroine then overpowered her, and throwing herself on her husband's bosom, she gave vent to her emotions in a copious flood of tears; while Richard found it utterly impossible, for a few minutes, to give utterance to a single syllable. Ben Binnacle, who was a rough, honest-looking seaman, left them to themselves for a short time, and the vessel was soon after pursuing its way.

"Oh, God be thanked!" at last ejaculated Mary, "that, for the present, we are safe; and let us hope that He will continue to favour us with his All-merciful protection. Oh, Richard! how much do we owe to Mr. Adams and this good man for the services they have rendered us; may Heaven bless them."

"Amen!" replied her husband, solemnly and fervently; "we can never repay them, my beloved Mary; but, alas! I fear that the time is not far distant when I shall fall into the hands of my enemies, and have to endure all the horrors of my fate."

"Oh, why give way to such dreadful thoughts?" said his wife, with a shudder of horror; "why——"

"Nay," interrupted Richard, "it would be cruel in the extreme to flatter you with any false hopes which I have too much reason to fear can never be realised. But think not that I fear death; were it not for the sake of you and this poor boy, I could meet my fate with calmness and resignation and without a murmur; but——"

He was interrupted by the sudden appearance of Ben Binnacle. Richard once more grasped his hand, and our heroine fixed upon him a look which expressed far more than volumes of words could have done the gratitude, the boundless gratitude she felt towards him.

"Mr. Binnacle," said Richard.

"Ben Binnacle," corrected the old seaman, "that is my name; but I know what you would say, and, as I am a plain-spoken sort of a man, whether I offend or please, I must enter my protest against it. What I have done is to oblige Mr. Adams, and my own conscience, and you are heartily welcome to it. I am sorry for your situation, Mr. Parker, and though I cannot exactly go the length that you and your shipmates have thought proper to do, I must say that I believe, and I know, you had plenty to complain of, and which ought to have been redressed."

"To complain of!" repeated Richard, warmly; "by the just God, we have endured that which was more than enough to turn the softest heart to stone. Insult heaped upon insult; outrage, brutal outrage, following each other in rapid succession, until the blood maddened in our veins, and we could endure it no longer. But who of all the oppressed has suffered half that which I have? Oh, it would harrow up your manly feelings were I to attempt to relate to you the horrors, the wrongs that have been inflicted upon me."

"Jack Adams has told me all," replied Binnacle; "and most sincerely do I pity you, and your poor wife and child. Mayhap you may yet find a friend, not to be exactly despised, in Ben Binnacle."

"Oh, sir," ejaculated Mary, with a burst of feeling which she found it impossible to control; "this disinterested kindness and humanity, this——"

"Say no more, madam, I beg of you," interrupted Binnacle; "whatever I have hitherto done, or may yet be enable to do, I am sure you are most heartily welcome to. So," he continued, addressing himself to Parker, "if I have heard aright, it is to Captain Arlington that you are indebted for the principal of your misfortunes?"

"To him, and him alone, the villain," answered our hero; "but for him I might now have been one of the happiest of human beings, instead of being a branded felon; a wretched, wandering outcast, with a disgraceful, an ignominious death staring me in the face at every turn. He has pursued me like a fiend of darkness, with the most vindictive feelings; he brought degradation and misery upon me, and made me hate myself as a man; but I have had my revenge, the revenge I so long panted to obtain, and I am in part satisfied!"

"Oh, Richard—dear Richard!" said his trembling wife; "talk not thus, I implore you; would that that deed of blood had never taken place; and then you might have been pardoned your other offences."

"Pardoned!" repeated Parker; "by Heaven, I would rather encounter a thousand of the most lingering deaths, than that the miscreant should have escaped me."

"Forbear! forbear!" said Mary. "I cannot, dare not listen to such words as those."

"Come, my friends," remarked Binnacle, "let us hope that better times are yet in store for you. Let us below, where I have prepared some refreshment for you, and of which, I am certain, you must stand so much in need."

Richard Parker and his wife made no reply, but followed their kind-hearted conductor, and soon found themselves seated before a table on which was spread a plentiful repast, with a goodly supply of wine, of which Ben Binnacle requested them heartily to partake. They endeavoured to comply with his request, but their minds were too violently agitated to suffer them to eat otherwise than sparingly, and Ben Binnacle again left them to themselves.

"Mary," said her husband, after a pause, "notwithstanding our present apparent safety, I feel sad at heart; but believe me, it is not any fears that I entertain for myself that give rise to the feeling; ah! no, it is the thoughts, the anxieties for you and my poor boy that make me suffer so acutely. Alas! should I be taken, and meet with the fate with which I am threatened, what will become of you, left alone, friendless, and without a protector, as you will be, in the wide world?"

"Dear Richard!" returned our heroine, "for the love of mercy do not give way to these dreadful, these distracting thoughts!—Heaven will look down with compassion upon us, and will not suffer you to be taken from us, and that in so awful a manner. Something will yet occur to save us, and we shall again be happy."

"Happy!" repeated her husband; "and think you that a poor, degraded, guilty wretch like me can ever again be happy?—Ought you not rather to loathe me—despise me—shun me?"

"Loathe you!—despise you!—shun you, Richard?" repeated our heroine, fixing upon him a look of mingled reproach and alarm.

"Yes," replied Parker; "for, however richly the villain Arlington merited the fate which I inflicted upon him, am I not in the sight of God and man a murderer? Oh, that I were dead!"

"Richard!—husband! you will drive me mad!—If you ever loved me—if you still love our tender offspring, oh, cease to talk thus, which cannot fail to engender the utmost feelings of horror in my breast! God will pardon you the crimes to which you were urged by wrongs, such as no human being, perhaps, ever before experienced; and I trust you will be yet many years spared to us, and enabled to forget the past.

"Oh, never—never!" returned Parker, with a look of despair; "it is stamped upon my brain in characters which nothing can ever obliterate! It would be in vain for me to seek to buoy myself up with delusive hopes! Mary, though dreadful is the task, we must endeavour to prepare ourselves for the worst!"

"Oh, no, no, no! I dare not—cannot think of such a thing!"

"There is no part of the kingdom, Mary," said her husband, "that I can fly to that my enemies will not pursue me. They are thirsting for my blood, and they will not rest satisfied until they have obtained it."

"Richard," said our heroine, reproachfully, "is this a specimen of the courage you have ever boasted of possessing, and in which I always placed the utmost confidence? But, no, I do not heed what you say; your mind is disordered, and you know not what you give utterance to."

"God knows my mind is indeed distracted," said Richard Parker; "but too well do I feel the force and truth of that which I have said. But think not, my beloved wife, that any feeling of cowardice has come over me.—Do not think that my courage has deserted me; death has no terrors for me; for what, besides your dear self and our innocent boy, have

I got to tempt me to cling to life?—No, my memory may be scandalised; my name may be handed down to posterity as that of one of the blackest monsters that ever disgraced society; but Richard Parker will die as he has lived—a man!"

"Die—die!" repeated the agitated Mary; "oh, fearful word!—it shocks my ears, and freezes the blood in my veins to hear it! You shall not perish thus, Richard! Heaven will not permit it!"

"And dare I appeal to Heaven," said our hero, "when my soul is stained with human blood?—Mary, I feel borne down by an overwhelming weight which I cannot resist, and which must ultimately press me to destruction! But more than all do I reproach myself for having united my fate with yours, and thus brought upon you such unexampled misery."

"Richard," said his affectionate wife, "have I ever given you reason to speak thus? Have you ever heard me utter one word of regret?"

"Oh, never! never!"

"Have I not always been studious of your happiness, and anxious to convince you how much I loved you?" demanded Mary.

"Always, best, and most faithful of women!" answered her husband.

"Then, why should you torture my feelings by remarks such as those you have just now made? By Heaven, I swear, that I would sooner have suffered ten thousand times more than that it has been my lot, in conjunction with you, to endure, than I could have resigned you; it would have been madness to me to have known that I no longer possessed your love. Oh, Richard, think of our early, halcyon days, and banish such thoughts from your mind. Remember all the misfortunes that have happened to us only as a fearful dream, and look forward to the future with hope."

"Beloved Mary," returned our hero, "if anything could sustain me, it would be your soothing, your gentle voice, which comes like heavenly balm to the careworn soul; but in vain would I endeavour to deceive myself, and to believe that my future path may be one of happiness, such as I once experienced. Ah! Mary, why do you remind me of the blissful days of my youth? All is

vanished! How fearful is the contrast which is now presented! I shudder when I think of it, and you——"

"No more, husband, I implore you," interrupted his wife; "calm the awful feelings that now disturb your breast, and put your trust in Him who is the searcher of all hearts. Come, Richard, let us on our knees supplicate His mercy."

"Oh, I dare not pray, Mary!"

"Dare not?"

"No, it would be worse than blasphemy, coming from lips like mine!" replied the unfortunate Richard Parker. "What hope can a murderer have of mercy from on high? And yet, was it not his cowardly villany and oppression that forced me to do the deed?"

"Oh, yes, yes!" eagerly returned our heroine, "and Heaven will pardon you for it. Come—come, let us proceed, while the opportunity of escaping is afforded us. The mercy of God will light upon the friendless and unprotected, and we shall be happy yet."

Richard Parker returned no immediate answer to his devoted wife, but beneath the eloquence of her affectionate arguments, his melancholy and despair were forced in a great measure to yield, and in the course of a short time he calmly resigned himself into the hands of Providence. Ben Binnacle now made his appearance once more before them, and the cheering observations which the honest-hearted man made to them, tended in no inconsiderable degree to alleviate the anguish and anxiety of their minds, and to inspire them with renovated hopes.

A storm, as we have before said, had been for some time threatening, and the vessel had not got far away from the shore, when it came on with great fury, and was sufficient, in the aspect it bore to excite terror in the breast of the fugitives, but more especially Mary and her child. It was then that our hero aroused himself, and sought to create a feeling of hope and confidence in the breasts of those so dear to him, and he succeeded even far better than could have been anticipated under the circumstances. Binnacle also exerted himself to the utmost to raise the spirits of Mary and her son, nor were his efforts thrown away. They could not be lost upon a mind like that of our heroine, and she viewed the raging of the tempest with what might have seemed to a mere superficial observer the utmost indifference, though her heart was full almost to bursting at the same moment. She thought more of the escape of her unfortunate husband from the cruel fangs of the law; and the knowledge that they were now far away from the land, and that at present there seemed to be no probability of their pursuers being able to track the course of their flight, sank the terrors of the storm into comparative insignificance.

"Providence, my dear Richard," she said, throwing her fair arms affectionately around his neck, "Providence, I am certain, will still watch over and protect us; and fearful even as the prospect now appears before us, the time is not far distant when we shall be restored to happiness and peace."

"To happiness, my Mary?" said Richard, with a melancholy and desponding sigh, and at the same time shaking his head in a doubtful manner. "Alas! alas!"

"Nay—nay, my Richard," returned our heroine, "why give yourself up to this abject and absolute despair? I say again, and I speak it in the full confidence of the goodness of the Supreme, that we shall shortly be restored to that happiness and peace of mind it was once our lot to experience, and when we shall be enabled to look back upon the trying past with feelings of the utmost complacency, nor entertain one pang of regret for the many bitters that have been poured into our cup of joy. Yes, my husband, even in the midst of all the horrors of the present raging tempest, even while a price is set upon your head, and the bloodhounds of justice are hot in pursuit of you, I feel hope animate my breast, and I am satisfied that those hopes will not be destined to be disappointed. We shall escape from all the dangers that at present surround us. We shall once more live in the calm retirement of rustic life, and experience the blessings of domestic peace and contentment. Once more, when the labours of the day are at an end, we shall ramble over the moonlit fields and verdant meadows, listening to the mellifluous notes of the nightingale, and recalling joyous reminiscences of our youthful days, before sorrow had ever cast one gloomy shadow across our path, and all was light and happiness, buoyancy and hope. Oh, that sweet spring-time of our life will assuredly again be restored to us, and the dismal past will vanish from our memory like a fitful dream. Cheer thee, my husband, my beloved Richard; shake off from your breast the heavy weight of care which now hangs upon it, and look forward with confidence and hope to the happiness which is dawning upon us."

"Excellent, best of women, and of wives!" said Richard Parker, "your words fall like the balm of Heaven upon the desolate heart. But, alas! how am I ever to hope that the bright visions of happiness you have so eloquently and vividly pictured can ever be realised? For the present, 'tis true, I may escape the merciless hands of the law, but can I avoid discovery altogether? Can I, a murderer, although the murderer of the miscreant who did me such monstrous wrong, flatter myself with the idea that I shall be able altogether to escape the penalty due to that crime? No, no, it would be madness to encourage such a thought, and still more monstrous to seek to encourage such a hope in you. My poor Mary! prepare your mind for the worst, I beseech you, for I know full well that my doom is sealed. For your dear sake, for that of my beloved boy, I could wish that it could be avoided, though from no love of life that I feel; for Heaven knows that I have experienced sufficient to render it now hateful to me. Oh, Mary, it will never be our lot to ramble again o'er those green fields and verdant meadows you have so beautifully described, in the richness of your heart, and the fulness of your affection. Haply, the green sob may cover my grave, bedecked with the flowers planted by your hands, and those of our dear boy, and watered by your tears; but—"

"Richard!" interrupted his wife, once more throwing herself, sobbing, into his arms, "for the love of God, do not continue to talk thus, for your words drive me to distraction. There is hope for the veriest wretch that ever disgraced humanity, and why not for you, whose errors have only been caused by the villany of others? Heaven knows that no one can more deeply regret the untimely fate of the guilty man, Captain Arlington, and that it should have been inflicted by your hands, than I do; but it was the just retribution of outraged Heaven that overtook him, and you ought not to reproach yourself so bitterly. Come, come, banish such fearful, such horrible ideas from your

RICHARD PARKER TELLS HIS TALE OF WRONGS TO MARY.

mind, and seek to reconcile yourself to the fate which it has been the will of the Supreme, whose acts we must not presume to question, to expose you to, and place your firm reliance on its future mercy and protection."

"Oh, Mary!" said our hero, "it is impossible! All hope has vanished from my mind, 'like the baseless fabric of a vision.' I feel myself, I know myself to be a doomed man, and I hate and despise myself as the wretch who has been the primary cause of plunging you, my devoted, my heroic wife, into such a vertex of inextricable misery. When I recall to my memory the scenes of your youthful innocence and joy—when your path was all flowers, the sun never set upon your artless enjoyments, when no clouds ever appeared in the horizon of your daily tranquillity—when I remember your bright smile, your joyous laugh, your happy recklessness and unconsciousness of the cares of the world, oh! how bitterly do I upbraid myself for having taken you from that haven of bliss, and committed you to the shoals and quicksands of life's stern realities. But for me, Mary, you might now have been that same happy, thoughtless, careless, jocund being; but accursed fate so willed it that I should be thrown in your path, and, like a pestilence, destruction and misery have followed in my track. Oh, Mary! would to God that we had never met!"

"Richard!" sobbed our heroine, her feelings almost overpowering her and choking her utterance, "do you love me? did you ever love me?"

"Do I love you! Did I ever love you!" repeated her husband. "Oh, my soul's idol, what a cruel question is that to put to me!"

"Then, if it be so," returned Mary, "and think not, my Richard, that I doubt your faith, why thus reproach yourself for that in which, if there was anything culpable, my heart was equally guilty with your own? It was the will of Heaven that we should come together; our hopes, our feelings, our virtues were assimilated, and with a cheerful heart, I am content to partake of those vicissitudes which it has been the will of God to visit us with. Richard, you shall never hear me murmur, or, if I do so, may that be the last breath I am ever destined to draw. No, my husband, you shall find your Mary all that your first fond hopes and sanguine expectations anticipated of her; faithful, fond, devoted, ready to encounter any difficulty, any trial, any danger, for your dear sake; the terrors that surround you may appal her, but you shall ever find her firm, ready to offer the soothing balm of consolation, and willing and anxious to share your fate, whatever that fate may be. As we have lived,

so, with the will of Heaven, will we die together!"

"Mary!" ejaculated our hero, clasping her at the same time frantically to his bosom, "can I listen to words of such pure, such genuine devotedness, without going mad? Oh, that your fate had been cast in another lot than what it is, for surely if ever mortal deserved all the blessings that Heaven, in its boundless mercy, can bestow, it is yourself. Again I say that it is unfortunate that we should ever have meet; for, had it not been so, you would probably have met with one more worthy of you, and who would never have plunged you into the troubles it has been my misfortune to do; but who, I am convinced, could never have loved you half so fondly, so devotedly as Richard Parker."

"Oh, no—no," exclaimed his wife, fervently, and the expression that beamed from her beautiful and intelligent eyes, attested the sincerity of what she said, and spoke more powerfully than the most eloquent language could have done; "that is impossible! Where could I have seen the man who I could love like the humble Richard Parker?—where have found one who equalled, much less surpassed him in virtue?—By the Almighty God, I declare that, notwithstanding all the troubles I have had to encounter, in the blissful confidence that I possessed my husband's love, I have been supremely happy; nor would I now, were it possible for me to do so, exchange my position for that of the proudest empress on the earth. Your heart, my Richard, is my kingdom; this dear child one of the brightest and most valuable gems in my diadem; and I hold all other treasures as nought whilst possessed of them!—Come—come! we will think—we will talk no more upon this dismal subject. In a short time, with the blessing of Providence, we shall be landed in a place of safety, till the storms which at present beset us have passed away; and, thanks to the disinterested kindness and generosity of Mr. Adams, we shall then be enabled so to disguise and conceal ourselves, that we may set detection at complete defiance!"

"But," said her husband, "can you be so sanguine, Mary, as to imagine that, although the Admiralty might be disposed, in that spirit of mercy and forbearance which I do not believe them to possess, to pardon me as the mutineer, they would ever forgive me as the destroyer of the life of Captain Arlington?—Oh, no! the bare idea is most preposterous, and it would be madness for me to encourage it, and cruel in the extreme to induce you to entertain it. For the crime I have committed, extenuating though may be the circumstances connected with it, my life is forfeited; and sooner or later, depend upon it, that life will have to pay the penalty. Mad Moll, as she is termed, spoke not unjustly or extravagantly when she prognosticated that an ignominious fate was in store for me; and, mark my words, for I feel them confidently, her prediction will be realised."

"Oh, horrible idea!" gasped forth our heroine, shuddering, and looking round her, as though she almost expected and feared to see that mysterious woman whom her husband had mentioned, standing at her elbow; "horrible idea! Why, my Richard, do you suffer your disordered and bewildered mind to entertain it? You are not superstitious, I know, and, therefore, it is impossible that you can place any reliance upon the wild and extravagant predictions of a wandering maniac."

"I would fain not do so, Mary," replied her husband, in melancholy accents, "but when I recall the dreadful past to my memory, can I any longer remain sceptical? Has not all that she formerly prognosticated been fearfully realised? Did she not say that I should become a seaman—that I should encounter manifold troubles—should meet with shame and degradation? And can you deny that all she foretold I have experienced to my most melancholy cost? Oh, God! the thought now distracts my brain, and drives me almost to madness. Methinks I feel again the burning lash upon my quivering flesh; the life-blood streaming from my gaping wounds, and trickling down in all directions. Methinks I see again the looks of savage exultation with which the miscreant whom my hands have slain, gazed upon my sufferings with fiendish mockery and exultation; and as I do so, I almost forget that I am a man, and feel as if I could do the work of the most diabolical

wretch that ever disgraced society, in the midst of my despair. Mary, this is no time to mince matters, or to disguise one's feelings; I feel, I know myself to be upon the very verge of a precipice from which I cannot escape, and down which I must be compelled to drag you and my innocent child, and I feel myself as one deserted by God and every hope."

"Oh, no, no, no!" sobbed our heroine, and at the same time looking in the face of her unfortunate husband with an expression of countenance which language must fail to give an adequate description of; "for the love of Heaven say not so, my beloved Richard."

"I must do so, Mary," replied our hero; "it would be madness, it would be worse than criminal, to do otherwise. Oh, why should I seek to buoy, to flatter you with hopes, which I feel satisfied are never fated to be realised? No, no, you had better prepare yourself for the worst, my sweet one, my devoted one, and endeavour to meet it with fortitude. There is no resisting the will of Heaven, and we must submit ourselves to it in all the spirit of meekness and resignation. The clouds that have so long been gathering over me, have burst at last, and I know that I am about to feel the full torrent of their fury; still, Heaven knows that I should be prepared to meet it as a man, were it not for the distracting thought as to what is to become of you and our tender offspring when I am no more. Oh, God, that thought! You will then be left to the world's scorn and contumely; you will become houseless wanderers upon the face of the earth! Where will be the helping hand that will be stretched out in friendship and humanity towards you? They will point at you, and say—'There is the widow and child of the mutineer and murderer, Richard Parker;' they will say——"

"Oh, hold! hold! in mercy," interrupted his wife. "I cannot bear this. Alas! Richard, how frightful, how horrible is the picture you have drawn. But it will no be realised, I feel confident that it will not. Heaven will never permit it, and, therefore, am I reanimated with hope. Let me implore you, as you love me and our child, to banish such terrible ideas from your mind, and to put your trust in that

Almighty Power, which ever looks with mercy and forbearance down upon even the most humble and erring of its creatures. Richard, the crimes, the brutal and unmerited oppressions of others have alone caused you to sin, and, as I have before said, and endeavoured so forcibly to impress upon you, the Supreme giver of all good will pardon you for what you have committed, and allay the fierce tempests with which your fate is at present beset. Oh, my husband! could I but impart to you the same feeling of hope which at present animates my breast, I should be comparatively happy. But let us drop this dismal subject, and seek to look forward to the future with fond feelings of expectation, which I sincerely and confidently hope are not destined to be disappointed."

"Dearest Mary!" ejaculated our hero, once more clasping her ardently to his throbbing bosom, "for your sweet sake I will endeavour to do so, though Heaven knows full well how faintly my hopes repond to yours. Oh, that I could recall the past, methinks how differently would I then act to what I have done!"

"And could you ever love me less, Richard?" demanded his beauteous wife, earnestly and anxiously, at the same time looking in his face with the deepest intensity of feeling.

"Love you less, Mary?" repeated her husband; "oh, why put such a cruel question to me? Were it possible, and especially after experiencing what I have from your unexampled devotedness and affection, I must love you ten times more. But, Mary, I fear, alas! that those days of happiness it was once our lot to enjoy are gone, never more to return. We shall never more ramble o'er the romantic scenes of our youth, strangers to care, and robust with health and contentment. No more shall we watch with the same feelings of tranquillity and delight that we were wont to do, the golden orb of day sinking in majestic glory behind the western hills; never again, I fear, will it be our fate to listen to the mellifluous warblings of the feathered songsters, as they breathed their sweet notes as if in admiration and rejoicing at our mutual and virtuous love; we shall never again listen to the soul-inspiring peal of our native village, as their tunes were borne upon the calm and balmy air. Oh, no, my Mary, I feel too well assured that those days of halcyon bliss are gone, never again to return; and, as the thought arises to my mind, a feeling of oppression and despair comes over my senses, which almost overwhelms me, and adds to the gloom of the dismal prospect which is now opened wide before me. Mary, could I but extricate you and my poor boy from the consequences of the fate which inevitably awaits me, methinks that I could meet that fate, however terrible and revolting it might be, with some degree of manly fortitude; but as it is——"

He was interrupted by the entrance of Binnacle, who, observing the manner in which Richard Parker and his amiable and devoted wife were engaged, drew back respectfully, and eyed them with feelings of the deepest sympathy and compassion. At length he said, addressing himself to our hero—

"Belay, mate; throw despair overboard for the sharks—it is fit food for them; but we'll go upon another track. Ere long, you will be safely landed, I hope, far away from the swabs who would alter your commission; and some day or other, and I think it is not far distant, you and your amiable mate here, with the little cock-boat, will meet old Ben Binnacle, and, I suppose, you won't know him then?"

"Not know you, sir?" replied Mary.

"No," replied Binnacle; "you will then see old Ben Binnacle in a new character, a d——d good fellow (axing your pardon, madam, for the *blasphemous*—don't they call it?) and——"

Richard Parker grasped his hand fervently, as he said,—

"Mr. Binnacle, I will not endeavour to thank you for the service that you have rendered us, for any language that I could call to my command must fail to express the gratitude that I feel towards you. May Heaven reward you as you merit!"

"And to that prayer," said Mary Parker, "I humbly, but most fervently respond. But the storm rages fearfully; I hear the winds howl; and I feel, from the motion of the vessel, that there is danger threatening. Oh! my husband! —my child!—my innocent boy!"

"Calm your feelings, my dear lady," said Binnacle; "it is only a bit of a squall, which myself and your husband understand perfectly well; it will soon blow over, and then ——"

At that moment a heavy sea almost placed the vessel on her beam-ends, and our heroine and her child rushed to Richard, and clinging frantically to him, looked on all that to their mind's eye was passing around them with the utmost despair and terror. Ben Binnacle, looking significantly at our hero, rushed hastily from the place upon deck, and Richard Parker would have followed, knowing full well the danger that prevailed, had it not been for the attention which it was necessary to pay to his wife and child in the painful position in which they were placed.

The storm indeed raged with the most fearful violence; the flashes of lightning were frequent and vivid; the peals of thunder deafening, and the howling of the blast as it swept over the ocean, mingled with the dismal bellowing of the billows, added to the horrors of the scene, and seemed to thunder despair in the ears of the unfortunate fugitives; but still our heroine struggled with her feelings, and behaved with far more fortitude than could have been expected under the alarming circumstances. The vessel was tossed about in the most violent manner, and it was quite evident that it had a difficult job to battle with the fury of the storm; and it was very doubtful whether, unless it shortly abated, she would be able to weather it. There were but two other men on board besides Binnacle and our hero, and the latter finding that the danger every moment increased, and that his wife remained firm and confident, could no longer continue inactive when his services were so much required, embraced Mary and his child, and bidding them be of good cheer, hastened on deck, and left her to her own reflections. Mary pressed her innocent boy to her bosom for a few minutes, and could not restrain the tears which streamed upon his cheeks.

"Do not cry, dear mother," said the little William, looking affectionately up in her face; "for Heaven is good, and will protect us through all the dangers of this tempest. I do not fear, dear mother, indeed i do not;—you see, I do not tremble, and, therefore, do not thus tor-

ture your mind for my sake. Oh, how often have I listened to the voice of the storm when poor father was far away at sea, until I became familiar with its terrors, and was fully prepared to meet those dangers I felt confident I must one day or other be exposed to. I am a sailor's son, mother, and you shall find that even young though I am, I possess all a sailor's spirit."

"My dear—my noble-hearted boy !" ejaculated the fond mother, again pressing warm kisses upon his cheeks. 'Oh, what an inestimable blessing it is that Heaven should have favoured me with a son like you! I will be firm, for your words are prophetic; and something seems to convince me, notwithstanding our present dismal prospects, that they will be realised. Come, my William, let us go down on our knees, and supplicate the mercy and protection of that Supreme Power, which never deserts the unfortunate in the hour of their need."

They both knelt down, and fervently Mary offered up her prayers to the Supreme, William responding with a heartiness and sincerity which could not have been expected in one of his tender years. They then arose, inspired with fresh confidence and hope.

The violence of the tempest, however, did not at all abate, but, on the contrary, it seemed rather to increase, and the rolling of the vessel was fearful and alarming in the extreme. It was dashed along at the mercy of the waves, and was driven completely out of her latitude, and it was impossible to steer her in the right course they were so desirous to pursue. They were driven far out to sea, and it seemed at present utterly impossible that they could reach the coast they wished, and unless Providence interposed to save them, their fate appeared to be almost certain. At length Richard Parker returned, anxious to know the condition of his wife and child, and he was much gratified to find them so much more firm and composed than he could have anticipated. Mary eagerly inquired of her husband whether the storm had in any degree abated, though it was too evident to her that it had not done so, but, on the contrary, had become still more violent even within the last few minutes.

"Alas, Mary !" replied her husband;

"it would be cruel for me to seek to deceive you, especially when I behold the exemplary fortitude with which you support the dangers by which we are surrounded. All at present wears the most threatening and dismal aspect; the lugger is driven about at the mercy of the waves; but she is a good craft, and I trust with the mercy of Providence we shall yet be enabled to weather the fury of the tempest, and at length reach the land in safety. Still, be of good heart, my dear Mary, and with the blessing of God I hope that all will yet be well."

"Oh, yes, my Richard," returned our heroine, throwing her arms around his neck, and looking affectionately in his face; "I will not despair, for Heaven, I trust, will hear the prayers that myself and child have offered up to it, and will not desert us in this, the hour of our imminent peril. But you look pale, fatigued, and care-worn; alas! I fear that this unusual exertion is too much for your strength to support."

"Nay, Mary," said Richard, "am I not inured to such dangers and hardships as these, and think you that I am not now fully prepared to encounter them? If I do indeed look pale and melancholy, it is only from the anxiety I feel for yourself and our child. But come, my beloved and devoted wife, let us banish such sad and gloomy thoughts from our mind, and meet the fearful dangers by which we are at present surrounded, but which I trust will not last long, with becoming fortitude."

"Richard," replied his wife, in accents which fully evidenced the sincerity of her observations; "you shall find me all that you could wish; Mary Parker will endeavour to prove herself worthy of being a sailor's wife."

"Nobly spoken, best of women!" ejaculated Richard; "your words inspire me with fresh confidence; and I feel the bright dawn of hope beam upon my mind."

"Continue to encourage the same feelings, Richard," remarked his wife, "and relying on the mercy of the Almighty, I trust that we shall not be doomed to be disappointed. But let me not detain you here, when your services are so much required on deck. Go,

my husband, and may Heaven's blessing attend you."

Richard Parker made no reply, but having once more embraced his wife and boy with the utmost tenderness and fervour, he again quitted them, and returned to the deck.

We should become tedious were we to seek to describe the various feelings of anguish, suspense, and anxiety which agitated the bosom of our heroine for some time after she was left alone with her child; but at length, by dint of great exertion, she became more calm, and endeavoured to await the result with patience and resignation.

The storm continued with scarcely any difference throughout the night, and it seemed wonderful, but most providential, how the vessel was enabled to battle against it; but towards morning it greatly abated—the wind became hushed —the thunder ceased to roar—the lightning no longer flashed across the heavens, and Richard Parker, with a bounding heart, hastened to his wife and child, and congratulated them upon their preservation from what for so many hours had appeared to be an inevitable and untimely death. They all three sunk upon their knees and earnestly poured forth their thanks to the Almighty.

"But where are we, dear Richard?" eagerly demanded his wife.

"We have been driven many miles out of our course," replied our hero, "but the wind having now changed, and the lugger not having received so much damage as might have been expected, I trust that we shall be enabled to reach the place of our destination in the course of a few hours."

"Ay," said Ben Binnacle, who at that moment joined them, "if I am not out in my reckoning, we shall reach the Essex coast by the evening at the latest. You have had a hard trial, Mrs. Parker, but you have supported it with the courage of a heroine, and I trust that Providence will reward you for it. Once landed, if your husband only follows the advice of my friend, Jack Adams, which I doubt not he will, he will be out of the way of all danger, and his enemies may search for him in vain, though, no doubt, they will leave no means untried to discover him. I shall see you again,

I hope, under happier circumstances; and one thing you may depend upon, and think not that I do not speak with all sincerity—you shall ever have the good wishes of old Ben Binnacle, and I hope that you will sometimes bestow a friendly thought upon him."

"Kind hearted man!" replied Richard Parker, cordially pressing the hand of the honest seaman; "we can never cease to remember you with feelings of the most unbounded gratitude, for are we not indebted to you for the disinterested kindness and services you have rendered us? May Heaven reward and prosper you for what you have done, for I fear, alas! that it will never be in our power to do so."

"Avast! avast! Mr. Parker," returned Binnacle. "I am but a plain-spoken, rough-spun sort of man; but what I say or do comes from my heart, I can tell you, and I feel amply satisfied. Lor' love you! what a pleasure there is in doing a good action! I seek no other reward. So let me request that you will make your mind perfectly easy upon that point."

"Mr. Binnacle," observed our heroine, "the sentiments you have expressed alike do honour to your head and heart, and must call forth the admiration and gratitude of all who know you. For my own part, I ——"

"Now, now, my good lady," impatiently interrupted the veteran tar, 'I must also lay an embargo on your thanks, for you flatter me far beyond my merits. Why, what a set of useless swabs we should be, how unworthy of enjoying the many blessings that Providence has sent us, were we not sometimes enabled to do a good turn for our fellow-creatures, and do it with a willing heart, too! But, come, I am not much used to palavering in this manner, so, if you please, we will drop the subject. There is one thing, however, I wish to say."

"And what is that, my good friend?" asked Richard.

"Why," answered Binnacle, "I consider, after all, that it is a fortunate thing this storm has taken place; for if your pursuers imagine that you have endeavoured to make your escape by sea, as it is not improbable that they will, they will most likely suppose that you have perished, and will, therefore, abandon their pursuit of you."

"Ah!" ejaculated Mary, "that is a very reasonable idea. Oh, Richard, I feel inspired with fresh hopes that we shall yet be enabled to elude the vigilance of our enemies, and may yet be permitted to pass our future days in peace!"

"Alas, my dear Mary!" returned her husband, "would to Heaven that I could encourage the same hopes, but I find that utterly impossible! For your sake, and that of our child, how glad should I be could they be realised; but, indeed, I cannot conquer the apprehensions I entertain that they are doomed to be disappointed. Had I been only a mutineer, I might have escaped, but as I have shed the blood of Captain Arlington, they will not fail to pursue me with remorseless perseverance, and they will not rest until they have got me in their power, and have wreaked their vengeance on my head! Peace! happiness! they are never fated again to be mine; and it would be the height of cruelty to endeavour to flatter you with any such hopes."

"Oh, my unfortunate husband," said Mary; "why will you thus give yourself up to despair? Has not Providence hitherto befriended us? and think you He will now desert us, while we put our trust in Him?"

"Mary," returned her husband, in a solemn voice, "am I not a murderer? And dare I look to that Supreme power you invoke, for mercy and protection?"

"Oh, yes," answered our heroine, "God is just, and never fails to look down with mercy upon even the most guilty of his erring creatures if they are truly penitent. Remember the brutal provocation, the wrongs you received from Captain Arlington, and surely you will no longer so cruelly and so bitterly reproach yourself, for that which has so unfortunately happened."

"'Tis true, Mary," replied our hero, "there are many circumstances that might be pleaded in extenuation of my conduct; but still nothing can excuse the shedding of human blood."

"It was in self-defence you acted, Richard," remarked his wife.

"You are right there Mrs. Parker," said Binnacle, "and if all be true that I have heard respecting the late Captain

Arlington, all I have to say is, that he was a most arrant villain, and richly deserved his fate, which was a just, though terrible judgment upon him. It is, to my thinking, a very good job that the world is rid of such a scoundrel; and had I been similarly situated to Mr. Parker, I do not hesitate to say that I should have done the same. Come, come, man, you must not give way to these gloomy feelings, which cannot be productive of any good, and will only serve to torture the mind of your faithful and amiable wife. Mark my words, Ben Binnacle is no prophet if this storm does not soon blow over, and you will live many years yet, and learn to bury the past in oblivion."

"Oh, no," returned Richard Parker, shaking his head, "that is impossible."

"Pshaw!" exclaimed honest old Ben Binnacle, impatiently. "I say it is no such thing; and if you love your wife and your boy as I believe you do, you will endeavour to think so too. Come, come, this is a dry subject, and I think it would be much better for you now to be engaged in partaking of some refreshment, for you must be rather exhausted after the exertions you have undergone during the night."

Parker and his wife returned him their heartfelt thanks, and Binnacle retired; but he was only absent for a few minutes, when he returned accompanied by one of the men, and bringing in an ample supply of the most delicate refreshments he had on board, which he placed before them, and urged them in the most cordial manner to partake of them as heartily as they could. He then once more retired from the place, thinking that they would wish to be alone, and left them to their own reflections.

Richard Parker, having, by dint of great exertions, succeeded in somewhat tranquillising his feelings, partook slightly of the repast which was spread before them, and a silence of several minutes ensued, during which time the thoughts of Mary arose fervently to Heaven for its mercy and protection. At length they both became more composed, and they then conversed with more freedom than they had been enabled to do for some time on their present situation, and the prospects of the future. The advice which Jack Adams had given them, they heartily approved of; and could they only succeed in acting up to it, they saw that there was every possibility of their yet being enabled to avoid detection, and that with the will Heaven they might ultimately escape the fate with which they were now threatened.

"Disguised as we shall be," said our heroine, "and living in the part of the country to which we are going, we shall stand every chance of escaping suspicion, and in time the excitement which the late startling events have caused, will have passed away, and we may live secure from all fear of our being again disturbed."

"God grant, for your sake, my beloved wife," said Richard, "that we may do so; for should I be taken from you and meet with an ignominious death (as I most assuredly should, if I were discovered) what would become of you and our poor boy?"

"Oh, Richard," said Mary, "do not talk thus; you make me shudder with horror when you give expression to such dreadful forebodings. Heaven will never permit you to meet with so terrible a fate! I feel convinced that it will not; and it is that thought which buoys me up with hope, and makes me look forward to the future with confidence."

"Oh, Mary," said her husband, "what sweet balm are your words to my afflicted soul!—What would become of me without your soothing voice?—I should become a miserable wretch, abandoned altogether to despair, and life would be to me an intolerable burthen which I could no longer endure! But now, for your sake, I will still endeavour to live—to repent—to forget the past, and to reward you for your generous, your unexampled devotion, with my most ardent love!"

"Richard—dear Richard!" returned his wife, "what joy your words impart to me! Oh! when these storms, to whose horrors we have been so long exposed, shall have blown over, we shall again be happy; and if the gloomy past should at any time recur to our recollection, it will only be remembered as a fearful dream!"

"May God grant that we shall thus find a kind oblivion to our manifold and terrible sorrows!" said Richard Parker, fervently.

"We shall — we shall!" ejaculated Mary, fervently, and her countenance was animated with an expression of increased hope. "Come, Richard, let us continue to encourage such thoughts, and the painful anxieties of our minds will find a speedy and wholesome relief."

Our hero returned no answer, but he

THE FLIGHT OF RICHARD PARKER AND HIS WIFE.

embraced his wife tenderly, kissed her fervently, and his looks expressed in far more eloquent language than words could possibly have done the feelings which predominated in his breast; and after a short pause, they were enabled to resume the conversation with much more calmness than they had hitherto done.

CHAPTER IX.

THE VOYAGE COMPLETED.—THE FUGI-
TIVES.—THE OLD TAVERN.—THE SE-
CRET CONVERSATION.—DANGER AND
ALARM.—A FRIEND IN NEED.

THE sun was just sinking to rest in
the bosom of the Western Ocean, when,
to the infinite delight of Richard Parker
and his wife, they came in sight of the
Essex coast, and their perilous voyage
was fast drawing to a termination.

"I shall be compelled to leave you as
soon as I have landed you safe on shore,"
remarked Binnacle; "for I have already
exceeded the time I promised myself.
About half a mile up the country you
will find a secluded tavern, kept by an
honest man, and where you may find a
secure shelter for the night, at any rate.
Remember the advice of Jack Adams,
and I have very little doubt that all will
go well with you. It may be some time
ere we shall meet again, if, indeed, we
should ever do so; but I heartily wish
you every success and happiness."

"Excellent man!" said Richard Parker, "your kindness overpowers me;
for what you have done for me, may the
blessings of Heaven overtake you."

"I hope it will, Mr. Parker, and all
of us," returned old Ben Binnacle;
"but I am perfectly satisfied that I have
been enabled to perform my duty towards a fellow-creature in misfortune.
This is about the safest point at which
I could land you, for it is quiet and
secluded; you are not likely to be known
or suspected, and it is more than probable that the events of the last few
days have not yet reached the ears of
any of the inhabitants."

"Oh!" ejaculated Mary, "that is
most fortunate; and the nearer we approach the place of our destination, the
more I feel my spirits revive."

Richard returned no answer, and the
lugger in a few minutes more was lying
close alongside the shore.

"I will not venture to land with you,"
observed Binnacle; "for I do not wish
to be seen. A little to the right yonder,
is a lane, and after you have traversed
that, you will come immediately upon as
comfortable an inn as any traveller could
wish to meet with; and kept by as
honest a man as ever ploughed the ocean
of life. There you may obtain every
accommodation, and have nothing to fear,
as the inn is seldom visited by any other
persons than the inhabitants of the place,
and it's a great chance if they have
heard anything of your affair."

"Alas!" returned our hero, still
unable to divest his mind of the melancholy doubts and forebodings that beset
it, "I fear the news has spread with
electric speed to all parts of the country."

"Avast, my lad," returned honest old
Binnacle, "you must not suffer yourself
to be cast on the shoals and quicksands
of despair. Depend upon it, your enemies will never think of searching for
you in this remote place; besides, especially disguised as you are, it is not
likely that any one here will be able to
recognise you. I am well known to
Master Worthington, the landlord of the
inn I have recommended you to, and
should you venture to reveal yourself to
him, I know that you will find in him a
friend, and one who will never betray
you. In a few days I shall probably
return here, and should you think proper to remain, we shall meet again, and
I will bring you intelligence from our
friend Adams, and you will probably by
that time have made up your mind as to
what course it will be most prudent for
you to pursue. Now, cheer up, my
friend, and my word for it that you will
be able to reach the port of happiness
at last."

"Excellent man!" said Richard, again
most cordially pressing the hand of the
veteran seaman; "such disinterested
kindness and friendship as this, towards
one who is an entire stranger to you,
completely overwhelms me, and I know
not how to express to you my gratitude.
I fear that it will never be in my power
to repay you, but I sincerely trust that
Heaven will reward you for the help you
have rendered to the unfortunate in the
greatest hour of their need. I will
follow your advice, and for the sake of
my poor wife and innocent child, I do
hope that the wishes you have so warmly
expressed may be realised."

"Enough, Mr. Parker," returned
Binnacle. "I am satisfied; and with all
my best and heartiest wishes for your
welfare, and with the earnest hope that
we may shortly meet again under more
prosperous and happier circumstances, I

now bid you God's speed, and fare-well."

Mary Parker and her husband would again have overwhelmed the warm-hearted man with their thanks, but his looks expressed how little he required them, and in a few minutes more they stepped on shore, and the lugger again put out to sea, old Ben Binnacle remaining on deck, and waving his hand to them, until the vessel was hidden from the sight in the distance.

Thus the unfortunate fugitives found themselves alone in a strange part of the country, and they stood for some time gazing upon each other with sorrowful looks, and without being able to give utterance to a syllable.

The prospect around them was dreary and cheerless enough, and its aspect was not at all improved by the grey shadows of evening which had now descended upon the earth, and veiled every object in dim obscurity.

"Oh, my beloved Richard," said his devoted wife, at length, "thank Heaven! we are now for the present in safety, and I trust that we shall finally be enabled to elude the vigilance of our pursuers. How greatly are we indebted to Mr. Adams, and this excellent man, for the invaluable services they have rendered us. But you look sad and hopeless, my husband; why will you still encourage those dismal forebodings and apprehensions you have suffered to take possession of your mind?"

"Mary," replied our hero, "deem me not weak when I declare, that, in spite of all my efforts, I cannot shake them off. Such, I am convinced, will be the vigilance of my pursuers, that they will never rest until they have discovered me, and wreaked their vengeance upon my head. I see no other prospect than an ignominious fate before me, and then, alas! what will become of you and our poor child, left alone and un-procted in the cheerless and unfeeling world, as you will then be? Poverty, misery, insult, contumely, persecution of the most merciless and harrowing description, can alone be your portion, and——"

"Oh, in mercy, Richard, forbear!" interrupted his heroic and devoted wife, with a shudder of horror; "how dread-ful is the picture which your tortured

imagination has drawn. I cannot bear to contemplate it, and will not believe that an all-merciful God will ever suffer it to be realised."

"Mary," returned her husband, in the same melancholy and despairing accents, "have I not offended against the laws of that Omnipotent Power to which you appeal?—Are not my hands stained with human blood?—And will you not in future be pointed at and stigmatised as the wife of a murderer?"

"Oh, why, Richard, will you persist in so cruelly reproaching yourself?" said Mary. "Can you remember the many wrongs you received from the late Captain Arlington, and yet find no extenuating circumstances for the deed into which his own rashness and villany unfortunately precipitated you? He would have sacrificed you to his vengeance, and you acted only in self-defence. Heaven surely will pardon you the fatal but unpremeditated deed!"

"For your sake, my faithful wife, and for that of our innocent boy, I would fain hope that it would," returned our hero; "but had we never have met, you would not have been involved in the misery which you are at present; but, on the contrary, you might have been the happy wife of some other man, equally, if not more deserving of you than myself."

"Oh, no, no!" energetically replied Mary; "never could I have loved any other man half so well as I do you, my husband! And have I any cause to regret the course which the strong impulses of my heart prompted me to take? You have been all that my soul could in the intensity of its love desire to me; and though it has been our fate to encounter sorrow and vicissitude, Heaven knows that it has caused in my bosom no feeling of regret, only such as was excited for you. I am still ready to meet any future troubles that may be in store for us with fortitude and without a murmur, so that I can be the means of cheering and sustaining you in your trials; and I must still indulge in the sanguine hope that we shall ultimately be rewarded by future happiness and peace! We shall be enabled to retire to some remote part of the country, where we are unknown; and there Providence will, in its infinite mercy, place us in some situation by which we may be enabled to support ourselves in comfort, if not in affluence."

"Oh, Mary, for your sake, would that the hopes you have just now so fondly expressed might be accomplished," said her husband; "but I dare not give them the least encouragement, for reason convinces me that they are, unfortunately, only doomed to be disappointed."

"Say not so, dear Richard!" remonstrated his wife. "But come, why do we tarry here?—You need refreshment and rest. Let us, then, hasten towards the house which the kind-hearted Mr. Binnacle has so favourably recommended to us, or we may be too late to receive that accommodation which we so much require."

Richard Parker returned no answer to this, but having embraced his affectionate and faithful wife with the utmost tenderness, he took her arm, and they quitted the spot, and took the direction which Binnacle had pointed out to them, our hero frequently looking back to see whether any person was watching them. But not a single individual was to be seen, and it was now completely dark, and therefore every object was rendered the more indistinct. At length they entered upon the lane which Binnacle had mentioned, and a gloomy place it was, a fit haunt for characters of the worst descriptions, and where any deed of darkness might have been perpetrated with impunity. It was of considerable length, but the fugitives quickening their speed, they at last came to the end of it, and emerged from it into a more open part of the country.

The lights which shone from the different casements, soon pointed out to them the inn which Binnacle had mentioned, and a comfortable and retired-looking house it was, well calculated for their purpose, with only a few straggling cottages near it. Here Richard Parker paused, and in spite of all his efforts to the contrary, still hesitated to proceed; but Mary, whose fortitude never for a moment forsook her, encouraged him by a look, as she observed—

"Nay, my dear Richard, do not suffer any groundless apprehensions to disturb your mind; what Mr. Binnacle said to us at parting, ought to inspire us with confidence. It is not likely that any person will know us here; and disguised as we are, I think it would be utterly impossible for even those who are intimately acquainted with us to recognize our persons. Come, come, let us proceed, and trust to Providence for the result."

They did so, and had arrived within a few paces of the house, when a burly, good-tempered-looking man, smoking his pipe with much gusto, appeared at the door, and they concluded from his appearance altogether that he was the landlord. He had observed them directly, and they, therefore, without any further hesitation, advanced towards him, and he greeted them with as much familiarity and cordiality, as if they had been intimately acquainted for years. His honest countenance and manners encouraged Richard, and he said—

"You are the master of this house, I presume?"

"Ay, master," replied the host: "I have been so for more than forty years, and though I say it that shouldn't say it, there is not a better house for accommodation in this part of the country. What can I have the pleasure of doing for you?"

"We are poor people," answered Richard in a feigned voice, "as you probably can see by our garb, with only limited means; but we have journeyed far, and are weary and tired; we need some refreshment, and a lodging for the night. Can you accommodate us?"

"To be sure I can, my friend," answered the landlord; "and that well and cheap; so walk in, and I will attend upon you directly."

"Can you oblige us with a private room?" asked our hero.

"Certainly," returned the host; "though there is no one in the house at present, except a few friends of mine, who usually spend their evenings here. This way, if you please."

With these words, the landlord led the way into the house, and our hero and his wife and child followed him, and they were quickly ushered into a small, but comfortable room, in which a cheerful fire was blazing. Having taken Richard's orders, the landlord was about to retire in order to execute them, when the former detained him.

"You will pardon me, sir, for making a request, which probably may seem a singular one, but I have my reasons for it, which, perhaps, it may be unnecessary for me to explain."

"Oh, certainly," returned the worthy host; "it is no business of mine to inquire into the private affairs of my customers—I have quite enough to do to look after my own. But what may be the request you have to make of me?"

"Merely, sir, that you do not make your guests acquainted with our arrival," answered our hero.

"Oh, certainly, my friend," assented the landlord; "nothing can be more reasonable than that."

He then retired from the room, but as he did so, Richard could not help observing that he eyed himself and his wife narrowly, and that caused some feeling of doubt and misgiving for a moment to enter his mind; but when he recollected the character which Binnacle had given of him, and the honest candour of the landlord's behaviour, it quickly vanished, and he turned to Mary with a look of renewed confidence and hope.

"Heaven be thanked, we are safely housed, my dear Richard," she observed. "The appearance and behaviour of this worthy man, fully realise the description which Mr. Binnacle gave of him; and here, I feel confident, that we are secure from every danger."

"God grant that it may be so, my Mary," answered our hero. "This place is retired, and every way adapted for concealment; and should the landlord prove to be all that he has been described to us, we might probably remain here until we hear again from our friend Adams, and receive his advice as to the course it will be best for us to adopt for our future conduct."

"True, my husband," she replied, "and something seems to assure me that we shall find a friend in the landlord of this inn."

"And yet it would not be prudent for us to make a confidant of him," observed our hero, "until we become better acquainted with his character. But, hush!—He comes."

The landlord now re-entered the room, bringing with him the refreshments they had ordered, and which he placed before them.

"There, my friends," he said, "enjoy yourselves freely, and do not trouble your minds about the reckoning; old Christopher Worthington never yet denied a meal and a lodging to those who stood in need of them, but who had not the best of means to pay for them; and he has never found himself any the poorer for it. When you have a wish to retire to your chamber, you have only to ring the bell, and I will conduct you to it."

"Oh, sir," said Mary, "you are most kind, and such behaviour towards strangers deserves our utmost gratitude."

"Don't mention it, my good woman," returned Worthington; "it is a duty incumbent on us all to assist one another when we have the power, and I only wish that that was a maxim more generally pursued by mankind; there would not be half the misery there is in the world at present. You are strangers in this part of the country?"

"We are, sir," answered Richard, "and have arrived from a distant part."

"And do you intend to stay here long?" asked the landlord.

"I do not think that is probable," replied Richard, who felt rather confused at the questions which Worthington put to him.

"Well, well," observed the host; "that, of course, is no business of mine, only all that I have to say is, that while you remain in this neighbourhood, I shall be most happy to accommodate you."

Richard again returned his acknowledgments, and Worthington again retired from the room, and left the fugitives to their own reflections. Having partaken of the refreshments, they were about to converse upon the prospects before them, when they were interrupted by voices which seemed to proceed from an adjoining apartment, and which they had no doubt were those of the guests to whom the landlord had alluded.

Richard had the curiosity to listen, and he started, and his agitation and alarm may be readily imagined when he heard his own name mentioned. Mary turned ghastly pale, trembled violently, and was obliged to cling to her husband for support. He motioned her to silence, and then placing his ear close to the wainscot, he continued to listen with the most breathless attention.

"It is a bad case—a very bad case," remarked one of the company, "and if they catch him he will be hanged, as sure as his name is Richard Parker, or Admiral Parker, as his partizans have thought proper to dub him."

"Very true, Master Ladbroke," said another of the guests; "and although he has managed to slip through their fingers for the present, it cannot be long before he is discovered and brought to justice."

"To be sure not," remarked the man who had been called Ladbroke; "the minute description given of his person, and that of his wife and child, will be sure to lead to his detection. He cannot possibly escape from the country, and the large reward which is offerered for his apprehension will be sure to find him. I only wish I had the good fortune to meet with him, it wou'd make a man of me, and I much need the money after the bad crops I have had this season."

"Oh, God!" gasped forth the terrified Mary, and clinging more vehemently to her husband.

"Be calm, Mary," whispered our hero, "for all now depends upon our prudence and firmness."

"For shame, Ladbroke," now observed another of the company, in whose voice they recognised that of the landlord; "and could you ever so degrade yourself as to wish to earn the wages of blood?"

"As for that, Mr. Worthington," replied Ladbroke, "I do not consider that I or any other man would be doing more than our duty by delivering so great a criminal up to justice. No proper-minded person, or loyal subject of his most Gracious Majesty, can have any sympathy with a murderer and a mutineer!"

"That may be your opinion, but it is not mine," returned Worthington; "I confess that I do sympathise with this unfortunate man, Richard Parker, not only for his sake, but that of his wife and child. If all be true that is reported, and I have very little doubt that it is, Parker has been a deeply injured and persecuted man, and the late Captain Arlington was a villain."

"But is that any reason why he should be murdered?" demanded Ladbroke.

"Why," remarked Worthington, "the sooner society is rid of such characters as him the better. But Richard Parker I do not consider to be a murderer."

"Indeed!" said Ladbroke, "how do you make that appear, pray? Did not Captain Arlington lose his life by his hands? Here is the whole account of it in the paper, and I can read, I suppose?"

"Captain Arlington made a cowardly and ruffianly attack upon him," returned the landlord; "and Richard Parker only accidentally slew him in his own defence."

"Well, that don't matter," remarked the pertinacious and loquacious Mr. Ladbroke; "it is murder to all intents and purposes; and they would hang him if he had a thousand necks. Besides, he is a mutineer, and his life is forfeited to the outraged laws of his country, if even he had committed no other offence."

"Well, all I hope is that they may not be able to discover him," replied Worthington. "I would be no cause of his apprehension, if even I knew where to find him this moment."

"You wouldn't?" demanded Ladbroke, in a tone of surprise and incredulity.

"No, I wouldn't," repeated the landlord, "for I should consider myself as an arrant rascal were I to do so, and should never be able to rest in my bed afterwards."

"Generous, humane man!" ejaculated Mary, fervently; "oh, Heaven be praised that we have fallen into such hands; you may yet be saved, my dear Richard."

Richard, who conquered his emotion as well as he could, again motioned her to silence, and then once more listened.

"I am surprised to hear you talk so, Mr. Worthington," observed Ladbroke, "for it is very little better than treason. Do you mean to say that if you knew where Parker was at the present time concealed that you would assist to screen him from the hands of justice?"

"I do not for a moment hesitate to say that I would," answered Worthington; "however, there is not much chance of my having it in my power to serve him in that manner, for it is not very likely that he will seek refuge in this part of the country."

"I don't know that," returned Ladbroke; "there is more unlikely places than this, so retired as it is. But it is not improbable, I think, if he could only find friends who had the power to assist him, that he has put out to sea, with the hope of being able to reach some foreign coast."

"And if he has done so," remarked the landlord, "it is equally likely that he has perished in the recent storm. Poor fellow, I sincerely pity him, for I believe from all that I have heard of his character, that had he had justice rendered to him he would have proved himself an ornament to society, and an honour to the British navy."

"Well," replied Ladbroke, "I must still maintain my opinion, and I cannot feel the least sympathy with any man who has been guilty of such a crime as that which Richard Parker has committed. Justice is justice, and if we offend against the laws of the country we must expect to pay the penalty. But it is getting late, and, therefore, it is time that we departed for home. Good night, friend Worthington."

"Good-night, Master Ladbroke," replied the landlord, "and I hope the time will come, when you will learn to temper justice with mercy."

What the answer was that Ladbroke returned to this, Richard could not catch, but directly afterwards he heard the guests take their departure, and that was the greatest relief to his mind. Mary sank in his arms, and the ghastly paleness of her countenance showed at once the extreme agitation under which she was labouring.

"Be firm, my love, my Mary," said her husband, "for on that depends our safety. It seems as if Fate had conspired against me and that there is no escaping the doom with which I am threatened. This neighbourhood is evidently no place of retreat for us, and we must depart again from it as soon as possible, if we have the opportunity. Alas! alas! what miserable, wandering outcasts we are."

"But still, fortune has been kind to us, my dear Richard," replied his wife, "in guiding our footsteps to this house. Should we be discovered, we may, from the observations we have overheard him make, calculate upon a friend in this excellent Mr. Worthington."

"Alas! I fear that his power to aid us, however great his will, would be limited," replied Richard. "But silence! I hear some one approaching, and doubtless it is he."

Mary hastily tried to compose herself, and the next instant the landlord entered the room. He hastily closed the door after him, and then looked at them stedfastly for a moment or two.

"Before you retire to rest, my friends," he said, "I must have a word with you. Do not alarm yourselves, for you have nothing to fear from me. You are not what you have represented yourselves to me."

"Ah!" exclaimed Richard Parker, starting; "this is a boldness, sir! What do you mean?"

"Nay," returned Mr. Worthington, "do not judge me hastily, for you may find me to be your friend. If I am not much mistaken, you are that unfortunate man, Richard Parker, for whose apprehension a large reward is offered."

"Ah! discovered!" cried our hero; "then my only course is one of desperation and determination."

"Again I request you not to agitate yourself," remarked Worthington, "and repeat, that you have nothing to fear from me. I felt satisfied that it was you the moment I saw you, notwithstanding your disguise."

"Oh, sir," ejaculated Mary, throwing herself at his feet, and looking up imploringly in his face; "you will not betray my unfortunate husband, and thus consign his wife and innocent child to the most indescribable, the most insupportable misery? Indeed, did you but know how deeply he has been injured, and what we have suffered, you would pity us."

"Rise, my good lady," replied the landlord, in his kindest accents; "I do, indeed, pity you, and am ready to offer you all the assistance in my power. Heaven forbid that old Christopher Worthington, after all the many years he has lived in the world, should now be guilty of an act of inhumanity towards his suffering fellow-creatures. I do believe from all that I have heard that your husband is not so guilty as he is represented; and although, unfortunately, he has destroyed the life of Captain Arlington, and thus rendered himself amenable to the laws of his country, that he only did so by accident and in self-defence, and that it was a just though terrible retribution on the head of that misguided and guilty gentleman."

"Oh, thanks—thanks, generous sir, for that opinion!" said our hero, grasping his hand. "But I must immediately depart from hence, and ——"

"Nay, not so," interrupted Worthington, "for, should you be seen in the neighbourhood, the utmost danger would have to be apprehended. If you can depend upon me, and I would sooner forfeit my life than act the part of a traitor, you may remain here concealed, until some arrangement can be made for your future safety; and you may by that means set detection at defiance."

"Generous man!" exclaimed Richard; "and is it possible that you will venture to run such risks for me, an entire stranger?"

"When you know me better, sir," replied Worthington, "you will find that there are no risks that I will not venture to run to save a fellow-creature in distress."

"May the blessings of Heaven light upon your head for this!" ejaculated Mary. "Oh, well did Mr. Binnacle depicture your character to us, and ——"

"Binnacle!" interrupted Worthington, hastily. "Do you allude to old Ben Binnacle, the master of the lugger, the Nancy?"

"The same, Mr. Worthington," replied Richard. "It was he who brought us to this coast from the scene of danger, and recommended us to your house, as the one in which we might be sure to be best accommodated, and be the least exposed to danger."

"What!" exclaimed Worthington, "and could he depart again without calling to shake the hand of, and take a glass with his old friend?—That was not right, at any rate, and ——"

"You will pardon him, I am sure, Mr. Worthington," observed Richard. "when you hear that he was pressed for time, and, moreover, he considered that it would not be exactly safe or prudent for him to come ashore."

"Ay—ay," replied the kind-hearted old man, "I see it all now clear enough, and commend him for the precaution which he used. A more noble-hearted fellow than Ben Binnacle does not exist, and he has done himself eternanl honour by this disinterested act of humanity."

"Yes," remarked our hero, " to him and another individual I owe a debt of gratitude, I fear I shall never be able to repay."

"And may I inquire the name of your other friend?" said the landlord.

"I feel that I can confide in you, sir, after what I have heard to-night," returned Parker, " and I therefore do not hesitate to inform you that the noble-hearted man to whom I am indebted for my escape, and who supplied me with the means for my present wants, is my old shipmate, Adams."

"What, Jack Adams of the Sandwich?" said Worthington.

"The same!" answered our here. "You know him, then?"

"Know him!" replied Mr. Worthington. "Oh, well, though it is some time since we have met. Jack Adams and I have had many a cheerful glass together, when he has been in this quarter, and the strictest friendship existed between us. Fate seems to have ordained that you should be guided hither, and that I should exert my myself to serve you; and if I do not do so to the best of my abilities, say my name is not Cristopher Worthington."

"Oh, sir," said Richard, "how can I express my thanks to you for this unexampled act of kindness? But no, it must not be. Should it be discovered that you secreted me or aided me in my escape, it would bring destruction upon your head, and why should I, a stranger to you, one whom you never beheld before, be the cause of exposing you to such infinite peril?"

"Say no more, my friend," remarked the kind-hearted old man. "I am fully prepared to brave everything sooner than see one who I firmly believe to have been so deeply injured, consigned to a fate so fearful and so ignominious. You could not possibly have a better place of concealment than this house. It is seldom that it is visited by strangers, unless it be a casual traveller, and I fancy that the officers of justice would never for a moment think of searching here for the object of their pursuit. No thanks, my unfortunate friends; what Christopher Worthington does, comes from his heart, and he will consider himself sufficiently rewarded in the certainty of having done his duty. So, here, then, you are welcome to remain as long as you think proper, and till some arrangements can be made for your

RICHARD CONSOLES MARY'S TERRORS DURING THE STORM.

future safety. There is no one but myself and my wife; besides, our friends, Adams and Binnacle, will be in the secret, and, therefore, there is no fear of detection."

"Mr. Worthington!" remarked Richard, grasping his hand more vehemently than before, "this noble act from one whom I never before saw, quite overpowers me, and I am totally at a loss to express my feelings. Believe me, that so many, so painful, and degrading are the trials to which I have been exposed, that I care little what fate might now overtake me; but for the sake of my poor and innocent wife and child, I would wish to live—for what would become of them if they should be deprived of my protection?"

"Horrible thought!" ejaculated Mary, with a shudder; "but an all-merciful Providence will never suffer it to take place. My dear husband, pray seek to banish such fearful ideas from your mind, and to look forward to the future with hope and confidence."

"True, Mrs. Parker," observed Worthington; "and depend upon it, as you put your trust in Providence, you will not be doomed to be disappointed. Dreary as your prospects at present are, the time will yet come when you will be restored to happiness; and I do trust your husband may yet be forgiven the offences he has committed, and be suffered to return once more to society."

"Oh, no, Mr. Worthington," answered our hero, "it would be madness for me to seek to flatter myself with any such fallacious hopes! Am I not considered in the eyes of the law a murderer, as well as a mutineer?—And what hope can I have of ever receiving any mercy or forgiveness?"

"Well, Mr. Parker," returned Worthington, "I am only glad that fortune has guided your footsteps hither, and we will talk upon this subject further, anon."

"But the man, Ladbroke?" inquired Richard.

"Ah! ejaculated Worthington, "you overheard the conversation that just now passed between us, then?"

"I did," answered Parker, "and can never feel sufficiently grateful to you for the kind sympathy you expressed in my fate. But is there not much to be feared from that man?"

"If he were aware that you were here there might be," said the landlord; "and yet, I do not think that there would either; he is only a busy, loquacious, thoughtless sort of individual. But I do not think there is any real harm in him after all. Besides, he can have no suspicion that you are here, and, therefore, you will have nothing whatever to fear from him. But the hour is getting late,

so, had you not better retire to rest? and to-morrow I will see you again, and we will further discuss this important subject. You need not, I repeat, be under the slightest apprehension, for you will be perfectly safe from any interruption."

"Indeed, my kind, disinterested friend," replied our hero, "I should be most ungrateful could I for a moment doubt you. Again I must be permitted to offer you my sincere and fervent acknowledgments for what you have already done, and——"

"Enough, my dear sir," interrupted Worthington; "again I assure you that I require no thanks; but should I see the whole of my wishes accomplished I shall be more than repaid for any trouble or inconvenience to which I may be put in seeking to serve one whom I believe to have been so deeply injured and so truly unfortunate as yourself."

"Ah, sir," returned Richard, "I have indeed been a cruelly wronged man. I have suffered tortures and indignities sufficient to harrow up the soul, and drive the brain to madness to think upon. Probably, sometime or other, if the opportunity is afforded me, I may make you acquainted with the melancholy facts of my history, and then will you not marvel that I should act as I have done, but you will, I think, wonder that my nature was not entirely changed, that every proper feeling was not extinguished in my breast, and that I did not, in fact, become the same demon in heart as that man from whom I have to date all my misfortunes, and who has at length had to pay the penalty of his crimes. But let me no longer detain you; I shall see you, I presume, in the morning?"

Mr. Worthington answered in the affirmative, and then taking up the lamp, he desired our hero and his wife, and the boy, William (who, overcome with fatigue, had fallen asleep during the best part of the time that this conversation was taking place) to follow him, and he then led the way up a back-staircase to the top of the house, and stopping at an old-fashioned oak-door on the landing, he opened it, and ushered them into an ancient, but comfortable, suite of chambers, which the worthy man had taken care, during the short time they had been at the inn, to prepare for their reception.

"These apartments are at your service as long as you like to remain here," he observed, "and being remote from any other part of the house, you need be under no apprehension of being intruded upon by any one but myself and my dame, who, although I say it, is as worthy a woman as ever drew the breath of life, and, what is more remarkable still," he added, with a smile, "she knows how to keep a secret, and no one can more deeply sympathise with the misfortunes of her fellow creatures than herself. I am so glad to think that Providence has guided your footsteps to my house, for nothing can give old Christopher Worthington greater pleasure than to be able to serve a fellow-creature in distress. Besides, you can have the range of the private part of the house without fear, and no doubt we shall be able to make every arrangement for your comfort and security."

"Generous-hearted man," exclaimed Mary, her eyes over-flowing with tears of gratitude, "may the blessings of a wife and mother light upon your head, for this noble act. Of what a weight of of care have you relieved my mind, and——"

"Pray cease, Mrs. Parker," interrupted Worthington, "for you quite overwhelm me by these numerous thanks for having done nothing more than performed my duty. Could I turn indifferently away from those who needed my aid, I should hate and despise myself. But enough of this. Should those who are in pursuit of you take it in their heads to pay me a visit and to search my house, which I do not think is very likely, you will still have nothing to fear, for I will show you the means of concealment; such means as must completely baffle them. Follow me for a minute."

They did so, and he led the way to a third chamber, and pushing the bedstead aside, showed them a secret door which opened by a spring, and then revealed to them a winding flight of stairs beyond.

"These stairs," he observed, "lead to some cellars or vaults below the house, and are only known to myself and wife, and, consequently, you would be there

as safe from detection, as if you were buried in the bowels of the earth."

Richard and his wife once more returned their acknowledgments, and having closed the door, and pointed out to them the way to open it, they returned to the room they had just before quitted.

"Thus you see, Mr. Parker," remarked the old man, "I did not exaggerate when I said that you could not have found a better place of security than my house, and Ben Binnacle acted a wise part in recommending you here. Now, now, I know what you would say, but do not distress your mind by any consideration of being under an obligation to me, but endeavour to make yourself as comfortable as possible. However, we have talked long enough at present. I will see you at breakfast in the morning, when I will introduce you to my wife, and I have no doubt that you will be pleased with her, and feel satisfied that she is every way worthy of your confidence. Good night, my friends, and may Heaven bring rest and comfort to your pillows."

Having thus spoken and cordially pressed their hands, without giving them time to return any answer, the good old man quitted the room, and left them to the free indulgence of their own thoughts and feelings. What the nature of those were, the reader may easily form a conception of; their hearts overflowed with gratitude to Mr. Worthington, and sinking on their knees, they fervently returned their thanks to that Omnipotent power that had hitherto so mercifully watched over their safety.

"Dear Richard," ejaculated his wife, throwing her fair arms around his neck, and looking with the utmost affection in his face; "banish from your mind the gloomy misgivings that have hitherto distracted it, and rest assured that those dark clouds that have so long obscured our path, are destined to pass away, and that happiness will again be ours. Providence has not yet deserted us, and I feel satisfied that it never will, while we continue to put our trust in it. Oh, my husband, with what different feelings shall we then be enabled to look upon the dreary past, to those we now experience; and how greatly shall we profit by the fearful lesson we have been taught.

Come, come, my Richard, do not look so sad and despairing, for improbable as it may now appear to be, something whispers to me, that all I have just now predicted will be realised."

"Ah! Mary," replied our hero, "your unexampled patience and fortitude under circumstances sufficient to break down the strongest spirit, unmans me more than all; and in vain I endeavour to struggle with the dreadful feelings that torture my mind; in vain do I seek to encourage the hopes you so affectionately try to inspire in my bosom. Alas! alas! what prospect is there of my ever escaping the awful and ignominious fate which is impending o'er my head? Can the mutineer, the murderer, expect any mercy? They will continue to hunt me like some wild beast until they have me in their power, and where can we long conceal ourselves? And can we expect for ever to be dependant on the bounty of strangers, and to involve them in the dangers by which we are ourselves surrounded? For your sake, my faithful wife, and that of our beloved boy, I would still cling to life; otherwise, so many are the troubles and vicissitudes I have experienced in it, so many are the unmerited persecutions to which I have been subjected, that I could hail death as a happy release, and with the hope of finding that rest and peace in another world which has been denied me here."

"Richard," ejaculated our heroine, "you torture and distract my mind to madness by talking thus. Let us place our reliance on the goodness and mercy of the Supreme, and bear the trials with which He has been pleased to visit us, with fortitude and resignation. The time will come, depend upon it, when these black and dismal clouds will pass away, when justice will be rendered you, and all will again be light and happiness around us. We ought indeed to be most grateful to the Almighty for having raised up for us at least these few staunch and disinterested friends in the midst of our difficulties."

"Oh, Mary," returned Richard, "and think you that I am indeed unmindful of the vast obligations we owe them? I should despise myself if I could; but I shudder to think what the consequences would be, should it be discovered that they aided me in my escape and concealment."

"Do not torture yourself, my husband," said Mary, "by any such apprehensions, for I feel confident that they will have to be groundless. If proper precaution be used, it is impossible that suspicion can light upon them. The observations of this excellent man, Mr. Worthington, have inspired me with fresh hopes; no place could be better adapted for concealment than this house; here then, please God, we can remain in security till such time as the excitement which at present prevails is abated, when we may make our escape to some remote part of the country, where we may live unknown and unmolested."

"How, Mary?" observed our hero; "what prospect have we of doing so, when we are entirely destitute of every means? God knows how willing I am to work; but where can I hope to find employment, friendless as I am, and branded with the name of felon? To be seen, to be known, would be to consign myself to an ignominious death. Alas! alas! what a cursed destiny it was that ever introduced me to you. It is I who have torn you from a parent's heart; from hope, from wealth, from every comfort, and I feel myself to be a villain, and that I deserve your curses and reproaches instead of the devoted affection you have ever bestowed upon me."

"For the love of Heaven, cease, Richard!" replied Mary, fixing upon him a look of terror and agony; "your words, I repeat, distract and torture me; think you I can ever love my husband less because of the misfortunes that have befallen him? Oh, I should indeed be unworthy of you could I do so. But your mind is distracted and bewildered by the many cruel sufferings it has been your hard lot so long to endure, and the anxiety you feel for myself and our child, and you know not what you say. Come, come, let us retire to rest, and by the morning, I trust, that your feelings will have become more composed, and you will see the necessity of acting with prudence, firmness, and resolution."

"Ah, my dear Mary!" returned Richard, "have I not a right to fear the worst, after the conversation we overheard to-night ? I feel that I am surrounded by dangers every moment we remain here."

"Nay, Richard," observed our heroine, "this is ungenerous and unreasonable; surely, after the candour and kindness with which he has already behaved to us, and the friendship that exists between him and Adams and Binnacle, you cannot doubt the sincerity of Mr. Worthington ?"

"Oh, no," answered Parker, "believe me I am not so ungrateful as that. I am satisfied that he is an honest and a humane man, who would willingly do everything in his power to serve a fellow creature in distress ; but why should I involve him in any trouble and danger on my account, who am a complete stranger to him ?"

"You will not do so, Richard," answered his wife, "for it cannot possibly ever be suspected that he has taken any part in your concealment; he, no doubt, will act with due precaution to prevent that ; but let us wait patiently till the morning, when we may consult him further upon the subject."

Fearful that he should increase the anguish of her mind, Richard Parker conquered his emotions as well as he could, and once more enfolding his wife affectionately to his bosom, he ejaculated—

"Dearest and best of women and of wives! pardon me, if any observation I have made use of should have caused you a single pang. 'Tis true, that trouble has so distracted and bewildered my brain, that at times I know not what I say ; but, henceforth, I will endeavour to follow your sweet advice in every respect, and to wait with patience, fortitude, and resignation, the fate which may be in store for me; but which, at the same time, for your sake, I pray to Heaven to avert. Come, my love, let us once more return our thanks to the Supreme for our preservation so far, and supplicate his mercy and protection for the future."

Mary returned no answer, but her looks spoke far more eloquently than words could have done what she felt, and again they all knelt down, and in accents of fervour and sincerity, they offered up their devotions to that Almighty power, who never deserts even the most humble and erring of His creatures, who put their trust in Him. This act of duty performed, they arose from their knees, and having once more listened, and found that all was silent in the house, they retired to rest, and endeavoured to obtain a temporary respite from their cares and anxieties in sleep.

CHAPTER X.

MARY'S DREAM.—CHRISTOPHER WORTHINGTON PROVES HIMSELF TO BE A REAL FRIEND.

WORN out with fatigue, and the extreme anxiety and excitement of mind he had so long experienced, Richard Parker soon sunk off to repose, but his faithful and affectionate wife for some time found it utterly impossible to gain a similar respite to her troubles. The dismal forebodings of her unfortunate husband, and the reason she had to fear that they would be realised, notwithstanding the hopes with which she had sought to inspire him, filled her mind with the most torturing and insupportable apprehensions, and she could not anticipate the future without a shudder of horror. She was compelled to acknowledge to herself that the fears he had expressed were too well founded, and that they were surrounded by the most imminent danger ; and although she placed the utmost confidence in the sincerity of the professions of Mr. Worthington and their other friends, yet she deeply deplored the painful necessity that compelled them thus to be beholden to the benevolence of others, and who, in seeking to serve them, might become involved in danger, and bring down upon themselves the vengeance of the law. It was too certain that the pursuit of her unfortunate husband would not easily be abandoned, and could he for ever escape detection? Alas, no! although she tried so hard to do so, she could not flatter herself with any such hopes, which she had too much reason to fear would prove delusive ; and should he be apprehended, could he expect any mercy from the law, charged with the serious offences that he was, and anxious as his enemies were to make a terrible example of him ? —He could not ; and when she reflected upon the awful doom which would be passed upon him, the blood froze with horror in her veins, and her fortitude almost entirely forsook her. The predictions of Mad Moll recurred to her memory with tenfold force, and when she considered the too great probability of their being fulfilled, her brain became distracted, and despair settled upon her heart. How great was her agony!—how powerful the feelings that tortured her breast, as she gazed on her sleeping husband, and noticed the fearful ravages which incessant care had made upon his handsome and manly countenance.

"And must this noble being," she reflected, "he, whose soul is the seat of every honourable and virtuous sentiment, be consigned to the awful and ignominous fate of the veriest criminal that ever disgraced society?—Must I thus cruelly be deprived of him who is far dearer to me than my own existence?—Forbid it, Heaven!—The very thought is sufficient to drive my brain to madness! But, oh, God! if it must be so, in thy mercy let me not live to witness his appalling fate! Oh, take, I beseech Thee, myself and my poor child to thy bosom! for what would become of us were we to be deprived of his protection, and by such revolting and awful means? Arlington, guilty and misguided man! thou art the cause of all this misery!—But for thee we might have been happy, strangers to every care! May Heaven pardon thee! And then, my father!—oh, surely, ere death shall overtake thee, thou wilt be awakened to reason, justice, and compunction, and have bitter cause to repent the unnatural conduct thou hast pursued towards me!"

She wrung her hands with agony as these painful thoughts occurred to her, and her tears flowed fast and unrestrained. In these moments of anguish she recalled to her memory in the most vivid colours all the scenes of her early days; the happiness that she and Richard experienced in each other's love; the ideal scenes of future bliss they had fondly pictured to themselves;—and when she contrasted them with the misery of the present, her feelings almost overpowered her, and she shrunk appalled from the contemplation of that which was yet in store for them. Again she fervently prayed to Heaven to avert the dreadful evils she apprehended, and that it would in its infinite mercy rather take them at once to itself than suffer her beloved husband to perish by such awful means as those with which he was now threatened.

At length, however, nature was completely exhausted, and sleep descended upon her eyelids; but it brought her no relief. The harrowing thoughts that had tortured her mind in her waking moments haunted her imagination in her slumbers. Visions of the most frightful description were presented to her imagination, and she frequently started up, the perspiration hanging in large drops upon her temples, and gazed around the chamber with terrified looks, as though she expected to encounter some fearful object. All, however, was silent as the grave; the rest of her husband remained undisturbed, and at length she again sunk beneath the influence of the somniferous god. And now a vision occurred to her of a more fearful description than any which had previously been presented to her imagination.

She imagined that it was night, and herself, her husband, and their child were wandering cheerless and wretched over a barren waste, in a strange part of the country, and where, as far as the eye could trace, there was not the least sign of a human habitation. They were miserably clad, and so much exhausted with want and fatigue, that it was with difficulty they could drag one limb after the other. The wind was piercingly cold, and the snow descended upon the earth in heavy flakes, rendering it difficult to proceed, and adding to the misery of their feelings. In this manner, Mary imagined, they continued to wander on for some time, without anything occurring to inspire them with hope, and the wind howling and bellowing around them in a manner that was quite frightful to listen to, and everything seeming to whisper to them horror and despair. At length the way became perfectly impassable, and, benumbed with cold, they became transfixed to the spot, and gazed around them with feelings of the most indescribable anguish, but still not the least prospect of relief appeared, and it seemed as if an awful and untimely death inevitably awaited them. At length, Mary imagined in her dream that her husband's fortitude and physical strength seemed entirely to have failed him, and with a deep sigh, and an expression of the eyes which it was awful to contemplate, he sunk upon the snow-covered ground, and it appeared as if his life were speedily about to depart from him. Frantically she called upon his name, with every endearing expression she could make use of, and sought to arouse him —forgetting her own sufferings in her efforts to do so; but it was all to no purpose; he fixed one glance upon her of the most intense emotion and affection, he tried to speak, but could not, and sinking back in her arms, his eyes seemed to close as if in death. Oh, the agony of that moment! So strong was the impression her dream had made upon her, that never, never from that moment could it be effaced from her memory. She threw her arms around his neck now, regardless of the cold, and in distracted accents called upon his name; but the echoes of her own voice were all that replied to her. The poor boy, William, also knelt upon the ground in the cold snow, by his father's side, and looking piteously in his pale face, rent the air with his cries. Suddenly these demonstrations of violent grief were interrupted by a strange, discordant, and derisive sound, and looking up, Mary Parker beheld the singular and mysterious being, called Mad Moll, standing before her, and pointing significantly towards the inanimate form of her husband.

"He lives," our heroine fancied in her dream that the old woman exclaimed; "fate has decreed that he should not perish thus; but nothing can avert the doom that is in store for him, and which I have predicted. For a time he will be spared to encounter fresh troubles, but that which is written in the Book of Fate must be fulfilled: he dies the death of a criminal!"

Mary thought in the agony of her feelings she tried to speak, and to sue to the woman for mercy; but she was deprived of all power to articulate a syllable; the form of the woman seemed gradually to melt away, and with a faint scream, our heroine awoke.

For a few moments she gazed vacantly and bewildered around the room, and could scarcely believe but that what she had seen was reality; but the position in which she found herself soon convinced her to the contrary, and she fixed her eyes with the most earnest attention upon the countenance of her husband, who still slept soundly, and she felt some little degree of relief. She pressed a kiss of the most unbounded affection upon his lips, and offered up a brief but earnest prayer to Heaven for his safety; but she did not attempt to wake him, lest what she had to communicate should only serve to add to the agony of mind he was already enduring. She threw herself back on her pillow, and notwithstanding all her efforts to the contrary, sleep once more overpowered her senses, and again her troubled imagination conjured up the following vision.

The scene was now changed. Richard and herself, and their child, were now in an open boat together on the wide ocean, and exposed to all the horrors of a furious tempest, in which it seemed to be impossible that they could save themselves from perishing. The sea ran mountains high, and the white surge was dashed to the summits of the loftiest rocks, with which the coast was bounded, and which stretched themselves far into the deep. Sometimes their frail vessel was tossed as it were to the clouds, and then again they were engulphed in the bosom of the raging billows and struggling desperately for life. The night was dark as pitch, save when the blue forked lightning shot across the angry sky, and rendered the horrors of the scene more distinct. To guide their boat was impossible, and they were driven about at the mercy of the waves, with no other prospect but a frightful death every moment before their eyes. No hope of assistance was nigh, all around them was madness and despair. In this manner they continued to struggle for some time, calling at intervals, in their frenzy, upon Heaven for mercy; but at length one tremendous wave swept over them, and the next moment they were struggling amid the wild and destructive element. Mary imagined in her dream that her husband had wildly and desperately clasped herself and her boy, but all his efforts were ineffectual; wave after wave drove with irresistible fury over them; the sky above them gradually faded from her sight; the waters hissed and gurgled in her ears; strange and frightful phantoms seemed to dance before her eyes, and all consciousness seemed to leave her. Still, it was only the unconsciousness of sleep, and once more her busy fancy was at work. Again the scene was changed, and she now beheld herself in a gloomy dungeon, and clasped to the bosom of her husband, whose limbs were heavily laden with fetters, while his emaciated features bore all the ashy and ghastly aspect of death. How solemn was the silence that reigned around, save when it was interrupted by their sobs of agony and despair, though they were neither of them able to give utterance to a word. Suddenly turning her gaze away for a moment from Richard, Mary again beheld Mad Moll standing before them, and gazing at them with mingled expressions of pity and exultation. Mary thought that she made an effort to give utterance to some words of supplication to her, but the power of speech was denied her, and the old woman in solemn accents ejaculated—

"The hour marked by fate has arrived; no earthly power can avert it; wretched, unfortunate beings, prepare yourselves to part for ever in this world. Richard Parker, the executioners await you."

"Oh, mercy—mercy! Spare my husband, for my sake, for the sake of his innocent child!" Mary thought in her dream that she screamed, but the woman only waved her hand, and the next moment the dungeon-door was opened, and several persons entered, whose ominous looks told too plainly the awful errand they had come upon. With frantic strength and the frenzy of despair, Mary still clung to him, and continued to shriek aloud for mercy, but her cries seemed to be unheeded, and they proceeded to force them from each other's arms. Richard struggled hard, but his efforts were all in vain, and he was forced from the dungeon, and along the various dreary and frightful passages to the outside of the prison, Mary following, and shrieking wildly for help on the way.

And now they stood on the deck of a man-of-war, arranged with all the awful paraphernalia of an execution, and it was evident that the last fatal moment had arrived. Mary was again clasped in the arms of her unfortunate husband; his demeanour was firm and manly, but his countenance was as pale as death, and the expression of his eyes, as they were fixed with melancholy earnestness upon her, was such as in her waking moments could never be effaced from her memory. It would be impossible to describe the agony that the sleeper endured at this time; again she shrieked aloud for mercy, but there was no one present to lend a pitying ear to her frenzied supplications. An officer now approached, and whispered something in the ear of Richard; he bowed his head in obedience, and then frantically kissing her and his child, and invoking a blessing on their heads, he gently placed them in the charge of a seaman standing by, whom she now recognised to be Jack Adams, and resigned himself into the hands of his executioners. She saw them remove the handkerchief from his neck, she beheld him mount the ladder, she noticed them adjust the fatal halter; she heard him say—

"Farewell for ever in this world, my beloved Mary and my poor boy, and may Heaven's blessings attend you. Richard Parker will die like a man!"

And with a piercing shriek she awoke.

The cry to which she gave utterance awoke her husband, and starting from the couch at the same moment that she did, he caught her in his arms.

"Hold—hold, monsters! forbear your murderous purpose!" she cried, gazing wildly around her, and not knowing where she was; "you shall not drag him from me to so hideous a death! Oh, Richard! my love! my husband, we will die together!"

"Mary! dear Mary!" ejaculated her husband, pressing her more closely to his bosom; "I am here! No danger has yet befallen me, love! For the love of Heaven, what means this wild emotion?"

But she could not answer him; the strength of her emotions had overcome her, and she swooned in his arms. The agitation of our hero was almost equal to her own, and again and again he imprinted kisses of the most unbounded affection on her lips, and endeavoured to recall her to animation; but for some time his endeavours were ineffectual, and he had a great mind to summon assistance.

Day was just beginning to dawn, and he could hear the inmates of the house beginning to stir ; he, therefore, exerted himself still more to recall his wife to her senses, for they might quickly be summoned to the morning meal, and he wished to obtain some explanation from Mary as to what occasioned her

THE VISION OF MARY PARKER WHILE AT THE INN.

such powerful alarm, previous to their entering the presence of Mr. Worthington and his wife.

He was not long kept in suspense, however, for in a few minutes Mary recovered, and opening her eyes, and beholding herself clasped in the arms of her husband, she uttered an exclamation of astonishment and delight.

"Richard ! dear Richard !" she ejaculated, " are you indeed still spared to me ? They have not torn you from me, and consigned you to that dreadful fate? Oh, God! I thank Thee for this expression of Thy mercy!"

"Compose yourself, Mary," said our hero; "you see I am perfectly safe, and that I clasp you to my bosom. Some frightful dream must have alarmed you thus."

"Oh, yes, thank Heaven, it was but a dream!" replied Mary; "but still so fearful was the description of it, that even now when I reflect on it I shudder with horror."

"Tell me, my love," said our hero, whose curiosity was greatly excited, "what was the nature of it that it should agitate you thus?"

"Do not urge me, Richard," she replied, "for I dare not repeat to you that which was presented to my disturbed imagination. Oh, God! surely it can never be Thy will that it should be realised."

"Nay, Mary," remarked Richard, "this hesitation does but increase my curiosity. But I pray you explain everything, for you shall find that I have firmness to listen to you, let the nature of it be whatever it may. Richard Parker is too well prepared for his fate to shrink from anything that may seem to relate to it."

Mary still hesitated, but after a few moments' reflection she mustered resolution, and in as few words as she could, and with as little emotion as she could help, she related to him the particulars of the extraordinary dreams that had occurred to her, and to which her husband listened with the most profound attention, and with mingled feelings of anguish and regret. When she had ceased, he gazed at her earnestly for an instant, and then heaving a deep sigh, he turned away from her, and with folded arms, paced the room for a few minutes, in a state of considerable alarm, and muttering incoherent words to himself. Mary watched him with considerable anxiety, but at length she advanced towards him, and placing her hand gently upon his arm, and looking up affectionately in his face, she said—

"It was, indeed, a fearful dream, dear Richard; but, for Heaven's sake, do not let it agitate you thus! It was that I feared it would do so, that made me hesitate to disclose it to you."

"Mary," replied our hero, "believe me, it is not for myself I fear, for I am fully prepared to meet any fate that may await me as a man! Richard Parker has too often faced death in the battle's heat and the tempest's fury, to tremble at it now! But it is for you, my wife, and our innocent boy, that my anxious thoughts are excited, and it is that which makes me shudder, when I reflect upon the probability of our worst fears—of those awful dreams being realised!"

"Oh, no, Richard," returned his wife, 'do not encourage such dreadful, such torturing thoughts. Those dreams will never be realised! I should go mad if I thought they would! It was only my disordered imagination that conjured them up. Let us endeavour to banish them from our recollection."

"Ah, Mary!" he said, fixing upon her a melancholy look, "it is impossible for me to do so; when I reflect upon all the unfortunate circumstances connected with us, I feel satisfied that, however my fate may be deferred, sooner or later it will overtake me; and, were it not for you, so tired am I of existence, I would no longer seek to avoid it."

"Terrible thought!" ejaculated Mary. "Oh! why will you persist in abandoning yourself to such feelings of despair? That Supreme Power which has hitherto so mercifully watched over our safety, will not now desert us, but in His own wise time will restore us to that happiness from which we have been so long estranged!"

Richard shook his head in a melancholy manner, as he replied,—

"Alas, Mary! happiness may yet again be the lot of yourself and our boy, and oh! how fervently do I pray to Heaven that it may be so; but it can never again be mine! I have drunk too deeply of the poisoned chalice of sorrow ever again to know peace; and there is that upon my mind that presses me down to the earth, and must ever render me one of the most miserable of human beings! When I am gone, you may find friends who will commiserate with and protect you, but while I remain ——"

"Cease, Richard!" interrupted our heroine, with a look of horror and gentle reproach; "such words as these are daggers to my heart, and if you love me sincerely, you will not repeat them. Oh,

God ! of what value would life be to me were I deprived of you?—you, on whom my heart's fondest affections have ever been placed!—Would not everything that this world contains then become hateful to me? It would!—Oh, Richard, you surely must doubt the sincerity of my feelings, or you could never have given utterance to such cruel words as these!"

"Pardon me, dear Mary," returned Richard, "if I have given expression to one word which may sound harsh and ungenerous towards you! Doubt your sincerity—the devoted affection you have ever lavished upon me?—I must, indeed, be a villain if I could do so. But——"

He was interrupted by a gentle knock at the room-door, and not doubting who it was, Richard and his wife hastily endeavoured to conquer their emotions, and the former then gave admittance to Mr. Worthington, who greeted them with increased cordiality, and inquired after their health.

"I trust that you have both enjoyed a good night's rest, my friends," he continued; "though, to tell the truth, you do not look much refreshed. However, there is nothing surprising in that, after the extraordinary anxiety of mind you have so long had to undergo. But the morning repast is now ready in my private room below, and I have made my old dame acquainted with all the particulars, so you can enter her presence without any embarrassment; she is most anxious to be introduced to you, and I know you will find her worthy of your confidence. Come—come, my friends! —to breakfast, and then to business."

Richard Parker and his wife returned no answer to these friendly observations, but followed Mr. Worthington down stairs into a back parlour, where they found a comely, good-looking old dame, a worthy counterpart of her husband, seated at the breakfast-table, and completing all the necessary arrangements for that meal.

She arose on their entrance, and being introduced by her husband, she greeted them, and welcomed them to "The Punch Bowl," in the most cordial manner.

"I am sure," said the loquacious old woman, as our hero and his wife took their seats at the table, "it quite wrung my heart when my good Christopher related to me the particulars of your sad story, and I said, and I repeat it now, and with all sincerity, too, that I am as glad that you have escaped from the terrible fate to which the law would have consigned you, and left your poor wife and child destitute and unprotected, Mr. Parker, and that Providence has guided your footsteps to the old Punch Bowl, as if we had a large fortune left us, for here you will be safe, and there is such a pleasure in doing good for our fellow creatures in distress, and I am certain that you are worthy of it."

"Oh, Mrs. Worthington," replied Mary, "this kindness of feeling towards us poor strangers is overwhelming, and never shall we be able sufficiently to evince our gratitude towards you for it."

"May the blessings of Heaven descend upon you and your husband for it," said Richard, emphatically, "and such disinterested kindness towards those who are completely unknown to you will surely meet with its due reward, though I fear, alas! that it will never be in our power to repay it."

"And I'm sure that neither myself nor my Chaistopher seek for any other reward than that we are sure to find in the consciousness of having performed our duty," said Mrs. Worthington.

"Bravo, my old lass," ejaculated her husband; "spoken like a trump as you are, and that is just what I told them."

"Ah, Mr. Parker," remarked the dame, and a tear trembled in her eye as she spoke, "I have reason to love a sailor, and to sympathise in his misfortunes, for my poor old father and my two brothers were all attached to the service, and three better or braver seamen never mounted a deck; may God rest their souls in glory, for they all three perished in the same engagement, by each other's side. It was a sad day for my poor mother and myself when we received the fatal intelligence. But let me not think of that now, for although it is many a long year since that took place, I never do so but it makes me sad at heart. Ah! poor thing," she continued, looking feelingly at Mary; "it is a pity that one so young, so fair, and delicate as you are, should have had to encounter so many troubles; and this poor child, too, he has, indeed, too early had to taste of the cup of sorrow."

"Nay, my good dame," replied William, his handsome countenance animated with the noble feelings his heart prompted him to give utterance to; "I am a sailor's son, and should learn to meet misfortunes like a man; I am young and strong, and will not murmur at any trouble I may have to encounter, if it will only please All-bounteous Heaven to preserve my poor father and mother; such are the prayers that I constantly offer up to the Almighty, and something tells me that they will not be unheard."

"My noble-hearted, my heroic boy!" exclaimed the fond mother, clasping him to her bosom. "What a blessing art thou to me and thy poor father in the midst of all our misfortunes! Kind Heaven will surely not turn a deaf ear to the fervent prayers and supplications of one so young and innocent."

"It will not, Mrs. Parker, depend upon it," returned Mr. Worthington. "Come, come, you must not despair; there are brighter days in store for you yet, take my word for it. But you look more pale and sad than you did when we parted yesterday evening; I am afraid that you passed but an indifferent night."

"'Tis too true, Mr. Worthington," said our hero; "my dear Mary's imagination was disturbed by dreams that have made a powerful and painful impression upon her mind."

"Dreams!" repeated Worthington. "Oh, they are but the offspring of a mind ill at ease, and should not be suffered to create a serious thought."

"For her sake, and that of our child, I would pray to Heaven that they might never be realised," replied Richard; "but, alas! the dreams that disturbed the imagination of my beloved Mary were of that ominous and fearful nature, that it is impossible that either her or myself can resist their influence."

"No—no," said our heroine, hastily, and struggling with her feelings, "I will not think of them; it is only natural that in my present distressed state of mind, such visions should haunt my imagination."

"True, Mrs. Parker," concided the dame; "but if it would not be troubling you too much, or would distress you by so doing, myself and my husband, I know, would like to hear you relate what occurred to you in your sleeping moments, so that we might offer you our humble advice upon the subject."

"No—no, my old lass," observed Worthington, "the recital of them would only serve to increase the anguish of mind under which Mrs. Parker is at present labouring; besides, that would appear to be taking a liberty that we are not justified in doing."

"No," answered Richard; "you are our friends, anxious to do all in your power to serve us, and we should have no secrets from you; besides, there is nothing in this that we should wish to conceal from you. Mary will relate them to you, and then you will be able to judge whether or not they are calculated to distress her mind."

Worthington and his wife offered no further objection, for, indeed, their curiosity was excited, and our heroine, in as few words as possible, related the particulars of the remarkable and painful visions that had occurred to her; shuddering as she proceeded, for, notwithstanding all her efforts to the contrary, she could not help feeling a sad and torturing foreboding that they would be realised.

The old people listened to her with the deepest attention, and it was evident from their looks that, although they tried to conceal their real feelings, the account which Mary had just given them had made a most painful impression upon them.

"They were, indeed, fearful dreams," at length remarked Mr. Worthington, "and I do not wonder that they should disturb you; but still, as I said before, they were no more that such as were likely to occur to a person placed in such distressing circumstances as yourself. But banish them from your thoughts, and try to look forward to a happy issue to your troubles, putting your trust in Providence."

"Ay," said the dame, "and I feel confident that it will never entirely desert those who have been exposed to such unmerited sufferings."

"You judge us kindly, Mrs. Worthington," remarked our hero, "and I can but repeat my thanks for the good opinion you have been pleased to form of us. Our wrongs have indeed been great and undeserved. Oh, did you but know all that I have had to undergo, the cruelties and indignities that have been heaped upon me by the villany of that man whose life I accidentally sacrificed in self-defence, you would not marvel at the feelings that were aroused in my breast. I am stigmatized by those who are prejudiced against me as a villain, a traitor to my king and country; but future history will do justice to my character, and the motives which guided my conduct; I have but sought justice for my fellow-men, who have braved every danger, encountered every hardship for their country's welfare, and in doing so have sacrificed myself; thank Heaven, if the truth be suffered to prevail, I feel confident that even his greatest enemies will not be able to point to a single blemish on the character of Richard Parker, whom they stigmatize as the mutineer and the cowardly assassin!"

"I believe you, Mr. Parker," replied Worthington; "and, rest assured, that there is no one who more deeply sympathises with you than myself."

"And yet," said our hero, "there is one thing with which I cannot help bitterly reproaching myself."

"And what is that?" inquired Worthington.

"It is the thought that I have involved one of the loveliest of God's creations in my own misery and misfortunes," replied Richard, "that I have torn her from wealth and happiness, to cast her forth into the wide and cheerless world, a wretched wanderer, with the curse of her offended parent upon her head. Oh, Mary, why did we ever meet! Oh, why did I, humble as I was, and so unworthy of you, ever presume to aspire to your love!"

"Richard, dear Richard, forbear!" ejaculated our heroine, "unless you would torture my brain to madness. It was Heaven that implanted that sacred and mutual passion in our breasts which nothing could ever eradicate, and which was as pure as it was holy; and has your conduct towards me ever given me one cause to regret the decision I came to? it has not, but, on the contrary, each day's experience has but given me reason

to love you more. In all the troubles it has been our hard lot to encounter, have you ever heard me murmur or complain? Oh, no, Heaven forbid that I should; but, on the contrary, if I could cheer you on in your dreary way, and if I could inspire you with the least ray of hope and consolation, I felt more than rewarded for all the vicissitudes I had to encounter. Why, then, will you persist in reproaching yourself so unjustly and so bitterly for that of which you have not been guilty?"

"Pardon me, Mary," said her husband, "if by what I have said, I have appeared for a moment to doubt the sincerity of your love, or the purity of your devotedness; but when I think of the horrors by which we are surrounded, the——"

"Think not of them, Richard," interrupted our heroine; "but rather look forward with hope to the time when we shall be surrounded with happiness, when we shall be restored to that peace and tranquillity from which we have so long been estranged."

"Ay, Mrs. Parker," observed Worthington, "that is exactly the advice I have to offer; we should indeed become wretched beings if we were to suffer ourselves to sink entirely into despair; for my own part, critical and alarming as I must admit your present situation to be, I cannot help thinking that the storm will yet blow over, and that justice will assert her right in your favour. Providence has protected you so far; here you are safe from discovery; in time, the excitement which now prevails will have abated, and you will be able to make your escape to some distant part of the country where you will be unknown and may remain unmolested. I have already arranged a plan for your better security, and one of which I think you will approve."

"But, my kind friend," said our hero, "why should we, who are entirely strangers to you, involve you in so much danger and trouble on our account? Should it be discovered that you have given shelter to me, and connived at my escape, it would bring ruin upon your head."

"Believe me," replied the worthy host, "I entertain no such apprehensions, and old Christopher Worthington is not the man to shrink from danger when he has made up his mind to perform a good action, confident as he is that Providence will assist and protect him through it. But hear me out. To remain entirely confined to this house might become irksome and tedious to you, and I have been thinking of a plan to obviate that, which I have no doubt will meet with your approbation. Only a short distance from this house I have a commodious cottage comfortably furnished, and which is at present unoccupied; thither I propose that your wife and child should remove, where she can remain in retirement, and without being annoyed by any impertinent curiosity; but as it might excite some suspicion were you to take up your residence there also, I would advise that you remain here, and so disguised that it would be next to an impossibility for any person to recognise you; and you will have daily opportunities of seeing your wife and son. What say you to my proposition?"

"My generous, disinterested friend," replied our hero, grasping his hand, "in what language can I express to you my thanks? I yield myself entirely to your will; I will follow your advice to the very letter, knowing that it will never be offered but for my welfare."

"Well said, Mr. Parker," returned the worthy host, "and believe me you will have nothing to regret in the confidence you repose in me. I further propose that your wife should assume widow's weeds, in order the better to drown suspicion; and should any inquisitive questions be put to me, as they probably may by such busy-bodies as Ladbroke, I will represent her as the Widow Sommerton, a distant relation of mine, who, having lately lost her husband, needed retirement, and had, therefore, availed herself of my offer to take up her residence in the cottage belonging to me."

"An excellent plan," ejaculated Mary; "you, my dear Richard, I know, must approve of it."

"Approve of it?" returned our hero. "Oh, how can I do otherwise? But, Mr. Worthington, how would you dispose of me?"

"In order to give you freer scope of action, and to give you an opportunity of personally observing all that passes, I have provided for that in a manner

which I think will afford you satisfaction," answered Worthington. "Listen to me. I have a nephew residing in the County of Kent, who is a single man, about your own age, whom I have long since invited to come and reside with me, in order that he might assist me in my business; but for some reason, which he has never satisfactorily explained, he has declined to accept of my offer. He has never been in this neighbourhood since he was a boy, and, consequently, he is entirely unknown to any of the inhabitants. Now, what I propose is, that you should represent him, and that you should be so disguised in rustic garb, and assuming all the rude and unpolished manners of the rustic, which I have no doubt you have sufficient abilities to do, that all suspicions as to your real character will be drowned. I will previously apprize my customers of your acceptance of my offer, and they will, therefore, be prepared to meet you as my nephew, Martin Worthington; from Maidstone, in Kent. Think you that you can enact the character I have set down for you?"

"Oh, yes," replied Richard Parker, "my anxiety for my beloved wife and child will enable me to do so. Again I must express my heartfelt acknowledgments for ——"

"No more—no more, my unfortunate friend," interrupted Mr. Worthington; "it is enough for me to know that you approve of my plan. The next thing is to put it into execution without the least delay. You will perceive that by this arrangement you will be allowed, as I said before, free scope of action, while, at the same time, you will have frequent opportunities of seeing your wife and child without exciting any suspicion, as they being supposed to belong to me, will be enabled to visit me as often as they think proper, without any particular notice being taken of it."

"Excellent man!" ejaculated Mary Parker, "how grateful ought we to be to Providence for having raised us such a friend as you in the midst of our difficulties! Cheer thee, my dear husband, for already I perceive that better prospects dawn upon us, and that the clouds that at present darken and obscure our path-way will be dispersed!"

"They will," said the good old dame,

"take my word for it; there is nothing which my Christopher has yet taken in hand for the good of his fellow-creatures which has not prospered; and I shall, indeed, be much disappointed if they fail to do so on the present occasion."

"I am confident they will not," said Worthington, positively; "and if I can only be permitted to be made the humble instrument to rescue Richard Parker and his wife from the difficulties by which they are at present surrounded, I shall consider myself one of the happiest of human beings. Well, so far, this important business is settled; to-morrow morning, at an early hour, and before any person is likely to be stirring about, I will conduct you to the cottage, when you will have an opportunity of seeing whether the arrangements I have made are likely to meet with your approbation."

"What, ho! Master Worthington! Where the deuce are you when you should be ready to attend upon your customers?" at that moment shouted a voice from an adjacent apartment, and which they all immediately recognised.

"It is that troublesome fellow, Ladbroke," observed Worthington. "Confound him!—what can have brought him here at such an unusual hour of the day?"

"Some danger, I fear, is afloat," said Richard. "I like not that man."

"Oh, you have no occasion to alarm yourself," returned Mr. Worthington; "for I do not believe that he would do any harm, though he is so fond of interfering with that which does not concern him. There is no fear of his intruding himself here, so you can remain, and you will be enabled to listen to the conversation that passes between him and me. My wife will advise you how to act."

Thus saying, Mr. Worthington quitted the room, and Richard and his wife placed themselves near the wainscot, so that they might the better overhear what passed between Worthington and Ladbroke, for it was only in the adjoining apartment where they were seated. And they were not long kept in suspense; but the dame motioned them to silence, whatever they might hear to excite their apprehensions, pointing at the same time to the door which led to their own apartment, and to which they could retire unobserved, if any danger should happen to threaten them.

CHAPTER XI.

MR. LADBROKE IMAGINES THAT HE HAS MADE AN IMPORTANT DISCOVERY.—A FLESH ALARM.—THE PURSUIT.—THE SEARCH.—THE SECRET DOOR.—DOUBT AND ANXIETY.

"WHAT, Master Ladbroke," they overheard Worthington say, "you are an early visitor here to-day; what important business has brought you to the Old Punch Bowl at this unusual hour?"

"Why," answered Ladbroke, "in the first place to take a jug of your best ale, and in the second to make you acquainted with something that I think may interest you."

"Indeed," observed Mr. Worthington; "what, have you then, in the course of your researches after the curious, made some fresh discovery of importance?"

"Why, I do not know whether or not you may consider it of any particular importance," answered Ladbroke; "but it strikes me that I have discovered sufficient to make me suspect that Richard Parker is concealed somewhere in this neighbourhood, and not far from this spot either."

Our hero started, and Mary turned ghastly pale and trembled, and could with difficulty repress an exclamation of terror; but her husband and Mrs. Worthington motioned her to silence, and she stifled her feelings as well as she could.

"Ha, ha, ha!" laughed Mr. Worthington, in reply to what Stephen Ladbroke had said, "that is a wonderful discovery truly; and I suppose you are in hopes that you will be enabled to earn the reward for his apprehension, and that has put you into unusual spirits?"

"Well, I should indeed be most happy to do so, Master Worthington," he replied; "but I am afraid that there is no such luck for me, though I think that there are others who will earn it, and that, too, before long. You may expect visitors here presently."

"What mean you?" demanded Worthington.

"Why," answered Ladbroke, "as I was leaving my farm a short time ago, I beheld a party of marines a short distance in advance of me; so I said to myself, 'something is up, as sure as my name is Stephen Ladbroke.'"

"And is there anything so remarkable in seeing a party of marines?" asked Mr. Worthington.

"Well, I don't know that there is," replied Ladbroke; "but I had the curiosity to follow them, nevertheless, and I was not altogether out in the conjectures I had formed in my own mind immediately on beholding them. I got near enough to them to catch portions of their conversation, and I overheard one of them mention the name of Admiral Parker distinctly."

Richard again started, and Mary again had the greatest difficulty to refrain from giving vent to her emotions.

"Well," observed Mr. Worthington, "and there was nothing extraordinary in that, either."

"Indeed, you may think so, Mr. Worthington," returned Ladbroke; "but there you and I differ in opinion. But, perhaps, you will judge differently when you hear all I have got to tell you."

"Well, let me hear it," said Worthington.

"Soon after I had heard the marine mention the name of Parker," continued Ladbroke, "and before I had time to listen to any more of their conversation, one of them turning suddenly round, and observing me, he called me to him, and requested that I would direct him to the nearest public-house, and, of course, I could not do better than to recommend them here."

"Curse your officiousness," returned Mr. Worthington; "I like not such customers as them, for they never know when they have given enough trouble, and are as independent and as saucy as if they were going to pay like princes."

"Well, I'm sure I am very sorry if I have done wrong, Master Worthington," remarked Ladbroke; "but I could not do otherwise than return a fair answer to a straight-forward question. They will not remain here long, I dare say;—they are in search of Richard Parker, no doubt. But you have nothing to fear, you know, for, of course, you are ignorant of his whereabouts, and can, therefore, give them no information."

"No," answered Worthington, resolutely and vehemently; "and if I could, damme if I would!"

"What!" demanded his companion, "and is it possible that you would run the risk of screening a mutineer and a murderer?"

"Richard Parker is no murderer!" replied the worthy host, warmly; "and it is a base and monstrous libel to call him so."

"Well," remarked the sapient Mr. Ladbroke, "if taking a man's life be not murder, I don't know what is, that's all I have to say about it."

"He did so in self-defence," returned Mr. Worthington; "and he has no cause to regret the deed, for he has rid society of a villain, and one from whom he had experienced the most cruel wrongs."

"Bless my soul!" said Ladbroke, "why, you seem to know all about it, Master Worthington. How did you acquire your knowledge?"

"It matters not," answered the latter. "I have heard those facts from a source which I cannot doubt."

"Well, it is no business of mine," said Stephen Ladbroke; "and perhaps I have no right to be inquisitive. I suppose, then, if you and Richard Parker were to meet accidentally, he would find a friend in you?"

"He would, and a sincere one!" answered Worthington.

"Well," observed the other, "I cannot say that I much admire your taste. But it will be lucky for him if he escapes detection, for if they should catch him, not all the influence in the world can save him from hanging."

"And you would exult in his fate?" said Worthington.

"Why," replied Ladbroke, "I don't know that I would do that; but justice is justice all the world over, you know."

"And if justice had been rendered the unfortunate Richard Parker," returned Mr. Worthington, "from all that I have heard, he would never have been placed in the situation he now is."

"Well," said Ladbroke, "I do not know anything about that, so, I cannot pretend to offer any opinion. But as I live, here come the mariners, so now we shall, probably, hear all about the business."

"Lost—lost!" ejaculated Richard, in low and despairing tones, and turning to his wife, who was pale as death,

and trembling convulsively in every limb.

"Silence!" said Mrs. Worthington, in low and cautious accents; "be firm! —you have nothing to fear!—Have you

THE DESOLATE SITUATION OF RICHARD AND HIS WIFE AFTER LEAVING THE LUGGER.

not the means of concealment, should these men really be in pursuit of you, and should persist in searching the house?—Listen!"

Richard and his wife did endeavour to calm their feelings as much as possible,

and listened attentively to what was passing in the next room. They heard the marines enter and greet the landlord, which he returned, with constrained politeness; and then one of them observed,—

"We shall only intrude upon your hospitality till to-morrow. We are in pursuit of Richard Parker, the mutineer, and murderer of Captain Arlington. No doubt, you have heard of the daring Admiral, as he is called?"

"True; I have heard of him," answered Mr. Worthington, with perfect composure; "but I have not the honour to be personally acquainted with the gentleman."

"A gentleman you call him, eh?" said another of the men; "one who has set the whole of the Lords of the Admiralty at defiance!—endangered the safety of the country, and murdered his captain!—However, gentle or simple, if he is caught, which he is almost certain to be, he will be strung up to the yard-arm as sure as his name is what it is!"

"I have not the least doubt of that," returned Worthington. "But have you any suspicion that he is concealed in this neighbourhood?"

"Not exactly a suspicion," answered the marine; "but parties are sent in pursuit of him all over the country, and we are sent here on the same mission."

"Very good."

"We have an unpleasant duty to perform," observed the man who had spoken before, "but we must obey our orders: we must search your house."

"Certainly, gentlemen," replied Worthington; "you are quite welcome to do that; and if you find Richard Parker concealed any where about my premises, I will give you leave to hang me the next moment to my own sign-post."

"And very fair and reasonable too," remarked Ladbroke; "but I'll answer for it, gentlemen, that you will have your trouble for nothing; Christopher Worthington is too loyal and honest a man to conceal a mutineer and an assassin; it is not likely."

"Well," replied the man; "we do not entertain any suspicion of him; but we must perform our duty, so the sooner we do it the better."

"Will you not partake of some refreshments first, gentlemen?" asked Worthington.

"No," answered the marine who had before spoken; "the business will not occupy us long, and we can then enjoy ourselves at our leisure. Corporal Twig,

you and one of our comrades keep watch outside the house, to see that no one passes that way, while I and the others will proceed with our examination of the premises. We will trouble you to escort us, Mr. Host."

"Certainly, gentlemen," replied Mr. Worthington; "this way, if you please."

"Quick! quick!" said the dame, in a low voice, "there is not a moment to be lost! To your chamber, and avail yourself of the secret door: you have nothing to fear."

Richard Parker took the arms of his trembling wife and son, and hurrying them from the room, ascended the stairs which led to the chamber with hasty and silent steps. They gained it in a moment, and closing the door, they paused for an instant to regain breath and to recover their composure.

"Oh, Richard," gasped forth his wife, "who would have thought that our pursuers would have been so soon upon our track? Where will this adventure end? All now depends upon the fidelity of Mr. Worthington."

"And that, my dear Mary," replied our hero, "we cannot doubt for a moment. Let us be firm, and, please God, all will yet be well. But we have not an instant for delay; come—come!"

With as little noise as possible he removed the bedstead, and without any difficulty opened the secret door, and entering, he drew the bedstead in its right position, and closing the door upon them, they were enabled to breathe more freely; but they did not venture to speak to each other, but awaited the result with the utmost anxiety.

Several minutes elapsed, and no sounds whatever met their ears; but at length they heard the door below close, and directly afterwards footsteps ascending the stairs. Their hearts palpitated violently against their sides, and it was a moment to them of the greatest excitement. They were not long, however, kept in suspense, for the room-door was opened, and the marines and Mr. Worthington entered.

"Well," observed the man who seemed to be the leader; "there are no signs of the fugitives here, at any rate, and there are no apartments beyond this, are there?"

"None whatever," answered Worthington.

"And I think we have now examined every part of your premises?" said the sergeant.

"You have, my friend," returned the landlord, "from the cellars to the attic; though perhaps you would like to take a range over the roof?"

"Oh, no," answered the sergeant, with a laugh, "there is no necessity for that; it is not very likely that we should see much there to gratify our curiosity, or to repay us for our trouble."

"Well," observed Worthington, "I hope you are satisfied, sergeat?"

"Perfectly so," replied the latter; "you, at any rate, do not harbour Parker and his wife at the present time, whatever you may have done before."

"And, of course, you do not suspect me of any such disloyalty or want of honesty?" said Worthington, drily.

"Oh, certainly not," returned the sergeant; "and if I did, it is not likely that you would confess the truth to me. But I am obliged to you for the civility with which you have acted throughout this unpleasant business, and if you have no objection, we will now go down stairs and have a cheerful and friendly glass together."

"With all my heart," replied Worthington, "and I think you will admit that a better glass of grog than I can serve you, you never had the pleasure of drinking."

The sergeant returned no answer, and they immediately quitted the room, and Richard and his wife heard them depart and descend the stairs with feelings such as it is needless for us to attempt to pourtray; though they did not yet venture to leave the place of their concealment.

"Thank God!" ejaculated Mary, fervently, "for the present we are saved. Oh, Richard, what do we not owe to the unexampled kindness and humanity of Mr. Worthington?"

"True, my beloved wife," observed our hero, "and may the blessings of Heaven reward him for that which he has done to serve us! Alas! but for him, what could have saved me from destruction?"

"I shudder with horror at the bare thought," said Mary. "Oh, my husband,

it is evident, notwithstanding the dangers by which we are at present surrounded, that Providence still watches over our safety."

"True, my Mary; but while these men still remain in the neighbourhood, we shall not be entirely secure from detection."

"While we remain here, under the protection of Mr. Worthington, we have nothing to fear," answered our heroine; "but, hush, some one is ascending the stairs; it surely cannot be our pursuers returned?"

Richard made no reply, and they waited with breathless anxiety and impatience to ascertain the truth. The next moment the room door was opened, and they heard a light footstep in the room.

"Hist! come forward, my friends, you have nothing to fear," said a well-known and welcome voice; "it is only I, Mrs. Worthington."

Richard immediately opened the door, and he and his wife and child issuing forth, threw themselves at the feet of the old woman, overwhelmed with their emotions of gratitude.

"Rise, my unfortunate friends," said Mrs. Worthington; "this is no posture for you to assume before me; I and my husband have performed no more than our duty, and I thank Heaven that our efforts have been crowned with success."

"The risks that you and your husband are running for our sakes, Mrs. Worthington," remarked our hero, "might involve you in ruin; and how, then, can we refrain from giving utterance to our feelings of gratitude for such unexampled kindness and friendship towards us, who are strangers to you, and who, for aught you know to the contrary, may be totally unworthy of your respect or sympathy?"

"Oh, no," replied the dame, "I can never believe that Richard Parker and his wife are unworthy of our esteem. But we have said enough upon that subject. I think you will agree that Christopher managed the business with the marines very cleverly?"

"Oh, yes," answered Parker; "nothing could have been executed with more ability; but that Mr. Ladbroke is a dangerous character, and it would not do to entrust him with the secret, especially as he appears, from some unaccountable cause, to be so prejudiced against me."

"Oh, you need be under no apprehensions, Mr. Parker," remarked Mrs. Worthington, "old Ladbroke is the last man in the world that we would trust with any secret of importance; and, of course, it is not likely that we shall confide this business to any one; but, as it happened, it was a fortunate thing that Ladbroke met the marines before they arrived here, or they would have taken us by surprise, and we might not have been able to have managed the matter so well as we did. But, thank God, you are now for the present safe, and have nothing to fear. The secret vaults with which these stairs communicate, are unknown to any one but ourselves, and, therefore, will at any time afford you concealment. The sergeant and his comrades are perfectly satisfied, and, therefore, all suspicion is removed from us."

"Are they still in the house?" asked Parker.

"They are," answered the dame, "and carousing right merrily. They will only remain here to-night, however, and they state that after they have prosecuted their inquiries in the neighbourhood to-morrow, they will take their departure; you will then be secure, for it is not likely that those who are in search of you will think it worth their while to take the trouble to visist this quarter again."

"Thank Heaven for that," exclaimed Mary, fervently; "in time, the vigilance of pursuit will be relaxed, and we may then be able to escape to some distant part of the country, where we may remain unknown and in security."

"You will," said Mrs. Worthington; "and in time, I trust, be able to forget the sorrows of the past."

"Alas!" said Richard; "willingly would I, but I dare not encourage such sanguine hopes. Even should we be able to elude detection, what means have we of procuring a bare subsistence? Cheerfully though I would perform the most menial labour, how can we save ourselves from destitution and want?"

"Banish such gloomy thoughts from your mind, Mr. Parker," observed the dame; "Providence will not desert you in the hour of need. You have two excellent friends in honest Ben Binnacle and Mr. Adams, and I'm sure that my husband and myself will only be too happy to render you all the assistance in our power."

"I know well the kindness of your hearts," said our hero, "for I have fully tested it during the short time we have been acquainted; but my soul recoils from the bare idea of being dependant on the benevolence of those upon whom we have no claim but that of humanity, and to whom it is not likely that we shall ever have it in our power to make any return."

"Why will you persist in talking thus, Mr. Parker?" said the kind-hearted dame; "what return, think you, my husband or myself require, but your friendship? and that, I know, we shall ever possess. We should indeed be unworthy to live could we see any of our fellow creatures in distress and not render them all the assistance in our power. Providence has been very bountiful to us, Mr. Parker; we are well to do in the world, we have no one but a nephew in the world to look to but ourselves, and, therefore, what greater enjoyment can we have than in making those comfortable who stand in need of it?"

There was an earnest simplicity in the observations of the good old dame that was perfectly irresistible, and Richard and his wife could but press her hand in silence, while the latter was moved to tears.

"Come—come, my good friends," said Mrs. Worthington; "there has been quite enough of this; and I hope that you will endeavour to compose your feelings as well as can be expected under the circumstances, and to acquire confidence; we now understand each other perfectly, I should imagine, and, therefore, there is no occasion to talk further upon the matter. I must now leave you, for my husband may require my services; you will, of course, remain here to day, and you may do so without any fear, for there is no danger of the sergeant making any further inquiries, as he is perfectly satisfied. When he and his comrades have retired to rest, which I imagine they will be compelled to do at an early hour, if they continue drinking at the rate they were when I left them, you may expect a visit from Christopher, and he will tell you all the particulars, and further advise with you how to act. For the present, good bye, and God bless you."

The kindness of the dame completely overwhelmed them, and they were unable to speak ; but Mrs. Worthington, without waiting to hear any reply, hurried out of the room, and left them to their own thoughts.

"Excellent woman!" ejaculated Mary, when she was gone, "such kindness and generosity of heart as she and her husband display is beyond all praise."

"True, my dear Mary," replied Richard, "and may the blessings of Heaven pursue them for it."

"They will, they cannot fail to do so," returned our heroine. "Oh, Richard, I beseech you to cast aside the heavy gloom which has so long pressed upon your spirits, for our prospects brighten, and the time will come when we shall be enabled to walk forth again in the broad light of day, and to fear the frowns and malice of no one."

"Never, Mary," replied her husband; "it would be cruel for me to deceive you ; for all hope of that is for ever banished from my breast. I am a boomed man, only struggling against the unerring decrees of fate for your sake and that of our poor boy ; the laws of my country have condemned me, whether justly or not, the Almighty Judge can bear witness !—The felon's brand is set upon my name, and though I may for a time evade it, as sure as my heart now beats with the palpitation of life, a felon's death will be my portion !"

"Oh, no, no, no!" cried Mary, with a look of horror, "it cannot—will not be ! The thought freezes the blood in my veins, and racks my brain to madness ! Kind Heaven, who know the cruel persecution you received—the monstrous injuries that were inflcted on you, will interp se to save you from a fate so awful, and to restore you to that position in society from which you ought never to have been removed. Oh, that you had never entered into the service of your country, since degradation, cruelty, and oppression have been your only reward !"

"Alas ! they have !" said Richard ; "and yet Heaven knows that no one ever more had the honour and welfare of his country at heart than Richard Parker ! Oh, when I recall to my mind all the bitter wrongs I have received, my brain burns with madness !—The wounds inflicted by the galling lash seem to open afresh, and I can feel again the hot blood trickle forth from every pore !— Once more, the fiendish looks of exultation with which the miscreant Arlington contemplated my maddening sufferings, are presented to my eyes, and I feel that if the wretch were again alive and standing before me, I could plunge my revengeful sword in his body, until I had drained every drop of blood from his hated carcase !"

"Oh, fearful thought !" exclaimed Mary. "Why, my dear husband, do you suffer them to haunt your imagination ?—Why do you not endeavour to look upon the past as a fearful dream, and —"

"Mary !" interrupted Richard, impatiently, "and think you that it is so easy to forget brutal wrongs, so unjustly received ?—to blot from the tablet of my memory the atrocities of that accursed wretch, from whom I have to date all my miseries, and the consequent sufferings to which you, my devoted wife, have been exposed ?—No, by Heaven, I cannot !—And when I reflect upon the poor, degraded being that I am, it renders me tired of life. And but for the consideration of what would become of you, I should long since have hurried myself into the presence of that Almighty Judge, whose laws I have never wilfully violated !"

"Forbear—forbear, Richard !" said our heroine, solemnly. "You speak in language that fills my breast with horror ! Oh ! reflect calmly, and you will be able to extinguish the fire which now burns up your brain, and consumes your reason !"

"Reflect calmly, my beloved Mary !" repeated our hero, looking upon her with an intense and melancholy expression of affection. "God knows how ardently— how anxiously I have sought to do so ! When sleep has closed your eyelids, and you were for awhile unconscious of the harrowing cares that racked your unfortunate husband's breast, how I have tried to think by what means I could haply rescue you from the sufferings by which you were surrounded; secure your future happiness, and place you beyond the persecution of the world!—But when I have gazed upon your care-worn features, once redolent of all that was lovely and contented — when I marked your emaciated form, the fearful wreck of all that once was beautiful and vigorous in health, and the thought has arisen to my mind—'But for me all this would not have been'—frenzy has seized upon my brain, and I have been compelled to rush away, lest in the desperation of the moment I should commit a crime which only fiends could contemplate—the destruction of you, my wife!—our child! and ——"

" Richard!" gasped forth the terrified wife, "what awful words are these! Reflect—reflect, I say again! and remember that there is a world beyond this—a dread eternity—against whose Almighty decrees there is no appeal!"

" Would that I were dead!" groaned the wretched man, striking his forehead in despair.—" I am but a curse—a burthen to you! Mary, were I gone, Providence would surely protect you from the horrors and the difficulties by which you are surrounded!—Our boy, too—our sweet and noble-hearted offspring, will live to be a man, and one that will prove an honour to his sex; he will protect, and prove a blessing to you, my wife, and fully replace the loss that you might sustain in me; and I know that you would sometimes shed a tear, and offer up a blessing to the memory of the unfortunate Richard Parker, even though that recollection should recall the ignominious death of a criminal.'

" Richard! husband!" cried Mary, throwing herself into his arms, and sobbing hysterically upon his bosom, "each word that you utter is worse than a thousand daggers to my heart!—You will drive me to distraction if you continue to talk thus!"

" Dear—dear father!" said the noble-hearted boy, clinging to his knees, and looking up, piteously and imploringly, in his face; " oh! do not, for mother's sake, talk in this fearful manner, and give way to such awful thoughts! God is good and merciful, and will preserve you many years yet to be a blessing to us! Let us offer up our prayers to Him with all devoutness and sincerity, and He will not turn a deaf ear to those who put their trust in Him! Come—come, beloved father!—it is your son, your William, who thus implores you; and I know that you will not turn away indifferently from him, however weakly his inexperienced language may be enabled to give expression to his feelings."

No language could possibly do justice to the feeling which animated the countenance of William Parker as he gave utterance to these pathetic and impressive words; the unhappy father might there have beheld a reflex of his own mind, and read at once the noble and honourable career he was destined in after life to pursue. And he did read it. What heart, however insensible, could have resisted the influence of language and argument coming from such innocent, such guileless lips? Certainly the heart of our hero was not the one to do so. His bosom swelled and heaved with manly emotion, and it was some moments ere he could give utterance to a syllable ; but at length, drawing his affectionate son to his bosom, in a voice half choked by the power of his feelings, he said—

"My boy! my boy! my sensible and affectionate boy—your observations have subdued me more than all the arguments of the greatest sages and philosophers could have done; bless you! bless you! for the advice which nature must have dictated to your young heart to offer. Dear Mary, pardon me for the rash and terrible words which in the very despair of my soul, and my anxiety for the future fate of yourself and our beloved son, I was prompted to utter; let us kneel, and offer up our supplications to that Almighty power, who alone can aid us and release us from the miseries and sufferings in which we are at present plunged."

They did kneel, and fervent were the prayers they offered up to the Supreme ; and, after some time passed in this act of devotion, they arose, and felt that sweet tranquillity of feeling which religion never fails to promote.

They sat down and freely conversed upon their present situation; the numerous difficulties that encompassed them—the most probable way of surmounting them, and their future prospects; and as they discussed these important topics, hope once more appeared to reanimate the breast of our hero, and that added to the composure of the mind of his devoted and faithful wife.

In this manner several hours passed away, when they were again visited by Mrs. Worthington, who brought them some refreshments, and they eagerly inquired of her how her husband and the marines were proceeding below.

"Why," answered the dame; "the fellows, I declare, drink like fishes, and are nearly done over. If you had, indeed, had any occasion or wish to escape from the house, it is almost impossible that a better opportunity could have been afforded you. In their drunken moments, too, they divulged many things that may be of importance to us in our future plans, and the knowledge of which will tend still more to baffle their attempts to discover you."

"Ah!" ejaculated Richard, anxiously, "and what are they?"

"Why," answered Mrs. Worthington, "in the first place, they have informed us of all the principal places to which it is suspected you have fled; and in the next place, they have disclosed most, if not all, of the plans that have been laid to entrap you, so that, at any rate, we can be on our guard, when they least suspect it, and use every precaution to frustrate their designs."

"Very true," coincided Richard; "and this information is most invaluable."

"By some parties it is imagined," said the dame, "that you are secreted somewhere in the neighbourhood where Captain Arlington lost his life; they cannot suppose that you could find those who had the means or would run the risk of assisting you to escape."

"That is also well," remarked our hero. "Then they have no suspicion, of course, of my friend, Adams?"

"They did not mention his name," answered Mrs. Worthington; "so I presume they have not. But leave Adams alone for that; he has his thoughts —from all I have heard my husband say —always too well about him to convict himself."

"True," returned Richard, "and knowing that he was opposed to me in

my proceedings at the Nore, it is not at all likely that they should imagine he would run any risk to save me, notwithstanding it was well known that in private matters we had been friends for many years."

"Certainly not," coincided the dame.

"And our friend, Ben Binnacle," asked Parker; "did you elicit anything from the sergeant and his comrades which might lead you to suppose that any suspicion was entertained of him?"

"We did not," replied Mrs. Worthington; "but that is still more unlikely than the other, for it was not even known that you and Binnacle were at all acquainted. No, believe me, Mr. Parker, all goes on as well as we could wish or expect it to do; and if you only wait with patience, and follow the advice of your friends, depend upon it you will yet be able to elude their vigilance, and remain for ever secure from the fate with which they threaten you, and which they are so anxious to inflict upon you."

"Heaven bless you for those sweet words of hope and consolation," said our heroine, earnestly; "there is truth and reason in them, and I trust, with the blessing of Providence, they will be verified."

"They will, mark my words, Mrs. Parker," observed Mrs. Worthington; "and I feel confident that we shall yet live to see the day when we shall all meet together under far different and happier circumstances, and when we shall be able to talk of the past as only a trial of your fortitude and resignation under the will of the Supreme."

"Mrs. Worthington," said our hero, grasping the old woman's hand; "your observations have indeed inspired me with fresh hope and fortitude, and never can I adequately express to you my gratitude for the kind and disinterested feeling which prompts them. Providence surely has not deserted us, or it would not have sent us such noble-hearted and indefatigable friends as yourself and your husband."

"Well, Mr. Parker," answered the dame, "I can only repeat that I am most happy to think your footsteps were guided hither, where you have such facilities for concealment and escape for had it not been so, even now you might have been in the power of those who are so anxious for your apprehension, and then your fate would have been certain."

"Oh, true, most true," responded Mary, "and I shudder with horror when I think of it. Dear Richard, how thankful ought we to be to the Supreme Disposer of all human events for the mercy which he has shown us."

"You should indeed," returned the dame, "and depend upon it, if you still continue to put your trust in Him, you will be restored to all that happiness and serenity of mind which you formerly enjoyed. But I must once more leave you to your own reflections, and sincerely hope that you may profit by the humble advice I have presumed to offer you, and the information I have been enabled to give you. You may expect my husband as soon as those men have retired to rest."

Richard and his wife once more warmly repeated their thanks, and Mrs. Worthington retired from the room.

———

CHAPTER XII.

THE STORM.—THE APPEARANCE OF MAD MOLL AGAIN.—THE CONFERENCE BETWEEN THE FUGITIVES AND CHRISTOPHER WORTHINGTON.—THE DANGEROUS INTERRUPTION.—THE DRUNKEN SERGEANT.—THE PERILOUS SITUATION OF RICHARD PARKER AND HIS WIFE.

THE day passed away in the same manner that we have described in the previous chapter, and evening spread its dusky mantle over the earth. At first it was clear and serene, and everything gave token of a fine night. Richard and his wife did not feel inclined to sleep, and, moreover, they were anxious to see Worthington, who they had no doubt would come according to his promise, and they, therefore, seated themselves in the window recess, William also taking his place by their side, and listening with the deepest interest and attention to the conversation that passed between them.

The window at which they were seated commanded an extensive view of the ocean, and the moon shining res-

plendently in the heavens, shed her lucid and silvery beams across the wide expanse of waters, and rendered everything as clear and distinct to the sight as if they had been presented in the broad sunlight of noonday. Countless myriads of stars twinkled in the skies, and were reflected again in the clear surface of the deep, as if in a mirror. The air was perfectly tranquil; and breathed a refreshing fragrance to the senses of the unfortunate fugitives, which seemed to revive their spirits, and to calm the painful feelings which had before agitated their breasts. Just off the coast several vessels were anchored, and others riding at a distance, whilst here and there a little fishing-smack met the eye, which appeared only like a speck upon the broad surface of the ocean. The scene was one which recalled the remembrance of the past vividly to the memory of our hero, and after contemplating it for some time in silence, he sighed deeply.

"Beautiful ocean!" he ejaculated at last; "what a multiplicity of conflicting thoughts does the sight of you engender in my breast. How varied are the scenes that I have witnessed, and taken an active part in, on your broad surface; and yet do I love thee with all the strength of fond affection that a mother feels for her first-born. My heart still clings to thee, and the brave men who peril their lives upon thy vast waters, in spite of the horrors with which my name and thyself are associated, with the same affection as when we first became connected. Why—why have I been thus cruelly estranged from thee, beautiful ocean? Oh, it would have been much better that I had long since slept at peace within thy mighty bosom, and that my name could have been blotted from the memory of all who are connected with me, and are dear to me!"

"Richard, dear Richard," said his wife, laying her hand gently but impressively upon his arm, and looking up affectionately in his face; "what dismal, what melancholy thoughts are these! I beseech you, do not give way to them."

"Do not give way to them, Mary?" repeated her husband, impatiently; 'and think you that I can so easily stifle the thoughts that arise to my mind, as I contemplate the scene which is now presented to my eyes? Think you that I have become so callous to every sense of feeling as to gaze upon that mighty element without a single pang of emotion? The whole history of my wrongs is stamped as vividly and dis-

MR. WORTHINGTON CONDUCTS PARKER AND HIS WIFE TO THE SECRET CHAMBER.

tinctly to my mind's eye upon its broad surface, as if it were depictured in a chart before me. It was on that mighty element that I fought and bled in the defence of my country's rights, and fondly hoped to carve my way to honour and fortune. Alas! how fearfully were those hopes doomed to be disappointed! What was the reward that the hardy seaman received for all the toils and dangers he had encountered?—Where was the encouragement to his future energies? Oh, the thought!—it maddens my brain!—it tempts me to curse myself and my fellow men!"

"Hold, Richard—for mercy's sake hold!" expostulated our heroine. "These painful reflections will but serve to drive you again into the frenzy of despair!"

"It was on that mighty ocean," continued Richard, apparently taking no notice of these observations of his wife, "that I first became degraded to the beast, and that villany was allowed to triumph over me, and to effect my ruin. Oh, God! the thought!—it paralyses every nerve, and makes the blood run burning, scalding hot throughout my veins!—And it was for this that I had periled my life, and never shrunk from the performance of my duty, when even surrounded by the greatest dangers; when confronting horrors that might have made even the stoutest heart quail! To be branded as a thief, and to receive worse than a thief's punishment!—And for what?—To gratify the deadly vengeance of that fiend in human form, whom I had outrivalled in the affections of one whose virtues rendered her so superior to him, and who could feel for him no other sentiment than one of unmitigated contempt and abhorrence! May his guilty soul linger in endless torments!"

"Dear Richard!" again remonstrated our heroine, alarmed at the excitement of his manner, and apprehensive of the consequences of which it might be productive; "again I beseech you not to give way to these violent emotions! The fearful wrongs of which you have spoken are past; they have been amply avenged by the death of their guilty author; and believe me that the time will yet come when justice will be rendered you."

"And what," demanded Richard, impatiently, and his fine countenance flushed with the powerful excitement of his feelings; "what can ever atone for the monstrous injuries that have been inflicted on me? What can ever remove from my remembrance the galling and degrading lash? Have I not suffered more than a thousand deaths? And what can render me compensation for that? Oh, no, Mary, there is no solace for my wounded spirit; day by day my misery feeds itself, and I feel myself more and more abject and hateful. And

you, too, I repeat, as I have often told you before, ought to look upon me with shame, with loathing and disgust."

"Oh, my husband," said Mary, "are you mad, that you can give utterance to such ungenerous words as these?"

"And if I am mad," replied the wretched and unfortunate man, staring at her wildly, "have I not had sufficient cause to make me so? Think you that all those gloomy retrospections can rush upon my brain without their maddening influence? I must, indeed, be less than man if they could do so."

"Then why not exert your energies, Richard," returned his wife, "and struggle against them?"

"It is impossible," he replied; "they are ever present to my imagination, in spite of myself; they haunt me constantly, like grim and ghastly spectres mocking, and exulting at my sufferings. They must, they will continue to pursue me to the last moment of my existence; oh, never shall I be able to obtain an oblivion to my sorrows."

"Oh, yes, my husband," said our heroine, "time and patience will bring it to you. But if you really love me, you will not thus utterly resign yourself to despair, and encourage thoughts, the bare expression of which fill my soul with horror."

"Mary, dear Mary, my devoted wife," said Richard, in the same melancholy and despairing accents; "I feel that I am a curse to you, and that but for me you might now have been happy, and can I help reproaching myself when I think of that?"

"How often have I tried, but in vain," replied Mary, "to stifle that painful and unnatural feeling in your breast? Have you ever heard me murmur or complain at the misfortunes it has been our lot to encounter?"

"Ah, no," returned her husband, "you have borne them far too patiently, too meekly, and it is that which has made me feel it far more severely than if you had heaped upon me your bitterest reproaches."

"No more of this, dear Richard," said Mary, "but let us remove from the window; the contemplation of this scene does but serve to increase the anguish of the sad and dismal thoughts that crowd upon your mind."

"No," said our hero; "I cannot relinquish the sight, gloomy though are the thoughts that it engenders in my breast. Let me be, dear Mary, I beg of you, and do not offer to interrupt me; reflection may tend more than all the arguments or persuasions that you can make use of to relieve the anguish of my mind."

Mary made no reply, but sighed deeply, and resuming her seat, suffered her unfortunate husband to relapse into silence. He continued for some time with his eyes fixed upon the ocean, and seemed to be communing with himself, but the expression of his features showed the deep anguish of mind he was enduring.

Suddenly the aspect of the heavens underwent a remarkable change; dark and ponderous clouds obscured the face of the moon which had lately shone forth so brilliantly; the stars retired, and a darkness almost impenetrable reigned on all around. The wind gradually arose and swept in hollow gusts around, and everything gave promise of an approaching storm. Mary again endeavoured to persuade her husband to leave the window, for the change that had now so suddenly and so unexpectedly taken place, she thought was still more calculated to increase the gloom and anguish of his thoughts; but he turned impatiently away from her as he observed—

"No, Mary, I have viewed it in the calm, and think you that I fear to contemplate it in the tempest? Oh, such a scene as now threatens to take place is in strict accordance with the feelings which at present occupy my mind."

"What madness is this!" remarked Mary; "will nothing persuade you to banish such torturning thoughts from your fevered brain?"

Richard retured no answer; but it was quite plain that nothing which Mary could say could have any very material effect upon him in the state of mind he was at that time. He continued seated at the window in the same attitude, and with his eyes fixed with an intense and earnest expression upon the ocean, while the horrors of the tempest appeared to afford him a kind of morbid satisfaction.

Every instant the storm increased in violence, and it was truly painful to contemplate it. An impenetrable darkness prevailed on all around, save when it was broken by the vivid flashes of lightning that ever and anon blazed in the heavens, and cast an awful and lurid glare across the broad and disturbed surface of the deep, and rendered the terrors of the night the more visible. Sometimes, between the pauses of the deafening thunder, might be heard the dismal signals of distress from many an unfortunate vessel; but, alas! it was a hopeless appeal; for it was totally impossible that any one could venture out to their assistance in such a tempest as was then raging; and inevitable destruction seemed too plainly to be the fate of all those unfortunate individuals who were exposed to its fury.

Mary Parker's heart sickened within her, and many were the fervent, though silent prayers she offered up to Heaven for the preservation of those unfortunate individuals who at that time were tossed upon the deep, with no other prospect but that of an awful and untimely death before them. Suddenly an exclamation from her husband aroused her from the partial lethargy into which she had fallen, and she gazed eagerly towards him, anxious and impatient to be made acquainted with what had happened to excite him in so remarkable a manner. She found that he had started to his feet, and was gazing earnestly upon some object in the distance, but which the intense darkness that reigned around would not suffer her at first to distinguish.

"What are you gazing so earnestly at, my dear Richard?" asked Mary; "what is it that seems to agitate you so much?"

"Look!" he replied, pointing in the direction of one of the rocks; "do you not behold that haggard form, which points derisively at me?"

"I cannot see anything, Richard," Mary replied, straining her eyes in the direction to which he pointed attention. "You must have been mistaken; besides, it is so dark, that it is impossible to distinguish objects at any distance."

"But I tell you again," said Parker, impatiently, "that I was not mistaken.

I saw it as plainly in the glare of the lightning as I see you now."

"And what was it you imagined you saw?" asked our heroine.

"It was the form of her who has predicted the fate that awaits me," replied Richard;—"Mad Moll. Even at such a distance the lightning enabled me not only to recognise her form, but likewise to recognise her features."

"Impossible, Richard!" remarked his wife; "what perfect folly it is to give way to such extravagant ideas as those. What should bring the woman of whom you speak to this part of the country? Besides, it is not likely that she can know you have sought refuge here, or that she could see you from the place to which you point."

"Mary," returned our hero, never for a moment removing his eyes from the rock, "it may seem impossible, and you may begin to imagine that the extreme anguish of mind it has been my lot for some time to endure has taken effect upon my intellect; but I tell you again I am positive, and not all the arguments in the world can remove the impression from my brain. I could almost swear that her eyes were fixed earnestly upon me, and that she waved her hand to me in token of recognition. And see, do you not now mark the truth of that which I have asserted?—Do you not behold her form?—You must—you must, unless you are blind. See, she comes this way!"

Again Mary strained her eyes in the direction of the spot to which her husband continued to point. The broad glare of the lightning, which now flashed more vividly than before across the heavens, enabled her to distinguish objects clearly, and she did then behold a shadowy form descend from the rugged rock, and advance with slow and measured steps towards the house, apparently quite regardless of the tempest, which, so far from abating, increased in violence every moment.

The form was that of a female; and after the assertions which Richard had made use of, and of which he seemed so positive, she could not but feel the greatest anxiety to ascertain who she was. She at last got to within only a few paces of the house, and there she paused, and folding her arms across her bosom, she looked up at the casement at which Mary and her husband were standing, as though she was aware that they were there. Again the lightning flashed full upon the face and person of the singular woman; and the astonishment and agitation of our heroine may be imagined, when she did, indeed, recognise the features of Mad Moll, whom she had never expected to behold again, and especially in this neighbourhood, and at such an hour.

"Good God!" she exclaimed, with much emotion, "what can this mean? What strange fatality has brought this woman here?"

"Are you not satisfied now that I was not mistaken?" demanded Richard. "Fate frowns upon us, and the appearance of this strange being in this part of the country, and at a moment when we are surrounded by such numerous and alarming dangers, betokens us no good."

"Nay, Richard," returned his wife, "it must have been accident alone that has guided her footsteps to this place; and as it is not likely that she is aware we are here concealed, we have nothing to fear from her."

"Ah!" ejaculated Richard, pointing hastily towards her, "do you not behold her actions, her strange gesticulations? She must perceive us, for see, she waves her hand significantly towards us, and by every means in her power seems to endeavour to make us understand that she is aware where we are."

The significant gestures of the remarkable woman were, indeed, enough to impart some degree of reason to the surmises of our hero; but when Mary reflected upon the utter improbability of her being able to recognise them in the peculiar situation in which they were placed, she immediately dismissed the idea from her mind, and also sought to banish the impression which this adventure and the extraordinary conduct of Mad Moll had made upon that of her husband. This, however, she found to be a task which it was not easy to accomplish; and he continued to watch the actions of Moll with the most intense anxiety and the deepest interest.

For several minutes the old woman remained in the same attitude, one arm erect, as though she were bidding defiance to the raging elements, and with her eyes fixed upon the window at which Mary and Richard were still standing; and it seemed as though she had not yet made up her mind as to the course she should pursue. The frequent flashes of lightning enabled our heroine and her husband to behold objects clearly for some distance round, and they had a full opportunity of watching all that took place. The cadaverous and haggard features and gaunt form of Mad Moll had undergone no perceptible change in the lapse of years; and as Richard and Mary once more contemplated the countenance of that woman whom they had never expected to behold again, and recalled to their memory the predictions to which she had formerly given utterance, and many of which had been so fatally fulfilled, they could not help shuddering with an instinctive feeling of horror, and Mary, notwithstanding all that she had said to the contrary, and the firmness with which she had tried so hard to support the many trials and dangers to which they had been, and still were subjected, was compelled to admit that the dismal forebodings which Richard had suffered to take possession of his mind, were neither unreasonable nor unfounded. She was, however, too much agitated in her mind to give expression to that which she so keenly felt, and she watched their mysterious visitor with the greatest anxiety. The wild form of the wanderer had a strange and impressive effect at that solemn hour of the night; and in the midst of that fierce warring of the angry elements it rendered the terrors of the scene complete. She looked not like a being of this world; and in spite of all the efforts of reason to resist it, our heroine could not help a feeling of superstitious awe stealing over her, and such as she did not remember ever to have experienced before.

"My doom is sealed, I know it well," said Richard, in a solemn and melancholy voice; "and see, she comes to remind me of it—to recall to my memory the prognostications to which she years ago gave utterance, and which I feel too well assured will be verified! But she has no occasion to do so; no, I have never flattered myself with false and delusive hopes; my enemies thirst for my blood, and they will not rest until

they have obtained the gratification of their wishes. But I will not shrink from the consequences of my past conduct; I do not regret for a single instant that which I have done; no, I have been avenged in the life's blood of the dastardly miscreant who was the cause of all the wrongs and indignities that were inflicted upon me; and Richard Parker is fully prepared to die, as he has ever endeavoured to live, namely, as a man."

"Oh, no, no, dear Richard," said his wife, throwing her arms around his neck, and looking up imploringly and affectionately in his face; "do not, I beseech you, talk in this horrible and awful manner; Heaven, in its infinite mercy, will avert the dreadful fate you apprehend. You will not be permitted thus to be taken from myself and our child. Dismiss such apprehensions, I once more say, from your thoughts, and——"

"Mary," interrupted our hero, hastily, "you advise me to do that which is impossible; does not everything point to the dreadful destiny which awaits me, and which, though probably retarded for awhile, I can never entirely escape? And now this woman comes as if to mock at me and exult in my sufferings—sufferings that are engendered in my breast on account of you, my faithful Mary, and our poor boy, and, believe me, not from any cowardly fear that I feel for myself. But see! she moves! What are now her designs? Does she contemplate my ruin?"

"No, no, Richard," replied Mary; "indeed you talk madly, and will persist in encouraging fears that there is not the least probability of being realised. Come, come, arouse yourself; it is not likely that this strange woman, whose intellects there cannot be any doubt are impaired, can know that we have sought shelter here, since no one but our friends, Adams and Binnacle, and Mr. and Mrs. Worthington, are acquainted with the secret, and, therefore, we are quite secure. But see; she is about to take her departure from the spot; accident, no doubt, has guided her footsteps hither, and it is more than probable that we shall never behold her again."

Richard returned no answer to these observations, and he and our heroine watched the woman narrowly, at least. as well as the darkness would permit them to do. Having cast one more eager glance towards the house, Mad Moll gathered her tattered cloak around her, and which but partially defended her bony form from the inclemency of the weather, and hurrying from the spot, was soon hidden from the sight in the darkness and obscurity beyond. Mary now again urged her husband to retire from the window; and after a time he did yield to her request, and throwing himself into a chair, he gave himself up to all the varied and painful thoughts that crowded with such overwhelming force upon his brain, and which his amiable and devoted wife did not for the present seek to interrupt, for she knew well that calm and deliberate reflection would be far more calculated to tranquillise his feelings than any argument it was in her power at present to make use of.

The storm continued to rage with unabated violence, and it was quite evident that the ravages it had committed were of the most alarming and frightful description. The thunder still pealed loudly at intervals in the heavens, and the flashes of lightning were terrific and appalling to behold. The howling waves, too, as they were dashed furiously against the rocks, and brought destruction to everything in their way, might be heard even above the voice of the thunder, and added to the terrors of the moment. A more awful night had scarcely been witnessed by human being; and it was well calculated to increase instead of abating the melancholy thoughts which had naturally taken possession of the bosoms of Richard Parker and his wife.

Our heroine at length ventured again to address her husband, and to arouse him from the lethargy of anguish and despair which he had permitted to obtain so powerful an ascendancy over him, and approaching him, and placing her hand gently upon his shoulder, she said, in her most persuasive accents, and which seldom failed to have their due effect upon him,—

"Richard, you must not suffer the remarkable adventure of this night to make too powerful an impression upon your mind, but try to arouse yourself from these gloomy thoughts and appre-

hensions, and to look forward to the future with the most sanguine expectations."

"And what cause have I," hastily demanded Richard, "to give encouragement to such hopes, situated as I am? Mary, your anxiety for me leads you to talk erroneously, and to endeavour to inspire me with hopes which I feel confident you cannot for a moment yourself indulge in."

"And did I not really feel those hopes animate my breast, Richard," replied our heroine, "life would become insupportable to me. Oh, yes, I do, indeed, feel a sweet assurance that, notwithstanding the troubles by which we are now surrounded, the time is not far distant when we shall be released from our difficulties, and restored to that happiness which we once so freely and abundantly enjoyed; and I do trust that my expectations will not be doomed to be disappointed. As I have said before, accident, you may depend upon it, has alone brought the woman whom we have just seen hither, and she must be ignorant of the place of our refuge. She has not the power to harm us, if even she had the will, which I do not believe she has; and while we have such a friend as Mr. Worthington, we may set detection at defiance. Come, come! not long since you promised me that you would be firm, and seek to combat all such gloomy fears, and torturing forebodings."

"True, Mary," he answered; "and fain would I do so if I could, for God knows what agony it causes me to see the sufferings to which it is your sad lot to be subjected; but that is a task which I find it is most difficult to accomplish, and continual cares and anxieties have almost prostrated all my energies. Oh, Mary, never again must we look forward to those days of halcyon bliss which it was once our happy lot to experience! Fate has ordained it otherwise, and we must endeavour to resign ourselves to that which I feel to be inevitable."

"Oh, my husband," said our heroine, "surely you cannot thus abandon yourself to such abject and overwhelming despair! But let us defer conversing upon this important and painful subject till the morning; we are neither of us in a fit state of mind to do so for the present. It is now late; Mr. Worthington will not visit us to-night, I should think, and as we both require rest, let us retire to bed."

"No, Mary," replied Parker, "my mind is too disturbed to suffer me to rest. Retire you with our boy, and I will watch by you, and offer up my supplications to the Supreme to protect and bless you."

Mary was about to return some reply, when they heard a footstep on the stairs, and they hesitated.

"There is nothing to fear, however," said our heroine, hastily; "it is doubtless only Mr. Worthington, who is coming to fulfil his promise."

She had scarcely given expression to this supposition, when there was a gentle knock at the door, and the worthy host immediately entered the room.

"So," he remarked, "you have not yet retired to rest? I was afraid you would have done so, for it is now late; but I could not get rid of the sergeant and his comrades quite so soon as I expected, and it would not have done to seem to hurry them, lest their suspicions might have been excited. But they are all safe enough now; in the morning they take their departure from the inn, and before the day has elapsed, they will be out of the neighbourhood altogether, and then you will be perfectly secure from future interruptions. It is necessary, however, that we should defer visiting the cottage where I propose that Mrs. Parker shall take up her future residence, until we have ascertained to a certainty that the marines have indeed quitted this part of the country."

"True, Mr. Worthington," observed Mary, "and I do hope that Richard may profit by your advice, and the affectionate arguments I have at my command, and to look forward to the future with hope and tranquillity."

"I need not assure you, Mrs. Parker," said the worthy old man, "that I most cordially respond to that wish, and it shall be no fault of mind if we do not succeed to the fullest extent of our hopes. This has been a fearful night, and many a poor soul, I apprehend, has met with a watery grave. God rest their souls in peace!"

"Ay, Mr. Worthington," replied Richard Parker, "it has, as you say, been an awful night; but nothing could be more strictly in unison with my feelings, and the racking thoughts which disturb my brain. But I have met with that which has added to my anguish, and filled my breast with doubts and apprehensions!"

Ah!" ejaculated Worthington, with a look of astonishment and curiosity. "What mean you?"

"From the window of this room," replied our hero, "I and my wife have beheld one, the sight of whom could not fail to excite a feeling of anguish and alarm in our breasts. Are you certain that no one besides the marines and Ladbroke have been at the inn since yesterday?"

"Certainly not," answered Worthington; "why do you put such a question?"

"There is no chance for any other persons but ourselves to be aware that I and my wife are concealed here?" interrogated Richard.

"Not the least," returned the worthy host. "I thought you were satisfied on that point before. But what has given rise to these questions?"

In as few words as he conveniently could, Richard related to him the particulars of the sudden and remarkable appearance of Mad Moll, and Mr. Worthington listened to him with the deepest attention.

"It is singular," observed the latter, when our hero had concluded; "but it is not likely that this strange woman can be aware of the place of your retreat, nor has she any means of discovering it. Accident has, no doubt, brought her to this part of the country, and she will have no opportunity of again crossing your path."

"But," remarked Richard, "when I recall to my memory the fearful prognostications to which she once gave utterance," replied Parker, "I cannot but look upon her appearance in this neighbourhood as an omen of some fresh calamity or danger that is in store for us."

"And is it possible, Mr. Parker," said Worthington. with a look of surprise, "that a man of your superior sense and experience in the world, can place the least confidence in the wild predictions of this old woman, whose intellect is evidently affected?"

"You may deem me weak and superstitious, my kind friend," replied our hero; "but when I reflect upon the horrors of the past, and remember how closely, even to the very letter, a portion of that which this mysterious woman prognosticated has been verified, think you that it is possible for me to banish from my mind altogether the impression she has made upon it?"

"Indeed, Richard," remarked his wife, "you are too ready to admit into your breast fears and apprehensions which have no foundation in reality. The observations of this woman, I repeat, are unworthy of a second thought, and we are all but criminal for permitting them to disturb us."

"Truly said, Mrs. Parker," observed Worthington. "I am decidedly of your opinion. But your husband will not suffer so unworthy a subject to disturb his mind, and, mark my words, surrounded even by so many obstacles as you now are, you will yet live to surmount them all. Of one thing you may rest assured, though I do not suppose there is any necessity for me to repeat the promises I have so often made, you shall find in me a friend who will adhere to you to the last, and who will consider himself more than amply rewarded in being enabled to contribute to your happiness."

"This assurance is most kind and disinterested on your part, my dear sir," returned Parker, "and believe me that I am fully sensible of the vast weight of obligation I am under to you."

Mr. Worthington was about to make use of some observation, when they were all astonished and alarmed by hearing some one ascending the stairs towards the apartment in which they were. There was not a moment to be lost.

"Quick—quick!" said Worthington, addressing himself to Parker in hasty tones; "to the secret-door, or you will be discovered. This must be one of the marines, and—silence."

As he thus spoke he placed his finger on his lips, and Richard, and his wife, and William, had only just time to secrete themselves again, when the sergeant of the marines entered the room, half undressed.

"How now, sergeant," demanded Worthington; "what does this mean? I thought you were in bed and sound asleep by this time."

"The fact of it is, my worthy friend," replied the sergeant, "that I did go to sleep for awhile, when I dreamt that I was still in your company, and that we were enjoying ourselves in the same manner we did this evening; but all at once I awoke, and I was so disappointed, that, for the life of me, I could not go to sleep again; so at last I thought I would just take the liberty of seeing whether you were still up, and I could prevail upon you to treat me with another glass of your excellent grog, just to tranquillise my feelings and to soothe me to sleep."

"It's rather a strange hour, Mr. Sergeant, to re-commence carousing," said Worthington, in reply; "however, I do not mind complying with your request, if you will only promise me that you will then retire to your chamber and do not disturb me again."

"Promise you?" repeated the sergeant; "to be sure I do, and I will keep my word, too; you are a good sort of a man, and have the heart that can feel for another, when he wants a glass of that which will do him good. But, I say, you'll pardon me; but as I came up the stairs it struck me very forcibly that I heard voices in this room conversing together."

"Voices!" repeated the landlord; "ha, ha! well, that's a good joke, to be sure. You must still be dreaming, I should imagine, sergeant."

"Oh, no," returned the sergeant; "I was as wide awake as I am at present. I could almost have taken an oath that I heard voices."

"Pshaw!" said Mr. Worthington; "what's the use of running away with such a ridiculous notion as that? You have seen all the people my house contains; my old dame has retired to her chamber, and I do not care how soon I follow her. As for the voices you fancied you heard, I suppose it was me humming a song to myself."

"Ah," returned the sergeant, "I shouldn't wonder; and yet 'tis very singular; it didn't sound like singing neither, and it struck me, too, that one of the voices was that of a female."

"Tut, tut, tut, man," said the land-lord, "do you know what you are talk-ing about? You are aware that there are no other rooms beyond this, and, therefore, where can all the company you supposed you heard have retired to?"

"True—true," replied the sergeant; "I did not think of that; I must have been mistaken, that's quite certain. But

PARKER LISTENING TO THE SEARCH AFTER HIM BY THE DRAGOONS.

come, my friend, be pleased to lead the way; one more glass of grog, and I will then positively bid you good night, for I think I shall be able to go to sleep com-fortably."

Mr. Worthington led the way, and the sergeant followed him. When they were gone, and the fugitives heard the room-door close below, our hero and his wife and son once more ventured from the place of their concealment, and having locked the door of the apartment to prevent all further interruption, they knelt down and returned their thanks to the Almighty for having so far aided them in their efforts to avoid detection, even when they were in the very same house with those who were in search of them. They listened for about a quarter of an hour, when they heard Mr. Worthington and the sergeant come from the room in which they had been seated, and bid one another "Good-night," which showed that they had at last separated, and Richard and our heroine felt more at ease.

The storm had considerably abated, and Mary had succeeded in partially banishing from the mind of her husband the dismal thoughts that had before tormented it. Being now exhausted with the cares and anxieties they had experienced during the day, and knowing that they were now secure from further intrusion, they sought their pillows, and being fatigued, it was not long ere they gained a temporary respite from their sorrows in a more tranquil sleep than they had enjoyed for some time.

They arose at an early hour the following morning, much refreshed, and after a short time passed in conversation, Mr. Worthington tapped at the room-door, and was immediately admitted.

"Well, my friends," he remarked, "I am glad to see you looking so much better after the few hours' rest you have had, and the alarm you met with last night. The sergeant's ears were much sharper than I took them to be, and if he had only been two minutes sooner, he would have discovered you, to a dead certainty. But I think I played my part pretty well, and managed to stifle his suspicions."

"You did, sir," returned Mary, "and to you we are indebted for our present safety."

"Well, well, that's all right," said the old man, "and I am extremely thankful to think that the business has terminated in the manner it has. However, you have nothing more to fear from the sergeant and his companions, Mr. Parker."

"Indeed!" said the latter. "Have they gone, then?"

"Yes," answered the landlord. "They took their departure from the inn as soon as it was daylight; and it is their intention, as I said before, to leave the town to-day. So, thus, you see, everything goes on as well as we could wish. Suspicion of your being concealed anywhere on this coast will be quelled, and you may then remain here under the disguise which I have suggested as long as you think proper, or till you have decided, with the help of your friends, what course it will be most prudent for you in future to adopt. As for the unfortunate woman of whom you have been speaking, I must say that it would show much folly and weakness to suffer her to disturb your mind, for her conduct proves her to be only some wretched maniac."

"And yet," returned Richard, "there is so much reason in her madness, that it cannot fail to excite more serious attention than you seem to imagine, Mr. Worthington. I am not prone to superstition, but it is impossible that I can forget the fearful manner to which many of the prophecies she uttered in the presence of myself and my wife some years ago have been fulfilled, and the reflection drives my brain to madness!"

"Do not think of them, dear Richard!" said Mary; "for the love of Heaven cease to remember those horrible events that have cast so fearful a blight upon your prospects!"

"Oh, Mary," he replied, "you talk in vain! Can I ever banish from my thoughts the recollection of wrongs so cruel, so monstrous, and unmerited? No; they are stamped upon my memory in characters of blood; characters that neither time nor circumstance can serve to efface, and which the contemplation of the sufferings you so patiently endure do but serve to increase. But, alas! the cup of your misery is not yet full to the brim. I feel that I am your curse, the very bane of your existence, and ——"

"Oh, cease, Richard!" interrupted his wife; "such observations as those seem to imply a doubt as to the sincerity of my love, while, at the same time, they only tend to increase the torture of your mind. Have you ever heard me murmur or complain of the troubles it has been my lot to encounter, but, on the contrary, have I not done all that I could to sustain you, and to raise your mind to hope?"

"Oh, yes, my beloved Mary!" he replied, "what language can do adequate justice to your unparalleled self-devotion? But still, when I consider what you have already suffered, and may still have to suffer for my sake, can I help regretting that Fate ever introduced us to each other?"

"Pardon me, Mr. Parker," said Worthington, "but this is sad conversation, and the sooner you put an end to it, it strikes me, the better. Your wife is a noble-hearted woman, and I honour and esteem her. But, come, the breakfast awaits us below."

Richard returned no answer, but composing his feelings as well as he could, he and Mary followed the old man down stairs, where they found the dame busily engaged in preparing the morning's repast, and she greeted them in her usual friendly and cordial manner. The meal passed over without any conversation taking place of sufficient importance to be recorded in these pages, and the arguments and remonstrances of our heroine at length had their due effect upon her husband, and his feelings became more tranquillised, and the painful and fearful impression which the unexpected and extraordinary re-appearance of Mad Moll had made upon his mind was gradually abated, if not entirely dissipated; for on mature reflection it did not appear at all probable that she had become acquainted with his place of concealment, and even if she had, he did not believe that she would betray him, seeing that he had never done her any injury, and she, therefore, had no reason to entertain any feelings of animosity against him. In this opinion he was further strengthened and encouraged by Mary; and Mr. Worthington also coincided in the arguments she made use of, and endeavoured to inspire him with hope and confidence.

"All goes on as well as we could wish, or have anticipated," he remarked: "Providence has watched over your safety so far; and, take my word for it, it will not now desert you, but enable you to surmount all the dangers and difficulties by which you are at present surrounded."

"Oh, yes," said Mary, "I feel satisfied that what you have said, Mr. Worthington, will be verified; and that something will yet occur to rescue us from the difficulties in which we are now placed, even much sooner than we

anticipate. As for this singular woman, we have nothing to apprehend from her, for she cannot be aware that we are here secreted, and she most probably by this time has quitted the neighbourhood altogether. Come, my dear Richard, think no more about it, but endeavour to look forward to the future with the most sanguine anticipations."

"For your sake, my faithful and beloved wife, I will try to do so," replied Parker, endeavouring to assume an air of composure and resignation he was, however, far from entirely feeling. "For your sake, I will humbly, but fervently beseech the Supreme to avert the terrible and ignominious fate with which I am threatened, and which would be the means of plunging you and our child into that state of misery which I shudder to think upon."

"Do not think upon it, my unfortunate husband," returned May, "for I feel a sweet confidence in the mercy of Heaven, and that none of the apprehensions you have so long and so naturally encouraged will be realised. I should indeed be a wretched being, tired of existence, could I think they would."

"Well—well," observed Worthington, "I trust that you will never be subjected to so painful, so insupportable a trial, Mrs. Parker. In time, the excitement which at present prevails will have abated, and you may then go whithersoever you may think proper, and set detection at defiance."

Richard Parker, the better to satisfy his wife, affected to agree with Mr. Worthington; though his feelings upon the painful subject were quite the reverse, for to him it did not seem at all likely that the search after him would be abandoned, and should he be discovered, then his fate would be certain, for he was well aware that he could expect no mercy at the hands of the law.

"And you say that it is the intention of the marines to leave the neighbourhood to day?" he said, addressing himself to Mr. Worthington.

"So they stated to me," replied the latter, "and I have no reason to doubt their word. We need be under no apprehension of a second visit from them, and I will lose no time in putting the plans I have formed for your future security into execution. To-morrow morning, before any one is abroad, I will take you to the cottage where I propose that your wife and child shall take up their future residence, and you will then see that I have prepared everything for their accommodation; my next task will be to introduce you to my guests as my nephew, Martin Worthington, of Maidstone, in Kent, mark that, and you will be so disguised, that it will be impossible for even those who are intimately acquainted with you to recognise you, or to entertain the least suspicions as to your real character. Do you think that you will possess sufficient confidence to enact the part I propose you to do?"

"Oh, yes," answered our hero, "the thought of how much depends on my conduct, my own life, and the happiness or misery of those who are more precious to me than my own existence, will aid and encourage me, and I do not doubt that I shall be enabled to conduct myself in such a manner as to quiet all suspicions that might otherwise be excited. But should your nephew at any time change his mind, and come here?"

"Oh, there is no fear of that," replied Mr. Worthington. "I will take good care that he does not do anything of the sort; and if he did, you need be under no apprehension whatever, for I would be sure to bind him to secrecy, and he would not be much inclined to disobey my wishes, I imagine. You know the character of old Stephen Ladbroke well enough, and will be on your guard against him?"

"I will," replied Parker; "though the less I have of that inquisitive gentleman's company the better."

"Ay—ay," returned Worthington; "he shall not trouble you much, you may depend upon that.

In conversation similar to that which we have described, but which it is unnecessary to particularise here, the remainder of the day passed away, and when the evening came, and the time at which Ladbroke and the other worthies who were accustomed to use the old Punch Bowl might be expected, Richard and our heroine bade Mr. Worthington and his dame good night, and retired to their own apartments, where they continued to discuss the prospects that

were now before them until a late hour, when they sought their pillow in much better spirits than they had hitherto experienced.

They arose at an early hour the following morning, and prepared to meet Mr. Worthington, and it was not long that they had to wait, for they heard a knock at the door, and directly afterwards he entered the room.

"Now, my friends," he remarked, "all is ready, and the sooner we depart the better; we are not likely to meet any one on the road at this early hour, and, therefore, we have nothing to fear."

"But I am afraid you are running yourself into great danger on my account," said Richard; "and should anything happen to you, I should never forgive myself."

"Pshaw!" returned the old man, impatiently, "what do you think is to happen to me? Providence will, I feel confident, protect me in performing my duty to my fellow creatures is distress. But, come, we do but waste time."

Richard did not make use of any further observation for the moment, and he and his wife, and the youthful William, followed the kind-hearted old man from the room, and quickly emerged into the open air. He looked anxiously around him, but as far as his eyes could stretch, the coast was entirely clear, and and they proceeded on their way without any apprehension.

In a few minutes they came in sight of a few straggling cottages, which Mr. Worthington had before described to them, and at length, apart from the rest, and situated in a most quiet and secluded spot, Mr. Worthington pointed out to them the one which he intended for the future residence of Mary. Its rural simplicity, and the retirement by which it was surrounded, were just suited to the taste of Richard and his wife, and they could not but again return their acknowledgments to him for his unexampled kindness; but the old man again interrupted them impatiently.

"Now, now, my dear friends," he said, "why will you persist in overwhelming me with your thanks, and which, I'm sure, I do not require? I think you will find this cottage just suited to your purpose, and here Mrs.

Parker can reside as the widow Summerton without the least fear of exciting any suspicion."

There was a small but well-arranged garden in front of the cottage, which greatly added to its prepossessing appearance; and it so reminded our heroine of some of the early scenes of her youthful days, before she knew what sorrow was, that she could scarcely refrain from tears; but Mr. Worthington having crossed the garden, followed by Richard and his wife, he unlocked the door with a key which he had brought with him in his pocket, and led the way into the cottage, which consisted of three rooms and a kitchen. Mr. Worthington had by no means exaggerated when he had said that it was commodious and comfortable; it far exceeded all the expectations which the fugitives had formed of it, and it was furnished in the most neat and handsome style, which showed the good taste of its benevolent proprietor. Everything that Richard and our heroine beheld excited their unqualified approbation and admiration; and they were at a loss for words to express the satisfaction they felt.

"Well," asked Mr. Worthington, at length, "what think you of the cottage?"

"Oh, my dear sir," answered Mary, "it is all that we could wish. Would that we might be permitted to pass the remainder of our days in tranquillity here; we should then have nothing left to sigh for, and the sorrows of the past, I trust, would be buried in oblivion."

"And so they will, my dear madam," replied Mr. Worthington; "of that I feel confident, and I would have you both to encourage the same hopes and ideas."

"I will do so," ejaculated Richard, pressing his hand with a warmth of feeling which could not be mistaken, "and should it please Providence to hear the prayers I will constantly offer up, the past will be deprived of its terrors, and I will look forward to the future with the fond hope that happiness will again be ours."

"Well said," returned Worthington. "But we had better return to the inn, before there is any one astir. To-morrow, if you please, Mrs. Parker, you can take up your residence here."

"I am most ready to do so, my kind friend," replied Mary; "but I shall not be separated from my husband long, shall I ?"

"Certainly not," answered Worthington; "you will have an opportunity of seeing each other every day, and that, too, without any fear of your real characters being suspected."

"I am satisfied," observed Mary; "and I will leave everything to your judgment and determination."

"Be it so," said the landlord, "and you may rest assured that neither you nor your husband will have reason to regret any confidence you may repose in me."

"I am well aware of that, Mr. Worthington," said our hero; "and like my wife, I am fully prepared to follow your advice in every respect."

They now quitted the cottage, and bent their steps towards the inn. They had proceeded for some distance without seeing any one or anything to create their alarm, when they were suddenly startled by hearing a rustling sound among the bushes on one side of the lane they were traversing, and the next moment a human form forced its way through the bushes, and confronted them. It was that extraordinary woman, Mad Moll.

CHAPTER XIII.

THE PROPHECY.—FRESH EXCITEMENT. THE FURTHERANCE OF THE PLOT.

THE sudden appearance of Mad Moll, and under such peculiar circumstances, as may be supposed, caused a deep sensation of astonishment and alarm in the minds of Richard and his wife, and the latter clung closely to him, and could not help giving utterance to an exclamation of terror, while Mr. Worthington contemplated the singular being before him with no little curiosity and anxiety. Moll, however, remained fixed in the same attitude she had assumed when she first appeared before them, and she fixed her small but piercing eyes upon the countenances of Mary and her husband with a mingled expression of pity and satisfaction.

"Richard Parker," she at last said, in a peculiar voice. He started, and it was impossible for him to prevent the expression of his emotions on hearing his name so familiarly mentioned.

"Ah!" he exclaimed, in tremulous and doubtful accents, "known?"

"Known! ay, Richard Parker," she retorted, with a half smile, "who knows you better than Mad Moll, as she is called?"

"Good God!" cried Mary, trembling convulsively in every limb, "what strange accident is it that has caused you to cross our path again, after the lapse of so many years?"

"Accident, do you call it, Mary Parker?" said Moll; "it is the will of a superior power that I should do so."

"You will not betray us?" said Richard, eagerly.

"No," she answered, "I am not your enemy, though I come to warn you, and to prepare you for that which must inevitably take place."

"Mysterious woman!" gasped forth the violently agitated Mary, "for the love of Heaven, have pity on us, and do not shock our ears and distress our feelings by giving utterance to your wild and fearful predictions."

"Ah!" ejaculated Moll, with a look of satisfaction, "you do then remember the prognostications which I uttered some years ago, and before the sun of your earthly happiness had entirely set? Answer me, Richard Parker: have they not any of them been fulfilled?"

"Woman, forbear!" cried Parker, gazing at her with a look of increased astonishment and alarm; "you torture me!"

"Have my predictions been fulfilled or have they not?" demanded the old woman, with a determined look.

"Alas! alas! they have, too fatally," groaned Richard; "but why art thou again sent hither to rack my brain to madness? You say you are my friend; why, then, do you seem to exult in my misery, and that of my innocent wife?"

"I do not exult, Richard Parker," she replied. "I merely give utterance to those fearful truths which are written in the Book of Fate, and the consummation of which it will be utterly impossible for you to avoid."

"But you will no longer seek to annoy me? You will not betray me?" again anxiously inquired our hero, and

he cast his eyes fearfully round, lest he should behold some person approaching.

"You have nothing to fear from me," answered the woman; "but I would have you not to flatter yourself with false and delusive hopes, but to prepare yourself for the worst. The prophecies to which I gave utterance some time since, I say again, have been partly fulfilled, and the rest will most assuredly be realised, though for a time you may elude the vigilance of your pursuers; the law will have its vengeance in your blood, and an ignominious death will close the career of the unfortunate Richard Parker!"

"Oh, horrible! horrible!" ejaculated Mary, clasping her hands together in the greatest agony of feeling; "strange, fearful woman, recall your words, and say that——"

"You supplicate in vain, Mary," interrupted the wanderer, and in a voice in which an expression of pity was mingled; "there is no averting the will of Heaven."

"Woman!" said Mr. Worthington, whose patience was quite exhausted, "who are you that pretend to penetrate into the mysteries of futurity?"

"I am no presumptuous pretender, old man," replied Mad Moll, with perfect coolness and composure, "as these unfortunate beings have already sufficiently experienced. They call me mad; but little do the ignorant know the extraordinary thoughts that are constantly passing in my mind. Richard Parker, you have heard what I have said, and rest assured that you cannot avoid the fate that is in store for you. Adieu! I have other, and equally solemn and important business to transact."

As the old woman thus spoke, she drew her tattered cloak closer around her bony form, and was about to hurry from the spot, when Richard Parker, in a voice half-choked by the power of his emotions, said—

"Stay—stay! you must not leave me thus. Whither would you go? Where may I again find you, should I need to consult you or ask your advice?"

"Whither I go, where I am concealed, or what are the motives for my actions, it matters not," replied the woman. "Who shall seek to penetrate my mysterious secrets? We doubtless shall meet again!"

"Nay—nay," said Richard, placing his hand on her arm, "I will not suffer you to depart until you have further satisfied me, and convinced me that I have nothing more to fear from you."

"You have nothing to fear from me, unfortunate man," returned Moll. "But do not seek to detain me, lest you should, indeed, have cause to repent it. Nay," she continued, in resolute accents, and releasing her arm from his hold, "you know me not thoroughly, or you would not thus presume. Remember my words, and begone!"

Thus speaking, and without giving our hero or Mr. Worthington time to return any answer, or to recover from their astonishment and confusion, Mad Moll forced herself again through the hedge by the way she had come, and was immediately hidden from the sight, leaving them gazing at each other with an expression of the most intense amazement and terror. As for Mary, so violent was her agitation that, had it not been for the support she received from her husband, she must have sunk upon the earth; and she gazed vacantly in the direction whence the old woman had disappeared, scarcely able to believe the evidence of her senses.

"Gracious Heaven!" she exclaimed, in a faint voice, "to what horrible words have we been compelled to listen?—What fresh sufferings are in store for us?"

"Come, Mrs. Parker," said Worthington, "I pray you to soothe the anguish of your mind, and not to pay any serious attention to the observations of this extraordinary woman, whose intellects are evidently deranged, and who knows not what she says."

"Ah, no!" ejaculated our heroine, wringing her hands in despair and agony. "In vain you strive to deceive me! Can I remember the fatal past without placing every confidence in her awful prognostications? Oh, Richard, my husband! speak to me—tell me that you are enabled to treat the words of this strange woman with contempt, and you will remove a weight from my bosom, which is almost more than human nature can support."

"My beloved—my devoted wife!" replied Parker, making a powerful effort to tranquillise his feelings, in order that he might quiet her apprehensions, "why should the words of this woman alarm and agitate you thus? She is only a human being like ourselves, and by what right can she presume to penetrate into the secrets of futurity? Let us endeavour to trust to Providence, and to submit to its will, whatever it may be."

"Well said, Mr. Parker," returned Mr. Worthington; "it would be the very height of weakness and folly to suffer the words of a wretched maniac to make any lasting or powerful impression upon you. But why did we suffer her to depart in the manner we did, and without binding her to secrecy? She says she is your friend, but I must say that she has a singular way of showing it. Should she betray you, and ——"

"Oh, horrible thought!" cried the distracted Mary; "Richard, unfortunate Richard, you are lost—you are lost! But it may not yet be too late to overtake her, and surely the tears and supplications of a wretched wife and mother will have some effect upon her, and cause her to keep the important secret she possesses closely confined to her breast. For the love of Heaven, Mr. Worthington, do follow her footsteps, and endeavour to prevail upon her to return."

"It is useless," answered Worthington, "for it would be a hopeless task to attempt to trace her footsteps; and even if we could overtake her, in what manner could we act? We must endeavour to satisfy ourselves with the promise she made you not to do you any harm, and leave the rest to chance."

"There is no other alternative," remarked Richard; "but alas! I fear there is but little hope for me. Fortune seems to frown upon me, and it is in vain for me to seek to avoid the fate which has been so long impending o'er my head."

"Oh, Richard!" again gasped forth the horror-struck Mary, and throwing her fair arms affectionately around his neck, while she looked in his face with an expression which showed the intensity of the anguish which corroded her heart.

"Come, Mr. Parker," said Worthington, "you must not give way to these feelings of despair. Fortune may yet smile upon you, and all may yet be well. But why do we stand here hesitating when we should return home with all possible speed, and before any one shall be stirring abroad, who may discover us?"

Richard Parker was with difficulty prevailed upon; but the anguish of his wife had its due effect upon him, and taking her arm, and gazing in her face with a melancholy look of agony and commiseration, with a heavy sigh, he followed Mr. Worthington, though he frequently looked behind him to ascertain whether any one was watching them, or if he could again see anything of the extraordinary woman who had created so painful a sensation in their breasts.

They conversed but little on their way home, and they soon arrived at the inn, where they found the dame waiting to receive them, having already prepared the morning meal. She soon perceived by the expression of their features that something had occurred to alarm and agitate them, and she eagerly inquired what it was. Her husband briefly informed her, and she expressed much astonishment and uneasiness at the circumstance.

"What a strange being this woman must be," she remarked; "but one thing is quite certain, I think, and that is, that she cannot be in her right senses, and it would be the height of absurdity to place any reliance in her wild observations."

"That is precisely my opinion, dame," returned Worthington; "and, although I must admit that this adventure is annoying and somewhat alarming, I would fain try to persuade Mr. Parker and his wife to think so, too."

"It certainly is somewhat alarming," observed Mrs. Worthington, "that accident should have guided her footsteps to this neighbourhood, and that she should have seen you. Should she either wilfully or by accident reveal what she knows——"

"Oh, terrible thought!" interrupted the agitated Mary; "I fear that all is lost! Our very lives are in that dangerous woman's hands; and should she betray us—Father of Mercy look down upon us, and avert the dreadful fate that seems to threaten us!"

"Oh, Mary!" sighed her husband, "ours is indeed an awful fate, and in vain may we try to extricate ourselves from the difficulties which surround us on every side. For myself, I am so worn and exhausted by the cares and anxieties I have had to encounter, that I care but little what becomes of me. Life has become an insupportable burthen to me; but were I no more, what would become of you, my devoted wife, and our noble-hearted and innocent boy? That thought maddens me! And then to meet with so awful and shameful a death! To be hanged by the neck like a dog! To——"

"Hold!" cried our heroine, in a hoarse voice, and her bosom heaving with convulsive emotion; "the frightful picture you have drawn, Richard, is more than reason can support! They shall not part us; they shall not, dare not consign you to a fate so horrible and unmerited. The just God above will not permit it; He knows the monstrous wrongs by which you have been urged to that you have committed, and that it sprang from no wilful or malicious act of your own, and he will not suffer you to fall a victim to the crimes and iniquities of others. Beloved Richard, we will live and die together!"

Her emotions overpowered her, and she sank sobbing on her husband's bosom, while he clasped her with the most indescribable affection to his heart, and was unable to give utterance to the agonising feelings that predominated in his breast.

Mr. and Mrs. Worthington were much affected by the scene which they witnessed, and suffered them to give free indulgence to their feelings for several minutes without offering to interrupt them; while the poor boy, William, clung to his parents' knees and looked up in their faces with all that deep affection and sympathy which his young heart so sincerely experienced.

"Be firm, Mr. Parker," at length said Worthington, "and give not way to these dreadful apprehensions, which only serve to render you miserable, and to distract the mind of your faithful and devoted wife."

"My good and generous-hearted friend," replied our hero, "and have I not sufficient cause for all the painful emotions I evince when I reflect upon the awful and critical position in which I am placed? Can you wonder at the anguish and anxiety I display, at the apprehensions I entertain, when you view all the terrible dangers by which I am surrounded?"

"True," returned Mr. Worthington, "it would be strange, indeed, if you could remain entirely unmoved under all

MR. LADBROKE IMPARTING HIS SUSPICIONS TO MR. WORTHINGTON.

the circumstances; but still I would persuade you not to abandon yourself entirely to despair, but to believe that, notwithstanding the present threatening aspect of your prospects, your fears will not be realised."

"Most gladly would I do so," remarked Richard; "but I find it is impossible; and I cannot but acknowledge the powerful and painful impression which the unexpected appearance of this singular woman in this neighbourhood,

No. 14

and her having beheld me, has made upon my mind."

"Well," answered Worthington, "it certainly would have been better had this circumstance not have taken place, though I do not believe that any harm will arise from it; from the observations she made use of, it would seem that she bears you no ill-will, and would not wish the predictions to which she gave utterance to be fulfilled."

"Oh, no," rejoined Mary, "I am certain she would not, and they should only be looked upon as the wild emanations of a disordered brain."

"That is exactly my opinion," coincided the dame; "besides, if she remains in this part of the country, my husband will probably be able to find out the place of her concealment, and then she may be persuaded to keep the knowledge she possesses a secret, and by an earnest appeal to her proper feelings, to abandon any sinister designs she might previously have had in contemplation."

"Exactly so," said her husband; "besides, this mysterious woman cannot possibly know me, and she must, therefore, remain in ignorance of the exact place in which you are concealed. Come, come, my unfortunate friend, let me again persuade you to banish these fears from your mind, and to rest assured that, with the aid of Providence, all will yet terminate as well as we could wish."

Richard Parker did struggle violently with the feelings that naturally agitated his breast, and in a few minutes became comparatively composed, and seated himself at the breakfast table, stifling as well as he could the thoughts that still continued to haunt his imagination, for he knew well what anguish it was adding to the mind of his wife, whilst the expression of his emotions was not at all calculated to effect any ultimate good.

"It is necessary," observed Mr. Worthington, "that we should complete our arrangements for your security without the least possible delay, and, therefore, I intend to-night to inform Ladbroke and my other guests of the expected arrival of my nephew in a day or two at the inn, and of his intentions to reside here in future, in order that he may assist me in my business. You

must, therefore, acquire all the coolness and confidence you can, Mr. Parker, to enable you to personate that character without suspicion."

"You need be under no apprehensions in that respect, Mr. Worthington," replied our hero; "anxiety for those who are so precious to me, will enable me to perform that task with all the ability that can be desired."

"Enough," returned Worthington, "I place every reliance on you; and disguised as I purpose that you shall be, it is almost impossible that you can be detected."

"I am satisfied," answered Richard; "and will be guided entirely by your advice, knowing full well the sincerity and integrity of your intentions; but still I cannot but feel the most painful regret at the thought of the trouble to which I, a complete stranger, am putting you to, and the danger in which your generous and humane exertions in my behalf may involve you."

"As for danger," returned Worthington, "I apprehended nothing of the sort; my plans are too well laid, and the just God above, who knows the purity of my motives, will protect me through the difficult task I have imposed upon myself. So let not that thought for a moment again disturb your mind, Mr. Parker, but look forward with hope and tranquillity to the future."

Richard and his wife pressed the hands of the kind-hearted old man in silence, and their looks expressed far more than any language, however eloquent, could convey. After they had passed some further time in conversation, as Mr. Worthington and his wife had some business to transact, which would occupy them the whole of the day, our hero and Mary retired to their own apartments, where they endeavoured to recover themselves from the excitement which their interview with the sibyl had caused them, and they so far succeeded that by the morning they were far more composed than they had been for several days before. As Mr. Worthington, however, had promised to visit them as soon as Ladbroke and his companions had taken their departure, they did not retire to rest; and much earlier than they had expected him, he made his appearance, and expressed his pleasure and satisfaction at the favourable change which had taken place in their appearance and manner since the morning.

"This is as it ought to be," he remarked; "and depend upon it that everything will turn out as well as we could wish it. I have apprized Ladbroke and the others of the intended addition to my family by the arrival of my nephew, and they are prepared to give him a hearty welcome. You will, therefore, be fully prepared how to act, and have nothing to fear. I have also promised to give them a bit of a jollification on the occasion of his arrival, the better to drown suspicion, and to enlist their goodwill in your favour; for I have not lived so long in the world as to be ignorant of the effect which a toast and a bottle or two of wine has upon such minds as Ladbroke's, and those of his companions. I have told them that in three days from the present my nephew may be expected at the inn."

"Enough, my generous friend!" replied Richard, "I will be upon my guard, and be prepared to perform my difficult task in such a manner as shall meet with your approbation, and the emergency of the case requires."

"You will be able to accomplish it," said Worthington; "and I don't entertain any fears as to the result. To-morrow morning I think it would be advisable that your wife and son should at once enter upon their residence at the cottage, and I have already procured for them such disguises as will enable them to look the characters they will assume. In order not to take them by surprise, I have also informed Ladbroke and his friends that I have let the cottage to my relation, the Widow Lamerton and her son; and thus I think that I have completed all my arrangements for your security in a most satisfactory manner."

Mary and her husband could but again return the good old man their hearty and grateful thanks; and after some further conversation, he left them to themselves, requesting them to be prepared to take their departure with him to the cottage at an early hour in the morning.

When he had quitted the room, they passed some time in conversing upon their future prospects; and Mary, as usual, exerted herself to the utmost to inspire her husband with hope, and in which she succeeded, taking all the melancholy and perilous circumstances by which they were surrounded into consideration, much better than could have been expected.

"The arrangements which the kind-hearted Mr. Worthington has made for our security offer every prospect of success," she remarked. "In time the vigilance of our pursuers will have relaxed; they will imagine that we have escaped to some foreign land, and will abandon all further idea of discovering us. We shall then be secure, and may make such final arrangements as prudence and circumstances may suggest."

"God grant, my dear Mary," replied her husband, fervently, "that your fond expectations may not be disappointed. Oh, there is no labour, however menial and degrading, no privations, however severe, to which I would not most cheerfully and without a murmur submit, if I am only permitted to live for your beloved sake and that of our poor boy. Even then, methinks, I could in time learn to forget the bitter and painful past, and apply all my energies towards the establishment of peace and tranquillity for the future."

"Blessed words!" exclaimed the fond and devoted wife, tears trembling in her eyes; "they fall like the dew of Heaven upon my soul, imparting to it sweet confidence and consolation. What care I for the stings of poverty, if you, my husband, are preserved to me? You shall never hear me murmur, but it shall be my constant task to study to cheer you on, and to banish from your memory the terrible wrongs and sufferings to which you have been subjected."

"I know it, my Mary," replied Richard, embracing her with all that ardour and affection which his feelings prompted; "and it is that which encourages me and makes me cling to that life which now possesses no other charms for me but those which are derived from you and our child. May the Almighty, in his boundless mercy, avert from me that awful and ignominious fate, with which the prognostications of that strange woman has threatened me!"

"Think no more of them, Richard," said our heroine, "for they are no more than the offsprings of a deranged intellect, and as such deserve only to be treated with contempt and indifference. I firmly believe that we have nothing to fear from her, for did she not solemnly declare that she would not harm us? What have we ever done to excite her animosity? And what can she possibly have to gain by our destruction?"

"True," coincided our hero; "but mankind are base and deceitful, and too often, without a cause, take delight to torture and to persecute their fellow creatures; and it is impossible for us to judge correctly what are the motives of this woman. Would to Heaven that we had not again encountered her; then I should not have entertained the doubts and fears that now beset my mind."

"Do not encourage them, my husband," said Mary; "for I feel assured they will prove to be groundless. This mad woman, I trust, will never annoy us again, and one thing is certain, that she is unacquainted with Mr. Worthington, or the place of his residence, and that she is, consequently, ignorant of the place where we are concealed."

"But a thought strikes me," said our hero, after a pause.

"And what is that?" eagerly demanded his wife.

"Should she still remain in this neighbourhood, and by any accident discover that you are a resident in the cottage?" replied Richard.

"Oh, there is no fear of that," said Mary; "I will keep myself confined to the place; at least, not venturing forth only at such times when I am not likely to encounter any person whom I should fear to meet. But I do not entertain any such apprehensions, and I would fain banish them also from your mind. Come, Richard, let us offer up our supplications to the Almighty, and I feel confident that he will not turn a deaf ear to them, but will protect us from all the dangers which we now apprehend."

They knelt down, and with upraised hands and devout and earnest hearts, implored the mercy of the Supreme. They then felt more composed and resigned, and retiring to rest, slept calmly and soundly till the first rays of the sun streamed in at their chamber-window in the morning. They then arose, and prepared themselves to meet Mr. Worthington. They had not to wait long, for almost immediately afterwards he entered the room, accompanied by his wife, who had come to bid our heroine adieu for the present.

"I shall visit you frequently, if you will allow me," said the good old dame; "and endeavour to impart such consolation to you as you may stand in need of in your lonely situation."

"Thanks, my kind friend," replied Mary; "and need I say how happy I shall be at any time to see you? Believe me, I shall be as happy and contented as circumstances will permit me, knowing how near I am to my beloved husband and those excellent friends to whom we are so greatly indebted."

"Well," remarked Worthington, "we do but delay time, and it is advisable that we should take our departure before any one is likely to be abroad to see us."

"True," replied Richard; "but should we again encounter that strange being who has already so greatly alarmed us?"

"Oh, fear not," said Worthington; "it is not very likely that she will again cross our path; and if she should, we must be prepared to meet her with firmness and resolution. We may be able to accomplish all we can wish by a little timely and prudent argument and persuasion. After the observations she made use of yesterday morning, I do not think it would be any difficult task to secure her secrecy and assistance even, if it be in her power to render any."

Richard Parker made use of no further observation, and Mary and Mrs. Worthington having bade each other a cordial farewell, they took their departure from the inn, and bent their way by the most unfrequented route towards the cottage.

Nothing particular occurred to them on the way, and in a very few minutes they arrived at the place of their destination, which they entered, and then considered themselves to be in safety. Mary looked eagerly round the neat apartment, and her gratitude to the benevolent Mr. Worthington increased. Since their visit to it the day before several additions had been made to its comforts, and Mr. Worthington had taken good care to place at her disposal an ample supply of provisions and other necessaries for the present, so that there was nothing left for her to require.

"You will also find up stairs a wardrobe for yourself and your son, suited to the characters you are to assume," remarked Mr. Worthington; "and you will then be so disguised that you may fairly defy suspicion."

"Such kindness as this is overwhelming," said our hero.

"Name it not," replied Worthington; "if all my wishes for your welfare are only gratified, I shall be satisfied. After what I have stated to Ladbroke and his friends, you need not fear any impertinent curiosity. Mr. Parker can visit you again to-night, and after he has been once introduced at the inn in the character of my nephew, he can do so as often as he pleases, and with perfect safety. But come, Mr. Parker, it is necessary that we should no longer remain here."

Short as was the time that they would be separated from each other, Richard could not help feeling the greatest reluctance, and emotions of the most melancholy description, at parting from his wife; and it was not until after they had embraced each other several times in the most ardent and affectionate manner that Mr. Worthington could persuade him to leave her, promising him, at the same time, that Mrs. Worthington should come to the cottage soon after their return to the inn, in order that she might pass the day with Mary. They then bade each other a fond adieu, as though they were about to separate for years, and Richard and Mr. Worthington left the cottage, our heroine and her son watching them from the casement till they were out of sight; and she then returned to the room, and she and William sinking upon their knees, implored the mercy and protection of Heaven.

Worthington and Richard regained the inn without meeting with any person on the road, and in a short time afterwards Mrs. Worthington departed for the retreat of Mary, and thus removed some of the weight of anxiety from her husband's mind.

The day passed away without anything particularly worthy of recording taking place, and in Worthington and Richard arranging their plans for the future; and the hopes of our hero gradually increased, and were not a little strengthened on the return of Mrs. Worthington in the evening, who informed them that she had done everything to the comfort of Mary and her son, and that they were as happy and contented as, under all circumstances, they could be expected to be.

"You may set your mind perfectly at rest, Mr. Parker," observed the dame, "for there is not the least fear of their being intruded upon. I have seen them in their sombre disguises, and it has made such an alteration in the appearance of them both, that it would be impossible, I think, for even those who are most intimately acquainted with them to recognise them."

"I cannot but repeat my thanks and admiration," said Richard, "for the excellent arrangements which yourself and your husband have made for our security. And the more I reflect on them, the greater is the confidence I feel in their success."

"Continue to encourage those hopes," returned Worthington, "and, depend upon it, you will not be doomed to disappointment. The next thing you have to do is to prepare yourself for your introduction to that busy and inquisitive gentleman, Mr. Ladbroke, and his friends."

"That I am already fully prepared for," answered our hero; "and I have no doubt, when I take into consideration the great stake I have in hand, I shall be able to accomplish my task to your satisfaction. I am, however, most anxious to hear again from my warm-hearted friends, Adams and Binnacle, for their advice will be necessary and valuable to guide me in my future conduct."

"Exactly so," remarked Worthington; "and I have no doubt that a few days will bring honest Ben Binnacle again to this coast, and then you will learn all the particulars from the seat of danger. Your friends, I think, cannot but approve of the course we have adopted."

"Undoubtedly," said Richard; "and how fortunate it was for me that Providence directed my footsteps hither where I have found a friend so ardent, and so disinterested, where I had the least right to expect to meet with one."

"Well," replied Worthington, impatiently, "a truce with all compliments, to which I do not feel myself entitled. A few days, I trust, will see your security firmly established, and then all those doubt, and fears, and anxieties which at present trouble you, will probably be removed from your mind."

As the time for Mr. Ladbroke, and his companions to arrive was now approaching, they thought it prudent for them to separate, and our hero retired up stairs, in order that he might collect his thoughts, and to await anxiously for the time to arrive when he might safely venture from the inn, and make his way to the new abode of the beloved partner of his sorrows and his misfortunes; for even the few hours that they had been separated appeared to him an age, and he felt wretched and uneasy until he was again in her presence, and well did he know how painfully she would reciprocate his feelings.

He seated himself at the window which commanded a view of the ocean, in order to endeavour to divert his mind, and again did his thoughts involuntarily wander to the fearful events of the past, whilst the dark shadows of the future cast their oppressive gloom upon his mind. It was in vain that he sought to resist their melancholy and powerful influence, for the more he did so, the greater became the effect of his doubts and apprehensions. It was impossible that he could really encourage the hopes with which Mary had sought to inspire him, and with which, in order to appease her anguish, he had affected to be animated; and now that he was alone, and there was no one to observe him, he gave free indulgence to his feelings.

"What madness would it be for me," he soliloquised, "to encourage the delusive hope that I can escape from the fate which the offended laws of my country have awarded me! Although the cruel wrongs I have endured will fully, in my own conscience, exonerate me from that which I have done, I can expect no mercy from man. They will continue to hunt me to the death like some wild beast, and will never rest until they have satiated their vengeance

in my blood. They will have no pity or mercy for my beloved wife and my unfortunate boy; they will look upon me only as a mutineer and a murderer, and as such will execrate my memory, and point at them the finger of scorn and hatred. Oh, God! how horrible, how torturing is that thought! It distracts my brain, and goads me on to madness! What will become of those innocent and friendless beings when I am no more? what will be the insupportable sufferings they will have to endure when they reflect upon my ignominious fate? And they will have no one now to sympathise with their maddening sorrows, or to aid them in their misery. They will become wretched wanderers in the wide and cheerless world, and their society will be shunned as though they were something loathsome and contagious. Great God! it would be a mercy for You to take them ere my shameful death is accomplished!"

He beat his breast in the agony and intensity of his feelings, and for a few moments he paced backwards and forwards across the room in a state of mind which it would be utterly impossible for any language to do adequate justice to. Then he resumed his seat at the window, and once more fixed his eyes upon the scene before him.

It was a fine, clear night, and all was calm and beautiful that his eyes rested on, and glistening in the silvery rays of Luna, who was shining with even more than ordinary brilliancy and grandeur in the firmament, undimmed by a single cloud. How ill did the feelings of the unfortunate man accord with the tranquillity of the hour; and in the power of his excited feelings, he could have unmanned himself and wept aloud.

"Beautiful ocean!" he ejaculated, "would that thy bright blue waters divided me and those so dear to me far from our enemies, or that we were now at rest in thy bosom! Oh, that the fates would waft us to some distant spot, where we might remain unknown and unmolested, never would I cease to pour forth my gratitude to the Supreme ruler of events for His mercy. But no, it will not be; I feel assured that there is no avoiding my doom; and I look forward to its approach with cowardice and terror, on account of those unfortunate beings whom I must leave friendless and unprotected behind. Great Heaven, I implore thee that the same day which consigns me to that awful and shameful fate which I feel impending o'er my head may also prove the termination of their existence! And yet, if it had not been for her unfortunate connexion with me, how happy Mary might now have been! But no, not for me; I accuse myself too severely and unjustly; it is from the miscreant Arlington that she has to trace all her misfortunes, all the sorrows which she is at present enduring. May the bitterest curses light upon his black and guilty soul! When I reflect upon the monstrous injuries and indignities I received from him, can I feel the least compunction or regret at the fate which I inflicted on him? No! By all my hopes, I glory and exult in the thought; and were he still alive, no earthly power should shield him from my vengeance, let the consequences to myself be whatever they might. But must my beloved wife and child be for ever exposed to such unexampled trials, when they have never done anything that should merit the retribution of Heaven? Have mercy on them, I beseech thee, oh, Heaven! Give them fortitude to support that which may yet be in store for them, and for myself I care not; I am content to die!"

Again he beat his breast, and groaned aloud in the agony of his mind, and it was some time before he could succeed in obtaining the least composure. Such were the thoughts that continued to harass his brain for several hours, and he never once removed from the spot where he was seated; but at last he made a powerful struggle with his feelings, fearing the effect his agitation might have upon Mary when he beheld her; and by dint of great exertion, he became comparatively calm, but still awaited the time when he might venture from the inn with the greatest impatience and anxiety. In a few minutes he beheld Ladbroke and his companions depart from the house, and soon afterwards Mr. Worthington entered the room, bringing with him a cloak, in which he intended our hero to enfold himself, so that his person should be more closely concealed from observation, in case he should meet any one on his way.

"Now, Mr. Parker," said Worthington, "my guests have all departed, and so you can hasten to the cottage without any fear. I shall not expect you to return to-night, of course, but I must strictly enjoin you not to delay leaving the cottage at the earliest hour in the morning."

"I will adhere strictly to your advice, my kind and excellent friend," repeated Richard; "you may expect me to return to the inn by daylight in the morning."

"That is enough," remarked Worthington; "and as your own safety and all that is dear to you depend upon the punctuality with which you keep your word, I shall place every confidence in you."

"You may—you may!" exclaimed our hero, eagerly. "Now, my beloved and faithful Mary, I hasten once more to enfold you in my anxious and affectionate arms!"

"Let me advise you," said the old man, "to be cautious how you behave towards her, and by no means endeavour to crush those hopes which probably predominate in her breast; for much, if not everything, depends upon your firmness and circumspection."

"Fear not," answered Richard; "I will control the real thoughts and feelings that agitate my mind all that is in my power, and act according to your wishes and suggestions."

"I am satisfied," returned Worthington, "and will no longer detain you. But wrap this cloak around you, which will conceal your person from notice, if you should happen to meet any one on your way, and God speed you!"

Richard Parker pressed the good old man's hand in silence, and then wrapping himself in the mantle, and pulling his broad-brimmed hat low over his brow, so as to the better concealment of his features, he followed him down the stairs, and Mr. Worthington having pressed his hand and bade him farewell, Richard made his way with hasty steps and a bounding heart towards the cottage, looking cautiously around him as he proceeded, but observing nothing that was at all calculated to create any alarm in his breast. In a very short time he arrived within sight of it, and the light which shone from the casement of the room above convinced him that his wife had not retired to rest, but that she was waiting most anxiously to receive him. The next moment he was locked fondly in her arms, and they breathed their mutual blessings upon each other's bosoms.

"Dearest Mary," at length ejaculated our hero, "again, for a few hours, we are permitted to enjoy each other's society in safety, and without the fear of interruption. Oh, what happiness is this! what a kind respite from the many cares and anxieties we have so long endured!"

"It is, my Richard," answered his wife, "and it glads my heart to see you so much revived in spirits and re-animated with hope. Oh, believe me, that dark as the prospects have been by which we have hitherto been surrounded, Providence will continue to watch over our safety; it will not desert us while we continue to place our confidence and fix our firm reliance on its infinite mercy."

"Best of women," returned Richard, "what consolation do your words impart to me! Yes, I will be firm, and trust that the Almighty will, for your dear sake, and that of our darling boy, avert the fate which has been so long impending o'er my head, and not suffer you to be plunged into that abyss of shame and misery which would inevitably overtake you should I be consigned to a death so awful and so ignominious."

"Do not mention it, my husband," she replied; "for the bare thought of it is quite sufficient to freeze the very blood in my veins with horror. But it will not be; the arrangements which the kind-hearted Mr. Worthington has made for our security must be crowned with success, and we may, with the blessing of Heaven, set detection at defiance. Oh, how much are we indebted to the disinterested friendship and unparalleled humanity of that excellent man!"

"We are, indeed, Mary," coincided Richard, "but for him and our other inestimable friends, Adams and Binnacle, I should ere this, doubtless, have been in the hands of my pursuers, and then the fate that would have overtaken me would have been certain. May Heaven's choicest blessings light upon their heads for all that they have done to serve us, for I fear, alas! that it will never be in our power to make them any other return than gratitude."

"And they seek no other reward, Richard, I am confident of that," answered his wife; "and yet I trust that the time will come when we shall have it in our power to make them some other acknowledgment than the mere expression of our grateful feelings."

"Ah, Mary," remarked Richard, "those are sanguine expections; and what prospect have we at present that they will ever be realised?"

"Encourage the hope that they will, my dear husband," Mary returned; "and endeavour to view the future on the brightest side."

"I will do so," said our hero, "but you must admit that we have many obstacles and difficulties to surmount."

"And we shall be able to surmount them, Richard," replied Mrs. Parker, firmly. "I feel a sweet assurance that there are brighter days in store for us, and that we shall again experience that happiness and tranquillity which no misconduct of our own has forfeited. The plans formed by our excellent friend Mr. Worthington, are admirable, and I cannot entertain the least apprehension that they will fail; and disguised as we are, and unknown as we are to any of the inhabitants of this place, I do not think it is possible that any suspicion can be excited against us.'

"There is but one man I fear," answered our hero, "and that is that busy, inquisitive individual, Ladbroke."

"Well," returned Mary, "I do not think it is very likely, with all his sagacity, that he will be able to recognise you by the description which is given of you in the advertisements, disguised as your person will be, and being introduced to him as the nephew of Mr. Worthington; but much, nay, everything depends upon the prudence and precaution with which you yourself act: for one unguarded word might betray you, and ruin everything."

"Oh, do not entertain apprehensions on that subject, Mary," answered her husband; "the thought of you and our son will sustain me, and I feel fully competent for the important task which will devolve upon me.   Heaven, surely, will not suffer me to fail."

"It will not," remarked our heroine, with increased confidence; "and here we can remain in safety, and daily meet each other, until we receive the advice of our friends as to what they consider will be the best course for us in future to adopt.   I have several times thought that if I made an appeal to my father, he surely could not turn a deaf ear to my supplication, but would forgive the past,

THE FUGITIVES GAZING ON THE NIGHT SCENE FROM THE INN WINDOW.

and assist us from the terrible difficulties and dangers by which we are surrounded."

"Oh, no, Mary," answered Parker; "it is madness even to think of such a thing.   The feelings that must ever continue to inhabit the bosom of your father are of the most implacable description. Nothing can ever divest his mind of the hatred and prejudices he encourages towards me, and those feelings will be increased by what has happened, and the death of Captain Arlington. Did he but know where I am concealed, I am satisfied that he would be the first to deliver me up to the vengeance of the law."

"Oh, it is impossible that he could be so cruel; that he could ever be the means of consigning to so awful and ignominious a fate the unfortunate husband of his own daughter."

"Ah, Mary, I could expect no mercy or commiseration from him. He must view me as the destroyer of his friend, and as such would exult at my fate, notwithstanding the consequences that would be sure to attend you. Should he discover where we are concealed, our fate would be certain. But let us not think of him, my beloved wife; we have nothing to hope, but everything to fear from him; let us rather put our trust in Omnipotence, and those kind friends on whom we can depend, and I do hope that we shall yet be able to surmount the dangers by which we are now surrounder, and be permitted in obscurity, that obscurity now so congenial to our feelings, to remain unmolested."

"Well spoken, my husband," said our heroine, "and again I must repeat how much it gladdens my heart to see you in this state of mind."

They again embraced, and after some further conversation, and having offered up their prayers to Heaven for its future mercy and protection, they retired to rest with much lighter hearts than they had experienced for some time.

CHAPTER XIV.

RICHARD PARKER IS INTRODUCED TO LADBROKE AND HIS FRIENDS.

OUR hero parted from his wife and son at an early hour the following morning, and returned to the inn without meeting any one on the road.

The whole of that day Mr. Worthington and our hero remained together. finally completing their arrangements for the introduction of the latter to the inn in his new character, while Mrs. Worthington again visited the cottage, in order that she might, by her friendly society, relieve the mind of Mary from those gloomy thoughts which might otherwise have occupied it.

"On the day on which I intend to introduce you here," remarked Worthington, "it will be prudent and necessary that I should pretend to meet you at the coach office, in order to escort you hither, and the better to prevent the least chance of suspicion, although I do not see how it is possible that any should be excited, if you only act your part well. On that occasion, therefore, you will remain at the cottage till I call for you, and we must make it appear as if you had just come off a journey."

"Very true, sir," answered Richard; "and I am fully prepared to act entirely by your advice. You shall find that I will act with firmness and caution."

"Enough," returned Mr. Worthington; "I am satisfied that the urgency and importance of the peculiar circumstances in which you will be placed will enable you to perform your task with ability and discretion; and you will have nothing to apprehend, for you will be so metamorphosed that it will be impossible for even those who are intimately acquainted with you to recognise your person. You must be upon your guard with respect to the answers you return to the questions which the inquisitive Mr. Ladbroke is almost sure to put to you; and should he mention your name, you must pretend perfect ignorance on the subject."

"I will follow your advice, my kind friend, to the very letter," answered our hero.

"Once introduced here in the character of my nephew," continued Mr. Worthington, "you will have no restraint put upon your actions, and will be in a better position to watch all that occurs and to act accordingly. I trust to Heaven that my efforts to serve you and to rescue you from the dangers by which you are now surrounded will prove successful; and if they are, I shall consider it to be one of the proudest moments of my life that introduced you and the amiable partner of your sorrows to me."

"Oh, Mr. Worthington," returned our hero, "no language that I can possibly give utterance to can adequately express to you the feelings of gratitude which your noble and generous conduct has inspired in my breast; but the time will come, I hope, in spite of the awful and critical position in which I am placed, when I shall have it in my power to convince you of the proper sense I entertain of the vast, the unspeakable debt I owe to you."

"Mr. Parker," he replied, "I am but a rough-spoken man, but I feel only too happy in being made the humble instrument in the hands of Heaven to serve my unfortunate fellow creatures in the hour of need; and the satisfaction of a good conscience is a far richer reward than all the wealth in the world can possibly bestow."

"But still," remarked our hero, after a brief pause, "mine is a fearful case; I am charged with being a mutineer and a murderer, and I must never again venture into society, for my life is forfeited to the offended laws of my country, and it would be madness for me to expect any mercy."

"I must admit," said Worthington, in reply, "that your situation is a desperate one, and it was a most unfortunate job that the guilty man, Captain Arlington, should have fallen by your hand, though it was entirely by accident, and his own rash conduct, I believe, that he did so; but still I cannot divest my mind of the hope that Providence will interpose to save you from the dreadful consequences of your offences, and that you will be permitted yet to end your days in peace."

"For the sake of those so far more precious to me than mine own existence, I would fain pray so," returned Richard, "but when I weigh all the circumstances in my mind—when I think of my destitute and helpless condition, the most gloomy thoughts come over me, and my heart sinks with despair."

"You must exert all your energies, Mr. Parker," replied Worthington, "and arouse yourself from those dismal thoughts. You may be able to retire to some foreign land, and there you will, at any rate, be completely out of the reach of danger."

"What prospect have I of doing so," said our hero, "poor and wretched as I am?"

"But you are not friendless," said his companion; "you have still those left who will willingly render you all the assistance in their power."

"And what right have I to expect it?" demanded our hero. "I feel that I have already placed myself under a weight of obligations, for which I can never make any adequate return; and why should I thus involve others in trouble and expense?"

"Pshaw! Mr. Parker," observed Worthington, "why will you persist in tormenting yourself by entertaining these delicate scruples? But there is another idea that has occurred to me, and which I think would be the means of placing you in a state of independence."

"What mean you, Mr. Worthington?" asked Parker.

"Were you to enter into the naval service of some foreign country, you—"

"What!" interrupted our hero; "desert the land of my birth; engage myself to raise my hand in deadly strife against my own countrymen! The thought is hateful and repugnant to my feelings; and I should despise myself if I could act with such base treachery, and should consider that there was no fate, however terrible and degrading, which I did not deserve to meet with. No, I have suffered wrongs, cruel, unmerited wrongs at the hands of those placed in authority above me; I have been lashed and degraded like a dog, in return for the perils and dangers I have encountered; but Heaven forbid that I should thus retaliate. Never will Richard Parker so basely disgrace that character he has always endeavoured to maintain, that of a true British sailor!"

"Well," returned Mr. Worthington, "I cannot but admire your sentiments; they do honour to your head and heart, and I hope you will pardon me for having, in the zeal of the friendship I entertain towards you, thrown out the suggestion I did. But we will talk further upon this subject at some future time. You know the feelings I entertain towards you and those so dear to you, and how anxious I am to serve you?"

"Oh, yes, Mr. Worthington," answered our hero, taking his hand, and pressing it vehemently in his own; "well indeed do I know your generous heart; the purity of your motives, the sincerity of the sympathy you express towards me and mine ; and I should indeed be a worthless scoundrel did I not duly appreciate them, and respect, nay, reverence you for them."

"Well—well," said Worthington, "I know your thoughts, and, as I said before, I honour you for the noble sentiments you have just now expressed. But, perhaps, as we are now alone, it will be as well for us to arrange about the disguise I propose that you should assume. I have it all in readiness, and I have no doubt you will approve of it when you see it."

Mr. Worthington then unlocked a chest which was in the room, and produced a variety of articles. They consisted of a rustic suit, and a wig of flaxen hair.

"There," observed the old man, "when you have assumed this disguise, if it is possible for any one to recognise in you Richard Parker, the seaman, why, I must admit that I am a bungler in such matters altogether."

"Yes," said Richard, "I feel confident that this dress will secure me from detection, if anything will ; and I flatter myself that I shall have firmness and ability sufficient to act up to the character."

"I do not think there will be any necessity for you to return from the cottage when you go there to-night, till I come to escort you to the inn," remarked Mr. Worthington ; "you will be quite safe there, for there is no fear of any one visiting the cottage. Before you leave here to-night, it would be as well for you to assume this disguise, just to see what effect it will have on your personal appearance."

"I will do so," replied our hero.

Some customers now arriving at the inn, Worthington hastened to attend upon them, and Richard retired up-stairs. Here he assumed the disguise with which the old man had provided him ; and so remarkable was the alteration it made in his appearance, that he was surprised at the metamorphosis himself.

The guests having departed, Worthington once more rejoined him, and he could not but express his satisfaction at the effect which the disguise had upon his person.

"It is even much better than I anti-cipated," he remarked ; "and it inspires me with redoubled confidence as to the success of our plans. Nothing could possibly be more complete than this disguise ; and I must confess that had I not been aware of it, and had accidentally met you, I should not have had the least suspicion as to who you were. So altered in appearance, I am certain you can remain in this neighbourhood, or go to any part of the country you think proper, without any fear of discovery. But for the present, at any rate, I would not advise you to depart from hence ; and I need not say, that taking into cosideration the deep interest I feel in your fate, I should feel more satisfied if you were near me, that I might watch over your safety, and give you my advice when required."

"My kind friend," answered Richard, "I have no desire to leave you while it may be safe for me to remain here, for the unexampled kindness and services I have received from you have excited the most lively feelings of esteem towards you in my breast ; and I need not say how much I value and require any advice that may come from you."

"I know it," said Worthington ; "and were you my own son, Mr. Parker, I could not feel more anxiety for your welfare, or sympathise more deeply in the misfortunes with which it has pleased Heaven to visit you. But I cannot help wondering at the extraordinary change which this disguise has effected. I am certain that if that old mad woman who so much alarmed you were to behold you now, she could not possibly know you."

"Nevertheless," replied Richard, "I sincerely hope that I shall never again encounter her."

"Oh," returned Worthington, "I do not think there is much fear of that, for I daresay she has quitted the neighbourhood ; and, besides, from what she said, she has no wish to do you any injury."

"And yet," observed our hero, "I cannot but feel some doubts and misgivings that she might by accident, if not wilfully, betray me."

"Nay," replied his companion, "such apprehensions as those, I am convinced, are entirely groundless. Who, think you, would pay any serious attention to the assertions of a woman whose intellects are evidently deranged ? But you must not let such thoughts as these disturb your mind, for everything now goes on as well as we could wish."

Thus they continued to converse for some time longer, when Worthington quitted him to attend to his business below, and he was left to his own thoughts.

When Ladbroke and the others had taken their departure at the usual hour from the inn, Richard, having bade Mr. Worthington good-night, and promised to attend to his advice in every particular, made his way to the cottage, where it was intended he should remain till the day on which he was to be introduced at the inn, and once more had the pleasure and satisfaction of clasping his faithful wife to his bosom, and was delighted to behold her looking much more contented and cheerful than he had seen her for some days. The alteration in his appearance filled her with as much surprise as it had done Worthington, while, at the same time, it added to the confidence she had before felt as to the success of their plans.

"Everything promises well, dear Richard," she remarked; "and I trust that the time is not far distant when all the dreadful anxieties and apprehensions which have so long distracted our minds will be abated, if not entirely removed."

"I would, indeed, hope so, Mary," replied her husband, in a hesitating and melancholy voice; "but, alas! I feel that it would be wrong to be too sanguine, for the disappointment would, if possible, be more painful to bear than the stern reality."

"But why should we give way altogether to despair?" demanded our heroine, "since Providence has hitherto been so merciful to us? Come, come, be firm; place your reliance on the justice of your cause, and depend upon it, black and threatening though our prospects be at present, we shall yet be triumphant. If we can only remain in concealment for some time longer, the excitement will have subsided; it will be imagined that we have long made our escape to some foreign land, and the pursuit will be abandoned in despair."

Richard shook his head, for, in spite of the arguments of his wife, and anxious as he was to quiet her apprehensions, he found it impossible to conceal the emotions that occupied his breast.

"The offences with which I stand charged," he remarked, "are of too grave a character to admit of any such a hope as that you have just expressed, Mary; they will still be indefatigable in their search after me; and if I do indeed escape, which I pray to Heaven that I may, it will only be by a miracle that I shall do so. However, we must leave everything to the wisdom and the will of Providence, and try to submit without murmuring to our fate, be it whatever it may, though, for your future happiness, I earnestly hope that it will be merciful to us."

"It will, it will!" ejaculated our heroine, eagerly; "I will not—cannot give way to despair, since the Almighty has hitherto so mercifully watched over our safety, and raised us up friends when we had the least right to expect to find them."

"Ah, yes," coincided her husband, "that is, indeed, most true; and sincere and earnest is the gratitude I feel. But I shall feel more contented and confident after I have been introduced to Stephen Ladbroke and the others at the inn."

"True," replied Mary; "but I do not believe that you have anything to fear; Ladbroke cannot have any suspicion of you if you only act your part well. Do you think that you will be able to accomplish your task?"

"Yes," answered our hero, "I have no doubt of that; the business is too important, and there is too much depends upon me, for me to shrink from it, or to render me doubtful as to my being able to go through with it satisfactorily."

"I am glad to hear you say so," remarked Mary, "for it convinces me more than ever that success will attend us."

Having partaken of some refreshment, as the night was far advanced, and they felt somewhat fatigued, they retired to rest, and forgot for awhile all their cares and anxieties in a refreshing slumber.

The next morning, soon after breakfast, Mr. Worthington made his appearance at the cottage, and was welcomed by Richard and his wife in the most earnest, though unaffected manner.

"I informed Ladbroke and his companions last night," he observed, "that I had received another letter from my nephew, and that he might be expected to arrive without fail at the inn to-morrow. I have invited them all to assemble at dinner in order to receive him, and they are most anxious for the time to arrive, for there are few persons that know how to enjoy themselves better than they do, especially when it costs them nothing. You may, therefore, expect me at the cottage to-morrow afternoon, when, of course, you will be in readiness to attend me."

"You will find me quite prepared, my dear sir," answered Richard, "and I do not care how soon the introduction is over."

"Above all things," observed Worthington, "you must not seem to have any anxiety on your mind, but to enter freely, and with all the vivacity you can, into the conversation that will take place."

"I will attend strictly to your advice," returned our hero. "You shall have no cause to complain of me."

"Well, well," said the old man, "I am satisfied, and place every confidence in you. You look the character you represent exactly, and have only got to take care that your conversation and manners are in accordance with it, and all will be well."

Richard Parker promised to be cautious in every particular, and after receiving some further instructions from Mr. Worthington, the latter took his leave, and left them to themselves.

The next day Stephen Ladbroke and his friends did not fail to make their appearance at the inn at the time they were invited, and seemed resolved to enjoy themselves.

"It is some years since you have seen your nephew Martin, is it not, friend Worthington?" asked Ladbroke.

"I have not seen him since he was a boy," answered Worthington.

"Ah! then, I suppose, you have not much recollection of him?" asked Stephen.

"No," replied the old man; "but if the accounts I have heard of him are correct, he is something superior in his manners and appearance to the usual class of rustics, and he has received a moderate education; so I expect he will take the shine out of some of us.

However, handsome is as handsome does, I say."

"True, true, friend Worthington," coincided Ladbroke; "and if he is only half as good a man as his uncle, why, you will have reason to be proud of him, and he will prove a valuable acquisition at the old Punch Bowl."

"Well, I have no doubt the lad will prove not unworthy of the name he bears," said the worthy host. "But I must leave you for awhile, my friends; it is near the time for the coach to arrive, and I must go to meet him, according to promise. I have no doubt you will be prepared to give him a hearty welcome."

This every one was most ready and willing to do, the more especially as old Christopher Worthington had made such ample arrangements for their entertainment.

"But," said Worthington, "this is only delaying time, which I flatter myself can be much better employed; so I will depart upon my errand, and in a short time you may expect me to return, accompanied by my nephew."

"Ay—ay, Master Worthington," remarked Ladbroke, "the sooner the better; for my own part, I am determined to enjoy myself to-day, if I should never have the good fortune to do so again, and so likewise are all our friends here; and if Martin Worthington only at all resembles his uncle, why, we shall not be disappointed, that's very certain."

Mr. Worthington now made his departure, and Stephen Ladbroke and his companions, who were all, like himself, in high glee, at the prospect of the day's pleasure before them, sat down to enjoy themselves during the brief period of his absence.

Our hero had been anxiously awaiting his arrival, and was fully dressed and prepared for the introduction, and in a short time, having had an affectionate parting with his wife and son, himself and Mr. Worthington were on their way to the inn, the latter giving him further instructions and advice as they proceeded.

They soon arrived at the inn, and having entered by a back way, Worthington ushered him into a back room, where he left him to collect his thoughts whilst he returned to Ladbroke and the others to announce his arrival and to prepare them for his introduction. In a few minutes he returned, and informed him that all was ready, and directly afterwards he found himself in their presence, and met with such a reception from them as he had a right to expect ; though the curious manner in which they all, but particularly Ladbroke, scrutinised him, could not but make him feel somewhat confused.

"Welcome, Master Martin Worthington, to the old Punch Bowl," observed Stephen ; "we are the particular friends of your esteemed uncle, and though I say it in his presence, a better man does not exist in the united kingdom ; and if you only the least resemble him in disposition, which, if I may be permitted to judge from your looks, I have no doubt you do, you will prove a most valuable addition to this establishment and our circle of friendship. My friends, bumpers all ! We must drink the health of our new companion, Martin Worthington, and welcome to the old Punch Bowl !"

This toast was received with the most lively and vociferous demonstrations.

"Mr. Ladbroke," replied Richard, "you will pardon me if I do not express myself in suitable terms, for I am a man of few words, and not much used to society ; but I thank you sincerely for the compliment you have just paid me, and the hearty welcome you have given, and I beg leave in return to drink one and all your good healths, and, at the same time, to express a wish for the cultivation of our future friendship."

"Bravo—bravo !" exclaimed Ladbroke ; "well spoken, young man. Oh, I can see that you are a true Worthington every inch of you. It strikes me, too, that there is a strong family likeness."

"Ha—ha—ha !" laughed the old man, good humouredly, and very well pleased to hear Ladbroke make use of these observations, while they inspired our hero with more confidence, "do you think so, friend Ladbroke ?"

"Do I think so ?" repeated the latter, "to be sure I do. What do you say ; my friends ?"

"Why, that we are of your opinion, Stephen," coincided the other guests.

"The eyes, and the expression of the features generally, are exactly alike," continued Ladbroke, "and Master Martin would pass as well for your son as your nephew, Christopher ; and I flatter myself that I am a man of some penetration and judgment in those matters."

"Very true," said Worthington, smiling, "and I have no doubt that you are right, for it was always admitted by those who knew us that a great resemblance existed between my late lamented brother and myself. But come, the dinner is ready, and the sooner we partake of it the better. There is nothing like good eating to add a zest to the pleasures of any festive occasion."

"Ah ! friend Worthington," returned Ladbroke, smacking his lips in anticipation of the banquet, "there again I must entirely agree with you in every particular ; and when we have despatched that part of the business, we will enjoy ourselves to our heart's content, or my name is not Stephen Ladbroke."

Christopher Worthington returned an answer in accordance with these observations, and then led the way to the room where the dinner was prepared, and himself, our hero, and the guests were soon seated at the table, and discussing the merits of the ample and excellent fare which the worthy host had provided for them.

Richard now felt himself perfectly at his ease, and entered into the conversation that ensued with the greatest freedom, for he saw that all the suspicions of the officious and inquisitive Mr. Ladbroke and his friends were quieted, if it had been possible under the circumstances for them to have entertained any, and he might, therefore, consider himself for the present, at any rate, in safety. Stephen was evidently much prepossessed in his favour, and he paid him many flattering compliments in the course of the conversation that took place ; but Richard was never once taken off his guard, and Mr. Worthington could not but feel perfectly satisfied at the manner in which he acted his part.

As the day advanced, the hilarity and conviviality of Mr. Ladbroke and his friends increased, and the joke and the song passed freely round, our hero, however, excusing himself as well as he could from joining in the harmony, but promising to do so on some future occasion.

At length, however, the boisterousness of the mirth somewhat abated, and they conversed upon different topics, in the whole of which Ladbroke, as usual, took a most prominent part.

"Well," at length said Stephen, addressing himself to our hero, "what is your opinion of that awkward business of Richard Parker's, or Admiral Parker, as he is more commonly called, Martin?"

Richard could not help starting, and feeling the greatest confusion at this unexpected question; but he quickly recovered himself, and having caught the eye of Mr. Worthington, he answered—

"Richard Parker!—I never heard of his name before."

"What!" exclaimed Ladbroke, staring at him with a look of astonishment and incredulity; "is it possible that you are a native of Kent, and not have heard of that which has caused, and is at the present time causing, such an universal sensation all over the country, namely, the mutiny at the Nore, and Richard Parker?"

"No," replied Richard, with the greatest composure, "I have heard nothing about the business, and I am not much in the habit of reading the newspapers."

"Well, you *do* surprise me!" remarked Ladbroke.

"Well, friend Ladbroke," returned Mr. Worthington, "he does not me; my nephew, I have no doubt, has found quite enough to do to trouble himself about that which concerns him not."

"Very true, uncle," answered Richard.

"But pardon me," observed the loquacious Mr. Ladbroke, "that is a business which concerns every one who is loyal to his king and country, and has a horror at the taking of human life. Parker is not only a mutineer, but an assassin; and notwithstanding he has at present contrived to escape, as a true lover of justice I hope that it will not be long before they apprehend him."

"I sincerely hope they may not," returned Worthington, "and I do not think they ever will."

"I am surprised to hear you talk so, Christopher," remarked Stephen; "why, any one would think that you knew Parker, and were a friend of his."

"I know him?" replied the old man; "that is not at all likely, I should think. But I have heard enough of him to believe that he is a deeply-injured man, and I sincerely pity him and his wife and son."

"Bless my soul!" ejaculated Ladbroke, "you astonish me more and more by hearing you make use of such observations as those. Pity one who has shed the blood of his fellow-creatures? It is impossible that you can do so. I only wish that I could meet with him."

"And what if you should?" demanded Worthington, hastily.

"What if I should!" repeated Ladbroke; "why, I should think that there cannot be a doubt I should consider it my bounden duty to deliver him up to justice."

"I cannot believe you," said Worthington.

"You entertain a strange notion of my ideas of justice, Christopher," he returned, "if you imagine that I would permit him to escape. I only wish I had the chance of earning the reward that is offered for his apprehension, that's all!"

"Well," observed Mr. Worthington, with a smile, "I do not think that there is much chance of the opportunity being afforded you of doing so. But this is not a very pleasant subject to discuss on the present occasion, and we will, therefore, change the topic of conversation, if you please. Come, come, replenish your glasses, my friends, and let us continue to pass the day in harmony."

Ladbroke and his companions needed no second invitation or argument to induce them to do this, and the remainder of the day was passed by them in the greatest conviviality, our hero participating in it with the utmost freedom, though he took good care to partake but sparingly of the refreshment, lest he might be thrown off his guard.

It was past eleven o'clock before the party broke up, and Stephen Ladbroke and his companions quitted the inn, entertaining golden opinions of the supposed Martin Worthington, and very well satisfied with the reception they had received.

When they were gone, Worthington complimented our hero upon the manner in which he had performed the difficult task attached to him, and congratulated him on the success of their plans.

"We have completely deceived that very busy and inquisitive gentleman, Stephen Ladbroke, and his companions," he remarked; "and you have now nothing to fear from them. It is impossible that they can ever have any suspicion of your real character, and,

MAD MOLL IN THE TEMPEST ON THE SEA-COAST.

therefore, all that weight of anxiety is removed from your mind."

"Yes," replied Richard; "and it is fortunate that I am totally unknown to Ladbroke; for it is evident, by the observations he made use of, that had he the opportunity of crossing my path, and of recognising me, he would not hesitate to deliver me over to the hands of the law."

"Nay," returned Mr. Worthington, "notwithstanding all that he has said,

I do not believe that he would be guilty of any such an act of cruelty. especially when he knew the friendship that exists between us, the manner in which I have implicated myself, and the deep interest I take in your fate and all so dear to you. So let not any such apprehensions trouble your mind. You have now got over one of the most difficult points, and I trust that everything will proceed as well as we could wish. I presume that you would wish to return to your wife to-night?"

"Oh, yes," answered Richard, " for she will be most anxious to know all that has taken place; and there is now no danger of my visiting her."

"True," coincided Worthington; "and, as the hour is now late, you had better not delay your departure any longer; you will return to the inn at an early hour in the morning, however?"

Our hero replied in the affirmative, and they then separated, Richard proceeding with a light heart and with more sanguine hopes than he had for some time experienced towards the cottage.

It was with feelings of the utmost satisfaction that Mary listened to the account of what had taken place that day at the inn, and they retired to rest, after returning thanks to Providence, with the most sanguine hopes that a favourable change had taken place in their prospects; and, notwithstanding the many and fearful dangers by which they had been so long threatened, they would yet escape them, and be restored to tranquillity, if not to complete happiness.

In this manner more than a week passed away, and nothing occurred to disturb their minds, and those apprehensions which had before distracted the brain of Richard were greatly abated, if not entirely banished, notwithstanding, from all that he could ascertain from the newspapers, the search after him was continued with unabated vigilance.

Mary had several times ventured to visit the inn, and was introduced by Mr. Worthington to Ladbroke as his relation, the widow Somerton, and was treated by him and his friends with the most scrupulous respect; so that now so much of restraint was removed from the unfortunate fugitives, they felt comparatively happy to what they had previously done.

They had neither seen nor heard any more of that strange being, Mad Moll, and they, therefore, concluded that she had left that part of the country; and possessing, as she had declared, no feelings of animosity towards them, that also removed a great portion of the weight of anxiety that had before disturbed their minds.

Our hero had become a great favourite with Ladbroke and his friends, and there was nothing which they would have hesitated to do to serve him. Mr. Worthington, too, by impressing more forcibly upon his attention the deep and cruel injuries which our hero had received, succeeded in banishing the prejudices he had before entertained towards him, and he now expressed a fervent wish that he might elude the vigilance of his pursuers, and ultimately be restored to liberty, though he might never more experience that happiness and tranquillity of mind which he had formerly once experienced before the black and ponderous clouds of misfortune had darkened the horizon of his prospects.

"Poor fellow," he would remark, when he and Mr. Worthington were conversing upon the subject, which the latter took care should never be in the presence of Richard, for he knew full well what bitter anguish it would be to his feelings; "his has, indeed, been a melancholy and untoward fate, and I cannot but hope that he may yet live to triumph. How terrible must have been the sufferings to which he and his amiable wife have been, and probably still are exposed."

"True, Stephen," replied Worthington; "and I am glad to hear you express so much sympathy for those unfortunates. You would not now betray them if you were aware in what particular spot they were concealed?"

"Heaven forbid!" ejaculated Ladbroke; "but, on the contrary, I would do all in my power to befriend them and to assist in their escape. You must not think seriously of what I said on former occasions when this subject was broached, for I must confess that I was prejudiced against poor Parker by the accounts which I had read of him in the newspapers."

"I do not doubt it," returned Worthington; "but all that I can say is this, and I need not tell you that I speak it fervently from my heart, that wherever Richard Parker and his wife and son are concealed, I sincerely hope that they may continue to remain in safety."

Ladbroke responded to that wish, and added—

"But what a noble-minded woman must the unfortunate Mrs. Parker be; how devotedly attached to her husband."

"No doubt of it," answered Mrs. Worthington; "and would it not be a monstrous thing for her husband to be consigned to so awful and ignominious a fate as that with which he is threatened, and thus to leave those who are so dear to him in the wide and cheerless world without a protector?"

"It would," coincided Ladbroke; "but I trust that Providence will avert so terrible a fate. If all that you have stated to me be true, and I have not the least reason to doubt it, the late Captain Arlington was a bad man, and he brought his fate upon himself."

"True," remarked Worthington. "I am convinced that a greater miscreant than Arlington scarcely ever existed, and that it was to gratify his deadly feelings of malice and revenge that he inflicted such brutal injuries and degradations upon Richard Parker. It was he who drove him to a state of madness and despair, and caused the blush of shame to mantle in his cheeks when he again beheld the beloved partner of his sorrows and afflictions."

"How is this, Mr. Worthington?" said Stephen, looking at him with an expression of surprise; "how is it that you, who are a stranger to the unfortunate individuals, should thus seem to possess so thorough a knowledge of all the particulars of their history?"

This question somewhat confounded and embarrassed Worthington; for he was afraid that he had spoken somewhat too freely and unguardedly; but he soon recovered himself, and said—

"It does not matter, for the present, by what means I have become acquainted with the facts I have just now mentioned; but you may depend upon their being correct; and, perhaps, at some future time you may know more: in the meantime, you express your good

wishes for Richard Parker and those connected with him?"

"I do," answered Stephen Ladbroke; "and that with all sincerity."

"And would you be willing to render them all the assistance in your power if the opportunity should be afforded you?" interrogated Worthington.

"I have before assured you that I would," returned Ladbroke, "and I believe I am not in the habit of speaking that which is erroneous in my serious moments."

"I believe you, Ladbroke," remarked Mr. Worthington, "and respect you more than ever for the sympathy you now express in the sorrows of these unfortunate persons."

After some further observations, the subject then dropped, and Mr. Ladbroke shortly afterwards left the house. We have said that the change which had taken place in the opinions and sentiments of Stephen Ladbroke afforded our hero and Worthington the utmost satisfaction—so much so, indeed, that they were almost induced to make him a confidant; but, upon more mature consideration, they thought that such a course would not be prudent, neither would it be necessary, unless something more particular should occur, or the suspicions of Ladbroke be excited, as they had already sufficient friends in Binnacle and Adams.

They were most agreeably surprised one evening, while they were sitting conversing together in a private room, by the entrance of the dame, and they could tell in a moment by the expression of her countenance that she had some agreeable news to communicate. Her husband eagerly inquired what it was; but before she could make any reply, they were startled by a well-known and welcome voice exclaiming—

"Christopher Worthington ahoy!— Where are you, my hearty?—Will you allow an old friend just to cast anchor for awhile, and——"

"It is Binnacle!" said our hero, starting from his seat, and with a look of the most unbounded satisfaction; and before he could give utterance to another syllable, the honest old seaman was in the room, and was firmly grasping the hands of Richard and Worthington.

"What, Christopher, my old veteran,"

he said; "it does my very eyes good to see you, and looking as spruce and as trim as a full-rigged seventy-four. And you, my poor friend! Oh, what a blessed thing it is to think that you have escaped the land-sharks hitherto; and have been wafted by the will of the Great Commander aloft to a port of safety. But your rigging is so altered, and there is such a change in the appearance of your figure-head, that, splice my timbers, if I should have been able to recognise you from Adam."

"My kind-hearted, generous friend," replied our hero, "how can I express the pleasure I feel at again beholding you? It was by your means that I was directed to the protection of this excellent man, and from whom I have experienced such kindness, attention, and friendship, that no language can adequately describe."

"And Heaven bless him for it," said Binnacle, fervently. "Christopher, my honest old tar, let me have another shake of your fin; I knew well that you would be one of the first to render all the assistance in your power to your fellow creatures in distress, and would never suffer them to founder for the want of a helping hand to rescue them from their difficulties."

"Binnacle," returned Worthington, "most warm-hearted and excellent of men, I cannot sufficiently express to you the pleasure I feel at seeing you, and at the very time when we stand so much in need of your advice. I have endeavoured to do my duty by our unfortunate friends, and I trust that I have not been altogether unsuccessful."

"Oh, Mr. Binnacle," remarked our hero, "I would fain do justice to the character of——"

"Now, now," interrupted the honest sailor, "avast! avast heaving, shipmate, if you please; old Christopher Worthington has a mortal dislike to compliments, I know, and requires no thanks for merely performing that which he considers to be his duty. But Richard —Mr. Parker, I mean—there is no one at hand to overhear us, I believe; how is the fair craft, and the young cock-boat, and——"

"Oh, they are as well as can be expected, Mr. Binnacle," answered our hero; "but Mr. Adams, the man to whom I am principally indebted for the preservation of my life, so far—tell me, how is he?"

"Quite well," returned Ben, "but anxious about the safety of yourself and your wife and child. He was fearful that we had all perished in the storm, but when he saw me, I, of course, quickly set his mind at rest. I bring despatches from him. But my old friend, suppose we get the grog aboard, for I have only arrived here about an hour, and I feel to want something. We will then explain everything, for there is much that I think it will be necessary for me to hear from you."

"Certainly," coincided Richard; "but tell me, has the excitement created by my escape at all abated?"

"Why, to tell you the truth, and it is no use deceiving you," replied Binnacle, "I do not think it has, and there is scarcely anything else talked about; however, I think if they discover and recognise you here, disguised as you are at present, it will be marvellous indeed."

"He is perfectly safe," remarked Mr. Worthington; "I feel confident of that; and I am only too happy to think I have been made the humble instrument of rendering him, and those who are so precious to him, that service. But I will return in a few minutes, and then we can discuss this important business at our leisure. Come, dame."

Thus saying, Mr. Worthington and his wife retired from the room, and for a short time left our hero and Ben Binnacle to themselves. Again did Richard give utterance to the feelings of gratitude that filled his bosom, and regretted that Mary was not present, that she might partake of the gratification which the re-appearance of Binnacle could not fail to engender; Ben, however, again requested him not to overwhelm him with his thanks, but rather to pour forth his gratitude to that Omnipotent being who was the supreme cause of his present safety, and on whose infinite mercy and goodness his future preservation depended. In the midst of this brief discourse, Mr. Worthington and his wife re-entered the room, bringing with them the necessary refreshments.

Having seated themselves, Binnacle stated all he had to explain, which we have already described; but he delivered into the hands of Richard the papers which he had brought from Adams, and which he stated would, no doubt, inform him of all he was anxious to know. He now requested that our hero would make him acquainted with all that had happened from the time they had parted, and with which he complied in as few words as possible.

"Nothing could have been better conceived or managed," remarked the old man, when he had concluded; "and poor Jack Adams cannot help being satisfied when he hears it. Christopher, my hearty old friend, you have performed your task to a miracle, and are deserving of every praise; it is not likely that Mr. Parker can be suspected in his present character, and, therefore, he need not be under any apprehension of his being detected whilst he remains here, if he only acts with proper precaution"

"True," said Worthington; "and I have no doubt he will do that; if he only proceeds in the same manner that he has done already, we shall have no cause to complain."

"Oh, fear me not, my friends," replied our hero; "I have too much at stake not to exert myself to the utmost; but think you my friend Adams will approve of these plans we have adopted?"

"To be sure he will," returned Binnacle; "how can he do otherwise? Besides, if you do not think yourself safe in remaining here, when this breeze is blown over, which I suppose it will be in time, I dare say we shall be able to contrive some means to convey you to some distant part of the country, where you may live unknown, and to look to your future security."

"But then the risks you run, and the consequences that would be certain to follow, should you and Adams be discovered to have connived at my escape," remarked Richard.

"Avast, avast!" replied Ben; "Jack Adams and myself are too old seamen to be so easily trepanned by the lubbers; so you may make your mind contented on that point. He felt perfectly satisfied when I informed him the part to which I had directed you; for he is perfectly well acquainted with the old commodore here, and knows that he is always one

of the first to fly to the rescue of any vessel in distress. Give us your fin again, my old tar, and believe me when I say there is not a man in existence who respects you more than old Ben Binnacle."

"I know it, my honest friend," replied Worthington, shaking the veteran's hand most cordially, "and I'm sure I need not tell you that I entertain the same feelings of respect and friendship towards you."

"Well, well," observed Binnacle, "belay all compliments, for we understand one another too well to require them. For my own part, I confess that I never felt so satisfied with any business in which I have been engaged as I am in the preservation of Mr. Parker, and there is no danger that I would not fearlessly encounter to serve him. My heart! what a glorious day it will be for us all when we shall see him completely clear of the shoals and quicksands of misfortune, and be able to walk the maindeck again without fear!"

"Ah, Binnacle," ejaculated Richard "how happy and how grateful to Providence should I be, could I rest satisfied that such would ever be the case; but can I ever expect any mercy from the offended laws of my country, and with so many enemies as I have got? And should I fall—oh, what would then become of my poor Mary and my boy?"

"Pshaw!" exclaimed the old man, hastily; "I tell you again that the fears you now entertain will never be realised. But should the worst come to the worst, which God forbid it should, your wife and son will never want for friends and protectors while myself and Jack Adams exist. But cheer up, Mr. Parker, and rest assured that we shall soon be enabled to steer you out of troubled waters."

"Mr. Binnacle," said Richard, "your words are sufficient to inspire me with hope, for well do I know that they spring from your heart. Still, when I look back upon all that has taken place, and weigh well in my mind the consequences attendant upon them, I cannot but give way to the most gloomy forebodings. But think not that cowardice shares any portion of my feelings. No! Richard Parker has many a time and oft faced death in all its most terrible shapes, and he would now bravely meet it, nor offer to murmur at the will of Heaven, if it were under different circumstances ; but to die the death of a dog—to leave those so dear to me behind, to the mercy of the world, with broken hearts, and to be pointed at by the vulgar finger of scorn and opprobrium as the connexions of a criminal ! Oh ! surely the bare thought is too horrible even for a moment's reflection !"

"Think not of it, Mr. Parker," observed Ben, "for it only serves to distract your mind, and to banish it from those hopes which, under all the circumstances that have so far attended you since your flight, you should encourage. Here are you, supported by friends who, though but humble, would willingly make any sacrifice to serve you ; and why, then, should you suffer yourself to founder altogether without a struggle ? But I must be going, and, therefore, I will at once deliver into your hands the papers of our friend Adams, and likewise this purse, the contents of which he expressed a wish might tend to help you through till you heard from him again."

Thus speaking, honest old Ben Binnacle placed in the hands of our hero the papers of which he had spoken, and a purse which was heavily laden, and rising from his seat, he was about to prepare for his departure, when Richard detained him, and grasping his hand, whilst a manly tear stood in his eye, he said—

"By Heaven this is too much, Binnacle ! What have I ever done to deserve this kindness, this unexpected generosity ? My heart recoils with shame at being thus behoven to the bounty of—"

"Bounty be d——d !" said the old seaman, interrupting him impatiently ; "is there any bounty in a man, especially one who is placed upon three-water grog, receiving a helping hand from his shipmate ? Bah ! may I never again go aloft, Parker, if I am not ashamed of you for the observation. But, however, enough has been said upon that subject ; so, if you please, we will postpone the revival of it to some future day, and when we are in a better condition to discuss it ; to-morrow night, after those persons that yourself and our friend Worthington have talked about, are likely to have quitted the inn, I will visit you again, and I then

hope to see your wife, so that we may all consult together after you have perused these despatches from our honest and esteemed friend, Adams. Good-by, Mr. Parker ; farewell, my old hearty, and remember, shipmate"— addressing himself to our hero—

" ' There's a sweet little cherub sits smiling aloft—

A sweet little cherub sits smiling aloft,' And cetera !' "

And without saying another word, but winking significantly at our hero and Mr. Worthington, and once more cordially pressing their hands, this genuine specimen of a true British tar abruptly quitted the room, and retired from the house, leaving them overwhelmed and surprised at the generosity and manliness of his conduct.

"Excellent man !" ejaculated Richard, after a brief pause ; "what return can I ever make to him for his conduct towards me, who am almost a total stranger to him ?"

"And I am sure, my dear friend," replied Mr. Worthington, "if you knew him as well as I do, you would be certain that he requires none. Ben Binnacle is every inch a sailor and a man, and many are the acts of kindness that I have myself experienced from him."

"I have no doubt of it," observed our hero, "for I am thoroughly convinced that the honest seaman would willingly render a service to any one, if it lay in his power : he has the heart that can feel for another."

"Ay, Mr. Parker," coincided his companion, "there you just spoke the sentiments of my mind ; and, therefore, as that is the opinion you entertain of him, of course you will not distress your mind by considering the weight of obligation you are under to him."

"And yet it troubles me to think of the danger he incurs by thus assisting me to escape."

"Pshaw !" returned Worthington ; "you must not give way to such thoughts ; Providence, I am convinced, will never permit him to fall a sacrifice to his humanity."

"And Adams, too," said Richard ; "oh, what do I not owe him for the manifold and unexampled acts of friendship he has evinced towards me ? But for him I should doubtless ere this have suffered the dreadful and ignominious fate which the laws of my country would have awarded me, and my poor wife and child would have been left destitute and heart-broken upon the world ; scouted from all society, as if they were something loathsome and contagious. How terrible, how distracting is that thought ! And may not such yet be their fate ?— My mind is racked with the fearful doubts that will, in spite of all my efforts to the contrary, rise upon it."

"Indeed," observed the dame, "you must not give way to them, Mr. Parker ; for, as Christopher says, I am certain that the Almighty will not suffer your fears to be realised, but will guide you safe through the dangers and difficulties by which you are at present surrounded. You should feel more confidence in His mercy ; and, depend upon it, if you put your trust in Him, He will not desert you, but will bring you safe at last to the haven of happiness."

"Right, right, my good old lass," said her husband ; "those are just the thoughts which I wish to inspire in the breast of Mr. Parker ; and he may depend upon it, if he encourages them he will not be doomed to be disappointed. But the papers from Mr. Adams, Richard—may I be permitted to inquire their contents ?"

"Certainly, Mr. Worthington," answered our hero ; "I should, I can have no secrets from you."

He then opened the letters and read them aloud. They were couched, as might have been expected, in the most friendly terms, but contained nothing of any particular importance, except some few valuable instructions as to his future conduct, an account of all that had taken place since his flight, and the most earnest professions of future friendship and of the deep interest which he took in his fate. They, however, imparted the greatest consolation to Richard, and renewed those hopes they sought to inspire.

"Those letters should, indeed, make you doubly confident, Mr. Parker," said Worthington ; "for they emanate from the heart of a sincere friend, and one who, I am certain, will never desert you."

"True, true," replied Richard ; "I should be base and ungrateful, indeed, if such were not the opinion I entertained of Mr. Adams. May Heaven reward him for all that he has hitherto done, and is still prepared to do, to save his unfortunate friend and former shipmate ! He well knows the wrongs I have suffered, and that it is from no fault of mine I am placed in the painful and critical situation I am in. Oh, my kind friends, did you but know half the injuries, the degradations that have been inflicted on me, you would not marvel that I suffer the anguish of mind that I do."

"We know sufficient to enable us to appreciate your feelings," replied Mr. Worthington, "and to sympathise with you. But why do you still give way to such painful thoughts, when the future presents so much brighter a prospect before you? All goes on as well as could be expected, and the time is not far distant, I trust, when all cause for doubt and apprehension will be removed"

"I thank you for your good wishes, my worthy friend," said Richard, "and will endeavour to think so. But I am anxious to see my dear Mary, in order that I may make her acquainted with what has taken place ; I know it will afford her much satisfaction to hear of the return of Binnacle, and from Adams."

"True," replied Mr. Worthington, "and, therefore, the sooner you depart to the cottage the better. It does not seen as if Ladbroke and his friends would pay me their customary visit tonight, and if they should, I can easily make an excuse for your absence. The night is not very cheerful, and the road you have to pursue is a dreary one, but the distance is short, and you have nothing to fear, for I do n t think we have any suspicious characters in the neighbourhood."

"Oh, I am under no apprehension that any one will molest me," returned our hero ; "so good-night, my worthy friends, and you will see me again at an early hour in the morning."

With these words, having pressed the hands of Mr. Worthington and his wife, our hero quitted the inn, and deeply immersed in thought, he made his way towards the cottage.

The night was, indeed, as Worthington had said, a cheerless one; it was dark as pitch, and the wind swept in hollow and mournful gusts around, whilst everything gave warning that a storm was fast gathering in the heavens. But our hero's mind was too much occupied with his own thoughts for him to take any heed of the weather, though, in spite of all his efforts to the contrary, he could not help giving way to the most dismal forebodings that something of a painful nature was about to happen to him. However, he endeavoured to arouse himself, and pursued his way with increased speed.

CHAPTER XV.

A NIGHT OF ADVENTURES.—THE AT-TACK IN THE COTTAGE.—MAD MOLL IS MORTALLY WOUNDED.—AND HER DEATH.

OUR hero continued to walk on for some distance further, still wrapped in meditation, when suddenly pausing and looking up, he found that he had deviated from the right path, and scarcely knew where he was ; and, to add to his annoyance, the rain began to descend in large drops, and everything betokened a tempestuous night. However, he quickly collected his thoughts, and soon found himself in the right road again, though the distance had never appeared so long to him.

It was so dark that he could scarcely perceive the way before him, and he was several times doubtful whether or not he had again mistaken the road. Penetrating through the darkness as well as he could, he started, for he imagined that he beheld a shadowy form moving stealthily in the distance before him; but it was quickly again lost to his vision, and he endeavoured to persuade himself that he had been deceived, and once more he hurried on his way, looking cautiously around him at intervals, to ascertain whether there was any one near him; but no one met his observation, and he chided himself for having permitted such cowardly fears for the moment to steal over him.

The rain now descended rapidly, and the storm which had been so long gathering now began to rage with all the vio-lence it had portended. Again Richard, as he strained his eyes to their utmost limits, imagined that he beheld the same shadowy form that had before alarmed him, and this time it was so palpable that he felt satisfied he was not mistaken, and he paused, in order that he might watch its movements and be prepared in case any danger should threaten him; but almost immediately it vanished from his sight, in what manner he could not imagine. But why should the appearance of this individual alarm or surprise him? he argued with himself. He was evidently retreating from him—wished to avoid him—and if he had any sinister design in view, it was apparently not against him. It was more than probable that he was only some traveller; and having come to those conclusions, our hero again pursued his way; but he had not proceeded far when he was startled by hearing his own name pronounced, and a form immediately afterwards crossed his path, which seemed to have sprung out of the earth as if by magic, and his surprise and alarm were not at all abated when he recognised Mad Moll, who was standing before him, with her eyes fixed upon him with their usual melancholy and foreboding expression.

"Strange and fearful woman!" he at last ejaculated, "what again brings you before me? What would you with me now?"

"To again warn you of the decrees of fate," she answered, "and to caution you not to encourage delusive hopes, but to prepare yourself for that fate which sooner or later must overtake you."

"Harbinger of evil," said the agitated man, "away! Why do you thus delight to torture me?"

"I seek not to torture you, Richard Parker," returned the old woman, in a solemn and earnest voice; "but, on the contrary, I pity you, and could I save you I would."

"Do you, indeed, speak sincerely?" interrogated our hero, eagerly.

"You need not doubt me," she answered; "but I have no power to avert your fate; it is sealed, unalterably sealed, though for a time you may escape it. The storm now rages violently in the heavens, but what is it compared with the tempest which will one day or other burst over your head?"

"Alas! alas!" groaned Richard, "and are there, indeed, no means of avoiding it? For the sake of my wife and child, may I not hope that mercy may be extended towards me?"

"From Heaven!" replied the old woman, in the same solemn tones, "but not from man! They thirst for your blood, and they will not rest until their revenge is satisfied."

MR. WORTHINGTON CONDUCTING RICHARD AND HIS WIFE TO HIS COTTAGE.

"Who are you?" demanded our hero, "and how do you presume to penetrate into the secrets of futurity?"

"It matters not," returned Mad Moll; "incredulous as it may appear to you and others, I do possess the power to penetrate into those dark secrets which are usually hidden from mortal eye. Many years ago I revealed to you and to that fair being who afterwards became your

No. 17.

wife, the fate which was in store for you; and have not my predictions partly been fulfilled?"

"Alas! alas!" sighed Richard, "too fatally they have. Fearful woman, why did I ever behold you?"

"I repeat, Richard Parker," she replied, "that I am your friend."

"And is it thus you evince it?"

"I should prove myself your enemy were I not to reveal what I know, and to prevent you from indulging in those hopes which can only end in bitter disappointment."

"What guarantee have I that you will not betray me?" demanded our hero.

"I swear that I will not," answered the singular being, raising her hand solemnly towards Heaven as she spoke. "Do you know where I am concealed?"

"Yes," she replied; "there is no action of your life, no step that you can take, that I am unacquainted with."

"Mysterious!" ejaculated Parker; "I can scarcely believe the evidence of my senses. But why do you linger in this neighbourhood? and where are you concealed?"

"It would serve you nothing to know," she returned; "but rest assured that so far from working you harm, I will give you timely warning should any danger threaten you. But again I solemnly enjoin you not to treat lightly that which I said to you, but to prepare yourself and your unfortunate wife for that which must ultimately take place."

"Oh, God!" groaned our hero, striking his forehead in the intensity of his feelings, "how agonizing is this! Is there no way to avoid that terrible fate?"

"None, none," answered the old woman; "that which Heaven decrees, it is impossible for erring mortals to avoid."

"Torturer!" cried the distracted man, as all the dread certainty of the realisation of her predictions rushed upon his mind, "begone! Your words madden me; I will hear no more."

"'Tis well," she returned, again fixing upon him a look of pity; "I obey you, Richard Parker; but remember, that as sure as the tempest now howls around us, will the predic-

tions I have uttered be fulfilled. Farewell; ere long we shall probably meet again."

With these words, before our hero could recover from his agitation and confusion, the mysterious woman hurried from the spot, and was in a moment hid from sight in the impenetrable darkness beyond.

For a few moments our hero stood rivetted to the spot, lost in amazement and confusion, and the varied feelings of emotion that agitated his bosom may be readily imagined. So deeply was his mind occupied by these distracting thoughts that he heeded not the storm, which had now increased in violence, and every word to which the singular woman had given utterance was stamped upon his memory in characters which nothing whatever could have the power to efface.

"Good God!" he at length exclaimed, starting and looking wildly round, as though he expected every moment to behold the officers of the law approaching him; "and must I, indeed, die a death of shame, and leave those so dear behind me to struggle with their awful fate?—Surely I have not merited this! And will not Heaven in its mercy prevent me from coming to so dreadful an end?—Ah! no; I see too clearly that my fate is inevitable, and I shudder with horror when I reflect on it. Oh, Arlington, guilty man! you have been the cause of all this. May eternal curses light upon your soul! But no; stay, my rash tongue, and do not let me give utterance to such guilty words; how can I expect mercy if I do not forgive those who have injured me? My poor Mary, my patient and devoted wife—my dear and innocent boy! great as have been the troubles it has been your hard and cruel lot to endure, how trifling are they compared to the sufferings that are still in store for you! And must all those fond hopes with which you have flattered yourself be doomed to disappointment? Terrible thought! it quite unmans me while it flashes upon my brain. But there is no flying from the fatal truth; there is no hope for me; and better, much better would it have been for me had I never been born."

Again he beat his breast in the agony of his feelings, and still he remained transfixed to the spot and totally regardless of the storm.

"And why was that mysterious woman," he resumed, after a pause, "ever permitted to cross my path, and to pour in my ears her fearful predictions? But for her I might still have indulged in hope, and that, at any rate, would have been some amelioration to my anguish. And shall I allow her wild observations to make any impression upon me? It is weak and unmanly for me to do so; I will arouse myself, and notwithstanding the darkness of my present prospects, in spite of all that has taken place, I will put my trust in the goodness and mercy of the Supreme, who will not suffer me to perish in so shameful and awful a manner."

These reflections somewhat calmed his agitation, and after once more looking around him, he proceeded on his way. One thing that alarmed and perplexed him more than all was, that Mad Moll should so easily have recognised him, notwithstanding his disguise; and his confidence in his security from detection was, consequently, greatly shaken; but still the improbability of his encountering any one that knew him personally somewhat quieted his apprehensions.

The storm had not at all abated, but, on the contrary, every moment added to its violence, the rain continuing to descend in torrents, so that he was completely drenched to the skin; he, therefore, increased his speed, and soon entered the lane which led to the cottage, the lights from which he could already perceive.

He was endeavouring to compose his feelings after his unexpected meeting with Moll, so that he might not alarm his wife, or excite her curiosity, for he felt that it would be a difficult and painful task to answer the questions which she would then naturally put to him, when he was suddenly startled by hearing loud cries for help in a female voice, and which, on being several times repeated, he was convinced came from the cottage.

"'Tis my Mary calls!" he cried; "what danger threatens us? What fresh troubles are in store for me?"

Again the cries for help smote his ears, and he was now more convinced than ever, if he could possibly any longer have entertained a doubt, that they proceeded from the cottage, and he flew with the speed of lightning towards it, and speedily reached the door, when the voice of his beloved Mary, in piteous accents of supplication and remonstrance, coupled with the cries of his son, and the bitter oaths and threats of a man, whose voice he had no recollection of, more distinctly burst upon his ears, and aroused his utmost alarm and indignation. In a moment he forced open the door, and entering the parlour, what was his astonishment and resentment at beholding the beauteous partner of his sorrows vainly struggling in the rude grasp of a powerful and repulsive-looking ruffian, while the poor boy William, on his knees with clasped hands, was piteously imploring the villain to forbearance.

"Miscreant!" exclaimed our enfuriated hero, tearing Mary from his grasp, and hurling the ruffian to the farther end of the room; "what means this daring and monstrous outrage? Mary, my beloved Mary, revive; it is your husband who now holds you in his arms, and who will protect you with his life."

"Oh, Richard! save me, shield me, from that savage man!" gasped forth our heroine in a faint voice.

"Confusion!" exclaimed the man, in a hoarse voice; "am I interrupted?—foiled? But I will, at least, have revenge upon the insolent intruder. Die, fellow! and thus every obstacle to the gratification of my desires shall be removed!"

As the villain thus spoke, he drew a pistol from his pocket, and presenting it at Richard, was about to fire, when at that moment a loud voice was heard to shout—"Hold!" the door was again burst open, and Mad Moll rushed in hastily, and interposing between Richard and the man, received the contents of the pistol in her side, and immediately sank to the ground, weltering in her blood. Mary uttered a loud scream of horror and astonishment, and overcome by her terrors, she fainted. The villain shouted forth a dreadful oath, and in an instant, and before our hero could recover from his surprise and confusion, ne hastily opened the window and leaped forth, thus making his escape without any one having the power to detain him, or to go in pursuit of him, in order that he might receive the full penalty of his atrocious crime.

It would be a fruitless task for us to attempt to pourtray the state of our hero's mind at this moment. The blood was flowing copiously from the wound which poor Mad Moll had received, and Richard, having placed his wife upon a sofa, and left her to the tender care of little William, turned his attention to the unfortunate woman, who was still alive, though quite insensible.

The origin of the scene we have described may be related in a few words. Mary and her son had been sitting in the parlour of the cottage from an early hour of the evening, anxiously awaiting the arrival of our hero, whom they had expected much sooner than usual, when the storm commenced, and which led them to suppose that he would not be able to venture there till it had subsided or abated, at any rate. Mary had been very low-spirited during the day, and the tempestuous state of the weather, as may be expected, served to increase her melancholy; but she was suddenly aroused from a dismal train of thought into which she had fallen, by hearing a knock at the door; and fully expecting that it was her husband, she started up and hastily opened it, but retreated again a few paces with surprise and disappointment on beholding a stranger, and one whose appearance was by no means prepossessing. He appeared to be about fifty years of age, with large black whiskers, a sunburnt visage, and coarse, forbidding features; and he was clad in a Guernsey jacket, and coarse canvas trousers.

Immediately upon seeing our heroine, he fixed upon her a rude look, which served to alarm her more than ever, and after eyeing her for a moment or two in silence, he said—

"Be not alarmed, missus; I am only a poor traveller, who, being overtaken by this storm which is now raging so desperately, I would request a shelter in your cottage for a few minutes, or till it has abated; and I'm sure you will not refuse a poor devil such a simple request."

There was something so vulgar and repulsive in the man's address and appearance, that Mary felt alarmed, especially as she was alone, and with no one near at hand to render her any assistance, in case she should require it; and she could not make any reply for a few moments, during which time the man continued to eye her with the same familiar looks.

"Am I to judge from your silence that you refuse me?" demanded the stranger; "well, well, I must say that is not very civil, at any rate, for I would not refuse shelter to a dog on such a night as this."

"I—I do not refuse you, sir," at length replied our heroine, in a hesitating voice; "but you took me by surprise—my husband has not returned home yet; but you are welcome to remain here till the storm has abated, though I cannot afford you any further accommodation."

"Thank you, ma'am," said the man, in the same rude and familiar accents; "you are very civil, and I have nothing but my thanks to return you."

Thus saying, the stranger walked unceremoniously into the room, and took a seat by the fire, and Mary, as she gazed upon his unprepossessing features, and considered the extreme delicacy, if not danger, of her situation, could not help trembling, and heartily wished that the storm would subside, so that he might take his departure; she, however, in order that she might conciliate his favour, and to conceal her own feelings, asked him if he needed some refreshments.

"Ay, missus," he answered, "by-the-by, I think a mouthful or two and a glass or so of spirits, if you happen to have such a thing in the house, would not do me any harm."

Mary immediately placed what he required before him, and filling a glass from the bottle to the brim, he tossed off the contents greedily, and finished a second in the same brief space of time, smacking his lips, in order to evince his entire approbation of the goodness of its quality. He then commenced eating voraciously, at the same time eyeing our heroine with a bold and vulgar expression of countenance, which greatly embarrassed and alarmed her.

"These are snug quarters of yours, marm," observed the man, after he had finished his meal; "and they are quite a treat to a poor fellow like me, who has been wandering about the country for some time past."

"Yes," replied Mary, in a faint voice, "thank God I am as well off as one in my humble circumstances can desire, and I wish all my fellow-creatures were the same."

"Indeed!" returned the stranger, looking first round the room and then at Mary; "well, that is very kind of you, and does you credit. For my own part, I must have money somewhere before long, or I shall starve, that's certain."

Mary trembled more violently than ever as the man uttered these words, and she turned very pale, for he seemed just the man who was capable of doing anything to gratify his wishes.

"If I could only come across Richard Parker, now," said the fellow, "the reward that is offered for his apprehension would make a man of me."

Our heroine started as she heard those words, and her agitation and terror were so great that she could not without the greatest difficulty refrain from giving utterance to a scream.

The man noticed it in a moment, and exclaimed—

"Why, bless me, marm, how pale you look! I hope the mention of the name of Admiral Parker, as he is called, does not alarm you?"

"No, no," replied Mary, in a confused and faltering voice, "the mention of such a name would not be likely to alarm me, as I—I never remember to have heard it before."

"Indeed!" said the man; "well, that is strange, however, since there is scarcely anything else talked about at the present time in all parts of the country. What's the use of Parker keeping out of the way? They are sure to nab him before long, and then they will string him up to the yard-arm as sure as his name's what it is."

The reader may well imagine the feelings of our heroine as she listened to this brutal speech, and she almost wished that her husband should not arrive at the cottage till the man had gone, lest he should be able to recognise him, even disguised as he was.

"I beg your pardon," said the stranger, after a pause, during which time he had been scrutinising her narrowly, "but did you not mention something about your husband being from home? How is it then, if you have a husband, living, that you should dress in widow's weeds?"

This was a question that confused and agitated Mary more than ever, and she knew not scarcely what to answer.

"My husband, sir?" she stammered out at length; "did I say my husband?"

"To be sure you did, marm," replied the fellow, impudently, "as plain as you could speak."

"Then," returned our heroine, recovering herself as well as she could, "I must have made a mistake; I meant my brother, who resides with me, and whom I expected home before now, had not this storm prevented him. I am a widow."

"Oh, a *brother*," said the stranger, with emphasis, and with a half sneer. "Well, I suppose you live very comfortably together?"

Mary nodded assent, for she could not return any verbal answer, and she walked to the window, praying most heartily that the storm would abate, and that her rude and inquisitive guest would take his departure. This, however, he seemed in no hurry to do, but remained silent for a few minutes, and gazing at her eagerly and stedfastly. The reader, however, may judge of her horror and disgust, when, suddenly turning towards her, he said—

"Well, it is a great pity, I think, for any woman to remain a widow, especially when she happens to be as good-looking as you are."

"Sir," exclaimed Mary, crimson blushes mantling in her cheeks, and her bosom swelling with indignation and offended modesty, "such language as that is bold and impertinent, especially proceeding from a stranger."

"Lor bless your pretty twinklers," said the unmanly ruffian, with a frightful smile, "we may soon become better acquainted, if you like; and I'm sure you ought not to feel offended at a compliment so deserving. I am such a man for compliments, that they flow from me as natural as my mother tongue."

"Sir," remarked our heroine, mustering up all her energy and courage, "such language as this is unpardonable to one who has treated you with hospitality and kindness; I must desire you to quit the cottage immediately."

"Quit the cottage," he repeated, "in such a storm as this! Oh, no, I could not think of such a thing; upon my soul I couldn't. But you are not offended at what I have said, I'm sure you are not."

"I am but 'a weak and unprotected woman," replied Mary, with more firmness than might have been expected; "but I will not listen to such insulting language as this. Again I desire, nay, command you to begone."

"Nonsense,' said the daring scoundrel, "I cannot think of such a thing for the present I own I am completely smitten by your charms, and I must have a kiss from those pretty lips, that I may carry something away in remembrance of you."

"Daring villain'" exclaimed the terrified Mary, retreating to the farther end of the room as he arose from his seat, and by his attitude and gestures seemed resolved to put his disgusting threat into execution. "Stand back and begone, or my cries shall bring those to my assistance who will punish you for your insolence!"

"Oh," returned the ruffian, with a laugh, "I have not much fear of that, in such a place as this. I am not to be thus intimidated from my purpose; so thus, my coy beauty, I take my demand."

As he thus spoke, he advanced towards her and attempted to seize her; but she struggled desperately, and shrieked aloud for help, whilst the poor boy joined his cries with those of his mother, and attempted to interfere between the ruffian and her.

"Your cries are in vain!" said the villain; "there is no one here to assist you. Out of the way, brat, or you will have bitter cause to rue it!"

As he gave utterance to these words, he thrust the boy rudely aside, and forcibly encircled her waist with his arms.

"God of Heaven!" exclaimed the unfortunate Mary, "what will become of me? Oh, help! help!"

Still she struggled desperately, and screamed as loud as she was able; but

she could not release herself from the cowardly miscreant's grasp, and her strength was almost becoming exhausted, and there is no knowing what the consequences might have been, had not Providence at that critical moment sent her husband to her rescue. What followed, the reader has already been made acquainted with.

Id a state of the greatest agitation our hero hastily bound up the wound which the poor old woman had received, as well as he was able, and endeavoured to stop the effusion of blood; but he feared that the injury she had received at the hands of the miscreant was fatal; and what grieved and perplexed him more than all was, that he was unable to procure the proper assistance she required.

Mary was soon restored to sensibility, and she was in a moment at her husband's side, and gazing with feelings of the deepest agony and sympathy in the pale face of the wounded woman.

"Oh, God!" she ejaculated, "what a terrible calamity is this, and what may not be the consequences that will attend it! Unfortunate woman, that she should meet with so terrible a fate as this. But what accident could have brought her to the cottage at such a critical moment?"

"I encountered her on my way from the inn," replied Richard; "and, doubtless, your cries attracted her hither. How shall we act in this dilemma?"

"I know not," returned his wife "I am completely lost and bewildered. We cannot obtain assistance, and what can we do with her, situated as we are? Alas! this fearful event may be the means of leading to our discovery. Heaven help us, and protect us from that danger which I now too painfully apprehend. Would that Mr. Worthington were aware of what has happened, for he would then immediately hasten hither to tender us his assistance and advice."

"Curses light upon the villain who has been the cause of all this," said Richard. "What fatal accident could have led him to the cottage?"

"He sought a temporary shelter here from the storm," answered Mrs. Parker, "and I dared not refuse him. Had it not been for your timely arrival, Heaven only knows what would have happened. But should he return?"

"Oh," remarked our hero, "after what has taken place there is not much fear of his doing that."

"I cannot think of him without feelings of the utmost terror," said Mary; "he expressed a savage wish to discover you, and——"

"Ah!" interrupted Richard, "did he, indeed, mention my name? Then we have good reason to fear that there is more danger to be apprehended from him. But he cannot possibly know me."

"Oh, no," replied his wife, "that is not at all likely; we have never seen the ruffian before."

"Not to my knowledge," returned our hero; "and yet from the hasty glance I had of his features, it struck me that I had some slight recollection of having seen them before."

"God forbid that you should have done so," said our heroine fervently. "But this poor old woman, I fear that she has received her death-wound, and that she will never more recover to sensibility."

"It is a deplorable case," remarked Richard, "and I fear that it is fraught with great danger to us. Should it become known to the authorities, a rigid investigation will, of course, take place into all the circumstances, and we being called as witnesses, it would be almost impossible for us to escape detection."

"Fearful thought!" ejaculated his wife, clasping her hands together; "may kind Heaven in its infinite mercy avert such a terrible calamity. But we must try to await patiently the issue of events, and probably Mr. Worthington may be enabled to advise us how to act."

They continued to watch anxiously by the side of the couch on which they had laid the form of the unfortunate woman, and tried every means in their power to restore her to consciousness, but in vain; though the blood had ceased to flow from the wound, and she breathed more freely.

They had taken good care to examine her clothes minutely, to see whether they could find any papers that might lead to the discovery as to who she actually was; but they saw nothing which was at all calculated to throw any light upon the subject, and they were compelled to wait with patience for her restoration to her senses, trusting that she would yet have strength sufficient to gratify their curiosity, and to set all their doubts at rest.

"Poor old woman," observed Mary, "it was quite evident that she bore us no animosity, or she would not thus have risked her life in our defence; and notwithstanding the eccentricity of her manners, we have nothing to fear from her."

"Very true," coincided Richard; "but I find it impossible to penetrate the mystery of her conduct."

"Should she survive long enough," returned Mrs. Parker, "no doubt she will explain everything."

"I trust that she will," said our hero; "but it is most unfortunate for us that this dreadful event has taken place."

"Do not give way to unnecessary fears, dear Richard," replied Mary; "for, after all, they may prove to be groundless."

They now secured the doors and the windows, to prevent any intrusion, and then anxiously awaited the arrival of morning, being determined then to send William to the inn to inform Mr. Worthington what had taken place, and to receive his advice and instructions as to the manner in which it would be best to act in the painful and important business; for it would be necessary that the utmost precaution should be used, particularly in regard to Ladbroke and the other frequenters of the inn.

The night wore tediously and drearily away, and in the course of it Richard informed his wife of the arrival of Ben Binnacle, and of all those other particulars with which the reader is already acquainted, and she could not but express the utmost satisfaction at the return of the honest old seaman, and at the intelligence which had been forwarded to them by their ardent friend Adams.

The wounded woman remained in much the same state during the night, and only by her low and difficult breathing gave any signs of life. As soon as daylight had dawned, William was despatched to the inn, and they awaited anxiously for the arrival of Mr. Worthington, for until they had consulted with him they were perfectly at a loss how to act. They had not to wait long, for in less than half an hour, Mr. Worthington made his appearance at the cottage, accompanied by the boy, and his astonishment at hearing all the extraordinary particulars from our hero may very well be conceived.

"Unfortunate woman," he exclaimed, as he gazed with an expression of pity upon her, "it is a terrible fate to meet with, and in so sudden a manner. But who can the villain be who has perpetrated this monstrous deed, and who committed such an atrocious outrage against your wife?"

"I cannot imagine," answered Richard; "but had I not arrived at the critical moment, there is no knowing what the consequences might have been."

"True," observed Worthington, "such a cowardly and heartless wretch would not scruple at the perpetration of any enormity in order to gratify his diabolical wishes; and it is likewise fortunate that Mrs. Parker was enabled to act with the firmness and fortitude she did. But it would not, I think, be safe to seek to detect him, for that might be fraught with danger. Should this unfortunate woman die, which I think in all probability she will, it will be necessary to keep the whole affair a secret, if possible."

"True," said Richard; "but I know not how that is to be accomplished."

"Leave everything to me," observed Worthington, "and I will contrive some means to make all secure. But I wish she would revive, in order that we may be able to elicit from her such particulars as we wish to know."

They now renewed their exertions to restore the unfortunate woman to consciousness, and at length they were crowned with success; she breathed more freely, and at last opened her eyes, and stared vacantly around her, not seeming at first to comprehend what had happened.

"What place is this?" she ejaculated with difficulty; "and how came I hither? All is strange and incomprehensible, and a mist seems gathering before my eyes. Ah! that pang! Can this be approaching death? Oh, I remember all now; the ruffian! it was he who fired the fatal shot, and—Ah! who are you that gaze so anxiously upon me?"

"Unfortunate woman," said Richard, "do you not know us?"

"Yes, yes," she replied, hastily, and fixing her glassy eyes now stedfastly upon him, "I know you now; you are the doomed man, Richard Parker, and this pale-faced woman is the hapless partner of your misfortunes. I know you too," she added, turning her gaze towards Mr. Worthington; "you are he to whom these wretched beings are indebted for concealment: but it is all useless, nothing whatever can save him from the dark and fearful fate that is impending o'er his head. He is doomed! he is doomed! and can only expect mercy from on high!"

"Oh, horrible!" groaned our heroine, and clasping her hands in agony.

"My good woman," Mr. Worthington ventured to remonstrate, "do not in this solemn hour indulge in such wild and fearful prophecies as these, but rather prepare yourself for that awful change which you probably are shortly about to undergo."

"Old man," replied the dying woman, solemnly, "I am prepared, and can leave this world, in which I have experienced so little of happiness, without one pang of regret. My career is fast drawing to a close; I feel that I am dying. Eternity opens upon my eyes, and with my latest breath, unfortunate Richard Parker, hear me repeat those predictions I have so frequently uttered to you."

"Oh, forbear!" cried the terror-stricken Mrs. Parker. "If you would not drive a wretched wife to madness, you will not repeat those fearful prognostications, which I can never reflect upon without a shudder of horror."

"Poor woman," she said, in a voice of the deepest melancholy, "I pity you, from my very soul I do, and with my dying breath I invoke a blessing on your head, and all connected with you. But who can avert the decrees of Omnipotence? Who shall dare to murmur at them, however terrible they be? May He give you strength and fortitude to support the heavy sorrows that are yet in store for you."

"Mysterious woman," said our hero, alarmed at the agitation of his wife, and deeply impressed with the solemn and awful words which the murdered woman had just spoken, "for the love of Heaven forbear, and rather devote your thoughts to that dread Eternity to which your soul is rapidly taking its flight. Presume not to know the secrets of futurity, which are hidden from all mortal eyes."

"I see it all!" said the extraordinary being, by a great effort of expiring strength raising herself on her pillow, and pointing with her long bony hand towards Heaven; "it is presented to my mind's eye as clearly as if it were reflected in a

MARY WATCHING RICHARD AND WORTHINGTON LEAVING THE COTTAGE.

mirror, and it is madness for you, Richard Parker, to seek to despise my words. But I grow weaker—my eyes become more dim; life's troubled scene is fast fading from my vision, strange thoughts flash upon my brain, and my soul yearns after things immortal; let me, then, use the few remaining moments that are left me in revealing all I know. Come nearer, Richard, and listen to that which I have to say."

Our hero and the others gathered

closer around the bed, and listened with anxiety to hear what the dying woman had to disclose.

"Richard Parker," she began, after a pause, and during which time she had apparently been trying to muster all the remaining strength she possessed for the task which she had imposed upon herself, "you, as well as others, I well know, have always thought me mad, in consequence of the solitary life I led, and the strange words of truth to which I have been accustomed to give utterance; but I was not so, though Heaven knows that I have experienced enough of the vicissitudes of life, and the treachery, the injustice, and the oppression of mankind, to destroy my reason. But it is all past now, and I freely forgive all those who have injured me, as I hope for forgiveness from that Almighty Judge in whose dread presence I must shortly appear. Richard Parker, did you ever in your boyish days know a female of the name of Rachael Melford?"

"Rachael Melford!" repeated our hero, starting; "that name is associated with all the happiest moments of my childish days; days of happiness, such as I can never hope to experience again. She was the old and faithful servant of my parents; but she disappeared suddenly without any cause assigned, and it could never afterwards be discovered what had become of her."

"True, true," said the poor old woman, "and that cause will never be known. Richard, look stedfastly at me, and see whether you can recall to your mind in these wrinkled and withered features any remembrance of that Rachael Melford to whom I have alluded."

Our hero did gaze more narrowly into the wrinkled countenance of the dying woman, and started back with astonishment, as he exclaimed—

"Good God! is it possible? and that I should never have noticed the strong resemblance before? Tell me, I beg of you, are you any relation to that much-esteemed woman?"

"I, Richard Parker," replied the old woman, "am that same Rachael Melford who nursed you in the days of your infancy, and who loved you as fondly as if you had been her own offspring."

"Gracious Providence! how wonderful is this! Rachael, respected but unfortunate woman, why did you not before reveal yourself to me?"

"Because," she answered with difficulty, "I had another object in view, and had I done so it would have been the means of foiling it. But listen to me, for my time is growing short, and I have more to reveal which it will be necessary for you to know before I die."

Richard and his wife and Mr. Worthington listened with the most breathless attention and anxiety; but it was not for a minute or two that the dying Rachael could gather sufficient strength to speak that which she wished, but at length she rallied a little, and resumed in the following words—

"You, Richard Parker, were the first-born of your parents, and great was the joy that pervaded their hearts when they gazed for the first time upon your innocent face, and I need not say that I most warmly participated in that feeling, for I had been in the service of your family from the time when your amiable mother was a child, and that I was as warmly attached to her as if we had been allied by blood. But you had not been born more than three days when your mother had a dream, which cast an everlasting gloom upon her mind, and destroyed all those fond anticipations she had so sanguinely indulged in, whilst, at the same time, it filled her breast with the most melancholy forebodings, which nothing could afterwards serve to dissipate. On the same night, too, to render it still more remarkable and impressive, I also had a vision which corresponded in every respect with that which had been presented to the imagination of your mother. In those visions, strange and incredible as it may seem to you, Richard, the whole of those terrible events were revealed to us as distinctly as they since have happened to you, and the future and awful fate that was in store for you was presented to our imagination in the most vivid colours. We saw you in your manhood writhing beneath the excruciating and maddening tortures of the galling lash; we witnessed the death of the villain Arlington by your hands; we saw you afterwards with your wife and child, wandering wretched in the cheerless world, pursued and hunted by the myrmidons of the law, and we beheld your lifeless corpse afterwards swinging from the yard-arm in the open air, while —"

"Oh, horrible! horrible!" interrupted Mary, with a groan of the most indescribable and irrepressible agony, "what fearful delusions have you suffered to take possession of your mind?"

"Be calm, my poor Mary!" ejaculated Richard, mustering all the fortitude he could, though, in spite of himself, his heart sickened with horror at the fearful nature of the observations which the dying woman had made use of; "there is a just God above, who will, I trust, look down upon us with mercy, and avert those dreadful evils with which we are at present threatened."

"They are no delusions, unfortunate woman," said Rachael, replying to the words of Mrs. Parker, and apparently taking no heed of what her husband had said—"they are no delusions; would to Heaven that I could convince myself that they were, it would, indeed, be a sweet consolation to me in my dying moments. But no; I feel too fatally satisfied that those terrible visions will be realised; thou art the doomed man, Richard Parker; and however you may seek to avoid your fate, there is no hope for you in this world. Nothing whatever could eradicate the impression that dream had made upon the mind of your mother, and from that moment she became a gloomy and wretched being, though you became, if possible, more precious to her heart than ever, and I need not remind you with what tender care and solicitude she watched over you, and the anxious and affectionate attention she paid to the cultivation of your mind, while, at the same time, her heart was breaking at the terrible anticipation of the future. But—but—my strength fails me—my moments are numbered—my end is rapidly approaching—darkness gathers around me! Raise me—raise me, gently!"

Richard and his wife did raise the poor old woman in the bed, and she gazed at them for a moment or two with the most intense looks of anguish and commiseration, but could not speak. She raised her hands, and seemed to be mentally invoking the blessing and protection of Heaven upon their heads, and she then sank back again upon her pillow quite exhausted, and breathing

with the utmost difficulty. The remarkable change which only within the last few minutes had come over her features was quite awful to contemplate; they were distorted with agony, and it was quite evident that only a few brief minutes would close the painful scene.

We will not seek to describe the feelings of Richard and his wife, for after what they had listened to from the lips of the dying woman, and the solemnity with which they had been uttered, they may be readily imagined by the reader. It was not without the greatest difficulty that our unfortunate heroine could sustain herself; and had it not been for the presence of her husband and Mr. Worthington, she must have sunk under the shock.

"The dread moment has come," at last old Rachael gasped forth; "my earthly troubles will soon be o'er, and I shall quickly be in the presence of that Almighty Judge, from whom I humbly but earnestly pray forgiveness for the sins I have committed. Bless you!—bless you! But remember my predictions, and prepare yourselves for the worst. Keep my death a secret; for the knowledge of it would only hasten your own fate. I wish not my old bones to moulder in the earth; I require no tablet to my memory; when I am no more, consign my body at midnight to the deep, and thus avoid all dangerous inquiry. Ah! 'tis darker and darker still!—I cannot see you, my friends—that pang!—I—I—Eternity—Oh!"

And thus, with one deep and lengthened groan, the soul of the mysterious woman took its everlasting flight from its frail tenement.

For some time after the breath had departed from the body of old Rachael Melford, Richard and his wife and Mr. Worthington stood by and contemplated the cold remains, deeply impressed with the awfulness and serenity of the scene they had just witnessed, but more especially with the words to which she had given utterance.

"Unfortunate woman," at length remarked Mr. Worthington; "her mortal career has terminated, and her spirit is now in the presence of its Maker, from whom I trust it will receive that mercy and forgiveness of which we all stand so much in need. How extraordinary it is that you should at the last moment have recognised in her one who was so closely connected with you in the days of your childhood. But still the singular conduct she has thought proper to pursue has not been satisfactorily explained, and, in spite of her assertions to the contrary, it seems to me more like that of an insane person than anything else."

"True," replied our hero; "but can I think upon her fearful predictions, uttered even with her latest breath, without a shudder?"

"Alas—alas!" groaned Mary; "my blood freezes in my veins when I reflect on them, and all the hopes with which I had previously flattered myself are banished from my mind. Good God! and is it possible that such a dreadful fate as that which Rachael has predicted, is indeed in store for you, my unfortunate and beloved husband?"

"Do not give way to any such torturing apprehensions, Mrs. Parker," said Worthington; "for Providence is too merciful to suffer them ever to be realised; your husband surely possesses more reason and confidence than to imagine they will."

"Alas! Mr. Worthington," replied our hero, "it is in vain that I attempt to banish from my mind the impression which the fearful prognostications of old Rachael have made upon it, and the more especially when I recall to my memory the manner in which many of them have already been fulfilled. The extraordinary dreams, too, which——"

"Nay, Mr. Parker," interrupted Mr. Worthington, "such superstitious feelings as these are unworthy of you, and I did not think it was possible for you to entertain them. What have you at present to apprehend? Does not everything proceed as well as could have been expected? You are now in security, and no suspicion can possibly light upon you, while you continue to act in the manner you have done already. 'Tis true that this unexpected event is sufficient to alarm you; but it is known only to ourselves and the villain who perpetrated the deed, and no danger, I believe, will arise from it to you."

"But the body," said Richard; "how can we possibly dispose of that without the knowledge of Ladbroke and the others?"

"The deceased has suggested an excellent plan herself," answered Worthington; "and we shall but be complying with her dying request by adopting it. When darkness has obscured the earth, and there is not likely to be any one about to observe our actions, we can consign the body to the deep, and thus all danger from inquiry will be at an end. It is fortunate that Binnacle is at present in the neighbourhood, for he will be enabled to manage all that business for us without any trouble. Come, come, arouse yourself; do not give way to any useless fears, and I have no doubt that you will soon be able to recover yourself from the shock which this event has naturally caused you."

"I will endeavour to do so," returned our hero; "though I much fear that when I take all the circumstances into consideration I shall find it a most difficult task to accomplish. But who can the ruffian be who has been the cause of all this?"

"It is impossible for us to form even the slightest conjecture," replied Mr. Worthington; "doubtless, he is a stranger in the neighbourhood, and after what has happened, it is not likely that you will behold him again."

"He may have associates," remarked Richard, "and, disappointed in his infamous designs against my beloved wife, and at my interposition, it is not at all unlikely that such a hardened miscreant as he evidently is will seek revenge. I tremble for the future safety of Mary during my absence from the cottage."

"Any such fears as these I believe are groundless, for it is not likely that he will again venture near the scene of his atrocious crime for fear of detection. But enough of this. I do not think that it would be prudent for you to leave your wife alone to-day after what has happened, and the state of agitation in which it has naturally placed her."

"Oh, no!" ejaculated Mary, "I tremble to be left alone with the ghastly corpse of this unfortunate woman. You will not leave me, Richard?"

"Oh, no, my beloved Mary!" replied her husband, "I could not for a moment think of doing so, let the consequences be whatever they may."

"I will form some satisfactory excuse for your absence from the inn to Ladbroke and the others, and by and by you may expect Binnacle and me at the cottage, when we will see at once to the disposal of the corpse. In the meantime, let me advise you to endeavour to tranquillise your feelings as much as possible; and depend upon it, notwithstanding all that Rachael has prophesied, you will yet be released from the difficulties which at present surround you."

"Heaven grant that we may!" exclaimed our heroine, fervently, "for should the fearful observations made use of by Rachael be fulfilled, what would become of myself and my child, destitute and friendless as we should then be, and with the dreadful reflection constantly upon our mind of the awful, ignominious, and unmerited fate which had befallen the unhappy partner of my affections?"

"It will not be, Mrs. Parker, depend upon it," returned Worthington; "the Almighty is too good and merciful to suffer such a fate to overtake your husband. Encourage every hope—look forward to the future with sanguine expectation and confidence, and rest assured that, however dismal your present prospects may seem to be, you will not be doomed to be disappointed."

After some further observations, Mr. Worthington quitted the cottage, and left our hero and his wife to their own reflections, which, as may well be expected, were of the most torturing and dismal description. With feelings of mingled anguish and regret they gazed upon the corpse of poor old Rachael; and so extraordinary and sudden were the circumstances which had brought about her fatal end, that it had to them more the appearance of a dream than reality. But the conduct which the deceased woman had thought proper to pursue during the latter years of her life was most extraordinary and unaccountable. Why should she lead the solitary life she had done, and what could be her reason for not revealing herself before to Richard? Her behaviour was certainly more that of an insane person than that of a rational being, and yet the observations she had made use of were such as could not fail to raise a doubt to the contrary in their minds. Her dying words had made an indelible impression upon them both, and it was in vain that they endeavoured by argument to view them with indifference.

"Would to Heaven," remarked Richard, "that we had never beheld this unfortunate old woman; it would have saved us much anxiety of mind; as it is, it is impossible that we can treat her prognostications lightly, especially after the fearful manner in which a portion of them has been verified. Oh, my poor Mary! what a cruel fate is ours; and how do I shudder with horror when I anticipate the dreadful sufferings you will be subjected to, should you be deprived of my protection in the awful and shameful manner with which I am threatened. To die a felon's death! Oh, there is something so revolting, so horrible in the thought, that the very blood freezes in my veins, as it seems to me, and I feel unmanned and hopeless!"

"Richard—Richard! dearest husband!" ejaculated our heroine, throwing her arms affectionately round his neck, and looking with the deepest emotion in his face; "you will drive my brain to madness if you continue to indulge in these cruel, these dreadful reflections. Die a felon's death!—Oh, never! never! What has Richard Parker ever done that he should meet with so untimely and ignominious a fate?"

"Mary," replied our hero, "grief has distracted your brain, and I fear that at times you scarcely know what you utter. You cannot forget that I am a mutineer, and in the eye of the law a murderer!"

"A murderer!" repeated Mary, with an expression of countenance which showed the deep emotions that were struggling in her breast; "oh, frightful word! how unjustly do you apply it to yourself!"

"Nay," he returned, "did not Arlington perish by my hands?"

"True," answered his wife; "and unfortunate is it that it is true. But you sought not his life: you slew him but in self-defence, and it was a just retribution on his head for the many crimes he had committed, and the injuries he had inflicted on you. Heaven surely will pardon you the deed, and not suffer you to become the victim of a fate so terrible."

"For your sake, my faithful wife," said Richard, "I humbly but earnestly hope that it will not. But still, when I view the circumstances calmly and deliberately, it is impossible that I can do otherwise than entertain the most gloomy apprehensions. Poor Rachael! yours has, indeed, been a strange and chequered career, and it is hard that you should perish in such a way, after all. I do not like the idea of not interring her remains with Christian burial, but consigning them to the deep; still, there is no alternative, situated as we are, and necessary as it is to keep the murder of the unfortunate woman a secret."

"True," coincided Mary; "should it become known, of course an investigation into the cause of her death would be sure to take place: we should be summonsed as witnesses, and detection would then not be at all unlikely to follow."

"Yes," said Richard, "that is but too probable. But the miscreant who committed this monstrous crime, and the outrage against you—who can he be?—I begin to suspect that it was not accident alone that led him to the cottage."

"Oh," replied Mary, "I think it is most improbable that it should be anything else; unless, indeed, he contemplated robbery, and he could not expect to get much in a humble habitation like this. But you say, Richard, that from the glance you had of his features, it struck you that you have seen him somewhere before?"

"It did," answered our hero, "but I cannot call to my mind where it was. His dress was that of a man who had been to sea; and it is not impossible that I have been his shipmate some time or other. It is strange, but I am almost positive that I have seen the villain before, and that impression becomes stronger upon my mind every moment."

He paused, and passed his hand across his forehead, in order to try to recall his thoughts, and to refresh his memory; but it was all to no purpose.

"I cannot think where it is I have seen him," he said; "and yet, the more I reflect upon them, the more familiar do his features become to me. Should he indeed have been my shipmate, and should recognise me, I am ruined!"

"Nay, Richard," remarked his wife, "it is useless for you to disturb your mind with such fears as those; it is quite clear that the ruffian did not recognise you, or he would at once have denounced you; you have nothing to apprehend from him; I feel satisfied that you have not."

Throughout the day they remained in much the same state of mind, and continued in the same room that contained the remains of the ill-fated old woman, reflecting deeply and seriously upon the important and exciting events that a few hours only had produced, and in speculating upon what was likely to be their future fortunes, though their present prospects were gloomy and hopeless enough. At length night set in, and Mr. Worthington and Binnacle arrived much sooner than they had expected them; the honest seaman greeting our heroine with the utmost respect. He had heard all the particulars from Mr. Worthington of the daring outrage that had been perpetrated against Mary, and the diabolical murder of poor old Rachael, and he expressed his feelings warmly upon the subject.

"Unfortunate old woman," he said, "it is a sad fate to meet with after living for so many years. What a blood-thirsty, cowardly miscreant the fellow must be who could be guilty of such crimes as these; I only wish that I had been present, he should not have escaped without a shot in his mizentop, I'll warrant. However, Mr. Parker, it was a fortunate job that you arrived at the cottage just at the critical moment of danger, or there is no knowing what might have been the consequences."

"Very true," coincided Worthington, "for there can be no doubt, after what has taken place, that he is a most desperate and determined ruffian, and that it would have been useless for Mrs. Parker to attempt to resist him."

"You say that he had the appearance of a sailor?" said Binnacle, addressing himself to our hero.

"He had," answered the latter; "and I cannot, somehow, help thinking that it is not the first time we have met."

"Indeed?" said Ben, with a look of astonishment and curiosity; "where do you think you have seen him?"

"I cannot imagine," replied Richard, "unless it was on shipboard."

"Ah!" remarked Binnacle, "that is very likely."

"If such be the case," said our hero, "he did not seem to recognise me."

"Why, no," returned Mr. Worthington, "I do not see how it was at all likely that he should, disguised as you are. You may consider yourself perfectly secure in that respect, if you only continue to act the character you have assumed with the same ability that you have hitherto done. But I have mentioned to our friend Binnacle all the facts connected with our plans for disposing of the body of the unfortunate woman, and he has made all the necessary arrangements for putting it into execution."

"I would that any other means could be adopted," remarked Richard, "for there is something very revolting to me in the idea of disposing of the remains of the poor old woman in such a manner."

"Well, but we have no other way of doing so, Mr. Parker," returned Ben Binnacle; "besides, I understand that it was her dying request."

"It was," said Richard.

"Then," observed the old seaman, "I don't see why you should any longer hesitate; and her bones will rest as well beneath the blue waters of the deep as if they were placed in consecrated ground. As she does not appear to have any relations living, it is not likely that any inquiries will be made after her, and, therefore, her fate will always remain a secret confined to ourselves."

"True," answered Worthington; "and it is not very likely that this ruffian, whoever he may be, will show himself in this part of the country again, or make any disclosure upon the subject. The body once removed, I trust that Mr. Parker and his wife will soon be able to recover from the shock which this awful event has naturally caused them."

Richard had nothing to say in opposition to this argument, and they continued to converse for an hour or two longer, when, imagining that there would now be nobody abroad to observe them, they made preparations to put their plan into execution, Mrs. Parker and her son being requested to retire to another apartment while they did so.

The corpse of poor old Rachael was now placed in a sack, which they had brought with them for the purpose, and Binnacle, with the assistance of our hero and Mr. Worthington, having raised it on his shoulders, and it being satisfactorily ascertained that the coast was perfectly clear, the old seaman and Worthington departed from the cottage, leaving Richard behind in order to protect his wife, in case any further danger should threaten, and promising to return as soon as possible.

Our hero watched them anxiously till they were hidden from the view by the clustering trees, and he then rejoined his wife, whom he found upon her knees, and solemnly and devoutly supplicating the mercy and protection of the Most High.

They waited most impatiently and anxiously for the return of Binnacle and his companion; and in little more than half an hour they made their appearance, and thus quieted their suspense.

"Well, that melancholy job is done," observed Ben Binnacle, "and we committed the remains of the poor old woman to the waves with all proper respect and solemnity. Heaven rest her bones, say I!"

To this they all responded most fervently and sincerely.

"The secret is now safe," remarked Mr. Worthington, "and you may safely set all detection at defiance, Mr. Parker."

"I trust to Heaven I may," replied our hero.

"Oh, there is no fear of that," said Ben; "nothing can be more complete than your disguise; I should never have recognised you if I had not been prepared for it. But come, it is late, and I think we had now better separate. I intend to stay with my friend Worthington at the inn to-night; and I shall see you again to-morrow, when we will consult further upon what is best to be done."

"You will return to the inn in the morning, Mr. Parker," observed Mr. Worthington, "and your wife and son can accompany you; for now that she, as well as yourself, have been fairly introduced to Ladbroke and the others, there is nothing to fear. In the meantime I would advise you both to exert yourselves to compose your feelings, lest it should excite the attention and curiosity of Ladbroke; who, as you well know, has a most penetrating eye upon all matters that do not concern him."

Richard promised to attend to his advice, and Worthington and Binnacle then took their departure from the cottage. Notwithstanding the lateness of the hour, however, our hero and his wife did not feel inclined to retire to rest just yet, but sat up for some time longer, conversing upon all the extraordinary circumstances of the last few eventful hours; at length, however, being tired, they arose from their seats and sought their chamber.

CHAPTER XVI.

SOME REMARKABLE EVENTS.—THE MURDERER AGAIN.—A PLOT.—MR. BUBBLE IN DIFFICULTIES.—THE BURGLARY.

IN order the better to work out the interest of his story, the novelist is allowed a wide licence to deviate from facts; and as it is necessary to the purposes of our plot, we shall take the liberty of availing ourselves of this privilege. The principal incidents of the mutiny at the Nore are, no doubt, familiar to most of our readers; but in order, as we before said, the better to develop our plot, we do not intend to adhere to them entirely, but to take a wider range, for the purpose of introducing some of the most extraordinary and romantic events into the pages of our narrative.

The search after our hero was kept up with unabated vigilance, but, as we have shown, without the least success, and not the slightest clue could be obtained as to the place of his concealment. By many it was imagined that he had contrived to make his escape out of the country, and there were not a few who sincerely sympathised in his misfortunes, and heartily wished that he might still be able to elude the vigilance of his enemies, and be restored to that happiness

of which he had been so long and unmeritedly deprived. That very sapient and extremely efficient individual, Mr. Timothy Bubble, was not of that number. He prided himself upon being full of loyalty to overflowing; the idea of anything in the shape of a mutineer was truly horrible to him, and for his own part he would have been gratified to have seen our unfortunate hero hanged, drawn, and quartered, so deep and ineffable, was the disgust he felt at his conduct; and that horror and disgust, as may be imagined, was not a little increased by the death of Captain Arlington, for whom, as it was perfectly natural he should do, he entertained the most profound respect.

As we have shown, Mr. Bubble had never been held in the highest esteem by the more respectable portion of his neighbours, and the prominent part he had played in the fatal business of which Richard Parker had been the hero, and the exertions he had made to lead to his apprehension, the reader may be sure did not serve to diminish that feeling; and there were many who would have felt a pleasure in drawing him through a horse-pond, or giving him a sound dubbing, if they could have done so without rendering themselves amenable to the law; and there was no one who would have been more ready to do so than his late servant, Dicky Chicken, who was now entered on the ship's books of the Sandwich, under the auspices and particular patronage of honest Jack Adams. Mr. Bubble, however, had some other business on his mind which greatly harassed and perplexed him; this was nothing less than a law-suit, in which he was defendant, and the decision of which involved a considerable sum of money. This caused him the greatest uneasiness and anxiety of mind; and he well knew, moreover, that he had the hearty good wishes of most persons who knew him that he might be defeated, which added to his vexation, doubt, and suspense.

It was about a month after the events that we have recorded in the previous chapter, and on a dark and cheerless night, that a man of the most ruffianly exterior and repulsive features might have been seen slowly making his way across a lonely and little frequented part of the country in the vicinity of the Isle of Grain. He seemed to have travelled far, and to have suffered much from fatigue and hunger. But we have no occasion to describe him farther when we state that he was the same desperate miscreant who had committed the brutal outrage against Mary Parker, and by whose hand the unfortunate old woman, Rachael Melford, had lost her life.

Having proceeded for some distance

BRUNSTON LURKING BENEATH THE WINDOW OF MARY PARKER'S ROOM.

further, he seated himself on a stone by the road-side, and gazed anxiously around him.

"Well," he growled to himself, "this is a confounded dismal place, sure enough; not a house or human being near, and I am so hungry and worn out with walking and the want of rest, that I know not how to proceed a step further. Well, Joe Brunston, you are now regularly done in the world at any rate, and you must adopt some desperate and determined course, or you will be lost altogether. It would not be lucky for any person who should happen to possess any money about him to encounter me just now. I only wish I could meet with some of my old companions, for I have no doubt that they would then effect a speedy change in my prospects; and if I have been informed aright, it is somewhere in this neighbourhood that they are located. They would be glad to see an old associate, I have no doubt; and I shouldn't wonder but they would find me some employment that would be suited to my present taste and habits."

He again paused, and having first taken a pistol from his pocket, and examined it carefully, he once more looked anxiously around him, as far as his eyes could penetrate through the darkness.

"An excellent spot this to commit a robbery," he said; "but the worst of it is, there is no one to rob. It is cursed vexatious for a man who is willing to do business, but cannot find any to do. What a slice of luck it would be for me if I could only stumble across Parker. I would never leave him till I had placed him in security and made sure of the reward that is offered for his apprehension. I have reason to know him well, for I was his shipmate, and he was punished for the robbery which I committed. I was a fool, however, to betray myself afterwards, and thus to subject myself to the same punishment and degradation which he had received. Bah! I cannot bear to think of that, and I feel gratified at the fate which Captain Arlington has met with, and which I would not have failed to inflict upon him myself if I had had the opportunity. That was a strange adventure that I had at the cottage of the widow, as she called herself; and I wonder if the wound I inflicted on the old hag who interrupted me proved mortal. I have no doubt it did, though; but it does not matter much, for I am safe enough now, and it is not very likely that I shall be detected. There was something in the personal appearance and the voice of the man, however, which were quite familiar to me, and I am almost certain that I must have seen him before, though where I cannot imagine. But it's no use sitting here; so I will e'en travel on in the best manner I can, and see what fortune will

send me. I must have money to-night by some means or other, and I am fully prepared to adopt any desperate course to obtain it."

With these words, the villain arose from his seat, and once more proceeded on his way, though he was totally at a loss in which direction to go. He had not advanced many yards, however, when, on turning an abrupt corner, he imagined that he perceived the shadow of a human form in the distance, and coming towards him; and straining his eyes to the utmost, he was satisfied that he was not mistaken, and that it was the form of a man.

"Ah!" he muttered to himself, "my wishes appear to be about to be gratified: should this individual happen to possess any money about him, it shall be transferred to my exchequer without delay. Let me be cautious, and there can be little or no doubt of my success."

He concealed himself behind the trunk of a tree by the road-side, and awaited the arrival of the traveller. In a few minutes he arrived at the spot, and paused to take breath, having apparently walked fast. It was Mr. Bubble, who, having been to a distant town upon certain business which had detained him longer than he had anticipated, was now returning home with all the haste he could.

"Well," he said, "I have settled that business in a satisfactory manner, at any rate, and have made twenty guineas by my bargain. That's not a very bad day's work, and I think I may indulge myself with a glass of wine when I get home, upon the strength of it. It is a gloomy and disagreeable night, however, and this is by no means a pleasant road to travel; so the sooner I proceed on my way the better."

With these words, Timothy Bubble walked on, and Brunston having started from his place of concealment, and crossed his path, confronted him. The little man staggered back a few paces in the greatest alarm, and trembled in every limb.

"God bless my soul!" he faltered out, "where did you spring from, my friend? and who are you?"

"Why," replied the fellow, "I am only a poor devil without a fraction in the world; and as, to judge by your countenance, you are a gentleman of the most amiable and benevolent character, I will take the liberty of borrowing a trifle from you."

" Ah! a robber! a highwayman!" ejaculated Mr. Bubble, his teeth chattering and his kneees knocking together; "let me pass; I am in a hurry, and must not be detained."

" When you have complied with my request you may do so as soon as you please," replied Brunston; " so, no more words about it, but do so at once."

" Let me pass, I say," returned the alarmed Mr. Bubble, " or it will be worse for you. I—I—I will call for assistance."

" If you are wise, and set any value on your life," answered the villain, presenting the pistol at his head, " you will do no such thing."

" No—no—no—don't !" stammered out the terrified Timothy, trembling more violently than ever, " I—I—I am rather nervous. A joke's a joke, but do not be so unreasonable. I have nothing to give—I am very poor—very poor, indeed, I assure you."

" What, after making a day's work of twenty guineas ?" said Brunston, with a sarcastic laugh.

" Twenty guineas !" repeated poor Bubble, in a faint voice. " God bless my soul! what an extravagant idea! It is a mistake of yours a most extraordinary idea. I—I—but ——"

" Come, come, no hesitation," interrupted the robber, impatiently. " The money I overheard you just now speak of. I must have it, and I have no time to waste with you in words."

Bubble dropped on his knees and supplicated for mercy in the most abject manner, but Brunston only replied to him with a derisive and contemptuous laugh, and proceeded, without any further ceremony, to ransack the pockets of his unfortunate victim ; and quickly depriving him of every farthing he possessed, together with a pocket-book, he politely bade him good-night, and immediately hurried from the spot.

Bubble had thrown himself on his face in a state of agitation and alarm that may easily be imagined, and groaned aloud for help; but at length, venturing to look up, he perceived that the robber was

gone, and in what direction he knew not.

" Here's a catastrophe !" he ejaculated ; " here's an event ! I am ruined ! All my money gone, and at the very moment when I was priding myself upon the good day's work I had made. Murder ! fire ! thieves ! murder ! oh !"

Thus wildly giving utterance to the expression of his terrors, poor Bubble started to his feet, and ran as fast as his legs and his fears would permit him towards his home. However, as the Admiral's Head was in his way, and he was too much terrified and agitated to proceed, he entered it, in order that he might inform the company of the misfortune that had befallen him, and probably obtain their assistance to go in pursuit of the highwayman. There were several persons assembled in the Admiral's Head, and among the rest were Jack Adams and Dicky Chicken, when Mr. Bubble staggered in, his clothes in disorder, and his features exhibiting the utmost terror.

" Oh, dear ! oh dear ! what shall I do ?" he exclaimed. " I am murdered ! I am ruined ! Fetch me a glass of brandy immediately, landlord, or I shall faint."

" What the devil's in the wind now, you old grampus ?" demanded Adams. " Have you seen the ghost of some person whom you robbed while living ?"

" Don't, don't, Mr. Adams," he replied ; " I can't stand it ! indeed I can't ! Those are very cruel words to a poor devil in my situation. I tell you again I am ruined !"

" Dear me !" remarked Dicky Chicken, with a satirical grin, " what a terrible calamity is that ; how extremely sorry I am to hear that, as I am certain everybody will be who is acquainted with the respectable character of Mr. Timothy Bubble."

" None of your jeers, you impudent varlet," said his late master ; " I know you entertain the most vindictive feelings towards me, and are gratified at any misfortune that may befall me. I verily believe that if you were to see me hanging to the branch of the nearest tree, you would not have the Christian charity to cut me down."

" Oh, no," returned Chicken, " I could not think of inflicting such an injustice on society."

" Base, ungrateful fellow," said the

unhappy Mr. Bubble, "after the kind and generous master that I have been to you. But you will come to a bad end, I am certain; you will be hanged or transported, mark my words if you are not."

"Avast! avast there, you old swab!" cried Jack Adams; "belay that lingo, or you will stand a chance of finding me athwart your hawser, and it strikes me that you would not have much cause to congratulate yourself then. What's the matter with you, and what has happened that you are making all this rumpus?"

"Oh, Mr. Adams," answered Bubble, "you are a sensible man, and I know you have a heart that can feel for another."

"I wish I could pay you the same compliment," remarked Adams; "but out with what you've got to say, and then weigh anchor as soon as you can, for the very sight of your d——d ugly old figure-head goes against my stomach."

"I have been robbed, Mr. Adams, cruelly, shamefully robbed," said Bubble; "I have been attacked by a desperate and murderous highwayman, and he has plundered me of no less a sum than twenty golden guineas."

"Well, it is only dog rob dog," returned Jack Adams, "and I have no doubt that your inventive faculties will find the means of making some one else pay for it."

"I, Mr. Adams?" said Bubble; "bless my soul, you do not suppose that I would be guilty of such a thing as that? You must be very ignorant of my real character, if you do. Twenty guineas—twenty guineas! What a sum! I shall never recover it. But do you not pity me? Will you not assist me in going in pursuit of the robber?"

"Not I, indeed," answered Adams; "I have other business to do, without troubling myself with such trifles as that."

"Trifles!" repeated Timothy; "do you call the loss of twenty golden guineas a trifle? Oh, dear—oh, dear! the thought of it will drive me to distraction."

"No, no, my much respected late master," said Dicky Chicken, in the same sarcastic tones as those to which he had before given utterance; "do not take on so, for if you were to be driven to commit suicide, only consider what an irreparable loss it would be to society."

"Unfeeling master!" said the indignant Mr. Bubble; "you have no more sense of humanity about you than a block of marble; you are a perfect savage; you are a crocodile, a—a cannibal, a—a——"

"Avast, you old lubber!" interrupted Jack Adams; "if I hear you speak another disrespectful word of my friend Chicken, I will pour such a broadside into you that will scatter your timbers to the devil. What are you, you old shark, that you dare to insult a gentleman in that manner? For my own part, I am glad that you have been made to deliver up part of your ill-gotten gold; and if I could only see the man who robbed you, damme if I wouldn't treat him to the best the house contains."

"Bless my soul!" returned Bubble, raising his eyes and hands with astonishment, "what a sinful world is this we now live in; there is no sympathy for the unfortunate, and——"

He was interrupted by the entrance of the landlord, followed by the man who was engaged by Bubble in the place of Chicken.

"Now, then, Matty," said his master, hastily, "what brings you here?"

"Why," answered Matty, "I thought you would have been at home before now, so I thought it was not unlikely I should find you here. Here is a letter for you, which arrived about two hours ago; and thinking it might, perhaps, contain something of importance, I—"

"Yes, yes," interrupted Bubble, impatiently; "give me the letter.—Ah! it is the handwriting of my lawyer. What's the matter, now?—Dear me, how I tremble: I am almost afraid to open the letter."

In an excited manner he did so, however, and he had scarcely perused the first line, when he uttered a loud groan, and starting to his feet, he paced the room backwards and forwards, and beating his breast with the most violent emotions.

"How now, you old gorgon!" demanded Jack Adams; "what's the matter?"

"The matter! the matter!" repeated the wretched little man; "I'm murdered! annihilated; ruined; beggared! The action is decided against me, independent of the costs. What will become of me? Oh, Bubble! Timothy Bubble! the sun of your earthly happiness and prosperity has set for ever, and you will henceforth become a wretched, wandering outcast in the wide and cheerless world!"

"It's very cutting!" remarked Chicken, with a look of mock solemnity and sympathy; "how sorry I am for you! But still you must not abandon yourself to despair altogether: to be sure, five hundred pounds is a large sum of money, but still it is no great deal, after all, to a man of your wealth."

"Wealth!" cried Bubble, staring at him with a most ludicrously melancholy expression of countenance; "I have no wealth now; I am beggared, I tell you again; I am a poor unfortunate victim of misfortune. Oh, Dicky Chicken, should I die of a broken-heart, I trust that, in spite of the bad feelings you have evinced towards me, you will sometimes drop a tear to the memory of your unfortunate master."

"Do not," returned Chicken—"do not so strongly appeal to my sensitive feelings. You know how tender-hearted I am, and that it drives me to madness to see you suffer in this manner. The kind sympathy you evinced for Richard Parker must have given every one the highest opinion of your character, and no doubt has endeared you to every heart; and they must, therefore, be extremely sorry that anything of so serious a nature should happen to you."

"You are an unfeeling monster!" groaned Timothy Bubble; "but, mark my words, a terrible retribution will some time or the other overtake you for the base ingratitude with which you have acted to me. Lead the way, Matty. Let me hasten to despair and solitude."

Thus saying, poor Bubble hastened from the house, Jack Adams and his companions laughing heartily.

In the meantime, the ruffian Brunston after the robbery having fled at the top of his speed, soon got to some distance from the spot, and considering himself to be in safety, he paused in order to take breath, and to congratulate himself upon the good fortune which had so suddenly overtaken him when he least expected it.

"This has made a man of me," he said. "Twenty guineas! it is a goodly sum for one night's work, and will encourage me to proceed in future. But it is no use standing parleying here; I must find some retired public-house if I can, where I can obtain some refreshment and a lodging for the night."

He hurried on his way, and after walking for about a quarter of an hour longer, he beheld lights glimmering apparently from the window of some dwelling at no great distance from where he was, and immediately made towards it.

He found it was a low, old-fashioned public-house, and thinking it was probably well adapted for accommodation and secrecy, he entered it, and sought the presence of the landlord. He was a coarse, hardy-looking man of muscular form, but no sooner did Brunston behold his countenance than he started back with an exclamation of astonishment, and he seemed to recognise him at the same moment.

"What, Will Hangsby!" cried Brunston, "is it possible I behold you? Well, this is a surprise, and it could not have taken place at a better time. It is many years since we have met."

"True, Joe," answered Hangsby, "and I have seen some strange things in that time. But you do not make a very respectable appearance; and I should think you haven't been very fortunate of late?"

"No," replied Brunston, "I have been very unlucky to be sure, until about an hour ago. But where are all our old associates?"

"There are several of them at present in this house," answered Hangsby, "so this way, Joe, and I will introduce you to them."

"Ay, I am anxious to see them," observed Brunston, "for we shall have much to explain to each other. But I must get you to supply me with some provisions as quick as you can, for it is many hours since I tasted food, and I am almost exhausted."

"Well," returned Hangsby, "it is fortunate that chance has led you hither, for I suppose you do not care to show yourself much amongst strangers?"

"Why, no," replied Brunston, "my appearance is not very prepossessing, and it would not be prudent or safe for me to venture into the company of strangers in this neighbourhood to-night, at any rate."

"Oh, then, have you been after some of your old tricks?" asked Hangsby.

"I should have thought you had no occasion to ask that question," replied Joe Brunston; "for you know that I never miss availing myself of any opportunity that is presented to me. But you seem to have changed your course of life."

"Not I," said Hangsby, with a grin; "but I do it now in such a manner as may defy detection. There is no person in the neighbourhood who can have the least possible suspicion of the real character of Will Hangsby, and those who resort to his house. But come, this is a waste of time. Follow me."

Completely astonished at this accidental meeting with one of his old associates in crime, and that at the very time when he so much needed his assistance, Joe Brunston made use of no other observation, but followed Hangsby from the room, and along a passage which seemed to lead to the back of the premises.

It may now be necessary to inform the reader that The Tankard, which was the sign of this house, was a place of low repute, and was never visited by any of the respectable inhabitants of the neighbourhood, while the landlord was looked upon with doubt and distrust, and certainly neither his manners nor personal appearance were of the most prepossessing description. It was well known that The Tankard was used by several men of rude and ferocious appearance; but for what purpose they congregated there, or what was the way in which they got their living, could not be imagined; the reader will, however, soon be enlightened on that subject.

The Tankard was situated in a lonely part of the country, and there was not another habitation near it; so that it was well adapted for those secret scenes which we shall presently proceed to show were so frequently enacted there. It was a very ancient building, probably of some two or three centuries standing, and the walls were thickly covered with ivy, which added to its venerable appearance.

Will Hangsby had been the proprietor of this hostelrie for some four or five years, but whence he came was not known to any one, though, from his general manners, it was believed that he had formerly been connected with a seafaring life.

Joe Brunston followed his conductor along the passage we have before mentioned, and through several apartments, which proved to him that the house was of much greater extent than he should at first have been led to suppose; and after at length descending a flight of steps, and proceeding through a range of vaulted rooms, they stopped at the door of one, from the crevices of which lights glimmered, and the voices of men, as if in noisy altercation, might be heard.

"Well," remarked Brunston, "this is certainly a singular building, and is well adapted for the transaction of any business which requires secrecy and security."

"Yes," coincided Hangsby, "and so you will say when you have seen all. But come, I will introduce you to some of our old associates, and whom you probably never expected to see again."

He opened the door as he spoke, and Brunston could not help starting back with amazement at the singular scene which presented itself. The room was of large dimensions, and lighted by two or three lamps suspended from the ceiling, and the walls were covered with various pictures of a rude description of painting. There were several large seamen's chests piled one upon another at one end, and in the centre of the room were two long tables, round which a number of men, of masculine forms, and coarse and determined features, were seated, carousing merrily, and indulging freely in the rude jest and boisterous laugh. They started up with some appearance of astonishment and dissatisfaction on beholding one whom they imagined to be a stranger; but their surprise increased on their recognising Brunston, who had been connected with most of them in many acts of villany several years before. A hearty and boisterous welcome was the consequence, and immediately Brunston was seated at the table, and enjoying himself to his heart's content; for, indeed, he had fasted so long that it would have been remarkably strange had he failed to do ample justice to the good fare before him.

"Well," he said at last, addressing himself to Hangsby, "you have, indeed, got a snug and convenient establishment here, and I have good reason to bless my lucky stars that guided me. But," he added, with a smile, "may I ask what particular profession our friends here follow?"

"Oh, they are clever tradesmen, I assure you," answered Hangsby, "and can turn their hands to anything: whether it be to address a gentleman on the highway, to crack a crib, or do a little in the smuggling line: they are the lads that are always ready for anything."

"Ay, ay, I do not doubt it," remarked Brunston; "in fact, I must be very silly to do so, as I am intimately acquainted with most of them, and I am glad to meet them again, for I was greatly in want of friends, and old Dame Fortune has been confoundedly perverse with me of late."

"To judge from your personal appearance, I should say she had, indeed," said Will Hangsby; "but you are right enough now you have met with us—that is, if you think proper to join our communion."

"And you may be very sure that I can have no objection to that," replied Brunston; "in fact, I was driven to my wits-end till about an hour since, when I was lucky enough to meet with an old gentleman, who, happening to have such a thing as twenty guineas about him, I took the liberty of *borrowing* it of him."

"Ha! ha! ha!" laughed Hangsby; "well done. But tell us all about it."

The ruffian Brunston complied; and while he was relating the particulars of the robbery of Mr. Bubble, the fellows laughed most heartily, and applauded him to the skies.

"From the description you have given of this individual," observed Hangsby, when he had concluded, "it strikes me that I know him; and if it be he whom I suspect, he is one of the most infernal old sharks in the country, and should

have been hanged years ago. But you say that you took a pocket-book from him; have you examined the contents?"

"No," answered Brunston; "but I will do so now, for it is not unlikely that it contains something valuable."

He opened the pocket-book accordingly, and carefully examined the contents, but found nothing but several papers that were of no use to any one but the owner; but the name of Timothy Bubble was written on the inside of the case.

"Ah!" ejaculated Hangsby, "the very man—the very old shark that I suspected. Joe Brunston, you have done a good thing to-night; for by robbing old Timothy Bubble, you have retaliated upon a villain who has plundered thousands of poor persons in the course of his infamous career—I say infamous, comrades, because I detest the hypocrite: consequently, his business can bear no possible comparison to ours. We are bold traders—we seek high game, and would scorn the idea of trafficking upon those who could not afford to lose it; it is their oppressors that we take delight to rob; and, therefore, I repeat that I am glad to think you have been fortunate enough, Brunston, to ease old Bubble of some of his superfluous cash. Here's success to all our future undertakings!"

Hangsby filled his glass as he gave utterance to these words, and the whole of the parties present responded to his toast in the most hearty manner, and applauded Joe Brunston to the skies for his predatory achievement.

"And this Mr. Bubble, you say," remarked Brunston, "is a man of substance?"

"A man of substance!" repeated Hangsby; "the old swab, no doubt, is as rich as a Jew by the rascally transactions in which he has been engaged for a long series of years."

"And resides in this neighbourhood?" said Brunston.

"Ay," answered Will Hangsby, "not more than half a mile from this house."

"I wonder, then," returned Brunston, "that you have never paid him a visit?"

"We should have done so, you may depend upon it, before now," said Hangsby, "had we seen an opportunity of doing so with safety. But it is singular that only this very night before your arrival we were devising a plan to enter his establishment, and we will now mature the same. I presume you will have no objection to lend a hand in the business?"

"You will find me at your service in anything you may think proper to propose," replied the ruffian Brunston. "You are well acquainted with his residence, I suppose?"

"Oh, yes," said Hangsby; "there will be no difficulty in obtaining an entrance; and there will be nothing to fear from any resistance that will be offered, for the old shark is too mean to keep more than a decrepit old man and woman in his establishment."

"That is fortunate," observed Brunston; "and, of course, it can be so managed as not to cause the least suspicion to light upon you or our friends here?"

"Certainly," answered Hangsby; "we shall be so disguised that it would be impossible for him to recognise us; and if he should happen to do so, there is an easy way of preventing any danger arising from it. You understand me, I daresay; the dead tell no tales, eh?"

"True," returned Brunston, "so that point is settled. When shall the business be settled?"

"The sooner the better," replied Hangsby. "To-morrow night. I have reason to believe, from all that I have been enabled to elicit, that old Bubble always keeps a large sum of money in his house, and, therefore, we shall, no doubt, be handsomely repaid for our trouble."

"Just so," said Brunston; "and it will be strange, indeed, if we cannot accomplish our task."

"There is no fear of a failure," said Hangsby, in reply. "Will Hangsby and his comrades never yet took anything in hand that they failed in."

"To-morrow night, then ———"

"We pay our respects to Timothy Bubble, Esq.," rejoined Hangsby, "and will take the liberty of easing him of any superfluous cash he may have in his establishment. I confess I long to be revenged upon him for the officious part he took in the affair of Richard Parker."

"Well," remarked Brunston, "as for that matter I don't know. I have not much reason to bear Parker any particular good-will, and I have only been anxious to discover him, for the reward that is offered for his apprehension is a large sum, and would be extremely handy at present."

"Very true," answered Hangsby; "but I must acknowledge I feel a sort of sympathy for the Admiral, as I consider he has been a very ill-used man; and although the reward is a very tempting thing, I should be loth to take any part in earning it. He has escaped for the present, and I hope he may do so altogether."

"Well," said Brunston, "there you and I differ in opinion, Hangsby; however, that matters not. Have you no suspicion as to where he has gone?"

"Not the least," replied Hangsby; "but he has managed his business very cleverly, and I wish him success with all my heart. However, we will talk no more upon that subject; it is decided that to-morrow night we transact this little business with Mr. Bubble, and it strikes me that we shall not come away without a rich booty."

"True," coincided one of the men; "and if fortune only smiles upon us, we shall have no occasion for business for some time afterwards. Push the grog about, comrades, and let us drink success to all our future undertakings, whatever they may be."

The glasses were replenished, and the rude jest and the boisterous laugh went merrily round, each of the ruffians by turns recounting the various daring exploits in which he had been engaged, and which elicited universal applause, until a late hour, when most of them departed from the house, and Hangsby conducted Brunston to the chamber in which he was to sleep; and after a few more observations upon the infamous plot they were to execute on the following night, he left him, exulting in the good fortune which had befallen him in having by accident been guided to the haunt of those desperate ruffians with whom he was so intimately acquainted.

"Joe Brunston," he soliloquised, "the fickle dame Fortune once more smiles upon you, and nothing can be brighter than the prospects now before you. This is an excellent retreat, and well suited to a gentleman of my peculiar habits and profession; and if I do not do honour to the respectable commntiny of which I have now become a member, may I never see gold again. I am not, however, exactly satisfied with the termination of my adventure at the cottage of that widow, as she called her-self. It strikes me rather forcibly that she is no widow at all, but that the man who interrupted me and foiled me in my designs was her husband. And then his features—they were so familiar to me,

MARY PARKER'S INTRODUCTION TO MR. LADEROKE.

that I could almost swear that I have seen him frequently before, but where, I cannot form the slightest conjecture. Of one thing, however, I feel confident, namely, that he was not the rustic cha-racter that he seemed to be. Curses light upon the old hag who came so awkwardly and so unexpectedly to the rescue, for he and I should, doubtless, otherwise have become better acquainted. But I will see him again, if possible, and then we will come to a proper understanding. I am certain I know him, but who he really is I am at a perfect loss to imagine."

Thus the villain Brunston continued to ruminate for some time longer; but at length he retired to rest, and what with the fatigue he had undergone, and under the influence of the drink of which he had so liberally partaken, he soon dropped off into a sound sleep, from which he was not likely to arouse for several hours.

Poor Timothy Bubble, on leaving the Admiral's Head and reaching his own home, was in that state of nervous excitement which may readily be imagined, and it was some time before he could at all recover himself or compose his feelings. He paced his room backwards and forwards, beating his breast, and muttering curses to himself in the most distracted manner; and it was in vain that he endeavoured to reconcile himself to the heavy shock which he had sustained.

"Timothy Bubble, Timothy Bubble!" he groaned, "what a poor unfortunate devil you are. This is the most dreadful night's work you ever experienced. There is no luck for the truly honest and industrious man; and of the truth of that you are a most melancholy example. Robbed of twenty bright guineas, defeated at law, involved in tremendous damages, all the earnings of many years of toil and anxiety gone at one fell swoop—oh, horrible! You are ruined, beggared! I don't suppose that you have more than a couple of thousand pounds left to bless yourself with. Deplorable case! What is now to become of you? There is no other prospect before you but the workhouse, that's very certain. And those wretches, Adams and Chicken, and the others, to laugh at my misfortunes; to exult at them, and absolutely to insinuate that it was a judgment upon me for the part I acted in respect to Richard Parker! Faugh! they have no breasts of humanity or common decency about them! I—I could commit suicide, only—only it is so much trouble, and would cause such a painful sensation in the world. But—but I will have revenge upon mankind at large for this. Oh, Timothy Bubble—Timothy Bubble!

it would have been better, far better for you had you never been born."

Thus the unfortunate little man continued to soliloquise for hours, and to traverse his apartment with hasty and disordered steps.

"I must quit this neighbourhood altogether," he said, after a pause; "every person in the neighbourhood has conspired against me, and I am not safe a moment while I remain. Yes, I will arrange my affairs as quickly as possible, and then, Mr. Bubble, the victim of untoward circumstances, will become *non est inventus.* But, poor as I now am, whither can I go? Where hide my distracted head? Alas, alas! I am driven to despair and madness!"

Such was the excitement of mind under which he laboured, that it was some time ere he could think of retiring to rest; and when he did so, it was long ere he could compose himself to sleep. Dreams of the most torturing description haunted his imagination, and he frequently started from his sleep in a state of the greatest agitation, fancying that there were persons in the house who had come to rob and murder him; and it was not without the greatest difficulty that he could banish the impression from his mind. Had he been aware of the designs that were formed against him, he would indeed have been in a more painful state of excitement and terror than he was; but as it was, his agitation of mind was of the most torturing and insupportable description. It was a great relief to him when daylight dawned, and he left the house in order to endeavour to drown the agony of his thoughts by rambling amongst the variegated scenery in the neighbourhood. This was all to no purpose, however, the more he reflected the greater became his anguish and despair, and he returned home, and locking himself up in his room, would allow no person to come near him. In this manner night approached, and his melancholy and despair had increased rather than abated. At last, after some time passed in gloomy meditation, he went to an iron-chest which was placed in one corner of the room, and unlocking it, took from it a large bundle of notes and a bag of gold and silver, which he spread on the table at which he was seated, and proceeded to count it carefully over, at the same time every now and then looking cautiously and fearfully around him, and starting at the least noise, imagining that some one was coming to rob him.

"Ah!" he ejaculated, "thank God that I am not quite ruined, after all! Here are five hundred and seventy odd pounds, and some twelve hundred more in my banker's hands, will keep me for a month or two from the workhouse; so, in spite of the dreadful misfortune that has so suddenly and so unexpectedly befallen me, I must endeavour to console myself with that assurance. It is very imprudent for me to keep so much money by me, however, and to-morrow, therefore, I will deposit the best part of this in my banker's hands also, and then make my arrangements for quitting this neighbourhood, of which I am now heartily tired, and retire to some part of the country where I am not known, for it strikes me that I am not held in that esteem here which my numerous merits entitle me to. Ah! what noise was that?" he added, starting from his seat, and looking fearfully around him. "I could almost swear that I heard footsteps on the stairs, and—Who's there?"

He paused, and fixed his eyes eagerly on the door, but no answer was returned, and all was perfectly silent.

"Ah!" he said, "it could only have been my imagination that deceived me; it is not likely that there can be anybody in the house besides myself and my servants, and they have retired to rest, I have no doubt, long since. How dreadfully nervous I am getting, to be sure. But it is not to be wondered at after what has happened to me. Let me return this money to the chest, and then, knowing that all is safe, I will retire to rest, and see whether or not I can sleep off the horrors and anxieties which at present disturb my mind."

He once more listened attentively, and finding that all was still, he replaced the money in the chest, and was about to lock it, when he was again startled by a sound which resembled that of footsteps upon the stairs, and he trembled so violently that he could scarcely support himself.

"That time," he said, "I am certain I was not deceived; if these were not footsteps, my name is not what it is. But it must be that booby Matty, or else old Deborah, who have not sought their chambers yet. What the deuce can they want wandering about at this time of the night? I would open the door and call to them, only I am afraid that I should appear suspicious, and that is a thing that I would not seem to be upon any account. However, I will question them minutely in the morning."

He now walked towards the window, forgetting to lock the chest in the confusion of the moment, and looked out, but he could perceive no one near the house, and he returned to his seat.

"All is safe," he said; "how foolish I must be to alarm myself in such a manner. There is no one who is likely to interrupt me here. No, I should think that I have had enough of misfortune for some time to come. I will go to bed, and try to sleep off these idle fears and fancies."

He was about to do so, when he was again startled, and more violently alarmed than before, for he now distinctly heard a door close below, and then an indistinct sound, as if of several persons moving about. The perspiration rolled from his forehead, and his knees knocked violently together, but he was too much agitated to give utterance to a syllable. In the excitement of the moment, and scarcely knowing what he did, he went to the door, and unlocking it, stepped on to the landing, and listened with breathless attention; but all was again still as death, and he partially recovered himself from the alarm into which he had been thrown, and returned to the room, neglecting to lock the door after him.

"All is quiet," he remarked. "What a silly man I must be to alarm myself in such a manner. It could only have been fancy, or perhaps the wind that blew one of the lower doors to. I wish it were morning, though, for in spite of all my efforts to the contrary, I cannot banish from my mind that most dismal forebodings that something of a terrible nature is about to happen to me. I have a good mind to go down stairs and see whether all the outer doors are secure; but then, if my servants should be about, and should happen to see me, I should look so ridiculous. No, no, I will rest myself contented, and I have no doubt that no harm will befall me."

He now cast another glance around the room, and then retiring towards the bed, he was preparing to undress himself, when the room door was cautiously opened, and what was his consternation to behold several men, who wore masks, and were otherwise disguised, standing at the door. Overcome with terror, the wretched man sank upon his knees, and attempted to call for help, but he was immediately surrounded, and Will Hangsby presenting a pistol at his head, said, in an assumed voice—

"Breathe not a word beyond a whisper, old man, as you value that worthless life of yours."

"Oh, dear!—oh, dear!" faltered out poor Bubble, "have mercy on me, good, kind gentlemen, I implore you! I am a poor, unfortunate old man, and——"

"Enough of that jargon," interrupted Hangsby, in fierce accents; "no whining will have any effect upon us, or move us from our purpose. We know you well, and it is not likely, therefore, that we can entertain any feeling of pity or consideration for you."

"Oh, dear!—oh, dear!" again stammered the terrified Timothy Bubble; "this is most cruel. What is your business with me, gentlemen?"

"I presume you can form a pretty shrewd guess," replied the ruffian; "however, in case you should not be able to do so, I will plainly inform you that we have come to ease you of what ready cash you may have in the house: and so, the sooner you deliver it over to me the better."

"Oh, murder! help! thieves!" cried Mr. Bubble, in a voice of the utmost alarm, and still continuing on his knees. Hangsby, however, again presented the pistol at his head, and threatened him with instant death if he persisted in creating any alarm; and that was sufficient to silence him.

"Now, pray, good gentlemen," he at length ventured to say, in a coaxing voice, "do not be rash; consider, I am an old man, and that I am actually as poor as a church mouse; I——"

"Very poor," sneered Brunston, who had fixed his eyes on the chest; "we are well aware of your poverty. However, this chest looks rather suspicious, and we will, therefore, just take the liberty of seeing what it contains."

"Oh, no—no—no!" exclaimed the old man, springing to his feet, and darting towards the chest, which, as we have before said, he had forgotten to relock: "not for the world! You will not be so inquisitive and so cruel!—That chest contains nothing, I assure you, but papers that are useless to any one but myself. Besides, I am full of trouble already: I have been robbed, and lost a law-suit. You surely would not wish to ruin me altogether?"

Brunston and the others, however, paid no heed to his supplications, but raising the lid of the chest, they took from it the money which old Timothy had deposited there only a short time before, and held it up exultingly before his eyes.

"So—so," observed Brunston, with a sarcastic laugh, "these are the papers that are no use to any one but yourself! They are remarkably interesting, notwithstanding, and we will, therefore, just take the liberty of borrowing them for a short time for our inspection."

"Oh, spare me—spare me! on my knees I implore you!" cried the distracted Mr. Bubble; "that is the hard savings of many years' labour and anxiety; it is every farthing that I possess in the world, and if you take that I shall be entirely ruined."

"We pity your case," replied Hangsby, "but I am sorry to think that we cannot comply with your request. Money was never intended to be hoarded up in a chest, just to gratify the eyes of the sordid miser occasionally; and fear not but we shall put it into proper circulation."

"For Heaven's sake, gentlemen," again supplicated the old man, wringing his hands in agony; "if you deprive me of that, I must starve."

"Well, we can't help that," returned Hangsby; "you may think yourself lucky that we do not take your life, and thus send you to the devil before your time. But we cannot stand parleying here with you; I suppose you have nothing else that we can carry away with us, so we will bid you good-night. We shall probably call to see you again before long."

The terrified and distracted Bubble was again about to call aloud for help, but Hangsby, once more placing the pistol to his head, said, in a voice which sufficiently bespoke his determination—

"Hold! unless you are mad, and value your money more than your life; but a word, and I will immediately stretch you a corpse at my feet. But your cries would be useless, for there is no one near at hand to fly to your assistance, and even if there were, of what use would it be for them to attempt to oppose such desperate and determined men as we are? Come, my lads, let us away, and leave this old shark to his own reflections, and to reconcile himself to his loss in the best manner he can."

Timothy fixed upon him a most melancholy and imploring look, but his feelings of anguish and despair were too powerful to suffer him to speak; and the ruffians having bowed to him with mock politeness, retired from the room, locking the door after them, and then making their way from the house with their booty.

It would be impossible to do adequate justice to the feelings of Timothy after they were gone; he remained on his knees the very image of despair, and was unable for a time to give utterance to a syllable; but when he did recover the use of speech, and cast his eyes towards the empty chest from which he had lost so large a sum of money, he shouted aloud for help in the intense agony of his emotions, and exhibited all the appearance of a madman. Then he arose from his knees, and rushing to the door, tried to open it, but finding that it was locked, he called aloud for assistance, and kicked against it with all the violence he could. No one, however, came to his assistance, and he began to think that Matty and his fellow-servant had probably been murdered by the burglars, so that his terror increased to a pitch that was almost beyond endurance. He threw himself on the floor in the most frantic and overwhelming grief and despair, and it was a considerable time before he could restore himself to anything like reason. He then kicked loudly at the door, and shouted at the top of his voice for help; but finding that no one heard him, or if they did they took no heed of him, he hurried to the window, and dashing it up, he renewed his cries for help with redoubled vigour, but with no better results.

"The whole world has conspired against me," said the unfortunate man, and at the same time beating his breast in the utmost agony of feeling; "there is not one of my fellow-creatures will pity or render me the least assistance in the midst of my difficulties; but, on the contrary, I know that they will much rather exult at my misfortunes, particularly that ungrateful rascal, Chicken, and that uncultivated savage, Jack Adams. I am ruined, totally ruined! This is my death blow! I—I shall go mad! But shall the robbers and murderers be permitted to escape with impunity? Will no one come to my assistance? Is everybody dead? Matty!—Deborah! Oh, help—help!"

He now laid hold of the bell and rang it so violently that one would have thought it would almost have been sufficient to arouse the dead, and he at length heard footsteps ascending the stairs, and directly afterwards the voice of Matty at the door inquiring what was the matter.

"The matter!" replied his master; "you lazy knave, why do you not open the door and see what's the matter? I am robbed—ruined—murdered!"

"God bless me!" ejaculated Matty, opening the door and appearing, with old Deborah by his side, in pretty well the same state of dishabille as they had just hurriedly left their bed. "God bless me, master, how you do frighten me, to be sure; how pale you do look, too; any one who beheld you now would verily believe you had seen a ghost!"

"Tell me, rascal," cried Bubble, hastily and impatiently; "have you seen anybody? Have you heard anything?"

"Seen! heard!" stammered forth the astonished and bewildered Matty and Deborah in a breath; "bless you, no! You—you—you must have been dreaming."

"Dreaming! you white livered-looking booby!" said the enraged and distracted Bubble, "if you dare to repeat those observations I will annihilate you! I tell you again the ruffians have been here not many minutes ago; are you not satisfied that I am speaking the truth after finding the door of my chamber locked on the outside? They have plundered me of all the money contained in my iron chest, and——"

"God bless us and save us!" exclaimed Matty, with a look of alarm.

"And," continued his master, with increased emotion, "yet you say that you heard nothing."

"Indeed, master, I have spoken the truth," remarked Matty, "as my friend Deborah, here, can testify."

"There has been some treachery in this," said Bubble; "it must be strictly investigated, and if I discover——"

"Discover what, sir?" interrupted Matty, still more alarmed; "surely you do not suspect me or Deborah with doing anything wrong?"

"How could the thieves have gained an entrance into the house?" demanded Bubble.

"I'm sure I can't imagine; and the thought makes me feel quite nervous," replied his man.

"Were all the outer doors secured before you retired to rest?" inquired Timothy.

"Oh, yes, I am positive that they were, for I and Deborah saw after them the last thing, didn't we, Deborah?"

"Ay, that we did, sure enough," replied the old woman.

"I shall go distracted!" cried poor Bubble, rushing wildly about the room, and tearing his hair; "this is the decision of my fate! I shall never more be able to hold up my head! It is a decided case! What will become of me? Oh, Timothy Bubble—Timothy Bubble, this is the severest blow, the greatest calamity it has ever been your lot to experience."

In this manner he continued to rave during the night, and it was in vain that Matty and old Deborah sought to compose him or to tranquillise his feelings. And as soon as it was daylight, he hastened from the house and made known the particulars of the burglary to the proper authorities, but without much chance of discovering the robbers, they being masked; and in the horror and confusion of the moment, his mind had been so fully occupied, that he was unable to give any description of their persons.

CHAPTER XVII.

MR. BUBBLE'S ABRUPT DEPARTURE.—THE CAROUSAL AT THE TANKARD.

THE news of the burglary at the house of Timothy Bubble soon spread over the neighbourhood, and caused no inconsiderable sensation, though it certainly could not be said that any one pitied him; but it was looked upon by most people as a judgment upon him for the many nefarious transactions in which he had been engaged, and by which he had been enabled to amass all the wealth he was supposed to possess. As for Bubble himself, he continued in the same state of distraction; and shutting himself up in his apartment, would not suffer any one to intrude upon him.

In the meantime, the burglars, in their secret retreat at the old Tankard, exulted over the success of their schemes, and gave themselves up to the most boisterous mirth and extravagant enjoyment, in which none of them played a more willing or active part than Brunston. The booty they had obtained was much greater than they had anticipated; and they could not but congratulate each other on the ability with which they had accomplished their task, and the security in which they were placed from discovery.

"The old rascal will break his heart over this job, I shouldn't wonder," remarked Joe Brunston; "ha! ha! ha! And how little does he suspect that those who have plundered him are such close neighbours of his."

"True," coincided Hangsby, "and it is not very likely that he will be able to discover us; but we must be careful how we act and what we say when we are in strange company; for the least word might betray us, and reveal the secret which we have so long and so successfully kept concealed."

"Ah, there is no fear of our doing that," remarked Brunston; "but we can afford to be merry after the good fortune that has attended us; and I suppose you have no objection to our enjoying ourselves as we like?"

"To be sure not," answered Hangsby; "am I not always one of the first for mirth and conviviality? So fill your glasses: do not stint yourselves of anything; the old Tankard has sufficient to supply your wants, let them be ever so extravagant; and he who flinches, shall be scouted from our community altogether. I will give you the health of Timothy Bubble, Esq., and may he always possess the means of supplying our wants in the same liberal manner that he has done on this occasion."

This rude toast was drunk with loud shouts of laughter and derisive applause; and the carouse had soon reached its highest pitch.

"But," observed Hangsby, suddenly changing the topic of conversation, "you have never yet told us the particulars of your adventure at the cottage of this widow, and which seems to have left so strong an impression upon your mind."

"Ay," answered Brunston, "that was, indeed, an adventure, and I cannot help thinking that it will be productive of something more than I can at present form any conception of."

"It seems, according to your own showing, that you were quite smitten with her?" said Hangsby, with a laugh.

"Well, I must confess that I was," replied Brunston; "and you would not wonder at it if you were once to behold her. Of one thing, however, I am certain, that she is no common individual."

"What, then, do you take her to be?" demanded the ruffian Hangsby, with a laugh; "some princess in disguise, eh?"

"Not exactly," returned the other. "But joking apart, Will, I feel confident that she is not the character she represented herself to be, and I am determined to see her again, if possible,"

"Well, well, I commend you for your determination. But explain all about it."

Brunston did so without hesitation, and they listened to him with the utmost attention and interest.

"And do you think that the person and features of the man who interrupted you are familiar to you?" said Hangsby.

"I do," answered Brunston; "but I have tried in vain to imagine where it is that we have met before. Of one thing, however, I feel positive, that he is not the individual he pretends to be, and that he has some particular motive for thus disguising himself."

"You do not, then, believe the assertions of the so-called widow," said Hangsby, "namely, that this man is her brother?"

"I do not," was the reply; "and I shall not be entirely satisfied until I have by some means or other been enabled to ascertain that fact."

"She said at first it was her husband whom she expected, did she not?"

"She did; and such I believe is the real relationship in which they stand to each other. Ah! a sudden thought now strikes me, which it is most extraordinary did not occur to me before. Surely the features of this man—this pretended rustic, bore a most extraordinary resemblance to those of Richard Parker; his figure corresponded, too, with his in every respect, and their ages would be about the same."

"Ah!" exclaimed Hangsby, "should that supposition turn out to be correct, and there is nothing improbable in it— the female who calls him her brother, too—she has a boy, you say?"

"True," answered Brunston.

"That makes the coincidence still more striking," remarked Hangsby. "We must see further into this business, Brunston; and yet, should they prove to be the fugitives, I should not like to lend a hand towards their apprehension."

"Why should you hesitate, Hangsby?"

"Because I believe that Parker is deserving of a better fate than that which inevitably awaits him if he should be discovered."

"But the reward, man—you must forget that."

"Yes, it is tempting, certainly," returned Hangsby; "but we will talk about this another time—this night is devoted to mirth and harmony; so push the grog about, my lads, and let us send all other thoughts to the devil!"

The ruffians required no further urging to induce them to comply with this invitation, and the rude entertainment was kept up with much spirit until the morning, when they separated.

But the villain Brunston found it impossible to banish from his mind the impression which had taken possession of it, namely, that the features of the man whom he had seen at the cottage bore a most remarkable likeness to those of our hero, notwithstanding his rustic garb, and that the colour of the hair was different to that of Richard's; and he determined to devise some means, and that as quickly as possible, of satisfying himself upon that important subject.

"There is no time to be lost," he said, when he was alone, "for should my conjectures really turn out to be true, they will probably not remain in any place long together, and should they depart ere I can obtain the information I am so anxious about, they would most likely escape altogether. But should my surmises prove to be right, the reward will be mine, and I must make an abrupt exit from this country, which is already almost too hot to hold me. People may talk about scruples of conscience—such things do not often trouble me; and if it be his fate to swing from the yardarm, why, it is no fault of mine; so I might as well earn the money for his detection as anybody else. However, I am afraid that there is no such luck for me."

In this manner the hardened ruffian endeavoured to argue with himself, and he found no difficulty, the reader may be sure, in forming a resolution in his own mind, and which he was fully capable of accomplishing.

Several days elapsed after the burglary, and Mr. Bubble had kept himself almost entirely confined to his own residence, and had been seldom seen by any one; and it was quite clear that the losses he had sustained, so suddenly and in so unexpected a manner, had made an impression upon the narrow and sordid mind of the little man, which he was not very likely soon to get rid of. The astonishment, however, of the inhabitants, when they found that the house had been privately sold, and that Mr. Timothy Bubble had secretly and abruptly quitted the neighbourhood, and had gone no one knew whither, was very great. But as he was held in such universal contempt, it was not at all likely that any person would take the trouble to inquire.

Having stated these few particulars, which were necessary to the better development of our tale, we will now return to our hero and his wife, whom we left filled with no inconsiderable portion of alarm, after the daring outrage committed by the miscreant Brunston, and the untimely death of that singular old woman, Rachael Melford. It was some days before they could recover themselves, and Richard, as may be expected, fell in a constant state of dread and suspense during the time he was compelled to be absent from the beloved partner of his misfortunes, his cares, and anxieties. But whenever they met, Mary exerted herself as much as possible to conceal her own feelings, and endeavoured to dissipate the fears that had taken possession of his imagination, and to try to impress him with the idea that, after the murder of Rachael, they need not be under any apprehension that the ruffian Brunston would again venture into the neighbourhood; and, indeed, it did not seem likely that he could entertain any further designs against them.

"I know not, my dear Mary," her husband would reply, "I have repeatedly said that the fellow's features are quite familiar to me, and should he happen to know us, you need not to be told that we should not be safe here one minute from another."

"Nay, Richard," urged our heroine, "do not give way to such ideas, for I think they are most improbable. Had this man have known us, and recognised us under our present disguises, he would have adopted a different course to that which he did. You must have been mistaken in supposing that you have seen him before."

"I would willingly persuade myself that I had if I could," answered Richard; "but I cannot; and the longer I reflect on it the more I am convinced that I am not mistaken in my conjectures."

"And you cannot form any idea where you may have been likely to have seen him?" said our heroine.

"I cannot," replied her husband; "I have been racking my brain in order that I might try to do so, but to no purpose."

"It is strange," remarked Mary; "but dismiss it from your thoughts, I say again."

"That is easier advised than accomplished," remarked Richard. He paused, and pressing his hand upon his forehead as if to endeavour to recall his thoughts, he paced the room to and fro for a few minutes, without giving utterance to a word; but suddenly stopping, and evincing the most powerful and uncontrolable emotion, he cried:

"Ah! what strange idea is this that flashes across my brain? Can it be? My heart recoils with disgust and horror at the thought, and—"

"For Heaven's sake, Richard," interrupted the agitated Mary, "what mean you? You speak in problems—

WILL LANGLEY WELCOMING JOE BRUNSTON TO THE TANKARD.

the strong emotion you also betray— Oh, do not keep me in suspense."

"The more I reflect, the stronger becomes my conviction," replied her husband. "Mary, my beloved, but unfortunate wife, whom do you suppose I take the miscreant who has created all this anguish and alarm in our bosoms to be?"

"Speak! tell me!" said our heroine,

anxiously and impatiently; "the words you have already spoken, and the agitation under which you labour, does but serve to increase my apprehension. Whom do you take the villain to be?"

"No other than the wretch through whom I first suffered shame and degradation" answered Richard Parker, in a hoarse voice; "he for whose crime I was scourged like a dog, and stigmatized, calumniated with the name of thief!"

"Oh, God!" exclaimed Mary, clasping her hands vehemently together; "can it be possible?"

"Yes, yes," remarked our hero; "I now feel satisfied that it is true; and that we have everything to fear from him, should he ever more cross our path. Oh, what feelings of horror does the recollection of that man engender in my bosom, whilst the purple current of life seems to be frozen within my veins. It must be he; no other man could possess his villanous features."

"How extraordinary is this!" said Mary. "But if it be indeed he, by what strange and fatal accident should he have been guided to this neighbourhood; and whither could he have been all these years?"

"I know not," replied Richard; "but I had hoped that the black-hearted scoundrel was either no more, or that he would never again torture me with his presence. All the horrors of the past now crowd upon my burning brain, and drive me to despair and madness. Once more I feel the galling and degrading lash; and I hate, I loathe, I despise myself!—Nay, Mary, fix not upon me such looks of affection and sympathy, for I feel myself to be unworthy of you, and wish that I were dead."

"Hold! Richard! husband!" cried our heroine; "talk not thus wildly, nor heap such bitter and unmerited reproaches on your head; after all, you may be mistaken as to the identity of this man, and even should it indeed be the villain whom you suspect, it is quite evident that he did not recognise us, and, therefore, that we have nothing more to fear from him. Be calm, and be upon your guard, lest in one inadvertent moment you should betray yourself, and thus frustrate all the excellent designs of our benevolent friends to serve us"

Richard returned no immediate answer, and folding his arms across his chest, he traversed the room for a few seconds, and seemed to be communing with his own painful thoughts. At length he said—

"'Tis all to no purpose. I cannot dismiss the torturing truth from my mind, and, therefore, how is it possible that I can keep entertaining anything but the most gloomy apprehensions? And then the terrors of the past!—how vividly does that villain recal them to my memory! They are all presented once more as distinctly to my imagination as if they had only taken place yesterday, and my heart is ready to break with the power of my emotions. God of Heaven! what a miserable, what a hopeless and despicable wretch am I."

Mary threw her arms around his neck, and fixing upon him one of her tenderest looks of mingled pity and supplication, she burst into tears, and was unable to speak a word.

"What a villain am I!" cried her husband with much emotion; "what a heartless wretch, thus to grieve and torture this gentle bosom. Can you forgive me, Mary, for words that are prompted only by the agony of despair?"

"Forgive you, Richard?" she replied, faintly smiling through her tears. "Oh, how sincerely, how fervently! if you will but endeavour to banish these dismal thoughts from your breast, and to seek to look forward to the future with hope, and firm reliance on the goodness of Providence."

"I will do so," said Richard; "and for your sweet sake, my beloved wife, I sincerely pray that I may not be doomed to disappointment."

They were now interrupted by the entrance of Mr. Worthington and Binnacle, who, being informed of the particulars of the conversation which had just taken place between our heroine and her husband, also added their arguments to hers to endeavour to banish from his brain the dismal forebodings that crowded upon it, and also to tranquillise his feelings, and was more successful than might at first have been expected.

"As Mrs. Parker has said," observed Mr. Worthington, "even should this man prove to be he whom you suspect, it seems quite certain that he did no recog nise you, as I do not see how it is possible he should have done, and, consequently, you have nothing to fear from him. It is not likely that one who has committed murder should venture again into the neighbourhood of his crime, and where his own destruction would be sure to follow."

"You are right, Master Worthington," coincided Binnacle, "and I only wish that our friend Parker, here, could contrive to get the weather-guage of fear and melancholy, and my word for it, he would soon find himself sailing with a favouring breeze towards the port of content and happiness."

"I thank you, my friends, for your excellent advice, and the kind solicitude which you feel in my fate," replied our hero; but it is not likely that I can reflect upon all the horrors and sufferings which the sight of that man recals to my memory, without experiencing the deepest emotion! Oh, no, by Heaven——"

"Richard," interrupted his wife, "I entreat you to forbear; did you not but just now promise me that you would not again mention those torturing facts, but try to look forward with calmness and hope to the future?"

"True, my love," he answered; "and difficult though the tssk will be to accomplish, for your sake I will persevere, and exert myself to the utmost to conquer my own feelings."

"Well said, Mr. Parker," returned Ben; "there is nothing like putting a bold heart upon the matter, and there is scarcely anything that we cannot accomplish."

They now changed the conversation, and continued together for some time longer, when Binnacle was compelled to take his leave.

CHAPTER XVIII.

MORE CAUSE OF ALARM.—AN UNEXPECTED VISITOR.—THE RECOGNITION.
—THE PRESS-GANG, AND MR. BUBBLE.

NOTHING of any particular importance occurred for two or three days, and Richard Parker, by the arguments and persuasions of his wife and Mr. Worthington, had become comparatively calm and tranquil, though he could not,

in secret, help entertaining the same dismal thoughts as regarded the reappearance of the villain Brunston (for he felt confident it was Brunston he had encountered at the cottage), and something seemed to whisper to him that he was yet destined to experience some dreadful calamity, through his guilty machinations.

Ben Binnacle had once more been compelled to take his departure from the neighbourhood, and our hero had forwarded to him a lengthy letter, in which he again expressed his gratitude for the unbounded kindness he had experienced from him, and he likewise expressed a hope that they should at some future time meet again, and that under far different and favourable circumstances than those by which they were surrounded.

Although he thus wrote, he could not entertain or encourage such hopes; for it would have been madness for him ever to expect to receive forgiveness from the offended laws of his country, and the only chance of his being able to avoid the ignominious fate that impended o'er his head, was, he considered, if he could succeed in escaping to some foreign country altogether, where he might continue to reside, in all probability, unknown. But even if he could accomplish this, in what manner was he to support himself and those who were so dear to him afterwards? His manly feelings of pride and independence revolted from the idea of continuing under a weight of obligation from those who had already lavished upon him so many favours; and as these reflections arose to his mind, he again could not help giving himself up to the most abject despair.

Matters went on much the same at the inn; it was seldom visited by strangers, and our hero was now quite at home with all the customers, and was a great favourite with them, especially Mr. Ladbroke, who would have done anything he could to serve him, and, of course, he could never for a moment entertain a suspicion of his real character.

One evening, as usual, Mr. Ladbroke and his friends were seated in the snug kitchen of the old Punch Bowl, when the former, having been talking about various matters in a garrulous way, suddenly observed—

"I hope, Master Worthington, that you will not be honoured by a visit from certain parties, who, I understand, are at present in the neighbourhood, for I should imagine you would be rather inclined to think their room more welcome than their company."

"Indeed," said the host; "to what parties do you allude, then? for there are very few persons who would not receive a hearty welcome at the Punch Bowl."

"Why," returned Ladbroke, "there are two or three pressgangs in the town, and several of the sons of our neighbours have already been forced from their homes."

"Pressgangs!" repeated our hero, starting, and turning pale.

"Yes," answered Stephen; "but, bless my soul, how agitated you seem to be, Martin; you are not afraid of falling into their clutches, are you?"

"Why, as for that matter," remarked Mr. Worthington, "my nephew is, I think, just the sort of man that would suit them; but it will be strange to me indeed if they have him; that's all I've got to say upon the subject. The system I consider to be a most cruel one, and that it should be resisted by every means in our power."

"True, friend Worthington," said Ladbroke, "I perfectly agree with you there; how can they expect men to make good seamen who are forcibly torn from their friends and home? As for the fellows who form the pressgangs, it is well known that they are composed of the very dregs of society; desperate ruffians, who are prepared for anything, however desperate. It would not do for them to be possessed of very sensitive natures. But, as you observe, I hope they will not favour me with a visit, for it would be anything but welcome."

The conversation here dropped, but our hero, as may be imagined, felt far from easy upon the subject, and when Stephen and the others were gone, he could not help expressing his feelings to Worthington, and acknowledging that the circumstance of the pressgangs being in the neighbourhood caused him considerable apprehension.

"Well," observed Worthington, "I should have been much more satisfied myself, had they remained away; but still I do not think that you have anything to fear; and should the fellows take it into their heads to pay a visit here, why, all that you've got to do, is to keep out of their sight as much as possible. It is not likely that any one should know you in your present disguise, even though they should have happened to be intimately acquainted with your features and person before."

"I trust not," said Richard; "but I hope, nevertheless, that they will not come here, and that I may not encounter them; for such a circumstance is fraught with considerable danger, and might be productive of the most fatal consequences."

Richard Parker said no more upon the subject, but he could not exactly reconcile it to his own mind, and he was determined to use the utmost precaution; but something was about to occur which was calculated to alarm and astonish him more than all.

It had been a gloomy, lowry day, and as evening advanced, the storm which had so long threatened commenced in a manner that seemed to promise to last long and violently.

Mr. Worthington and his good dame were seated by the blazing fire in their comfortable parlour, our hero being occupied in some other part of the house, when they were aroused from the conversation in which they had been indulging by the voice of a stranger, and going into the adjoining room, they beheld two individuals of rather an eccentric appearance, and who seemed to have travelled some distance in the rain, for they were drenched to the skin.

"Have you pretty good accommodation here, Mr. Landlord, for a gentleman?" asked one of the travellers, who appeared to be the master, for the other was a clownish looking man, who was habited in a suit that bore some resemblance to livery, and who carried a portmanteau on his shoulder.

"Good accommodation, sir?" replied the worthy host; "ay, that have I. I'll warrant there is no better to be found in any part of the country."

"You will pardon me, sir," said the

stranger, "if I should appear to be inquisitive, but have you many customers to this house?"

"Why, no," answered Worthington, "I can't say that I am much overburdened with business in that respect, and what customers I have are very select."

"I am glad of that," remarked the traveller; "for I wish so be as private as possible while I remain at your house. Do you know that I have a remarkable dread of robbers?—a dread that I have had good reason to give way to latterly."

"Indeed?" said Worthington, "I am sorry to hear that."

"Ah!" sighed the stranger, "I have been a terrible sufferer, and the only thing which surprises me is that I am able to support it with the fortitude I do."

"Well, sir," returned Worthington, "I can assure you that you will have nothing to fear while you remain here. But I will show your attendant into another room, if you please, and perhaps you will require some refreshments, sir?"

"Oh, certainly," he answered. "In the first place let me have a stiff glass of brandy-and-water, as hot as you can make it, for I am wet to the skin, and a nice hot supper of the best you have in the house, for I am as hungry as a hunter. But I must not forget my faithful man. I say, landlord, suppose you give him a pint of ale and some bread and cheese and onions."

Worthington nodded assent, and beckoning the man to follow him, and having seen his master seat himself comfortably by the fireside, he left the room. On his return, Richard accompanied him, but no sooner had he fixed his eyes upon the figure and countenance of the traveller, than he started back with confusion, astonishment, and alarm, when he recognised the features of his old enemy, Mr. Timothy Bubble.

So great was his agitation, that he could not help betraying it, and Mr. Worthington, who, of course was ignorant of the cause, looked surprised; but at the same time he was satisfied that it was something particular that excited him in so remarkable a manner, and by a significant glance he enjoined him to compose himself and to act with that due precaution which might be necessary under the circumstances. Our hero, however, wished that he had never entered the room, especially when he observed the small but penetrating eyes of Mr. Timothy Bubble fixed inquiringly upon him.

"Good evening, young man," he remarked at last; "you look timid and confused; but never mind me, bless your soul, I am a gentleman without the least pride, so do not suffer my presence to awe you."

"You are very kind and condescending, sir," remarked Worthington; "this is my nephew, and you will find him civil and obliging, though he is a little retiring in his habits."

"Oh, I see," returned Timothy, again eyeing Richard narrowly; "rather rustic, eh?—Ah, well, he is none the worse for that; I like modest and unassuming people; I am very modest and unassuming myself. But, dear me!—surely I have had the pleasure of seeing this young man before."

Richard was more alarmed than ever, and could not help starting and changing colour as he stammered out:

"Seen me before, sir? Oh dear, no; you must be mistaken; I do not remember ever to have had that honour."

"Well, well," observed Bubble, "perhaps I am mistaken; and yet it is very singular, very singular indeed; your features are quite familiar to me, and the longer I look at you, the stronger becomes the impression on my mind. I would not appear to be inquisitive, but pray has this young man resided long in this part of the country?"

"Not many weeks," answered Mr. Worthington, who felt vexed and uneasy at the questions which his guest put to him; "I sent for him from his native place, Maidstone, to assist me in my business."

"Ah, humph!" said the inquisitive Mr. Bubble, thoughtfully; "but really, now, the longer I look at him, the familiarity of his features becomes more striking."

"Well," observed our hero, in as composed a tone as he could assume, "it is remarkable, certainly, but I have not the least recollection of you, sir; you must be labouring under a wrong impression. Do you require my attendance here, uncle?"

"No, Martin, you may retire," replied Worthington, shrewdly guessing the motives that rendered him so anxious to do so, and heartily wishing that his guest had never entered his house. Richard bowed, and retired from the room; Mr. Bubble still following him with his eyes, and appearing to be far from satisfied.

When our hero had gained his own private room, he gave free indulgence to the agitation of his feelings, and could not but encourage the most powerful apprehensions of the danger by which he was surrounded.

"A fatal spell seems to rest upon me," he said; "what cursed ill-fortune has guided the footsteps of that dangerous man to this place? Should he be able to recal my features to his recollection, I am lost. What is to be done in this painful and terrible emergency? It is no use trying to avoid my fate; I see it as plainly before me as if it were reflected in a mirror. The predictions of that mysterious woman, old Rachael, will be realised, and the future misery of my unfortunate wife and child is inevitable. Alas, alas! Richard Parker, why did cruel destiny ever introduce you to one so innocent and so worthy of a different fate? It is no longer safe for me to remain here, but whither can I fly? where conceal myself? I am bewildered and distracted."

He beat his forehead, and for some time he continued to pace the room in the most disordered manner.

In the meantime Mr. Worthington remained in the room with his guest to attend upon him, and Timothy Bubble did full justice to the ample provisions that had been supplied to him, conversing freely all the time.

"This is rather a retired spot," he remarked, "but the accommodation is excellent, and I do not know but that I may be induced to stop here for a day or two."

"You do me great honour, sir," returned the landlord, though, after the agitation which our hero had evinced, he was far from thinking what he said

"Oh, not at all," observed Bubble, "not at all; I have been very unfortunate of late, and I have scarcely made up my mind where I shall fix my future residence. This is a sinful world, sir, and there is very little luck for the really honest man."

"Very true, sir," replied Worthington.

"Ah!" added Bubble, "I have lately experienced the truth of that to my cost. Everything has gone wrong with me; I have been half ruined by the law, and plundered into the bargain."

"I am sorry to hear that, sir," said Worthington.

"Ah," remarked Timothy, with a sigh, "it is a sad thing; but it is no use lamenting it. However, I cannot help thinking of your nephew; his features are so familiar to me, I repeat, as if I had been acquainted with him for years. Ah! now I have it!" he added after a momentary pause, during which he seemed to be endeavouring to recal something to his memory; "but there is no such luck for me, or it would make up in some measure for the loss I have sustained; how foolish I must have been not to have thought of that before. What an extraordinary resemblance, to be sure!"

"To whom, pray?" demanded Worthington, eagerly, though with as much composure in his demeanour as possible.

"Why, to Richard Parker," answered Bubble.

"What, Richard Parker, or Admiral Parker, as he is commonly called, the mutineer, about whom there is so much talk at present?" interrogated Mr. Worthington, who could with difficulty conceal the agitation into which the observations of his guest had naturally thrown him.

"The same," answered Bubble.

"Nonsense," remarked Worthington, with an assumed laugh, "what a singular idea to compare my rustic nephew to a weatherbeaten seaman."

"You may think so," returned Bubble, "but I am not often led away by the force of my imagination, and I mean to say that if your nephew was dressed in seaman's clothes, I could almost swear that Richard Parker stood before me"

"Ha! ha! ha!" laughed Worthington, with difficulty repressing his alarm; "pardon me, my good sir, but I cannot help thinking that such an idea is rather extravagant and preposterous."

"It may be so in your opinion, sir," observed Bubble, "but it is not in mine. There is no knowing what disguise Parker has assumed with the hope of concealing himself from detection; and he is just as likely to take that of a peasant as any other. I still maintain that the likeness is a most extraordinary one."

"Well that may be," replied Worthington, "and there is no accounting for it; but there is not much chance of finding Richard Parker here, I should imagine."

"I wish there was," returned Timothy. "You know there is a large reward offered for his apprehension, and it would be no bad thing for you and I, Mr. Landlord, to share it between us— Eh?"

"Why, for the matter of that," replied Worthington, "I am quite contented with the little money I have managed to accumulate by honest industry, and I have no wish to add to my fortune by any such means as that."

"You seem to be a most particular man, my worthy friend," observed Bubble; "but, to tell the truth, I must confess that I entertain no such delicate scruples as those you have expressed."

"You seem to know this Richard Parker, then?" said Worthington.

"Know him?" repeated Bubble. "Ay, well; and as I am an honest man, I must say that I think he fully merits the fate that is in store for him, should he be apprehended, which I have very little doubt that he will be some time or the other, and, perhaps, sooner than he expects."

"Well," returned Mr. Worthington, "I do not pretend to know much about the business, so I do not feel any interest in it; still, I trust that I am charitable enough to view the errors of my fellow-creatures with mercy. If every man had his deserts, there would not be so many rascals in the world as there are at present."

Mr. Bubble rather winced under these observations; but concealing his real thoughts and feelings as well as he could, he said—

"That's very true, my friend; and for my own part, it quite shocks me when I think of the depravity of the world. But I have been travelling some distance, and feel rather tired; I will, therefore, trouble you to show me to my chamber."

"Certainly, sir," answered Worthington, taking up the light; "this way, if you please."

Bubble bowed very politely, and following the landlord out of the room, was conducted to his chamber, where Worthington, having bid him good-night, left him. Mr. Bubble, however, sat himself down after he was alone, and ruminated.

"I am not altogether satisfied," he muttered to himself; "there is something superior in the manner of this nephew of the landlord's, notwithstanding his rustic dress; and then the very extraordinary resemblance which his features bear to Parker; he seemed to be about the same age, too; and I could not help noticing that he seemed quite confused when he saw me. I must have something more to say to him before I leave here, and examine him more narrowly. What a remarkable thing it would be if I should be destined to discover Richard Parker; and I don't know how it is, but a strange notion runs in my head that I shall do so. I only wish that I may not be disappointed; but it shall be from no want of exertion or ingenuity on my part if I am. They may talk about pity and mercy if they like, but that is all nonsense; is he not a murderer and an assassin?—And what pity or mercy does he deserve? Such weak and childish notions, thanks to his good sense, never enter the breast of Timothy Bubble. He has a mind that soars above all such folly."

Having indulged in reflections such as these for some time longer, the worthy gentleman sought his pillow, and was soon wrapt in the arms of Morpheus.

Mr. Worthington, after having seen Bubble to his chamber, hastened to the apartment of our hero, whom he found in a state of the greatest excitement, and traversing the room with disordered steps.

"Mr. Worthington," he said, fervently grasping his hand, "fresh danger stares me in the face, and I fear there are no means of avoiding it;

what terrible misfortune could have directed the footsteps of that man here?"

"Be calm, my unfortunate friend," said Worthington, "and all may yet terminate much better than your fears now anticipate. You know him, then?"

"Know him!" repeated Richard; "alas! too well. He is the very man of whom you have heard me speak so often; one of my worst enemies, though I never gave him any cause for offence; it was he who betrayed me, and led to the death of the villain Arlington."

"What, the man, Bubble?" asked Mr. Worthington.

"The same," answered our hero.

"The rascal," exclaimed Worthington; "now should I feel a pleasure in clipping off his ears, or drowning him in the nearest horsepond."

"It is evident from his observations, and the manner in which he scrutinised me, that he had a strong recollection of me, in spite of my disguise," said Richard. "What conversation passed between you after I quitted the room?"

Mr. Worthington informed him, and his agitation increased.

"It is no more than I expected," he said; "should he again see me he will put such questions to me that I shall be unable to answer without at once betraying myself."

"Do not give way to any unnecessary alarm," returned Mr. Worthington; "such an opportunity must not be afforded him; you must keep out of his sight while he remains here, which I do not suppose he will do long; and should he be inquisitive, I can easily invent some story or the other to satisfy him that business of a particular nature has compelled you to leave the inn for a few days."

"Alas!" replied our hero, "I fear his suspicions are too strongly excited to be thus easily quieted. I see no alternative but immediate flight."

"Nonsense, Parker," ejaculated the old man; "why will you suffer your fears to obtain such a strong hold of you? Wither would you go? Would you now abandon me, after the deep interest which I take in your fate?"

"It is the danger in which I may involve you, my kind and excellent friend," said Richard, "that urges me on. Why should I, who am almost a stranger to you, thus avail myself of your generosity, when, should it be discovered that you have connived at my escape, it would plunge you into inevitable destruction?"

"Fear not, Richard," answered the old man; "Providence will protect me, and assist me in my good intentions. Wait patiently till to-morrow, and all will yet be well."

Richard was about to return an answer, when he was prevented from doing so by hearing a confused noise from below stairs, and he started and looked more alarmed than he had done before; and that was strengthened, when the voices of several men speaking in loud and coarse accents saluted his ears.

"Fear not," remarked Mr. Worthington, "they are only travellers, I dare say; though it is rather a late hour of the night. Should any danger, however, threaten, you will know where to conceal yourself, and, as you have proved before, you will have no reason to apprehend discovery. I will ease your doubts as soon as I can."

"Some fresh danger threatens, I am afraid," said our hero; "would to Heaven that I was with my beloved Mary and my poor boy, that I might be convinced they were in safety. But why this cowardly feeling? Am I not a man and a sailor? and shall I coward-like shrink from danger? No, let me boldly face it; for nothing can be half so torturing as this terrible state of suspense."

"Hold, Richard!" exclaimed Worthington, "are you mad? Why will you thus persist in anticipating danger? I will return to you in a few minutes, and I have then no doubt that I shall be able to quiet your apprehension."

He then quitted the room, and left our hero in the greatest impatience and anxiety of mind. He listened at the door, and he heard the coarse voice of several men as if in noisy altercation; and several oaths to which they gave utterance, gave him no very good opinion of the respectability of their characters; but he could not understand the nature of their conversation distinctly. At length he heard some person ascending the stairs, and closing the door cautiously and silently, he prepared to rush to the secret panel in order to conceal himself, when he was arrested in his intention by hearing the voice of Mrs. Worthington at the door of the room, and he immediately opened it.

"How, now, my good dame," he demanded, breathlessly, "what is the matter? You look alarmed and agitated."

"The press-gang," faltered out the old woman in a faint voice.

"Ah!" ejaculated Richard, "the press-gang, say you?"

MR. BUBBLE AND MATTY ESCAPING FROM THE INN.

"Yes," she answered, "the ruffians are below, and are determined to search the house. Quick, conceal yourself!"

Richard made use of no observation, but immediately hurried to the secret door, entered, and closed it after him, and then awaited the result in the most breathless suspense.

In the meantime, while this was going forward, Mr. Bubble, who was aroused from his sleep by the noise which prevailed below, and supposing that there were thieves in the house, or that the premises were on fire, jumped out of bed in a state of the greatest alarm, and hastily throwing on his clothes in the best manner he could, was considering in which way he should make his escape, when his chamber door was forced open, and the men who composed the press-gang entered the room, followed by Mr. Worthington, and much to the consternation of poor Nr. Bubble, who, imagining they were robbers, sank on his knees, and in piteous accents sued for mercy.

"Get up, you swab!" said one of the fellows, "and let's look at your figurehead. Ha! ha! ha! here's a pretty specimen of a man! What a capital powder-monkey he would make, to be sure! Shall we send him on board, comrades?"

"Oh, no, no, no, not for the word, good gentlemen," supplicated the terrified Mr. Bubble. "I—I—I am only a poor devil who would not be the slightest use to you. Besides, I am an old man, and——"

"Old?" interrupted another of the gang, with an oath; "well, what if you are? You are tough, and will do as well as the best man in the fleet to be shot at."

"Surely, surely, gentlemen," cried Timothy, in a voice half stifled with fear, "you do not intend to go to such terrible extremities? There is a young man in the house who will just suit you—the landlord's nephew, as he is called; but his real name is Richard Parker, or I never saw two faces more alike."

"Richard Parker!" cried the whole of the men in a breath, and looking earnestly and impatiently at Worthington.

"Nonsense!" said the latter, with as much calmness and fortitude as he could assume; "you surely do not take any notice of what this foolish man says? Is it at all likely that I would venture to conceal Richard Parker here? It was my nephew that he saw, and he left the house a short time afterwards upon business, and I do not expect him to return for a few days."

"Don't believe him, gentlemen," said Mr. Bubble; "the man he calls his nephew is as much like Parker, whom I know well, as two peas in a pod, and I firmly believe that it is him in disguise."

"If it should indeed be true what this lubber says," observed one of the men, 'it will be a good night's work for us. At any rate, we must search your house, old gentleman."

"That you are quite welcome to do," said Worthington; "and I am fully prepared to abide by the consequences should you find that this gentleman has spoken the truth; but he must be mad, or else he has been dreaming.,'

"It will be a good job for you if he should prove to be so," said the captain of the gang; "but come, my lads, let's to business; and as for you, if you have deceived us, we will give you good cause to repent it."

"Th—th—thank you, gentlemen," stammered out the bewildered Mr. Bubble, and the men then departed from the room, followed by Mr. Worthington.

When Bubble was satisfied that the coast was clear, he fumbled his way down the stairs, and finding Matty, who had hid himself in a sly corner, and having secured his portmanteau, they silently quitted the house, and, in spite of the time of night, made their way from the spot as fast as they could.

In the meantime the men strictly examined every room, without meeting with anything to gratify their curiosity, and at last they entered the apartment of our hero, who stood within-side the secret door, and listened to all that took place in the most breathless trepidation.

"Well, there is nobody here, at any rate," remarked one of the gang; "neither Richard Parker nor anybody else."

"There is not, gentlemen," replied Mr. Worthington; "and as you have now examined every part of my premises, I hope you are satisfied?"

"Yes," answered the man, "that swab has deceived us, and we will reward him for it as he deserves. Come, my lads, we must see to this; then we will just trouble the landlord for a glass or two of grog, and depart."

"You are welcome to the best my house contains," remarked Worthington, "and, of course, after what you have seen, you will think no more of what that old man has said?"

"Oh, no," answered the man; "we have seen quite enough to satisfy us that he has either attempted to deceive us, or that he was drunk or mad. But lead the way, landlord, and let us test the quality of your grog, for our time is limited."

"This way, gentlemen," said Worthington, and they immediately followed him out of the room, and our hero, much to his relief, heard them descend the stairs, and he then once more ventured from the place of his concealment. But his mind was still far from being easy. Mr. Bubble was still in the house, and the assertion he had made fully convinced him of the danger he had to apprehend from him, and to lead him to imagine that he would yet take the earliest opportunity of making his suspicions known to the authorities, who would be sure to institute a rigid investigation of the truth or erroneousness of his information, which might lead to his apprehension. The easy manner in which Bubble had recognised him, destroyed his confidence in the success of the disguise he had assumed, and consequently convinced him of the imminent danger by which he was surrounded.

"How unfortunate it is," he said to himself, "that accident should have guided that officious and dangerous man hither, or that he should, at any rate, have seen me. I know his character too well to suppose that he will fail to betray me into the hands of justice, should he have the opportunity to do so, if it were only with the hope of obtaining the reward, as well as to gratify those vindictive feelings which from some unaccountable cause he has ever evinced towards me, and, therefore, I am not safe one moment from another, but——"

He was interrupted by hearing a noise from below, and going to the window, he was gratified to behold the press-gang depart from the inn, and they were soon hidden from the sight in the darkness of the night.

"Thank God for that," said Richard, fervently; "but, oh, what scenes of the past, what bitter scenes of misery does the sight of those men recall to my memory, and with what dismal forebodings of the future, that is in store for me, does it fill my breast. Well do I now remember that fatal evening, when I and my beloved Mary were residing in humble, but contented poverty, soon after our marriage, that the cruel press-gang tore me remorselessly from her arms, from my poor, but happy home—from all that was precious to me, and dragged me on board the vessel, commanded by my most deadly and implacable enemy, Captain Arlington, to endure such wrongs, such cruelties, and degradations as make the heart shudder to think of them. That was the forerunner of all my troubles. God of Heaven! how could I ever find fortitude to support such manifold and unparalleled horrors as it has been my hard lot to encounter? Why did I not die an honourable death in the service of my country? It would have been a mercy to me; and my Mary, though I know it would have been impossible for her ever to banish me from her memory, would have learnt to resign herself to my fate, and might haply now have been the wife of one who, though he could not possibly love her with that intensity of feeling that I do, would

have done all in his power to render her happy and contented, and to have protected her from the cares and injustice of the world."

He paused, overcome by the anguish of his feelings, and at that moment he heard a footstep ascending the stairs, and directly afterwards Mr. Worthington entered the room. Richard hastily grasped his hand, as he ejaculated:—

"Ah, my excellent friend, what a night of anxiety and suspense has this been! But I see plainly that it is useless to struggle with my fate, and, therefore——"

"Talk not thus, Mr. Parker," interrupted Worthington; "for it is useless, and only torturing yourself to no purpose; the men are gone, and you are safe."

"But that fellow, Bubble?" said our hero, eagerly.

"On our entering his chamber, we found that he had also abruptly made his exit," answered Mr. Worthington

"Then," observed Parker, "I have everything to apprehend. Could he have been secured, some means might have been contrived to enforce his silence; but as it is, he will doubtless lose no time in making the discovery he imagines he has made known to the authorities, and such steps may be taken as will render my escape impossible. We must part, my good friend; I see that there is not a moment to be lost! I must immediately to my poor Mary and my boy, and then take to instant flight!"

"Rash man!" exclaimed Worthington, "know you what you say? Whither would you fly? Where can you be more safe than here? Come, come, you must not give way to this excessive agitation. Besides if even this man should denounce you, who do you think would believe his extravagant tale?"

"I would fain think as you suggest, Mr. Worthington," said our hero, "but when I recollect the eagerness of my enemies for my apprehension, and how much they thirst for my blood, I cannot do so. They will not neglect any opportunity that may occur to discover me."

"It will be impossible for them to do so while you remain here concealed," replied Worthington.

"But it will be impossible for me to continue to act the part I have assumed," observed Richard "and appear openly at the inn as your nephew; for should this man inform against me, and revisit the inn, accompanied by the officers, I shall be at once detected, and all hope of escape will then be at an end."

"We will devise some means to prevent

that," returned Worthington; "but rest yourself contented; remain here to-night, and—"

"Oh, no, that is impossible," interrupted our hero; "consider the dreadful state of suspense that my beloved Mary will already be in at my prolonged absence; I must immediately away to her, be the consequences whatever they may."

"But should you encounter any one on the road?" suggested Mr. Worthingtrn.

"I must, I will run every risk," said our hero; "the distance is not great, and a very few minutes will bring me to the cottage."

"Would that I could persuade you to remain here," said Mr. Worthington, "and I will go myself to the cottage and apprise your wife of what has taken place, and of your safety."

"No, no," returned Richard, impatiently' "nothing will satisfy me unless I see her myself, and consult with her upon what is best to be done in the midst of our difficulties; so do not detain me, my kind friend, for every moment of delay appears to me an age."

"Well," replied Worthington, pressing his hand, "I will offer no further opposition to your wishes; but I would much rather you would do as I desire; I do not know how it is, but a melancholy feeling has within the last few minutes come over me, that something is this night about to happen to me, and——"

"Heaven forbid!" interrupted Richard, fervently. "But come, my dear friend, you must banish such gloomy ideas as these. What should happen to you, unless it be some danger that threatens you for the part you nave taken in my escape?"

"No, Parker," said the old man, "believe me I do not apprehend anything of the kind. But enough of this: perhaps it is only a weakness after all. You will return, as usual, at an early hour in the morning?"

"Should nothing occur to prevent it, you may depend upon me," answered our hero, who noticed with regret the melancholy expression of Mr. Worthington's countenance, and was at a loss to account for it. "But should it be ordained," he added, after a pause, "that we should never meet again, may the choicest blessings of Heaven descend upon your head, and that of your amiable wife, for all the manifold and disinterested kindnesses you have bestowed upon myself and those so dear to me. Good night, my amiable, my esteemed friend and protector."

Mr. Worthington returned the pressure of his hand with equal warmth and sincerity; and Richard, having thrown a large cloak over his form, the better to conceal his person from observation, took his departure from the inn, and striking into the most secluded path. hurried on his way to the cottage.

———————

CHAPTER LX.

A SCENE OF HORROR.—THE DESTRUCTION OF THE INN.—THE AWFUL DEATH OF MR. AND MRS. WORTHINGTON.—MR. BUBBLE AGAIN.—THE DENOUNCEMENT, AND THE ESCAPE.

BUT as our hero proceeded on his way, in spite of the other conflicting thoughts that distracted his brain, he could not help recalling to his mind the last observations of Mr. Worthington at parting; and when he recollected the gloom which had evidently pervaded his breast, he could not help feeling uneasy and apprehensive, and he regretted the necessity which had compelled him to leave the inn, though he feared he should be in no condition to have sought to banish the gloomy presentiments from his mind. Such were the various doubts and forebodings that crossed his brain, that he could not help pausing two or three times and looking back upon the old inn, as though he was never more going to return to it, at least for many a long day; and when it was hidden from his sight altogether, a heavy sigh escaped his breast, and his thoughts became more dismal and oppressive than ever.

"But how is this?" he ejaculated; "what is the meaning of this sad feeling coming over me? What is there to apprehend? Providence will surely shield that good old man from any danger that may threaten him, and will not permit him to suffer for his unexampled acts of humanity towards his fellow creatures. My misery would be tenfold more great should I find that I have been the cause of bringing trouble upon the head of that venerable and excellent man. But no, it will not be; I feel a blest assurance that it will not, and I will therefore banish such melancholy and painful forebodings and misgivings from my mind."

He now proceeded on his way, and meeting with no obstruction, he very soon afterwards arrived at his cottage door. A candle was still burning in the up-stairs room, and convinced him that Mary had not yet retired to rest; and knocking at the door she speedily opened it, and rushed into his arms.

"Dearest Richard," she said; "how glad I am you have come, for I was afraid. when the time had so far advanced, that I should not see you to-night, and that would have filled me with the most painful doubt and anxiety. But you look pale, and even more agitated than usual; tell me, love, and do not keep me in suspense, has any fresh circumstance occurred to disturb you?"

"Alas! Mary," he replied; "ours is a dismal, a hopeless fate; but what agony does it impart to my mind, to be compelled at all times, to be the harbinger of misery and evil to you."

"What has happened?" repeated Mary, more anxiously than before; "does any fresh danger threaten us?"

"Would to Heaven, for your sake, that there did not," replied Richard.

"This suspense is insupportable," she cried; "I beg of you, Richard, at once to remove those doubts to which it naturally gives rise in my mind."

"I have been discovered! recognised!" answered our hero.

"Discovered! recognised!" repeated Mary, turning very pale, and looking earnestly in his face for an explanation; "impossible!"

"It is too true," returned her husband, with a melancholy expression of countenance, which fully corroborated his words.

"By whom?" demanded our heroine, breathlessly.

"By him who formerly betrayed me," said Richard; "by that man, whose sordid and wicked mind would lend him to do anything for money."

"Ah!" she ejaculated; "I know who you mean; good God! what could have brought him into this neighbourhood?"

"I know not," answered our hero; "but he put up for accommodation at the inn, he saw me (you may guess my feelings when I beheld him), and notwithstanding my disguise, he almost immediately recognised me."

"Alas! alas!" sighed Mary, wringing her hands in the terror and anguish of her feelings; "this is, indeed, alarming; oh, my husband, but still they shall not tear you from me! Kind Heaven, in its mercy, will not suffer you to fall a sacrifice!"

"Mary!" replied her husband, "it is useless to blind ourselves to the fearful truth; the hopes I might once have entertained are now all annihilated. We must prepare ourselves for the worst; for but a few hours will probably be suffered to elapse ere I shall be torn from your arms by the myrmidons of the law, and thrust into a loathsome dungeon to await the fate that must inevitably overtake me."

"Horrible thought!" gasped forth his distracted wife; "oh, no — no — no —

it will not, it cannot, be realised! But calm your feelings, my unfortunate husband, and tell me the particulars of this alarming and unexpected event."

Richard paused for a minute or two, and having, at last, succeeded in somewhat quieting his emotions, he complied with the request of his wife, and she listened to him with the most breathless attention.

"Oh, my dear Richard," she ejaculated, when he had concluded, "unfortunate though it is, it is not half so alarming as I expected it would be; had the press-gang, indeed, discovered you, your fate would have been sealed; but as it is, his assertions will not be believed, and you have nothing to fear, while you act according to the advice of Mrs. Worthington."

"And think you then, Mary," returned her husband, "that this fellow, Bubble, as he is called, will so easily abandon his designs, when he is so positive that he is right, and with the temptation of the reward which is offered for my apprehension before his eyes? We must leave this spot, and that with as little delay as possible."

"Alas!" sighed the hapless Mary; "and must we leave those friends who have acted with such unexampled kindness towards us?"

"There is no alternative," replied her husband; "should we remain here, something assures me that even perhaps before many hours have elapsed, I shall be in the hands of those who seek me, and then the dreadful and revolting fate which awaits me is certain."

"But whither can we go?" demanded our heroine, in a voice which bespoke the extreme anguish of her feelings; "where can we seek a shelter from the terrible storms of adversity by which we are pursued?"

"We must trust to fate, Mary," said our hero.

"Alas! cannot this be avoided?"

"It cannot; there is but one way of doing so, and of escaping from the trouble and anxiety to which we have been so long subjected."

"Oh, name it, dear Richard," eagerly cried his wife.

"It is," answered our hero, "by at once delivering myself into the hands of those who seek me, and boldly meeting my fate."

"Richard!" exclaimed his wife, looking into his face with a mingled expression of horror and reproach, "can you really love me, to give expression to such frightful, such unnatural observations as those, or has madness seized upon your brain?"

"Yes, yes," replied Parker, wildly, "I am mad!—distracted! when I reflect upon all the circumstances of my dismal history, and look upon your pale face— your wretched attenuated form, my poor Mary, and feel how utterly hopeles it is for me to attempt to restore you to that happiness from which I have torn you! But, perhaps, it is better that we should part. Why should you any longer follow my gloomy fortunes. Remain here, then, (Providence will probably protect you and our child) and let me forth alone, and——'

"Oh, God!" interrupted Mrs. Parker, "this is most cruel. Richard, what have I done that you should make use of such language towards me? Suffer you to leave me—abandon you to your fate—oh, never, never! I must be a wretch unworthy of the name of woman, if I could. We will never, never part, till death shall separate us; and then I hope that the same blow which shall strike you may also lay me low!"

Her emotions overpowered her as she thus spoke, and bursting into tears, she threw herself upon his bosom, and could only give utterance to convulsive sobs.

"Oh, Mary," said her husband; "to witness your emotion, and devoted affection, and yet, to know how ill-able I am to requite your love distracts me more than all. But—but, he added, in a hoarse voice, gently disengaging himself from her embrace, and looking wildly around the room, there is still one way of ending this insupportable misery, and of escaping the ignominious fate which otherwise awaits me, and——"

"Richard! Richard!" interrupted his terrified wife; "what dreadful meaning do your words convey?—What is it that you contemplate?—Your looks are wild and awful! There is something terrible brooding in your mind. Oh, speak! speak!"

While she was thus addressing him, he had gradually retired to a remote corner of the room, and feeling in his bosom, he drew forth a loaded pistol, which he had brought from the inn, in order to defend himself in case he should be attacked on the road, and presenting the muzzle towards his head, he exclaimed:

"Thus! thus! do I end at once all my earthly misery! Thus does Richard Parker escape a death of ignominy!—Mary, my child! farewell for ever!"

"Forbear! forbear! rash, unfortunate man," shrieked our heroine, as she rushed suddenly towards him, and wrenching it from his hand, discharged its contents in the air. "Oh, great God of Heaven! what is it you would do?— Richard! Richard! bethink yourself; would you thus recklessly commit a deed which would, probably, consign your soul to perdition?"

He looked at her stedfastly for a moment or two, and then uttering a deep groan of agony he sunk into a chair, and covering his face with his hands, abandoned himself entirely to the agonizing feelings that distracted his mind, whilst the unfortunate Mary stood by and anxiously watched him, for the power of her emotions was too great to suffer her to give utterance to a word.

At length Richard started suddenly to his feet, and looking in the same frantic manner upon his wife, he exclaimed':

"Why am I not to put a period to that existence which so many wrongs and misfortunes have rendered hateful and wretched?—Is there no way in which I may be permitted to avoid that death of shame which is impending over me? Away! I will not be thwarted in my plans!"

"Richard!" remonstrated our heroine, laying her hand impressively on his arm, and tears starting to her eyes; "for the love of Heaven, struggle with your feelings, and arouse yourself from this dreadful state of despair. Think of me and your child, and let that once more awaken you to reason. Alas! I shudder when I think of the rash and desperate crime you would have perpetrated."

"And were it not better that I should perish thus than die the death of a felon?" demanded Richard Parker, in a hoarse voice, and fixing upon his affectionate wife a look of the utmost despair.

"Oh, my beloved husband," replied Mary, "you must not, you shall not thus die a death of shame; but I tremble at the idea of your thus rushing unbidden into the presence of your maker, and were we to be deprived of you, what would then become of me, and our noble-hearted, innocent boy? I implore you, Richard, if you love me and your child, to banish such dreadful thoughts from your mind, and not thus to abandon yourself entirely to despair; the Almighty has hitherto protected us through all the terrible dangers by which we have been surrounded, and He will now forsake us."

"You have subdued me, Mary," said the unfortunate man, once more clasping her to his bosom; "oh, forgive me for the guilty act which, in a moment of frenzy, I contemplated. Yes, for your dear sake I will still struggle with my desperate destiny, and try to be firm. But——"

He was interrupted by an exclamation of mingled surprise and terror from his wife, and he required no explanation as to the cause of her excitement, for at that moment the room in which they were was illuminated by an unnatural light, and looking towards the window, he saw that a lurid glare overspread the Heavens, which every instant became more intense and awful. They rushed to the window, and then beheld dense clouds of smoke, and columns of sparks ascending into the skies, and presently terrific flames rose from behind the trees, only a short distance from the cottage, and seemed to spread far and wide into immeasurable space.

" A terrific fire is raging and that at no great distance," said Mary; " and see, great Heaven! it is in the direction of the inn."

" It is," cried Richard, with a look of the deepest emotion and horror ; " the dismal forebodings of our friend, Worthington, I am afraid are being realised. But why do I remain inactive here? See, the conflagration increases in fury; everything threatens destruction. I must away, and see if I can render any assistance."

" Oh, this is, indeed, most awful and unexpected," ejaculated our heroine ; " our unfortunate friends ! But this suspense is dreadful, I will accompany you, Richard."

" No, no," answered Richard, " it would not be safe for you to do so ; besides, you can render no aid. I will return as soon as possible and let you know the result."

" Be it so, Richard," said his wife ; " away, then, and may Heaven, in its infinite mercy, preserve those to whom we are so much indebted. Oh, do not delay !"

Our hero was too much agitated to return any answer, but his looks expressed, more than words could have done, the nature of the feelings that agitated his breast, and having hastily embraced his wife, he rushed from the cottage, and hurried towards the fearful scene of the conflagration in a state of mind which we need not attempt to describe."

It was too true that the fire was raging at the inn, and when our hero came in sight of it the whole of the building was enveloped in flames, from the base to the roof, and several persons were assembled, and endeavouring, but in vain, to extinguish it. It was truly an awful sight to behold the red flames doing their work of devastation ; to see the dense clouds of smoke that curled up into the atmosphere ;

the dense columns of sparks that shot up into the heavens ; to hear the crackling timber as it became a prey to the devouring element; and the loud shouts of the persons assembled as, despairing, they rushed about and sought to extinguish the fire, but with not the least chance of success; for, although it was only a few minutes since it had broken out, so rapid had been its progress, that it was almost impossible to approach near it, in consequence of the tremendous heat, and the total destruction of the building seemed to be inevitable.

Richard hastily and anxiously inquired of the bystanders after Mr. Worthington and his wife, and his horror may be readily conceived when he was informed that they were both in the burning pile, but whether or not they had yet fallen victims to the devouring element they had no means, of course, of ascertaining.

" Good God, then !" exclaimed Richard, " there is not an instant to be lost. My friends, my unfortunate friends, I will save you or perish with you."

As he thus spoke, he was about to rush into the burning house at all hazards, when he was prevented from doing so by two or three of the persons assembled arresting him.

" Hold, master," said Stephen Ladbroke, whom our hero now recognised for the first time, " would you rush upon certain destruction? It is impossible to enter the house, which, you see, is now one mass of flames. Alas! I fear that the unfortunate Mr. Worthington and his wife have perished."

" Do not detain me, Ladbroke," said Richard, hastily ; " I will save them at every risk. I must be a wretch, indeed, could I stand idly by and see those who have proved themselves to be my best friends, perish in so frightful a manner."

Again he was about to rush into the midst of the flames with the hope of being able to rescue those to whom he was so much indebted, when his attention was diverted by a loud shout of horror from the persons assembled, and looking up, what was the intense agony of his feelings, when he beheld Mr. Worthington and his wife standing at the window of one of the upstairs rooms, and shrieking for help! But, alas! it was utterly impossible to render them any assistance, the whole of the lower part of the premises being enveloped in flames, which were rapidly extending to the room in which they were, and the horrible fate that was in store for them was but too apparent.

It would be a fruitless task to seek to

describe the feelings of our hero at that moment, or the excitement which prevailed amongst all present; and the gestures of the unfortunate, aged couple, showed their utter despair. Several of the persons present called upon them to throw themselves from the window; but they did not seem to heed the advice, and even had they done so, their immediate death must have been inevitable. Nearer and nearer approached the flames to the place in which they were and they were almost hidden from sight by the dense clouds of black smoke which gathered around on every side. Suddenly there was a loud, crackling noise, which was followed by clouds of sparks and smoke, and when that had, in some degree, dispersed, the unfortunate Mr. and Mrs. Worthington had disappeared. The flooring of the room in which they had been standing had sunk beneath the influence of the flames, and there could be no doubt that they had both perished by that most horrible of deaths.

Who shall attempt to depicture the anguish of our hero at that fatal moment? But for a moment or two he stood completely paralysed to the spot with horror, and gazed vacantly and wildly towards the place where he had lately beheld the unfortunate Mr. Worthington and his wife standing, and from which the destructive flames were now pouring forth in torrents, and rapidly making their way to the roof; the work of destruction was soon complete—the roof fell in with a terrific crash, and nothing was left of the inn but a heap of smoking ruins.

Completely distracted, and scarcely knowing what he did, Richard was about to force his way into the ruins, in spite of the danger, when he was again withheld by Ladbroke.

"Do not be rash, Master Martin," he said; "it is useless now; alas! the fate of my poor friends, Worthington and his wife, is too certain."

"Gracious Heaven!" exclaimed Richard; "can this, indeed, be true, or am I only labouring under some fearful delusion? Unfortunate old people, to meet with so frightful and untimely a death; surely your numerous virtues deserved not so cruel a destiny."

He was interrupted in the midst of this melancholy soliloquy by hearing a voice near him, the tones of which were familiar to his ears, and looking round, his confusion and alarm may be imagined when he beheld Mr. Bubble, who was eyeing him narrowly, and who seemed to have been watching his actions for several minutes; at the same time he was not a little uneasy to behold several of the men who had composed the press-gang, and who also seemed to be surveying him with equal curiosity.

"By Jupitor, it is he!" cried Bubble, at the same time rubbing his hands with much apparent satisfaction; I was certain that I could not have been mistaken; oh, this is a slice of luck! I say, Mr. Richard Parker, you have played your part with great skill, but it won't do for me; I am not to be deceived; so you may as well deliver yourself up quietly into my custody."

"Richard Parker!" exclaimed two or three of the men, in a breath, and staring more eagerly and earnestly at our hero.

"Yes," said Mr. Bubble, "I repeat that the man whom I have addressed is no other than Richard Parker, the mutineer, and the murderer of Captain Arlington."

He had scarcely got the words out of his mouth when he was felled to the earth by a blow from our hero, and the men were then about to rush upon him and to seize him, when he drew a pistol from his pocket, and levelling it at them, whilst he stood in an attitude of determination, he exclaimed—

"Stand back! I will not be thus easily taken, the first man who ventures to approach me, shall pay for his temerity with his life!"

The men were quite paralyzed, as it were, with the boldness of his demeanour, and did not offer to obstruct him. Taking advantage of their confuson, he rushed from the spot, and fled with all the precipitation he could, and he had got some distance before they had recovered themselves, when then rushed after him in pursuit; but he quickly distanced them, and finding that the coast was clear, he paused to collect himself, and to consider what was best to be done. The horrible events of the night had, as may be expected, affected him, and his brain was feverish and bewildered; but there was not an instant to be lost; he was now discovered; his friends had been brought to an untimely end, and it was evident that nothing was left for him but immediate flight, and he therefore made his way with all the despatch he could towards the cottage, where he knew that his faithful Mary would be waiting his return, in a state of the greatest anxiety.

"Oh, God!" he cried, as he proceeded on his way, "can I ever banish from my mind the dreadful events of this night? My unfortunate friends, little did I ever expect that you would meet with so awful and untimely a fate as that which has befallen you. Oh, surely Providence should have been more merciful to those who were possessed of every virtue."

He could not repress a groan in the agony of the feelings which this thought

excited, but fearful that his pursuers might overtake him ere he could reach the cottage, he quickened his speed, and soon arrived at it, and found our heroine standing at the door, herself and Will'an both

THE ROBBERY OF TIMOTHY BUBBLE.

with their eyes fixed upon the skies, which were still illuminated by the reflection from the conflagration. He rushed distractedly towards them, and the paleness of his features, and the extreme agitation of his

demeanour fully convinced them that the worst had taken place."

" Alas! alas!" she sighed; "dear Richard, husband, I dread to ask you the dreadful truth; and yet I am anxious that this terrible suspense should be removed. Our unfortunate friends; tell me have they escaped?"

"Escaped!" repeated Richard; "alas, no, they have both perished in the devouring and merciless flames, and—"

"Both perished!" replied Mary, with a look of horror; "Oh, God! is it possible? This is, indeed, a terrible blow. But what brings you hither with such breathless speed, Richard? Why do you cast your eyes around you with such expressions of terror and anxiety? There is something more than you have yet informed me of."

"Mary!" replied her husband, in a voice half stifled by the power of his emotions. "We must leave this spot immediately!"

"Leave it?" she repeated; "what necessity is there for that, even though death has deprived us so suddenly, and in so awful a manner, of the two most valuable friends we had?"

"I have been betrayed again by that fellow, Bubble," said Richard; "I am discovered, and my pursuer will probably be here before many minutes have elapsed, and then my fate will be sealed."

"Alas! alas!" groaned the distracted wife; "what fearful intelligence is this! But whither can we go? And must we, indeed, abandon this place, where I had fondly hoped we might have been permitted to remain in security?"

"We have no other alternative," said our hero; "unless you would rather see me resign myself into the hands of the law; and perhaps that would be as well, and would at once put an end to the care and anxiety it has so long been my lot to encounter."

"Oh, Heaven forbid!" said Mary, with a look of terror, and throwing herself into his arms; "how terrible is that thought. But surely such dreadful calamities as those which have now befallen us, are almost too much for human fortitude to endure. But where can we now direct our lonely footsteps? Where can we conceal ourselves from the vengeance of the law?"

"I know not," answered Richard, "and after the dreadful events that have taken place this night, I am perfectly reckless as to the fate which may befall me. But come; we do but delay, and but a few minutes more and all may be too late."

"Alas!" sighed Mary, looking round the comfortably furnished room with an expression of sorrow and regret; "I had hoped that here we might, for the present, remain in safety, and receive the friendly counsel and advice of those kind friends whom we have now lost for ever, and in so awful a manner; but the fates seem to

have conspired against us, and it appears as if happiness was never again fated to be ours."

"Happiness!" repeated Richard; "oh, no, it would be madness to expect such a thing. But are you prepared to accompany me, while we have yet the opportunity to escape? There is no knowing how soon my pursuers will be here, and then all will be lost."

"I yield," sighed Mary, hastily putting on her bonnet and cloak; and then having packed up a few trifling necessary articles, and all the money they possessed, with sad heart; they quitted the cottage, having secured the door after them, and were soon hurrying on, they scarcely knew whither.

They had not proceeded far, however, when they were alarmed by hearing the confused sound of several men's voices, and which seemed to be proceeding from the direction in which they were going; and not doubting but that they were in pursuit of Richard, they struck into a path in a contrary direction, and in which, being very lonely, they trusted that they should not encounter any one.

Mary was so shocked and bewildered by what had happened, that she was scarcely conscious of what she was about, and for some distance they proceeded in silence, though the anguish of mind they were both enduring may be readily imagined.

"Oh, Richard," at length said his wife, "what a terrible event is this; what a dreadful and insupportable fate is ours. Poor Mr. and Mrs. Worthington to perish in so shocking a manner."

"The thought freezes the very blood in my veins," said Richard in reply; "what can ever replace the loss we have experienced in them? But why should I thus continue to struggle against the fate which must ultimately overtake me? Let me rather resign myself to our pursuers, and thus end at once my misery."

"Oh, no, my unfortunate husband," replied our heroine, "you must not abandon yourself to despair altogether; the time will yet come when the black clouds that at present obscure our prospects will have passed away, and we shall then be once more permitted to experience that peace and content from which we have lately been so much estranged."

"It is a futile hope, my Mary," he returned; "and do not, therefore, indulge it, for you will only be doomed to be disappointed. We are now again wretched wanderers; and Heaven only knows what will be the next that will befal us. But we cannot expect to remain long undiscovered, houseless, friendless as we are, and after the description that will probably be given as to my present personal appearance."

"Do not say that we are entirely friendless, dear Richard," answered his wife, "although the loss we have this night sustained is irreparable; have we not Mr. Adams and his friend Binnacle, who I am certain would willingly do everything they could to serve us?"

"True," coincided her husband; "but we may never see them again, since this has happened; and we cannot receive any assistance from them without involving them in danger. Alas! I know not what will become of us."

"Be firm, Richard," she returned, "and Providence, depend upon it, notwithstanding the untowardness of our fate, will yet watch over our safety."

Richard shook his head mournfully and hopelessly, and returned no answer, and again they proceeded on their way, not knowing what course to adopt, and almost careless what became of them.

"But whither are we going, dear Richard?" at length asked our heroine, looking anxiously and inquiringly into the pale and careworn face of her husband.

"I know not, Mary," he answered; "it is a matter of almost utter indifference to me; but if I would for the present escape from the hands of my pursuers, it will be necessary that we should quit this part of the country as quickly as possible. But how do I pity you and my poor boy, to behold you put to such a severe trial as this: to be thus driven from that place which you had been led to look upon as your home, and at such an hour; it is more, I fear, than you will be able to find strength to support."

"Oh, do not give way to such anxiety on my account, dear Richard," she returned; "for Providence will, I humbly hope and trust, sustain me. Come, let us proceed; and, perhaps, we may be able to meet with some place where we can obtain an hour or two's rest."

"Ah! Mary," said her husband, "but a few hours since, little did I anticipate the dreadful events that were destined to take place this night. The awful fate of those excellent old people, to whom we owe such an immense and incalculable debt of gratitude, can never be effaced from my memory; and whenever I recal it to my mind, it must freeze the very blood in my veins with horror."

"Ill-fated beings!" said Mary; "it was, indeed, a fearful catastrophe. But are there no means of saving them?"

"Alas, no!" replied our hero; "for had there been so, you may rest assured that, at the hazard of my own life, I would have rescued them. I could not have lost a life which has long been hateful to me in a better cause."

Mary returned no answer, and they continued on their way, taking the most lonely and least frequented route, and without encountering any one. It was some time past midnight, and dark, cold, and cheerless; there was no moon, and not a star to be seen, and it was quite evident that a storm was gathering, which, of course, added to the misery and uneasiness of the wanderers. The boy, William, bore up with the most heroic fortitude; and the whole of his anxiety was for his parents, whom he at intervals endeavoured to console by his simple but earnest conversation.

Much as our heroine regretted the painful necessity that had compelled her to leave the cottage so suddenly, she felt the greatest satisfaction at the escape of her husband at the very time when his fate appeared certain; and she could not avoid indulging in the hope that something would yet occur to change the current of their fortunes, and to place them in peace and serenity, if they could not hope for happiness.

"Dear Richard," she remarked, after a pause, during which brief interval she had been weighing the above thoughts in her mind, "we shall not be permitted by an All-wise and Merciful Omnipotence to sink altogether, depend on it; this is but a trial of our patience and fortitude, and the time will come when we shall be enabled to look back upon the past only as a painful dream."

"I dare not think so, my unfortunate wife," returned Richard, "for reason too plainly and forcibly tells me that such hopes will never be fulfilled. What is the prospect that is now spread before us? Is it not one of the most dismal description? Are we not wretched outcast—wanderers in the wide and cruel world, without a home or shelter? And are we not every minute threatened with shame and misery of the most insupportable description? My poor boy, too! Oh, it is indeed hard and cruel that his young days should be thus exposed to such severe trials and sufferings!"

"Dear father," replied William, and his handsome and intelligent countenance fully expressed the sincerity of his feelings, "do not, I beseech you, disturb your mind about me, for although I am but young, I feel fully prepared to meet any danger and vicissitude it may be my lot t) have to undergo. There is a just God above, I know, who will look down with an eye of pity upon my beloved, but unfortunate parents, and who will not suffer them to sink altogether in despair."

"My brave boy!" cried our hero, pressing his hand, and much moved by the fervour and simplicity of his manner; "may the fond hopes to which you have given utterance never be doomed to be disappointed. But you look tired; and I fear that you will suffer much from being thus disturbed, and put to such extraordinary exertion."

"No, my father," said the boy, "indeed I feel very well, and shall be able to undergo any fatigue so that I only know that you are free from danger."

Our hero and his wife again embraced their noble-hearted boy, and they then continued to journey on, but without meeting with a human habitation or a single individual.

It now began to rain heavily, and the fugitives looked with melancholy expressions of anxiety around them with the hope of beholding some cottage or other place of shelter; but nothing of the sort met their eyes, and they were soon completely wet to the skin, and felt truly cold and wretched. Still no word of regret or complaint escaped the lips of the devoted wife and her son, and they wandered on amidst the raging storm, their minds fully occupied in the contemplation of the dismal prospects before them. In this manner they must have walked more than an hour, and they were certainly in a most miserable state from the effects of the storm, but the fortitude of Mary and her son never seemed for a moment to forsake them, and they sought all that they could to raise the hopes, and console the mind of Richard; but in this effort, however, they were far from successful; when he beheld the sufferings to which those he so dearly loved were exposed, he could not but feel doubly wretched, and it would have been utterly impossible for him to get rid of the painful impression, under the particular circumstances in which he was placed. They had now got a considerable distance from the neighbourhood in which they had recently resided, and the aspect of the country through which they were travelling was particularly wild and unprepossessing; and being wet, weary, and wretched, they found some difficulty in proceeding. However, when they had travelled on a little further, the scene changed, and became much more favourable than it had been before, though they

did not yet behold any signs of a human habitation. An old out-house, however, the door of which was hanging off the hinges, at length met their observation, and was indeed a welcome sight to them. Having entered this place, they found some straw in one corner, on which, no doubt, some poor traveller like themselves had before laid; they secured the door as well as they could, and then sinking on their knees, they fervently returned their thanks to the Supreme for having thus far protected them from the danger which had threatened them, and earnestly and devoutly they supplicated His assistance for the future; and then felt more contented and confident.

"Here we are not likely to be disturbed," remarked our heroine; "a few hours' rest will refresh us, and by the morning we shall, perhaps, be able to come to some decision as to the course it will be most prudent for us to adopt."

"I know not what will become of us," returned Richard, in the most melancholy accents; "the trifle of money we at present have will soon be exhausted, and how then can we contrive to live? Where can we we look for assistance?"

"Oh, do not view everything on the darkest side, dear Richard," said our heroine; "but rather trust to Providence, and my word for it, He will not forsake us. We may settle in some part of the country where we are not known, and you may find some means of communicating with Mr. Adams, or Binnacle, and there is no doubt but that we shall have their speedy advice and assistance on the subject."

"Oh, yes," answered our hero; "I have not the least doubt of the continuance of their friendship; but I feel repugnant to place myself under any further obligation to those from whom I have already received so much; and should it be discovered that they have taken any part in my escape, you are well aware that the consequences would be fatal to them."

"Yes," said Mary, "I know that full well; but there is no fear of anything of the kind taking place; how is it likely that any suspicion can attach to them? Be composed, my beloved husband, and I beseech you not to anticipate troubles half way."

"Ah, Mary," he observed, "and do you think that I can so easily remove from my mind the impression it has received from the terrible shock it has sustained this night? Think you that I can ever forget the awful fate of those two excellent individuals from whom we have experienced such unexampled favours?"

"Oh, no, Richard," replied our heroine, "I do not expect anything of the kind, for I know it would be impossible; but I would have you not to give way to this melancholy any more than you can possibly help, for, while it can do no good, it will unfit you to encounter the many difficulties it may yet be our lot to experience. Need I assure you how painful is the effect which the shocking death of Mr. and Mrs. Worthington has had upon me?"

"Oh, Mary," said Richard, "had you but seen the poor old couple as they stood at the window of the room in which they were, and supplicating for that assistance which it was totally impossible to render them, you would never have forgotten it. Then to see how the bellowing and kissing flames rapidly advanced towards them; to——"

"Oh, forbear, dear Richard," interrupted his wife, "the picture is too frightful for me to contemplate; I need no description to present it to my imagination. But enough of this dismal subject to-night; you require rest, and here, it seems, we may take it without any fear of interruption. We must resume our journey by break of day—that is, if this storm has subsided."

Richard made no particular reply to this, and after some few more observations, the unfortunate fugitives, wet as they were, stretched their weary limbs upon the straw, and after a short time they fell asleep. How long they had slumbered they knew not, but our hero was suddenly aroused by his wife, who in a faint voice said—

"Hark, Richard; do you not hear anything?"

"Hear anything?" he replied. "No; What was it you thought you heard?"

"Why," returned our heroine, in the same low tone, "I could almost have sworn that I heard some one trying the door, and a muttering of voices."

"Oh, you have only been dreaming, my love," said Richard, "or else it was the storm, which I hear has not yet abated."

"I do not think I could have been so deceived, Richard," remarked Mary; "however, I will not be positive; so we will try to compose ourselves to sleep again."

Richard was about to make some reply, when he was prevented from doing so by distinctly hearing such sounds as his wife had described, and he started to his feet and listened attentively. It was quite evident that some person was trying the door, and he could also hear the voice of a man muttering curses to himself. Mary

trembled, and clung to her husband, whilst William stood firm and undaunted, and evinced a courage and determination of spirit that could not have been expected at his age. Richard drew forth a pistol, which he had in his coat-pocket, and was fully prepared for the worst that might take place.

He had not to wait long; the door was burst open, and the figure of a man entered, which the darkness of the night prevented him from observing distinctly. He did not perceive that there was anybody in the place besides himself, and Richard and our heroine drew in their breath, and resolved to watch his conduct. He moved to the opposite corner of the place, and seemed to be trying to examine where he was.

"It's confoundedly dark," he said; "you can't see your hand before you in this place; however, I can see to go to sleep, and this is no bad shelter from the storm."

"Ah!" thought Richard, "that voice! Surely I have heard it before."

"I soon cut the connection with Will Hangsby and the others," continued the intruder, after a pause; "however, I have no doubt, now that I have got a fair starting, I shall do much better on my own account. What a strange discovery is this that I have made to-night in passing by the scene of the conflagration of the old Punch Bowl; namely, that the female whom I formerly saw at the cottage was no other than Mrs. Parker, and that her pretended brother was Richard himself. What a confounded fool I must be not to recollect him; and yet his features seemed to be so familiar to me. He has made his escape again, but I do not think it is very likely that he will be enabled to avoid detection much longer. Now, if fortune would only place him in my way, I should be one of the luckiest fellows in existence."

Mary's horror was now so great that she found it impossible to repress a scream, and the man starting, and looking anxiously about him, exclaimed,—

"Hallo! what the devil was that? It sounded remarkably like a scream."

"Who are you?" demanded Richard, in a determined voice, and stepping forward and grasping the man by the collar with one hand, while he held his pistol to his head with the other; "speak, and tell me your business here, or I fire!"

"Ah!" cried the man, "what's in the wind now? Some one here before me; well, you're not the master of the place, I suppose, but have only, like me, sought a shelter from the storm; so there's room enough for me, I imagine."

"Ah, villain!" cried Richard, grasping his collar more firmly than before, "I know you now; you are he who committed the daring outrage at the cottage, and shed the blood of an unfortunate old woman!"

"Yes," replied the ruffian, with a dreadful oath, "I am that man, and you, then, are Richard Parker, mutineer and murderer, and my prisoner!"

In a moment he grasped the arm of our hero, and a desperate struggle ensued. Mary being so overpowered by terror that she was paralysed to the spot, and could not give utterance to a syllable. It lasted for only a few minutes. In the scuffle, the pistol, the muzzle of which was pointed towards the body of the ruffian, was accidentally discharged, and with a dreadful oath he sank bleeding to the earth, Mary and her son gazing on with mingled expressions of astonishment and consternation.

"Oh, curses of perdition light upon you for this," said the miscreant, in a hoarse voice. "My account is settled, I feel, plain enough; but to die by the hand of Richard Parker—oh, that is more torturing than all."

"Wretched, guilty man," said our hero, "who are you, and why do you mention my name in the manner you have done? Who are you, I repeat?"

"One whom you have sufficient cause to remember," replied the wounded man; "one for whom you once suffered the degradation of the lash; and that thought, at any rate, affords me some satisfaction."

"Ah!" cried Richard, with the utmost surprise, "can I hear aright? Let me examine your features. No, 'tis so dark that I cannot distinguish them. Your name is——"

At that moment a flash of lightning darted across the wounded man's features, and our hero, starting back in astonishment, exclaimed—

"Astonishment! Do my eyes deceive me? No; it is, it is the villain, Brunston! This is, indeed, retributive justice."

"Ay, Parker," gasped forth Brunston, "it is, indeed, your turn to triumph now. Again I say, may the curses of hell light upon your head; but think not to escape the fate that is in store for you, for it will as surely overtake you as that you are now standing before me. You will die the death of a dog, and that assurance is some consolation to me at the present moment."

"Wretched, guilty man," ejaculated our heroine, "forbear those awful words; and rather employ the last few minutes you probably may have to live in prayer and penitence."

"Prayer! Penitence!" replied the hardened ruffian, with a frightful laugh; "bah! to me that is all idle cant and mockery; but—oh, that pang—Parker, you have, indeed, done for me. Curses—curses!—Would that I had recognised you in time; then would the triumph have been mine; the reward that is offered for your apprehension would have fallen into my hands, and your wife would have been made to yield to those passions with which she had inspired me immediately on so accidentally beholding her."

"Wretch!" exclaimed the disgusted and indignant Richard; "dare you, in such an hour as this, and when the dew of death is fast gathering on your brow, give utterance to such language as this? Have you no sense or shame of feeling that——"

"Hold!" interrupted the ruffian, and his features frightfully distorted with the mingled feelings caused by pain and rage, "let me not be annoyed by listening to your ridiculous jargon. Oh, I could, even at this moment, had I the strength to do so, plunge my knife into your heart, and then be content to die since you would perish with me. But your fate is sealed; you cannot escape it, though you may flatter yourself that you will, and that affords me some satisfaction. Yes, I see the doom that is in store for you as clearly as if it were passing in reality before my eyes; you will die the death of a dog—the death of a dog; ha! ha! ha!—Your lifeless corpse will swing in the air, amid the shouts and execrations of those who witness it. Mark the words of Joe Brunston, who falls by your hands, and rest assured that they will be verified."

As the remorseless ruffian thus spoke, the expression of his coarse and repulsive features was quite hideous to look on, and at the same time it was evident that he was suffering the most excruciating agony. We need not attempt to describe the feelings of Richard and his wife, as they listened to him, and gazed upon him. Notwithstanding all that had taken place, however, and the abandoned and villanous character of the man, our hero could not but feel almost regret that he should have fallen by his hands, and he would willingly have endeavoured to staunch the wound which he had given, and to save his life, if possible; but he saw plainly enough that it would be fruitless for him to seek to do so, and fearful of the consequences that would be almost certain to follow should he be discovered where he was before the death of Brunston, who would be certain to denounce him; he saw no other alternative but immediate flight, and to leave the villain, Brunston, to his fate; as it was impossible to venture to call in any assistance, if even such could have been obtained.

Brunston appeared to read his thoughts, and raising himself up with difficulty, and glaring frightfully upon him, he cried:

"So, you would abandon me to my fate?—You would leave your victim to perish, and perhaps to fix the blame of my murder upon an innocent man. Oh, coward—dastardly coward! but, be it so. I scorn to receive any aid at your hands. No, I would sooner die. I—I feel that there is no chance for me, and so it is no use murmuring about the business. Joe Brunston will die as he has lived—hardened and reckless in spirit, and regardless of the future. But with my dying breath again I curse thee, Richard Parker, for this, the deed of thy hands!"

As he thus spoke the blue lightning glared across his ghastly and distorted features, and the effect was more awful than ever, for death was evidently rapidly approaching, and the wretched, guilty man, although he tried to conceal it, it was quite clear was suffering the most insupportable pain. Mary gazed at him, appalled, and clung still closer to her husband, who was petrified and bewildered, and was undecided how to act.

"'Tis coming!" at length ejaculated Brunston, in a hollow voice, and staring wildly around him. "I feel it's very touch! The blood freezes and stagnates in my veins—my sight grows dim—yet—ah! what are those frightful forms that dance before my imagination, and strike horror to my soul? Away—away! I tremble to gaze upon ye, and Brunston never trembled before. Quench those flames!—they gather round me—I burn—I burn! Parker, curses—oh!"

One frightful pang convulsed his whole frame; he fixed his glassy eyes upon the countenance of our hero with an expression that thrilled his very soul, and which he could never forget, and the next instant he fell back a ghastly corpse.

For some moments after the close of this fearful tragedy, Richard Parker and his wife and son, stood transfixed like statues to the spot, and gazed with feelings of the most inexpressible horror upon the lifeless body of the unfortunate, but guilty man; but at length our heroine found strength sufficient to ejaculate,—

"Oh, God, Richard, what a terrible adventure is this! Wretched man! why were you fated again to cross our path? But—but you are not to blame—you only acted in self-defence, and it was by accident that he met his death. He would have denounced you, too—betrayed you into the hands of the law, and all to gratify his sordid feelings, and a spirit of revenge which he felt towards you. But why do we remain here? Should we be discovered, and in such a situation, our recognition would be almost sure to follow. Oh, let us fly whilst yet there is time and opportunity to do so."

"Fly!" repeated Richard, with a look of despair. "Alas! whither can we go? How avoid the fate which is in store for us, and which Brunston has predicted? A terrible spell is upon us, and I feel convinced that it is no use struggling against my destiny; why then should I longer seek to live in this state of misery and suspense? No, I will at once resign myself into the hands of justice, and——"

"Richard!" interrupted his devoted wife, with a look of terror; "are you mad? You cannot know what you say or do, or you would not talk thus. Have you no thought for me or your son that you would thus rashly throw away all chance of escape, and resign yourself to so cruel and ignominious a fate? Come—come, let us not delay, for every moment that we do so is fraught with danger; let us immediately away, and hasten from this neighbourhood altogether."

As she thus spoke she placed her hand upon his arm, and drew him towards the door, and he not knowing what he did, offered no resistance; though, as they passed the corpse of the guilty man, Brunston, they could not help shuddering with a sensation of horror, such as the nature of the circumstances that had taken place were calculated to inspire. On gaining the door, a loud peal of thunder shook the Heavens, and a flash of lightning darted across their path, and caused them to start back, appalled, while it nearly blinded them. In fact the storm had increased in violence, and the night was of that terrific description that it was sufficient to daunt the stoutest heart. The rain descended in one complete sheet, the wind howled and bellowed at intervals vieing with the deafening sound of the thunder, and the lightning was incessant, and of the most awful and alarming description.

"It is impossible that we can go forth in such a storm as his," said our hero; "we must e'en remain here and run the risk of the consequences."

"Remain here!" gasped forth his wife, with a look of terror, as her eyes again wandered to the ghastly face of the corpse. "Oh, Heaven forbid! Come—come, my Richard, my husband; if you have any regard for me or your child, you will no longer hesitate. I fear not the storm, and Providence will, I trust, soon guide us to a place of shelter and security."

"Oh, do, dear father," supplicated William, "do not suffer my poor mother to plead in vain; I tremble for the consequences every moment that we remain here. The raging tempest has not half such terrors for me."

"My poor boy," said our hero, greatly moved by the earnestness of his son's entreaties, "how it agonizes me to be the cause of introducing you to such revolting and terrible scenes as this. Oh, surely the Supreme, in His mercy, should spare you and your unfortunate mother, who are both innocent, such severe and insupportable trials to which you have been so frequently subjected."

"This is not the time or the place, dear Richard," said Mary, "to talk upon such a subject. Again I implore you not to delay a moment here, in spite of the violence of the raging elements, or all may be lost."

"And this poor, guilty, but unfortunate wretch," remarked our hero, pointing to the body of Brunston, "must we leave him here?"

"What would you do with his lifeless remains?" demanded Mary.

"I know not; but still I would dispose of them in such a way that they would not be likely to be discovered, and thus prevent the possibility of any innocent person being charged with, or suspected, of murdering him."

"Oh," returned Mary, "there is not much fear of that; he is most likely a stranger in this part of the country, and who could be suspected of his murder? It is more likely, under all the circumstances, that it will be imagined he has committed suicide. It is an unfortunate thing that you encountered him at all."

"Yes," coincided her husband; "it would have been much better had it not have happened; however, he has got his deserts, and it is but a just retribution on his head. He it was who was the first cause of my degradation, and—"

"Nay, dearest Richard," interrupted our heroine, "torture not yourself by thoughts such as those, but rather act with promptitude. It fills me with feelings of dread and horror while I remain here; oh, for Heaven's sake do not longer hesitate, but let us away with all the precipitation we can, and braving the terrors of the storm, we may in a short time reach a place of shelter and safety."

Richard Parker embraced her fondly, and by his looks fully evinced how duly he appreciated the feelings that dictated the observations she had made use of, and then having cast one more fearful glance towards the corpse, he yielded to the persuasions of his wife, and they issued from the place.

They were again in the midst of the terrors of the tempest, and fiercely, indeed, did the elemental strife continue to rage. Nothing can be more truly frightful than the scene which presented itself on every side from the effects of the storm, which had blown a perfect hurricane, tearing trees up by the roots, whilst others were split by the lightning, which still ever and anon flashed its forked fury, and threatened destruction to all those unfortunate beings who were exposed to it.

In spite of all her endeavours to conceal it, Mary Parker could not but feel greatly alarmed; but the boy, William, bore the horrors of the night with the most extraordinary fortitude, and never once gave utterance to a word of complaint. Richard walked on in gloomy silence for some distance, but it was evident that all his fears were for his wife and child, and that as for himself he was totally indifferent what might become of him. He drew them closer to him, and tried to shelter them as much as possible from the furious pelting of the rain with his cloak, but it was not likely that in such a tempest as was then raging it could have much, if any, effect, and their condition was as truly wretched as it would be possible to imagine. In vain they looked for some place of shelter, or even the signs of a human habitation; nothing of the kind met their view, and it seemed as if there was not the least chance of their being enabled to escape from the terrors of the night, or that the storm would in the slightest degree abate. Our hero ever and anon between the pauses of the blast looked around him, fearful of pursuit, and then all the horrors that he had just encountered rushed upon his brain with tenfold force, and he could almost imagine that he again beheld the ghastly and repulsive features of Brunston, as they appeared in death; and so strong was the impression on his mind, that he found it the greatest difficulty in the world to conquer it.

For more than half an hour they continued to travel in this manner, and no change came over the weather, nor did it seem at all probable that there would. Mary had struggled as long as she could against the difficulties and miseries by which they were surrounded, but at length her strength failed her. and she was compelled to lean on the arm of her husband

MR. BUBBLE SEEKS SHELTER IN THE FARM HOUSE FROM THE STORM.

for support, or she must have sunk upon the earth.

"My Mary, my beloved Mary," cried our hero; "alas! alas! your strength fails you beneath this severe trial; and your poor limbs refuse to perform their office. All is desolation and horror around; oh, God! what will become of us?"

"Fear not, my dear husband," replied his devoted wife, in a faint voice, and endeavouring to smile encouragingly in his face, "it is only a temporary weakness, arising from the unusual fatigue and anxiety of mind I have for the last few hours undergone. I shall be better soon."

"Oh, no!" returned Richard; "in vain you seek to inspire me with confidence; it is not possible that you can much longer bear up against the fury of this terrific tempest; and our poor boy, too—oh, God! how torturing it is to witness the sufferings to which you are both exposed, and I have no power to relieve you."

"Fear not for me, my father," said the noble-hearted boy; "I am young and fully able to endure fatigue; besides, I know that God will give me more than sufficient strength to endure all the trials to which I may be exposed, especially in so sacred a cause as the preservation of my unfortunate and beloved parents."

"My sweet boy," ejaculated our heroine, clasping him to her bosom in a transport of affection; "may Heaven bless you, as I am sure it will, for those generous and dutiful feelings. Come, Richard, I feel renewed strength now; so let us proceed; Providence surely will at last bring us to a place of shelter."

"Mary," returned her husband, "my hopes are completely crushed, and I feel as though I could lay myself down and die. It is impossible that I can do otherwise than abandon myself to entire despair."

"Say not so, Richard," observed his wife; "but rather view everything on the brightest side. We are now far away from the scene of danger, and there, at present, seems to be no fear of our pursuers being able to track our footsteps."

"I do not see the smallest chance of escape," said Parker, "now that it has became once known that I have been concealed in this part of the country. No doubt that persons are dispatched to every locality, and it would seem, after what has taken place, that no disguise can conceal my person from their knowledge. Unfortunate Mr. Worthington, in you and your amiable wife I have lost two of my best and most devoted friends; and never can I cease to deplore your awful and untimely fate."

"And in that feeling, need I say that I most cordially and sincerely participate?" said our heroine. "It is indeed, true that in those two excellent old people we have experienced a most irreparable loss; but we must not, nevertheless, give way to despair. Ah! again that death-like faintness!"

Once more her countenance became ghastly pale, her limbs trembled convul-

sively, and it was not without the greatest difficulty that she could prevent herself from swooning in her husband's arms. Nothing could possibly be more miserable than the condition they were in; they were completely drenched to the skin; their limbs were shivering with the cold, and they were so worn-out with suffering, that that their spirits were quite broken, and they abandoned themselves to the most abject despair, notwithstanding Mary Parker tried all that she could to conceal the real feelings that agitated her breast. But still the storm did not in the least abate, and there was nothing to impart to their minds the least ray of consolation. Slowly they proceeded on their way, though they knew not whither they were going, and the features of the country presented the same wild aspect that it had previously done.

"My patience is completely exhausted," said Richard at last, and at the same time striking his forehead; "the further we proceed, the more terrible and dismal become our prospects. It would have been better for me not to have offered any resistance, when that man denounced me. You, at any rate, my poor wife and boy, would have been spared all this misery."

"And at what a cost!" answered Mary. "I shudder to think of it. Oh, better that we should run every risk, encounter every misery, than that you, my dear husband, should be consigned to so dreadful a fate. But let us not tarry here; I do once more feel revived; I will exert myself to the utmost to shake off this painful feeling."

Richard returned no answer, but he sighed deeply, and taking the arm of the faithful partner of his sorrows, they again proceeded on their weary and dismal way, but without the least alteration for the better in their prospects; nor was there any cessation in the fury of the tempest. Several times, when the thunder for a brief space of time ceased to roar, they started, and looked back timidly, as they almost imagined that they heard the voices of men; but as far as their eyes could penetrate through the dense darkness which predominated on everything around —except when the lightning at intervals flashed across the sky—they could not perceive any person, and they, therefore, concluded that they must have suffered their imaginations to deceive them, which was not at all unlikely or unnatural, considering the excitement of mind under which they now laboured. Our heroine, however, exerted herself to the utmost of her power, and bore up with much greater strength and fortitude than might have been anticipated. And now the tempest became less violent, and it seemed not at all unlikely that in a short time it would subside altogether. The thunder moved off in the distance, until its voice could scarcely be heard, and the lightning ceased to blaze in the Heavens, adding fresh terrors to the fearful scene which had so long prevailed.

"Courage, Richard," said our heroine, in her sweetest accents, and looking with the most unbounded tenderness in her husband's face ; "Providence has heard our prayers ; the storm will shortly cease, and we shall be able to meet with a place of safety and shelter."

"Mary," replied Richard, "and know you not the danger there might be in seeking relief, if even we should meet with a human habitation? If the description of our persons should have reached this part, or wherever our footsteps may be guided to, which it is not at all unlikely that it will, we can scarcely fail to be immediately recognised."

"You give too much encouragement to apprehensions such as those you have just now expressed," remarked Mary ; "but, for my own part, I do not believe that they will ever be realised."

"The appearance of yourself and our boy," continued Parker, "would probably be enough to excite suspicion, and it is, therefore, not without good cause that I encourage the fears which you blame me for."

Mary tried all that she could by argument to persuade him to the contrary ; but finding that it was all to no purpose, she abandoned the effort, and they walked on for some distance in silence. The storm had now quite subsided, and, notwithstanding the extraordinary fatigue and suffering she had undergone, Mary felt her strength revive, and she looked forward to the future with renewed hope, although there certainly was not much to encourage it at present.

CHAPTER XX.

THE FUGITIVES CONTINUE THEIR FLIGHT. — THE HEATH. — THE PARROW ESCAPE. — A SIGNAL TRIAL.

They travelled on for some time longer, without meeting with anything to cheer their hopes, and Mary was worn out, that in spite of the powerful exertions she made, it was not without the greatest difficulty that she was enabled to support herself at all. But it was most remarka-

ble to witness the fortitude and self-endurance evinced by the courageous and intelligent boy, William. With the exception of the effects produced by the tempest, he showed very little signs of fatigue, and never once gave utterance to a word which could be construed into a murmur of complaint.

They now found themselves on a wild heath, which appeared to be of considerable extent; and, still, not the least signs of a human being or habitation met their observation, and it seemed as though the fates had conspired against them. What added to their embarrassment was, that they, being entire strangers to the country, where totally ignorant as to the way in which it would be most advisable for them to direct their course, and where they would be more likely to meet with the relief they sought. However, they mustered all the resolution they could, and kept on their way, though they were necessarily compelled to proceed with less speed than they had done before, in consequence of their strength being almost exhausted. It was now more than three hours after midnight, and it would soon be daylight, when they were afraid it would not be safe for them to travel, as their pursuers would be on the alert ; and yet they at present saw no prospect of meeting with any place where they might conceal themselves.

Our hero was in the same melancholy and helpless state of mind, and his amiable wife saw that it would be useless to attempt to arouse him from it at present ; she, therefore, contented herself by exerting all her energies to sustain herself, so that her husband, witnessing her fortitude and resignation, might possibly become more calm and resolute. The heath, however, proved not to be of that extent which they had at first imagined it ; and having crossed it at the nearest point, they found themselves in a more agreeable part of the country than they had hitherto traversed, and their spirits in some slight measure revived.

"No doubt," remarked our heroine, "we shall now soon meet with some human dwelling, and be able to obtain that temporary relief of which we so much stand in need."

"And should we be known?" remarked Parker.

"Nay," replied his wife, "why will you still persist in giving way to such apprehensions, as those you have just now uttered? Although I am bound to acknowledge that we have had some narrow escapes, and have met with many misforᵗᵃnes, Providence has hitherto not deserted us, and, therefore, we should still continue to put our trust in Him."

"Dearest Mary, I will strive to do so," said Richard; "though I much fear whether I shall be able to succeed. Without you, my beloved and devoted wife, I must have become the victim of despair altogether; and must long since have fallen into the power of those who thirst for my blood, and who will yet have their wishes gratified; though for a time fortune may favour my escape."

"Still those sad, those terrible thoughts will haunt your imagination, Richard," said our heroine; "will nothing serve to banish them from your mind, and to excite in your bosom some feeling of hope and confidence?"

"Well, well, my beloved Mary," he observed; "we will say no more about it for the present, since it can only serve to engender painful and conflicting thoughts in our bosoms. I sincerely pray that the dismal forebodings which I have suffered to take possession of my mind may not be realised; not for my sake (for, believe me, I am tired of existence) but for thine, my Mary, and that noble-hearted boy, who promises so well to be an honour and a comfort to you in your declining days, and when I, no doubt, shall have long since mouldered to dust."

"Oh, Heaven forbid!" exclaimed Mrs. Parker fervently; "God grant that you may yet live for many years to come, my husband, to experience that happiness and content of which you have been so long deprived, and, that when it may please that Supreme Being, at whose decrees we must not presume to murmur, to take us to Himself, the same hour that consigns your soul to eternity may also prove the close of my mortal career. But let us not dwell on subjects that can only serve to add to the melancholy and anguish which already disturb our minds. We must try to assume all the composure we can, so that those whom we may have to encounter should not be excited to any feeling of suspicion."

"Very true," coincided her husband; " I know full well the force and justice of your observations; but I am afraid I shall find what you advise a most difficult task to accomplish."

They still continued to advance, and after crossing one or two fields, and traversing a long lane, they came in sight of a small, but comfortable looking farmhouse. And now our hero paused, and again hesitated to approach it, fearing that they might either be considered as intruders, and repelled accordingly, or that they

might otherwise meet with those who under the cloak of benevolence and hospitality might deceive and betray them. But Mary combated all his objections, and reminding him of the distance they were from the place where the awful occurrences which gave rise to the cause of their flight had happened, and of the improbability of their meeting with any one who was acquainted with them, he became more calm and confident.

"And yet the hour is so early," he remarked, "the first break of day is only just appearing in the east, and the inmates of the farm will probably think us bold in venturing to disturb them."

"Oh, no," answered our heroine; "when they remember the storm which has only just ceased, and which they must have heard, if they have a spark of humanity within their breasts, they will not refuse us that temporary relief which we seek."

"True," said Parker, conquering his scruples, "and you, Mary, and our poor William, I am convinced, in spite of your endeavours to conceal it from me, must be so fatigued with the unusual exertions you have undergone, and the excitment of your feelings consequent upon the circumstances that have taken place, that it would be utterly impossible for you to proceed further. I will e'en arouse the inmates, and appeal to their benevolence and humanity; but, mark me, we must assume the rustic manners that our appearance would lead any one to suppose should belong to us."

"Exactly so, Richard," answered his wife. "I will leave everything to you, and be guided entirely by what you say."

"Enough," remarked our hero, and they then advanced to the farm, and opening the gate, which they found no difficulty in doing, they walked up to the house, and Richard then rang a bell by the side of one of the doors, and awaited the issue in doubt and anxiety. To the first application there was no answer, and our hero, therefore, again pulled the bell more violently than before; and presently afterwards they beheld a window just above the door-way slowly opened, and a man's head, ensconced in a night-cap, protruded itself, and after two or three yawns demanded, in no very agreeable tones, probably in consequence of his having been suddenly and unexpectedly aroused from his slumbers, who was there and what they wanted?

"I be a poor man," answered Richard in as broad accents as he could assume, "who with my sister and her child have travelled for many miles. So we be hungry, and footsore, and quite wet to the skin from the storm, which has only just ceased."

"Well," interrupted the man, again yawning, "and what be that to do wi' I? It be a main sheame that a poor man can't have his nat'ral rest arter working hard all day."

"Well," returned Richard, "I ask your pardon for disturbing you, I'm sure, but all I want is an hour or two's rest for myself and my sister, and her son, and then we shall be better able to resume our journey, for we have got a great deal further to go."

"Well," said the man, after a pause, "your tale do sound som'at like th' truth, sure enough, so I'll just hear what measter has to say about it, and will let you know directly."

Richard thanked him, and the man retired from the window. They were only kept in suspense a few minutes, when they heard a heavy footstep descending the stairs, and directly afterwards the door was opened, and a rough looking countryman, partly undressed, and bearing a lamp in his hand, made his appearance, and scrutinised Richard and his wife and William narrowly.

"Well, you do look tired, to be sure," he said, after he had thoroughly surveyed them; "and how wet you be; I had no idea it had been such a storm, for I generally sleep pretty sound. I suppose it be all right, so measter told me to show you in, and he will be wi' you directly. This way, this way."

Richard again thanked him, and the simple rustic having made some reply, which meant them to understand that he was by no means a lover of compliments, they followed him into a room beyond, in which, although it was so early, there was a rousing fire, a very cheerful sight to our poor fugitives, who were shivering with cold, wet, and miserable.

"There, my friends," remarked the man, "you will find that fire a comfortable companion, I imagine, in your condition, so I will leave you to enjoy it, and you will see measter in a few minutes."

"And who be your master, my good man?" asked Richard.

"Why, Farmer Judkins, to be sure," replied the servant; "and a better man there does not exist in any part of the country, although I say it. But you will be best able to judge for yourself, for that matter, when you see him."

With these words, the man once more left them, and they then had an opportu-

nity of communicating their thoughts to each other.

"Fortune has, I think, again favoured us," remarked Mary; "if all be true that this man has said of his master, we could not have fallen into better quarters."

"True," coincided her husband; "no doubt it will answer our purpose for the time we remain here, which must not be many hours; but we must act with the strictest precaution, for we don't know any one till we have tried them."

"Certainly not," agreed our heroine; "you will find me, as usual, on my guard. I will be guided by what you say in everything, and I cannot but approve of the character you have assumed, and the way in which you have represented me."

"It would not have been prudent to have done otherwise, considering the dress you wear," replied Richard. "But hush," he continued, in a low voice, "some one is coming; it is the farmer, I suppose."

The next instant the door was opened, and a stout, good humoured looking man entered the room, and Richard and his wife rose to greet him with proper respect, but the farmer prevented them.

"No thanks, my friends," he said. "I am a plain sort of man myself, and I like plain-dealing people. My man, Giles, tells me that you have been travelling a long way, and overtaken by that storm which raged so long and so violently?"

Our hero replied in the affirmative.

"And wet and tired enough you seem to be. Well, I am very glad you have come to my house, for there is no one who ever goes away, who is in want of it, without being relieved and accommodated; so, I will send you some refreshments, and after you have partaken of them, Giles will conduct you to your chambers, and I will see you again when you have rested yourselves. You are a labouring man, I presume, by your dress?"

Richard again replied in the affirmative.

"And from what part of the country may you come?" asked Mr. Judkins.

"From the adjoining county, sir," answered Richard, again assuming the dialect.

"What, Kent?" said the farmer.

"The same," returned our hero. "Myself and my sister, who you may perceive is a widow, and under my protection, are now travelling to a distant part of the country, in order to join a relation, who is pretty comfortably off, and where I hope to obtain work. We were strangers about this quarter, and lost ourselves, and were overtaken by the storm, and were compelled to be out in the whole of it, for we could not find out any place where we might obtain a shelter until we beheld your house."

"Ay," observed Mr. Judkins, "this is rather a wild part of the country round about here, and there is not much accommodation for travellers. However, it is a good job you found your way here, or there is no knowing what might have been the consequences to you, wet as you are. Make yourselves quite at home here, for you are heartily welcome."

Having thus spoken, without giving Richard or his wife time to reply, the farmer quitted the room, and left them to their own reflections, which, on the whole, were of a satisfactory description. The urbane, free, and hospitable bearing of the farmer, could not fail to make a favourable impression upon them, and to inspire them with confidence ; and Mary again congratulated her husband on the good fortune which had once more attended them, in guiding their footsteps to a place of security, and to one who, apparently, entertained no suspicion as to their real characters, and who, if he should even by any means discover them, they had a right to imagine, from the disposition he had already evinced, would not be likely to betray them. Richard could not, however, go to the same length as his wife in these sanguine expectations, although he endeavoured to assure himself that there was no fear of any discovery taking place. The extraordinary, important, and exciting events of the last few hours—the awful and untimely fate of Mr. Worthington and his wife—their unexpected meeting with the hardened ruffian, Brunston, and his death, had naturally tended to imbue his mind with a painful feeling of awe, which it would not be easy to eradicate ; and the longer he reflected upon them, the more uneasy became his feelings.

"It would seem," he remarked, "as if misfortune were destined to attend all those who in any way become connected with us, or befriend us. A curse follows in our path. Unfortunate Mr. and Mrs. Worthington! so good and amiable, but for us they might probably now be alive and happy."

"Nay, my love," returned his wife, "it is surely wrong and unreasonable to arrive at such a conclusion as that. The death of those inestimable beings to whom we are so largely indebted, was, undoubtedly, a terrible and lamentable visitation of the Almighty, but in what way can we possibly attach blame to ourselves for the calamity? Come, Richard,

you must arouse yourself from this dismal train of thought, and learn to look forward to the future with hope."

"Ah, Mary," said our hero, "how can I do so when I contemplate the many fearful and painful dangers by which we are surrounded? Are we not now friendless wanderers, outcasts from society, pursued by the myrmidons of the law on every side, and what is to become of us, how are we in future to exist, when the limited means we at present have in our possession shall have become exhausted? Oh, that thought drives me to distraction!"

"Try to banish it, my dear Richard," replied Mary, "and trust to the goodness and mercy of Providence."

"Alas!" he ejaculated, "I have long and earnestly tried to do so, but I find that to be impossible. Already my tortured imagination pictures to me the sufferings and privations to which yourself and our poor boy, I fear, are doomed to be exposed when I am no more, and as the fearful picture rises to my imagination, madness almost seizes upon my brain. I behold your emaciated forms sinking upon the earth, worn out with fatigue, and care, and hunger ; I see your pale and ghastly countenances, your hollow, sunken eyes ; I hear your low moans of anguish, and see the multitude standing around you, gazing callously upon you, and mocking your sufferings. I hear them, whilst pointing the finger of scorn at you, call you the wife and offspring of a murderer, and remind you of my ignominious death, and——"

"Hold! hold!" interrupted our heroine, in a hoarse and agitated voice ; "the picture you draw is too frightful for the imagination to support. It will not be realised—I dare not believe that it will; why, then, will you persist in torturing yourself with such terrible thoughts ?"

"Because reason too forcibly convinces me of their probability," he replied ; "and it is in vain that I seek to persuade myself to the contrary. My being discovered in the neighbourhood from which we have just flown, will put my pursuers doubly on the alert, and they are probably now spread all over the country, and ready to prevent our egress at every point. Where, then, is it possible that we can conceal ourselves, and especially when our money is all exhausted? Besides, our present personal appearance is probably by this time well known, and we have now no other means of disguising ourselves. I see nothing but the most imminent and unavoidable danger in whatever direction I turn my eyes. The meeting with Brunston, too, and his death, have filled my mind with additional alarm; and it seems all to be an augury of the fate which is in store for me."

"Oh, why so, Richard?" demanded his wife; "it can never be discovered that you encountered or was acquainted with him, or that he lost his life through your means; and, therefore, what have you to fear? You are not to blame; it was a just retribution on his head; besides, you ought to feel grateful and satisfied that we had been fortunate enough to escape from the cottage before he arrived at it, or the consequences might have been fatal to us. And how doubly thankful ought we to be that he did not recognise you on that fearful night which first introduced the villain to me, for your apprehension might then have been unavoidable. Cheer you, Richard, my husband, for we have, even under all the painful and trying circumstances that have attended us, much to congratulate ourselves upon."

Our hero did not at that time make use of any further observation, but his looks sufficiently testified the real feelings that inhabited his breast, and how little he participated in the hopes which Mary seemed to entertain. Having partaken of the refreshment with which Mr. Judkins supplied them, they felt much revived, and by the genial warmth of the fire; and in a few minutes afterwards the man Giles re-entered the room.

"Well," he observed, "you look much better now, and I am glad to see it. It was a lucky job that you were conducted hither, for you will find that my master is one of the most hospitable of men; and he is always ready and happy to do a good turn for his fellow-creatures who may stand in need of it."

"Believe me, my honest friend," replied our hero, "that I feel most grateful to your worthy master for the kindness he has shown us in the time of need; and should it at any time be in power, we shall not forget to make some return for it."

"Oh, as for that, master," returned Giles, "you may rest yourself quite contented. Farmer Judkins is well off in the world, and he does not require any return for any act of kindness it may be in his power to perform. But you seem tired, and, therefore, if you please, I will conduct you to your chambers."

Richard thanked him, and Giles, having taken up the lamp from the table, led the way into a suite of apartments at the back of the premises, and only a little above the round floor, in which there were beds,

and everything for their accommodation; and after having exchanged a few more observations with them, he bade them good-night, and retired.

Richard and his wife, on finding themselves alone, could not help sinking on their knees, and offering up their thanks to the Supreme for the protection which had hitherto been awarded them, and for the security in which they seemed at present to be placed; and they then took a more minute survey of the apartments in which they found themselves. They were spacious, and furnished comfortably, though in an old style of fashion, and opened into each other. The blinds of the several windows were drawn down, but on raising them, they perceived that they opened upon the back part of the farm-yard, and commanded, as well as the darkness would permit, a view of the country beyond, which, especially at that solemn hour of the night, presented anything but a cheerful aspect. In the ceiling of the inner-chamber, was a skylight, which seemed to communicate with the roofs of some of the outer buildings, and which, from some unaccountable reason, attracted the attention of Richard more than anything else. But in spite of their present apparent security, and the improbability of any person from whom they had cause to apprehend danger intruding upon them, our hero could not entirely divest his mind of the fears and forebodings that occupied it; and having first listened at the door to ascertain whether or not all was still in the house, he threw himself into a seat, and hesitated to go to bed. The storm which had for some time subsided, now re-commenced, and the rain soon rattled down with the same impetuosity, and the thunder roared, and the lightning flashed with equal violence to that which it had done before. Mary Parker could not help shuddering as she witnessed its terrors, but at the same time how grateful did she feel to Providence for granting them a shelter from its fury, and she once more sought, with all the energy at her command, to raise the drooping spirits of her husband.

"Come, my dear Richard," she observed; "we have already suffered enough from the anxieties and trials we have for the last few hours experienced; let us, then, seek to obtain at least a temporary respite from our cares in sleep."

"I do not feel inclined to sleep, my dear Mary," replied our hero, "and, notwithstanding our present apparent security, I cannot resist the apprehensions that cross my mind. Let you and William, however, retire to bed, and I will sit up and watch, in case that any danger should threaten."

"Oh, Richard," she returned; "surely this is most unreasonable and uncalled for; what can there be to fear?"

"I know not," answered her husband; "but I find it impossible to divest my mind of the torturing impression."

"All is quiet in the house," said our heroine; "and we have no reason to doubt the integrity of the farmer; he knows us not, and even if he should, I do not believe, from what we have already seen of him, that he would seek to do us any harm. Come, come, away with such gloomy thoughts as these; and with the bessing of Heaven, at an early hour in the morning we will be far from this locality, and probably safe beyond the reach of our pursuers."

"Would that I could think so," remarked Richard; "but fresh danger seems to enclose us on every side, and whither can we direct our steps? I see nothing but inevitable destruction before us; and for myself, I am resigned, and fully prepared to meet my fate; but for you, my poor devoted wife, and our delicate child— oh! how it tortures my brain to think of the dreadful hardships you have already endured, and those to which it is but too certain you will yet be exposed. This terrible agony and suspense is insupportable."

"Learn to conquer it, dear Richard," said Mary, "and you will yet find that all those torturing forebodings and apprehensions to which you now give indulgence are groundless. I am firm in hope, and would fain inspire you with the same feeling."

"I know well the sincerity and affection that prompt your observations, my Mary" returned her husband, in the most melancholy accents, but at the same time gazing with the most indescribable affection in her pale but beauteous face; "but it is useless for me to seek to deceive and flatter myself and you with any such delusive hopes. The doom that hangs over my head is unavoidable. How fearfully the storm rages; Heaven in its thunder seems to warn me to prepare for that fate which the offended laws of my country will inflict upon me."

"Oh, do not give way to such awful ideas," said Mary; "they freeze the very blood in my veins as I hear you give utterance to them. Consider the lateness of the hour—remember that we shall have but a short time for repose, of which we both stand so much in need after the fatigue we have undergone, and let us immediately retire to bed."

Richard returned no answer to her earnest solicitations, but they seemed to make no impression upon him, and he continued to listen to the voice of the tempest with the most mute, but solemn attention, and the apprehensions that beset his mind appeared to suffer no abatement. Every moment the storm gathered strength, and the flashes of lightning and deafening peals of thunder were fearful and incessant. The loud voice of the heavenly lion seemed to shake the very house to its foundation, and Mary found it so impossible to conquer her fears, that she was frequently obliged to cling to the arm of her husband for support. A silence of several minutes ensued between them, and they gazed with vacant looks of terror in each other's countenance; but it was wonderful the fortitude and self-possession which the boy, William, maintained. At length our hero, as if some sudden fear had seized him, started to his feet, and advancing to one of the windows, hastily drew up the blind, and gazed out upon the night. Mary hastily followed him, and grasping him by the arm, demanded what it was that alarmed him.

"I thought I heard voices in the pauses of the storm," he replied, "and they seemed to be approaching this way."

"Oh, it could only have been imagination," she said; "you see there is no one here. Oh, why will you suffer these fears to have such a powerful ascendancy over your mind? Come away from the window, and let us seek our couch; all have evidently retired to bed in the house, and there is nothing to apprehend."

She had scarcely given utterance to these words, when the bell at the gate was rang violently, and they both started and looked at each other alarmed.

"Ah!" exclaimed Richard; "you see that my apprehensions were not without foundation; some danger threatens, I am convined. Who can that be?"

"Compose yourself," replied his wife. "Most probably it is only some traveller or travellers, like ourselves, who seek shelter from the storm."

At that moment Giles appeared in the yard with a lantern, and made his way towards the gate, and Richard, partly opening the window, listened with breathless attention, whilst his wife was in a state of the greatest suspense; and although she sought to conquer them, and to conceal them as much as possible, her fears were as great as those of her husband. They soon heard the voice of Giles, as if in noisy altercation with several persons, and their apprehensions increased. Mary hastily concealed the light in an obscure part of the room, and then with silent, but earnest gestures, endeavoured to persuade Richard to leave the window, but

he remained obstinate, and fixed his eyes upon the gate as well as the occasional flashes of the lightning would permit him. They were not long kept in suspense; the gate was opened, and the next moment they beheld several persons advancing towards the house, bearing something

THE DEATH OF MAD MOLL.

heavy on their shoulders, which seemed to be a human form, and preceded by Giles with a lantern.

"Ah!" ejaculated Richard, as they approached nearer, and he could more

distinguish them; "by Heaven they are some of our pursuers; we are betrayed, we are lost. It is a human form they bear, too; should they have discovered the body of Brunston?"

"And if they should," replied Mary, "what matters it? It is then most likely that they have merely brought it to the nearest house until a coroner's inquest be holden upon it. Did he not die before we left him? And, therefore, our secret was safe. The farmer knows us not, and, therefore, after all, we have nothing to fear."

"What, not while our pursuers are under the same roof with us?" said our hero, hastily; "we must endeavour to make our escape, or we shall be discovered, and destruction will then inevitably follow."

"Nay, be firm and confident," said Mary, "and all will yet be well. The farmer will not have occasion to describe us, for it is not likely that they will make any inquiries about us. Come, let us away from the window, and listen, for the men have now entered the house."

Richard drew down the blind, and then, in a state of the greatest agitation, himself and his wife approached the door, and listened attentively. For a few minutes, however, all was silent, but at length they heard a confused sound of several voices, among which they recognised that of the landlord, and they were so distinct, that they seemed to proceed from the adjoining room. Richard and his wife drew in their breath, and listened with the utmost anxiety, and the reader may judge of their terror when the following conversation reached their ears:—

"Here the body of this unfortunate man must remain," said one of them, "until such times as a proper investigation has been entered into by the authorities. We found him in an old out-house some distance from this place, and we were in search of far different prey, and which, if we are not much mistaken, will very soon fall into our hands."

"Really, gentlemen," remarked the farmer, "this is a very disagreeable business for me, to have a corpse in my house, and——"

"Well," replied the man who had before spoken, "it cannot be helped, and it is not in our power to relieve you. We must perform our duty, you know."

"True," coincided Mr. Judkins; "but was this unfortuate man quite dead when you discovered him?"

"No," answered the officer.

Richard and his wife trembled, and looked at each other with an expression of the utmost alarm; but they then listened breathlessly to hear what would follow.

"We thought him dead when we first discovered him," continued the man, "but on examining him more minutely we found that he still breathed, and by dint of great exertion he was at length able to speak."

Our hero and his wife could scarcely repress a groan when they heard these words; but they conquered their emotions as well as they could, and awaited with the most torturing anxiety to hear the result of this conversation between the farmer and the officer.

"Well then," said the farmer, "I suppose he was enabled to inform you of the manner in which he came by his death?"

"He was," answered the man; "he declared to us with his dying breath that Richard Parker, the man of whom we are in search, was the author of his death, and, therefore, we are certain that he must be concealed somewhere hereabouts. Have any persons sought shelter from the storm in your house?"

The farmer seemed to hesitate, and the agony of our hero and his wife may be imagined.

"It is useless for you to seek to evade the question I have put to you," remarked the officer; "Richard Parker is a mutineer, a traitor to his king and country, and a murderer; there is a reward offered for his apprehension, as your are probably aware, and you as an honest man, which I take you to be, can have no wish to shield him from justice, I presume?"

"Certainly not," replied Judkins, much to the consternation of our hero and Mary; "to tell you the truth, then, I have given shelter to-night to some persons, whom I imagined were what they represented themselves to be, namely, poor travellers who were overtaken by the storm; and they are at present in the house."

"Ah!" ejaculated the officer, "and what is their description?"

"A man, and a female, and a lad about fourteen years of age," answered Judkins.

"The man attired as a peasant, and the female in widow's weeds?"

"Exactly."

"Ah!" cried the officer, in accents of exultation; "by Heaven, fortune smiles upon us. They are those we seek. In what part of the house are they?"

"In those chambers yonder," replied the farmer.

"Betrayed! destroyed!" gasped forth Richard Parker, unable any longer to control himself; "but I will not be taken alive! Mary, William, farewell for ever upon this earth!"

"Hold!" ejaculated our heroine in a

low hollow voice, and grasping his arm as he drew a pistol from his pocket and was about to present it at his head; "what would you do? It may not be too late to escape. Listen!"

Our hero did so, and the following words from the officer then met their ears:—

"Comrades, let us immediately secure our prisoner."

"Nay," interposed the farmer; "there is surely no occasion for so much haste, now that you know they are secure, and that it is impossible for them to escape you. They are probably now asleep, and in the morning you can capture them without difficulty. I do not suppose that you have any wish to leave the house to-night in such a storm as that now raging?"

"Very true," replied the man. "I will e'en take your word for it, for I should think you are rather too wise to deceive me; so I will just place a couple of sentries at the door of their chamber, and not disturb them till the morning. What a disagreeable surprise it will be for them when they behold us."

The farmer made some reply which Richard and his wife did not catch, and then they heard them move from the room in which this conversation had taken place, and all was again hushed in silence.

The perspiration stood upon the brow of our hero, with the painful excitement of his feelings, but he quickly recovered himself, and breathed more freely again when he found that there was no immediate danger to be apprehended, and he looked at his terrified wife as he ejaculated in low accents—

"There is not a moment to lose; we must quit this house immediately, and make our escape, if possible. Oh, what a fortunate thing it is that we had not retired to rest, for then nothing could have saved us from the power of our enemies. Come, my beloved Mary."

He advanced with noiseless steps to the windows as he thus spoke, but found that they were secured by bolts outside; however, he remembered the one which he had partially opened, and immediately he raised it with as little noise as possible; and having first looked out to be certain that no one was near the spot, he raised Mary in his arms, and safely landed her in the yard below. William sprang after her, our hero followed, and the next instant they were hurrying towards the gate with the speed of lightning, heedless of the storm. but looking back ever and anon with sensations of terror. fearing that they might be pursued. They reached the

gate, however, in safety, and they then fortunately discovered that Giles had, in thoughtlessness, no doubt, left the key in the lock after admitting the officers, and opening it, they were at once at liberty. Mary rushed into the arms of her husband. and sobbed hysterically upon his bosom; but they were both too violently agitated to speak, and having hastily recovered themselves, and called all their strength and energies to their aid, they hurried on their way by the most gloomy path, never once pausing to take their breath, until they had got a considerable distance from the farm, and they imagined that all danger of any immediate pursuit was at an end; and then our heroine, clasping her hands vehemently together, exclaimed,—

"Father of Mercy, I thank Thee for this ! Oh, Richard, my unfortunate husband, from what a terrible danger have we again escaped ; and ought we not now to feel more confident than ever that Providence will not desert us?"

"For the present, we have, indeed, escaped, my beloved wife," replied her husband. "But Heaven only knows how soon the terrible fate which I seek to avoid may overtake me. It seems as though there is no place where we can long conceal ourselves without our pursuers being upon our track ; and I fear that the time will come when we shall find it impossible to save ourselves from falling into their hands."

"Oh, say not so, dearest Richard," returned Mary, "for fortune would now seem to smile upon us; and let us make the best use of the few hours that will be allowed us ere our escape can be discovered to pursue our flight."

"But in what direction can we go?" said Parker, in a despairing voice. "In what part of the country can we hope to find a secure asylum? What a cursed misfortune it was, that the ruffian, Brunston, still survived, and that our pursuers should be led to the very place in which he was. His death will increase the vigilance of the search after us; and so well as the description of our persons is now known, there appears to be scarcely any chance of our long remaining undetected. And here we are again exposed to all the horrors of the night, without the least prospect of our being enabled to obtain a shelter. My beloved wife, and poor boy, it is impossible that you can much longer bear up against such unexampled trials; and I tremble to reflect upon the consequences that must, in all probability befal you."

"Distress not yourself, Richard, on m

account, or that of our boy," answered our heroine. "The thoughts of the danger with which you are threatened will sustain us, and give us strength to endure the trials to which we may be exposed. Come, let us proceed."

"Ah! whither?" said Richard, again beating his forehead in despair; "where can we fly that the myrmidons of the law, so eagerly as they thirst for my blood, will not detect us? Every step that we take may bring them upon us. I am weary of this fruitless struggle for that life which is no longer worth the preserving, and car not what becomes of me."

"And is this the noble Richard Parker, whose boldness and heroism in the hour of danger have been so much talked about?" said his wife, with a look of gentle reproach. "Oh, shame, my husband! I thought not you could so degenerate. But no, I will not upbraid you, for well do I know that fear has never yet found admission to your breast, and that it is only your intense anxiety for myself and our son that causes you thus to give way to anguish and despair. I beseech you let us not delay, for I feel too painfully that every moment is fraught with danger; should our flight from the farm by any accident be discovered before the morning, an immediate pursuit will be sure to ensue, and the fatigue we have already undergone may render it impossible for us to escape."

"But how will you again be able to support the terrors of the tempest?" demanded our hero, in a voice of the deepest emotion; "your poor limbs are already shivering with the cold and wet, and I feel convinced that you must soon sink exhausted. The elements seem to conspire against us, and the wrath of Heaven to pursue us. The storm increases; and there is no place of shelter in his wild part of the country. Oh, God help us in this terrible hour of adversity. And when the daylight dawns, which anon it will, where, oh, where can we conceal ourselves from the penetrating eye of scrutiny and suspicion? Wretched outcasts as we are, we dare not meet the gaze of our fellow creatures, nor seek that relief which our urgent necessities require. Despair! despair! this is more torturing than death itself."

"Exert your energies, dear Richard," again supplicated his wife, "and however fearful and hopeless our prospects may at present appear to be, we may yet be able to surmount all difficulties, and—But why do you thus start? What means that look of terror? Oh, tell me what fresh cause of misery thus seems to distract your brain?"

"Distraction!" exclaimed Richard, with looks of the most agonizing despair, and at the same time hurriedly examining his pockets; "we are ruined, irretrievably ruined! Oh, God!"

"What mean you?" demanded Mary, eagerly; "oh, for the love of Heaven keep me not in suspense!"

"The purse—the purse," gasped forth her wretched husband, "which contained the principal portion of our little money, is gone!"

"Gone?" repeated our heroine, turning ghastly pale, and trembling in every limb

"Yes, yes," replied Richard; "I have lost it; I must have dropped it somewhere about the farm in the hurry and confusion of our flight."

"No, no, it cannot be," said our heroine, in tones of the most indescribable anguish; "you have overlooked it, Richard; Providence surely would not be so unkind to us in this the hour of our adversity. Examine your clothes again, and—"

"No, no," he interrupted; "it is useless to do so; here are but the few shillings that I had loosely in my pockets; the purse is gone. Fate conspires against us. Now we are indeed completely destitute, and have nothing left but to lay us down and die."

Poor Mary, overwhelmed by the agony of her feelings, threw herself into her unfortunate husband's arms, and sobbed convulsively upon his bosom. It did, indeed, seem as though Providence had deserted them, and, notwithstanding all her efforts, she could not help giving herself up entirely to despair. The contents of the purse was their sole dependance in their difficulties; they had now but a few shillings in the world, which must soon become exhausted, and then what was to become of them? The thought was terrible, and it was no wonder that Mary's usual heroic strength of mind for the moment sank beneath it; but she exerted herself to the utmost, and was soon enabled to recover herself, and again sought to impart hope and consolation to her husband.

"Arouse yourself, my beloved Richard," she ejaculated; "terrible as this misfortune is, we may yet, by perseverance and firmness, be able to surmount it, and something may turn up that will render the loss of our money a matter of indifferance. We have yet sufficient for our present necessities, and the All-merciful God, who watches over the humblest of His creatures, will not suffer us to perish of want."

"What other prospect is there before us?" hastily and impatiently demanded our hero ; "are we not going amongst strangers who cannot sympathise with our misfortunes? and who will relieve us ? Oh, God ! this is the severest blow of all ; better had I remained at the farm, and resigned myself to my fate."

"Oh, no," cried Mary, "those are dreadful words, and they thrill my heart with horror as I listen to them. Be firm, be firm, and all may yet turn out more fortunate than we can now at all possibly anticipate. Let us no longer tarry here, for it is useless, and every instant that we delay does but increase the horrors of our situation."

"Oh, I am sick at heart," groaned Richard, clasping his burning temples with despair, "and I know not what to do."

At that moment William, who, during the principal part of the time that this melancholy conversation was going forward, had wandered some short distance from them, hastily approached them with looks of terror imprinted upon his features.

"Oh, hasten, my beloved parents," he ejaculated ; "I see lights moving in the distance as if proceeding from lanterns or torches ; they come in this direction, and I fear that our pursuers are upon our track. Oh, let us immediately away, or we are lost !"

"No," said our hero, folding his arms, and his looks expressive of a firm determination; "let them come. I am resigned to my fate, and will endeavour to meet it as a man."

"Richard," cried his distracted wife, "are you mad? Have you no regard for me or your child? For the love of God, do not stand thus when such danger threatens. And see, the words of William are verified; the lights approach nearer, and are evidently carried by human hands; it must be those who are in search of us, and but a few moments' delay may render all chances of our escape futile. Come, come—thou shalt not tarry here. I will exert all my woman's strength, and drag thee from the spot."

She seized his arm as she spoke, and with the strength of frenzy and despair, forced him away, William following. The lights every instant advanced nearer upon their track, and they could no longer entertain any doubt that their flight from the farm had been discovered, and that those were the officers in pursuit. They turned abruptly into another track, and then they were hidden completely from their view. As fast as their weary and exhausted limbs would permit them, they pursued their way ; but so great were the sufferings to which they had been exposed, and such was the terrible anxiety of their minds, that they could not proceed with the speed they wished; and after a short time they were compelled to pause to rest themselves, and to collect their thoughts. Fiercer and fiercer howled the tempest, and the situation of the unfortunate fugitives, as may be expected, was most deplorable. It was not without the greatest difficulty that Mary could support her cold and weary limbs; but she exerted herself to the utmost for the sake of her wretched husband and her child, and she succeeded much better than, under the painful circumstances, could have been expected. They again proceeded on their way, they knew not whither, frequently looking timidly back, fearful that their pursuers might have gained upon them; but as far as their eyes could penetrate through the darkness they could see nothing of them, and Mary, therefore, began to hope that they had eluded them altogether, and fresh courage nerved her heart. But most wild and dismal was the part of the country they were traversing, and there was not the least prospect of their obtaining a shelter from the storm; and even if they could have met with one, they considered that it would be hardly safe to avail themselves of it, as they might there be discovered by those from whom they were endeavouring to escape. It is astonishing what the human frame is capable of enduring when placed in similar circumstances to our hero and his wife. Richard, indeed, had entirely abandoned himself to despair, and cared not what became of him ; but Mary, although drenched to the skin, and worn out with fatigue, kept up her fortitude in the most extraordinary manner, knowing the desperate and dangerous situation in which her husband was placed, and succeeded in sustaining and consoling him, when he must otherwise have sunk completely, and at once become a victim to the awful fate which was impending o'er his head. The boy, William, too, exhibited the most remarkable firmness for his age, and never did a murmur of complaint escape his lips; his only anxiety being for his parents, and feeling as though he could encounter anything, however terrible, for their dear sakes. In this manner, then, the unfortunate fugitives travelled on their dreary way. What were their feelings or sufferings upon that melancholy occasion, it would be a fruitless task for us to attempt to describe, for the reader may easily imagine it; and, indeed, as Richard in his despair had observed, the elements seemed to have conspired against them, for never had raged a more terrific storm than that which vented its fury on this the night of their dismal wanderings. Persons placed in ordinary circumstances it would have appalled, but they were so completely absorbed in their own sufferings that they were almost indifferent to it, and our hero being urged on by his devoted wife, and perfectly reckless as to what became of him, they continued to hurry forward, nearly unconscious of the frightful storm that battled around them.

But although Mary murmured not, notwithstanding she uttered no word of complaint, merely to reanimate the energy and fortitude of her unfortunate husband, need we attempt to pourtray to the reader the bitter anguish of soul which that heroic woman endured? We are confident that we need not. All the horrors and hopelessness of their situation were presented to her imagination in the most vivid and torturing colours, and she looked forward to the dreadful future with the most painful apprehension. She reviewed in her own mind all the circumstances in which they were placed, and she shuddered with horror and despair as she could not deceive herself into the hope that the predictions of that most extraordinary woman, old Rachael, would not be realised. How was it possible that her wretched husband could escape for ever the awful doom that was impending o'er his head, hunted, pursued as they were? Whither could they go? Where find a shelter, moneyless, friendless as they were? She felt satisfied that the course they were now pursuing was only retarding, but could not avert the dreadful catastrophe which must ultimately befall them, and her heart sickened at the thought, and it was, indeed, only by the most powerful and extraordinary efforts on her part that she could sustain herself, or give the least semblance to firmness, confidence, and resignation.

It was an awful thing to see those poor victims of misfortune, those wretched outcasts from society, wandering through the darkness and the storm on that fearful night; to behold the look of despair expressed on the wan and careworn, but still handsome and manly features of the hero of our tale; to mark the emaciated form of his devoted wife; her mild, but melancholy countenance, and ever and anon the looks of anxiety and affection which she fixed upon her husband; and then to observe the heroic firmness and

patience of the noble-hearted boy, William, as he hurried on by their side, braving with more than manly fortitude the fury of the tempest that howled and bellowed around them, and ever and anon casting a fearful glance around him, to see whether they were pursued. But we have no occasion to draw the picture which must be so vividly presented to the imagination of the reader.

Cold, wet, and weary as they were, their progress was necessarily slow and tedious, and had their pursuers been upon their track, they could scarcely have failed to overtake them. The way they travelled was one of the most dismal that could well be conceived; the road was broken and uneven, and, consequently, rendered their task the far more arduous and toilsome, and several times they were compelled to stop in order to rest themselves, and to enter into a brief consultation with each other as to the best course it would be for them to pursue. All, however, was dark and obscure, and it seemed to them that whichever way they might turn it would be almost a matter of impossibility for them to extricate themselves from the terrible difficulties that encompassed them on every side. They were perfectly at a loss to arrive at any satisfactory conclusion.

They had been for some time traversing a long and dreary lane, but they now emerged from it, and found themselves on a wild and barren moor, which presented even a more cheerless aspect than any part of the country they had hitherto journeyed through, and there was nothing whatever to shelter them from the pitiless pelting of the storm. Richard suddenly stopped, heart-sick and despairing, and fixed a melancholy look upon the pale and careworn features of his partner in misfortune, as he said—

"Let us proceed no further; my heart is full to bursting with these dreadful trials, and all my manly fortitude forsakes me. It is evident that Providence has deserted us, and left us to our fate, and of what use is it, weak mortals as we are, for us to struggle against it? Here, then, enclosed in each other's arms, we will remain, and pray for the speedy arrival of that death which will be such a happy release to us from all our earthly sufferings."

"Oh, Richard," replied our heroine, mustering all her firmness, and looking in his face with an expression of the most unutterable affection; "if you love me and our child as fondly as I believe you do, I beseech you not to talk in this wild and desponding manner. Arraign not the mercy of that Supreme who has hitherto protected us through all the terrible difficulties that have obstructed our path, but rather supplicate to him for an extension of His goodness, and I feel a blessed assurance that such prayers will not be unvailing. Oh, I can scarcely believe that it is my husband. that it is Richard Parker, who never yet was daunted at the most imminent peril, whether in the battle's heat or on the stormy waves, who has just addressed me. Arouse, arouse, my beloved husband, and, with a bold front, look forward with confidence to the happy termination of our sorrows."

"And what is there at present to inspire me with any such hopes?" demanded our hero, impatiently, and at the same time fixing an earnest look upon her countenance. "Are we not driven to the last extremity? Houseless, penniless, wandering without any place of destination, and soon shall we not be reduced to starvation? Can I look on the sufferings of yourself and our noble-hearted, uncomplaining boy, think you, without feeling at once the maddening horrors of our situation? Can you expect me to be calm, and patient, and hopeful in the midst of all this? Oh, I must, indeed, be less than a man if I could be so. It is true that I have been engaged in all the bloody horrors of the deadly conflict; that I have, unnerved, been exposed to all the terrific violence of the stormy ocean; but what were those terrible trials compared to that which I now experience, the cruel, the unexampled sufferings of all I hold valuable and precious in life? Nothing; mere trifles, scarcely worthy of a serious thought. You tell me to look forward with a firm reliance on the goodness of Providence for a happy termination of our sorrows; but what have I to inspire me with any such hopes? They are all fallacious, and the only termination that I can see to our troubles is death."

"Death!" gasped forth Mary, and fixing upon him a fearful look.

"Ay, death, Mary," replied her husband, in a hoarse and hollow voice, grasping her wrist with more than usual violence, and at the same time fixing upon her an expression which made her shudder and shrink appalled to contemplate; "what is there left for such poor, friendless, unfortunate wretches as us to live for? Had we not better at once terminate our misery? But a moment, this pistol will do its deadly office, all will be over, and the voice of the tempest will howl a requiem o'er our remains. Come, come, some instinctive Power, which I know not how to resist, urges me on, and I am fully prepared for

the deed. One solemn prayer, then, to Heaven for mercy, and let those words be the last that we shall utter in this world."

"Richard!" exclaimed our heroine, fixing upon him a look of astonishment and horror, "madness surely must have seized upon your brain, or you could never give utterance to words such as those with which you have just now shocked my ears. Would you become a murderer? Is it thus you would repay my devoted affection towards you? But no, no, I cannot, I will not believe that it is the spirit of my husband that speaks. Some fiend has taken possession of your senses, and would urge you on to the destruction of your eternal soul. For the love of mercy, and by all your future hopes, do not give way to such horrible thoughts as those which you have just now expressed. Why do you fix that awful look upon me, and grasp my arm with such vehemence? For the first time in my life, Richard, my husband, I shudder to gaze upon you. Release your hold; becalm yourself, and supplicate the mercy and forgiveness of Heaven for the guilty thoughts you have, in the frenzy of your despair, entertained."

"Mary," returned the wretched man, in the same fearful, and almost unearthly accents, and still retaining his hold of her arm; "you appeal to me in vain; monstrous though it may seem to be, reason and humanity prompt the deed I would commit. Why should we thus linger on in misery, and with nothing but the prospect of horrors too great for contemplation before us, when we have the ready means of terminating our sufferings? Heaven will in its infinite mercy pardon the deed, and thus then——"

"Hold! madman!" cried Mary, in tones of desperate firmness, which were sufficient to thrill and paralyse his very soul, and at the same time arresting his arm, he having as he spoke presented a loaded pistol at her head; "what would you do? Oh shame, shame! For the first time in my life I am shocked and horrified at the monstrous guilt of your own conceptions. Put away that deadly weapon, for whilst you hold it in that threatening manner towards me, I can scarcely believe that it is my husband who stands before me."

"Father, dear father," supplicated the poor boy, in the most impressive accents, and throwing himself on his knees at the feet of his distracted parent; "oh, forbear! Dear mother and myself are prepared to endure any sufferings with which it may please Heaven to visit us, firm and unmurmuring, but you will not, cannot commit so cruel a deed as to sacrifice our lives."

The simple, but earnest appeal of his son completely paralysed the unfortunate man, he dropped the pistol from his hand, and for a few moments he stared upon them with vacant looks, without being able to give utterance to a syllable; but at length clasping his burning temples, he exclaimed:

"Great God! what a monster I am; to what a fiendish act was I about to commit myself. I must indeed be mad, or such horrible thoughts could never for a moment enter my imagination. Mary, my poor, suffering, devoted Mary, I scarcely dare look upon you, for you must view me now as a miscreant of the blackest dye, and——"

"Oh, no, no, no," interrupted his wife, and throwing herself at the same time into his arms, "you are still my husband, and you shall find me the same devoted, uncomplaining partner in your troubles that I have hitherto endeavoured to prove myself."

"And can you forgive me, Mary?" he asked, looking in her pale face with an expression that told far more than words could have done the poignant, the almost insupportable anguish of his feelings. "Can you pardon me for the dreadful, the diabolical thoughts that, in the anguish of despair, I suffered to take possession of my brain?"

"Forgive you, Richard?" she answered, and her looks sufficiently told the earnestness and sincerity with which she spoke. "Oh, yes, freely, gladly, most heartily; and never—oh, never will I repeat what has this night taken place."

"Best, most generous, most amiable of women," cried our hero, clasping her with the fondest transport and gratitude to his bosom, "how shall I ever be able to repay you for this unexampled act of forbearance and mercy? I shudder at myself when I think of the awful and guilty act which in my madness I was about to perpetrate, and dare scarcely look you in the face. Yielding, then, to your will, I will still struggle with my evil destiny, and endeavour to acquire firmness and resignation by your bright example."

"A noble resolution, my beloved husband," said our heroine, returning his fond embrace with equal order; "your words inspire me with fresh fortitude and confidence, and the sufferings we are experiencing sink into comparative insignificance before my imagination. Come, my love, let us again on our weary way, and with the hope that we may shortly find some relief. We are now several miles from the farm, and those who were in pursuit of us have evidently lost our track."

"But, alas!" sighed Richard, as he gazed dismally around him, "our prospects are still no brighter than they have hitherto been. The storm continues with unabated violence, and unless we find immediate relief, which in this wild place we are not likely to do, it is impossible that you and our child can much longer bear up against the horrors it is our fate to encounter."

"Oh, fear not for me, dear Richard," repeated his wife, with a faint smile, and concealing her own sufferings as well as she could; "I feel revived, and endowed with fresh strength and vigour to brave every hardship we may yet have to experience. Let us proceed, and soon, I trust we shall arrive at some place of shelter.

Richard Parker returned no answer, but taking the arm of his wife within his own, he proceeded on his way across the gloomy waste. It was now about four o'clock in the morning, but it being at the latter period of the year, there were yet no signs of daylight; but that was a thing which disturbed them not, and, in fact, they almost dreaded its approach, lest they should be seen by any one who might then be about, and recognised. As the tempest had abated nothing whatever of its fury, their deplorable condition may well be imagined, fatigued, too, as they were with travelling and anxiety of mind, but still Mary remained firm, and never once uttered a complaint. The moor was of great extent, and there seemed to be not the least chance of obtaining any relief there, for it was not likely that they would meet with any human habitation in such a wild and dismal place. They, however, travelled on, and at length a vivid flash of lightning revealed to then a large dark shadow in the distance, which, as near as they could ascertain from the slight glimpse they were enabled to obtain of it, appeared to be a building of some description.

"Providence has heard our prayers," said Mary, "and at length, I trust, we shall be enabled to obtain a shelter and a rest from the fury of the battling elements. That surely is a human habitation?"

"And if it should be," returned our hero, "how can we hope to obtain any relief at this early hour of the morning?"

"Oh," replied his wife, "there surely cannot be those so destitute of feeling as to refuse us."

"I know not," remarked Richard, "it

is hard to have to trust to the humanity and benevolence of strangers. Besides, situated as we are, may there not be danger in applying to them? Should we be recognised——"

"Nay," interrupted our heroine, "do not give way to any such apprehensions; it is not likely that anyone will know us in this strange place, where we have never been before, and I trust that the description of our persons has not yet reached them."

ARMER JUDKINS GIVES THE WANDERERS SHELTER FROM THE STORM.

"After the many disappointments and narrow escapes we have experienced," returned her husband, "it is not surprising that I should feel doubtful."

"At any rate," observed Mary, "we must be prepared to run the risk, and I feel confident that the Almighty will take compassion on our deplorable condition, and not suffer us again to be exposed to that danger from which we have just escaped. Let us proceed with all the haste we can, and if we can succeed in obtaining a few hours' rest and shelter, we shall be the better prepared to collect ourselves, and to pursue our way to some probable place of safety."

"Alas!" ejaculated our hero, "with what hope, what prospect, can we do so, almost penniless as we now are? What a cursed misfortune it was for us that we lost the money we possessed, and which would have furnished us with the means of existence for some time to come."

"Well, my dear Richard," answered our heroine, "it is useless now to regret it, and Heaven, I hope, will not suffer us to be sacrificed altogether."

"But what is to become of us, without means, or a friend to whom we can apply for assistance?" said Richard.

"Do not entirely despair," returned his wife; "should we be fortunate enough to meet with some place where we can find even temporary security, we shall be able to communicate with our friend, Mr. Adams, and he will, no doubt, again strain a nerve, and forward us all the assistance in his power."

"No," said her husband; "I cannot think of it; we already owe that excellent man a debt of gratitude we shall never be able to repay. Besides, if I were even so disposed, how could I venture to communicate with him, when by so doing I might not only betray myself, but likewise involve him in the most imminent danger?"

"Well, Richard," remarked his wife, "it is useless to discuss this point at present, but let us hope for the best, and proceed at once to this building, in which we may probably find the relief we seek."

They increased their speed, and as they did so, the outlines of the building, for such it evidently was, were more distinctly visible to them, and it appeared to be of a more extensive description than the ordinary character of dwellings.

"Should it prove to be a nobleman's mansion," observed Richard, "our hopes of relief will be at an end, for it is but seldom that the wealthy have any sympathy or commiseration for unfortunate creatures in our destitute condition."

"It is a most unlikely spot for a gentleman's mansion," returned our heroine, "and even should it prove to be so, I will not judge so uncharitably of its inmates as to suppose that they will refuse us at least a shelter from the storm."

Richard returned no answer, and hurrying on, they soon arrived at the object which had attracted their attention, and which they were surprised to find was the ruins of some mansion, apparently of great antiquity, and which had evidently been left for many years neglected, and to moulder into decay. Its walls were covered with ivy, and it had altogether a most gloomy and solemn appearance; the oaken door had fallen from its hinges, and large fragments of stone had fallen across the porch, and nearly obstructed the entrance.

Richard and his wife stood for a minute or two and surveyed this ancient edifice in silence, and they hesitated to venture to enter, lest, in spite of the unlikeliness of its appearance, it should be inhabited by some persons of questionable character, and who might give them anything but a welcome reception.

"It is a gloomy place," observed Richard, "and in such a lonely part of the country as this, it would form an excellent retreat for persons of bad character. I almost fear to enter it."

"Oh," replied Mary, "indeed I do not think there is anything to apprehend; ruinous as this building is, it would form but an indifferent retreat for those who might need concealment. Come, Richard, let us at once enter the ruins, for they will at least afford us a shelter until the storm has subsided, and after resting ourselves we shall then be able to proceed with our journey, and probably arrive at some village or town, where we may be enabled to obtain some relief to our present necessities."

Richard still hesitated, and looked up at the different broken casements of the building, and all was involved in darkness, and there were not the least signs of its being inhabited by any human being. He then advanced to the porch and listened attentively, but all was buried in the most profound silence, and regaining courage, he took the arm of his wife, and clambering with much difficulty over the broken fragments of stone, they entered the gloomy ruins.

CHAPTER XXI.

THE ADVENTURE IN THE RUINS.—THE SURPRISE.—THE HIDDEN MONEY.—THE FUTURE FORTUNE OF THE FUGITIVES.

ALL was buried in profound darkness, except at intervals, when the lightning flashed through the different apertures which the ravages of time had made in the walls, and they, therefore, had to grope their way with caution, and without being able to distinguish much of the character of the place. The broken pavement was thickly strewn with fragments of loose stone, and they were frequently in danger of falling, and the task to them in their present fatigued state was one of the most laborious description. However, they persevered, and after having traversed several ruinous apartments, into which the rain poured in torrents, they at length found themselves in one which was not in such a state of decay as the rest, and where they might obtain that shelter from the storm of which they stood so much in need. Here they seated themselves upon fragments of the broken stone, and as well as the darkness would permit them, gazed upon the objects by which they were surrounded, but which were not at all calculated to excite the least interest.

"Thank Heaven," said our heroine, after a pause, "we are here secure and sheltered from the storm, and although the place is a gloomy one, and calculated to inspire anything but pleasant thoughts, under all the circumstances we aught to be grateful to Providence for having conducted our footsteps hither."

"It is, indeed, a dismal place," remarked Richard, "but it is in strict accordance with the sad thoughts that at present occupy our minds. What will be the termination of this alarming adventure?"

"I trust a happy one," replied our heroine; "at any rate, we have eluded the vigilance of our pursuers."

"For the present," said her husband; "but we know not how soon they may overtake and detect us, for it is not likely that they will abandon their search, as they will feel confident that we cannot have proceeded far, exhausted as we were, and exposed to such a storm."

"These apprehensions, I do believe, are groundless," said Mary, "for it is not likely that they can form the least conjecture of the particular route we have pursued, or they would have overtaken us before this. It was fortunate that we discovered them when they were upon our track. And I wonder that they were so imprudent as to carry lights with them, for they might be certain that they would betray them to us, and cause us to change our direction."

"Alas!" ejaculated our hero, "I fear that our escape is but temporary, and I am completely lost and bewildered to know in what way in will be most prudent for us in future to act."

"Dismiss all fears from your mind," returned Mary, "and I have no doubt that we shall yet be enabled to find a friend, who will take compassion on us, and afford us that relief and protection which we so much require."

Ah, Mary," replied her husband, "I fear that you are too sanguine in your hopes; what assistance can we expect to find amongst strangers? Indeed, I shall hesitate to apply to any one lest I should be detected, and not again have an opportunity to escape. In vain I seek to shake from my mind the melancholy impression which has gained such a strong hold on it; it is too probable, far too probable to be removed, and every moment does but serve to increase its influence. I feel that my days are numbered, and that the day is not far distant when we must be parted for ever in this world, and what will then become of you, my beloved Mary, when you are left alone, destitute, and unprotected? The thought is surely one that is sufficient to drive me to madness."

"Then exert all your energies, dear Richard," returned his wife, "and banish it. Oh, what anguish does it impart to my mind to behold you give way to such fearful forebodings. Conquer it, my husband, and view the future on the brightest side."

"It is impossible, Mary," he returned; "there is nothing whatever that can induce me to cling to hope. But try to compose yourself to sleep for a short time, which will serve to refresh you, and I will sit by and watch over your safety."

"Oh, no," answered our heroine. "I cannot sleep in this dismal place; but the rest will refresh me, and I shall be prepared to resume the journey when the storm has ceased."

"I am completely at a loss which way to pursue," remarked Richard; "but all paths are alike to me; for each is fraught with danger, and I fancy that every eye will be fixed upon me with suspicion."

"You must conquer those feelings, Richard," she replied, "or you will betray yourself to those who would otherwise probably not have the least suspicion of you."

"Too well I know the necessity of it, but much I fear that I shall not be able to accomplish the task."

"Oh, say not so," returned Mary; "remember how much you have at stake, and for my sake, and that of our son, try to be firm. If we can only succeed in reaching some distant part of the country, we shall be secure, and in time all further pursuit of you will be abandoned as hopeless."

"But how are we to gain a distant and obscure part of the country without money?" demanded our hero; "and should we even succeed in doing so, what is then to become of us? how are we to support ourselves?"

"Providence will furnish us with some

means of doing so," answered Mary; "and, therefore, let us not abandon ourselves entirely to despair."

"Alas!" sighed her husband, "have we not too much painful reason to do so? What other prospect is there before us than that which my distracted imagination pictures? But it is useless to talk thus; try to compose your feelings, and depend upon it, while I have the power it shall be my constant care and anxiety to watch over your safety."

Mary returned no answer, and a dismal silence of some minutes ensued, during which interval the most melancholy thoughts occupied both their minds.

The wind howled mournfully through the dilapidated chambers of that ancient place; the heavy peals of thunder threatened to shake the crazy ruins to the earth, and the vivid flashes of lightning darted in at numerous fissures, and rendered everything around them still more awful. The limbs of poor Mary trembled with the wet and cold, and she felt a faintness and deadly sickness at heart which was quite overpowering. But still she endeavoured as well as she could to conquer it and to conceal her emotions from her husband, knowing full well how much it would add to the anguish of mind he was enduring. As for Richard, he sat in moody silence, and it was evident that his anguish had increased instead of having abated.

The boy, overpowered by the extraordinary fatigue he had undergone, had fallen asleep. But suddenly Richard and his wife were aroused by hearing a sound which resembled that of approaching footsteps, and they looked at each other with mingled feelings of fear and amazement.

"Some one comes," said our hero, in a low voice; "should it be those who are in pursuit of us we are lost. Hark!"

"Be calm," said Mary, "for after all we may be mistaken, though I certainly thought that I heard the sound of footsteps."

"There again," said our hero, as the sounds more distinctly than before saluted their ears; "there is no mistaking that; some one is in the ruins, and they are coming this way."

Nearer and nearer the individual, whoever it was, continued to advance, and they now beheld a light glimmering through one of the crevices in the wall. Richard, having aroused his son, looked hastily around him, and he then beheld a deep recess at the farther end of the apartment, before which stood the broken remains of a pillar, which offered a fitting place of concealment, and they immediately retired into it, and awaited with anxiety the result of this adventure. They were not long kept in suspense, for almost immediately afterwards the form of a man, bearing a lantern in his hand, made its appearance, and he gazed cautiously around him, while our hero and his wife had a full opportunity of scrutinising his features and watching his actions.

He was a short old man, with long white hair, and shrivelled features, and his eyes had a sinister expression, which it was anything but pleasant to look upon. He carried under his arm a small box, which he seemed to hug to him, as though it contained something precious, and which he was loath to part with, and having finished his survey, he placed the lantern on the ground, and sitting himself down upon one of the stones that the fugitives had just quitted, he seemed for a minute or two absorbed in meditation. Richard and his wife, as may be supposed, watched him with the greatest wonder and curiosity, and scarcely dared to breathe, lest the sound should reach his ears, and discover them; and they were at a complete loss to conjecture what could be his errand in the ruins, at such an unseasonable hour, and in such a storm; but their curiosity was soon gratified in the most extraordinary way. Having again surveyed the ruinous apartment, but apparently not noticing that part of the ruins where they were concealed, the old man muttered in a low, but chuckling tone of voice, the following words:—

"There is no one here, though I need not have expected there was, for these ruins are avoided by most persons with a feeling of superstitious awe, and I, therefore, need not fear any interruption or discovery. The money I have with me, I will conceal beneath the stone where I have so often deposited other cash, and never found it disturbed. It is not likely that it would be, for who would think of finding buried money in such a place as this? It will be safer here than in my own house, for I am inclined to think that there are suspicious characters in the neighbourhood, so if they think to rob me they will find themselves mistaken, ha! ha! ha!—Let me see that I have brought it all away with me."

He opened the box as he spoke, and proceeded to count over his gold, while the astonishment and excitement of Richard and his wife may be much better imagined than described.

"Five and twenty guineas," the old

man said at length ; "it is all right, and I only wish it was double the sum ; however, it will not be long, I dare say, before I shall be able to add to the hoard. Now, then, to conceal it."

He stooped down close to where he had been sitting, and taking a large clasp knife from his pocket, he proceeded to rake the dirt from around a stone of a dark colour, and which he at length raised, and having made a hole in the mould underneath, he deposited the box in it, and then replaced the stone carefully over it. He arose from his knees, and once more looked cautiously around him to be certain that no one was watching him, and an expression of satisfaction and exultation was upon his forbidding features as he ejaculated :

"There all is secure, and I need be under no apprehension that any one will discover it. It is an excellent idea of mine to conceal my money there. Ha! ha! ha! But now to return home, for I confess that these ruins always excite feelings of dread in my mind whenever I behold them."

Having thus spoken, the old man quitted the room, and his footsteps might be heard as he stumbled over the broken fragments in his way. It would be almost impossible to give any idea of the emotions of Richard Parker and his wife at the extraordinary scene they had witnessed, and when they were convinced that the old man had quitted the ruins, they issued from the place of their concealment, and advanced eagerly towards the spot where he had buried his money, and for a few minutes they were so much astonished at all they had seen that they could not give utterance to a word, and, in fact, they could not without difficulty persuade themselves that they had not been labouring under the influence of some extraordinary dream.

"What have we witnessed, Richard?" at length said Mary, and looking earnestly and with an expression of mingled feelings in her husband's face.

"That which has caused me no less gratification than astonishment," answered our hero. "It was the All-wise will of Providence which directed us to these ruins, and placed us in the way of redeeming that money we had lost, and of which we stood so much in need."

"But," said his wife, in a hesitating tone, "think you that we should be justified in appropriating the hidden gold of this old man to our use?"

"Yes," replied Richard ; "you know, Mary, that my soul revolts from the bare idea of committing a dishonest act ; but surely, destitute and desperately circumstanced as we are, the Almighty will pardon us for securing that money which it seems that its sordid owner stands so little in need of, or he would not have disposed of it in the manner he has done. Oh, Mary, this circumstance, so remarkable and so unexpected, has indeed revived my hopes, for had we not received some timely relief, what would have become of us? How could we have existed ?—It does indeed seem as if the Almighty had not altogether deserted us, and terrible though the dangers are by which we are surrounded, I will endeavour to banish that absolute despair which had before taken possession of my mind."

"Oh, how it glads my heart, my beloved Richard," said our heroine, "to hear you talk thus ; still persevere in encouraging the same ideas, and, depend upon it, you will not be doomed to disappointment. But this remarkable old man—oh, what will be his feelings when he discovers his loss?"

"Mary," he replied, "it is useless for us to trouble ourselves upon that subject; it will be a just punishment to the sordid miser ; and, if we may judge from his observations, the loss of this sum of money will not be of any considerable consequence to him. But come, I must not delay. Let me secure the gold, lest the old man should change his mind, which is not at all improbable, and returning to the ruins, remove it again from the place where he has deposited it."

Mary made no reply, and our hero stooping down, in a very few minutes had removed the stone, and had the box in his possession. With eager haste he opened it, and having satisfied himself of its glittering contents, he deposited it in his pocket with a look of satisfaction.

"This money will supply our wants for some time to come," he remarked ; "and should we be able to elude the vigilance of our pursuers for only a short time longer, we may succeed in escaping to some remote part of the country, where we can remain unknown."

"Oh, yes," ejaculated Mary, confidently, "Providence will indeed assist us, and we shall, I am convinced, ere long be released from those troubles by which we are at present surrounded, and once more restored to that happiness to which we have so long been strangers."

"I would fain think so," returned our hero ; "but, alas ! when I reflect upon the melancholy circumstances of my fate,

I cannot expect that real happiness can ever again be mine."

"Say not so, Richard," observed his wife, " but, on the contrary, look forward with hope to the future, and try to bury the painful past in oblivion."

"Oh, that is impossible," replied Richard ; "what must ever be the anguish of my mind, as the dreadful transactions of the past crowd upon my memory, and I reflect upon the almost unexampled sufferings to which you, my faithful wife, have been subjected, and all through your fond devotion to one who I fear has never been enabled to prove himself worthy of you ?"

"Richard," ejaculated our heroine, with a look of gentle reproach, "your words astonish and pain me. After all the many years that we have been acquainted, and those in which we have been united to each other, tell me, what has there ever been in my conduct towards you to warrant such observations as those you have just now made use of ? Has it not been my constant aim, my most anxious care, to endeavour to prove to you the truth and sincerity of my attachment—to cheer you in the hour of affliction, and to inspire you with hope ? Have I not participated in all the misfortunes and vicissitudes it has been our painful lot to encounter without one murmur of complaint? And do you not believe me when I declare that I am still prepared to brave every danger we may still be called to experience, nay, even willingly to lay down life itself for your dear sake ?"

"Oh, yes, my beloved Mary, best and most amiable of wives and of women," replied our hero, energetically, and at the same time clasping her to his bosom with a fervour that expressed much more powerfully than words could possibly have done the sincerity of his feelings ; "too well do I know that; and when I reflect upon it, it only serves to prove to me more than all my own unworthiness. Mary, what is there that I am not prepared to do to evince to you my unbounded, my inexpressible gratitude to you for all the sacrifices you have made for my sake ?"

"Richard," replied his wife, "I am surprised to hear you still persist in giving utterance to observations such as these. What have I done more than my duty ? and I should indeed be unworthy of the name of woman, could I have acted differently to the manner in which I have done. But away with such gloomy and torturing thoughts as those which you have permitted to take possession of your mind ; although I am ready to admit that the peculiar and extraordinary events and horrors we have within the last few hours only experienced, have been sufficient to excite you, and to prostrate your energies. But let us be thankful to that All-merciful Power who has given us strength and fortitude to support them."

"True, my Mary, he returned, "we should indeed be most grateful ; but the storm has somewhat abated, and it is necessary that we shoul quit these ruins with as little delay as possible ; for something might induce the old man to return to ascertain whether his gold be still safe in the place where he deposited it, and—Ah! what mournful sound was that ?"

Mary heard it at the same moment as her husband, and started, trembled, and listened attentively. It was repeated, and sounded like the cry of some person in pain, and gradually approached nearer towards the ruins.

" What can be the meaning of this?" said our hero; "there! did you not hear cries for help? Some unfortunate person has probably met with some accident, or has perhaps been waylaid and ill-treated by ruffians. The sounds seem advancing this way. What is to be done ? Where will the remarkable and extraordinary events of this night terminate ?"

"Be cautious, Richard," said his wife, " or there is no knowing in what danger we may involve ourselves. The sounds evidently become more distinct, and are approaching nearer towards the ruins. Let us conceal ourselves, and await with patience the result of this singular adventure."

"Should any danger threaten us," said our hero, "I am most fortunately armed. You will be prepared to act with your usual firmness, I am convinced, Mary."

"Oh, yes," she answered, " you may depend upon me. But still I trust that we, at any rate, have no danger to apprehend."

A deep and painful groan, more distinct than any they had before heard, now struck their ears, and it seemed as if it proceeded from only a short distance from the ruins. Richard motioned his wife to silence and firmness, and then made his way to the entrance to the ruins, and looked eagerly beyond as far as his eyes could penetrate through the darkness, but he could not perceive any object, and all was now again as still as death, save the hollow murmurings of the storm as it rolled off in the distance. Richard returned to his wife, and they looked at each other surprised, and with expressions of bewilderment.

Mary was about to make some reply,

when she was prevented from doing so by the sound of approaching footsteps, and it was evident that some person or persons had entered the ruins. Richard hastily grasped the arm of his wife, and hurried her and their son into the place where they had formerly concealed themselves; and they had scarcely done so when two men entered the dilapidated apartment in which they were, and one of them opening a dark lantern which he had with him, looked anxiously around the place, and our hero and his wife had a distinct view of their persons and features. They were dressed as labouring men, were of tall and muscular proportions, and their features were particularly coarse and repulsive.

"This is not one of the most cheerful looking places in the world, Ralph," remarked one of the fellows. "Well, we have made but a sorry night's work of it, I am afraid. The old fellow not to have a single coin about him. Well, so much the worse for him; I think we have settled his business."

"Yes," coincided the other; "and what have we gained by so doing? Murder is all very well, if you only get paid for the trouble and the risk you run."

"Well, well," returned his companion, "we do not know yet whether or not we shall reap any benefit. The old fellow, in the agony of his terrors, declared that he had only just buried some money in these ruins, and should he have spoken the truth, we shall not have much cause to complain. Let us see whether we can find the spot which he described to us."

Mary and her husband shuddered as they listened to this brief conversation between the villains, for it was quite evident from it that the unfortunate old man whose money was in their possession, was the victim alluded to, and they could not help feeling the deepest commiseration for the fate which had too probably befallen him. They, however, remained silent, and watched the motions of the ruffians narrowly. They now proceeded to examine the broken pavement of the room, and at last their eyes rested upon the spot beneath which the miser had deposited his gold.

"Ah!" exclaimed one of the men; "this must be the stone which he mentioned, and see, it has evidently been but recently removed. Quick, and let us see what fortune will send us."

They immediately proceeded to raise the stone, which they quickly accomplished, and having gazed eagerly into the hole beneath, they gave utterance to the most dreadful oaths when they perceived that it was empty.

"D—n!" cried Ralph (as his companion had called him), "the old wretch has deceived us!—There is nothing here!—May perdition seize his soul for this. We have had all our trouble for nothing."

"Curses light upon it!" exclaimed his companion; "but we have had some revenge. Let us return to him, and if he still survives we will put a period to his existence."

Our hero was so horror-struck and disgusted by all that he had heard, that he could scarcely contain himself, and was about to start forward from the place of his concealment, and to confront the murderers, when his terrified wife convulsively detained him, and they awaited in silence, but the greatest anxiety, the departure of the miscreants.

"Come, Ralph," said his companion, after they had both for several moments been giving vent to their fierce feelings of rage and disappointment, in the most frightful and disgusting maledictions; "it is no use for us to remain here, and we may only involve ourselves in danger by doing so. We must endeavour to make the best of this. Worse luck now, better another time. Come, it will soon be daylight, and we had better not be seen lurking about in this neighbourhood, especially should the body of the old fellow be discovered, for it is not at all unlikely, from our anything but prepossessing appearance, that we might be suspected."

"True," said Ralph, "but it is d—d vexing that we should be thus deceived and disappointed."

"Well," returned the other, "it can't be helped, so it is no use grumbling about it."

Ralph made some reply, which our hero and his wife could not hear, and the ruffians then retired from the place, and having satisfied themselves that they had quitted the ruins altogether, they ventured from their hiding-place, and for a few minutes were so much overpowered by their feelings of horror and excitement by all that they had heard, that they could not give utterance to a syllable.

"Good God, Richard!" at length said our heroine, "what a terrible adventure is this. The unfortunate old man; alas! I fear, from what these wretches said, that an awful fate has befallen him. And we have got his money. Oh, I dread that we should appropriate a single coin of it to our use after what has occurred."

"Nay, Mary," replied her husband, "your scruples, though natural, are unjust. Accident has placed it in our possession, and surely, situated as we are, it is better that we should have it, than the brutal miscreants who sought to obtain possession of it by such inhuman means. It seems to be a just retribution of the Almighty, and——"

"But," interrupted our heroine, "should the unfortunate man be no more, his body will soon be discovered, a hue-and-cry will be raised in pursuit of his murderers, and wandering about in our present wretched condition, might we not be apprehended on suspicion? and the money being found upon us, how terrible might be the consequences. Oh, I shudder to think of them. Let us deposit the money where we found it, and trust to Providence to extricate us from the difficulties by which we are at present surrounded."

"Mary," returned our hero, "it is little short of madness to talk thus, when we are driven to such a state of desperation and destitution. Leave that money which will supply our present necessities, and probably serve to remove us from danger, here buried in the earth, useless to any one? The idea is preposterous, and much as I am ever ready to yield to your judgment and advice, I cannot entertain it for a moment. Come, my love, arouse yourself, and let us depart from here, for I do not consider that it is safe for us to remain her any longer. We have but to exert ourselves for a short time longer, and most likely we shall find some place where we may obtain that rest and refreshment of which we so much stand in need, after the extraordinary and almost unparalleled exertions we have undergone."

"Unparalleled, indeed," said Mary; "so many terrible and exciting events occurring within a few hours, seem to be almost incredible."

"True," coincided her husband; "but let us endeavour to subdue their effect upon our mind. The storm has at length again ceased; let us then away, and trust in Heaven for protection."

Mary returned no answer, and she was glad to see the fresh hopes and courage that had sprung up in the bosom of our hero; and he having first looked cautiously out to see that no one was near the sept, they emerged from the ruins, and proceeded on their way, taking the direction from whence they had heard the cries of distress.

The grey mists were now fast dispersing, and the first streak of day was just appearing in the eastern horizon, so that they had a better opportunity of distinguishing the objects around them. The aspect of the country was, however, still gloomy and cheerless enough, nor did they as far as their eyes could penetrate discover any signs of a human habitation. Notwithstanding the unequalled fatigue, both of body and mind, which the unfortunate fugitives had undergone, they felt somewhat refreshed by the temporary rest they had had at the ruins; and as the storm had ceased, their situation was, of course, not half so miserable and hopeless as it had been before. The fortitude with which our heroine and the boy William supported the trials to which they were subjected, was most remarkable; it seemed almost incredible, and the heart of Richard Parker overflowed with gratitude to the Supreme Being who had given them strength to sustain an accumulation of terrors and difficulties, under which ordinary individuals must have sunk. They had not proceeded far from the ruins, however, when they perceived some object, which appeared to be the form of a human being, stretched upon the earth, at no great distance from them, and their fears anticipating what it was, they hastened towards it, and were horror-struck at discovering it to be the lifeless body of the unfortunate old man who was the subject of their thoughts. He had received several dreadful injuries, apparently from blows and kicks, his face was covered with blood, his features terribly disfigured, and he was quite dead. Mary shuddered, and could not repress a groan at the appalling spectacle, while Richard gazed on the lifeless form of the ill-fated old man, with feelings of the deepest commiseration and regret.

"The inhuman wretches," he exclaimed, "may the terrible vengeance of Heaven pursue ye, as undoubtedly it will, for this hideous crime. Alas! had it not been for his sordid avarice, he might have been spared this untimely and fearful end."

"What a terrible sight is this, Richard," said his wife, again shuddering; "the blood freezes in my veins as I contemplate it. May his brutal murderers be detected, is my fervent prayer, and brought to that condign punishment which they so richly merit. But let us hasten from this dreadful scene, for should we be discovered here, we shall be suspected of being his murderers, and nothing can then save us from destruction."

"True, Mary," returned our hero; "and we can do no good by remaining here; the body of the ill-fated man will, no doubt, soon be discovered, and his inhuman assassins pursued, and, I trust, brought to justice. Come, Mary, seek to banish the painful impression which this

THE OLD MISER VISITING THE RUINS TO BURY HIS MONEY.

awful event must naturally have made upon your mind, and let us proceed on our way, with the hope that we may shortly find that relief which we so much need."

They turned one melancholy look of pity upon the mutilated remains of the poor old man, and then striking into a contrary path to that which they had hitherto been pursuing, hurried on their way. Still, there was nothing to inspire them with any hope, or the prospect of relief; they met not a single human being, and it would appear as if they were travelling in some wild and uninhabited part of the country altogether. They kept up their spirits, however, much better than could have been anticipated, and exerted themselves to the utmost, conversing but little on their road, their minds being too busily occupied by the thoughts that engrossed them, and which were a source of such anguish and anxiety to them.

In this manner they continued to travel for more than an hour, and by that time it was broad daylight, and the effects of the late tempest were fast disappearing beneath the influence of the sun, which had arisen in full splendour in the eastern horizon, and whose golden beams imparted an aspect of cheerfulness even to the dreary scenery which met their gaze as far as their eyes could stretch.

"Alas!" said Richard, at length, pausing, and looking despairingly around him; "how tedious and insupportable is this. Fate seems to frown upon us altogether, and no prospect of relief appears before us. My poor suffering wife and boy, what will become of you? It is utterly impossible that you can proceed much further, dreadfully exhausted as you are, and it is indeed a miracle that you have been able to bear up in the manner you have."

"My dear Richard," Mary answered, "I beseech you not to agitate and distract your mind respecting me, but rather to seek to maintain your own fortitude. Indeed, I feel not so fatigued as you imagine; Providence has already supported me through the horrors of the night, and I feel confident that it will not now desert me, when it is so necessary that I should exert myself to the utmost. It affords me the greatest satisfaction to think that we have been enabled to elude the vigilance of our pursuers. They must now have lost all trace of us, and if we can only bear up for a short time longer, I trust that we shall find ourselves in some place of safety."

"Ah! would that I could think so," replied our hero; "but too much cause have I to fear that there is no place of safety for us; and I almost dread to encounter a human being, lest we should be recognised. Could we but procure other disguises, I should be more confident, but as it is, it would be useless for us to attempt to conceal from ourselves that we have everything to apprehend."

"Why will you persist, dear Richard, in viewing everything on the darkest side of the question?" said Mary; "it is thus that you torture your mind and unfit yourself for acting with that prudence and determination that are so necessary in our dangerous and painful situation."

"I feel the full justice of your observations, Mary," replied her husband, "and would fain endeavour to act in accordance with them; but when I weigh all the circumstances in my mind, how is it possible that I can do so? Could I but see yourself and our son placed in security, and with a prospect of your being protected from future misery and danger, I should care little what might become of myself."

"Richard, husband," returned Mary, looking at him with a mingled expression of sorrow and reproach, "know you what you say? If you have no regard for your own safety, in which all my hopes of happiness are involved, you have none for me. Think you that I could endure to live another hour should cruel fate deprive me of you? Oh, no; life would, under such dreadful circumstances, become an intolerable, an insupportable burthen to me, and nothing whatever should prevent me from ridding myself of it by the readiest means in my power."

"Mary," ejaculated our hero, fixing upon her a look of the most inexpressible horror, but unbounded affection, "give not way to such terrible thoughts, which unman me to listen to."

"And what then, think you, must be my feelings at those which you have expressed?" demanded his wife; "are not our fates linked together by ties the most indissoluble? and—"

She was interrupted in her observations by hearing the tinkling of bells a short distance off, and looking hastily over the hedge, they perceived a waggon coming slowly along the highroad, in the direction they were going, and they paused, and looked at each other for a second or two in silence.

"This is a fortunate circumstance," said Richard at length; "this waggon will probably stop at the nearest town, and if we can only induce the driver to convey us, we shall obtain rest, security from discovery on the road, and no doubt all that we require when we arrive at the place of his destination. I will speak to him, for I do not suppose that we have anything to fear from him; at any rate, we are driven to the last extremity, and must chance it."

Having thus spoken, Richard Parker handed his wife and son over a stile into the high road, and awaited for the waggon to come up, being determined to put the question to him. The driver, who was a stout, red-faced, simple looking rustic, came whistling on his way, and soon arrived at the spot where the unfortunate fugitives were standing, and whom he scrutinised with no small degree of curiosity.

"Good morning, friend," he said, addressing himself to Richard; "you look tired; have you been travelling far?"

"Yes," answered Richard, "many weary miles, all night, and exposed to the storm. We are quite exhausted, and being strangers in this part of the country, we know not where to find a place where we may obtain rest and refreshment."

"Well, that be a bad job, measter, to a certainty," remarked the waggoner; "I be going to stop for a short time at the nearest town, Bilston, which is about three miles from here, and where there is good accommodation."

"Would you, then, convey us thither?" asked Richard; "and I will reward you for your trouble?"

"To be sure I will, measter," replied the countryman, "and willingly too, for I do not like to see any one put to it as you seem to be. There is no one in my waggon, so jump up, and we will be jogging on our way."

Richard returned his thanks to the kind rustic, and handing Mary and the boy into the waggon, he followed himself, and it then proceeded on its way at the same slow pace as before. Mary and her husband now felt much more easy in their minds, and felt grateful to Providence for the prospect of relief which was before them. The waggoner continued whistling on his way by the side of his team, and they were, therefore, left to the uninterrupted indulgence of their own thoughts and conversation.

"We are now released from the many hardships and severe trials we have had to endure on this eventful night," remarked Richard; "and I trust that we shall be able in a short time to obtain that rest and refreshment of which we stand so much in need, and we shall then better be able to collect our thoughts and to arrange our plans for the future."

"Yes, my dear Richard," replied his wife, "and I trust to God that, however dismal our prospects may seem to be at present, our troubles will soon be at an end, and that Richard Parker may yet again be able to show his head in the broad light of day, without having anything to apprehend from the myrmidons of the law."

"Ah, Mary," returned our hero, "would that I could entertain any such sanguine expectations, but I dare not. I may succeed for a time in concealing myself, but I can never hope to receive forgiveness from the offended laws of my country. But we have talked sufficiently upon that painful subject already, and we had better seek to divert our thoughts into some other channel."

They did so, and by the time that the waggon had arrived at the clean little town of Bilston, they had succeeded in becoming perfectly composed and collected. The town was situated in a retired spot, and was not of any extent, and at that early hour of the morning there were but few persons stirring, and they were too busily occupied with their own affairs to take any notice of strangers. The inn itself was a small old-fashioned place, and the fugitives received a favourable impression from its appearance, and alighting from the waggon, Richard again thanked the driver, and offered him some trifling recompense, but the honest fellow, judging from their appearance that they were as poor as himself, declined to take anything, and told them that they were heartily welcome to the little favour they had received from him. They then entered the house, and walking into a small, retired room, the door of which was standing open, Richard rang the bell, and the landlord, who was a little, sharp, intelligent-looking old man, immediately made him appearance, and with much civility, inquired their pleasure. Richard, who had not lost his presence of mind, and who acted the part necessity compelled him to assume, to perfection, informed him that they were poor people who had been travelling all night, not being able to meet with any place of shelter, and requested to have some refreshments as quickly as possible, and to know whether they could be accommodated with a lodging till the following day.

The landlord replied in the affirmative, and added—

"You will always find the best of fare and accommodation to suit every person's pocket, I assure you; but is it possible that you have been travelling all night, and in such a storm, too, that I thought Heaven and earth were coming together?"

"It is true, sir," answered our hero; "and you may, therefore, very well imagine that we are now quite exhausted, and that we need a few hours' rest."

"Exhausted?" repeated the landlord; "yes, I should think you were; why, I would not have been exposed to the fury of such a tempest for the best twenty guineas that could be placed before me. But I will not waste that time which you should be employing in so different a way. I will fulfil your orders immediately."

Richard returned his acknowledgments, and the landlord departed from the room.

"Again we are fortunate in meeting with one who seems to be an honest and kind-hearted man," observed Mary, "and I think we may rest ourselves contented here for a short time, at any rate, for we seem to be in a place of safety, and where we are not likely to meet with any one who will recognise us."

"That may be, Mary," said her husband; "but it still will be necessary for us to act with the greatest caution, and during the time we remain here, which must be brief, we must not be seen by any more persons than possible."

"True," coincided Mary; "I am ready to agree with you that we cannot be too cautious, though I hope and trust that we shall find no cause for apprehension."

The landlord now re-entered the room, with a plenteous and comfortable repast, which he placed on the table before them, and after some little conversation with them of not much importance, and in which he did not exhibit much of that disagreeable and impertinent curiosity which is characteristic of many of his fraternity, he desired them to ring for him when they required his attendance again, and once more quitted the room.

The fugitives, who had had nothing to eat for so many hours, were, of course, very hungry, and, therefore, partook heartily of the repast, and when it was concluded, they felt newly invigorated, and much refreshed, and could talk more calmly on their situation.

"I do not consider that we are for a moment safe in any of this part of the country," remarked Richard; "especially after the events that have recently taken place, and which are sure to add to the excitement that now prevails. To-morrow morning, after we have taken that necessary rest which we require after the fatigue and anxiety of mind we have undergone, we must depart from here."

"So soon?" said Mary; "had we not better (if we see nothing to excite our suspicions) remain here for at least a day or two, until we have quite recovered ourselves, and arranged our plans?"

"No," answered Richard; "any delay might be fraught with the most imminent danger, and bring ruin upon us."

"From this place you might communicate with Adams," observed our heroine, "make him acquainted with all that has happened, and receive his friendly advice in return, of which we stand so much in need."

"I need not tell you, my dear Mary," said her husband, "how anxious I am to do so, but I must defer my wish until some other and more fitting occasion: for I again say that I consider we are still not remote enough from the scenes of the late important and fearful events to imagine ourselves in safety."

"Terrible events they have been indeed," ejaculated Mary Parker; "and when I recall them to my memory, they smite my heart with horror. The awful fate of the unfortunate Mr. and Mrs. Worthington—the death of the villain Brunston— our narrow escape from our pursuers at the

farm-house—the murder of the old man whom we beheld in the ruins—surely such circumstances as these to take place, and all within the short space of a few hours, is unparalleled, and have more of the character of some wild and extravagant creation of the imagination than reality."

"True, Mary," coincided our hero; "and I marvel not that you should feel so excited about them; I only wonder that you should have been enabled to endure them with that unexampled fortitude which you have evinced. Our noble boy, too; oh, how justly proud ought we to be of him for the extraordinary heroic and patient behaviour which has characterised him through so many trials and difficulties for one of his tender years, and which were sufficient to try the stoutest heart. William, my beloved boy, receive a father's blessing, and may it never be your fate to experience the cruelty and injustice it has been his hard lot to endure."

William knelt down, and our hero, raising his hands above his head, fervently invoked the blessing of Heaven, in which solemn prayer the fond mother earnestly and devoutly joined.

"Thanks, my beloved parents, for this your affectionate regard and solicitude in my welfare," said the boy; "and, oh, may Heaven teach me to realise your fondest hopes, and do honour in my years of maturity to that name which, as a child, I am proud to bear. God grant, too, that the heavy sorrows which now afflict you may soon be at an end, and that you may yet live many, many years to come, to experience a sweet reward for all the numerous and almost insupportable sufferings it has been your cruel destiny to encounter."

The affectionate parents raised the noble boy from his knees, and clasped him with the fondest transport to their bosoms, being too much overpowered for a moment or two by their emotions to be able to speak.

"Child of misfortune," at length cried his father; "what language can express the full nature of my feelings as I hear you speak thus, and picture to myself what you will be when manhood shall be stamped upon your brow. Alas! would that I might be permitted to live to see that day; but it must not be; I feel convinced of the fatal truth; many years before that time shall arrive, your father's bones will have mouldered into dust, and, happily, the memory of his wrongs is misfortunes, his errors, and degrad.... may be forgotten."

"Oh, Richard," exclaimed our heroine,

"what awful thoughts are these which you suffer to haunt your imagination and continually to distract your brain. But divest your mind of them, and I am fully satisfied that the time will yet come when you will find that all I have in my anxious and affectionate anticipations predicted, will be verified."

"Mary," said her husband, "to hear you talk thus, one might imagine that you had forgotten the heavy crimes with which I stand charged, and the prejudice which exists in the minds of those whom I have cause to dread, against me. Alas! it is painful, it is most torturing, to see you encourage such delusive hopes; how dreadful will be the shock when you are doomed to disappointment, and my ignominious doom——"

"No more," hastily interrupted Mary, with a ghastly look, and shuddering; "I cannot listen to the fearful words you would give utterance to. But it is useless to attempt to alter the impression which has taken such firm hold of my mind. In spite of our present dismal prospects, I will still believe that you will be able to surmount the difficulties by which you are at present surrounded, and that you will escape the awful and shameful fate with which you are now threatened. But why do we venture to talk upon that subject here? Should we be overheard, we should bring destruction on our heads. But tell me, Richard, have you no present idea of the course it will be most safe and prudent for us next to pursue?"

"Yes, Mary," he answered, "I have been thinking that could we by any means cross over to the other side of the coast, we might baffle those who are in pursuit of us, and be more secure than we can possibly be in this part of the country."

"Well," remarked our heroine, "I should think there would be no difficulty in accomplishing that; the offer of a reward would, I have no doubt, induce some poor fisherman, whom we shall be sure to meet with, if we travel near the coast, to convey us."

"Yes, if he had no suspicion as to who we were," said Richard. "But I am afraid the painful particulars connected with me have become too well known, and the large reward that is offered for my apprehension is a temptation that few would have the power to resist."

"At any rate we must run the risk," said Mary; and if we only act with firmness and precaution, I do not entertain but very little doubt that we shall be able to accomplish our wish. One thing,

however, must be done at the earliest opportunity."

"And what is that?" demanded our hero.

"Mr. Adams must be made acquainted with all the particulars that have taken place," answered his wife; "for on his advice and assistance our sole dependance now exists."

"True," coincided Richard; "and should we reach any place where we may remain in security for a time, I will take the earliest opportunity to communicate with him; though we are already under such a heavy weight of obligation to him, that I feel reluctant to try his benevolence again."

"Nay, Richard," replied Mary, "I am certain that you have no occasion to entertain any such scruples, though I duly appreciate your feelings, and fully participate in them myself. Mr. Adams will only be too happy to aid us, and never will he, we may rest assured, remind us of the vast obligations we owe him. His generous nature would scorn to do so."

"True, Mary," coincided Richard; "you do our excellent and disinterested friend, Adams, no more than justice by expressing such an opinion of him."

"Enough," observed our heroine; "then rest your mind contented upon that point."

"It is impossible for me to do so exactly, Mary," returned her husband, "when I recollect the imminent risk that he runs in taking the active interest he does in our fate. But we delay that time which should be occupied in rest, after the great fatigue we have undergone."

Mary made no reply, and Richard having rang the bell, the landlord made his appearance, and requested to know their pleasure.

"I have before informed you that we have been travelling all night, and are consequently exhausted with fatigue," replied our hero; "can we retire to rest for an hour or two?"

"Certainly," answered the worthy host, "there is every comfort and accommodation at my inn, although I say it, and I am glad to think that you had the good fortune to come here, for, if I may judge from your appearance, you would not have been able to travel much farther, and your wife and boy seem to have suffered much already from what they have undergone."

"True, sir," returned Richard; "such fatigue as they have experienced is but little adapted to their delicate natures."

"Your business, methinks, must have been of a most urgent nature," observed the landlord, "to compel you to journey all night and in such a storm?"

Our hero did not much like these remarks, but he overcame his confusion as well as he could as he replied—

"True, sir, our business was rather urgent; but still, we would gladly have put up for the night, could we only have met with a place of shelter."

"Ay," returned the host, "the part of the country you say that you have journeyed through is certainly most wild and inhospitable. But if you will attend me, I will conduct you to a chamber."

Richard and his wife returned their thanks, and without making use of any further observation, they followed the landlord from the room, and after ascending several flights of stairs, they were ushered into comfortable chamber, where the landlord left them to themselves.

Richard having secured the door on the inside, in order to prevent any sudden intrusion, they seated themselves, and for a few minutes remained silent, and gave themselves up to the busy thoughts that naturally occupied their minds. However, as they had already spent sufficient time in conversation, and as Mary and William were quite worn out with fatigue, they shortly retired to rest, and our heroine and her son being so much exhausted, soon fell asleep, and for a while obtained a temporary respite from their cares and anxieties. But the stirring and alarming events that had taken place within the last few hours, had made too powerful an impression upon Richard to suffer him for some time to compose and resign himself to the influence of the drowsy god, and he lay tossing about and restless, and reflecting upon every particular with the utmost anxiety. In spite of all his efforts to the contrary, and the arguments and persuasions of his faithful and affectionate partner in misfortune, he could not but be painfully alive to the extreme danger and misery of his situation, and the hopes he would fain have formed were overwhelmed by despair. The possibility of his ultimate escape from the awful fate which was impending o'er his head, he could not for a moment imagine, taking all the circumstances by which he was surrounded into consideration, and that conviction was of itself enough to render him one of the most truly wretched beings in existence. He could not contemplate the troubles that would succeed to his unfortunate wife and their child when he was no more, without feelings of the most unbounded and in-

supportable horror, and the thought completely unmanned him. He beat his breast, and starting from the bed, on which he had merely thrown himself in his clothes, he paced the room with disordered and uneven footsteps, and in vain sought to obtain the least composure. The death of the excellent Mr. Worthington and his wife had completely annihilated the hopes he had formed; in them he had lost the most inestimable of friends, and nothing, he was fully convinced, could ever replace them. Powerful as might be the wishes of Adams to serve him, and he could not for a moment doubt their sincerity, he would be deprived of the means, as the vessel to which he was attached must shortly sail from England, and thus all chance of their communicating with each other would be at an end; and exposed as he would be to innumerable perils, the possibility was that they might never meet again. He would then be entirely friendless and destitute in the world, and the fate that must necessarily overtake him, seemed to be inevitable. Had he been alone in the world—had he possessed no one who was dear to him, he could have viewed the doom with which he was threatened with comparative indifference; for after all the troubles it had been his had lot to experience, life possessed no charms for him; but to leave those so precious behind him friendless and unprotected, the thought alone was sufficient to rack his brain to madness, and the blood seemed to freeze in his veins with horror, as the dark and fearful picture presented itself to his imagination. With what bitter anguish of feeling did he gaze upon the pale and careworn features of his wife, and when he reflected upon all the unexampled troubles she had encountered for his sake, without one murmur of complaint, his heart seemed full to bursting, and it was in vain he sought to tranquillise his emotions in the smallest degree. He continued in this manner to pace the room for some time longer, while his wife and son slept soundly and calmly, and that circumstance did, indeed, afford him some consolation.

In order to endeavour to divert his thoughts, if possible, from the dismal channel in which they had so long been wandering, he walked to the window, and for a few minutes contemplated the wild but picturesque scenery commanded from it, and to which the bright rays of the morning's sun now imparted a degree of cheerfulness. He perceived but few persons about, and such as he did seemed merely rustics going to their daily labour.

There was no noise or bustle stirring in the inn, and that afforded him some satisfaction, as it did not appear that they were likely to receive any interruption, and at length exhausted with thinking, and the fatigue he had for so many hours experienced, he again threw himself upon the bed, and weary nature at last found relief in repose ; though the agonized mind never at rest, he frequently started up alarmed, as dreams of the most painful nature arose to his disturbed imagination.

CHAPTER XXII.

THE HONEST WAGGONER.—THE FUGITIVES PURSUE THEIR JOURNEY.—THE FISHERMAN'S HUT. — ANOTHER SURPRISE.—AN UNEXPECTED RECOGNITION, AND THE CONSEQUENCES.

THE unfortunate wanderers did not awake until the afternoon had somewhat advanced, and they felt much refreshed and invigorated by the undisturbed rest they had enjoyed. They arose, and the first thing they did was to throw themselves on their knees and to pour forth their heartfelt gratitude to the Supreme for the protection He had hitherto vouchsafed to them, and to supplicate His merciful interposition in their behalf for the future. This sacred duty performed, they felt more composed than they had done for some time before, and endeavoured to connect their thoughts as well as they could, to enable them to form some plan for the future.

"This inn seems to be retired and little frequented," remarked Mary; " the landlord, also, evidently entertains no suspicion of us, and I still cannot help thinking that we might remain here with confidence until we can communicate with our friend, Mr. Adams, and receive his valuable advice as to the course it will be most prudent for us to adopt."

"I should like to do so," replied our hero, "for I need not tell you how anxious I am to hear from Adams; but, still, I cannot divest my mind of the impression that we are not safe for a moment, however favourable circumstances may at present appear to be, while we remain in this part of the country. Could we gain the other side of the coast, my mind would be somewhat more at ease."

"And why so?" demanded our heroine, "is not the excitement consequent upon your escape likely to be as great there as here ? It is more than probable that our pursuers

are on the alert in all parts of the country."

"It is too true," answered Richard, "and it is that conviction which the more forcibly shows me the uselessness and hopelessness of struggling against my fate. I am only for your sake retarding it for a time, but I cannot avert it."

"Still despairing, Richard," said our heroine ; "oh, would to Heaven that I could arouse you from these dismal thoughts, and persuade you to look forward to the future with confidence. Consider how kind and merciful the Supreme Power has already been to us, and depend upon it that while we put our trust in Him, He will never forsake us."

"May the hopes you so warmly and so fervently express, my beloved Mary, be not fated to be disappointed," said her husband ; "but, alas ! the prospect that ever presents itself to my contemplation is of the most gloomy description. There is no place to which we may go, where we shall be secure. Reason, and all the torturing circumstances by which we are surrounded, will not suffer me to blind my eyes to the fearful truth. I am lost, distracted, and bewildered, and know not how to act."

"Exert all your energies, my dear Richard," returned his wife, "compose yourself, and seek to reflect calmly, and you will, I doubt not, be able to come to some wise and prudent decision in this our hour of need. I have often thought that were I to address a letter to my father, appealing to his feelings in such eloquent terms as the circumstances would dictate, that he surely could not resist it; he would forget the past, and assist to extricate us from the dreadful dilemma in which we are involved."

"Appeal to your father, Mary !" replied our hero ; "inexorable of heart as he has proved himself to be, and especially after what has recently happened, the thought is preposterous ; I am convinced that nothing whatever can dissipate the prejudice, the absolute hatred and feelings of revenge with which Mr. Mason views me, and that so far from aiding me in my escape, he would be only too ready to consign me to the fate with which I am threatened."

"Oh, it is impossible that he could be so cruel, so unnatural," ejaculated Mary ; " for my sake, and that of our child, he would stifle the unfortunate feelings that have so long held possession of his mind, and recal the curses which in the moment of his blind excitement he invoked upon my head."

" Never, Mary," remarked her husband, " it is useless to entertain any such idea. Should he by any means become acquainted with the place of our concealment, we should have reason to apprehend the worst. He would not for a moment hesitate to betray me, of that I feel as satisfied as that I am now addressing you."

" He must then, indeed, have become totally insensible to every feeling of humanity and nature if he could," said Mary ; " but notwithstanding the manner in which he has behaved to us, I cannot entertain any such opinion of him."

" And have you not too much reason to do so?" demanded our hero ; " has not the conduct he has for so many years pursued towards you, fully proved that he has discarded you from his breast? Had he been inclined to assist us in our terrible emergencies, he would not have required any appeal to his sympathies to induce him to do so ; but has he not left us to all the miseries of want and destitution? and the death of his friend, Captain Arlington is not at all calculated to soften his feelings in our favour. No, Mary, we must abandon all thoughts of appealing to him, and, on the contrary, we must take the utmost care to prevent his becoming acquainted with the place where we are concealed, for if he should obtain any such knowledge, my destruction would be inevitable."

" Ah, how agonising is that thought," said Mary, tears starting to her eyes. " Oh, my father, if your heart does indeed still remain closed and inexorable towards me, may Heaven in its infinite mercy forgive you for your cruel injustice towards that unhappy daughter who ever viewed you with the utmost affection and reverence."

" Enough of this, my beloved wife," said Richard, after a brief pause, during which time he endeavoured to conquer his emotions as well as he could ; " let us proceed below, and perhaps we may be enabled to elicit from the landlord some information that may be of service to us. I understood from the honest man who brought us hither, that he would stop here again to-morrow evening, and probably we may be enabled to agree with him to carry us to the place where he is going, and we shall be safe from discovery in his waggon, while at the same time we shall not be exposed to the fatigue of travelling, or to the inclemency of the weather, as we have hitherto been."

" Exactly so," remarked our heroine, " that is a good thought. The waggoner is very civil and obliging, and he does not seems to entertain any suspicions of us."

" No," replied her husband ; " he is a poor simple fellow, and it is not likely that he would. It is not improbable that he never heard my name mentioned, and if he has, I do not expect that he has penetration enough to recognise me according to the description of my person in the placards that are circulated about."

They now left the chamber, and having first listened to hear whether all was quiet in the house, they descended below, and made their way to the room in which they had been ushered on their arrival at the inn, and in which they found the worthy host seated alone, and enjoying his pipe and his glass of grog. He arose on their entrance and greeted them with the utmost respect, which our unfortunate travellers returned with equal cordiality.

" I am glad to see you, my friends," he said ; " and hope you feel refreshed after the few hours' rest you have had."

" We are obliged to you, sir, for the accommodation we have received, and of which we stood so much in need," answered our hero ; " it has, indeed, revived us, and will enable us to resume our journey with renewed vigour."

" Well, I hope so," observed the landlord ; " but I suppose you do not intend to leave the inn to-night ?"

" Why, no," replied Richard ; " I do not think we shall be exactly in a condition to do so, though our business is rather urgent."

" And have you much further to travel before you can reach the place of your destination?" inquired the landlord.

" Yes, several miles," answered our hero, hesitating, " we wish to get further up the coast ; the place we have to go to is principally inhabited by fishermen, where we have some relations living, but by some strange accident we have forgotten the name of it."

" Indeed," observed the landlord ; " that is singular, too. The nearest place of that description to here is M———"

" That is the name," said our hero, catching eagerly at the idea ; " how far is it from here, pray ?"

" Why, a matter of fourteen miles," replied the host ; " do you intend to journey on foot?"

" Why," answered Richard, " we would rather not do so, if we could get any cheap conveyance, for I suppose we need not inform you, as you may judge from our appearance, that our means are rather limited?"

" Well," returned the landlord, " I dare

say that can be managed; young Daniel, who brought you hither, goes to within half a mile of the place, and so if you do not mind remaining here till to-morrow evening, he will stop here with his waggon on his way there, and I have no doubt that you will be able to strike a bargain with him."

"I am obliged to you for this information, sir," said Richard Parker, "and will gladly avail myself of it. The waggoner seems to be an honest man, and we are

THE FLIGHT OF THE WANDERERS.

muck indebted to him for the timely assistance he rendered us."

",Oh, yes," returned the landlord;" "a more honest or better-hearted, though simple fellow than Daniel does not stand in shoe leather, and he is much respected by all who know him."

"But there is one favour I wish to ask you."

"And what is that?"

"While we remain here," answered our hero, "that you will suffer us to remain as private as possible, for we have business of importance to ourselves to settle, and, indeed, we are in no circumstances to mix in company."

"Oh, certainly," replied the landlord ; "I can have no reason to refuse to comply with your request. You can be as private as you think proper, and no one will attempt to interrupt you. I always endeavour to accommodate my guests according to their tastes as far as is in my power."

Richard again returned his thanks, and the worthy host having finished his pipe and glass, arose to depart, having first inquired whether they required any further refreshments. Our hero replied in the affirmative, and the former then quitted the room, and Richard and his wife were then once more left to the free indulgence of their own thoughts.

"It is a most fortunate job that this man Daniel, as the landlord has called him," remarked Mary, "is going to the place which has been indicated ; for probably amongst some of the fishermen who inhabit that part, we may be enabled to find one who will be willing, on the offer of a trifling reward, to convey us to the opposite side of the coast."

"Yes," answered her husband, "and when we are landed there I shall feel much more at ease, and more confident than I am at present. The landlord of this house appears to be a worthy and considerate man, and by no means inquisitive, so during the short time we remain here, I do not think we are likely to excite any suspicion."

"Oh, no," remarked his wife, "that is not at all probable. Act with the same prudence and presence of mind that you have hitherto done, and I firmly believe that we are perfectly secure from discovery. We cannot be too grateful to Providence for the manner in which it has as yet enabled us to elude the vigilance of our pursuers."

"True," replied our hero; "and for your sake, my devoted wife, may it still not desert us. If we can only manage to avoid them until after we have communicated with Adams, we may be able to reach some remote part of the country where we can at least remain for some time concealed."

"For some time, Richard?" ejaculated his wife, anxiously; "oh, I trust, for ever. In the course of a little while the excitement which now prevails will be abated, if not subsided · it will be imagined that we

are either no more, or that we have been enabled to reach some foreign land, and we shall then be suffered to remain safe from discovery. I feel my hopes gain strength every moment, our future prospects seem to brighten upon my imagination, and I am comparatively happy."

"And may nothing, my beloved Mary," observed our hero, "may nothing occur to disappoint those hopes, for how terrible and insupportable would then be the trial to your feelings. But I will try to be firm, for on that I know alone depends everything."

"True, Richard," answered his wife; "and, therefore, do I fervently pray that Heaven will enable you to act as you desire."

Richard was about to make some reply, but at the moment they heard the landlord at the door, and directly afterwards he entered the room, bringing with him the refreshments which had been ordered, and of which our hero and his wife and son partook with a good appetite, the worthy host remaining in the room during the time to see whether they had any more orders to give. Richard, however, felt somewhat uneasy, when he saw that, although he said nothing, he was observing them narrowly.

"You will pardon me," he said at last, "but there is something in your appearance and manner that leads me to imagine you do not naturally belong to the humble class of individuals that you would now seem to do by your dress."

"Indeed, sir," replied our hero, trying to conquer his confusion as much as he could, "you flatter me, by such an opinion; but, indeed, I am humble enough, and poor enough, God knows."

"That may be," remarked the landlord, "and more's the pity ; but no dress, however miserable, can conceal the gentleman, and I still cannot help thinking that you have at one time occupied a very different station from that which you now seem to do."

"'Tis true, sir," returned Parker, after a pause, and during which time he was considering what answer it would be best for him to make, "I am of respectable birth and connexions, but misfortune has come upon myself and my family, and I have for some time been only able to obtain a scanty subsistence by the sweat of my brow."

"Well," remarked the landlord, "it is a sad reverse of fortune, but it cannot be helped, and all the harm I wish you is that the times will shortly mend with you. I know what it is to experience misfortune, and can, therefore, feel for my fellow-creatures."

Our hero thanked him, and returned no further observation, trusting that the landlord would drop the subject.

"You must not deem me inquisitive, by what I have said," remarked the latter; "I never seek to pry into that which does not concern me, for I find quite enough to do to attend to my own business; but I will leave you to yourselves, for my presence may seem an intrusion, and I have not the least desire to interrupt you. Whenever you wish to retire to your chamber you can do so, and my servant will call you at any time you may desire in the morning."

With these words the landlord again quitted the room, and Richard and his wife felt much relieved by his departure, for the questions he had put to them had greatly served to confuse and agitate them, as may be expected.

"Our host is much more inquisitive than I at first supposed him to be," remarked our hero; "and I did not like the curiosity with which I noticed him observing us."

"Oh," returned Mary, "it is not worthy of a serious thought, in my opinion; he is not likely to have any suspicion as to who we really are, or he would probably have mentioned it at once; the answer you returned to him was a very proper and prudent one, and he seemed to be perfectly satisfied with it."

Richard did not return any immediate answer, and he remained for some time silent, and buried in deep thought.

"That fellow Bubble," he said, at length, "I wonder what has become of him."

"Oh, that is a matter of perfect indifference," answered our heroine; "I do not suppose that he will ever again cross our path."

"I hope not," remarked our hero; "for it is quite evident that we have everything to dread from him. The fellow seems to take an unnatural delight in the misery of his fellow-creatures. Whenever he appears, some mischief is sure to follow, and yet I never did him any injury either by word or deed. It was truly unfortunate his making so sudden an appearance at the house of the late Mr. Worthington, and our escape after he had denounced me was most miraculous.

"True," coincided his wife; "and no doubt he was greatly chagrined and disappointed at it; but Providence seldom fails to thwart the designs of such evil and malicious individuals as that man has proved himself to be, and—"

She was interrupted by hearing the sound of the guard's horn, and looking hastily along the high road, of which the window of the room in which they were sitting commanded an unobstructed view, they beheld the mail-coach approaching rapidly towards the inn, and in a second or two it arrived so close that they could distinguish the passengers who were outside, and their alarm and astonishment may be imagined when they recognised among them the mischievous little individual who had formed the subject of their recent discourse. They drew aside for fear he should observe them, and the next moment the coach passed the window, and they heard it draw up to and stop at the door of the inn, no doubt to change horses, and to afford the passengers time to obtain some refreshment. The agitation of Richard and his wife may readily be conceived, and for a moment or two they were unable to speak, and could only gaze at each other with looks of bewilderment and alarm.

"What a terrible misfortune is this," gasped forth Richard, at length; "what cursed accident has brought that dangerous man to this place? He follows us like a shadow."

"Do not unnecessarily alarm yourself, Richard," said his wife; "he will probably not be here many minutes, and will have no opportunity of seeing us."

"But should he put any questions to the landlord," observed our hero, "which, from his busy and inquisitive nature, he is not at all unlikely to do, he may learn sufficient to excite his suspicions, and our discovery would then be certain."

"Nay, Richard," returned Mary, "that is most improbable. But let us wait with patience and firmness, and all will, I trust, yet be well."

Our hero returned no answer, but he listened with the most breathless and painful attention, expecting every moment to hear the voice of Bubble, or to see him enter the room, notwithstanding the landlord had promised him that no one should intrude upon him during the time that they remained in the house; but all continued silent, and the courage of Parker and his wife revived. Several minutes more elapsed, when they again heard the sound of the guard's horn, and the noise of the coach-wheels as it was driven from the inn, and their minds were relieved from an almost insupportable weight of alarm and anxiety.

"The coach is gone," remarked Richard, "and I trust that the object of our fears has gone with it, or we are indeed lost. But hush! some one approaches."

The next moment there was a knock at the room door, and the landlord entered, and did not seem to notice their agitation and confusion.

"Pardon me," he said, in his usual tones of civility, "but I thought you rang."

"No, sir," replied Richard, "I did not. Was not that the mail-coach which just now stopped at the inn?"

"Yes," returned the landlord, "to change horses, and well loaded with passengers it is."

"Have any of them remained at the inn?" asked Richard.

"No," replied the host, "there was no such luck for me this evening. However, they all partook of refreshment, which, as is usually the case on such occasions as these, they had not time to finish. But there was one busy and eccentric little gentleman among them, who, having made up his mind, I presume, not to be done, put up the remainder of his meal in a pocket-handkerchief, and carried it away with him; and all the time he was eating, he kept putting a number of impertinent questions to me, as to the amount of business I have; whether I stood at any great expense for my establishment; the number of years I have been here; how many servants I keep; what guests I have at present staying here; who they are, and what description of persons they might be."

"He was, indeed, an inquisitive gentleman," remarked our hero, affecting to laugh, though, at the same time, he felt far from easy or satisfied; "but I presume you did not think proper to gratify his curiosity?"

"Certainly not," replied the laddlord; "for it is always a maxim of mine to mind your own business, and I am confident that you will find enough to do."

"Very true," coincided our hero; and the answer of the worthy host had relieved his mind from the most intense apprehension.

"I would not have given the value of the smallest copper coin for that man to have become my guest," remarked the landlord, "for I am certain, from his manners, that he would have given me much more trouble than he would have been worth. But is there anything that you require?"

"Nothing," answered Richard; "we will, if you please, again retire to our chamber, for my wife feels rather indis-

posed, and a few hours' rest will do us all good."

"Very true," concided the host, "you have had sufficient, after your exposure to the inclemency of the weather last night, to wear you out, and you cannot do better than to get all the rest you can previous to your again resuming your journey; so, if you please, I will attend you."

Richard bowed, and they then once more followed him, and were conducted to their chamber, where the landlord bade them good evening, and immediately made his exit.

"Thank Heaven!" ejaculated our hero when he was gone, "we have again had a most providential escape from detection. Had Bubble remained here, the worst consequences might very reasonably have been apprehended."

"Very true," coincided Mary, "and this last circumstance ought to convince us that Providence still continues watch over our safety. The landlord, too, is also a man upon whom we may depend; had he answered the impertinent questions of that dangerous man, I shudder to think what might have been the result."

"Why," returned Richard, "it would have been impossible for us to escape, and my fate would have been at once sealed. I wonder whither Bubble is going? God forbid that we should ever again encounter him, for we should probably not then be so fortunate as we have just now been."

"I do not entertain any such fears," observed his wife, "and should we only succeed in reaching the opposite side of the coast, we shall probably then be out of the reach of all those whom we have cause to dread."

"True," replied our hero; "for a time, at least. I wish to-morrow morning had arrrived, for I am all impatience and uneasiness till we have got away from this place, where, in spite of all my efforts to persuade myself to the contrary, danger seems to stare us in the face at every turn."

"I do not indulge in the same apprehensions, Richard, indeed I do not," said our heroine, "though I confess that I am still as anxious as yourself to reach some place which may offer more security than this part of the country. But you will not delay any longer than is possible, communicating with Mr. Adams?"

"Certainly not," answered our hero; "as soon as ever we reach a place where we are likely to remain for a short time, it shall be my first task to write to him, for he must, I am sure, be most anxious to hear what has become of us, especially if he is made acquainted with the late startling events, and the frequent narrow escapes that we have had."

"And he is sure to have heard all the particulars," remarked Mary Parker; "and no doubt will send an answer immediately on the receipt of your letter, in which he will give us all the necessary advice we require as to the course we must in future adopt. Have you any idea where to go, should we succeed in reaching the opposite coast?"

"None whatever at present," replied her husband, "all places are alike to me so that they will but offer me the means of present security from the vigilance of my pursuers."

"Could we make our way to France," remarked our heroine, "we should there, I think, be free from all danger; you would find no difficulty in entering into the French navy, Richard, and——"

"Mary," he interrupted hastily, and at the same time fixing upon her a look of gentle reproach, "know you what you say?—Can this be my Mary who talks thus? Think you that Richard Parker, notwithstanding the cruel injustice he has received, could ever be so base as to engage himself to fight against his own countrymen? Sooner would he perish by the ignominious fate with which he is threatened. The very idea is revolting, and calls the blush of shame upon my cheek."

"Pardon me, Richard," said his wife, "if in the anxiety of my feelings for your welfare I have been led to give utterance to observations repugnant to your feelings. Well do I know the honorable sentiments that occupy my husband's breast; but, alas, how badly has he been rewarded."

"True, Mary," returned our hero; "I have received the most cruel wrongs—the foulest degradation, for the blood I have shed it the defence of my country. And what am I now? Hunted as a felon and a murderer, my own countrymen thirst for my blood, nor will they rest satisfied until they have wreaked their vengeance on my devoted head. The thought is madness; and as it flashes upon my brain, my heart sickens, and I feel that I am encompassed by a fearful destiny from which, in spite of all my struggles, I shall never be able to extricate myself. The dreadful fate which is in store for me is presented as vividly to my imagination as if it were already about to be consummated; I behold the awful preparations for my execution; I see——"

"Hold! hold! Richard, husband, for Heaven's sake!" interrupted our heroine, shuddering with horror as she listened to his observations, and too painfully felt their force and truth; "to hear you talk thus appals my very soul, and unfits me for that task which I wish to perform. Do not, I again implore you, give way to such frightful apprehensions; but, on the contrary, look with confidence to the successful issue and happy termination of all our troubles. Everything depends upon your firmness, and knowing how much you have at stake, I cannot but believe that you will act with prudence and determination, and by such means you will be enabled ultimately to surmount all those difficulties by which we find ourselves at present surrounded."

"I should be unworthy of your love and devotion, my Mary," he replied, "did I not seek to the best of my ability to follow your advice. But still, when I reflect upon all the painful circumstances connected with my fate, is it at all to be wondered at that I should be unable entirely to divest my mind of the dismal forebodings and apprehensions that cross it? But enough of this; to-morrow evening we shall depart from hence, and when we have reached some other place of security, I shall feel my mind much more at ease and confident."

"Yes, Richard," remarked our heroine; "something seems to assure me that the time is not far distant when the dark clouds which at present obscure the horizon of our happiness will be dissipated, and that we shall be permitted to pass the remainder of our days in tranquillity. Humble though our circumstances may be, and hard though the struggle may be that we shall have to make to support ourselves, so that you are secure from the dreadful fate with which you are now threatened, I can endure it all without a murmur of complaint, and you shall find me, as I have ever been, most anxious to ameliorate your sufferings, to blot out from your memory the sorrows of the past, and to direct your thoughts alone to peace and content."

"I know it, my beloved Mary," returned her husband; "could I for a moment doubt the sincerity of your words, I should be unworthy of that unbounded affection and devotion which you have ever bestowed upon me."

Richard embraced his wife as he spoke, and they remained for some time afterwards silent, and giving free indulgence to the various thoughts that crowded upon their minds, and which filled them with alternate hopes, and doubts, and fears.

In this manner they sat till the shades

of evening descended upon the earth, and Mary and her son were then persuaded to retire to rest, but our hero, who did not feel at present disposed for sleep, remained up, and sat watching his wife, who was soon wrapped in the arms of slumber, with looks of the most painful, yet affectionate solicitude and anxiety, whilst all the numerous vicissitudes and startling events of his past life rushed upon his memory in rapid succession.

As he gazed upon the pale features and the emaciated form of the affectionate partner of his troubles, it was impossible that he could help feeling the deepest anguish and regret; and when he reflected upon the troubles that were probably yet in store for him, he shuddered with horror, and could almost have prayed that Heaven would take her to itself, rather than that she should be exposed to fresh miseries that were almost too dreadful to contemplate.

"Alas, my poor Mary," he sighed to himself, "you are but a fearful wreck of what you once were. It is dreadful—it is heart-breaking, to view the frightful ravages that sorrow has made upon you, and to know, at the same time, that it is not in my power to assist you or to release you from them. God, I beseech You, to look with an eye of pity upon this unfortunate woman, and not to suffer her to perish altogether."

He clasped his hands vehemently together, and raised his eyes fervently towards heaven as he spoke, and it would be a task far too difficult for our pen to accomplish to attempt to describe the emotions which at that moment were passing in his mind.

He started at the least sound that occurred in the house, and listened attentively, fearful that some danger might threaten, but all remained perfectly secure, and, by degrees, he became more confident, and endeavoured to reflect calmly upon the course it would be most prudent for him to adopt for his future safety. Various were the plans that occurred to his busy imagination, but which he rejected almost as soon as they were formed, and he was unable to come to any fixed determination, for the longer he reflected, the more bewildered became his brain.

The sleep of our heroine, however, was far from being undisturbed; she frequently started, and gave utterance to incoherent words, which showed plainly that her imagination was haunted by painful visions; and her husband continued to watch her with the most intense anxiety, and he did not feel at all disposed to retire himself to rest. His mind was too much agitated,

he knew, to suffer him to sleep, and he traversed the room with disordered steps, and gave free indulgence to the variety of conflicting thoughts that held their powerful dominion over his brain. He stood for some minutes by the window, and endeavoured to divert his ideas from the dismal channel in which they had been so long wandering, by gazing at the scenery beyond, now lighted by the pale rays of the moon; but there was nothing in its rude features which was at all calculated to soothe his feelings, and his mind continued in the same restless and moody state.

"What a hopeless struggle is this," he said, at last; "of what use is it for me to combat with my fate? I cannot avert it; the dreadful hour must come, sooner or later, and, therefore, there is nothing left for me to do but to prepare myself to meet it with the courage of a man. Courage! alas, how can I hope to obtain it when I reflect upon the terrible situation in which my wife and child will then be placed? Will they not be left entirely destitute and unprotected? Will not the cruel and ungenerous world brand them with infamy, and continually remind them of my ignominious fate? And to whom can they then look for consolation and sympathy? That thought alone is sufficient to distract me. Oh, Mary, how little have your numerous virtues deserved such a cruel return as this. Why were we ever permitted to meet? Had we never have known each other, you might now have been one of the happiest of human beings, and no care or anxiety would at all have beset your mind; but as it is, you are doomed to perpetual misery, and I see no prospect of your being released from it. Surely I have proved a curse to you, and I cannot but reproach myself for it, although, Heaven knows, how fondly, how sincerely, I have ever, and still love you, and how willingly I would lay down my own life to save yours, and to restore you to that happiness, that prosperity and peace of mind from which you have been so long and so undeservedly estranged."

He was interrupted in the midst of this gloomy soliloquy by hearing an exclamation of terror from his wife, and at the same instant she started from the bed, clasped her hands to her temples, and stared wildly and vacantly around her, apparently for the moment unconscious as to where she was.

"Mercy! mercy!" she exclaimed, in frenzied accents; "you will not be so monstrous as to break the promise so solemnly given? Oh, God! spare my husband! Ah, no! it is too late! The terrible decree is sealed ! His awful fate is accomplished ! And see, his ghastly corpse is swinging in the air, whilst hundreds gaze coolly and exultingly on at the frightful spectacle ! Richard ! husband ! thou art torn from me for ever ! God of Heaven, then, hear my prayer, and let me also immediately perish !"

"Mary, dear Mary !" ejaculated her husband, enfolding her affectionately in his arms, and looking anxiously in her pale face ; "oh, what mean those terrible words ? Why do you tremble so violently, and gaze so wildly around you ?"

"Ah !" she cried, frantically straining him to her bosom ; "you here, my beloved, but unfortunate husband ? Am I labouring under some strange and powerful delusion ? Do I indeed hold you in my arms ? It was, then, but a frightful dream. Oh, Heaven be thanked for this !"

"Calm yourself, my love," returned our hero ; "some painful dream has, indeed, disturbed your imagination ; but tell me what was the nature of it, that it should thus so powerfully agitate you ?"

"Oh, Richard," replied his wife, "it was, indeed, a fearful dream ; the blood freezes in my veins when I think of it. I dare not give utterance to it."

"Nay, Mary," returned Richard, "to keep me in this state of suspense is more torturing than all. Relate the facts to me. I am prepared to hear everything."

"Alas !" sighed our heroine, "what bitter, what insupportable anguish, my beloved husband, must it impart to your mind to listen to it. Oh, spare me the painful task."

"Mary," said our hero, "think you that I am so weak as to shrink from listening to the recital of a dream, however fearful it may be ? Confide the facts to me, and you shall find me act with firmness, but to be thus kept in a a state of doubt and suspense, I repeat, is most torturing."

Mary still hesitated, and her husband became more anxious and impatient, and urging her further, she at length said:

"Oh, Richard, fain would I conceal from your knowledge the dreadful vision that has been presented to my imagination, for well do I know the agony of feelings that it will cost you, and the despair to which you will in consequence abandon yourself. But you have urged me earnestly to communicate the facts to you, and I am compelled to comply; but I beseech you to listen to me with calmness and patience, and not to attach too much importance to that which in fact has only

originated from the disturbed state of my mind, and my anxiety for your preservation."

"Proceed, Mary," said our hero; "I am fully prepared to listen with firmness to all you have to relate."

"Methought, then, Richard," she commenced, "that you had been apprehended, that you were the inmate of a dismal cell, and that you had been tried, convicted, and condemned to—to death. Oh, I cannot proceed ; pray excuse me, my dear Richard, but the bare recollection even of that which my disordered fancy conjured up, fills my breast with horror, and I feel as though the awful facts had really taken place. Be satisfied with what I have already related, and suffer me to proceed no further."

"Mary," replied our hero, "why this hesitation, after the assurance I have given you? It does but torture me the more. Proceed, proceed."

"I imagined in my dream, Richard," continued his wife, after a brief pause, "that myself and our poor boy visited you in the gloomy and loathsome cell, and oh, what was the anguish, the maddening anguish of that interview? It is impressed upon my memory with all the overwhelming force and intensity of reality, and I tremble with terror when I think of it. How ghastly pale were your cheeks; what unutterable despair marked the expression of your eyes, and how sad were the observations that you made to me. Your form and features were so altered altogether, that it was scarcely possible to recognise in you the same individual. Premature old age and decrepitude seemed suddenly to have overtaken you, and I could not gaze upon you without feelings of the most indescribable agony and horror.

"But suddenly the scene was changed, and I found myself travelling at night and alone, across a dreary heath, as I imagined in my dream, on my way to London, having determined to endeavour to obtain an interview with the king, and on my knees to supplicate him to spare your life. And with what desperate courage and perserverance did I proceed on my almost hopeless errand, for there was not a moment to be lost, as the awful sentence of the law was to be carried into execution on the following day. How vividly did my imagination picture to me the sufferings I endured on that melancholy journey; but I surmounted all the difficulties by which I was surrounded, and by daylight I found myself standing before the gates of the palace. By what means I achieved the object of my painful mission

I know not; but suddenly I found myself in the presence of the sovereign, and on my knees was making a most eloquent and earnest appeal to him for mercy. At first I imagined that he listened to me with a stern expression of countenance, and turned a deaf ear to all my supplications; but, at length, my tears and entreaties seemed to make some favourable impression on him, and after a pause, he commanded me to rise, and I heard the blessed words proceed from his lips:

"'Away, woman! it is not revenge we seek; for your sake your husband's life shall be spared, and may he, as he does not abuse our clemency, receive mercy from the king of kings.'

"Again I imagined in my dream that I was travelling alone on my return to the place where you were confined, but it was now with a light heart, and a bosom overflowing with gratitude to the Supreme, for I held in my possession the precious pardon of the king, and methought that your life was saved, and that but a few short hours would restore us to each other's arms, and that we should again be happy. I reached the place of my destination, as I thought, only a short time before the execution was fixed to take place; the yards of the various vessels were manned, and there was a vast multitude of persons assembled on the shore to witness the awful spectacle. What a terrible moment of horror and suspense was that to me! With difficulty I procured a boat, and put off towards the vessel, on board of which the last fearful sentence of the law was to be carried into effect, shouting aloud in the extreme agony of my feelings—'Hold! stay the execution! He is saved! he is saved!' The loud report of a signal gun drowned the sound of my voice, and oh, horror! the next moment I beheld the writhing body of my husband hanging from the yardarm of the Sandwich. I had arrived too late! Your awful fate was decided, Richard, and in the terror and indescribable excitement of my feelings I awoke."

"It was indeed a frightful dream, my poor Mary," said our hero, after a pause, with all that agony of feeling which may be imagined, upon all the circumstances she had related; "and I marvel not that it should make the powerful impression upon you that it has done. It is but a timely warning sent to us by the Almighty to prepare ourselves for the worst, and not to bury ourselves up with false and delusive hopes, which can only end in fearful disappointment.'

"But, oh, my beloved and unfortunate husband," returned Mary, at the same time shuddering with horror, "it will never be realised; I cannot, dare not believe that it will; the Almighty who knows the many injuries you have received, and the unparalleled sufferings to which you have already been exposed, will not permit you to come to so awful and untimely a fate. Come, my husband, let us endeavour to banish this frightful dream from our memory, and to place every reliance in His goodness and mercy."

"Ah, Mary," replied our hero, "I dare not encourage any such hopes, for well convinced am I that they will never be gratified; is it possible that, with the heavy charges brought against me, I can for a moment expect forgiveness, or that the slightest mercy will be extended towards me? No, Mary, should I be apprehended, the fate which awaits me is inevitable, and there is nothing left for me to do but to resign myself to it."

"Oh, horrible thought!" ejaculated our heroine; "would to Heaven that I could banish it from your mind."

"Alas!" returned her husband, "it is a fruitless task to endeavour to do so; it is the stern but all-wise decree of the Supreme, and we must not presume to murmur at it. The predictions of old Rachael I feel satisfied, and have ever done so, will be fulfilled, and that, although I may retard my fate for awhile, I cannot avoid it. Be firm, my poor Mary, and console yourself with the belief that, although we may shortly be separated from each other in this world, we shall meet again in heaven."

"Oh, agony most insupportable!" gasped forth our heroine, and at the same time clasping her burning temples; "I cannot, dare not make up my mind to any such dreadful thoughts as those which you seem to entertain. My husband, the father of my child—he to whom my whole soul is devoted, and from whom I have experienced such unbounded affection—to be taken from me by such awful means; it is impossible! the very thought is enough to drive my brain to madness. Oh, Richard, say that you do not yet abandon yourself entirely to despair, and it will at least afford some portion of relief to my agonized mind."

"It would be cruel to deceive you, Mary, by any such assertions," replied her husband; "and reason at once points to the folly of indulging in any such flattering and delusive ideas. But let us be firm, and leave everything to the wisdom and mercy of Omnipotence. Should it indeed be decreed that I am to be taken from you, I trust that He will give you strength to bear the dreadful trial with fortitude and resignation, and that He will protect you and our child from every danger when you are left alone in the wide world."

"Alas! alas!" sighed Mary, wringing her hands, "how can I be firm or resigned, Richard, while I hear you give way to such dismal forebodings? No, should it indeed be the stern will of the Supreme that I should be deprived of you

THE DISCOVERY OF JOE BRUNSTON IN THE OLD COTTAGE.

in so awful a manner, I swear, by all my future hopes, that I will not survive you many hours; that I——"

"Oh, hold! hold, Mary!" interrupted our hero. "Know you what you say? Give utterance to no rash vows. You

must continue to live for the sake of the poor boy, who will have no other protector than yourself; and, young as he is, what would become of him were he to be left alone in the world?"

"Richard," returned our heroine, "I

am distracted. Oh, God! should you indeed be taken from me, what would there then be left for me to wish to cling to life for? Heaven grant that, if you must perish, we may all die together. Would that I had kept this fearful dream concealed from you; for too plainly do I perceive the painful and fatal impression it has made upon your mind."

"Mary," remarked our hero, "although I am ready to acknowledge that it has made a powerful impression upon me, it has not in the least degree altered the opinion I had previously entertained. When we come to take all the melancholy circumstances connected with us into consideration, it would be little use short of madness to encourage the fallacious hopes with which you would fain inspire me. For awhile I may elude the vigilance of my pursuers; but as to escaping from them altogether, or to expect to receive any mercy from the offended laws of my country, that is impossible. Would to God that, for your dear sake, I might be spared, then, indeed, might I flatter myself with the fond hope that, in the course of time, we might be restored to that peace and tranquillity to which we have been so long strangers."

Mary returned no immediate answer, but threw herself, sobbing, on her husband's bosom, and gave unrestrained indulgence to her feelings, whilst he endeavoured by every means in his power to impart consolation to her; but of that, however, he stood in equal need with herself. At length, however, she did become somewhat more calm, and he then tried to persuade her to again return to bed, and after a short time she yielded, and worn out with thinking and anguish of mind, she soon again sunk into repose, and Richard was gratified to perceive that her sleep was now comparatively calm and tranquil. Still, however, he did not feel inclined to retire, and sat for some time longer reflecting seriously, and with the deepest emotion upon all the circumstances of Mary's fearful dream, and which had made an impression upon his mind too powerful for him to conquer. In that vision he read the whole history of his fate, and his very soul shrank appalled at the bare contemplation of the awful doom that awaited him. But not for himself did he tremble; no, he felt convinced that had he been alone in the world, so completely weary was he of its miseries and injustice that he could have met death with fortitude, even under such revolting and ignominious circumstances as those with which he was threatened; but when

he thought of his wife and child, and the horrors to which they would be consigned after he was no more, his courage naturally failed him, and he gave himself up to the blackest despair.

"Oh, God!" he groaned, as he beat his breast in the intense agony of his feelings; "surely it would be a mercy to me, and to those who are far more precious to me than my very existence, if you were to take me to yourself this very night, and spare me the violent and shameful death which is at present impending o'er my head. In pity to their feelings, to the feelings of those so innocent and so virtuous, listen to my earnest prayer, and suffer me to expire ere the cruel and remorseless myrmidons of the law can get me in their power; to that I can calmly and patiently resign myself, but I cannot, dare not contemplate the other awful doom without trembling and horror."

Thus he continued to reflect for some time longer, and he was unable to obtain the least consolation and hope.

It was now midnight, and all was hushed in the most profound silence, and the solemnity of the hour, and the death-like stillness which reigned around, added to the gloom and misery of the unfortunate Richard Parker's mind. He continued to gaze upon his sleeping wife and child for some time, and as he did so, and pictured to himself the terrors which he was certain awaited them, the most fearful thoughts beset his mind, and again the awful idea of self-destruction flashed upon his brain; but in a moment he aroused himself from it, and he felt appalled at himself for having entertained it.

"Would it not be base cowardice in me to commit such a deed, and thus to leave those who are so dear to me at once destitute and unprotected?" he said. "It would; no, rather let me still struggle on against my fate to the last, and trust to Providence for the result. The chances of escape are yet before me, and why should I in the frenzy of my despair thus madly reject them? I must, I will be firm, for on that depends everything."

As these thoughts occurred to him he became more calm, and at length completely exhausted with fatigue, and the anxiety of mind, he sought his couch, and sleep at last came to his relief.

The unfortunate fugitives did not awake until a late hour on the following morning and although they felt somewhat refreshed by the sleep they had obtained, the anguish of their mind was still as intense as ever. Mary's frightful dream continued to haunt their imagination, and it was in vain that they sought by every means in their power to banish the painful impression it had made upon them. Richard, however, exerted himself to the utmost to appear calm and resigned before his patient and devoted wife, but he could not cenceal from her keen and penetrating eye the deep anguish of his despair, and that added to her misery, and increased her dismal forebodings.

"Alas, Richard!" she ejaculated; "too well can I perceive the dreadful thoughts and feelings which you have permitted to obtain such powerful ascendancy over your mind. Oh, why did you urge me to relate to you my dream, since it has been productive of such terrible effects?"

"Nay, Mary," answered our hero, "it could not add to my despair, for I have long made up my mind as to the certainty of my fate, though it would perhaps have been far better could I have concealed my real thoughts from you. It is impossible, when we consider all the horrors and the dangers by which we are surrounded, to deceive ourselves; let us rather prepare ourselves for the worst, and then the shock, however terrific and overwhelming' will not come so awfully upon us."

"Richard, my husband," returned his wife, "what unspeakable horror do your words convey to my mind; can you suppose me to have become so totaly insensible to all feeling as to calmly contemplate that which you predict? I must indeed be less than woman if I could, and entirely unworthy of your love. But no; I will not drive myself to despair and madness by entertaining any such dreadful thoughts; that just God, whose holy laws we neither of us ever wilfully outraged, will in mercy look down upon us, and preserve you from a fate which is far too frightful and revolting to contemplate. We shall still be able to elude the vigilance of our pursuers, and in some part of the world, far remote from danger, be permitted to pass the remainder of our days in peace and tranquillity. We shall then be able to bury the painful past in oblivion, and to look back upon the numerous and almost unequalled troubles it has been our hard lot to encounter, with indifference."

"Would to Heaven that we might," said Richard Parker, fervently; "what a comparatively happy man I should then be; how grateful should I be to the Supreme for His infinite mercy. But alas! I cannot flatter myself with any such sanguine hopes and expectations, and it would be wrong for me to encourage that in you which can only end in such bitter and cruel disappointment. No, Mary,

peace and tranquillity, I fear, can never again be ours, and the longer I reflect upon all the circumstances by which we are surrounded, the more thoroughly convinced I am of it. There is a dreadful spell upon us, from which we cannot release ourselves; but, methinks, could I but see you calm and resigned, and be certain that you and our poor boy would not be left entirely destitute and unprotected in the world, I could meet even the revolting and ignominious fate with which I am threatened, without a murmur."

"For the love of Heaven," said our heroine, fixing upon her husband a look which penetrated his very soul, "Richard, oh, talk not thus. You must not, you shall not be taken from me by such awful means; Providence will hear my fervent prayers, and spare your life. We shall again be suffered to breathe the pure air of Heaven, and to wander forth into the broad light of day without dread, and not remain as we are at present, like hunted wild beasts. Surely what we have endured already, is more than sufficient punishment for any sins which we may have committed. It would be cruel to suppose that such a dreadful fate as that which you apprehend should overtake us."

"It is, indeed, awful, my poor Mary, to reflect upon," answered our hero, "and yet, what prospect is there before us that we shall be able to avoid it?"

"Again I implore you to be firm and confident, Richard," said his wife; "and in spite of all, notwithstanding the difficulties in which we are now involved, I cannot divest my mind of the belief that we shall be able to surmount them all, and to be admitted again into that society from which we are now estranged. Come, my love, say that you will endeavour to think as I have expressed myself; exert all your energies, and I shall then be comparatively happy."

Richard embraced his wife affectionately returning no verbal answer, but his looks expressed much more than words could have done, and after some further observations, they left the chamber, and made their way to the same room which they had occupied on the previous day, and where they again found the landlord, and the morning's repast spread upon the table. He greeted them in the same friendly manner as he had done on the previous day, and they returned his compliments with equal sincerity.

"I hope you are now quite recovered from the effects of the fatigue you had undergone, and the violence of the storm," he remarked; "have you quite made up your minds to resume your journey in the evening?"

"Yes, sir," answered our hero, "I am sorry that the urgency of our business will not permit us to avail ourselves of your hospitality any longer; but we must ever feel obliged to you for the civility and attention we have experienced from you, during the short time we have been your guests, and——"

"Oh, as for the matter of that," interrupted the landlord, impatiently, "I do not know that you have anything to thank me for particularly; I have done no more than my business required of me to do; but I am happy to think I have been able to accommodate you, and should you at at any time be passing this way, I hope you will not forget to give me a call."

"I shall be proud to do so, sir," returned Richard.

"Excuse my curiosity," observed the worthy host, "but is it your intention to settle at M——?"

"I know not at present," replied our hero, hesitating; "but why do you inquire?"

"Simply for this reason," returned the landlord, "that somehow or other I have taken quite a fancy to you and your wife, and as I am frequently over that way, I should like to call upon you, and take a cheerful glass with you."

"You do me too much honour, sir," said our hero, in a faltering voice; "but I am rather doubtful whether I shall remain many days with the relations I am going to see, and if they cannot assist me to anything, I must travel on further in search of employment."

"Well," said the landlord, "you know your own business best, and I wish you success with all my heart. I am much mistaken, as I said before, if you were ever born to fill the humble situation you now seem to occupy."

"I have before informed you, sir," replied Richard, with some confusion, and the more especially as he beheld the looks of the landlord fixed upon him with much curiosity, "that I was respectably born, but reduced by untoward circumstances to my present condition. However, it is no use to murmur, for there is many a better man than myself who has suffered a similar reverse of fortune, and I shall be perfectly contented if I am only enabled to get an honest living by my own industry."

"Well spoken," observed the landlord; "there is no disgrace in poverty, where it is not brought on by our own improvidence and vicious habits. A clear conscience is

everything, and renders the toils of labour light."

"True, sir," coincided Richard, and at the same time he earnestly wished that the landlord would change the topic of conversation, for it was becoming by far too interesting and embarrassing to him; the worthy host, however, seemed by no means inclined to do so, and did not offer to leave the room. He had been reading a local newspaper when Richard and his wife entered the room, and having now glanced his eye over a particular paragraph, he observed:

"I see, according to this paper, that the government has increased the reward by a hundred guineas, which is offered for the apprehension of Admiral Parker, the mutineer; poor fellow, his mind must be in a dreadful state, hunted about as he is, and with nothing but a shameful death staring him in the face, and no doubt he would gladly exchange situations with the humblest individual that breathes."

Mary turned sick at heart, and trembled violently, as the landlord made use of these observations, and the agitation of her husband may readily be imagined; but he conquered his emotions as well as he could, and said:

"This Admiral Parker, as he is called, is, I believe, an unfortunate man, and has received many injuries."

"Well," returned the host, "there may be some truth in that to be sure; but still nothing can sanction the conduct he has pursued; mutiny is a serious offence, especially when conducted on such a scale of magnitude as his designs were; besides, he is charged with a double murder."

"A double murder?" replied our hero, in a faint voice.

"Yes," answered the landlord; "the death of Captain Arlington in the first instance, for which crime there was probably some excuse to be offered, as it appears from all that I have read of the matter that he was merely acting in self-defence; but he is now accused of a second murder."

"A second murder?"

"Yes, on the night before last. Here are the whole particulars of it given in this paper, and I think you will agree when you have perused them, that Parker stands in a much more critical and questionable position than he did before. Read it, and judge for yourself."

With these words the landlord placed the paper in the hands of our unfortunate hero, pointing out to him the paragraph to which he had alluded, and the reader may easily form a conception of his feelings when he read the particulars of the death of the villain Brunston, and the full particulars of the dying declarations he had made to the men who discovered him. He fixed a keen glance upon the countenance of the landlord, to see whether he could discover anything which might lend him to imagine that any suspicion as to his identity had entered his breast, but perceiving nothing, he became more composed and collected, and said:

"This is indeed a bad job for this unfortunate man, Parker; but still it would not be right to condemn him altogether until the whole of the particulars are brought to light."

"True," coincided the landlord; "and notwithstanding that circumstances at present appear so strong against him, I cannot help pitying him. I think, however, that it is almost impossible for him longer to escape detection; for it is supposed that he is entirely destitute and friendless, and where can he conceal himself? However, for my own part, I hope he may be enabled to elude the vigilance of his pursuers, and to live to repent, and I should be sorry to have any hand in his apprehension, if even I knew where he was. We none of us know what we may come to, and I cannot help pitying my fellow-creatures even if their misfortunes should be brought upon themselves."

"The sentiments you have just now expressed do honour to your head and heart, sir," replied Richard, encouraged by his observations: "and I cannot but most cordially agree with them myself."

"Well, I may be wrong," said the worthy host, "and many persons might laugh at me for what they might be pleased to call my misplaced and mistaken sympathy; however, I hope I shall ever entertain the same feelings, which I am fain to flatter myself are far from discreditable to me. But I am intruding upon you, and having other business to attend to, will bid you good morning for the present."

Richard and his wife returned the compliment, and the landlord then made his exit, much to their relief.

"It is now too evident," remarked Richard, "that every moment we remain here is fraught with the most imminent danger, and that our pursuers have not relaxed anything in their vigilance. The observations of the landlord have filled me with doubts and apprehensions, and should he really have detected us, which from the description of our persons given in this paper, it seems almost impossible he should fail to do, we have everything to dread, and I know not in what manner to act."

"It is most unfortunate and embarrassing," replied Mary; "but still I cannot help thinking that we have nothing to fear from the landlord, should he even have recognised us, which I am inclined to think he has not. The sentiments he has expressed ought to inspire us with confidence, and I do not believe that he would be the means of doing us any injury."

"Ah, Mary," returned our hero, "I know not; money is a very tempting thing, and when the large reward which is offered for my apprehension is taken into consideration, we have, I am certain, every reason to dread the worst."

"I cannot, I dare not entertain the same apprehensions as you do, my dear Richard," observed his wife, struggling with her feelings as well as she could, although it was impossible for her not to be fully alive to the danger by which they were surrounded; "the landlord, depend upon it, suspects us not, or he would at once have accused us; besides, in a few hours we shall leave this place, and I feel satisfied in my own mind, that Providence will not forsake us, but that something will shortly occur to brighten our prospects altogether, and to aid us in our ultimate escape from the myrmidons of the law, if you only continue to act with the same precaution that you have hitherto done."

Our hero shook his head doubtfully, but he returned no immediate answer. He saw plainly enough, in spite of all his wife had said, that their danger increased rather than abated, and he could not help almost entirely abandoning himself to despair; but fearful of alarming her, and of rendering her incapable of the arduous task they had to perform, he struggled with his feelings as well as he could, and affected to conquer those apprehensions which he had previously expressed. Thus the day wore on, and nothing more particular occurred to excite their fears, and the behaviour of the landlord towards them was sufficient to inspire them with confidence; they saw him frequently in the course of the day, and he entered freely into conversation with them, never again alluding to the subject that was so embarrassing to them; but, on the contrary, he expressed his regret that they were about to leave him so soon, and heartily wished them success in their future undertakings. During the day, Richard and his wife made such trifling preparations as were necessary for the resumption of their journey, and they then awaited the arrival of the evening with impatience and anxiety. Presently, at the time mentioned by the landlord, the waggon stopped at the inn, and the man, Daniel, was once more introduced to our hero and his wife, and greeted them in his usual rustic and simple manner, but apparently with much sincerity.

"Master Hatfield has been telling me," he remarked, "that you want to go to M——, and as I have no one travelling in my waggon, and I am going to within a short distance of the place, if you have no objection, I will willingly take you there."

"I thank you, my good man," replied our hero, "and gladly avail myself of your kind offer; but as you see I am only a poor fellow like yourself, I cannot afford to pay you very liberally."

"Oh, as for that, master," returned Daniel, "I dare say we shall not fall out; I do not care if you do not give me a farthing; it is no trouble to me, and I should be ashamed of myself if I could refuse to give any poor people a lift to help them on their way to any part to which I might be going."

Richard again thanked the honest rustic for his kindness, and after they had partaken of some slight refreshment, they prepared to depart. Our hero having also expressed his thanks to the landlord for the kind attention they had received from him, requested to know what he was indebted to him for the accommodation he had received from him.

"You are poor," replied the landlord, "and are, therefore, welcome to all that you have received from me, and I am glad that it was in my power to accommodate you; any time, if you should be passing this way, I hope that you will not neglect to give me a call, and you shall always find a hearty welcome."

"My dear sir," returned Richard, "how can I ever sufficiently express to you my acknowledgments for your disinterested friendship and kindness towards those who are entire strangers to you? Believe me if at any time I should have the opportunity, I will not fail to call upon you, and to evince to you how highly I appreciate the favours I have received from you."

"I am perfectly satisfied, and require no thanks," answered the worthy host; "I should despise myself if I could refuse to render all the assistance in my power to those who stand in need, and who I am convinced are deserving of it."

"Now, sir," interposed Daniel, and addressing himself to our hero, "all be ready, and the sooner we be jogging on the road the better, for we have a good fourteen mile to travel, and I must be punctual to my time at the place where I am to stop."

Richard and his wife cordially bade the kind host adieu, and then quitting the inn, they entered the waggon, and were soon proceeding on their journey, with hearts somewhat lighter than they had been previously; Daniel walking by the side of his team, and whistling merrily on the way. The shadows of evening had now fallen thickly in silvery splendour, myriads of twinkling stars lent their lustre to the sky, and everything betokened a fine night. There were few persons about, and as they were completely concealed from observation, our hero and his wife felt quite at their ease, and they became more tranquil than they had been for some time before. The part of the country they were now travelling through presented a by far more cheerful aspect than any they had lately seen, yet it seemed to be but little frequented, a circumstance which was highly gratifying to them, as they had no cause to fear any interruption, and, in spite of all that had taken place and the many difficulties they had to surmount, their minds felt far more at ease.

"Heaven is yet kind and merciful to us," observed Mary, "in sending us such kind and generous friends in the midst of our adversity, and notwithstanding the dark and ponderous clouds that have hitherto obscured the horizon of our happiness, our prospects begin to brighten. We are much indebted to Mr. Hatfield for his behaviour towards us, and that ought to be sufficient to divest our minds of any suspicion that he had recognised us; nay, even if he had done so, I feel satisfied that he possesses too generous and humane a heart to betray us. Come, Richard, do you not feel hope revive within your breast?"

"Yes, Mary," answered her husband, "I must confess that I feel more at ease after what has happened, and we have obtained this conveyance from the scene of our immediate danger; but yet it is necessary that we should act with the greatest precaution, for the least imprudent step on our part might be productive of the most serious consequences."

"True, Richard," coincided our heroine; "but while we bear in mind what we have at stake, there is not much fear of our doing that. But should we not be able to obtain a temporary shelter at the place where we are going, what course do you mean to adopt?"

"Circumstances will most likely suggest that," replied Richard. "But I have little doubt that the offer of some adequate reward will induce one of the fishermen to convey us to the opposite side of the coast, and then I shall imagine that we are, for the present, at any rate, free from danger. I will then communicate with our friend Adams, and abide entirely by the advice he may think proper to forward us. Oh, my beloved Mary, could we indeed reach a place of safety, where we might remain undiscovered and unmolested, even though we should be destined to encounter the severest trials of fortune, how happy should I be."

"And it will be so, Richard," said his wife, and looking up calmly and confidently in his face; "there is something whispers to me the sweet assurance that it will, and all the difficulties it may yet be our lot to encounter sink into comparative insignificance. We have already endured trials enough, and the Almighty will now extend His mercy towards us, whilst we put our trust in Him, and will not suffer us to fall victims to misfortune altogether."

Richard embraced his wife, and a silence of some minutes ensued, and they resigned themselves entirely to the various and conflicting thoughts that crowded upon their minds in such rapid succession, and to which the many stirring and startling events that had recently taken place naturally gave rise. They continued on their journey at the same slow and steady pace, and nothing worthy of notice occurred to them, Daniel never offering to interrupt them in their cogitations, but still continuing to whistle merrily as he proceeded on his way.

There was but little diversity in the scenery amongst which they travelled; but the road now passed near the sea coast, and they could catch occasional glimpses of the ocean, whose broad surface was silvered by the moonbeams; and here and there, but far apart, a straggling cottage or two met their sight, and which, from their outward appearance, seemed to be inhabited by the poorest of persons.

"Beautiful ocean," ejaculated our hero, as he gazed upon it, "would that we were far beyond thy bright waters, and in some place of security, free from the power of those who so anxiously seek to shed my blood, methinks that then, in spite of all the sufferings that I have undergone, notwithstanding all the manifold wrongs I have endured, I could be contented and resigned, let my future fate be whatever it might."

"Fear not, dear Richard," replied his wife, "your prayers will be granted, and that the time is not far distant when we shall be removed from these dangers and difficulties by which we are at present surrounded. My hopes gain strength every moment, and I feel myself fully prepared to encounter any further troubles it may yet be our lot to encounter, so that I can see you act with firmness and resignation."

"I will exert myself to the utmost to do so, Mary," returned her husband, "and I hope that Heaven will give me strength to act according to my wishes."

"Well said, dear Richard," replied his wife; "it glads my heart and inspires me with fresh courage to hear you talk thus. I cannot but predict a fortunate and happy result to the termination of our journey."

"Should your predictions be verified, Mary," remarked our hero, "what an inconceivable debt of gratitude shall we owe to the Supreme."

"Ah, Richard," returned Mary, "why should we resign ourselves entirely to despair, after the many hairbreadth and miraculous escapes we have already had? They should at least convince us that, however dark our destiny may at present seem to be, Providence has not deserted us, that it still continues to watch over our safety, and, therefore, that whilst we continue to pursue the right course, we may look forward to the time when we shall be extricated from our present deplorable and torturing situation, and be restored to that position in society which we formerly occupied."

"No, Mary," returned our hero; "I can't go so far as to anticipate all that you have expressed; though we may be permitted to live in humble obscurity, we can never hope to be restored to that position in society from which we have now been so long estranged; nor, I must candidly confess, do I scarcely wish it; the many misfortunes I have experienced, render retirement to me far more inviting than the busy walks of life, and I can only hope by that means to find that consolation and tranquillity which I am so anxious to obtain."

"Be it so, my husband," said Mary, "I perfectly appreciate your feelings, and shall only be too contented and grateful should your wishes be gratified, which I trust to Heaven that they will."

Richard returned no answer, and they again sank into silence, and gave themselves up to their own reflections for a few minutes; but they were suddenly aroused from their lethargy of thought by beholding at a distance, and advancing in the direction that the waggon was proceeding, the shadows of several human forms, and as they advanced nearer they could plainly distinguish, by the light of the moon, that they were those of men. Richard and our heroine felt alarmed, for the idea of some approaching danger immediately presented itself to their imagination. They might be some of the men who had been sent in pursuit of them, and should they have called at the inn, they might have elicited from Mr. Hatfield, the landlord, all the information they required, and then, indeed, their danger would be imminent. As they advanced nearer, and they had a more distinct view of their persons, their suspicions became strengthened, and they were almost positive that they were some of those men whom they had so much cause to dread.

"Good God!" ejaculated Richard, "what is to be done in this fresh dilemma? Should these persons really prove to be the men who are sent in pursuit of us, our discovery is inevitable. We have not the least means of escape; and see, they are gaining fast upon us."

"Be calm and firm, Richard," said his wife, "and, after all, your fears may turn out to be unfounded. Do you not think that we may trust to Daniel?"

"And how can he assist us," demanded our hero, "if even he should have the will to do so?"

"At any rate, you had better speak to him," answered Mary; "there is no time to be lost."

Richard immediately put his head from the waggon, and called the driver to him.

"Well, master," said Daniel, "what be the matter now? Is there anything I can do for you?"

"Yes, my good friend," answered Richard, "you have it in your power to do us a great favour."

"And what may that be, master?" asked the waggoner.

"Why," replied Parker, "for particular reasons, that are of no interest to any persons but ourselves, we do not wish to be seen by any one on the road. You see those men that are coming this way?"

"I do," replied Daniel.

"Should they speak to you," continued our hero, "when they come up to the waggon, and put any questions to you, will you be kind enough not to acknowledge that you have any one travelling in your waggon, and to deny that you have seen any one answering our description on the road to-night?"

"Well," said the simple countryman, after a pause, "I don't mind doing so, though it is a strange request to make. And, if you do not wish to be seen, you will find plenty in the waggon with which to conceal yourselves."

Richard thanked him heartily, and Daniel again left them, and urged on his horses. The men had now arrived to within a few yards of the waggon, and the suspicions of Richard and his wife were confirmed, for they perceived that they were a portion of the men whom they had seen at the farm, and who, no doubt, had received sufficient intelligence to give them some idea of the route which they had probably taken. Mary trembled, and the alarm of Richard may be conceived without our attempting to describe it. There was not an instant to be lost, however; all depended upon the integrity of the waggoner, and should he fail to keep his word, but, on the contrary, betray them, their fate was certain and inevitable. Hastily they concealed themselves beneath the hay and straw, and then awaited the result, in a state of the most breathless and painful suspense. It was not long that they were kept so; they heard the footsteps of the men as they approached, and the different observations they exchanged with each other, which all served to confirm their suspicions, and the next instant they had come up to the waggon, and were addressing themselves to Daniel.

"Good evening, my friend," said one of them; "you seem to be rather merry."

"Ay, master," answered the waggoner, carelessly; "what's the use of being sad? It be a poor heart that never rejoices, you know; and I have nothing that should particularly trouble me, I believe."

"Well, that's a good job," remarked the man; "I should, indeed, judge from your countenance, that you and sorrow are not on very intimate terms together. plenty to eat and to drink, I suppose, moderate wages, and very little labour?"

"Ah, master," said the simple-hearted and good-natured countryman, "you may say that, master; why, bless your soul, there is not a happier man in the universe than myself. I consider myself as well off as a prince; but then, you see, I have got a contented mind, that is one great thing, you know."

"True," coincided the officer—"a contented mind is a very essential thing. But are you travelling far?"

"Why, yes," replied Daniel; "I expect that my journey will take me all night to accomplish."

"And have you no one in your waggon?" asked the man.

"No," returned Daniel; "I have no room for passengers, as you will perceive, if you just look how my waggon is loaded."

"Right," remarked the officer, looking into the waggon; "you have a tidy load. Have you met any persons on the road?"

"Two or three," answered the countryman.

DANIEL HAWTHORN ALLOWS THE WANDERERS TO RIDE IN HIS WAGGON.

"Have you seen a man, dressed as a countryman, tall, and good-looking; and a woman, having the appearance of a widow, together with a young lad, as you have come along?"

"Why," answered Daniel, "they must be the persons whom I saw about a quarter of an hour ago, and who inquired of me the road to Hemisford Marsh."

"Ah," ejaculated the officer, eagerly,

"those must be the very individuals we seek. Which is the road to Hemisford Marsh, my friend?"

"Yonder, to the right," returned the cautious countryman.

"And it is about a quarter of an hour, you say, since you saw them?" asked the man.

Daniel answered in the affirmative.

"Then we have not a moment to lose," said the man, addressing himself to his companions; "and if we are quick, we shall doubtless overtake them; we are on the right scent at last. Come, lads. Good night, my friend, and thank you for the information."

"Oh, you are welcome to it," replied Daniel, drily, "if it is of any use to you."

"Useful to us, my good fellow!" repeated the officer; "indeed it is; but we have no time to stop conversing longer. Good night."

"Good night," said the waggoner, chuckling in his sleeves, and the men hurried away, taking the road to which he had directed them, and were almost immediately out of sight. What a weight of apprehension were the unfortunate fugitives released from when they heard them depart, and how grateful were they to the honest waggoner for the sagacity and presence of mind which he had evinced. They now ventured to come from the place of their concealment, and Richard having again called Daniel to him, they poured forth their thanks to him in no very measured terms.

"Oh, my good friends," returned the kind-hearted rustic, "I don't want any thanks for the trifling service I have rendered you; if you do not wish to see them, I have sent them far enough out of the way, I can tell you, and you have nothing to fear from them."

Richard again thanked him, and then added,—

"But I suppose that the request I have made of you, has appeared strange to you, and that it has excited your curiosity?"

"No," replied Daniel. "I can tell you, master, that I am not a man of that description; your reason for acting in the manner you have done is your own business, and I have nothing to do with it."

"You are an honest man, I am convinced," remarked Richard.

"Well," returned the countryman, "as for that matter, I cannot say much, though I know I try to be as honest as the world will let me."

"Have we much farther to go?" asked our hero.

"About four miles, or better," answered Daniel; "and I think we have made pretty good speed, considering the road, which is not one of the best in the world."

"True," coincided Richard; "and I shall be very glad when we have arrived at our journey's end."

"I dare say you will, master," said the waggoner; "but have you any particular place to go to when you get to M——?"

"Why," replied Parker, after a moment's reflection, "I had some relations residing there, but whether they have quitted the neighbourhood or not, I am not certain."

"And what might their names be, master?" asked the waggoner. This was rather an embarrassing question for our hero, but he quickly recovered himself, and replied,—"Melford."

"Melford," said Daniel; "I never heard of the name before, and there is scarcely a person at M—— whom I do not know—for I was bred and born there. I am inclined to think that you will not find them there, my friends."

"It will be most unfortunate if we should not," said Richard; "but if it should turn out that we shou'd not be able to do so, do you know any person there who can accommodate us with a lodging for a day or two?"

"Yes," answered Daniel, "my own brother, Harry, who, although I say it, that perhaps shouldn't say it, is as honest a man as ever drew the breath of life. He is only a fisherman, with a wife and one daughter, poor thing! but he is better to do in the world than some of his neighbours, because he has, perhaps, been more prudent and careful. He has a couple of huts of his own, and he will gladly accommodate you, I know, if you say that I recommended you."

"I am much obliged to you," said our hero, "and shall probably avail myself of the opportunity, if it would not be putting him to any inconvenience."

"Not in the least," returned the waggoner.

"But how shall I find him?"

"I would accompany you," said Daniel, "but time will not permit me; however, you will be sure to find him, for his is the second dwelling as you enter the place."

Richard again thanked him, and the waggoner then left him, and returned to his horses.

"We have again been fortunate, Richard," said his wife, "in meeting with this honest countryman. His having put our pursuers on the wrong scent, and the shrewd replies he made to them, has saved is from detection; and from his brother, according to the description he has given of him, we shall probably be enabled to obtain all the assistance we require."

"Yes," observed Richard, "and if we can only prevail upon him to convey us to the opposite side of the coast, we may succeed in eluding the vigilance of our pursuers for some time longer, if not altogether."

"I trust that we shall be able to escape altogether, dear Richard," said his wife; "at any rate, there is at present everything to inspire us with hope, and to encourage us to persevere."

"I will try to do so," returned her husband, "and if I fail it shall not be from any want of exertion on my part."

"Now does my husband indeed speak like himself," ejaculated the faithful and devoted wife, "and I feel buoyed up with the most sanguine hope."

"May the fond hopes you have formed not be doomed to be disappointed," said Richard; "but we must act with caution, for the least inadvertency on our points would betray us to immediate destruction."

"Oh, fear not," answered our heroine; "Providence will assist us in the accomplishment of our task; we have too much at stake to be thrown for a moment off our guard. I see the dawn of future prosperity, notwithstanding all the sufferings we have experienced; our troubles, depend upon it, are nearly at an end."

Richard Parker thought very differently to his wife, but he took great pains to conceal his real feelings from her observation, for he well knew the anguish it would inflict upon her mind, and without accomplishing any useful purpose. The remainder of the journey they performed in comparative silence, meeting with no further adventure which was calculated to cause them any excitement; they approached nearer and nearer the sea coast, without perceiving any human being on the road, and at length they beheld several lights glimmering at a distance, which Daniel informed them proceeded from the windows of the inn at which he was going to stop, and where he would be compelled to leave them, as his route lay in a different direction to that which they had to go.

"You will not have more than half a mile to walk, however," he said, "and you will have no difficulty in finding out my brother Harry, who will gladly afford you all the accommodation in his power."

In a very few minutes after this the waggon stopped at the door of the inn, and Richard and his wife having first satisfied themselves that there was nothing to fear, walked into the house in order that they might obtain some refreshment and settle with Daniel for the service he had rendered them. Their orders were promptly attended to, and they were shortly afterwards rejoined by the waggoner, who informed them that his time was up, and that it was necessary for him to pursue his journey.

"Well, my friend," said Richard, "for your kindness towards us, I cannot but return you my most sincere thanks. We are greatly indebted to you, and I am afraid that, poor as we are, we shall not be able to reward you adequately for your services, but if—"

"I tell you what it is, master," interrupted Daniel; "I am only a plain-spoken simple sort of a fellow, but I trust that I am none the worse for that; I do not think that what I have done for you is worth talking about, and as for any reward, I do not wish to offend you, but I should be ashamed of myself if I could take anything at all from persons who are so poor as you appear to be. No, master, keep your money, and put it to a much more useful purpose; I am quite sufficiently paid for my services by the person who employs me, and I require no more."

"Nay," said our hero, lost in admiration at the noble sentiments which the simple and illiterate rustic expressed; "this is too generous, and I must insist upon your taking at least some trifling recompense for your trouble."

"Not a farthing," returned Daniel, determinedly; "and if you offer it me you will offend me, though I don't suppose that would be of much consequence. You will find plenty of other ways for what trifle of money you may have, I have no doubt; but, if you do go to my brother Harry's, and stop with him for a day or two, I shall most likely see you again."

"I shall be most happy to do so, my friend," answered Richard; "but, before we part, there is one thing I have to request of you."

"Name it," said Daniel.

"It is merely that you will not say anything to your friends or acquaintances about me, for I have particular reasons for not making the place of my destination known at present."

"You may depend upon me," replied Daniel, "what has passed between yourself and me I shall never reveal, for I am not one that is fond of talking about or prying into that which don't concern me."

Richard once more returned his acknowledgments to him, and after some few more observations of no importance, and having received from him all the necessary directions as to the nearest road to M———, Daniel took his leave, and left the fugitives to themselves.

As it was now past ten o'clock, the landlord tried to persuade them to stop all night at his house, but Richard having told him that the business they went upon would not permit of any delay, but concealing from him the fact that they had but a short distance to go to reach the place of their destination, settled for what refreshments they had had, and immediately afterwards left the house, and took the road which the waggoner had pointed out to them, looking cautiously around them at the same time to see that no one was watching them, but there was not a person near the spot. In a very short time they came in sight of the village or hamlet, which consisted only of a few fishermen's huts of no very general inviting appearance, and from which could be commanded an extensive view of the ocean, which was now calm and beautiful, and glittering in the bright rays of the silvery empress of the night. They paused for a minute or two to gaze upon it, and to indulge in the reflections to which the scene gave rise, but, at length, they turned away, and sought out the residences of Daniel's brother. They were not long in discovering them from their neat and cleanly appearance, which presented such a striking contrast to the others, and they perceived lights from the parlonr window. Richard hesitated for an instant, and he then advanced towards the door, and listened, but all being quiet within, he ventured to knock.

The door was quickly opened by a decent middle-aged woman, with a lighted lamp in her hand, and on beholding Richard and his wife and the boy, she started back in evident amazement and confusion, and hastily inquired what their business might be.

"I beg your pardon, my good woman," answered our hero, "for our seeming rudeness; we are only poor people who are bent to a certain place, and we were informed that we might be able to obtain from your husband and yourself accommodation for a day or two, for which we are willing to pay you, as far as our limited means will allow us to do."

"Indeed," said the woman, civilly, but with some expressions of astonishment, and scrutinising them narrowly at the same time; "from whom could you have received this information?"

"I believe your husband has a brother named Daniel?" replied our hero.

"He has," returned the woman; "and was it he who directed you hither?"

"It was," said Richard; "we have not long left him, and he brought us here in his waggon from the Golden Lion."

"Oh, then, it is all right, I have no doubt," remarked the female. "Yes, we certainly can accommodate you, as the next hut belongs to us as well as this, and we have only one daughter; so walk in, and make yourselves quite at home. My husband is at present absent, but I expect him to return every minute, and I have no doubt you will be able to arrange everything in a satisfactory manner with him."

The fugitives thanked her, and walked into the clean and neatly furnished parlour, in which a cheerful fire was blazing, and before which the female placed chairs for them, and invited them to seat themselves, and not to make themselves shy.

"Have you travelled far?" asked the woman, still eyeing them with more curiosity than was agreeable to their feelings.

"Yes, ma'am," answered Richard, "we have been travelling several days, and have endured much fatigue. We wish to get to the opposite side of the coast, and would not mind paying any one as fair a sum as our poor means will allow us to do to who would convey us there."

"Well," observed the female, "there will not be much difficulty in doing that; and, I have no doubt, you will be able to come to some arrangement with my husband about it. But you need some refreshment, and I will, therefore, immediately place them before you."

Richard, however, informed her that they had already partaken of some, and the woman was about to address some observation to them, when she was interrupted by a knock at the door, and rising from her seat, she said,—

"That is my husband returned, no doubt; do not disturb yourselves, you will find him an agreeable man, who is always ready to do a good turn for any of his fellow-creatures who may stand in need of his assistance."

Thus saying, she went to the door, which she opened, and gave admittance to a man about the middle age, stout and robust, but whose features our hero and his wife had not an opportunity of distinguishing immediately in the dim light. He greeted his wife in tones of simple but honest affection, and then walked into the room in which the fugitives were sitting, but started back in some confusion and amazement on beholding strangers there.

Richard Parker and his wife arose, and the good woman who had so kindly received them was about to explain to her husband, when the light, falling full upon their features, he no sooner beheld them, than he seemed to recognise them in a moment, and started back with astonishment, and uttered a mingled exclamation of pity and pleasure. Richard Parker turned pale and trembled, for he also appeared to recognise the fisherman immediately. Mary looked fearfully, anxiously, and inquiringly upon both of them ; and the fisherman's wife was evidently completely bewildered at the emotion they evinced, but offered not a word.

CHAPTER XXIII.

ANOTHER SURPRISE AND RECOGNITION.—
WHO THE FISHERMAN REALLY IS.—
OLD FRIENDS AND ASSOCIATIONS.

"RICHARD!" at length exclaimed the fisherman, gazing still more intently upon him; "is it possible?"

"Hawthorn!" cried our hero, in a faint and faltering voice.

"Unfortunate man," said the fisherman; "how is it after the lapse of so many years that we meet again, and when you are placed in such painful and dangerous circumstances? What has guided your footsteps hither?"

"Accident, pure accident," replied Parker; "but oh, Hawthorn, you surely will not betray me?"

"Betray you!" repeated Hawthorn, in tones of sincerity; "Richard, think you that I have become so despicable and ungrateful a scoundrel? Betray you? No, damme, if Harry Hawthorn would not suffer himself to be hung up like a dog first."

"Known!" said Mary, looking doubtfully and anxiously, first at her husband and then at Hawthorn.

"Yes," replied the latter; "but here you have nothing to fear. I am a friend; I pity your misfortunes; I am glad that you have hitherto been able to elude the vengeance of your pursuers, and that Providence has directed your footsteps hither. This is such a surprise that I can scarcely believe the evidence of my senses; but be seated, for Heaven's sake, for you look completely exhausted with fatigue and anxiety of mind; and Alice, do you see immediately to the comfort and necessities of these unfortunate persons."

"What does all this mean?" asked Alice, eagerly, and looking with astonishment upon her husband; "explain yourself, Harry."

Richard grasped the worthy fisherman's hand cordially, and expressed his gratitude by his looks, for he could not do so by words.

"Alice," said Hawthorn, in reply to the anxious inquiries of his wife; "you have often heard me speak of the excellent farmer who many years since acted the part of the good Samaritan to me, when I was friendless, houseless, and starving?"

"Yes, yes," answered Alice; "and you must ever think of him with feelings of the most unbounded gratitude and respect."

"And you well know that I do, Alice," returned her husband, "he is now no more; may God rest his soul; but this is the son of that excellent man."

"Richard Parker!" ejaculated Alice, with a look of increased astonishment and almost incredulity.

"The same, Mrs. Hawthorn," replied our hero; "I am the unfortunate man over whose head an ignominious death is impending, and who, by a strange dispensation of Providence, is thus led to throw himself, with his wife and child, upon the charity and benevolence of yourself and your husband."

"Say no more about it, Mr. Parker, I beg of you," said the good woman; "charity, benevolence!—it is a duty that we owe to all our fellow-creatures, and I know that you will find no one more ready to perform that duty than myself and my husband. But, dear me, why do I stand talking here, when you so much need refreshment? Oh, Mrs. Parker, you can't imagine how much I pity you and your husband, and this poor boy, too; it is hard for him to be exposed so early to such misfortunes. How glad I am that you should happen to have met with Daniel."

"We owe him much," returned Parker; "and I shall never forget the disinterested kindness with which he has acted towards us."

"Ay," remarked Hawthorn, "Daniel is a good, kind-hearted fellow, though simple and illiterate, and I know that he would do all the good in his power for any of his fellow-creatures who might happen to be in misfortune."

"Indeed," returned Richard, "we have most amply experienced that; but, how is it, Hawthorn, that after so many years, I find you here?"

"Why," replied Hawthorn, "you know that after I had recovered myself from my difficulties, through the unexampled benevolence of your father (Heaven bless his memory, but for him I must have perished), I again went to sea, having previously married my present wife; and many years of peril and persecution I encountered, till at last I became disgusted with the service, and retired from it. My only child, my Flora, was then a lovely maiden, fast blooming into womanhood, and the admiration of all who knew her; but now, poor thing, alas! alas! she——"

His voice was choked with emotion, and he could not finish the sentence; Alice sighed deeply, and covered her face with her hands, and Hawthorn hastily dashed the manly tear from his eyes. Richard and his wife were deeply affected, and looked on in silence. A pause of a few moments ensued, but at last Hawthorn said—

"Oh, I have much to tell you, Mr. Parker, and you will then find that I have not been without my heavy misfortunes as well as yourself. But this is not the time for explanation; you need rest; to-morrow we will, if you please, talk all these important matters over, and then we will advise together what is best to be done. I have often thought of you, and trembled for the fate which was impending over your head; but I rejoice that you have hitherto avoided it, and Heaven grant that you may be able to escape it altogether."

"Oh, Hawthorn," returned our hero, again pressing his hand, "need I tell you how grateful I am to you for this kind expression of the sympathy of your feelings towards me? But do you blame me for the part I have acted?"

"Blame you, Parker?" replied Hawthorn; "oh, no, you must be well convinced that I do not, for you were driven to it by the basest persecution and tyranny; I only regret that you should have made so great a personal sacrifice. However, I sincerely hope that you will yet be duly rewarded for it, and that Providence will not desert you in the midst of your misfortunes."

"Oh, Mr. Hawthorn," ejaculated Mary, while the tears started to her eyes; "how can I express my feelings for these kind sentiments in our favour? Providence has, indeed, been most bountiful and merciful to us, in thus raising us up so many friends in the midst of our adversity."

"Enough, Mrs. Parker," observed the fisherman, "for what it may be in my power to do for you, yourself and your husband will be heartily welcome, and I shall only be too happy to have the opportunity of serving you. But it grows late, and it will be better for you to seek rest, after the fatigue of your journey, as soon as possible. You will find everything necessary for your comfort in my adjoining hut, and you need be under no apprehension of danger, for it is not likely that any one will think of searching for you here. Alice, go you and kindle a fire, and make all the necessary preparations, and then we will part with our unfortunate friends for the night."

Alice nodded assent, and then left the room for that purpose. During the short time she was absent, our hero entered into a brief explanation of all that had occurred to him up to the time of their arriving there, and Hawthorn listened with the most profound attention, evidently deeply interested in the romantic and startling particulars.

"Well, Mr. Parker," he observed, when Richard had concluded, "you have certainly experienced some most terrible misfortunes and adventures, and have had the most miraculous escapes. The villain Arlington met with the fate that he deserved, as did also the ruffian Brunston. I know Adams and Binnacle well, and although I could easily convey you in one of my fishing smacks to the opposite coast, I would advise you to remain here for a short time, where you will be perfectly safe, and until you have made them acquainted with your present situation, and received their advice upon the subject."

"I will be guided by you, Hawthorn," returned our hero; "and have no wish to act until I have communicated with them."

"Well," said Hawthorn, "we will talk this matter fully over to-morrow. I cannot express to you properly how glad I am to see you, and that it is in my power to serve you. Such misfortunes as those you have met with are worthy of the deepest sympathy."

Richard Parker was about to make some reply, when he was interrupted by the appearance of Alice, who announced that everything was in readiness at the hut for their reception.

"Then," remarked Hawthorn, "we will separate for the night; and I wish you tranquillity and repose after the many trials that you have experienced. Good night. In the morning we will meet again, and then we can calmly and patiently discuss the many important matters in which we are so deeply interested."

Richard Parker and his wife again returned their heartfelt acknowledgments, and pressed the hand of the kind-hearted fisherman vehemently.

"My wife will conduct you to the hut," said the latter, "which I hope you will find in every way suited to your convenience. Farewell, till we meet again ; we shall have much to converse about to-morrow."

"Good night, Hawthorn," responded our hero, "and may Heaven reward you for your kindness to me."

Hawthorn pressed his hand in silence, and Mary, taking the hand of William, they followed Alice out of the cottage.

On entering the hut in which they were to repose, they were struck with the neatness and comfort of its appearance, which was quite in keeping with the character of the one they had just quitted ; and Alice soon after showed them into a clean and well-furnished chamber, in which the good woman had kindled a cheerful fire, which gave the room a still more comfortable appearance, especially to persons placed in the melancholy situation of our hero and heroine. They warmly thanked Mrs. Hawthorn for the attention which she had paid ; but she stopped them impatiently by saying—

"What I have done, my unfortunate friends, I consider nothing, and I, therefore, do not require any acknowledgments. Here, I trust, you will repose comfortably, and endeavour in some measure to recruit your spirits by the morning ; here, at any rate, you may be sure that you are in safety. Good night !"

"Good night !" repeated our hero and his wife, and Mrs. Hawthorn then took her departure. As soon as she was gone, Mary and her husband rushed into each other's arms, and embracing affectionately, they gave vent to the emotions which struggled in their bosoms, in sobs and tears. They then sunk upon their knees, and poured forth their thanks to the Supreme for his wonderful interposition in their favour, and it was several minutes ere they could sufficiently compose their feelings to converse rationally and calmly.

"For the present, thank Heaven, we are again saved," at length ejaculated Mary, fervently; "Providence still watches over us, dear Richard, and raises us up friends where we least expected to find them. How singular, and yet how fortunate it is, that we should be guided to the very residence of those who are acquainted with you, and who are, at the same time, so warmly disposed to serve us all that lays in their power."

"It is, indeed," replied her husband;

"and we cannot but acknowledge a special Providence in it all."

"True," coincided our heroine ; "and that should doubly inspire you with the hope that we shall yet ultimately escape."

"I will endeavour to think so, my dearest Mary," returned Richard ; "and be grateful to that Almighty who has hitherto so mercifully preserved us. Heaven knows that we have already suffered enough from the terrible anxiety of mind which it has been our hard lot to experience."

"We have, indeed, Richard ; and I wonder how, under all our heavy afflictions, we have had the strength to support them with the fortitude and patience that we have. Mr. Hawthorn seems to be a kind-hearted man, and I think we may depend upon his promises."

"Oh, yes," returned Richard ; "I know his character well, and, therefore, can place every confidence in him."

"And if I may judge from his observations," said Mary, "he is under some weight of obligation to you."

"To my late lamented father he is," answered our hero, "and therefore is it that he respects me, and sympathises with me in my misfortunes."

"May I inquire what the particular nature of those obligations were ?" said Mary.

"They may be briefly told," replied her husband ; "therefore, listen."

Mary did so, with much attention, and Richard went on as follows :

"It is now about four-and-twenty years ago, as near as I can recollect—for I was, as you must be aware, quite a boy at the time—that I was sitting in company with my parents, before a blazing fire in the parlour, listening to the different wonderful and romantic stories that my father was telling, in order to while away the time. It was night, and a bitter cold and tempestuous night it was, in the midst of winter ; the snow descended in large flakes, and the wind rattled with such violence, that, at intervals, it seemed to shake the very house to its centre. It was a terrible night for those poor creatures who were exposed to its fury, and who had no means of shelter, and many were the prayers that my excellent parents offered up to Heaven for those who were not so fortunate as to possess the blessings that they themselves enjoyed. I do not remember such a dreary and inclement season, and I do not think I shall ever forget it the longest day I may have to like. Every window in the old farm-house rattled, as if from the effects of an earthquake, and the wind howled in such frightful gusts, that it frequently made my parents start from their seats, and look around them in alarm.

"Suddenly they were aroused from the conversation in which they had been engaged, by the appearance of one of the servants, who seemed, from the excitement of his manner, to have something of a particular and melancholy description to communicate.

"'Well, Ralph,' said my father, 'what brings you here so abruptly? You seem agitated.'

"'Yes, zur,' replied Ralph, 'I be, indeed, agitated; poor fellow! such a sight —such an object of pity, I never did see. We have taken him into the kitchen, and tried to get some warmth into his poor limbs; but they are frozen quite stiff with the cold, and I do not wonder at it, seeing as how he be almost naked. I really do think he will die.'

"'Who—what do you mean?' demanded my father, with impatient curiosity. 'Why do you not explain yourself, man?'

"'Oh, ye-es, zur,' returned the simple, but good natured Ralph; 'I ax pardon; I had almost forgotten, but I am so confused and agitated, that I really hardly know what I say. Well, then, you must know, zur, that while I and two or three of the other servants were seated in the kitchen, and listening with feelings of horror to the storm without, we were all startled, by suddenly hearing, between the pauses of the wind, the groans and moans of some poor human creature, as if in great distress; and continuing to listen with great attention, we heard them several times repeated more distinctly than before. We looked at each other in consternation, and no one offered to move; but at last I mustered up resolution, and said: —This be some poor unfortunate creature who is exposed to the fury of the storm, as sure as my name be Ralph, and here are we all seated comfortably around a blazing fire, with (thanks to our good master) plenty to eat and to drink before us. This won't do, lads; come, let us go and see who it is that may require our assistance, for I know we shall not be blamed for rendering aid where it is needed.

"'So, with that,' continued Ralph, 'I took the lantern, and we all moved towards the spot from which the sounds had seemed to proceed, and we had scarcely got from the door, when we perceived something lying on the ground, and

which, on examining it more closely, proved to be a human form, and that of a man, half covered with the snow. We raised him up, and then found that he was quite insensible, was half naked, and was evidently half perished to death with the cold. Oh, master, he was such a miserable-looking object, that it quite wrung all our hearts to gaze at him; so, as we knew very well that you would not be offended, we took him into the house, placed him before the kitchen fire, as I have said before, and did all we could for him, but we have been unable to restore him to sensibility; so we thought it was better to let you know.'

"'Poor fellow,' said my father, compassionately; 'you have acted perfectly right, Ralph; Heaven forbid that I should refuse a shelter and relief to any unfortunate creature who is exposed to the horrors of such a night as this. Come, dame, we must attend to this sufferer directly.'

"My mother needed no second request to urge her to comply, and my curiosity as well as sympathy being also excited, I followed them to the kitchen, where we found the unfortunate stranger, stretched, as Ralph had described, before the fire, and the servants doing all that humanity could suggest to restore him to animation, but without effect.

"And certainly a more pitiable or emaciated looking object could not very readily have been imagined, and we could not help starting back aghast when we beheld it. He appeared to be a man little more than twenty, though want and suffering made him look much older; his face was ghastly pale and livid; his features fixed, his eyes set and glassy, and he seemed to be dying. The tattered garments that hung from his stiffened limbs could scarcely conceal his nakedness, and altogether he formed one of the most frightful spectacles that could possibly be witnessed.

"Seeing that there was not a moment to be lost, my father despatched one of the servants to the nearest medical man, and immediately had the unfortunate stranger conveyed to a warm bed, and himself and my mother never left his bedside for a moment, until they should know the result of their humane efforts. On the arrival of the doctor, he applied such remedies as the urgency of the case required, but it was some time ere any symptoms of returning life were discovered, and then his recovery to sensibility and to speech was extremely slow. By the steady attention of the doctor and my parents, however, he was so far restored by the following afternoon that he was enabled to converse, and he then informed them that his name was Henry Hawthorn, that he had no relations living, with the exception of an only brother, and he did not at the time know where to find him. He further added that he had been apprenticed to the sea when a boy; that he had suffered many vicissitudes abroad, and that the

THE DEPARTURE OF THE FUGITIVES FROM THEIR FRIEND, JACK ADAMS.

vessel to which he had belonged, and which was returning home, was wrecked a few months previously off the coast of Ireland, every soul on board of her, with the exception of himself, perishing, and he lost everything he possessed in the world; he could obtain no relief, with the exception of such scanty trifles as he was enabled to beg from the charitably disposed, and, consequently, he was reduced to the most awful state of destitution and want, and was almost starving.

"In this deplorable condition, he set forth, with the forlorn hope of endeavouring to find his brother, but to add to his misfortune, a highway robbery having been committed in the neighbourhood where he was travelling, he was apprehended on suspicion of being the thief, and after undergoing several examinations before the magistrates, and remanded to prison, he was discharged, without any relief being afforded him, and left to resume his dreary journey in the same miserable and destitute condition. Many miles he traversed with no better success; and during which time he experienced sufferings which it would harrow up your very soul, my dear Mary, to listen to, but of which I know you can form an adequate conception, till at length, starving, and completely exhausted, he sunk down in the manner I have described, and had not Providence fortunately guided him to the residence of my parents, he must unquestionably have died.

"You may guess how sincerely moved my father and mother were at this melancholy story; and they redoubled their attentions to the unfortunate man. In a few days so unremitting had been their exertions, that he was completely restored to convalescence, and having been properly clothed, he appeared a robust and good-looking young man. As he had no wish to change his situation at present, my father offered him an asylum in his house, on the condition that he would endeavour to make himself useful; and you may well imagine how gladly he accepted of the proposal. He remained under our roof for several years, during which time my parents treated him in the same manner as if he had been their own brother, and it is but due to him to say, that he took every opportunity that was in his power to evince his gratitude, and never once gave my parents cause to regret the kindness they had bestowed upon him. At length, however, having formed an attachment to a young woman, who resided some few miles from the farm, he married her without the knowledge of my parents, and receiving what he considered to be a favourable offer, he once more went to sea, and we heard no more of him.

"Such, Mary, are the particulars of Mr. Hawthorn's history, as far as I am acquainted with them, and you will now perceive that he was indeed under a heavy weight of obligation to my parents, which it would have been most ungrateful in him not to have endeavoured to repay to their son, if it should ever lay in his power."

"Most true, Richard," replied his wife;

"and I feel confident that he will try to do so. Poor man, he has had his share of misfortunes; but how exraordinary that you should meet again in so singular a manner after the lapse of so many years."

"It is," coincided our hero; "and also that we should recognise each other, so great, too, as must be the alteration that time has worked in our features. On him I now greatly depend, and I do not believe that he will disappoint me in my anticipations."

"Oh, no," returned Mary, "he must be, indeed, ungrateful were he to do so. But I will not for a moment encourage such a thought, but endeavour to look forward to a speedy alteration in our fate for the better."

"God grant, my beloved and faithful wife," said Richard, "that your expectations may be realised; for Heaven knows that the sufferings to which we have been already subjected, are almost too much for human nature to endure. But it is now late, therefore, let us once more offer up our prayers and supplications to the Supreme Ruler of all, and than retire to rest."

Mary complied most willingly and fervently with this request; and this sacred duty performed, they arose more tranquil in mind than they had been for some time, and our hero having fastened all the doors to prevent any intrusion, they retired to bed, and being more composed in their mind, and fatigued with the excitement of the remarkable and startling events of the last few hours, they soon dropped off to sleep, and did not awake till the morning, when they found themselves much refreshed, and in better spirits than they had been for a considerable time previously.

They had scarcely dressed themselves when they heard a knock at the outer door, and Richard, looking cautiously from the window, saw that it was Mrs. Hawthorn; so he hastened down stairs, and immediately admitted her.

Mrs. Hawthorn greeted them with much kindness and friendship, and the alteration in their looks and general appearance evidently afforded her much satisfaction. She inquired anxiously how they had passed the night, and on being informed without anything occurring to disturb or alarm them, she repeated her gratification, and congratulated them on the favourable change which only a few short hours had made in their apppearance.

"I have no doubt, my good friends,"

she continued, "that your troubles are not destined to continue much longer; and believe me that nothing will afford myself and my husband greater satisfaction and delight, than to see you be able to surmount the numerous difficulties by which you are at present surrounded."

"I cannot sufficiently express to you my thanks, Mrs. Hawthorn," replied our hero, "for your kind wishes, which, I feel convinced, emanate from your heart."

"You do me no more than justice by that opinion, Mr. Parker," said Alice. "But come, will you attend me to the other cottage? Breakfast is waiting, and my husband is most impatient to see you, for you have much important business to transact to-day, and the sooner some of your plans for the future are arranged the better."

Richard Parker and his wife agreed with this, and without making use of any further observations, they accompanied Mrs. Hawthorn from the cottage, and entered that in which she and her husband resided.

Mr. Hawthorn arose at their entrance, and extended his hand to them, which they then pressed warmly, and he put the same questions which his wife had done to them, and which they answered accordingly; but the attention of Richard and Mary was quickly attracted to another object which was seated at the breakfast-table. and which soon engrossed their whole curiosity and interest.

This was the graceful form of a beautiful young girl, apparently scarcely twenty, and who, they concluded, was the daughter of Hawthorn and his wife, of whom he had spoken so feelingly, and in such melancholy terms on the previous night. Never had they, they considered, gazed on a more beauteous being, and yet there was something mingled with the expression of her beauty, which could not fail to excite the most painful sensations of pity and regret in the breast of the beholder. It was evident that her mind was a wreck, and it was sad, indeed, to behold one so young and so lovely in such a deplorable condition. There was a melancholy history in her wild and expressive features, and as Richard and his wife continued to gaze upon her, they felt their curiosity increase, though they hesitated to put any questions to Hawthorn respecting her, which, they feared, might wound his feelings.

The poor girl seemed not at all confused or disconcerted at the appearance of strangers, but smiled vacantly upon them, and then averted her looks, and seemed to be altogether lost to every surrounding object in the contemplation of an artificial rose which she held in her hand, and played with like a child.

Hawthorn saw the earnestness and interest with which Richard and Mary gazed at her, and in a low voice of deep emotion, he said,—

"It is my poor child; alas! her mind wanders, and—but we will speak of her another time. I am glad to find you looking so refreshed, and trust that you are satisfied with the accommodation it is in my power to afford you."

"Satisfied, my friend!" replied our hero, "oh, yes; we must, indeed, be ungrateful and unreasonable were we not. We are already much indebted to you for the sympathy and friendship you have shown us."

"Oh, as for that, Mr. Parker," said Hawthorn, "I need no acknowledgments for having performed no more than my duty, and I am only too happy to think that it is in my power to do so, and that Providence has directed your footsteps to my dwelling. I have often thought of you, and been most anxious to see you, but knew not where to find you; and when I heard of the unfortunate position in which you were placed, I need not tell you how deeply I sympathised with you, and deplored the awful fate that seemed certain to overtake you; but, thank God, that you have hitherto so providentially been able to avoid it, and it shall be no fault of mine if you do not escape from it altogether."

"Hawthorn," replied Parker, "this feeling towards myself and my devoted and beloved partner in misfortune, does you honour; and, believe me, that I place the utmost reliance in your friendship; but you must be aware of the danger of harbouring me, and should any harm befal you in consequence, I cannot tell you how deeply I should regret it."

"Mr. Parker," returned the fisherman, "let not any idea of that sort trouble you, for I apprehend no danger of the sort, I can assure you. Here you are, I am convinced, perfectly safe as long as you think proper to remain; for your pursuers will not think of searching for you here; I will be constantly on the watch, and should any danger really threaten you, you have here the means of immediate escape. It was a good thought of my brother Daniel to put those men upon the wrong track; but you say you did not reveal to him who you really were?"

"I did not," answered our hero; "for, although I liked the simple honesty of his manners, of course, you will admit that it was no more than prudent of me to act with caution."

"True," coincided Mr. Hawthorn; "but still you might safely have placed every confidence in him; for I know that Daniel would sooner suffer anything than he would have been guilty of a single act which he might afterwards have cause to regret, or to reproach himself with."

"I believe you, Hawthorn," said Parker, "for there was that in the behaviour of your brother which convinced me that he possesses a heart of the strictest integrity and humanity. It was a most fortunate and extraordinary thing that we happened to meet with him, or I might, ere this, have been in the power of those who are so anxious to get possession of me. We are under great obligation to him, and likewise to Mr. Hatfield, the worthy landlord of the Golden Lion, who behaved to us with the greatest kindness and hospitality, during the brief time we remained in his house, and would receive no remuneration for it."

"Hatfield is, I know, a worthy and kind-hearted man," observed Hawthorn; "he, of course, did not discover you?"

"Not that I am aware of," returned our hero; "though, from his manner and several observations he made, I could not help imagining that he had some suspicion of me. He alluded most pointedly to Richard Parker, and appeared to sympathise in his misfortunes."

"I have no doubt he did," said the fisherman, "and you might have reposed confidence in him, had you been so disposed, with safety. However, you acted with becoming prudence and precaution in not doing so, to one who was an entire stranger to you. You informed him that you were coming hither, did you not?"

"I did," answered Richard.

"Well, there was no danger in doing that," remarked Hawthorn, "for I do not believe that he would answer any inquiries that might happen to be made after you; especially as you say he seemed to suspect who you were and to sympatise in your misfortunes."

Flora, who had been conversing in a wild and unconnected strain with her mother, now suddenly arose from her seat, and running up to her father, embraced and kissed him with all the simple fondness of a child, and then taking the arm of her mother, she quitted the room. Mr. Hawthorn sighed deeply as she retired, and pressed his hand upon his forehead; and Richard and his wife could not help also feeling deeply affected.

"Poor lost child!" ejaculated Hawthorn, in a voice of the greatest emotion; "what a terrible wreck you have now become; better would it be for you were you in your silent grave; and yet it would surely break my heart to lose you."

"Alas!" said our heroine; "what terrible misfortune has reduced the poor girl to this deplorable state?"

"Villany!" replied Hawthorn, vehemently, and his countenance flushed with the excitement of his feelings; "the blackest, basest villany! Oh, my friends, had you known how pure, how innocent, how lovely she once was, you must indeed pity her and regret the destruction which has come upon her."

"Indeed," said Richard, "we do most sincerely pity her. But what fearful history is connected with her? It is lamentable to behold one so young and so beautiful thus reduced to misery and insanity."

"A fearful history!" repeated Hawthorn, "you may well call it so; it is one that should wring the most insensible heart to listen to. May eternal curses light upon the wretch who has thus destroyed one of the most lovely of Nature's works. Would that I could encounter him; by all my hopes I would revenge myself in his heart's blood, and rid the world of one who has so disgraced society and outraged humanity."

He beat his breast, and paced the room with hasty and disordered steps as he thus spoke, and Mary and her husband were more deeply affected than before. The words of Hawthorn convinced them of the whole painful truth; Flora was the unhappy victim of some heartless and unprincipled seducer.

"Ah!" sighed Hawthorn, after a brief pause; "it is, indeed, a terrible blow for me and her poor mother, and many are the hours of bitter anguish and useless regret that her melancholy and deplorable fate costs us. Had you known her in her innocence and pride of beauty but three years since, how deeply must you deplore her sad fate, and reprobate the brutal author of it. Oh, what a cold-hearted villain must he be to crush me of the fairest flowers that ever blossomed."

"He must indeed," said Richard, "and Heaven will surely punish him for it. But is he still living?"

"I know not," answered the fisherman; "but I believe he is. Having achieved his guilty object, coward-like he fled, and I have never been able to discover him; but I trust that the day will yet come when I shall again meet with him; and should Providence thus place him in my power, let the consequences to myself be whatever they may, I will not suffer him to escape me until I have wreaked such a terrible revenge upon his head that his crimes merit."

"Would it be too great a trial to your feelings, Mr. Hawthorn," asked our hero, "to relate to us the particulars of your unfortunate daughter's melancholy history? For after what you have said, I need not tell you how deeply interested myself and my wife feel in it."

"It is a sad tale," replied Hawthorn, "and I know not whether I shall find fortitude to relate it. However, knowing how much you will sympathise with me and my poor child, I will endeavour to do so. I also wish to relate to you many other facts connected with myself, with which you are not already acquainted, and you will then see that I have not been without my full share of misfortunes as well as yourself."

"I do not doubt it, my friend," said Parker ; "and you may rest assured that no one can more sincerely pity you than myself."

Hawthorn returned no answer ; and after a short pause, during which interval he seemed to be endeavouring to collect his thoughts, he commenced his narrative.

CHAPTER XXIV.

THE FISHERMAN'S STORY.

"MINE has been a chequred life, as you know, but Providence has never deserted me, and were it not for the dismal fate of my poor child, I should now consider myself happy. I lost both my parents in childhood, and not having a friend in the world, myself and my brother, who is some years younger than myself, were placed in the workhouse, from which I was apprenticed to the sea ; and the many perils and acts of injustice that I there experienced, I need not recount to you, for you are already acquainted with them ; and I will, therefore, confine myself to what occurred to me after I had quitted the house of your excellent parents, which you are aware was in consequence of my private marriage. That union, however, I have never had any cause to regret, for there could not have possibly been a more affectionate or faithful wife than Alice has been to me.

"We had only a few pounds to begin the world with, and I not being able to obtain any employment, and not liking to apply to your father. Richard, though I knew well that he would not refuse me that was soon exhausted, and it became necessary that I should adopt some immediate means of getting an honest living. But at length, having failed in all my efforts to obtain employment, and what I considered a favourable opportunity presenting itself to go again to sea, I resolved to avail myself of it ; though it grieved me much to have to separate from my young and affectionate wife, who at that time was far advanced in pregnancy ; but I had no means of avoiding it, and mutually invoking the protection of Heaven, we parted, and I was soon again exposed to all the vicissitudes of a sailor's life.

"I did not expect to have been absent more than two years ; but the war broke out, and the vessel on board of which I was, was engaged in all the hottest of it, and being at length captured by the enemy, we were taken prisoners, and were exposed to the most terrible hardships and inhumanity ; but I suffered more from anxiety of mind, fearing that I should never more behold my wife, and forming all kinds of torturing conjectures as to what would become of her and her child.

"Myself and four others at length made a desperate attempt to escape from the place in which we were confined, but we were re-captured, and cruelly flogged almost to death.

In this wretched and deplorable situation I remained for a period of several years, and I had resigned myself entirely to despair, and hourly prayed for death to release me from my misery, when the war suddenly terminated ; prisoners were exchanged, and I was restored to liberty, and shipped on board a vessel that was homeward bound.

"You may guess what my feelings were on that occasion ; but still the most painful doubts and apprehensions occupied my mind that my wife was no more, or that, thinking me dead, she had become united to some other man. The ship arrived in England ; I was paid off, and, with a palpitating heart, I hastened to the neighbourhood where I had resided before I returned to sea, and had the happiness of finding my wife living in the same place, where she had managed to support herself and her child in comfort, by her own industry, and had never abandoned the hope that we should meet again.

"You may readily imagine how great was the joy of our meeting ; but I am not possessed of language sufficiently powerful to describe it. With what feelings of ecstasy did I, for the first time, gaze upon the lovely and innocent features of my child, my little Flora! who was then all that the most glowing imagination can depicture; and after all the troubles and vicissitudes, and disappointments I had experienced, I now considered myself one of the happiest men in existence.

"I had a large sum of prize-money to take, and with that I resolved to embark in something, and to go no more to sea, for I could not for a moment encourage the thought of being again separated from my wife and child, so at last I settled myself where I now am, and in the same calling as I am at present, and in which, thanks be to Providence, I have prospered even far beyond what my most sanguine expectations could anticipate.

"I endeavoured to find out your parents, Mr. Parker, that I might convince them of my gratitude for the many favours I had received from them; but I ascertained with the deepest regret that they were both no more, and that you, having married, and being reduced to great distress, had gone to sea, for which I knew you had from a boy always had an inclination. I heard no more of you till the unfortunate affair of the mutiny, and you may well imagine the deep regret I felt at the awful situation in which you were placed; I prayed to Heaven that you might escape from the fate with which you were threatened, and lamented that it was not in my power to render you any assistance; but little did I expect that we should so soon meet again, and under the singular and extraordinary circumstances that we have done. But I am digressing.

"For several years my wife and myself continued to enjoy the most uninterrupted happiness; and our whole attention was devoted to the culture of our daughter's mind; who, as she increased in years, improved in beauty, and virtues, and accomplishments. Oh, how innocent and affectionate she was! Heaven surely could never have created a more beauteous being, or one who was in every way so calculated to captivate. She was the delight of all who knew her, or beheld her. Alas, alas! what is she now?—How terrible is the change which the most consummate villany has wrought in her! Oh, may the curses of the Almighty pursue the wretch to destruction, and wring his black heart to madness!"

Overcome by the power of his emotions, Mr. Hawthorn was compelled to pause in his narrative, and Richard and his wife did not offer to interrupt him in the indulgence of his thoughts. But at length he again resumed.

"Flora was now about sixteen, and notwithstanding her youth, several overtures were made for her hand, and from persons who were placed in a far higher position in life than herself; but she rejected them all, for she had not yet seen the youth on whom she could place her affections, and myself and my wife considered that she was yet too young to enter into the state of matrimony.

"How happy and contented was her mind at that time, and with what pride and delight did we gaze upon her. No child could possibly be more affectionate and dutiful; and she endeavoured by every means in her power to study our wishes and to contribute to our happiness. Little did we think that at that time the storm was brooding which would overwhelm us with its fury and destroy all our hopes, or we must have sunk under the anticipation.

"One night it came on a dreadful storm, and soon it blew a complete hurricane, and the ocean was quite frightful to look upon. The waves ran mountains high, and dashed against the rocks with the most tremendous and deafening violence; and it seemed impossible that anything could live on it. Myself and several of my neighbours hastened to the cliffs, and there we had not stood many minutes, when we heard signals of distress, and immediately afterwards beheld a vessel at some distance, tossing about amid the waves, and threatening to founder every instant. It was an awful sight; but I need not seek to describe it to you, Mr. Parker, for you have doubtless witnessed many such scenes in the course of your experience; but what made it the more melancholy was the fact, that it was impossible to render the unfortunate ship any assistance, and it would have been madness for any one to have ventured forth on such a sea as was then raging. Her fate seemed to be inevitable, and we returned to watch her with the utmost anxiety, expecting every moment to see her go to pieces. We were not long kept in suspense. One moment the ill-fated vessel was tossed to a tremendous height, and the next instant she was buried in the waves, and we saw no more of her. Still we waited for some time longer on the cliffs, to see whether there were any unfortunate beings floating from the wreck, to whom we might be able to render any assistance; and supposing that all had perished, we returned with sad hearts to our habitations.

"I found Flora and my wife anxiously watching at the window, and when they learnt the fate of the unfortunate ship, the former could not help sheddding tears. Alas! little did she then anticipate the dreadful consequences of which the shipwreck would be productive to her.

"After the lapse of two or three hours the storm abated, and at length entirely subsided, and I then went to the shore in order to see whether any of the bodies or portion of the wreck were washed upon it. I found several others there on the same errand as myself, and happening to cast my eyes a short distance along the coast, I perceived some large object lying on the beach, and hastened towards it, accompanied by two or three of my neighbours. On arriving at the object which had attracted our attention, we perceived that it was a large sea-chest, on which was stretched the body of a man, dressed, or rather partially dressed, as a private individual, and not as a seaman. He was young and extremely good looking, but he seemed to be quite dead; on the lid of the chest was inscribed the name of Alfred Mowbray, and we concluded that it belonged to him.

"Stooping down to examine the unfortunate man more minutely, I found that he still breathed, and, therefore, hoping still to be able to preserve his life, I had him conveyed without delay to my hut, and such remedies were applied by myself and my wife as the urgency of the case required, while Fora stood looking on with the most painful anxiety, while the greatest compassion was depicted in her countenance.

"It was some considerable time ere we could make any impression on him, but at length our efforts were crowned with success; he breathed more freely, and opened his eyes and stared vacantly around him for an instant, but it was evident that he was still unconscious, and we immediately conveyed him to bed, and myself and my wife continued to watch anxiously for his complete recovery, grateful that we had at least been able to save one individual from the fatal wreck. Would to Heaven that he had perished, then my poor girl might still have been as innocent and happy as she once was."

"And was this man the author of her misfortunes?" asked our hero.

"He was! he was!" answered Hawthorn with a burst of agony. "Curses light upon him, and hunt him to perdition! From that fatal night I date the origin of all those misfortunes which I have now so much to deplore. But let me proceed. By the morning, through the exertions of myself and my wife, the shipwrecked stranger had so far recovered

that he was enabled to speak, and he then inquired where he was, and to whom he was indebted for his preservation. We informed him, and he was then most unbounded in his professions of gratitude for the inestimable service we had rendered him.

"He informed us that the chest belonged to him, and that the name on it was, therefore, his. He added that the name of the vessel was the Neptune, bound for London; that he was a single man, who had resided for several years in the West Indies, but was on his way to England, in order to take possession of some property that had been bequeathed to him; and he then reiterated his acknowledgments for the humanity we had evinced towards him. Having seen that he had everything that his situation required, and thinking that a few hours' sleep would revive him, we retired from the room, and left him to himself.

"We found Flora, anxiously awaiting us below, and she eagerly inquired after the condition of the shipwrecked man, and nothing could exceed her gratification when we informed her that he was recovered, and related to her all the facts as he had stated them to us. I saw that this adventure had made a more than usual impression on her, but taking all the circumstances into consideration, I did not feel much surprised at it.

"In the course of the day Alfred Mowbray had so far recovered that he was able to leave his bed and to walk down stairs, and on being introduced to Flora, she appeared to be no less struck with him than he was with her, and she blushed deeply, and seemed to tremble when he addressed himself in the most bland accents to her.

"He was indeed a handsome man, and possessed of the most insinuating address; but there was something in the expression of his eyes which I did not like; and I felt somewhat embarrassed in his presence. He again expressed to us his gratitude for what we had done for him in most unbounded terms, and begged to know in what manner he could reward us; but I informed him that I did not require any reward, and that what I had done for him he was quite welcome to.

"We passed some hours in agreeable conversation, and I found that he was a young man of considerable intelligence; and seemed to possess an almost inexhaustible fund of information upon almost any topic. However, Flora seemed to engross the principal portion of his attention and his thoughts, and I frequently caught him bestowing the most earnest glances of admiration upon her, while the crimson blushes mantled in her cheeks, and she hesitated and faltered whenever he addressed himself to her. However, I did not take any particular notice of this, for, of course, I could not think that any harm could come of it, and I did not wonder that the youthful and superior charms of my daughter should excite his admiration.

"Before we separated in the evening, as Mowbray wished to retire early to bed, he desired me to inform him where he could obtain accommodation for a few days, in the neighbourhood, so that he might have time to arrange his affairs previous to his departure to London, and I told him that the cottage adjoining also belonging to me, I should be happy to do so, if it would suit him.

"He seemed delighted with this offer; and I could not help noticing an expression of pleasure pass over the features of Flora; but still it was not possible that any suspicion should enter my breast. Mowbray instantly accepted my proposal, and we then separated for the night.

"When he was gone we sat for some time conversing upon all that had taken place, and my wife was most eloquent in her praises of the handsome person and elegant manners of Mowbray; and Flora seemed to listen to her warm eulogiums with pleasure, though she offered no observation.

"'Ay, Alice,' I remarked, 'this young man whom you so warmly eulogise, seems well enough, and to possess no inconsiderable share of information upon different subjects; but you know we must not always judge from appearances ; and it too often happens that those who are the most bland and insinuating in their manners possess a villanous heart, and should be shunned as something loathsome and contagious.'

"'That may be true, Harry,' replied my wife; ' and I have no doubt that to a certain extent it is ; but still I am sure you are not ungenerous enough to judge all your fellow creatures by the same rule; and I am much mistaken of this young man is not fully deserving of all the praises I have bestowed upon him.

"'Well,' I returned, 'I hope he may be so; though it can be no matter of consequence to us whether he is or not; I am happy to think that I have been the means of preserving his life; but in a few days he will depart from here, and it is not at all likely that we shall ever see him again.'

"A sigh escaped the bosom of Flora as I gave utterance to these words, and I was surprised to see that she was otherwise considerably agitated.

"'Why, Flora, my dear child,' I said, 'what is the matter with you? You sigh, as though you had some heavy care and anxiety on your mind; and you look as sad as if something painful had happened to you. What is the cause of this?'

"Flora looked greatly confused, but hastily endeavouring to recover herself, and affecting to smile, she said—

"''Twas nothing, my dear father—it was only a dull and foolish thought that came over me. I do not feel exactly well to-night, and will, therefore, if you please, retire to my chamber.'

"Her mother and myself embraced her affectionately, and bidding us good night, she quitted the room. We remained for some time longer conversing together, but at length we also sought our chamber. But in spite of all my efforts I could not banish the remembrance of the agitation of Flora from my mind; and I lay thinking about it for some time after I had retired to bed.

"At the usual hour the next morning Alfred Mowbray joined us at the breakfast table, and he was then completely recovered from the effects of the shipwreck, and seemed to be in high spirits, and entered into conversation with great animation and vivacity; displaying, as he proceeded, a most remarkable versatility of talent, and which could not fail to excite admiration in all who listened to him. He frequently addressed himself to Flora, but her answers were returned in the same hesitating and fluttering manner that they had been the day before, and it was quite evident that she felt uneasy and embarrassed. I watched her and Mowbray narrowly, and frequently beheld him gazing at her with looks of the most earnest admiration; and whenever her eyes met his, crimson blushes suffused her cheeks, and her whole demeanour testified the agitation she experienced.

"I felt far from satisfied; yet there was an irresistible charm about the conversation of Alfred Mowbray that won me against my will; and I could not, therefore, feel surprised that it should make such a powerful impression upon a young girl of the susceptible temperament of my daughter. Oh, he was formed every way to allure and deceive, and few persons, I am convinced, would have been able to resist the powerful fascination of his arts. It was, indeed, a cursed misfortune that introduced him to us, but, of course, it was impossible for us to foresee the fatal consequences that were to ensue from it.

Little might any one have imagined that so fair and plausible an exterior could conceal the mind of the basest villain. And yet, as I have said before, in spite of his tongue, and the glowing and prepossessing character of his demeanour, that created certain doubts and suspicions in my mind, for which I could not exactly account; and it was, therefore, that I felt jealous and uneasy at the marked attention which he paid to my daughter, and the powerful impression he had evidently made upon her. But my wife did not entertain any such ideas, but, on the contrary, she was charmed with the eloquence of his conversation, and the elegance of his manners, and flattered by the admiration he bestowed upon poor Flora, of whom I need not say she was doatingly fond.

"During the course of the day Alfred Mowbray made us acquainted with a few more particulars as regarded himself, and informed us that he had lost both his parents when he was very young, and had been left under the guardianship of an old and bosom friend of his father, who being an East India merchant, hence the reason of his having been resident so many years abroad. That gentleman was now also dead, and had left him a considerable fortune ; but he was grown tired of an eastern climate, and was anxious to return to his native land. The death of a distant relation in England, who had bequeathed him some large property there, had decided him in his determination, and having arranged his affairs in India, and appointed a trustworthy agent to superintend them, he had embarked on board the Neptune, which quickly set sail for his native shores. The voyage was prosperous until they approached the English coast, when they encountered heavy gales, which for some days they weathered, but at length the vessel became a total wreck, as I have described, and every soul on board, with the exception of himself, had perished. When he was washed overboard, he added, after rising again upon the crest of the angry billows, being an excellent swimmer, he made a desperate and determined struggle for life, and battled with the waves manfully, endeavouring to reach the shore, from whence he could perceive the lights which myself and my companions carried, but his strength was nearly exhausted, and he must also have perished undoubtedly, had he not in that terrible and critical moment fortunately beheld a chest floating near him, which was tossed about by the violence of the waves like a straw. With much difficulty, and by the dint of great exertion, he succeeded in reaching it, and throwing himself upon it, worn out and helpless, he breathed a hasty, but an earnest prayer to Heaven, and resigned himself to his fate. The result I have shown to you. The chest fortunately proved to be his own, and he consequently lost but little of any value in the wreck.

" 'My escape was, indeed, most miraculous and providential,' he added, in conclusion ; ' but to you, Mr. Hawthorn, I may say, that I owe the ultimate preservation of my life, and I am under a weight of obligation to you in consequence, which I fear it will never be in my power adequately to repay.'

" The heartless hypocrite! what was the return he made for it? The destruction of one of the most beauteous and innocent beings that Heaven ever created ! Oh, how my brain burns, and what feelings of indignation agitate my breast when I think of it ! But let me proceed, and

not suffer my feelings thus to overpower me.

" 'Mr. Mowbray,' I answered, 'you have already overwhelmed me with your acknowledgments, and I assure you that I require no other return for the service I have been so fortunate as to render you, but your respect.'

" 'My respect?' he repeated ; 'oh, that you must ever possess ; and I can never regret the accident which has introduced me to such excellent and amiable friends. I am sorry that necessity compels me to leave you so soon, but I trust that you will suffer me to renew your acquaintance shortly, and that I shall be honoured by your future friendship.'

"1 saw that the eyes of Flora sparkled with more than usual vivacity, as Mowbray made use of these observations, and and that her features expressed the greatest anxiety for my answer.

" 'Of course, I cannot but help feeling highly flattered by your friendship and esteem, Mr. Mowbray,' I at length replied ; ' but the difference of our stations in life will, of course, necessarily preclude that intimacy which might otherwise take place between us.'

" 'Difference of station, Mr. Hawthorn?' he returned ; ' oh, why raise such an objection as that? All men are equal whose virtues and actions correspond. Wealth cannot alter them, nor rank add to their value. It is I who would be honoured by your friendship, and I sincerely trust that you will suffer me to visit you frequently, after I have arranged my affairs. I have no acquaintances in England, and I wish not to enter into any terms of intimacy with those on whom I know not whether I can rely. But what says the fair and gentle Flora ? Will she not plead for me ?'

" Flora blushed deeply, and was evidently much confused by this unexpected question.

" 'I must be guided entirely by my parents, sir,' she at last answered, in a timid voice ; ' but who, I have no doubt, will at all times feel proud and happy to receive Mr. Mowbray with that respect and welcome that is due to him.'

" The eyes of Alfred glistened with delight at this reply, and he fixed even more powerful looks of admiration upon Flora than before, as he ejaculated : —

" 'Thanks, thanks, Miss Hawthorn, for this most gracious answer to my question, which, I cannot but flatter myself, will have due weight with your excellent parents. Of one thing, I can confidently and sincerely assure them, namely, that I will never abuse the friendship they may be pleased to bestow upon me.'

" You will perceive as I proceed," continued Hawthorn, "what a consummate scoundrel he must have been thus to make use of those observations and protestations, when probably, even at that early period, he contemplated the villanous part he afterwards played with such fatal success! I had my misgivings at the time; however, I returned some evasive answer to his remarks, and then changed the subject of the conservation, which became more general, and passed off altogether in a more agreeable manner than might have been expected. Flora became more free, though at the same time she blushed deeply whenever Mowbray addressed himself to her, and she could not conceal the emotions that were struggling in her breast.

"I was not sorry when the time arrived to separate for the night, and Mowbray retired to the cottage adjoining. Flora also sought her chamber almost immediately afterwards, and myself and my wife were left alone.

" ' What a prepossessing, and apparently amiable young man is this Alfred Mowbray,' observed Alice; ' I declare that I feel quite flattered by his professions of friendship and esteem, and am delighted that accident has introduced him to us.'

" ' Ah, Alice,' I replied, 'you must not be so ready to judge from appearances, for they are, at times, very deceitful, and cover the basest minds. Mowbray, I confess, has a most prepossessing exterior, and insinuating manners, but, at the same time, I cannot go to the full extent of my admiration of him that you do; and there is something about him which makes me view him with doubt and suspicion, and, for my own part, I do not care how soon he leaves this neighbourhood, nor have I any wish to behold him again.'

" ' Oh, Hawthorn,' she said, with a look of surprise, ' surely you do this young man an injustice by these uncharitable surmises, and I must say that it is unworthy of you. I cannot see anything about him that should authorise such suspicions, and I have no doubt that you will yourself be convinced, in time, how much you have erred in judgment on this particular occasion.'

" ' Well, Alice,' I returned, ' I hope that I may; but I suppose I need not tell you how much it behoves us to be upon our guard, so that we may avoid any evils that might arise by placing too much implicit confidence in one who is an entire stranger to us, and who has been introduced to us under such peculiar circumstances.'

" ' Your fears appear to me to be ridiculous,' Alice observed, with some degree of warmth. ' What motive could Alfred Mowbray possibly have for wishing to deceive us? What has he to gain by doing so?'

" ' Mankind have often many sinister motives that guide them in their conduct, Alice,' I answered; ' and it, therefore, behoves us to look upon those who are unknown to us with jealous eyes, especially when we have that to guard which might be insidiously assailed, and which is far more precious to us than our own existence.'

" ' I do not understand you, Hawthorn,' she observed.

" ' Our daughter is young, innocent, and beautiful,' I returned; ' and is she not, therefore, likely to be exposed to the dark designs of the systematic and unprincipled seducer?'

" ' True,' she coincided, ' but Heaven forbid that our dear child should be exposed to any such danger. She has, however, too much virtue and strength of mind to become the victim of any such villany. But what has all this to do with Alfred Mowbray?'

" ' I liked not the bold and ardent looks of admiration which he bestowed upon her, Alice,' I answered; ' and the agitation of Flora's manner convinces me that he has made a powerful impression upon her.'

" ' And is there anything surprising in that,' demanded my wife, ' when the graces of his mind and person are taken into consideration?'

" ' But it must be checked, Alice, or it might lead to the most fatal and lamentable consequences,' I observed.

" ' Well,' she ejaculated, ' I cannot help still thinking that you entertain the most groundless apprehensions. It would have been strange, indeed, if one so young as Alfred Mowbray could help entertaining feelings of admiration for one so fair and innocent as our dear child. Come, come, husband, you must banish all such erroneous thoughts and false prejudices as those you have just expressed from your mind, and endeavour to entertain a better opinion of our guest.'

" ' I would fain do so,' I answered, ' but I must confess that I do not care how soon he takes his departure from hence, and I have no particular wish to see him again.'

" 'How extraordinary is this feeling, and how unlike you.'

" 'It may appear so, but I cannot conquer it ; though Heaven forbid that my fears should be realised, for then, Alice, all our happiness would be destroyed for ever.'

" 'Oh, it cannot be ; the very thought is torturing and revolting,' she said ; 'but what if an honourable passion should spring up in the bosom of Mowbray towards our daughter, and she should return his love ?'

" 'If an *honourable* passion should spring up in *his* breast, Alice ?' I repeated, and shaking my head doubtingly.

" 'Ay,' she returned, 'is there anything improbable in that ?'

" 'You forget that Alfred Mowbray is rich, and our daughter is comparatively poor, and of humble origin,' I remarked ; 'it is not often that the wealthy will make such, what they consider to be, sacrifices for the gratification of their passions, however worthy, and virtuous, and beautiful, the object may be. And we have as yet no reason to suppose, unacquainted as we are with his real character, that Alfred Mowbray is any exception to the general rule.'

" 'I cannot entertain the same opinion of the young gentleman as you seem to do,' said Alice ; 'and I am greatly surprised at the observations you have made regarding him. I am greatly deceived if he is not strictly honourable, and would be ashamed to do anything which he might afterwards be ashamed to acknowledge.'

" 'Well,' I returned, 'I sincerely hope that he may prove to be all that you believe him ; for I should be sorry to wrong any one by entertaining erroneous opinions of their character.'

" 'The statement he has given of himself is plain and straightforward, and bears the impression of truth about it ; and he must be an ungrateful and heartless villain indeed could he contemplate anything wrong towards those who have rendered him so inestimable a service.'

" 'True,' I agreed ; 'but you cannot be ignorant of the fact, Alice, that there are such villains in the world. Flora is yet young, and there is yet time enough for her to think about changing her condition, and I must repeat that I would much rather see her place her affections upon some worthy young man who is placed in the same humble station of life as herself.'

" 'Fear not, Hawthorn,' returned my wife, 'our daughter will never fail to act with prudence and precaution, nor without our advice and sanction. But you view this matter in too serious a light ; Flora has never been used much to society, and it is only natural that a young man possessed of such accomplishments as those of Alfred Mowbray, should make a sensible impression on her, or that he, on the other hand, should admire her for her virtues and accomplishments. As for us to deny him our friendship till he does something which might render it absolutely necessary for us to do so, it would, it strikes me, be both ungenerous and unreasonable.'

" 'And I have no wish to do so,' I replied ; 'but we will discuss this subject no farther at the present, though I say again it is our duty to keep a watchful eye over the safety of our daughter.'

" 'It is so, Henry,' coincided my wife, 'and we can never be found neglecting to do that. Dear Flora is the pride of our hearts, and the admiration of all who know her ; and should anything happen to her, our happiness will be annihilated for ever, and life would become an intolerable burden to us, which we would be most anxious to be released from as soon as possible.'

" 'It would,' I returned ; 'but God grant that all such evils may be averted, and that nothing may occur to disturb the happiness and tranquillity which we now enjoy.'

" The conversation here dropped for the present, and shortly afterwards we retired to bed ; but my thoughts were again so busy, that I found it impossible, for some time, to go to sleep. I lay reflecting upon all the observations which Mowbray had made use of, and his demeanour towards Flora ; and I could not divest my mind of the doubts and suspicions that had taken possession of it. There were many of the remarks which I remembered him to have made, which, I considered, were couched in rather ambiguous language, and they increased the prejudices which—I scarcely knew why—I entertained towards him. I could not help regretting the circumstances which had introduced him to us, though I felt thankful that I had been made the means of saving the life of a fellow-creature ; and I was anxious for him to take his departure as soon as possible, for there seemed to be some danger threatening while he was near.

" I must acknowledge that these surmises and suspicions may seem unreasonable, unjustifiable and extravagant, but circumstances afterwards too fatally proved to me how well they were founded in truth. Alas! it was a cursed hour which introduced him to my residence, and bitter cause have I ever since had to regret it. But for that I should have nothing to disturb the happiness and tranquillity which I once enjoyed, and my poor child would have been as pure, innocent, and contented as she formerly was; but now—oh, let me not think, or I shall go distracted!

"The next day passed away in much the same manner as the previous one had done, though Alfred Mowbray himself appeared more agreeable, if possible, than he had hitherto; and it pained me to observe that he hourly seemed to gain more and more influence over the feelings of Flora, and that she replied to the observations he so frequently made to her, with scarcely any of the embarrassment that she had done previously, and seemed to feel the greatest delight and admiration in listening to him. And yet all his remarks were couched in the most delicate, scrupulous, and respectful language, and he did not utter a word that I could reasonably find fault with.

"Several more days elapsed without anything particular or worth recording occurring; a fortnight passed away, and still Mowbray said nothing about departing; and it was now quite evident, if there could even for a moment have been any doubt in my mind upon the subject, what was the magnet that attracted him, and made him so loth to leave the place. I took every opportunity to keep my daughter out of his society, but it was seldom that I could do so, and I must confess that there appeared to be no just grounds for my using any such coercive measures, and I hesitated at present to converse with Flora upon the delicate subject, though I was fully resolved to do so at the earliest opportunity. I was perfectly satisfied, from all I saw, that Mowbray had made a tender impression on her heart, and the pain and regret it cost me were great, indeed ; but still I hoped that time, and the advice which I should feel it my duty to offer her, would have a proper effect upon her mind.

"Alice and myself had frequent conversations upon the subject, but nothing could banish from her mind the favourable and flattering opinion she entertained of Mowbray, and all my arguments were completely lost upon her. Fatal delusion! what bitter cause has she since had to regret it.

"At length Mowbray, much to my relief and satisfaction, announced the time of his departure, and I could perceive in a moment the powerful effect it had upon the feelings of Flora.

"'I am fearful that I have intruded upon your kindness and hospitality too long,' continued Mowbray ; 'but I must confess that I feel extremely loth to separate from the society of such excellent friends, and I can but again assure you, Mr. and Mrs. Hawthorn, of the high and grateful sense I entertain of the favours you have shown me, and which it is impossible that I can ever forget.'

"'We have done nothing, Mr. Mowbray,' I replied, 'to merit so many acknowledgments ; and if we have been able to serve you, you are welcome to it, and the knowledge of having done so affords us sufficient satisfaction.'

"'I hope, Mr. Hawthorn,' he observed, 'that you will not consider me an intruder if I call upon you again in a few weeks, for I have business that will bring me this way.'

"I noticed the agitation of Flora at this question, but I was so confused that I scarcely knew how to answer.

"'If the dwelling of Hawthorn, the fisherman, be not too humble for a gentleman of Mr. Mowbray's standing in society,' I at length replied, 'of course I must feel myself honoured by his visit.'

"'The dwelling of the preserver of my life, and to whom I owe so much,' he repeated, 'too humble for me? The thought is preposterous, and I should despise myself could I for a moment entertain it. But you have by far too modest an opinion of yourself, my good friend, believe me, and it is I who must ever feel flattered and honoured by your friendship, though, I trust, when you know me better, that you will find I am not undeserving of it.'

"I bowed assent, and after a brief pause, during which time his eyes wandered to Flora, he continued:

"'I expect that the business I am coming upon will detain me some weeks in this neighbourhood, and, therefore, it will be necessary for me to put up at the nearest inn where I can be accommodated. I anticipate much pleasure in being able to resume our acquaintance, which I hope may continue for many years.'

"An expression of delight passed over the features of Flora, which was not unobserved by Mowbray, and evidently afforded him the utmost inward gratification, whilst my uneasiness and confusion increased, and I could with the greatest difficulty conceal the real state of my feelings from his observation.

"'I am afraid, Mr. Mowbray,' I remarked at last, 'that you will find but very indifferent accommodation in this neighbourhood, which is principally inhabited by very poor people.'

"'Well, well,' he returned, carelessly, 'that is not a matter of much consequence, and I can put up with it during the short time that I shall continue here. There is one favour, however, that I have to request of you, Mr. Hawthorn, and your good wife and daughter, and which I shall feel very much disappointed if you do not comply with.'

"'And what is that, sir?' I demanded eagerly, and with some degree of surprise.

"'Why, it is this,' he answered, 'namely, that when I have settled my affairs, you will do me the honour to pass a few weeks with me at my country mansion, where it shall be my study to make you some return for the hospitality you have shown me.'

"'You will pardon me, Mr. Mowbray,' I replied, 'if I decline this invitation, for it is out of no disrespect to you : but we are not accustomed to leave our home, where business calls us ; we have been used to an almost secluded life ; besides, we are far too humble to become the guests of such a gentleman as yourself.'

"He looked vexed and disappointed at this answer, and Flora could not conceal the emotion which it caused her.

"'The excuse you offer, you will pardon me for saying, Mr. Hawthorn,' he remarked at last, 'is anything but a reasonable one ; but, however, I will content myself by not arguing that point for the present ; and I hope that you will change your mind by the time we meet again."

"'I cannot make any promise to do so, sir,' I returned ; 'though, at the same time, I am obliged to you for the invitation.'

"He returned no immediate answer, and after some further conversation of no importance, he left the cottage, and shortly afterwards Flora, who was evidently much depressed in spirits, made some excuse and retired from the room.

"'I cannot but regret the departure of Mr. Mowbray, who has made himself so agreeable during the time he has been residing with us,' observed my wife, when we were left alone, "and I am at a loss to conceive for what reason you declined his polite invitation.'

"'For the best of reasons, Alice,' I answered; 'because, in the first place, we are no fitting society for a person in his station of life, and should only excite impertinent observations from jealous persons; and, secondly, because I cannot divest my mind of the impression that some danger might accrue from our visit.'

"'How uncharitable is this supposition, Hawthorn,' said Alice; 'what is there in the conduct of Mr. Mowbray that should give you cause to suppose he intends us any harm?'

"'I am more convinced than ever,' I returned, 'that the charms of our daughter have created some powerful passion in his breast, and that he also has made a favourable impression upon Flora's heart. Did you not notice her agitation when he announced the time of his departure? His wealth and rank preclude all chance of her ever becoming his wife, and, therefore, it is necessary, if we study her future happiness and prosperity, to endeavour to stifle her hopeless passion in its infancy.'

"'But should Mowbray make honourable proposals for her hand?' said my wife.

"'That I do not believe he will ever do,' I answered; 'the pride of rank and fortune will prevent him; and I again declare that I have no other ambition than to see our daughter united to a worthy man of her own position in society, whom she can love, and who will do his duty by her.'

"'I cannot see the force or reasonableness of your arguments, Hawthorn, although humble, I consider that Flora by her virtues is a match worthy of the proudest nobleman in the universe.'

"'That may be,' I remarked; 'but it is seldom that pure happiness arises from such ill-assorted unions, and Heaven forbid that we should be guided by avarice in the future settlement of our beloved child. Come, Alice, I am certain that you will be of my opinion when you come to reflect calmly and reasonably upon the subject. The idea of this young sprig of fashion entertaining any feelings of regard towards our daughter, seems to have almost turned your brain; but, for my own part, I am sorry that we have ever seen him, and I regret sincerely that it is his intention to return to this neighbourhood so shortly.'

"'Well, Hawthorn,' she said, 'I really have scarcely any patience to hear you talk so ; Mr. Mowbray professes the warmest friendship towards us, and, in spite of all you have said, I cannot see that we have any reason to doubt his sincerity.'

"'I should deeply regret were I to wrong him by my suspicions,' I returned, 'though I have experienced too much of the world, and of the deception of mankind, not to be upon my guard. I will keep a strict watch over Flora during the time that he remains in the neighbourhood, and should he contemplate any such a thing, I will prevent, if possible, his taking any advantage of her innocence and inexperience.'

"My wife expressed in the warmest terms her disapprobation of my surmises, and all my arguments failed to convince her, or to have the least effect upon her; so we again dropped the subject for the present, and I had firmly made up my mind as to the manner in which I would act.

"Flora avoided our society as much as possible during the remainder of that day, and that convinced me that I was right in my conjectures as to the nature of her feelings. When we saw her again, she was extremely low spirited, and it was in vain that we endeavoured to draw her into conversation. We did not, however, make any allusion to Alfred Mowbray, who, we were convinced, was the subject of her thoughts, for we thought that a more appropriate opportunity would present itself. I was also much gratified that he did not make his appearance again that day, and had no doubt that he was making all the necessary preparations for his departure.

"The morning on which Alfred Mowbray was to leave at length arrived, and we breakfasted at an earlier hour than usual, in order to enable him to be in time for the coach, which would pass near the neighbourhood in which we resided at eight o'clock. Flora had excused herself from being present on the plea of being indisposed, and Mowbray evinced much disappointment at her being absent; but I well guessed the reason of being so, and was pleased at the resolution she had come to, though at the same time it the more convinced me, if possible, of th e fatal and unfortunate passion which was engendered in her breast, and showed me the double necessity there was for my using the utmost precaution, in order to prevent the consequences which I so much, and, as circumstances afterwards proved, so justly dreaded.

"As I before stated, the vexation and disappointment of Alfred Mowbray at the non-appearance of Flora were quite evident, though he tried to the utmost to conceal his real feelings, and merely expressed his regret that he had not the opportunity of my daughter's being present at his departue, to bid her adieu, as it was caused by illness, and trusted that her indisposition would be brief, and not attended with any serious conseqnences.

"My wife (poor, simple w oman, as she was at that time) it needed no very keen penetration to perceive, was as much chagined as himself, and notwithstanding the significant looks which I fixed upon her, she gave utterance to her feeelings with her usual volubility; thus, on her part, giving, without serious thought, some encouragement to his hopes, and his bold advances.

" ' I cannot but repeat my acknowledgments, Mr. Hawthorn,' he said, after some previous observations, ' for the uniform kindness I have received from yourself and your amiable wife, since I have been under your roof, and it is that which renders me the more anxious to resume our acquaintance at as early a period as possible.'

"I bowed in acknowledgment for this, but returned no answer, and he went on—

" ' I, therefore, feel highly gratified that I must so soon return to this neighbourhood, and I trust that that circumstance will be the means of ripening an acquaintance auspiciously begun into a friendship the most fervent and endurable.'

"I was about to reply, but Alice interposed.

" ' I am sure, Mr. Mowbray,' she remarked, ' that my husband, as well as myself, must feel highly flattered and honoured by the friendship of such a gentleman as yourself, and that he will do all in his power to mark his due and proper sense of it.'

"I perceived a smile of satisfaction pass over his countenance as she uttered these words, and I felt vexed and embarrassed at the observations she had made use of. However, I concealed my real feelings as well as I could, and after a pause, I said—

" ' Mr. Mowbray, I am sure, will do me the justice to suppose that I duly appreciate the friendly feelings he has expressed towards us, and it shall be my task to convince him that I deserve them. But you will pardon me, sir, I am but a simple, humble man, unused to compliments, and you will, therefore, be pleased to accept the will for the deed.'

" ' Say no more upon that subject, Mr. Hawthorn,' he returned, at the same time pressing my hand, ' I am satisfied of the genuine goodness of your heart, and that surpasses all the surperfluous flattery of the tongue. I must beg of you to give my best respects to your fair daughter, and express to her my sincere regret at the circumstance which prevents her from being present at my departure. But there is one thing more that I wish to observe, and I hope you will not feel offended with me for so doing.'

" ' Name it, Mr. Mowbray,' I replied, anxious to hear what it was that he had to say.

" ' I have put you to much trouble and inconvenience, I fear, since I have been here,' he resumed, 'and I, therefore, beg that you will, at least, accept of this purse, as some trifling acknowledgment of the obligations to which I feel myself under to you.'

" ' Nay, Mr. Mowbray,' I answered, pushing back his hand, 'this is quite unnecessary and uncalled for. Thank Heaven, I am in comfortable, if not affluent circumstances, and even if I were not, I could never think of receiving any pecuniary reward for performing a common act of humanity.'

" ' You possess a noble heart, Mr. Hawthorn,' he remarked, 'and deserve to move in a far different station of life to that in which you are at present placed.'

" ' I am perfectly contented with my lot,' I returned, 'and my ambition does not soar beyond it. I have an excellent wife, an amiable and affectionate daughter, prosperity has attended all my exertions of late years, and what more can I, or should I require?'

" He was about to make some reply, when at that moment the coach was heard approaching along the road, and he hastily prepared to depart. He repeated his thanks to myself and Alice ; pressed our hands fervently, and apparently with much sincerity of friendship, and then left the cottage, we following him to the door. As he hastened towards the coach I perceived that he cast an anxious look up at the window of the room in which he knew Flora was, and waving his hand, I felt vexed, for I concluded that she was at the window to witness his departure. The next moment he had taken his seat in the vehicle, and it was driven off rapidly, and was soon hidden from the sight.

" We returned to the room, and I felt a weight taken off my mind, now that Mowbray was gone, and notwithstanding what he had said, I heartily wished that we might see him no more."

CHAPTER XXV.

HAWTHORN CONCLUDES HIS STORY.—THE
BETRAYER AND HIS VICTIM.

" ' WELL,' said my wife on our return to the room, 'I am sorry that Mr. Mowbray has gone, for he is one of the most affable and agreeable young men that I ever met with, and I wish him success wherever he may go to. We shall feel quite dull without him ; but I am glad that he will have to return to the neighbourhood shortly.'

" ' I cannot entertain the feelings that you express, Alice,' I replied, ' and I should be much better satisfied if our acquaintance were to end where it is.'

" ' You astonish me,' observed Alice ; ' what has there been in the conduct of Mr. Mowbray since he has resided with us, that you should entertain such ungenerous prejudices against him?'

" ' Well, probably I may be wrong,' I returned, 'for his conduct has certainly been most friendly and flattering towards us since he has been here ; but still I cannot help having some misgivings as to his real character, and I liked not the very marked attentions which he paid to our Flora.'

" ' Nay,' said Alice, 'this is sheer nonsense, Henry. He behaved no more towards our daughter than common courtesy and gallantry demanded at his hands, and we ought to feel ourselves highly flattered by the admiration which she excited in his breast.'

" ' Ah, Alice!' I returned, shaking my head, 'admiration in one of his station is often fraught with danger; and it, therefore, behoves us as parents to keep a watchful and jealous eye over the safety of our child, who, I am afraid, is already too strongly prepossessed in Mowbray's favour.'

" ' Well, for the life of me,' she said, in a tone of vexation, 'I cannot see the least cause that you have for entertaining these suspicions and apprehensions of Mr. Mowbray. To me he appears one of the most amiable and honourable of young men, and let me tell you that a match between him and Flora would—'

" ' Pshaw ! Alice,' I interrupted, impatiently ; 'you talk absurdly, and at random ; I have experienced too much of the world, and seen too deeply into the characters of mankind, to suppose that a man placed in the position of Mr. Mowbray could be likely to entertain any serious or honourable thoughts of making a poor girl like our Flora his wife ; therefore I say again that there may be danger in his attentions towards her, which it is our bounden duty to be on guard against. I am glad that Flora was not present at his departure, though I am fully convinced from the close observations I made that he has made an impression upon her heart which it will not be easy to eradicate, and at some future opportunity I shall consider it my duty to question her narrowly, and advise her on the subject.'

" Alice returned no answer, but I could see plainly that she entirely dissented from my opinion and still entertained the same

RATFIELD POINTING OUT TO PARKER THE REWARD FOR HIS APPREHENSION.

sanguine and preposterous idea which she had before so often expressed. Unfortunately, she was inexperienced in the world, and her judgment was, therefore, too apt to lead her astray. How fatally it did so on the present occasion will be seen by the sequel of my tale. Alas! alas! what bitter cause have I not now to lament the realisation of my forebodings. My poor child! cursed, most fatal was the hour that ever introduced Alfred Mowbray to you. Would to Heaven that he had perished in the storm, you might now have been as innocent and happy as you once were. Villain! villain! may the curses of Heaven light upon your head for the fearful destruction you have caused."

Here Mr. Hawthorn was so greatly excited that he was compelled to pause in order to give vent to his feelings, and Richard Parker and his wife were scarcely less deeply affected than himself. At length he resumed his melancholy narrative in the following words:

"The conversation between myself and my wife shortly afterwards teminated, and I visited the apartment in which Flora was, for the purpose of inquiring after her health, though I was before all but confirmed in my suspicions as to the real cause of her absenting herself on the departure of Mowbray.

"I found her seated by the window, her head reclining pensively on her hand, and she was evidently buried in deep thought, and was weeping. She arose hastily, and with some confusion on my entrance, and endeavoured to conceal her emotion ; but it was no use, and advancing towards her, I took her hand, and looked tenderly and sympathisingly in her face, while I said:

"'In tears, my dear child—how is this? Surely, my beloved Flora, who has been hitherto so light-hearted and so happy, cannot now have anything to distress her?'

"'Pardon me, my father,' she replied, in a faltering voice, 'for this foolish display of weakness ; but a melancholy feeling has for the last few minutes come over me, for which I cannot in any other way account than by indisposition.'

"'And think you candidly, Flora,' I interrupted, at the same time looking earnestly in her face, 'think you that this emotion emanates from no other cause than indisposition?'

"'What mean you, my dear father?' she returned in a hesitating voice, and trembling slightly.

"'Alfred Mowbray has departed,' I replied, significantly. A deep blush suffused her cheeks as I thus spoke, and she trembled more violently than before It was evident that I had touched upon one of the most tender chords of her heart ; but she made a powerful effort to struggle with her feelings, and at length said—

"'I am aware of it, father, for I witnessed his departure from the window.'

"'He expressed much disappointment, Flora, at your not being present for him to take his leave of you,' I observed.

"'Ah! did he?' she ejaculated eagerly, and her eyes glistened, but she quickly checked herself, and continued—'I trust he will not consider me unkind for absenting myself, but I really felt too ill to leave my chamber.'

"'I am glad that you did not, Flora,' I remarked ; 'but now that Alfred Mowbray is gone, may I ask what is your candid opinion of him?'

"She blushed deeply at this question, and was evidently more confused than before.

"'Why, my dear father,' she at last answered with apparent ingenuousness, 'there is no denying that Mr. Mowbray is a gentleman of the most amiable and prepossessing manners, and I cannot feel otherwise than glad that you were made the means of rescuing him from so awful and untimely a fate.'

"'That I was made the humble instrument of saving a fellow creature from death, affords me much gratification,' I observed ; 'but at the same time I cannot but regret that it did not fall to the lot of some other individual than myself, or that Alfred Mowbray was ever introduced to us.'

"'What mean you, my dear father?' she demanded in a tremulous voice, and looking anxiously in my face ; 'surely you cannot justly apprehend that any ill consequences will arise from that circumstance?'

"'Flora,' I said in serious accents, 'you are young and innocent, and inexperienced in the world, and it, therefore, cannot be expected that you can penetrate the human character with that nice discrimination that I can. I must candidly acknowledge that, in spite of the plausibility and urbanity of his manners, there is something about this Alfred Mowbray which I do not like, and which excites my suspicions.'

"'Oh, my dear father,' she returned, eagerly, and the expression of her features showed the agitation of her feelings, 'surely you do Mr. Mowbray an injustice by encouraging those surmises derogatory to his character ; his behaviour towards us, while he has been residing with us, has been most respectful and gentlemanly; and I am convinced that one who bears so amiable an exterior, can never possess a bad heart.'

"Her eyes brightened as she spoke, and her whole demeanour was animated in the extreme, and if I could before have entertained any doubt as to the state of her mind, I must now have been thoroughly convinced of it.

"'Flora,' I said, solemnly, 'you cannot conceal the fact from me, and I have observed it with the deepest regret and apprehension, that this Alfred Morbray has made a powerful impression upon your young and susceptible heart.'

"'Oh, my father!' she ejaculated, and crimson blushes again suffused her cheeks.

"'Nay, Flora,' I interrupted, 'it is useless for you to deny it, for your whole conduct, and your present agitation, confirms it. But beware, my dear child; there may be danger in your encouraging such feeling, though I neither feel surprised, nor am I going to reproach you for entertaining them. The base deceiver often assumes the most plausible and flattering disguise, in order to further his nefarious and diabolical designs, which his unhappy victim discovers when too late. Remember the difference of station there is between yourself and Mowbray, and you must then at once see the necessity of your exerting yourself to the utmost to stifle any passion with which he may have inspired you in your breast.'

" She burst into tears, and sobbed bitterly as I thus spoke, and was for several minutes unable to return any answer. The violent emotion of her manner was sufficient to convince me of the real nature of her feelings, and I was scarcely less agitated than herself. I, however, approached her affectionately, and endeavoured, by every means in my power, to soothe her into composure.

" 'My dear child,' I observed, ' do not give way to this emotion, nor deem me harsh for the observations I have deemed it my duty to make to you. You know full well that they were dictated only by my anxiety for your welfare, for should anything happen to my darling Flora, how great and terrible would be my misery and despair.'

" 'Flora Hawthorn,' she replied, in a firm voice, and looking up through her tears, 'will never be guilty of anything that will disgrace herself or the parents who are so dear to her.'

" 'I know that, my dear child,' I replied, embracing her; 'but there are villains enough in the world who are ready and anxious to take advantage of an unguarded moment, and it is against such as those that I would protect you. Nothing would afford me greater pleasure than to see you place your affections upon some worthy young man in your own station of life ; but, tor the reasons I have before stated, I would enjoin you to endeavour to cease to remember Alfred Mowbray with any other feelings than those of respect.'

" 'I cannot, I will not attempt to deny, my father,' returned Flora, in a hesitating voice, ' that the amiable manners and brilliant accomplishments of Alfred Mowbray have excited my admiration; but surely that sentiment cannot be misconstrued into love?'

" 'Beware, Flora,' I said, seriously; 'it is love; your looks, your every word and action betray it. Alfred Mowbray is no match for you. Fortune has placed him above you, and, therefore, to encourage any such futile hopes would be fraught with such imminent danger that I fear to contemplate.'

" 'And why, my dear father,' demanded Flora, 'should you entertain such powerful prejudices against the character of Mr. Mowbray as those you have expressed ?'

" 'I scarcely know how to answer that question, Flora,' I returned; 'but I cannot banish them from my mind, and I would, therefore, have you bear constantly in your mind the advice I have given you, and to shape your conduct towards Mr. Mowbray accordingly, should he ever again visit us; which, although he has promised to do, I hope he will not.'

" Flora sighed deeply, and I could plainly perceive that she was far from coinciding in my wishes.

" ' In all things, my dear father,' she at length said, 'consistent with virtue and reason, you will ever find me most dutiful; and I trust that upon this delicate point I shall not be guilty of anything that can cause you the least pain or regret. Flora Hawthorn can never do anything that she should be ashamed to acknowledge, and that, too, without a blush.'

" 'Spoken like my own sweet child,' I ejaculated, embracing her most affectionately; 'continue in this same state of mind, and all will yet be well. But I will urge you no more upon this subject for the present, but will leave you to the indulgence of your own feelings and reflections, satisfied that they will guide you to a right conclusion.'

" 'I will endeavour to do as you desire me, father,' she returned, 'though I will not forbear candidly acknowledging, that until something may occur to change that opinion, Mr. Mowbray must ever possess my warmest esteem; and I trust that you will yet find that your suspicions, as to his real character, are unfounded.'

" ' Well, my dear child,' I answered, ' I sincerely hope that I may; for I should be sorry to treat any of my fellow-creatures with an uncharitable feeling.'

" With these words I once more embraced her, and left her to herself, descending to the room in which my wife was seated, and whom I found anxiously awaiting my return, and about to hasten to the chamber of Flora also. She eagerly questioned me as to the state of our daughter, and what had taken place between us at our interview; and I replied,—

" 'My surmises were correct, Alice; the person and accomplishments of Mowbray have made an impression upon the susceptible heart of our child, and she is absolutely in love.'

" 'Bless my soul!' exclaimed the simple woman, 'is it possible? However, I am not at all surprised, and it is no more than I expected, considering the numerous attractions of this young gentleman. I am much mistaken, too, if he is not equally struck with her.'

" 'Unfortunately, I fear that is the case,' I returned.

" 'Unfortunately, say you?' Alice repeated; 'what, and he a rich gentleman, too, and able to make our Flora a lady, and to place her in that station of society to which her numerous merits entitle her? I am surprised to hear you talk so, husband.'

" 'And is it possible, Alice,' I demanded, 'that you are so bedazzled by rank and station? What are riches, if not accompanied by happiness?'

" 'And if they sincerely love each other, must they not be happy as man and wife?' she returned.

" 'No, Alice,' I replied, 'that does not always follow—seldom so when the female whom a wealthy man marries is of humble origin. Regrets and reproaches are almost sure to follow when the first heat of passion has subsided, and they become wretched, and miserable, and hateful to each other. Besides, how many instances do we hear of innocent damsels being betrayed to ruin by the artful seducer under the promise of marriage? Such heartless villains are, alas! too plentiful in the world; and we should have bitter reason never to forgive ourselves were we not to be upon our guard against this same Alfred Mowbray, whatever his professions may be.'

" 'You wrong him, I am convinced,' said Alice; 'but I see that you are so strongly prejudiced against him, though for what reason I cannot imagine, that it is almost worse than useless to argue with you upon the subject. Poor Flora, I dare say you have wounded her feelings severely at this interview, and I must see her without delay, and endeavour to console her.'

" 'I caution you, Alice,' I said, seriously, 'as to what you say to her, and how you endeavour to counteract the advice I have given her, which was dictated by truth, duty, and affection. She has promised to submit to my will, and on her doing so, I feel confident, depends her happiness. Remember how fearfully you will have cause to reproach yourself should you, by holding out to her any false hopes, which may only end in disappoint-

ment, be the indirect means of plunging her into that ruin which I so much dread.'

" 'Why, gracious me, husband,' she ejaculated, 'you talk as seriously upon this subject as if that which you dread was on the eve of inevitably taking place. God forbid that I should do anything which might at all tend to bring misery upon the head of our dearest child, who is the sole prop and blessing of our declining days. But again I tell you that I am convinced that your fears are groundless, and that ——'

" 'I sincerely hope that they may prove to be so,' I interrupted; 'but I strictly enjoin you, as you fear my displeasure, to bear in mind all that I have said, and act accordingly.'

" 'I will do so,' she replied; 'but, for my own part, I see nothing whatever to apprehend. We can safely depend upon the wisdom and strict virtue and integrity of our daughter, to guard her from the insidious artifices of the tempter, and as for Mr. Mowbray, I am no judge of human nature at all if he be not a gentleman of the greatest honour, and most estimable qualities of heart.'

" 'I hope we may find him to be so,' I returned; 'but enough upon this delicate subject for the present. You can go to Flora, but I again caution you to remember what I have said to you.'

" Alice made no reply, but quitted the room, and I was left to my own reflections. The confirmation of my fears in the acknowledgment of the sentiments which Flora bore towards Alfred Mowbray, filled my mind with the greatest anguish and anxiety, and I could come to no other decision as to the manner in which it would be best to act in order to guard my beloved child from the dangers which I apprehended. But I am becoming tedious. Flora did not leave her chamber that day, and I learnt from my wife that she continued in much the same state of mind as when I had seen her in the morning. The next day, however, she rejoined us in the room where we usually sat; but, although she evidently made a strong effort to appear tranquil, and even cheerful, she singularly failed, and it was quite clear that her mind was a prey to the utmost care and anxiety. Myself and my wife took good care never once to allude to the name of Alfred Mowbray; but I was satisfied, from the frequent absence of mind she betrayed on several subjects upon which we conversed, that the whole thoughts of Flora were fixed upon him.

" Two or three days elapsed in this

manner, and the depression of Flora's spirits increased, and it was in vain that myself and her mother endeavoured to arouse her from it. She avoided our presence as much as she possibly could, and was frequently from home, and on more than one occasion I discovered that her walks were extended to those spots which had been the favourite places of resort of Mowbray during the time he had resided with us, and which had consequently endeared them to her.

"On these occasions I always gently, yet seriously remonstrated with her on the folly and danger of her conduct; but it seemed to have little or no effect upon her, and I saw with the most indescribable grief and anxiety, that she found it impossible to stifle the unfortunate passion which Mowbray had engendered in her breast.

"I now more than ever dreaded the return of Mowbray to the neighbourhood, but made up my mind when he should do so, to take some decisive and important step on the subject which was of such vital interest to me.

"Another week passed away, and I began to hope that Alfred Mowbray had abandoned his design, and that we should, in all probability, not behold him again, when all doubts upon that subject were removed by our receiving a letter from him, in which, after expressing in the most eloquent terms the warm friendship he entertained towards us, he apprised us that he should return to the neighbourhood in which we resided in three days from the date of his letter, when he hoped to have the pleasure of seeing us again, and of frequently enjoying our society. He expressed himself in the most ardent manner towards Flora, which could leave no room to doubt the real nature of his feelings, and increased my alarm, if not indignation.

"I would willingly have kept the contents of this letter a secret from Flora, but that was impossible; and on hearing them, I could not but notice with regret the pleasure they seemed to impart to her, although she endeavoured to conceal her real feelings from my observation. From that hour the heavy depression which had before weighed upon her feelings entirely vanished, and she entered as freely and cheerfully into the conversation as she had formerly done; but she took every opportunity of being alone, notwithstanding, no doubt to indulge in joyful anticipations of the return of Alfred Mowbray. Upon one of those occasions I obtruded myself suddenly and unexpectedly upon her, and

overheard some observations that fell from her, in which she mentioned the name of Mowbray in terms of the warmest affection. She turned pale and trembled violently upon beholding me, and I fixed upon her a mingled look of pity and gentle remonstrance.

"'Flora,' I said, 'has, then, all the advise that I have given you been thrown away upon you? Have you so soon forgotten the promises you made to me? You still love Alfred Mowbray with all the ardour of a most intense passion, and I shudder to think of the consequences that may accrue to you from it. Pause, my dear girl, and reflect calmly and reasonably, ere you plunge yourself into that misery from which nothing can extricate you.'

"'Oh, my father,' she ejaculated in a voice of the deepest emotion, 'what can I say to you? How can I answer you?'

"'Acknowledge the truth, Flora,' I replied; 'for I know that you must ever hate and despise yourself, could you become an hypocrite. You love Mowbray?'

"She covered her face with her hands and sobbed heavily, as she replied in a faint voice—

"'Alas! I do. But Heaven knows, my dear father, that it is with a passion as pure and holy as ever took possession of maiden's breast. I have sought to follow your advice, to obey your injunctions, and I have tried to stifle the unfortunate passion in my breast; but all my efforts have been in vain, for the more I think of him, the greater becomes the influence that he has obtained over my affections. Nothing can possibly eradicate my feelings unless I could banish his image from my memory, and that I feel to be so hopeless a task that it would be madness to attempt it; but pity me, my father, and do not reproach me for that over which I have no control.'

"She looked eloquently and supplicatingly in my face as she thus spoke, and I could not, indeed, help feeling towards her the greatest commiseration, though, at the same time, I was mad at the influence which Mowbray had so unfortunately obtained over her, and dreaded the consequences that might ensue, if she should not be able to stifle her fatal passion in her breast; for I still could not help entertaining the strongest suspicions that Alfred Mowbray was not the honourable individual he represented himself to be.

"Perhaps you may deem me uncharitable and unreasonable for encouraging those prejudices against one who was almost a stranger to me, and who had certainly never yet given me any cause to suspect the integrity of his character; but, alas! what bitter cause have I since had to be convinced of the truth of my conjectures.

" ' My dear Flora,' I at length said, in reply to the observations she had made use of, ' think not for a moment that I have any wish to reproach you for that which I know is so natual to so young and innocent and inexperienced a maiden as yourself, and who is also possessed of the same tender susceptibility of feeling as you are. You know full well that your future happiness and prosperity are far more precious to me than my very existence, and it is that which makes me look with fear and caution upon the advances of any man who may seek to obtain a hold on your affections, and to endeavour to penetrate into the sincerity of their professions. I must again assert that my mind is not altogether satisfied with Alfred Mowbray.'

" ' Strange and unaccountable prejudice,' said Flora, with a look of emotion, regret, and disappointment; ' what was there ever in the conduct of Mowbray, during the time that he resided here, that you should thus have reason to doubt him ?'

" This question was a most reasonable one, and I must confess that I scarce knew how to answer her.

" ' Flora,' I said at length, ' you then acknowledge that Mowbray has made an impression upon your heart ?'

" She blushed deeply, averted her looks from mine for a moment, and hesitated. I repeated the question, and she then replied, in a faltering voice :

" ' Alas! it is useless for me to deny that I consider Mr. Mowbray the most agreeable and interesting young man whom I have ever seen, and that since he has been introduced to me, my heart has felt a sensation which it never before experienced. It is in vain that I have endeavoured to stifle the feeling in my breast, for hourly it gains strength, and ——"

" ' Fatal passion !' I interrupted; " my mind too fearfully anticipates the misery of which it may be productive. Oh, my dear child, let me beg of you once more to make a powerful effort to conquer it, and to fix your affections upon some other youth who may be worty of your numerous virtues, and whose whole study it may be to render you happy.'

" She shook her head and sighed, as she replied,—

" Ah, my dear father, that is impossible; what other youth can ever make the powerful impression upon my heart which Alfred Mowbray has done?'

" ' But remember, Flora,' I urged, ' how far he is placed above you by station, and you must at once perceive the folly of aspiring to his hand, if even you should have excited any sentiments of affection in his breast. Beware, beware, my child, for the feelings you at present entertain are fraught with the most imminent danger, and one unguarded moment, one moment of weakness on your part, might give the tempter an advantage which would end in your destruction.'

" ' Oh, my dear father,' she ejaculated, with a look of the most extreme agitation, ' what fearful meaning do your words convey? What is it against which you would so solemnly warn me?'

" ' Flora,' I answered, ' I have experienced much of the world, and I have been accustomed to study and to penetrate the characters of mankind. Mark me, there are those who have the art to assume the most specious and prepossessing exterior, in order to accomplish their nefarious designs, and to delude their innocent and unsuspecting victims. Alas! how many a bright and innocent spirit has fallen into the snares of the unprincipled libertine and seducer! It is against such miscreants as those that I would guard you; for virtue, however pure, is not always proof against their base and brutal artifices. Would to Heaven, I repeat, that we had never seen Alfred Mowbray.'

" ' And what has there ever been in his behaviour during the short time that we have known him,' Flora demanded, ' to cause you to doubt the integrity of his character? All his actions and observations have gone to prove him to be a man of honour.'

" ' It may be so,' I returned; ' but I trust and hope sincerely that nothing will ever occur to disappoint you in the favourable opinion you have formed of him.'

" ' And can my father,' said Flora, at the same time blushing deeply, and fixing a look of gentle reproach upon me, ' form so indifferent an opinion of my virture as to imagine that I will ever be guilty of that which I should be ashamed to acknowledge?"

" ' No, my child,' I answered, ' I should be ashamed of myself could I for a moment entertain so uncharitable and unnatural an idea; but, alas! what young and unsuspecting damsel can be sufficiently on her guard against the designs of the experienced and systematic libertine? It is the difference of the stations of life which you occupy which leads me to doubt whether

Alfred Mowbray can ever entertain any serious ideas of making you his wife, and it is, therefore, that I would have you seek to conquer that passion which he has engendered in your breast, and to repel those advances which might otherwise lead to such serious consequences.'

"'Ah! my dear father,' replied Flora, 'you impose upon me a most arduous task, and one which I much fear it will never be in my power to accomplish. Again do I candidly acknowledge the powerful influence which the manly accomplishments and manners of Alfred Mowbray have gained over my heart; and although I am ever anxious to act in the strictest accordance to your will, I fear that nothing can ever eradicate the impression he has made upon me.'

"'Oh, my poor child,' I ejaculated, in a voice of the deepest emotion, 'how torturing is that declaration to a parent who is so anxious for your welfare. Alas! I fear that there is some trouble in store for us which we should shudder even to contemplate.'

"'Do not, my dear father,' returned Flora, 'entertain any such dismal apprehensions, which, after all, may prove to be entirely groundless.'

"'God grant that they may,' I exclaimed; 'but let me beg of you, Flora, to reflect calmly and maturely upon this painful and important subject, and I know that your good sense will lead you to struggle against the feelings that have so unhappily taken possession of your mind, and to come to a right conclusion. Surely amongst all the young men of your own humble station, who are ambitious to pay their addresses to you, you may find one on whom you could place your affections, and who would be anxious to render you happy?'

"'Ah, no!' she replied, shaking her head, 'there is not one that I have seen who can ever inspire any warmer sentiment in my breast than esteem and friendship. Oh, how greatly do they suffer by comparison with Alfred Mowbray.'

"'Foolish, headstrong girl,' I cried impatiently; 'what a terrible weakness is this that you display, and how fatal may the consequences be to you should you not persevere to triumph over it.'

"'You wrong me, my dear father, and Mr. Mowbray also, I am certain,' Flora returned, in a voice of gentle remonstrance, 'by encouraging any such idea. Flora Hawthorn will never be guilty of that which can bring shame and disgrace upon her parents' heads, nor do I believe that it is in the nature of Alfred Mowbray

that he could even for a moment entertain a dishonourable thought against myself or you.'

"'How!' I exclaimed, fixing upon her a keen and penetrating glance, 'so enthusiastic in his praise, and yet you have been so shortly acquainted that it is impossible you can form a just opinion of his character?'

"'At any rate, father,' she retorted, in a tone of reproof, 'I have yet seen nothing in his behaviour towards myself or you that should prejudice me against his character. It has, on the contrary, been marked by the utmost respect and condescension, and he has evinced a proper sense of gratitude for the service you were so fortunate as to be able to render him.'

"I felt confused, and somewhat abashed by her reply, for I could not deny the force of it, and for a few minutes I scarcely knew what answer to return; but at last I said,—

"'Flora, all that you have said only goes to prove the justice and the necessity of the injunctions I have given you, and I warn you, as you value your future happiness and that of the parents who have ever behaved to you with such unlimited affection, not to disregard them.'

"'I have never done so yet, my dear father,' she returned; 'and it is not at all probable that I shall do so now; but I am convinced that you have arrived at wrong conclusions on this important and delicate matter, and I would humbly but earnestly implore of you to suspend your judgment of the character of Mr. Mowbray until you become better acquainted with him, and not to condemn him altogether.'

"'I should be sorry to do so, Flora,' said I, 'without a just cause; but I would have you give no encouragement to his advances, for that might be the means of involving you in a dilemma which you can now but little anticipate, and from which you would find it a difficult task to extricate yourself.'

"'Alas!' she sighed, 'I know not how to promise you, for my heart revolts from the task.'

"'Ah! say you so?' I ejaculated with a look of anger; 'nay, then, I must adopt some other means to avert the evils which I apprehend. Mr. Mowbray must not be permitted to visit us again, and I must despatch a letter to him immediately to that effect.'

• "'Oh, my dear father,' cried Flora, turning pale and trembling, 'you surely will not be guilty of such an uncalled-for and unreasonable act of discourtesy towards a gentleman who has given you not the slightest cause for it? You will think better of this, I am sure, and abandon any such idea. You shall have no cause to complain of any want of prudence and discretion on my part while Mr. Mowbray may remain in this neighbourhood, and why, then, should you resort to any such means as those you have mentioned?'

"I hesitated, for there was too much reason in her arguments for me to return any immediate answer to them, but at length I said—

"'Well, well, perhaps upon second consideration it would seem wrong of me to do so, after the numerous professions of friendship he has made, and I will, therefore, consent to abandon the idea; but remember, Flora, what I have said, and also recollect that I shall keep a strict watch upon your conduct, and should anything occur to justify me in so doing, I shall not fail openly to denounce it, and to adopt such measures as may seem best to prevent its recurrence.'

"'I submit to your will, my dear father,' replied Flora, 'and you shall find no cause to complain of me. I will never be guilty of anything which can show me unworthy of the virtuous name I bear.'

"I embraced her affectionately, and having made use of all the arguments at my command, and given her such advice as I considered the occasion required, the interview endeed, and I left her.

"I have been thus particular in detailing this conversation, merely to show the powerful influence which Mowbray had gained over my poor girl's affections, and also to prove how fatally the conjectures I had formed were afterwards realised. But notwithstanding the promise which I had given to Flora, I was still undecided as to whether or not it would be my duty to prohibit the visits of Mowbray, and, at any rate, I was determined that while he remained in the neighbourhood where I resided, he should be in her society as little as possible, and then not without my being present; but, alas! how vain were all my precautions; how well did the villain contrive his plans; may the vengeance of Heaven pursue him to his dying hour!

"I looked forward to the time at which Mowbray had stated in his letter he would arrive in the neighbourhood with the utmost anxiety and fear, and I sincerely hoped that some accident would occur to prevent his doing so. Flora, I could perceive, was, also, all anxiety and impatience, though she endeavoured to conceal her real feelings from my observation; and it was quite evident that the sentiments she entertained towards Mow-bray increased every hour instead of abated.

"The day at last came, and Flora was up at an unusually early hour in the morning; and from her agitated manner, and her flushed countenance, she was evidently on the tiptoe of expectation. It was not, however, till towards the afternoon that a servant came to our cottage to inform us that his master, Mr. Mowbray, had arrived at the inn, and that, with our permission, he would do himself the honour of visiting us in about an hour.

"The eyes of Flora sparkled at this message, and it was impossible for her to conceal the otherwise agitation of her manner; and my wife did not attempt to disguise the pleasure she felt at the return of Mowbray, though I endeavoured by my looks to check the expression of her feelings.

"The hour came, and with it that man whom, from some unaccountable cause, I so much dreaded and doubted, and I received him with much formal politeness, though he was most profuse in his compliments; and the looks he bestowed upon Flora when he greeted her, and those of mingled pleasure and embarrassment which she exchanged with him, increased my jealous doubts and fears, and made me even more reserved and distant in my manner towards him than I should otherwise have been. He was looking better than ever, and I must confess that I could not wonder at the admiration which he had excited in the bosom of my unfortunate daughter. I was anxious for her to retire from the room, but there was no chance of her doing that, and, of course, out of common politeness to Mowbray, I could not openly desire her to do so; but I sat all the time in a state of the greatest uneasiness of mind, the more especially as he addressed his conversation to her as often as he could, and passed the most flattering compliments upon her, which she seemed to receive with much pleasure.

"'The business which has brought me to this neighbourhood again,' he said, after a pause in the conversation for a short time, 'will, I expect, detain me here for five or six weeks, a circumstance which I must say I cannot regret, since it will give me an opportunity of being in the society of those whom I so much esteem. But I should be doubly gratified, Mr. Hawthorn, if I could prevail upon you, and your wife and daughter, to accompany me for a few weeks on my return to Mowbray Hall, which you would find a charming place, and a most agreeable change from the dull and

THE AFFECTING SCENE BETWEEN FLORA AND HER FATHER.

monotonous life that you lead here. What say you, Miss Flora? Will you not endeavour to persuade your father to comply with my request, and to accept of my invitation?'

"Flora blushed deeply, and in other ways evinced the confusion she felt at this question.

"'You will pardon me, Mr. Mowbray,' I said; 'I am obliged to you for your kindness and condescension, which I had no right to expect; but upon that point I am immovable; my business will not permit me, as I before told you, to accept of your invitation; we have also been so long used to our present course of life that we should be completely taken out of our element if removed from it; and, besides, our humble station——'

"'Nay, Mr. Hawthorn,' he interrupted, 'indeed I cannot listen to any excuses or apologies of that description; I recognise no distinction in our stations, and the great service you have rendered me, and the uniform kindness and attention I have experienced from you since we have been acquainted, must cause me ever to look upon you with the utmost friendship and esteem.'

"'You flatter me, Mr. Mowbray,' I returned, 'by the feeling you so warmly express towards me; but I am gratified sufficiently by the assurance that it has been in my power to serve you, and I require nothing more.'

"'Well,' he observed, 'I suppose I must yield to you, but I trust that I shall yet be able to prevail upon you.'

"'I can make no promise of the kind,' I answered, 'for it is out of my power to comply with it. I am, however, I again assure you, fully sensible of the kindness of your intentions, and hope that you will find me worthy of them.'

"He bowed to this, though it was clear that he felt far from satisfied, and the topic of conversation was changed. In this manner the day passed away, which appeared to me a most tedious and irksome one, though my wife seemed to be more and more delighted with the manners and conversation of our visitor, and replied to the observations which he at different times addressed to her, in the most fulsome and extravagant strain, notwithstanding the significant looks which I at times fixed upon her.

"Mowbray seemed loth to depart, and it was not until the evening had far advanced that he arose from his seat to do so, and I could then plainly discern the regret and agitation which were expressed in the countenance of Flora, particularly when he respectfully raised her hand to his lips in bidding her farewell. The ardour of uncontrollable love betrayed itself in her every action, and I saw at once that all my efforts to conquer the feelings which she had imbibed within her breast would be unavailing; and I could not without the greatest difficulty conceal my real thoughts from the observation of Mowbray.

"'I presume,' he said, on leaving, 'that I shall not be considered intruding if I repeat my visits every day during the time I continue in this neighbourhood; for I am most anxious to snatch as much of your agreeable society as I possibly can.'

"'Of course,' I replied, 'I shall feel most proud by a visit from Mr. Mowbray at any time; though I should be sorry for him to neglect the business he is upon to do so.'

"'Oh,' he rejoined, 'as for that, it will not at all interfere with it, and I shall not forget to avail myself of the kind permission you have given me.'

"'I made no reply to this, and he directly afterwards took his leave, much to my relief, for the increased attentions he had paid to Flora, and the observations he had made to her, had strengthened my doubts and suspicions, and I felt uneasy and embarrassed in his company. Flora requested permission to retire soon after he had departed, and I, well judging of her feelings, raised no objection, and myself and my wife were left alone.

"'Mr. Mowbray appears more amiable and agreeable,' she remarked, 'every moment that we are in his society, and I declare that I am quite enraptured with him. I should think, Harry, after what has taken place this day, you must be inclined to change the opinion you formerly expressed of him?'

"'No, Alice,' I answered, 'indeed, I am not; for I am not to be so easily deceived by outside show, and I am still strongly of opinion that there is not that sincerity about Mr. Mowbray which you seem to imagine he possesses.'

"'How can you possibly be so unreasonable and uncharitable?' demanded Alice, with a look of vexation. 'I am sure I have watched him as narrowly as you could possibly have done, and I could notice nothing about him which should at all authorize such a suspicion of his character.'

"'My opinion is, Alice,' I returned, "that Mowbray has some other object in view in returning so soon to this neighbourhood than the one he has stated.'

"'What mean you?' she demanded.

"'Our daughter loves him,' I answered, 'and of that her every look and action, and observations, must convince him.'

"'Well,' said my wife 'and what if she does? Could she bestow her affections upon one more worthy of her?'

"'Yes,' I replied, 'I firmly believe that she might. And it shall be my task to endeavour to fathom out his real designs, and to counteract them. Such an alliance, even though his intentions should be honourable, is most strongly opposed to my wishes and inclinations. I have already, as you are aware, made Flora acquainted with my mind, and if she acts wisely, she will not fail to attend to and obey the advice I have given her. I heartily wish that this Alfred Mowbray had never been introduced to us, or that he was now far away from the neighbourhood of our dwelling.'

"'Well,' remarked Alice, impatiently, 'I see plain enough that you and I shall never agree upon this subject. You seem to view this young gentleman in the same light as if you already knew him in the character of a most consummate villain. This must surely be wrong, Henry, and is so unlike you that I can scarcely believe the evidence of my senses when I hear you talk so.'

" ' Well,' I returned, ' I may be wrong, and we will not, therefore, argue any further upon this subject for the present ; but, at any rate, I am determined to keep a strict eye upon his conduct, and likewise to guard our daughter, as far as lays in my power, against any evil designs which he may contemplate against her.'

" My wife returned no immediate answer, and the conversation dropped, and shortly afterwards we retired to our chamber.

" I will not tire your patience by detailing all the circumstances that took place while Mowbray was in the vicinity of our residence.

" He never missed a day visiting us, and every time he come, he appeared more ardent in his friendship towards me and my wife, and redoubled his attentions to Flora, which, in spite of all that I had said to her, she received with apparent pleasure, and evinced scarcely any of the embarrrassment when she was in his society that she had formerly done. Poor girl, he had completely triumphed over her heart, and she could never for a moment doubt him, or suspect the real villany of his character, and the diabolical designs he had in contemplation against her. No doubt he well perceived the power he had gained over her, and exulted at the prospect of success which seemed to await his nefarious designs. Whenever he was later in arriving at the cottage than usual, she evinced the greatest anxiety and impatience, and when he did make his appearance, the smiles with which she greeted him could not be misunderstood. You may judge of the uneasiness which this cost me, and there where times when I could scarcely endure the presence of Mowbray with any degree of patience, or help betraying to him the real thoughts that inhabited my breast. I often conversed with Flora upon this subject, and questioned her particularly as to whether Mowbray had made any confessson of love to her, or elicited from her an acknowledgment of a return ; but she always replied in the negative to my interrogatories, and I could not for a moment suspect that she would attempt to deceive me. Nevertheless, I was several times half resolved to prohibit his visits, or to demand from him an explanation as to the sentiments he entertained towards her.

" Mowbray had now returned to the neighbourhood more than five weeks, and there yet seemed no likelihood of his departure from it, and whenever I questioned him upon the subject, he always returned some evasive answer, which was anything but satisfactory, and only served to strengthen my suspicions. But I now come to one of the most important parts of my narrative. Mowbray had missed visiting the cottage one day, and Flora was in a state of the greatest agitation in consequence, though I rebuked her rather sharply for it, and reproached her for not having fulfilled the promise she had made to me. She left the presence of myself and her mother as soon as she conveniently could, and retired to her chamber, I had no doubt to give free and uninterrupted indulgence to the feelings of emotion that agitated her bosom.

" Alice was scarcely less uneasy than our daughter, and formed all kinds of conjectures as to what could be the cause of Mowbray's absenting himself ; but for my own part I felt satisfied at it, and was not without the hope that something of importance had caused his abrupt departure, and that he had not even had time to communicate it to us.

" The following morning Flora did not make her appearance at the usual hour at the breakfast table, and after waiting for her some time in vain, my wife, thinking that she had probably overslept herself, hastened to her chamber in order to arouse her. In a few minutes she returned with alarm depicted on her countenance, and then informed me, in reply to my eager inquiries, that Flora was not in her chamber.

" This somewhat astonished me, but I did not feel much alarm, for I concluded that she had merely taken an early walk, as she was sometimes accustomed to do before breakfast, and had been induced by the fineness of the weather to ramble farther than she had at first intended. However, when more than an hour had passed away and still she returned not, I became uneasy, and determined to start forth in search of her.

" I traversed all her favourite walks, and inquired of my neighbours to endeavour to ascertain whether any one had seen her, but to no purpose, for I could neither see nor hear anything of her, and I now became seriously alarmed, and the most dismal forebodings crossed my mind that something had happened to her. I stood for a few minutes and hesitated how to act, but at length a sudden thought occurred to me, and I determined to go to the inn at which Mowbray had been staying, in order to ascertain from him whether he had seen anything of her. I hastened thither accordingly, and was there informed, to my astonishment and dismay, that Mowbray had departed suddenly from the inn before daylight in the morning, in a private carriage which had been brought there the evening before for his use.

"A feeling of dread now came over me on receiving this intelligence, and my worst fears were all but confirmed. I hastily inquired of the innkeeper if he knew the place of Mowbray's destination; but he declared that he did not, and unable to obtain any further information from him, I returned hurriedly towards my home, giving myself up to the most dreadful and torturing apprehensions. For some time after I had received this information from the landlord of the inn, I was so completely thunderstruck, bewildered, and agitated, that I was unable to speak or to move; but at length, aroused by the violence of my fears and suspicions into action, I put some more questions to the landlord of the inn, with the view of eliciting whether or not he knew anything of the destination of Mowbray, but without being able to gain any further intelligence from him which could throw the least light upon the subject. I quitted the house, and with a heavy heart I made my way towards home, but still inquiring as I proceeded of all whom I met whether they had seen anything of my unfortunate daughter; but, in every instance, I was doomed to the most bitter and torturing disappointment; and I could come to no other conclusion than that my worst fears were realised, and that my poor unsuspecting Flora, influenced by the violence of her passion, had fallen a victim to the insidious artifices of Mowbray. His abrupt departure from the inn, and the sudden disappearance of my daughter at the same time, all but confirmed those painful surmises, and as I walked on my way home, I could not help breathing curses upon his head, and vowing a terrible revenge should I by any chance encounter him again.

"In this state of mind, I arrived once more at my cottage, and found my wife in the greatest state of anxiety and alarm, for Flora had not returned; and when she saw me come back unaccompanied by her, she could not but entertain the most terrible fears that something of a fatal nature had happened to her. She eagerly inquired of me as to the result of my search; and when I informed her, she wrung her hands in despair and was completely overwhelmed with grief. I was equally as much agitated as herself, and for some time I paced the room, giving utterance to my emotion in incoherent sentences, and at intervals invoking the most bitter maledictions upon the head of Mowbray.

"'My poor Flora,' sobbed my wife; 'alas! what has become of you? What can be the cause of your absenting yourself from us in this sudden and mysterious manner? Surely you can never have been so cruel and undutiful as to abandon us altogether.'

"'Yes,' I returned, in accents of mingled grief and reproach, 'you now see that the suspicions which I entertained, and which you so totaly disregarded and ridiculed, are all but confirmed. The villain Mowbray has triumphed in his diabolical designs, and the innocence of our child is destroyed for ever. May the retributive vengeance of Heaven pursue him, and by the most torturing and unceasing future remorse, in some degree punish him for the crime of which he has been guilty.'

"'My God!' exclaimed Alice, again wringing her hands, 'surely it is impossible; it cannot be; Flora could never so far forget the virtuous principles we have instilled into her breast, and Mowbray could never become the black-hearted wretch as to be guilty of the crime which you have imputed to him. She will return, and at once banish all our fears and suspicions.'

"'Still credulous,' I returned, passionately and impatiently; 'had you taken my advice, and not been dazzled by the accomplishments and apparent sincerity of this man whom Fate so unfortunately sent to throw a blight upon our happiness, this might not have happened. But you derided all my arguments; was flattered by his fulsome compliments and supposed wealth; gave every encouragement to the fatal passion of Flora, whose inexperience and confiding nature were so apt to lead her astray, and you now see the consequences. Oh, Alice, foolish woman, you have, alas, yourself much to blame!'

"'Oh, my husband,' she sighed, in a voice completely broken by the violence of her emotions; 'do not, I implore you, so harshly reproach me; for I acted only from the impulse of my heart, and affectionate regard for what I considered to be the welfare and happiness of our poor child. I may have been to blame, but I have erred not wilfully; and I could not help thinking that the suspicions you expressed of the real character of Mowbray, were unfounded and uncharitable. But even now I cannot come to the dreadful conclusion that he has acted so monstrous a part, or that Flora, our innocent and affectionate Flora, has suffered herself to be thus cruelly betrayed. God of Heaven, hear my prayer, and avert so terrible a calamity.'

"I returned no answer, but again traversed the room in a state of mind which it would be useless for me to attempt to describe, and continued at intervals to invoke the heaviest curses upon the head of Mowbray, whilst Alice threw herself in a chair, and covering her face with her hands, gave herself up to a paroxysm of the most violent grief.

"In this manner another half hour passed away, and still Flora did not return, and now both myself and Alice were worked up to a pitch of the most complete anguish and despair. It seemed quite evident that our most painful conjectures were correct, and that our unfortunate and too-confiding child was the companion of the flight of Mowbray, and if so, her ruin was certain. Oh, how agonising was that thought; and how fatally was it destined to be realised. But after a short time we somewhat aroused ourselves, and resolved once more to examine the chamber of Flora to see if we could discover anything to confirm our fears. We entered it with sad and foreboding hearts, and the melancholy desertion of the place served but to increase the depression of our spirits. The bed had evidently not been entered, but had only been reclined on by Flora, and we discovered that a small cabinet in the room was open, and several of the principle articles of wearing apparel were taken from it. This was a more fatal proof of the truth of our surmises than anything we had yet seen, and we again gave vent to our feelings of despair.

"'It is too true,' I ejaculated; 'she has gone—she has deserted us; wretched girl, thou art ruined—lost for ever! Oh, God! to think that after all the care and affection we have bestowed upon you it should come to this!'

"'Alas! alas!' groaned Alice, and the tears streamed rapidly down her cheeks, 'I can scarcely bring myself to believe the fatal truth. Flora could never so have forgotten every feeling of virtue and duty as to resign herself to the will of the tempter, and abandon us to misery and despair. We wrong her by the supposition—I am convinced that we do; she has only wandered beyond her usual limits, and will yet return, and remove

the terrrible doubts that now distract our minds.'

"'Cease, Alice,' I returned, impatiently; "to encourage any such futile hopes is erroneous, and can only end in disappointment. It is too evident that she is gone, and that she is the companion of the villain Mowbray. Poor deluded girl, into what shame and misery have you plunged yourself and your unhappy parents!'

"I was turning towards the window, when, happening to cast my eyes upon a small table that stood by the side of it, I beheld a letter, and hastily snatching it up, I saw that it was in the handwriting of Flora, and addressed to myself and her mother.

"'Ah!' I exclaimed, 'this is enough; this will, doubtless, explain and confirm all.'

"Read, read!" cried Alice, in a voice of extreme emotion and anxiety.

"With a trembling hand I unfolded the letter, and in a faltering voice I read aloud the following words, which were frequently rendered almost illegible by the tears which Flora had evidently shed in writing them:—

"'Beloved Parents,

"'With a trembling hand I venture to address these few lines to you, in order to explain the apparent undutifulness and culpability of my conduct, and with the faint hope of receiving your forgiveness for the step I have taken, and to which I have been urged by the power of an affection which, in spite of all your arguments, advice, and injunctions, I have found it impossible to conquer. Oh, my dear parents, did you but know the anguish and anxiety of mind I am at present enduring, methinks you would pity me. By the time you receive this letter I shall be far away from that home which has ever been so dear to me; but I trust to God that I shall soon be permitted to return to it, and to receive your blessing and forgiveness for this my first and only act of disobedience to your will. Almost from the first moment that we beheld each other, a passion has sprung up between myself and Alfred Mowbray as fervent as it is sincere; but you, my dear father, disapproved of it, and I was driven to despair, though I found it was impossible for me to stifle it within my breast. The more I sought to do so, the more powerful became the influence it had over me, and I felt that my whole hopes of future happiness were centred in Alfred Mowbray. He confessed his love, and drew from me an acknowledgment in return. He would have disclosed his sentiments to you, and asked your consent to pay his addresses to me, but I, knowing the prejudices which you so unfortunately entertained against him, prevented him. He then proposed to me a secret marriage, but I at first shrunk from such a proposition from the repugnance I felt at such an idea, but he urged his suit with such eloquence that I could no longer doubt the honour and sincerity of his intentions, and I at last yielded to his wishes. May God forgive me if I have acted wrong, but I can never believe that my beloved Alfred will deceive me. At an early hour this morning, he is to have a carriage ready to receive me, and we then hasten to be united in the indissoluble bonds of matrimony. Probably by the time your eye peruses this epistle I shall have become his wife, and I place too much confidence in the love of my revered parents to believe that, when they have maturely and calmly reflected upon all the peculiar circumstances in which I have been placed, they will reproach me for the course which I have taken, and on which my future happiness so entirely depends. In a short time you shall hear from me again, and I will then inform you where you may communicate with me and my husband. God grant that you may be willing to receive us both as your children, and that you will not reproach us for that which then cannot be recalled. Farewell for the present, my beloved parents, and pity and forgive your ever affectionate daughter,

                                'FLORA.'

"'Wretched! rash, misguided girl!' I exclaimed, when I had finished the perusal of this letter; 'you are lost, eternally lost! You have fallen into the snares of the base and heartless deceiver, and brought disgrace and misery upon yourself and your too fond and indulgent parents. Oh, what a crafty, designing wretch is he to whom you have sacrificed your innocence and your love. May all the curses that retributive Heaven can heap upon him, descend upon his head.'

"'Oh, hold, my husband!' remonstrated Alice, shocked and alarmed by the vehemence of my manner; 'do not thus cruelly condemn him until you have had ample proof of his duplicity. Our poor child places the utmost reliance upon the honour of his intentions, and I do not think she will be deceived. He will make her his wife, and——'

"'His wife!' I hastily interrupted; 'and think you that I am so inexperienced in the world that I am to be thus cajolled by his flattering professions, and

empty promises? Is it all a delusion, and a snare. The villain has triumphed in his well-laid designs, and Flora is ruined and degraded for ever. And this is the return that we receive for the affection and indulgence we have bestowed upon her. Alas! ungrateful, disobedient girl, you will have bitter cause to repent of this.'

"'Forbear, Henry,' ejaculated Alice, 'do not judge our poor child so harshly, or reproach her so severely. A short time only, I trust, will elapse, and you will then be convinced that your fears are unfounded, and Flora will be restored to us, to render our future days those of happiness and content.'

"'No, Alice, no,' I answered, in a tone which showed the despair under which I laboured; 'it would be next to madness to encourage any such an idea. All hope of that is past for ever. Our child has become the victim of a heartless scoundrel, and that innocence which has hitherto been our pride and admiration is superseded by shame and misery. Make her his wife! It is false as his own black heart; but so great is the fatal power that he has gained over her affections and her unsuspecting nature that he, no doubt, has found but little difficulty in persuading her. Oh, Flora, unfortunate, misguided, imprudent girl! why did you not listen to the advice I so properly tendered you? Into what a dreadful abyss have you precipitated yourself; and from which it is now impossible to extricate you!'

"I beat my breast in anguish and despair as I gave utterance to these words, and my wife was, if possible, more agitated than myself. It was quite evident that she now saw plainly the force of my arguments, and participated in my apprehensions, though she endeavoured to conceal her real feelings from my observation, and tried to persuade me to think differently to the manner in which I had expressed myself.

"'Come, my dear husband,' she ejaculated, stifling her emotion as well as she could; 'do not give way to this abject despair, but let us seek to put our trust in the goodness of Providence, who surely will protect our daughter from the fate you apprehend. I cannot persuade myself that Mowbray could be the atrocious miscreant to seek to destroy the innocence of that poor girl who loves him so fondly, and who has placed every confidence in his honour and integrity.'

"'Talk not thus preposterously, Alice,' I quickly returned, 'for I have not patience to listen to you. Had the intentions of Mowbray been honourable, he would not for a moment have hesitated to reveal his mind to me, and have scorned to act in the shameful and clandestine manner he has done. His motives are too transparent to be misunderstood by any one who has had any experience at all in the world. He is a systematic and practised libertine, and now, alas! Flora is added to the long list of victims who, doubtless, have fallen beneath his guilty stratagems. Ere this she has probably become a poor lost and degraded being, and has brought disgrace upon our hitherto unblemished name. For soon she will find the ruin into which she has plunged herself, and her seducer having triumphed in his diabolical designs, will cast her from him, and will leave her to shame and sorrow.'

"'Oh, horrible thought!' exclaimed Alice; 'it surely can never be realised. Alfred Mowbray must, indeed, be one of the most consummate villains that ever disgraced society if he could be guilty of such atrocities as those to which you have alluded. But you must lose no time in searching for them, and——'

"'Oh, no,' I interrupted, shaking my head in a despairing manner; 'it is too late; the fatal deed, it is too probable, is by this time accomplished; and whither is it possible for me to direct my footsteps in pursuit of them? She is lost—she is lost! and nothing, alas! can save her from the evils which I apprehend. But, by all my hopes I swear, that, should I ever again encounter him, I will have a most terrible revenge, let the consequences to myself be whatever they may.'

"Alice was too deeply affected to make any reply, and we at length quitted the chamber, and descended to the room down stairs, where we gave the most unrestrained indulgence to our grief. Oh, what a wretched day was this to us; we had never before experienced such a one, and every moment our despair and anguish increased instead of abating. Our neighbours, who quickly became acquainted with what had happened, deeply sympathised with us in our misfortune, and endeavoured to console us, but their efforts were crowned with little or no success, and the longer we reflected upon all the melancholy circumstances of the case, the greater became the violence of our grief. Many were the curses that I continued to invoke upon the head of Mowbray, while, when I reflected upon the probable fate of that poor child on whom I had ever bestowed so much affection, and in whose future happiness and welfare all my principal hopes had been fixed, I could have

wept like a boy; and I saw plainly that all the bright prospects I had so fondly indulged in, were annihilated for ever.

"Several days passed away, and still we heard nothing more of our unfortunate daughter, or the villain with whom she had eloped; and this silence on her part could not fail to add to our despair, and to convince us of the truth of our apprehensions. I had made the most minute inquiries for miles around the neighbourhood, but I could get not the least intelligence of them, or gain any clue to the place of their concealment. I had not the least doubt that Mowbray had imposed upon her by a false marriage, and that he had not failed to adopt every precaution to prevent her from corresponding with us. Had he acted the honourable part he had professed to do, he would not have delayed a moment in banishing our anguish and suspense, either by writing to inform us where they were, or by presenting himself and Flora to us, and seeking our forgiveness for the clandestine step they had taken. There was the damning stamp of villany and treachery upon all his proceedings, and I saw at once that our misery was complete.

"'Alas!' I ejaculated, 'what a cursed fate it was that introduced him to us; why did he not perish in the storm, rather than be preserved to inflict upon us the cruel injuries that he has done? Oh, Flora, my unfortunate child, little did I dream that you would ever come to such a fate as this. Better, much better, would it have been for you and us had you died in your infancy. And what art thou now? A thing of shame, whom the world will point at with scorn, and shun you as though you were something contagious.'

"'Oh, Harry,' said my wife, with a look which sufficiently bespoke the nature of her feelings, 'I shudder to contemplate it. My poor girl! may Heaven watch over and protect you from the dreadful fate which we apprehend has befallen you. Alas! what could ever have induced you to abandon your too fond and indulgent parents! But I cannot yet resign all my hopes that you have had virtue and fortitude to resist the temptations of that man who has so unfortunately gained such powerful influence over your affections; and that you will yet be restored to us as pure and unsullied as when you left us.'

"'Alice,' I replied, impatiently, 'what madness is there in that thought. Did she not willingly resign herself to the protection of Mowbray, and place the most unlimited confidence in his honour, and think you that he has not ere now succeeded in accomplishing his infamous and brutal designs? If you can persuade yourself as your words would seem to imply, you must be far more credulous than I could ever have believed you to be.'

"'Alas!' she returned, 'is there no reason to hope? And shall we never behold her again?'

"'Alice,' I answered, 'it would be better for us not to do so; for how could we bear to gaze upon the fearful wreck of that which was once so lovely? Oh, God, the thought drives me to madness, and I could almost curse the hour she was born.'

"'Forbear, Henry,' remonstrated my wife; 'I must not hear you give utterance to such words as those. Flora may have fallen, though Heaven forbid that she should have done so, but we can never forget that she is our child, and that she has been the unfortunate victim of the most consummate villany.'

"'Had she followed my advice,' I remarked, 'and obeyed my injunctions, as it was her duty to do, she would never have met with the degrading and miserable fate which has doubtless now befallen her. Oh, Alice, although you may naturally enough endeavour to excuse her, she has been much to blame, as I fear she will too soon find to her sorrow; and you have yourself been guilty of the most culpable error in encouraging her in the indulgence of that passion, which I saw too plainly would be attended with the most fatal consequences, if it was not stifled in its infancy. But I will not now reproach you, for Heaven knows that you have already enough to torture and distract your mind.'

"'Alas! I have indeed,' sighed Alice; 'little did I ever anticipate that it would come to this; and what was there in the conduct of Mowbray that should cause me to suspect him? Oh, would that Flora would write to us again, to ease the terrible doubts and suspense that at present distract our minds, and to make us acquainted with the place where herself and Mowbray are now residing.'

"'It is not likely that her betrayer will fail to take every means to prevent her from doing so,' I answered; 'and shame and remorse will also restrain her. Alas! alas! how terribly has one of the loveliest of God's creatures fallen; and what can ever compensate us for the loss we have sustained, and the brutal injuries that have been inflicted on us? The miscreant Mowbray, no doubt, is now exulting in the diabolical triumph he has obtained over his too credulous and confiding victim,

and when he has fully gratified his unholy passions, he will cast her from him, and leave her to all the misery of despair and remorse.'

"'Heaven forbid that your fearful prognostications should be realised,' ejaculated Alice; 'but he can surely never prove himself so abandoned a miscreant. But should our poor child really have fallen in the manner you anticipate, surely you would not refuse to forgive her, and to receive the poor unfortunate to your bosom with all the affection you ever bestowed upon her?'

"'Oh, Alice,' I returned, 'how painful is the question you have put to me, and I know not how to answer you. How could I ever trust myself to look again upon her, when I knew her degradation? My heart would surely break, or madness would seize upon my brain.'

"'For the love of Heaven calm your feelings, my husband,' said Alice, 'and endeavour to hope that all will terminate much better than you can now anticipate. I cannot yet bring my mind to believe that Mowbray will fail to fulfil the promises he has made, and that Flora is not now his wife.'

"'Pshaw!' I retorted impatiently, 'how wildly and ridiculously you talk, Alice; does not his silence confirm my worst suspicions? Had he fulfilled his promises, would he not have informed us of it without delay, especially when he must be fully aware of the dreadful state of anxiety and suspense we are in? There is not the least room for us to hope: and every moment can but serve to add to the misery of our feelings.'

"'But you will not abandon your search after her?' said my wife; 'it might not yet be too late to save her, and——'

"'Alas!' I interrupted, 'it is a hopeless task. Whither can I direct my steps where I may be likely to find her? The villain Mowbray will be sure to keep her closely concealed.'

"'At any rate it is your duty to make inquiries at Mowbray Hall,' observed my wife, 'and if they are not there, you may, in all probability, be there able to obtain information where to find them.'

"'I will do so; I will depart for there to-morrow,' I answered; 'but I fear my task will be a hopeless one.'

"The next morning, with a heavy heart, I took my departure on the coach for the neighbourhood in which Mowbray had informed us the hall was situated, and on the way I firmly resolved in my own mind to have a terrible revenge on Mowbray if I should meet him, and discover that

FLORA HAWTHORN MOURNING THE RETURN OF MOWBRAY.

my suspicions of the villanous part he had played were correct. Nothing particular or at all worthy of recording occurred on the journey, and in the course of a few hours I arrived at the place of my destination. But in vain I searched for the hall; there was no such a building in that neighbourhood, and Mowbray was completely unknown to every one of whom I inquired; and thus were all the apprehensions and surmises I had from the first entertained, realised, and my agony and despair were rendered complete. Flora had, indeed fallen a sacrifice to the artifices and guilty machinations of one of the most consummate villains that ever disgraced society, and it seemed but too probable that I should never behold her again. I had now no doubt but that Mowbray was nothing more than an experienced adventurer, and that the story he had told me and my wife regarding his family connexions and the wealth he possessed was entirely false; and that conviction, if possible, excited my indignation the more. Again I invoked the most terrible maledictions upon his head, and had I at that moment encountered him, I verily believe that I should not have hesitated to make an attempt upon his life, such was the terrible state of my excited feelings.

Having failed in my object, I lost no time in returning home, and the despair and anguish of my wife on learning the result of my journey, you may readily conjecture. She was now satisfied that all my suspicions were correct, and for some time she was completely overwhelmed with grief, and quite inconsolabe. The fate of Flora now seemed certain, and our hearts were almost broken; especially when we thought that we should probably never behold her again. It was a dreadful blow for us, and I know not how we could find strength to support it with the fortitude we did. Day after day, and week after week elapsed, and we could gain no information that was at all calculated to quiet our suspense and anxiety; and the most terrible fears continually haunted our imaginations; and among others was the one that Flora had perished by the hands of her betrayer, who, having gratified his wishes, would in all probability be anxious to rid himself of his unfortunate victim, and so conceal his shame from the world. I need not tell you the anguish that this fearful idea cost us, and every hour it increased in strength. After what had taken place, I could not help believing that Mowbray was capable of anything. But I must hasten to the conclusion of my melancholy story, which has already occupied more of your time than I thought it would.

"Three months elapsed in this dismal manner, and Alice took the loss of her daughter so much to heart, that she was for some time in a most dangerous state, and I began to fear that I should also be deprived of her. As for myself, I was a prey to the utmost misery and despair, and for some time I was rendered totally incapable of following my usual employment; but at length, by a powerful effort, I was enabled partly to arouse myself, and I exerted myself to the utmost to calm the feelings of Alice, in which I but indifferently succeeded.

"The winter season had now set in, and the weather was very severe. There had been a succession of storms for several days past; and there seemed to be not the least prospect at present of any favourable change taking place.

"It was night, and myself and Alice were seated in the parlour of our cottage, listening to the dismal voice of the tempest which raged so violently in the heavens, and at times conversing upon the melancholy subject that was nearest our hearts.

"'What a fearful night it is,' said my wife, 'and how greatly are those unfortunate beings to be pitied who are exposed to its fury. Alas! where, in this awful hour, is our poor fallen child?—Perhaps she is wandering a wretched, friendless outcast in the world; with no place where she can seek a shelter, or look for pity and relief. My God! how torturing is that thought! How terrible is the fate which has befallen her!'

"'And what curses ought we not to invoke upon the head of her brutal destroyer?' I ejaculated vehemently. 'Never could greater villany disgrace society; and may the most terrible retribution of Heaven pursue him for the misery he has caused.'

"'And it will do so, my dear husband,' returned Alice, 'you may depend upon that; for the Almighty will never suffer one who has been guilty of such an enormous crime as that which Mowbray has committed, to go unpunished."

"Fiercer and fiercer raged the storm, and seldom do I remember a more awful night either at sea or on land. The voice of the howling wind was perfectly terrific, and shook our habitation to its very centre; rain, and snow, and hail seemed to emulate each other in the fury of their wrath, and the roaring of the angry ocean might be heard even above the voice of the blast. My wife gazed at me with mingled looks of awe and terror, and I must confess that I could not help feeling a sensation of dread as I listened to the battling of the elements, and a foreboding of something fearful about to happen took possession of my mind.

"A silence of several minutes ensued, for both myself and Alice were too much confounded and appalled by the unusual horrors of the night to speak; but at length I walked to the window and gazed more minutely upon the tempest which was raging without; and frightful indeed was the scene which, as well as the almost impenetrable darkness would permit me, met my sight. I will not attempt to describe it; for I should fail if I were to do so, but I will rather leave it to your imagination. I returned to Alice, who was trembling in her chair, and muttering prayers to herself.

"'Oh, Harry,' she said at last, ' what a truly fearful night is this; how many a poor creature will be hastily summoned to the presence of its Maker, with all its sins upon its head. God help those who are this night exposed to the mercy of the infuriated elements.'

"'Amen!' I solemnly returned; 'God help and protect the hardy mariner, and the houseless wanderer.'

"'Our poor child!' ejaculated Alice, in a broken voice, and the tears started to her eyes. "Oh, what an agonizing pang shot through my heart at the mention of that name, and I groaned aloud, and beat my breast in the anguish of my despair.

"'Wretched, deluded, too confiding girl!' I exclaimed; 'alas! too well do I predict the fate to which you are now exposed. Probably despised, deserted by that man on whose truth and honour you so entirely and fatally depended, and left to wander a wretched and degraded being, without one person in the world to look down on you with an eye of pity, or to afford you any assistance.'

"'My God!' gasped forth my wife, 'the picture is too horrible! Our Flora— our once beauteous and innocent Flora exposed to all the horrors of such a night as this; with no place to shelter her head, no sympathising breast to administer to her wants or soothe her sorrows; it cannot be! The Almighty in His infinite mercy will never permit this. Alas! what has become of her? Why has she not written to us, to ease the terrible doubts upon our mind, and to inform us of her real situation?'

"'Ah! Alice," I answered, 'shame and remorse would not suffer her to do so, and probably the heartless villain to whom she owes her destruction would take good care to prevent her. She is lost to us for ever; one of the most lovely of nature's creations is taken from us by the fell destroyer who assumed so hypocritical a disguise to accomplish his diabolical designs, and there is nothing left for us but to mourn her fate, and to pray to Heaven to pardon her for that of which she has been guilty. But may curses, tenfold curses light upon the head of the wretch who has been the cause of all this misery and ruin, and may his death-bed be attended with all the horrors of remorse and despair."

"I clenched my fists, and struck my head violently as I thus spoke, and the convulsive sobs of overwhelming anguish that escaped the bosom of my wife were quite pitiable to hear. Again a pause for some minutes took place, and we continued to listen to the storm in the same state of awe and terror, and without being able to console or advise each other under the dismal circumstances.

"In this manner more than an hour must have elapsed, and no change took place in the weather; there was not the least prospect of its abating, and we shuddered as we still thought upon the awful destruction to human life which must that night take place. There was, however, a temporary pause in the howling of the blast, and I suddenly started to my feet, and looked earnestly at my wife, as I imagined I heard a plaintive and wailing sound borne upon the air towards our dwelling, as if it proceeded from some human voice; and Alice evidently had heard the cry also.

"'Ah! what sound was that?' she ejaculated; 'it was not the wailing or whistling of the wind, I feel convinced; did you not hear it, Henry?"

"'I did,' answered I; 'it appeared to me like the voice of some unfortunate human being in distress. Hark! 'tis there again!'

"The cry was indeed repeated, and that time much more distinctly than it had been before, and it seemed to proceed from no great distance from the cottage.

"'It must be some wretched creature who is exposed to the fury of the storm,' said Alice, 'and whom we may be the means of rescuing from death. Come, my husband, do not let us delay exerting ourselves in the cause of humanity.'

"She was prevented from proceeding further by a loud noise as if of something falling heavily against the door of our cottage, which was burst open by the violence of the shock, but the torrent of hail and snow which burst into the room on the opening of the door so confused us, that we were unable for a moment or two to ascertain the cause. When, however, we had in some measure recovered from our surprise, we perceived a human form, and that, too, of a female, stretched insensible half way across the threshold. With trembling but hasty footsteps we advanced towards it, but stood appalled at the sight which presented itself to our gaze. The tattered garments which the unfortunate creature wore could scarcely conceal its nakedness, and those were drenched and covered with the snow, and the limbs appeared to be completely frozen with the cold. A terrible foreboding flashed across my brain, and I almost feared to touch the insensible wanderer, lest my worst apprehensions should be verified; but at length I stooped down, and ventured to raise the inanimate form, while my wife held the lamp to her face, in order that we might more readily be enabled to observe her features; but no sooner did the light fall upon them, than we uttered a simultaneous cry of the most indescribable horror! Oh, God! it was her whom we had so long mourned; it was her of whom we had been so basely, so cruelly deprived; it was our poor ruined, unfortunate, and once innocent daughter.

"I must pause for a few moments to recover myself from the anguish which the remembrance of the horrors of that hour creates within my brest, and you, my hind friends, will, I trust, bear with me, aud sympathise with me in my feelings."

Richard and his wife, who were deeply affected by the narrative, returned no answer to this, but their looks sufficiently expressed what they meant, and Hawthorn retired to another part of the room, where, covering his face with his hands, he resigned himself for a few minutes to the dismal and torturing thoughts that crowded upon his mind, and endeavoured, as well as he could, to regain his composure. At length, having apparently recovered, he once more seated himself, and resumed his story in the following words:

"Yes, it was, indeed, our wretched child, whose insensible, cold, and emaciated form, I now held in my arms; but, oh, Heaven, how awful and deplorable was the wreck of what once was so beautiful and so innocent, that we now gazed upon. Her countenance was ghastly and cadaverous—her features haggered and careworn—her eyes sunk deep into her head, and her cheeks hollow as that of a corpse! Her hair was hanging wild and dishevelled over her shoulders; the grace of her person had fled, and the bones seemed all but protruding through her skin! You may well judge of what the distracted feelings of her hapless mother and myself must have been as we gazed on this truly frightful spectacle, and read at once the whole history of her sufferings. It was wonderful that the fearful shock did not cause our immediate deaths.

" 'My child! my wretched, betrayed child!' I exclaimed, with a burst of agony, which I feel it utterly impossible to describe. "Oh, God! and has it, indeed, come to this? May the tortures of perdition pursue the diabolical miscreant who has been the cause of this!'

" 'Heaven help us, and have mercy on us!' cried Alice, as again and again she kissed the ghastly cheeks of our daughter; 'my Flora!—my only one!—my—Oh, God! she is dead! Fate has but guided her footsteps hither to perish in our presence! My child! and wilt thou never look upon or speak to us again? I shall go mad!'

" 'No, no,' I returned, hastily, as I carried the poor girl to the fire, and placed her in a chair; 'she is not dead, she still breathes! The Almighty will surely aid our efforts, and once more, in His infinite mercy, restore her to us. For Heaven's sake, compose yourself, Alice, and let us see to her recovery.'

"In a state of the most indescribable agony, my wife chafed her frozen limbs, and applied all such other remedies as we could think of, but although she still breathed, she gave no signs of returning consciousness. We now placed her, with as little delay as possible, in a warm bed, and having called in one of the female neighbours to the assistance of Alice, I hastened, regardless of the storm, to the nearest medical man, whose attendance at my cottage I procured with the least possible delay, and who somewhat abated our alarm by giving it as his opinion, that, although she was in a most deplorable and precarious situation, that there were strong hopes that, in consequence of her youth, she would ultimately recover, though it would require time, and the utmost care, to enable her to do so.

"I need not tell you with what painful care and anxiety myself and my wife continued to watch by the bedside of the sufferer during the night; but although we had succeeded in imparting some of their natural wamth to her limbs, and she breathed more freely, she exhibited no signs of returning consciousness, and, as you may imagine, we were still not without our most torturing doubts and apprehensions.

"On divesting her of her tattered garments, we discovered in her bosom a letter, which fully confirmed our worst surmises, and proved at once, if we could have doubted for a moment, the heartless villany of Mowbray. It was couched in the following language, and you may judge of the anguish and disgust of myself and Alice as we persued it:—

" 'Dear Flora,—for dear you must ever be to me while life remains, notwithstanding the present apparent cruelty of my conduct—I write you these few lines with a heavy and desponding heart, to bid you farewell for ever! I have deceived you, Flora, but I was impelled by fate and unfortuitous circumstances to do so, and I trust that Heaven will, if you cannot, forgive me. Our marriage was but a mockery, for there are circumstances connected with me, independent of my limited means, for I am but a poor man, which prevent me from venturing upon the hazardous sea of matrimony, though so great and powerful was the passion with which your manifold charms had inspired me, that I could not resist the temptation into which I have been led, and which has unfortunately placed you in such a delicate and melancholy position. I know that I shall be considered a villain, but I cannot recall the past; and believe me, Flora, that no one is more deeply stung with remorse than yours faithfully till death,

'ALFRED MOWBRAY.'

"This letter was addressed to 'Flora H—, The White Farm, Sanbury,' and I determined, as soon as Flora might be out of danger, to hasten thither, and endeavour to ascertain all the particulars I could.

"'The heartless miscreant!' I cried, when I had read this letter aloud to Alice; 'the shameless hypocrite! Oh, what a brutal, an unmanly advantage has he taken of the confiding innocence of our unfortunate child. And then to abandon her thus! Good God! how terrible must have been the sufferings she has endured to be reduced to such a dreadful state as this. But by all my hopes, I will search him out, and will not rest until I have had a terrible revenge for the irreparable wrongs he has inflicted upon us.'

"'The tale he told too about his wealth is all erroneous,' said Alice; 'in this letter he admits himself to be a poor man.'

"'Yes,' I returned, 'he is, as I always suspected him to be, an unprincipled adventurer. What a cursed fate it was that introduced him to us. Why did I not persist in forbidding his visits to our cottage after he had once quitted it?'

"'Do not reproach yourself, my husband,' remarked Alice, 'for indeed you have not been to blame; little did I suspect that one possessed of such a plausible exterior could inherit so base a heart. Our poor child, what a melancholy fate is hers; but thank God that she is restored to us, even the poor blighted flower that she is; and should she recover, it must be our task, as it is our duty, not to reproach her for what has happened, but to endeavour to console her under her misfortunes.

"'True, Alice,' I replied; 'but alas! I fear that nothing will have the power to afford her consolation under the awful circumstances in which she is placed. Her brain will be distracted by shame and remorse, and I have too much reason to apprehend that the villain Mowbray has struck the fatal blow which will hasten her to a premature grave!'

"'Oh, say not so,' ejaculated Alice, 'but rather let us hope for the best. Providence will not visit us with so terrible a calamity,

and poor Flora will yet be restored to peace and resignation, if not to happiness.'

"I shook my head doubtingly, and the conversation terminated, and we returned to the chamber of our daughter, and continued to watch by the side of her couch with unabated anxiety and anguish, but no particular change took place during the night, though the doctor pronounced it as his opinion that all danger was past.

"It was not till about the middle of the next day that Flora was restored to anything like life; when she opened her eyes, she gazed wildly around her, did not seem to recognise any one, and was evidently unconscious of where she was, those who surrounded her, or what had happened. Oh, how terrible was the anguish that my wife and I now experienced; affectionately we hung over her, wept upon her pale cheeks, and called upon her name, but she knew us not; stared vacantly upon us, uttered a few wild and incoherent words to herself, and then relapsed into a state of insensibility. We augured the worst from these ominous symptons, and were completely inconsolable. Two or three days confirmed our apprehension, for although she had recovered sufficient strength of body to be enabled to leave her bed, it was but too painfully evident that her reason was gone, and there seemed at present but little chance of its being restored to her.

"With what feelings of poignant agony did we gaze upon her, as she was seated in the same room with us, and how ardently did we strive, by every fond endearment, to recall her to recollection, but without effect. She seemed perfectly conscious of our kindness and attention, and to be grateful for it, but yet she knew us not, and her disordered imagination seemed to wander to far different objects, thus annihilating our hopes, and increasing our misery.

"What a terrible change was now wrought in that which was once so beautiful and innocent. It is true that the pale and careworn aspect of her countenance had disappeared, and her form had assumed many of its former graces; but still there was a wildness in the expression of her eyes, which told of the wreck of reason and destruction which had taken place, and there was that about her laugh which was rather calculated to excite awe and trembling than that unbounded sensation of pleasure which it could not fail once to impart.

"Sometimes we fancied that she had a dreamy recollection of us, and in those moments how eagerly did we endeavour to arouse her, by all the means that could suggest themselves to us ; but it was all to no purpose ; an idiotic laugh would, perhaps, be the only return we met with, and all was again darkness and insensibility.

"I now lost no time in repairing to the place to which the letter from the villain Mowbray to Flora was directed, and had no difficulty in finding it out. It was a small farm-house, inhabited by a Mr. Dewsbury and his wife, and two daughters, and immediately making known to them the object of my visit, they expressed the utmost sympathy with me in my misfortunes, and readily offered to furnish me with all the information in their power. They began by acquainting me that they had no knowledge of Mowbray whatever, prior to his introducing himself to them at the farm, which he had done a few months previously, and stating that he was a gentleman, and but recently married, unknown to his friends and relations ; he had a wish to reside with some respectable and private family for a time in retirement until he could effect a reconciliation with his friends. He added that the former was above all other places best suited to his wishes, and was most anxious that we should be able to come to some arrangement.

"'His manners were so prepossessing,' added Mr. Dewsbury, 'and the circumstances he stated were so reasonable, that myself and my wife could not have the least suspicion, and as we had every convenience, we immediately came to terms, and the next day Mr. Beaumont (which was the name he had introduced himself to us by) and your daughter, whom we supposed to be his wife, took up their residence with us at the farm, and their conduct was of that exemplary description that they quickly gained upon our friendship. Mrs. Beaumont, as we believed her to be, particularly won our admiration, for we thought her one of the most amiable and charming young women we had ever met with, and we looked forward with regret to the time when they should think proper to depart. They appeared to be doatingly fond of each other, though your daughter at times seemed to labour under a melancholy depression of spirits which she could not conquer. but the cause of which we, of course, did not venture to inquire into. Mr. Beaumont for some time paid her the greatest attention, and only seemed happy when in her society, and nothing whatever transpired to give us cause to surmise that they were not united ; but suddenly there was a change took place in his habits, though his affection towards her seemed to suffer no abatement. He fre-

quently absented himself from the farm, and would be gone for hours together, and on those occasions your daughter would lock herself in her own apartment and would not be seen by any one. At length he was absent for a whole day, and when night arrived, and still he did not return, the agitation of your daughter you may readily imagine. That night wore heavily away, and Beaumont was still absent, and in the morning your unfortunate daughter was in a state of mind bordering upon distraction, for it seemed but too evident to her that something of a serious nature had happened to him. We endeavoured to quiet her fears and to re-assure her, but with little effect, and we sent round the neighbourhood to make inquiries, but with no better success, for we could hear nothing of him.

"'Towards the afternoon a man arrived at the farm with a letter, which he said he must not deliver into the hands of any one but the young lady who was staying there, and, as it required no answer, he immediately took his departure, and before we could put any questions to him.

"'Your daughter no sooner saw the superscription on the letter than she turned very pale, and uttered a faint scream, and her agitation was in other respects so powerfully evinced, that our curiosity and alarm were excited, though we forebore, from motives of delicacy, to put any questions to her. With a trembling hand she broke the seal, and proceeded to peruse the contents, but she had, apparently, scarcely read the first line or two, when she uttered an exclamation of horror, and sank insensible on the floor.

"'Our curiosity and anxiety, as you must be well aware, were more than ever excited ; the letter was lying open before us, and in order to solve at once this painful mystery, I determined to peruse it. The contents of that epistle revealed everything, and I perceived at once that your unfortunate daughter had been betrayed, and that the pretended Beaumont was a heartless scoundrel, and most consummate hypocrite.'

"'Alas! my good sir,' I ejaculated, 'you have but justly designated him, and the curses of enraged Heaven will assuredly yet pursue him to destruction. Oh, had you but known my poor child in her innocence and purity, you would doubly pity her, and deprecate the monster who could bring about the destruction of what was once so lovely.'

"'I do, indeed, pity her, Mr. Hawthorn,' replied the farmer, 'from the very bottom of my soul. for it is evident that she has fallen a victim to the artifices of a villain only from the strength of the love she bore him, and through placing too implicit a reliance in his integrity and honour. But he will be punished, depend upon it, for the heinous crime of which he has been guilty. Your daughter was immediately conveyed to her chamber, and attended by my wife and my two girls, who were greatly attached to her, but throughout the night she remained in a state of insensibility, and the following day, when she was partially recovered, she raved deliriously, calling wildly upon the name of her seducer, and we found it impossible to pacify her, or to bring her to any degree of reason. We now found ourselves placed in rather a delicate and awkward position ; for we had no idea with whom our unfortunate guest was connected, and there was no chance of obtaining any information from her while she remained in the same deplorable condition that she was at present.

" She underwent but little or no change for more than a week, and it was quite melancholy to behold her sufferings, and you will believe me I am certain, Mr. Hawthorn, when I assure you that myself and my family paid every care and attention to her that sympathy and humanity could suggest. But at length her reason returned, and she was enabled to leave her chamber, but she was still in such a precarious and deplorable condition, that we feared to interrogate her, lest she should relapse into that delirious state, which, if it was not abated, threatened to be attended with such fatal consequences. She was almost constantly bathed in tears, and seemed anxious to avoid all society ; but from this morbid state of feeling we sought to arouse her as much as possible, though it was with but little, if any effect.

" 'At length I seized the opportunity when she was more calm than usual, to question her, and to beg of her to inform me who she really was, that I might communicate with her friends, and inform them of her unhappy situation; but the question only threw her into a paroxysm of grief and anguish, and she declared that she could sooner die than she could again venture to meet those amiable parents upon whose heads she had brought shame and misery. It was in vain that I remonstrated with her in as gentle and persuasive a manner as I could; I could make no favourable impression upon her, and I was compelled to abandon my efforts for the present, and was at a loss what course to adopt in the painful position in which I found myself placed. I suffered two more

days to elapse, when I determined once more to try the power of argument and persuasion with her, but on the morning that I had resolved to put my design into execution, we were surprised that she did not make her appearance at the usual hour at the breakfast table, and imagining that she had perhaps overslept herself, I sent one of my daughters to her chamber to arouse her. In a few minutes she returned to the parlour with surprise and alarm depicted on her countenance, and informed us that Flora was not in her chamber, that her bonnet and cloak were gone, and that it seemed quite evident she had quitted our house.

" 'You may imagine the surprise and consternation that this intelligence caused us,' continued Mr. Dewsbury, 'and I lost no time in going in search of her, and making every inquiry after her, but I could ascertain nothing of her, and the day passed away without her returning, or our being able to form any conjecture as to what had happened to her, though I entertained the most painful apprehensions, considering the deplorable state of mind in which she was, that she had, in her despair, been induced to lay violent hands on herself, and I redoubled my exertions to remove the terrible doubts that had taken possession of my mind, though without success, and at length I abandoned my efforts in despair.

" 'Your daughter had left nothing behind her which might afford the least clue to unravel the mystery, and I could only, therefore, leave it to chance, though of that there appeared at present to be but little probability. Thus, Mr. Hawthorn, I have told you all I known. I trust that you will acquit me of all blame in this painful business ; I am glad that your daughter is restored to you, and I cannot but repeat my sincere sympathy in the fate of your unfortunate child, and express my thorough disgust and hatred of the villain who could bring it about.'

" I thanked the kind-hearted farmer warmly for the candid and lucid explanation he had given me, and likewise for the sympathy he so ardently evinced ; and yielded to his pressing invitation for me to delay my departure from the farm on my return home to the following day, and we entered into a long conversation od the painful subject, I making him acquainted with the particulars of the manner in which Mowbray had so unfortunately been introduced to me, and what had afterwards taken place.

" 'The more I hear of him,' observed Mr. Dewsbury, 'the greater villain does he appear in my sight, and the more utterly do I loathe him for the misery he has caused. But depend upon it, Mr. Hawthorn, such black crimes as those of which he has been guilty will not be suffered to go unpunished, however he may be able to escape the punishment for a time; the retribution of offended Heaven will at last assuredly overtake him.'

"'It will, it must!' I replied; 'for it would be monstrous to suppose that such a miscreant will be suffered to escape with impunity. But my poor child; is it not dreadful to see her suffer in the manner she is now doing? Her reason is, I fear, alas! gone for ever!''

"'Say not so, my dear sir,' returned the farmer, 'I trust that Heaven will look down with pity upon her, and yet arouse her wandering senses.'

"'And if it should,' I observed, ' oh, how terrible and insupportable will be her feelings of shame and remorse. Will she not know herself as a degraded being, and life, which once presented every charm, will become a burthen to her.'

"'Hope for the best, Mr. Hawthorn,' said my companion, 'and rest assured that Providence will not desert you and your daughter in the midst of your misfortunes.'

"I thanked him for the goodness of his wishes, and the hopes with which he sought to inspire me, but which at present I found it impossible to encourage, and we continued in conversation till a late hour in the evening, when we bade one another good-night, and I was conducted to a chamber.

"I need not tell you that I slept but little, for you may well guess what the nature of my feelings must be after the account which Mr. Dewsbury had given me, and which exposed the systematic villany of Mowbray in a still more odious point of view than ever.

"I repeated again and again my curses upon his head, and with a heavy heart the following morning I departed from the farm, bearing with me the most sincere sympathy of the worthy owner, and determined to continue to use every effort in my power to discover the wretch who had inflicted so much misery upon me and mine, so that I might wreak my vengeance upon his head.

"I returned to my home, now made so wretched, and found my unfortunate child in the same deplorable condition that I had left her. Alice listened to my repetition of the sad account which Mr. Dewsbury had given me with mingled feelings of disgust, indignation, and sorrow, and for some time her emotions were so great and overpowering that she could do nothing but wring her hands, and give vent to sobs of the most bitter and poignant description of anguish.

"'Wretched, unfortunate child,' she ejaculated; 'alas! what a cruel victim hast thou been made to treachery of the blackest and almost unparalleled description. How fatally have all thy fondest hopes been annihilated, and that, too, by one who appeared to be the very soul of truth and honour. Curses the most dreadful must surely pursue him for conduct so monstrous and so odious.'

"'They must,' I exclaimed, 'and a terrible day of retribution must sooner or later arrive, when he will have reason to curse the hour he was born. Oh, that it may be my fate to encounter him, old as I am, he shall then find what an injured parent's vengeance can induce him to do. There is no atonement he can make for the monstrous wrongs he has inflicted on those who rescued him from death, and bestowed upon him even more than the rights of hospitality.'

"'He must indeed be insensible to every proper feeling,' remarked Alice, ' if he is not at last awakened to a full sense of his own enormity, and the remorse of conscience will be a terrible and sufficient punishment to him.'

"In this manner we continued to converse throughout the day, and nothing whatever could serve to ameliorate the bitter anguish and despair of our feelings.

"Day after day passed away, and still had there no change taken place in our unfortunate daughter, although, as you may be certain, we tried every means in our power to recal her wandering senses. She would sit for hours together laughing and weeping alternately, and giving utterance to the most wild and incoherent sentences, which were quite torturing to hear. Sometimes we imagined she had some slight recollection of us, and we would seize upon such moments with the most painful avidity, and seek by all the means that could suggest themselves to us, to re-kindle the dormant spark of reason within her brain; but, perhaps, a wild laugh, or some frenzied laugh was our only reward, and she would quickly relapse again into darkness. Oh! what a sad—sad spectacle was this for parents who loved her so fondly, and who would willingly have laid down their very lives to have restored her to happiness; but the fatal blow was struck, and we gave ourselves up to all the misery of despair.''

MRS. HAWTHORN PLEADING THE CAUSE OF MOWBRAY TO HER HUSBAND.

CHAPTER XXVI.

THE MANIAC GIRL.—THE RE-APPEARANCE AND THE DEATH OF THE BETRAYER.

IN these words Mr. Hawthorn concluded his interesting, though melancholy narrative, and he remained for some minutes afterwards silent, Richard and his wife not offering to interrupt him, but suffering him to give free indulgence to the feelings which they were satisfied must at that moment be agitating his breast. At length he recovered himself sufficiently to observe—

"My tale of sorrow is over, Mr. Parker, and I think you will now be fain to acknowledge that you are not the only one in the world who has had the greatest troubles to encounter with."

"True, my kind friend," returned our hero; "and believe me when I say that I sincerely sympathise with you. But let us hope that your unfortunate daughter may yet recover from the dreadful malady with which she is at present afflicted, and that she will live to be a comfort and a blessing to you in your declining years."

"Ah! no!" replied Hawthorn, "I dare not encourage any such hope. All the efforts that we have hitherto made have failed, and it seems to me but too clearly that her reason is fled for ever."

"What a villain must this Mowbray be, to have been the cause of so much ruin and misery!" observed Richard.

"A villain!" repeated Hawthorn; "oh, a baser could never possibly have disgraced humanity. May every curse attend him, and hunt him to destruction."

"But have you never yet been able to meet with him?" asked Richard; "or to discover who he really is?"

"I have not," answered Hawthorn; "and I now begin to fear that I never shall. He will take good care to avoid me, for he would be sure that I would not fail to wreak my vengeance upon his head, let the consequences to myself be whatever they might."

"Heaven forbid that you should encounter each other," said Mr. Hawthorn, "for that I fear would only be the means of increasing the misery we now endure. The Almighty will not suffer one who has acted so basely to escape unpunished. Prosperity can never attend him, and the horrors of remorse will sooner or later drive him to despair and madness."

"May he suffer an earthly perdition," said Hawthorn, vehemently; "for he has spread misery and desolation where happiness and contentment alone once presided."

"It is quite evident," remarked our hero, "from what you were enabled to ascertain from Mr. Dewsbury, that he had in the first instance grossly deceived you, and that he was not what he represented himself to be.

"True," coincided Mr. Hawthorn, "he acted the part of the deceiver throughout, and that from the moment when he first beheld our unhappy daughter, he had marked her for his victim. And yet his manners were so plausible and so prepossessing, that they were almost sufficient to deceive any one. It is evident that he was nothing more than an unprincipled adventurer, and that Fortune and he were strangers to each other."

"But how came he on board the vessel from the wreck of which you saved him?" said Richard.

"That is impossible for me to conjecture," answered Hawthorn; "and I have never found any means of ascertaining, though I have made every inquiry. But,

hark! my poor child is returning to the room."

The door opening on to the staircase now opened, and the poor maniac girl walked into the room with a light but solemn step, and after staring wildly and vacantly for an instant upon the persons present, she seated herself in a remote corner of the room, and Richard and his wife watched her with increased interest and compassion. Alice and her husband walked towards her, and each of them taking a hand, called her affectionately by name; she looked at them earnestly for a moment, smiled sweetly upon them, passed one of her fair hands across her forehead, as if endeavouring to recollect something, and then relapsed into apathy, and seemed to take no notice of anything.

She had encircled her brow with a wreath of faded artificial white roses, which gave a more melancholy and painful expression to her features, and our hero and Mary were deeply affected, the latter so much so that she could not refrain from tears, but Mr. Hawthorn motioned them to silence, and they seated themselves on the opposite side of the room, and watched the poor girl with the deepest attention and interest.

For some time she remained almost as inanimate as a statue, and muttering unintelligble words to herself, but at length she heaved a deep sigh, which seemed to come from the very bottom of her heart, and without once raising her eyes from the floor, on which they had been fixed, in the most impressive and melancholy accents, she ejaculated,—

"Ah's me! ah's me! He does not come; and it is past the hour when he promised to meet me; what can detain him so long from me? He was wont to be more punctual, and seemed to live only in the presence of his Flora. But why am I so impatient?—He will be here anon, and cheer my drooping heart with his honeyed accents, and looks of affection. Oh, yes, Alfred loves me too fondly to deceive me. Hark! hush! I surely hear his footstep on the staircase; let me then dry my tears, and meet him with my usual smiles of love and welcome. He comes! he comes! Alfred, dear Alfred!"

As she thus spoke, she partly arose from her chair, and gazed eagerly towards the door as though she expected the appearance of the subject of her wanderings; but a cloud of melancholy and disappointment almost immediately overspread her features, and with a deep sigh she reseated herself, and covered her face with her hands.

" No, it is not he," she said again; "he is still absent, and time wears apace; cruel, cruel Alfred, thus to tarry, when you know how anxious I must be to see you again. How unlike yourself is this neglect. Methought that happiness alone was yours when you were in the presence of your young wife, and yet you now leave her to mourn in silence and alone. But he will come—oh, yes, I know he will come soon, and we will be so happy. I have encircled my brow with his favourite wreath of white roses, in which he led me to the altar, and in which he always said I looked so beautiful, and I know he will be delighted to see me in it. Oh, how fondly, how ardently, how sincerely, he loves me; and I must be base and ungrateful, indeed, could I believe that he would ever deceive me. No—no; he will be here—he will be here shortly, and then, oh, then, what happiness will be ours."

"Poor girl! poor girl!" cried her agitated father, addressing himself to our hero and his wife; " in those melancholy words is told the sad story of her wrongs, and the diabolical part which her seducer has acted towards her. Alas! Mr. Parker, is not the contemplation of such a scene as this enough to break a parent's heart?"

" True, my friend," coincided Richard; "and duly do I appreciate the feelings that must agitate your breast at this moment; but I pray you endeavour to compose yourself, to trust in the goodness and mercy of Providence, and to yet hope for the best."

Mr. Hawthorn shook his head despairingly, and they again relapsed into silence, and watched the conduct of the beautiful maniac with the most painful anxiety and attention. She was now once more seated almost as inanimate as a statue, with her eyes fixed upon vacancy, and apparently lost in meditation. But suddenly she aroused herself; her features relaxed their fixed expression, and she burst forth into a song of such wild, such melancholy, and such plaintive melody, that its tones penetrated to the very soul, and rivetted the attention as if by enchantment. Mr. Hawthorn and his wife, our hero and Mary, listened with breathless silence to every note and word that fell from the lips of the maniac till the tears started to their eyes, and they found it impossible to restrain the emotions that were so powerfully excited in their bosoms. But at length she ceased, and for several minutes remained as still as death, and her countenance re-assumed all the torturing anguish of despair.

"No, no, no," she sighed at length;

" he will not come—why, then, should I sing since he is not here to listen to me? Cruel Alfred, I little thought that you could ever treat me thus. Can I have done anything to offend him? Oh, no; I love him by far too fondly to do so, and —but let me to my room and watch his coming, for surely it cannot now be long ere he hastens to rejoin me."

As she thus spoke, she arose from her seat, and slowly moved towards the door, without taking any notice of any one, and Mr. Hawthorn and his wife did not offer to interrupt her, for they well knew the ill-effects it would have upon her in her present state of mind, and she quickly disappeared by the door, and they heard her light footsteps ascending the stairs towards her own chamber.

"Poor girl," said Mrs. Parker, " hers is indeed a melancholy fate; and it must be a truly insensible heart that could not feel for and pity her. The miscreant Mowbray has much to answer for in having caused the wreck of one so lovely and innocent."

"He has, indeed, Mrs. Parker," said Hawthorn; " and can you wonder after the heart-rending scene you have just now witnessed, at the feelings of hatred which I bear towards him?"

"No," replied our heroine; " it is only natural that you should do so; but he will be punished for his crimes, depend upon it, both in this world and hereafter; and I trust that your unfortunate daughter will yet be restored to the light of reason, and be enabled to support her melancholy fate with fortitude and resignation,"

"Alas!" returned Mr. Hawthorn, " I dare not encourage such a hope as that, for what prospect is there under all the dismal circumstances of its ever being realised? The reason of my poor ruined child has fled for ever, and it will in future be my hard lot to gaze alone upon the awful ruin of that which was once so lovely and so innocent."

" Say not so, Mr. Hawthorn," remarked Richard; " for Providence is good and merciful, and will not suffer you always to be subjected to so much misery. Hope for the speedy dawning of better days."

"I feel obliged to you for your commiseration, Mr. Parker," replied Hawthorn, " for I know full well that it comes sincerely from your heart; but I cannot, at the same time, conceal from myself the madness of encouraging any hopes, which I have too much reason to fear can only end in the most bitter disappointment. Heaven be thanked for restoring my daughter to my arms even in her present deplorable condition; for I had at one time almost despaired of ever beholding her again."

"Ay," said our hero, "that is indeed a melancholy consolation ; and you aught to feel yourself greatly indebted to Mr. Dewsbury for his kindness."

"I do, indeed," replied Hawthorn, "and have ever since experienced from him the utmost friendship and solicitude. But let us drop this subject, which is of such a painful nature to me. Do you feel satisfied with the accommodation I have been able to afford you?"

"Oh, yes," answered Richard; "how is it possible that I can be otherwise ? And I must ever feel grateful for the providential circumstance which guided my footsteps hither."

"Yes," observed Mr. Hawthorn; "here I feel confident that you will be perfectly safe from discovery as long as you think proper to remain. You see, Mr. Parker, that amidst all the troubles and difficulties by which you have been surrounded, Providence has never yet deserted you, and that ought to inspire you with the hope that you will ultimately be enabled to escape the fate with which you have so long been threatened altogether."

"For the sake of my wife and child," returned Richard, "I would fain think so; but it is not to be supposed that my enemies will at all relax in their endeavours to discover me; and unless I can find the means of retiring from the country, and of obtaining my livelihood in some place where I am unknown, I do not see the possibility of my long evading their vigilance."

"That opportunity, no doubt, will be afforded you," observed Hawthorn, "but before you proceed to act, it will be necessary and prudent for you to communicate with your friends, Adams and Binnacle, and to receive their advice."

"True," coincided our hero; "I will lose no time in doing so; and I have no reason to doubt the continuance of their friendship and exertions in my welfare. But still I am already under such a weight of obligations to them, that I know not how I shall ever be able to repay it."

"Let not that trouble you for a moment," said Hawthorn; "for I know both Adams and Binnacle too well not to be confident that they will feel themselves amply rewarded by the success of their efforts to serve you."

"You do them no more than justice by expressing that opinion, Mr. Hawthorn," answered Richard; "and I should indeed feel most grateful to Providence for raising me up such friends in the midst of my difficulties."

"Yes, Richard," remarked his wife, "it would be ungrateful for you to repine, or to abandon yourself entirely to despair. We have met with friends where we least expected to find them, and, therefore, that is a satisfactory proof that Providence has not yet deserted us, and to lead us to hope that something will yet occur to deliver us from the dangers by which we are at present surrounded."

"My affectionate, my devoted wife," exclaimed Richard, fondly embracing her; "oh, what would have become of me, had it not been for your consoling voice and sympathising spirit ? What can surpass your noble and heroic conduct in the midst of dangers that were sufficient to daunt even the firmest heart?"

"Richard," she replied; "why thus advert to that which is worthy of no more than ordinary consideration? What more have I performed than my duty? And had I not done so, I should have been unworthy of your love, and must have hated and despised myself."

"Ah! Mrs. Parker," observed Hawthorn, "how happy should that man consider himself who possesses such a wife as you ! And I trust that you will not go unrewarded for your affectionate devotion."

"The safety of my husband is all I seek," said our heroine; "and should it please the Almighty to secure that, I shall indeed be happy. Something has always assured me, too, that my hopes will not be disappointed, and that all the dark clouds that at present o'ershadow our fate will be dispersed, and that we shall once more be restored to happiness and tranquillity."

"Well spoken, Mrs. Parker," said Hawthorn, "and I perfectly coincide in your prognostications, however gloomy your prospects may at present appear to be. Come, come, Richard, you must arouse yourself, my worthy friend, and not give way to those feelings of despair which have too long inhabited your breast. My word for it, that happier days are yet in store for you, and that Providence will never suffer you to fall a victim to so awful and ignominious a fate as that to which you are doomed by the laws of your country."

"The observations of my wife and yourself, Mr. Hawthorn," replied our hero, "inspire me with fresh fortitude, and I will endeavour to look forward to the best. But something must be done, and that shortly, for any delay in my future plans might be fraught with the most imminent danger."

"True," coincided Mr. Hawthorn, "but there is no necessity for any delay. However, there is one thing I would advise."

"Name it," said Richard.

"In order to prevent any suspicion as to the hand-writing of the letter which you are about to forward to your friends," replied Hawthorn, "I propose that I should write the superscription, and then there will be no fear of its not reaching the place of its destination in safety."

"A very wise and prudent precaution, Mr. Hawthorn," said our hero; "it shall be so, and I feel obliged to you for the suggestion. To-morrow, then, I will be prepared with my communication, and I shall await an answer with the utmost anxiety and impatience."

"No doubt that Adams will not long keep you in suspense," remarked Hawthorn, "and that he will be prepared to send you such advice as the urgency of the case requires. Make your mind completely happy and contented, and all will turn out better than you can now anticipate. At any rate, those who are in pursuit of you can have no suspicion that you are secreted here."

"Very true," agreed Mary, "I do not see how it is possible that they can do so; and we should, indeed, bless the good fortune which introduced us to your kind-hearted brother, Mr. Hawthorn, and thus guided our footsteps hither. But I am fearful that we shall put you to great inconvenience."

"Do not mention it, Mrs. Parker," replied Hawthorn; "what inconvenience can it possibly put me to? and I am only too happy in having it in my power to serve the son of that excellent man to whom I am under such a weight of obligations. How providential it was that we should meet again, after the lapse of so many years, under such peculiar circumstances."

"It was, indeed," returned our hero, "and I can never feel sufficiently thankful for it. We are both the victims of misfortune, Mr. Hawthorn, and can, therefore, sympathise with each other."

"True," said the fisherman, "but let us hope that we shall shortly meet again under happier circumstances, though I have too much reason to fear that my poor girl's unfortunate and awful malady will never be removed."

"Do not give way to despair, Mr. Hawthorn," observed our hero; "for something convinces me that your daughter will again be restored to the light of

reason, and that happiness will once more be hers."

"Happiness!" repeated Hawthorn, shaking his head dismally; "ah! no, that I fear is impossible. Her wandering senses may be restored, and we may exert ourselves to the utmost to compose her, but think you it is possible that she can ever forget the gloomy past, or banish from her memory the base treachery of that man on whom she had placed her whole soul's affections, and in whose truth and honour she so fatally confided? Terrible must indeed be her remorse, and bitterly would she reproach herself."

"And yet you would not upbraid her, sir?" said our heroine.

"Upbraid her, Mrs. Parker?" replied Hawthorn; "no, Heaven forbid, for indeed she was not to blame. The villain Mowbray was the cause of all; and adopting the artifices he did towards one so young, so susceptible, and inexperienced as Flora, I wonder not that he should triumph in his diabolical designs. The wretch, would that I had him now before me, old as I am, I would not rest satisfied until I had fully avenged my wrongs upon his head, and, regardless of the consequences to myself, rid the world of such a heartless scoundrel."

"Be calm, my husband," remonstrated Mrs. Hawthorn; "it makes me shudder with horror to hear you talk thus."

"Be calm?" repeated Hawthorn, impatiently; "oh, how can I be calm when I think of the monstrous conduct of that man, and the irreparable misery he has brought upon us? It is madness to advise me thus. Remember what our ill-fated child was, before cursed ill-fortune introduced the wretch to us; how beautiful, how innocent, how happy; turn from that picture, and look upon her now; remember who it is that has wrought that terrible change, and then marvel, if you can, that I, her father, should feel this deadly hatred and ungovernable spirit of revenge towards him."

"The retribution of Heaven will most surely overtake him," said Alice; "and you should not presume to seek more. For my own part, I fervently hope that you may never be fated to encounter each other again; for I shudder to think of what the consequences would then be."

"Alice," said her husband, impatiently, "the sentiments I have expressed were dictated by reason and justice. What else but a terrible revenge can at all atone for the fearful and irreparable wrongs that have been inflicted upon our unfortunate girl? Nothing! and by all my hopes, I swear that I will have it, should the opportunity ever be afforded me. But enough of this ; I am sick at heart, and no longer in the humour to discuss this painful subject to-night."

He threw himself into a chair as he thus spoke, and resigned himself to the most gloomy and torturing thoughts, and no one offered to interrupt him, for they thought that any observations they might make use of would probably be only calculated to increase his anguish.

The supper passed over with but little conversation taking place, and that only upon indifferent subjects, and as it was now getting late, our hero and Mary arose to depart, and bidding Mr. and Mrs. Hawthorn good-night, they separated, deeply interested and affected by all that the fisherman had related to them, and at the deplorable situation of the youthful and beauteous Flora.

"Poor girl," said our heroine, compassionately, "what a dreadful fate is hers, and I wonder not at the anguish of her parents. Surely it is a terrible affliction."

"True," replied her husband ; "and most deeply do I sympathise with them in their misfortunes. As for the scoundrel Mowbray, there is no fate he can meet with which could be too bad for him."

"He must indeed possess a heart insensible to every feeling of humanity," observed Mary ; "and should remorse ever reach his guilty soul, as it can scarcely fail to do, how terrible will be his sufferings."

Richard coincided in this opinion, and after some few more observations, they retired to rest, and satisfied of their present security, and encouraging hopes of the future, they slept more calmly and soundly than they had done for some time before.

Our hero arose at an early hour in the morning, and proceeded to write his communication to Adams, in which he related as briefly as possible all the particulars of what had happened to him since he had last heard from him ; expressed his confidence in a continuance of the friendship he had ever evinced towards him, and requested a speedy answer with his advice as to how it would be most prudent for him in future to act. This task accomplished, they repaired to the cottage inhabited by the fisherman and his wife, whom they found anxiously awaiting to see them, and who greeted them in their usual friendly and cordial manner.

The morning repast being over, Richard placed the letter in the hands of Hawthorn, and asked his opinion of it. The fisherman perused it with much care and atten-

tion, and having concluded, he expressed his entire approbation of it.

The letter was then folded and sealed, and Hawthorn having written the address, they were about to despatch it, when they were interrupted by hearing a knock at the outer-door, and Mrs. Hawthorn opening it, they were agreeably surprised by seeing Daniel Hawthorn enter. Our hero and his wife greeted the honest waggoner most cordially, and Daniel expressed no less pleasure at seeing them again.

"Dang it now," he said, "if I didn't think that I should find you here ; for I knew that if you saw my brother Harry and his dame, you would meet with a right hearty welcome Well, I be main glad to see you, and hope that you be quite well?"

"To you, my good friend," said our hero, "I am more indebted than you can think, for in your brother I have found an old friend and acquaintance, whom I never expected to see again ; and had it not been for your kindness, I should probably never have had that opportunity."

"Well, dang it now," said Daniel, "that be strange, sure enough. Old friends !— why, who'd a thought it ?"

"Daniel," remarked Hawthorn, "I know I can depend upon your prudence and secrecy on any subject in which the happiness and safety of your fellow-creatures are involved, and I will, therefore, with the permission of my unfortunate friend here, explain everything to you."

"Depend upon me, Harry ?" said his brother ; "yes, I should think you could, too ; there be not many who could keep a secret better than I can, I warrant, and especially when it is to do any person a good turn, or to screen them from danger.'

"I know it Daniel," returned the fisherman. "Now listen to me, and as you value everything, do not let a syllable by accident escape you to anybody else."

"No fear of that," said Daniel ; "you know, Harry, I wouldn't do so for the world."

Mr. Hawthorn then related to his brother who our hero and his wife were, and all the misfortunes that and befallen them, and the simple waggoner listened to him with mute astonishment and attention.

"Egad !" he exclaimed, when his brother had concluded, "now this be strange, sure enough ; this be Master Parker and his wife ! Dash my old wig, now, if I didn't half suspect as much as soon as I saw 'em, though I didn't like to say so. Well, I can only say, that I am very sorry for 'em, and I wish it was in my power to assist 'em."

"Thank you, heartily, Daniel, for your

good wishes, which I know come from your heart," said our hero, pressing his hand ; "we already owe you much for services you have rendered us, and had it not been for you I should probably not have been introduced again to my old and esteemed friend, your brother."

"As for what I have done for you, Mr. Parker," said Daniel, in reply, "that is nothing, and I only wish it was in my power to do twice as much. I am only a poor, foolish, simple fellow, I know, but I flatter myself that I do not possess one of the worst hearts in the world ; but only to think that Harry should be an old acquaintance of yours, and that you should meet in such a manner! How very fortunate, to be sure."

"Yes," replied Richard, "it was, indeed, Daniel, and for it I am entirely indebted to you. Besides, but for your kindness and ready wit on the road from the Golden Lion, I should probably now have been in the hands of those who are in pursuit of me."

"Ha! ha! ha!" laughed the honest countryman ; "that were not a bad trick o' mine, were it ?—I baffled the fellows nicely, I've a notion, and put them on a fool's errand—ha! ha! ha! Oh, for gulling the knowing ones, when he sees occasion for it, there be not many that can bang Dan Hawthorn, I can tell you. I be going to the Golden Lion how, for my team be waiting there, only as I were near my brother's I thought I might as well call and ask him and his good dame how they be, and how poor Flora was. Ah, poor lass !—poor lass !"

The fisherman pressed the hand of his brother in gratitude for the sympathy he so fervently expressed.

"Have you heard any inquiries after me at the inn, Daniel, since I left there?" asked our hero.

"God bless you, no," answered Daniel, "though there has been talk enough about you, and every one that I have heard mention your name have seemed to pity you, and expressed themselves glad that you have hitherto been able to escape."

"Heaven bless them for it," ejaculated Mrs. Parker, fervently.

"And has Mr. Hatfield talked about me?" interrogated our hero.

"Oh, yes," replied Daniel, "frequently; and he has two or three times told me that he thought you were not exactly what you represented yourself to be, for your manners were so much like those of a gentleman."

"And do you think he has any suspicion as to who I really am?" asked Richard, eagerly.

"Why, to tell you the truth, Mr. Parker," said Daniel, "I have a strong notion that he does, though he never hinted as much to me."

"But do you think he would reveal anything, if he should be questioned about me?" said Richard.

"Reveal anything?" returned Daniel ; "God bless you, no ; not for the world, Master Hatfield is a very different man to that, I can tell you, as my brother Harry, here, knows; he would sooner do all in his power to assist you, or any other of his fellow-creatures in distress, wouldn't he, Harry?"

"Yes, he would indeed," replied the fisherman ; "he possesses an excellent and humane heart, and if I were placed in your situation, Mr. Parker, I would not hesitate a moment to make him my confidant."

"I can believe you," observed Richard, "for his manners showed it, and he acted with the greatest kindness towards me during the short time that I remained with him."

"Ay," said Daniel; "a better man than Master Hatfield never stood in two shoes, and I know he would hate himself if he thought he could betray any man placed in the unfortunate situation that you are, Master Parker. But may I make so bold as to ask what you intend to do now?"

Our hero told him without reserve.

"And a very good plan, too," said Daniel, "and I wish you success in it, with all my heart."

Richard once more thanked him, and they then sat down and discussed the business for some time, and as Daniel was going to the inn, it was considered most expedient to entrust the letter to him to be forwarded to the place of its destination, he undertaking not to commit it to the care of any one but on whom he might depend.

"But leave me alone for that, Master Parker," observed the worthy fellow, "I always know my customers, and when I have a person to serve, in-course I entrust them."

"I place every dependance on you, Daniel," returned our hero, "for I feel confident that you will not deceive me. I need not enjoin you to be on your guard should you hear anything respecting me, and——"

"But," interrupted Daniel, "should Master Hatfield question me upon the subject, do you think I need hesitate, after the character my brother Harry has given of him, and what you have yourself experienced of him, to tell him the truth?"

"Mr. Hatfield," observed the fisherman, "as I have said before, is a man of the strictest integrity and humanity, and if my friend, Mr. Parker, will take my word, he will answer in the affirmative to your question, Daniel."

"I should be most ungenerous were I not to do so, after the kind behaviour I have received from him, and what you have said of his character," replied Richard Parker. "I leave everything to your discretion, Daniel, and am satisfied that you will not act imprudently."

"Oh, no," returned the waggoner, with a little bit of an egotistical chuckle, which, under all the circumstances, was pardonable; "Daniel Hawthorn knows what's what, depend upon that. Take my word for it, Mr. Parker; if we put our heads together, we shall bring you clean out of this unpleasant business; and Master Hatfield will be one of the first, when he knows all about it, to render you all the assistance in his power."

"Yes, that I'm sure he will," replied Mr. Hawthorn; "and there is no doubt that we shall find him an able anxiliary. Are you satisfied with this arrangement, Mr. Parker?"

"Perfectly so," answered the latter; "how can I be otherwise?"

"Then as far as that part of the subject goes," remarked the fisherman, "it is settled."

"True," coincided our hero, "and should anything reach the knowledge of our friend Daniel, which may seem to threaten me with danger while I remain here, I have no doubt that he will apprise me of it at his earliest convenience."

"Trust me for that, Master Parker," said the countryman; "I will be upon the 'lert, don't they call it? But I must be going, for my time is up. I am dumb to every one but Mr. Hatfield, by your permission, and if you find me deceive you, I will be quite willing to be hung up, like a dog to the branch of the first tree you can meet with."

"I do not doubt you, my honest friend," said Richard, again pressing his hand; "and depend upon it that I entertain a full sense of your kindly and manly feeling, and should it ever be in my power to return it, no one will feel more happy than myself in doing so."

"Oh, as for that, Master Parker," returned Daniel, "the least said about it the better; I want no return for what it may be in my power to do for you, but your good will and friendship; for I con-

sider that what I have done, and what I may still be able to do, is no more than performing my duty as a man towards my fellow creatures. God bless you, Mr. Parker; the cause you have struggled in, I know, is a just one; God bless you, Mrs. Parker, for your devotion to your husband proves that you are a woman, every inch of you; and God bless the little boy, for I can see plain enough that he is a chip of the old block, though I hope it may never fall to his lot to meet with his father's misfortunes, and—why, I don't know that I can say better in conclusion, than, God bless everybody that deserves it. Ha! ha! ha!"

As the worthy fellow thus eloquently delivered himself, he burst into such a hearty laugh, that could only emanate from one of the most generous of breasts, and shook hands with every person in the room, by way of sealing the truth and sincerity of his intentions.

Richard Parker and his wife were completely overpowed by this natural display of good feeling, and could not find words to express the sentiments they wished, and which they felt were so justly due to the simple rustic, Daniel Hawthorn; and his brother could only press his hand vehemently, and evince by his looks how warmly he appreciated and admired his manly feelings. In Daniel Hawthorn was displayed the true nobility of nature, and it is, therefore, that we have thus particularised it, as a bright example to others, which it would be well for them to copy and to follow.

"But," observed Daniel, after a short pause had taken place, and rather hesitating before he expressed himself; "you will pardon me, I know, Mr. Parker, for what I am about to say, for I assure you it is all done in friendship, and I think my brother Harry can answer for me on that point; you have had a great many difficulties to contend with, and, perhaps, you may yet have many more; all these sort of things are very expensive, I believe, though I have never experienced them myself, and—and—dang it! I am a poor silly fellow, and don't know how to express myself as I ought to do; but the long and the short of it is, I have got a guinea or two by me which I can very well spare, for I've no one to look to but myself, and if you will do me the favour to accept of them I shall feel so much obliged, you can't think. Now, do not be offended, I beg of you, for I do it all in good part, as brother Harry knows, don't you, Harry? Here they are, all bright, golden guineas of his Majesty, his most gracious Majesty,

I should say, King George the Third, as fresh as when they first came from the mint. I always keep 'em about me, in this canvas bag, for I can't afford to have a banker, you see; and as I do not know any particular use to put 'em to, and could do very well without 'em myself, why, do take 'em, Mr. Parker, and God bless and prosper you with 'em, I say."

As the poor fellow thus spoke, he drew forth from his breeches pocket a long canvas bag, and uncoiling about three yards of

MOWBRAY'S VISIT TO FLORA HAWTHORN.

whip-cord from around the neck, he was proceeding to count the contents into the hand of our hero, when the latter, who was quite overwhelmed with such unexampled and disinterested generosity, prevented him, and in a voice which showed the sincerity of his feelings, he said—

"Excellent, generous-hearted man, this act of kindness towards a stranger is too much, and I should despise myself were I to take advantage of it. I cannot find terms sufficiently strong enough for me to express to you my gratitude; but I cannot think of accepting your liberal offer, for at

No. 37.

present I require it not. Believe me, that although I thus decline, it is from no feelings of empty and ridiculous pride, and that I shall ever entertain a grateful remembrance of the noble feelings that have prompted you to make this offer."

"Yes," said Daniel, with a look of disappointment, and still fingering the bag in a fidgety manner, "I have not the least doubt that you will, Mr. Parker, but I should be much better pleased if you would only condescend to oblige me, for I know pretty well what travelling expenses must be, 'specially situated as you are. Now do take a few of 'em, if it's only ten or twenty or so."

"Not one, my kind friend," replied Richard; "though at some future period, it is not at all unlikely that I may tax your liberality."

"Well," remarked Daniel, reluctantly returning the bag to his pocket, "I hope you may never have any occasion to do so, though if you do, you know where to apply to; that's all the harm I can wish you."

"Nobly spoken, Daniel," said his brother, again cordially shaking him by the hand; "the sentiments you have expressed do honour to your head and heart, and I feel proud of you as a brother. Mr. Parker, I am satisfied, duly appreciates your feelings, and although he declines your generous offer, experiences the same sense of gratitude towards you as if he accepted it."

"Oh, yes," remarked our heroine, who was moved to tears by the conduct of the kind-hearted Daniel; "I can answer for my husband that he does, and allow me, Mr. Hawthorn, to add my simple tribute of gratitude to his for this unexampled and spontaneous act of generosity, and noble and manly feeling. Heaven be praised for raising us up such friends in the midst of our adversity."

"And Heaven will raise you up more powerful, though not more sincere friends still, Mrs. Parker, depend upon it," returned the fisherman; "and you will be restored to that happiness and peace of mind from which you have been so long estranged. That is my fervent wish, and my most sanguine prediction, and something seems to convince me that I shall not be disappointed."

"Thank you for expressing those hopes, my kind friend," said Mary, "for I know that what you say comes from your heart, and I feel the kindness the more keenly, knowing the effect that such observations, and coming from such a source, must have upon the mind of my unfortunate hus-

band. Why should we indeed resign ourselves entirely to despair, since Providence has already shown such mercy towards us, and supplied us with warm-hearted and disinterested friends where we least expected to find them? What say you, Richard?"

"I am overwhelmed with the power of my emotions at all that has recently taken place, and know not where to find words that will adequately express my feelings on the occasion," replied Richard; "I should be unworthy of the regard of these excellent friends did I treat with indifference their arguments and opinions, which I know full well are given in so generous a spirit. I can only repeat that I am grateful for them, and whatever may be the fate in store for me, to the latest moment of my existence I shall continue to feel for them that honour and respect which my tongue fails to give utterance to."

"Well," said Daniel, after a brief pause had ensued, "I must be going, for my time is quite up; and I only wish I could stay with you a little longer. I will see that this letter is forwarded safe to where it be directed, and I hope it may bring you good news, Mr. Parker. If you do not leave here shortly, I shall be this way again in a few days, and then I will bring you all the news I may have heard. Good bye, Harry, good bye, dame, good bye all."

Mr. Hawthorn, his wife, and the others heartily responded to the good wishes of honest Daniel, and after having once more shaken hands with him, he took his departure from the cottage.

"What a noble generous hearted man is your brother, Mr. Hawthorn," observed our heroine, when the waggoner was gone; "oh, if all were like him, how little of misery would there be in the world."

"Very true, Mrs. Parker," coincided Hawthorn; "Daniel is a simple but an excellent-hearted man, and, uncultivated though he is, he would do honour to a far higher position in society than that which he at present occupies. I feel proud of him as a brother, as I told him; and I can never cease to rejoice that you fell into his hands in the dangerous circumstances in which you were placed, for it has been the means of enabling me to make some return for the many services which I received from the late Mr. Parker."

"Those services, my dear friend," returned Richard Parker, "are more than requited already, and I beg you will no more [....] them. But where is your [....]? I hope that she is not ill, as she has not made her apperance this morning."

"No," replied Hawthorn, "nothing, I believe, affects her but her unfortunate malady. She seemed to have an inclination to remain in her chamber to-day, and we think it always best to humour her inclinations."

"Very true," said Parker; "poor girl! how sincerely do I pity her; and fervently do I hope that Providence will restore her to reason and to happiness."

"Alas!" sighed Mr. Hawthorn, "I feel convinced that happiness can never more be hers, and that should the light of reason again dawn upon her, her sufferings will be more acute than they even are at present, for then she will be tortured by all the horrors of remorse, and her life will become an insupportable burthen to her."

"Oh, no," said our hero, "endeavour to think differently."

"I cannot do so," answered Hawthorn; "and this morning my mind is oppressed with dismal forebodings, which, although I have struggled hard, I find it impossible to dispel."

"Melancholy forebodings?" said Mrs. Hawthorn, looking anxiously at him. "What mean you?"

"Something of an important nature, it is the impression on my mind, is about to happen," returned her husband, "and I cannot banish it from my thoughts. You may deem me weak and foolish for the thought, but I cannot forget a strange and painful dream I had last night, and which appears to be a forewarning of that which is about to take place."

"A dream?" repeated his wife; "and is it possible that a mere idle vision can have made such an impression on your mind?"

"You may deem it idle if you think proper," returned the fisherman, somewhat impatiently, "but it is, nevertheless, true, and I am not ashamed to acknowledge it."

"It is strange," ejaculated Alice, with a look of surprise; "but what was the nature of the dream that has taken such strong hold upon your senses?"

"I fancied myself upon a dreary waste," replied Hawthorn, "and in the midst of a wild tempest, the awful power of which seemed to deprive me of all my faculties, and to dash me about at its mercy. Oh, how hoarsely roared the thunder, and how terrifically the lightning flashed! while a deluge of rain descended from the heavens and seemed to threaten the world's destruction. It was night, and so dense was the darkness, that my eyes could not penetrate it, save when the lightning flashed across the sky, and that only rendered the horrors of the scene more palpable to me. Suddenly, in the pauses of the thunder, a piercing and terrific shriek in a female voice vibrated in my ears, and seemed to proceed no great distance from me. I tried to move in that direction, but, as I said before, all my faculties failed me, and I seemed as though I were rivetted to the spot. Again the lightning blazed on high, and straining my eyes in the direction from whence the cry had proceeded, I beheld at no great distance from me a couple of human forms, but so momentary was the light afforded me, that I had no opportunity of observing them distinctly. A second and a third shriek rent the air, and seemed to penetrate to my very soul, and then the lightning blazed more vividly, and the objects that had before attracted my attention were revealed to me as plainly as if it had been in the broad light of day. Judge of my agony, when I beheld Flora struggling, and almost exhausted, in the arms of the villain Mowbray, and vainly screaming aloud for help!"

"Ah! is it possible?" demanded Alice, who now felt her interest excited in a most painful degree; "but proceed."

"It is true," answered her husband; and now I think you will be ready to admit that the impression made upon my mind by this extraordinary vision is not at all surprising. I could see the countenances of them both distinctly. That of Flora was expressive of the utmost terror and despair, but the features of Mowbray were distorted by various disgusting passions, and were quite hideous and appalling to gaze upon. I tried to shout and call upon him to forbear, but I could not; my tongue cleaved to the roof of my mouth, and not a sound beyond a whisper escaped my lips. And then I endeavoured to rush towards them, but all in vain; my limbs seemed paralysed, and I was rivetted to the spot, and immovable as a statue. 'Father! father!' I heard our daughter shriek, 'will you not save me from the demon who would drag my soul to perdition?' Another powerful effort I made to rush towards the spot, but all to no purpose, and a number of supernatural and invisible beings seemed to shout and mock in my ears. I imagined that I was wrougt up to a pitch of frenzy, but the more agitated I became, and the more I struggled to rush to the rescue of my child, the louder became the shouts of mockery and exultation of the demons in my ears. More vividly the lightning flashed, and more distinct was the view I had of my daughter, and the wretch with whom she struggled. Suddenly the expression of her countenance underwent an awful change; it became ghastly and livid as that of a corpse; gradually the flesh seemed to roll away from her features, and that which but so recently was life, stood revealed to my appalled gaze a ghastly skeleton! Horrorstruck, I imagined in my dream that I turned my eyes from her, and gazed upon the form of her distroyer; but still more frightful was the metamorphosis that he had undergone. His face had become black and hideous. His eyes gleamed like balls of fire; his hair seemed changed into twisting snakes, and his form had lost all affinity to anything human. Still he retained his hold of the ghastly skeleton which I had so lately recognised as my daughter, and between the pauses of the thunder I could hear him shout in fiendish exultation. More fiercely raged the storm—the thunder sent forth its deafening peals, shaking the very earth to its foundation—and the lightning's blue fires seemed about to set the world in one universal conflagration. Again did I endeavour to rush from the spot, but I was as powerless to move as ever, nor could my tongue give utterance to a syllable. Oh, the horror of my feelings at that moment! How shall I describe it? I feel myself incompetent to the task; but still the impression is as vividly stamped upon my mind as if it had been reality. Suddenly as I gazed towards the spot on which the forms had been standing, they were gone, and in their place, flames of fire seemed to blaze from the earth, and an unearthly voice shouted in my ears: 'Man! man! there is no hope for thee! Thy daughter has yielded to the tempter, and she is lost to thee for ever!' A thousand shouts of supernatural derision seemed to follow those words; the earth trembled beneath my feet—everything appeared to dance before my eyes—hideous faces seemed to grin upon me from every side—my brain was on fire! My heart seemed ready to burst from its tenement, and in the horror of the moment I awoke."

Mr. Hawthorn ceased, and such was the impression he had made upon his hearers by the account he had given, that they stood for some moments and gazed with mingled feelings of awe and astonishment upon each other, and were unable to give utterance to a single word.

"It was indeed a frightful dream," observed Alice at length; "but still you must not suffer it to make such a powerful impression upon your mind."

"And think you I can help it?" demanded Mr. Hawthorn, impatiently, "when I recal all the awful circumstances of it to my memory?"

"It was the agitation of your mind probably, that conjured it up to your imagination," remarked Richard.

"No," returned Hawthorn, "it is impossible that I can think so. I feel certain that something of an important nature is shortly about to happen."

"What should we fear?" demanded Alice; "surely the Almigty is too merciful to visit us with any fresh calamity."

"Yes," said our hero; "believe in that, my good friend, and endeavour to compose yourself."

"I have tried, but in vain," replied the fisherman; "I cannot banish it from my thoughts. The words I heard the invisible being utter, still seem to sound in my ears, and I shudder with horror when I think of them."

"I am surprised to hear you talk so," observed his wife; "for it is a weakness of which I do not think that even I could be guilty."

"You may affect to treat my observations with indifference, Alice," remarked Hawthorn; "but mark my words, I am satisfied that something of an appalling nature is destined to happen to us."

"Oh, what madness it is thus to torture yourself with these apprehensions," returned his wife; "what calamity have we cause to dread?"

"The sudden death of our child," replied Hawthorn, in a faint and hollow voice.

Alice started, and turned ghastly pale, trembling violently.

"Good God! husband," she exclaimed, "what awful thoughts are these you have suffered to take possession of your senses? Why should we apprehend so terrible an affliction as that? Flora is at present in more than her usual health, and, please Heaven, she will continue so. Come, come, arouse yourself, and do not give way to these gloomy and frightful thoughts. I never saw you in such a mood before."

"No, Alice," said her husband, "you know that I am not apt to give way to the weaknesses of superstition; but this was a dream of no ordinary description, and I find it difficult to banish it from my memory, or to do away with the impression it has made upon me."

"You will pardon me, Mr. Hawthorn," remarked our hero, "but, really, I must be of the same opinion as your wife, namely, that, although it was certainly a most remarkable dream, it is unworthy of the painful importance which you attach to it; and that it was doubtless only conjured up to your imagination by the disorder and anxiety of your mind, probably increased by the recollection of the wrongs inflicted upon your ill-fated daughter; and I, therefore, regret that you should have been put to the pain of reciting them to us."

"Nay, my friend," returned Hawthorn, "there needs no apology of that kind from you; the recital of the melancholy facts to a sympathising friend, must afford me some relief, and such a friend I know I have in Richard Parker."

"You have, indeed, Mr. Hawthorn," replied Richard; "I could not feel more sincerely for yourself and your afflicted daughter, were you my own relations, and I am satisfied that in that sentiment my wife also most warmly participates."

"I do, indeed," observed our heroine; "and most heartily do I deprecate and abhor the conduct of that bad man in whose honour and fidelity she so unfortunately placed too much confidence."

"Oh, he was a monster of the blackest dye," said Mr. Hawthorn, vehemently, and the expression of his features showed the power of the feelings that were passing in his mind; "a baser scoundrel could never have been permitted to disgrace and outrage society; and surely he will not, sooner or later, if he still survives, be suffered to escape that most terrible retribution which is so justly his due."

"Depend upon it that he will not," returned Richard Parker; "and if he is not entirely callous to every sense of proper feeling, his conscience must ere this have become a most terrible monitor to him."

"His conduct proves," remarked Mr. Hawthorn, "that he is a man whom remorse is not likely to reach, inured to profligacy and crime; on the contrary, he probably exults at the success of his diabolical schemes, and Heaven knows how many more have since fallen the victims to his infernal artifices. May every curse attend him and render his future days those of incessant torment, for it would be no more than a just punishment for the terrible crimes he has committed, and which stamp him as a villain of the most enormous description."

"True—true," coincided Mrs. Hawthorn, "and no one can attempt to extenuate his conduct; but we must leave everything to the will of the Almighty, who, no doubt, in His own wise time will see that justice is done to those whom he has so severely injured, and avert those

evils which you now so painfully apprehend. But let us for the present drop this torturing subject, for you are evidently in no state of mind to discuss it. I will see to Flora, and with the blessing of Heaven, I hope that no future trouble is in store for her and ourselves."

Mr. Hawthorn returned no answer to this, for he seemed at that moment to be completely absorbed in his own dismal thoughts, and Mrs. Hawthorn quitted the room, in order to repair to the chamber of Flora.

Hawthorn remained silent for several minutes, buried in deep meditation, and evidently experiencing great agitation of mind, and Richard and his wife did not offer to interrupt him, for they were indeed most forcibly struck with the strange and ominous character of the fearful vision which had occurred to his imagination, and could not help in some measure participating in the apprehensions he had expressed, though they sincerely hoped that such melancholy forebodings might not be realised.

In a few minutes afterwards, Mrs. Hawthorn returned to the room, and to the eager and anxious inquiries of her husband, she replied that she found their daughter in much the same state as she usually was, and that she could not perceive the least signs of her suffering from any bodily indisposition, but, on the contrary, she appeared to be in more than usual good health.

"Therefore, my dear husband," continued Alice, "I do trust that you will no longer continue to give way to the dismal thoughts and forebodings that at present disturb your mind; but endeavour to forget the strange and fearful dream which has so unfortunately made such a powerful impression on you."

"Ah, Alice!" replied Hawthorn, "it is far easier to offer such advice than to follow it; notwithstanding all that you and our friends here have said, I feel a melancholy depression of spirits, which nothing seems to have the power to dissipate, though most happy should I be if I could do so. I am confident that something of an important and painful nature is shortly about to happen."

"What a strange and unfortunate infatuation is this," said Mrs. Hawthorn; "indeed I can see no sufficient reason for encouraging it to the extent that you do. But let us not continue the subject; let us endeavour to divert our thoughts to something else."

"Ay," remarked Parker; "it is no use to give way to such dismal feelings as these; for I feel confident that the calamity which Mr. Hawthorn so unfortunately apprehends is not fated to take place."

Mr. Hawthorn shook his head doubtfully.

"Would to Heaven that I could think as you have expressed yourself, Mr. Parker," he said, "but I feel that to be impossible. There was something too awful and impressive in the circumstances of my dream to be easily forgotten."

"I admit, my good friend," returned our hero, "that they were of a most strange and painful character; but what are dreams but the mere creation of a disordered imagination? And were we at all times to give way to the idea that they were certain to be realised, what miserable beings should we become."

"True," answered Hawthorn; "and yet how many instances do we see of Providence giving us a forewarning of that which is about to happen to us through the medium of them?"

Richard Parker did not offer any reply to this, and after awhile the subject was changed, and Hawthorn gradually seemed to become somewhat more composed. Thus the day wore away, and the unfortunate Flora kept herself confined to her own room, and never once made her appearance below. As the evening approached, however, the weather, which during the day had been fine, and clear, and frosty, suddenly changed; dark and heavy clouds obscured the horizon, the wind began to below in the rocky cavaties around, and everything gave warning of a coming storm.

"It will be a fearful night, I see plainly enough," observed Hawthorn; "the storm is fast gathering in all its fearful power, and will soon burst upon the earth with overwhelming fury."

"Thank Heaven we are under shelter," returned Alice, "and safe from exposure to its horrors. Would to God that all our fellow creatures were as well off as ourselves."

"Ah! Alice," remarked her husband; "who knows the frightful calamities which this night may produce? Again I feel a dreadful presentiment of something about to happen."

"Why will you suffer yourself to give way to this weakness?" said Mrs. Hawthorn; "surely there is nothing yet to sanction such dismal forebodings. What should we apprehend?"

"I know not," answered Hawthorn; "but the feeling has obtained so strong a hold upon my mind, that I feel totally incapable of conquering it."

"Nay, Mr. Hawthorn," remonstrated our hero, in a friendly way, "I must confess that I feel surprised at you. Exert yourself to banish such melancholy and agonising thoughts from your mind."

"Alas!" sighed Hawthorn, "the task is far less easy than you seem to imagine, Mr. Parker, and I doubt not that if you were placed in the same situation as myself, you would think as I do."

Mrs. Hawthorn, our hero, and his wife again exerted themselves to the utmost to re-assure him, but it was with little or no success, and they abandoned the effort, and a dismal silence of some minutes ensued; but it was quickly interrupted by the voice of the storm, which, so long threatening, now commenced with even greater violence than they had anticipated, and it was evident that a terrific and long continued war of the elements was about to take place. Mr. Hawthorn folded his arms across his chest, and walking to the window, looked out upon the dismal scene beyond, in moody and painful silence, which showed at once the torturing nature of the thoughts that were passing in his mind. Alice once more retired upstairs, to see after her daughter, and shortly returned, and informed them that Flora had gone to bed, and was wrapped in a calm sleep, and apparently quite unconscious of the storm which was raging around.

"And God grant," continued Alice, "that her sleep may continue undisturbed during the night. Come, my husband, arouse yourself from those gloomy thoughts which I perceive occupy your mind, and endeavour to dissipate the dismal effects of the night in conversation upon other topics."

"I would fain do so, Alice," replied her husband; "but in spite of all my efforts to the contrary, these sad thoughts I feel every moment to increase upon me. Would to Heaven that this night were past, for I feel certain, notwithstanding all the arguments you have made use of, and the weakness of which you may accuse me, that there is some fresh trouble impending o'er our heads, or that there is something of a most exciting and important nature about to take place."

Mrs. Hawthorn looked at her husband with a melancholy and foreboding look, and in spite of all she had said, and notwithstanding all her efforts to shake off the feeling, she could not help somewhat participating in his apprehensions. Hawthorn at length walked once more to the fire, and seating himself, sunk into a state of the most gloomy meditation, from which it seemed almost impossible for any one to arouse him.

The tempest was now at its height, the rain and snow and hail descended with terrific violence; and the wind howled in such fearful gusts that it was quite frightful and appalling to listen to it. The windows rattled in their frames, and the cottage seemed to be shaken to its very foundation. The persons present drew themselves closer to the fire, and for some time sat looking at each other in solemn silence without exchanging a word. In this manner more than half an hour elapsed, and the storm grew fiercer every moment. It was evident that it was set in for the night; and it was awful to think of the destruction that would in all probability take place during the time that it continued. Mary Parker felt alarmed, and drew her chair closer to that of her husband, and although she was unable to utter a word, the looks she fixed upon him sufficiently told the anguish of mind she was enduring. Richard whispered some words of comfort in her ear, and endeavoured to tranquillize her feelings, though it was with but little effect, and they continued for some time in the same painful state of suspense, as though something of an awful nature was about to take place.

It was now night, and darkness reigned around, which rendered the horrors of the scene more appalling; but still every one seemed too busily occupied with their own gloomy thoughts to have any wish to enter into conversation, and the time wore slowly and drearily away. At length a gust of wind more fearful than any they had yet heard, and which seemed to threaten to level the cottage with the earth, aroused them from their lethargy; and they all started to their feet, and gazed at each other with looks of terror and fearful expectation, but without being able to give utterance to a single word. Gradually it died away in long and sullen moanings, and then the rain and the snow came down with redoubled violence, and rattled against the windows with such fury, that they threatened every moment to be forced in by the violence of the shock.

Mr. Hawthorn had been for some moments pacing the room backwards and forwards with folded arms and disordered steps, muttering incoherent words to himself, though it was plain enough to be seen the agitation of mind he was enduring. At length he re-seated himself by the fire, and after a few minutes passed in reflection, he said—

"It is, indeed, a fearful tempest, the fiends of destruction seem to ride upon the blast, and to threaten all mankind with vengeance. What poor weak mortals we are, and how quickly might we all be crushed and annihilated, like so many insects. And this is the life that we so much covet, and struggle, and battle to retain."

"What fearful and dismal thoughts have you suffered to take possession of your brain, my husband," said Alce; "for Heaven's sake do endeavour to conquer this torturing and morbid feeling."

"No," replied Hawthorn, "it is useless for me to endeavour to do so, and is not the contemplation of this scene more than sufficient to cast a gloom over the most buoyant spirits, and the minds of those even who have never yet experienced what misfortune is ?"

"I agree with you in that respect, Mr. Hawthorn," observed Parker; "but still it behoves us to do all in our power to banish such ideas from our breasts, and to leave everything to the wisdom and will of the Supreme, who does everything for the best ; and whose Almighty decrees what poor puny mortal shall presume to question? His omnipotent power now speaks to us in the voice of the tempest; and where is the individual who must not bow down with awe and trembling before Him ?"

"True," coincided Hawthorn; "and there is no one who is more ready to acknowledge His omniscient power than myself. But hark! how the storm increases in violence. It was just such a fearful night as this when our poor, wretched, ruined child was restored to us; and you, my friends, may, therefore, be able to form some idea of the sufferings she must have endured in her lonely wanderings. Oh! that night can never be effaced from my memory, and even now when I think of it, the blood curdles with horror in my veins, and my brain is driven almost to distraction."

"Calm your feelings, my husband," said Alice, "and do not continue to torture yourself with such reminiscences. Thank God that she was restored to us ; for had not Providence mercifully guided her footsteps to our dwelling, she must have perished by a frightful death, and we might ever have remained in ignorance of the fate which had befallen her."

"Very true, Mrs. Hawthorn," observed our hero; "and that reflection ought at least to afford you some comfort and consolation in the midst of your misfortunes."

"Alas!" sighed Hawthorn, "but to see her so awfully changed from what she once was—to witness the dreadful and hopeless malady with which one so young, so beautiful, and once so innocent, is afflicted, surely is enough to torture even the most insensible breast; and how can I, her parent, be expected to be calm when I reflect on it? And this, too, now I remember, is the anniversary of the very night when she was restored to us. Three long and dismal years have elapsed since that fearful time; three years of the most unspeakable suffering to myself and my wife, and the wretch who has been the cause of all this misery has hitherto eluded me. Would to Heaven that he would once more cross my path, that I might wreak my vengeance upon his head, and, in some measure, obtain satisfaction for the cruel wrongs we have experienced at his hands."

"Heaven ordains everything for the best," remarked Alice, "and for my own part I sincely hope that we may never behold the villain Mowbray again; fear not but he will not be suffered to escape punishment for the crimes of which he has been guilty, and the injuries he has inflicted on us."

"True, Mrs. Hawthorn," said our hero, "I quite agree with you in that opinion; the Almighty is too just to suffer one who has so basely outraged every sacred law to escape with impunity, and you must be satisfied to leave the work of retribution in his hands. Come, my good friend, try to compose yourself, and to encourage the hope that there are better times in store for you yet, and that, too, before long."

"Ah! no, Mr. Parker," returned Hawthorn; "I have often tried to flatter myself with such ideas, but to no purpose; for reason convinces me to the contrary. My poor child's reason is fled for ever, and what happiness is it possible that I can ever experience, while I contemplate her melancholy and deplorable condition?"

"Something may yet occur," said Mary, "when you least expect it, to restore your unfortunate daughter from the awful malady with which she is now afflicted, and she may learn to look back upon the dismal past with calmness and resignation."

"Alas! that can never be," returned the fisherman; "it would be next to madness for me to give way to any such idea. And if indeed my poor girl should recover her senses, how tenfold must be her sufferings, when she reflected upon her degraded and forlorn condition, and thought of the monstrous treachery with which that man to whom she had devoted her whole affections, and in whose truth and sincerity she placed every confidence, had acted towards her. I shudder even to think of it, and though it may appear a strange contradiction to the feelings I have expressed, I would much rather that she should remain as she is, than be subjected to additional suffering. Ah, my friends, there is but little hope for me, let me view it in whatever light I may."

Richard Parker and his wife returned no answer to this, for they could not deny the truth and force of what he said, and they more deeply sympathised with him in his misfortunes than ever.

The night advanced on rapid wings, and the storm still continued to rage with unmitigated fury; in fact, it seemed rather to gain in strength than to offer any signs of abating, and the persons present in the fisherman's cottage relapsed into dismal silence, and gave themselves up to the melancholy thoughts which the weather naturally created in their breasts. Alice had several times re-visited her daughter's chamber, and found her still wrapped in the same sound and tranquil sleep, and that circumstance did in some measure seem to alleviate the anguish of Hawthorn's mind, and to quiet the apprehensions that had taken possession of it; but still he traversed the room to and fro with disordered steps, and ever and anon looked out upon the storm, as though he expected something particular to happen. Suddenly he started, and turned his eyes eagerly and anxiously towards the door, and Alice hastily inquired what was the matter, and what had occurred to alarm him.

"Did you not hear that?" he replied.

"Hear what?" demanded his wife.

"That cry," returned Hawthorn, "that dismal cry; it sounded like the voice of some unhappy wretch in his last groans."

"I hear nothing but the wailing of the wind," observed our hero; "you must have been mistaken, Mr. Hawthorn."

"No—no," returned the latter, impatiently; "it was not the wind, and I was not mistaken. I heard it distinctly."

They returned no answer, and all of them listened with breathless attention.

"There again!" ejaculated Hawthorn, and once more starting; "surely, you must have heard that?"

They had, indeed, heard it, and looked at each other with surprise and anxiety. It sounded like the groaning of some person in the greatest agony, and seemed to be approaching nearer the cottage; but in a very few moments all was again silent

THE DISTRESS OF FLORA'S PARENTS ON FINDING THE LETTER.

and they heard nothing but the howling of the tempest, which at that moment was perfectly terrific.

"Some poor unfortunate needs our help," observed Alice; "and it must not be withheld from them in such a dreadful hour as this. Hasten, Henry, for not a moment is to be lost, and Mr. Parker will probably accompany you?"

"Most willingly," replied our hero, "and I hope that our efforts in the cause of humanity may be crowned with success."

Mr. Hawthorn hastily put a light in a lantern, and himself and Richard advancing towards the door, opened it and issued forth into the open air. The wind blew with such tremendous gusts, and the rain and snow descended so violently, that they could scarcely keep their feet, and they were at a loss which way to go, for there was now no sound to direct them; but still they proceeded, feeling confident that they could not all have been mistaken, and that some poor unfortunate, overtaken and exhausted by the fury of the storm, must be at no great distance off. They shouted aloud several times, but no answer was returned to their cries, and they remained in the same state of bewilderment and uncertainty as before.

"I am afraid we are too late," said the fisherman; "and that death has already overtaken the unfortunate traveller, whoever he may be."

"No," replied Parker, "we must not thus give up in despair. The sounds evidently proceeded from no great distance from the cottage, and whoever it is, he probably has only fainted from exhaustion. Let us continue our search."

Mr. Hawthorn, of course, assented, and they struck out into another direction which they had not yet examined. They again shouted at the top of their voices, but still they received no reply, and their hopes again began to fail them. Then they carefully examined the snow on the ground as they proceeded, to see whether they could discover any human foot-prints, but nothing of the kind met their sight, and this added to their hopelessness of being able to discover the object of which they were in search.

"It is most strange," remarked Hawthorn, "it seems impossible that we could all of us have been mistaken, and yet we can discover no signs of any human being here. If he has fainted he must soon perish, for it is impossible he could long survive a storm like this in such a condition as we have a right to suppose this unfortunate stranger to be."

"True," said Parker, "but we must not give up the search while there is even the slightest chance of success. Let us take this direction."

They now turned another way, and the fisherman holding the lantern towards the ground, they examined every step they took with the greatest minuteness, but still with no better success than that which had hitherto attended them.

"It is all useless," remarked Hawthorn. "Fate seems to baffle all our exertions, and we are not permitted to gratify our humane wishes. The poor fellow must doubtless by this time have perished. May Heaven have mercy upon his soul, whoever he may be."

Our hero fervently responded to this prayer, and he felt grieved and disappointed at the failure of their efforts, for that some wretched and ill-fated individual had met with an untimely end he felt certain, and it would have afforded him the utmost satisfaction had they been permitted to rescue him. They had now, however, no other alternative but to return to the cottage, which they did by another route, and they continued to examine the ground as they proceeded, with the faint hope of still being enabled to discover the object of their search.

They had arrived within sight of the cottage, and the fisherman, who was a little in advance of his companion, was still holding the lantern towards the ground, when his foot suddenly came in contact with something, and he stumbled and fell, and the lantern being dashed out of his hand, the light was extinguished, and they were left in total darkness.

Hawthorn quickly gathered himself up again, and they both proceeded to grope about the spot where he had fallen, and their hands immediately came in contact with a human form, which was stretched at full length upon the earth, and was almost covered with snow.

"Ah!" exclaimed Parker, "fortune has at last directed us to the object of our search. It is evidently the form of a man, and I can feel that he still breathes. Poor wretch! But let us not delay a moment, Hawthorn; it may not yet be too late to save him."

Hawthorn made no reply, and raising the insensible form of the stranger on their shoulders, they proceeded with all the haste they could towards the cottage, where they arrived in a very few seconds.

Alice had been awaiting their return with the utmost anxiety, and when she beheld them enter the cottage with the unfortunate stranger upon their shoulders, he exhibited the greatest agitation.

"Poor fellow!" she ejaculated; "is he dead?"

"No," answered Hawthorn, "but I fear he will soon be, if the remedies we shall apply to him do not succeed. Quick! quick, Alice, and get such restoratives as you may consider necessary and most efficacious."

They now placed the form of the unfortunate stranger upon a sofa, and proceeded to examine him more particularly. His apparel was of the meanest description, and his whole appearance indicated the utmost poverty and wretchedness. His features were so covered with dirt, and otherwise disfigured, that they presented scarcely anything human; but still there was something about them that Hawthorn could not help imagining he had seen before, and he felt a strange sensation steal through his breast as the idea occurred to him, for which he could not at the moment account. On examining him more minutely, they perceived the marks of blood upon his clothes which seemed to have proceeded from a wound in his side, and this the more created their curiosity and anxiety. He was, as we have stated before, quite insensible, but he still breathed, and Alice, therefore, hastened to apply such remedies as she had at hand, with the hope of recovering him ; and having done so, she proceeded to remove some of the dirt from his face, so that they might the more distinctly discern his features. She had no sooner done so than she and her husband started back with an expression of the utmost amazement and agitation ; and the former, in a horse voice, exclaimed—

"Powers of darkness! is it possible? or is it some ghastly phantom called forth from the other world to tortue and bewilder my senses ? No, by all my hopes, it is no mockery! Those features can never be banished from my recollection, until memory shall blot out the remembrance of my wrongs, which can never be; —it is—it is the villain whom I have so long sought after in vain ;—it is the monster, Mowbray !"

"Mowbray !" repeated Richard Parker and his wife, with unaffected astonishment ; "is it possible ?"

"Alas !" sighed Alice, "it is, indeed, that wretched, guilty man ! But, oh, what a terrible change has taken place in him. What can have reduced him to this awful condition? and why has his footsteps again been directed hither ?"

"Hah !" exclaimed Hawthorn, and the whole expression of his features showed the extreme excitement of his feelings ; "my dream! the wretch ! the deceiver ! the fiend ! do I indeed again behold him? Retribution has at last overtaken him ; but he must not perish thus ; he must not die until I have poured into his ears my heaviest curses and reproaches, and gratified the implacable feeling of hatred and revenge which his acts of villany have created in my breast. Arouse ! seducer ! fell destroyer of all that once was pure, and lovely, and innocent ; and once more meet those whom you have so deeply injured."

As Hawthorn thus spoke, his eyes flashed with the excitement which the recollection of his wrongs had rekindled in his breast ; and his whole demeanour evinced the powerful emotion by which he was agitated.

"For Heaven's sake, my dear husband," remonstrated his wife, "be more calm, and—"

"Calm !" interrupted Hawthorn, passionately ; "how think you I can be calm when I once more behold the fell destroyer of my child before me, and recollect the monstrous wrongs of which he has been guilty towards us?"

"But remember his present abject and helpless condition," replied Alice, " and do not give way to these bursts of feeling. It would be worse than cowardice to seek to take any advantage of the wretched guilty man under such circumstances ; if we may judge from his deplorable appearance, he has already been most terribly punished for the atrocious crimes of which I must admit he has been guilty."

"Yes," remarked Richard ; " he has no doubt suffered much; and probably it is remorse that has brought him hither ; exert yourself to restore him to consciousness, and then you may at least listen to the explanation he may have to offer."

"What explanation can he give?" demanded Hawthorn, impatiently ; " how can he excuse his conduct ? What atonement can he possibly make for his villany? Oh, as I gaze upon the hateful features of the monster who has destroyed my child, and brought us all to shame and misery, my brain is fired with madness, and I could plunge my knife in his heart, and—"

"Oh, horrible !" ejaculated Alice, placing her hand upon his arm, and looking imploringly in his face ; " be calm, be calm, I again supplicate you."

"Yes," continued Hawthorn, in the same tone of bitterness and anguish of feeling ; "here abject and fallen reclines the once proud and gallant Mowbray ; he whose prepossessing manners and honeyed accents so well aided him in his diabolical designs, and unconsciously, unsuspiciously led his unfortunate victims into the cruel snares which he had laid for their destruction. Miscreant ! how does the warm blood curdle in my veins as I gaze upon thee, and curses loud and deep must continue to escape from my indignant breast. Should you recover, how will you dare to meet the gaze of those whom you have so cruelly, so irreparably injured?"

Mrs. Hawthorn returned no answer to this, but she redoubled her exertions to recover the unfortunate but guilty Mowbray, though for some time with but little succes, for he gave scarcely any signa of returning life. Our hero and his wife stood by and watched the proceedings with the deepest anxiety, and they awaited the possible restoration to his senses with no small degree of impatience and curiosity. The wretched appearance of the unfortunate man struck them most forcibly, and notwithstanding the heinous crimes of which he had been guilty, and the misery and disgrace he had caused, they could not help feeling some little degree of pity for him, when they saw his utterly helpless and deplorable state.

"Misguided man," remarked Richard; "he does present a terrible example of the retribution which is certain, sooner or later, to overtake the guilty. To judge from his appearance, and his emaciated form, he must have suffered all the horrors of remorse, and want, and destitution."

"I trust sincerely that he has," said Hawthorn, bitterly; "the wretch! what misery is there too great for him to suffer for the wrongs he has inflicted, and to whom he was bound by every tie of gratitude? Think of the melancholy situation of my poor child, and then imagine what my feelings must be on beholding again the author of it all."

"Yes, Mr. Hawthorn," returned our hero; "believe me I can duly appreciate your feelings, and that I deeply sympathise with you, and deprecate and loathe the heartless conduct of this guilty man. But it has pleased heaven to visit him with its wrath, and you should be satisfied. But he is wounded, and that the more excites my wonder and suspense; how has he received this wound?"

"Doubtless," answered Hawthorn, "in the attempt to commit some other act of villany. There is no crime, however atrocious, of which I do not now consider him capable. But the wound he has received is apparently only slight, and he has evidently suffered principally from want and the inclemency of the weather. Oh, how impatient am I for him to recover his senses, that I may pour in his ears my curses and reproaches. Oh, God! what must be the sufferings of my poor Flora, should she again behold the heartless destroyer of her innocence, and the annihilator of her hopes; and should returning reason enable her to recognise him? I shudder even at the thought. See! he breathes more freely, and some degree of warmth is imparted to his limbs. He will recover, and I shall have the satisfaction of reproaching him with his villany, and heaping my maledictions upon his guilty head. My dream again recurs in the most vivid colours to my memory, and I feel satisfied that it was not remorse which brought him into the neighbourhood of

this cottage, but in order to endeavour to accomplish some other infamous design against that unfortunate girl on whom he has already inflicted such monstrous and irreparable wrongs."

"Oh, no," said Alice; "indeed your excited feelings cause you to judge him too harshly; he must be a monster of the blackest dye if he could contemplate that of which you suspect him."

"And has he not already sufficiently proved himself to be entirely callous to every sense of proper feeling?" demanded her husband. "What is there that a wretch like him would hesitate to do, after that which he has already committed? There is no plot, however brutal and hideous, of which we have not just cause to suspect him. Oh, the longer I gaze upon him, the greater becomes my horror and detestation; and the wrongs which our ill-fated daughter has suffered rush with tenfold and overwhelming force upon my memory; and I felt as though I could embrue my hands in his blood, and even exult in the execution of the deed."

"What dreadful words are these," said Alice, fixing upon her husband a mingled look of amazement, incredulity, and gentle reproach; "I could not have believed you capable of entertaining such fearful thoughts, and even now I must suppose that anxiety of mind has bewildered your brain, and that you know not what you say."

"No, Alice," replied her husband; "you judge wrong if you suppose that I am not perfectly conscious to everything which I give utterance to; and truth and justice prompt the thoughts that I have expressed. What else can sufficiently wash out the stain of a beloved daughters, shame and dishonour, but the death of her destroyer?"

Hold!" ejaculated Alice, with increased looks of alarm; "I cannot hear you talk thus; for it chills the very blood in my veins to listen to you. The soul of the misguided Mowbray will probably shortly be summoned into the presence of the Almighty, to whom he will have to render up an awful account for all the crimes he has committed, and who will judge him accordingly. Who shall presume to arrogate to themselves that power which rests with the Supreme alone?"

"True, Mrs. Hawthorn," remarked Richard, "and doubtless your husband, when he comes calmly to reflect, will be ready to admit the truth and force of your arguments. It would be worse than cowardice to take advantage of this wretched, misguided man, in his present helpless condition. Should he be restored to consciousness, how bitterly must remorse sting and torture his guilty soul !"

"No," said the fisherman, impatiently, "he possesses too hardened and insensible a heart, I am convinced, to be moved to repentance ; besides, what atonement can all the remorse he may feel, make for the cruel wrongs of which he has been the guilty and detested author ? Can he restore his unfortunate victim to that state of innocence and happiness which she once enjoyed ? Can he wipe out the indelible stain of infamy and degradation which he has fixed upon us ? He cannot; and with such a conviction, is it not worse than mockery to argue in the way that you are doing ?"

Mrs. Hawthorn returned no answer to this, but sighing deeply, she renewed her exertions to restore the guilty Mowbray to sensibility, while her husband, having again fixed a look of the most unspeakable agony and detestation upon the pale and ghastly features of the once handsome and volatile Alfred Mowbray, folded his arms across his chest, and he walked to the farther end of the room, and seemed to be entirely lost in the reflections that crowded upon his brain.

Mrs. Hawthorn was scarcely in a less state of agitation than himself, but, nevertheless, she continued to apply such remedies to the unfortunate Mowbray as the urgency of the case required, and her own judgment dictated ; but they seemed to have but very little effect, though he certainly breathed more freely, at the same time that he gave no symptoms of returning life, and Mrs. Hawthorn was anxious to call in the aid of some medical man, though she did not like to venture to offer such a suggestion to her husband.

The storm continued with unabated violence, and nothing whatever could exceed the horrors that reigned around, and which were calculated to add to the dismal thoughts which the extraordinary and exciting events of the night had created in their breasts. Hawthorn again returned to the place where the insensible form of Mowbray was lying, and once more, with folded arms and knitted brows, he stood and contemplated the pale features of the man whom he had so much reason to hate ; muttering incoherent sentences to himself, and evidently awaiting his recovery to consciousness with the utmost impatience and anxiety.

Richard and his wife were now, as may be imagined, deeply interested, and awaited the result of this adventure with much curiosity ; but as there were no signs at present of Mowbray's being restored to sensibility, and observing that their presence seemed to place the fisherman under some feeling of restraint, they arose from their seats, and bidding him and Alice good night, they retired to the cottage which they inhabited during their stay in that neighbourhood, where they could without restraint or interruption give free indulgence to the thoughts which the events of the night had naturally excited in their breasts.

"How extraordinary it is," remarked our heroine, "that the guilty Mowbray should be once more guided to the dwelling of those whom he has so deeply and irreparably injured ; and that, too, under such peculiar and painful circumstances."

"It is," coincided our hero, "and I am anxious to see what the result will be. Hawthorn is painfully excited, and I do not marvel at it, when I take into consideration the fearful and cruel wrongs which he has suffered at his hands ; but should Mowbray be restored to sensibility, I hope that he will be able to exercise some influence and control over his feelings, and to listen patiently to the explanation of the wretched man, whom I feel convinced has been led to the cottage by feelings of remorse and repentance."

"Yes," replied Mary, "that is decidedly my opinion ; and it is quite evident from his wretched and emaciated appearance that he has suffered much, and has received a just, though terrible punishment for the crimes he has committed."

"True," coincided her husband, "and he affords a terrible and striking example of the awful consequences of guilt. The retribution of the offended Supreme, is certain sooner or later to overtake all those who outrage His laws. Poor Flora, what a melancholy fate is hers, and how awful must be the effects of conscience upon the mind of her destroyer, should he ever recover to be made acquainted with her present deplorable condition."

"It must, indeed," returned our heroine ; "but her parents will surely be careful not to suffer her to see him, which, in her present diseased state of mind, must be productive of the most disastrous consequences."

"They will be certain to avoid any such circumstance," replied Richard, "for it is not likely that it would be productive of any good. The dream which occurred to the imagination of Mr. Hawthorn was a most extraordinary one; and the strange event of this night proves that his forebodings were not altogether without foundation."

"True," coincided his wife, "and so I could not help thinking at the time he related it to us; though, seeing the powerful impression it had made upon him, I refrained from giving utterance to my real feelings. The ways of Providence are wonderful, as has been fully exemplified in our own instance, Richard; and it is that which inspires me with confidence, and convinces me that, notwithstanding the many misfortunes it has been our lot to encounter, and the difficulties by which we are at present surrounded, the time will yet come, and that, too, I trust, before long, when the heavy clouds that are at present impending over us, and the dismal character of the prospects that are spread before us, will be dispersed, and that we shall again be restored to happiness and tranquillity."

Richard Parker shook his head. It was a subject upon which he was not now at all inclined to enter, for, in spite of all that had recently taken place, and the arguments that had been made use of by his wife and his friends, he could not entirely banish from his mind the dismal forebodings that had so long held possession of it.

"Ah, Mary," he observed, after a brief pause, "would that I could be so sanguine on that painful subject as you profess to be; but when I reflect upon all the circumstances connected with my unfortunate fate, it is impossible that I can help having my misgivings."

"Become more firm and confident, Richard," said his wife, "for has not the Almighty hitherto been most kind and merciful to us, in enabling us to elude the vigilance of our pursuers, even when they were immediately on our track, and in raising us up honest and ardent friends where we least expected to find them?"

"Most true," replied our hero; "but I fear that something will yet occur to betray me into the hands of my enemies, and if so my fate would be indeed sealed, and you and our poor boy would be left to all the horrors of poverty, misery, and despair. Oh, my fond, devoted wife, need I seek to describe to you the poignant anguish of my feelings as these ideas present themselves to my distracted imagination?"

"For Heaven's sake, my beloved husband," returned our heroine, throwing her arms around his neck, and looking affectionately in his face, "do endeavour to banish such gloomy thoughts from your mind, and to look forward with hope and confidence to the best. You have staunch friends in Adams, Hawthorn, and Binnacle, and I feel certain that, with their assistance, we shall yet be able to elude the vigilance of those who are in pursuit of us, and to settle ourselves in some part of the country where we may remain unmolested. Endeavour to await patiently until you receive a reply to the communication you have despatched to our friend Mr. Adams, who, no doubt, will furnish you with the best advice how to act, and I entertain but little, if any, fear as to the result."

"I will do so, dear Mary," returned our hero, "but still I cannot help feeling the deepest regret, when I reflect upon all the dangers in which I hourly involve those to whom I am so much indebted, and who, if they should be discovered to have befriended me in the manner they have done, would be sure to be plunged into ruin."

"Do not agitate yourself with these fears," returned Mary; "for I trust that they will prove to be entirely unfounded. Providence will never permit those to suffer who have acted with such unexampled humanity towards their unfortunate fellow creatures in distress. Come, Richard, endeavour to think as I have expressed myself, and something seems to assure me that my hopes and anticipations will not be doomed to be disappointed."

"God grant that they may not," fervently ejaculated Richard; "but come, the night wears apace; let us retire to rest, and see what to-morrow will produce."

"Ah!" replied our heroine; "I am most anxious to learn what will be the result of the meeting between the guilty Mowbray and Mr. Hawthorn, should the former be restored to sensibility."

"I fear that the excited feelings of Mr. Hawthorn will be too much for him to control within the bounds of reason," remarked Richard; "at any rate, the meeting cannot fail to be a most painful one. It would have been better had the wretch Mowbray never again have been guided to the dwelling of those whom he has so greatly injuried."

"True," coincided our heroine; "but no doubt he has been urged on to do so by the remorse of conscience, and, by convincing them of his sincere repentance, offer them the only atonement in his power. Poor Flora, what an unfortunate thing it was for her that Fate should ever have introduced her to one who was destined to act with such base treachery towards her. Surely he has much to answer for, and terrible must be the agony of his dying moments, if he is awakened to a full sense of the enormity of the crimes he has committed. Alas! alas! what a lovely and innocent being have his accursed arts destroyed."

"They have," returned Richard; "and most deeply do I sympathise with his unfortunate and too confiding victim. But I sincerely hope that the light of reason may once more dawn upon her brain, and that she may be restored to peace if she cannot be to that happiness which she once enjoyed."

To this wish Mrs. Parker most cordially responded, and after some further conversation, they retired to bed, and sought to gain a short respite from their cares and anxieties in sleep.

The terrors of the night were not at all diminished; the wind howled with unabated fury, and the rain and snow descended as violently as it had done all the evening. Mrs. Hawthorn continued unremitting in her exertions to restore the wretched Mowbray to animation; but he remained in a complete state of lethargy, and it seemed to be very doubtful, indeed, whether he would ever again revive, Hawthorn continuing alternately to watch him anxiously, and with looks that sufficiently expressed the feelings that were passing in his mind, and to pace the room backwards and forwards, muttering unintelligible words to himself; and it was in vain that Alice endeavoured, by all the arguments she could make use of, to calm his feelings, though, in fact, as might naturally be expected, she was scarcely in a state of less excitement than himself, and awaited the recovery of Mowbray with much fear and anxiety. She several times sought to persuade her husband to retire to rest, but to that he would not listen with any degree of patience, and she, therefore, ceased to urged him.

"What!" he said, hastily, "and think you that I could rest, while my mind is in this state of anxiety and suspense? Should the villain Mowbray die, before I have had an opportunity of breathing my curses in his ears, I——"

"Oh, forbear," interrupted Alice; "your observations quite shock me. Guilty though this misguided man has been, he will no doubt shortly be summoned before that dread tribunal at which we must all some time or other appear, and you should not pursue even the most abandoned wretch with such vindictive feelings in his last moments."

"And think you," demanded Hawthorn, impatiently, "that I can ever forgive the wretch who has blighted all the hopes, and destroyed the happiness of our young and beautiful child? She who was the only pride and comfort of our declining days? By all my hopes, this thought is preposterous; and even as now gaze upon him, and think of the over-whelming misery he has brought upon us my brain is almost excited to madness and curses, ten-fold and terrible curses rise upon my lips, and would heap themselves upon the devoted head of the heartless miscreant. Oh, what a fiendish work has he accomplished! And yet you seem to wonder that I should now view him with feelings of disgust and detestation."

"No, my dear husband," replied his wife, "I do not marvel at the feelings you have so warmly expressed, yet I would have you control them within the bounds of reason. Neither do I attempt to extenuate the conduct of this unhappy and guilty man, for it would be unjust and unreasonable for me to do so; but situated as he now is, it behoves us, at least, to show some mercy and forbearance towards him, and to leave his fate in the hands of the Almighty. If we may judge from his careworn, haggard, and emaciated appearance, so different to what he once was, when we unfortunately first became acquainted with him, he has suffered much, not only from remorse of conscience, but misery and destitution; and his punishment no doubt has been as severe as the fate which seems to await him will be terrible."

"Oh," exclaimed Hawthorn, "what adequate suffering can he possibly have experienced for the wrongs and misery he has inflicted on others? What punishment can be half sufficiently terrible for a guilty wretch like him? Think of our poor witless child, and ask yourself what should be the reward of the heartless wretch who has been the cause of her destruction — he, the fiend, who under the most specious guise of honour and virtue, betrayed to shame and misery one of the most lovely of Nature's works? By Heaven, my brain burns to madness when I think of it; and there is no argument which reason can make use of that can convince me of the injustice and undue severity of my feelings."

Alice felt too much the truth and force of these observations to offer any reply; and her husband, beating his breast in the agony and excitement of his feelings, again paced the room with disordered steps, and seemed to resign himself entirely to despair.

In this manner hour after hour elapsed, and still there appeared to be little or no change in Mowbray, and but for his breathing, any person to have gazed upon him would have supposed him to have been a corpse. How fearful was the change that had taken place in that wretched, guilty man since the last time they had seen him, and what a dismal tale of suffering, remorse, and dissipation did it indicate! In spite of all the crimes of which he had been guilty, Alice could not help gazing upon his haggard and cadaverous countenance—his sunken eyes—his dishevelled hair, and attenuated form, with some feelings of pity and regret, and she redoubled her exertions to revive him, notwithstanding she anticipated with dread the scene that would be sure to take place between him and her husband.

"Miserable young man," she ejaculated ; " alas ! how shamefully have you abused the manifold gifts with which Providence has so bountifully supplied you, and which, had they been put to a proper use, would have rendered you an honour instead of a scourge to society. Was there no friendly voice to withdraw you from the brink of the fearful precipice on which you so long tottered ?"

"No," observed Hawthorn, hastily, " all advice and remonstrance would have been lost upon one whose heart was perfectly insensible to every proper and virtuous feeling. All the most evil passions that can possibly disgrace mankind were inherent in him, and he delighted only in working the misery and ruin of his fellow creatures. Curses light upon the fatal hour which first introduced him to us ; for but for that, Flora would now have been innocent and happy, and our declining years would have been spared the heavy sorrows which now have descended on them."

"But let us not quite despair, my husband," said Alice, "for Providence will yet view us with mercy and compassion, and, perhaps sooner than we expect, restore us to that peace of mind to which we have so long been strangers."

"Oh, no," returned Hawthorn, impatiently, "I can encourage no such ideas, for I feel satisfied that they can only be doomed to disappointment. My poor child! Oh, if the light of reason still beamed upon your brain, and you were aware that the villain to whom you owe all your misery is again under this roof, what would be the anguish of your feeling ?"

" It is a mercy to her," observed Alice, "that she is unconscious of it; and not for the world would I that they should encounter each other."

" The sight of his unfortunate victim must strike the monster Mowbray dead, if he is at all capable of feeling!" exclaimed Hawthorn, violently. " He must be a wretch indeed if he could gaze unmoved upon the terrible work of his guilty hands."

Alice only sighed, for she was unable to make any other reply, and Hawthorn, throwing himself into a chair, again relapsed into silence, and seemed to abandon himself altogether to the gloomy thoughts that crowded in such rapid and tumultuous succession upon his mind.

As the morning approached, Alice, leaving her husband alone in the room with the insensible Mowbray, hastened to the chamber of Flora, to ascertain the state of her daughter's health.

Hawthorn, on finding himself alone, walked up to the sofa on which the insensible form of Mowbray was stretched, and for a few minutes he contemplated it with mingled expressions of revenge and gratification. Then he placed his hand upon the heart, and feeling it throb, he ejaculated—

" Yes, he still lives, and may yet revive. I hope to Heaven that he may, that he may hear from my lips the bitter reproaches which his diabolical conduct towards me and mine so richly merits. The miscreant! what could have emboldened him to venture hither? Is it to gaze on the ruin and desolation caused by his hands, and to taunt and mock at me with his triumph? By Heaven, it were well for him that it should not be so, for he can but little calculate what the revenge and indignation of an injured parent might incite him to do. But no ; it is not with that purpose that he comes hither. His ghastly and emaciated appearance convinces me of that, and at the same time assures me of what he must have suffered. Want, misery, and destitution are stamped upon his features, and satisfy me that the just retribution of offended Heaven for the many crimes he has committed has at last overtaken him, and I triumph at the downfall and misery of my most bitter enemy. He is justly punished, and the terrible wrongs he has inflicted on my poor child, will not go wholly unavenged. Where is now the gay gallant who once could so easily lure and betray the too confiding and innocent maiden by his dangerous fascinations? The change is no less fearful than it is extraordinary, and I glory in it. Oh, Mowbray ! how base and brutal must be thy nature, to have incited thee to perpetrate the hellish deeds thou hast done. What a pity that youth and manly accomplishments should be thus perverted. Revive ! and listen to the tale of ruin and misery thou hast caused, and then, if thine heart is not quite insensible to every feeling of humanity and justice, how bitterly must thy conscience upbraid thee in thy dying moments, for thy countenance convinces me that they are numbered."

As he thus spoke, Hawthorn still continued to gaze with looks of hatred and revenge at the wretched, guilty man, and with the utmost anxiety he watched to see him revive, with the hope to pour in his ears the expressions of his indignation, and the bitterest curses that could suggest

THE RETURN OF FLORA TO HER HOME.

themselves to him. Never before had such feelings entered the breast of the warm-hearted fisherman ; but when all the cruel wrongs that had been inflicted upon his unfortunate daughter are taken into consideration, and he saw the guilty author of them all stretched out before him, can his excitement be wondered at?   He was interrupted in the midst of his gloomy and painful meditations by the return of Alice to the room, and he eagerly inquired of her the condition of Flora.

"She has risen," answered Alice; "and appears well, but she seems to entertain the same fancy to remain in her chamber, and it shall be my care to induce her to remain there during the day."

"That is well," remarked Hawthorn; "on no account whatever must she be permitted to enter here, for should she behold the cruel destroyer of her hopes, her innocence, and her happiness, how terrible would be the consequences."

"True," said Alice; "alas! poor girl, what a dreadful fate is hers."

"Yes," said Hawthorn, passionately, and the expression of his countenance fully testified the torturing feelings that inhabited his breast; "and there lies the wretch who has been the cause of it all. May Heaven's curses pursue him both on this earth, and in that dread eternity into which he will doubtless shortly be summoned. Oh, as I gaze upon him, I can scarcely control the feelings of hatred, disgust, and vengeance that inhabit my breast, within the bounds of reason."

"Forbear!" remonstrated his wife; "the helpless and deplorable condition of the wretched and misguided man ought to restrain your passions, and excite your pity."

"Pity!" repeated Hawthorn, impatiently, "pity for the miscreant who has destroyed the hopes, the innocence, and the happiness of that poor child to whom we looked as our only comfort in the downhill of life? It would be a bitter mockery to talk of such a thing. What! would you have me kiss the hand of the fell destroyer, and honour him for that which he has done?"

"No, Henry," replied Mrs. Hawthorn, "you misunderstand me grossly if you imagine that such thoughts or wishes could for a moment enter my breast, for it is impossible that you can feel more just abhorrence and indignation against the betrayer of our ill-fated daughter than I do; but still I cannot help feeling a sentiment of pity and regret at his fallen condition, and to lament that human nature should ever so degrade itself as he has done. What a tale of suffering does his wan and emaciated features express."

"And what can be all the sufferings he may have experienced, compared with those he has inflicted on us?" demanded Hawthorn, hastily; "has he not by his crimes brought all his misery on himself? Had he endured all the torments of perdition, he would have experienced no more than a just punishment."

"And I am satisfied," observed Alice, "that the tortures of remorse he has endured have been terrible and severe. He must indeed have been totally insensible to every proper feeling of humanity, could he for ever have remained indifferent to the crimes he had committed, and the cruel injuries he had inflicted on his unsuspecting fellow-creatures. It must have been the upbraidings of his conscience, and his wish to make all the atonement in his power, that guided his footsteps here."

"Atonement!" repeated Hawthorn; "it is impossible for him to make any—for the evils of which he has been the guilty and fatal cause, can never be remedied. Oh, as I gaze upon him, and think of all the base treachery and ingratitude with which he has acted towards us, the feelings of detestation and indignation which swell my breast are almost too powerful for utterance. Would to Heaven that he would revive, that I might at once give vent to my torturing thoughts, and show the libertine what the resentment of an injured parent is."

"Nay, Hawthorn," replied his wife, "again I must expostulate with you, and once more beg of you to endeavour to restrain the passions which have taken such powerful possession of your breast. The wretched situation in which we now behold this unfortunate and misguided man, should stifle all vindictive feelings against him, and rather excite our pity and regret."

"Pity!" reiterated Hawthorn, with a look of impatience; "pity for the miscreant who has brought our unhappy daughter to the miserable, hopeless, and degraded situation she now is in? Alice, there is no reason or justice in what you say, and how do you think it possible that it can make any impression on me? By all my hopes, I should despise myself if I could view him with any other sentiments than those of the most unbounded hatred and disgust. The part he has acted is that of the most black and heartless villany, and there is no punishment here or hereafter which can be too terrible for him."

Alice was prevented from making any reply by the entrance of our hero and his wife, who expressed their anxiety and regret at seeing Mowbray in the same condition as he had been the night before, and the former could not help suggesting the prudence and necessity of calling in the assistance of some medical gentleman.

"No," replied Hawthorn, with an impatient look; "I will call in no such aid for one who has acted so monstrous a part as he has done towards me and mine.

It would be little better than pandering to his crimes, and would——"

"Nay," Mr. Hawthorn," interrupted Richard, "you will pardon me, but common humanity I should think ought to induce you to do all you can to save the life of this guilty young man, that he may at least have time for repentance."

"Mr. Parker," returned the fisherman, " you have never experienced that which I have done, or you would not talk thus. But something seems to assure me that remorse has never yet entered the hardened breast of the miscreant who is now stretched before us, and that the contemplation of the accomplishment of some further villanous design has alone been the cause of his coming again to this neighbourhood."

"Oh, no," replied Richard ; " that is impossible ; he must indeed be an abandoned miscreant if such could have been his designs. But his miserable and deplorable condition—his ghastly and haggard features, and the utter appearance of want and wretchedness he evinces, prove at once the fallacy of such suspicions. He has evidently suffered much, and I am much mistaken if remorse alone has not brought him once more to your dwelling ; and a wish to assure you of his repentance, and to seek your forgiveness for the many wrongs he has inflicted on you before he dies."

"Forgiveness !" returned Hawthorn, bitterly ; "and can he ever expect that I can forgive the monster, who so basely abused my friendship and hospitality, and took advantage of an innocent, unsuspecting, and inexperienced girl to betray her, destroy her happiness for ever, and to bring shame and misery upon the heads of her parents? The bare idea is preposterous and unreasonable ; and, although I am not naturally of a vindictive disposition, I have not patience to encourage it for a moment."

"I must admit, Mr. Hawthorn," said our hero, " that you have had sufficient to excite your feelings, and to make you view this misguided man with disgust and hatred ; but surely if he evinces a proper feeling of compunction, and acknowledges the great injuries he has done you, you will not refuse to him your forgiveness in his dying moments, and when he is about so soon to be summoned into the presence of the Almighty, to render up a terrible account of all the crimes he has committed?"

"True, Mr. Parker," said Alice, " you express exactly the same sentiments as I entertain, and I trust that my husband will

exert himself to control his feelings, and to restrain his excitement within due bounds. At any rate, it is necessary that we should wait calmly and patiently th , restoration of Mowbray to his senses, that we may hear the explanation he has to offer. I must confess that the wretched appearance of the misguided young man has excited my deepest interest and curiosity, and I am most anxious to hear by what means he has fallen into his present condition, and who he really is. He seems to have suffered much from want and destitution, and anguish of mind."

"He does," remarked our hero, "and, notwithstanding his numerous vices, and the crimes he has committed, that at least entitles him to some small degree of commiseration. But how has he received this wound?"

"No doubt in the attempt of some act of villany," answered Hawthorn,

"Do not judge too uncharitably of him, husband," said Mrs. Hawthorn, "nor suffer that prejudice, which the great injuries he has undoubtedly inflicted upon us has naturally excited in your breast, too powerfully to prevail."

"After what we have experienced from him," returned Hawthorn, "have I not a right to believe him capable of any crime? There is nothing whatever that can plead for him with me in extenuation of his conduct, and the longer I reflect upon it, the more inveterate must I become against him. It would have been much better had fate ordained I should never behold him again."

"Most true," coincided his wife, "and I regret the circumstance that has brought the unfortunate though guilty man here. But still, we must do all in our power that humanity can suggest to restore him, and leave the retribution which is due to his crimes in the hands of the Supreme."

Mr. Hawthorn saw plainly that it was useless to attempt to argue the painful and important point with his wife, and he, therefore, returned no answer to this, and a silence of some minutes ensued, he seating himself opposite to the place where Mowbray was reclining, and watching him with looks of mingled anxiety and resentment. Richard and his wife, however, at length endeavoured to divert his thoughts from the painful subject that engrossed them, by engaging him in conversation upon other topics, and in which they partly succeeded, while Alice redoubled her efforts to restore Mowbray to sensibility, without, however, for some time their being attended with any visible effects. The time wore tediously away, and the afternoon arrived without any change taking place, and they all began to think that the wretched man would never again awaken to consciousness, when suddenly they were all startled by hearing a deep groan escape him, and Mr. Hawthorn started to his feet, and hastened to the sofa on which he was reclining, in eager expectation of that which was about to take place. Gradually Mowbray seemed to revive from the deep and death-like stupor in which he had been so long wrapped, and attempting to raise himself, which he was enabled to do with the assistance of Alice, he opened his eyes, and stared wildly and vacantly around him, but apparently without being enabled to distinguish any person or object in the room. The expression of his hollow, sunken eyes, and the convulsive distortion of his features, were awful in the extreme, and all awaited with the most breathless anxiety and suspense to know what would be the result of this painful scene.

"Away! fiends of darkness, away! Ye shall not yet drag my guilty soul to perdition," at length cried the unhappy man, in a hoarse and fearful voice, and still glaring upon vacancy; "I dare not, must not yet meet the terrible punishment which is due to my crimes. Give me time to repent, and to endeavour to make some atonement to those whom I have so cruelly injured. Let me live a little longer, for how can I meet the presence of the Almighty Judge with all this overwhelming grief upon my soul? Ah! they mock at me with their glaring eyes, and their hideous looks; and, now, see the form of the gentle and innocent Flora appears before me, and reproaches me with looks that penetrate to my conscience-laden soul, and bid me despair! Ah, I can bear anything but this! Flora, I own that I have been a villain of the blackest dye; but have I not been fearfully punished for the crimes I have perpetrated? Away!—away! I cannot, dare not gaze upon you!"

Once more giving utterance to a groan of agony, the dying man threw himself back on his pillow, and seemed to be quite exhausted. Hawthorn gazed upon his ghastly features, and the convulsive writhings of his body, with mingled expressions of satisfaction and horror, and Richard and his wife remained silent, and watched with the most painful attention the issue of this exciting scene.

"Unfortunate man," said Alice; "it is now evident that the horrors of remorse have long preyed upon his guilty soul, and that he has been severely punished for the many heinous offences which he has committed. May Heaven pardon him, for awful, indeed, is the situation in which he is now placed."

"Pardon!" repeated Hawthorn, in an agitated voice, and totally unable to control the violence of his feelings; "there can be none for such a diabolical miscreant as he has proved himself to be; and the sufferings he is here enduring, are but a prelude to the tortures he is doomed undoubtedly to experience hereafter."

"Hold," said Alice, with a look of horror; "the words to which you have but just this moment given utterance, Hawthorn, surprise and shock me. Be calm, I beseech you, for this is not a time to give utterance to your excited feelings, or to give expression to your revengeful thoughts to that unhappy man, who so shortly will have to appear at the judgment seat of his Maker."

"And think you," demanded Hawthorn, "that I can behold the monster who has destroyed the hopes, the happiness, and the prospects of one of the best of children, without giving vent to my feelings of indignation and disgust? By Heaven! I should be unworthy of the name of a man and a father if I could do so, and I should have just cause to hate and despise myself. Mowbray! libertine! seducer! look up; arouse yourself, and meet the bitter reproaches of the father of your unfortunate victim, whose innocence you have destroyed, and whose once bright mind you have made a dismal blank for ever."

As he thus spoke, he approached still nearer the place where the ill-fated man was lying, his whole frame powerfully agitated with the violence of his feelings, and his countenance flushed with rage, and grasped the arm of Mowbray, notwithstanding the looks of remonstrance which Alice fixed upon him. Mowbray, however, seemed to have sunk again into a state of torpor, and evidently heard him not, and was unconscious of all that was passing around him. Richard and his wife gazed upon the painful and solemn scene with feelings of the deepest interest and suspense, but did not venture to make use of any observation, as they thought that any interruption on their part might appear intrusive and impertinent, and could not possibly be productive of any good. Hawthorn having continued to gaze upon the countenance of the wretched Mowbray for some moments in the same excited manner, folded his arms across his chest, and paced the room backwards and forwards with the most disordered steps, and evidently lost in meditations of the most torturing and conflicting description. Alice continued her humane attentions towards the ill-fated Mowbray with unremitting assiduity, though it appeared quite evident to her that his earthly career was fast approaching to a termination, and it seemed doubtful whether he would ever again revive to consciousness. In this manner about another half hour passed away, when Mowbray again gave some signs of returning life, and once more by a violent and convulsive effort raising himself upon his elbow, he glared around him.

"Where am I?" he ejaculated, in a hollow voice; "what frightful dream is it that has so long held its potent spell on my senses? Am I still living? Oh, that pang! Can this be the agony of death that is upon me? Ah! yes; I remember now, when driven by despair and want to desperation, I sought to commit that dreadful crime on the wild heath, but was foiled in my villanous attempt, and the weapon of my intended victim penetrated my breast! But where am I now? What is it holds me down?—and what strange and fearful forms are these that seem to present themselves to my distracted imagination? Flora! deeply injured Flora, shall I not be permitted to see you once again before I die, and to crave your forgiveness?"

"Mowbray! guilty, wretched man!" ejaculated Hawthorn, in a voice of deep solemnity and agitation; "look up and behold those on whom your diabolical crimes have inflicted so much misery."

"Ah!" exclaimed the dying man, starting convulsively, and glaring more wildly and eagerly around him; "that voice! where have I heard it before? and what is the meaning of the torture it imparts to my soul as it vibrates in my ears? Horror! horror! the mist is removed from my eyes; terrible recollection resumes its sway; I know ye now! What accursed fate has caused this? The parents of my wretched, my unfortunate, and innocent victim stand before me, to heap their curses upon my devoted head in my dying moments! Away! away! I do confess my guilt, but I cannot, dare not gaze upon you!"

"Mowbray!" said Hawthorn, bitterly, and unable to control the violence of his feelings, "you do, indeed, behold the parents of that unfortunate, too confiding girl, whom your black-hearted villany destroyed; well may your conscience smite you for the monstrous part you have played. Oh, how fair, how lovely, how young, and innocent was she before accursed Fate introduced you to her; and your hypocritical, base, insidious allurements, won upon her susceptible heart! With what heartless and cold-blooded ingratitude have you acted towards those who rescued you from death, and treated you with every kindness and hospitality; and can you marvel that I should now feel the utmost gratification in witnessing the retribution that has at last overtaken you? Would to Heaven that we had met under different circumstances; oh, how terribly would I have avenged my own and my daughter's wrongs upon your guilty head! But your moments are numbered; eternity, that awful eternity which you should so much dread to meet, is opening upon you, when you must render up a full account to the Almighty Judge of all the dark and hideous deeds of which you have been guilty, and——"

"Hold—hold!" gasped forth the wretched man, interrupting him, and his ghastly features frightfully convulsed with the agony of his feelings, "forbear! Mr. Hawthorn, for mercy's sake spare me, and pity me, if you cannot forgive me. I do admit my guilt; I own that I basely deceived you from the first; that I imposed upon you by a fictitious name, and a false representation of my character and circumstances; I acknowledge that I took advantage of the confiding affection and innocence of your daughter; but such was the overpowering influence that her superior, her superlative charms had obtained over my passions, naturally warm and ungovernable, that I found it impossible to resist the temptation, and even though I knew that I had not the means of acting an honourable part towards her, I suffered myself to be hurried headlong through the stream of guilt to her destruction; but oh, how terrible has been the remorse of conscience I have suffered since. No language that I have at my command could describe it properly. The curse of offended Heaven has pursued me ever since, and life has been an insupportable burthen to me, though I feared to rid myself of it."

"Oh, villain—villain!" exclaimed Mr. Hawthorn, his feelings wound up to a pitch of agony which was almost insupportable; "think you that I can gaze upon you, and know you for the author of all the misery that has fallen upon me and her whose happiness is far more precious to me than my own existence, without feelings of hatred and revenge, and exulting in your present sufferings? The curse of Heaven is, indeed, upon you, and the feelings of remorse you now express can offer no atonement for the cruel, the dastardly, and brutal wrongs you have committed."

The wretched, guilty man, covered his face with his long bony hands, and groaned aloud in the overwhelming agony of his feelings, and Alice, and Richard and his wife, were deeply impressed and affected by the scene, and watched the result with the most breathless and painful anxiety.

"Oh, God!" at length gasped forth Mowbray, with the greatest difficulty, "too well do I feel the truth of all that you have stated, Mr. Hawthorn; and how sincerely do I hate and despise myself; but I am lingering on the threshold of eternity; I feel that my moments are indeed numbered, and do not, therefore, I implore you, pursue me with malice to the grave. Oh, pardon me, and lead me to hope that there is yet mercy and forgiveness for me from that dread tribunal before which I must shortly appear."

"Can hideous crimes like yours expect forgiveness?" said Hawthorn, and he still continued to fix the most reproachful glances upon the poor dying wretch before him; "oh, no, it were a base libel upon the justice and wisdom of the Supreme to hold out any such hopes, and never shall my tongue give utterance to that which my reason condemns."

"Horror! horror!" groaned Mowbray; "am I then indeed shut out from the pale of every hope? And if so, why is she not here to intercede for me, and to witness the sincerity of my repentance?"

"And dare you," demanded Hawthorn, in a hoarse voice, "dare you again meet her whom you have destroyed? If so, your heart must indeed be callous to every proper feeling of shame and compunction. Yes, Flora still lives, but what a fearful wreck of what once was so lovely and so innocent have your infernal arts now made her! Madness has seized upon her brain—it, perhaps, may be a mercy that it has done so—the light of reason is extinguished for ever; a poor maniac is all that is left of that which was once perfection's self, and this, this is all the accursed work of your hands. Think of this, Mowbray, and be the reflection the cause of tenfold more horror to you in your dying moments."

The unfortunate man fixed upon him one look that was more than sufficient to penetrate to the most insensible soul; he tried to speak, but the words were stifled, and rendered inaudible in his throat, and sinking back on the sofa, his features and body became frightfully convulsed. Mr. Hawthorn and the others were greatly shocked and terrified at the scene, and the former, drawing her husband aside,

endeavoured to calm the violent excitment of his feelings, and to expostulate with him on the severity of his observations towards the wretched man, whose existence seemed to be so fast drawing towards a close.

"Forbear, my dear husband," she said, in an under, but impressive tone; "forbear thus to add to the agony of his last moments, and leave him to the mercy of that Almighty Power in whose dread presence his soul must so shortly appear. It is unworthy of your character, notwithstanding the heinous offences of which he has been guilty, to pursue him with this vindictive feeling to the last."

"My daughter's wrongs rise paramount to my thoughts," he replied; "and completely supersede every other feeling within my breast."

He was about to proceed further, when he was interrupted by an appalling groan from Mowbray, and with a strength which could not have been expected in the condition in which he was, he started up on the sofa, and with every limb convulsed, and every feature distorted with dying agony, he exclaimed, in a voice which struck terror to the hearts of all who heard it:—

"He comes! the grim tyrant approaches! already I feel his icy fingers upon me, and there is no avoiding him, or escaping from the terrible and everlasting doom that awaits me! My brain is on fire! my eyes grow dim; and yet, what are those awful forms that dance before me, and grin in fiendish mockery upon me? Oh, save! oh, save me from them! Let me not die until I have had time to repent! What is it that clings around my throat, and prevents me from breathing? I—I shall be choked! Will no one have pity on me, and relieve me? No, you all stand tamely by, and mock at my sufferings! Oh! this is most cruel! I am but mortal, and have not others sinned as well, and as atrociously as me? Again that pang! Christ of Heaven, have mercy upon me! And this, oh, this then is death!—Flora Hawthorn, all whom I—Oh!"

With a groan more appalling than before, he sunk back on the sofa; a frightful expression passed over his features, he fixed one indescribable gaze upon the countenance of Hawthorn, and his eyes closed for ever.

"It is all over," ejaculated Alice, in a voice of much emotion; "he is dead; may God pardon and receive his guilty soul!"

Mr. Hawthorn stood fixed and inanimate as a statue for a few minutes by the side of the sofa, and gazed on the ghastly face of the corpse with an earnestness that showed the intensity and emotion of his feelings, and for some time he seemed to imagine it all a dream, and was unable to give utterance to a word; while Richard Parker, our heroine, and Alice were affected in a manner which we need not attempt to describe. At length Hawthorn somewhat aroused himself, and still gazing on the pale face of the corpse, he said—

"So, such is the end of the once gay and accomplished Alfred Mowbray; he whose honeyed accents have deceived and flattered so many, and who would fain have appeared the very paragon of honour and virtue, while under the alarming disguise, he concealed the heart of a fiend, and exulted in the misery of his fellow creatures. Oh, how many has he, by his base artifices, consigned to shame, to anguish, and despair. Such is the death of the heartless libertine, who doubtless flattered himself with the idea that his guilty and diabolical career would never be brought to a termination. Such are the last moments of the fell destroyer of our child; he has blighted all her hopes, and rendered her the most wretched and afflicted of human beings. Oh, it is a terrible, but just retribution, and as I gaze upon his livid features in death, I cannot but exult, and——"

"Oh, hold! my husband!" interrupted Alice, with a look of horror and astonishment; "is it possible that you can thus exult over the dead? But you know not what you say, I am convinced of it, or you could not thus give utterance to such dreadful words. The wretched and misguided Mowbray has paid the penalty of all his crimes, and forgetting the wrongs he has inflicted on us, we ought rather to offer up our prayers to Heaven for the repose and forgiveness of his soul."

"Forget the injuries we have received from him," repeated Hawthorn, impatiently, and with looks that shewed the excitement of his feelings; "and think you that I can continue to gaze upon the sufferings of our unfortunate daughter and cease to curse the memory of the author of them all? No, it is a bitter mockery, and a libel upon my affection towards our child to expect me to do so."

"If you cannot forgive others," observed Alice, "how can you expect mercy from the Supreme—that mercy of which we all stand so much in need? Oh, Hawthorn, reflect calmly upon this, and reason will dictate to you better. It is true that our poor Flora is at present a great sufferer; but I hope that time will restore her to the light of reason, and that——"

"Restore her to the light of reason!" repeated her husband; "oh, no, there is no hope of that; and it would be a mercy to her, if it should not; for how tenfold more horrible would be her sufferings, should she ever again become conscious of the shame and degradation into which she has fallen, and to know the utter hopelessness of her ever again being looked upon as the amiable and innocent being she once was. By Heaven, I would sooner see her in her grave than that such should be the fate in store for her!"

"Oh, Hawthorn," said Alice, "how your words agonise me. Surely Heaven, if we put our trust in it, will avert the dreadful evils that you apprehend, and look down with mercy upon us and our poor child."

"I am past all hope," replied Mr. Hawthorn; "we have already suffered too much to make me look forward to anything but misery."

"Nay, Mr. Hawthorn," interrupted our hero, "you must not, indeed, give way to any such feelings as these; for something will yet transpire, when you least expect it, to restore you to tranquillity and peace, if not to happiness. With the death of this misguided man you should endeavour to forget the many wrongs he has inflicted on you; and you should also feel thankful that your daughter was not present when he was brought to the cottage, or to witness his death, for then there is no knowing what the dreadful consequences might have been to her."

"Very true, Mr. Parker," coincided Alice; "and my husband must admit the force and reasonableness of your observations when he comes to reflect calmly and seriously upon them. Oh, what a fearful scene would it have been, had she been present at his death! I shudder to think of it. It must be our task to endeavour to conceal it from her—though her reason is too much affected to suffer us to entertain any apprehensions upon that point. Would to Heaven that Providence had not guided him here to die, for then we should have been spared the pain and excitement which his death has caused us."

"Nay!" exclaimed Hawthorn; "I am satisfied that it did so, for it has given me ample cause for triumph in witnessing the bitter agonies and remorse of a guilty conscience, experienced by the villain in his last moments."

"Those are cruel and awful words, Hawthorn," remarked his wife, "and it shocks and grieves me to hear you give utterance to them. But I once more implore you to endeavour to banish all such thoughts from your mind, and to reflect upon all that has happened with calmness and reason. Providence has sent the guilty Mowbray here to die ; he has apparently neither friends nor relations to whom we can apply, and it is, therefore, our duty to perform for him the last sad offices of the dead."

"Were his carcase left to rot in the open air, it would be no more than his villany, while living, merited," said Hawthorn, bitterly ; "the wretch! As I gaze upon his corpse I feel the blood curdle in my veins, and my hatred of the fell destroyer increases every moment."

"Hawthorn," observed his wife, "you disgrace yourself by giving expression to such feelings as those over the ghastly remains of the dead, and I can scarcely believe the evidence of my ears when you give utterance to them. But come, come, arouse yourself from this morbid and gloomy state of mind, and let us, at least, perform that duty which has devolved upon us—burying the past, for the present, at any rate, in oblivion. The corpse of the unfortunate Mowbray must be removed to some other room until such time as we can make arrangements for the interment; and care must be taken that Flora does not become acquainted with what has happened, or behold the corpse of her seducer ; for we may very well guess what would be the consequences were she to do so."

Mr. Hawthorn returned no answer to this, but still continued with his eyes fixed upon the cold and ghastly remains of the once gay and handsome Mowbray; and Richard and his wife thinking that their presence, under the circumstances, might probably be considered an intrusion, made some excuse, and retired from the cottage to that which they themselves occupied, deeply impressed and affected with all that had happened.

————

CHAPTER XXVII.

THE IDIOT GIRL AGAIN.— THE DISCOVERY OF THE CORPSE.—THE TEMPORARY RETURN OF REASON, AND THE FEARFUL SCENE WHICH FOLLOWED.

OUR hero and his wife did not return again to the cottage of Hawthorn that day, but sat together conversing upon the remarkable events that had taken place within the last few hours, and their own future prospects.

"The death of Mowbray is an awful example of the retribution of offended Heaven," remarked Richard, "which sooner or later never fails to overtake the guilty."

"True," coincided Mary ; "he has doubtless suffered much from the horrors of remorse ; and I cannot but think it was harsh and cruel of Mr. Hawthorn to express such feelings of hatred and exultation towards him in his last moments."

"And yet we can scarcely wonder at it," replied her husband ; "when we take into consideration the many wrongs which he has experienced from him, and the deplorable state of his beauteous daughter, who but for him might still have been innocent and happy. Ah ! Mary, the man who could thus heartlessly destroy that which was once so lovely and so pure has, indeed, much to answer for."

"He has," answered our heroine ; "and think not that I will, for a moment, endeavour to extenuate his conduct ; but vengeance, my dear Richard, you know is for Heaven ; and I know that if you were similarly situated you could not entertain any such feelings."

"Well, probably not," returned her husband ; "but still I must say that I consider that every allowance should be made for the excitement which Hawthorn has evinced ; and it only proves more powerfully the strength of the affection which he bears towards his daughter. Poor Flora ! it is truly melancholy to behold one so young, and so greatly endowed by nature with every charm to captivate, thus destroyed, and rendered but a wreck of what she once was."

"It is," agreed Mrs. Parker ; "and I know you will believe me, Richard, when I assure you that there is no one who can more deeply sympathise with her than I do ; or who more sincerely hope that the time may yet come when she will be restored to reason, and with the aid of an all merciful Providence may be enabled to bury the dismal past in oblivion."

"In that wish I most heartily join," said Richard ; "though I have too much cause to fear that it will never be realised. The fatal malady seems to have taken too strong a hold on the intellect of the unfortunate girl, to lead to the hope that she will ever recover from it ; and even if she should, it is quite impossible, at least, so I should imagine, to suppose that she can ever forget the shame and misery that has fallen upon her, or the brutal wrongs she has received from that man to whom she had devoted her whole soul's affections, and in whose honour and fidelity she placed every confidence."

"Hers is, indeed, a deplorable case,"

remarked Mrs. Parker; "and I wonder not at the anguish of mind which Mr. and Mrs Hawthorn experience when they see all the fond hopes, which once they had cherished, thus cruelly and fatally annihilated. You see, Richard, that great though our troubles have been, there are others who have experienced equal trials and misfortunes to ourselves, and we should not, therefore, resign ourselves en-

FLORA WANDERING THROUGH THE COTTAGE IN QUEST OF MOWBRAY.

tirely to despair, or murmur at the just decrees of the Supreme Being, however severe they may appear to be."

"I agree with what you say, Mary," returned her husband, "but still it is impossible at all times to bear with fortitude and resignation the heavy trials to which we may be subjected, and Heaven knows that we have had our share of them, and there is no knowing when or where they may yet terminate."

"Hope for the best, I again urge upon

you," said our heroine, "and, depend upon it, that you will not be doomed to be disappointed. At present we are much indebted to the goodness of Providence for having enabled us to elude the vigilance of our pursuers, and, I trust, it will not abandon us for the future, should we require its aid."

Richard Parker could not but express the same hope, and, after some further observations, he said—

"I wait with no little impatience and anxiety an answer from Adams; for from that I shall be able to judge how it will be best and most prudent for us to act, as I place the utmost confidence in his friendship and advice."

"Very true," replied Mary; "Mr. Adams is, indeed, most sincerely your friend, and there is nothing that he would not do, I am certain, to serve you."

"Yes," observed our hero, "I am under an immense weight of obligation to him, and I do not feel at all easy at the risk which he himself runs to serve me."

"Oh, fear not that he will use every precaution," answered Mary; "and I do not see that there is much reason to fear a discovery of the part he has acted to serve you. The same reliance, too, I believe, can be placed on Mr. Binnacle."

"No doubt of it," returned her husband, "for a more honest or worthy fellow never breathed, and he and Adams are on terms of the warmest intimacy and friendship. But should the letter not arrive safely?"

"What fear is there of that?" demanded our heroine; "honest Daniel has given his word to see it forwarded in safety, and as no suspicion, from the superscription, can arise as to who it comes from, there is no danger of its being intercepted, so you may rest your mind perfectly easy on that point."

"Well," remarked Parker, "I think I may, and in the mean time, until we receive some communication advising us how to act, I imagine we shall be perfectly safe where we are."

"Quite so," returned Mary; "that is, if we do not venture abroad; it is almost impossible that those who are in pursuit of us can have any idea that we are concealed here; and I am quite confident that we may place every reliance upon the friendship and sincerity of Mr. Hawthorn and his wife, and brother."

"Oh, that is most true," coincided our hero, "and we must be ungrateful, indeed, could we think otherwise. Oh, my beloved and faithful Mary, when I reflect upon all the narrow and remarkable escapes we

have had, it seems to me to be hardly credible."

"It is those that should inspire you with confidence," observed Mary, "and do away with all the apprehensions you entertain, for I feel satisfied that they are completely groundless."

"Yes," answered her husband; "I will try and do so, for certainly our prospects, upon the whole, do appear to brighten."

"Yes," said our heroine, "and ere long the heavy clouds that have so long obscured the pathway of our life will be dispersed, and I doubt not but that we shall once more experience all that happiness to which we have been strangers for so many months."

"If I am still permitted to live to protect and cherish you and our poor boy, my beloved Mary," replied her husband, "my happiness will, indeed, be unspeakable; though we may have to struggle with poverty, and to suffer many privations."

"Oh," I care not for poverty," ejaculated Mary, fervently, "so that the life of my beloved husband be spared to me; but should he perish, and that in the fearful manner with which he has been so long threatened, life will become hateful and disgusting to me; and I shall pray that Heaven will, in its infinite mercy, take me and our poor boy to itself."

"Dearest Mary!" cried Richard, embracing her with the most unbounded affection, "let no such dreadful apprehensions torture your breast; for I will endeavour to believe that they will not be realised. For your sake, and that of our child, I do, indeed, pray that the Almighty will extend His mercy to me, and permit me yet to live; though I confess that there are times when the most dismal forebodings cross my mind, which I find it most difficult to conquer."

"Make a resolute effort, Richard, and banish them, and I am certain you will succeed. In a few months, if we can only elude the vigilance of our pursuers, the excitement will greatly have abated, if it has not subsided altogether; it will be imagined that we have been able to make our escape to some foreign land, and all further inquiry after us will be abandoned."

"But the relations and friends of Captain Arlington will never give up the pursuit; for they, doubtless, consider me in the light of his murderer, and are anxious that I shall expiate my offence upon the gallows."

"They will, I trust, find all their efforts unavailing," observed Mary; "for although I deeply regret the late Captain Arlington should have perished by your hands, it was not premeditated by you, and was alone caused by his own head-strong villany and folly ; and the wrongs and cruel persecution and degradation you had received from him was fully deserving of so terrible a retribution."

"Very true," returned Parker; "but those from whose power I am flying will entertain no such opinions upon the subject, but will continued to pursue me with the most deadly feelings of hatred and revenge, and will exult, indeed, should they at last succeed in securing me."

"If such are their savage hopes," said our heroine, "and I have no doubt that they are, I most sincerely and ardently hope that they will be disappointed ; and they will be so—of that I feel as confident as if I received the confirmationfrom Heaven itself. But come, Richard, let us converse no more upon this subject at present, but try to look forward to the future with the most joyful anticipations."

"I will do so, my dear Mary," he replied, and then embracing her affectionately, the conversation dropped, and they retired to rest. In the morning they repaired to the cottage of Hawthorn, and found him and his wife sitting in the parlour as usual, waiting their arrival to breakfast, and looking somewhat more composed than they had done the day before. They looked around the room, and then perceived that the remains of Mowbray were removed; and Hawthorn noticeing the curiosity they evinced, said—

"I see, plainly, what you mean, Mr. Parker; you are anxious to know what has become of the corpse of the guilty Mowbray. Of course it would not have been proper to have suffered it to remain here, and so we have removed it to a small outhouse at the back of the cottage, until we have made some arrangement for the funeral. It will put us to great inconvenience, and we have good reason to regret that accident should ever have brought him hither, though, I must confess, that I felt much gratification in witnessing the last dying moments and sufferings of the villain from whom I have experienced so many miserable and unpardonable wrongs."

"He is no more, Mr. Hawthorn," returned Richard Parker, "and let his faults rest with him."

"True, Mr. Parker," remarked Alice, "that is my solemn opinion, and it is the advice which I have also given my husband. His last moments showed how bitterly he was stung with remorse, and

his emaciated appearance proved how terribly he must have suffered, and surely that is sufficient to excite in our breasts some feeling of pity towards him."

"Pity!" repeated Hawthorn. "Alice, you know full well that I am not vindictive or uncharitable ; but can you repeat that I can entertain any other sentiment towards Mowbray than one of disgust and hatred ? Ah, no ! I must, indeed, be callous to all our daughter's sufferings and the injuries that have been inflicted on her if I could be so. I can never think of the name of the seducer of our child without invoking a curse upon his memory."

"Time will, I trust, banish those feelings from your breast, Hawthorn," said Alice, "which, I must acknowledge, are unworthy of you."

"Well," returned her husband, "it may do so, but I doubt very much whether it will. However, I scarcely know how to act as regards the funeral of this guilty man ; it is hard that the expenses should fall upon me, who have suffered so much from his crimes."

"Common humanity demands that you should do it," said Alice ; "and you surely cannot turn a deaf ear to its pleadings in behalf of one who seems to have been completely friendless and destitute."

"Did you not find anything about his person," inquired our hero, "which might lead you to conjecture who he really is ?"

"Nothing whatever," answered the fisherman ; "not the slightest document which might be the least clue upon the subject. It seems as if he had been anxious to carry the secret with him to the grave, though for what reason I am at a loss to conjecture. His manners, and the superior education he had evidently received, would incline me to think that his birth must have been respectable, and, as it is more than likely that he has some friends and relations living, I have been half-inclined to advertise his death, with a full description, and the way in which he was introduced to me, in the newspapers, with the hope that some one will, at least, come forward to own him."

"Oh, no," observed Alice; "I do not like the idea of that, for it will be only giving greater publicity to the shame and misery of our poor child, without, as I conceive, being attended by any beneficial results."

"That is exactly the idea I form of it," said Richard; "and for the sake of your daughter, and your own peace of mind, Mr. Hawthorn, I would advise you to abandon any such design. The inconvenience which the funeral will put you to will be but trifling, and that once over, it will be the means of relieving you from many painful thoughts."

"Well," returned Hawthorn, after a pause, "perhaps it will be better that I should do so; though it seems rather unnatural and revolting that I should bury the remains of the base destroyer of my daughter's happiness. Had he died the death of a dog it would have been no more than the fate which was due to his diabolical villany."

"True," coincided Parker; "his crimes were very great, and they can never be sufficiently deprecated, or abhorred; but he was, no doubt, at last sincerely penitent, though he died before he make that atonement it was probably his wish to do."

"Atonement!" repeated Hawthorn, "oh, no; his crimes were too great to admit of any. It would have been nothing better than mockery for him to attempt to do so; and in my opinion it would have been an aggravation of his guilt."

"Well," remarked Parker, "I will not attempt to controvert your opinion, though I would fain have you banish such thoughts from your memory, which can only serve to add to the anguish of your feelings, without effecting any good. But how is your unfortunate daughter?"

"She is much the same as usual, poor girl," replied Mrs. Hawthorn; "and I expect that she will leave her chamber today; so that I presume I need not caution you not to let fall a word in her presence which might cause her to suspect what has happened; and on no account mention the name of Mowbray at all; for, although her brain is disordered, she might yet be able to comprehend what was said, and the consequences would, probably, be most painful."

"You may depend upon us, Mrs. Hawthorn," replied our heroine; "you will ever find us on our guard. Most fervently do I hope that the time is not far distant when the poor girl will be released from the dreadful malady with which she is afflicted."

"And should she be so," said the fisherman, "with what insupportable horrors will her return to reason be accompanied. Indeed, it would be almost a mercy that she should not, though it is heart-rending to see her in the deplorable condition she now is. She would then awaken to all the absolute horrors of her situation. She would know herself for a poor, degraded, unfortunate creature, and she must loathe and despise herself in consequence. Oh,

no; it would be better that the light of reason should never again dawn upon her than that she should have to endure such additional and insupportable horrors."

"But," observed Parker, "I trust that Providence will give her sufficient strength of mind to bear her cruel fate with fortitude and resignation. She will have nothing to reproach herself for, for Mowbray was all to blame, and she placed every confidence in his affection, honour, and sincerity."

"Yes," said Hawthorn; "and the knowledge of his treachery would be sufficient to break the poor girl's heart. I know not what to think, or how to act for the best."

"We must leave everything to the mercy of Heaven," replied Alice; "and it will probably come to our relief when we least expect it. But hush; I thought I heard our daughter's footstep on the stairs, and I need not say again that we must be cautious in her presence. I will go to meet her."

Mrs. Hawthorn quitted the room as she spoke, and Mr. Hawthorn, our hero, and Mary, waited with some anxiety the appearance of the poor, benighted, mindless girl. The next moment she was led into the room by her mother, and after fixing a half playful, and half vacant glance upon the persons present, and smiling with a sweet, but melancholy smile, she took her seat in a remote corner of the room, still bearing in her hand the faded chaplet of artificial white roses, and without taking any further notice of any one, she seemed to be totally occupied in the contemplation of it, and her own wild thoughts. Richard and his wife again watched her with the greatest interest and sympathy, and Mr. and Mrs. Hawthorn seated themselves at the further end of the room, and it needed no keen eye to penetrate the violence of the emotions that agitated their bosoms.

For a few minutes the hapless maniac remained perfectly silent, and scarcely ever removed her eyes from the chaplet she held in her hand, but suddenly she burst forth into a song of such plaintive and thrilling melody, that it was almost enough to move the listeners to tears; these were some of the words:—

"Weep not maiden, he is faithful,
    Loving, honourable, and true ;
Sooner could he die, fair maiden,
    Than break those vows oft breathed to you.

Scorn the envenom'd voice of scandal,
    Rumours false, oh, ne'er believe,
Cans't thou think that he thou lovest,
    Beauteous girl! could thee deceive?"

"No, no, no," continued the unfortunate girl, in the most wild and impressive accents; "Who dares to tell me he is false?—that the love he once vowed for me is all extinguished in his breast, and that he will abandon me to shame and despair? It is all false! I know my Alfred better; he is the very soul of honour and of truth, and he would despise and hate himself if he thought he could ever deceive me. He will be here anon; I know he will, and I shall again bask in the sunshine of his smiles. He false to me! ha, ha, ha! It is a monstrous falsehood; they are only jealous and envious of my happiness. But let them beware what they say, lest he should visit them with his vengeance and indignation. Ah, me! what a time he tarries; and yet he was always wont to be so punctual before. This is his favourite chaplet of roses, with which he entwined my hair on the morning of my marriage; and I know he will be delighted to see me wear it, for he always said it was an emblem of my own purity; and yet, 'tis strange, how faded are these roses that once bloomed so fresh and fair. What can be the meaning of this? I am not faded. No—no—no!"

As she uttered these words she continued playing with the chaplet; then throwing it petulantly away from her, she relapsed into silence, and once more seemed buried in the most profound thought. It would be impossible to describe the anguish of the fond parents as they listened to the melancholy and impressive observations of their afflicted child; and they were almost affected to tears.

"Wretched child!" ejaculated the fisherman, in an under tone to his wife, "thou art, indeed, faded, and never canst thou bloom in innocence and purity again. Oh, curses, the bitterest curses light upon the memory of the miscreant who has been the cause of this. May his soul suffer for everlasting in perdition, and may—"

A look of horror and remonstrance from Alice prevented him from completing the sentence, and their whole attention was soon again absorbed in contemplating and listening to their unhappy daughter.

"Still absent!" she ejaculated, in even more melancholy accents than before; "why does he not come, according to his promise, when he knows the impatience and anxiety with which I shall be waiting for him? What can be the meaning of this? Has some other damsel detained him from my presence with her syren smiles, and has he resolved to abandon me to my fate? Oh, frightful thought! How could it ever enter my brain? It cannot

be. No, no, I do but wrong him by such a supposition, and surely I cannot know what I say. Alfred could never, never deceive his fond and devoted Flora; besides, am I not his wife? his lawful wife—and he is bound to be faithful to me and to protect me. He is now most likely on his way hither, eager to embrace me, and to seal the assurance of his truth and constancy on my lips; and I am much to blame for giving encouragement to such childish fears. I will go forth to meet him—I will go forth to meet him; and with looks of the fondest love I will escort him to his lady's bower."

As she thus spoke, without taking the least notice of any one in the room, the poor maniac slowly arose from her chair, and still holding the chaplet of roses in her hand, she walked towards the door which led to her own chamber, and opening it, and quitting the room, she was heard ascending the stairs, no one attempting to interrupt her.

Our hero and Mary were no less affected than Mr. and Mrs. Hawthorn by what they had seen and heard of the unfortunate girl, and for a few minutes after she had quitted the room, they were unable to utter a word, and remained buried in deep thought.

"Poor, unfortunate girl," observed Mrs. Parker, "it is really quite lamentable to behold one so young thus blighted in prospects and in mind. Heaven assist her, and grant that she may yet be restored to you in all her pristine happiness, reason, and tranquillity."

"Oh, no, Mrs. Parker," ejaculated the afflicted father; "grateful though I am for the kind sympathy which you and your husband express in the welfare of our unfortunate daughter, I feel too well convinced that the wishes you have thus so fervently and sincerely expressed, and knowing full well that they spring from your heart, that they can never be realised. The rude and cruel tempest that has broken with such overwhelming and destructive violence upon the sunshine of her hopes will never be subdued. The blow, the terrible blow which seals her doom for ever is struck, and there will be no future peace for her but in the silent grave."

"Alas! what melancholy thoughts are these, my dear friend," replied our hero; "you must endeavour to conquer them, for indeed they can only be productive of the most painful consequences."

"Mr. Parker," returned the fisherman, "how easy, how very easy it is to talk; but have I not, when I consider all the dismal facts, a right to look on the darkest side of the subject? What room is there for me to hope? None, none whatever. Can you marvel when you behold the awful wreck of all that was once so lovely and innocent which the villain Mowbray has made, that I should curse his memory?"

"I wonder not, Mr. Hawthorn," said Richard, "that your feelings of indignation should be excited to the utmost degree against the baseness of his conduct, which has been productive of such deplorable consequences; but now that he is no more, and has gone to answer for all the injuries he has done to you and yours, you should endeavour to stifle the violence of your feelings, and to leave him to the mercy of that Supreme Judge whose wisdom and whose justice we erring mortals must not presume to arraign."

"Well said, Mr. Parker," remarked Alice; "and although there is no one who can more strongly condemn and abhor the cruel conduct of the late Alfred Mowbray than I do, yet now that he is no more I would suffer the crimes of which he has been guilty, and which have entailed such heavy sorrows upon us, to rest with him, and not to follow him with any vindictive feelings to the grave, which cannot be productive of any good to us, but which, on the contrary, can only increase, instead of ameliorating the anguish of our mind. Unhappy, misguided man, if we may judge from his awful and emaciated appearance, he has been punished on earth severely for the numerous vices of which he has doubtless been guilty."

"No punishment he may have received can be any way adequate to the vices of which he has been guilty," said Hawthorn. "Nay," he added, seeing our hero was about to interpose some observation; "it is useless to seek to combat my arguments, for nothing whatever can alter my opinion upon this torturing subject, and, therefore, it is but a waste of time, and the cause of unnecessary anguish to discuss it. The longer I reflect upon the innocence and happiness which once our poor Flora possessed, and contrast it with the wretched and hopeless condition to which the brutal and treacherous conduct of Mowbray has reduced her, the more do my feelings of shame and indignation increase, and I feel that the wrongs which he has so heartlessly inflicted have not been half avenged. Believe me, Mr. Parker, that I am not naturally of a vindictive disposition, and there are few enemies whom I could not forgive; but the name and the memory of the seducer of my child, must ever be held in the utmost detestation by me. Was

not the scene you just witnessed sufficient to wring your heart, and to convince you of the fond and fatal confidence which the hapless Flora placed in that man who from the first moment that he unfortunately beheld her, had evidently marked her for his victim, and who was never content until, by the most consummate and diabolical artifices, he had effected her destruction?"

"True, my friend," coincided our hero, "and most deeply do I deplore the accident which first introduced him to you. But death has now sealed the penalty of his crimes, and you have nothing more to fear from him; and let us hope that time will serve to remove the dreadful malady with which your daughter is now afflicted, and that with care and attention she may be restored to tranquillity, if not indeed to complete happiness."

Mr. Hawthorn shook his head dismally.

"Would to God that I could think so," he observed; "but that is impossible. Her reason is fled for ever, or should it indeed ever return, her sufferings will be even far more terrible than they are at present. In whichever way I view this fearful subject, I see not the slightest reason to hope; all is darkness and despair, and the late startling events have but served to increase the anguish of my mind. But, hark!"

They did indeed listen, and that, too, with the most breathless attention, for again they heard the melancholy, impressive, and plaintive voice of the poor maniac singing in tones that were enough to move the most insensible heart to pity and emotion, the following simple words

" And can he ever cease to cherish
    Her whose soul is all his own?
No! ah, no! he'd sooner perish
    Than so base a feeling own.
Vows so often fondly plighted,
    Love so pure and true as mine,
Never can by him be slighted,
    Sacrificed on treachery's shrine.

" Hand to hand, and heart to heart,
    Through life's sunny scenes we'll stray,
Truth and virtue taking part,
    Gathering flowers all the way:
Flowers redolent of beauty,
    Oh, how blest will be our lot!
Flowers rich in hue and perfume,
    Heart's-ease and forget-me-not!"

There was something so wild and simple in the words of this little ballad, yet so strictly in keeping with the unfortunate malady under which poor Flora laboured, that they could not fail to make the most powerful and painful impression upon all who heard them, and they continued to listen with the most breathless attention until the last note of them had died away, and all was again wrapped in silence. Mrs. Parker was moved to tears, and went to another part of the room in order to conceal that emotion which was too powerful for utterance. Mrs. Hawthorn was also deeply affected, while her husband, pressing his hands to his forehead, paced the room backwards and forwards with rapid and uneven footsteps, and the convulsive sobs that escaped him spoke much more eloquently than words could possibly have done the agony of the feelings which at that moment were passing in his bosom.

"Can you listen," he said at length, turning to Richard and his wife, " to the wild strains of my poor unconscious girl, and not fully appreciate the feelings of detestation I entertain towards the memory of her fell destroyer? Can you contemplate the ruin of all that was once so lovely, and good, and marvel at the agony I endure? Oh, no ; I feel that it is impossible. Wrongs such as those I have received can never be forgotten or forgiven."

"Indeed, Mr. Hawthorn," replied our hero, "you have much to lament, and no one can more deeply and sincerely sympathise with you than I do ; but there is one consolation left for you still, namely, that it was from no neglect of duty or prudence on your part, that your daughter became the victim of that man whose life you had saved, and whom you treated with every kindness and hospitality."

"Yes, the miscreant," returned Hawthorn, bitterly, "and how did he repay me? Oh, the heart sickens with disgust and indignation to reflect upon his cold-blooded treachery. Would that he had perished in the storm in which so many of his fellow creatures met with a watery grave ; what a fortunate release would it have been to society to have rid the world of such a villain ; and my poor child might now have been innocent and happy, and the honest wife of some man on whom she could have bestowed her heart's purest and warmest affections, and whose virtues should have rendered him worthy of her. But now, how dark and drear are all the prospects that are spread before her. What sombre and ponderous clouds have obscured the sunshine of her youthful days ! What have we ever done that our peace of mind should be thus cruelly invaded? How have we ever deserved so heavy a curse to light upon us?"

"For Heaven's sake, my dear husband," expostulated Alice, "do endeavour to calm your feelings ; these violent bursts of emotion will but serve to increase the anguish of your mind without effecting any good."

"Of what use is your advice to me, Alice?" replied Hawthorn, testily ; "I have not patience to listen to it. Talk to me of calmness, while I witness the sufferings of her who should be dearer to us than our very existence ! it is impossible. But hush ! she comes again. Oh, how it will rack my heart to see her, and to know at the same time that the corpse of him who has been the author of all her misery is at present beneath our roof."

He covered his face with his hands as he gave utterance to these words, and gave vent to his feelings in half-stifled sobs. No one offered to interrupt him, but they awaited with impatience and anxiety the appearance of poor Flora, whom they heard descending the stairs. They had not to wait very long, for she quickly entered the room, her eyes staring upon vacancy, and her whole demeanour solemn, affecting, and impressive in the extreme.

She had changed her apparel during her absence, and now wore a dress of virgin white, decorated with artificial roses, while a long white flowing veil depended from her head, and fell far over her shoulders. In her hand she still carried the chaplet of white roses, and ever and anon she pressed it alternately to her lips and to her heart. She seemed to take no notice of any one, but walking slowly to one corner of the room, she seated herself, and seemed to be deeply wrapped in thought, while they watched her with the most mute attention, and did not offer to breathe a syllable, lest it should interrupt her. A silence for some moments ensued ; but at length the unfortunate maniac said—

"I wish he would come, for methinks he would now be doubly delighted to see me, since I have arrayed myself in his favourite dress, the one in which he led me to the altar, where those fond and sacred ties were plighted, which he had so often breathed in my ears. Oh, what a day of bliss was that to me ! When I was satisfied that Alfred, dear Alfred, was mine for ever, and that nothing but death could e'er again separate us. But they have dared to hint to me that he has deceived me—that his vows were faithless, and that he will, ere long, desert me for some other damsel whom he considers far more worthy of him than the humble fisherman's daughter. Oh, how base and monstrous are such aspersions on the character of one whom my heart assures me is the very soul of virtue, truth, and honour ! Besides, is he not mine, indissolubly mine ? And what shall deprive me of him ? They are false and treacherous who get up these vile calumnies, and are only envious of our happiness, and soon will Alfred be able to hold them up to shame and infamy. But he promised to return home long ere this, and I never knew him to break his word before. What can detain him ? Would — oh, would that he would come back, for my poor heart is so lonely and wretched when he is away !

"Come, dearest youth, to her who lonely
    Sighs to meet thy fond embrace ;
Whose bliss is centred in thee only,
    Come, and all marks of grief efface.
Surely none thou lov'st more dearly
    Can tempt thy truant heart to stray ?
Loving thee, oh, how sincerely,
    Judge my grief when thou'rt away !"

The last words died away in her throat, and resting her head disconsolately on her hand, melancholy sighs escaped her bosom. Still, she seemed to be quite unconscious of the presence of every one, and to be entirely absorbed in her own gloomy thoughts. Mr. Hawthorn and Alice, and our hero and his wife, drew themselves apart from where she was sitting, and watched her with the deepest interest, emotion, and solicitude, and it was not without the greatest difficulty that the fisherman could control the expression of his feelings, which, of course, were excited to the utmost degree by what had already taken place.

At length Flora again arose from her seat, and moving towards the window, appeared to look from it with the utmost anxiety and impatience ; then, after a brief pause, she ejaculated, in the most melancholy accents—

"Ah, me ! How tedious is the time, when all that is light, and joy, and happiness to me, is absent from my sight, and I cannot listen to the music of his voice—the charms of his conversation ! Oh, Alfred ! this is most cruel and neglectful of you, and what I never imagined you could have been capable of. It is long, very long, since you left me, and you promised to return soon ; but you have forgotten your promises, and appear to be regardless of the sufferings that your poor Flora must be enduring at the uncertainty of what has become of you. My heart is heavy and sad with dismal forebodings, and my brain begins to grow distracted. Can what they have so often whispered to me be true ? Is he false to me ? And

does he love another ? No, no, no ; away with all such hideous thoughts ! Alfred Mowbray would despise and loathe himself, could he be guilty of such monstrous deceit towards one who loves him so fondly, so ardently, sincerely, and who has made such sacrifices for his sake ! Besides, am I not his wife—his lawful wife ? And who shall dare to tear us asunder ? No, no, no !—he is not false —he is not false ! it would be a gross libel upon human nature to believe him so. He will be here anon, and I shall again be happy."

The poor girl again relapsed into silence, but continued by the window, and still watched anxiously, as though she expected the arrival of her betrayer. The emotion of the fisherman and his wife increased and it was with difficulty they could repress the convulsive sobs that struggled for vent in their bosoms.

Richard Parker and our heroine were equally affected by the mournful wanderings of the wretched maniac, while the boy, William, who was present on this painful occasion, could not refrain from tears. They none of them, however, attempted to interrupt the poor girl, and they awaited the result of this trying scene with the greatest anxiety.

For some time she continued in the same position, and her countenance underwent no change. But suddenly she burst into tears, and the heart-breaking sobs that escaped her bosom were quite pitiful to hear. Her mother now ventured to approach her, and placing her arm tenderly round her neck, she uttered her name in her softest and most affectionate accents. The poor girl started, alarmed at her touch, and stared in her face, and did not appear to know her.

"Dear Flora," she said, "why do you weep ? Are not all those that you love present, and only too anxious to contribute to your happiness ?"

"All that I love !" repeated the maniac, hastily, and still staring vacantly in her mother's face. "No, no, no—you do but mock me. He is not here ! All that I love is away, and how can I be happy ? But who are you, that gaze so intensely upon me, and breathe those words of derision in mine ears ? What right have you to obtrude upon the privacy of my sorrows, and to court me from my sad, sad thoughts ?"

"Do you not know me, dear Flora ?" interrogated Alice, in a voice half choked with the power of her emotion, and fixing an earnest and anxious look upon the

THE ALARM IN HAWTHORN'S COTTAGE AT THE VIOLENCE OF THE STORM.

agitated countenance of her unfortunate child.

"Know you?" replied the poor girl, in the same wild accents. "Know you?" she repeated. "No; how should I? for I never beheld you before. You seek to pry into the secret of my heart, and, like the rest, I suppose, would taunt me with the infidelity of my husband. Away! I want no further converse with you; I am waiting for him who will be here pre- sently, though he should have returned long ere this. Begone--begone! You are an aged woman, and should know better. Away, I say, and annoy me not!"

"Oh, how torturing is this," ejaculated Mrs. Hawthorn, wringing her hands; "will nothing impart the light of reason to her disordered and wandering senses? Look at me, my beloved and unfortunate child. Listen to me;—I am your mother—your own, fond mother."

The maniac burst into a wild and hysterical laugh, and gazed more vacantly at her than she had done before,

"Mother!" she cried; "what a bitter mockery is there in that word. Shame on you, old woman, for using it so lightly and irreverently. I have no mother, though I had one once; yes, and a fond father, too, who would have done anything that could contribute to my happiness; but they are lost to me now—lost to me for ever, and I must never behold them again. Leave me, old woman, for I am not to be deceived—I am not to be deceived!"

Reluctantly Mrs. Hawthorn withdrew her arm from around her neck, and retired to a few paces from her. The agony that her and her husband experienced at that moment was indescribable, and they watched in silence the future conduct of their unfortunate daughter. For some minutes she continued at the window, with her eyes earnestly fixed upon the prospect beyond, and muttering incoherent words to herself. But at length, as a sudden thought seemed to strike her, she exclaimed—

"No—he will not come. He is regardless of the anguish I must suffer, and leaves me here to wretchedness, loneliness, and suspense. Cruel, cruel Alfred! how have I deserved this? Have I not ever studied to convince you of the intensity of my love, and placed every confidence in your truth and sincerity? Surely I merited a far different return to this. You cannot love me as you have ever vowed to do, or you would not treat me with this cold and cruel neglect. Ah! and are, then, the tales that have been whispered in my ears of his treachery and deceit true? Has he betrayed me, and now abandoned me for another? Oh, horrible thought! Alfred Mowbray false to me?—false to her who was willing to lay down her life for his sake? No, no—it is impossible! He must be a villain of the blackest dye, could he be guilty of such conduct. Besides, has he not sworn at the altar, and in the presence of the Almighty, to love and cherish me for ever? He has, and he would not dare to break those solemn and sacred vows. Oh! Alfred, keep me no longer in this terrible state of suspense, but return to me, and give me the blest assurance that your heart is still as fondly, as faithfully, and as ardently attached to me as ever. I will not chide you for this delay, for well I am convinced that some unavoidable accident has alone detained you, or you would have been here long ere this!"

She again paused, and the powerful excitement of her poor disordered brain seemed to increase in intensity. Her eyes had an expression more than usually wild, and her bosom heaved with convulsive emotions. Her unhappy parents gazed at each other with melancholy and significant looks, and sighed deeply; but not a word passed between them, and they scarcely knew in what way to act under the painful circumstances.

In a few minutes more, Flora suddenly started from the spot on which she had been standing, and dashing the chaplet from her hand upon the floor, she exclaimed, in tones that thrilled to the hearts of all who heard them—

"Away! away!—thou art now worthless and hateful to me; for he who bound it round my hair, and used to be so delighted to see me wear it, has deserted me, and no longer loves me. I am awakened from a terrible dream, and see at once the full extent of my misery. He has deceived me, betrayed me, abandoned me; and now another basks in the sunshine of that love, which he so often and so solemnly vowed was mine alone. Oh, God! why have I lived to experience this cruel annihilation of all my hopes? How cruelly and fatally have I deceived myself! But who could ever have suspected that such apparent virtue and honour could conceal the heart of a hypocrite? But I am his wife, and he shall not be permitted to desert me thus! I will pursue him to the farthest extent of the earth, and never rest till I have discovered him. Surely, when he again beholds me, he must take pity on me; his conscience will be stung by remorse, and he will be anxious to make me all the atonement in his power for the wrongs he has done me. Ah! methinks I see him now, lavishing his fondest affections upon some other damsel, and giving utterance to those vows of constancy he has so often and so solemnly repeated to me. Heed him not, fair damsel, for he seeks to betray you, and when he has accomplished his purpose, he will abandon you to misery and despair, as he has done me, his lawful wife. Alfred—Alfred, do you not hear me? Has not my voice the power to arrest you in your unholy purpose, and to awaken you to remorse? Oh, remember, that a terrible curse will most assuredly pursue such a crime as this! Ah! he sees me, and smiles ironically and scornfully upon me. Great God of Heaven this is surely too much for human nature to endure. Mowbray! deceiver! libertine! villain! it is thine injured wife—thy too fond, confiding Flora, who calls upon you and commands you to desist! No! he mocks me still; he laughs at my agony; and now he clasps the form of the damsel in his arms, and lavishes upon her his fondest endearments! My eyes flash fire! a tempest of uncontrollable passions rages within my breast! the blood runs scalding hot throughout my veins! a hundred serpents seem to entwine themselves around my heart! My brain—oh! God!"

The strength of the unfortunate maniac was exhausted, and she sunk insensible in the arms of her mother, who had rushed forward to receive her. Every one present was completely horror-struck with what had taken place, and Mr. Hawthorn could restrain the expression of the agony of his feelings no longer.

"Oh, God!" he exclaimed, in a hoarse voice, "what a terrible trial is this for parents to have to endure. Oh, my poor child! how little conscious art thou of their present agony, and that which they have so long had to experience in witnessing thy sufferings, and deplorable and hopeless condition! May perdition seize the soul of the heartless monster who has been the cause of this!"

"Alas! alas!" sighed Alice, as she supported the inanimate form of her daughter in her arms, "what will be the end of this? My darling child, what an awful fate is thine, and how little didst thou ever deserve to suffer in the manner thou art doing now! God of Heaven, be merciful to her, for, without Thine aid, oh! what will become of her?"

"My dear friends," said our hero, "endeavour to compose your feelings as well as you can; although I am ready to admit that these wild paroxysms are sufficient to alarm you, and to excite the utmost emotions of anguish in your bosoms, I trust that Providence will yet, ere long, effect a favourable change in the mind of your unfortunate daughter, and that she will be restored to some degree of tranquillity and resignation, at least."

"No, no," replied Hawthorn, impatiently; "there is no prospect of it, and it would be folly for us to delude ourselves with any such hopes. Her fate is sealed for ever, and it would be much better for her were she now resting in the cold and silent grave."

He sighed deeply as he gave utterance to these words, and then approaching his beauteous and insensible daughter, he imprinted the most affectionate kisses upon her pale lips, and tried but in vain to give full vent to his feelings.

Alice now removed the insensible form of her daughter from the room, and conveyed her to her own chamber, in order to see to her recovery; and Mr. Hawthorn, throwing himself into a chair, covered his face with his hands, and resigned himself entirely to the agony of his feelings. Richard Parker and his wife seated themselves in another part of the room, and conversed in whispers upon the extraordinary and affecting scene they had just witnessed, and which had made a painful impression upon their minds, which they would find it difficult to eradicate. At length Mr. Hawthorn aroused himself from his lethargy, and rising from his seat he traversed the room for some minutes in a state of great agitation, and did not give utterance to a syllable.

"I beg of you, Mr. Hawthorn," at length our hero ventured to observe, "not to give way so entirely to this intense agony of mind, which can do no good, but, on the contrary, may be productive of the worst consequences. After the interment of the remains of the misguided man, Mowbray, your excitement will, I trust, be somewhat abated; and that you will be enabled to banish his name from your memory."

"Mr. Parker," returned Hawthorn, "you talk extravagantly; if I could bury the past in oblivion, I must possess a heart insensible to every proper feeling. Will not the sufferings of my afflicted daughter, and such paroxysms as the one we have just witnessed, constantly remind me of it, and torture me to distraction?"

Mrs. Hawthorn now returned to the room, and prevented Parker from making any reply, and her husband eagerly inquired after the condition in which she had left their daughter.

"She has revived," replied Alice, "though she seems very ill and much exhausted. I have persuaded her to retire to bed, and I hope that some refreshing sleep will have a most beneficial effect upon her."

"God grant that it may," said Hawthorn, "though I fear that the awful malady with which she is afflicted is for ever fixed upon her brain, and that we shall thus daily have the anguish of witnessing her wild paroxysms. How fearful must have been the consequences, had she been present at the time when the villain, Mowbray, was brought to our cottage."

"If she had recognised him," replied Alice, "they would, indeed, and I am satisfied that Providence did not permit her to be witness of that which might have been fraught with so much danger. Poor girl;

how agonising were the wild ravings to which she a short time since gave utterance!"

"Ay," returned her husband; "callous indeed must that heart be to every sense of proper feeling, that could have remained unmoved at the painful scene. Oh, had her betrayer been alive, and enabled to witness it, how bitterly must his conscience have reproached him for the destruction he had caused!"

"True," coincided Alice; "but, thank Heaven that we have been spared the additional anguish of such a scene. I shudder to think what would have been the sufferings of our poor afflicted girl had she encountered Mowbray ere he died, and had recognised him."

"True," replied Hawthorn; "and she could scarcely have failed to have done so, for what is more likely to recall the wandering senses of the sufferer than the sight of the guilty man who was the author of all her misery? And had he seen her, how doubly acute must have been the anguish of his last moments—how tenfold more poignant the horrors of his remorse!"

"Far better is it as it is," remarked our hero, "for such a meeting might have terminated fatally with your unhappy daughter. Now that the destroyer of her peace is summoned to answer for all the crimes which he has committed, you should, I humbly suggest, endeavour to banish him from your mind, and to forget that such a being ever existed."

"No, no," said Hawthorn, impatiently; "how utterly useless is it to advise me thus ! It is impossible that I can ever forget him, or cease to bestow upon his memory feelings of the utmost disgust and abhorrence. Can you remember the scene you but recently witnessed with my poor child, and yet marvel at the sentiments I have so frequently expressed regarding her heartless seducer ?"

"It is a torturing subject, Mr. Hawthorn," observed Mary, "and it would be much better that you should not dwell upon it more than you can help. After the interment of the remains of the misguided Mowbray, you may probably be able to arrive at a calmer and more resigned state of mind."

Mr. Hawthorn shook his head, and it was quite evident that his feelings had not and were not likely to undergo any change. The conversation then dropped, and for the remainder of the day our hero and his wife endeavoured to divert the thoughts of Mr. Hawthorn to some less dismal subject, although, notwithstanding all their efforts to the contrary, they succeeded but indifferently.

Poor Flora did not leave her chamber again that day, and according to the account of her mother, she continued in much the same state of mind, and frequently her wild ravings were quite heart-rending to listen to. Thus the day passed away, and in the evening Richard and his wife retired at an earlier hour than usual, in consequence of the latter feeling slightly indisposed.

The next morning, on visiting the cottage, they found that Mr. Hawthorn was absent from the room, and fearful that he might be ill, after the extraordinary excitement he had undergone for the last few days, they eagerly inquired of Alice the cause of his absence.

"My poor husband is more than usually melancholy this morning," replied the old woman, "and he is at present in the shed which contains the remains of Mowbray, no doubt brooding over all the painful events of the past. Would to Heaven that the funeral had taken place, for there is no chance of his being able to conquer the excitement of his feelings while the corpse remains under the roof. But I wish you would accompany me to the place where he is, Mr. and Mrs. Parker, for our presence might be most useful in his present state of mind. It is a most gloomy spectacle to gaze upon, but I fear the effect it may have upon the senses of my husband, if he should be permitted often to indulge his morbid feelings alone."

"True," coincided Richard; "he must be drawn from it, if possible; and myself and my wife will most willingly attend you, if you think that we should not offend him by our presence, or seem to be impertinent or obtrusive."

"Certainly not," replied Alice, "he has too warm a friendship for you to entertain any such feelings towards you. Come, then—I will conduct you."

Mr. and Mrs. Parker readily assented, and Mrs. Hawthorn led the way to the outhouse where the remains of Mowbray had been placed, and they paused at the door, for the voice of Hawthorn smote their ears, giving utterance to the most melancholy observations.

"I am fearful," remarked Richard to Alice, in an under tone, " that, in the state of mind he at present appears to be, he may consider our intentions as taking an unwarrantable liberty on his privacy, and that our appearance will only tend to increase the excitement of his feelings. We had better retire, and leave you alone to counsel with and endeavour to console him."

"Nay," replied Mrs. Hawthorn, "on such sad occasions my arguments and persuasions have seldom succeeded in having much effect on him, and should he be left alone to indulge in this mood, there is too much reason to fear that it will lead to the most melancholy consequences. Come, let us enter."

Richard and our heroine nodded assent, and all being now again silent, they cautiously opened the door, and entered the building. All was buried in the most sombre gloom within, for there was but one small aperture by which light was admitted, and that was at present covered with a blind. The coffin which contained the remains of the unfortunate Mowbray was placed on tressels, at the further end of the place, and before it, with folded arms and in gloomy contemplation, stood Mr. Hawthorn; and so deeply did he seem to be wrapped in his own dismal and torturing meditations, that the noise of their entrance had not in the least disturbed him, and he was not aware of their presence. They approached him nearer, and still he heard them not, and they then perceived that the lid of the coffin was removed, and that the corpse was consequently exposed. The sight had a sickening and melancholy effect upon Mary, and she pressed the arm of her husband, and looked up in his face with an expression which he could not fail to understand.

"Yes," soliloquised the fisherman, in tones which showed the bitter anguish and excitement of his feelings, "there lie the cold and ghastly remains of the once gay and accomplished Mowbray; he who so fatally ensnared the affections of what was all so fair, so young, and innocent, and, demon-like, rested not until he had plunged his unsuspecting victim in shame and misery. I gaze upon the corpse of the destroyer of my child; his guilty soul is now arraigned before the Judgment-seat of that Almighty Power whose laws, while living, he so grossly, so recklessly outraged, and I feel that I am, at least, partly avenged. Oh, how base must that heart have been that could thus work the destruction of her who was so good, and who placed, in her purity of soul, so much fond confidence in his truth and honour! My poor child! what a terrible wreck art thou now of what thou once was; and what can ever restore thee to that state of innocence and happiness which thou once enjoyed? Thou art lost, lost for ever, and in the bitterness of my soul, I can but curse the memory of him who has been

the cause of all. May the wrath of the Almighty——"

"Oh, my husband," interrupted the shocked and agitated Alice, approaching close to him, and placing her hand upon his arm, "for the love of Heaven forbear, and do not give utterance to such fearful words as these over the cold ashes of the dead, who has gone to answer at that dread tribunal, before which we must all one day appear, for the sins he has committed!"

Mr. Hawthorn started hastily round as she spoke, and the ghastly and care-worn expression of his countenance was such as to make the most painful impression upon the minds of all those who beheld it.

"Ah!" he ejaculated; "you here? Why am I interrupted in my gloomy meditations over the remains of that man who has inflicted such terrible wrongs on me as nothing whatever can atone for? And yet I am glad that you have come. Come forward, Mr. Parker, and gaze upon the corpse of that man who, in life, was the base author of crimes that should make human nature shudder. See, the proud and heartless libertine, the fell destroyer of innocence and virtue, is brought low at last; and but for the father of her whom he has so basely wronged, his ashes, might remain to rot in the open air and——"

"Mr. Hawthorn," interposed our hero, "let me beg of you to calm the excitement of your feelings, and not to give way to such dreadful and revolting thoughts as these. However much they may have injured you in life, you should not visit the dead with your vengeance, but rather to hope that they may receive that mercy from the Supreme Being which they denied to their fellow-creatures."

"Hope for mercy for him who so cruelly abused my kindness, hospitality, and friendship?" repeated Hawthorn, vehemently. "No! There is mockery in the bare idea; and, by all my hopes, the longer I gaze upon him the more bitter become the feelings I entertain towards him. It is useless, Mr. Parker, to talk to me, or to remonstrate with me, for nothing whatever can remove from my mind the remembrance of the heavy wrongs he has inflicted on me; and can you wonder at my feelings when you call to mind the deplorable situation of my poor child, and reflect how happy and innocent she might now have been had it not been for him? The recollection drives me to madness, and I feel convinced that nothing can ever remove the terrible impression from my mind that has now taken possession of it."

'Oh, do not say so, Mr. Hawthorn," observed our heroine. "Time and perseverance will ameliorate the violence of your grief and despair, your daughter will yet be restored to reason, and you, learning to bury the painful past in oblivion, will yet be happy."

"Bury the past in oblivion?" repeated Hawthorn, impatiently. "Oh, that is impossible! I must be callous to every sense of proper feeling if I could do so; and as for my poor child, her fate is sealed for ever. No more will the light of reason dawn upon her mind; and surely it would be almost a mercy if it were not to do so, for how terrible would then be her sufferings—how bitter and overwhelming her self-reproaches, when she should be aroused to a full sense of her misery and degradation! Degraded, too, by him to whom alone her heart was ever devoted, and upon whose honour and sincerity she so unfortunately and faithfully relied. Oh, villain—villain! how terrible are the crimes for which you have to answer!"

"Retire from this gloomy place," said Alice, "for the contemplation of the remains of this unfortunate, but misguided man, can but serve to add to the anguish of your thoughts, and to increase the fearful impressions that have taken such strong hold on your mind. Come, come—you will be persuaded by one who is, at any rate, so sincere a friend to you as Mr. Parker."

"Yes, Mr. Hawthorn," said our hero; "the advice of your wife is dictated by truth and reason, and I feel convinced that you will yield to it. Why should you persist in torturing yourself thus, when it can be productive of no possible good?"

"No," answered Hawthorn; "I cannot make up my mind to retire, for the contemplation of the livid corpse of the villain who has wrought all the misery I I have ever experienced is, at least some little gratification to my wounded feelings, and it is not long that I shall be permitted to indulge in them. Where is now the gay and accomplished libertine, whose deceptive allurements were so irresistible to all those unfortunate victims who came beneath the influence of their fatal fascinations? Cold, cold, and senseless; revolting to the sight, and loathsome to look upon. But would that he had lived to feel a father's vengeance—what tenfold gratification would it not have afforded to my soul! But may my bitterest curses pursue him to eternity!"

"Oh! this is horrible!" ejaculated Alice. "Hawthorn, husband, have you gone mad? You surely must, for you talk not like yourself!"

"Mad!" repeated the fisherman, and he looked wildly round upon her; "yes, yes—I am mad; and is it not enough to make me so when I reflect upon all the wrongs that this villain has done me? Should I not be insensible to all the proper feelings of a man and a father, could I reflect with indifference upon all that has happened, and not curse the memory of the wretch who could basely be the cause of all? You talk to me in vain; justice and reason dictate all that I say and do, and the longer I reflect on it, the more convinced I am of the irreparable injuries that have been inflicted on me and mine, and the stronger becomes my abhorrence of the author of them."

"Again let me persuade you to quit this place," said Richard; "and to let reason once more predominate in your mind. Such thoughts as those you have given utterance to, allow me to declare, are very unbecoming, to say the least of them."

"Ah! Mr. Parker," replied Hawthorn, "you cannot duly appreciate my feelings, or you would not thus express yourself. Who can marvel at my excitement, when they reflect upon all that my poor girl has suffered, and the awful and hopeless situation in which she is now placed?"

"True," coincided our hero; "it is, indeed, a most melancholy one, and there is no person who can more deeply sympathise with her and yourself than I do; but still, it is useless to give way to these wild paroxysms of despair, which can only increase instead of diminishing the evil; and it is therefore that I urge you to exert all your fortitude to conquer the feelings that have taken such strong and painful hold on you."

"Ah! Parker," returned Hawthorn, "how easy is it for those to advise who have never experienced that which I have done! Heaven knows that I never possessed any vindictive feelings towards my fellow creatures, but there are wounds which pierce so deep, that they defy human patience or forbearance to resist them, and such is the nature of the wounds which I have received, and the remembrance of which, I am convinced, nothing can ever eradicate from my mind. Can you forget the wrongs you have received from your enemies, and which have been the cause of all the misery you have and are now enduring?"

"Alas! my friend," sighed Richard Parker, "surely my misfortunes have been greater—far greater, if possible, than those which you have experienced; and yet I struggle all that is in my power to bear up against them, and to encourage hope. Have I not suffered wrongs and degradations which should make the human soul recoil with disgust and horror? Am I not, with my poor wife and child, a wretched, wandering outcast, with no other means of existence but such as I receive from the bounty of strangers, and with an ignominious and untimely fate every moment staring me in the face? And yet you talk to me of inexperience, and seem to doubt my want of proper sympathy with my fellow-creatures in misfortune. But this is not the time or the place to converse upon such melancholy subjects as these, and we had better, therefore, waive them, and depart from here."

"Ay," remonstrated Alice, "pray be persuaded by what Mr. Parker says, and do not longer remain here. I confess that the contemplation of this dismal scene shocks my feelings, and I dread almost to look around me. Death is, indeed, most solemn under any circumstances, and it must be doubly so to persons unfortunately situated as we are. Come, my husband, do not remain thus foolishly obstinate."

"I yield," replied Hawthorn, turning reluctantly away from the corpse, "and may Heaven grant me fortitude to support the weight of sorrow which it has been pleased to burthen me with. Would to God that the footsteps of the guilty Mowbray had never been directed here to die; I might then have been spared the heavy sorrow, and anguish of mind which I now experience."

"True," said Alice; "but this is not the proper place to converse upon the subject, and your agony of mind can only be increased while you remain here. Let us depart."

Mr. Hawthorn made no reply, and they were all about to quit the place, when the door suddenly opened, and the fisherman and his wife started back in amazement and consternation, when poor Flora made her appearance, and before they had time to prevent her, she advanced hastily towards the spot where the coffin which contained the remains of the destroyer of her happiness stood.

Her appearance was more than usually wild and impressive; her eyes glared vacantly upon all present; her countenance was ghastly pale, and her hair dishevelled. She looked, indeed, as if she had just awakened out of some frightful dream, and it confused and appalled her parents and Richard and his wife to gaze upon her. For a minute or two she stood in the same attitude, and continued to gaze wildly around her, but at length Mrs. Hawthorn advancing towards her, in her most gentle, persuasive, and affectionate accents, said—

"Dear Flora, what brings you here? Why have you quitted your chamber? The morning air is cold, and it will have the worst effect upon your tender frame. Come, my poor child, let me persuade you to return, and I will accompany you, and endeavour to console and amuse you in your loneliness!"

"You—you! Ha—ha!" repeated the unfortunate girl, with a wild laugh, and gazing earnestly upon her mother. "Who are you that thus presume to question me and to dictate to me? Away—I know you not!"

"Alas—alas! my wretched—my ill-fated child!" cried Hawthorn, with much emotion, "that Fate should ever direct your footsteps hither! Oh, begone, I beseech you, and avoid the sight which is here to shock your feelings!"

"And you, too, old man!" said the hapless maniac. "Who are you that thus obstruct me in my purpose? You are a stranger to me, and should not dare to interfere with me. I come to seek him who has long been absent from me—my husband, my truant husband; and who shall dare to detain me from him? I dreamt that he had arrived, and was anxious to see me, and to crave my forgiveness for the length of time he has been away, and the anxiety and misery he has caused me; and who shall prevent me from seeing him? Oh! he looked so beautiful, and so kind and affectionate, as he appeared to me in my dream; and he smiled upon me just as he used to do when we first became acquainted. Oh! he was so fond and loving then; and I know that he is faithful to me now, though there have been those who have whispered in my ears that he was false and treacherous, and that he had deserted me. But that was false. I know my Alfred's heart too well to believe that he could ever act towards me with such cruelty and ingratitude. But he should have returned to me before, and I must chide him well for it when I see him. Stand aside, I say, and let me approach him!"

"Oh, God!" exclaimed Hawthorn, beating his breast, "how torturing is this! What is to be done? Flora, my poor child, if there is one spark of reason still left to you, be persuaded by your mother, and leave this dismal place!"

"Mother—mother!" repeated the ill-fated girl, still gazing vacantly upon them.

"What mean you? Such a word is a stranger to me. I have no mother now, though once I had; but she has abandoned me, and I seek no other companion now but my husband. He is here, and who shall dare detain him from me? Back—back, I say! I will not be obstructed in my purpose. He is waiting for me. I know he is here; and he will think me, indeed, unkind, if I do not hasten to meet him."

"You cannot proceed," said Hawthorn, grasping her arm in the agony and fear of his feelings, and scarcely knowing how to act. "Flora, child, you labour under a painful delusion; it is no more than a dream you have had. Away—away from hence, I beseech you, and get you gone once more into your chamber!"

"Ah!" cried the maniac, wildly, and her eyes seemed to flash fire, "do you still dare to detain me from all that I hold most precious on earth? Do you seek to separate us, and make me appear false to him? Release me, I say, or I will invoke the curses of Heaven on your head, and exult in the retribution it will not fail to inflict upon you. Let go your hold, I say, for I am resolute, and you may have bitter cause to repent your boldness and presumption. Alfred—dear Alfred—I come —I am here!"

And with these words, with an effort of strength which only madness could give her, the wretched girl released herself from the hold of her father, and thrusting him and her mother aside, she advanced hastily still nearer towards the coffin, before which she now stood, and gazed upon it wildly and vacantly. The agony and suspense of Mr. Hawthorn and his wife may readily be imagined; but it was now too late to prevent the consequences thus dreaded, and they stood silent and appalled.

Flora remained in the same attitude for several minutes, and seemed undecided whether to advance or recede, but at length, in the most melancholy accents, she exclaimed—

"He is not here; and yet I cannot doubt the truth of my vision. Where is he? Oh, Alfred—dear Alfred! this is most cruel to torture me thus, and to keep me in such suspense. What have I done that you should thus neglect me? But what is this?—What fearful thoughts are these that come over me? A coffin!—The emblem of the dead! Let me penetrate this dreadful secret!"

"Hold—hold! wretched, unfortunate girl!" exclaimed her father, again catching hold of her arm, and endeavouring to withdraw her from the ghastly sight;

"thine eyes must not gaze here! Forbear —forbear, or you will drive me mad!"

"Release me, I say, old man!" cried the poor girl, and at the same time struggling violently; "who are you that thus take such unpardonable liberties with me? Strange, wild thoughts flash across my bewildered brain; and yet I am not mad! No, I am not mad! Ah! I have escaped you, and now—"

She again burst frantically from her father's hold, who buried his face in his hands in despair, and approaching close to the coffin, she stood fixed and inanimate as a statue, and gazed upon the livid features of the corpse. The agony and suspense of all present at that awful moment was almost insupportable. Suddenly a dawn of reason seemed to light upon the wretched maniac's brain, and in a voice that completely appalled the souls of all who heard it, she shrieked—

"Ah! those features, but now so pale, so ghastly, and distorted! 'Tis he—my Alfred—my husband! He is dead—he is dead! They have murdered him! Oh! who has done this? Husband—dear husband—thy faithful Flora is here! She hastens to join you in death!"

And with these words, the unfortunate maniac girl threw herself frantically on the corpse, and all consciousness seemed to forsake her.

CHAPTER XXVIII.

THE MELANCHOLY STATE OF THE MANIAC GIRL.—THE ARRIVAL OF BINNACLE.— THE DANGER, AND DEPARTURE OF THE FUGITIVES FROM THE COTTAGE OF HAWTHORN.

"Oh, God!" groaned Mr. Hawthorn; "what a terrible misfortune is this! My poor child, what fresh troubles are in store for you? This shock will surely be the death of her, since it is plain that she has recognised the features of her seducer, and my dream will at length be verified. What cursed fate guided her footsteps hither?"

"Alas! alas!" sighed Alice, "what will be the end of this? Oh, why did you not hasten the interment of the remains of Mowbray? and then the knowledge of his fate would never have reached her. Never can this awful scene be effaced from my memory! But see, she has fainted; we must remove her without delay, and see to her recovery."

"Ah, no!" ejaculated Hawthorn; "she will never revive again; and the cup of our misery is now filled to the

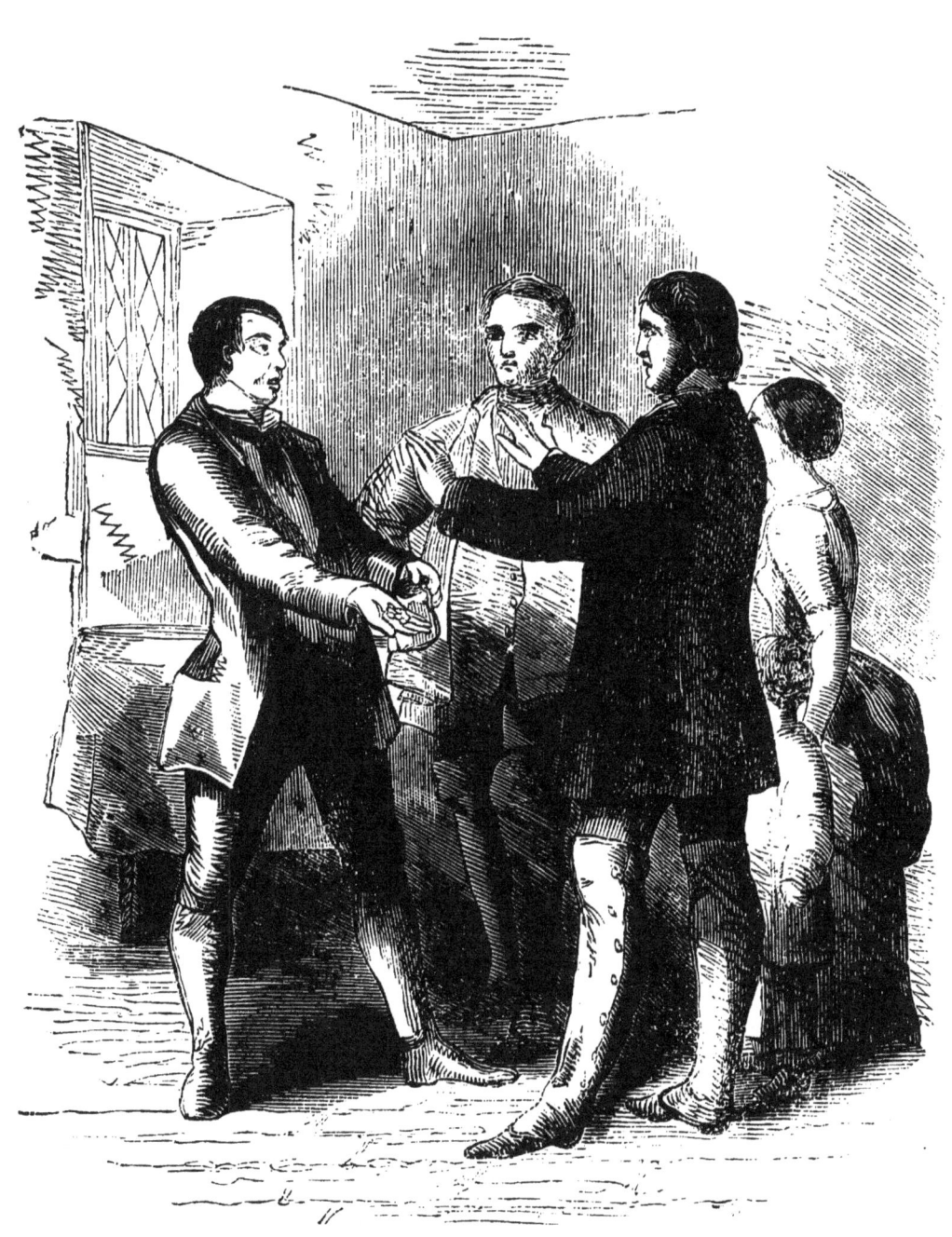

RICHARD PARKER REFUSING THE MONEY PROFFERED HIM BY DANIEL.

brim, and it would be better for us both if it would please Heaven to take us also."

"No no!" remonstrated his wife, who struggled with her feelings as well as she could ; " we must not give way to this agony of despair ; for, terrible as our prospects are, everything may yet turn out much better than we can now possibly anticipate."

"True," observed Richard, who, as well as his wife, had been much shocked by all that he had witnessed ; "it is an unfortunate occurrence, and it is a pity that fate ever directed Mowbray again to this cottage. But there is no time for delay ; your daughter must be removed, and attended to immediately ; for should she recover, and again behold the corpse of Mowbray, there is no knowing what the fatal consequences might be."

"True," coincided Alice ; "come, come, my husband, arouse yourself, and assist me."

Hawthorn obeyed, though it was with a sad heart that he did so, and removing the senseless form of poor Flora from the corpse, on which she had thrown herself, they conveyed her into the cottage, and placing her on a sofa, they immediately proceeded to adopt such means as reason suggested for her recovery, at the same time it is quite needles to describe the agony of their feelings. Richard and his wife also watched the poor sufferer with the greatest anxiety and compassion, and entertained the worst apprehensions as to the consequences, when she should be restored to consciousness.

"Whatever could have induced her to wander to that fearful place?" said our hero, "and at the very time when there was nothing to obstruct her entrance?"

"Heaven alone knows," replied Mr. Hawthorn; "but I fear the final blow is struck that annihilates our few remaining hopes for ever. Should she recover, that which she has seen, I feel satisfied, can never be eradicated from her memory."

"Say not so," returned Richard; "you must endeavour to persuade her that it is all some frightful dream, and——"

"Ah! no," hastily interrupted Hawthorn, "any such attempt would be useless. Of what avail would it be to seek to reason with one whose brain is already so dreadfully affected? I see nothing but misery and despair before us, and dread the moment of her recovery as much as if the fatal result were already revealed to me. Oh, God! this is surely too much for human nature to endure."

As he uttered these words, he wrung his hands in the agony of his feelings, and he continued to watch his unfortunate daughter with the utmost anxiety. Her face had all the livid appearance of a corpse, and it was only by a slight breathing that she showed any signs of life. Her mother continued unremitting in her efforts to restore her to animation, but for some time there seemd to be little or no symptoms of her being enabled to do so, and their fears and suspense became almost insupportable. But at length her breathing became more free; her features somewhat relaxed their rigid expression, and heaving a deep sigh, she once more opened her eyes, and stared vacantly around her, as if for the moment unconscious of everything, or where she was. With a strength, however, which could not have been expected, she suddenly started to her feet, and fixing her eyes as though upon some ghastly object, she clasped her hands together, and in the most piteous accents she said—

"See! there he lies, so pale and rigid! His once handsome and manly features distorted frightfully, and those eyes that lately beamed such expressions of love and intelligence, are fixed in death! He will never speak to me more; I shall never again listen to the music of his voice. Alfred! beloved Alfred, who has done this? Couldst not thou escape the murderer's knife? Monsters! where are they? Let me behold them, and I will wreak a terrible revenge upon their heads."

We should become tedious were we to dwell at any unnecessary length upon the melancholy subjects we have just dilated upon. We need not say how much affected Richard and his wife were by the startling and impressive events which they had so recently witnessed, and how deeply they sympathised with Mr. Hawthorn and his wife in their misfortunes, and tried to impart consolation to them, and to inspire them with hope; but that, as might naturally be expected, under all the trying and painful circumstances, was almost a fruitless task, and they exhausted all their arguments in vain to accomplish it. They were both, especially Mr. Hawthorn, quite inconsolable; and certainly when they hourly contemplated the deplorable situation of their unfortunate daughter, and could come to no other conclusion than that her doom was sealed, and that the last circumstance had given the final blow to any hopes they might previously have entertained of her ultimate recovery, they had enough to make them so.

The remains of Mowbray having been consigned to the earth, their whole attention was devoted to the hapless sufferer, and many were the anxious hours they passed in watching her, and observing with thoughts which may be well left to the imagination of the reader to conceive, the progress of her malady, which seemed hourly to increase in intensity. For hours she would remain in a state of lethargy, with her eyes glazed and fixed on vacancy, and not a muscle of her countenance seeming to move. In fact, to gaze upon her in such moments as these, it was almost difficult to imagine that she was a thing of life, so perfectly inanimate and statue-like was her attitude, and so pale and haggard were her features. In such moments as these, which were, if possible, even more painful than her most delirious ravings, Mr. Hawthorn, overpowered by his emotions, and unable to contemplate the awful wreck of that which was once so lovely, and so innocently happy, would be compelled to leave the room, and at such times he was usually followed by our hero and his wife, who liked not to leave him alone, when by their praiseworthy efforts they might in some measure succeed in tranquillising the anguish of his feelings.

It was on one occasion of this kind that Hawthorn was more than usually agitated, and he gave vent to his feelings in the most bitter lamentations.

"To behold her suffer thus," he ejaculated, in the most melancholy tone of voice; "she who was the prop of my declining days—the one fair thing whom I prized and cherished beyond all earthly beings, and on the future of whose life I had fixed all my fondest hopes; oh, surely this is too much—far too much for human nature to endure. Oh, God! methinks I would much sooner see her laid peacefully in her coffin, than to behold her in the deplorable, the heart-rending condition she now is in."

"For Heaven's sake, my dear friend," remonstrated Richard, "do not give way to such dismal and agonising thoughts as these; but endeavour, even gloomy as the prospect is, I own, before you, to hope for the best."

"Hope for the best!" repeated Hawthorn, impatiently; "oh, how easy is it to advise! Mr. Parker, had you ever experienced that which I have, you would not talk thus."

"And have I not experienced my full share of the misfortunes of life?" replied Richard; "has not my cup of sorrow and suffering been almost filled to the brim? And is not my situation, if possible, even now far more deplorable than your own?"

"No, no," returned Mr. Hawthorn, hastily, "that is impossible; there is not the slightest hope for me, and it would be worse than madness for me to encourage it."

"And what hope is there for me?" demanded our hero; "am I not, with my poor innocent wife and child, a wretched, wandering outcast from society—a branded criminal, with a price set upon my life? And although I have hitherto eluded the vigilance of my pursuers, can I expect to escape altogether? To me the idea appears to be preposterous; and whenever I am taken, I can expect no mercy from the stern laws of my country; nothing but an ignominious death upon the gallows awaits me, while the faithful and devoted partner of my life, she who has shared in all my troubles and vicissitudes, with a fortitude and heroism unparalleled, and my poor and unoffending boy, will be left destitute and friendless in the unfeeling world, and pointed at with

opprobrium and mockery by the finger of unrelenting malice and scandal."

"Oh, Richard!" cried his wife, with a look of the most unspeakable anguish, "why will you persist in giving way to these fearful thoughts, when you know the insupportable torture they must inflict upon my heart?"

"Because," replied Parker, "in spite of all my efforts to the contrary, reason tells me that they will be realised, though for a time I may be able to avoid the fate which is impending o'er my head."

"No, Mr. Parker," observed Hawthorn, "Providence has protected you hitherto, and I feel satisfied that he will not now desert you. But as for me, there seems to be no hope; every day the sufferings of my poor girl increase in intensity, and I see plainly enough that her reason has fled for ever. And she was once so innocent, so lively, and so happy. All was sunshine wherever she appeared. Whose smiles were half so gay, whose laugh so jocund as hers? But what is she now? A wretched maniac, whose wild ravings are sufficient to strike terror into the most insensible breast, and whose looks appal where once they used to charm and fascinate. Oh, how deplorable is the change! And think you that I can contemplate it with the calmness you would advise? I must be less than man, and unworthy of the name of parent, if I could."

"But, Mr. Hawthorn," said Mary, "of what use is it your giving way to these violent paroxysms of grief, which can only serve to increase the trouble of which you so justly complain? In time the malady which now afflicts your unfortunate daughter will probably wear itself out, and the light of reason may once more dawn upon her distracted intellect."

"Ah! no," returned Mr. Hawthorn. "How delusive is such an idea! And I can scarcely dare wish that it may be fulfilled, for with returning reason would come all the torturing remembrance of the past, and her sufferings, if possible, be even tenfold more horrible than they are at present. She would be awakened to a full sense of the extent of her misery and shame; and what could serve to console her, or ameliorate the anguish of her hopeless situation? In whichever way I direct my thoughts, nought but the grim form of the gaunt demon of Despair presents itself to my imagination. Would to Heaven that I had ever been childless, then should I never have experienced those bitter and insupportable troubles it has been my lot to encounter, and which have cast such a dark shadow upon my path, crushed all my hopes and prospects, and rendered life itself a misery to me!"

He averted his looks from Mr. and Mrs. Parker as he thus spoke, and burying his face in his hands, to conceal the intensity of his emotion, he walked to the other end of the room, and gave himself up entirely to the misery and anguish of the feelings that at that moment agitated his breast, and our hero and his wife, who could not but duly appreciate his sufferings, did not offer to interrupt him.

In a few minutes, he aroused himself from this lethargy of grief, and returning to the spot he had quitted, he said—

"Oh, what a fearful scene was that when my wretched child discovered the corpse of her destroyer, whom in her unconconscious madness she still imagined to be living, and to be all that is good, and honourable, and faithful to her! Can I ever erase it from my memory? Ah! no —it is utterly impossible; and the more I think of it the greater becomes the anguish of my mind, and the more must I deprecate and detest the memory of the villain who has been the cause of so much misery. Surely an eternity of punishment awaits his guilty soul for the heartless crimes he committed while living."

"It is a pity," remarked Richard, "that the remains of the unfortunate, but misguided man were not consigned to the earth before; then your daughter might ever have remained in ignorance of the fate which had befallen him, and her recovery might not thus have been retarded."

"And why did fate ever again guide the footsteps of the villain to my dwelling?" said Hawthorn, vehemently. "It seemed as though it were but in mockery of my misery, and the ruin and desolation which his crimes had caused. Oh, when I beheld him, such was the natural excitement of my feelings, that I could have buried my fingers in his throat, and thus at once have wreaked that deadly vengeance upon him which his diabolical crimes and the cruel injuries he had inflicted upon me, so richly merited."

"Nay, Mr. Hawthorn," returned our hero, "I am surprised to hear you express such sentiments as those, but which I am confident, notwithstanding, do not spring sincerely from your heart. It is our duty to forgive and to show mercy to even those who have injured us most, and to leave their punishment in the hands of that all-wise and beneficent supreme, whose will we must not presume to arraign, and who orders all things for the best."

"Forgive and show mercy to the fell and heartless destroyer of my child?" ex-

claimed Hawthorn, hastily; "oh, it would be worse than a bitter mockery for me to affect to do so, and never can I act the hypocrite. No, Parker, in spite of all the arguments you may bring forward to persuade me to the contrary, my sentiments upon this torturing subject must remain the same, and I must ever curse and abhor the memory of the wretch Mowbray. Oh, he has done that which nothing can ever repay. You have but to look upon the sufferings of my poor child to be convinced of the truth of what I say. Is not the contemplation of the wreck of one of the loveliest of the works of nature sufficient to rend the stoutest heart?"

"True, true," coincided Richard Parker, "her situation is most melancholy, and it is impossible to help entertaining feelings of the greatest disgust against the guilty individual who has been the cause of bringing her to such a condition, when she might otherwise have been so happy in the affections of some worthy man, who would have sincerely loved her, and have cherished with his very heart and soul the treasure which had been bestowed upon him."

"Then," exclaimed Hawthorn, "if such is your opinion, Mr. Parker, what think you must be my feelings as a father, when I view the sufferings of my hapless child, and know how bright might now have been the summer of her life, had she never known that villain whom a cursed fate introduced to my humble dwelling? Oh, with what base ingratitude did he return the hospitality and friendship that I bestowed upon him! My heart sickens, and my feelings of disgust know no bounds when I reflect on it."

There was so much truth and reason in that which Hawthorn said, that our hero felt himself at a loss to return any reply, and a silence of some minutes ensued, which was, however, at length interrupted by loud and mournful cries from the room upstairs, which they well knew proceeded from poor Flora, and they listened with the most painful attention.

"The delirium of her madness is at its height again," said Hawthorn; "oh, is not this enough to rend a parent's heart, unless it were composed of the most stern and insensible materials? I cannot remain here, and listen to here wild and melancholy ravings. Heaven help her, for without its aid, what, alas! will become of her?"

"Had you not better stay where you are?" suggested Richard; "the contemplation of her sufferings can but add to your own anguish, without enabling you to afford her any relief."

"No," replied Hawthorn, "it is impossible that I can do so; to listen to her mournful lamentations, without beholding her, tortures me more than all. My poor child! my poor child! oh, what will be the result of this?"

He sighed deeply as he thus spoke, and hastened from the room, and Richard and his wife, considering that their presence might probably be required, also followed.

On entering the chamber, they found that the unfortunate girl, who was dressed, had arisen from the couch on which she had previously been reclining, and was supported in the arms of her mother, who was exerting herself to the utmost to soothe her into something like composure, but with little or no success, and she seemed to take no notice of them when they entered the room. Her appearance was wild and melancholy in the extreme, her fine silken hair was hanging dishevelled upon her fair shoulders, and the expression of her eyes was quite painful to look upon. Mr. Hawthorn stood at some short distance from her, and contemplated her with feelings of the keenest anguish, but which we will not attempt to describe, and Richard and his wife could not but gaze upon the painful scene with pity and regret, though they offered not to say a word. Suddenly the maniac girl released herself from the hold of her mother, and fixing her eyes upon her with a mingled expression of curiosity and anger, she cried—

"Away! who are you that seek to hold and detain me thus? Am I not my own mistress? and think you that I am that weak idiot to be thus controlled? Away, I say! I know you for one of those who would deceive me, and lead me astray, when I would hasten to meet him who holds possession of my heart, my lord, my husband! Who dares to tell me that he is false to those vows which he has so solemnly plighted to me? It is false!—false as the minds are base that could concoct so atrocious a libel! Oh, Alfred—dear Alfred!—never, I am certain, could you seek to deceive that fond girl who has placed so much confidence in you, and who would willingly lay down her life to serve you. But why is he not here? Why does he leave me here alone to mourn his absence, and to form all kinds of fearful conjectures as to the cause of his being away? Ah! what demon is that who whispers in my ears that he is dead? That they, the wretches who were jealous and envious of our happiness, have murdered him? Horror! horror! It cannot be. And yet did I not but just now gaze upon his pale and ghastly corpse? Yes. I saw the pale and livid hue of death upon that loved face which once possessed such manly beauty. Those eyes were closed for ever which once gazed upon me with such looks of affection; that voice was stilled, whose softest tone awoke my very soul to rapture. Oh, God! surely it could only have been some frightful dream, or my senses must be wandering. Alfred! why do you not hasten to my arms, to remove this terrible suspense, and to banish from my mind the strange and awful delusion that has taken possession of it? Ah! what ghastly form is that which rises to my sight, and gazes so solemnly upon me? It is he, the phantom of my husband, in all the awful cerements of the grave! He stands before me—he waves his hand mournfully towards me, but he does not speak. See—see!—he beckons me to follow him. Alfred!—husband!—I come! I come! In life we were united by every tie of affection, and in death we will not be separated. Ah!—he fades from my sight!—he is gone! I am again left here alone to mourn his fate. My heart-strings burst! My brain is on fire! Oh, horror! —horror!"

With these words the wretched and unfortunate girl sank insensible in the arms of her mother; and Mr. Hawthorn clasped his forehead, and groaned aloud in the agony of his feelings.

"It is too plain," he said, "alas! that what she has seen has made an impression upon her disordered and wandering senses, which nothing whatever can eradicate. My God! how torturing it is to witness her sufferings, and to listen to her wild and delirious ravings, without being able to relieve her! Oh, what bitter curses should rest upon the head of the guilty miscreant who has brought her to this!"

"Retire, Henry," said Mrs. Hawthorn, "and endeavour to compose your feelings, while I see to the recovery of this poor girl. Alas! it is, indeed, most painful, most heart-rending, to witness her sufferings, and to know that we have not the power to assist her, or to convince her of the deep sympathy which we feel for her in her misfortunes. Retire, and Mr. and Mrs. Parker will, I dare say, accompany you, and endeavour to tranquillise your feelings."

"Tranquillise my feelings?" said Mr. Hawthorn; "oh, how hopeless is such a task as that. There are no means of composing myself when I think of the miserable, the unmerited fate of my poor child.

Alas! alas!—here is, indeed, a spectacle to rend a father's heart!"

"Come, my friend," said our hero, in a soothing voice, and laying his hand gently on his arm, "let me persuade you. You can do no possible good by remaining here; the attentions of your wife will do everything for the restoration of your unfortunate daughter."

Hawthorn cast one glance of anguish towards his insensible child, and then, with a deep and heavy sigh, he suffered Richard and his wife to conduct him from the room, and they returned to the apartment which they had previously quitted. Here he threw himself into a chair, and for a few minutes resigned himself entirely to the power of his emotions, and Richard and his wife stood by and watched him in silence, and with feelings of the deepest commiseration, but did not offer to interrupt him in his gloomy meditations. At length he arose again from his seat, and traversed the room with rapid and uneven steps, while the expression of his countenance fully testified as to the agony of mind he was at that moment enduring.

"Oh, God!" he ejaculated at last, "this is surely too much for human fortitude to endure. My ill-fated child, when will your miseries have an end?"

"Something, Mr. Hawthorn, I hope, will occur much sooner than you now anticipate to alleviate the sorrows which you now so naturally experience, and to restore your daughter to health and tranquillity, if not to happiness."

Hawthorn shook his head despairingly, and again sighed, as he replied—

"Ah, no! I have endeavoured to think so, and to buoy myself up with that hope, till my heart has sickened, and the utter wretchedness of my fate, and all who are connected with me, has become the more apparent, and quite overwhelmed me in the anguish of my mind. Death alone will close the miseries of my darling Flora; and I ought to hail it with gratitude, as it would be a mercy to her in her present deplorable condition. As for her ever being restored to happiness, the thought is little better than madness."

"You must not think so, Mr. Hawthorn, indeed, you must not," remarked Mary, "for you know there is a just power above, who will never desert those who put their trust in Him."

Hawthorn returned no answer, and another interval of silence ensued, which no one seemed inclined to interrupt. At length it was broken in upon by the sudden appearance of Alice, and her husband eagerly inquired after the condition of the fair sufferer.

"Thank God," replied Alice, "she is much better now; I succeeded in recovering her, and in persuading her to retire to bed, and she is now wrapped in a calm sleep, which I trust will have the most beneficial effect upon her."

"Heaven grant that it may," said Hawthorn, vehemently, "though I much fear that it will not. Oh, Alice, is it not awful to see her suffer thus, and to have to anticipate what must be the ultimate result?"

"Yes, my husband," replied Alice; "it is, indeed, most painful, and I know I need not tell you that I feel it as keenly as you can possibly do; but still we must hope for the best, and I trust that we shall not be disappointed."

"I would fain think so, Alice," replied her husband, "but find it impossible to do so. The longer I reflect upon it, the more dismal does the prospect before me appear to be."

"You must try to arouse yourself from this feeling of despair and anguish," observed his wife; "for it can effect no possible good, and may be attended with the worst consequences. But I must return to the chamber, and keep watch by the bedside of the poor girl. You had better remain here, for your presence can do no good, and the sight of her will probably only serve to increase your anguish."

Hawthorn returned no answer, and Alice having bade Mr. and Mrs. Parker good-night, for it was not likely that she would see them again, retired from the room. Richard and his wife remained in conversation with Mr. Hawthorn some time longer, and he becoming more tranquil, and the hour getting late, they bade him adieu for the night, and returned to the cottage which they themselves inhabited, deeply impressed with all that they had seen.

"I do not feel comfortable in remaining here," said Richard; "Hawthorn and his wife have already sufficient trouble and anxiety upon their minds, without being bothered with us. I wish that I could receive some communication from our friend Adams, advising us how to act, for I do not think it possible for us to stay here much longer. It is strange that we do not hear from him; surely my letter must have miscarried; something particular has happened, or, perhaps he finds the necessity of abandoning the idea of rendering me any further assistance."

"Oh, no," returned Mrs. Parker; "I do not believe that of Mr. Adams; his friendship for you is too sincere and too ardent; you alarm yourself unnecessarily, Richard. You will hear from him before long, depend upon it; he will only be too anxious to render you all the assistance in his power, depend upon it. As for Mr. and Mrs. Hawthorn, we have no reason to doubt their friendship, since they have ever behaved to us with such uniform kindness and attention. Besides, here you are perfectly safe; no one but those who are your friends can form the least conception of the route you have taken, and why, then, should you make yourself so uncomfortable?"

"For no other reasons than those I have mentioned to you," answered Richard. "I must be ungrateful, indeed, could I doubt for an instant the sincerity of the friendship of Hawthorn and his wife, who have given such unexampled proofs of their goodness of heart since we have resided with them; but such a thought never entered my mind; still, you must be aware that their whole attention and anxiety is required for their ill-fated daughter."

"True," coincided our heroine; " it is quite heartrending to see the dreadful malady under which the poor girl suffers; but I hope that with proper care and attention she may yet to restored to reason."

"No," observed her husband; "to me, I must confess, it does not seem at all likely; her brain, I fear, has suffered by far too great a shock for her ever to recover from it. It is most melancholy to behold one so young and so lovely so awfully afflicted."

Mrs. Parker could not but agree with this; and after some further observations the conversation dropped, and they retired to rest.

Two more days passed away without anything more particular taking place, and Flora remained in much the same situation, though there were, indeed, times when some slight degree of reason seemed to dawn upon her disordered intellect, and her parents exerted themselves to the utmost to arouse her; but those favourable changes were only temporary, and the paroxysms that succeeded them were only more violent than ever.

Still, no communication arrived from Adams, and the apprehensions and uneasiness of Richard at the circumstance naturally increased, and he formed all kinds of torturing and perplexing conjectures as to the cause. Daniel had been to the hut, and to the eager questions which our hero put to him, he replied that the letter had been forwarded with all due precaution, immediately, by Mr. Hatfield, who, he assured him, took the deepest interest in their welfare, and was anxious and willing to do all he could in his power to serve them.

"I can assure you, Mr. Parker," remarked Daniel, " that Master Hatfield is a man, every inch of him, and no one is ever more ready to serve a fellow-creature in distress than himself. You may safely depend upon his sincerity and friendship."

"What my brother says is true," said Hawthorn, "for I know the character of Mr. Hatfield well, and I am certain he would sooner suffer anything than be the means of increasing the misery of his less fortunate fellow-creatures."

"After the character that yourself and your brother have given of him," said Richard, "I cannot, of course, any longer doubt the character of Mr. Hatfield, or suspect that he would betray me; but still you must admit that I have a right to feel uneasy at the time which has elapsed without my receiving any answer from my friend Adams."

"True," replied Hawthorn, "I did expect that you would have received a communication from him before this; but you may depend upon it that he is still as zealous in your cause as ever, and that he is only waiting until he has arranged some certain plans for your future security. However, in the meantime, you may set your mind at rest, for here you are in perfect safety."

"I would fain believe so," returned Parker; "but I fear that we are putting you to much trouble and inconvenience, and——"

"I must again beg of you not to mention that," interrupted Hawthorn, "or to make your mind at all uneasy about it. You must, I am sure, be well aware that you are most heartily welcome to all that I can do for you, and that I am only too happy to have it in my power to serve one to whose late lamented father I am under such a weight of obligation."

Richard Parker pressed the fisherman's hand cordially, as he replied:—

"I know it, my kind friend, and believe me, whatever may be the fate that is in store for me, I must ever entertain a most lively sense of gratitude for the kindness which I have experienced from you. Could I but ultimately escape from the fearful dangers by which I am at present surrounded, for the sake of my wife and child, of whom, deprived of my protection, I know not what would become, oh, how happy I should be!"

"And you will do so, depeed upon it," said Hawthorn, confidently ; "I feel certain of it, and I hope that at some future time we shall meet under far different and happier circumstances."

"I trust to Heaven that we shall," said Mr. Parker ; "and that the dark clouds that at present hang over your fate will then have passed away, and that your daughter will be restored to that reason and peace of mind from which she has been so long unfortunately estranged."

Mr. Hawthorn shook his head mournfully.

"Alas !" he said, "I would willingly, but dare not encourage such a hope ; the fatal malady which affects my poor child has, I feel convinced, taken too deep root in her brain ever to be removed ; and can you wonder at the agony I endure, when I reflect on this ? Oh, it is indeed a most dreadful trial to a parent's feelings, and it quite unmans me when I witness her sufferings."

"It is, indeed, a severe trial for you," observed Mrs. Parker, "but you must endeavour to support it with fortitude."

"I have struggled hard," replied Mr. Hawthorn, in a voice of the deepest emotion ; "but all my efforts have been of little or no avail.   Heaven help her, for without its aid I know not what will be the result of it."

Richard and his wife made no reply, and after awhile they changed the topic of conversation, and talked upon indifferent matters.

Our hero had latterly indulged in short rambles not far from the cottage early in the morning, when there were not many persons about, or in the shade of the evening; and as he was disguised, he did so without much fear of his being recognised by any person whom he might meet. This gentle exercise he found to recruit his health, which was naturally considerably impaired from long anxiety of mind, at the same time that it afforded him an opportunity of indulging in his meditations without interruption, for his wife never accompanied him, as he considered it would not be exactly safe for her to do so. Mr. Hawthorn always cautioned him not to go too far, in case he should happen to encounter any one who, even under his disguise, might recognise him, and Richard had ever been most careful to follow his advice until the occasion of which we are about to write, when, his mind being completely absorbed by the reflections which crowded upon it, he unconsciously wandered beyond the extent of those limits which he usually allowed himself, and,

suddenly aroused to recollection, he looked up, and found himself in a part of the country which he never remembered to have seen before, but which, as it seemed lonely and unfrequented, did not create any alarm in his breast; and feeling somewhat tired, from the unusual length of his ramble, he seated himself on a mound of earth, which rose just before a majestic tree, whose wide-spreading branches formed a pleasant canopy over his head, and continued the chain of thoughts that had previously occupied his mind.

It was evening, and the bright orb of day had not long since retired to rest in the western horizon, the traces of his departing glory still remaining in the heavens.   It was a lovely evening, and all was calm around, a gentle breeze being wafted from the ocean at a short distance, which came refreshing to the senses, and was enough to impart some degree of consolation and hope even to the most care-o'erladen mind.   Although but a few days only had elapsed since the dreary inclemencies of winter had reigned around, all now seemed to be, as if by magic, clothed in the vernal and refreshing aspect of spring, and the human mind could scarcely conceive or believe in the wonders of the extraordinary change. And now the bright moon arose in all her chaste glory, shedding a silvery light upon the earth that added beauty and lustre to the wondrous works of Nature, and rose the soul in awe and admiration to the Almighty Creator of all.

Richard Parker sat for some time, and gazed upon all that met his eyes with feelings of admiration, though his mind at the same time was occupied and tormented with other thoughts of a far different description.   In spite of all that his wife and Hawthorn had said to him, he could not but help entertaining the most serious doubts and apprehensions as to the cause of his not having received any communication from Adams, and likewise the most dismal forebodings crowded upon his brain that something was shortly about to happen to him, which would at once annihilate all the hopes he might at any time have entertained, and precipitate that fate which he had so much reason to dread. He felt confident that Adams was too sincere in the professions he had made him, and was too anxious to serve him, to have delayed so long in rendering him all the assistance in his power, had not something of a particular description occurred to prevent him ; and he was fearful lest he should have been betrayed, and involved in any danger by the part he had already so

HAWTHORN'S DENUNCIATIONS OVER THE DEAD BODY OF MOWBRAY.

generously taken in aiding his escape from the dangers surrounding him.

"Kind-hearted man," he soliloquised; "how deeply grieved should I be, were the fears that I too reasonably entertain be realised; for should it be discovered that you have not only connived at, but aided me in my escape, I know full well that it must end in your destruction, and that would render my last moments even more bitter and poignant to know that I had been the cause of bringing an excellent and innocent man to ruin. Alas! alas! it seems to be my fate to bring misery upon the heads of all those who become in any way associated with me, and who take an interest in my welfare. Cruel destiny! how can I possibly escape from it? Would to Heaven that I had never been born, since it seems that I am doomed to endless misery and anxiety of mind, and Heaven knows full well that it has not been my own seeking, but that it has been brought upon me by the villany, persecution, and injustice of others. And you, my poor wife and child—oh, how terribly do you share in my misfortunes, and how much do I fear that you have yet to suffer. Mary, dear Mary ! most devoted of women, and affectionate of wives, why did Fate ever make us acquainted? You might now have been happy, and moving in that proud and distinguished station in life to which your numerous virtues and accomplishments so justly entitle you ; but now what are you? A wretched wanderer, never free from care and anxiety, and all those bright prospects that were spread before you for ever crushed, while the future you have to look to, is too awful even to contemplate in imagination. And yet Heaven knows how fondly and sincerely I have ever loved you, and how anxious I have been for your happiness. What is to be done in this dreadful emergency? Teach me, great God, for I know not how to act."

He paused, and striking his forehead with his hand, for a few moments became again completely lost in bewildering and racking thought.

"Oh, Richard Parker, unhappy man," he said, at length ; "what a wretched fate is thine, and of what use is it you struggling against it? It is impossible that you can escape from it ; and my blood freezes in my veins with horror, when I think of the ignominious fate which, sooner or later, awaits you."

"Ay," said a voice near him, "and it strikes me, friend Parker, that it will not be long ere that fate overtakes you, so you might as well resign yourself to it as not."

The reader may imagine with what astonishment and alarm our hero started on hearing these words, and looking hastily up, his surprise and consternation increased, when he beheld that officious and mischievous individual, Mr. Timothy Bubble, standing before him, and gazing upon him with vindictive and petty looks of triumph. He sprang hastily to his feet, and for some moments he contemplated him with looks of the utmost confusion and incredulity; but at length he said—

"Ah, you here? Am I then discovered ?"

"Nothing so sure, Richard Parker," replied the little wretch, with a malicious grin ; "I thought I should have the good fortune to meet with you again some day or other, in spite of the clever manner in which you have contrived to conceal yourself for so long a time; but now that I have done so, you might as well let me get the reward for apprehending you as anybody else. So, if you will just be kind enough to take my arm, I will escort you into custody with all the politeness that any gen-

tleman placed in your situation can possibly require."

"Insolent reptile !" exclaimed our hero, indignantly ; "dare you thus boldly address me? Are you not afraid that you will bring my vengeance upon your head? Suffer myself to be taken by such a despicable thing as you ! Oh, what a shameless mockery is this ! Begone, begone, while you are safe, and, as you value your life, dare not to mention to any one that you have seen me, or that you have any idea of the place where I am concealed."

"Now—now, Mr. Parker," said Bubble, "let me advise you not to be obstinate; of what use is it resisting the law? I do not wish to act violently, but——"

"Cowardly knave !" interrupted Richard, unable to control the violence and exasperation of his feelings, at the cool impudence of Bubble ; "think you that Richard Parker will ever suffer himself to be taken by such a fellow as you? Begone, I say, while you are safe, and as you value your life never let me behold you again, lest the consequences that ensue to you should be far more dangerous than you seem to anticipate."

"Oh," returned Timothy, with much effrontery, "I am not to be intimidated in that sort of a manner, I can assure you, although I am a little man, and you are the self-styled Admiral Perker, the mutineer and murderer, who——"

"Wretch! villain !" exclaimed our hero, passionately, and at the same time seizing him by the collar, "since, then, you will not be advised, take the consequences !"

"Now—now, Mr Parker," stammered out Bubble, trembling, and trying to release himself; "don't be rash! I—I—upon my soul, you'll choke me, if you do not take your hand off my throat—I—I'll call for assistance ! Murder ! help ! treason ! Oh—oh—oh !"

"Busy, malicious fool !" cried Richard, "you call in vain. Down with you, and learn prudence and mercy."

As Parker thus spoke, he dashed Mr. Bubble violently to the earth, and his head coming in contact with the stump of a tree, he was so stunned by the violence of the shock, that his senses completely left him. Our hero, as may be imagined, did not wait to see the result, but first looking around him to ascertain whether or not the coast was clear, he hurried away from the spot, in the road which he considered to be the way home, in a state of agitation of mind which we need not attempt to describe. He had proceeded to some distance before he ventured to stop, when he was compelled to do so in order to take breath, and in some measure to recover himself from the state of surprise and consternation into which this unexpected adventure had thrown him; and he looked anxiously and fearfully around him, to see whether any one was watching him; but there was no one at hand, and finding himself in a secluded place, and knowing the condition in which he had left Bubble, he considered himself, for the present, at any rate, perfectly safe.

"Who would have thought of meeting with this mischievous fellow again in such a place, and at such a time?" he soliloquised; "thank Heaven that there was no one at hand to assist him, and that I have escaped from him. It must have been accident alone that brought him to the spot, for had he known where I am concealed, it is not at all likely that he would have failed to have adopted some means to apprehend me ere this. But I wish to Heaven I had not seen him, for it will not be safe for me to remain any longer in this part of the country; he will be sure to make known to the authorities that he has seen me in this neighbourhood, and a strict search will be immediately made for me. Cursed misfortune! the Fates have conspired against me, and I know not how to act. Oh, Mary, what will be your alarm and agitation when you hear of this! I almost dread to make you acquainted with the circumstance. The fears and forebodings I entertained, then, it seems too evident were not without some foundation. The busy fool! what can make him pursue me with such vindictiveness, since I never did him any injury? Oh, what a wretched life is this to lead; to be hunted like some wild beast, and unable to find any place of shelter from those who are in pursuit of me, and who thirst for my blood. I had better, much better be dead, than to have to endure this constant state of anxiety and misery. It is useless for me to seek to to avoid that fate which seems too surely to await me. And yet my wife and child; oh, what will become of you when I am no more, and especially if I come to the awful and ignominious end with with I am threatened? My heart trembles to contemplate it. No, I must, for their beloved sakes, still struggle to escape it, and trust to the goodness and mercy of the Supreme, who knows full well that I have been sinned against much more than I have sinned myself, to aid me in my efforts. But why do I tarry here, when danger threatens me, and my Mary will be so alarmed at the unusual length of my absence from home? There is no one to observe me, but Bubble might recover his

senses, and obtaining assistance, enter into a pursuit of me ere I have time to escape. Let me begone, while I have yet the opportunity in my power."

As he said this, he once more looked anxiously and cautiously around him, and then hurried on his way, his mind still distracted and tortured by that which he had seen, and undetermined in which way it would be most prudent for him to act.

He was not long in arriving at the cottage which himself and his wife inhabited, and rushing breathlessly into the parlour, where he found her, as he had expected, most anxiously awaiting his return, he threw himself hastily into a chair, and was so much overcome by the power of his emotions that he could not give utterance to a word. Quickly noticing the agitation of his looks, Mary advanced eagerly towards him, and taking his hand, and looking anxiously in his face, she said—

"For Heaven's sake, dear Richard, what is the meaning of this powerful emotion, and what has occurred to detain you so long? Tell me, I pray you, and at once remove the painful suspense which now agitates me."

"Mary," said her husband, "I fear we are discovered, and that every moment we remain here is fraught with the most imminent danger."

"Discovered!" repeated our heroine, with a look of alarm; "oh, you surely cannot mean what you say; explain yourself at once, I beseech you."

"It is too true," answered Parker. "Oh, I have had a narrow escape."

"But is it possible," demanded Mary, "that any one can have recognised you, disguised as you are?"

"Yes," answered our hero; "but a short time since I encountered that mischievous and dangerous individual, Bubble, the lawyer."

"Ah!" ejaculated his wife, with a look of alarm; "oh, where?"

"In a lonely and secluded spot some short distance from hence, and he immediately recognised me, and had he had any one with him to render assistance, I should probably have been in custody."

"Alas—alas!" ejaculated Mary; "how unfortunate and alarming is this. What can have brought him to this part of the country?"

"I know not," replied Richard; "unless it was that he had some suspicion that we were concealed here. However, it is evident that we are no longer safe here, and that we must depart from hence without delay, Heaven only knows whither, and without waiting to receive the communication from our friend Adams."

"Oh, no, say not so; I trust there will be no necessity for that. But think you this dangerous man had an opportunity of watching whither you went?"

"No; for I hurled him senseless to the earth; but being now fully aware that we are secreted somewhere in the neighbourhoood, he will be sure to make it known in the proper quarter, and a strict search will be immediately made in the neighbourhood, which can scarcely fail to be crowned with success. Surely I must by some means, through the letter which I forwarded to Adams, have been betrayed, and that accounts for my not receiving any answer."

"No," observed our heroine, "you must not entertain any such ideas and apprehensions, Richard; for had it been known that we had sought refuge in this place, is it at all likely that immediate and certain steps would not have been taken to apprehend you? Be calm, and still hope for the best."

"How can I do so," demanded Richard, "under all the circumstances? Every moment the impossibility of my escape from the awful fate which is impending o'er my head, seems to be the more certain, and my breast is filled with the utmost anguish and despair; but, believe me, that it is more on account of you, my beloved and faithful partner, and our poor boy, than myself; for I have been so long harassed and tormented, that life has become a complete burthen to me, and did I not fear what would become of you when left friendless and alone in the cruel world, without a protector, I should court death with pleasure, as a release from those sufferings it has so long been my hard lot to endure."

"For Heaven's sake, Richard, do not talk thus," said his wife, "for it tortures and distracts my brain to hear you. Kind Providence will yet avert that dreadful fate you so much apprehend, and which you so little deserve; and something convinces me that the time will come, and is probably not far distant, when we shall once more be restored to that happy position in society from which we have been so long unfortunately estranged."

"Ah, no!" returned Richard, disconsolately. "I have too long endeavoured to think so, but reason convinces me of the folly of so doing. Am I not charged with two of the heaviest crimes known to the laws of my country?—and is it likely that they will show me any mercy, especially when they are so prejudiced against me?

They will not rest, depend upon it, until they have discovered me, and wreaked their vengeance upon my devoted head."

"Oh, why will you give way to this black despair?" sighed Mary, in a voice of agony and gentle remonstrance. "Heaven, who knows the cruel injuries you have received, and how little you deserve such a fate as the one with which you are threatened, will save you from it, and not suffer your cruel enemies to triumph. But you must not again venture to wander from our place of concealment until this affair has in some measure blown over, and you have received some communication from Mr. Adams, advising us how to act."

"I do not now expect to receive any letter from Adams," replied Richard, "for it is my firm belief that mine has miscarried, or that something of a serious nature has happened to him through the part he has taken towards me."

"Oh, no!" remarked our heroine; "such fears are, I trust, groundless; for had it been as you apprehend, we should have been sure to have heard of it ere this. Heaven forbid that he should suffer for the disinterested friendship he has shown towards us."

"Need I say that I most heartily concur in that prayer?" said her husband; "but, at the same time, I cannot but fear that there is too much reason for the misgivings that cross my mind. But where is Mr. Hawthorn? Think you that he has yet retired to rest?"

"I do not," answered Mrs. Parker, "for it is early yet, and I saw him but a few minutes before you returned."

"I must see him," observed Richard, "to consult with him what is best to be done in this most painful and alarming business."

"It will be better for you to do so," said his wife, "and I have no doubt that his opinion will coincide with that I have expressed to you."

"Come, then," returned Richard; "let us at once visit him, for my mind is quite uneasy and doubtful until I have received some further counsel and advice upon the subject."

Mrs. Parker made no reply, and she, having first looked out to ascertain whether or not there was any one at hand, and finding the coast was quite clear, placed her arm in that of her husband, and retired with him to the cottage of Mr. Hawthorn, whom they found sitting alone, buried as usual in deep thought. Aroused by their entrance he arose, and advancing towards them, said—

"So, Mr. Parker, you have returned; you acted imprudently, I think, in remaining out so long, and must have wandered beyond your usual limit, I should think."

"True," answered our hero; "being wrapped in meditation, I certainly rambled unconsciously farther than I had intended, and now regret that I did so."

"What mean you?" demanded Hawthorn; "you look alarmed. Has anything particular happened?"

Richard Parker replied in the affirmative, and then briefly related that with which the reader is already acquainted, and to which Hawthorn listened with much attention and the deepest interest.

"This an unfortunate occurrence," said the fisherman, when our hero had concluded. "But you say that the fellow had no opportunity of watching whither you went?"

"He had not," answered Richard; "but I fear that now he has once seen me in the neighbourhood, it will be no longer safe for me to remain here, for he will be sure to make the circumstance known, and those who are in pursuit of me will lose no time in endeavouring to discover the place of my concealment."

"No," observed Hawthorn; "I do not believe that, if you only act with circumspection, you have anything to fear. No one can have any suspicion that you are secreted here, and this Mr. Bubble, as you call him, will naturally conclude that you have immediately made your escape from the neighbourhood after you had seen him. You are perfectly safe here, if you only act with due precaution, and do not again venture out."

"That is my opinion, and what I have told him, Mr. Hawthorn," remarked our heroine; "and I have also endeavoured to persuade him not to unnecessarily alarm himself."

"Very true," coincided the fisherman, "it is, however, fortunate that this man was alone, or the consequences might have been fatal."

"When I weigh all the circumstances in my mind," said our hero, "I cannot but entertain the worst doubts and apprehensions. I see plainly that it is useless for me to struggle against my fate, and had better at once resign myself to it, than to be kept in this constant state of doubt and suspense."

"Are you mad, Mr. Parker, that you talk in this manner?" remonstrated Hawthorn. "What have you yet to fear? Has not Providence hitherto protected you from discovery, and baffled all the efforts of your enemies to get you in their power? And it is my firm belief that it will ultimately bring you safe out of the difficulties with which you are at present surrounded. Come, come, my friend, you must not give way to these melancholy and despairing thoughts, but view everything on the sunniest side. In me, I think, you are fully aware that you have a sincere friend, who will do everything in his power to serve you, and who will only be too happy, when these storms of adversity have passed over, to see you once more restored to your proper position in society."

"Oh, yes, Hawthorn," returned our hero, grasping his hand; "believe me, well do I know the sincerity of your heart, and the disinterested friendship with which you act towards myself and those who are far more precious to me than my own existence; but still I cannot divest my mind of the sad forebodings that have so long taken possession of it; and the longer I reflect upon all the circumstances, the more thoroughly do I feel convinced that they will be realised, and that I am a doomed man. My enemies will never relax in their vigilance till they have discovered me, and when once they shall have done so, I know that my doom is sealed, and that I can expect to receive no mercy from them."

"Away with such thoughts," said Mr. Hawthorn, hastily, "for I have no patience to listen to them. Have you not friends who will remain staunch to you to the last? And with their assistance you will be able, with your wife and child, to retire to some distant part of the country, where you may remain undisturbed and unmolested."

"And why should I involve so many in danger for my sake?" demanded Richard; "whoever shall be discovered to have shielded or befriended me, will be sure to bring down upon themselves the vengeance of the law, and that must end in their destruction. Already I fear that something of a fatal nature has happened to my esteemed friend Adams, and that the part he has acted in my escape has been discovered, for in no other way can I account for his not answering my letter."

"No," returned Hawthorn; "I do not believe that there is the least ground for any such apprehension; for the letter being confided to the parties it was, would be sure to reach him safe, and you may rest assured that Mr. Adams is only waiting till he has matured his plans to assist you, to return an answer to it. As for this busy fool, Bubble, I do not think, after all, that you have much to fear from him. It will puzzle him to detect where you are, if you do not venture forth abroad again, which it would be very imprudent of you to do at present ; and when he finds that there is no chance of accomplishing them, he will abandon his designs. Come, come, my friend, arouse all your energies, and my word for it you will yet live to triumph over all the difficulties in which you are at present involved."

"Right, Mr. Hawthorn," remarked our heroine ; "I feel confident that all will yet terminate as you seem to anticipate, and that my unfortunate husband will not be suffered to fall a victim to the terrible fate which he apprehends. Richard, you used to be more firm under dangers of the most trying description, and why, then, do you not now exert yourself, when so much depends upon your fortitude and prudence ?"

"Because," replied her husband, "I am worn out with constant anxiety of mind; and surely there is every allowance to be made for one who is placed in my fearful situation."

"True," replied Mr. Hawthorn ; "but by abandoning yourself thus entirely to despair, you cannot hope to better your condition, but, on the contrary, will only unfit yourself to act as prudence should dictate. It is fortunate, I again say, that this man was alone, or I shudder to think what the consequences might have been. Very likely you might now have been the inmate of a prison."

"Oh, yes," said Mrs. Parker; "that is most certain ; and Providence be thanked for averting so dreadful a calamity. That ought to convince you, Richard, that it has not yet deserted you."

"I believe in its mercy," returned our hero, "and am grateful for it; but still I find it impossible to banish from my mind entirely the gloomy apprehensions that have taken possession it, and which, when I think of the fearful situation in which you would be placed should anything happen to me, completely weighs me down."

"Think not of it, dear Richard," said the devoted wife, tenderly. "Banish all such torturing ideas from your mind, and look forward to the future with the most sanguine feeling of hope, which I sincerely trust will not be doomed to be disappointed."

"Alas!" sighed Richard, "the task you would impose upon me is a most difficult one, and I fear that I should fail in attempting to accomplish it."

"There is no knowing what energy and perseverance can effect, so

"and I would, therefore, urge you to follow the excellent advice of your wife, Mr. Parker. A day or two, I trust, will bring us some news from Mr. Adams, and then we shall the better be able to judge how it will be best for you to act."

"No," returned our hero; "his silence has been so long that I now despair of hearing from him again. I still cannot help fearing that something particular has happened to him, or he would certainly have communicated with me ere this, knowing, as he must do, how anxious I must be to receive an answer to my letter. Heaven save him from danger, for I should never forgive myself should I be the means of bringing any trouble upon him."

"Do not encourge any such apprehensions," remarked Hawthorn; "for, depend upon it, they will prove to be groundless. Who has Adams to fear? There is no one acquainted with his secrets but honest old Binnacle, and I know his character too well to suspect that he would ever be the means of injuring his fellow creatures, especially one whom he esteems as he does his friend, Adams. No, no, Parker; take my word for it that you have nothing to fear on that score. You may make your mind perfectly easy ; and as for this adventure of to-night, I should not trouble myself to think anything more about it, though you may think yourself fortunate that it has ended no worse."

"True," coincided Mary ; "and I cannot be sufficiently grateful to Providence that it has not. But come, Richard, it is getting late, and probably our friend, Mr. Hawthorn, wishes to retire to rest; we had better depart and see what to-morrow will produce."

Our hero offered no objection to this, and having bid Mr. Hawthorn good-night, he and his wife quitted the cottage. On their arrival home, however, they neither of them felt disposed to retire to rest, and they sat conversing for some time upon the events of the evening; and, notwithstanding all that his wife and Mr. Hawthorn had said, and the arguments which they had brought forward to dissipate the apprehensions which his unexpected meeting with Bubble had excited in his mind, he found it impossible to help feeling very uneasy upon the subject; for he well knew the dangerous and malicious character of the little lawyer, and urged on by those feeling, but more especially by the idea of the reward which was offered for his apprehension, he would be sure not to fail to use every means in his power which might lead to his detection. It was in vain that his wife endeavoured to combat these fearful apprehensions; and, in fact, although she took good care to conceal her real thoughts from Richard, Mary could not but enter greatly in some measure into the doubts and misgivings that caused him so much uneasiness.

"But still," she remarked, "I do not believe that there is so much danger to apprehend, after all. It is evident that this man could have had no suspicion whatever as to where we were concealed, or he would have lost no time in betraying us into the hands of our enemies, and thus at once securing the reward. He had no opportunity of watching you, and I should imagine that this is the last place where they would think of searching for us; besides, after what has taken place, they would make sure that we should lose no time in abandoning this part of the country, and they will be puzzled to form a conjecture as to the course we have pursued. Banish your fears, Richard, and take my word for it, that, if you do not again venture from home, you will still remain perfectly safe, and that we shall ultimately be enabled to elude their vigilance altogether."

"No," replied Richard, "I find it impossible to be so sanguine upon this subject as you appear to be; such are the vindictive feelings with which the friends and relations of the late Captain Arlington will no doubt pursue me, that they will never rest until they have discovered me and wreaked their vengeance on my head. I can expect no mercy from them."

"But from that Almighty Power which has hitherto protected us, even at the very moment when we were surrounded by the greatest danger, you may," returned Mary, solemnly, but confidently. "Believe me, dear Richard, that He will not desert you while you put your trust in Him, and that He will not suffer you to perish in so untimely and ignominious a manner, especially after the many trials, vicissitudes, and persecutions you have so undeservedly undergone. Endeavour to wait patiently; act with prudence and precaution, be firm, yield not to despair, and depend upon it, dismal even though our prospects may at present seem to be, we shall ultimately surmount all the terrible difficulties by which we are now, and have been for so long surrounded."

"I would fain hope so," said our hero; "and I should be unworthy of your affection and heroic self-devotion did I not endeavour to follow your advice. Oh, how grateful, how unspeakably, how boundlessly grateful should I be to that Providence who has given me so fond, so vir-

tuous, and so devoted a partner as yourself; for had it not been for your soothing voice, and affectionate sympathy, how could I ever have found fortitude sufficient to support with becoming firmness the many and severe trials to which I have been subjected? Could I only hear from our friend Adams, the doubts and apprehensions which I cannot help now at times entertaining would be removed, and I might then indeed look forward to the future with hope and resignation. But his long silence alarms me, and I know not what to think."

"We have already argued that point sufficiently, my dear Richard, I think," answered Mary; "and I must confess that I do not feel so much astonished and uneasy at the silence of Adams as you seem to do. He probably is only maturing his plans, and most likely does not think it prudent to communicate with you until he has fully arranged everything for your final escape. He will never abandon your cause, depend on it, but, on the contrary, will only feel too anxious to serve you to the utmost of his power."

"I do not doubt him," remarked our hero; "but still, should it be discovered that he has connived at my escape, his destruction would be inevitable; and I should never forgive myself if I should unfortunately be the means of bringing so much misery upon the head of a worthy and innocent man."

"Oh, fear not, my husband," rejoined Mrs. Parker. "Such a fate will never, I trust, be allowed to overtake our generous-hearted friend, Mr. Adams; and I hope that at some future time we may all meet again under far different circumstances to those under which we parted, and when we shall be able to look back upon the past, without any of those corroding pangs of regret which at present torture us."

"God grant that your wishes may be realised," cried Richard, fervently; "for surely the troubles and sufferings we have already endured, have been more than sufficient."

"True," coincided our heroine; "the trials we have already experienced, have been as severe as they were unmerited; but let us hope that they will yet have a happy termination, and that the fears you now entertain will prove to be, as I firmly believe they will, entirely groundless. But come; the time is advancing, and it would be much better for us to retire to rest."

The conversation here dropped, and they then sought their couch, but although our hero soon sunk off to sleep, his slumbers were broken and disturbed by troublesome dreams, which seemed to him to forebode no good, and in his waking moments excited a variety of the most conflicting thoughts in his mind. He was far from being satisfied with the adventure of the previous evening, and in spite of all that his wife and Mr. Hawthorn had said upon the subject, he could not help still at times apprehending that some danger would ensue from it ; for it did not appear likely after Timothy Bubble had once more encountered him, that he would readily relax in his efforts to capture him, so that he might secure the reward to himself, and such precautions might be taken by the authorities, upon his information, knowing that he was still in the country, as would render his escape impossible.

These thoughts tortured and bewildered him, and it was in vain that our heroine sought to banish such apprehensions from his breast, and, in fact, she could not but secretly admit to herself, that his fears were not altogether without some reasonable foundation ; though, of course, she was careful that he did not become acquainted with her opinion upon the subject.

Thus two more days elapsed, and nothing more occurred to alarm them. Richard had been careful not to venture his usual walks, for the present, at any rate, and he began to hope that he should experience no further annoyance from the circumstance of his having again met the officious fellow, Bubble, who evidently had no suspicion as to the place where he was concealed, and that he would, therefore, see the inutility of remaining in that part of the neighbourhood, with the hope of apprehending him.

Still no communication arrived from Adams, and the doubts and uneasiness of our hero increased, and he formed all kinds of conjectures upon the subject as to the cause.

A more favourable change had now taken place in the condition of the unfortunate Flora; the paroxysms of her malady were less violent than they had formerly been, and at times she seemed as though a faint ray of reason were again dawing upon her intellects, and that she had some shadowy recollection of her parents; but it was soon gone, and all was again darkness and obscurity. But when the name of her seducer flashed across her disordered brain, and she remembered that she had so lately gazed upon his livid and ghastly corpse, her wild ravings and piteous lamentations, would become as violent as ever, and it required the greatest

energy and exertion on the part of her agonised parents to pacify her, or to restore her to anything like a degree of composure. She was now enabled to leave her chamber, and would sit for hours in the same room in which her parents and our hero and heroine were assembled, talking to herself, and in the most impressive and melancholy accents mourning the fate of Mowbray, whom she supposed to have been murdered, and against whose imaginary assassins the wretched maniac invoked the most terrible curses of the Supreme.

"See! see!" she would exclaim, in the most wild accents; "the path is stained with blood! Ah! it is the blood of the noble, and the generous; the blood of my Alfred, my own beloved and affectionate husband! Monsters! what had he done, that ye should thus so remorselessly have sacrificed his life? Was it because you envied me the possession of one so good and honourable? Oh, that I had ye here! how terrible should be the retribution which I would bring down upon your accursed heads for the frightful, the fiendish crime you have perpetrated. Hark! and now what demon is it that whispers in my ear that he was false to me—that he deceived me—that he never loved me? Wretches! you know that it is a monstrous lie, and I must be mad to believe ye, or entertain any such suspicion against that beloved being who was willing at any time to lay down his life to serve me. Libellers! begone! I will not listen to ye, or be led astray by the base and infamous libel! But, he is dead! Yes—yes! But a short time since I gazed upon his pale cold features; but where is he now? Oh, Alfred, my husband! shall I never behold you more? Is thy image for ever torn from my gaze? Must I no more listen to thy voice as it breathed such vows of ardent affection? No! no! Thou art dead—thou art dead—and Flora hath now no other wish, no other hope, but to follow thee! Away, then, with this mortal coil! What is life now to me, but a dreary and hateful blank? My soul pants to join the spirit of my husband in the realms of eternity! Oh, Alfred! Alfred! who shall dare to detain me from you? Off! off! I say! Husband! dearest, but ill-fated husband, I hasten to join thee!"

As the poor girl gave utterance to these words, she hastily rose to her feet, and with clasped hands, and mournful and impressive aspect, she advanced towards the door, but before she could reach it, her strength seemed to be entirely exhausted, and overcome by the power of

THE DEATH-BED RAVINGS OF MOWBRAY.

her excited feelings, she swooned in the arms of her father, who was standing near her.

"Alas! my unfortunate child," he ejaculated, as he placed her fair form on the sofa; "how piteous—how truly heart-rending it is to hear you give utterance to these wild ravings and wanderings. Your husband! Oh, poor innocent victim, could you but be sensible of the truth, how bitterly must you curse the memory of the wretch who could so cruelly, so heartlessly deceive you. Heaven help you, for it alone knows how this will terminate."

"Alas!" observed Mrs. Hawthorn; "it is indeed most agonising to a parent's feelings to behold their only offspring, and that fond and gentle being on whom they had placed all their brightest hopes, reduced to this deplorable condition, and to know that we have no power to relieve her. Oh, Mowbray! wretched, misguided, guilty man, you have indeed much to answer for."

"Curse him!" exclaimed Hawthorn, vehemently, and his countenance fully showing by its expression the power of the emotions that were struggling in his breast; "may the endless torments of perdition seize upon his black and guilty soul, and——"

"Oh, hold! hold, Hawthorn," hastily interrupted his wife; "such awful words as these proceeding from your lips surprise and shock me. He has gone to answer for all, before the presence of the Almighty Judge, and in His hands it is your duty to leave him, and not presume to question His heavenly will. But hush; see, she recovers."

Flora, with the assistance of her mother, now raised herself on the sofa, and pressing her fair and delicate hand upon her forehead, as if to recall her recollection she looked vacantly around her, as, after a brief pause, she said—

"Where is he? Why has he gone? But now he stood before me, and beckoned me to follow him; and oh, how beautiful he looked!—But I do not see him now! Why has he left me? Could it be only a dream?—Yes, yes! I remember now! Oh, horror! what black despair lights upon my heart, as the thought recurs to my memory!—He is dead! dead—and cold! I gazed upon his corpse in all the awful and ghastly cerements of the grave. I called upon his name, but he answered me not! No! no! his voice is hushed for ever, and I have no one now to love me!"

"Dear Flora," said her mother, in her most tender and impressive accents; "oh, look at me, speak to me, and your wretched father. No one to love you now? Oh, Flora — Flora, my poor, unfortunate, and darling child, this is surely more torturing than all!"

"Flora," repeated the poor maniac girl, and staring wildly upon her mother; "who calls me by my name? It is not his voice; ah—no! alas! that will never more gladden mine ears. Who art thou that gazeth so earnestly upon me?"

"Flora, beloved child!" exclaimed the old woman, throwing her arms around her neck, and straining her affectionately to her bosom; "your words go to my very heart, and seem to pierce it like so many daggers; do you not know me, I once more ask you? Look narrowly into my features, and in me behold your mother!"

"Mother!" repeated the unfortunate girl, with an idiotic laugh; "away! think you I am mad, that I am likely to be so easily imposed upon? Begone, and mock me not; you are a stranger to me!"

Mrs. Hawthorn turned away from her afflicted child with a deep sigh, and the emotion which was evinced by her husband was equal to her own. Richard and his wife did not offer to say anything, but, as may be expected, they watched the affecting scene with the deepest interest and sympathy.

Flora once more relapsed into silence, and at length, as a sudden thought seemed to strike her, she started to her feet, and without taking the least notice of any person in the room, she retired with a solemn step, and her mother slowly followed her.

"Poor girl," said our heroine; "how sad, how melancholy, and how touching is it to listen to her wild wanderings. How sincerely and deeply is she to be pitied for the dismal fate which has befallen her."

"Alas! Mrs. Parker," replied the fisherman, with a sigh, "you may well say that. And is it at all wonderful that my mind should be filled with all the agony of despair as I contemplate her, and feel more and more convinced of the hopelessness of her condition?"

"True," said Richard; "I duly appreciate your feelings, my good friend; and, as I have frequently assured you before, I deeply sympathise with you; but it is the will of Omnipotence, and however painful the trial, you must learn to support it with fortitude and resignation."

"Yes," returned Hawthorn; "it is most easy to give advice; but mine are no ordinary troubles, and to meet them with that fortitude and resignation which you would urge, Mr. Parker, is almost impossible. However, we have talked sufficiently upon that painful subject before, and I am not at all disposed to discuss it now. One thing, however, appears to me more certain than ever, namely, that all chance of my ill-fated daughter ever being restored to reason is at an end, and nothing seems likely to occur to lighten the misery which the melancholy malady with which she is afflicted has created in my breast."

"Seek to hope differently, Mr. Hawthorn," said Mary, "and I trust sincerely that Providence will not suffer you to be disappointed."

Hawthorn shooked his head, as he answered—

"I am sorry I cannot entertain the same idea as that you have expressed, Mrs. Parker. I have endeavoured to hope till my heart sickens, and my patience and fortitude almost sink beneath the trial. But enough, enough, I must try to submit; for it is useless for us to murmur against that over which we have no control."

Richard and his wife saw that he was in no humour to enter upon the painful subject that day, and they, therefore, changed the topic of conversation, and the day passed away without anything more particular occurring.

Flora had retired to bed, and the evening having turned rather cold, Hawthorn and his wife, and our hero and heroine, had gathered around a cheerful fire, conversing about those important matters that more immediately interested them.

"Another day, you see, has elapsed," remarked Richard; "and still I hear nothing from my friend Adams. You must admit, Mr. Hawthorn, that this continued silence is sufficient to make me feel doubtful and uneasy."

"Why," answered Hawthorn, "it is rather strange, I must admit. I thought that Adams would have returned an answer to your letter ere this, or that we should have seen or heard something of honest old Ben Binnacle. However, Mr. Parker, after all, I should not make myself the least uncomfortable, for no doubt they are doing everything for the best, and have your interest and safety constantly at heart."

"I cannot doubt the sincerity and honesty of their motives," returned our hero; "but still, when all the circumstances are taken into consideration, I cannot help thinking that my anxiety is excusable."

"Certainly," coincided Hawthorn; "but something seems to strike me that it will not be long before your suspense is at an end."

"Well," observed Richard, after a temporary pause; "I know not how it is, and probably you may only smile at me when I tell you; but there has been an impression on my mind all this day, that something of a particular nature is about to happen, and that some danger threatens me."

"Nonsense!" returned Hawthorn, with a smile; "what reason have you to entertain strange thoughts like these?"

"I know not," answered Parker "but still I cannot dismiss them from my mind."

"I am surprised at you," remarked Mr. Hawthorn. "However, we will not argue this subject further, as it does not seem likely to me that we shall be able to come to any satisfactory conclusion. This is not a very cheerful night, and the wind howls dismally without. I am afraid we shall have some rough work at sea."

"Yes," coincided our hero; "and Heaven help all those who are exposed to its perils. I sincerely hope that they may never meet with the wretched fate that has attended Richard Parker."

"Do not distress yourself by thinking of of it now, dear Richard," said his wife. "God grant that such troubles as you have already experienced you may never have to encounter again, but that the time is not far distant when we shall be restored to that peace and tranquillity to which we have so long been strangers."

"I fear," answered Richard, "that we must never look for that again. I know not how it is, but I find it impossible to dissipate the melancholy sensation that has taken possession of my mind, and every instant the certainty of my forebodings being realised seem to gain strength."

"Well," said Mr. Hawthorn, "this is certainly very extraordinary; but, at the same time, I certainly should struggle against the feeling if I were you, Mr. Parker. Probably, it is the dulness of the night only which has taken this effect upon your spirits, and you should try to arouse yourself out of it."

Richard shook his head, and a pause in the conversation ensued. The wind still continued in the same boisterous quarter, and howled dismally around, at times seeming to shake the cottage to its foundation, and making the windows rattle in their frames in a manner that was anything but agreeable to the ears. While they were thus seated, they were suddenly startled by hearing a loud knock at the outer door; and Richard started, and turned pale, and his wife was evidently also alarmed, and clung to him, as he stood and gazed anxiously and fearfully towards the door.

"Psha!" ejaculated Hawthorn, rather impatiently; "what is there to fear? It is probably only a neighbour, or some one who seeks a shelter. Retire into the next room while I inquire who the intruder is."

Richard and his wife hastily did so, and closed the door cautiously after them, and listened. They were not long kept in suspense; an exclamation of mingled surprise and satisfaction escaped Hawthorn; a well-known voice immediately afterwards greeted their ears, and rushing from the room, Richard and his wife had the satisfaction of shaking honest old Ben Binnacle by the hand.

We need not attempt to describe the meeting, which was so welcome to all parties; but the first greeting over, Richard eagerly and impatiently inquired after his friend, Adams, and the reason of his having remained so long silent.

"Ah," replied Binnacle, "we thought you would be rather anxious to receive an answer to your letter, which reached us quite safe; but it could not be helped, as some unforeseen circumstances prevented him from doing so. However, I have brought you a letter from Jack now, but—but——"

"But what?" hastily demanded Richard. "You seem agitated. Has anything happened?"

"Why, yes," returned Binnacle, hesitating, "I am sorry to say there has."

"Ah!" cried Mrs. Parker, alarmed, "what mean you? What has occurred?"

"The fact of it is, that, by some accident or other, it has become suspected that you are secreted somewhere in this neighbourhood. That confounded little land-shark —Timothy Bubble, don't they call him?— has signalled to the Lords of the Admiralty that, while he was cruising off this coast, he came athwart of you, and that it was only by a marvel you were enabled to escape him; and, in consequence, I have not the least doubt that a party will be sent here in pursuit of you without any delay."

"Oh, Heaven!" exclaimed our heroine, clasping her hands together in an agony of grief, "what will become of us?"

"Be calm, Mrs. Parker," said Binnacle, "I beg of you. You are safe enough at present; but one thing is certain—namely, that you must depart from hence with as little delay as possible. If you could only reach one of the Channel Islands, you would, no doubt, be free from danger. You will perceive by the letter of Adams, that such is the advice he gives you, and it is for that purpose that I came here. My lugger is in the creek, and if this wind would only take a favourable turn, the sooner we were off the better."

"And must we so abruptly quit our kind friends here?" said Richard. "It is, indeed, most provoking."

"I regret, Mr. Parker, that it seems we must so soon separate," replied Hawthorn; "but your safety demands it, and I must not raise any objection. I trust that we shall meet again, and that then all those troubles and dangers by which you are at present surrounded will be removed. But Mr. Binnacle will probably relate to us the particulars of this unfortunate discovery, which no doubt has all been made through the over-officiousness of that fellow, Bubble."

"No doubt of it," returned Binnacle; "and if I should ever have the good fortune to come athwart his hawse, I will teach him such a lesson for his pains as he will not easily forget. But I have related all the facts that I know, and it will be time enough to enter into further explanation when we are on board the lugger,

which must be at daylight to-morrow morning at the latest, for there is no knowing how soon your pursuers may be here."

"Oh, how much am I indebted to you and Adams for this generous endeavour to save me!" remarked Richard.

"As for the matter of that, Master Parker," answered Binnacle, "you know you are heartily welcome to anything we can do to serve you; and, therefore, the least said the soonest mended. If we can only succeeded in reaching the place of our destination, you will have nothing to fear. Myself and Adams have mustered you up some more cash, which perhaps will serve you for some time, and any further assistance that we can render you, you shall be sure to receive from us. There, then, you can enter into some way of business, and will be unknown and unmolested."

Richard cordially pressed the hand of the kind-hearted old man, and they then seated themselves at the table, on which Mrs. Hawthorn had spread the evening repast.

"But think you," said our hero, addressing himself to Binnacle, "that my pursuers are acquainted with the exact place where I am concealed?"

"No, I do not think that very likely," answered Ben, "as you say that Bubble had not an opportunity of watching you."

"He had not," returned Parker; "for he was stunned by the fall I gave him, and was in a state of insensibility when I left him."

"That was fortunate," observed Ben; "however, I shall not consider you safe until we are on our voyage. As I said before, I think it would be advisable for us to set sail before daylight. Have you any particular preparations to make?"

Our hero answered in the negative, and he then added, addressing himself to Mr. Hawthorn and his wife—

"You see, my kind friends, that my forebodings were not quite so groundless as you imagined them to be. So we must separate, then, much sooner than I expected. I cannot sufficiently express to you the weight of gratitude I feel under for the many favours I have received at your hands; and should we never meet again, belive me that I shall, as long as I may live, entertain the most lively sense of the obligations I am under to you."

"Mr. Parker," replied Hawthorn, "I should imagine that by this time you know my character well, and you must, therefore, be aware that I require no thanks for that which sprang spontaneously from my heart. I sincerely hope that the clouds which at present obscure your prospects will be dispersed, and that you may be permitted again to enter into that society in which you are so well calculated to shine."

Our hero and his wife could only once more repeat their grateful acknowledgments to the generous-hearted fisherman, and then they proceeded to talk more freely upon what they considered would be the most prudent and the safest course for them to adopt; and Richard read the letter of Adams aloud, which he found was couched in the most friendly language, and tendered him some excellent advice as to his future conduct, and the most likely way of avoiding detection.

"For my own part," remarked old Ben, "I do not see how it is possible that any of these plans can fail, when we are only once clear of this coast. Let your pursuers come, then, if they please; we shall be far out of the reach of them then, especially if the wind should be in our favour. It is a pity that you should be put to the inconvenience of having to depart so suddenly, Mr. Parker, but it cannot be helped, and I hope and believe that, after all, it will turn out for the best."

"For the promptitude which you, my generous friend, have shown in apprising me of my danger, and in flying to my rescue, I am much indebted to you," answered our hero; "all that I regret in having to quit this place so abruptly is the necessity of my sudden separation from those excellent and disinterested friends, who, ever since we have been here, have behaved to us with so much kindness, and whom we fear we have put to much trouble and inconvenience."

"Do not mention it, Mr. Parker," remarked Hawthorn. "I am sure that both my wife and myself feel only too happy and grateful to Providence, who has enabled us to serve our fellow creatures in misfortune. I hope that the time is not far distant when we shall meet again, and that the clouds which at present darken and obscure your fate will have dispersed, and that you may be permitted once more, without fear, to mingle in that society from which you are now estranged."

"I thank you most cordially for those wishes, which I know are sincere," said Richard, "and most grateful to Providence shall I be should your hopes be realized; but I must at the same time confess that I have my doubts upon the subject. I fear that the vigilance of my enemies will now be redoubled, and that they

will not rest until they have discovered me."

"Avast there, Marter Parker," said Binnacle; "you must not give way to such thoughts as these; in a few hours, if all goes on well, we shall be far away from this spot, and let us but reach the place of our destination in safety, and you may then, I have no doubt, set those who are in pursuit of you at defiance."

"Yes, Richard," remarked our heroine, "what Mr. Binnacle says, I believe to be perfectly reasonable, and I have but very little, if any, doubt, but that his words will prove true. You must, therefore, dismiss from your mind all useless fears, and look forward to the future with firmness and confidence."

"Well," replied Richard, "I will try to do so, and for your sake, my Mary, and that of our poor boy, I sincerely trust that we shall not be doomed to be disappointed."

"And now, my friends," observed Ben, "had you not better endeavour to snatch an hour or two's rest previous to our departure? As I said before, it will be necessary for us to leave this place at the earliest hour in the morning, lest anything should occur to prevent us, and thus to thwart our plans. There is no knowing how soon those who are sent in pursuit of you may arrive in this neighbourhood, and then all chance of escape might probably be at an end."

"Oh, Heaven forbid!" ejaculated Mary; "but Providence will not suffer our wishes to be disappointed, and our plans frustrated. Of that I feel certain. Come, Richard, let us retire and prepare ourselves for our departure from this place, where we have experienced so much hospitality and kindness."

They now bade Mr. Hawthorn and his wife, and old Ben Binnacle good-night, and promising to be at the cottage at an early hour on the following morning, they departed. The minds of Richard and his wife, however, were too much excited to think of retiring to rest, and they determined to occupy the time which must intervene prior to their commencing the voyage, in making such preparations as were necessary.

"I cannot but regret that we have so soon to leave those esteemed friends from whom we have experienced so much kindness and attention," said our heroine; "and that we are compelled to go amongst strangers."

"Ay," returned Richard, in a sad tone, "this is no more than I expected, after my meeting with Bubble; I felt assured that he would quickly divulge the whole circumstances, and that it would be no longer safe for us to remain here. What a wretched, restless, wandering life is ours, Mary, and I see no chance of our escaping from it, notwithstanding all the arguments that yourself and our friends have made use of to convince me to the contrary."

"Why will you persist in thus giving way to despair?" said our heroine; "your fears, I feel most confident, will prove to be unfounded, and that we shall yet be restored to that peace of mind, of which the most untoward circumstances have deprived us. The promptitude and wisdom with which Mr. Adams and Binnacle have acted, will, I trust, be the means of saving us, and of placing us beyond the reach of that danger with which we have so long been threatened."

"You are most sanguine in your expectations, my dear Mary," returned her husband; "and God grant that you may not be disappointed; but——"

"Ah!" interrupted Mary, "I know full well what you would say, but cannot listen with any degree of patience to your dismal forebodings. The Almighty has hitherto most mercifully watched over our safety, and He will not now desert us while we put our trust in him. Come, come, you must, dear Richard, as I have often before enjoined you, arouse yourself from this state of mind, and, mark my words, gloomy even as our prospects may at present seem to be, the time is not far distant when we shall again be happy, and be enabled to look back upon the gloomy past with calmness, if not without regret."

Our hero shook his head doubtfully, but returned no answer, and Mary exerted herself to the utmost to change the topic of conversation, and to inspire him with the same hopes as to the future as those that animated her own breast; but she only succeeded indifferently. Thus hour after hour passed away, and Richard and his wife never once thought of retiring to rest, so busily were their minds occupied with the thoughts of the future, and so impatiently did they await the time for their departure from the cottage to arrive. Their little preparations were soon made, and they now endeavoured to pass away the tediousness of the time in conversation.

The wind which had hitherto roared so boisterously, now went down, and their apprehensions of tempestuous weather were dissipated. Richard, however, could not help but feel most anxious for the time to arrive when they should be safe on board the lugger, and far out at sea, lest those in pursuit of him should arrive in the neighbourhood, and they should have happened by any means, which he considered to be not at all improbable, to have discovered the place of his concealment. He listened to catch every sound, and frequently walked to the window and looked out, as though he expected to see those whom he had so much cause to dread. Mary well knew the thoughts and feelings that were passing in his mind, but she was far from participating in them, and she sought all in her power to calm his apprehensions.

"There is, I am certain," she observed, "no cause whatever for these fears. It is not likely that our enemies can have discovered the actual place of our concealment, or they would doubtless have been here before. The dangerous man whom you encountered, fortunately, was not in a condition to watch whither you went; therefore, there is nothing to fear from him."

"I am not exactly satisfied of that," said Richard. "At any rate, I shall be more contented when we have taken our departure from this place."

Mary still tried to reassure him, and she at last succeeded, much better than might have been expected; and thus the time passed away until the first flush of dawn appeared in the eastern horizon, and immediately afterwards a knock was heard at the outer door; and Mary, putting her head cautiously out of the window, perceived that it was Mr. Hawthorn, and she, therefore, immediately admitted him, and he greeted them with even more than his usual warmth of feeling.

"My dear friends," he observed, "the time has now come for your departure. There is no person about at this early hour whom it might be dangerous for you to see, and Ben Binnacle is waiting at the cottage to conduct you to his lugger. The weather is favourable, and, therefore, I trust that, before many hours have elapsed, you will be far removed from every danger, and that you will shortly be placed in a situation in which you will again experience that happiness of which you have so long been deprived."

"I thank you most gratefully for your kind wishes," said Parker, cordially pressing his hand, "and most deeply do I regret being compelled to leave one who I have so much cause to esteem, and to whom I am under a weight of obligation which I fear it will never be in my power to repay."

"Pray do not mention that, Mr.

Parker," replied Hawthorn; "for you well know, I believe, that I require no thanks for that which it has been so fortunately in my power to do for you, and that I only rejoice that Providence guided your footsteps to me in the hour of your emergency. I need not, I think, again assure you how much I regret the necessity of our separation; but I sincerely hope that happiness and prosperity may attend you wherever you go, and that at some future period we may meet again, under far more auspicious circumstances than we do at present. But come; we do but delay time, and Binnacle, in consequence of the favourable state of the weather, is most anxious to depart."

Our hero and his wife offered no further observation, but, accompanied by the lad William, they followed Mr. Hawthorn from that place in which they had found so secure a shelter, though it was with sad hearts that they did so, when they reflected how soon they must separate from those kind friends to whom they were so much indebted. On reaching the cottage of Hawthorn, they found Ben Binnacle ready equipped for the voyage, anxiously awaiting them. He greeted them in his usual cordial and honest way, and then added—

"All is in readiness; the weather is in our favour, so the sooner we depart from here the better. Master Hawthorn, I suppose, will accompany us to the lugger?"

"Certainly," replied Hawthorn; "and I hope that, though this separation has taken us by surprise, and was quite unexpected, at least, so suddenly, that our meeting again will be equally the same."

In this wish our hero and his wife, it is almost needless to say, perfectly coincided, and having bid Mrs. Hawthorn a most kind adieu, they accompanied Binnacle and the fisherman from the cottage, and made their way towards the lugger, which was anchored in a small creek only a short distance off. The hour was so early, as we have before stated, that there were no persons about, and they were not long in reaching the place of their destination, and were soon on board the vessel of old Ben Binnacle, and, for the present, at any rate, in safety. It is useless to enter into all the particulars as to what took place at the parting between Richard and his wife and Hawthorn; it is enough to say that it was all that might have been expected from the warmth of friendship that existed between them.

"I hope that you will communicate with me, as soon as you get settled," remarked the fisherman, "and let me know all the particulars as to how you are getting on; for I need not tell you how anxious I shall be to hear."

"You may depend upon that, Mr. Hawthorn," replied our hero; "I must indeed be ungrateful could I treat with neglect that man who has proved to me my best friend; and who has put himself to so much trouble and anxiety for the sake of myself and my wife."

"Enough," said Hawthorn; "I know your heart, and will not, therefore, entertain a doubt of your sincerity; but one thing I must impress upon you strongly, and that is, not to run any risk, in writing to me, of a discovery, but endeavour to adopt some means of security."

"You may rest assured that I shall be upon my guard," replied Parker. "I have too much at risk not to be careful to act with the greatest precaution."

"True," coincided Hawthorn; "and now, my friends, farewell; and that Heaven may prosper you and release you from the troubles it has so long been your hard lot to encounter, is the sincere wish of myself and my wife."

"I believe you," replied our hero, cordially pressing his hand; "and I shall never cease to remember with feelings of the most ardent description, while life shall exist, the names of Mr. and Mrs. Hawthorn; and should it ever be in my power, which I fear it never will, to reward you for——"

"Hold! Mr. Parker," interrupted Mr. Hawthorn, hastily, and with a look of mild reproach, "unless you would offend me. You know full well that even were I placed in those indigent circumstances which, thank Heaven, I am not, I would never accept of any reward for doing that which I consider to be no more than my duty towards my fellow creatures."

"Pardon me, my esteemed friend," replied Richard; "I meant not to insult you; but when a man is placed under that weight of obligation which I consider I am to you, it is difficult to give proper expression to the feelings. May your unfortunate daughter be restored to reason, that she may prove a comfort and consolation to you in your declining days."

"Alas!" returned Mr. Hawthorn, with a sigh, "I fear there are but little hopes of that, for the fatal malady with which my poor child is afflicted seems fixed upon her intellect. But this is neither the time nor the place to talk upon that dismal subject, and we will, therefore, if you please, waive it."

"Yes," interposed Binnacle; "and I only wish to remind you that we delay time, and that the sooner we get away from this coast the better."

With this every one agreed, and after another most friendly and ardent farewell, Mr. Hawthorn was escorted to the shore in one of the boats of the lugger : in a few minutes afterwards the anchor was weighed, and our unfortunate fugitives were once more cast upon the ocean of destiny, mingled fears and hopes springing up in their breasts. But our hero felt no inconsiderable relief from the anxieties and apprehensions that had before agitated his breast now that they were fairly on the ocean, and at present there seemed to be nothing likely to prevent their escape, while the eyes of his devoted wife sparkled with a mingled expression of satisfaction and gratitude, now that they had, for the present, at any rate, escaped from the dangers that seemed to be impending o'er them.

The little vessel was soon far away from the coast, and impelled by a favouring gale, was steering rapidly on its course to the place of its destination ; and, overwhelmed by the power of their feelings, Richard Parker and his wife and child sunk upon their knees upon the deck, and poured forth, in the most eloquent terms, their gratitude to the Supreme for their deliverance, and earnestly besought His protection for the future, while old Ben Binnacle stood by, and watched them with looks of admiration and feelings of esteem. After a while, they retired below, escorted by Binnacle; and there they found that every preparation had been made for their comfort and accommodation, and they could not but again express their gratitude to Binnacle, in terms of the utmost ardour and sincerity.

CHAPTER XXIX.

THE VOYAGE.—THE STORM.—THE WRECK.
—THE MIRACULOUS ESCAPE OF RICHARD
AND HIS WIFE AND SON.—MELANCHOLY
DEATH OF BEN BINNACLE.

THE little vessel proceeded swiftly on its way, and nothing occurred to damp the spirits of our hero and his wife. The weather was remarkably fine, and they passed a great part of the day upon deck, and inhaling the bracing and refreshing breeze which was wafted from the broad waters of the ocean; and Binnacle remained with them with few intervals, conversing with them on the past, and holding out to them the most sanguine hopes and prospects of the future.

"I am much mistaken," said the old man, "if you have not now completely eluded the vigilance of your pursuers; and if the present favourable weather only continues, we shall soon arrive at the place of our destination, and then you may make your minds perfectly easy."

"Oh, Mr. Binnacle," ejaculated Mary, "how greatly are we indebted to you and that excellent man, Mr. Adams, for the great and inestimable service you have rendered us, and the disinterested friendship and kindness you have at so much cost and trouble to yourselves ever evinced towards us. I can but faintly give expression to the feelings with which your conduct has inspired me, but, believe me, that I must, as well as my unfortunate husband, under all circumstances, ever entertain the warmest and most sincere sentiments of gratitude towards you."

"I know that, Mrs. Parker," replied old Ben, "and I am perfectly satisfied. As you know, I am only a simple, rough-spun old tar, and not much used to compliments; but I can say this here, and that too without any fear of any one wishing to overhaul my log-book, that you are quite welcome to all it is in my power to do to serve you, and that I only wish it was ten times more. But that's neither here nor there ; you've slipped through the fingers of your enemies once more, and I am much mistaken if they will not be baffled this time entirely."

"But should you or Adams get into any trouble on my account," said our hero, "your destruction would be inevitable, and how could I, even under under any circumstances, then, ever again be happy?"

"Psha !" answered old Binnacle, impatiently; "do not let such ideas as that trouble you, for there is not the least danger of their ever being realised. How is suspicion likely to fall upon Adams or myself, seeing that we have managed the business so secretly and with such precaution? We are safe enough, never fear, and will remain staunch and true to you to the last."

"But I fear that I am distressing yourself and Adams," said Richard ; "by accepting those frequent sums of money which I have had from you."

"Distress us !" repeated honest old Ben, in accents that fully bespoke the sincerity of his heart; "lor love you, not in the least ; it will do you good, for I know you will put it to the best advantge ; but, if we had not bestowed it upon you, it's a great chance if it would not have been squandered in waste, so say no more upon that subject, if you please, Mr. Parker,

ALICE REPROVING HAWTHORN FOR EXULTING OVER THE BODY OF MOWBRAY.

unless you wish to offend old Ben Binnacle, which is not an easy task to accomplish, I can tell you."

"God grant that it may some day be in my power to return it," replied Richard Parker, "though I fear it never will."

"As for any return," observed Binnacle, "neither myself nor Jack Adams require any; though I am much mistaken if it will not be in your power to make it. The money you have by you, and the little more we shall probably find it in our power to forward you, will enable you to follow some honest and respectable pur-

suit; time may wear away the prejudices which in some persons' minds are entertained towards you; interest and persuasion may accomplish the rest, and who knows but a free pardon may be extended towards you, and that you will be permitted to return to your native country, and to pass the remainder of your days in peace?"

"Oh, yes—yes," cried our heroine, her eyes sparkling, and her bosom heaving with the powerful emotion of her feelings; "it must, it will be so. Oh, how I thank you, my kind friend, for that suggestion."

No. 45.

"Nay, Mary," returned her husband, "do not flatter yourself with any such false and delusive hopes. A free pardon for one who is charged with murder and mutiny?—Oh, that is impossible. It would be sheer madness to entertain any such an idea. No, my only chance of escape is by concealment, for should I once fall into the power of my enemies, they would not rest until they had gratified their vengeance in my blood."

"Fearful thought!" cried Mary, "why will you suffer it still to torture and haunt your imagination, Richard? Have you no reliance upon the goodness of the Almighty, who has hitherto guarded us through the many and fearful dangers by which we have been surrounded? Be firm, and do not suffer yourself to give way to any such terrible forebodings."

"You still continue to advise me, my beloved Mary," replied her husband, "to that which is most difficult to accomplish. But I will not dwell upon the painful subject, nor seek to crush the ardour of your hopes, which for your own sake, and not mine, I fervently pray to Heaven may be realised."

Thus did they continue to alternate between hope and fear; but the gentle, persuasive arguments of the faithful and affectionate wife had their due effect upon our hero, and he became more calm, patient, and resigned.

The day passed away without anything particular occurring; the weather remained unchanged, and they were all of them most sanguine in their hopes and spirits. At an early hour Richard and his wife sought the little cabin which was allotted to them, and were soon soundly wrapped in the arms of sleep.

How long they had thus slumbered they knew not, but they were suddenly aroused by the violent motion of the vessel, and starting from their berths in confusion and amazement, they found to their dismay that a fearful storm was raging, and that the little vessel was tossed violently about at the mercy of the waves, and seeming to threaten each moment to founder. Mary was so terrified at this sudden and unexpected change, that she flew to the arms of her husband, and trembled convulsively in every limb. He was also so much bewildered and confounded, that for some moments he was unable to endeavour to quiet her apprehensions, or to impart to her any degree of consolation. The storm was of the most terrific nature, and Richard could not but feel the most dismal fears and forebodings as to the result. The frequent peals of thunder were completely deafen-

ing, and mingling with the roaring of the waves, and the howling of the wind, rendered it doubly awful. Mary looked aghast in the face of her husband, and it was quit evident, from the expression of her features, the anguish, the almost insupportable anguish of mind she was enduring.

"Oh, Richard!" she ejaculated, "what a frightful change is this! Wha—oh! what will be the consequences of this storm? God of Heaven! how the vessel reels and pitches! Surely she will never be able long to withstand such a tempest as this. The fates conspire against us, and just at the time when everything seemed to be going on so favourably. Lost—lost!"

"Be firm, Mary," said our hero, "and give not way to the fears which I admit this storm is well calculated to create. Put your trust in that Providence which never deserts the innocent and virtuous even in the hour of the greatest danger and horror. But I must on deck. Be calm, I say again, and this tempest may probably soon abate, and we shall then be rescued from the danger which threatens us."

"You will not leave me, dear Richard?" said his wife, in fearful accents: "you will remain here to——"

"Nay, Mary," interrupted her husband, "you seem to forget that I am a seaman, and that, should I shrink from performing my duty upon such an emergency, I should disgrace myself. I must on deck, I say again, and see what assistance it is in my power to render. Remain here, my love, and rest assured that, should any particular danger threaten, I will lose not a moment in hastening to you, and rescuing you, if possible."

"I must—I will seek to conquer my terrors," said Mary. "Go, then, my husband, and God grant that the efforts of yourself and the others who will be with you may be crowned with success."

Richard embraced his wife and the boy, and hurried away from the cabin, and hastened on deck, where he found Ben Binnacle and the limited crew of the lugger exerting themselves to the utmost to avert the fate which seemed to threaten them. The scene, even to the experienced eye of the old sailor, was of the most appalling description, and Richard could not contemplate it without a feeling of dread. It seemed to be almost impossible that such a change should have taken place in so short a space of time. It was quite dark, and that rendered the effect of the scene—lighted up as it was, at intervals, by the vivid flashes of lightning—still more terrific. The waves rose to a frightful height, and every one seemed to carry destruction in its foam-covered crest. The ocean hissed, and bubbled, and fermented like the contents of some huge cauldron; the thunder pealed still louder than before, and, in fact, the whole scene was one which, if any person had been permitted to contemplate it at a distance, and in a place of safety, he could never more, by any possible means, have forgotten it.

"What think you of this, Mr. Parker?" inquired old Ben Binnacle, in his usual cool and collected manner. "Some hundreds of poor souls will find a watery grave this night. God protect us, I say, though I know not that we more deserve it than any others of His creatures."

"It is indeed a fearful storm," replied Parker; "and is a sad disappointment to us, after the favourable and promising weather which we previously experienced. But still we must exert ourselves to the utmost, and we may yet be saved."

"My little craft is a tough one," remarked Binnacle, "and has stood many a severe storm before; but I must say this is one of the worst I ever remember to have witnessed for years, and we must not be idle if we mean to save her or ourselves."

"You will find me ready to render all the assistance in my power," returned Richard; "but there is not a moment to be lost."

"True," agreed Ben; "but where is your wife?"

"In her cabin, with our son," answered our hero. "They would only be in the way if they were suffered to come on deck, and the contemplation of such a frightful scene as this would naturally excite a tenfold feeling of horror in their breasts, and probably be attended with the most painful and fatal consequences."

"Right!" again coincided old Binnacle. "But, come, to business."

The few hands that were on board the lugger exerted themselves with the most praiseworthy energy, our hero taking the most active part in the more hazardous and dangerous part of the business; but all their endeavours were of little or no avail in such a storm as that, and their danger seemed every moment to increase. The lugger was tossed about at the mercy of the waves like a straw, and it appeared to be almost impossible for her to weather it; but the courage of Ben and the crew appeared to be undaunted; nay, on the contrary, it seemed to increase as the

horrors and the dangers of their situation become more evident. What added to their danger was, that they were driven completely out of their course, and knew not where they were, nor could old Ben Binnacle, notwithstanding his long experience, form the least conjecture.

In the meantime the situation of Mrs. Parker and her son, in the cabin, may be easily imagined; but the youthful William displayed that same degree of firmness which had always characterised him in moments of the most imminent danger. Mary listened to the loud voice of the roaring tempest with feelings of the greatest consternation, and the most dreadful apprehensions, under all the circumstances, could not fail to take possession of her mind. She clasped her hands in agony, and trembled in every limb.

"Heaven look down with mercy upon us," she ejaculated in a tremulous voice; "for without its merciful interposition, nothing but an untimely and awful fate most assuredly awaits us. Oh, my husband! my child! and must we, indeed, perish thus, after the many dangers we have passed through?"

"Dear mother," said William, looking up tenderly and imploringly in her face; "I beseech you to be calm, and to hope for the best. The Almighty will not desert us while we put our trust in Him, and we shall yet be saved."

"My darling boy!" cried the fond mother, straining her child to her bosom, and imprinting a fervent kiss upon his forehead; "it would indeed be hard were your noble spirit to be thus nipped in the bud. But as I listen to the horrors that reign around, my heart misgives me, and the untimely fate which awaits us seems to be inevitable."

The vessel now gave a fearful lurch, and the voice of the thunder became more terrific in its violence. Mary trembled more than ever, and her countenance became ghastly pale. Her agitation was not in any way diminished, when a loud and confused sound from on deck saluted her ears, and instantly the vessel seemed to be more agitated than ever. She again clasped her son in her arms, and for a few minutes she was so overcome by her emotions of horror and despair, that she was transfixed as a statue, and was unable to utter a syllable.

"My God!" she exclaimed at length, "will nothing interpose to save us? But why do we stay here when death stares us in the face, like some grim demon exulting o'er his defenceless victim? Come, my boy, let us instantly rejoin your father, and if we must die, at least let us perish together. Come—come."

"Pray, dear mother," again urged the boy, and he looked up in her face with an expression which it would be a difficult task for language to describe; "pray, dear mother, do not thus agitate yourself. God is good and will not suffer us to die thus. My father's aid is required on deck, and should we join him we should only interrupt him in his duty. Let us remain here and await the will of Heaven."

"My noble-minded boy!" cried our heroine, again pressing him to her bosom; "oh, it would indeed be hard were you, so young and promising, to be thus snatched off ere your numerous virtuous qualities have had time to expand and to shed a lustre upon your fellow-creatures. God of Heaven! to what severe trials do you put us."

Distracted with the various torturing thoughts that crowded so rapidly upon her brain, she covered her face with her hands, whilst convulsive sobs escaped her bosom. More terrific every moment became the storm, and the confusion that prevailed on deck increased to such a degree that it might be heard even above the voice of the tempest, and showed plainly the frightful danger that was apprehended. The little vessel rolled about in the gurgling waters like a top, and crash after crash, as its masts and rigging fell, showed too plainly how rapidly the work of destruction was going on, and was sufficient to strike horror and despair into even the stoutest heart. Mary still held her son (whose firmness remained unshaken) in her arms, and looked wildly and vacantly around her. Her brain was bewildered; various frightful images crowded upon it, and she scarcely knew where she was. The terrific flashes of lightning that darted across the dark sky were awful, and every succeeding peal of thunder seemed to increase in fury.

"There is no hope," cried our heroine, clasping her hands in an agony of feeling that was perfectly indescribable; "the fiat of Heaven has gone forth, and our last moment is rapidly approaching. Oh, Richard, husband, where are you?"

At that moment the cabin door was burst open, and our hero, pale and disordered in his looks and dress, from the extraordinary exertions he had undergone, rushed into his wife's arms.

"Oh, Richard, dear Richard," she exclaimed, "tell me, is not all hope at an end? This frightful storm—your wild and despairing looks!—oh, yes, the fatal truth is too fearfully apparent;—we must perish!"

"God's will be done," said Richard, solemnly; "it is, indeed, a frightful storm, and I fear that unless some speedy and miraculous change takes place, our little vessel will be unable to weather it. But, Mary, my beloved and devoted wife, in this solemn hour let us endeavour to be calm, and commit ourselves to the protection of the Almighty, whose will we must not presume to arraign. My poor boy— so young, too—oh, this is indeed a moment of trial."

"Oh, Richard," sobbed our distracted heroine, clinging fondly to her husband, and looking up despairingly in his face; "and after all the many painful struggels we have had to contend against, must we at the very moment when the prospect of safety dawned upon us, die thus? You bid me be calm, but, oh, the very idea is madness! Are there no means of averting our fate? Come—come, exert yourself; let us abandon this frail vessel, and committing ourselves to the mercy of the infuriated waves, save our lives, or perish together."

"Mary," replied her husband, looking at her with bewildered astonishment, "know you what you say? Why should we thus rush precipitately on our fate? Be calm—be calm, I again implore you, and let us try to await patiently the issue of this dreadful night. The storm may abate, and we may yet be saved."

"Ah, no," returned Mary, "it is useless to seek to buoy me up with any such hopes; for I see by your looks, although you may endeavour to conceal the awful fact, that they are futile. Oh, Richard— Richard, it is for you and our poor child that I feel more—much more than myself. This frightful scene! it shakes my every nerve, and I——Despair—despair! my brain is racked to madness!"

"My poor wife!" sighed Richard, as he clasped her frantically to his bosom; "to see you suffer thus is far more torturing than all. Great God of Heaven, I beseech your mercy, if not for myself, at least for those poor innocent and helpless beings who are far more precious to me than my own existence. But why do I tarry here when my assistance is so much needed? I must again on deck. Mary, I must leave you; for awhile farewell, and you, my noble boy. Heaven bless and protect you both. In a short time, I hope we shall meet again, when all danger shall be at an end."

"No, Richard, husband!" ejaculated our heroine, still frantically clinging to him, and fixing upon him such looks that penetrated to his very soul; "you must not, shall not leave me; I will accompany you, and witness, and try to brave the worse. In life we have shared all the perils that it has been our hard lot to encounter, and if it be the will of Heaven, we will perish together, and in each other's arms."

"For the love of Heaven, Mary," he returned, "remain here. Why should you increase the agony of your mind by gazing upon all the horrors of this scene? and your appearance on deck may only serve to obstruct those who are so ardu ously exerting themselves to rescue us from the fate which is at present impending o'er our heads. Should all hope be at an end, fear not but I will immediately fly to you, and save you and our boy, or perish together."

"No! no!" replied Mary, with a look of wild determination; "it is useless to attempt to persuade me; to remain here would be far more torturing to my feelings than any of the horrors which I can witness. I will go with you, and at least share with you all the dangers that may arise."

Finding that it was useless to seek to expostulate with his wife, Richard took her arm in his, and hastened with her from the cabin, followed by the boy William, whose extraordinary and almost incredible fortitude and self-possession must have excited wonder and admiration in the minds of all who beheld it.

Notwithstanding that our heroine was prepared for the worst, on arriving on deck the scene of horror that burst upon her sight made her start back appalled, and she was obliged to cling to her husband for support. All was one terrific din of noise and confusion. The hurried yet energetic actions of the men on board seemed scarcely those of human beings, such was the extraordinary effect which the danger of the moment imparted to all their exertions. Yet in their looks was stamped in the most vivid characters all the horrors of despair, and it was plain to every one who cast their eyes around the appalling scene that it was not without ample cause. The storm was now at its full pitch; the pealing thunder, the hoarse voice of the wind, and the frightful roaring of the angry billows, which seemed to rise to the very clouds, were completely deafening, and were sufficient to distract and bewilder the firmest mind. The darkness was impenetrable, save when at intervals it was broken by the lurid glare of the lightning, which only served to render the

horrors of the scene more visible, and pointed out the hopelessness of human beings endeavouring to avoid that fate which was evidently approaching them with rapid strides. The appearance of the little vessel was melancholy in the extreme; and it seemed impossible that it could weather the awful dangers with which it had to contend for any length of time. Every mast was gone, and finding that it was useless to attempt to manage her, the unfortunate crew could do little more than leave her to the mercy of the waves, anticipating death every moment, and most of them quite exhausted with the great exertions they had already undergone, and the sea dashing over them every instant with overwhelming fury.

All this time old Ben Binnacle never for a moment lost his fortitude and presence of mind, but gave his directions to the crew with the same degree of coolness as if nothing unusual was taking place. On seeing our heroine and William come upon deck, he approached them, and with a look of sympathy and intense feeling which could not be mistaken, he said—

"Alas! Mrs. Parker, this is a terrible scene for you and your child to be exposed to, and it grieves old Ben Binnacle's heart to see it. I had hoped that our voyage would have been performed with safety and success, and that I should have been able to have landed you securely at the place of our destination; but Fate seems to have willed it otherwise, and Heaven only knows what will be the result of it. God protect us, for without His merciful aid we are lost."

"Alas! alas!" sighed Mary, wringing her hands, and fixing upon the old man a look of the utmost agony, "and is there no hope? Must we indeed meet with so untimely a fate as this?"

Binnacle shook his head, and then begged of our heroine again to retire below, and to endeavour to calm her feelings.

"Ah, no," she replied; "I must remain here till the last moment; I cannot, I dare not again be separated from my husband."

"Oh, Mary," said her husband, "what can I do, what can I say to comfort you in this fearful moment? Better—far better had we remained where we were, and run the chance of discovery, than have exposed ourselves to these horrors."

"Nay, then,' said Binnacle, with a look of gentle reproach, "do you blame me for advising you to that to which I was dictated by feelings of friendship and sympathy?"

"Oh, no, my kind friend," replied

Parker, eagerly, "indeed you misunderstand me; I must indeed be an ungrateful scoundrel, and unworthy of the many acts of kindness which you have shown me, could I entertain such a thought. But when I think of the awful situation in which my fond and faithful wife and my poor boy are placed, my brain is racked to madness, and I scarcely know what I say. But there is nothing left for us but to resign ourselves to the will of Heaven, and to implore its mercy and protection in this the terrible hour of our need."

Neither Mary nor Ben returned any answer to this, but their looks expressed much more than words could have done. They all of them clasped their hands together, and fervently supplicated the interposition of the Supreme to rescue them from the terrible fate which seemed too surely impending o'er their heads; and Richard having placed his wife and child in as secure a part of the deck as he could find, he and Binnacle returned to superintend the crew, and to see if anything could be done to relieve them in their deplorable situation.

It was wonderful how well the lugger battled with the fury of the watery element, but such were the injuries she had already sustained, that it was quite evident, unless the storm speedily abated, or some assistance should arrive, that she could not last much longer, and the dangers by which she was surrounded seemed to increase every minute. The oldest seaman could scarcely ever have witnessed such a storm as that, and it was enough to appal the stoutest heart to gaze upon it. The lugger had made so much water that two or three of the crew were obliged to be kept incessantly working at the pumps to prevent her from sinking, and, in fact, they were in as wretched a situation as it is possible to imagine, or for language to describe; and there was not a soul on board that little craft who did not fully expect death every minute. It was so intensely dark, that they had no opportunity of forming the least conjecture in what direction they were being driven, nor could they tell whether or not they were any where near land.

In this manner more than another hour of the most indescribable suffering passed away, and there was no change for the better in their situation.

To describe the sufferings of poor Mary Parker would be impossible; but her anxiety was more for her husband and child than herself, and it was in vain that our hero endeavoured to console her. But at length a wonderful and Providential

change took place, and hope suddenly sprung up in the minds of the whole of the unfortunate individuals on board. The wind went down, the thunder ceased to roar, and the lightning no longer blazed in the heavens, as if by magic, and every symptom of a coming calm was apparent. Overpowered with joy and gratitude at such a miraculous deliverance from what had appeared to be certain and almost immediate death, the whole of the unfortunate persons on board the lugger fell simultaneously upon their knees, and returned their heartfelt thanks to the Supreme for His merciful interposition, and most of them were affected even to tears. Richard and his wife rushed into each other's arms, and the former exclaimed, as he clasped her to his bosom—

"Heaven be praised, my Mary—we shall yet be saved!"

"Oh, Richard," replied his wife, while tears started to her eyes, and her bosom heaved with emotions that were too powerful for utterance, "what a relief is this to my heart! Should we fortunately be near the land, we may yet be rescued from our perilous and awful situation."

"Ay," observed old Ben Binnacle, who had immediately joined them, "and the darkness will disperse shortly, I have no doubt, and then we shall, probably, be able to discover where we are, and to see whether we are likely to obtain any assistance; for our vessel is in such a crazy condition, from the buffeting she has received, that I doubt much whether she will be able to wear it out much longer. Had you not better retire again to the cabin, Mrs. Parker, and endeavour to obtain a little rest, and to compose your feelings after the extraordinary fatigue you have undergone?"

"Oh, no," answered our heroine. "I feel reanimated with fresh health and spirits now that the principal danger is past, and will remain here. My husband," she added, looking affectionately in his face, "Providence has not yet deserted us; and I trust that, before many hours have elapsed, we shall again be in safety."

"God grant that we may," returned Richard, fervently; "and never can I be sufficiently grateful to him for giving you sufficient strength to support this additional trial, which was enough to try the fortitude of even the stoutest heart."

Mary earnestly responded to this, and she and her husband once more embraced, and endeavoured to tranquillise their feelings. The storm had now entirely subsided, and the change which had so suddenly taken place was scarcely credible.

The waves were comparatively calm, but still the vessel leaked so much that the men were compelled to be kept constantly at work at the pumps ; and the fatigue they had undergone was so great that their duty was rendered most difficult. Another hour elapsed, and the lugger did not seem to make much way, and the patience of all on board was almost exhausted ; but at length the intense darkness which had so long obscured the horizon gradually dispersed, and daylight began to dawn. All strained their eyes eagerly towards the eastern horizon, with the hope of beholding some vessel which might render them assistance, or to descry land; but for some time their hopes were disappointed, and they had nothing left but to steer their own shattered vessel in the best way they could, and to trust in Providence to deliver them from their still dangerous and critical situation. At length there was a loud cry of "Land ahead!" and Richard and his wife starting up, strained their eyes in the direction indicated, and beheld the dark shadow of land upon the horizon, but which seemed to be at some considerable distance from them. Several ponderous articles were now thrown overboard, in order to lighten the vessel, and a signal of distress was hoisted at the fore, in the hope that it might meet the observation of some persons on the shore, who might despatch them assistance. Fortunately, the wind was in their favour, and drifted them in the direction of the land ; but still the lugger made but little way, and every moment her condition became evidently more critical.

"Would that our signal might be seen by some humane individuals on the land we descry," remarked Binnacle, "that they might forward us some assistance, for our situation is most desperate, and I am afraid that our vessel is in such a crazy condition that she will never be able to reach the land."

"Oh, God !" exclaimed our heroine, in a voice of agony, "and should all the fond hopes which the discontinuance of the storm has excited in our breasts even now be doomed to be disappointed !"

"Cheer thee, my Mary," said her husband. "I trust to Heaven that such a fate as that which you anticipate is not in store for us, but that we may yet reach the land in safety. Binnacle, this is not the time to deliberate. I feel keenly for the heavy loss you will sustain, and all in endeavouring to serve me; but since it is evident that the lugger must quickly go to pieces, having sprung another leak, had

we not better construct a raft without delay, and abandon it to its fate?"

"My poor lugger, which has served me for so many years!" said Ben, in a melancholy tone of voice. "But it can't be helped, since Fate has so ordained it; therefore, I accept of your suggestion, Mr. Parker, since it seems the only means of saving our lives. All hands to work immediately."

The order was promptly obeyed, and everyone set to work to form a raft from such spars and planks as they could find ; and it was scarcely completed when the lugger sprung another leak, and filled so fast that it was evident she must sink almost immediately. Quick as lightning it was thrown overboard, and the crew, who were in a state of desperation, were about to leap upon it, when Binnacle rushed hastily before them and prevented them.

"Avast!" cried the old man, in a commanding voice. "Are ye men? Richard Parker, your wife and boy."

"No, no," answered our hero, "I can never look to their safety even before yours, old man. To the raft first, and we will follow."

"Do not hesitate," said Ben, "for I am determined; on to the raft, Mr. Parker, I say, for the lugger is fast sinking, and I will hand you your wife and boy, and follow myself ; even if I should meet with a watery grave, I do not know that it would be of much consequence ; but those who are so precious to you, with yourself must, if possible, be saved. Quick ! quick !"

Richard Parker offered no further observation, though he was overwhelmed with the noble conduct of the old man, but sprang on to the raft immediately, and William followed his example with astonishing rapidity ; Binnacle then handed Mary over the side of the sinking vessel, and he had no sooner done so, than a sudden gale of wind sprang up, and the raft was drifted with the greatest impetuosity far away from the unfortunate lugger, and of course our hero had not the least power to stop its progress. A loud cry of horror and despair arose from the unfortunate beings on board, and immediately several of them threw themselves frantically overboard with the hope of being able to swim to the raft, but quickly sank to rise no more. Our hero, whose agony of feelings may well be imagined, beheld poor old Binnacle still on the deck of the lugger, apparently straining his eyes in despair after them ; but it was only for an instant, for almost as quick as thought the lugger had disappeared beneath the dark blue waters, and the fate of the unfortunate old man was certain. Our heroine uttered a piercing shriek as she witnessed the appalling sight, and immediately fainted in the arms of her husband, who turned away with a sickening sensation of horror which we find it impossible to describe.

"Unfortunate, noble-hearted old man," ejaculated Richard, with a burst of feeling which can readily be imagined; "that such should be thy fate in the cause of humanity! Oh, God! surely Thy decrees are too severe."

He cast his eyes eagerly towards the spot where the vessel had sunk, but not the least signs of it met his gaze, and the raft was drifted with such speed, fortunately in the direction of the land, that he was soon far away from the scene of the calamity. He now turned his attention to his wife, and pressing a fervent kiss upon her pale lips, he offered up a prayer to Heaven for their future preservation. He now endeavoured to steer the raft as well as he could, and rapidly approached the land, which seemed to him to be an island, and in his efforts he was assisted by the boy, William, with an energy which could not have been expected from a boy of his years, and especially after the great fatigue he had already experienced. As well as they could see, however, no human being appeared upon the land, and Richard began to fear that they were driven to some wild part of the coast where they might be unable to procure any relief or assistance. However, they must trust to Providence for that, though anyhow their situation was most desperate, as they had lost nearly all the little stock of money they possessed in the wreck, and they were thus rendered completely destitute. These painful reflections passed rapidly in the mind of Richard as the raft was drifted on its way, but his attention was quickly wholly occupied in reaching land, and perceiving a small creek, where he thought he might effect a more easy ascent to the higher land, he made his way towards it, as well as he could. Fortunately, the wind was in his favours and he was driven directly towards it, and in a very few minutes he found himself entering the creek, and the raft quickly afterwards became fixed in such a position that he had no difficulty in landing. Raising the form of his wife in his arms, for she was still insensible, he stepped from the raft on to the shore, followed by William, and easily ascended a small rocky eminence, which led like a flight of steps to the higher part of the land, and soon

found himself on a wild barren space of considerable extent, but the appearance of which was cheerless in the extreme. Still supporting the form of his wife in his arms, he gazed around him with feelings of despair, and for some minutes his mind was so bewildered that he was scarcely conscious whether he was awake or dreaming, or what had happened to him.

"Thank God!" he exclaimed at last, as he pressed a fervent and affectionate kiss upon the pale cheek of his wife, "thank God that you, the faithful and devoted partner of my sufferings, are saved from an awful and untimely fate. But you, poor gray-headed old man, alas! that you should perish thus, in the cause of humanity. Oh, I am a spell and a curse to all those who unfortunately become in any way connected with me. But where am I? In what strange place has Fate cast me now? My boy!"

"I am here, dear father," replied William, approaching him; "it is a wild spot, but thank Heaven that you and my beloved mother are preserved from the wreck; and God will yet direct us to some place of shelter and safety."

"My brave boy!" said our hero, much affected; "oh, it is indeed hard that one so young should be subjected to such misfortunes as those which you have experienced. The thought of it drives me mad."

"Pray, dear father," returned the affectionate child, "do not agitate yourself thus on my account. I am young, but God has blessed me with strength beyond my years, and I do not murmur at what I have to undergo. But poor mother, she is still insensible; oh, pray let us exert ourselves towards her recovery."

As the poor boy gave utterance to these words, his unfortunate mother breathed a deep sigh, and immediately afterwards opening her eyes she stared vacantly around her.

"A fearful dream," she uttered; "it was too dreadful to be reality; methought that my husband and my poor boy had perished in the ravenous deep, and that I was left alone in the pitiless world. But—but, where am I?"

"Mary—my beloved Mary!" cried our hero, pressing her delicate form still more warmly to his heart. She started at the sound of his voice, and looking with an indescribable expression of delight and affection in his face, she exclaimed—

"Ah! my husband! Thank Heaven, then it was but a dream! But this wild place! oh, say, where are we now?"

"Thank Heaven!" replied her hus-

FLORA IN DEEP THOUGHT ON MOWBRAY'S PERFIDY.

band, "that we are saved from the fate with which we were threatened."

"But the old man?" said Mary, in a tremulous voice, and looking anxiously in her husband's face. He could return no other answer than a heavy sigh, and the melancholy expression of his features told too plainly the fatal truth.

"Ah!" gasped forth our heroine; "I remember all now; the wreck! the fatal wreck!—The poor old man, he perished with it."

"Alas!" replied Richard; "it is too true. Unfortunate old man, he sacrificed his own life to save ours. What terrible misfortunes do I ever bring upon those who become in any way connected with me."

"Oh, God!" cried our heroine, wringing her hands, "it was a terrible sight; methinks I now see the poor gray-headed old man as our raft drifted from the sinking ship, pacing the deck with despair, and raising his hands in supplication for that help which no one but the Almighty could render him. And then the remorseless waves gathered around him, and overwhelmed him and the frail vessel on which he stood. Oh, surely it was hard that one so aged, so noble-hearted and virtuous should meet with so untimely a fate."

"Peace to his soul," said Parker, solemnly, "it is a melancholy and awful subject to dwell upon; endeavour to banish it from your memory, Mary."

"Banish it from my memory!" she repeated; "oh, that is impossible! But where are we now? This place so lonely and so wretched—oh, what is to become of us now?"

"Alas!" replied her husband, "I know not. But you, my dear wife, you are weak and exhausted; oh, how can I afford you any relief?"

"Think not of me, Richard," ejaculated the devoted and affectionate wife; "you are saved from a watery grave, and I care not what becomes of me. It would be a happy release for me, were I permitted this moment to perish in your arms."

"Oh, for Heaven's sake talk not thus," said Richard; "or you will drive me to distraction. Surely the Almighty will not entirely desert us, but will afford us some speedy relief. And yet this place, so wild and so barren, I fear that it is not inhabited, and if it be not, we have only been rescued from one death to meet with another still more terrible."

"I feel faint and exhausted," said our heroine, in a weak voice; "I must rest myself; let me recline for a few minutes on the earth, and I shall probably revive."

"I will support you in my arms, my beloved," said Richard, whose bitter anguish of feelings need not be described. "Heaven help us, for without its aid, I know not what will become of us."

"Oh, my poor dear mother," said William, as he fondly and tearfully approached her; "how pale she looks; she will die, unless she has speedy relief, and in this desolate place where is it to be obtained?"

"My child," said his mother, smiling faintly upon him, "be not alarmed; I shall soon recover; I am better now."

"Alas! alas!" groaned our hero, striking his breast, "a bitter curse pursues us. Oh, God! surely thy decrees are too severe!"

"Nay, Richard," returned his wife, fixing upon him a look of gentle remonstrance; "murmur not at the will of the Supreme, who does everything for the best. We must put our trust in Him, and He will not desert us in the hour of need. I will endeavour to be firm, and you shall not hear me complain, let whatever may betal me, and however severe the trials may be that are allotted to me."

"Noble, best of women, and most devoted and affectionate of wives!" cried our hero, straining her still more rapturously to his heart, "oh, where can I find language to express to you the feelings with which you inspire me? Would to Heaven that we had never quitted the hospitable and friendly roof of Mr. Hawthorn."

"And had we not done so," replied his wife, "ere now you would probably have been the inmate of a prison. I shudder with horror to think of it."

"And even if I had," said Richard, with a look of despair, "could our fates have been more awful than that with which we are now threatened? Oh, Mary, the cup of our misery is nearly full, and I again see the madness of seeking to fly from that destiny to which the Supreme Judge has doomed me."

"Richard," said our heroine, fixing upon him a solemn and expressive look; "you betray a weakness and an error of judgment by giving way to these thoughts. Be firm, be firm, and desperate and gloomy though our prospects may appear at present to be, something will yet occur when we least expect it to relieve us. Have you no idea where we are?"

"Alas!" answered Parker, "none whatever; how can I? But this is a dreary, desolate place, and I fear it is uninhabited, and if so, destitute as we are, what is to become of us?"

"Give not way to despair," she replied, arousing herself by a powerful effort. "We must examine the place more minutely. I see trees at a distance, and probably beyond them we may find some signs of human habitation."

"Ah!" ejaculated Richard, looking eagerly in the direction to which she had pointed; "strange I did not see them before. Rest you here, my dear Mary, till I return; no doubt you will be safe. William will remain with you, and I will go and search for that of which we stand so much in need."

"No," answered Mary; "I am better now, I feel my strength revive, and I will accompany you. I could not remain in this place alone."

"Be it so, then, dear Mary," he said; "and Heaven grant that our errand may be successful. Lean on me, my wife, and we will take our leisure. Surely Providence will not suffer our hopes to be disappointed. Come, come."

Mary returned no answer, but took the arm of her husband, and gathering up all her strength, she suffered him to lead her from the spot, followed by William.

CHAPTER XXX.

WHAT BEFEL THE FUGITIVES. — THE SEARCH, AND ITS RESULTS.

MRS. PARKER was, however, so weak from the effects of the great exertion and excitement she had for some time been subjected to, that she was only able to proceed at a slow pace, and had it not been for the support of her husband she could not have accomplished the task at all. It would not only be tedious, but useless for us to seek to describe the agitation and excitement of the feelings under which they both laboured, but which was rendered, if possible, still more painful by the efforts which they made to conceal them from each other, and certainly their present forlorn and almost hopeless condition, and the terrible calamity which had befallen them, coupled with the melancholy and untimely death of the poor unfortunate old Ben Binnacle, was more than enough to fill their minds with despair. Still they proceeded across the dreary waste towards the spot which had attracted their attention as well as they could, though our heroine was so weak from the extraordinary exertion that she had undergone, that, as we have before stated, it was rendered a task of great difficulty, and she was frequently compelled to pause in order to rest herself; and at such times they would both strain their eyes to their fullest extent with the hope of perceiving some signs of a human being or habitation, but at present nothing of the kind met their gaze, and they could not but begin to fear that their wishes would end in disappointment.

"Alas!" sighed Mary, "what a terrible fate is ours, to be cast upon such a wild and desolate place as this, and where there is at present no prospect of our being enabled to obtain any relief. Oh, Richard, unless kind Heaven in its infinite mercy shall interpose to save us, I fear, indeed, that we are lost."

"What can I say, what can I do?" returned her husband, with a look of the most intense anguish. "How can I seek to inspire you with hope, when all around us bears nothing but the aspect of the blackest despair? Fate seems to have conspired against us, and better would it have been for us had we all perished in the wreck, than to be exposed to the horrible and lingering destiny which is probably in store for us. But, come, my poor wife, let us endeavour to arouse ourselves, and seek the relief in which we at present stand so terribly in need. Could we but meet with some human beings, we might yet be saved; though our present situation and prospects are indeed most desperate. Our poor boy, too; alas! this is a trial far too great for his strength to bear."

"My beloved parents," replied the noble-hearted and courageous lad; "fear not for me; for though I am young, yet God will, I trust, give me strength and fortitude sufficient to brave all the hardships which it may be our lot to have to encounter, and you shall never hear me murmur or complain."

Richard and his wife were so deeply affected by these observations of their child, whose firmness under such manifold and awful trials was most extraordinary, that they could only again fondly press him to their bosoms without being able to return any reply, and after a brief delay, they again proceeded on their way, without anything particular occurring to strengthen those hopes which they sought to encourage. Their progress, as we have before said, was but slow, but as they approached nearer towards the trees that had attracted their attention, the prospect began to assume a less cheerless aspect, and again the hope was renewed in their bosoms that they would probably in a short time come within sight of some friendly dwelling or dwellings, where they might obtain that relief and information of which they at present stood so much in need. Cold and cheerless, and sick at heart, they wandered on; and as they did so, all the painful occurrences of the past arose with redoubled force to their memory, and, coupled with their present wretched situation, rendered their anguish of mind tenfold. Still, all that they gazed upon was entirely strange to them. Richard had not the slightest recollection of the place, and was unable to form even the most remote idea of the part to which the ill-fated vessel had been driven previous to going to pieces. To add to their misery, the sky again became obscured by black and ponderous clouds, which gave but too plain a token of a speedy renewal of that storm which had ceased for some time. The thunder began to murmur at a distance, and the lightning to flash in the heavens, and soon the rain descended in large drops, which as quickly increased to torrents, and everything gave fearful warning of another war of the elements, if possible, more violent than that which had so recently taken place.

The unfortunate fugitives were again compelled to pause, and to gaze despairingly around them; and as they contemplated the utter desolateness of the situation in which they were placed, and the horrors that were so rapidly gathering around them, their hearts sank within them, and while they could not help shuddering with feelings of the most indescribable dismay, they looked upon each other with expressions of despair. It, indeed, required more than human fortitude to support the misery to which they were exposed, especially after all the severe trials and hardships which they had already encountered, and without the prospect of any relief being afforded them.

Notwitstanding all the efforts of our heroine to the contrary, her strength fast failed her, and as her husband gazed upon her pale features, her sunken eyes, and shivering and attenuated form, the intense anguish of his mind may be much better imagined than described. For several minutes she seemed as if she were about to sink into a state of insensibility, and Richard felt his own strength almost exhausted; but exerting himself to the utmost, he supported her in his arms, and gazed upon her with an expression of countenance which plainly told the overwhelming feelings of anguish and despair that pressed upon his heart, while the poor boy, William, stood by, with clasped hands, and looked upon his unfortunate mother's pale face with all the agony of mind which was in accordance with his affectionate nature.

"Great God of Heaven!" cried our hero, as the storm every moment increased in violence, "what will become of us, without any prospect of relief or shelter being at hand?—What, oh! what will become of us? Try us not beyond our strength, I humbly beseech Thee, but take pity on us, and afford us some speedy help in this, the terrible hour of our emergency. My wife, my beloved Mary! oh, how heart-rending is it thus to view the miseries to which you are exposed, and to know that I have no power to aid you in the midst of your sufferings! Your strength is almost exhausted, and you are fast sinking beneath the weight of those trials that are far too much for your tender frame to bear, exposed to the many months, the years of suffering that it has already been. Oh, despair—despair! I shall go mad! Mary, my faithful and devoted Mary! oh, look up and speak to me, and do not drive me altogether to distraction!"

She did indeed look up in his countenance with a most touching and expressive look of affection, and tried to speak, but for several moments she was unable, and her husband could but strain her still more fervently to his bosom, and press the warmest kisses of affection upon her pale cheeks.

"Oh, my Mary!" he again ejaculated, "where can I find language sufficiently powerful to express to you the agony of my mind at this moment, when I see you exposed to such sufferings that, under any circumstances, would be so torturing to behold? This fearful storm, and no prospect of pity or assistance at hand—our fate is surely most frightful to contemplate. All-merciful Father, look down with pity and compassion upon us, or there is nothing left for us but destruction."

"Dear Richard," ejaculated Mary, in a faint voice, "oh, do not thus give way to despair, fearful and agonising though our situation at present is; God will not entirely forsake us in this, the awful hour of our need, of that I feel convinced. I—I am better now, and you shall not find me murmur. But let us proceed, and we may yet find that assistance of which we both stand so much in need."

Again our unfortunate heroine exerted herself to the utmost, but her trembling limbs again almost failed her, and she sunk nearly helpless on the arm of her husband.

The storm was now raging in all its fury, and the appearance of the heavens and all around was most awful to look upon.

"It is impossible that you can walk, my poor Mary," said our hero, "I see it plainly, and how, oh! how can I express to you the intense, the insupportable agony of mind which I am enduring? The heavens, too, appear to have conspired against us, and you are already drenched to the skin, and your pale and exhausted looks are quite heart-rending to look upon. Alas—alas! how little do you deserve to meet with such a fate, my faithful, my devoted wife, as that which now so plainly threatens us. My God, speedily send us some relief, if not for my sake, at least for that of my innocent wife and child, and if it be your will, visit me alone, I implore you, with your wrath, and not those who are far more precious to me than my very existence."

"Richard," again ejaculated our heroine, in a voice that was scarcely audible, "do not speak thus, for the manner in which you seem to reproach yourself agitates me more than all. If it is the will of Heaven that we should thus suffer, we must endeavour to submit, however arduous the task may be; for, weak mortals as we are, how shall we presume to murmur? I—I—oh, Heaven!"

"Mary—Mary!" cried her distracted

husband, looking with an expression of the most indescribable terror and anguish in her countenance, as she again sank completely exhausted in his arms, "this trial is too much for you, and in vain do you endeavour to bear up against it. I see it plainly, and my fortitude forsakes me. The curse of Heaven most assuredly pursues me wherever I go, and it is useless for me to endeavour to avoid that fate which, sooner or later, must overtake me. But why do I linger here, when my beloved wife's life is in such imminent danger, and there may yet be relief at hand much nearer than we can possibly anticipate? Come, my beloved Mary, I will support you in my arms, and we will again put our firm reliance on the goodness and mercy of Providence, and endeavour to find out some place of shelter, and in which we may meet with that compassion and assistance wich we so much require."

"No, my husband," replied our heroine, again by a most extraordinary effort arousing herself from the state of exhaustion into which she had sunk; "you have already undergone sufficient exertion, and I can, with the assistance of your arm, walk; let us proceed, for fresh hope reanimates my bosom, and I firmly believe that Heaven will hear our prayers in this solemn hour, and that we shall not be doomed to be disappointed. Come, Richard, come."

As she thus spoke, it was astonishing to see the energy with which the amiable and heroic woman exerted that strength which but a moment or two before had seemed to be completely exhausted, and her husband, after having fondly embraced her, without saying a word, took her arm, and they again moved slowly from the spot towards the more woody part of the island.

But it required the utmost courage and perseverance to stand against the violent storm that was now raging with the most frightful fury, and the unfortunate fugitives could not possibly view it without shuddering with horror. The reader may well imagine the misery of their situation, wet and shivering with cold as they were, and after having suffered so much from the wreck, and it was indeed wonderful how they, but more especially Mary and her son, could withstand it with all the firmness that they did.

In this manner they had arrived within a few paces of the wood, when they were startled by the sudden appearance of a man, who emerged from it, and who on beholding them, stood and gazed upon them apparently with no less astonishment than that which they themselves experienced. He was a tall, stout, and muscular looking man, clad in the garb of a seaman, and from all that they could distinguish of his features at the distance from which they gazed at them, they seemed to be harsh and forbidding, and were by no means calculated to inspire them with hope, though the sight even of a human being in that desolate place was a relief to them, and presented to them at least some chance of their meeting with some place in which they might find shelter and assistance in the numerous difficulties by which they were surrounded. They advanced towards him, and, as they did so, the man came forward to meet them, and was quickly standing before them, scanning them minutely from head to foot with a scrutinizing, but anything but a prepossessing glance. From his features and dress, however, he appeared to be an Englishman, and their confidence revived.

"Who are ye? and what brings you hither?" he demanded in peremptory accents.

"Misfortune," answered Richard. "The fact of it is, we have been shipwrecked off this island, and having had a most miraculous escape, we seek such kind assistance as persons placed in our unfortunate situation require."

"Humph!" ejaculated the man, and once more eyeing them narrowly. "Have you any money?"

"Alas!" returned our hero, "but a sorry trifle, indeed. Nearly all that we possessed was lost in the wreck."

"Then you stand but little chance of any aid here, I can tell you," said the man, gruffly. "I have quite enough to do to look after myself, and have nothing to spare. But it is not very wise or pleasant to stand here talking in the storm. I have business to attend to, so I wish you good-day."

"But surely," said Richard, looking appealingly in his face, "common humanity will not suffer you to leave us thus."

"Psha!" returned the man, impatiently, "I tell you again that I have nothing to give you, so what is the use of talking of humanity to me?"

"Is there no town or village near this place?" eagerly demanded our hero.

"Yes," replied the man; "about seven miles through the wood you will meet with a village or hamlet, but I much doubt whether you will find assistance from any of the inhabitants, for they are all as poor as myself, and have nothing to give away."

"Alas—alas!" sighed Mrs. Parker, and at the same time wringing her hands in the anguish of her feelings, "on what inhospitable shore has fate now cast us?"

"Why," answered the man, "if it will be any gratification for you to know, you are on the coast of Cornwall."

"Cornwall!" repeated Richard, in surprise. "Is it possible that the unfortunate lugger should have been driven by the lugger so far out of its course? But for the sake of my poor wife and child, stranger, who you may perceive are completely exhausted with the dreadful sufferings they have already undergone, I implore you to render us some assistance, and to guide us at least to some place of shelter from this raging storm."

"There," said the fellow, in the same uncouth accents as before, "I have already told you that I have business to attend to, and cannot waste my time in standing here parleying with you in the storm. I am already drenched to the skin, and not in any of the best of tempers in consequence. So again I wish you good-day, and I have no doubt that you will be able to find some sort of a shelter in the wood."

With these words, the man turned abruptly away from them, and walking at the top of his speed, had soon got to some distance from them, leaving them in a state of the greatest disappointment and agitation.

"Is there, then, no hope for us?" said our hero, striking his forehead in the anguish of his feelings, and gazing upon his unfortunate wife with an expression of the deepest emotion. "Unfeeling man, how different is his conduct to that we have hitherto met with from those to whose humanity and benevolence we have had occasion to apply! A distance of seven miles before we can reach any human habitation, and in such a storm as this! Alas—alas! my devoted wife, you will never be able to perform such a journey, for even now your limbs fail you, and——"

"Courage, courage, dear Richard," she interrupted, in a faint voice. "I am not so bad as you apprehend me to be—indeed I am not. In the forest we may find some temporary place of shelter from the storm, and where we can rest ourselves until it has subsided, and I have no doubt that I shall be able to reach that, even fatigued as I am—at least, I will try. Oh! droop not, my husband, for Omnipotence will watch over us yet."

"Patient sufferer!" exclaimed our hero, with a burst of feeling which he could not restrain, "your fortitude is a bright example for mankind at large to follow. Come, then, my own one; let me once

more guide your tottering footsteps, and I will endeavour to dispel the dismal apprehensions that have crowded upon my mind. Heaven protect us, and direct us to some place of safety!"

Poor Mary made no answer, and her husband again supporting her as well as he could, and followed by their son, they once more resumed their toilsome journey through the horrors of the tempest, which was now at its height, and soon afterwards they entered the wood. It was a gloomy and intricate place, and they were at a loss which way to pursue, for all were alike devious, and presented no prospect whatever to gratify their hopes. But at length Richard discovered a part that was more open than the rest, and that way he took, avoiding the trees as much as possible, for fear of their attracting the lightning, which still blazed awfully in the sky.

In this manner they continued to journey on slowly for some distance, but without meeting with any place which was at all calculated to afford them even a partial or temporary shelter, and the trembling limbs, and pale and languid features of Mary, plainly showed that it would be impossible for her to proceed much further. At length, she was again compelled to pause, and looking up with the deepest feelings of emotion and regret in her husband's countenance, she said—

"Alas! my strength fails me, and I find that I cannot proceed. Oh, God! what a terrible trial is this! What will become of us? But—but leave me here to my fate, Richard, and yourself and our poor child seek to save yourselves!"

"Mary—Mary," cried our agitated hero, "you will drive me mad if you make use of such observations as these. Leave you here, my dear one? Abandon that gentle being who has ever clung to me through every danger with all the strength of woman's fondest love? Horrible—unnatural idea! Oh, what a monster must I be could I ever be guilty of such a hideous crime as that! Something seems to convince me that we are even now not far from some place of shelter, and I have strength sufficient left to bear you in my arms. Come, then, my unfortunate wife; the anxiety of my mind will make me deem the burthen but light."

She tried to speak, but nature was quite exhausted, and she sank helpless and fainting into her husband's arms.

"She will die!" he ejaculated, with a burst of agony, and looking in her face as if his heart would break. "She can never survive this dreadful trial, and I shall be deprived of the only being who renders life to me at all endurable, or worth the struggling for. All merciful Father, either, I beseech you, avert so fearful a calamity, or at least suffer us all to perish together! But there is not a moment for delay. I feel endowed with redoubled strength on the painful emergency of the occasion; and I will yet save her or die with her. Heaven—oh, Heaven assist me in my efforts!"

With these words, he raised the form of his wife in his arms, and with a strength and speed that could not have been expected in his exhausted condition, he hurried with her through the wood. He had proceeded in this manner for some distance without perceiving anything to gratify his hopes, when, pausing for a moment or two to rest himself, and straining his eyes as far as he could in the direction immediately before him, he beheld what appeared to be the shadow of some building at a short distance, and his hopes revived.

"Ah!" he exclaimed, "the Almighty has heard my prayers; should this building prove to be inhabited by any human being, who may not be destitute of every proper sense of feeling, we may yet be saved. Let me immediately away. Dearest Mary," he added, pressing an affectionate kiss upon the pale lips of his wife, "Providence, I trust, has not yet deserted us."

Again he raised her in his arms, and hurried towards the building, which had so fortunately attracted his attention, and before which he shortly arrived. It proved, however, somewhat to his disappointment, to be merely the ruins of what appeared to have been an ancient tower, but which had evidently been deserted and left to decay for many years; yet there seemed to be plenty of it sufficiently sound to afford them a shelter from the tempest, and that, under all the painful circumstances in which they were placed, was most fortunate. He entered the ruins at a low door, which was partly off its hinges, and found himself in a small court, which was overgrown by rank grass, and the pavement of which was covered with huge masses of stone, which had fallen from different parts of the building. Here there was not the least shelter from the storm, and he, therefore, proceeded, as well as he could, into the more interior parts of the tower, and after ascending, with no inconsiderable difficulty and danger, several flights of broken steps, he at length succeeded in gaining a small gothic apartment, which seemed to have suffered scarcely anything from the ravages of time. Here he placed his wife upon a large block of stone in the

centre of the room, which seemed to have formerly been the basement of a pillar which had supported the roof, and paused to take breath, after the extraordinary exertions he had undergone, and to collect his thoughts, while William stood by and watched his mother with the deepest emotion and anxiety.

"Thank God!" ejaculated our hero, at last, "for directing us even to this place of rest and shelter; for had we been much longer exposed to the violence of the storm, the most fatal consequences must have followed. Oh, my poor wife, how fearful are the sufferings you are fated to endure. May the Almighty send us some speedy assistance, or I fear that your tender frame, already worn out by the many sufferings to which it has been subjected, will sink under it."

He pressed the warmest and most affectionate kisses on her lips as he thus spoke, and hung over her with the deepest emotion and anxiety.

"But what can I do to revive her?" he said; "this insensibility alarms me, for I fear that she has already undergone more, much more than her strength can bear; and should this only prove the mournful prelude to death! Horrible thought! Forbid that it should be realised, All-merciful Heaven! How pale, how ghastly, and how careworn she looks, poor thing. Alas! what an awful change has a few years wrought in what was once so blooming, so cheerful, and so lovely. And it is through her fatal love for me that all this has taken place. Would to God that we had never met; how happy and how prosperous might she now have been. Surely fate must have frowned upon our union, or she would never have been subjected to such a cruel destiny as this. But, hush! she revives. God be praised for this, what a relief it is to me. My beloved Mary!"

The unfortunate woman opened her eyes, and gazed curiously around her.

"Where am I now?" she ejaculated, in a faint but eager voice; "what fresh and remarkable changes am I destined to encounter? Ah, Richard, my husband, you here? Then I am safe; kind Heaven I thank you."

"Mary," said her husband, anxiously, "I have found a place of shelter from the fierce tempest to whose fury you have been too long exposed, and here we may rest in safety till it has subsided, when I trust Providence will guide us to some hospitable dwelling, where you may obtain that assistance which you so much require in your present exhausted condition."

"But what place is this, Richard?" said

our heroine, again looking anxiously around her.

"It is the remains of some ancient building," answered her husband, "which seem to have been for many years deserted, and where I should imagine that we have no couse to fear any interruption. But how do you feel now, my love? How pale and ill you look; I fear that the terrible hardships that we have for the last few hours experienced are for too much for your delicate frame to support."

"Be not alarmed, dear Richard," she replied, "for I am better, oh, much better now. But alas! that such a dreadful calamity should befal us. Where can we now direct our footsteps, deprived of our excellent and unfortunate friend, and cast upon this strange place?"

"Oh, give not yet way to despair, my dear Mary," replied our hero, "for notwithstanding the present gloominess of our prospects, I trust that we shall still not be abandoned by Heaven, but that it will release us from our present difficulty, and direct us to some place of safety. But try to compose yourself to rest for an hour or two, for that may serve to revive you."

"No," returned Mary, "I do not feel at all disposed for sleep, and would this storm but subside, methinks that I could find strength sufficient to proceed on our dreary journey. That strange uncouth man whom we met informed us that there was a village some distance off, did he not?"

"He did," answered her husband; "but he said that it was about seven miles distant, and it would be almost impossible for you to proceed so far in your present weak and exhausted condition."

"And what is to become of us if we remain here?" demanded Mary.

"Alas! I know not," said Richard; "I am completely bewildered. I cannot but be fully sensible of the horrors of our situation. We are now nearly destitute, and unless Heaven sends us some timely aid, I know not what our fate will be. I shudder to think of it. And then the untimely fate of one of our best friends, poor Binnacle!"

"Alas! unfortunate old man!" sighed Mrs. Prker; "surely he was deserving of a far different fate to that which he met with. Never, never shall I be able to efface from my memory that awful scene."

"True," coincided her husband, "it was a most appalling sight; and again I cannot help regretting that we ever quitted the roof of our kind friend, Mr. Hawthorn."

"Say not so," returned Mary, "for you know well the danger that threatened, and long ere this you might have fallen into the power of onr enemies. The thought is too torturing to think upon."

"And had I done so," remarked our hero, "the life of poor old Binnacle and many others would have been saved."

"Richard," gasped forth his wife, and fixing upon him a look of mingled astonishment and reproach, "can you talk thus calmly and unconcernedly upon a subject of such awful and vital importance to us both? If you would not torture me to distraction, you will never again make use of such thoughtless and painful observations. If you had been taken a prisoner, what would have become of myself and our poor boy?"

"True," said Richard; "I was wrong in doing so; but my brain is so bewildered by the various and conflicting thoughts that crowd upon it, that I scarcely know what I say. For your dear sakes, and that alone, I will still endeavour to avoid the awful and ignominious fate which has so long been impending o'er me."

"And in this distant part of the country," added Mary, "there is no fear of our being discovered by those whom we have cause to dread; and had we but the means of present existence, we might safely remain, until we had an opportunity of making our friends acquainted with what has happened, when they would, no doubt, lose no time in forwarding us advice and assistance."

"Alas!" returned her husband, "I dread making Adams acquainted with the fearful calamity which has taken place, for I know that he will be so deeply affected at the death of his old and esteemed friend, poor Binnacle, that he will be inconsolable. And I am already under such a heavy weight of gratitude to him, which I feel assured I shall never be able to repay, that I do not like again to intrude upon his kindness and benevolence. It is our destitute and dependant state which tortures me more than all; and I feel convinced that, however good the will of Adams to assist us further, that he cannot do so without distressing himself; and why should I do so? Oh, Mary, ours is a sad life to lead, and methinks it would be better for us all were we rid of it."

"Richard, what fearful talk is this? Why will you give way to such gloomy thoughts? But cheer you, my husband, and try to believe that the time is not far distant when a favourable change will take place in our circumstances, and that we

HAWTHORN MEDITATING OVER THE DEAD BODY OF MOWBRAY.

may be restored to tranquillity, if not to happiness."

"If I could persuade myself to even the probability of that," answered our hero, "I should be comparatively content; but, alas! when I weigh all the circumstances in my mind, I find it impossible to do so. Oh, Mary, little did I expect when I became your husband that I should ever be the means of consigning you to the miserable fate which it has been your hard and cruel lot to experience."

"Richard," replied our heroine, "you must doubt the sincerity of my love if you believe that I can ever reproach you for that which Providence has ordained, and over which you had no control."

"Doubt the sincerity of your love, my Mary?" he returned: "oh, that can never be. How many are the fond and ardent proofs I have had of your unexampled devotion to me! Have you ever murmured or uttered a word of regret when you have had to encounter sufferings that might appal the stoutest heart? and I must be an ungrateful scoundrel could I thus return the noble, the generous affection you have bestowed upon me."

"Then never more allude to the subject, dear Richard," said his wife, "for it can only be the cause of anguish to us both."

Richard embraced his wife affectionately, and a silence of some minutes ensued, for they were both of them too much occupied with their own thoughts to offer any observation. At length Mary arose, and taking her arm, he led her to one of the broken casements of the ancient apartment, in order that they might watch the progress of the storm, and thus judge how it would be best for them to proceed. It still continued to rage with unabated violence, and nothing could possibly be more cheerless and disheartening than the aspect it imparted to the otherwise gloomy scene. Night had not yet approached, yet it was almost dark, save when at intervals the lightning flashed across the sky, and that only served too add to the horrors of the scene.

"It is indeed a fearful tempest," said our heroine, "and at present there seems to be no probability of its abating. Must we remain in this gloomy place, and without the opportunity of making those further inquiries which are of such immediate importance to us?"

"We have no other alternative, my dear Mary," answered her husband, "for it would be madness to venture forth again in such a tempest as this. And yet, it is many hours since we tasted food, and you must be faint and exhausted for the want of it.

"No," returned our heroine; "my mind is too much occupied to make me feel inclined to eat. Fear not for me, for I am content to endure anything, so long as I know that you are in safety."

"Come then, my love," remarked her husband, "let us retire from the window; the contemplation of this dismal scene will but add to the melancholy and anguish of your mind."

Mary made no reply, and he led her again to her seat, and taking his place by her side, they continued to converse for some time longer, only pausing alternately to listen to the voice of the tempest. In this manner the time passed drearily away, and at length night set in, and the darkness that prevailed was impenetrable, and rendered the gloom of the apartment in which they were more complete. It was quite evident that they must remain there till the morning, for even if the storm had subsided, they did not consider it would be safe for them to venture forth at that hour,

and in such a strange and gloomy place. They, therefore, made up their minds to remain there for the night, thinking that they were quite safe; but before they ventured to seek a few hours' repose, of which they both stood so much in need, Richard thought it most prudent to make secure the door of the room as well as he could, in order to prevent any sudden intrusion, and this he managed to accomplish pretty well, by piling against it such rubbish as he found in the room. This done, they committed themselves to the care and protection of the Supreme, they arranged their outer garments on the floor, and then stretching their weary limbs upon this rude couch, overpowered by the extraordinary fatigue they had for so many hours undergone, they soon fell asleep, and for awhile had a temporary respite from their cares and anxieties.

How long they had thus reposed, it was impossible for them to conjecture, but they were suddenly aroused by hearing a loud and confused noise from below, and which seemed to proceed from immediately underneath the room in which they were. They started up hastily, alarmed, and listened with the most breathless attention, at the same time looking at each other in amazement and consternation. The storm had almost ceased, so that they were enabled to hear anything more distinctly than they could otherwise have done. The noise was repeated, and then they were almost certain that they heard persons moving about, and the voices of men. Mary turned pale and clung to her husband, who was, in fact, little less alarmed than herself, though he tried to conceal it.

"There are other persons in the ruins," she said; "they might be robbers, and should they discover us——"

"Nay," interrupted Richard, in a low voice, "do not terrify yourself; they are probably only travellers, who are seeking a shelter from the storm, like ourselves. Set us remain still and listen."

Mary returned no answer, and her husband having knelt down, placed his ear to a crevice in the flooring, and listened attentively. He was soon convinced that he had not been mistaken, for he not only plainly distinguished the voices of several men in earnest conversation, but likewise beheld a light glimmering through the crevice, and which all but confirmed the surmises of his wife. The dialogue that took place satisfied him of their real character, and showed him the danger in which they were placed. They were wreckers, and evidently otherwise men of the most desperate character.

"Well, Hawlet," said one of them, "it was as well to put the poor devils out of their misery, as they were nearly dead when they were washed ashore. The storm has been a good friend to us to-night, for it has sent us a rich booty, and greatly added to the wealth we had already accumulated."

"Ay, you may say that," returned another; "but come, let us deposit it in our secret cavern below, and then we must again to business."

The ruffian who had first spoken made some reply, and then the light disappeared, and our hero heard them depart. Mary, who had been as attentive as her husband, had heard all the conversation that passed, and her terror may be well imagined.

"Good God!" she exclaimed, "into what fresh danger have we been led? Should these ruffians discover us here, desperate as their characters evidently are, we know not what may be the consequences. They would suspect us of being spies upon their actions, and probably sacrifice our lives to their vengeance."

"Be firm, Mary," answered our hero; "there is not a moment to be lost; we must depart from these ruins immediately, and while these fellows are in their secret cavern below."

"But should they encounter us on our flight?" remarked his wife, in a tremulous voice.

"Oh, fear not," replied Richard, "they will probably be detained some time in secreting their booty. We must be firm, for this is a moment that demands not only that, but all our presence of mind. Come, Mary, your hand. William, keep close to myself and your mother, and tread as softly as you can."

Mary and her son obeyed the injunctions of our hero, and he having previously removed the rubbish from the door, they silently and cautiously quitted the room; but they had scarcely descended more than two or three of the stairs, when the light which they had before seen, again appeared, and they heard a sound as if proceeding from the hasty falling of a trap-door. Instantly they started back into the room, but in doing so, they had a momentary glance of the men below, and which was quite sufficient not to prepossess them much in their favour; and foremost among them they recognised the very man whom they had met in the storm, and who had behaved to them in such an abrupt and uncouth manner. Their alarm, however, would not suffer them to pause, and on regaining the room, they stood and looked at each other with expressions of apprehension and anxiety.

"We are too late!" gasped forth our heroine; "these men, whose desperate characters the conversation we overheard too well convinces us of, will discover us, and if so, we are lost."

"Hush!" ejaculated our hero, in a low tone, "should our voices reach their ears, we should indeed be lost. Having accomplished their object, they will no doubt immediately quit the ruins, and then we shall be again safe. Let us be firm and cautious. Hark!"

They now heard the men conversing below, and silently approaching the door, they listened attentively to endeavour to catch what they said.

"Well," said one of them, "we have deposited our treasure safe enough among our other hoard, and, as the storm has ceased, we may as well hasten to our rendezvous, and regale ourselves, after our night's success. If we go on at the rate we have done lately, we shall soon become as rich as princes."

"True, Jack Hawlet," returned another of the fellows, "we have no cause to complain of the frowns of Fortune, who has been most kind and generous to us for some time past. Oh, there is nothing beats the wrecker's life, after all."

At this moment a sudden movement of Mary, in her agitation, caused her foot to come in contact with part of the rubbish which her husband had piled up against the door, previous to their retiring to rest, to prevent them from sudden intrusion, and it fell with a loud lumbering noise on the floor, which reverberated through the ruins. They started with dismay, and Mary turned pale and trembled violently, looking at the same time aghast at her husband. By his looks he endeavoured to calm her agitation, and motioned her to silence, and they then again listened with breathless attention, anxious and fearful as to what would be the result of this unfortunate accident. The noise had evidently startled and surprised the ruffians, and they heard one of them exclaim—

"Ah! what noise was that? It proceeded from the room above; it strikes me that there is some one in the ruins besides ourselves, and should any daring intruder have ventured here to penetrate our secrets, by all the infernal host, it shall cost them dear for their daring."

"Ay," remarked another of the men, "should any one have been so bold they shall never leave this place alive. Come, let us search the room, and ascertain whether or not our suspicions are correct."

"Oh, God!" groaned the terrified Mrs. Parker, clinging to her husband, "we are lost—destroyed!"

"Be firm!" said her husband, with breathless haste, and in an under tone. "We may yet be saved!—Ah—see! yonder recess, behind the broken pillar—with the aid of All-merciful Providence, it may serve to conceal us. Quick—quick! for they have begun to ascend the stairs."

Quick as thought the unfortunate fugitives hurried into the dark recess which was so situated that it might serve to shield them from immediate observation. They compressed themselves into the smallest possible compass, and then awaited the result, in a state of agitation which the reader will be easily able to imagine. They had not to wait long, for they immediately heard the heavy footsteps of the men ascending the stairs, the rays of the light which they carried streamed into the room through the different crevices, and directly afterwards the door was thrown open, and they entered. There were four of them in number, and their appearance fully corresponded with their character, for it was of the most ruffianly and savage character imaginable, and their repulsive features plainly showed them to be men who were capable of committing any atrocious or desperate deed. The foremost of them, who carried the lantern, raised it above his head in order to accelerate the view, and they all of them gazed eagerly and minutely around the room. Fortunately, the light did not fall upon the place where our hero and his wife and child were concealed, and their hopes began in some measure to revive, especially when one of them observed, after he had cast a scrutinising glance around the room—

"There is no one here; our suspicions were unfounded; what fools we are to have been so easily alarmed; see, it was nothing more than the falling of some of this old rubbish, brought down by the wind, which caused the noise we heard."

"Ay," said another of the men, "that must have been it, and we might have guessed that without giving ourselves so much unnecessary alarm. These ruins are not a very likely place for any one to venture into. Come, let us depart, for time wears apace, and our comrades will be anxious for our return."

"Come, then," said the man who had first spoken, "it is useless for us to delay here."

They cast another hasty glance around the room, and then retired; and when Richard and his wife heard their footsteps retreating down the stairs, they felt a weight removed from their breasts which was almost insupportable. They ventured from their place of concealment, and hastening to the window, they beheld the ruffians emerge from the ruins, and they quickly vanished from sight in the distance. Overpowered with their feelings of gratitude, our hero and his wife sank upon their knees, and with clasped hands they poured forth their thanks to Heaven for their fortunate deliverance from the critical danger which had just threatened them.

"God be praised!" ejaculated Mary, fervently, "we are once more saved from the most imminent peril. Oh, Richard, had those desperate men discovered us, our destruction would have been inevitable. I shudder to think of it."

"Compose yourself, my dear Mary," said our hero; "for we are now, for the present, at least, out of danger, and may safely rest here for awhile, until we have in some measure recovered ourselves from the excitement which this adventure has naturally occasioned us. It is not yet daylight, and you have not sufficient strength to proceed on our weary and uncertain journey at present."

"Oh, yes," replied Mary; "I feel much better now, and think that I should be able to proceed with less difficulty than you seem to imagine. These ruins, especially after what has occurred, inspire me with feelings of dread, which I cannot conquer. Come, let us depart."

"Nay," returned Richard; "why in such haste? We have nothing now to fear, and should we venture forth just yet, we might chance to encounter these ruffians who have already caused us so much alarm, and then the consequences would probably be of the most terrible description. Let us wait here patiently for an hour or two; Heaven knows how you will be able to support the want, privation, fatigue, and anxiety to which you are exposed."

"Fear not for me, Richard," said the patient wife, "for Providence will yet give me strength to support all the trials to which we may be subjected, could I but see you safely delivered from the numerous dangers by which you have so long been surrounded, and restored to that position in society which you have ever ornamented, and from which, had it not been for the villany of that man from whom we have to date all our misfortunes, you would never have been estranged."

Richard shook his head mournfully as he replied—

"I would fain hope so, my Mary; but,

alas! when I come to take all the circumstances of my fate into consideration, I find it to be a task which it is impossible for me to accomplish. The fearful calamity which has cast us upon this strange and wild place, is one of the most terrible misfortunes which has hitherto befallen us; and the fate of poor old Binnacle, in his humane and christian efforts to endeavour to serve us, has made an impression on my mind which nothing can ever eradicate."

"Alas! poor old man," ejaculated Mary, "it was, indeed, awful that, after living for so many years, and performing so many noble and virtuous deeds, he should perish thus. But let us not dwell upon the painful subject, Richard, for it was the will of Providence, which we must not presume to question."

"True," answered our hero: "but yet the decree seems cruel and severe. But, alas! it seems to be ordained that I should bring ruin, misery, and destruction upon all those who interest themselves in my welfare."

"Banish all such ideas from your mind, Richard, and try to view all the unfortunate circumstances with which our fate is surrounded with different feelings. God's will be done, and I sincerely hope that, notwithstanding the gloomy prospects that are at present spread before us, the time is not far distant when we shall experience a happy change, and at least be restored to some degree of tranquillity."

"Tranquillity, I fear, will never again be mine," answered our hero; "I could endure everything myself with the fortitude and resignation which become a man, but to see you and our poor boy suffer, completely everpowers me, and almost drives me to distraction. But come, we will no longer dwell upon this mournful subject; let us endeavour to rest ourselves for an hour or two, and then we will proceed on our way, with the hope that Providence will afford us some relief. Surely we shall meet with some benevolent person who will take compassion on us, and at least afford us some temporary assistance, till we can make up our minds what course it will be most prudent for us to pursue, in the painful and bewildering difficulties by which we are surrounded."

"We are destitute, Richard," said his wife, with a sigh, "and in a strange place, where we are unknown to any one. I much fear that we shall find it a difficult, if not an almost hopeless task to move the hearts of any one in our favour. Alas! did my inexorable father but know the dreadful sufferings to which we are and have been so long exposed, his heart must be moved to pity, and he would no longer hesitate to relieve and forgive us for that to which we were alone urged by the love we entertained for each other, and his unjust opposition to our wishes."

"Ah! no, Mary," said her husband; "it would be little short of madness to think of such a thing. Too well do I know the implacable disposition of your father, and the hatred and feelings of revenge which he bears towards me, to believe that he will forgive us; but, on the contrary, did he but know the place where I am at present concealed, he would be the first to denounce me, and to betray me into the hands of the law. Never can he forget the death of his favourite, Captain Arlington, and viewing me only in the character of his murderer, he thirsts for my blood, and would exult to see me mount the gallows."

"Horrible thought!" exclaimed Mary; "inexorable even as I know him to be, he cannot be so entirely lost to every proper feeling of humanity. And yet, when I think of the manner in which he discarded me, his only child, from his breast, and invoked a curse upon my head, my heart sinks within me, and the worst fears crowd upon my brain. Oh, my father, how little have I deserved such cruel treatment at your hands, for Heaven knows how much I studied to prove to you the affection I bore towards you, and how ardently I sught to promote your happiness."

"True, my Mary," said our hero, "and you have nothing whatever to reproach yourself with. But it is strange what has become of your father; for he has retired for some years from Exeter, and although we have every reason to believe that he is still living, we have no idea where he is at present residing."

"No," said Mary; "and it is that which tortures me more than all, for did I but know where he is now residing, I would write to him, and surely the appeal which I would make to his feelings would move him to mercy and compassion."

"It is a vain and delusive hope," said our hero; "banish it from your mind, my dear Mary, for, rest assured, that no appeal that you could make to his feelings would induce him to relent. There is one gentle being of whom I greatly feel the loss, and the mystery of whose fate often tortures my mind."

"To whom do you allude?" asked Mary.

"To my fair and amiable cousin, Amy Parker," answered Richard. "In her, I am certain, that we should ever find a kind and sympathising friend."

"Oh, yes," said our heroine ; "poor Amy, how much are we already indebted to her ; and her sudden disappearance from her native place, without any cause assigned, is a mystery which I have never been able to penetrate. Alas! I fear that she must have met with some strange and untimely fate, or she surely would have corresponded with us in our misfortunes, and have made us acquainted with all that had happened to her."

"The more I reflect on the circumstances," remarked Richard, "the deeper am I involved in perplexity. But I hope that, if she be still living, we shall meet again, and that all will be explained."

"God grant that it may," ejaculated Mary; "oh, how greatly do we stand in need of such a gentle friend and adviser in the midst of our troubles."

"From the observations of the ruffians from whom we have just now so providentially escaped," said our hero, after a pause, "there are numerous treasures buried beneath these ruins. Could we discoved the secret trap, and gain access to them, we should probably find the means of releasing ourselves from our present desperate situation, and——"

"Nay, Richard," interrupted his wife, "suffer not such a thought to retain possession of your mind; are they not the proceeds of the most heartless, the most diabolical villany, the plunder of the dead? and to touch them would be putting ourselves upon a level with the wretches who so surreptitiously obtained them. No, I can endure every misery rather than that we should be guilty of that. But come; see, the morning dawns; I feel greatly recovered from my fatigue now. Let us depart."

"Alas! I fear that you overrate your strength," returned her husband, "and that you will never be able to perform so long a journey. Besides, see, the skies are again lowering, and, ere long, I fear, we shall have a renewal of the storm. You remain here, Mary, with our boy, for you have nothing te fear, and I will hasten and endeavour, with the slender means which I possess, to procure some provisions, of which you stand so much in need."

"Oh, no," answered our heroine, "I dare not think of such a thing; to remain here alone in this dismal place, and after what has happened, would be more than I could endure. We must not separate, dear Richard, but share whatever dangers may be in store for us together. Come, I am fully prepared for the journey, and

God grant that no fresh calamity may befall us."

It was truly wonderful, under all the circumstances, the fortitude which our heroine displayed; and Richard, finding that it was useless seeking to persuade her, yielded; and, having once more invoked the protection of Heaven, they prepared to leave the room, having first looked forth from the window to ascertain whether or not any of the ruffians whom they had so much cause to dread were still lurking about the ruins. The coast, however, was quite clear, and they then descended the stairs, Mary leaning on the arm of her husband, for, in spite of all her efforts to conceal it, she still felt so weak and exhausted, that she could with difficulty support her tottering limbs. When they reached the lower part of the ruins, our hero paused, for he still felt the most anxious curiosity to discover the secret entrance to the cave or vault in which the wreckers had deposited their booty ; and in spite of the remonstrances of his wife, he stooped down and examined the broken pavement minutely, but not the least traces of any secret trap could he perceive, and he was involved in doubt and perplexity.

"It is most strange," he remarked ; "a secret trap must be somewhere here concealed, that it may defy discovery."

"Come, come," said Mary, impatiently, "why do you seek to penetrate that which does not concern you? Let us away from these dreary ruins, for there may be danger threatening us while we remain here."

Our hero returned no answer, but yielding to his wife's persuasions, he again took her arm, and they emerged from the ruins, and having first looked around them to see that they were not watched by any one, they proceeded on their way, using the precaution, however, of taking a different route to that which they had perceived the wreckers to take.

CHAPTER XXXI.

THE FURTHER SUFFERINGS OF THE WANDERERS.—THE APPEAL FOR HELP.— THE COTTAGE.—THE BRUTAL HUSBAND. —HOSPITALITY REFUSED. — ANOTHER NIGHT OF HORROR.

ALTHOUGH their progress, in consequence of the weak condition of our heroine, was necessarily slow, they at length got to some distance from the ruins, and were compelled to pause and rest themselves. It was a cold bleak morning, and dark clouds had long been gathering in the sky, which portended another approaching storm ; and it was not long ere some large drops of rain began to descend, and gave sufficient warning as to what the wretched wanderers had cause to expect. There was little or no change in the prospect ; all was sad and cheerless, and as yet they had not seen any signs of a human being or habitation, and they were at a loss which way to proceed. The paleness of Mary's looks, and her trembling limbs, alarmed her husband, and he looked around in despir, with the hope of discovering some place where they might obtain relief, for he thought it would be utterly impossible for her to proceed much further; but nothing of the kind met his observation, though he strained his eyes in every direction, and he was at a loss what to do.

"Alas ! my poor wife," he ejaculated, " how torturing is it to me to witness your sufferings, and I have not the power to relieve you. What will become of us? It is in vain that you strive to deceive me ; it will, I am convinced, be impossible for you to proceed much further, and we seem to be no nearer to relief than ever we were."

"Do not agitate yourself thus," she replied, " but trust to Providence to support me throughout this trial. Ere long, I hope, we shall meet with some friendly dwelling, and those who are willing to assist us ; let us then seek to await patiently and with resignation."

' Patience and resignation !" repeated Richard; " oh, is not this a severe trial to them both? Dear Mary, you may seek to conceal from me the real state of your feelings, and to inspire me with hope, but I am satisfied that unless some speedy relief presents itself, you will never be able to bear up against the anguish of mind and the fatigue of body to which you are subjected."

"Nay—nay, say not so," replied Mary, with a faint smile; "indeed, you do but unnecessarily alarm yourself, for I am better now; come, Richard, I feel myself enabled to proceed with fresh strength and courage."

"Heroic woman !" exclaimed her husband, "how cruel it is to think that your energies should be put to such a test."

As he thus spoke, he once more supported her delicate and exhausted frame, and they again proceeded on their way, though it was with but slow and faltering steps, and without meeting with anything to reanimate their hopes.

The rain now came down in torrents, the wind blowing at the same time fiercely, and being but thinly clad, they were soon drenched to the skin, and were shivering with the cold. Our hero was scarcely in any better condition than his wife, although he tried to struggle against it to the utmost of his power, and it was with difficulty that he himself could proceed and support the devoted partner of his misfortunes on her way. Their situation was certainly one of the most deplorable that could well be imagined, and it was wonderful how they were enabled to support it as they did. The conduct of the boy, William, under the peculiarly trying circumstances, was beyond all praise; he bore himself up in the most courageous manner, and never once uttered a word of complaint; but it was quite evident that, unless some speedy relief should present itself, he could not long remain proof against such extraordinary exertions as those which they had to undergo.

In this wretched manner about half an hour passed away, and, of course, in the state they were in, they had not been able to make much progress, and the storm rather increased than abated, so that they had everything to render them wretched and despairing. They now almost regretted that they had quitted the ruins, and yet how was it possible that they could have survived there many hours longer without food, of which they had not partaken for so long a time?

At length, on suddenly emerging into a more open part of the forest, their eyes were gladdened by the sight of a neat but humble cottage, from the casement of which gleamed the reflection of a cheerful fire, and they could not help giving utterance to an exclamation of satisfaction.

"Thank God !" cried our hero, fervently, "our prayers have been heard. Now, if this cottage does but contain some kind and humane being, we may at least hope to find some temporary relief. Come, my dear Mary, let us at once test the hospitality of the inhabitant of this humble but welcome dwelling."

Mary returned no answer, but she breathed a secret prayer to Heaven that their hopes might not be disappointed, and suffered her husband to lead her towards the cottage, at the door of which they stopped, and listening, heard the voice of a female singing some simple ballad, in tones that were far more noisy than musical. Parker knocked gently at the door, but the woman still continued with her song, and did not seem to have heard it; so he repeated the knock still louder than before, and the voice then ceased, and immediately afterwards the door of the cottage was opened, and a female presented herself, and started back with an expression of surprise on beholding strangers.

She was a woman about the middle-age, and attired in the most humble apparel; but her countenance was rather expressive of kindness and simplicity than otherwise. She seemed to look upon the miserable appearance of Richard and our heroine with some degree of sympathy, but was too much confused and surprised to say a word, and Parker, therefore, was the first to speak.

"My good woman," he said, "no doubt you are astonished at seeing strangers; but you need be under no apprehension, I assure you. We are unfortunate individuals who suffered shipwreck in the storm the night before last: we are wet, hungry, and fatigued, and would solicit your humble assistance, if it is in your power to render us any."

The woman hesitated for a minute or two, and then, in a broad, Cornish accent, she replied—

"Why, you see, my friends, that my heart's good enough to do it, but I am afraid; for, should my husband come to know it, he is such a strange man that he would never forgive me for it. He has little pity for his fellow creatures; but he is now from home, at his business in the wood, and as you do look sad enough, poor things, I will e'en venture it, though it is little enough, God knows, that I have got to offer you. So come in—come in, and warm and dry yourselves by the fire."

Most warmly did Richard return his thanks for the generous hospitality of the woman, and taking the arm of his wife, they walked into the cottage, which they found to be remarkable for its cleanliness and the neatness of its humble furniture. The woman invited them to take their seats by the fire, with which they readily and gratefully complied, and the sudden change had such an effect upon our heroine that it almost overpowered her, and it was not without difficulty that she could prevent herself from fainting. Richard, however, exerted himself to the utmost to revive her, and the woman seemed to view her with increased compassion.

"Poor thing!" she said, "you seem to have suffered much, and are evidently very ill. Have you no friends about here?"

"Alas! no, my good woman," answered Richard. "We are complete strangers here, and have not the slightest knowledge of the country. Every soul on board the ill-fated ship, with the exception of ourselves, perished, and since then the sufferings we have undergone have been awful. If you can grant us some temporary relief, let it be ever so humble, we shall be most grateful. My poor wife is, as you see, reduced to the last extremity."

"Ay, poor soul, so she seems to be," returned the woman, compassionately. "I have not much to offer you, for I am only the wife of a poor woodman, but such as it is you are heartily welcome, for my own part, though I would not have my husband know it for the world; for, as I said before, he is such a strange man, gruff and uncouth in his manners, and he looks upon all his fellow creatures with suspicion and dislike. God forgive me for saying so, but it is the truth, as I know it to my sorrow."

"Then there is no hope of our being accommodated in your cottage for a day or two, I fear," said our hero.

"Accommodated here?" repeated the woman, with a look of surprise and consternation. "Lor bless you, no. Why, we have scarcely room for ourselves; and if you were even to hint such a thing to my husband, I verily believe that it would drive him frantic."

"Is there no town or village near this spot," said Richard, "where we can hope to obtain some relief?"

"Yes," replied the cottager; "there is a little village about a mile and a half from here, but it is inhabited chiefly by wreckers and the worst of characters, and there is not much chance of your obtaining either pity or relief from them."

"Alas—alas!" sighed Mary, wringing her hands, "then, indeed, is our condition most deplorable and hopeless."

"Nay, say not so, my good woman," remarked the cottager, "for Providence is good and merciful, and will come to your aid. I am sure I would relieve you if I could; but it is not in my power, and Robert is not one to make any impression on. But try to compose yourself as well as you can, and I will get you such refreshments as my poor dwelling affords."

Our hero and his wife again returned their warmest thanks to the kind-hearted woman, and she bustled about, and soon placed before them such humble provisions as she had, and which consisted principally of fish, a few vegetables, and some coarse brown bread, which, to the hapless wanderers, however, in their present famishing state, was extremely welcome, and they partook of it heartily. The cottager, however, produced a bottle containing some cordial, of an agreeable

RICHARD PARKER'S ENCOUNTER WITH BUBBLE.

favour, of which Mary and her husband partook; and that, and the warmth of the fire, served to revive them more than all. The repast over, the woman removed the things, and then, taking a seat near the fire, she seemed to eye them with much curiosity and sympathy.

"Well," she said. "I hope you feel better, now. Ah, shipwreck is a dreadful thing, and they must possess bad hearts, indeed, who cannot pity those who suffer by it."

"True, my good woman," returned Richard, "and the sentiments you express do you honour."

"Ah," said the cottager, "I only wish my husband was of my way of thinking: it would make me a much happier woman than I now am. But, however, it is no use complaining, and, perhaps, it is wrong of me to speak thus of my husband: that's neither here nor there. Have you come from far, friends?"

"Yes," answered Richard, evading the question as well as he could, "a long distance from here, and we have lost nearly all we possessed in the wreck, and Heaven only knows what will now become of us, in a strange place, and without a friend to whom we could apply. I care not for myself, but it is my anxiety for my poor wife, and this unfortunate boy, my son, that distracts me."

"Believe me, my unfortunate friends," said the cottager, "that I pity you, and only regret that it is not in my power to serve you more than I have done. But I have not the means, and should Robert come home, and find you here, though I do not expect him till night, I should have to suffer for it most severely."

"We should deeply regret your having to do so," returned Richard, "and although the task we have to perform is an arduous one, and Heaven only knows how we shall accomplish it, after you have permitted us to rest ourselves awhile, and till the storm shall in some measure have abated, we will resume our wretched and hopeless journey. But, alas! know you of no place where we may be likely to obtain a shelter for the night?"

"Not any," answered the cottager, "unless you should be able to obtain relief at the mansion of Squire Melborough, of Melborough Hall, which is situated about two miles beyond the village I have mentioned to you; and it is not at all unlikely but you might; for although the squire is a very eccentric gentleman, and keeps himself almost secluded from the world, I believe he is far from being uncharitable."

"But I fear that he would consider it a boldness in individuals so humble as ourselves to apply to him for relief," said our hero.

"Then he must possess no true charity in his heart, if he could do so. But you must excuse me, my friends; I have got a little business to perform in the next apartment, and, as I dare say you can dispense with my society, I will leave you to yourselves."

She then departed from the room, and Richard and his wife were left to indulge in such conversation as this adventure was calculated to give rise to.

"Oh, Richard," sighed our heroine; "how dismal are still our prospects. Where can we find a shelter and relief? Whither can we direct our footsteps?"

"Alas!" he replied, "I know not; the fates have evidently conspired against us, and all our efforts to extricate ourselves from the difficulties by which we are on every side surrounded are completely unavailable. It is impossible that you can ever find strength sufficient to support this extraordinary demand upon your energies: and should you sink beneath the blow, there is nothing left for me but to rush upon my fate, for life would then become insupportable to me."

"For Heaven's sake cease to make use of observations such as these," said Mary, "for it tortures my soul to listen to you. Severe as the trial is, I feel convinced that I shall yet find strength sufficient to endure it, and I will still hope that something will shortly occur to extricate us from the many troubles in which we are at present involved."

The woman now returned to the room, and again expressed a hope, in her plain and simple way, that her unfortunate guests were better, and her deep regret that it was not in her power to accommodate them to the full extent of her wishes and inclination.

"Believe me, my good woman," returned Parker, "that we fully appreciate your kindness, and that we shall ever entertain a lively sense of it. But think you that your husband is so entirely insensible to the dictates of humanity as to refuse a temporary shelter in his cottage to unfortunate individuals placed in the situation of ourselves?"

"Oh, yes," she answered; "I grieve to say that his heart is entirely insensible to pity; his disposition is selfish and suspicious; and should he return home and find you here, he would not only abuse me, but no doubt would insult yourself and your wife grossly."

"I fear, then," remarked Mrs. Parker, "if that is his disposition, you have but a sorry life with him, and it is a pity that a woman who possesses the kindness of heart which you seem to do, should ever have been united to one so unworthy of you."

"But Robert was not always the same character that he is now," said the cottager; "there was a time when he was gentle, kind, and generous, and there was no one more rejoiced than he was whenever he had the opportunity of serving his fellow creatures."

"What could have wrought so strange and painful an alteration?" said Richard. Before, however, she could return any reply, there was a loud knock at the cottage door, and the coarse voice of a man called upon the name of "Maud," and with an oath, demanded why she kept him waiting in the rain. She turned pale and trembled as she listened to this, and in a faint voice, she ejaculated to Richard and his wife—

"It is he, and you here; oh, dear, what will become of me?"

"Why, Maud, I say!" cried the husband, again knocking loudly at the door, "where the devil are you? Are you asleep, that you do not hear me? or is it your intention to keep me here all day? Open the door, I say."

Tremblingly, poor Maud obeyed, and gave admittance to her uncouth and savage husband, who entered the room with a bundle of faggots on his shoulder, which he tossed on to the floor, and then turning to his wife, for he did not at first perceive that there was any one in the cottage but herself, he again with an oath demanded the reason she had kept him waiting outside so long; to which she returned some evasive answer, with which he seemed to be far from satisfied.

He was a tall and muscular man, apparently about fifty, and the rude and savage expression of his features fully indicated his character. There was a sinister expression about his eyes that was particularly repulsive, and Mary as she gazed upon him could scarcely help shuddering.

"I shall do no more work to day," he said; "for such weather as this is not fit for a dog to be out in; stow them faggots away, do you hear? and—Oh! who have we here?" he added, starting, as he suddenly beheld Richard and his wife; "strangers! intruders! What is the meaning of this?—Explain!"

"Pardon me, my friend," replied Richard, calmly: "we are sorry if we have intruded upon your hospitality, but we have lately suffered shipwreck, are poor, destitute, and wretched, and happening to wander near your cottage, we took the liberty of asking for shelter from the storm."

"Which, I suppose, my wife was fool enough to give you, forgetting altogether that we are as poor as church mice, I suppose, and that I have to work early and late to be able to get a bare existence?"

"I beg you will not blame her, sir," remarked our hero; "for she acted, I am convinced, only from the purest motives of humanity."

"Humanity be d——d!" said the ruffian, fiercely; "such beggars in the world as we are cannot afford to be humane; I have enough to do to look after myself, and those who would accept of anything from my table, I look upon as nothing better than common robbers."

The bosom of our hero swelled with feelings of indignation and resentment at these insolent observations, and rising proudly from his seat, and fixing upon the brutal fellow a look of reproach, he said—

"Sir, such remarks are uncalled for, and unmerited by those who have been unfortunately driven to accept of a trifling favour at your hands, and, allow me to say, reflect the greatest discredit upon any one who can make use of them."

"Bah!" said the fellow, impatiently: "it is not likely that I am going to submit to be thus schooled by a stranger and intruder in my dwelling; and, therefore, to be candid with you, the sooner you depart from here the better."

"Oh, Robert, Robert," remonstrated his wife; "have you no feeling for——"

"Hold your tongue, fool!" interrupted the vulgar wretch, "unless you would exasperate me more than you have done already. Why should I submit to have my place intruded upon by every idle vagrant who passes this way? I want no further explanation with you, my man," he added, seeing that Richard was about to speak. "Be satisfied with what you have already obtained, and leave this place immediately."

"Alas—alas!" sighed Mary, "and while the storm continues to rage thus violently? Do not close your heart entirely to every feeling of pity."

"I have said the word," returned the woodman, in the same fierce and disagreeable tones. "Why am I thus annoyed in my own dwelling?"

"Come, my Mary," said Richard, taking the arm of his wife, and fixing upon the woodman a look of the utmost disgust and contempt; "it is useless to remonstrate with such a man as this. His heart is evidently callous to every proper feeling. We must again put our sole dependance on the Almighty, and He, I trust, will be more merciful than man. To you, my good woman, we owe our best thanks for your kindness, and believe me that we shall ever remember you in the prayers we offer up to the Supreme."

Maud looked her feelings, but she was afraid to make any reply, for fear of the more exciting the wrath of her savage husband; and our hero, taking the arm of his wife, and fixing upon Robert, the woodman, a look of mingled reproach and scorn, the wretched wanderers slowly retired from the cottage, and once more entered the open air, exposed to all the pitiless pelting of the storm, and without knowing whither to direct their steps, where they might meet with those who would compassionate their deplorable and destitute situation.

The rain had not in the least abated, and the wind was so cold and bleak, that it seemed to penetrate to their very hearts, and to freeze up every faculty. But for some short distance they walked on, and were so overwhelmed by the various feelings that crowded upon them that they could not exchange a single word with one another.

"Oh, God!" at last ejaculated Mary, "of what have we ever been guilty that we should be doomed to suffer thus? Hope seems to have vanished from us altogether, and in whatever direction we turn ourselves, nothing but misery and despair present themselves to our metal vision. And then to be insulted—to have our feelings wounded as they have just been, that can but add to the torture it is our hard lot to endure."

"The heartless wretch!" exclaimed our hero. "There was a time when, had he thus have dared to insult Richard Parker, I would have felled him to the earth, and given him ample cause to repent of his audacity. But whither can we now go? Where can we hope to find sympathy and relief? It seems, alas! but too painfully evident that there is none for us. Mary—Mary, it is evident that I am accursed of God and man, and that I have involved you in the same ban as myself. I am a wretch unfit to live; and why should you——"

"Forbear—forbear!" interrupted his wife. "Such fearful words as those you have just now uttered are uncalled for, and can but serve to shock my feelings. You have nothing to upbraid yourself so severely with, for the misfortunes that have come upon you were not of your own seeking, but were brought about by the villany and injustice of others. Let us, then, still seek to bear up against it with redoubled fortitude, and to struggle against our fate as long as we can, with the hope that we shall be able to surmount every obstacle that is thrown in the way of our happiness."

Richard was too overpowered by his feelings to be capable of speaking, and they proceeded for some distance farther in gloomy silence, our hero endeavouring all he could to shield the delicate form of his wife from the wind and the rain, though his efforts to do so were crowned with little or no success, and they were both shortly again wet to the skin. The short time they had been at the woodman's cottage, and the refreshments of which they had partaken, had served to revive them; and, therefore, they were better enabled to withstand the inclemency of the weather than they would otherwise have been; but still the continual excitement and anxiety of mind they had for so many months experienced had naturally made such inroads on their constitution, that it seemed impossible they could do otherwise than sink under their effects, should they be exposed to them much longer.

At length, the curling smoke from the different chimneys convinced them that they were near approaching some village; and their hopes in some measure revived, for they thought that they should surely, notwithstanding all that they had heard of the character of the inhabitants, be able to meet with some place where, for the small sum of money they had in their possession, they should be able to procure some assistance; or, at any rate, that the village might contain some public-house, where they would be almost certain to obtain accommodation. Inspired with these hopes, they pressed on their way with renewed vigour, and soon came within sight of the village, which consisted of about twenty straggling wooden huts or cottages, which had anything but an inviting appearance, and bespoke either extreme poverty or neglect. The hearts of the wanderers sickened as they gazed upon them, and for a moment or two they hesitated, and were almost inclined to continue their journey; but there was no time for delay, and Richard, still supporting the weak and trembling form of his faithful partner, and William walking by their side, approached the door of the first, and again paused and listened before he ventured to knock. There was a strong smell of tobacco-smoke from within, and, as the fugitives approached the door, loud laughter saluted their ears, followed by the coarsest language, which showed plainly the character of the inmates, and fully corroborated what Maud had told them.

As Mary listened to these disgusting sounds, she shrank back in terror, and said, in a low voice to her husband—

"Oh, no—do not make any application here. It is evident that those who inhabit the cottage are not the sort of individuals from whom we might expect pity or relief, and we should only get insulted. I would sooner remain exposed to the terrors of the storm than venture to seek their aid. Let us begone."

Richard could say nothing in opposition to this, for it was too reasonable, and they walked again from the hut, and proceeded to the next, where their ears were saluted with similar sounds; and so it was with several others, but at last they arrived at one which seemed to be more quiet than the rest, and here our hero ventured to knock, and the door was immediately afterwards opened by a man of the most forbidding aspect, who stared rudely and narrowly upon them, as he demanded—

"How now—what do you want here?"

"A shelter from the rain, my good man," replied Richard, "and——"

"Ah," interrupted the man, "beggars! Begone, or, mayhap, I may find the means to make you do so much quicker than you came here."

With that the ruffian shook his fist at them in a threatening manner, and then banged the door abruptly in their faces.

"Oh, let us away from this wretched place," cried Mary, bursting into tears. "It is useless to expect any relief from here, and we know not what danger may threaten us while we remain."

"And whither can we go, my unfortunate wife?" said Richard. "You are now completely worn out, and our prospects are as gloomy and hopeless as ever. If we could only meet with some inn, or public-house, notwithstanding our means are so limited, we surely could procure that accommodation of which we stand so much in need. Heaven only knows what our fate will be, though I cannot but anticipate the worst. Come, my Mary, we must e'en proceed on our dreary way as well as we can, and pray to the Almighty to assist us in the midst of all these our difficulties."

Our heroine sighed, but returned no other answer, and suffering her husband to lead her away, they slowly quitted the wretched village. Wet, weary, and heart-broken, they crawled on, for their limbs now almost refused to perform their office, and every step they took they became weaker; while the ghastly paleness of their careworn countenances, and the expression of despair which was settled in their eyes, was quite painful to contemplate. There seemed to be not the least likelihood of the storm subsiding, and whichever way the unfortunate wanderers turned their eyes, nought but misery and despair met them. At length, when they had got to some distance from the village, they came in sight of what appeared to be the remains of a cow-shed, but which would afford them a partial shelter, and Mary, in a faint voice ejaculated—

"Dear Richard, I have struggled with my feelings as long as I could, but nature is exhausted; my limbs fail me, and I can proceed no further at present. Here, then, we must stop, and leave our future fate in the hands of Providence. Alas! I fear there is another night of horror in store for us."

"Heaven forbid!" returned Richard; "surely we shall not much longer be permitted to be exposed to this misery. The mansion which the woodman's wife mentioned, should we be able to reach that, and as she said it was only about a mile and a half from the village, we cannot be far from it, we probably might obtain relief. We can remain here until the storm has passed over; by that time you will, perhaps, have in some measure recruited your strength, and you will be enabled to resume your journey."

They sheltered themselves in the shed from the rain as well as they could, and huddling themselves close together for the sake of warmth, they awaited the result with heavy hearts. Above an hour passed away, and no change came o'er their situation; the rain still came down in torrents, and the wind continued to howl with unabated violence. Night gradually set in, and the dreariness of their situation became more intense and insupportable.

"Would to Heaven that this storm would abate," said our hero; "but even then, my poor Mary, I fear that you would not find strength sufficient to proceed; and the night wears on apace. If the storm abates not shortly, we shall stand no chance to meet with a shelter at all. Oh, how agonising is this suspense."

"Give not way to this state of excitement, Richard," remonstrated his wife; "for it can answer no purpose, and may only serve to aggravate the anguish of our condition; you shall find that I will still remain firm under the most trying difficulties; and I will yet place my dependance upon the goodness and mercy of the Most High."

"Oh, Mary!" ejaculated Parker, at the same time he fixed upon the pale, but still lovely features of his wife, a look of mingled affection, admiration, and regret; "what a noble and heroic soul do you possess, which thus enables you to combat with the most unparalleled misfortunes—misfortunes that are sufficient to daunt even the stoutest heart. How little do you deserve to be put to the severe trials that you have been; and to know that I have no power to relieve you, or to afford you the least room for hope or consolation, tortures me more than all."

"Richard," replied Mary, and her looks fully told the sincerity of her feelings, "oh, how well do I appreciate the sentiments that throb at your bosom, and believe me that I murmur not at the destiny which it has pleased Providence to mark out for me; my whole anxiety is for yourself and our child, and to see you exposed to all these sufferings racks my soul to madness. But hope is not yet extinct within my breast. Dark and dreary though our prospects at present are, I feel convinced that the time is still not far distant when we shall be restored to tranquillity, if not to complete happiness."

"Sweet soother!" exclaimed Richard, again embracing her fondly, "I should be unworthy of your love and faithful devotedness, did I not endeavour to be calm, and to support you through this awful trial; but still when I think of the utter misery and loneliness of our situation, is it not enough to fill my heart with despair? Another night of horror is before us, and yet no prospect of relief presents itself to us. Oh, could we but reach the mansion of this gentleman, somethings seems to convince me that we should meet with that timely assistance which we so much require in this the terrible hour of our emergency."

"Would to Heaven that your words might prove prophetic," observed our heroine; "and yet," she added, after a brief pause, "I almost dread to venture thither."

"And why, my Mary?" eagerly interrogated her husband.

"It is strange and unaccountable," answered his wife, pressing her thin, fair hand upon her forehead, "but a dismal foreboding presents itself to my mind that we should there encounter something that would add to our anguish, and perhaps plunge us into that immediate danger which we are so anxious to avoid."

"Nay," said her husband, "surely those fears are groundless and premature, and you would do well to banish them from your mind. What should we apprehend? It is not likely that there is any one who knows us in this place, or who can have the slightest motive for doing us any harm."

"True," coincided our heroine; "and the fears I have expressed may seem ridiculous, but still I cannot get rid of the impression. Alas! alas! our fate is most terrible and uncertain, kind Heaven take pity on us. How dark and dreary is all around; and it is so cold, so very cold."

She shuddered as she spoke, and had it not been for the support of her agonised husband, she must have sunk to the earth. With what poignant feelings of anguish did he hold her in his arms, press her to his bosom, and try to shield her delicate form from the pattering rain which the wind blew fiercely into the frail shelter to which they had betaken themselves. But every moment her strength seemed to fail

her more and more, although she struggled against exhausted nature with an energy that was truly wonderful. How frequently did Richard strain his eyes through the darkness, with the hope of seeing some individual who might probably take compassion on them, and guide them to a place of shelter and security; but nothing appeared to cheer his prospects, and as he gazed upon the increasing horrors of the night, his agony of mind became the more intense. The boy William, too, it was evident, notwithstanding all his efforts to conceal it, was fast sinking with fatigue; and it was wonderful that one so young should have been able to support such unexampled hardships as those to which he had been exposed so long, and with such remarkable fortitude. Thus did the time wear tediously and drearily away, and still no prospect of deliverance from their present painful situation presented itself. Richard exerted himself as much as possible to revive the exhausted nature of his wife, and to inspire her with that feeling of hope, which, although he affected it, he was far from experiencing himself; but his efforts were crowned with little or no success, notwithstanding Mary herself did all that she could to combat with the effects of the dreadful fatigue and exertions, as well as the intense anxiety of mind, she had for so long a time undergone. Every moment the perils of their situation became greater, and the brain of our unfortunate hero was worked up to a state bordering upon madness.

And thus another hour passed away, and Mary was so much worn out that she was incapable of speaking, though the melancholy looks which she fixed upon the countenance of her husband spoke a language much more powerful than words could have expressed, and affected him more than all. He pressed his hand upon his burning forehead, and as he gazed still more despairingly upon the horrors around him, he could not help groaning aloud in the agony of his feelings.

"Our doom is sealed," he exclaimed; "all hope of succour is at an end; the curse of Heaven is upon us, and in vain may we seek to avoid its terrible decree. What a frightful destiny is this to have to undergo! What a state of lingering death, without one compassionate friend at hand to sympathise with or console us. And must we, indeed, perish thus? Are there no means of averting the fate which is at present impending o'er our heads? My God—my God! I humbly, but most earnestly beseech Thee to have mercy upon us, and not to permit us thus to suffer horrors which are greater, far greater than human nature can endure. Mary, my beloved, my devoted, my suffering, my heroic wife, you are sinking fast. The fearful truth is too apparent to me for me to suffer myself to be deceived, or to flatter myself with any false and delusive hopes; and yet you seek to conceal it from me. Alas! what can I do? What possible means can I adopt that are at all calculated to relieve you? For myself I care not; but you and my child, to see you suffer thus, is agony most unspeakable—most insupportable!"

Mary aroused herself as well as she could, and, fixing upon him such a look of tenderness as was sufficient to make a powerful impression upon even the most insensible heart, she with difficulty said—

"Torture not yourself thus, I implore of you, dear Richard, for it is the will of Heaven to subject us to this dreadful trial, and, however hard the task, I will endeavour to submit without a murmur. I—I shall be better soon; this storm will abate, my strength will be renewed, and we shall be enabled to proceed; and should we be fortunate enough to reach the mansion to which we have been directed, something seems to assure me that we shall there find that relief of which we both stand so much in need. Come, come, be calm, and do not abandon yourself entirely to despair."

"Ah!" said our hero, with a sigh, for he was completely unnerved, "how can I help doing so, under all the awful circumstances in which we are placed? This, indeed, amidst all our sufferings, is the most awful night that we have ever experienced. The warring elements—everything frowns upon us, and too plainly show that our doom is sealed, and that nothing whatever can rescue us from the horrors by which we are environed. Had we perished in the wreck, it would have been much better for us than to have to endure this state of lingering suffering."

"Say not so, Richard," returned his wife, in a faint voice, "but, rather, seek to dissipate from your mind the present painful impressions, and to look forward to the future with more sanguine expectations."

"Alas! Mary," he said, "how useless is it for you to talk thus! What room is there for us to hope, when hitherto every one that we have formed has been doomed to be disappointed? It is in vain that I may seek to follow your advice, though, at the same time, I feel thoroughly convinced that, in your heart, you cannot really think as you express yourself, since it is opposed to all reason or probability."

Mary tried to answer him, but she could not. The little strength she had exerted herself to display failed her, and she again sank back almost fainting in her husband's arms, while the ghastly expression of her features was sufficient to inspire him with the most poignant feelings of alarm. He pressed her with the deepest anguish more closely to his bosom, and again he gazed anxiously forth into the darkness with the vain hope of perceiving some chance of assistance; but none whatever presented themselves, and every instant their situation became the more awful. Still the tempest raged, if possible, with increased violence, and there appeared to be not the least chance of its abating, and the cold was so intense, that, wet to the skin as they were, they trembled in every limb, and presented altogether a spectacle that was quite painful and melancholy to contemplate. But they were suddenly aroused from the lethargy of despair into which they had naturally fallen, by hearing the voice of a man at some short distance off, who, notwithstanding the miserable state of the weather, was indulging himself in a song, and seemed to be, from the gusto with which he sang—or, rather, vociferated it, in the most cheerful state of mind.

"Ah!" ejaculated our hero, "thank Heaven some one at last approaches this way from whom we may obtain information and assistance. That man can possess no bad heart who can give utterance to such jovial sounds as those in such a dismal time as the present. Arouse yourself, my dear Mary, for something convinces me now that relief is not far distant."

"Oh, yes," replied our heroine; "we shall yet be saved. Hark! The man, whoever he is, approaches nearer. God grant that he may be some humane individual who will be moved to compassion at our distressed situation, and have it in his power to aid us in the midst of the difficulties by which we are at the present moment surrounded."

The sound of the voice now became more and more distinct, and it was evident that the man was approaching the spot where they stood, and their hopes were strengthened every instant. They both looked most anxiously towards the spot from whence the sounds proceeded, and at length, through the darkness, beheld the tall shadow of a human form, which gradually approached nearer, until it arrived to within a short distance of the place where they stood. It was that of a young man, clad in the humble garb of a rustic, but who, from what they could distinguish of his features, possessed an expressive, intelligent, and prepossessing countenance. He continued to sing merrily as he proceeded, and seemed to be completely regardless of the storm. He was, however, about to turn off in a contrary direction, when Richard called aloud to him, and he paused, apparently taken by surprise; but he quickly recovered himself, and immediately, directed by Richard's voice, advanced towards them, and was evidently struck by the melancholy sight which our hapless fugitives presented.

"Kind stranger," said our hero, "I implore your aid for my unfortunate wife and child, if it is in your power to afford us any. We are exhausted with long suffering and privation, and, strangers in this part of the country, we have no place in which we can seek a shelter from the storm."

"Poor creatures," said the man, feelingly, "your looks show much more than language could describe it, the sufferings to which you have been subjected, and I pity you from my very heart. This is a terrible night for any one to be exposed in, and Reuben Goodson will never refuse to assist his unfortunate fellow creatures when it is in his power. Poor woman, how weak and ill she looks; and this little boy, too. Oh, what can have brought you into this miserable situation?"

"Misfortunes of the most unexampled kind," replied Richard. "We were shipwrecked on this coast the night before last, and ever since have been wandering about without being able to meet with any one to assist us; if it is in your power to do so, our gratitude must be unbounded, and Heaven will most certainly reward you for your kindness and humanity."

"Well," returned the stranger, "I am but a poor man, yet I think I can assist you in the way you require. Not far from this spot is Melborough Hall, belonging to Squire Hallerton, who, though somewhat eccentric and austere in his manners, is nevertheless a good man, and has never yet refused assistance to those of his less fortunate fellow creatures who might stand in need of it. My mother lives housekeeper at the hall, and I am now going there; so, if you will accompany me, I will conduct you there, and I will undertake to say that you will not be turned away without that assistance which you evidently so much require."

"Oh, many thanks for this, kind stranger," ejaculated our heroine, fervently, and completely overwhelmed with gratitude; "Heaven will reward you for this important service rendered to those who are at present in so wretched a situation,

and who are almost worn out from the long sufferings with which it has been the will of Providence to visit them."

"No thanks, my good woman," replied Reuben, "for I require them not. You are most heartily welcome to anything which it may be in my humble power to do for you. But you are weak, and I fear that you will find it a difficult task to walk to the hall; however, I will assist you, and, as I before told you, it is at no great distance from this place. So come, my good friends, let us at once proceed."

Richard again returned his acknowledgments to the kind-hearted man, and then he and his wife and child quitted the shed, and Reuben having tendered his arm to Mary, which she accepted, supported by him and her husband, she proceeded on the way to the hall, taking now but little notice of the storm, which had not at all abated. As they walked on, Reuben expressed the gratification he felt at having met with them, and warmly eulogised the liberality and generosity of Squire Hallerton's character.

"He is a strange and reserved man," he continued, "and there are not many who would be prepossessed in his favour from first appearances; but he possesses a warm and humane heart beneath a rough exterior, and many are the acts of unostentatious charity which he is constantly in the habit of performing. He has no family, has only a young lady, who is somewhat related to him, I believe, residing with him, and is very rich; yet he is averse to society, and avoids it as much as possible. No doubt he has his reasons for it, and it is imagined that he has met with some severe misfortunes in the world, which have rendered it hateful to him; however, be that as it may, it is no business of any one."

"True," coincided our hero; "but I am afraid that he will consider us, poor and wretched as we are, bold in obtruding upon his hospitality."

"Not so," answered Reuben; "on the contrary, I am certain that he will feel highly gratified in affording assistance to those who so much require it."

Richard and his wife were satisfied with this assurance, and they proceeded on their way with renewed strength, and with hope revived in their bosoms, and Reuben encouraging them by all the observations he could make use of. In about an hour they came in sight of the hall, which was a large and ancient looking building, but which had anything but a cheerful or inviting appearance, and it was situated in a gloomy and retired spot, which was in

THE PARTING BETWEEN PARKER AND HIS WIFE AND MR. HAWTHORN.

strict accordance with the character which Reuben had given of its eccentric owner. There were lights in the lower apartments of the hall, which showed that the whole of its inhabitants had not retired to rest; and Reuben having led his companions to a side door, rang a bell, and they there anxiously awaited to see what the result would be, our heroine, in spite of her efforts to the contrary, feeling some doubtful misgivings and forebodings, for which, however, she found it impossible properly to account. They had not to wait long, for the door was almost immediately opened by an old woman, who by her features they at once concluded was the mother of their conductor. She seemed much surprised at seeing them, though it was evident that she beheld their distressed appearance with compassion, and looked to Reuben for an explanation.

"You see, mother," he said, ' I met these poor people on my way here; they are strangers in this part of the country, and in great distress, and being in want of a place of shelter, I thought I should not be acting wrong in bringing them here."

"Certainly not, my dear boy," said the old woman, "and it is a fortunate thing you happened to meet with these poor people, for they seem to be reduced to the last extremity. Walk in, my friends, and rest assured that you will meet with every kindness and hospitality here at Melborough Hall; those who stand in need of it, have never to apply here in vain for aid. Poor things, you seem to have suffered much."

"We have indeed, my good woman," said Richard, "and had it not been for the timely arrival of your son, Heaven only knows what would have become of us. Many thanks to you for your kindness, and for the commiseration which you express for our misfortunes."

"Enough," said the old woman; "I am only performing my duty, and my master would be much offended with me were I not to do so. He has retired to his chamber, or I would have introduced you at once to him. But we delay; follow me."

Our hero and his wife gladly obeyed, and the old woman led the way down stairs into a cheerful and commodious kitchen, in which a large fire was burning, and the sight of which seemed to reanimate Mary immediately. Having handed them seats before it, she bustled about and quickly placed before them a goodly supply of provisions, of which she invited them to partake heartily.

"You seem much distressed," she said, compassionately, "and no doubt are hungry, so do not be afraid; you are sincerely welcome to anything which I can do to serve you."

"This is a kindness which we had little right to expect," remarked our hero, "and I know not in what language to convey to you our deep sense of the weight of obligation we are under to you. Without your friendly succour I know not what would have become of us this night; for, as you must perceive, we are completely worn out by the suffering we have for so long a period had to undergo. Through unforeseen and unavoidable misfortunes we have been reduced to the greatest state of destitution, and compelled to leave our native place through circumstances which it may be unnecessary for me to explain; we were shipwrecked on this coast, and every soul on board the ill-fated vessel, with the exception of ourselves, perished."

"You have, indeed, been unfortunate," returned Mrs. Goodson, "and I most sincerely pity you. Here you are welcome to remain for the night; in the morning I will introduce you to my master, and I have no doubt that when he hears the melancholy statement which you have just made to me, he will relieve you."

"Heaven bless you for your kindness and humanity, my good woman," ejaculated Mary; "our fate is indeed a severe one, and God only knows how we have found strength to support it."

"Say no more, my unfortunate friend," said Mrs. Goodson; "I can fully appreciate your feelings, under the melancholy circumstances in which you are placed, and I hope that the time may not be far distant when your misfortunes will be alleviated, if not entirely removed. But you are very weak and ill; what can I do to relieve you?"

"Oh, madam," answered our heroine, "this goodness is completely overwhelming, and I know not in what language to express my acknowledgments. I am, indeed, quite exhausted with fatigue and anxiety of mind, but I am better now, and probably a night's rest will serve to revive me. But my husband and my child—alas! their sufferings have been as great as mine."

"Do not agitate yourself, Mary," said her husband, "respecting us; we shall probably soon recover from the effects of the fatigue we have lately experienced, and a night's repose may restore us. But to this good woman and her son we are indebted in a manner which I fear we shall never be able to repay."

"Do not mention it, sir," replied Mrs. Goodson; "for I can but repeat that you are sincerely welcome to anything which I can do to serve you, and I am only glad that I have had the opportunity to do so. But to-night it is useless to waste time in conversation; whenever you feel disposed I will conduct you to a chamber, and I hope that the morning will find you better."

"But I am afraid that we are intruding, strangers as we are to you, and that your master will blame you for having afforded us the shelter which you propose."

"Oh, no," answered Mrs. Goodson, "do not let such thoughts trouble you; I have already assured you of the benevolence and hospitality of my master's disposition; he delights in being able to afford assistance to his unfortunate fellow creatures, and he will be gratified to find that I have acted up to his wishes on such an occasion as this."

"Oh, he must be an excellent man to entertain such truly christian and charitable feelings as these," said our heroine, warmly; "how few are there in the world who possess the same noble qualities."

"And yet," remarked Mrs. Goodson, "he has his peculiarities, which might prejudice many persons, who are not acquainted with his real character, against him. He is gloomy, reserved, and austere; but he has experienced certain misfortunes and disappointments in life that have rendered him so."

"Ah, then," said Richard, "I can fully appreciate his feelings, and sympathise with him. But pardon me, my kind friend, it is late; myself and my wife are too much fatigued to prolong this conversation, and we must, therefore, request that you will permit us to retire."

"Certainly," answered Mrs. Goodson. "If you will follow me, I will conduct you to a chamber."

Our hero and his wife again thanked her, and having bade Reuben good-night, they followed Mrs. Goodson from the room. Having ascended two or three flights of stairs, she stopped at a door which seemed to open into a room in the back part of the building, and having opened it, she ushered them into a clean and commodious chamber, where, after a few observations, and promising to see them in the morning, she bade them good-night, and left them to themselves.

When she was gone, they were so much confused and surprised at all that had so unexpectedly taken place, and the difference of the situation in which they found themselves, that they could not utter a word; but at length, overpowered by their feelings, they sunk upon their knees, and most fervently returned their thanks to Heaven for the timely relief which had been afforded them when they stood so much in need of it.

"Providence has not yet deserted us, my dear Mary," observed her husband; "and I sincerely hope that this will be the precursor to a favourable change in our circumstances."

"God grant that it may," replied the former ; "and yet I know not how it is, but I cannot help feeling some sad misgivings that this adventure will not terminate so happily as we could wish."

"Nay, Mary," he remonstrated, "this is surely wrong and unreasonable. What should we have to apprehend? We have heard the character of the owner of this mansion, and, consequently, we have nothing to fear from him ; on the contrary, we may find him a friend of the greatest value and importance in our present circumstances. How thankful we ought to be that Providence has guided our foot-steps hither, for had we remained exposed to all the terrors of the night, I shudder to think of what the consequences must have been."

"Oh, yes," returned our heroine, "they would indeed have been awful, for my strength was almost exhausted, and although I exerted myself to the utmost, I could not, I am convinced, have borne up against it much longer. Dear Richard, surely the sufferings we have already undergone are more than a sufficient punishment for any sins we may have committed, and I pray the Almighty that He will now have mercy upon us. Could we but find a friend in this gentleman we might yet be able to extricate ourselves from the difficulties by which we are at present surrounded."

"True," coincided Richard ; "and yet it would be almost unreasonable to expect that he will interest himself for those who are complete strangers to him, and whom he cannot know whether they are worthy of his sympathy. But come, Mary, it is late, and we waste time that should be devoted to rest in talking here. Let us seek our couch, and hope that the morning will produce some favourable change in our circumstances."

Mary assented to this, and after having once more supplicated the protection of Heaven, they retired to bed ; and, worn out by the long fatigue and anxiety of mind they had endured, refreshing sleep shortly descended upon their eyelids.

CHAPTER XXXII.

AN UNEXPECTED MEETING.—A PAINFUL SCENE.—THE ABRUPT DEPARTUE OF THE FUGITIVES FROM THE HALL.

RICHARD and his wife continued to sleep soundly till the morning, when they awoke, much refreshed, and far more cheerful and buoyant in spirits than they had been for some time before. They arose, and awaiting till they should be summoned down stairs by Mrs. Goodson, as she had promised to do on the night before, they sat themselves down, and entered into a conversation upon the remarkable and trying events that had happened to them lately, and their future prospects.

"I trust, Mary," said her husband, "that this adventure will be the means of relieving us from some of the miseries with which we have been for so long a time overwhelmed. If this gentleman is, indeed, the benevolent individual he has been represented to us, he will doubtless be moved to compassion when he hears of the misfortunes we have undergone, and we may find in him a friend who will be ready to assist us as far as is in his power from the difficulties by which we are surrounded, and to afford us an asylum until such time as we shall be able to come to some decided arrangement as to the future."

"God grant that those sanguine hopes may not be doomed to be disappointed," replied Mary. "But, although I would not damp the ardour of your expectations, I must confess that I cannot altogether entertain the same ideas that you seem to do upon the subject. We cannot venture to confide to this gentleman the whole particulars of our history, for, probably, he might be prejudiced against us when he became acquainted with them, and then the danger in which we should be placed would be most imminent."

"Indeed," returned her husband, "I do believe that your fears are groundless, and that, if Mr. Hallerton possesses the humanity and charitableness of heart which we have been informed that he does, we shall have nothing to fear from him. Banish those apprehensions from your breast, my dear Mary, and endeavour to hope for the best results."

"I would fain do so, Richard; still I know not how it is, but I cannot help feeling a certain dread to meet this gentleman, and I would that the interview were over."

"Nay," said our hero, "surely these fears and misgivings are unfounded. What should we have to apprehend from him? Come, come, arouse yourself from this state of despondency, and depend upon it that something is yet in store for us to relieve us from a deal of that anxiety which now besets our minds."

"I will try to do so," answered Mary, "and, perhaps, it is wrong and foolish of me to give way to such ideas as those which I have expressed. Oh, Richard, should we, indeed, find in this gentleman the friend that you anticipate, what important service might he not render us in the midst of the numerous difficulties by which we are surrounded."

"True. But what I principally wish is that I may have an opportunity of communicating with our friend Adams to inform him of all which has so unfortunately happened, and to receive his advice as to the future, though I must acknowledge that I almost dread to make him acquainted with the melancholy particulars, and the death of poor Binnacle, for I well know what anguish of mind it will cause him. Unfortunate old man, it was hard that he should have met with the untimely fate

that he did, and in performing an act of such remarkable and Christian humanity."

"It was, indeed," observed our heroine, "and never shall I forget it even to the last moment of my existence. May Heaven rest his soul, and reward him for the many deeds of virtue which he performed throughout his long and valuable life."

"To that wish most heartily do I respond," said Richard: "but Heaven will do so. Alas! had it not been for that fatal catastrophe, and we had been enabled to reach the place of our destination, we might now have been in safety; but as it is, until I can receive some advice from Adams, I am at a loss to imagine in what way it would be most prudent for us to direct our steps, especially moneyless and destitute as we are."

"Our situation is a sad and disheartening one," remarked his wife, "but we must endeavour to bear up against the misfortunes with which we are constantly beset, with all the fortitude that we can, and to trust to Providence to avert those evils that seem to be constantly impending o'er our heads. Oh, how grateful ought we to be that we were so unexpectedly rescued from the horrors to which we were exposed last night, for had we not been so, I shudder to think what the consequences must have been."

"True," answered our hero; "it was a most fortunate deliverance, and to Mrs. Goodson and her son we must ever feel most greatly indebted; the kind sympathy, too, which they have since expressed in our misfortunes, demands our gratitude. And how, my dearest Mary, can I ever sufficiently express my admiration of the patience, fortitude, and resignation with which you have ever endured those bitter trials that were sufficient to daunt even the firmest spirit? Without you, my friend, my wife, my consoler and adviser, what would have become of me and our poor boy? My fate must long ere this have been certain. To your devoted affection I am indebted for everything."

"And have I performed more than my duty?" interrogated Mary. "I should have been unworthy of the name I bear, and of your love, could I have done less."

Richard embraced his wife, and was about to make some reply to her affectionate observations, when he was prevented from doing so by hearing a gentle knock at the door, and immediately opening it, Mrs. Goodson presented herself. She greeted them with the same warmth and familiarity as if they had been acquainted for years, and expressed her gratification at seeing them look so much refreshed after their night's rest.

"Come," she continued, "breakfast is already prepared and waiting for you below, and that will serve to revive you. I would not disturb you before, though it is rather late, for I well knew how much you required rest after the numerous exertions and privations you have undergone."

"How kind is this, and to those who are complete strangers to you!" said our heroine. "But for you, God only knows what our fate would have been; and we can never find language sufficiently powerful to express to you our gratitude for the unexampled kindness and attention you have evinced towards us. May Heaven reward you for it, for I fear that we shall never have the power to do so."

"And think you that I seek any reward for merely performing that which common humanity demanded?" said Mrs. Goodson. "No. I should be ashamed of myself if I could do so, and I am only too happy to think that I have had it in my power to serve you. But come—let us below; we will talk more of this subject anon. My master has not yet left his chamber, but when he does so I will make him acquainted with what has happened, and then I will introduce you to him; and, take my word for it, when he finds your distressed situation, he will be ready to render you all the assistance that is in his power."

"I can but repeat my thanks, my good woman," observed Parker, "and——"

"Enough," interposed Mrs. Goodson. "I am satisfied, and require to hear no more. Follow me."

Our hero and his wife, and William, did so, and they were once more escorted by her to the kitchen, where they found a plentiful and refreshing repast prepared for them, and to partake of which they sat down with lighter hearts than they had experienced for some time. During the time this was going forward, Mrs. Goodson entered more particularly into the character of her master, which she lauded most warmly, and showed by her observations how much she admired and was attached to him.

"He has not resided here more than three years," she continued, "and I have been in his service ever since. Although I know that some heavy misfortunes have afflicted him, and in some measure soured his temper, and made him look upon mankind with a cautious and suspicious eye, I have never been able to learn the particulars of his history, though I have no doubt it is a melancholy one. He will sometimes keep himself confined to his room for days together, and will suffer no one to approach him, and after that he is generally more calm and tranquil."

"It is a pity that one who possesses the noble and generous qualities which you have represented him to have should have experienced misfortune," said Richard.

"True," returned Mrs. Goodson; "but time, probably, may serve to ameliorate the anguish of his mind, and enable him to look with calmness and resignation upon the past."

"I hope that it may," remarked our hero. "But you say that he has a young lady residing with him. Is she in any way related to him, pray?"

"Not in the least, I believe," answered Mrs. Goodson. "He has adopted her in the place of one who should have been dearer to him, but who, from all that I have been able to ascertain, has been the principal cause of his sorrows. He is very much attached to her, and there is no doubt but, at his demise, she will come into the possession of the whole of his property."

Mary and her husband felt deeply interested in the facts which Mrs. Goodson related, and there was something connected with them which excited an almost painful sensation in the breast of our heroine.

"Miss Amelia," continued Mrs. Goodson, "is very handsome and accomplished, and very kind and attentive to her guardian, whose every wish and will she studies with the most scrupulous care; but I am sorry to say that she is not without her bad qualities, which are sometimes displayed in a manner which is highly prejudicial to her, and painful to those who witness it; she is proud and haughty, and often gives way to bursts of passion, which distort her character, and can alone excite pity and regret. But I am perhaps wrong in speaking thus, and will, therefore, say no more upon the subject."

Mrs. Goodson now ceased, and a silence of some minutes ensued, during which time Richard and his wife reflected deeply upon what she had said, and they felt the greater curiosity to behold Mr. Hallerton, though at the same time Mary could not help still encouraging a feeling of doubt and apprehension as to the result of the interview, for which she was completely at a loss to account. The gentleman's bell at length rang, and Mrs. Goodson left them to attend to the summons, and they awaited her return with some anxiety.

"You look pale and agitated, Mary," observed our hero, gazing earnestly in her face; "has anything occurred in the conversation which has taken place between ourselves and Mrs. Goodson to excite any unpleasant feelings in your breast?"

"Why, Richard," she replied, "the description which she has given of the *protege* of Mr. Hallerton, and the manner in which they are associated, I confess has given rise to some strange thoughts and speculations in my mind, and render me still more fearful to meet him. She said that he had adopted this young lady in the place of one who ought to have been more dear to him; and who, she believes, had been the principal cause of his misfortunes. His daughter, perhaps; and surely if that is the case, it bears a most painful similarity to my own."

"Banish such thoughts from your mind, Mary, for they are idle and erroneous."

"Nay, Richard, call them not so; have I not a right to be forcibly struck with the similarity? Have I not been discarded, abandoned, by my father, because I could not act in accordance with a will so repulsive to my feelings; and, knowing his disposition so well, was he not likely to act in a similar manner to that which it seems this gentleman has done? Oh, God! what terrible ideas crowd upon my brain! Would to Heaven that this interview were at an end, that the strange suspicions that present themselves to my imagination were either confirmed or dispersed."

"This is most strange and unaccountable," said our hero; "you seem to be labouring under some extraordinary infatuation or delusion, Mary, which I am at a perfect loss to comprehend."

"I may, in this instance, appear weak and ridiculous to you, my husband," she replied; "but so powerful is the impression which all the circumstances have made upon my mind, that I find it almost impossible to eradicate it, and——"

She was interrupted by the reappearance of Mrs. Goodson, who, taking no notice, apparently, of her agitation, said—

"My good friends, I have explained all the circumstances of your arrival here to my master; he has expressed the greatest sympathy for your distressed and deplorable condition, and is most anxious to see you; so, if you please, I will conduct you to him."

Richard nodded assent, and taking the arm of his wife, they followed Mrs. Goodson from the room to the study of Squire Hallerton, where he was waiting to receive them, and our heroine trying to regain her firmness and composure as they proceeded, though she succeeded but indifferently. On arriving at the apartment, they stopped at the door, and Mrs. Goodson, having knocked, and received permission to enter, opened it, and ushered our hero and his wife into the room. The gentleman's back was towards them on their entrance, and Mrs. Goodson, advancing towards him, said—

"My honoured master, these are the unfortunate individuals whom you have permitted me to introduce to you, and to claim your sympathy."

He turned hastily round as she spoke, but no sooner did Mary behold his features than she uttered a mingled cry of astonishment and alarm, and sank almost swooning in the arms of her husband.

It was her father!

"Mr. Mason!" exclaimed Richard, breathlessly. "My wife—my Mary—oh, look up! Courage—courage, for if one spark of natural feeling remains in the bosom of the author of your being, he must pity you in your misery, even though he condemn you!"

"Her father!" exclaimed the astounded Mrs. Goodson.

"No!" cried Mr. Mason, hoarsely, and the most fearful emotion agitated and convulsed his frame. "She is no daughter of mine. I know her not. My malediction is upon her head, and all—just Heaven, it is evident, from her present wretched condition, has sanctioned the decree. What cursed fate has guided her footsteps hither to annoy me by her presence, accompanied by him who seduced her from her duty—Richard Parker, the mutineer and the murderer?"

Mrs. Goodson clasped her hands together, and raised her eyes towards the ceiling with astonishment; and at that moment the room door opened, and a young female entered, whom our hero no sooner beheld than he exclaimed, in a voice of the deepest agitation—

"Amelia Arlington!"

"Yes, wretch—villain!" cried Mr. Mason, furiously, "the niece of your murdered victim, now my adopted daughter, in the place of her who proved herself to be so unworthy of that name. Villain, I say again, does not your conscience smite you as you gaze upon her, and remember the hideous crime for which the gallows awaits you?"

"Mr. Mason," replied our hero, with a firmness that could scarcely have been expected under the circumstances, "I can

bear with your reproaches and vitupera-
tion, however unjustifiable they are, for
my conscience acquits me of all that black
and cold blooded villany which you lay
to my charge. Captain Arlington rushed
upon his own fate, and it was no more
than the just retribution of outraged Heaven which overtook him for the brutal and
cowardly wrongs he had inflicted upon an
innocent man, who never injured him.
Denounce me, call me wretch, miscreant,
villain, whatever you please; I say again,
that I can bear patiently with it all, and
make every allowance for the prejudices
which I know you always entertained
against me; but it is for this poor unfortunate sufferer that I plead. In the name of
High Heaven, in the name of all that is
pure, is just, and virtuous, aged sir, I implore you to think of that gentle, that
amiable being who bore her, and you cannot surely forget that she is your child,
your only child, who has ever loved you
with a daughter's fondest affection and
devotion."

Mr. Mason for a minute or two seemed
to be completely staggered by the energy
and eloquence of Richard's manner, and
was unable to speak a word, though the
wild and truly ghastly expression of his
features showed plainly the agitation of the
feelings which at that moment agitated his
breast. Miss Arlington stood by a silent
spectatress of the scene, and various were
the emotions which struggled in her bosom.

"'Tis false!" at length exclaimed Mr.
Mason, glaring fiercely upon our hero and
the form of his daughter; "she is no child
of mine; she has severed for ever the ties
that bound us by uniting herself to a villain, and I have long discarded her! Remove her from my sight, for she is now
odious to me! Richard Parker, I would
not have your blood upon my head; but if
you would not precipitate that ignominious
fate which ere long must most assuredly
overtake you, you will immediately leave
this place, and never again disgust me with
your presence or that of her who is now
the partner of your guilt. Away, I say."

"Father! father! Mercy! mercy!"
shrieked our heroine, frantically tearing
herself from the arms of her husband, and
sinking on her knees at the feet of her
excited parent. "You will not, cannot
surely thus close your heart to every feeling of pity towards me. Oh, reflect, reflect,
ere you act thus harshly, and take compassion on me. I might have been wrong
in opposing your will, but my feelings
revolted from the bare idea of that which
you would have imposed upon me. Say
that you forgive me, and although you

may never again acknowledge me for your
daughter, if that you do not invoke the
maledictions of Heaven upon my head, I
will endeavour to resign myself to my fate,
severe and cruel even though it may be."

"Forgive you!" repeated her inexorable
parent, and still gazing with the most excited expression of countenance upon her
features; "never! The more I look at you
the greater become my feelings of disgust
and indignation against you, and again
that curse arises to my lips which I have
before invoked upon your head. Begone,
I say! lest in my wrath I spurn you like
something loathsome and hideous from my
feet, and consign to death that man whom
you now call your husband!"

"Oh, God!" groaned the wretched Mrs.
Parker, tears gushing to her eyes, and
streaming in scalding torrents down her
pale cheeks, "what a dreadful trial is this!
Will nothing move him to compassion?"

"Mary, dear Mary," ejaculated her
husband, raising her from the floor, "you
appeal to him in vain; 'tis plain that his
heart has become insensible to every feeling of pity. Mr. Mason, I fear that you
will have bitter cause to repent this unnatural severity. I plead not for myself, for
I am now perfectly indifferent to the censure of the world; but the time will come,
depend upon it, when you will remember
that this poor suffering woman is your
daughter, and you will most keenly reproach yourself for the manner in which
you have treated her when too late."

"Away!" exclaimed Mr. Mason, impatiently; "I will no longer listen to you,
and the sight of you is odious to me. Begone, I say, and let me endeavour to forget that I have ever again beheld you."

"I go, sir," said Richard, boldly, and
fixing upon him a proud and reproachful
look; "but remember well what I have
said, and rest assured that all which I have
predicted will be verified. Come, my
love, my Mary, this is no place for us; be
firm, Heaven will not yet desert us; let
us again wander forth, and trust to its
mercy for its future disposal of us.'

Poor Mary endeavoured to speak, but
the power of her emotions choked her utterance, and fixing upon her father such a
look as must have penetrated to his heart,
she suffered her husband to lead her from
the room, and they were quickly followed
by the compassionate Mrs. Goodson, who
was deeply affected by the unexpected and
painful scene which she had witnessed.

"Accompany me below," she said; "it
may not yet be too late to arrange this painful and melancholy business. From the
bottom of my soul I pity you, and there is

nothing that I would not do to serve you. Come, come."

"No," replied Richard, "we must not remain here beneath the roof of that man who has cursed us, and who views us as something monstrous and loathsome. Oh, would to Heaven that our wandering footsteps had never been guided hither. Mary, arouse yourself, and we may yet find that relief and sympathy which we cannot hope to meet with here. Let us again away, for there is danger while we remain here."

"Alas! alas!" groaned our heroine, "what will become of us? Cruel father! is this the treatment which you should bestow upon your only and unfortunate child? But—but I will be firm, and trust in receiving that mercy from Heaven which it seems I cannot hope to meet with here. I am ready, dear Richard. I will muster all my strength and fortitude. Let us away—let us away!"

"Nay," urged Mrs. Goodson, "you must not leave here while you are in this excited condition; a short time will probably serve to compose your feelings, and your father may repent, when the excitement naturally consequent upon his sudden and unexpected meeting with you has abated. Attend me, I beg of you."

They had now reached the bottom of the stairs, and were standing in the hall, and Mrs. Goodson again urged them to accompany her to the kitchen.

"No, no," said Richard, resolutely, "I am much obliged to you for your kindness, and must ever entertain a lively sense of gratitude towards you; but I cannot consent to remain another minute here after what has happened. I know not to what length Mr. Mason's malignant feelings of revenge may carry him. Should he betray and denounce me, we are lost."

"Oh, dreadful thought!" exclaimed our heroine, with a shudder; "let us not delay a moment, Richard. I am ready, quite ready. Come—come, I tremble with apprehension while we tarry here."

"But whither can you go?" said Mrs. Goodson; "you are poor and friendless, and there is no house where you are at all likely to meet with any accommodation within five miles of this hall. Again let me persuade you."

"Ah, no," answered our hero, "we should but bring down upon you the anger of your master were we to yield to your solicitations. Farewell, and may Heaven bless you for the kindness and humanity you have shown towards us."

At that moment they heard the bell again ring from Mr. Mason's room, and it was, therefore, clear that there was no time for delay.

"Hark!" said Richard, "you are summoned; there is no time for you to waste with us. Adieu, and should we never meet again, I beseech you to remember us in your prayers, and not to be prejudiced by anything you may hear against us."

"Ah, no," returned Mrs. Goodson, "you may depend upon that, and that I pity you sincerely and fervently. But you are pennyless, and without means; what is to become of you? This purse may relieve your present wants; take it, and may Heaven watch over and protect you."

With these words, the generous-hearted woman thrust a well filled purse into the hands of Richard; the bell rang again, and before he had time to reply, she hurried up the stairs to attend the impatient summons of her master.

Richard and his wife stood for a minute or two unable to speak a word, and uncertain what to do, and then our hero, taking the arm of his unfortunate partner, opened the door, and the wretched fugitives were again wandering cheerless and hopeless in the open air.

CHAPTER XXXIII.

THE EXCITEMENT OF MR. MASON.—EXPLANATION.—THE WANDERERS.

It may perhaps be unnecessary to describe particularly the agitation of Mr. Mason, after this unexpected and painful meeting with his daughter and her husband. When they had quitted the room, he threw himself in a chair, and covering his face with his hands, gave himself up entirely to the distracting thoughts that crowded upon his brain. Amelia Arlington was scarcely less agitated and astonished than he was; but in spite of the feelings of prejudice which she entertained against Mary and her husband, the extreme wretchedness of their appearance could not fail to make a powerful impression upon her mind, and to excite some small degree of pity in her breast.

Amelia Arlington was just three and twenty, and independent of a tall, graceful, and commanding figure, she possessed a countenance which might justly be termed beautiful, though there was a haughty expression about her mouth and in her eye which greatly detracted from its charms. In her manners she was elegant and accomplished, but she possessed several bad qualities which rendered

MARY ATTEMPTS TO ROUSE HER HUSBAND FROM HIS DESPONDENCY.

her a dangerous individual to offend, and one whose friendship it was no easy task to conciliate. The implacability of Mr. Mason gratified her, for it served her interests, as will be shown by the explanation which we purpose giving presently.

Mr. Mason at length looked up, and finding that Richard and his wife were gone, he exclaimed—

"What cursed fate has brought about this event to torture me? I had hoped that I might never more behold her, or the wretch with whom she has associated her destiny, the murderer of your unfortunate uncle, my Amelia. And yet," he added, after a brief pause—" how pale, how careworn, and how wretched she looked—she who was once loveliness itself. Surely, my heart should have been moved with some feeling of compassion towards her."

"Pardon me, my dear sir," said Amelia; "but has she not by her own misconduct brought all this misery upon herself? Is it not a just punishment for her disobedience to your will—her guilty obstinacy in throwing herself away upon a man who has proved himself to be a villain, and thus brought disgrace upon your name?"

No. 50.

"True, true," he returned; "she has indeed brought it all upon herself, and why should I pity her? No, I ought rather to despise and loathe her. But would to Heaven that she had never again crossed my path, for it has once more aroused all the anguish of my soul in its greatest bitterness. But away with these thoughts! She is no child of mine, and why, then, do I not banish her from my memory altogether? But her guilty husband, he who shed the blood of your unfortunate relation—I should not have suffered him to escape; justice demands that he should pay an awful penalty for his crime, the penalty of death."

He rang the bell violently as he thus spoke, and his excitement increased.

"I invoked a malediction upon her head," he exclaimed; "and did she not deserve it? Oh, yes! What punishment is sufficient for her for the disgrace which she has brought upon my name?"

"True, my dear sir," coincided the crafty and malicious Amelia; "and why then should you agitate yourself thus?"

At this moment Mrs. Goodson entered the room, and Mr. Mason, turning hastily towards her, demanded—

"Where are they? Let them not depart; that man is a mutineer and an assassin; he has too long escaped detection, and now——"

"They have left the hall, sir," interrupted Mrs. Goodson, disgusted with the unfeeling and unnatural observations that her master had made use of, "and I sincerely hope that something will occur to release them from their present wretched situation, poor things; for I am sure they are to be sincerely pitied, and my heart really bleeds for them."

"Why, how now, Mrs. Goodson?" said Mr. Mason, hastily, and fixing upon her a look of anger and astonishment, while Amelia could not conceal her vexation; "this is rather bold language to address to me. Pity! Should it ever be bestowed upon such worthless wretches as these?"

"For shame, sir," remonstrated Mrs. Goodson, who was unable to control her feelings of honest indignation; "and is it possible that you can thus speak of your own daughter?"

"My daughter!" repeated Mr. Mason, passionately; "no, she is no child of mine; my heart spurns the idea. She abandoned me years ago, and fled to the arms of the villain who has brought all her present misery upon her. But why should I condescend to talk to you thus? Your words are insolent, woman; quit the room."

"Most willingly, sir," answered Mrs. Goodson, coolly, and fixing upon him a look of mingled contempt and disgust; "and since I have now discovered your real disposition, I do not care how soon I quit the hall altogether."

"Mrs. Goodson, are you mad?" said Amelia, angrily. "You seem to forget that you are addressing your master."

"No, miss," replied Mrs. Goodson, "indeed I do not; but I will never give my sanction to feelings so revolting to nature and humanity."

"This is unbearable!" exclaimed Mr. Mason, with increased resentment; "leave the room, woman, I say again."

Mrs. Goodson did not condescend to make any reply, but immediately retired from the apartment.

"The observations of this woman have annoyed me," said Mr. Mason, when she was gone. "I never heard her so bold before. Curses light upon the accident, I say, which brought these wanderers to the hall. I had hoped to remain here in seclusion and unknown."

"Endeavour to calm your feelings, my dear sir," said Amelia, "and to forget what has happened. It is not likely that you will ever behold them again; and, therefore, you have no reason to fear that they will annoy you. Richard Parker will be only too anxious to conceal himself, that he may escape that punishment which his crime so richly deserves."

Mr. Mason returned no immediate answer, and after a little more conversation Amelia retired from the room, and left him to his own reflections. In spite of all his efforts to the contrary, his anguish of mind increased, and he could not help secretly upbraiding himself for his harsh and cruel conduct towards his unfortunate daughter.

"Alas!" he soliloquised, "what a strange and awful change has come over her since last I saw her! And yet, how beautiful, how innocent, and how happy she once was! Surely I acted with too much severity towards her in banishing her from my breast, and it is in vain that I try to reconcile my conscience to it. How many hours of misery has that thought cost me! And the oftener it occurs to my mind the more torturing becomes its effect. But did she not obstinately oppose my will, and set me at defiance? She did; she brought disgrace upon my name, and she is but justly punished for it."

In this state of excitement he continued throughout the day, and kept himself secluded in his own chamber. But we must now proceed to explain a few facts which may, perhaps, be necessary to the more easy development of our story For some time after the elopement of our heroine, Mr. Mason was a truly wretched man, wavering and undecided. That she should have set his authority at defiance, and become the wife of one so poor as Richard Parker, sadly mortified his pride, and he could never forgive her; but still there were moments when Nature prevailed, and he could not help feeling that she was still his child, notwithstanding the manner in which he had discarded her from his breast, and the curse which he had invoked upon her head, and he regretted the painful circumstance which had deprived him of her. But still these feelings seldom lasted for any length of time, and one of indignation and vindictiveness against her and her husband was the one which usually predominated in his breast. His sordidness of disposition completely overwhelmed his sense of justice, and in the comparative poverty of Richard Parker, he entirely overlooked the intrinsic virtues, and strict integrity and honour of character which he possessed. Captain Arlington was rich, and was likewise connected with some of the most aristocratic families in the kingdom; therefore the reader may easily imagine how much the pride of Mr. Mason was mortified by this clandestine marriage. In fact, he felt that he could never forgive his daughter for the step she had taken, and as for her husband, he could not even think of him without feelings of the bitterest hatred and malice arising in his breast.

"The presumptuous beggar!" he would exclaim, when he was alone, "to dare to aspire to the hand of one who was so much his superior, and to supplant the man on whom I had fixed my mind in her affections. And she, the disobedient, thus obstinately to oppose my will, and to throw herself away upon a beggar. Never, never can I forgive her; but she will be amply punished, and so will he with whom she has united her fate. Let them never more cross my path, for they are now both loathsome in my eyes, and should they do so, again would I invoke the heaviest maledictions upon their heads, and I know not what the consequences might be."

Possessing such unnatural and vindictive feelings as these, the reader may well imagine the indifference, or rather the exultation with which the misguided gentleman heard of the difficulties and privations that Mary and her husband were unfortunately so soon doomed to suffer, and, in fact, instead of its moving him to pity, it only afforded him gratification to his revenge.

But how shall we describe the mortification and disappointment of Captain Arlington, when he found how completely he was foiled in the designs he had formed by the man whom he so thoroughly despised and detested? Although he was well aware that his real character had been penetrated by Mary, and that she viewed him with repugnance, if not with absolute abhorrence, he had nevertheless flattered himself with the idea that she would be compelled to yield to the wishes of her father, and that he would yet triumph over his rival in obtaining possession of her hand, if he could not her heart. Proud, haughty, and entertaining a most superlative opinion of his own superior merits, personal, intrinsic, and pecuniary, he could not for a moment brook the idea of a rival; and, notwithstanding the candid and decided manner in which our heroine had ever rejected his addresses, he still flattered himself that the time would come when he should not only overcome every difficulty, but likewise to win the respect of Mary, if he could not obtain her love. He had contrived so to insinuate himself into the good graces of Mr. Mason, who believed him to be a very paragon of all that was good and honourable, that he thought it was impossible for him to fail in his designs, and he was, therefore, inclined to view Richard Parker with feelings of contempt as well as those of hatred.

Entertaining such feelings as these, we need not attempt to describe his rage and disappointment when he found all his proud and ambitious hopes annihilated by their elopement and clandestine marriage. For some time he was in a state bordering upon madness, every one was afraid to approach him, he uttered the most terrible curses upon their heads, and vowed, let the consequences be whatever they might, to have a fearful revenge; and how well he kept his word has been shown.

As soon as he had become somewhat more calm, he sought an interview with Mr. Mason, and together they gave vent to their feelings of rage, and threatened to pursue Richard and his wife with their vengeance at every opportunity. Time passed on, and these guilty resolutions gained strength instead of decreasing, and the oftener they heard of the privations which it was their lot to encounter, the more they exulted. It would seem that Mr. Mason was entirely led astray by some strange and fatal prejudice or infatuation, and that he had completely stifled every feeling of nature in his breast. Captain Arlington possessed every power over him, and could persuade him to anything he thought proper, a fact which could not have been more forcibly exemplified than in that which we are about to relate.

Captain Arlington had for some time had under his protection the only daughter of his late brother, who from the dissipated life which he had led since the death of his wife, had died poor, and, consequently, it was the wish of Captain Arlington to aggrandize his niece as much as he could without infringing upon his own property, for in addition to all his other bad qualities, he possessed that mean and miserly spirit, which is generally one of the characteristics of a narrow mind. In Mr. Mason, especially after the conduct of his daughter, he perceived a ready means of accomplishing his wishes, and he determined to avail himself of the opportunity.

Amelia Arlington was young, and very beautiful, proud, crafty, ambitious, designing, and vindictive to a degree, but when she had any particular object to serve, she could become one of the most irresistibly fascinating beings in existence, and so well could she assume the hypocrite, that she might have deceived the most experienced and penetrating eye, and made them believe her to be a very paragon of perfection. It will not be wondered then that she should so easily have insinuated herself into the good opinion of Mr. Mason, that he believed her to be completely faultless, and after the elopement of his daughter he was never happy but when she was at the hall, and, in fact, he soon began to look upon her in the same light as that unfortunate and much-injured child whom he had so cruelly and unnaturally discarded from his breast.

We need not state the satisfaction with which Captain Arlington viewed the success of his plans, and he now perceived that his revenge was likely to be gratified to the fullest extent; but still he was determined so to get our hero in his power that he might wreak upon him the full weight of his malice and hatred, and degrade and punish him for the manner in which he had frustrated him in his designs against Mary; and it was not long ere he found an opportunity of putting that wish into execution. It may scarcely be necessary to state that it was by his means that Richard was seized by the press-gang, as related in the early part of our narrative, and when he was drafted on board of the ship which he commanded, his triumph was complete, and it has been seen how cruelly and basely he took advantage of

the opportunity which was afforded him of gratifying his cowardly and implacable feelings of deadly revenge.

During the time that her uncle was at sea, Amelia took up her residence at the hall, and such was the power that she had gained over the misguided Mr. Mason, that he studied her every wish, and could not perceive a single fault in her. He considered her in the character of his daughter, and was determined that she should possess that fortune to which Mary would have been entitled had she not incurred his wrath.

The conspicuous part which Richard Parker played in the mutiny at the Nore, and the consequences which he considered it was sure to bring upon his head, afforded him much gratification, and his stern heart could never be moved to pity for the sufferings to which he was aware his unfortunate and unoffending daughter must be exposed.

"The disobedient," he would often soliloquise to himself; "it is a just punishment for her obstinate opposition to my will, and the disgrace she has brought upon my name, by uniting herself to one who was so much beneath her. Why should I feel any remorse of conscience? Did she not set my authority at defiance? She did, and let the consequence be upon her head!"

So he endeavoured to think, but in spite of himself there were times when the unnatural severity of his conduct became so apparent to him, that he could not reconcile it to his conscience, and he became restless and miserable. It was those feelings that prompted him to retire to some part of the country where he might live more secluded and unknown, and he, therefore, much to the surprise of every person in the neighbourhood where he resided, abruptly quitted his paternal estate, and retired to the mansion in which we have introduced him in the preceding chapter, under the assumed name of Hallerton, and where his habits became very different to what they had formerly been. Mrs. Goodson had given so correct, though laconic, a description of them in her statement to our hero and his wife on their introduction to her, that we have no occasion to particularize them. From that account the reader will perceive, from his reserved and secluded conduct, that, although he struggled hard against the enemy, he could not resist the qualms of conscience, and that his natural good qualities frequently predominated over his evil ones, and thus it was that he could never resist the appeal of those in distress.

though, by a strange perversion of feeling, the misery of his own unhappy child could make no impression upon him, or move him to relax one iota of his resentment towards her.

The critical position in which our hero was placed, materially caused him the greatest excitement, and he read the daily accounts in the public journals with the deepest interest, in which Amelia equally participated, and by the most insidious means she cherished the animosity of Mr. Mason against his daughter and her husband, while at the same time she affected to extenuate their conduct, a piece of hypocrisy she played with so much ability, as completely to deceive her misguided benefactor, and to increase his admiration of her supposed noble and generous conduct.

The revolt on board the Sandwich, the pursuit of Richard Parker, and the death of Captain Arlington, with the subsequent escape of our hero, were events which naturally caused the greatest sensation in the minds of Mr. Mason and Amelia, particularly the former, and, if possible, it increased the feelings of hatred and revenge which he had against Richard, whilst it more and more steeled his heart against his own unfortunate daughter; while the manner in which they had been enabled to elude the pursuit which had been made after them, disappointed and enraged them.

Amelia Arlington had now no other protector than Mr. Mason, and he at once adopted her as his daughter, and made her the sole heiress of his fortune, excluding Mary from the receipt of a single shilling. Thus matters stood at the time we have introduced our hero and his wife at Melborough Hall, and the reader will, therefore, not be surprised at the reception they met with. But to the crafty and revengeful Amelia it was a complete triumph, and while she pretended to sympathise with them, and to extenuate their conduct, she insidiously fanned the flame of Mr. Mason's excitement against them, and would have been glad had they not been suffered to escape, for then the destruction of Richard Parker, and the utter misery and despair of his wretched wife, would have completed her revenge for the death of her uncle.

For several hours after the departure of Richard and his wife from the hall, Mr. Mason kept himself locked in his own apartment, and gave free indulgence to his feelings, alternately wavering between remorse, hatred, and revenge; but nothing whatever could abate the excitement of his mind. He paced his room with hasty and uneven footsteps, and various and conflicting were the thoughts which crowded upon his brain. One moment he reproached himself for the cruelty of his conduct towards his unhappy daughter; then again he upbraided himself for his weakness in feeling the least commiseration for her, and invoked the bitterest curses upon the head of herself and her husband. Altogether, the tumultuous and conflicting thoughts that crowded upon it, rendered his mind a complete sea of torment, and he could come to no complete decision.

"Would to Heaven that they had never again crossed my path!" he soliloquised; "then I should not have been subjected to the torturing thoughts I now experience. But why should I pity them, after the manner in which they have disgraced me? Are they not justly punished? It is the retribution of offended Heaven that is overtaking the murderer and the recreant from her duty. And yet," he added, after a brief pause, "how pale, how wretched and how careworn she looked—she that once was so lovely, so innocent, and so happy! Alas—alas! what a sad change has time and circumstances wrought in her! And still the resemblance of her who bore her is so strongly stamped upon her features, that—that——Away with these thoughts, for they will drive me mad, and render me weaker than a child! She has basely committed herself, and she richly merits the fate she has met with. As for her husband, he is an assassin, and a traitor to his country, and he deserves a murderer's doom!"

At that moment there was a knock at the door, which aroused him from his reflections; and hastily demanding who was there, he was answered in the voice of Amelia Arlington, who had been listening to all that he had said. He immediately admitted her, and she advanced towards him with the greatest semblance of affection and sympathy, and taking his hand, said—

"My dearest friend, my only earthly benefactor and protector, oh! why do you thus seclude yourself from my society, and deny me the indulgence of that sympathy in which you stand so much in need? 'Tis true the unexpected meeting you have lately experienced is sufficient to excite you; but still I must beseech you to endeavour to calm your feelings, and to remember that to whatever misery and wretchedness this Richard Parker and his wife, your—your daughter, are reduced, they have brought it all upon themselves."

"My daughter!" repeated the misguided

man, hastily. "Call her not so; I disown her; she is no child of mine. You—you, my sweet Amelia, are my only daughter, and the comfort of my declining years; the dear consoler to me in the midst of all my heavy afflictions. What should I do without you? Oh, had she been possessed of your numerous virtues, how happy should I have been in acknowledging her for my child!"

"My dearest guardian," said the deceitful Amelia, throwing her arms with mock affection around the old gentleman's neck, and assuming one of her most insinuating looks, "how little deserving am I of the flattering encomiums which you bestow upon me! But if I can in any way replace her who is lost to you for ever, I——"

"Name her not!" passionately interrupted Mr. Mason, "for her name is odious to me, and I marvel that the thought of her should excite me thus. Alas! what must have been the feelings of horror, my dear Amelia, that agitated your gentle breast, on beholding the murderer of your late lamented uncle, who has hitherto unfortunately evaded the ignominious fate which his atrocious crime so justly merits! Noble-hearted Arlington! that you should perish in such a manner, and that, too, by the hands of him who had inflicted so much misery upon you, and so deeply injured you by the disappointment of your hopes!"

Amelia affected to weep, and in a voice of emotion replied—

"My poor dear uncle, how deeply do I deplore his fate; for he was all that was good and virtuous. But never can I be sufficiently grateful to Heaven that has raised me up such an invaluable friend, a more than parent in his place, in you."

"Sweet innocent!" ejaculated the deluded old man, embracing her, "how worthy have you proved yourself of all the affection which I can possibly bestow upon you! It is I who should be most grateful to the Supreme for sending me such a blessing in the midst of all my troubles. Away with dismal thought! I have nothing to reproach myself with. You, my Amelia, are now my only solace —my only hope and comfort in my declining years. Bless you, my child, for I acknowledge no other daughter but you."

Amelia returned his embrace, and secretly exulted at the power which she had over him, and which would enable her to carry out her ambitious and selfish wishes to the fullest extent.

"But come, my dear benefactor," she said "let us retire from this room, and endeavour to forget all that has taken place. It was accident alone, doubtless, that brought the fugitives here, and I trust that you will never behold them again, since the meeting with them seems to cause me so much excitement."

"No," exclaimed Mr. Mason; "Heaven forbid that they should ever again cross my path, for I know not what then might be the consequences."

Amelia coincided with him, for it was her policy to agree in everything he said, and taking his arm, they quitted the room in which this conversation had taken place, and hastened to the study, where Amelia, fearful of the effect which too much excitement might have upon him, for reasons very well known to herself, sought to change the topic of conversation. But, notwithstanding all that he had said, and the arguments which the designing Amelia Arlington had made use of, Mr. Mason could not close his ears to the voice of conscience, which told him that, in whatever different light he might endeavour to view it, he had acted towards his unfortunate daughter, and still was acting, with the most unnatural cruelty, and that every sense of feeling and justice must condemn his inhumanity of conduct towards one who had ever been to him one of the most affectionate of children.

He threw himself into a chair on their entrance into the room, and for several minutes, with his face buried in his hands, he resigned himself to the most gloomy and torturing reflections, which Amelia did not think proper to interrupt. All the innocent actions of Mary's childhood passed in rapid but vivid review before his memory; he recalled to his recollection all the many proofs of the dutiful affection she bore towards him, and which she had at all times taken such pains to evince, and his conscience upbraided him more and more. To his conscience-stricken imagination the spirit of his departed and amiable wife, whom his poor child so much resembled in features and disposition, seemed to frown upon him, and to breathe reproaches in his ears; and at length, overpowered by his feelings, he started from his chair, in a state of the greatest agitation, and staring wildly around him, he exclaimed, in a voice that made Amelia start and took her by surprise:

"I am a wretch! an unnatural monster! to act in the manner that I have done, and the curse of Heaven must pursue me for it. Is she not my own child, whom it was my duty to love and cherish, and I have abandoned her to misery and despair? Oh, what a heart of stone must I possess to be able to resist her pathetic appeal to me for mercy, and to spurn her from me in her wretchedness. What happiness can such a villain as myself expect to experience?"

"My dear sir," remonstrated Amelia, in her most persuasive accents, "why do you thus unjustly reproach yourself? Be calm, I beseech you, and reflect dispassionately upon all that you have done, and truth and reason must convince you that you have nothing whatever to blame yourself for, and that however great the sufferings of Mrs. Parker may be, she has brought them all upon herself, by her unnatural disobedience to your will in uniting herself with a man who has since proved himself to be a villain. Had it not been for the fatal and guilty step which she thought proper to take, my poor dear uncle might still have been living and happy."

"True! true!" cried the weak-minded gentleman; "she has been the indirect cause of all these calamities, and why should I regret the wretched state to which she is reduced? She deserves it all, and justice demands that I should for ever discard from my breast, and disown for a daughter, the wife of an assassin. Oh, Amelia, what bitter cause have you to look upon her with loathing, and to heap your curses upon her head and that of her guilty husband. I will endeavour to forget her; I will cease to remember that such a being ever existed."

Amelia was about to make some reply to this cruel speech, when she was prevented from doing so by a knock at the door, and on its being opened, Mr. Goodson entered the room. She was dressed as if for a journey, and Mr. Mason and Amelia gazed at her with no little surprise.

"Why, how is this?" demanded the former; "what is your business here, Mrs. Goodson, and why do you appear so excited?"

"My business is soon told, sir," answered Mrs. Goodson; "I come to bid you good-bye; I am going."

"Going?" repeated Mr. Mason and Amelia in a breath, and gazing with still more astonishment upon her.

"Yes," she returned, "I am going to leave you. After the scene I have witnessed to day, and the sufferings of that poor lady and her husband, I can never consent to remain in the service of a gentleman who can act with such unnatural cruelty towards his own daughter, spurning her from him in her wretchedness and adversity, and leaving her and her unfortunate husband in all probability to starve."

"Can I possibly hear aright?" exclaimed Mr. Mason, passionately; "this from my own servant?"

"No, sir," answered Mrs. Goodson, "I am no longer servant of yours. I discharge myself, and sincerely hope that you may be brought to a proper sense of feeling, Mr. Mason, for that I understand is your name, and that you will yet endeavour to make all the atonement in your power for the past."

"This is unbearable!" said Mr. Mason, in a voice of great agitation; "you are not going to leave me in this manner, Mrs. Goodson, without giving me fair warning?"

"Indeed, but I am, though," replied Mrs. Goodson, pertly; "there is no occasion for any warning between us. You are welcome to the wages that are due to me, for, thank God, I am not without a pound or two that has been honestly earnt."

"Mrs. Goodson," said Amelia, "you forget yourself, and your language is most unjustified and insolent."

"It may be so," retorted Mrs. Goodson, "it may be so, in your opinion, miss, but it is such as my feelings prompt me to make use of, and I do not retract a single word of it. You may reconcile it to your feelings, if you can, to usurp the place of this gentleman's daughter, while she and her husband are left to misery and destitution, that is your business, not mine; but I must say that I do not envy you the feelings that must take possession of your breast some time or other."

The bosom of the haughty Amelia swelled with indignation at this homethrust, and she frowned angrily upon Mrs. Goodson, as she exclaimed—

"This insolence is not to be borne; Mr. Mason I appeal to you; am I thus to be subjected to be lectured and upbraided by this woman?"

"Mrs. Goodson," observed her master, in a faltering voice, "your language and conduct is most reprehensible and unjustifiable. I demand that you immediately make an ample apology to Miss Amelia, and——"

"I have no apology to make, sir," interrupted Mrs. Goodson. "I have spoken my mind, and I do not regret a single word that I have uttered. You yourself will some time or other, or I am much mistaken, have bitter cause to repent of your cruel conduct towards your daughter, whose only crime has been in giving her hand to the man who alone possessed her affections;

and for that you have discarded her from your breast, disowned her, left her to all the horrors of want and misery of the most insupportable nature. You could witness her sufferings unmoved, and turn a deaf ear to her supplications for mercy, for pity, and forgiveness; oh, shame—shame! I should despise myself were I to continue in the service of one who could so unpardonably commit him, and of whose character I had heretofore entertained so different an opinion. But I have nothing more to say, than to bid you farewell, and I only hope that you may meet with another who will serve you as faithfully as I have done during the time I have been with you."

"Stay, Mrs. Goodson," said Mr. Mason, much agitated, and feeling himself most keenly and justly rebuked by the observations she had made use of; "will you not listen to reason? You surely are not going to leave me thus?"

"Yes," replied Mrs. Goodson, "my mind is made up, and no persuasions can induce me to alter it; my conduct may appear strange and unreasonable, but it is nevertheless dictated by my conscience. Dear me, never shall I be able to get that poor lady, your unfortunate daughter, and her husband, and their innocent child, from my sight, and I only hope that I may again meet with them, that I may afford them all the assistance in my power; they shall never want an asylum while I have the means of providing one. Good-day, sir, and God grant that your heart may yet be moved with compassion towards them, and that as some atonement for the past you will endeavour to release them from the dreadful difficulties by which they are surrounded at present."

With these words Mrs. Goodson dropped them a formal curtsey, and then immediately quitted the room, leaving Mr. Mason and Amelia completely overwhelmed with astonishment and confusion.

"This is worse than all," exclaimed Mr. Mason, at length; "the words of that woman have sunk deep in my heart, and rendered me wretched. To be thus insulted and upbraided by my own servant! And yet my conscience cannot but acknowledge the force and truth of her observations, and I feel that I have acted with the most unpardonable severity towards my unhappy daughter. Would to Heaven that I could recall the past; that I could once more behold her and assure her of my forgiveness. Oh, how could I so heartlessly reject her pathetic supplications! I shall go mad!".

He struck his forehead passionately as he spoke, and paced the room in a state of the most violent excitement.

"And is it possible, my dear sir," observed Amelia, who was, in fact, scarcely less excited than himself, "that you can so unjustly condemn yourself? Why will you suffer the insolent remarks of this woman to make such an effect upon you? Surely this is betraying a weakness that I thought you incapable of. Come, arouse yourself; you have nothing to blame yourself for. Mrs. Parker defied your authority—brought misery and disgrace upon you—treated you with the basest ingratitude, and thus severed every tie that bound you together. She is unworthy of a second thought, and as for her husband, the murderer of my unfortunate uncle, can you, do you pity him for any sufferings he may have to endure?"

"Oh, no," answered the deluded man; 'he richly merits any fate, however severe, which may overtake him. But my mind is distracted, and I scarcely know what to say; Heaven teach me how to act, for I know not."

"You have acted only as any other parent would have done under similar circumstances," said Amelia; "and may, therefore, set the scandal of the world at defiance. Let me again beg of you to try to tranquillize your feelings, which have been naturally excited by the strange and unwarrantable conduct of Mrs. Goodson, and you will soon learn to forget the event which has this day so unexpectedly taken place."

"Would to Heaven that I could do so." returned Mr. Mason; "but painful thoughts will crowd upon my brain in spite of myself, and render me restless, dissatisfied, and undecided. Would to God she had never been born, then I should not have been subjected to this constant state of misery."

"Nay," said Amelia, "banish her from your memory; if you persevere, I am certain that you will be able to do so; and I will endeavour by every means in my power to alleviate the anguish of your mind, and to supply the place of that daughter who is now lost to you for ever."

"I know you will, my Amelia," said Mr. Mason, at the same time imprinting a kiss upon the forehead of the deceitful beauty; "I know you will, for you have ever done so, and had it not been for your soothing voice of sympathy, Heaven only knows what would have become of me in my solitude. Would to God that she had been half so good as you."

"Oh, my beloved benefactor, my only earthly friend," ejaculated his companion,

THE WRECK OF BEN BINNACLE'S LUGGER.

fixing upon him one of her most affection-ate looks, and speaking in such silvery accents that were enough to deceive and fascinate the most insensible heart; "do not give me that flattering praise which I know is so little my due. How can I ever evince by conduct towards you, my sense of the gratitude I owe you for the heavy weight of obligation I am under to you, for the unexampled, the more than paren-tal kindness which you have ever shown towards me? Believe me, it is the con-stant study of my life to convince you of the esteem and reverence which I bear you,

and when I shall cease to do so, discard me from your bosom, and endeavour to forget that there was ever such a being as Amelia Arlington in existence."

"Sweet girl!" returned Mr. Mason, completely overcome by her manner, "that is impossible; my Amelia, whom I now look upon as my own child, will never do anything that can forfeit my affection, and I have to thank the Almighty, who has sent me such a blessing in the midst of my affliction. But the abrupt departure of Mrs. Goodson from the hall vexes and annoys me. She was a good servant, and

I shall feel her loss greatly ; besides, who knows the scandal she may spread abroad to my prejudice?"

"Do not entertain any apprehensions upon the subject, my dear sir," remarked Amelia, "for you are proof against all that the voice of slander may think proper to promulgate. No reasonable person can blame your conduct towards your daughter, after the manner in which she forfeited all claim to your affection and consideration."

"Well," said Mr. Mason, with a sigh, " it may be so; but let us drop this painful subject, and endeavour to be calm."

"Well spoken, my dear sir," replied Amelia, "and most happy shall I be in being able to contribute to the tranquillity of your mind."

Mr. Mason returned no answer, but again became immersed in deep thought, and it was plain from the expression of his countenance that the agitation of his mind was far from suffering any abatement. Amelia withdrew herself to the window, where she could indulge in the various thoughts that also agitated her breast unobserved, and a long silence ensued, which neither of them seemed inclined to interrupt. Amelia reflected upon all the observations which Mrs. Goodson had so candidly made use of, and while she could not but acknowledge their truth, she felt extremely mortified, and was apprehensive of the effect which they might have upon Mr. Mason. She regretted that accident had ever guided the footsteps of Mary and her husband to the hall; for the wretched condition in which they were had, in spite of all her efforts to the contrary, excited in her breast some feelings of pity and remorse, when she knew the part she had acted in strengthening the prejudice which her father entertained towards her.

At length Mr. Mason again rose from his seat, and advancing towards her, said—

"My dear Amelia, why should I tax your patience thus? This is a melancholy duty for you to have to perform, and I should be ungenerous and unreasonable to wish to detain you longer in my society, in my present gloomy state of mind. Leave me, my dear girl; I wish to be alone, and I will endeavour to regain my composure, and, if possible, to forget what has happened. Leave me, Amelia."

"I will do so, my benefactor!" said Amelia; " thought I would fain remain with you, and endeavour to assist in tranquillising your feelings ; for nothing can cause me more pain and regret than to see you unhappy."

"Bless you, Amelia," he replied ; "I know full well the sincerity of the words you utter, and no one can feel more grateful than myself; but probably the free and uninterrupted indulgence of my own thoughts may tend more to bring about the object you have so much at heart, than anything else. We shall see each other again shortly, and then I hope that I shall so far have recovered myself as to be able to converse on what has taken place with calmness."

He embraced her, and she then retired from the room, and he was once more left to his own thoughts, which, as may be supposed, were of the most conflicting and torturing description. It was in vain that he tried to reconcile himself to the arguments of Amelia, or to acquit himself of cruelty and injustice towards his ill-fated daughter; her pale and emaciated features and attenuated form were still present to his imagination, and the more he called to mind her pathetic appeals to him for mercy and forgiveness, and the stern refusal he gave to her supplications, the more did he condemn and reproach himself, and the greater became his agitation.

"Surely all who hear of my conduct," he observed, " must say that I have acted with the greatest inhumanity, and pity and commiserate that unfortunate being whom nature should have prompted me not only to pardon, but likewise to cherish. I have acted with too much precipitation, and do now most sincerely regret that I should have been unable to control the excitement of my feelings. The observations of Mrs. Goodson were true, and I find it utterly impossible, in my own conscience, to deny that they were so. What will now become of her, friendless and destitute as she is? But why does my mind thus waver? Had she acted in obedience to my will, she might now have been happy, and I should have been spared all the years of anxiety it has been my lot to experience. She has brought all her troubles upon herself, and she deserves to suffer. Can I ever again take to my bosom or acknowledge as my daughter the wife of a murderer? No, reason and Nature revolt at the idea. Let me be firm, and no longer give way to those emotions which only serve to keep me in a constant state of torture. I must try to forget her, and to place my whole affections upon the amiable and gentle Amelia, who has ever performed the part of a daughter towards me, since she has been under my protection."

He paused, and again deeply ruminated, but in spite of all his efforts, he found it was impossible to obtain that tranquillity and firmness of mind which he was so anxious to accomplish. In this restless and agitated state he continued throughout the day; and when he again met Amelia, all her efforts to compose him were nearly unsuccessful. But we must leave him to follow the footsteps of the unfortunate Mary Parker and her husband.

It would be impossible to do adequate justice to the feelings that distracted their bosoms, as they departed from that mansion in which they had experienced so unexpected and painful a meeting, and after the cruel and remorseless reception they had met with from Mary's father. Her brain was racked to madness; his curses still seemed to ring in her ears, and she scarcely knew what she did. Overpowered by her feelings, her fortitude nearly forsook her, she was almost sinking, and it was wonderful how, even with the support of her husband, she was enabled to proceed. The poor boy was nearly heartbroken at what he had witnessed and the sufferings of his parents; and his tender and youthful frame was almost exhausted by the extraordinary fatigue he had undergone; but still he bore up as well as he could, and tried to conceal his real feelings from his parents as much as possible. Where were they now to go? They knew not, and they wandered slowly on they knew not whither.

Like the others that had preceded it, it was a most cheerless day, and the cold blustering wind penetrated keenly through their thin apparel, and added to the misery and wretchedness of their condition. But at length they were compelled to stop, and Mary cast one sad and lingering look towards the Hall, which might still be seen between the trees, and sinking on the shoulder of her husband, and looking piteously in his face, she ejaculated—

"Oh, God! this is, indeed, a more dreadful blow than any we have yet experienced. What cursed fate directed our footsteps to that place? Oh, my misguided father, surely, in the serious moments of your reflection, your heart must condemn your cruel and inhuman treatment of your unfortunate daughter, especially when you beheld her again after the lapse of so many years, and under such wretched and heart rending circumstances! Never—never can I efface from my memory his fearful looks—his words—the hatred with which he spurned me from him, and denounced me as an alien to his breast; and the recollection will surely drive me to madness!"

"Alas! my deeply-injured and suffering wife," replied Richard, in a voice of the deepest emotion, "what can I say to you—how endeavour to console you under this dreadful trial? My heart bleeds for you, while at the same time I know not in what language to condemn the inhuman conduct of your father, who could behold your sufferings unmoved, and could turn a deaf ear to your fervent and powerful appeals to him for mercy and forgiveness. Surely his heart must have become insensible to every proper feeling, or he could never have acted thus. But remorse must sooner or later overtake him, and then he will bitterly repent the unnatural length to which he has suffered his feelings of indignation and revenge to carry him. But, oh! my poor Mary, endeavour to arouse yourself, and to forget that this torturing meeting has ever taken place."

"Forget it?" repeated our heroine; "oh, that is impossible. It is stamped upon my memory in characters of fire, that must pursue me to my grave. He cursed me, too, and it still seems to ring in my ears, and fills my soul with horror. My God! better would it have been had I been dead, ere I could have experienced such a terrible trial as this!"

"And I have been the cause of all," said her husband, "and upon my head alone should the vengeance of Heaven fall. But come, my beloved Mary; let us endeavour to proceed, and we may yet providentially be able to meet with some kind beings who will take compassion on us."

"Alas!" sighed Mary, "my strength is almost exhausted, and I know not how I shall be able to proceed much further; and oh! whither can we direct our footsteps?—where can we now expect to find relief in this strange, wild place, where all mankind seem to be our enemies?"

"My unfortunate partner, say not so," returned our hero. "At least, there is one who, though a stranger to us, has proved that she has a heart that can sympathise with us in our misfortunes. I mean Mrs. Goodson, to whom we are indebted for our present means of relief."

"Oh, yes," ejaculated his wife; "I had forgotten her. She has, indeed, been most kind to us, and may Heaven reward her for it."

"It will," observed Richard, "and all those who view with an eye of pity and charity their less fortunate fellow creatures. But there is danger while we remain here. Possessing the feelings of malice and revenge that your father does towards me, he might send those in pursuit of me who would, for the sake of the reward which is offered for my apprehension, only be too happy to get me in their power."

"Oh, no," gasped forth Mary, "surely he could never be so lost to every feeling of shame and humanity. And yet, after the interview which we have had with him, what have we not a right to expect? We must away; and yet I am so weak and faint—my limbs fail me—my heart seems to sink within me, and——Almighty God, assist us, for without Thine aid I see nothing but utter destruction before us !"

"Come, come," said Richard, in the most tender accents, and encircling her waist with his arm, "lean on me, and I will support your feeble footsteps to some place of safety, which I trust to Heaven we shall encounter before long. I feel a nameless sensation of horror and disgust while we remain within sight of that mansion."

Mary shuddered and sighed deeply, as she once more cast her eyes towards the hall.

"Farewell, cruel father!" she ejaculated in a melancholy and solemn voice, "and may Heaven soften your heart, which is now, alas ! so invulnerable to the tender appeal of nature and humanity. My poor boy! oh, what a dreadful trial is this for one of your tender age."

"Dear mother," replied the noble-hearted boy, endeavouring as much as possible to conceal his weak and exhausted condition, and looking up affectionately in her face, "fear not for me, for I am yet strong, and shall, I hope, be able to struggle against all difficulties. Come, come, let us begone, and I trust that we shall, ere long, meet with some place of shelter."

The fond parents could not reply, but embraced him affectionately, and then, Richard supporting his wife, the unfortunate fugitives moved slowly from the spot, and took the first path that presented itself to them, and which seemed the most likely to lead to some place where they might obtain the assistance of which they stood so much in need. But it was indeed a most painful and arduous task for Mary; her strength every moment failed her more and more, and what with fatigue and terrible anxiety of mind, her husband was scarcely in a better condition than herself.

The wind now blew almost a complete hurricane, and that also greatly impeded their progress, while their limbs were nearly benumbed with the cold, and the terrors of their situation every moment became the more apparent. They looked anxiously around them, but there was little or no change in the lonely and dismal aspect of the scene, and they could not perceive the least signs of a human habitation. For a few minutes they were again compelled to pause, in order to endeavour in some measure to recruit their exhausted strength, and Richard, as well as he could, sought to shield the delicate frame of his wife from the piercing wind, and looked with the utmost anxiety and apprehension upon her pale and careworn features, and her sunken eyes, which plainly told him that unless kind Providence should send speedy relief, what little remaining strength she possessed must entirely give way.

"Alas!" she sighed, in a faint voice, and as she looked dismally around her, "what a wretched place has cruel fate cast us upon, as if in mockery of our sufferings. The further we proceed, the dreariness of our prospects seem to increase, and dark despair frowns upon us on every side. Oh, my beloved, but unfortunate husband, what will become of us? In spite of all my efforts, I feel that it is impossible for me to proceed much further. The dreadful hardships to which we have been so long exposed have been too much for my strength to bear, and——Oh, All-merciful God, help us!"

"Oh, my dearest, my devoted wife," cried Richard Parker, in a voice of the deepest emotion, "how torturing, how indescribably torturing it is to me to witness your sufferings, and to know that I have not the least power to relieve you. Heaven I beseech you to look down with pity upon us, and not to put our fortitude to too severe a test."

Again they moved slowly on their way, but it was with sad and despairing hearts that they did so, for every step they took seemed but to increase their difficulties, and cruel Fate did, indeed, seem but to mock their sufferings.

And now the wind changed; black and heavy clouds seemed to obscure the horizon, and everything betokened similar tempestuous weather to that which had prevailed for the last few days. Soon those ominous clouds discharged their contents; down came the rain, first in large drops, which quickly merged themselves into one huge and immeasurable sheet of water, descending upon the earth with overwhelming violence. Then the wind ceased altogether, and was succeeded by the sullen rumbling of thunder in the distance, like the snoring of some intoxicated giant in his sleep. If we may be permitted to follow the simile, the giant's slumbers were disturbed by the vivid lightning's flash; and, as though excited to wrath by the circumstance, he gave free vent to his passion in two or three successive roars that seemed to shake the very earth to its centre, and to utter one terrific malediction upon the human race. Nothing whatever could exceed the terror of the elemental warfare which now ensued. Peal after peal succeeded the lightning's flash, the earth trembling, and the sturdiest trees quivering, as if beneath the influence of an earthquake. Then came down the rain in still more deluging torrents, and blinded by its violence, confused and horror-struck by the frightful scene which prevailed around them, our unhappy wanderers became transfixed as statues, and were compelled to cling to each other to prevent themselves from falling. It was truly a moment of horror, which might have tried the stoutest nerve, and it will, therefore, not be wondered, after the many hardships they had had to encounter, that they should become completely subdued.

They looked into each other's countenances with an expression of despair, which showed at once the poignant agony of soul they were enduring, and, for a few minutes, quite overwhelmed by the horrors of the tempest, which, as we have before stated, had completely paralysed their faculties, they were unable to utter a word.

The elemental warfare continued; in fact, it seemed rather to increase in fury than to abate, and it would have defied the most eloquent pen to describe, or the most skilful artist to have depictured on canvas, the combined terrors of the scene which prevailed.

Although so early in the day, the black and ponderous clouds that hung upon the horizon (save when broken at intervals by the glare of the lightning) gave it all the appearance of the darkest midnight, and, if possible, added to the horrors of the scene. Richard Parker, as we have said before, was too much overpowered by his feelings to be able to speak; but when he looked in the ghastly countenances and fast-sinking faculties of his heroic and devoted wife and child, and knew how utterly incapable he was of rendering them any assistance, or of offering any observation which might at all be calculated to inspire them with consolation or hope, he mentally and devoutly offered up a prayer to Heaven for mercy and protection, though at that awful moment their fate seemed to be inevitable.

For a few brief minutes the storm abated, as if it had exhausted itself, by its extraordinary and powerful exertions, and was compelled to pause for the purpose of recruiting its strength, and our hapless fugitives, who, as may be expected, were drenched to the skin, and presented the most wretched objects of misery conceivable, looked at each other with countenances of despair and agony, but still, for a few moments, were unable to communicate their thoughts to each other. Our heroine was ready to sink to the earth, and so enfeebled was the condition of her husband by the remarkable exertions he had undergone, and the appearance of fortitude and composure he was compelled to assume, that it was not without the greatest difficulty he was enabled to support her. As for the poor boy, William, he clung closely to the side of his mother, and looking up with an intensity of feeling into the face of both his parents, attempted to make use of no observation, but seemed to resign himself to the will of Providence. Although so young, he possessed the heart of a hero, as his conduct throughout the whole of the numerous hardships which they latterly, in particular, had to encounter sufficiently testified.

"My wife, my Mary!" at length our hero formed strength sufficient to articulate, as he pressed her more closely to his bosom, "what can I say, what can I do to relieve you from the miseries which you are enduring? Oh, God! this trial is too severe, and quite unmans me. How pale, how ghastly you look; how weak your tender limbs become, and my fast failing strength——Heaven, I earnestly beseech thee to have mercy on us! This hideous tempest, even more awful, if possible, than any of those which we have hitherto experienced, and no prospect of shelter at hand—what is to become of us? Speak to me, Mary, if but one word to——"

He was prevented from finishing the sentence, by the terrific flashes of lightning that darted from the heavens, followed by peal after peal of crashing thunder, the effect of which was indescribable. Several trees in the vicinity in which they were standing were rent asunder, and fell with a loud crash; the earth trembled beneath them; the rain again descended in overwhelming torrents, and Mary, uttering a faint shriek, sunk insensible in the arms of her husband.

What was now the terror of the wretched wanderers' situation? No language, however powerful, could adequately pourtray it, and, therefore, we must leave it to the imagination of the reader.

Appalled, and almost reduced to the same deplorable situation as herself, our hero held her inanimate form in his arms, and gazed with the most indescribable feelings of anguish and despair in her ghastly countenance, while the boy hung despairingly over her, and fearful that she was dying, if not already dead, he was unable any longer to control the agony of his feelings, but called frantically upon her name, and wept aloud.

All the time the storm continued to rage with the most terrific violence, and there was no short cessation of its fury to afford them even a temporary relief. Thunder, lightning, and rain, seemed to be trying their various powers of destructiveness, and it would be difficult to decide which had the supremacy.

"Father of mercy help us!" at length exclaimed Richard, raising one of his hands solemnly towards the angry heavens, which seemed to frown despair upon them, "for without your aid we must perish."

"Dear father," said William, "I thought that, by the last flash of lightning, I saw something like a building yonder," (indicating where he meant); "could we convey poor mother there——"

"Ah! child!" interrupted our hero, as his eye caught the object to which his attention had been directed, "I see it now; and although it bears not the form of a human habitation, it may at least afford us some temporary shelter from this fearful storm, and in the meantime, if God so will it, some better relief may be afforded us."

The object which had attracted the boy's attention was, as well as our hero could distinguish, an incongruous mass of stone or brickwork, which took no definite shape whatever, but still, anything that offered the least prospect of a shelter from the tempest was indeed most welcome, and raising the insensible form of his wife in his arms, at the same time breathing a prayer to Heaven to aid him in his efforts to preserve the lives of those so precious to him he hurried as fast as his almost exhausted limbs would permit him towards it It was not many minutes before he reached it, and pausing for a moment to rest himself, he contemplated it with some degree of surprise and interest.

There was a vast quantity of ruins lying mouldering about it, that seemed, as far as could be gathered from their heterogeneous description, in far remote ages, to have formed some church or monastery, and there could be little doubt that this was a mausoleum attached to it. In fact, there were portions of a tablet, with fragments of a Latin inscription, that denoted the same. It was very lofty, and bore the traces of having originally possessed much

architectural beauty. It was overgrown with ivy, and although much of it had crumbled into decay under the remorseless scythe of Time, there was enough of it left to afford a shelter from the storm. Yet as our hero contemplated it, and the insensible form of the beloved being whom he supported in his arms, he could not help feeling a shuddering sensation, almost amounting to horror; for the awful idea occurred to him, that he was conveying her into her final tomb, as there was scarcely any signs of life remaining in the cherished being whom he held in his arms. But there was no time to hesitate, fiercely as the storm was at that time raging, and solemnly invoking the mercy and protection of Heaven, he entered this gloomy place, followed by his son. The interior of the place confirmed the opinion he had formed of it. There were the remains of the statue of a knight in armour, and several inscriptions on the walls, which Time had nearly effaced, but of which sufficient remained to denote that it had been a place devoted to the interment of the remains of some noble family, though all traces of any coffin were gone, and the earth was completely overgrown with rank grass and noxious weeds.

The roof of this place, however, was comparatively sound, and it, therefore, afforded the wanderers the shelter which they wanted, though the effect of the lightning, as it darted in at the opening through which they had entered, and the rattling of the thunder, which seemed to threaten every moment to bury them in the ruins, was, if possible, still more awful than it was in the open air, and made our hero shudder with a sensation of the most uncontrollable dread. He, however, seated himself on a large block of stone which he found in the place, and holding his unfortunate wife to his bosom, endeavoured by every means in his power to recall her to animation, while William knelt at their feet, and clasping one of his mother's cold hands in his, looked up anxiously and affectionately in her pale face, and was unable to utter a word, such were the powerful emotions that agitated his bosom. But not the least signs of returning consciousness for some time appeared in poor Mary Parker, and her unhappy husband was worked up to a state almost bordering upon frenzy, fearing that she would never recover. Again and again he pressed his lips upon her cold cheek, and calling frantically upon her name, endeavoured, though in vain, to arouse her from this death-like state of torpidity.

" Alas !" he sighed, " how torturing, how truly heart-rending is this horrible state of suspense. My wife, my poor suffering Mary, oh, will you never again speak to me? Has, then, the grim destroyer at last overtaken you? Forbid it Heaven, for to perish thus were horrible indeed, and if I am deprived of you, what remains for me but to hasten the decree of Fate, and to end a life which for so long a period has been a burthen to me?"

" Oh, my dear father," said the boy, looking earnestly and appealingly in his face; " I pray you do not talk in this sad manner, but put your trust in Heaven, which will not desert us in this dreadful trial. Were I to lose both of you, my beloved parents, oh, what would become of me, left as I should be without a friend in the world, or any one to whom I could look for protection?"

" My poor boy," replied his father; " in consideration of you, and the noble, the heroic fortitude with which you have supported such heavy trials for one of your tender age, I ought not to have spoken what I did; but my mind is so agitated and bewildered by the terrible hardships we have had to encounter, and the awful dangers by which we are at present surrounded, that I scarcely know what I say. For your sake, and that of your unfortunate mother, I will seek to bear up against the misfortunes by which we are surrounded as well as I can, and pray that the Almighty will shortly grant us some amelioration to our misery."

The poor boy kissed his hand with a fervour whice fully evinced the feelings he had not the power or the language to give utterance to, and a dismal silence ensued, which was only interrupted by the voice of the tempest, which continued to rage with the most unabated fury. It was truly frightful to gaze from that awful place upon the horrors that prevailed around, and every moment seemed to threaten them with destruction. Still for some time longer did our heroine remain in the same state of utter unconsciousness, and it was only by the low palpitation of her heart that life was at all perceptible. It would be impossible for us to do ample justice to the feelings that agitated the bosom of our hero during this awful and agonising period. He found it impossible to control them, and bitter sobs of agony, and prayers to Heaven for mercy, escaped him alternately. Again he renewed his efforts, with redoubled energy, to recall to life the beloved partner of his misfortunes; and at length they were crowned with something like success, for she breathed

more freely, and again vehemently pressing his lips upon her cheek, he called affectionately upon her name, and tried every possible means to arouse her to recollection. At length she opened her eyes, and gazed wildly around her, and a weight was removed from his heart which was almost too heavy to bear.

" My Mary, my dear suffering Mary!" he ejaculated, pressing her form still closer to his heart; " oh, thank God that you are not yet taken from me; oh, look up and speak to me; it is your husband who holds you in his arms, and who has been watching your recovery from this fearful trance with such torturing anxiety."

" Richard," gasped forth Mary, in a faint voice, and fixing her eyes earnestly upon him, " you here; this strange place— where have I been, and where are we now?"

" Compose yourself, my dearest," replied our hero; " we have at last obtained a temporary place of shelter, and when this furious tempest shall fortunately have abated, we shall, I trust, be able to discover some house where we shall find that assistance of which we stand so much in need."

" God grant that we may," replied our heroine; " but I am so weak and sick at heart, and this awful storm is such, that it strikes terror to my soul, and seems as though High Heaven frowned upon us, and threatened us with some awful doom."

" Be firm, my Mary," returned her husband, embracing her affectionately, " and all will yet, I trust, be well, notwithstanding the dismal prospects with which we are at present surrounded."

Mary did endeavour to control her emotions, but was unable to return any answer to the observations of her husband, and she was so faint and exhausted that she had scarcely strength to move a limb, and in spite of the efforts which he made to conceal it, Richard's emotion was so great that he could with difficulty sustain himself.

So far from the storm subsiding, it every moment became more fierce and terrific, and our hero could not gaze upon it without feelings of the utmost dread and horror. Inclement as the weather had been for some time past, it even now exceeded all that it had ever done, and the imagination was worked up to a pitch of excitement and awe, which was almost insupportable. And thus more than a couple of hours passed away, without any particular change taking place, and there still appeared but little signs of the storm abating; and even if it should, their prospects would be but little better, for they knew not what direction to take where they were likely to find a place of refuge, and in the present deplorable state of Mary, it seemed almost impossible that she should be able to travel.

Richard was in a state of despair; and what made his sufferings the greater was the powerful and arduous efforts he was compelled to make to conceal them, so that he might not increase the agitation of his wife; but notwithstanding her distressed condition, and the apparent hopelessness of any relief from it, she bore it all with the most exemplary patience and fortitude.

"Alas! Richard," she observed, looking anxiously upon him, "how pale, how careworn and exhausted you look. In spite of your efforts to conceal it, I perceive but too clearly that your strength is fast failing you, and that, unless we meet with some speedy relief, you will be unable to bear up much longer, and then, indeed, our situation will, indeed, be too awful to think upon."

"Do not alarm yourself, my dear Mary," replied our hero; "fear not for me, for I trust, with the goodness of Providence, that I shall yet find strength and fortitude to support the heavy troubles by which we are at present surrounded; but you, so worn down with fatigue and anxiety of mind, I fear, alas! will never be able to recover from the severe shock which your system has received."

"I am better now," said Mary, struggling with her feelings, and endeavouring to arouse herself from the depressed and languid state in which she was, though the task was one which was almost impossible of accomplishment. "I feel much better now, and would but this fearful storm subside, I trust that I should revive altogether, and should, with your assistance, be able to proceed; but, alas! how gloomy and cheerless is the prospect before us; whither, oh, whither can we direct our footsteps?"

"I know not, Mary," answered her husband, in melancholy accents; "but kind Heaven in its infinite mercy will surely direct our footsteps to some hospitable dwelling, where we may hope to meet with assistance, which, thanks to the generous-hearted Mrs. Goodson, we are supplied with the present means of purchasing. We surely cannot be far from some town or village, amongst the inhabitants of which we may find some humane person who will take compassion on us."

"God grant that you may not be disappointed in your expectations," said our heroine. "They must indeed possess a hard heart who could refuse to assist poor unfortunate creatures in our wretched condition. Oh, surely my unnatural parent must be stung with remorse, could he but form the slightest conjecture of the sufferings to which we are exposed, and he would by his future conduct seek to make some atonement for the past."

Richard shook his head doubtfully, as he replied—

"Think not of him, Mary; it will only serve to agitate you more than you are at present. We shall, I hope to God, be able yet to rescue ourselves from our present difficulties without his assistance."

Mary said nothing in reply, but she exerted herself to the utmost, and in a short time became more firm and calm than could have been at all expected under the circumstances. The storm now decreased in violence, and enabled them to proceed on their melancholy journey. The lightning ceased to dart its forked fury; the thunder gradually rolled off into the distance, until its voice could no longer be heard; and the rain did not descend with that violence as it had done heretofore. This fortunate change in the weather greatly tended to reanimate their spirits, and Mary felt her strength revive, which was soon apparent in the different aspect of her countenance, and which we need not say was a source of the most infinite gratification to our hero, who had previously almost resigned himself to despair. In a short time the storm ceased altogether, and there now remained no further obstacle to their proceeding, which they thought it would be better for them to do as soon as possible, and before night set in. Richard looked at his wife anxiously, and she guessing what he meant, said—

"Let us resume our weary journey, dear Richard; this rest has served to revive me, and I have no doubt that, with your assistance, I shall be able to proceed without much difficulty."

"Thank God for that," he replied, embracing her, "and I hope that we shall not have to proceed far before we shall meet with some place where we shall be able to meet with some place of accommodation where we can remain for a few days until we have recovered ourselves from the fatigue and terrible anxiety of mind which we have for so long a period undergone."

Mary did, indeed, arouse herself, and was soon ready for starting on their way; and having first devoutly implored the assistance of Heaven, Mary leaning on

THE STRANGER EMERGING FROM THE WOOD.

her husband's arm, whilst the affectionate boy, William, supported her as well as he could on the other side, they issued from the gloomy place in which they had so fortunately found a shelter from the storm. The air was piercingly cold, and as their progress was necessarily slow, they suffered much from its effects; but still they endured it with much more fortitude than might have been expected, and notwithstanding the gloominess of the prospect before them, they were not without the hope that they should ere long meet with some relief, and it was that confidence

which inspired them with more determination than they would probably otherwise have experienced.

They, however, wandered on to a considerable distance without anything at all appearing to gratify or realise their expectations, and the aspect of the country remained much the same, as they had hitherto found it, namely, wild and cheerless in the extreme, and it would seem as if it were entirely deserted by the human race, for they did not meet with a single individual on their way; no one from whom they might have the means of obtaining the information they so much required. In this way upwards of two hours were exhausted, and although they had been frequently obliged to stop, and their progress, as we have before said, was necessarily slow, they had traversed a considerable distance of ground, and notwithstanding all the endeavours she had made to bear herself up against the difficulties that they had to encounter, our heroine felt herself so weak and languid, that she feared she would not be able to continue the weary journey much longer, and her husband saw plainly what the consequences were likely to be, and his courage almost forsook him entirely. Still with a heroism most remarkable, and beyond all praise, she persevered, and they continued on their way, inwardly beseeching the Almighty to assist them in the midst of their accumulating difficulties.

And now the day began to close, and they were fearful that they should have to pass another night without a shelter, in which case they foreboded too well what the consequences must be.

"Alas!" said Richard, "it seems that all in vain are our efforts; Providence has deserted us, and all our hopes appear to be futile. What is to be done? My mind is racked to think of it. Oh, surely we have never deserved to suffer thus."

"It is the will of Heaven, my dear Richard," returned his wife calmly, "and however severe the trial, we must learn to submit to it with patience and resignation. It is certainly a wild and desolate place, but still something seems to assure me that, if we persevere a little longer, we shall yet be able to meet with some place of refuge. I will continue to exert myself to the utmost for your sake and that of our innocent child, whose fortitude under such trying circumstances is as extraordinary as it is beyond all praise. Come, let us again pursue our way."

"Excellent woman!" exclaimed our hero, "best and most devoted of wives! what can ever sufficiently repay you for such heroic, such exemplary conduct as this?"

"Richard," returned his wife, "this praise is unmerited; I have performed no more than my duty, and I should feel ashamed of myself if I shrunk from it. But let us away, for we waste time which is now so precious to us in the coming darkness."

Richard again embraced her, and still supporting her on his arm, he led her from the spot, and they continued on their way, though they knew not what direction to take for the best. Gradually the twilight disappeared, and night set in, veiling the earth in complete darkness, for there was no moon, and not a star to be seen, and nothing could be more dreary than the scene before them. They were now travelling through a woody part of the country, and the wind, which had now arisen to its full height, swept in hollow gusts among the branches of the tall trees, and tended, by its mournful sounds, to add to the depression of their spirits. Mary sighed, as her eyes penetrated through the darkness of the night, with the hope of being able to discover some means of shelter, but none appeared; and although she struggled resolutely with her feelings, under all the painful circumstances of their situation, she could not help abandoning herself to despair, a feeling in which her husband but too painfully participated.

"This continued disappointment is most torturing," he observed, "to be thus left shelterless in the darkness of the night. I know not now how to proceed, or what plan to adopt for the best. And you, my beloved Mary, who have continued to sustain yourself with such wonderful heroism; what will become of you, since all prospect of our receiving any relief seems to be at an end? It is impossible that you can bear up against the coldness of the night, and in such a dismal scene as this."

"Torture not your mind so much about me, Richard," replied the patient woman, "for Heaven will yet give me strength to struggle against the fate to which we are so unfortunately subjected."

"Ah, no," returned our hero, "in spite of all that you have said to quiet my apprehensions, I feel convinced that it is impossible you can do so, and it is only marvellous to me that you have so long been able to endure hardships against which the most robust constitution might not have been proof. This is a most dreary place, and as I view the scene around me, my heart is filled with despair."

Mary, by a look, endeavoured to reassure him, but this was no easy task to accomplish, and it was with sad and heavy hearts that they resumed their uncertain way. They had not proceeded far, however, and had entered a more open part of the country, when, casting their eyes before them, their hopes were again raised by perceiving lights at a short distance, which seemed to glimmer from the windows of some human habitation or habitations.

"Thank God!" exclaimed Richard;

" our prayers have at last been heard. We are near the dwellings of some human beings, from whom we may be able to obtain that pity and relief which we so urgently require. It is most likely that we are near some town or village, where, having fortunately the means in our possession, we may at least be able to procure a shelter for the night, and such information as may guide us how to act."

"Oh, welcome sight!" cried Mary, clasping her hands vehemently, and her heart palpitating with hope; "our exertions have not been in vain, and surely our hope will not be doomed to disappointment."

"Heaven forbid," answered Richard; "but surely common humanity cannot resist our supplications. Come, let us not delay, for you need immediate rest, and the lights which we see are sufficient to convince us that the inhabitants of those dwellings have not yet retired for the night."

Mary made no reply, and still leaning on the arm of her husband, they moved towards the spot from whence the lights issued; and as they approached them nearer, they perceived several small habitations, but the lights that had attracted their attention proceeded from the windows of what was evidently a public-house, and which offered to them the most probable means of accommodation. They were not long in arriving at it, and they then perceived that it was a small old-fashioned building, but that it presented anything but a cheerful and inviting aspect; however, in the present deplorable condition of the unfortunate fugitives, it was, indeed, most welcome. They hastily approached the door, which they found to be fastened, but they heard voices from within, so that they were satisfied the inmates had not retired to rest, and peeping in at one of the parlour windows, they had an indistinct view of several men, who seemed to be enjoying themselves over their pipe and their glass. Richard now ventured to knock at the door, and it was almost immediately opened by a middle-aged man with a lamp in his hand, and whose aspect and general appearance was anything but prepossessing. He thrust the light rudely in their faces, and scrutinised them narrowly, and seeming not much to fancy their appearance, he demanded in an abrupt manner—

"Well, and what is your business here, eh?"

"We are travellers who are tired," replied Richard, "and we need some refreshment and a shelter for the night; can you accommodate us?"

"Have you any money to pay for it?" interrogated the man.

"We are poor," replied our hero, "but still I dare say we can find sufficient to satisfy any reasonable demands you may make upon us."

"Ah, if that's it," said the man, "that will do; I can accommodate you; so come in."

Richard thanked him, and Mary, who could not help entertaining a sensation of fear at the uncouth appearance of the man, took the arm of her husband, and leading her son by the hand, they followed him into the house.

CHAPTER XXXIV.

RICHARD PARKER AND HIS WIFE ARE IN DANGEROUS QUARTERS.—THE HEARTLESS ROBBERY.—THE DEPARTURE.

ON entering the passage, and hearing the rather noisy voices of the men whom they had seen seated in the parlour, our hero inquired of the landlord whether he could not accommodate them with a room to themselves, as they wished to be alone.

"Oh, yes," he answered; "I have accommodation here to please every taste, and my guests would not much like the intrusion of strangers, I know. So, come this way."

Richard bowed, and the man conducted them into a small room of not very cleanly appearance, at the back part of the house, and placed the lamp upon a table. Richard and his wife seated themselves, and the landlord said—

"Now, I suppose, you want something to eat and drink, for you look hungry enough, that's certain."

Our hero answered in the affirmative, and ordered such provisions as their limited means would afford.

"Very good," said the host, "you shall be supplied with what you want immediately."

He then quitted the room, and our hero and his wife were left to themselves."

"Thank Heaven we are safely housed at last," observed Richard, when he was gone; "and we shall be able, I hope, to obtain that rest of which we stand so much in need."

"And yet," returned Mary, "there is something about the appearance of this man which I do not like. His countenance is far from pleasing, and his manners are coarse and repulsive."

"True," coincided her husband; "but still we must not at all times judge from appearances, and he may be a worthy man after all, in spite of his looks, and the vulgarity and uncouthness of his behaviour. At any rate we have nothing to fear from him, so you had better make yourself easy upon that point."

Mary was about to make some reply, when she was prevented from doing so by the return of the landlord to the room, bringing with him the refreshments that had been ordered, and which he placed on the table before them.

"There," he remarked, "I will defy you to get better fare than that in the whole county of Cornwall. Now then, I will trouble you for the money; short reckonings make long friends, and I always make it a rule to be paid on delivery."

Richard drew forth the purse which had been given to him by Mrs. Goodson, and presented him a piece of gold, out of which he desired him to take his demand, and to give him the change.

It did not escape their observation, that he gazed at the purse and its contents with a greedy eye, and that made them feel anything but satisfied or comfortable.

"Ah!" he said; "that is the way to do business. Let me see—what shall I charge you? You are poor people, and I suppose you cannot afford much, and I always like to be as moderate as I can. Three shillings for the refreshments, and two shillings for your lodging, that's just a dollar, and I suppose that won't hurt you?"

Richard nodded assent, and the landlord having given him the change, they expected that he would leave the room, but he lingered behind, and seemed to eye them with much vulgar curiosity.

"You are strangers in this part of the country, are you not?" he inquired.

"We are," answered Richard; "and were only brought here by accident."

"Have you travelled far?" asked the landlord.

"Yes," returned our hero, laconically, for he did not like his inquisitiveness.

"And where are you going?"

"We are as yet uncertain."

"Humph!" ejaculated the host. "However, it is no business of mine, and, therefore, I have no right to inquire. If my customers pay their way that's all I have to do with them; so I will leave you to yourselves; when you wish to retire, you have only to ring the bell yonder."

Richard thanked him, and he then left the room, much to their relief, for the impertinent questions he had put to them had much annoyed and bewildered them.

"That man's vulgar curiosity has increased my prejudice against him," said Mrs. Parker, "and I do not feel at all satisfied with the place to which chance has led us. Heaven grant that no harm may come of it."

"Nay," replied Richard, "what harm can possibly come of it? We are strangers to him, and consequently, I do not suppose we have anything to fear from him. We ought to feel thankful that we have at last reached a human habitation, for, in truth, I began to despair of our doing so, and I shudder to think of what the consequences must have been, had we been compelled to wander in the cold all the night. But let us finish our repast, and then the sooner we retire to rest the better."

Mary complied with his request, and they then partook sparingly of the coarse provisions with which the landlord had supplied them, and having finished their meal, Richard rang the bell, and the host immediately again made his appearance. He stood for a moment or two, and eyed them rudely and narrowly as he had done before, and Mary could not help her prejudice against him increasing, from his unprepossessing appearance, and uncouth and vulgar manners, while her husband, although he endeavoured to conceal it, felt far from easy in his presence, and entertained a very little, if any, better opinion of him than our heroine.

"So," he said at last, "you have finished your repast, and now, as the time is getting late, and you seem rather fatigued, I suppose you wish to retire to rest?"

Richard replied in the affirmative.

"Ah!" added the landlord "you will find excellent accommodation here. Here, mother!"

The latter words were shouted in a loud voice, and obedient to the summons, an old woman entered the room, whose appearance was, if possible, even more repulsive than that of the landlord. She eyed Richard and his wife with a scrutinizing eye, and the latter shrunk from her gaze with a shuddering sensation, which she had a difficulty in concealing, and heartily wished that they were far from the place, for she could not help foreboding no good from this adventure.

"Well, Bill," said the old woman, addressing the landlord; "what do you want?"

"Show these people to the vacant room up stairs," replied the man; "they sleep here to night. You understand?"

"Oh, yes," returned the old woman,

and Mary fancied that she observed her exchange a significant look with the host as she spoke; "this way, if you please," she added, taking up the lamp and pointing to the door. Richard and his wife arose, and prepared to follow her.

"Good night," said the landlord, with a half ironical smile, "I shall see you in the morning, and I wish you pleasant dreams."

Richard, although he did not like his manner, and was not without entertaining similar misgivings as those of his wife, returned his thanks, and they then followed the old woman out of the room, and up several flights of stairs, until they stopped at length before a low and crazy looking door, which their conductor having opened, introduced them into a chamber of small dimensions, and the appearance of which was by no means cheerful or comfortable. A bed and bedstead, and a couple of broken chairs, were the only articles of furniture it contained, and the walls and ceiling were black and decaying with neglect and age.

Having ushered them into the room, the old woman departed without saying a word, and our hero and his wife were left to themselves. Mary cast one anxious glance around the chamber, and the expression of her features showed the feelings she experienced. Richard by a look endeavoured to encourage her, though he could not but fully participate in her feelings, and the coarse manners and personal appearance of the landlord and the old woman, whom he supposed to be his mother, had left the most unfavourable impression upon his mind.

"This is a wretched looking place," remarked Mary, "and is quite in keeping with that of the landlord and the old woman who has just left us. I would much rather we had not come hither, for I cannot help foreboding that no good will arise from it."

"Nay," replied Richard, "why should you suffer such feelings as those to take possession of your mind, my dear Mary? What can we possibly have to fear? Even if the character of this man is of the worst description, surely our condition is too wretched for us to hold out any temptation to him, and I do not see that we have any reason to apprehend that he entertains any evil designs against us. Come, you must try to dismiss those gloomy thoughts, for although the accommodation is not of the best description, under all the circumstances in which we were placed, we ought to be thankful that we have met with it, for completely worn out as you

were, what might not have been the consequences had we been exposed another night without a shelter?"

"Alas! alas!" sighed Mary, "ours is indeed a most miserable fate, and Heaven only knows what will be the result of it. I shudder when I think of it."

"Providence surely will at last take pity on us," returned her husband, "for we have had more than our full share of misfortunes, and Heaven only knows how doubly great has been my anguish to witness the sufferings to which yourself and our poor boy have been exposed, and the unexampled fortitude and resignation with which you have endured them. Such heroism under trials that were sufficient to bear down the stoutest heart, cannot but excite the most enthusiastic admiration, and must ultimately meet with its due reward."

"Oh, Richard," replied his wife, "I have been, and am still prepared to endure everything for your sake; but when I see the gloominess of our prospects, I must confess that it makes me feel the utmost despair."

"Again I beg you to try to banish these thoughts from your mind, Mary," said our hero, "and still continue to seek to support the heavy trials which it has been our hard lot to encounter, with fortitude and resignation. But, come, we waste that time which should be devoted to rest, for we shall probably have to resume our weary wanderings in the morning. All is now silent in the house, so that the guests have most likely departed, and the landlord and the old woman retired to their chambers; we have nothing to fear; so calm your feelings, and try to look forward to the future with hope."

Mary shook her head, and it was quite evident that she found it impossible to conquer the dismal forebodings that had taken possession of her mind. Her husband now went to the room-door with the intention of fastening it; but was somewhat bewildered and alarmed, when he found that there were no means of securing it, for there was neither key nor bolt, and, notwithstanding his endeavours to conceal it, his fears and suspicions were nearly equal to those of his wife. Mary had followed him anxiously with her eyes, and when she perceived that there was nothing to prevent intrusion into the room, she could not but consider that her suspicions were all but confirmed, and she turned more pale than before, as she ejaculated—

"Ah! this is a sufficient proof that my fears are not without foundation, and that some danger threatens us. Would to

Heaven that our footsteps had never been guided to this place, or that we were now safely out of it."

"Be calm, Mary," replied her husband; "what can we possibly have to apprehend? We can, I dare say, so secure the door as to prevent any person from intruding upon us without arousing us. Besides, what design can the inmates of this house possibly have against persons who are placed in our wretched condition?"

"I know not," answered Mary, "but still I cannot divest my mind of the impression that some evil is intended us. The suspicious looks and observations of this man are vividly stamped upon my memory, and I feel confident that he is a man who would not hesitate at the perpetration of any outrage. I shudder with fear while we remain here. All seems at present quiet in the house, and we might probably make our escape from it without being observed. Come, come, let us not delay, for every moment may be fraught with danger."

"What!" exclaimed Richard, "leave this place at such an hour as this, and in your present exhausted condition again expose yourself to the cold and cheerlessness of the night, when it is quite evident that you have not strength to travel until you have obtained that rest in which you so much stand in need? It is impossible; you talk madly, my dear Mary. I pray you become more firm and confident."

"Oh," returned our heroine, "there is no fatigue which I am not prepared to encounter, rather than remain here. It is impossible that I can rest with all these doubts and suspicions upon my mind."

"Depend upon it," said Richard, "that they will prove to be without foundation. All is still, the inmates of the house have doubtless retired to rest, and being now wrapped in sleep, will have no thought of disturbing us. An hour or two's repose will serve to recruit your strength, and then we can again proceed on our journey, with the hope of at length meeting with more hospitable shelter."

"I yield to your persuasions, Richard," said his wife, "for I see that you are worn out with the fatigue which you have undergone, though it is with a melancholy and foreboding heart that I do so."

Richard embraced her affectionately, and having again endeavoured to inspire her with confidence, he set about trying to secure the door as well as he could, by placing a chair against it, so that he thought no one could attempt to enter the room without making a sufficient noise to disturb them. They then knelt down, and having

supplicated the protection of the Supreme they stretched themselves upon the bed without undressing, so that they might be ready in case of any emergency. Our hero was so completely worn out both by the exertions of the mind and the body he had undergone, that notwithstanding be endeavoured to prevent it, until his wife might have composed herself to rest, he found it was impossible for him to resist the influence of the drowsy god, and in a very short time he was sound asleep. But the fears of Mary kept her awake, and she listened with breathless attention to catch the least sound which might be moving in the house; but all was silent as the grave, and she consequently became more composed and confident. For about half an hour she continued in the same condition, but at length nature was completely exhausted, and sleep descended upon her eyelids.

How long she had slept she had no means of forming any idea, but she was suddenly aroused by hearing a confused noise in the chamber, and starting up in the bed, and rubbing her eyes, she immediately fixed them in the directed from which she imagined the noise to proceed. The light had burned out, but from that which was admitted through the window, for the day was just beginning to break, she imagined that she could behold the dark shadow of a retreating form at the farther end of the room, and so strong was the impression on her mind that she could not repress a scream, and starting from the bed, she aroused her husband.

"For Heaven's sake, my dear Mary," he said, observing the ghastly paleness of her looks and her trembling limbs; "what is the matter?—what has alarmed you?"

Our heroine was so violently agitated that she could not reply for a moment or two, but continued with her eyes fixed with trembling suspicion upon that part of the chamber where she imagined she had seen the form, and her husband repeated his question with more anxiety than before.

"Some one has been in the chamber, I am convinced of it," she answered at length.

"Impossible," returned her husband, "for you see the door remains secured in the same way that I left it. You must have been dreaming, my love."

"Oh, no," said Mary, "it was no dream, I was aroused by an indistinct noise, and could swear that I beheld the shadow of a human form retreating in that direction. Some danger threatens us, and I tremble with fear until we have safely quitted this place."

"How improbable is this," observed our hero; "you must have suffered some painful dream to delude your senses. There are no means of entrance or egress from this room but the door, and that has evidently, as I said before, not been disturbed. Compose yourself, Mary, and reason must convince you how much you have been deceived."

"Nay, Richard," replied his wife, "it is useless to attempt to persuade me; it was a human form I saw as plainly as I see you now, and it vanished from my sight in yonder direction. There must be some secret entrance to this room."

"That does not seem at all likely," remarked Richard, "however, we can soon ascertain the truth or fallacy of that conjecture."

He now examined the wainscot in that direction of the room where our heroine imagined she had seen the form disappear, minutely; but not the least sign of anything appeared to confirm her suspicions, and he again endeavoured to compose her feelings.

"It is quite evident," he said, "that you must have been mistaken, Mary; there are no secret means of entrance to the chamber here, and no person could have entered by the door without disturbing that which I had placed against it to secure it, and that remains the same as when we retired to rest; besides, what could have been their motives for doing so?"

"I know not," answered our heroine, "unless it were robbery."

"Robbery!" repeated Richard, "that idea is preposterous. What could they expect from persons in our wretched and destitute condition?"

"Ah! I noticed the greedy any scrutinising glances of the landlord, when you produced the purse which Mrs. Goodson was so kind as to give us, to pay him," replied Mary; "and at the moment I believed his cupidity was aroused by the sight of its ample contents, and from that moment my suspicions and prejudices against him were strengthened. Feel in your pockets, Richard, and see whether or no you have that purse still in your possession."

Startled by her suggestion, and a secret fear coming over him, Richard did as she advised, and feeling hastily in all his pockets, he exclaimed—

"No, by Heaven it is gone! There is nothing left but these few shillings which I had accidentally removed from it, and placed in another pocket."

"Ah! then," ejaculated his wife, "I was not deceived; my worst suspicions are confirmed! We are in a den of wretches who are capable of any crime, and I shudder to think what will become of us. Let us endeavour to make our escape, lest some further calamity should befall us."

"Compose yourself, Mary," said her husband, "for, if our suspicions are correct, our most prudent course will be to endeavour to submit to our loss, however deplorable it is in our present desperate situation, and to appear to be ignorant of it; then we may be permitted to leave the house without any further molestation."

"I tremble with fear every moment that we remain here," replied our heroine, "and dare not encounter that repulsive-looking man again. There seems to be no one now moving in the house, and we could probably, therefore, depart without being observed. Oh, let us not delay an instant, dear Richard, for I tremble to think what the consequences may be should we stay. Alas! how rapidly do our misfortunes follow upon each other."

"No, Mary," returned her husband, "strangers as we are to the intricacies of this house, it is impossible that we can effect our escape. But we have only to act with firmness and precaution, and all will probably yet be safe, and the wretches having secured all that they want, will most likely suffer us to depart without attempting any act of violence. But the whole affair is so mysterious, that it seems to be almost incredible. How could any one have obtained admission here, if not by the door? And after all may we not have been mistaken? I may have dropped the purse somewhere here among the bed-clothes. Let me search."

He did so, carefully and minutely, but all in vain; it was nowhere to be found, and it appeared but too evident that it had been abstracted from his pocket by some surreptitious means, while he was asleep, and the excitement of himself and his wife increased.

It was now daylight, and they had not the least doubt but that the inmates of the house would shortly be stirring, though all was now perfectly silent. Richard sought to calm the agitation of his wife, but he only slightly succeeded, for her fears as to what would be the ultimate result of this adventure were undiminished, and she fervently wished that they were far away from the house. He again examined the wainscot minutely, but no signs of any secret door met his observation, and he became involved in still greater doubt and perplexity.

"How strange is this," he remarked; "I find myself quite incapable of fathoming the mystery with which the whole of this adventure is surrounded. It seems impossible that anyone could have entered this room, and yet the purse is gone; but may I not have dropped it instead of returning it to my pocket, before we quitted the room below?"

"Oh, no," answered Mary, "I am certain that I was not mistaken; it was a human form that I beheld retreating from the chamber, I am confident. Would to Heaven that we were safely away from this place."

"We must await the result with firmness," said Richard, "and, as I before observed, appear to be innocent of the loss we have sustained, or we know not what danger may attend us."

"Alas!" sighed our heroine, "I cannot but apprehend the worst, after what has happened. I dread to meet this forbidding-looking man again; there seems to be no one now stirring in the house, and surely we should not miss such an opportunity of escaping without being observed. Come, Richard, let us at once depart."

"Nay," answered the later, "it would be imprudent to attempt to do so, for although all is so silent in the house, there probably is some one on the watch, and should we be observed, we might plunge ourselves into greater danger than that which we wish to escape from. If we act with due precaution, they will probably offer no obstruction to our departure."

"And what is now to become of us in this strange part of the country," said Mary, "and deprived as we are of the little means of present support with which Mrs. Goodson had so generously supplied us? Surely never were human beings before subjected to such cruel and successive misfortune as we are."

"Do not despair, Mary," observed her husband; "although I am compelled to acknowledge that you have already experienced enough to make you do so. We shall yet, I hope, with the blessing of God, be relieved from our misery; we shall again be able to find those who will sympathise with us in our misfortunes, and render us that assistance which we so much require. But hark! there is some one stirring in the house. Be firm, exert all your strength which has been so much tried of late, and before many minutes have elapsed, we shall probably be safe away from this place, in which we have experienced so much to alarm us."

"Alas!" ejaculated our heroine, "the task you would impose upon me, dear Richard, is a difficult one to accomplish. Would that we could have departed from this house without again seeing this man."

"I do not believe that we have anything more to fear from him," returned our hero; "but should he have the boldness to attempt to molest us, I have yet strength sufficient left to defend you and our poor boy. Be calm, be calm, and you will find that your apprehensions are groundless."

Mary did endeavour to struggle with her feeling, and succeeded much better than might have been expected, and Richard taking her by the arm they descended the stairs to the room below, in which they found the landlord and the old woman seated. Mary could not help shuddering when she beheld them, for their countenances seemed to bear a more repulsive aspect than before; but she quickly recovered herself, and the landlord and his mother on perceiving them enter, immediately arose, and the former advancing towards them, said, with a half-ironical grin upon his countenance—

"So, you have risen betimes. I should have thought, from the plight in which you seemed to be last night, you would have felt inclined to indulge yourselves with another hour or two's rest this morning. Of course, you have nothing to complain of your accommodation?"

"No," replied Richard, composedly; "but we wish to resume our journey early, for no doubt we shall have some distance to travel. We will, therefore, wish you good morning, and will, if you please, immediately depart."

"Why, you are in a hurry," said the man, still eyeing them narrowly; "but will you not take some breakfast before you go? You will find no other house for some distance from this."

"No," answered our hero; "it is yet too early, and, besides, we do not feel disposed for eating. We thank you all the same."

"Well, you know best," he remarked, in his usual coarse and vulgar manner, "though there is nothing like laying a good foundation before you commence a journey. Good morning, and I hope, if you should ever again be passing this way, you will not forget to give us a call."

"It is not likely that we shall do so for some time, at any rate," returned Richard, in the same composed manner, "but if we should, we will not fail to avail ourselves of your invitation."

The landlord made no answer, but seeing

THE WRECKERS ALARMED AT THE NOISE MADE BY PARKER.

them to the outer door, which he unfastened, the fugitives took their departure, much to the relief of our heroine, who had been in a state of fear and suspense all the time they had been talking to him.

CHAPTER XXXV.

THE FUGITIVES STILL CONTINUE THEIR DREARY WAY.—ANOTHER SURPRISE AND UNEXPECTED MEETING.

THE morning, like all the others had been since the shipwreck, was cold and cheerless, and it seemed to be not at all unlikely, from the dark and heavy clouds that hung upon the horizon, that there would shortly be a resumption of the storm which had raged with such fury for the last few days. But the minds of our unfortunate fugitives were too much occupied by other thoughts to suffer them to take much heed of the weather, and they proceeded as fast as they could from the tavern, though, on once turning their heads, they perceived the landlord and the old woman watching them from the door, and that circumstance only served to add speed to their footsteps, lest any further danger might menace them; and having at last lost sight of the house, and proceeded to some considerable distance, they stopped to rest themselves and to collect their thoughts for a few minutes.

"Thank God!" ejaculated Mary, "that we are now away from that house, which I am well convinced is the resort of ruffians of the worst character. The looks of that man, and the old woman whom we suppose to be his mother, were enough to satisfy us, if we could before have entertained any doubt, that he was the heartless thief who plundered us of our little property, and we may thank Providence that we slept so soundly, for had he met with any resistance in the execution of his purpose, our lives might have fallen a sacrifice to his vengeance."

"Most true," coincided Richard; "and you now see that we acted with prudence in following my advice. He seemed to have no suspicion that we were aware of the robbery."

"He did not," returned our heroine; "but, oh, how desperate and deplorable is our situation now. We are now again left almost destitute, and strangers as we are in this place, without a friend to whom we can apply for assistance, what is to become of us? I shudder to think even of the horrors by which we are surrounded."

"Let not the contemplation of them torture you thus, for that will only make your condition the worse," replied Richard. "We have yet a few shillings left, and before that is exhausted, we may meet with some other means of relief. I am afraid, however, that your strength must at last entirely yield to these painful and trying exertions, and that you will not be able to support the severe trials and hardships that may yet be in store for us."

"Fear not for me," said Mary, in reply, "for although I have suffered much more than I ever thought my delicate frame could endure, I trust that Providence may yet enable me to bear up until some favourable change may take place in our fortunes, and we may be restored to tranquillity, if not to complete happiness."

"Heaven grant that your hopes may not be doomed to disappointment, my beloved Mary," said her husband, fervently; "for surely such heroic firmness and resignation as that which you have displayed throughout the numerous vicissitudes to which we have so long been exposed, is deserving of a reward. But let us proceed; the road before us may probably conduct us to some town or village where we shall again be

able to obtain some rest and refreshment, and such information as we require."

"Alas!" sighed Mary, "that fatal shipwreck, in which poor old Binnacle lost his life, was almost sufficient to annihilate all our hopes. To what place can we now direct our steps?"

"Could we meet with some kind and benevolent friend, who would take pity on us, and where we might stop for a few days, I might communicate with Adams, and I know that he would not delay a moment in adopting some plan for our future relief."

"I know well the goodness of his heart," said our heroine, "for have we not amply experienced it? But I fear that we have already exhausted his means, and that, however good his will, he has no longer the power to assist us. Oh, my father, how insensible must your heart have become to every feeling of pity and humanity, to turn a deaf ear to my supplications, when you saw the wretchedness and deplorable situation to which we are reduced. May Heaven show more mercy to you, than you have evinced towards us."

"Think no more of him, Mary," said her husband; "endeavour to forget the painful scene in which we acted such prominent parts at the Hall."

"Forget it!" repeated our heroine, and tears started to her eyes; "oh, that is impossible; it is imprinted upon my memory in such vivid characters that nothing whatever can efface them, and the longer I reflect on them, the more does my agony increase. Oh, surely I little deserved to meet with such cruel and heartless treatment from that parent towards whom I had ever evinced the greatest reverence and affection, and whom it was my constant study to endeavour to please."

"You did not, indeed, my Mary," replied our hero, "and the time must yet come when he will be awakened to a full sense of the unnatural severity and injustice of his conduct, and when he will be stung with remorse. But let us talk no more upon that painful subject, but hasten on our journey with all the strength we can."

Mary complied with this request, and leaning on the arm of her husband, she proceeded much better than, under all the circumstances, could have been expected. The road into which they had struck seemed to be of some extent, and the surmises that Richard had formed that it would lead to some town or village, appeared not at all unlikely to be realised, and they, therefore, hurried on with increased hope, thinking that they probably should meet with some individual who might direct them; but they saw nothing of the kind, and they, therefore, continued on their way in perfect ignorance as to whither it would lead them. The cold every moment became the more intense, and notwithstanding that Mary struggled as well as she could against it, her limbs trembled from its effects, which greatly impeded her progress; but the storm still kept off, and that afforded them some consolation, for they dreaded to encounter again those horrors to which they had but so recently been exposed, and which had tended so much to add to their misery.

The road at length terminated in a long, gloomy, and narrow lane, overshadowed by lofty trees on either side, and their prospects of a town or village were as hopeless as ever. However, they entered the lane, and proceeded some distance along it; but the footsteps of Mary every moment began to grow more feeble, and her husband's fears were again excited, lest she should sink exhausted on the road. Reaching a small mound of earth, they sat themselves down to rest for awhile, and looked anxiously around them, for nothing could appear more gloomy and cheerless than their prospects.

"How tedious is this wandering," remarked our hero at last, "and the further we proceed the more hopeless our prospects seem to be. My poor Mary, I fear that you are almost exhausted, and that it will be impossible for you to proceed much further. The paleness of your cheeks and your trembling limbs convince me of that, and I am completely bewildered and at a loss how to act."

"Quiet your anxiety respecting me," replied our heroine, "for a few minutes' rest will, I trust, shortly recruit my strength; and surely it will not be long ere we shall meet with some place where we may find a shelter."

"Heaven send that we may," said Richard, "ere the storm commences which has so long hovered o'er our heads; but this dismal lane offers no prospect of such a wish being realized."

He was interrupted in the midst of this speech by hearing the sound of horses' feet approaching in the direction of the place where they were sitting, and starting hastily to his feet, he gazed eagerly before him, and soon afterwards beheld a man, apparently a farmer's servant, mounted on a strong waggon-horse, advancing slowly that way. In a few moments he came up to them, and seemed to eye them with some curiosity and surprise; but he immediately stopped his horse, and Richard addressed him.

"My good friend," he observed, "as you may perceive, we are poor travellers, who require rest and refreshment; can you direct us to any place where we may obtain them?"

"Why," replied the man, in a broad dialect, "the nearest village is about five miles from this place; but there be a snug inn enough little more than two miles off, where I dare say you can get what you want."

"No nearer than that?" said Richard, looking anxiously at his wife.

"No," replied the man; "this be rather a lonely place, and, that be the nearest and the likeliest house that you can meet with."

"And which way can we go to it?" inquired our hero.

"Why," answered the man, "you must go straight along this lane till you come to the end of it, get over the stile to the right, cross over the hundred-foot field, bear a little to the left, and then to the right again; turn the corner, go straight for'ard afore you; turn again to the left, then to the right, right ahead, and you will come upon it in no time at all."

This was certainly not a very explicit direction, but our hero thanked him, and the countryman then departed on his way.

"Come, Mary," said her husband; "you will exert yourself, I know, and if we can only reach this inn before the storm commences, we shall be most fortunate."

"I shall be able to do so now, I know," replied Mary, "with the support of your arm. I am ready, Richard."

He raised her from the ground, and supporting her with his arm, he conducted her from the spot, and they proceeded on their way along the lane as fast as they could, for the storm seemed every moment about to burst, and they feared what the consequences might be after what they had already undergone. They had scarcely, however, emerged from the lane, and entered into the open field which the countryman had directed them to, when the rain suddenly came down in overwhelming torrents, so that they were completely drenched to the skin in a few minutes.

"How unfortunate is this," said our hero, "and the direction which the man gave us was such a confused one, that I scarcely know which way to turn."

"Providence will guide us," replied Mary; "so let us proceed as fast as we can, and probably we shall be much sooner there than we expect."

They hurried on through the storm as well as they could, and endeavoured to follow the countryman's direction, but it was such a confused one, that it was a difficult and almost hopeless task to accomplish. They crossed several fields, turned two or three corners to the right and to the left, as he had directed them, but without seeing any signs of the house he had spoken of, and they began to despair of finding it, and to think that he had practised some cruel hoax upon them; and they were now so cold and wet, that the wretchedness of their situation may easily be imagined. At this, moment, however, when they stood uncertain how to act, they were greatly relieved from their suspence by beholding a man approaching them, and they eagerly hurried towards him, and inquired whether he could direct them to the place they sought.

"Why, yes," he replied; "but you have come at least a quarter of a mile out of your way; and it is fortunate that is the very place I am going to, so, if you please, I will conduct you there."

Richard and his wife thanked him heartily.

"Come on then, my friends," said the man, "for it is no time to stand talking in such a rain as this, and you, like myself, seem to be drenched to the skin. You are strangers in this part, I presume?"

Richard replied in the affirmative; and then, to prevent any further questions, he asked him the name of the person who kept the house to which they were going.

"Why, it is old John Milsom," replied the stranger; "and a worthy sort of a man he is, and has resided where he is for the last thirty years."

"We are very poor," observed Richard, "for we had the misfortune to be shipwrecked only a few days ago, and lost nearly everything that we had in our possession. Do you think that he will accommodate us?"

"To be sure he will," said the man; "for Johnny Milsom never yet refused to assist those who stood in need of it, as far as was in his power. I am sorry for your misfortunes, and I hope that you will be shortly able to recover yourselves."

Richard again thanked him, and they then increased their speed, and entering a short lane, our unfortunate wanderers were gratified to behold a comfortable-looking inn at the end of it, and a sign-board swinging between two trees described it as "The Jolly Sportsman."

The door was standing wide open to welcome any guests that might chance to arrive, and Richard and our heroine followed their companion into the house, and entering a room to the right of the passage, they beheld a comely-looking old man and woman seated before a blazing fire, and who seemed to be engaged in conversation; but they immediately arose on their entrance, and advancing towards them the landed said—

"What, my friend, Blowden, who would have thought of seeing you on such a day as this. But who are those good people you have brought with you?"

"They are strangers to me, Master Milsom," answered Blowden, "whom I accidentally met with on my way here. They are poor travellers, who have suffered shipwreck a few days ago, as they tell me, and they wish to know whether you will accommodate them?"

"Accommodate them!" repeated Mr. Milsom, "to be sure I will, and with pleasure. I should be a brute if I would not, on such a day as this. So walk in, my friends, and make yourselves quite at home. Seat yourselves by the fire, for you are miserably wet, and I will soon bring you something that will revive you, I'll warrant. Come, bustle, bustle, dame, and see what you can do for this poor woman and the little boy,"

"This kindness is most unexpected, sir," said Richard, "and I thank you most fervently and sincerely for it. But I must inform you that we are very poor, and that we have not the means to pay for any extravagant accommodation."

"Hold your tongue, my good friend," said Mr. Milsom, "and leave everything to me. But first of all you require some refreshment, and that I will hasten to procure you. Dame, you do all that you can for the poor woman, during my absence, for you see how miserably wet she is, and the paleness of her looks shows how much she has suffered."

With these words Mr. Milsom darted from the room, and left his wife in busy attendance upon our heroine, who was so overcome by this unexpected kindness that she was affected to tears.

"Oh, madam," she ejaculated, "how can I express my feelings at this humane conduct towards a poor friendless stranger? My emotions overpower me, and I cannot give utterance to what I wish."

"Do not agitate yourself, my good woman," replied Mrs. Milsom; "you have no one here but friends, and I am only glad to think that you should happen to have been guided here. You seem to have suffered much."

"We have indeed, madam," replied our hero; "and Heaven only knows how we have found strength sufficient to support it. Had not Providence guided us hither, I know not what would have become of us; for my unfortunate wife was, as you perceive, quite exhausted, and must shortly have died on the road, for we knew not where to go."

"Ah! poor thing," remarked Mrs. Milsom, compassionately, "she is, indeed, in a sad condition, and I sincerely pity her; but I hope that, with the blessing of God, we shall soon be able to revive her."

Richard and his wife were about to return some reply, when Mr. Milsom re-entered the room, bringing with him a goodly supply of refreshments, which he spread before the unfortunate wanderers, and invited them to partake heartily.

"Come, my friends," he continued, "do not be bashful, for I assure you, you are most cordially welcome to all that my house can afford. John Milsom always had a heart to assist such of his fellow-creatures who stood in need, as far as his means would allow, and when he shall cease to do so, he will no longer acknowledge his name."

"I need not tell you, sir," replied Richard, "how fully I appreciate this great kindness of yours towards those who are complete strangers to you; but as I before told you, we are extremely poor, and I am afraid that we shall never be able to repay you as amply as your generosity deserves."

"Say no more about that, my good friend," returned Milsom, "for you are sincerely welcome, and so is any other who requires it. Thank God I am not so poor as to be unable to perform a good action, and I know well I shall always have the heart to do it. So make yourselves quite at home, and partake freely of such humble fare as I am enabled to supply you with, for, I repeat, you are most heartily welcome."

Richard and his wife again thanked the kind-hearted man, and then seating themselves at the table, they partook freely of the provisions with which he had so liberally supplied them, and which, having been so long without, they enjoyed heartily, and felt much refreshed. The kind attentions of Mr. Milsom and his wife, who continued in the room, quite overpowered them, and they were at a loss for words to express their acknowledgments, but Mr. Milsom again assured them that they had no occasion to trouble themselves, as they were welcome to all that he could do for them.

"You are unfortunate, my friends," he remarked, "and your appearance convinces me that you have suffered much, and therefore do I sincerely pity you. You seem to have travelled far."

"We have indeed for the last few days," replied our hero, "exposed to all the inclemency of the weather, and being complete strangers in this part of the country, you may imagine what we have had to undergo, destitute as we are, and when I tell you that you are the first person whom we have met with who has taken compassion on us. Heaven only knows how my poor wife and child have been able to support trials which were sufficient to try the stoutest heart."

"Poor things," said Mr. Milsom, compassionately, "and whither are you now going?"

"That we scarcely know," answered Richard, hesitating, "but we are anxious to reach some place where we can obtain a temporary shelter, until we can communicate with some friends, who we have no doubt will render us all the assistance in their power."

"I am extremely sorry for you," observed Mr. Milsom, "but as my house at the present time is nearly full, I am afraid I shall be unable to accommodate you; however, you can remain here for to-night, and we will see what to-morrow produces. If I find that I can then make convenience for you, and you are willing to accept of it, I am sure I will do so most freely."

"Oh, sir," replied Richard, "this is indeed most kind; but I am afraid we shall put you to too much trouble, and being strangers to you, of course, we have no claim upon your hospitality."

"Say not so," returned Mr. Milsom, "for being in distress, you have every claim upon my humanity, and God forbid that I should ever become insensible to that feeling."

Our hero and his wife could but repeat their thanks, and the conversation then took a different turn, and they discoursed upon various subjects; but what satisfied Richard more than all was, that Mr. Milsom evinced no impertinent curiosity, and put no questions to him which he could at all hesitate to answer; though from the candour and strict integrity of his manner he was convinced that he should run no danger in confiding everything to him. At length Mr. Milsom and his wife retired from the room, and left them to themselves, and when they found themselves alone they gave vent to their feelings in the most unrestrained manner.

"Oh, how fortunate is it," said Mary,

"that chance has directed our footsteps hither. Kind Heaven has not yet deserted us, dear Richard; the behaviour of this man and his wife shows at once the benevolence of their hearts, and convinces me that we shall find in them that sincerity and warmth of friendship which we have so little right to expect from strangers."

"True, my love," returned Richard, "and most grateful must we feel to them for it. Had we been still exposed to the horrors of the storm, Heaven only knows what would have become of us. It would have been impossible for you to have survived it, so completely exhausted as you were. How it gladdens me to see the favourable change which the short time we have been here has wrought in you. Should we be permitted to remain here for a few days, you will, I trust, be quite recovered, and we can then find some means of communicating with our friend Adams, who will be sure to lose no time in forwarding us all the assistance in his power under the many difficulties in which we are placed."

"Yes, Richard," returned his wife. "And yet," she added, after a pause, "the future presents to us but a dreary prospect. Whither can we go, destitute and wretched as we are, and what means can we adopt for our future support and safety? Oh, it was most cruel of my father to turn a deaf ear to the appeal I made to him, seeing the wretched condition in which we are. It is that which tortures me more than all."

"Alas!" said our hero, "and what can I say to comfort you? How remove those dreadful forebodings from your mind in which I also so painfully partake. Ours is indeed a wretched, a deplorable destiny, and could I but see you and our poor child in safety and happiness, I would not care what became of me."

"Oh, Richard," returned his wife, "I beseech you not to talk thus; for to hear you thus give way to despair, wrings my heart more than all; I am ready still to endure anything for your sake, and you shall never hear me utter a murmur of complaint; were I to lose you, oh, what would become of me? Who should myself and our dear child then have to look up to for protection? But we shall not be suffered thus to sink entirely. I feel confident that we shall not, and that the time will yet arrive when we shall be restored to peace, if not be that complete happiness which we once experienced."

"Heaven grant, my beloved Mary," replied her husband, "that the anticipations you have so sanguinely expressed may indeed be realised. Could we succeed in reaching some foreign land, where we should be unknown, we might indeed escape, and Providence would, I trust, supply me with some means of supporting us; but while we remain in this country, and are compelled to the wandering and wretched life we have lately led, it is useless for us to try to conceal from ourselves the imminent dangers by which we are every hour — nay, every moment surrounded; and it is painful to be thus dependant as we are upon the charity and benevolence of strangers."

"True, most true," coincided our heroine; "but still, amidst all the many dangers and miseries that we have had to encounter, we ought to feel grateful that we have met with so many individuals who have sympathised with us in our misfortunes, and have rendered us all the assistance in their power. Such disinterested friendship cannot be too highly praised."

"It cannot, indeed, my Mary," replied our hero; "but it is painful to be thus compelled to place ourselves under such a weight of obligation to those on whom we have no claim, and it is not at all likely that, unless the Almighty should mercifully interpose in our behalf, we can much longer continue to exist in this manner."

"Let us not view our prospects on the darkest side, Richard, for we know not what yet may be in store for us. My father——"

"Endeavour to banish him from your thoughts, Mary, for it can only serve to increase the anguish of your mind when you reflect upon the unnatural severity of his conduct."

"But surely he will yet be brought to a full sense of the injustice and cruelty of his conduct towards me," said our heroine; "and to restore me once more to his parental bosom."

"Deceive not yourself with any such hopes," replied Richard, "for to me it appears to be most improbable that they will ever be realised. Your last meeting with him ought to convince you of the obduracy of the feelings he entertains towards you, and which feelings I am convinced, from what we have heard of her character, and the manner in which she has succeeded in supplanting you in his affections, will not fail to be encouraged by Miss Arlington, whom the death of her uncle has doubtless prejudiced so strongly against myself and you. No, my dear Mary, we must put our whole dependance on the goodness of Heaven, from which alone can we hope for a deliverance from the dangers and the troubles by which we

are at present, and have been so long surrounded."

Mr. Milsom now re-entered the room,
and the conversation, of course, dropped.

"My friends," he observed, "I hope
you are satisfied with the accommodation
I have hitherto been enabled to afford you,
and if there is anything more that you require, you have only to mention it, and if
it is in my power, I shall feel a pleasure in
complying with your request."

"My dear sir," answered Richard,
"this is, indeed, most kind; but we are
already indebted to you far more than we
have any right to expect, and are unable
to make any other return for it than our
gratitude."

"I seek no other return," replied Mr.
Milsom; "to what I have done, and may
still be enabled to do, you are most heartily
welcome, and I feel most happy to think
that chance conducted you to my house,
for you would otherwise have had to have
wandered to some considerable distance
before you would have met with any other
place where you might have procured that
shelter and assistance which you so much
required."

"And that, in the exhausted condition of
my wife and child, it would have been almost impossible for us to have done," remarked Richard."

"True," returned Milsom; "and even
if you had, I question much whether you
would have found that relief of which you
stood in need. There are a number of
the most disreputable characters who inhabit this part of the country; desperate
and heartless wretches, wreckers, men
who are insensible to every feeling of pity,
and who are ready to perpetrate any
crime, however cruel, in order to gratify
their thirst for plunder. The consequences
might have been fatal had you fallen into
their hands, even poor and destitute as you
appear to be; in all probability your wife
and yourself would have been subjected to
the most brutal insults."

Mary shuddered.

"Ah, Mr. Milsom," said Richard, "I
have too much reason to believe what you
have stated, and cannot feel too thankful
to think that we have been saved from
such danger. To you we are indebted for
all, and——"

"Do not mention it," interrupted Mr.
Milsom; "for there is not so much credit
due, to me after all, for merely performing
an act of common humanity. But I see
you are fatigued, and require rest; therefore, if you please, I will conduct you to
a chamber. The storm still continues
to rage with unabated fury, and Heaven

protect all those poor unfortunate destitute
creatures who are exposed to its violence,
I say."

Richard and his wife most heartily responded to this humane wish, and having
again thanked Mr. Milsom for his kind
attention, they followed him from the
room, and ascending the stairs, he ushered
them into a clean and comfortable-looking
chamber, and which was further enlivened
by a cheerful fire that was burning in the
grate. Here he bade them good-night,
and desiring them not to disturb themselves
until what hour they liked in the morning,
he quitted the room.

Not feeling inclined to retire to bed just
yet, Richard and his wife seated themselves before the fire, and again entered
into conversation upon their present and
future prospects, while they listened at intervals to the voice of the tempest which
raged so fiercely without, and could never
feel sufficiently grateful for the shelter
which was so providentially afforded them,
and the disinterested kindness which Mr.
Milsom had already evinced towards
them.

"Should we be permitted to remain
here for a few days," observed Mary, "it
will recruit our strength, and you can probably have time to communicate with our
friend, Mr. Adams, and to receive his
answer, for he will not fail to use the
greatest promptitude in so important a
business."

"True," answered her husband; "and
how great will be his excitement when he
hears of what has happened, and of the
melancholy and untimely fate of his old
and much esteemed friend, poor Binnacle.
Alas! that fatal wreck, and the loss of one
upon whose friendship and assistance we
could so much depend, is one of the greatest calamities that has befallen us, and I
cannot help thinking upon it without a
shudder of horror. Had it not have taken
place, we should now have been in safety,
and our future prospects would have been
such as to make us look forward with
hope."

"It was, indeed, a terrible misfortune,"
remarked Mary; "but it was the will of
Heaven, and we must not murmur at its
decrees; perhaps, after all, it was ordained
for the best."

Richard shook his head disconsolately.

"Alas!" he said, "how prolonged are
our sufferings; and no sooner does hope
begin to dawn upon us, than it is ended by
some cruel disappointment. It seems as
if we were marked out to be the sport of
Fate."

"Let us endeavour to struggle on with

patience and fortitude," returned our heroine, "and we may yet be able to overcome all our difficulties, notwithstanding insurmountable as they may at present seem to be."

"My dear Mary," said our hero; "your sweet voice is ever ready to offer me consolation and hope, and I should be unworththy of you did I not seek by every effort in my power to follow your tender example. Come, then, we will, indeed, exert ourselves to battle with our misfortunes, and to look forward for happier times. We should be most grateful to that All-merciful Omnipotence who has hitherto enabled us to elude the vigilance of those who are in pursuit of us, notwithstanding we have so many times been on the point of falling into their power."

"Oh, yes," said Mary, "and that plainly shows that Providence has not yet deserted us."

"True," returned our hero; "but come, Mary, let us retire to rest, for the time is now getting late, and rest is what we all much require."

Our heroine complied, but first of all they knelt down, and supplicated in devout and fervent terms the protection of the Supreme, and were then about to rise from their knees, when they were startled by the loud report of fire-arms, and which seemed to proceed from the direction of the lane which led up to the house. They started to their feet and hastened towards the window, and at the same time they heard Mr. Milsom and his wife moving in the house, being evidently alarmed.

"What is the meaning of this?" said our hero ; "some danger threatens, I fear. We must be upon our guard; it is well that we had not retired to rest."

"Nay, Richard," returned Mary, "what danger can we have to apprehend? We are safe enough here ; but I fear that some terrible outrage has been committed near the house. Some unfortunate, defenceless traveller probably waylaid and murdered by some of the desperate wretches who, it seems, infest this part of the country."

"I must see Mr. Milsom," said Richard, "and endeavour to ascertain the fact. You remain here, and I will soon return." — "No," said Mary, "I will accompany you, for I cannot remain here in this state of doubt and suspense."

Richard offered no further objection, and the boy William being fast asleep, they quitted the room, and hastened towards the parlour, in which they heard Mr. Milsom and his wife stirring.

On entering it, they found the host and hostess, and one or two strangers who were staying at the inn, assembled, and in earnest conversation upon the circumstance that had taken place, and on seeing our hero and his wife enter the room, Mr. Milsom advanced towards them, and addressing himself to Richard, said—

"Ah, then you have been alarmed?"

"True," replied Richard; "what can be the cause of this?"

"I know not," returned Milsom, "for it is a very unusual thing here; I am afraid that some dreadful crime has been committed, and I and my friends here were just going to see whether we could ascertain the fact, and probably to render assistance, before it is too late, to the unfortunate victim of any outrage that may have been committed. Will you accompany us ?"

"Certainly," answered our hero; "for the more of us there are, the less fear is there of any danger, and should murder have been committed, it may not be too late to detect and apprehend the brutal perpetrators of it."

"True," agreed Milson, "and there is not a moment to lose. Here is a gun, myself and my friends are also armed, and we shall probably, therefore, be a match for any enemies whom we may chance to encounter."

Mary Parker could not help feeling some degree of fear, at the danger into which her husband might be precipitated; but, of course she could offer no opposition to his going, and having provided themselves with a lantern, the whole of the party issued forth from the inn, leaving Mrs. Milsom and our heroine together.

"The report seemed to proceed from the farther end of the lane, which is a lonely spot," remarked Mr. Milsom, "and thither we must direct our steps. Be cautious, my friends, or we may be taken by surprise."

They returned no reply to this, and all proceeded in silence along the lane, and listening to catch any sounds that might reach their ears, but all was perfectly still, save the voice of the storm, and as far as their eyes could stretch they could perceive no signs of a human being. They had not reached the end of the lane, however, when they heard the hasty sounds of horses' hoofs, and they stood prepared for anything which might be about to occur. The next instant a horse, without a rider, galloped past them with great speed, and before they could attempt to stop it, it had got far beyond their reach.

"That is a plain proof that my worst fears are too true," observed Mr. Milsom:

THE WANDERERS COME IN SIGHT OF THE VILLAGE.

"murder has been committed. Follow me, my friends."

They did so, and emerging from the lane, entered upon the dreary place which Mr. Milsom had mentioned, and opening the lantern, looked eagerly around them, but could discover nothing whatever to gratify their anxious curiosity.

"It is strange," said Milsom; "but I am satisfied that the report came from this direction, and that we cannot be far from the object of our search. Hark! did you not hear something?"

"I did," answered our hero, "and it seemed like the low moaning of some person in agony. We cannot be far from the unfortunate individual, whoever he is, and it may not yet be too late to save him."

The groans were now repeated more distinctly, and they hurried towards the spot from which they seemed to proceed, holding the lantern towards the ground in order to facilitate their search; and soon a stream of blood met their gaze, which guided them almost immediately to the body of a man stretched upon the earth, weltering in his gore, and apparently lifeless. His pockets were turned inside out, and his clothes much disordered, plainly showing that a robbery had been committed; but their first object was to scrutinise the unfortunate individual more minutely, and they discovered that he yet breathed, though it seemed certain that he had received such desperate injuries that he could not long survive. His face was completely deluged with blood, so that it was impossible to recognise his features, but there was something in the peculiarity of his dress which struck our hero as being familiar to him, and a sensation almost approaching to dread shot through his veins, though why it should do so he could not account.

"This is a shocking sight," said Milsom. "Poor fellow! I am afraid it is all over with him, for he appears to have been shot through the head. However, there is not a moment to lose : assist me to convey him to the inn, where I will send for the nearest surgeon, who, however, resides four miles off."

They now raised the inanimate form of the unfortunate stranger from the ground, and proceeded with him as fast as they could on their return to the inn, where in a few minutes they arrived, and the horror and alarm of our heroine and Mrs. Milsom on beholding so frightful a spectacle may readily be imagined. Mr. Milsom immediately despatched one of his servants on horseback to the nearest surgeon, telling him to make all the speed he possibly could, and they then set about rendering the stranger all the assistance in their power, though all hope of his recovery seemed to be completely futile, from the awful nature of the injuries that he had evidently received. He still breathed, but that only faintly, and it appeared to be utterly impossible that he could survive until the surgeon had arrived. They bound the wound in his head as well as they could, and having washed the blood from his face, they all eagerly gazed at his features ; but no sooner did Richard and his wife behold them than they uttered a cry of mingled astonishment, horror, and alarm, which startled the other persons present, and drew their immediate attention towards them.

The emotion of our hero and heroine will not be at all wondered at when they recognised in the features of the wounded man those of their old enemy, Bubble! Had they encountered the most ghastly spectre, they could not have been more excited, and it was in vain that they tried to conceal their feelings from Mr. Milsom and his friends.

"Why, how is this?" demanded the former, addressing himself to our hero;

"why are you and your wife so violently agitated? Is this unfortunate man known to you?"

"No—no," replied our hero, hastily, and much confused; "but—but the ghastly expression of his features shocked us, and we could not help giving expression to our feelings of horror."

"True—true," returned Milsom; "it is a fearful sight, and I only regret that the wretches who have committed this bloody and inhuman deed have for the present escaped; but I trust that they will yet be detected, and brought to that punishment which they so richly merit. No time must be lost in making the authorities acquainted with what has happened, and, of course, the evidence of all of you will be necessary to state the manner in which we found him, and all the circumstances of the awful case."

The agitation of Mary and her husband increased at this intimation, for they could not help at once perceiving the danger with which it was fraught to themselves, for should they appear before any magistrate, it was not at all improbable that they would at once be detected, and then their destruction would be inevitable, for all chance of their escape would be at an end. Their attention was, however, now directed to the unfortunate Bubble. A few convulsive emotions agitated his frame ; he opened his eyes, and glared wildly around him with a ghastly expression; closed them again, and uttering one deep and agonising groan, sunk back on the couch.

"Poor fellow!" said Mr. Milsom, in accents of the deepest compassion; "it's all over with him; he is dead!"

The persons present looked at each other, with feelings of horror, and Mary trembled so violently, that had not her husband been by her side, she could not have saved herself from sinking to the floor. By a look he endeavoured to reassure her, and she struggled with her emotions as well as she could, and conquered them much better than might have been expected.

"This awful event is too much for the feelings of my wife to endure, in her present delicate situation," observed Richard, "and as we can render no further assistance, we will, if you will permit us, retire, Mr. Milsom."

The latter offered no objection to this, and Richard taking the arm of his wife, led her from the room.

On once more regaining the chamber, and sinking into a chair, Mary for some moments abandoned herself to all the excitement of her feelings, Richard being in a very little better condition than herself.

"Oh, Richard," she said, at length, "what a strange and terrible event is this. What could have brought that unfortunate man into this part of the country?"

"Heaven only knows," answered our hero, "and it seems as though some fatal spell were upon us. So great was my emotion on recognising him, that it was a wonder that I had not betrayed myself."

"Had the murdered man ever have recovered to consciousness, he would at once have discovered us," said Mary; "but what are we to do now?"

"I know not," answered Richard; "this unexpected event has crushed all the hopes we had formed. It is impossible that we can remain here; for should we be compelled to go before the authorities to give evidence, which we shall be certain to be, I should no doubt at once be discovered, and then my fate would be sealed."

"Alas! alas!" sighed our heroine, "how agonising is this, and at the very moment when we thought we had found a safe asylum for a few days. But whither can we go? How depart from this house without being observed? It is impossible; we must remain, and chance the consequences."

"No, Mary," returned her husband, "that must not be; should we remain here till to-morrow, it may be too late. In a short time the inmates of the inn will probably have retired, and we may then depart without any fear of being observed. But, oh, how madly I talk! How is it possible that you can again support such fatigue and anxiety, my beloved wife, after all the terrible trials you have already experienced? No, we will remain here, and run the risk of everything. I see that it is useless for me to seek to fly from my fate, and the sooner that this misery is terminated one way or the other, the better I——"

"Oh, for Heaven's sake, cease!" cried our heroine, in a voice of the greatest emotion, "do not talk thus, or you will drive me to distraction. Have you then so little regard for me or our child, that you would thus rush upon destruction, and leave us alone and unprotected in the world? No, no; you cannot mean what you say; if you do indeed apprehend the danger you have mentioned from remaining here, I am ready to depart whenever you please, though it grieves me to leave those from whom we have already experienced so much kindness so abruptly, and which must leave a most unfavourable impression on their minds regarding us. But I will say no more, dear Richard, I will

yield entirely to your will; and although I have already suffered so much, Providence will, I trust, yet give me strength to support that which I may yet be fated to undergo."

"Most heroic of women, exclaimed Richard, clasping her to his bosom; "oh, how different is the fate to which you should have been exposed. Need I tell you, Mary, how deeply I participate in your feelings of regret at being compelled to leave the benevolent-hearted Mr. and Mrs. Milsom in so clandestine a manner? But this unfortunate and unexpected occurrence has rendered us no alternative. Why did Fate guide the footsteps of this unfortunate man hither?"

"It is indeed most unfortunate for us that it did so," remarked Mary; "and, in spite of the feelings of enmity and malice which he ever evinced towards us, I cannot but deeply regret the dreadful and untimely fate which has befallen him. Oh, Richard, while such wretches as those who have perpetrated this inhuman crime infest this part of the country, to what dangers may we not be exposed in pursuing our weary and helpless way?"

"No, Mary," he answered, "our miserable and destitute appearance will protect us. We have nothing to fear from them. But my principal fears are for you; for how is it possible that your tender frame, already so much exhausted, can again bear up against the fatigue of travelling, and the inclemency of the weather?"

"Oh, agitate not yourself thus," said Mary; "for what is there that I shall not yet be able to endure for your sake? The Almighty surely will ere long send us some permanent relief after the patience and resignation with which we have endured the sufferings to which he has been pleased to subject us."

"We must try to hope so, dear Mary," replied Richard, "and something seems to assure me that we shall not be doomed to disappointment. When all, then, is hushed in silence in the house, we must endeavour to depart, and once more commit ourselves to the will of Fate; and may it smile far more propitiously on us than it has hitherto done. Thank God the storm seems to be subsiding."

"Yes," said our heroine, "and our poor boy having slept soundly for this last hour or two, will be much refreshed, I hope, and better prepared to resume the fatigues of our uncertain journey. Alas! if we could have remained here for a few days, we might have had some prospect of relief. But I will not murmur; danger seems to threaten you, my husband, and I must do as your judgment may suggest to avoid it. There are no difficulties and hardships which I may have to encounter shall daunt me from the execution of my duty."

Our hero again embraced her fondly, and they then again endeavoured to muster up all their fortitude for the arduous task which they had to perform. They earnestly supplicated the aid of Heaven, and then feeling somewhat more composed and resolute, they awaited anxiously for the time to arrive when they thought it would be safe for them to attempt to depart. The awful death of Bubble, however, had made an impression upon their minds which they felt certain that they should not be able readily to get rid of, and they could not but feel the greatest pity for the unfortunate man, and to hope that by some means or other his brutal assassins would be discovered and brought to punishment. More than an hour passed away, when they heard Mr. and Mrs. Milsom, as they supposed it was, retire to their room, and soon afterwards the house was wrapped in profound silence, and Richard and his wife prepared for their departure; they aroused William, and, although they did not tell the poor boy the particulars of what had happened, he expressed himself ready to depart, though he could not but feel surprised at the necessity of this abrupt resolution. For fear that any one should be left to watch the corpse, our hero had determined to try to depart by the back of the house, and having cautiously opened the door, and listened attentively, but without hearing any sounds stirring, they noiselessly descended the stairs, and turning round to the right when they had got to the bottom of them, and traversing a short passage, they found themselves at the back door, which was bolted but not locked. Richard had some difficulty in removing the bolts without making a noise sufficient to alarm any person who might be up; but at last he succeeded, and they then found themselves again in the open air. Our hero closed the door again as well as he could, and then taking the arm of his wife, he hurried her away from the spot as fast as her feeble strength would permit her; but Mary could not help looking back upon the house, and when she remembered the great kindness they had experienced from Mr. and Mrs. Milsom, during the short time they had been with them, she could not repress a sigh of regret at the circumstances that had compelled them to leave them in so uncourteous a manner.

"What must be their opinion of us," she said, "when they discover our abrupt departure? They must form all kinds of suspicions to our prejudice."

"I sincerely hope not," replied our hero; "but the hasty course we have been obliged to adopt was unavoidable. The murder is sure to excite the greatest sensation; a strict investigation is sure to take place, and had I remained to be examined as a witness, I am afraid that I should have been so agitated and bewildered by the questions that might have been put to me, that even if I had not been recognised, I should have betrayed myself. No, Mary, we could not have acted more prudently than we have done, and I hope that it will not be many hours, at any rate, before we shall meet with some other place of safety."

Mary returned no answer, but suffered her husband to lead her from the spot, and they proceeded to some distance in silence. It was quite dark, and their way was, therefore, dismal and cheerless enough, and sufficient to add to the heavy depression of their spirits. The storm had, however, entirely subsided, but the air was piercingly cold, and the unfortunate fugitives felt it the more after the comforts they had so recently enjoyed at the inn. The scenery was extremely wild and dreary through which they were travelling, and after what had that night occurred, they could not help feeling some slight sensation of dread, and every now and then they cast their eyes anxiously around them, fearful lest some danger should threaten them, though they surely had nothing to fear from robbers, poor and destitute as they were. They had now got a considerable way from the inn, and without seeing anything which was at all calculated to cheer their spirits, or to open to them the prospect of relief; but Mary supported everything with the most exemplary fortitude and resignation, and did not seem to experience that weakness and fatigue which, under all the circumstances of the case, might have been expected; though it was evident that she sought to conceal her own feelings as well as she could, so that she might not agitate her husband any more than possible. The way at length became somewhat less dreary, and that tended in a great measure to revive their spirits, but still, although Mrs. Parker continued to struggle with her feelings in the same heroic spirit which she had done all along, it was quite evident that it was only by the dint of extraordinary exertion on her part that she could bear up against the many hardships they had to encounter at all. The strength of the poor boy, too, was nearly exhausted, and altogether their miseries and difficulties rapidly accumulated upon them, and were sufficient to annihilate what little hopes they had suffered alternately to take possession of their breasts. The extraordinary meeting with, and awful fate of Bubble continued to haunt their imaginations, and in spite of the many annoyances they had received from him, and the vindictive feelings he had ever, without a cause, evinced towards them, they could not help sincerely pitying him; and at the same time they sincerely regretted a circumstance which had compelled them to leave the house of the kind-hearted Mr. and Mrs. Milsom so abruptly; when they might have expected so much friendship, kindness, and solicitude from them in the time of their need.

"What must be the opinion they will form of us?" observed Mary; "what suspicions must not our strange conduct excite in their breasts? I am half inclined to think that it would have been better for us to have remained at the inn and have braved the result."

"No, Mary," replied her husband, "we had no other alternative than to act in the manner which we have done, under all the peculiar circumstances. You must admit the danger that I must have run in appearing before the authorities. It is more than probable that, so vigilant as my pursuers have been, a description of my person has been forwarded to the most distant parts of the country, and that I should have been immediately recognised and arrested."

"And is it not probable that Mr. Milsom, in his examination, will state the peculiar circumstances under which we arrived at his house," said our heroine; "our sudden and mysterious departure, and that, coupled with a description of us, will naturally excite suspicion, and a pursuit being set on foot for us, in a strange place as we are, and destitute of any means of concealment, how shall we be able to escape? It would have been a much better course for us, I cannot help thinking, to have confided our secret to Mr. Milsom, who might have been depended upon, and he would probably then have taken compassion upon us, and formed some excuse for your not appearing in this painful and dangerous affair at all."

"Alas!" returned Richard, "I only acted as prudence seemed to dictate, and I am completely bewildered, and know not what course to adopt. This continual anxiety almost wears me out, and when I witness the sufferings to which yourself and our poor child are constantly exposed, my fortitude nearly forsakes me. Where

I alone I would not shrink from anything which I might have to endure, and so completely tired am I of this painful state of anxiety and suspense, that I would no longer seek to avoid a fate which it appears but too clearly to me must sooner or later overtake me. But why do I talk thus, knowing the anguish it must cost you? Come, dear Mary, let us still endeavour to exert ourselves, and to bear up against the many troubles to which we are exposed, with the hope that kind Heaven will, ere long, afford us some relief."

"Well spoken, my dear husband," replied Mary; "we will endeavour to do so, and I sincerely trust that in our hopes we shall not be doomed to be entirely disappointed. In spite of the many difficulties and dangers it has hitherto been our lot to encounter, Providence has enabled us to surmount them, and that, at least, is a guarantee that it has not entirely deserted us. I cannot divest my mind of the impression that before long a favourable change will take place in our circumstances; that we shall reach some place of safety, and be able to avoid those dreadful evils which we have so long had reason to apprehend."

"God grant that we may," said our hero, fervently; "could I but see you again happy, my Mary, how much would I endeavour by my future conduct to evince my heartfelt gratitude to Heaven for the mercy shown us. But you are very ill, Mary, I know, although you try to conceal it; such painful exertions as you have for some time had to undergo, are too much for your tender frame to support, and I wonder how you have had strength sufficient to endure them so long."

"Let me but see you firm and confident, Richard," she answered, "and I shall then have courage and strength, I am sure, to endure much more than that I have hitherto experienced. God grant that we may ere long meet with some other humane persons who may take compassion on us."

To this wish Richard most fervently responded, and they again proceeded on their way as well as they could, though, in spite of all her efforts to the contrary, the strength of our heroine was fast failing her, and as nothing appeared to cheer their prospects, the anguish of her feelings, as may naturally be expected, increased.

It was still quite dark, and the wind having arose, was howling around them in fearful gusts, the cold was most intense, nor were they enabled to proceed fast enough to combat in any measure against its severity. The pale and care-worn features, the sunken eyes, and attenuated forms of the unfortunate fugitives, must have excited a feeling of pity in the most insensible breast; but they had hitherto met with not a single individual on their way; and, indeed, at that early hour of the morning, it was not at all likely that anyone would be abroad, unless they were poor wanderers like themselves; so on they slowly went, sad at heart, and looking with feelings of despair at the dreary scene around them. They were now travelling over a barren waste, with nothing whatever to shelter them from the piercing wind, and their limbs shivered with the cold, while every step that they proceeded they became the more exhausted. It would seem that this wild part of the country was entirely deserted, and, in fact, so cheerless was it, that it appeared quite unfit for human habitation. Richard looked anxiously in the pale face of his wife, and his fears increased. Her progress became slower and slower, and at length she was compelled to stop, and to lean upon the arm of her husband for support.

"Alas!" he sighed, "what is to be done? I see that it will be impossible for you to proceed much further, and there are no signs of any place where we are likely to obtain a shelter. This is most torturing, and I am completely at a loss how to act."

"Do not agitate yourself, Richard," she replied, in a faint voice; "I shall be better soon, I trust. Let me rest awhile on your arm, and then I shall be able to recover my strength."

"Ah, Mary," returned our hero, disconsolately, "it is in vain that you try to deceive me; I see that you are sinking fast, and when I know that I have not the power to relieve you, it drives me almost to distraction."

"Oh, why should you torture yourself in this manner?" returned the devoted wife; "you have nothing to blame yourself for; you have performed your duty towards me faithfully and affectionately, let the consequences be whatever they may. Perhaps it would be better if kind Heaven would take me to itself, for I feel that I am now only a useless burthen to you."

"Such words as these, Mary," said her husband, fixing his eyes upon her with a look of gentle reproach, "oh, they are most cruel, and how greatly do they add to the agony of my mind. Deprived of you, the beloved and devoted partner of my troubles, oh, what would become of me? What would become of our poor child? But no, Heaven in its infinite mercy will not inflict such a terrible calamity upon me."

"Pardon me the words I uttered, dear Richard," replied our heroine, looking in his countenance with a melancholy expression of affection; "my anxiety for yourself and our poor boy so bewilders and distracts my mind, that I scarcely know what I say. I will exert myself, and banish these melancholy thoughts from my breast. I am better now, so let us on our way, and God grant that we may speedily meet with some relief."

Richard embraced her, and they then pursued their journey, though they were only enabled to do so at a slow rate, and were frequently compelled to stop in order to enable Mary to recruit herself. They at length came to the end of the waste, and then, if possible, entered upon a scene still more dreary, being a kind of woody glen, whose leafless trees seemed to frown despair upon them, and where the darkness seemed to be more intense than it had been before. Mary could not help shuddering as she gazed upon this frightful place, and clung still closer to her husband, who was himself in a very little better condition than she was, though he tried to conceal it from her, and by his looks to compose her feelings and inspire her with confidence.

"This is a dismal place," she observed, "and as I gaze upon it, it imparts a melancholy sensation to me which I cannot resist. Come, Richard, let us hasten from it as fast as we can."

"We shall soon emerge from it, my love," answered our hero, "and then I hope that the prospect before us will begin to brighten; still, I trust that we have nothing here to fear."

They now again resumed their journey, but they had not proceeded far when they were startled by hearing footsteps and voices behind them, and hastily looking back, they beheld, as well as their eyes could penetrate through the darkness, several men approaching that way.

"Ah!" said Richard, "these men are probably peasants going to their daily labour, from whom we may be able to obtain some information. We will question them."

"Not so," returned Mary, with a look expressive of the alarm which she unaccountably could not help feeling; "there might be danger in meeting them, until we have endeavoured to ascertain better what their characters are. They probably have not yet observed us, so let us step aside until they have passed, and we can observe them more distinctly."

Richard could not deny the prudence of

this suggestion, he therefore complied with the request of his wife, and they therefore stepped into a dark part of the glen, where they could conceal themselves, and at the same time have a distinct view of the men. They approached, and as they did so, by the loudness of their tones, and two or three words which reached their ears, they appeared to be quarrelling. At length they approached to within a yard or two of where the travellers had concealed themselves, and there they stopped, as if to settle their differences, and Richard and his wife had a distinct view of their persons, which did not give them a very high opinion of their characters.

There were three of them, and from their dresses they seemed to belong to that desperate class of men who infested that part of the country, and from what they could see of their features, they were coarse, repulsive, and ferocious, and Mary could not help shuddering with an instinctive feeling of fear as she gazed upon them, and which was increased when she heard the observations that escaped from them.

"He had more money about him, I am certain, than you think proper to acknowledge, Sam," said one of them, "and as we all shared alike in the danger, so we ought all to share alike in the booty."

"Why what a d—d dissatisfied fellow you are, Wildfire," returned the other ruffian, "I am sure you ought to be satisfied with what you have got, for the old fellow bled well, much better than we had a right to expect from his appearance. And what if I have taken a little extra to myself, I'm sure I earnt it, for was it not I that shot him, and at any rate, you have not got that on your conscience."

"Conscience be d—d!" said Wildfire; "what matters it who shot him? we were all out for the same purpose, and we are therefore all equally guilty, and should share the same fate if we were to be discovered. Fair's fair, and as old pals we oughtn't to endeavour to cheat one another."

"So I say," observed the other fellow, "and so, whether you are or not, Wildfire, I am determined to have my rights. Sam took a purse from the traveller after he had shot him, and the contents of that I expect to be shared amongst us."

"Well," replied the man whom they had called Sam; "we will have no more words about it, since you seem to be so determined. We will settle this business when we get to the rendesvous."

"Agreed," said Wildfire, " and I think we ought to be very well satisfied, for we have not made such a bad night's work of

it. The old fellow must have had pretty good courage to travel at such an hour of the night, and with so much money in his possession."

"He must," coincided Sam ; "but it is just such customers as he that we want to meet. I wonder if he is dead.'."

"No doubt of it," answered Wildfire, "for the shot seemed to pass right through his head. However, it does not matter much whether he is or no, for there is no fear of our being discovered. The report of the gun no doubt alarmed the inmates of the inn, and we acted wisely in making our exit as quickly as we did, for old Milsom knows us well."

"True," said Sam, "but come, let us hasten on our way, for I confess that I require a glass or two after this night's business, and it is no use our standing talking here upon the subject."

To this the other ruffians agreed, and without any further observations they hurried from the spot, and were almost immediately out of sight. Richard and his wife looked fearfully at each other, and we need not attempt to describe their feelings at the observations they had heard.

"These wretches then, are the assassins of that unfortunate man," said Mary, with a shudder of horror.

"There can be no doubt about it," replied our hero, " after what we have heard, and I sincerely hope that they may not escape the punishment they merit for their inhuman crime."

"It is fortunate that they did not observe us," remarked Mary; "for had they been aware that we were listening to them, we know what we might have expected from such desperate miscreants."

"True," coincided her husband; "but come, Mary, let us no longer tarry in this dismal place. Probably we may ere long meet with some place where we may obtain that relief of which we stand in need, though our means are so limited."

Having first looked eagerly in the direction which the villains had taken, for fear they should be still lurking about, but seeing nothing of them, our hero took the arm of his wife, and they prepared to traverse the glen, anxious to emerge from it as quickly as possible.

Daylight was now first beginning to dawn, and, therefore, the aspect of the country did appear a little more cheerful, and proceeding as fast as they could, they at length emerged from the glen and came upon a less wild part of the country than they had hitherto travelled through. Having crossed one or two fields they entered upon a narrow lane which was only of limited extent, and upon leaving that they found themselves on the highroad.

They proceeded with renewed spirits, and the wind having abated in its violence, they did not feel that inconvenience which they had previously done, though it was still exceedingly cold, and from the appearance of all above, it seemed as though they were likely before long to have a renewal of the storm which had raged almost incessantly for the last few days, and from which they had already experienced so much to annoy and distress them.

They had advanced along this road for about half a mile when it took a winding turn, and stretching their eyes before them, they perceived smoke ascending to the clouds at a short distance, which seemed to issue from the chimney of some dwelling in the vicinity, and it was a most welcome sight to them, exhausted as they were with the distance they had already travelled, and so much as they stood in need of some refreshment.

"Thank Heaven," said Richard, "that we have yet the means, however small, of procuring present aid, and we must trust to Providence for the future. A few hours rest will serve to revive you, I hope, Mary, and there is no knowing what may then transpire."

"True, Richard," replied our heroine. "Oh, we must not yet despair, for Heaven knows what favourable change may yet be in store for us."

They hurried on as well as they could exhilarated by these hopes, and at length came in sight of a small hamlet, composed of wooden huts of the most humble, if not, wretched appearance, and from the chimneys of one larger than the rest, and which seemed to be used for the purpose of a pot-house or tavern, the smoke issued which had first attracted their attention. They hastened towards it, and by the time they had arrived at it, a middle-aged man, of not very prepossessing appearance, emerged from the door, and taking him to be the proprietor of the establishment, our hero advanced towards him, and addressing him, requested to know if they could be accommodated in his house for a few hours with rest and refreshment. The man eyed them narrowly and apparently suspiciously for a moment or two, without returning any answer, but at length he said—

"Why, I dare say we can, that is, if you have got the means of paying for it; but I must tell you, master, that we cannot afford to give anything away in charity here."

A feeling of shame and mortified pride flushed the cheeks of Richard Parker for a moment, and his wife felt abashed and alarmed, but knowing the urgency of the case, they quickly recovered themselves, and the former said—

"We are poor, but as far as our means will allow us, we will pay you for what we may have."

"Well, that's enough," returned the man, "so follow me, and I'll see what I can do for you."

Thus saying, he led the way into the house, and conducted them to a room which had a much more comfortable appearance than the exterior of the house would have led them to expect, and in which, although at that early hour of the morning, a cheerful fire was already blazing. The landlord having directed them in somewhat more civil terms than before to be seated, now said—

"I suppose you will take some breakfast; for, if I may judge from your appearance, you stand in need of it?"

Richard replied in the affirmative, and nodding his head, he left the room.

"How much this man resembles, in his manners, those of the landlord of the house in which we were robbed," observed Mary; "I fear we have again got into bad quarters; what an uncouth set of individuals there are in this part of the country."

"True," coincided our hero, "but still, Mary, you must not always judge from the manners of a man, and certainly our present miserable appearance is not the most prepossessing. If we can remain here for a few hours it will serve to refresh you, and we may be enabled to obtain such information as we require."

Mary was about to make use of some observation when the landlord re-entered the room, and brought with him a substantial breakfast, though it was composed of the coarsest viands, and our hero having paid him his demand, which was pretty moderate, after having again scrutinised them narrowly, he said—

"Have I never seen you before, young man?"

Richard was somewhat startled by this abrupt question, and the look which the landlord fixed upon him in putting it, but he quickly recovered himself, and replied—

"Not to my knowledge, sir, and we are strangers in this part of the country."

"Have you never been a seaman?" questioned the landlord, with a still more scrutinising glance.

Richard was startled by this interroga-

MRS GOODSON INVITES PARKER AND HIS WIFE TO TAKE BREAKFAST.

tory, and his wife was so a'armed that she could with difficulty conceal her agitation. Our hero hesitated, for he dreaded telling an untruth, but necessity compelled him to do so, and at last, he answered --

"You are mistaken, sir, I have not been a seaman, though myself and my wife have suffered shipwreck on this coast, on our way to one of the Channel Islands."

"Well," said the landlord, "I suppose I must be mistaken; though I could almost have sworn that you was an old shipmate of mine, one Richard Parker, who I believe has made some little stir in the navy lately. But now I look at you again, you are a different complexioned man to him, and not quite so tall, though the features are still very much alike. You will excuse me for the liberty I have taken, but you know we are all liable to mistakes in our time."

"Very true," replied our hero, as composedly as he could; "and there needs no apology."

The landlord made no reply, and immediately afterwards quitted the room, greatly to the relief of Richard and his wife.

"Alas!" sighed Mary, after he was gone, how unfortunate is this; we must depart from here as soon as possible, for I tremble with apprehension while we remain. Every moment is fraught with danger."

"Silence, dear Mary," enjoined Richard, in an under tone, "and subdue your feelings; the landlord has acknowledged that he was mistaken, though he says that my features resemble the man he takes me for; we have only to act with prudence and precaution, and all will be well. In a short time we will be far away from this house."

"Oh, yes," said Mary, "and the sooner the better. But have you no recollection of this man?"

"None," answered her husband; "though, from his observations, it is evident that he has seen me before, and that frequently."

"Would that we were far away," said Mary, "for he may, by reflection, become convinced of your identity, and then I shudder to think of what the consequences would be sure to be. It seems as though we were fated to be in a constant state of alarm and agitation."

Richard exerted himself to the utmost to compose her feelings, but he succeeded only indifferently, and, in fact, although he strove to conceal it, the observations of the landlord, so pointed, had excited him very little less than herself, and he felt anxious to be away from the house. They partook but sparingly of the meal which the landlord had brought them, for their minds were too much agitated to suffer them to eat, and they were still engaged in conversation when they were interrupted by hearing a confused noise in the house, and immediately afterwards the door was opened, and three men entered the room, followed by the landlord. The alarm of our hero and his wife may be imagined when in the persons of those individuals they recognised the three men whom they had seen in the glen, and who by their observations had acknowledged themselves to be the murderers of Bubble. Mary turned very pale and trembled violently, and it was not without the greatest difficulty that our hero could conceal his agitation and alarm. The men eyed them narrowly, and with no pleasant expression in their countenances, and then turning to the landlord, one of them said—

"Strangers here! How is this, Bolton? I thought this room was always reserved for our use?"

"We ask pardon if we have intruded," said Richard, rising, "we are merely travellers who seek a temporary shelter here, but probably the landlord can accommodate us with another room during the brief period we intend to stop?"

"Ay," answered the host, "I have no doubt I can make it agreeable to the gentlemen, who, you see, are regular customers of mine, and I suppose have private business to transact; so, if you will accompany me, I will conduct you to another room."

Richard nodded assent, and glad to escape from the presence of these desperate men, they followed the landlord out, and he ushered them into another apartment, which seemed to be adjoining the one they had just quitted. Here he left them, and for some moments after he was gone they remained without uttering a word.

"Oh, Richard," said his wife, "let us immediately depart; chance could not possibly have led us to a more dangerous place than this. The sight of those ruffians has filled my breast with horror. Did they but know that we had overheard them in the glen, our destruction would be inevitable, and——"

"Hush!" interrupted Richard, cautiously, "speak low, for should we be overheard we should immediately bring upon us that danger which we now apprehend. They can have no suspicion of us, and we can remain here until we have sufficiently rested ourselves to proceed. Should we depart immediately we might excite suspicion which might prove dangerous to us."

"Would that we were away from this part of the country altogether," remarked Mary, "for it seems that some fresh danger besets us wherever we direct our steps."

Richard returned no answer, for his attention was directed to the men in the next room, whom he heard conversing, and immediately afterwards he was startled by hearing his own name mentioned by one of the ruffians, and placed his ear close to the wainscot in order that he might hear more distinctly what was said. Mary also listened attentively, and nothing could exceed the agitation and alarm of her feelings.

"Yes," observed one of the men, in reply to the observations of his companions, "it is rather extraordinary that this Parker should have succeeded in eluding the vigilance of his pursuers so long, especially considering the large reward that is offered for his apprehension. He must have more friends than is exactly known, and it is my opinion that he is not now in this country."

"How is it possible that he could have left it, so closely as every seaport is watched?" demanded another. "It is my belief that he is secreted somewhere in London, for that is the place where he is more likely to remain in safety, after all. I only wish that one of us had any chance of arriving at the knowledge of his whereabouts, for the reward would be no bad thing to handle, and it is not our business to stand nice about trifles."

"You say right," answered Wildfire, for our hero and his wife could recognise his voice in a moment; "and I don't suppose that any one would make any particular inquiries into our characters if we should happen to apprehend him."

"Certainly not," observed Sam; "but I am afraid that there is not much chance for us; it is not very likely that he will find his way to this part of the country."

"No," replied another, in whose voice they recognised that of the landlord; "but did you not ce the stranger who was in this room just now?"

"I did," returned the man; "poor devil, him and his wife, for I suppose she is so, seem to be in great distress; but what of him?"

"Why, you must know that some years since I served on board of the same vessel as Richard Parker did, under the command of Captain Arlington, with whose murder he stands charged."

Mary could scarcely suppress a cry of terror when she heard the landlord give utterance to these words, and her husband was scarcely less agitated than herself, but he motioned her to composure and silence, and they again listened attentively to this important conversation.

"You know him, then?" said one of the men.

"Certainly I do," was the answer, "and when I first saw this stranger I was most forcibly struck with the strong resemblance which his features bore to Richard Parker's."

"Ah!" exclaimed the men in a breath.

"But, on a closer inspection," continued the landlord, "I was convinced that I was mistaken; Parker was a much darker man than he; four or five years younger, I should say, and two or three inches taller."

"Well," observed Wildfire, "that alters the business altogether."

"Oh, yes," observed the landlord, "I am certain that I was mistaken, although their features are so much alike. It would have been a bad job for Parker had he accidentally fallen into my clutches, for I would not have failed to earn the reward, you may depend on that."

How Mary shuddered as the landlord uttered these words, and she looked at her husband with the most painful anxiety, but he was much more composed than could have been expected, and he again, by a significant look, enjoined her to silence. Once more they listened with the most breathless attention, but the remainder of the conversation was conducted in so low a tone that they could not distinguish a single syllable, and soon afterwards they heard the men arise and quit the house, which was a great relief to them.

"Oh, Richard," said his wife, "what is it we have heard? Should we remain here much longer the landlord's first suspicions may be confirmed, and I tremble to think what would then be the consequences. Let us not lose a moment in departing from this place which is so surrounded with danger."

"Be calm, my love," replied Richard, "for we have nothing now to fear; but should we appear in any hurry to depart, the landlord's suspicions might be excited, and then all the fatal consequences which you now apprehend might take place. It is strange that chance should lead us to a place the landlord of which should happen formerly to have known me. But time and suffering have evidently wrought such a change in me that he imagines he is now mistaken as to my identity. It is fortunate that we have overheard this conversation, for now I shall be upon my guard should he put any questions to me. These ruffians have quitted the house, so that we have nothing to apprehend from them. Try to compose your feelings, I say again, and take that rest which may befit you to resume your journey."

"I am quite prepared for it now," replied Mary, "for this conversation has made me uneasy and alarmed while we remain here. When shall we find a place of security? The Fates have evidently conspired against us, and we are kept in a continual state of dread and suspense."

"And yet let us not despair," said our hero, "for a favourable change may take place in our circumstances much sooner than we expect."

"Alas!" returned Mary, "after the many bitter disappointments we have experienced, I dare not entertain any such hopes."

Richard still endeavoured to console her, and to inspire her with fortitude, but he succeeded only indifferently, and Mary still expressed the same anxiety to depart. While they were still conversing the landlord entered the room, and in more civil accents than he had yet spoken, inquired whether there was anything more he could do for them. Richard thanked him for his attention, and replied in the negative.

"We are very poor, sir," he continued, "having nearly lost everything we possessed in the shipwreck. We are now on our way to the nearest seaport, where we hope to meet with friends to assist us, and who will enable us to reach the place of our destination."

"You seem to be a man who has mixed in good society," observed the landlord; "from what part do you come?"

"From London," answered our hero, "with much presence of mind; "for many years I was a principal clerk in a merchant's office in the city, but on the failure of the firm I was, of course, thrown out of employment, and having a promising offer at Guernsey, I was on my passage there with my wife and child when this misfortune took place."

"Well, it was a bad job for you, sure enough," remarked the landlord; "but yourself and your wife do not seem in a very good condition to travel just yet, so, if you like to remain here for a day or two I can accommodate you, I dare say."

"No, I thank you," answered Richard; "I am anxious to get on my way, for my business is urgent, and my means are limited."

"Well," returned Bolton, "of course you know best. But the more I look at you the more am I struck with your great likeness to Richard Parker; had your complexion been different, and your age a few years younger, I should have taken you to be the very man."

"Indeed?" said our hero, in a tone of the utmost indifference, and affecting a smile; "it is no great honour, and rather dangerous, I take it, to bear a likeness to such a man."

"You have heard of him, then?"

"Certainly," replied our hero, with the same composure; "and I wonder that he has escaped so long."

"Yes," coincided the landlord, "he has managed his business remarkably well, and I do not think that he will ever be taken now; it is my opinion that he has contrived to get out of the country, and if so he may set the law at defiance."

"Well," remarked Richard, "I think that is not at all unlikely. But you say you knew this unfortunate man?"

"I did," answered Bolton; "he was formerly my shipmate, and a trim sailor enough he was, and one who I believe would, at that time, have done a good turn for anybody. I never thought he would have turned out as he has, though I know he had much to complain of both against

Captain Arlington (who was never over scrupulous in applying the lash), and the Lords of the Admiralty. However, if they catch him now they will hang him up as sure as his name's Parker."

"And would you be the means of betraying an old shipmate, should you ever chance to come across him?" asked our hero.

"Why, for the matter of that," answered the landlord, "as times are now it will not do for a man to be over particular, and I might as well earn the reward which is offered for his apprehension as anybody else. However, I do not expect it will ever come to my chance, for I am not one of the lucky ones; so it is no use talking about it. You decline my offer then?"

"I do," returned Richard, "thank you all the same; for, as I said before, my business is urgent, and my means are limited. I will, however, remain here for another hour or so, and as myself and my wife have some private business to discuss before we resume our journey, I should feel much obliged to you if you would allow us to have this room to ourselves."

"Very well," said Bolton, "you need not fear any intrusion, for I am not troubled with many customers at this hour of the morning."

Richard again thanked him, and he then quitted the room. During the time this conversation had been going on Mary, as might have been expected, was in the greatest state of fear and trepidation, and she was surprised at the firmness and presence of mind which her husband displayed, especially after the observations the landlord had made use of, and she felt her mind greatly relieved when he quitted the room.

"All is safe, dear Mary," observed our hero, "when the landlord was gone; "we have nothing to fear; this man is convinced that he was mistaken, and we can quit the house at the time I have mentioned without any suspicion."

"And why should we at all postpone our departure, dear Richard?" she anxiously inquired; "I feel much refreshed now, and ready to resume our journey. Before long we may meet with some other place of accommodation, and I am in a state of dread and suspense while we remain here."

"Nay, Mary," replied our hero; "there is no necessity for this; another hour's rest will do you good; besides, it seems to threaten us with another storm presently, and we had better remain for awhile to see whether it clears off."

Mary found it was in vain to offer any

further objection, and they sat conversing upon their future prospects for some time longer, her impatience to be gone increasing every moment.

The dark and ominous clouds which had so long obscured the horizon at length cleared off, and it was evident that the storm which had for some time threatened would not take place for the present, so that Richard could no longer raise any opposition to the wishes of his wife, and they arose to depart. On seeing the landlord, they thanked him for the accommodation he had afforded them, and the attention he had shown them, and having bade him good day, they once more resumed their cheerless and uncertain journey. They passed through the village without seeming to excite the curiosity of any one, although there were several persons about, and thinking it would be more prudent to avoid the main road, under all the circumstances, they struck into the open fields, and proceeded for some distance on their way in silence, though their thoughts were busily occupied. The sun having now obtained full power, they did not feel the cold so much as they had done before, and they journeyed on much refreshed with the rest they had obtained. In this manner they continued to travel for more than a couple of hours, only stopping for a short time at intervals, and the aspect of the country was not so dreary as that they had journeyed through the day or two previously. But at length dark clouds again obscured the horizon, which every moment became more dense, and it was now quite evident that a renewal of the storm which had so long threatened, would shortly take place. They increased their speed as much as they could, with the hope of meeting with some place of shelter before it commenced; but, although they strained their eyes in every direction, nothing of the kind appeared to gratify their wishes. It seemed as if a spell were upon them, and that they were doomed to perpetual disappointments and misery. Mary tried to conquer her emotions, but with continual anxiety of mind, and disappointment, she was completely worn out; she felt sick at heart, and she looked in the face of her husband in despair, while at the same time a melancholy presentiment crossed her mind that there was some fresh misery in store for them. It was, indeed, wonderful the manner in which she had borne up against such accumulated sufferings as had fallen to their lot for the last few days so well. Our hero felt most keenly for her and their son, who had supported the many severe

and overwhelming trials to which they had been so long subjected with a fortitude and perfect heroism which was truly surprising for his years, and he knew not what to say to impart consolation or hope to them. He tried to encourage them with a look, and Mary, who, of course, perfectly well understood his feelings, and duly appreciated them with that generous self-devotedness which formed so noble and prominent a feature of her character, uttered not a murmur of complaint, but taking his arm, suffered him to guide her footsteps forward on their hopeless and desolate track as well as he could, mentally supplicating the Almighty to assist them in the midst of the terrible difficulties by which they were on every side encompassed, and to which there really now appeared to be no end. Slowly and with sad hearts they proceeded, straining their eyes in every direction with the hope of beholding some dwelling where they might apply for and obtain the relief they so much required, or to see some person who might furnish them with such information as would assist them in the midst of the many difficulties by which they were surrounded; but still nothing of the kind appeared, the way became more wild and dreary, and the only prospect before them was one of the utmost misery and despair.

And now the black and ponderous clouds which had so long threatened, suddenly burst, the rain began to descend in a manner which must soon drench them to the skin, while the wind blew a perfect hurricane, and added to the misery of their situation, rendering their progress difficult, and, in fact, almost impossible. Mary's remaining strength almost failed her, and had it not been for the support of her husband, she must have sunk to the earth.

"Alas! my poor Mary," he said, in a voice of the deepest anguish, and looking in her pale face with despair; "what can I say to you? how comfort you under this dreadful trial? The elements seem to mock at our sufferings; and it would appear that cruel Fate had decreed that no relief, no hope, should come to our aid. What is to done in this terrible emergency? It is impossible that you can long bear up against the tempest which every moment increases in fury. Oh, what bitter, what insupportable agony does this impart to my very soul."

"For Heaven's sake, calm your feelings, dear Richard," expostulated his wife, "for to see you suffer thus much tortures me more than all. True, it is a painful trial, and I know not how we have deserved to be subjected to such unexampled suffering, but still we must submit to it with all the patience and fortitude that we can, and——"

"Patience! fortitude!" interrupted our hero; "oh, surely this is enough to put the firmest feeling to the test, and to make even the stoutest heart sicken and droop with despair. And what prospect is there before us of any relief? None whatever. In a strange place, friendless and destitute, what is to become of us? Better would it be to end at once this insupportable suffering, by abandoning all hope of escape from the fate which has been so long impending o'er my head and resigning myself into the hands of the law."

"Oh, forbear, Richard," remonstrated our heroine, with a look of terror, "talk not in this manner, for it makes my heart shudder to hear you. But surely continual anxiety of mind has disordered your reason and you know not what you say. Resign yourself into the stern hands of the law—heedlessly sacrifice that life which is so precious to me—and to meet with such a fearful, such an ignominious death—horrible thought! It freezes the very blood in my veins as it occurs to me. If you indeed love me, and pity me, you will not again repeat those words, but will by your example endeavour to animate me with fortitude and hope to still struggle against the terrible misfortunes it is our cruel lot to encounter."

"Pardon me, dear Mary," said her husband, embracing her, "I was wrong in speaking as I did, but long suffering and disappointed hopes have, indeed, bewildered and distracted my brain, and there are moments when I am little better than a madman, and I know not what I say. But can you wonder at it when you see the dreadful misery to which we are exposed, and the little prospect there is of our being released from it? This storm, too, and in the situation in which we are placed, can but add to my anguish and despair; and your pale features and trembling limbs too plainly convince me that unless some means of relief speedily present themselves to us, that you must sink under it. Oh, believe me, I could bear even all that I have had, and may yet have to endure, without a murmur, but to witness the sufferings of yourself and our poor child, is the most exquisite torture to my soul, and the more so because I know it is not in my power to afford you the least help or consolation."

"Cease to torture yourself any longer, Richard," said the affectionate wife, "and

I will exert myself to the utmost, and Providence will, I trust, yet enable us to surmount all the painful difficulties which Fate has thrown in our way, until a favourable change shall have taken place in our circumstances, and we may be placed beyond the reach of danger. Surely it cannot be long before we shall meet with a temporary shelter."

"Alas!" sighed Richard, as he cast his eyes anxiously around, "there seems to be no prospect of it at present. You are already wet to the skin, and the tempest rather increases than abates in violence. There is no chance of its abating for some time, and it is impossible that you can much longer withstand its pitiless raging. Heaven help us, for without its merciful interference, I know not what will become of us."

Mary returned no answer to this, for she knew not what to say, and they still continued to journey on as fast as their trembling and exhausted limbs would permit them, but still without any prospect presenting itself to them to at all gladden their hopes, and the most eloquent pen would be perfectly inadequate to describe the poignant anguish of their feelings.

The wind and the rain continued unabated in their violence, and the wretched situation of the unfortunate wanderers may be much more easily conjectured than described. Wet to the skin, and shivering with the intense cold, it was a wonder how they were enabled to proceed at all, and the poor boy William was, if possible, in a still more deplorable plight than his hapless parents, though with an energy which was surprising in one of his tender years, especially after what he had already suffered, he still struggled against every difficulty, and endeavoured to conceal as much as possible his exhausted condition, so that it might not add to the anguish of mind which he knew too well his father and mother were at that time enduring.

At length they found themselves in a narrow road, banked on either side, and enclosed by leafless trees, and there they were in some slight degree sheltered from the wind and the rain, but not sufficiently to deserve any particular notice. They had not advanced far along the road, however, when their eyes were gladdened by the sight of a lonely cottage, and from the chimney of which the smoke was curling in the wind.

"Thank Heaven!" exclaimed Richard, "if the inmates of this humble dwelling possess but the common feelings of humanity, they will not refuse us a shelter;

seeing the deplorable condition in which we are placed."

Mary made no reply to this, but her looks sufficiently bespoke her feelings, and they having arrived at the cottage, Richard advanced to the door, supporting his wife, and knocked. Almost immediately it was opened by an elderly and homely-looking female, of kindly aspect, who started on beholding strangers, but observing their distressed condition, she evidently viewed them with feelings of compassion, and that encouraged Richard to speak.

"My good woman," he said, "you see the wretched condition in which we are, and I, therefore, have to request that you will grant us a temporary shelter in your cottage from this fearful storm, to whose fury we have been long exposed."

"Ah! God forbid that I should ever refuse such a simple request to any of my fellow creatures in distress," replied the woman; "so walk in and welcome, and accept freely of such accommodation as I can afford you."

Richard and his wife were about to return their thanks, but she stopped them with a significant look, and having motioned them they followed her into the cottage, in the neat and cleanly little parlour of which a cheerful fire was blazing. The old woman took off the wet cloak of Mary without any further ceremony, and she then desired them to take their seats by the fire, whilst she still contemplated their distressed condition with increased looks of compassion.

"Dear me," she observed, "you are indeed in a most wretched plight, and I do not wonder at it, considering the frightful storm to which you have been exposed. Have you travelled far?"

"Yes, my good woman," answered our hero, "many miles; and having for some time been exposed to the greatest misfortunes and being poor and destitute, you may imagine how much we have suffered."

"Ah, poor things," remarked the old woman; "you must, indeed, and I pity you sincerely, and only regret that it is not in my power to assist you, for I am only a poor widow, and am depending entirely upon the earnings of my son, who labours early and late, poor lad, to support me; and then there is the good lady at the villa assists me greatly, for she is very benevolent and humane, and Heaven will, I trust, reward her for it. But make yourself quite at home, I beg of you, while you remain here; this fire will soon dry your clothes, and I hope the storm will quickly subside."

"Your disinterested kindness, my good woman, is entitled to our warmest thanks," said Richard; "my wife and child, as you see, are quite exhausted, and I know not what would have become of them, had not Providence fortunately guided our footsteps to your humble but hospitable dwelling. But I regret that I am unable to reward you for——"

"Do not mention it, my good man, I beg of you," interrupted the cottager; "God knows it is little enough that I can do for you, but such as it is you are heartily welcome to. It is a good job that you were led here, for there is not another dwelling for more than a mile from this place, and that is Ashton Villa, where the good lady who is so kind to me resides; there you would have been sure to find assistance I know, for she and her husband never turn any one away from their house without relief who stand in need of it. But you want some refreshment; my fare is only humble, but you are welcome to it with all my heart, so I will go and get you some without delay."

"This is indeed most kind," ejaculated Mary, who was completely overwhelmed by the unaffected benevolence of the old woman; "but I am afraid we shall put you to too much inconvenience by troubling you in this manner."

"Not at all," answered the cottager; "I shall never be any the worse off, I dare say, for anything I can do for those who are in need, so do not trouble yourself about it. I will return in a few minutes."

With these words the kind-hearted woman quitted the room, and left Richard and his wife to themselves. For a moment or two after she was gone they were so overpowered by their feelings that they could not speak a word, but at length Mary said,—

"Oh, Richard, we ought still to be most grateful to Providence even amidst all the troubles it has been our lot to experience; Providence has not yet deserted us, but has again raised us up an humble but sincere friend in this good woman; and who knows that this may be merely the prelude to some further and permanent relief?"

"True, my love," coincided her husband, "the shelter of this cottage is a most seasonable relief, and I had begun to despair of meeting with any. But the benevolent lady whom this good woman mentioned; if the character she has given of her be a correct one, we might by applying to her, and making our distressed situation known to her, obtain some assistance, and——"

"Ah, Richard," interrupted our heroine, "what can we expect from her, strangers as we are to her? Alas! my heart revolts at the idea of our thus reducing ourselves to a complete state of vagrancy."

"Vagrancy!" repeated Richard, and his face coloured as he spoke; "did I ever think that such a term could be applied to Richard Parker and his wife? And yet it is most painfully true. Alas! to what a wretched and degrading situation has cruel Fate reduced us."

"Pardon me the observation, Richard," said his wife; "I meant not to wound your feelings. Let us think no more about it, but bear up against our painful destiny as well as we can."

Our hero was prevented from making any reply by the return of the old woman to the room, and she placed before them such humble fare as her cottage afforded, inviting them cordially to partake of it. Encouraged by the kindness of her manners, they did so, and during the time they were making this humble, but welcome repast, the good woman busied herself about the place, and made everything in it as comfortable for them as she could.

Having finished their meal, Richard and his wife and their child felt much refreshed, and again most fervently and sincerely returned their thanks to their generous hostess for the disinterested friendship and benevolence she had displayed towards them.

"My good people," returned the cottager, "I do not require any acknowledgment for the little kindness and assistance that I have been enabled to bestow upon you, for I consider it is a duty we owe to each other, and I only wish it was in my power to do more; but, as I said before, I am a very poor woman, and were it not for the industry of my son, God bless him, and the many favours I receive from the benevolent Mrs. Ashton, who delights in doing good towards her fellow creatures, I know not what would become of me."

"This Mrs. Ashton, then, to whom you say you are so much indebted, is a married lady?" interrogated our hero, who was much interested by the observations she had made use of respecting her, and whose curiosity was likewise excited.

"She is, sir," answered the cottager; "but although she has, I believe, one of the best husbands in the world, and who I am certain doats upon the very ground she walks upon, I am afraid she is far from happy."

"Indeed?" said our hero, "and can you at all account for that?"

"Why you see," answered the old woman, "Mrs. Ashton is young and very beautiful, and her husband is old and deformed, and, though I say it, that shouldn't say it, I do not believe that their marriage could have been one of affection, on her side, at any rate. It is my opinion that she has something heavy on her mind, and that she has been crossed, or disappointed in love."

"Poor lady," said our heroine, "and has she and her husband long resided at the villa you have mentioned?"

"Yes," answered the cottager, "some years, and much good have they done since they have been there. Any person who is in distress they are always ready to relieve, and, in fact, they delight in acts of Christian charity."

"The character you give of this lady interests me," said Richard; "she must be a most excellent woman, and it is a pity any sorrow should afflict her mind."

"True," coincided the old woman, "but I am afraid it is of that description that time and circumstances will not readily remove. But, pardon me, you say you are distressed, and indeed your appearance sufficiently proves the truth of your words; have you been long in Cornwall?"

"Not many days," answered our hero, "and it was accident alone that brought us hither where we are complete strangers, and have not a friend or acquaintance to whom we can apply for assistance. Oh, my good woman, myself and my devoted partner have indeed drunk deep of the cup of sorrow, and it is wonderful how we have been able to support the many trials and vicissitudes to which we have been subjected, so well as we have done. Time was, when sorrow was unknown to us, and happiness and prosperity showered their blessings upon us; but fearful calamities, which I may not mention, suddenly came upon us, and we were compelled to leave our native place, and to wander destitute, we knew not whither. Providence raised us up a friend, and our prospects brightened. We were on our way to one of the Channel islands, where we hoped to obtain some permanent relief; but the little vessel in which we sailed with our friend was wrecked off this coast, and every soul on board, with the exception of ourselves, perished, thus blighting all our hopes, and leaving us destitute."

The old woman was affected almost to tears, and it was some moments ere she could make any observation, but at length she said, and her looks and the tone in which she spoke sufficiently proved the sincerity of her feelings on the occasion—

"It is a melancholy tale, and I feel convinced of the truth of it. Poor things,

THE REMORSE OF MARY'S FATHER ON THINKING OF HER SUFFERINGS.

you are, indeed, much to be pitied; and I only regret, and that most deeply, that it is not in my power to relieve you, for your manners and appearance assure me that you have been placed in far different circumstances to what you are at present."

"Oh, that is most true," returned our hero, "and most deeply, most sincerely am I indebted to you for the sympathy you express towards us."

"Unfortunately," observed the cottager, "sympathy is all I have to bestow, but thank God that I have the heart to feel for the misfortunes of my fellow creatures. But where are you now going? and what course do you intend to adopt?"

"Alas! we know not," answered our hero; "for, as I said before, we are left completely destitute; but we have still a friend left, who resides some distance from this place, and could we only reach him, or find some temporary relief till we could communicate with him, and make him acquainted with our present melancholy and wretched situation, I am certain that he would promptly and willingly render us all the assistance in his power."

"I wish it were in my power to accommodate you," said the kind-hearted cottager, "but you see my limited means, and, therefore, you will be at once aware how incompetent I am to act according to my wishes."

"Oh, yes," replied Mary, gratefully pressing her hand; "I am fully convinced of the goodness and generosity of your heart, and we can never forget the kindness you have shown towards us. But were it even in your power to assist us, we have no right to expect it from you, who are a complete stranger to us."

"It is the duty of every one," replied the old woman, "to assist their fellow creatures in distress, as far as their means will allow them to do; for we none of us know what we may come to; but now I think of it, the benevolent Mrs. Ashton would, if she was aware of your situation, although you are unknown to her, willingly afford you some relief, and probably shelter you in her house until you could communicate with your friend, and make some arrangement for the future."

"Oh," returned Richard, "how could we expect that the lady, however benevolent she may be, could interest herself in the behalf of such humble individuals as ourselves, and who are perfect strangers to her?"

"But," remarked the old woman, "I know her character too well to believe for a moment that she would refuse you, or treat you with indifference. Had it no been for this storm, she would most likely have called upon me to-day, and then I could have introduced you to her; but you are welcome to remain in my cottage for a few hours until you have somewhat recovered yourselves, and I tell you what it is, if you have no objection, when the storm has subsided, I will accompany you to Ashton Villa, and make your melancholy case known to her."

"Kind-hearted woman," ejaculated our hero, with much emotion; "what can I say in acknowledgment for such disinterested friendship as this? But——"

"No more," interrupted the cottager, "I know well the objections you would raise, but there is no necessity for them, for I am certain that Mrs. Ashton would be much hurt if she was prevented from performing an act of charity which is so much in accordance with her own heart. Will you agree to my proposal?"

Richard hesitated for a minute or two, for he was completely overwhelmed and bewildered by such unexpected generosity on the part of a stranger, but at length he observed—

"What words can I find sufficient, my good woman, to convey to you a sense of the feelings which your kindness has created in my breast? I—I will agree to your proposal, especially after the character you have given to me of this lady, and may Heaven reward you for your humanity towards we poor unfortunate wanderers."

"Say no more about it, I beg of you," returned the old woman, "for I require no thanks; I shall be only too happy if I can succeed in obtaining for you that relief of which I am convinced you are so well deserving, and I know that I shall not be disappointed in my wishes. A more amiable woman than Mrs. Ashton does not exist, as I said before, and she will feel herself most happy to be afforded the opportunity of being able to render assistance to any of her fellow creatures, placed in the unfortunate situation in which you are. Endeavour to make yourselves contented, therefore, and when the storm has subsided, which I trust it will shortly do, we will, if you please, depart to Ashton Villa, and make known to the lady the facts of your case."

Our hero pressed the old woman's hand in silence, for he was so completely taken by surprise that he knew not what to say, and something like a feeling of hope sprang up in his breast. The cottager evidently read his feelings, for, after a brief pause, she said,—

"I know quite well what you would say, but there is no necessity for any further remarks upon the subject, as I think that you must be convinced that what I do, is dictated alone by the proper feelings of my heart, and that the satisfaction I feel in performing my duty is a sufficient reward for me. But I will leave you and your wife to yourselves for a short time, for you may have something to communicate to each other which it may not be prudent for me to hear."

Our hero and his wife again returned their most fervent thanks, and the old woman then retired from the room, and left them to their own reflections.

"Oh, Richard," ejaculated Mary, when she was gone, "what an excellent, what a kind-hearted woman is this. How grateful ought we to feel to the Almighty for the manner in which he has befriended us in the midst of all our difficulties. From the character which she has given of this benevolent lady, and which I have no doubt is a correct one, I cannot help encouraging the hope that something will occur to relieve us, which we can now but little anticipate."

" God grant that your expectations may not be doomed to be disappointed, my dear Mary," replied her husband fervently; " and yet my heart feels a repugnance in thus appealing to the benevolence and charity of one who is an entire stranger to us."

"It is stern necessity that compels us to do so," remarked our heroine, " and we must submit to it, for our case is desperate, and without some speedy relief what is to become of us ? For my own part, I feel the most anxious curiosity to be introduced to this lady, and I know not how it is, but an impression has fixed itself on my mind that we shall meet with some surprise of an agreeable nature."

" It is strange," observed Richard; "that such a singular idea should occur to you is unaccountable."

"I admit that it is so," answered his wife, "but still I cannot dismiss it. To this good woman, however, who has so kindly received us, and who so sincerely sympathises with us in our misfortunes, we are much indebted, and I hope that the time will yet come when we shall have it in our power to make some grateful return to her, and all those who have so generously assisted us in the midst of our adversity."

" Alas, I fear," said Richard; "that will never be. What prospect is there that we shall ever be released from the numerous and terrible difficulties by which we are at present surrounded?"

"Say not so," returned Mary, "but let us rather hope for the best. I feel my fortitude and confidence revive, and something tells me that in spite of the heavy clouds that have so long obscured our prospects, a happy change in our circumstances is in store for us."

"Could I ever hope to receive mercy from the laws of my country," remarked Richard, "I might encourage the same feelings, but at present I cannot. A terrible fate is hanging o'er my head, and which, I fear, must sooner or later overtake me."

" Oh, Richard," returned our heroine, " how it agonises my mind to hear you talk thus. But kind Heaven will, I feel certain, avert the calamity which you apprehend, and not suffer you to fall into the hands of those from whom you can expect no mercy."

Richard shook his head, and was about to make some reply, when the old woman re-entered the room and prevented him.

"I hope I do not disturb you," she said, " but having completed the business I had to perform, I could not help returning to you. You seem revived, and I am glad to see it."

"Oh, yes," replied Mary, "thanks to your kindness, I am much better now, and trust that I shall soon be enabled to resume our dreary journey."

"Not till you have seen Mrs. Ashton," returned the cottager, "and I feel confident that some good will result from the interview. The misfortunes of yourself and your husband cannot fail to excite the sympathy of that excellent woman."

"But her husband?" said Richard, doubtfully.

"Oh," answered the cottager, "he is as kind and charitable as herself, and cannot disapprove of anything she does ; but he is at present from home, and as I understand, is not likely to return for some days. The storm rages with less violence than it did, and I trust it will soon subside altogether, and then, if you please, we will depart to the villa, which, as I before told you, is only about a mile from here."

Richard was about to make some reply, when he was prevented from doing so by hearing a knock at the door, and the old woman started to her feet.

"It is my son, I dare say," she remarked; "I wonder he did not return before, for it is impossible that he could work in such a storm. Do not disturb yourselves, for he will not be cross to find you here."

As she spoke these words, the old woman went to the door, which she opened, and a young man of decent appearance entered the cottage, but started and looked rather confused on beholding strangers.

"These poor people have merely sought a shelter from the storm, Philip," said the old woman, " and, of course, it is not likely that I could refuse them."

"You are right, mother," replied the young man, "and it would not have been like you if you had. It has, indeed, been a violent storm, and I was compelled to leave off work more than an hour ago, but was forced to stand up on the road home for shelter, and that has delayed me so long. You are welcome here, my friends, as my mother, no doubt, has told you, and I only wish it was in our power to accommodate you better."

Our hero returned his thanks, and Philip took a seat.

"You appear to have suffered much," he said, again addressing himself to our hero and his wife.

"We have, indeed," returned Richard;

"we are poor friendless wanderers, who suffered shipwreck on this coast a few days ago, and we are now left entirely destitute, and know not where to go."

"It is a bad job," said Philip, compassionately; "and myself and my mother are so poor that we have not the power to render you much assistance, which we would willingly do if we could. But have you not had any refreshment?"

"Oh, yes," answered Richard; "your mother has behaved to us with a kindness which we had no right to expect from a stranger, and one placed in her humble circumstances. We regret that we have not the means of making some return for what we have received from her."

"Do not mention that," said Philip, "for you are heartily welcome, and so is every one who requires it, to all that it is in our humble power to do for them. You are strangers, then, in this part of the country?"

"We are," replied our hero, "and know not whither to go, for we are entirely destitute."

"Ah!" ejaculated Philip, "I am sorry to hear that; and I only wish that I had the means to do something for you."

"I have proposed to introduce these poor people to Mrs. Ashton," said the old woman, "and I have not the least doubt that she will do something to relieve them, for you know the benevolence of her disposition, Philip."

"Know her benevolence!" he replied; "oh, yes, for who has experienced it more than we have done, mother? She is a most excellent and amiable woman, and the poor are greatly indebted to her and her husband."

"You say right, Philip," returned his mother, "and Heaven will surely reward her for her many acts of Christian charity."

"True," observed Philip; "and are these good people agreeable to accompany you to Ashton Villa?"

"They are," answered the old woman, "and I do not entertain the least doubt as to the result of the interview, when Mrs. Ashton is made acquainted with their present melancholy circumstances."

"No," remarked her son, "Mrs. Ashton never yet turned a deaf ear to those who have had occasion to apply to her for aid."

"I have no doubt of the excellence of her character, after what yourself and your mother have said," returned our hero; "but still I must say that I feel tenacious in appealing to the benevolence of a stranger."

"You have no occasion to feel any delicacy upon the subject," said Philip, "for Mrs. Ashton is a lady who does everything with a free heart, and will have the strictest regard for your feelings. I most earnestly wish you success, and hope that before long a favourable change will take place in your circumstances, which appear to be bad enough at present."

"This from a stranger is most kind," observed Richard, "and I thank you sincerely for it. We have indeed suffered most terrible misfortunes, and Heaven only knows how we have had fortitude to support them in the manner we have done."

Philip and his mother returned no answer to this, and they then retired from the room for a short time, and again left Richard and his wife to their own reflections.

"The kindness of these poor people is quite overpowering," remarked our hero, "and we can never cease to remember it with feelings of gratitude; but still, notwithstanding all they have said respecting this Mrs. Ashton, I cannot help feeling some hesitation in applying to a stranger for relief."

"And why should you entertain any such scruples, Richard," said his wife, "situated as we are?"

"She will naturally put such questions to us as we may find it difficult to answer," returned our hero, "and should she by any means discover who we really are, would she not be sure to be prejudiced against us?"

"Oh, no," answered Mary, "not if she is the humane individual she has been described to us. Besides, you have only to use your usual prudence and precaution, and she will be unable to elicit more than we want her to know. I feel most anxious to see her, and have the greatest confidence as to the result of the interview."

"Well, Mary," he said, "I sincerely hope that everything may turn out just as you anticipate. Could we only find some place where we could remain until we had an opportunity of communicating with our friend Adams, and receiving his answer, I should be content, for I have no doubt that he would then suggest something which might tend to our future security."

"And who knows but that we may find a friend in this amiable lady?" said our heroine.

"Not to the extent which you seem to expect, I fear," replied Richard; "for it is impossible that we can make her acquainted with all our circumstances, and it is not to be supposed that she will take so deep an interest in the welfare of those who are unknown to her. For my own part I must confess that I am not altogether sanguine as to the result of this visit."

"If Mrs. Ashton is indeed the amiable being that she has been described to us, we have everything to hope," said Mary.

Philip and his mother now returned to the room, so the conversation was, of course, brought to an end.

"The storm has now subsided," said the latter, "so are you ready to accompany me, my friends?"

Richard replied in the affirmative, and again returned his thanks to the cottager for the kindness and attention she had shown to them; but she hastily stopped his acknowledgments, and prepared herself to depart from the cottage, again expressing her regret at not being able to accommodate them, or to do more for them than she had already done. Having shaken hands with Philip, who wished them every success, they followed his mother from the cottage, and they proceeded along the road she said led to the residence of Mr. and Mrs. Ashton, conversing all the way in a most friendly manner, and as if they had been on the most intimate terms for years. In a very short time they came in sight of the villa, which was a handsome building, and which even in its exterior showed the refined taste of its inhabitants.

"You had better remain here for a few minutes," said the cottager, "while I will go alone to the villa, and make Mrs. Ashton acquainted with the cause of my visit. I do not fear what the result will be, and she will be pleased, I know, to think that I did not suffer any persons in your unfortunate situation to go away without making her acquainted with it. I will soon return, and then I will introduce you to the lady."

Richard and his wife thanked her, and she then hastened to the house, and ringing a bell at the door was immediately admitted. Our unfortunate travellers awaited her return with much anxiety, and Mary became more sanguine in her expectations every moment; and she could not divest her mind of an impression that had got hold of it that something of a particular and favourable nature was about to happen to them, though why she should entertain such an idea she could not understand. Richard still felt doubtful and irresolute, for he could not but consider it degrad-

ing and humiliating to appear in the character of a beggar before one whom he had never seen before. They were not, however, long kept in suspense, for they saw the door of the villa opened, and the old woman appearing at it, beckoned them forward. They advanced to the house accordingly, and the cottager said—

"I have seen the good lady, and told her all about you. She was very much moved by your distress, and wishes to see you immediately, so, if you will follow me, I will introduce you to her directly, and you will then find that I have not misrepresented her in the character I have given you of her."

Richard thanked her, and they then followed her into the house, and ascending a flight of stairs they stopped at a door, and here the heart of our heroine palpitated, and she felt otherwise agitated in a manner for which she was not able to account. They had not many minutes for reflection, however, for the old woman knocked at the door, and a gentle, but melancholy voice, immediately desired her to enter. Mary Parker started, and pressing her hand upon the arm of her husband, said—

"Ah, Richard, that voice, surely it should be familiar to us?"

The old woman heard not what she said, and before Richard could make any reply, she had opened the door, and they were ushered into an elegant apartment, in which the graceful form of a lady was seated, but who arose immediately on their entrance, evidently moved to compassion by the extreme wretchedness of the unfortunate fugitives appearance, and advanced towards them, observing—

"My unfortunate friends, I deeply regret to see the deplorable condition to which you are reduced, and shall feel most happy in affording you all the assistance that is in my power. Mrs. Robinson has told me all the particulars of the manner in which you were introduced to her cottage."

At the tones of Mrs. Ashton's voice, our hero and his wife suddenly raised their eyes towards her, but they all started, and uttered a simultaneous exclamation of astonishment on beholding each other.

It was that amiable being whom they had lost sight of for so many years—she who was once Amy Parker, the cousin of the unfortunate hero of our tale.

CHAPTER XXXVI.

THE AFFECTIONATE MEETING.—THE EX-
PLANATION.—AMY'S SORROWS.—BLIGH-
TED HOPES.—HER NARRATIVE.

OVERCOME by the power of her emotions and surprise, Amy sank back in the
chair on which she had been seated on
their entrance, and was unable to speak a
word. Richard and our heroine gazed at
her with feelings of astonishment and agitation which we need not seek to describe,
and could scarcely believe the evidence of
their senses. But they, too, were completely astounded by such an unexpected
and providential meeting, after so many
years absence, with one whom they had
every reason to view with feelings of the
most profound regard, that they were
unable to give utterance to a word, but
continued still to gaze upon her with emotions of the most unmitigated astonishment.

But what a melancholy change had
time wrought in the appearance of Amy.
Although she was still the same gentle
and amiable-looking being that she had
ever been, her pale features, and the
melancholy expression of her countenance
altogether, showed but too plainly that
she had drunk deep of the cup of sorrow
since last they had met her. Premature
age seemed to have stolen upon her, and it
was evident that the cankerworm of care
and no common sorrows had corroded her
heart, and had left those feelings of anguish
behind which time might ameliorate, but
could not entirely remove. At length
Amy somewhat recovered herself from the
surprise which this unexpected meeting
with her unfortunate relatives had occasioned her, and rising from her seat, and
addressing herself to Mrs. Robinson, she
said—

"I must request you to retire, my good
woman, for a short time; these unfortunate persons are not altogether unknown
to me, and I am obliged to you for the
kindness with which you have behaved to
them, and for having introduced them to
me. I would have a few words with them
in private."

Mrs. Robinson, who seemed not a little
surprised and confounded by what had
taken place, curtsied, and immediately
withdrew; and no sooner had she done so
than Amy rushed to the arms of Richard
and his wife, burst into a passionate flood
of tears, and was so overpowered by the
violence of her emotions, that she could
not give utterance to a word.

"Amy, dear Amy," exclaimed our hero
at length, "oh, what an extraordinary

meeting is this, after the lapse of so many
years. How can we properly express the
agitation of our feelings, placed in the
melancholy and deplorable situation in
which we are?"

"Alas! my unfortunate relations," sighed
Amy; "how deeply it agonises my heart
to see you in your wretched condition, to
think of the dreadful sufferings it has
been your hard lot to experience, and to
know the bad opinion you must have
formed of me, from my long silence, and
apparent want of communication with
you, in the terrible sorrows and afflictions
with which it has pleased the Almighty to
visit you. But when you know all, and
the painful trials which it has also been
my lot to experience, I am certain that
you will make some allowances for me,
and that you will not consider me so much
to blame."

"Ah, no, dear Amy," said Mrs. Parker,
"we know your gentle and affectionate
heart too well, to suppose that any want
of sympathy in our misfortunes, or a
wish to disown your connexion with us,
has been the case of your long silence.
Thank Heaven that we have now met,
though it is under circumstances which we
must all most painfully regret."

"Alas!" returned Amy, "I scarcely
know what to say, I am so completely
overpowered by my feelings at this unexpected event. Heaven knows how deeply
I have felt for the dreadful misfortunes
that have overtaken you, and how much I
wished to relieve you all that was in my
power so to do; but circumstances which I
cannot this moment explain, and which
made me feel ashamed of myself, prevented
me, and I knew not wh re or how to communicate with you after your flight."

"But, oh, Amy," said Richard, "must
you not be prejudiced against me, after
what you have doubtless heard? Must
you not blame me, condemn me, and look
upon me with feelings of disgust?"

"Oh, Heaven forbid!" replied Mrs.
Ashton, fervently, "how much you wrong
me, Richard, by such a supposition. For
well do I know the wrongs that have been
heaped upon you; and how sincerely does
it grieve me when I think of the terrible
sufferings you must have undergone.
Thank God, that you have hitherto been
enabled to escape, and I trust that, now we
have so fortunately met, some certain
means may be adopted for your future
security."

"But what a melancholy change h s
come over you, Amy," remarked our hero,
"since we last beheld each other. Your
pale and careworn countenance too plainly

convinces me that your misfortunes have been great."

"Ah!" sighed Mrs. Ashton; "they have indeed ; and time may soften but can never banish from my mind the remembrance of them, or the bitter feelings of regret and self-reproach which they have left behind."

"Say not so, my dear cousin," returned Richard, looking in her face with an expression of the deepest, and most fervent compassion. "But you have a husband, Amy?"

"Yes," she replied, in a faint voice, and with downcast eyes; "I am indeed united to one who is old enough to be my father, and whom, though I must ever esteem him for the kindness and urbanity of his disposition, it is impossible that I can ever love. Ah! no!" she added with a deep sigh, while her lips quivered, and crimson blushes mantled in her cheeks; "he who possessed my love, was treacherous, cruel, and—but let me endeavour to think not of him now, for it is sinful for me to do so, and he is unworthy to be remembered with any other feelings than those of disgust and detestation. Oh, how grateful ought I to feel towards my husband for the affection and unremitting attention he has ever bestowed upon me, although he knew all. If it had not been for him what would have become of me? I must at this time have been a wretched and despised wandering outcast upon the face of the earth, unless I had been urged by despair to have rushed unbidden into the presence of my maker."

Richard and his wife were deeply affected by what she had said, and by which they could partly read her melancholy history.

"But," observed the former, after a pause; "will not your husband ref se o pity us prejudiced as he must be against us from what he has heard?"

"Oh, no," replied Amy, "you can judge but little of his real character, if you entertain that imagination. He has been informed of all the particulars of your history from me, and he has ever expressed the deepest commiseration in your misfortunes, and the wrongs that have been inflicted upon you, and his utmost abhorrence of the character of the late Captain Arlington. He is now away from home, and I do not expect him to return for a few days, but when he does, you may expect every kindness and welcome from him, and I know that he will feel a pleasure in doing all he can to serve you in the difficulties by which you are at present surrounded. But you need refreshment, therefore I will leave you for a few minutes to procure them, and to dismiss Mrs.

Robinson, who, I suppose, has no idea who you really are?"

"Oh, no," replied Richard ; "though I think, from the little we have seen of her, and from the kindness of her disposition, that even if she were, she would not betray us."

"She is a most excellent woman," said Amy, "and I am sure she would not; but still it would. perhaps, be as well to keep her in ignorance of the facts. I will return shortly, and in the meantime you and Ma y will probably somewhat have recovered yourselves from the surprise and agitation into which this unexpected event has thrown you."

With these words Mrs. Ashton quitted the room, and for some moments after she was gone, Richard and his wife were so overpowered by the various feelings that rushed tumultuously through their breasts, that they could not give utterance to a syllable, but stood gazing at each other with looks of stupified amazement. They at length rushed to each other's arms, and Mary, as her eyes filled with tears, and sobs of the most powerful emotion almost choked her utterance, ejaculated,—

"Oh, Richard, what an unexpected, what a fortunate meeting is this! We are not yet abandoned by the Almighty, and here, under the protection of Amy and her husband, we may remain safe from danger until we have made some permanent arrangement for the future, which, no doubt, with their advice and assistance, we shall speedily be able to do."

"Yes," answered our hero; "how fortunate it was that chance guided our footsteps to the cottage of Mrs. Robinson, to whose kindness and humanity we are indebted for all that has happened."

"Most true," coincided Mary; "and you see, my dear Richard, that the singular presentiments I entertained that some unexpected surprise was in store for us have been most wonderfully realised."

"They have," returned her husband; "but how it grieves me to see the melancholy change which Time has wrought in the appearance of poor Amy; it is but too plain that, like ourselves, she has been subjected to the most painful misfortunes."

"May Heaven give her strength to banish them from her memory," said our heroine, "and to look forward to the future with hope and cheerfulness."

Richard was prevented from making any observations in reply to his wife, by the entrance of a female servant, with such a repast as it had not been their good fortune to partake of for many months past, which she placed before them, and eyeing them rather with an expression of sympathy than impertinent curiosity, she retired from the room, and was almost immediately followed by Amy, who seemed to have greatly composed her feelings during her temporary absence.

"Come, my dear cousins," she said, "partake freely of the provisions before you, of which I am satisfied you must stand so much in need, and do not stand upon ceremony. Oh, how thankful I am to Providence that we have met again, and that I have the means to assist you in the terrible difficulties and dangers by which you are now surrounded. But we have much to communicate to each other, and I am most anxious to be made acquainted with all that has happened to you since we last met. When I have fortitude sufficient, I will also relate to you my melancholy history, and although you may and must condemn me for many things, still I am certain you will almost pity me for my misfortunes, and when you shall hear all, you will no longer marvel at the care which you see settled upon my brow, and the deep feelings of anguish and regret which ever occupy my breast."

"I am certain, my dear Amy," replied our hero, "that there is no part of your conduct which we can justly condemn, and who is there that can more deeply sympathise with you in your misfortunes than myself and Mary? But I hope that happier days are in store for us all."

"God grant that there may," replied Amy, fervently, "but for myself I have very little hope. Nothing whatever can banish from my memory the dismal and torturing past. It has cast a shadow on my path which has clouded all my future prospects, and which, the longer I reflect on it, the more am I convinced that nothing can remove."

"Say not so, Amy," remarked our heroine; "give not way to those feelings of despair, but endeavour to review everything on the sunniest side, and I feel no doubt that you will yet be restored to tranquillity, if not to complete happiness."

Amy shook her head doubtfully, and after a pause, during which brief interval she seemed to be struggling with some painful feelings, she said,—

"Alas! I have tried hard, as Heaven knows, but have never been able to encourage any such hopes. But why should I trouble you with my sorrows, when you have so many of your own upon your minds? Partake of the refreshments before you, and probably by that time we shall all of us have been enabled sufficiently to recover ourselves as to converse more freely."

Richard and his wife returned no answer, and Amy taking her seat in another part of the room, suffered them to partake of the ample and delicate repast with which she had supplied them, without interruption. Their minds relieved of a great part of the insupportable weight of care which had previously pressed upon them, and hope once more re-animating their breasts, they partook freely of the provisions that were spread before them, and it was, indeed, many months since they had so much enjoyed a meal. It seemed to impart new life and spirits to them, and when they had concluded, they returned their thanks to the Almighty most fervently and sincerely.

The female servant having removed the cloth, and Richard and his wife having partaken of a glass of wine, Amy drew her chair closer to them and said—

"It gratifies me to see you already looking so much better, and I trust that, with the care and attention which myself and my husband will bestow upon you, you will ere long be enabled to regain something like your former tranquillity, and to avoid that fate with which you have so long been threatened. But I am most anxious to be made acquainted with all that has happened to you since we last met, and the circumstances which have so fortunately led you hither, and, therefore, if the recital will not pain you too much, I should feel obliged to you for it."

"Alas!" replied Richard, "it is a sad history, and I am afraid it will only wound your gentle and susceptible heart to hear it, Amy; but as it must afford me some relief to confide my sorrows to a sympathising breast, I will comply with your request, and then I am certain that you will wonder we have had the fortitude to support that which it has been our lot to undergo."

Richard paused for a minute or two to recollect himself, and to prepare himself for the painful task which had devolved upon him, and he then commenced relating to Amy those dismal particulars with which the reader is already acquainted. Amy listened to him with the most profound attention, but she was frequently compelled to interrupt him to give expression to the heartfelt sympathy which the many hardships the unfortunate fugitives had had to encounter excited in her breast; and to express her wonder that they had ever had the fortitude to support them, and to struggle against them in the man-

PARKER INVOKES THE PROTECTION OF HEAVEN FOR HIS HELPLESS WIFE.

ner they had. When he had concluded, she said—

"Alas! my dear cousin, now terrible and unmerited have been the misfortunes that have fallen to your lot, and how miraculous have been the numerous narrow escapes you have had. It is evident, notwithstanding the numerous and heavy trials you have had, and the manner in which Fate seemed to frown upon your hopes, and to trample all your prospects under foot, that the Almighty has ever watched over your safety, and I feel con-

fident that He will yet extricate you from all your difficulties."

"Heaven grant that your hopes may be realised, my dear Amy," returned our heroine; "now that we have so providentially encountered you, I feel much more sanguine as to the future. But think you my unfortunate husband has been much to blame for the conduct he has pursued? or that he is deserving of the fate to which his enemies would most undoubtedly consign him, if he should ever unfortunately fall into their power?"

"Oh, no," answered Amy, "terrible are the wrongs that have been inflicted upon him, and which principally originated in the villany of the late Captain Arlington, and he fully deserved the fate which he met with, and which he brought upon himself. It would, perhaps, have been better had he fallen by any other hands than those of Richard, although it was a just retribution of offended Heaven."

"Very true," coincided our hero, "and I deeply regret that he should have fallen by my hands; though I cannot consider that I was so much to blame after all, for I only acted in self-defence."

"Certainly," agreed Amy, "and I would not suffer the remembrance of it to torture my mind, but try to look forward to that which is to come with the most sanguine expectations."

"I would fain do so, Amy," replied Richard; "but when you take all the circumstances into consideration, you will not marvel that I find it a most difficult task to accomplish."

"Very true," returned his cousin, "yours is a most peculiar and cruel destiny, and it requires the strongest energy to bear up against it. However, you cannot but feel grateful to that Omnipotent power which has enabled you to avoid the ignominious and untimely fate to which you were doomed. Your prospects brighten, and I trust that the time is not far distant when you will be completely released from those dangers that have been so long impending o'er you."

"Dear Amy," observed our heroine, "how cheering and consolatory are the hopes which you thus so warmly, and sincerely, I am confident, express towards us. Now that you are restored to us, we have indeed every reason to look forward to the future with the most sanguine expectations. But my misguided father; oh, surely nothing whatever could justify the conduct he has pursued so remorselessly towards myself and my unfortunate husband!"

"No," answered Amy, "he has been most severe, unjust, and unnatural; but he has, no doubt, been greatly biassed and influenced by the artifices of Amelia Arlington, who, from all that I have heard, is envious, proud, crafty, and in every respect, so far as disposition is concerned, exactly resembles her uncle."

"True," remarked Richard, "such I believe to be her real character; and there can be no doubt but that she has, from interested motives, obtained the greatest power over Mr. Mason, and succeeded in prejudicing him still more strongly against us; otherwise he could never have found the heart to discard his own child from his breast, and to supply her place with one who is not at all allied to him."

"But she may yet defeat her own plans, and Mr. Mason may, notwithstanding his present obduracy, still be brought to a full and proper sense of the cruelty and injustice of his conduct, and be stung with feelings of remorse."

"Alas!" sighed Mary, "after what took place at our last interview, I fear there is but little chance of that. But where you aware that he resided in this part of the country?"

"I was not," replied Amy; "or I should certainly have ventured to see him with my husband, and to have interceded with him for yourself and Richard."

"Your efforts would, I am sure, have been unsuccessful, and would probably only have subjected you to insult, you being a relation of mine, and so deeply connected with the clandestine marriage of myself and Mary," said Richard; "I am thoroughly satisfied, from all that I have seen of him, that he is completely invulnerable to argument or persuasion. If he could resist the pathetic appeal of my unfortunate wife at our last interview, it is quite evident that he must be perfectly insensible to every proper and natural feeling."

"Too true," coincided Amy, "but let us drop that painful subject for the present, which, by dwelling upon it, can only serve to add to the anguish of your feelings. How much you are indebted to this Mr. Adams for the generous kindness which he has shown you in the midst of all your troubles; and the numerous friends whom you have met with in the course of your melancholy wanderings."

"Ah, yes," returned Richard; "and to no one more than poor old Binnacle, who met with such an untimely fate in his endeavour to serve us."

"Ay," replied Amy, "it was a great misfortune, and I sincerely regret that one so worthy should come to so untimely an end; but he will be rewarded for the humanity and disinterested kindness which he showed towards his fellow creatures. But you say that Mr. Adams is unacquainted with these sad particulars, or what has become of you?"

"Certainly," returned Richard; "for I have hitherto had no opportunity of communicating with him; but now that Providence has been so kind as to direct us hither, I will take the earliest opportunity of doing so. But still, Amy, are you certain that your husband will not be angry with you on his return for having received us?"

"Angry?" repeated Amy; "oh, no, for he possesses a generous and humane heart, and he too deeply sympathises in your misfortunes, and deprecates the wrongs which he feels satisfied has been inflicted on you, to blame me for what I have done; on the contrary, I know that he will be happy to think that chance has so fortunately led your footsteps to the Villa, and will gladly render you all the assistance in his power. So make your minds perfectly easy on that point."

"We will do so," said Richard; "but will not the curiosity of Mrs. Robinson be excited at our remaining here, and being on such intimate terms with persons whom she has a right to suppose are quite unknown to you?"

"No," answered Amy, "Mrs. Robinson is a kind-hearted woman, and will express no curiosity upon the subject; besides, it will be easy to satisfy her with some plausible tale, accounting for your remaing here, and to enjoin her to secrecy, should any inquiries happen to be made after you, which it is not likely there will be. Here you will, for the present, at any rate, be perfectly safe, and when my husband returns, we will lose no time in adopting some plans for your future security. Take courage, my dear relations, for depend upon it your troubles are nearly at an end."

"Oh, how kind and considerate are those observations," ejaculated Mary, raising Mrs. Ashton's hand to her lips; "and what fond hopes do they impart to my breast. Take courage, my dear Richard, the Almighty God has not yet abandoned us, and the fate which we have so long dreaded will be yet avoided."

"Yes," returned her husband, "I should be unreasonable, and unmindful of the kindness of Amy, were I not to endeavour to do so. Oh, what a sudden and happy change is this in our circumstances."

"And it is, I trust," remarked Amy, "only the precursor of that which is to follow. Terrible, indeed, have been your misfortunes, and you deserve an ample reward for the patience and fortitude with which you have borne them. Ah, my dear friends, and what have not been the vicissitudes, the cares, and disappointments that it has been my lot to encounter since last we met? It makes me shudder to think of them, and Heaven only knows how I have been able to bear up against them with the fortitude and resignation that I have done."

"How greatly does it grieve me, dear Amy," said our hero, "to hear that you also have been a sufferer. What can be the nature of the misfortunes that have cast such a deep gloom upon your mind?"

"Alas," answered Mrs. Ashton, with a sigh, "they have been of the most overwhelming description; and in their terrible course have completely annihilated all my hopes, and have rendered me one of the most wretched of human beings."

"Nay, say not so," expostulated Mary; "you say that your husband behaves to you with affection?"

"Oh, yes," replied Amy, "he treats me with far more affectionate kindness and consideration than I fear I deserve. But my heart is not his, he who possessed it took advantage of my innocent confidence, and left me to misery and despair."

"And may the curses of Heaven light upon him for it!" exclaimed Richard, vehemently.

"Oh, hold!" hastily ejaculated Amy; "say not so; I would not that any misfortunes should befal him, great even as are the injustice, the cruelty, and the misery he has inflicted on me. Oh, Charles! Charles! after all the solemn vows that you pledged to me, how little could I ever imagine that you would have deceived me in the manner you have done. May Heaven forgive you, for, oh! how much do you stand in need of it."

She covered her face with her hands as she thus spoke, and convulsive sobs and tears choked her further utterance.

Our hero and his wife were greatly affected, and they watched her with silent compassion for a few minutes, and did not offer to interrupt the ebullition of her grief, although their curiosity was much excited by what she had said.

"And does he of whom you complain still live?" interrogated Richard, at last.

"I know not," answered Amy, tremblingly looking up through her tears; "but if he is, I fervently pray that we may never meet again, for Heaven only knows what would then be the consequences."

"Unburthen the whole of your sorrows to us, dear Amy," said our heroine, "for that might afford you some relief, and you may depend upon our sympathy and consolation."

"Oh, no," she answered, "not at present I cannot; I feel myself totally inadequate to the task; but at some future time I will reveal everything to you, and then I am satisfied that you will pity me, if even you cannot help blaming me."

"Blame you, cousin?" said Richard; "oh, no, I am certain that you cannot deserve that, so well do I know the virtue and strict integrity of your character. You reproach yourself without a cause."

"Alas," returned Amy, "I fear that you will alter your opinion when you have heard all. But my feelings at present overpower me, and I must retire for a short time, and endeavour to recover myself. I will return before long, and then I trust that I shall be in better spirits to meet you."

Richard and his wife pressed her hand in silence, and she then quitted the room.

"Poor Amy," said Richard, compassionately, when she was gone, "I fear that she has suffered some wrong of the most lamentable description."

"Alas," returned his wife, "it is but too evident that she has done so, and most sincerely do I pity her; and am anxious to be made acquainted with her melancholy history."

"Her misfortunes, whatever they are," remarked Richard, "seem to have made an impression upon her mind, which it will be difficult to eradicate. It is evident that the man upon whom she had placed her affections, basely and cruelly deceived her, and annihilated all her hopes; and I am only fearful that something of a more serious nature has happened to her."

"Oh, Heaven forbid," said Mary; "he must be a black-hearted scoundrel indeed who could be guilty of such a crime as that which you insinuate."

"And yet experience convinces us that there are too many such villains in the world," observed her husband; "is not the melancholy case of Alfred Mowbray and poor Flora Hawthorn a deplorable instance of it?"

"It is too true," replied Mary; "and from what we have been enabled to gather from the observations of Amy, hers is a similar case. God grant that she may not indeed have met with the same fate. But I cannot believe that she has done so; one so strictly virtuous could never so have fallen."

"Alas! what will not the artifices of man accomplish, when they are badly disposed?" said our hero.

"But we must not prejudge her case," observed Mrs. Parker; "but wait patiently till we have had the disclosure of the whole particulars from her own lips. I fear, that notwithstanding all that she has said respecting the character of her husband, this marriage is anything but a happy one."

"Where there is such a difference in the ages of the parties coming together," replied Richard, "it is impossible that it should be so; especially after the manner in which the fondest hopes of poor Amy have been blighted. But still it is a consolation to hear that Mr. Ashton behaves with so much affection and attention towards her, and that she can esteem him, if she cannot love him."

"Most true," agreed his wife; "but oh, how thankful am I to think that we have met with her, and at the very moment, too, when despair seemed to close upon us on every side. We are now in a place of security, and need entertain no apprehensions that we shall be unable to procure that assistance which we so much require to forward us in our future plans."

"It will be as well not to be too sanguine upon that subject," remarked Richard, "lest we should be disappointed. I cannot help feeling anxious and uneasy to know what kind of a reception Mr. Ashton will give us on his return."

"Oh, we cannot entertain any doubts upon that subject," answered Mary, "after the description which Amy has given us of her husband, and the sympathy which she says he feels in our misfortunes. Come, Richard, you must not suffer these misgivings to take possession of your mind, for there is no occasion for them; and I flatter myself that everything will even turn out much better than we can now anticipate."

"Heaven send that it may," returned her husband; "for my patience is almost exhausted, by being kept in this continual state of suspense, and the many disappointments that we have experienced at the very moment when we though that our prospects had begun to brighten."

"At any rate," said Mary, "our prospects were never so flattering as they are at the present time; and it would be a folly and a weakness for us to anticipate evils, when there is no occasion for it."

"True," coincided Richard; "and I will endeavour to hope for the best. It is, however, a source of deep regret to me to see Amy a prey to such secret grief. What a melancholy change have time and care wrought in her appearance."

"Alas, they have, and it is sad to contemplate it; but were you ever aware that Amy's affections were fixed on any particular object?"

Richard replied in the negative, and expressed his surprise that, so intimate as they were, she had never made himself or Mary a confident.

"But probably delicacy prevented her from doing so," he added; "or, perhaps, the attachment might not have been formed until after our separation."

"True," replied Mary; "but we must suspend all judgment upon the subject until after she has given us the explanation she has promised, and which, probably, she will be able to do before long."

"Her abrupt departure from Exeter fills me with strange misgivings," observed Richard; "which I only hope may turn out to be groundless; but whichever way it may turn out to be, I am certain that Amy is more to be pitied than condemned."

"Oh, no doubt of it," returned Mary, "and you do her no more than justice by the supposition, Richard. Was she not ever good, and innocent, and amiable?"

"She was," replied her husband; "but her artless and unsuspicious disposition only rendered her the more likely to become the victim of the unprincipled and designing. Heaven grant that it may not be so; but still it must be something of a very fearful description to have made such a powerful impression on the poor girl's mind."

"It must," agreed our heroine, "but still it may not be to that degree of turpitude which you apprehend. But, hush! I hear her ascending the stairs; we must reserve our remarks upon the subject to a future occasion."

The door was now opened, and Amy re-entered the room, and seemed to be much revived in spirits, and the expression of her countenance evinced much less agitation and excitement than it had done before she retired.

"I fear," she observed, with a faint smile, "that you will find me but a dull companion, and one but little calculated to arouse you from the contemplation of your sorrows; but I will exert myself to the utmost, and hope that I shall be able to succeed much better than I now anticipate."

"To know that we possess your warmest sympathy, dear Amy," replied our heroine, "will afford us the greatest consolation; and I hope that when you shall have made us acquainted with the cause of your secret sorrow, that we also shall be enabled to impart that consolation to you, which you have done to us."

"Thank you, thank you most cordially for your kind wishes," said Amy, returning the warm pressure of Mary's hand; "but, alas! I fear there is but little hope of consolation in this world for me. The fatal blow is struck which annihilates all my hopes for ever."

"Nay, Amy," said her cousin, "give not way to such sad thoughts as these, for you know not how soon something may occur to brighten your prospects."

"Ah! no!" replied Amy with a deep sigh, "it would be little less than madness for me to indulge in any such delusive hopes as these; for I feel convinced that they can only end in disappointment. What can possibly occur to work such a happy change in my prospects as that which you have hinted at? Is it possible to recal the past, or to blot out its sorrows and its errors from the memory? It is not; and, therefore, I have nothing to look forward to but despair and misery. But wait patiently till I can find sufficient courage to unfold all that which now presses so heavily on my heart, and you will then discover that it is not without a cause that I abandon myself to this agony of feeling, which Heaven only knows how I have been able to support so long."

"Well, my dear cousin," observed Richard, "we will no longer press you upon a subject which is the cause of so much pain to you, till you feel yourself in a better condition to confide your secret to us."

"Thanks," said Amy, in reply; "I do not feel myself at all capable of performing that task to-day; but probably to-morrow I shall find sufficient fortitude to do so. Come, we must endeavour to banish these dismal subjects from our minds, for the present, at any rate; and to divert our thoughts and attention to something else. If you have no objection, I will conduct you over the villa, and then you will be the better able to judge of the comfort and even luxuriance by which I am surrounded."

She said this with a faint smile; and Richard and his wife readily assented, for their own curiosity was somewhat excited, and Amy leading the way, they followed her out of the apartment. The villa was built in the semi-gothic style, and possessed considerable architectural merit. Its rooms were spacious, lofty, and elegantly furnished, and, in fact, nothing had been left undone to contribute to the comfort and convenience of its inmates. Our hero and his wife could not but express their warmest admiration of all they saw, and it was quite evident that the master of this place, as well as being in affluent circumstances, was a person of the most refined taste, and as such his mind, at any rate, whatever might be the disparity of their years, must be in unison with that of Amy.

But what more particularly attracted the attention of Mr. and Mrs. Parker was a rather extensive picture gallery, the arrangements of which were in admirable keeping with the other portions of the building, and was lighted by a large dome in the roof of the house. Here were paintings of every description, the choicest productions of the most celebrated ancient and modern masters, and which could not fail to draw forth the most unqualified admiration of all who inspected them. Landscapes, historical subjects, and portraits profusely decorated this handsome apartment, and whichever way the eye turned there was something to delight and rivet the attention. It also cont. . . some very fine works of sculpture.

But what more particularly struck our hero and heroine was a full length portrait of Amy attired in a bridal dress, and which presented such an admirable likeness of the fair original, that, at the first glance, it might almost have been taken for herself, and seemed to be imbued with life and animation. But there was the same melancholy expression of features which marked the original, and which seemed to be so out of keeping with the character of a youthful bride.

Richard and Mary long contemplated this portrait, and again and again praised the remarkable skill of the artist who had executed it; but while they did so, Amy turned away her head, sighed deeply, and seemed to be suffering some deep emotion, which they perceiving, reluctantly averted their looks from it, and refrained from making any observation. They now turned their attention to the opposite side of the room, and their eyes immediately became fixed upon a painting of such a remarkable description, that they could not remove them from it.

It was the portrait of a venerable man, of at least seventy years of age, and the general expression of whose features was so disagreeable, that it almost approached to absolute ugliness. The form was also diminutive and misshapen, and altogether it was a matter of surprise to Richard and his wife that such a portrait should find a place among so many rare works of art, unless it was to present a contrast, or as a specimen of the painter's skill in portraying the grotesque.

Their curiosity excited, they turned towards Amy to make some inquiry, when they found her weeping bitterly; but finding she was observed, she dried her tears hastily, and endeavoured to appear composed.

"Dear Amy," said Richard, who could not refrain from putting the question;

"pray, whom may this extraordinary portrait represent?"

"My—my *husband!*" replied Amy in a faltering voice, and she cast her eyes towards the floor, and a heavy sigh escaped her bosom.

"Your husband?" repeated our hero and heroine in a breath.

Amy nodded assent, and they said no more, for they were so completely taken by astonishment that they could not. Here, then, was at once partially explained the cause of the sorrow that pressed so heavily upon her heart, and they could not but feel for her the most acute sense of pity. Again they fixed their eyes upon the portrait, and the longer they did so, the more forcibly the ugliness of the individual it represented struck them. What a strange partner for such a woman as Amy! And yet there was something in the expression of the eyes, which seemed to testify to the natural goodness of heart which the original possessed, and which could not fail to excite a feeling of esteem and reverence in the breast of the beholder.

Perceiving how deeply affected Amy was, they at length turned away from the portrait, and after having minutely examined the various other pictures, they followed Amy out of the gallery, and were conducted by her into the library, which was also of considerable extent, and contained all the most celebrated English, French, German, and Italian works; a rich store for the mind to dwell upon, and to luxuriate among. Here Richard and his wife (whose literary taste was of the first order) could have lingered for hours, and here they determined that, with the permission of Mr. and Mrs. Ashton, they would pass much of their time during their stay at the villa.

Having inspected the whole of the apartments, all of which possessed much to admire, and the grounds attached to the villa, which, however, at that time of the year could not be seen exactly to advantage, they returned to the room which they had lately quitted, and in which they found dinner prepared for them. Much gratified with all that they had seen, they sat down to the table in much better spirits than they had experienced for some time, and Amy seemed to have nearly regained her composure. The meal passed off without many observations, and when it was over Richard and our heroine could not help paying the most flattering compliments to the skill and taste of those who had superintended the arrangements of the villa.

"I'm sure, my dear Amy," remarked Mary, "that it is a perfect little palace, and," she added, forgetting herself, for the moment, "it delights me to see you so happy and comfortable."

"Happy! comfortable!" repeated Amy, with a melancholy look and a deep sigh, "alas! it is impossible that I can ever be so again. Those heavy clouds have obscured my peace of mind, and darkened my prospects, which nothing can ever disperse."

Mr. and Mrs. Parker thought of the portrait of her husband, and they, independent of the painful secret which weighed upon her heart, wondered not at her observations.

"But you must not give way to those feelings of despondency, my dear cousin," said Richard, at last; "for, however gloomy your prospects may appear to be at present, there is no knowing how soon a favourable change may take place, which will place you in that state of happiness and tranquillity which I am certain from your numerous virtues you so richly deserve to experience."

"My virtues!" repeated Amy, with a shudder, and blushing deeply, "oh, Richard, you know not all, or you would not thus flatter me, for, indeed, I deserve it not."

"Amy," ejaculated our hero, with a look of astonishment and incredulity; "what mean you by thus disparaging yourself? You surely know not what you say?"

"Alas!" sighed Mrs. Ashton, and tears again started to her eyes; "I do too well, and while I make the degrading admission, a pang shoots through my sered heart which is almost overwhelming. But ere long you shall know all, however much you may afterwards despise me, and then you will be convinced of the ample cause I have for the most heartfelt grief, remorse, and self-reproach."

"It is impossible," observed Mary. "Amy could never have been guilty of anything that she should be ashamed to acknowledge."

"Alas!" returned Amy, "would to Heaven that your opinion were a just one, then I should not be the poor miserable being that I am at present. But surely, after all, I am not so much to blame; no, I have been cruelly, basely deceived, and upon him who has been the cause of it should the retribution of offended Heaven descend. Oh, Charles! Charles! if you still live, and you have not become insensible to every feeling of shame, how bitter must be the pangs of conscience you are now suffering!"

Sobs choked her further utterance, and she arose from her seat in the greatest emotion, and paced the room for several minutes, muttering some incoherent words to herself, and Richard and his wife, who sincerely and deeply felt for her, did not offer to interrupt her. She at length returned to her chair, and drying her eyes, she said,—

"Pardon me for this emotion, but when sad memory recalls the past, I cannot help feeling all that anguish of mind which its painful reminiscences naturally engender."

"But you must try to bury the past in oblivion, Amy," returned our hero, "and to look forward to the future with a cheerful and confident spirit."

"Alas!" replied Amy, "that is a task which, although I have struggled hard, I find it impossible to accomplish. Torturing memory will still cling to me, in spite of myself, and the more I reflect, the darker does all appear before me."

"Ah, Amy," said our heroine, "and what think you then must be the feelings of myself and my husband, when we recall the past to our memory, and reflect upon the danger, the misery, and the almost utter hopelessness of our present condition, wretched wanderers as we are, and afraid to meet the light of day?"

"Yours is indeed a hard destiny," replied Mrs. Ashton, "and you have much to cause you the bitterest anguish of mind, but still your condition is not entirely hopeless, since Providence has been so kind as hitherto to preserve you from the many and imminent dangers by which you were surrounded, and to conduct you hither. You may yet be restored to happiness, but for me there is no hope."

"It grieves me, Amy," said her cousin, "to hear you talk in this melancholy strain. But time and perseverance will, I hope, ameliorate your grief, and you will learn to look back upon the past without regret."

"Without regret?" repeated Amy; "oh, how is it possible that can ever be? But you can form but little idea of what I have suffered, or the extent of my present misery, or you would not talk thus. Oh, Richard, you have seen the portrait of my husband, and however amiable and affectionate he is, and which I most readily admit him to be, think you it is possible that I can love him, or be happy when I look at him and think of him to whom my youthful heart was devoted, in whom all my hopes and wishes were centred, and who so cruelly deceived me?"

"True," said Richard, "I admit the force of all your observations; but how came you to become the wife of such a man as Mr. Ashton?"

"I was wretched, houseless, destitute,

heart-broken," answered Amy, " when chance guided me to his dwelling. I had not had a morsel of food within my lips for several hours, and exhausted with grief, and travelling for many weary miles in the most inclement weather, I sank over-powered on the threshold of his door, and—"

"Good God!" interrupted Mrs. Parker, "and is it possible that you were ever re-duced to such a state of extreme wretched-ness as this?"

"Alas! I was, and oh, much greater than I can now find courage to describe. Mr. Ashton took me in; he had compas-sion on me; he befriended me; watched me with the same care and solicitude as if he had been my father. Can you then wonder that he should excite in my breast feelings of the most unbounded gratitude, esteem, and reverence, when but for him I must have perished?"

"No," replied Richard, "he did indeed perform the part of the good Samaritan, and may Heaven's blessings light upon him for it."

"Ah! better would it have been for me," continued Amy, "far better had I perished; then should I have been spared the insup-portable misery which it is now my lot to experience."

"Oh, say not so," remonstrated Mary, "for there is yet many days of happiness in store for you."

Amy shook her head, and she then pro-ceeded.

"The kind treatment I had received from Mr. Ashton, urged me to comply with his request to make him acquainted with my history, and the mournful facts which had reduced me to that deplorable state of wretchedness, and placing every confidence in him, I concealed nothing from him, though it cost me many a heart-rending pang, and a blush of shame to reveal it. He heard me with the deepest emotion; expressed his warmest sympathy, and his disgust and detestation of the man who had been the cause of all my miseries, and from that time his care and attention to me increased, and he seemed never happy but when in my presence, and en-deavouring to alleviate the poignancy of my grief, and to impart to me that conso-lation of which, Heaven knows, I stood so much in need. Destitute even as I was, I would have quitted his house, and left my fate in the hands of Providence, for my heart revolted from the idea of being thus heavily beholden to a stranger, especially when I well knew that it would never be in my power to make him any return for his benevolence; but he would not hear of such a thing; did all he could to quiet my

objections, urged upon me to make his house my future home, and redoubled his attentions towards me. I had not to ex-press a wish that remained ungratified, and he seemed to be never so delighted as when he thought he had done anything that afforded me pleasure or tended to my comfort."

"Excellent man!" exclaimed Richard, "how much he is to be admired. Oh, that there were many more like him in the world, then would there not be half the misery that there is at present."

"Most true," coincided Amy; "and it must be an insensible heart, indeed, that could not reverence him for his humanity. In the manner which I have described, time passed on, and I had now been two months at the house of Mr. Ashton, when his attentions to me assumed so marked and peculiar a character, that I became uneasy and embarrassed, and scarcely knew what to understand from them; but I was not long kept in doubt or suspense upon the subject, for at length he acknow-ledged that I had inspir d him with warmer sentiments than those of mere sympathy and respect, and made me a formal offer of his hand and fortune. As you may imagine, I was completely startled at such an unexpected proposal, and from such a man, and I then for the first time regretted that I had laid myself under such heavy obligations to him, and which had led him to encourage hopes, which at that time I thought it was impos-sible that I could ever gratify. He took me so by surprise, that I was at a loss at first what to reply; but when he again urged his suit in still more eloquent and persuasive language, I candidly acknow-ledged that the great disparity of our years and other circumstances, would pre-clude the possibility of my ever consent-ing to become his wife, and though I must ever most warmly esteem him for the un-exampled kindness I had experienced from him as a stranger in the time of my greatest misery, I could never love him with that strength of affection which a woman ought to feel towards her husband. He combated all my objections with great ingenuity, and continued to urge his suit with the greatest vehemence, but he made little or no impression on me, and I begged of him to desist as he valued my peace of mind, and would not have me alter the favourable opinion I had hitherto formed of him. He seemed almost distracted at my firm rejection, and I could not help pitying him, though the idea of becoming the wife of a man old enough to be my father, was revolting to my feelings, and I

THE OLD WOMAN CONDUCTING THE PARKERS TO THEIR BED-CHAMBER.

could not encourage it for a moment. He begged of me at last to reflect for a few days calmly upon his proposal, promising during that interval not to disturb me by his presence, and I at length consented to do so, though I held out no hopes to him that anything could make me alter my determination. When I was alone, I reflected with astonishment and emotion upon this singular circumstance, and I could scarcely bring myself to believe that it had taken place; but the bare thought was revolting to me, as I said before, and my heart sickened as it occurred to me.

I considered that I had been much to blame in remaining so long under the roof of an entire stranger, and accepting so many favours from him, and I almost resolved secretly to depart from the place. But whither could I go, destitute, penniless, friendless as I was? And surely to leave the house in so clandestine a way would appear like treating Mr. Ashton with unkindness and ingratitude after the many favours I had received from him; and I, therefore, resolved to remain till the time which I had promised to consider of his proposal had elapsed, at any rate, though, at that time, I did not believe it possible that anything could persuade me to give my consent to that which appeared to me so unreasonable and unnatural; and when I thought of him on whom I had bestowed my love, and the cruel manner in which he had betrayed and deceived me, my heart was full to bursting. After the first shock which this surprise to my feelings was over, I did begin to reflect upon the proposals of Mr. Ashton more calmly and seriously, and although it was impossible that anything could alter my sentiments towards him, when I took all the circumstances of my desperate and deplorable situation into consideration, my mind began to waver, and I was, in truth, bewildered how to decide. Should I reject the offer which had so generously been made to me by Mr. Ashton, knowing, as he did, every particular phase of my unfortunate history, it was impossible that I could any longer remain, with common prudence or delicacy, under his roof ; and, as I have before stated, I considered whither I was then to go? Where could I apply for protection and sympathy, poor and completely friendless as I was? I had seen enough of his character to convince me of his excellent and amiable qualities, and to rest satisfied that his principal object in wishing me to become his wife, was one of pure philanthropy, to give him a legal right to the office of my protector, and that he would act towards me both the part of a father and a husband. He in whom I had placed every confidence had basely deceived me, and abandoned me to misery. I could not expect, nor would accept any terms of reconciliation with him; he had crushed my hopes, and was worthy, therefore, only of my scorn and detestation. Why, then, should I longer hesitate between a prospective good and a certain evil? Some portion of the unthinking world might censure and ridicule me for the step I had taken, but surely I had been too deeply schooled in the vicissitudes of life to heed such sequences? These were the arguments that I weighed maturely in my mind, imploring the Almighty to assist me in coming to a right conclusion, and at last I came to the determination, after all the most deliberate and careful analysis of the peculiar and painful circumstances in which I was placed, to yield my consent to become the wife of that excellent man, who had been my sincere and Christian friend in the hour of my greatest affliction, when all else despised me, and mocked at my sufferings. Can you, my dear relations, blame me for the decision to which I came?"

"Blame you, Amy?" replied our hero, who had, together with his wife, listened with the profoundest attention and deepest interest to every word which had passed from the lips of the unfortunate woman. "Oh, no ; you acted alone as prudence and gratitude should have dictated, and from what you have said of the conduct of your husband towards you since your marriage to him, you have had no cause whatever to regret the decision which you came to?"

"Regret?" returned Amy; "oh, no; on the contrary, I have every day, every hour, had more reason than ever to admire the generous, the honourable, the kind, the considerate character of him to whom I have united my fate, and Heaven knows how strictly I have endeavoured to perform my duty towards him as a wife, and prayed to it for blessings upon his head. Old and deformed he may be, repulsive to the sight, as perhaps the portrait of him which you have just seen may lead you to suppose ; but there is no deformity of the heart or mind, it is as pure as that of the new born babe, and, therefore, worthy of all honour, all love, all respect."

"True, true, dear Amy," observed Mary, "and the Almighty has, indeed, been most kind and bountiful to you, in sending you such a protector in the midst of your adversity."

"Oh, yes," replied Amy, "and most grateful am I to Him for it. He alone knows what would have become of me, had I not been guided to him, when my circumstances were in that awful state that, in the frenzy of my despair, I should probably have been led to the perpetration of some desperate and guilty act, and thus have plunged my soul into perdition. All these things, you may be certain, I weighed maturely in my mind before I could come to the decision I did, and they did but serve to strengthen me in my resolution. It was more than a week after the time which I have described, before I again saw Mr. Ashton, he having absented himself from the house, when he returned, and requested, through the medium of a female servant, about my own age, whom he had deputed to attend upon me ever since I had been under his protection, to know when it would be convenient for me to see him? I named the following day, and in the interim how earnestly I supplicated the Almighty to give me strength to go through the delicate and important task which was imposed upon me, I am sure I need not describe to you. But I had weighed every point and every argument so maturely in my mind, that my determination was fixed, and I felt confident that I should only act as prudence, reason, and gratitude to my benefactor dictated. The day appointed arrived, and I arose in much more cheerful and hopeful spirits than I had been in for some time before, for my conscience told me that I was acting right, and that I should have no cause to regret the decision I had come to. About an hour after I had risen, my waiting-maid came to me with a message from her master to know whether it was my pleasure to attend him at breakfast, and I instantly expressed my willingness to do so, and when she had gone to deliver my answer, I fell upon my knees, and again most earnestly implored the Supreme to give me confidence in the course I was about to adopt, and to guide me to do that which was just to myself, and towards that excellent man to whom I was so much indebted. I felt fresh courage after this prayer, and immediately made my way towards the apartment in which I knew Mr. Ashton was so anxiously awaiting me. He met me at the door, and greeted me most respectfully and affectionately, and I could plainly see the anxiety and suspense of mind he had suffered si ce he had been away, and the doubt and apprehension he was then enduring. He took me by the hand and led me into the room without saying a word, and I could not help trembling while he did so, and a nameless feeling came over me, which I found it impossible, for the instant, to control; but I speedily recovered myself, and with more confidence than I though I could have mustered, I took my seat by his side at the breakfast-table.

"A silence of several minutes ensued, during which time he seemed uncertain and tenacious how to begin, or what to say; but at the same time he kept his eyes earnestly fixed upon my countenance, and seemed anxiously endeavouring to read the thoughts that were passing in my mind, and which I am certain that my blushes, and the agitation of my manner altogether, must have revealed to him. At length he said—

"'Amy, I trust that I have paid proper respect to the delicacy of your feelings in this important matter, and given you due and reasonable time to come to a decision, which so immediately concerns the welfare and the happiness of us both, but more especially of myself. Oh, believe me, my dear girl, that the anxiety of mind which I have suffered since we last met, has been intense and painful. I am an old man, I know, and a portion of mankind might

consider me either as an old idiot, or to act from selfish motives, in seeking the hand of one so much my junior in years, and whom I cannot expect to rivet her heart upon me in the true sense of the word. But rest assured, Amy, that whatever your determination may be, and I am ready to submit to it, whatever the anguish and disappointment it may cost me, no such feelings guide me in my present conduct. Providence has thrown you in adversity upon my path; I have long been a lonely man, wretched and restless, because I have had no one to care for me, or to look upon me with esteem, if they could not with love. You are just the fair and gentle being that has presented itself to my imagination when my mind has been wandering in that direction. Treachery and villany have made you their victim, and abandoned you to misery. You need a protector—one who can love and honour you—one who would perform the duties of a parent as well as a husband to you, and endeavour to impart consolation to you for the heavy and cruel wrongs you have received. To that blissful office have I the presumption to aspire. I seek not your love, for that I know it would be preposterous in me to think of obtaining; I require but the respect and esteem due to me, according to my conduct towards you. But the world is censorious; and I would, therefore, to stifle the voice of scandal, give you a legal claim upon my protection. This is the moment which decides my fate, Amy, and I wait with anxiety the most intense, yet not without hope, to hear your determination.''

"What could I say in reply to this address, so forcible and so reasonable?" continued Amy; "for a minute or two I hesitated, and casting my eyes to the floor, my heart palpitated so violently against my side, that I could scarcely support myself. But the treachery of the man on whom I had fixed my hopes, and the dismal prospect before me, if I should reject the offer now made to me, together with the generous and reasonable propositions of Mr. Ashton, presented themselves most vividly before me, and at once decided me. I felt fresh courage, and presenting him my hand, I said in a timid voice,—

"'Fate seems to will it—I cannot doubt the honour of your proposals, my dear sir, after what I have experienced from you; I am indebted to you to an extent which I fear it will never be in my power adequately to repay, but if my hand, my future esteem and reverence are considered by you as acceptable to you, in part liquidation of the obligations I am under to you, they are yours.'

"He uttered an exclamation of mingled gratitude and rapture as I uttered these words, and sinking on one knee, he raised my hand to his lips, and kissed it fervently, but respectfully. I felt my heart relieved of a heavy burthen, and my conscience approved of the course I had adopted, and assured me that I should have no reason to regret it. We did not remain together many minutes longer, when he suffered me to retire to my own apartment in order that I might collect my feelings, after so delicate and important an interview as that which had just taken place between us. When I found myself alone, I again sank on my knees, and supplicated the mercy and protection of the Supreme, and by degrees I became more calm, and could not but feel satisfied in the justice and wisdom of the decision to which after so long and painful a struggle with my feelings I had come to. The next day I was enabled to meet my future husband with perfect composure, and nothing could exceed the respect and affection with which he received me. We talked over our future prospects with earnestness and calmness, and he made such arrangements for my settlement as could not but meet with my approbation, and further convince me of the honour and generosity of his intentions. Before we separated that day the time was fixed for our nuptials, which on the appointed day were solemnized as privately as possible, and I became the wife of that man who had taken compassion on me, and acted almost more than the part of a parent towards me when I had no other friend in the world. Thus have I explained to you the manner in which this important epoch in my life was brought about; but the further and more painful portion of my history I must reserve to a future time, probably to-morrow, though I almost tremble to make the disclosure. Now, tell me, can you blame me for having agreed to form an union apparently so ill-assorted and unnatural?"

"Oh, no, my dear Amy, I say again, that is impossible," replied her cousin; "placed in the precarious situations in which you were you could not have acted more wisely or prudently. You secured for yourself the legal protection of an honourable man, to whom you owed an incalculable debt of gratitude for the generous services he had rendered you, when you must otherwise, probably, have perished, and I am certain that you have never given him cause to regret the course he adopted."

"Heaven forbid that I should," said Amy, sincerely; "it has been my constant study to perform the sacred duties of a wife towards him to the very letter, and I will continue to do so while the current of life circulates through my veins. I have nothing whatever to reproach myself with in that respect, and that conviction affords me the greatest consolation in the midst of all my troubles. All that I regret is that I am unable to bestow upon him that ardent love which should be required from a wife."

"Considering the disparity of your ages, and all the circumstances of your peculiar fate, Amy," observed our heroine, "that can hardly be expected. And your husband is contented, I presume, and never offers a word of complaint?"

"Oh, never!" replied Mrs. Ashton; "on the contrary, it is his constant study to make me happy, and to endeavour to remove from my mind, by every means in his power, the heavy sorrows that oppress it, and to inspire me with hope and consolation."

"From the excellent character you have given me of him, my sweet cousin," said Richard, "I am prepared to esteem and admire him. You say that he will not be angry at your having received us in the manner you have done?"

"Oh, no," answered Amy; "he always possesses the heart to sympathise with his fellow creatures in misfortune, and I know full well that it will afford him the greatest gratification to find that Providence has guided your footsteps hither, and that he is enabled to render assistance to those who have suffered so many unmerited wrongs. So, once more I beg of you to rest your mind easy upon that point, and you will find that in all that I have said to you, notwithstanding his unprepossessing appearance, I have not at all exaggerated in my description of his character."

"I believe you, Amy," returned our hero, "and feel more happy and buoyant with hope for the future than I have for many a day."

"It gratifies me to hear you say so, Richard," remarked Amy, "and you may depend upon it that there shall not be anything wanting on my part to keep you in the same state of mind. But night is now advancing, and we had better separate, for I am certain that you must require rest. In the morning I hope that we shall meet again, refreshed, and in better spirits than it has been our lot to experience for some time past. I will conduct you to the apartments I have prepared for you, and in a cabinet you will find a decent change of apparel for you both, of which you at present stand so much in need."

"Oh, my dear Amy," ejaculated Mary, "how shall we ever be able to repay this considerate kindness? what——"

"Hold, Mrs. Parker," interrupted Amy, "that which I am enabled to do for you is dictated by my heart, and requires no thanks. But let us talk no more upon this subject to-night. Here, at any rate, you may sleep in safety, a thing you probably have not been able to do for many a day."

"Most true," said Richard; "for however kind and friendly has been the reception where we have sought shelter, still the individuals being strangers to us, always naturally left a doubt upon our minds; and had we not, indeed, been cautious, and always on our guard, I have no doubt that we should ere this have fallen into the hands of our pursuers, for, as I have informed you we have had many perilous and hairbreadth escapes."

"No doubt of it," answered Amy, "and terrible indeed must have been the privations and constant anxiety of mind you must have suffered. But will you attend me?"

Our hero and his wife nodded assent, and Amy taking up a lamp led the way from the apartment, followed by her unfortunate relations. Having conducted them up a flight of stairs, she ushered them into a commodious suite of chambers, handsomely furnished, and which for the comfort and accommodation they afforded presented quite a novelty to the hapless wanderers. They could not refrain from again expressing their thanks to Amy in the warmest manner; but she stopped them shortly, and said—

"Why will you persist in returning thanks where they are not required, and not deserved? Am I doing any more than my duty towards my fellow creatures, especially those who are so nearly related to me?"

"May Heaven bless you, dear Amy," said our heroine, "and speedily remove from you that heavy weight of care and sorrow that now oppresses your mind."

"Alas!" sighed Mrs. Ashton, "that I can never hope for; but we have said enough upon that dismal subject for the present. Good-night; and may you gain a sweet respite from your cares and anxieties in refreshing sleep."

"Amen, my sweet cousin," fervently responded Richard, raising her hand to his lips; "we shall meet again in the morning, and till then farewell."

Amy now quitted the chamber, and no sooner had she gone than the wanderers threw themselves on their knees, and in the most earnest tones, they poured forth their gratitude to the Supreme for the mercy He had shown them, and supplicated His farther protection from any dangers that might assail them. Their hearts were so full with the mingled feelings that now took possession of them, and especially at the sudden and unexpected change that had taken place in their prospects, that for some time they could not give utterance to a word, but could only weep upon each other's bosom, while the poor boy William's emotions were, if possible, even more powerful than their own, and he continued on his knees, with clasped hands and upraised eyes, and with all the innocent simplicity of childhood, he poured forth his thanks to that Almighty power who had supported them throughout so many dangers and hardships.

"Dear Richard," said his wife at last, "this is indeed a change in our circumstances, as fortunate as it is unexpected. From the friendship and sympathy of Amy and her husband we may expect much; and I cannot but flatter myself with the hope, however sanguine it may appear to be, that our troubles are now nearly at an end, and that we shall ultimately be enabled to entirely avoid those dangers that have been so long impending o'er us."

"God grant that your hopes may be realised, Mary," replied her husband, "and I must confess that our prospects certainly are much more flattering than they were even only a few hours ago; but still it is better for us not to indulge in those anticipations to which circumstances have recently given rise too freely, lest they should be doomed to disappointment. Notwithstanding the character which Amy has given of Mr. Ashton, and the many amiable qualities he doubtless possesses, still he might hesitate to run the risk of sheltering us, well knowing the penalty that would be sure to attend any one who should have been discovered to have done so."

"Nay," observed Mary, "after what Amy has said, I cannot think that he will do so; I do not believe any idea of danger will intimidate him from the performance of what he must consider to be a Christian duty. Besides, what has he to apprehend? All traces of the course we have taken in our flight are evidently lost, we have eluded the vigilance of our pursuers, and it is not at all likely that anything like suspicion can attach to Mr. Ashton, a gentleman placed in the circumstances in which he is, and ignorant as any one must be that we are at all related to him."

"Well, my dear Mary," returned our hero, "it is not at all unlikely to turn out as you anticipate, and I will not attempt to dampen the ardour of your expectations. Heaven knows we have already suffered sufficient, and surely we may at last look forward to the merciful interposition of Omnipotence in our favour. One thing, at any rate, affords me the greatest satisfaction, and that is, that we shall at last have the opportunity of corresponding with our friend Adams, who must be so anxious to hear from us; and from the answer we shall doubtless promptly receive from him, we shall be enabled to come to the conclusion as to what course it will be most prudent and secure for us in future to adopt; and I trust that we may safely calculate upon every humane assistance from Amy and her husband."

"Oh, yes," said Mary, "we may depend upon that. Poor Amy, it grieves me to see her thus the victim of some secret sorrow, which must have been of the most painful description to have made such a powerful and melancholy impression upon her."

"Very true; and I am most anxious to hear the particulars of her history, though, from the observations she has made use of, I am apprehensive that the trials it has been her lot to experience have been of no ordinary description. But let us await patiently till to-morrow, and probably we shall then be made acquainted with everything."

With renewed hopes, and minds more at ease than they had been for some time, they now retired to rest, and sleep soon descended upon their eyelids. They arose at an early hour in the morning, much refreshed, and having attired themselves in the clothes which Amy had provided for them, they awaited impatiently the summons to attend Amy in the breakfast-room. The sudden change from the most abject and hopeless misery to comfort and present security, had the most powerful effect upon them; re-animated their spirits, and inspired them with hope. Again and again did they return their thanks to Heaven for the mercy and protection that had hitherto been extended to them, and most earnestly they supplicated a further extension of it, at the same time they felt a sweet confidence that their prayers would not be unheeded, and they begun to look forward to the future with the most bright and sanguine expectations.

At length a servant knocked at the door, and informed them that her mistress awaited them in the breakfast-room, and Mary and her husband immediately accompanied her thither, and were received by Mrs. Ashton with every kindness and affection. They were glad to see her looking so much more cheerful than she had done the day before; and she expressed her gratification at beholding them appear so much refreshed.

The morning repast was despatched in the most comfortable and happy manner, and the friends conversed freely, during the time, upon subjects of general interest.

"I cannot help thinking," remarked Amy, at its conclusion, "that this is but a prelude to your future happiness, my dear cousins, and that the dark and heavy clouds that have so long obscured the sunshine of your hopes and prospects, will quickly be dispersed, and that you will receive an ample reward for the many trials and vicissitudes it has been your hard lot for so many years to experience."

"Heaven bless you, Amy," returned our heroine, "for your kind wishes, which we know to spring so warmly and so purely from your heart. How thankful are we to Providence for directing our footsteps to you, whom we never expected to meet again. God grant that you too, ere long, may be able to banish those cares and sorrows which now weigh so heavily upon your heart, and that you may be restored to peace and tranquillity, if not to complete happiness."

Amy sighed and shook her head, as she replied—

"True happiness, my dear friends, I can never expect to meet with again, for when I reflect upon the dark and dismal past—and what can ever banish it from my memory?—anguish, regret, and self-reproach must ever be mine. Mine have been no ordinary sorrows, and so you will admit, when you are made acquainted with them; but I must confess that since our meeting, I do feel some small degree of hope revive in my breast, and I am more calm and resigned than I have been for many a day."

"Oh, how glad am I to hear you talk thus, Amy," replied Richard; "and most sincerely do I wish that the time is not far distant when you will be enabled to acquire even greater firmness, and to look back upon the past with far less anguish and regret than you do at present. Communicate to us the particulars of the misfortunes that have befallen you since we last met, if it will not be too great a trial of your fortitude to do so, and I am sure I need not assure you of our warmest sympathy, and that we will most gladly exert ourselves to afford you all the consolation in our power."

"Ah! my dear cousin," replied Amy, "well do I know that, and although the task will be a most painful one, I will endeavour to comply with your request. But, alas! I have too much reason to fear that you will condemn me in many respects, though I have been most cruelly deceived, and my fondest hopes blighted by one in whom I had placed every confidence, and whose truth and sincerity I could never for a moment suspect. I shall have to reveal that which I should blush to acknowledge, and for which I fear you must too justly condemn me. But I claim your pity and indulgence, when you shall have the opportunity of taking all the melancholy circumstances of my hard case into consideration; and I feel confident from the respect and affection which you have ever evinced towards me, that you will not refuse them to me.".

"Oh, no, Amy," answered her cousin, "you may depend upon that; and we feel certain that you have nothing justly to reproach yourself with so keenly as you appear to, and that whatever misfortunes may have befallen you, they have been brought about by the treachery and villany of others."

"That is most true," remarked Amy, "but would to Heaven I could acquit myself altogether. However, I will reveal to you all the dismal facts, concealing nothing, and then leave you to judge for yourselves. My mind may experience some relief in unfolding its sorrows to those whom I know can sympathise with them, and will put the most charitable construction upon my conduct."

Mary and her husband returned no answer, and Amy having paused for a few minutes to collect her thoughts, and to gain composure and firmness for the task she had imposed upon herself, commenced her narrative, as will be found in the succeeding chapter.

CHAPTER XXXVII.

A TALE OF WOE.—WOMAN'S LOVE.—SUNSHINE AND SHADE.—THE DECEIVER AND THE DECEIVED.

"It is quite needless, my dear friends," began Amy, "for me to enter into the particulars of my early history, which was marked by nothing of any importance, for you are already acquainted with them;

but it may be, perhaps, necessary for me to mention that the sudden death of both my beloved parents, within a short time of each other, was the first and most melancholy calamity which I had ever experienced, and that it has cast a shadow over all my future days. Prior to that my life had been one continual round of happiness, peace, and contentment, and sorrow was known to me by name alone. I had been nursed in the lap of indulgence by the fondest and most affectionate of parents; and there had not been a single wish that I might entertain which could long remain ungratified; therefore, how painful was the change which I now experienced, and it was some time before I could find the least consolation under my dismal and irremediable bereavement.

"From their economical and prudent habits, my poor parents had been enabled to save a few pounds, which, of course, at their death came into my possession, and which was sufficient to keep me for some time, or until I had obtained some means of procuring a permanent livelihood, which I hoped to do by the industry of my own hands, as I was skilful at my needle and had the respect and promise of patronage of many influential families in the neighbourhood where I resided, and who had known me from childhood. I know full well, Richard, that I might have made the house of your parents my home, and that they would have behaved to me with the same affectionate care and attention as if I had been their own daughter, but nothing could induce me to quit that cottage in which I was born, and where my beloved parents had drawn their last breath, and I well knew how much they were reduced in circumstances, and I could not think of becoming a burthen to them when I considered I had the means of supporting myself; and it was that feeling which made me decline all the offers they made to me in that respect, though I must ever esteem and feel grateful to their memory, for the many acts of kindness which they bestowed upon me.

"In this manner two or three years passed away, and I need not tell you how great was the interest which I felt in the love of yourself and Mary, and how deeply I regretted the opposition which it met with from Mr. Mason. I saw plainly that there was no hope of his relenting, prejudiced as he was in favour of the late Captain Arlington, and especially when misfortunes, over which you had no control, Richard, and which were occasioned by no imprudence or misconduct of your own, had reduced you to a state of comparative poverty ; and I could not but apprehend that you would have to experience some severe trials and disappointments, for I was convinced that you could never banish from your hearts the affection you entertained towards each other. What subsequently took place I need not repeat here. Your frequent appeals to Mr. Mason, and his stern rejection of your suit, your elopement and clandestine marriage, with the misery which followed, must be ever too vividly fresh in your memory, and it would be painful to animadvert upon those dismal circumstances; my present business is only to explain that which has happened to me since we last met, and I will, therefore, hasten to the relation of those facts as speedily as possible. The villany of Captain Arlington, who caused your seizure by the press-gang, and the sufferings of Mary, when you were thus cruelly separated from her, may also be passed over briefly. She well knows that I did all that I could to console her, and endeavoured to make her as comfortable as possible ; but she could gain but very little peace and resignation, and I saw plainly that she was the more miserable and desponding because she considered that she was a burthen to me, and that she should never have the means to return it. But Heaven knows that such thoughts never for a moment entered my mind, for I need scarcely say that I looked upon her with the same affection as if she had been my own sister, and that there was nothing in my power which I would not willingly have done which could at all contribute to her happiness."

"Oh, yes," observed Mary, "how much have I experienced that, my dear Amy, and never can my gratitude cease towards you for it. But I could not conquer the feelings that came over me, and that accounts, or may probably account for my subsequent conduct."

"And yet I cannot tell you, Mary," resumed Amy, "how much I was hurt, when I found that only a few weeks afterwards you had absconded from my cottage, and without leaving me any information as to whither you were gone, or what course you proposed in future to adopt."

"I doubt it not, Amy," replied our heroine ; "but I knew not then myself, and my mind was so bewildered that I was scarcely conscious of what I was about."

"I made the most anxious inquiries after you in every direction where I thought I was likely to obtain any information," continued Amy, "but without meeting with any success, and there were many times when I was apprehensive that you had been urged by despair into the perpetration of some rash and desperate act, and my mind was in a continual state of uneasiness and anxiety about you, but still I was in hopes that Providence would watch over and protect you in the midst of your misfortunes, and that we should yet meet again under happier circumstances. Being now left alone, my time passed away in the most tedious and melancholy manner, and my thoughts were continually occupied with the images of my late beloved parents, and I could not but look upon myself as a most miserable and unfortunate being, who was left withou. a friend in the world, or any one to care for me, or to commiserate with me. I had no acquaintances, and I might be said to lead a life of complete seclusion, and to experience such a change in my circumstances as I never expected would have fallen to my lot, especially in my youthful days; but still I sought to bear with it with all the patience and resignation I could, and to hope that the time would come when the clouds which at present obscured the horizon of my peace would pass away, and that I should be restored to tranquillity, though I could never expect again to know that real happiness which I had once enjoyed. Little, however, did I anticipate that this was only the dawning of the miseries that were in store for me.

"It happened that, one afternoon, I had occasion to take a dress home which I had been making for a lady who resided two or three miles from the cottage in which I lived, and on my return the darkness of night overtook me before I was aware of it, having been detained longer than I expected, and being alone, and in rather a dismal and unfrequented spot, I could not help feeling rather timid and alarmed, and I therefore quickened my speed, but without appearing to make much progress in my journey.

"My way lay through a dreary lane, in which I had heard that many robberies and outrages had from time to time been perpetrated, and the recollection of which increased my fears, and I heartily wished myself at home. I hurried on as fast as I could, but the lane seemed to have no termination, and I was compelled at last to pause and take breath, and I looked anxiously back upon the way I had come; but I saw nothing to increase my fears, and I endeavoured to regain my firmness, and once more started on my way; but I had not proceeded far when I was startled

THE PARKERS ALARMED AT THE SOUND OF FIRE-ARMS.

by hearing the sound of hasty footsteps behind me, and looking back, you may judge of my alarm, when by the faint light of the moon I beheld two men rapidly advancing towards me, and who seemed as if they were in pursuit of me. My heart sunk within me, and I tried to redouble my speed; but my limbs seemed suddenly fettered, and I could make scarcely any progress at all, while the men seemed to be gaining fast upon me, and it was evident they were endeavouring to overtake me, for what purpose I shuddered to think. I looked anxiously before me, but I could perceive no one to render me any assistance in case I should stand in need of it, which it seemed, from the conduct of the men, not at all unlikely to be the case, and in that suspicion I was almost immediately afterwards confirmed, by their calling upon me in a loud voice to stop.

"My terror was now inexpressible, and I gave myself up for lost; still I made one more desperate effort, and heedless of their shouts, with which I now heard them mingle oaths, I redoubled my speed; but the men gained faster and faster upon me, and as they did so my strength completely failed me, and I was brought to a dead stand-still, and clasping my hands together, I supplicated the protection of the Almighty; for I could no longer doubt that the intentions of the strangers were of the basest description. I was not long kept in a state of suspense, for the next moment they came up with me; and rudely seizing me, one of them said, in a coarse voice—

"'So, you thought to escape us, did you, my girl? Why did you not stop when we called upon you to do so?'

"They were two ferocious-looking men, meanly attired, and carrying thick sticks in their hands; and when I beheld the savage and threatening looks they fixed upon me, and considered the lonely spot in which they had encountered me, the blood almost chilled in my veins, and I gave myself up for lost, which fear was not in the least diminished, you may be certain, by the observations which were made use of by the companion of the ruffian who had at first addressed me.

"'She is not a bad-looking wench, Mark,' he said, 'and it is quite refreshing to one's eyes to look at her. This is rather a lonely place, and an awkward time of the night, my girl, for you to be taking your rambles.'

"I was ready to sink into the earth with terror, and it was not without the greatest difficulty that I was enabled to gasp forth—

"'For the love of Heaven, what do you want with me? Strangers as you are to me, why do you stop me thus abruptly? Unhand me, I beg of you, and suffer me to proceed.'

"'Not so fast, young woman,' returned the man who had first spoken; 'we cannot part with you so easily. In the first place, have you any cash about you?'

"'Ah—robbers!' I ejaculated, with a look of inexpressible alarm.

"'Ay,' returned the ruffian, with a disagreeable grin, 'gentlemen of the road, more politely speaking. Circumstances will not allow us to be very particular, so the sooner you hand us over what money you may happen to have about you the better.'

"'I am but a poor, friendless girl,' I replied, in a faint voice, 'and what can you, therefore, expect from me? But here; take the trifle I have in my possession, and for pity's sake leave me, and suffer me to pursue my way unmolested.'

"With these words, I delivered into the hand of the man who had made the demand the few shillings which I had received in the evening, and awaited in the utmost anxiety and trepidation the result of this fearful adventure.

"'And is this all the money you have in your possession?' demanded the fellow, fixing upon me a savage look of doubt and suspicion.

"'Every farthing, I assure you,' I replied. 'Now that I have complied with your demands, I once more implore you no longer to detain me.'

"'Before we agree to your request,' returned the villain, 'we must each of us have a kiss from those pretty lips, and then——'

"As the cowardly and brutal ruffian thus spoke, he threw his arms rudely around my waist, and endeavoured to put his disgusting threats into execution; but I struggled violently, strengthened by the desperate and dangerous situation in which I was placed, and shrieked aloud for assistance.

"'Stop her cries!' ejaculated the other ruffian, 'though there don't seem to be much chance of her obtaining any assistance in this place.'

"Again I screamed for help, and struggled more violently in the embraces of the highwayman than before; but of what use were all my efforts when opposed to the strength of such desperate and determined wretches as these? Terror and despair completely overcame me, and I fainted.

"How long I had remained in this situation I knew not, but when I was restored to consciousness I found myself tenderly supported in the arms of a stranger, and that the two villains who had caused me so much alarm were gone. I gazed at the unknown with mingled feelings of hope and terror, and on my opening my eyes, he uttered an exclamation which seemed to express satisfaction, and gazed eagerly, and apparently with compassion upon me. Crimson blushes suffused my cheeks, and a nameless feeling agitated my heart, as I gazed upon him.

"He was a young man, apparently not more than twenty-two years of age, fashionably and elegantly dressed, and of graceful and commanding figure. His features were regular, striking, and handsome, and there was something in the expression of his dark eyes, which it seemed impossible for anyone to gaze upon without admiration. Surprised and confused, I hastily, but gently, withdrew myself from his arms, and in a faltering voice I demanded—

"'Ah! where are the cowardly villains by whom I was robbed and insulted?'

" ' I was attracted to this spot, fair lady,' replied the stranger, in accents of kindness and respect, which immediately made a favourable impression on me—' I was attracted to this spot by the cries you uttered for help, and, on arriving at it, found you struggling in the arms of two men, at whom I fired, but without the shot taking effect, and they instantly released you from their hold, and took to flight. I am a stranger in this part of the country, staying for a brief period at the inn in the town; but I am most happy to think that I was fortunate enough to be near the spot at the time when you so much needed assistance from the power of villains of evidently such desperate character.'

" During the time that he was speaking, my heart fluttered with a nameless emotion, and I scarcely knew what answer to make; but at length I said—

" ' Oh! sir, I know not how to return to you my thanks for the service you have rendered me. Had it not been for your timely arrival to my rescue, Heaven only knows what would have become of me in the hands of such heartless miscreants. I can but express to you my gratitude.'

" ' And may I make bold enough to inquire who is the fair being whom it has been my good fortune to rescue?' he interrogated, anxiously, and fixing upon me a look of admiration, but at the same time of respect. I blushed still more deeply than before, and hesitated what reply to make; but his manner and appearance inspired me with confidence, and at length I said—

" ' I am but a poor, friendless girl, sir, residing not far from here; business having called me to a town a mile or two from hence, I was detained longer than I had expected to be, and was overtaken by the darkness in this lonely and unfrequented spot, when I was attacked by these ruffians, who robbed me of what trifle I had about me, and grossly insulted me likewise.'

" He seemed to dwell with pleasure upon every word that I uttered, and his eyes continued fixed upon my countenance with an expression which I could not misunderstand, and which increased my confusion.

" ' The cowardly miscreants!' he said at length. ' Could they have no respect for your sex? But it was most providential that accident led me hither, and I shall ever reflect upon the circumstance with feelings of satisfaction. But there may still be danger while we linger here. Allow me to see you to your dwelling, fair damsel—that is, if you are not afraid to entrust yourself to the protection of a stranger.'

" It was impossible that I could refuse this polite and reasonable request, though I could not but feel the utmost confusion and emotion in the company of the handsome stranger; and allowing him to take my arm, we moved from the spot, and proceeded to some distance on the way to my cottage, without making use of any observation, though my heart fluttered all the time with a sensation which was entirely new to me, and I could not help considering my deliverer one of the most handsome and prepossessing young men I had ever seen.

" At length he became more free, and entered into conversation with me in the most familiar, but at the same time respectful manner, and put several questions to me, which I answered with diffidence; but there was something in his manner which satisfied me he was a perfect gentleman, and I could not resist a wish which I felt to become better acquainted with him. Fatal prepossession! How dearly has it cost me! In the course of the conversation I elicited from him that he was a gentleman who had been on a visit to London, and was now returning to his seat in a distant part of the country: that himself and an only sister, two or three years his senior, had been left orphans some time before, and that his name was Charles Cecil. I treasured all these things in my memory as though I had something particular depending upon them, though for why I did so I never stopped to inquire of myself, and it was not at all likely I should ever behold him again, and shortly afterwards we arrived at my cottage-door.

" ' Dear lady,' said Charles, after having respectfully raised my hand to his lips, ' I shall probably not leave the inn where I am at present staying for two or three days, and may I not be permitted to call upon you, to pay my respects to you, and inquire after your health?'

" I hesitated. This was a delicate question to put to a young girl placed in my situation, and I scarcely knew how to answer. But surely there was nothing unreasonable in the request from one who had rendered me such an important service, and whose manners convinced me that he was a perfect gentleman and a man of honour, and at length I timidly gave my consent; and appearing highly delighted with my compliance, he returned his thanks to me, bade me good-night, and immediately afterwards he departed, and I re-entered the cottage, in a very different state of mind to that which I had before experienced. I threw myself on a seat, and resigned myself entirely to the various thoughts which the events of the evening had created in my breast, and every moment my agitation increased.

"As I said before, I could not but consider Charles Cecil one of the handsomest and most interesting men I had ever seen; my heart felt grateful to him for the service he had rendered me, and I was anxious to behold him again. I remembered every word he had uttered to me, every look he had fixed upon me, and my heart fluttered with emotion as I did so, and I was unable to account for the extraordinary feelings he had excited in my breast. Love had hitherto been a stranger to my heart, or I should have known that the first seeds of that passion were already planted in my breast, and had my experience of the world caused me to penetrate his real character, I should have seen at once the brink of the fearful precipice on which I stood, and have avoided it in time. But, alas! how little did I then dream the fate which was in store for me. But I felt surprised that one whom I had never seen before should create such a powerful interest in my breast, and I almost regretted that I had given him permission to visit me again, and I could not but imagine that, considering all the circumstances of my situation, I had acted with some imprudence. On my retiring to my chamber for the night, the form of Cecil still continued to haunt my imagination, and the longer I reflected on him the more my admiration of him increased, and the higher opinion did I form of his character. When I slept, I dreamt of him, and he seemed in this remarkably short space of time to have taken entire possession of my soul.

"I awoke in the morning, anxious and restless, and I took more than usual pains with my toilette that morning, though I scarcely knew for what reason I did so; and I still felt in a state of the greatest anxiety and perturbation.

"The day passed away, and Cecil did not again make his appearance, and I felt vexed and disappointed, for I could not help thinking that he had only made the request of me in a moment of thoghtlessness, and would think no more about it. But the idea that I should never see him again, caused me a pang of anguish and regret which I could not restrain, and I could not entirely make up my mind to it. Alas! it would have been fortunate for me had my fears been realised, for I should not have suffered those pangs of sorrow

and remorse which it is now my lot to experience, and I might have looked back upon my past life without the feelings of regret and self-reproach. But Fate had set its spell upon me, and it seemed as though it were impossible that I could escape the destiny that was in store for me.

"I rested but little that night, and various were the thoughts that crowded upon my brain, and rendered me doubtful, uneasy, and miserable. And yet why should one who was a stranger to me make so remarkable and powerful an impression upon my mind? Why should I be so anxious to see him again? I was at a loss to answer these queries, though it was not long ere I was destined to understand them too well, and to acknowledge their influence, though I had not the power to resist them.

"The next day my agitation had rather increased than abated, and I sat by the window of my cottage, and looked anxiously on the road beyond, with the hope of seeing the object who so fully occupied my thoughts approaching. In this manner two or three hours passed away, and still Cecil came not, and I now began to give up all thoughts of seeing him in despair, when I suddenly beheld the form of a man emerge from round a corner, and on approaching nearer, I distinguished that it was Charles Cecil. I need not attempt to describe to you what my feelings were, and I hastily withdrew from the window, and endeavoured to compose my feelings, and to conceal my confusion, previous to his arriving at the cottage. In this I succeeded much better than I could have expected, and soon afterwards he knocked at the door, and I opened it and admitted him with a trembling hand. I cast my eyes to the floor, and feared to look up at him on his entrance; but he greeted me with the utmost kindness and respect, and at the sound of his voice I trembled more violently than before, and I scarcely know what answer I returned.

"'I have to apologise, Miss Amy,' he observed, 'for not having called upon you yesterday, for I was anxious to see you to inquire whether you had recovered from the fright you had received on the previous evening; but I had some particular business to attend to, and that prevented me. However, I am most happy now to perceive that it has been productive of no ill-effects.'

"I thanked him as well as I could, and he then seated himself, remained silent for a few minutes, though whenever I ventured to raise my eyes towards him, I perceived that he was gazing at me with looks of admiration, and that could not fail to increase the emotion which fluttered at my heart; but I gradually became more composed by the delicacy and gallantry of his manner, and I awaited him to commence the conversation with some degree of anxiety.

"'I am afraid, Miss Amy,' he said at last, 'that you will consider me bold and intrusive in thus calling upon you, stranger as I am to you. But I assure you that I do so with the utmost respect, and I could not resist the desire which I had to see you at least once again, before I quit this neighbourhood, which I expect will be in a day or two at the farthest.'

"'There needs no apology, sir,' I replied, in a timid voice, ' and I cannot but feel happy in seeing my preserver from outrage, and thus have the opportunity afforded me of expressing to him my warmest acknowledgments for the service he has rendered me.'

"He seemed pleased at my observation, and immediately replied—

"'Indeed, fair lady, all acknowledgments for the little I have done are quite unnecessary, and I shall ever esteem it as one of the most fortunate events of my life when I was able to rescue one so young and innocent from a situation of such imminent danger. Should circumstances at any future time cause me to take up my residence in this neighbourhood, may I hope that myself and my sister may have the honour of your friendship?"

"This was a question which I was at a loss at first to answer, and I hesitated; but at length I mustered resolution, and said—

"'Ah, sir, I fear that a gentleman placed in the situation of society in which you are, would but ill become himself were he to accept the friendship of a poor girl like me. It is an honour that I must not aspire to, although I will acknowledge that from the obligation which I am under to you, I cannot help remembering you with esteem.'

"'You entertain too humble an opinion of yourself, Amy,' he returned; 'virtues and accomplishments such as I am certain you possess, entitle their owner to the friendship and regard of the most proud and wealthy; and I cannot but hope that the time will come when we shall be more intimately acquainted.'

"He fixed his eyes still more earnestly on my countenance as he gave utterance to these words, as though he would penetrate my every thought: I felt more embarrassed, and was at a loss what answer to make. But still his manner, and the observations he made use of, imparted a sensation to me which I had never before experienced, and I could not help dwelling with a feeling almost approaching to rapture upon every word he uttered. By degrees, however, my confusion somewhat diminished, and the captivating and varied description of his conversation, coupled with the respectful language in which it was couched, gradually won upon me, and I discoursed as freely with him as if we had been acquainted with each other for years. The loneliness of my situation excited some remarks from him, and he elicited from me, in the course of conversation, the particulars of my simple history, with which he seemed to be deeply interested; and I could not but perceive that his admiration for me increased—a conviction which, I am bound in truth and candour to acknowledge, imparted to me a feeling of the utmost gratification. And yet I could not but consider that my situation was a most delicate one, and that, should it become known to any of my neighbours that I had given encouragement to the visits of a young gentleman who was almost a stranger to me, it might give subject for the voice of Scandal, and be the cause of much annoyance and uneasiness to me hereafter. Yet surely I could not be so much to blame in granting him the simple request to pay his respects to me after the important service he had rendered me; and no harm could arise from it when he was so shortly about to quit the neighbourhood, and it was not at all likely that I should ever behold him again. The latter thought caused in my breast a feeling which it would, perhaps, be wrong in me to call by any other name than regret, and I could not help secretly hoping that something might ere long occur to bring us together again, and to make us better acquainted; though, from the difference of the station, I supposed, that we held in society, I feared that there was very little probability of that. Fatal prepossession! Oh! could I have foreseen the fearful consequences it would have been productive of, I would have struggled with my feelings, and stifled it in my breast. Could I but have read the real character of Cecil, how different would have been the sentiments I entertained towards him! But young, inexperienced, and unsuspicious as I was, how was it likely that I should do so? And thus did he possess every advantage over me, which he no doubt soon perceived, and immediately determined to avail himself of it at the earliest and every opportunity.

"He remained for two or three hours at my cottage, and seemed loath to depart. We by degrees conversed with less reserve upon a variety of subjects, and I was surprised and fascinated by the extent of his knowledge, and the depth and force of the arguments he made use of. I could have listened to him for ever, and he unconsciously won upon me every word he uttered. Oh, Charles—Charles! why were you formed so well to deceive, and to lead the minds of those upon whom you had unfortunately fixed your nefarious designs astray? Alas—alas! why did Fate ever cause us to meet, since by so doing it has been the cause of all that has befallen me, and the heavy sorrow which is at present corroding my heart?

"At length he arose to take his leave; and after expressing the great pleasure and gratification he had experienced in my society, and his regret at being compelled so soon to leave the neighbourhood, he requested that I would grant him permission to visit me once more before his departure. I hesitated, but still my heart pleaded in his favour; and never for an instant suspecting that any harm could come of it, I gave my consent, and having raised my hand respectfully to his lips, and fixed upon me such a look as I could never afterwards forget, he took his leave. I returned into the cottage, and placing myself at the window, I watched his fine, manly form, until it was completely out of sight, while my feelings were in that state of agitation which I never remember them to have been before. I recalled to my mind every observation he had made use of—the expression of every look that he had fixed upon me; and as I did so, my emotion gradually increased, and now that he had departed, I felt more lonely and wretched than I ever remember to have done before. Certainly, I could not help thinking him one of the most amiable and agreeable young men that I had ever seen before; and a suspicion that such a thing as hypocrisy formed any portion of his character, never for a moment entered my breast; and I would have treated those with scorn and reproach, as falsely prejudiced persons, who might have hinted such a thing to me. Alas! at that time he appeared to my eyes all perfection, and most deeply did I regret that the time must so quickly arrive for him to leave the neighbourhood, for I did not think it was at all likely, from the distance he resided, that I should ever see him again.

"And yet I could not help blushing, and even secretly chiding myself, when I reflected upon the powerful impression which this young gentleman had made upon me; though at that time I was at a loss thoroughly to understand the meaning of the feelings that had taken possession of my breast. My heart overflowed with gratitude to him for the services he had rendered me in rescuing me from the power of the robbers; for, had it not been for his timely and fortunate arrival at the spot, and the courage and determination he had displayed, there could be little doubt as to the fate which would have befallen me.

"The remainder of that day passed dismally away with me, for now that Cecil was not present, and I could no longer listen to the charms of his conversation, I felt truly miserable. It was, indeed, most astonishing that he should have been able to make such a powerful impression upon me in so short a time, and I was unable to account for it; but every moment the feeling gained more and more strength, and all other thoughts but such as were connected with him were banished from my mind.

"I retired earlier than I was accustomed to do to my chamber, but my mind was too busily occupied to suffer me for some time to sleep, and when I did so, the form of Cecil was constantly presented to my imagination; and all he had said was repeated in my ears as plainly as when he had given utterance to it. I arose in the morning restless and dissatisfied, and scarcely knowing what to do. It seemed to me as though I had been guilty of something culpable, and yet I tried in vain to recollect any part of my conduct which was deserving of censure. Surely there could be nothing wrong in entertaining feelings of esteem and gratitude towards one who had rescued me from outrage, and who had probably been the means of preserving my life; and it was not at all likely that anything serious could arise from my encouraging these feelings. Alas! could I but have penetrated to the real character of him in whom I was so deeply interested, I should have seen at once the danger by which I was surrounded, and prudence and virtue would have snatched me from the brink of the precipice on which I stood; but, unfortunately, it was my fate to experience the most poignant anguish, shame, and disappointment, and I had no friend at hand to counsel and forewarn me, or I might have been saved from that which afterwards befel me.

"My mind was in a constant state of

anxiety and suspense the following day, for I expected to have seen Cecil again; but he did not make his appearance, and I began to think that he had repented of the promise he had made, when he ascertained the humbleness of my position, and that he would not condescend to visit me again. I could not but feel vexed and mortified as these thoughts occurred to me; but I quickly banished them from my mind, and tried to hope that he would not fail to keep his word, more especially from the pleasure he had expressed and evinced at our last interview; but still why I should be so anxious upon the subject, I was at a loss exactly to understand. I tried to divert my attention from the subject, which had so completely engrossed it for the last day or two, by reading; but it was all to no purpose that I did so, for my thoughts were too fully occupied with the image of Cecil, to suffer them to dwell on anything else, and I threw the book aside in disgust, and resigned myself entirely to the reflections that crowded so rapidly and so tumultuously upon my brain. But why should I thus tediously dwell upon that which can be in no way interesting to you, my dear friends, and which can only serve to create in my own breast feelings of the deepest regret and self-reproach?

"The next morning I was seated by the parlour window of my cottage, and, buried in deep ruminations, was gazing listlessly at the scenery before me, when, happening to cast my eyes anxiously in the direction of the road, I beheld Cecil approaching the cottage. A heavy weight seemed to be removed from my mind, and my heart palpitated violently; but I withdrew from the window lest he should see me, and endeavoured in some measure to regain my composure previous to his arrival at the cottage. This, however, was no easy task to accomplish, and I am certain that he must have perceived the agitation and embarrassment of my manner on his entering the room. He greeted me with the greatest gallantry and respect; and I returned it as well as I could, though my heart fluttered as I did so. I could not help thinking that he looked handsomer than ever, and that his manners were, if possible, more fascinating, and by degrees I felt less restraint, and entered more freely into conversation with him, and he seemed to dwell with feelings of the most unaffected pleasure upon all that I said. He informed me that he had found it necessary to defer his departure from the inn at which he was at present staying, for a week or a fortnight, and hoped that he might frequently be permitted to pay his

respects to me during that interval. This announcement afforded me the greatest satisfaction, and I could not conceal from Cecil's observation, I am certain, the pleasure I felt. I replied however, as well as I could, and remarked that I could not feel otherwise than highly complimented by the polite attention which Mr. Cecil paid me.

"A smile of satisfaction beamed upon his countenance as I made use of these observations, and he being now encouraged, entered more familiarly into conversation with me than he had ever done before; and I replied to him with less timidity and bashfulness of demeanour. Oh, had I but imagined the danger in which I had placed myself, how quickly should I have endeavoured to extricate myself from it; but a spell, some strange infatuation had taken possession of me, and it seemed as though nothing whatever could save me from the gulph of ruin and misery upon the brink of which I was standing. His conversation charmed me more than ever, and the time had never appeared to fly so quickly, though Cecil seemed to be in no hurry to go, and I could not by any means find the resolution of hinting to him the propriety of his doing so. But throughout the whole time his manners were most respectful, and there was nothing at all in his language or demeanour that could offend the most delicate or fastidious person, or give rise to the slightest suspicion as to the base and hypocritical part he was acting. From his conversation it was evident to me that he had seen an immense deal more of the world than could have been expected for one so young, and one thing likewise was certain, that he had amply profited by the experience he had had, and improved and cultivated his mind by it. Certainly, as I said before, he was one of the most accomplished young men that I had ever seen, and it will therefore, perhaps, not be altogether a matter of surprise to you that he should have made such a powerful impression upon me; although our acquaintance with each other had been for so brief a period.

"In the course of the conversation he took the opportunity of highly eulogizing the character of his sister, whom he represented as one of the most gentle and amiable of beings; and expressed his conviction that I only wanted to behold her to be charmed with her. He also hoped that, at some future period, he might have an opportunity of introducing us to each other, adding that he was certain his dear sister, Clarissa, would be delighted in cultivating the friendship of so charming a young lady as Miss Amy.

"Cecil, as you will perceive, well knew how to flatter, and unsuspicious and inexperienced as I was, it is not to be wondered that it should have all the fatal effect upon me that he wished it to have. I felt completely fascinated, and could only reply by my blushes, and the expression of my eyes, which, however, spoke a language that he too well understood, and which, no doubt, afforded him room for the greatest exultation, and which encouraged him to persevere in the guilty designs he had formed in his own mind. When he departed that day, he had left an impression upon my heart of a far more powerful and irresistible description than before, and it would have been all to no purpose at that time, however much I might have called reason to my aid, to have endeavoured to restrain it. I only looked forward to the time when he should depart from the neighbourhood in which I resided, and to the probability that we might never meet again, with the utmost anguish and anxiety; and I dreaded it to approach. Such was the unfortunate state of my feelings at that period, and which led to all the fatal circumstances that afterwards befel me, and which I am about to relate to you. But I must claim your indulgence for a short time, while I collect my thoughts, and endeavour to compose myself for the task I have imposed upon myself."

Our hero and his wife could, of course, raise no objection to this, and Amy retired from the room, leaving them deeply interested by what she had related, and most anxious to hear the remainder. They were not long kept in suspense; for in a few minutes Amy returned to the room, and being now apparently fully prepared for her task, and quite composed, in a short time she resumed her eventful and interesting story, in nearly the same words as the reader will find it in the next chapter.

CHAPTER XXXVIII.

THE TALE CONTINUED.—THE TRIUMPH OF GUILT.—THE FEARFUL DISCOVERY.—THE COINERS.

"Not a day passed over after this during his stay in that part of the country, without Cecil calling to visit me, and passing several hours in my company, and I began to feel little or no restraint in his society, but to look upon him as an old and particular friend, and I felt unhappy when he was absent. He entered more fully into family matters; again eulogized his sister in the most glowing terms; described the beauty of his paternal estate, and the romantic scenery by which it was surrounded, and expressed a hope that he should yet have the unspeakable pleasure of receiving me there as the guest of himself and his sister, adding that she would be really delighted in having such a charming companion, and that he was certain I should never again fancy my present solitary life, when I had once experienced so great a change.

"All this appeared so reasonable that I could offer not the least objection to it, and secretly I could not help entertaining a wish that an opportunity might soon be afforded me of testing the truth of Cecil's statement.

"At length the day prior to the one on which Cecil was to take his departure arrived, and it was one of the greatest uneasiness and anxiety to me. I could now no longer deny to myself that Cecil had made a much more tender and powerful impression upon my heart than such as could be caused by mere esteem and gratitude; and I could not but give every encouragement to the passion which had so insidiously stolen into my breast. The looks, the demeanour of Cecil too, and the observations that frequently inadvertently escaped him, convinced me that the feelings he entertained towards me were of a warmer and more enthusiastic nature than those caused by admiration, and created a most pleasurable sensation in my breast. Could this be love? I asked myself. Oh, yes, it appeared but too evident to me, even unacquainted as I was with the tender passion, that it was, and my heart throbbed with emotion as the thought occurred to me. But of what use was it my encouraging that fatal passion, when our stations in life were so different, and we were so soon about to be separated, most probably never to see each other again? The idea seemed to be preposterous, and it made me truly wretched. I found it impossible to conquer my emotion in the presence of Cecil, and it was evident that he observed it, and understood its meaning, and an expression of satisfaction passed over his features which I could not help remarking.

"'Dear Miss Amy,' he said, after a short pause, during which time he seemed to have been consulting with himself how it would be best for him to express what he wished; 'I cannot sufficiently explain to you the regret I feel at being about to separate from that fair being from whom I have derived so much pleasure, and by

THE ROBBERS DISPUTING ABOUT THE BOOTY.

whose friendship and esteem I feel so highly honoured.'

"'Mr. Cecil,' I replied, timidly and modestly, 'I am unused to flatter or to be flattered, but this I may be permitted to say, that I have felt extremely honoured by the friendship you have bestowed upon so humble an individual as myself, and the polite attention you have shown towards me. Mr. Cecil must always possess my esteem and gratitude, though it is most improbable that we shall ever meet again.'

"'Oh, say not so, Amy!' ejaculated Cecil, with more warmth than I had yet heard him express himself with; 'never meet again! There is something in that thought which is repugnant to my feelings, and I would discard it from me altogether. I trust that we shall not only meet again, and that I shall have the opportunity of introducing you to my dear sister, but tha .

something will occur to cement that friendship that accident has introduced between us.'

"This was rather a difficult speech to reply to, and I was bewildered, and hesitated; but at length I returned such an answer as prudence dictated, though my feelings were of a far more warmer nature. Cecil lingered as long as he could, and seemed loth to depart, and the agitation of my mind might have been fully observed in the expression of my countenance. I felt such dismal forebodings and such a depression of spirits, that I could scarcely contain myself; but at length the painful moment arrived, and Cecil in a melancholy tone of voice, and looking tenderly in my face, said—

"'The time has arrived, Amy, when I must say the ward adieu, and believe me when I assure you that I have never done so with feelings of deeper regret. May I hope that when I am gone, Amy Parker will sometimes bestow one friendly thought upon him?'

"'Believe me, Mr. Cecil,' I answered, 'that, as I have before assured you, I shall ever remember your name with respect, gratitude, and friendship.'

"'Oh, thanks for this,' said Cecil, fervently, and with apparent sincerity; 'but there is still another favour that I would ask of you.'

"'Name it, sir,' I requested, in a timid voice, and with my eyes partially cast towards the ground; 'if there is nothing unreasonable in what you require, I shall feel myself bound, under all the circumstances, to grant it.'

"'This is indeed most kind,' he returned; then, after a minute or two's hesitation, he added, at the same time taking my hand, he produced something from his waistcoat pocket, 'take this simple ring; it is of little value, but still the motive that prompts the giver is all the same. Will the fair and gentle Amy condescend to wear it for my sake, and as a mark of my esteem, when we shall probably be separated by many, many miles?'

"How my heart palpitated at this unexpected request, and I trembled so violently with the emotion of my feelings, and blushed so deeply, that Cecil could not but observe it.

"'Mr. Cecil,' I at length replied in a faltering voice, 'believe me, that it is out of no feeling of disrespect that I beg to decline this handsome gift; I need nothing whatever to remind me of the respect that is due to the preserver of my life in all probability.'

"'Nay, then,' he returned, with a look of disappointment, 'you decline this simple token of my regard, Miss Parker, and, therefore, seem to entertain a doubt as to the motives with which it is given. I regret that I have been unable to impress you with a better opinion of me.'

"'Oh! no, Mr. Cecil,' I returned, hastily, and with considerable emotion. "You wrong me greatly if you think that I entertain any such opinion of you as that which you have insinuated. I should, indeed, be ungrateful and uncharitable, did I judge you thus. I—I will accept your proffered gift, to remove all doubts from your mind, and I will ever treasure it most carefully as a mark of friendship and esteem.'

"His countenance brightened with satisfaction as I spoke these words, and taking my hand, he placed on my finger a handsome diamond ring; then raising my hand to his lips, he kissed it with the utmost fervour, yet respect. What my feelings were during this time you may easily imagine, and it was a wonder how I could conduct myself with the composure I did. But at length the important moment arrived, and we parted, and I fully expected never to see Cecil again. Had I, indeed, never done so, what indescribable misery would it have saved me! Having watched his receding form till it was hidden from my view in the distance, I threw myself on a seat, and covering my face with my hands, I burst into a violent paroxysm of sobs and tears. The whole truth was now out: he loved me, and I loved him in return; but misery and despair fell upon my heart when I thought of the improbability of our ever meeting again. I now, for the first time in my life, knew what it was to experience a sincere, yet apparently hopeless passion; and the power of my emotions was almost greater than I could support. I saw at once that this was only the commencement of my troubles, though what the nature of those troubles might be I had not the means of forming the slightest conjecture of. I could never for a moment doubt the honour of Cecil, whom I believed to be all that could be good and to be admired in mortal being, and that he could not harbour a single thought which might be to the prejudice of his fellow creatures. Oh, how fearfully—how cruelly was I deceived in him!

"The longer I reflected, the more the anguish of my feelings increased, and the greater became my fears that I should never more behold that dear object who had made so powerful an impression upon my heart, and whom I now felt to be so necessary to my happiness. I pressed the ring he had given me again and again to my lips, and my tears flowed faster than ever, though they afforded some relief to my overcharged bosom. That night, you may depend upon it, sleep never once came to my relief, and the morning found me in a most deplorable and melancholy state, which was the more insupportable to bear as I had no one to whom I could communicate my thoughts, or receive from them advice and consolation. In this dismal manner, day after day passed away, and without any change taking place in my prospects, or anything occurring to inspire me with hope, and my hopeless passion increased in strength instead of diminishing. I became so ill that I could with difficulty leave my chamber; and had it not been for the few pounds I had by me, but which were getting very short, I know not what would have become of me. My thoughts were continually fixed on Cecil, and many were the tears I shed when I remembered the amiable qualities he seemed to possess, and his fascinating manners; and fervent were the prayers I offered up to Heaven for his preservation from every danger, and that we might meet again. The observations that Cecil had made use of on our parting were ever fresh in my memory, and, in spite of everything, I could not but think at times that something would yet occur to cause us to meet again, and that, notwithstanding the obstacles that seemed to be at present thrown in the way, not only might we freely indulge in the sentiments we entertained towards each other, but that we might also look forward with the most sanguine expectations to the consummation of our hopes of happiness.

"The secluded life which I had hitherto led, and in which I had felt so sad an enjoyment, since the death of my parents, now became irksome to me; and I would frequently be away from home for hours together, and ramble about I scarcely knew whither, for my mind was completely occupied with the most gloomy and torturing thoughts, and I was generally quite unconscious of everything around me.

It was on one of these occasions that I had been wandering ever since the morning, and at an advanced period of the afternoon I found myself in a romantic but lonely spot, a considerable distance from home.

"The day was very hot and sultry, but independently of that, I felt tired and faint from the distance I had walked, and as there was no one near the spot to interrupt me, I seated myself on a small mound

beneath the shade of two or three trees, and in spite of all my endeavours to arouse myself from it, sleep gradually stole over me, and I remembered no more for some time.

"When I again awoke, I was astonished and alarmed to find that it was completely dark, and being unacquainted with the immediate locality in which I was, I was afraid that I should find it a difficult matter to be able to retrace my footsteps towards home; and I knew not by what danger I might not be surrounded, in such a dreary place as the one in which I was. I now blamed myself for having been so thoughtless as to wander so far, but there was no time for these reflections; it was evidently very late, and all that I could do was to proceed in the best manner I could, and endeavour to find my way into the main road, when I might probably proceed without much difficulty or fear of danger. I looked around me with a sensation of alarm, but I could perceive no one near me, and taking fresh courage, I proceeded as fast as I could in what I imagined to be the right direction, though I was very uncertain about it.

"I suppose I had walked on in this way without any interruption for about a quarter of an hour or twenty minutes; but I saw no further chance of discovering the right track than I did at first, and all was dark and dismal around me. I paused, and consulted within myself what was best to be done; but without being able to hit upon any plan; and, therefore, mustering up all the resolution I could, I once more hurried on my way. I was just about to emerge from a dismal avenue of trees, by which I had been for some time traversing, when I was suddenly startled by hearing the indistinct sound of footsteps upon the grass, and almost immediately afterwards three men crossed my path, and brought me to a dead stand-still, with astonishment and terror. Before, however, I had time to utter a single word, one of the men advanced towards me, and opening a lantern which he carried in his hand, the light gleamed full upon my face, and in a voice of mingled satisfaction and surprise, he exclaimed,—

"'Ah! by all that's fortunate, it's the very girl we seek! 'Tis Amy Parker!'

"His companions now also gave expression to an exclamation of astonishment; and I then perceived that they were all three coarse and powerful looking men, two of them having stout bludgeons in their hands, and the other being armed with a gun. You may imagine my feelings at this moment, but I was so completely taken by surprise that I was rivetted to the spot, and for a minute or two could not give utterance to a syllable. The men, however, did not suffer me to remain silent or inactive long, for advancing towards me, and rudely grasping my wrist, one of them observed,—

"'Ah! this is most fortunate! We have been looking for you at your cottage, young woman, and were rather disappointed at not finding you at home; however, this accidental meeting makes up for it. You must go with us.'

"'Oh, God!' I exclaimed, trembling with terror; 'what mean you? Who are you? and what can possibly be your business with me, unless it be robbery?'

"'No,' answered the man who had before spoken, 'that don't happen to be it this time; but it is no use for us to enter into any explanation here. You will know everything before long. Come, we must away.'

"I shrieked aloud for help as the ruffians seized me, and struggled to release myself; but as you may well imagine, my efforts were all quite useless, and throwing a large cloak over my head they stifled my cries and hurried me along. Overcome by the terror of my feelings, as you may very well imagine, I fainted, and remember no more till I found myself being carried along at a rapid rate, and rubbing my eyes, and looking eagerly around me, you may judge of my unspeakable astonishment to find myself the occupant of a closed vehicle of some description, and which was proceeding as fast, apparently, as the horses could convey it.

"At first my brain was so confused, and I was so excessively alarmed at this unexpected and fearful change in my situation, that I did not notice that there was anybody but myself in the carriage; but I now perceived that a form, which, as near as the faint light would permit me to distinguish, was that of a man, was sitting opposite to me. On finding that I was restored to consciousness, he came over to me, and without any further ceremony took his seat by my side, and attempted to encircle my waist with his arm. I uttered a loud scream, and drew back in terror, when he said—

"'Be not alarmed, beauteous Amy, for you are with one who loves you too well to harm you,"

"'Gracious Heaven!' I exclaimed, starting and gazing eagerly towards the speaker; 'that voice! it is——'

"'Cecil!' he added, and revealing himself more distinctly to me; 'that Cecil who has been so fortunate as to obtain your friendship and esteem, but who would gain your love in return for that he entertains so ardently for you, and who——'

"'Oh, villain! villain!' I interrupted, tears at the same time streaming from my eyes.

"'Nay, Amy,' he returned, 'it is not so; you judge me too severely, and accuse me of being that which I am not. It is the fervour of my love, and the fear of not being able to overcome your objections, that have alone urged me to this desperate course. But you have nothing to fear. I would merely convey you to a place of safety where I——'

"I heard not the finish of the sentence, for my fears again overcame me, and I once more became totally insensible.

"When I recovered, my situation was again changed, and I could scarcely believe the evidence of my senses, though my brain was so bewildered that I almost imagined all that had happened to me to be some frightful dream; but I was soon convinced to the contrary. I now found myself in bed, in a strange room, and a lamp glimmering on a table which was placed behind the curtains. At first I thought there was no one in the room besides myself; but raising myself in the bed, I perceived a middle-aged woman, who seemed to have been seated at the table. On seeing that I was restored to consciousness, she advanced to the side of the bed, and inquired how I was?

"'Ah!' I exclaimed, with breathless eagerness, 'who puts that question? Where am I? and what has brought me here?'

"'You are the inmate of an inn, not much frequented by strangers,' answered my unknown companion; 'as for the other part of your question, Mr. Cecil will probably explain to you by-and-by.'

"The whole fearful truth now rushed upon my recollection, and clasping my hands tohether, I groaned in the intense agony and terror of my feelings.

"'Gracious Heaven!' I cried, 'and is it possible that any one can have dared to commit this brutal outrage? Oh, Cecil, how have I been deceived in your character! But I will not remain here! Let me begone! You dare not seek to detain me!'

"'Nay, my poor girl,' said the woman who was in attendance upon me, in rather persuasive and gentle accents, 'you had better be calm, and see what expostulation and remonstrance will effect. I do not believe that any harm is intended you.'

"'Then why am I thus torn from my humble dwelling?' I demanded, 'and that, too, by the command of him whom I thought was the last man from whom I had cause to apprehend any danger? Tell me, I beseech you, who is he?'

"'I know nothing of him,' answered the woman, 'than from seeing him stop here on two or three occasions, and that his name is Cecil; but I believe that he is a gentleman.'

"'He is a villain!' I exclaimed, vehemently, and unable to control my feelings, 'or he could never have been guilty of such a deed as this, and towards one who had been induced to place every confidence in him, and did not believe him capable of such an atrocity. But I will not remain her, I say again,' I added, spring from the bed on which I had been reclining in my clothes, 'who shall dare to detain me here against my will?'

"'Pray, young lady,' said my attendant, 'do try to be more patient, and you may perhaps obtain your wishes. I will, with your permission, make Mr. Cecil acquainted with your recovery, and probably he will then see you, and enter into a satisfactory explanation of his conduct.'

"'A satisfactory explanation!' I repeated, indignantly, 'and think you it is possible for him to do that? But I must, and will see him, and demand from him that atonement which it is necessary he should make for the outrage he has committed against me.'

"'Very well,' replied the woman, 'I will inform him of your wish, and will return shortly with his answer; but in the meantime you must remain here'

"I made no reply, for I was too much agitated, and my heart was too full to suffer me to do so; and the attendant quitted the room, fastening the door after her, and leaving me to my own meditations.

"For a few minutes after she was gone, I was so agitated that I could not collect or arrange my thoughts. Was it possible, I at last reflected, that Cecil could so heartlessly deceive me? Was this indeed the man who had gained such a stronghold on my affections, and whom I had thought so good, so amiable, so honourable? It could not be; it seemed to me like some torturing dream; but little did I even then imagine how soon I was to be convinced of its reality. What could his motives be when he could adopt the determined, the heartless, and unlawful course he had taken? What regard could he have to my feelings, or my character? And what must be his real principles when he could have any connexion with ruffians such as those who had seized me? I

shuddered to think; and yet such was the influence which he had contrived to obtain over my heart, that, in spite of all that had happened, I felt that I could forgive him, if I was satisfied with the explanation he had to give me. Still, if he really loved me, ought he not to have confessed that passion in an honourable way, and depended on me for a favourable reception of his vows? Oh, yes, view it even in the most lenient light I could, his conduct was, to say the least of it, most reprehensible, and I was at a loss to imagine what excuse he could make.

"These reflections passed rapidly and tumultuously in my mind during the time the woman was absent, and I remained in a state of the greatest uncertainty, uneasiness, and suspense until her return. I went to the window, which I tried, but found it strongly secured, and that increased my alarm and suspicion. The scene which met my observation was wild and cheerless, and in the distance I caught a view of the ocean. I saw several persons passing and repassing, but all seemed to be intent on business, and if they had not been it was not likely that I could draw their attention to me, or expect any assistance from them, and even if I might I should have hesitated to have done so, until I had seen Cecil, and had some explanation from him, for even now I could not persuade myself that he would act towards me in the dishonourable manner that the present rash course he had adopted might induce me to believe. Alas! it was that want of suspicion, that fatal confidence which led to my destruction. At length the woman returned to the room, bringing some refreshments, and to my eager inquiries she replied,—

"'Mr. Cecil sincerely regrets that he should have put you to any inconvenience, Miss, but he has requested me to assure you that you need not alarm yourself, as no harm is intended you, and in a short time he will have the honour of an interview with you, when he hopes to be able to explain everything to your satisfaction.'

"'Oh, how can he do that?' I ejaculated, 'what can ever excuse the conduct he has pursued towards me? It is most cruel, it is most unjust.'

"'Do not condemn him unheard, Miss,' returned my attendant; 'for I feel certain that he will be able fully to justify his conduct.'

"'Justify his conduct towards one who is almost a stranger to him, towards a poor friendless girl, of whose lonely and unprotected situation, he has taken such an unlawful advantage?' I answered. 'Oh, how utterly ridiculous it is to talk thus; it is impossible that he can do so. Little did I expect from what I had previously seen of him, and the plausibility of his manners, that he could never have acted as he has done. Alas! my dear parents, I feel your loss more severely now than I have ever done before.'

"I burst into tears as I thus spoke, and the woman returned no answer, but she seemed to view me with some degree of compassion, and did not offer to interrupt me by any impertinent observation. It was in vain, however, that I tried to compose my feelings, for the more I did so, the greater my anguish increased, and I awaited the appearance of Cecil in the greatest suspense.

"'And am I to be detained here a prisoner?' I at length demanded.

"'I do not suppose that you will remain here long,' answered the woman, 'but it is not likely Mr. Cecil will suffer you to return home after all the trouble he has been at to obtain possession of you.'

"'But he dare not detain me,' I returned, 'poor and friendless though I am, he dare not.'

"'Well, Miss,' said the woman, 'you had better wait with patience till you behold Mr. Cecil, and hear what he has to say to you. I have nothing to do with the business, and, therefore, cannot interfere. I will leave you to the indulgence of your own thoughts.'

"With these words she again quitted the room, and I was once more left to the solitude of my own thoughts, the nature of which I need not attempt to describe to you. About a couple of hours elapsed, without any one appearing to interrupt me, when I heard footsteps ascending the stairs, and soon afterwards the room door opened and Cecil stood before me. I darted upon him a look of indignation and reproach, and for a minute or two he seemed to be confused and abashed, and at a loss how to address me.

"'Mr. Cecil,' I at last demanded, 'what is the meaning of this outrage? Why have you dared to tear me forcibly away from my home? and why am I detained here?"

"'Dear Amy,' he replied, sinking upon one knee, and looking up in my face with an expression of mingled affection and of supplication, 'may I be permitted to crave your pardon for that to which I have been alone impelled by the ardour of the love with which you have inspired me, and the fear that you would reject my suit? Yes, beauteous Amy, from the very first moment I beheld you, my heart was taken

captive by your superior charms, and every interview that I had with you did but serve to convince me of the virtues of your mind, and to strengthen my passion. Believe me I am no hypocrite, but that I speak sincerely the sentiments of my mind. My intentions towards you are strictly honourable, and, oh, if I could but obtain from you a return of my love, I should be one of the happiest men in existence.'

"'No more,' I said, though I must confess that his words had made a great impression on me, and I could not but feel a secret pleasure to think that I had obtained possession of his heart: 'no more, Mr. Cecil. What excuse have you to offer for the conduct you have pursued towards me? What opinion have I a right to form of your intentions, in thus forcibly seizing upon me, and bearing me away I know not whither? If you would make any atonement for conduct so outrageous and entirely unwarrantable, you will immediately restore me to my humble home, and no more seek to annoy or interrupt me.'

"'Fair Amy,' he repeated after a pause, during which time he seemed to be hesitating what to say, 'again I implore your forbearance and forgiveness for what I have done, and which, I repeat, has only been caused by the violence of the love with which you have inspired me. I pitied your lonely situation, and was determined at all hazards to place you in one to which your superior virtues and accomplishments entitle you, and there would I fain endeavour to win your love, and contribute all in my power towards your happiness; but I felt satisfied that, had I made such a proposal to you, your natural timidity and delicacy of disposition would have induced you to decline it, and, therefore, was I urged to act in the manner which you consider to be so reprehensible, but from no other wish than for your future advantage and welfare. I would wish you to accompany me to my home, where I trust you will find an asylum worthy of you, and in my sister a sincere friend, companion, and adviser.'

"His manners were so candid and so plausible, and, as I have before said, he had made so powerful an impression upon me, that I confess I hesitated and scarcely knew what answer to return. Fatal irresolution! it was that which favoured his guilty designs, and led to my ultimate ruin.

"'Ah! Mr. Cecil,' I at length answered, in a faltering voice, 'what can I possibly think of one who has acted in so strange, so bold, and clandestine a manner, but that he seeks to deceive me, and has some sinister design against me?'

"'Say not so, Amy,' he returned; 'oh, surely, even after all the circumstances, it is uncharitable for you to form such an opinion of me, when again I swear that I would sooner perish than I could encourage one dishonourable thought towards you. Oh, Amy, did you but know the power of the sentiments with which you have inspired me, could you but read my heart, and discover how fondly, how firmly your dear image is stamped thereon, how different, I am convinced, must be the sentiments with which you would view me. But, alas! I see that Amy views me with scorn and abhorrence, and that conviction seals my doom, and renders me one of the most wretched beings in existence.'

"He struck his forehead in apparent despair as he gave utterance to these words, and I could not help being moved by the agitation and anguish of his manner. My heart palpitated violently against my side, and while burning blushes crimsoned my cheeks, and I trembled, I cast my eyes to the ground, as I thus replied in a faint voice—

"'Mr. Cecil, have you no consideration for the delicacy of my feelings? I must not, dare not listen to such observations as those which you have just now made use of.'

"'Heaven forbid!' he answered, with energy, 'Heaven forbid that I should say anything to offend you or to wound your feelings; ah, no! I respect you too much for that, Miss Amy; but your coldness tortures me; say that you do not hate and despise me, and I will for the present, at any rate, endeavour to be content, and to live in hopes that the time will yet come, when my conduct may induce you to view me with a much more tender sentiment.'

"Weak, foolish girl that I was! I felt my resolution failing me beneath the apparent eloquence and sincerity of his words, and I could not help replying—

"'Mr. Cecil, I should appear ungrateful were I to deny that I esteem you for the service you have rendered me; but is not your present conduct sufficient to prejudice me against you?—and what can I possibly apprehend but the worst, when you have thus forcibly seized upon my person, and refuse to restore me to my home?'

"'I implore you, Amy,' he returned, 'to suspend your judgment to the future; and believe me, dear girl, that you shall have no cause to regret the generous confidence you may repose in me. I would bear you to comfort and happiness. Try me, and I promise you—faithfully promise

you, that if you are dissatisfied, or find any cause for complaint, that I will restore you to your home, uninjured, and as innocent as you now are. Say, will you not yield to my request?'

"My resolution failed me more and more, and he must have observed it, and taken every advantage of it.

"'Alas!' I at length returned, in a faint and faltering voice, 'what can I say, delicately situated as I am? I would fain entertain the same opinion of you, Mr. Cecil, that I have hitherto done. Oh! tell me—may I, indeed, confide in your honour?'

"'You may, dear Amy,' he replied, fervently. 'If I deceive you, may the heaviest curses of offended Heaven descend upon my head! Say, then, do you consent?'

"Again I hesitated; but the earnestness and anxiety of his looks and demeanour overpowered me, and in a faint and tremulous voice I answered in the affirmative.

"'Generous condescension!' he ejaculated, in tones of rapture: 'you have made me one of the happiest of human beings; and if ever I abuse the confidence you have reposed in me, may Heaven forsake me!'

"'If I have acted imprudently,' I observed, 'I hope that Heaven will pardon me, and not allow me to suffer for my inexperience. Oh! Mr. Cecil, remember my friendless and unprotected situation, I beg of you, and do not attempt to deceive me!'

"'Never—never—by all my hopes!' he answered, energetically. 'I must, indeed, be a consummate villain could I attempt to do so. It shall be my constant study to contribute to your happiness. In an hour or two, then, we will depart from hence, and by the evening I have no doubt that we shall arrive at my mansion, where you will find my amiable sister ready to receive and welcome you.'

"Strange and fatal was the influence that he had obtained over me, and I gradually felt the confidence which I placed in the honour and integrity of his intentions increase in strength, and I listened to his conversation with a degree of pleasure which I could not conceal. He remained with me for some time longer, and by degrees I conversed with him more freely, and became more and more convinced of the nobleness of his character, and my heart throbbed with sensations that it had never experienced before. He pictured to me, in the most glowing colours, the beauty of his residence, and the amiable character of his sister; and I own that I was quite enraptured with his description, and was anxious to have an opportunity of proving the truth of what he stated. He must have perceived the impression which he had made upon my heart, and no doubt he considered his triumph was all but complete. Foolish, thoughtless girl that I was! little could I perceive the brink of destruction upon which I stood, or how well the deceiver had laid his infamous plans to betray me. At length he left me to make preparations for the resumption of our journey; and being now left alone, I gave myself up to all those thoughts that so naturally, under the peculiar circumstances in which I was placed, crowded upon my mind. One moment I blamed myself for the assent which I had given to resign myself to the protection of one who was comparatively a stranger to me, and then again I placed more confidence in him, and looked forward to the future with hope and impatience.

"'He loves me!' I said; 'he has acknowledged that he does, and in that assurance I ought to feel supremely happy. Oh, I am certain that he possesses that true nobility of soul which should win the esteem and admiration of all his fellow-creatures; and why, then, should I hesitate to acknowledge the sentiments with which he has also inspired me? And yet, why should I venture to encourage the passion which he has created in my breast, when he is placed so far above me in station, and I can never hope to become his? Alas! I am placed in a most painful and delicate situation, and scarcely know in what way to act.'

"These thoughts continued to harass and perplex my mind, and I remained in a state of doubt and fear. But at length Cecil returned, ready equipped for the journey, and informed me that a post-chaise was waiting at the door of the inn, if I felt myself in a condition to proceed. Again I hesitated, and almost regretted the compliance I had given, but Cecil, who read my feelings, quickly quieted my apprehensions, and taking my hand he led me from the room, and conducting me from the house, assisted me into the vehicle, which was standing at the door, and following himself, it was driven off at a rapid rate, and had soon got far away from the inn.

"My mind was so bewildered and agitated that for a few minutes I was quite unconscious of everything, but Cecil soon aroused me from this lethargy, and such was the tenderness and eloquence of the language he addressed to me, that it completely rivetted my attention, fascinated me, and held me in a kind of spell. I could have listened to him for ever, and

every moment greater became the power which he obtained over me. But I will not tire your patience by detailing all the particulars of the conversation which passed between us, or the artifices he made use of to accomplish his designs; it is enough for me to say that he succeeded too well, that I was too weak and credulous to withstand the arguments he made use of, and before the completion of the journey, he had drawn from my lips a fatal confession of the truth, namely, that he had created in my breast a passion as powerful as that which he professed to feel for me. His triumph was now certain! he appeared to be enraptured; again and again he embraced me, and pressed the most ardent kisses upon my lips, and I could offer no resistance to his caresses; in fact, my senses were bewildered, and I scarcely knew what I was about.

"'Beauteous Amy!' he exclaimed, 'how can I express the feelings of transport with which this fond acknowledgment has inspired me? No language could do adequate justice to them. Amy loves me, and that blessed assurance renders me one of the happiest of human beings. If ever I abuse the generous and affectionate confidence you have reposed in my honour, may the heaviest curses that can descend upon mankind, pursue me.'

"'Alas!' I sighed, passing my hands across my forehead to recall my scattered recollection, "what have I done? What has my rash tongue given utterance to? Oh, Cecil! let me recall my words, and forget that I ever spoke them, for I knew not what I said.'

"Recall your words, dearest Amy?' he replied; 'oh, not for the world, for on that assurance rests my only happiness. But I know you cannot sincerely wish to do so, for I feel confident that it came from your heart. Amy, you shall have no cause to regret the acknowledgment you have made to me, but, on the contrary, you shall find it to be my constant study to render myself worthy of your love; my only hope of happiness must in future be centred in that of Amy.'

"What could I say? There was truth and candour in his observations, and I could not for a moment doubt him. The fatal confession had passed my lips, and it was useless for me now to attempt to withdraw it, and my heart would not suffer me to do so. I had placed myself completely in his power, but, unsuspicious as I was at that time of his real character, I could not, of course, for a moment imagine the consequences that were likely to ensue from

THE WANDERERS ARRIVE AT THE ROAD-SIDE COTTAGE.

it. Rash imprudence! How bitterly have I since had cause to repent of it.

"By degrees however, as we proceeded on our journey, I became more composed, and conversed more freely with my companion, who, finding that any allusion to the sentiments which existed between us, for the present, confused and embarrassed me, with a consideration which excited my gratitude, changed the subject, and conversed upon a variety of topics that were calculated to amuse my mind, and in this manner two or three hours passed away, when we stopped at an inn to change horses, and to procure some refreshment. Here I was allowed a few minutes for the indulgence of my own thoughts, the nature of which I need hardly attempt to describe. One moment I blamed myself for having been too precipitate; and the next I felt a degree of pleasure that the confession had been made, and that that weight was off my mind; and I resolved to trust to Providence for the result. That Cecil would ever attempt to deceive me, or to take advantage of the power which he now knew he had over me, I could not imagine for a moment, and I, therefore, rested myself happy and contented upon that point. But what would those who knew me think of my abrupt and mysterious disappearance from the cottage? This was a reflection that perplexed me much, and I knew not to what conclusion to come to upon the subject. Having partaken of a repast, we resumed our journey, and my embarrassment more and more diminished the further we proceeded, and I listened to the conversation of Cecil with increased pleasure. His fund of information seemed inexhaustible, and he conversed with a degree of eloquence which I had never heard equalled, much less surpassed. He described the different scenes we travelled through most graphically, and I dwelt with rapture and admiration upon every observation he made. The country we travelled through was very romantic, and of the most diversified character, and that served to amuse my mind; but still I was most anxious for us to arrive at the place of our destination, and to be introduced to the sister of Cecil, of whom he spoke so highly, and to see what kind of a reception she would give me.

"'My dear Amy,' observed Cecil, 'I assure you that you have nothing to fear on that score. I have already made my sister fully acquainted with your character and the sentiments I feel towards you, and she is prepared to welcome you with the same affection and cordiality as if you were some dear relation.'

"'But did you make your sister acquainted with the means you had adopted to get me to accompany you?' I inquired, eagerly.

"'No,' he answered, with some little embarrassment; 'I merely told her that it was my intention to endeavour to persuade you, and that I entertained the strongest hopes, as your present situation was so lonely, that you would comply with my request. Believe me, Amy, you will find her to be all that I have represented her to be, an agreeable companion, and a sincere friend.'

"'But will she not consider me an intruder?' I demanded.

"'An intruder?' he repeated; 'oh, no; on the contrary, she cannot fail to be charmed with you, Amy, and will thank me for having afforded her the pleasure of such a companion.'

"I returned no answer to this, but my hopes increased, and my confidence gained strength. I fear, however, that I am becoming tedious by thus entering into minute details, and I will, therefore, pro-

ceed with my narrative to the conclusion, as fast as I can.

"It was not until the sun was just sinking to rest in the western horizon, that, after we had emerged from an extensive wood, Cecil informed me we were fast approaching the place of our destination, and in a few minutes afterwards we came in sight of a large building, which Cecil told me was his family mansion; but the scenery by which it was surrounded by no means answered the glowing description which he had given me of it.

"It was evidently a building of great antiquity, and its walls were almost entirely covered with ivy. It stood alone, and there did not seem to be another house near it for some distance. It was inclosed all round by a high wall, which added to the heaviness and gloominess of its appearance; and its situation was one of the most cheerless description.

"I confess that I felt disappointed, and somewhat uneasy, which Cecil perceived, for he observed—

"'Do not judge too hastily, dear Amy, I beg of you. I own it is somewhat retired, but you see it under every disadvantage, and when you become better acquainted with it, you will find that it fully realizes the description I have given of it.'

"'But is there no other habitation, or town or village near it?' I interrogated.

"'There is a town or village about half a mile from it,' he answered, and the conversation here dropped, for the carriage had stopped before a pair of large folding gates, and the servant having rung a bell, they were immediately opened by an old man, who had the appearance of a porter. The vehicle was then driven into the grounds which the walls enclosed, and soon stopped before a lofty portal, and Cecil having assisted me from the vehicle, led me into the hall, which was very spacious, and, like the rest of the building, bore all the appearance of great antiquity. Having traversed this, preceded by a man who was dressed in the livery of a footman, Cecil ushered me into a large and elegantly furnished apartment, where he handed me a chair, and taking my hand, and pressing it to his lips, he said—

"'My dear Amy, welcome, thrice welcome to Bramblington Manor, in which I hope you will find your future home, and never have cause to regret your having come to it. But I must apprise my sister of our arrival, for she will be most anxious to receive you. I will leave you for a few minutes for that purpose.'

"I returned no answer to this, and he

immediately quitted the room. When he was gone, I stared around me with stupified amazement, and could scarcely imagine where I was, so great was the change. But my heart palpitated violently in my bosom, and I could not but feel a sensation of doubt and apprehension come over my mind. The apartment I was in was, as I said before, one of the most spacious dimensions, and was furnished with the greatest elegance and taste; showing clearly that the owner of this mansion must be a person in a superior station of life.

"'And can I ever hope to become the wife of one so far above me?' I ejaculated to myself; 'the thought seems to be unreasonable, and if so, have I not acted imprudently in accepting of his protection, and placing myself under his roof? I fear that I have done wrong, and my heart misgives me. But why should it do so? What is there yet to give rise to any apprehension on my part? Cecil will never deceive me; oh, no! I feel convinced that he possesses too honourable a heart to do that; and it would be most uncharitable in me to suspect him.'

"These thoughts made me feel more composed, and I awaited the return of Cecil, accompanied by his sister, with the utmost degree of anxiety and impatience. I had not to wait long, for soon afterwards I heard footsteps approaching along the hall towards the apartment in which I was, and the next minute the door was opened, and Cecil entered, leading in his sister, whom I had risen to meet, and upon whom I timidly fixed my gaze, which she returned with a smile of welcome, and a look of admiration.

"She was a remarkably fine and handsome woman, though I confess that I could not discover the least resemblance between her and Cecil. Her figure was tall, commanding, and graceful, and she was attired in the first style of fashion, which added greatly to the dignity of her appearance. I own I felt somewhat abashed, which she observing, smiled upon me more graciously and encouragingly than before, and Cecil taking my hand within his, said—

"'My dear Amy, allow me to introduce yourself and my sister Clarissa to each other, and to hope that this will be the commencement of a friendship as fervent as it is lasting.'

"'My dear Miss Parker,' said Clarissa, in the most bland accents, 'I heartily and sincerely welcome you to Bramblington Manor; and feel proud and happy to think you have accepted the invitation of my brother. If my future friendship should be acceptable to you, you are welcome to it, and I trust that you will not consider me unworthy of a return.'

"What could I say in answer to a welcome apparently so cordial and sincere? My embarrassment was quickly dissipated, and at last I replied—

"'My dear madam, how can I sufficiently express to you my thanks for this kind welcome to an entire stranger? I am but an humble individual; but if you will not deem me presumptuous, I shall feel but too happy in bestowing upon you all that friendship which my heart is susceptible of.'

"She took my hand in hers, and with a playful smile she said—

"'Well, now all these preliminaries are settled, and we all seem to understand each other, let us do away with all formalities, and endeavour to pass an agreeable hour or two together—that is, if Miss Amy is not too much fatigued after her journey to enter into conversation. Upon my word, Charles, I can never be sufficiently grateful to you for having provided me with one who promises to prove to me such an agreeable companion.'

"'Yes, Clarissa,' returned Cecil; 'and I can never feel grateful enough to Providence for having introduced me to her. Bramblington Manor will now become a perfect Elysium, since we shall be honoured by her presence.'

"I need not say how confused I felt by these fulsome compliments, and the deepest blushes suffused my cheeks. I found it impossible to return any answer; and Clarissa, noticing my confusion, again smiled encouragingly upon me, and Cecil, taking an arm of each, conducted us up a wide staircase, and ushered us into a kind of saloon, which was brilliantly illuminated, and where a sumptuous repast was prepared.

"I was completely dazzled and thunderstruck by all I saw, and could scarcely believe the evidence of my eyes; but Cecil handed me to a seat in silence, and then I had an opportunity of taking a full survey of all around, and my wonder was more and more increased the longer I gazed.

"It was, indeed, a noble apartment, and lighted by several chandeliers and candelabras; the walls were hung with mirrors, which, reflecting back the lights, gave to the whole scene a most dazzling effect; the furniture was of the most elegant description, and, in fact, it was an apartment altogether which was fit for the noblest palace.

"Cecil and his sister noticed my astonishment and admiration at all I saw, and they seemed satisfied ; but, for my own part, my brain was bewildered, and I could not without difficulty persuade myself that it was not all some strange and delusive dream.

"'Oh! whither have you brought me?' I at length said: 'my brain turns giddy at the sight of such unusual splendour.'

"'Collect yourself, dear Amy,' replied Cecil: 'you will soon get used to such scenes as this. You now find that the descriptions which I gave you of my mansion were not altogether exaggerated.'

"'Oh, no,' I returned ; 'but still, it ill-becomes one of my humble station to mingle in scenes of such magnificence as this.'

"'Say not so, Amy,' said Cecil, 'for what scene is there to which you must not add a lustre by your presence? But come, the repast awaits us, and you must stand much in need of some refreshment after our journey.'

"I was so completely taken by surprise, that I was almost unconscious of what was passing around me ; but at length, by the assiduous attentions of Cecil and his sister, I somewhat regained my composure, and joined them in the repast which was spread upon the table. This over, Clarissa and her brother endeavoured to engage me in conversation, in which they succeeded to some little extent, and I was quite captivated and astonished at the accomplishments which she displayed.

"In that respect, she fully equalled her brother, and I did not know which to admire the most. At length, finding that I evinced some signs of being fatigued, and as it was getting late, Cecil proposed that we should separate; and after bidding me an affectionate good-night, I left the room, accompanied by Clarissa, who informed me that it was her intention to sleep in the adjoining apartment to me, a fact which I was very glad to hear, as it would remove from my mind any doubt and uneasiness I might otherwise have experienced.

"The chambers, like all the other apartments I had yet seen in the Manor, were furnished with every taste and comfort, and I could not but wonder still more at all I saw. Clarissa again engaged me for a short time in conversation, and passed many flattering compliments upon me, and made numerous professions of future friendship, and having bid me good-night, she retired into her own chamber, which opened into mine, and I was left alone. As soon as she was gone, I sank upon my knees, and earnestly supplicated the Supreme to guide me in my future conduct,

and to grant me His protection: and I then seated myself on the side of my bed and endeavoured to reflect calmly upon all the extraordinary events that had occurred to me within the last few hours, and to try to imagine how it would end. But the longer I reflected, the more my brain became bewildered, and the deeper was I plunged in amazement. The splendour which I had witnessed in the Manor was such as I had never seen before, and firmly convinced me of the great wealth of Cecil, and filled my mind with doubts and apprehensions, as to the sincerity of his love for a poor, friendless girl like me; still, the kindness and attention of both himself and Clarissa was quite overwhelming. Yet had I not acted with the greatest imprudence in accepting the offer of Cecil, and thus placing myself entirely in his power? Notwithstanding all my efforts, I could not exactly reconcile it to my mind, but still I could not doubt the honour and integrity of Cecil, for he must be a villain, indeed, if he should seek to deceive me. The behaviour of Clarissa had greatly prejudiced me in favour of her, and I could not but rely with confidence upon her professions.

"At length I retired to rest, and all that had happened to me was reconjured up to me in dreams. In the morning when I awoke, I found Clarissa already sitting in my chamber, and apparently watching me with much anxiety. On seeing me awake, she saluted me with the greatest kindness, and inquired how I had rested.

"'For my own part,' she added, 'I have done little else but dream about you, so much have you interested me.'

"'Ah! madam,' I answered, 'I am afraid you flatter me beyond my deserts. I am but an humble individual, and unworthy of the attention paid me by yourself and your brother, who are placed so much above me.'

"'Nay, Amy,' remarked Clarissa, 'you entertain too mean an opinion of yourself, indeed you do. It is myself and my brother who should feel honoured by your friendship. But still my brother Charles is a noble-hearted youth, and I feel proud of him.'

"Every word that she uttered in praise of him, went to my heart, and I could not but coincide in all she said. Oh, little did I suspect the wretched dupe they were both making of me, or that one who wore so fair a mask as Clarissa did, could possess so base a heart. But the time was soon to come when my eyes were to be opened, and I was doomed to behold myself a wretched and degraded being.

"Clarissa having assisted me to dress, she conducted me to the breakfast-room, where we found Cecil already waiting to receive us, and who greeted us with the greatest warmth of feeling. This day was one of the happiest that I had ever experienced, and Cecil and his sister seemed to make it their whole study to render me contented. Nothing could possibly be more kind, indulgent, and respectful than their behaviour to me, and it was quite impossible that I could entertain the least suspicion of the treacherous part they were acting towards me. Every minute Clarissa, by the urbanity of her manners, insinuated herself more and more into my favour, and I believed her to be one of the most amiable of women. She and her brother seemed to be very much attached to each other, and she also seemed to be fully aware of the sentiments that existed between us, and to approve of them, for she lost no opportunity of eulogising Cecil, seeing that such observations afforded me the utmost gratification. When we retired to our chambers for the night, being now as familiar with one another as if we had been acquainted for years, we got into conversation upon the subject, and in the course of which she elicited from me the true state of my heart, and which she seemed to hear with the most unfeigned delight.

"'Ah, my dear Amy,' she observed, 'I am certain that there is no other damsel whom my brother has seen whom he can love like you, and his whole hopes of future happiness are centred in you; you are worthy of one another; Fate seems to have destined you for each other, and what then shall prevent you from coming together? I must confess that nothing could possibly afford me greater pleasure, and I sincerely hope that the day is not far distant, when those wishes will be gratified.'

"Oh, Clarissa,' I answered, 'how you flatter me by the observations you have just made? How can I return my acknowledgments for them? But alas! the difference of our stations will preclude the possibility of your brother and myself ever coming together.'

"'And why so?' demanded Clarissa. 'Who is to control his will? Is he not master of his own actions? And who is there who shall take the liberty of questioning his conduct? Come, my dear Amy, you are far too delicate and scrupulous upon this subject. Charles, I am convinced, loves you for yourself alone, and your numerous virtues and accomplishments render you every way worthy of

him, or even the proudest nobleman in the land.'

"'Oh, Clarissa,' I returned, 'how little deserving am I of the flattering eulogiums you have thus lavished upon me!'

"'It is no flattery, Amy,' she replied, 'but no more than an humble tribute which is due to your merit. My brother's whole hopes of happiness, as I have before observed, are centred in an union with you; and I do trust that, when you become still better acquainted with his character than you are at present, and are thoroughly convinced of the fervour and sincerity of the love he bears you, you will not condemn him to disappointment.'

"'To Mr. Cecil I am greatly indebted,' I remarked; 'and,' I added, with a blush, 'I must be devoid of candour did I not confess that he has made the most favourable impression on me; though, at the same time, I cannot but say that the course he recently adopted—so strange and so precipitate—was naturally calculated to alter the good opinion I had formed of him.'

"'True, I admit that it was,' replied Clarissa; 'but I trust that you are now ready to attribute it to the impetuosity of his love, and that you cannot but believe his intentions towards you are strictly honourable.'

"'True,' I answered: 'I should be sorry to do your brother an injustice, and I will, therefore, place every reliance in his honour.'

"'Spoken like a sensible girl,' said Clarissa, embracing me with much show of affection and esteem; 'and you will find, depend upon it, that you will have no cause to regret the confidence you may repose in him.'

"Alas!" continued Amy, "how brutally was I deceived by this crafty woman!—how little did I suspect her real character, or the heartless and wicked designs that she and Cecil had against me! But, alas! they had entrapped me into a snare, from which it was almost impossible to escape; and, inexperienced as I was in the artifices of mankind, what a ready victim did I become in their hands! Every day and every hour the attentions and affection of Cecil and Clarissa towards me appeared to increase, and they seemed to make it their constant study to contribute to my pleasure and happiness. They anticipated my every wish, and lost not an opportunity of gratifying it to the fullest extent. I became perfectly contented and happy, and the fatal passion with which Cecil had inspired me daily increased in strength, and I received his addresses with all that warmth of feeling which h^ evinced towards me. And yet I must acknowledge that there were times when I had my misgivings, and there was something in the behaviour of Cecil and Clarissa towards each other at times which excited some suspicions in my breast; but those thoughts were quickly banished, and I reproached myself for ever having encouraged them. The respect with which I was invariably treated, and the great deference which was at all times paid to my wishes, convinced me more than all of the honour and integrity of his intentions, and I resolved to make my mind perfectly at ease, and to look forward to the future with the most sanguine hopes and anticipations. Day after day elapsed, and I had now been about a month at Bramblington Manor, and had begun to feel myself quite at home. Cecil now became more urgent and persevering in his suit; he was in my company at every opportunity; in fact, he never seemed happy but when he was in my presence, and at length he urged me in the most earnest and impassioned language to allow him to name a day when I would consent to become his wife, and thus to set at once to rest any doubts that I might still entertain as to the strict honour and sincerity of his intentions. What could appear more generous and honest than this? How could I any longer doubt him, or hesitate as to the course I should adopt? Alas! such was the fatal influence he had succeeded in obtaining over me, that it was impossible for me to do so, and I yielded to his solicitations, and the day was appointed which he said was to unite our fates for ever. He seemed enraptured at his success, again and again embraced me, and called me by the most affectionate names, declaring that I had made him one of the most happy of individuals, and declared that it should be the constant study of his future life to convince me how worthy he was of the confidence I had thus reposed in him, The hypocrite! oh, that I could have read his guilty thoughts at that moment! But little could I suspect that such base deceit and treachery could lurk within the breast of a human being, and especially in that of one who had made such fervent and honourable professions. In order that it might not excite any undue or unpleasant curiosity, Cecil proposed that the nuptials should take place as privately as possible, and said that he had a friend who would perform the ceremony in the Manor, his sister being my bridesmaid, and one or two other most intimate friends of his acting as witnesses. With this arrange-

ment, I expressed myself perfectly satisfied, and thus everything was decided, and the triumph of Cecil might be said to have been complete.

"From that fatal moment the affectionate attentions of Cecil and Clarissa towards me were redoubled, and they sought to inspire me with the most blissful anticipations of the future. But I must confess that there were times when I felt the most strange misgivings cross my mind, and I almost regretted that I had so readily given my consent to the solicitations of Cecil, and without giving myself longer time to reflect more maturely upon the important subject. But what had I to fear?—I at last argued with myself—were not the proposals of Cecil honourable?—and in strict accordance with the feelings of my heart? They were so, and surely I must be wrong in suffering anything like doubt to enter my breast. I endeavoured to reassure myself, and prepare myself for the solemn change which was so soon to take place in my circumstances. As the wife of Cecil, I must surely be one of the happiest of women, for to me it seemed evident that he loved me with an ardour and sincerity which nothing could ever abate, and I returned his passion with all the strength which the human heart is capable of experiencing. Had I not, therefore, a right to look forward to an union with the most sanguine and blissful expectations, rather than encourage those doubts and apprehensions which I had at times permitted to take possession of my mind? I determined to struggle against such erroneous feelings, and to look forward to the future with confidence. As the time, however, approached, I became greatly agitated, and my mind wavered between doubt and fear. A few days previous to the day fixed for the nuptials, the friends who were to be present at the ceremony, arrived at the manor, and were introduced to me in due form by Cecil and his sister. These consisted of two ladies and three gentlemen, among the latter of whom was the clergyman who was to perform the marriage rites, and who seemed to be a most amiable man, indeed, and endeavoured to inspire me with confidence, holding out to me the most promising prospects of the future, and passing many flattering eulogiums on 'his dear and respected young friend, Mr. Cecil,' whom he said he had had the pleasure of knowing, and being on terms of intimacy with, from childhood.

"There were considerable preparations for the wedding; there were great additions made to the splendour of the saloon, and a spacious apartment was fitted up as a chapel, in which it was arranged that the ceremony should take place. Nothing could seem more fair and reasonable that the arrangements that were made, and all doubts and apprehensions were now removed from my bosom. Fatal delusion! what bitter cause have I since had to regret it. But, alas! I must have been blind and infatuated at the time, and when all the circumstances are taken into consideration, and the artful contrivances that were resorted to to deceive and entrap me, can it be wondered at that all suspicion should be stifled in my breast? I had fallen into the hands of those who were adepts in the artifices of the world, and I had no one to advise or put me on my guard.

"The important day at length arrived, and Clarissa was in attendance upon me at an early hour, and sought to hold out to me every encouragement, and lavished upon me the most unbounded marks of her esteem. I need not describe the state of my feelings at that time. My heart palpitated violently, and I could not entirely resist some dismal and painful forebodings that would at times flash upon my brain; and there were moments when I could not but regret that I had been so premature in giving my consent to a secret marriage with a man with whom I had been for so short a time acquainted, and who had taken such a strange and questionable course to press his suit. However, these thoughts were at length dissipated, and, accompanied by Clarissa, I entered the room where Cecil and his friends were waiting my arrival. Nothing could exceed the apparent warmth of affection with which he received me, and the looks of admiration that he bestowed upon me, and the deep blushes of maiden modesty suffused my cheeks, and I became more agitated than before. After a choice repast, the bridal procession was formed, being brought up in the rear by those whom I supposed to be the servants at the manor, and we moved slowly and solemnly towards the spacious apartment in which the ceremony was to take place; and the nature of my feelings at that time it is needless for me to seek to describe to you. We entered the room; the supposed reverend gentleman took his place behind the temporary altar, and the ceremony commenced, and was gone through with due form and solemnity, and I supposed myself to be the wife of that man, who had gained such fatal power over my affections. But my brain suddenly turned giddy—a sickly sensation came over my heart, and overpowered by my feelings, I swooned in the arms of Cecil. Would that it had been the everlasting sleep of death; for then what indescribable misery would it have saved me, and the cruel designs of him into whose hands I had so unfortunately resigned my fate, would have been defeated; but I soon recovered, and quickly regained my composure, beneath the influence of the too persuasive and eloquent voice of Cecil, who seemed to view me with feelings almost amounting to adoration, and again and again pressed me with transport to his bosom, and pictured to me in the most glowing colours the happiness which was in store for us. Alas! I was but too ready to believe him, and thus I was deluded, deceived, and betrayed, and without the least chance of saving myself. The day passed away with much festivity, considering the limited number of the guests; and it was not until a late hour that we separated. That night proved the consummation of my misery, and the complete triumph of Cecil! Oh, let me not dwell any longer than possible upon it, for the thoughts it creates are maddening. But in the morning, I must confess that the same gloomy forebodings that had before tortured me again beset my mind, and I could not but look upon what I had done with a feeling fast approaching to dread. But it was too late now to repent, and Cecil quickly re-assured me, and I reproached myself for having for a moment entertained any doubts upon the subject.

"In a few days after the marriage, the guests took their departure from the manor, and myself, Cecil, and Clarissa, were again left to ourselves. Charles seemed to lavish upon me the fondest affection that man could bestow, and he was never absent from me only at a brief interval at a time. In fact, nothing could exceed the attention which he and Clarissa bestowed upon me, and I considered myself to be supremely happy, and constantly prayed to heaven for blessings upon his head. Oh, God! how could he ever have the heart so cruelly to deceive me, and to plunge me into that irremediable shame and misery which he has done? My brain is distracted, and I shudder with disgust and horror when I reflect on it."

Here Amy was obliged to pause for a few minutes in order to give vent to the feelings of emotion that took possession of her bosom, as the painful reminiscences of the past arose to her memory, and our hero and heroine, who, as may naturally be expected, deeply sympathised with her, did not offer to obtrude upon her sorrows by making use of any observations. But at length she resumed her story in the following words: —

"Weeks, months passed away, and I had no cause to regret, or to suspect that all which Cecil had stated was correct. He continued to pay me the same affectionate attention that he had ever done, and I had no wish which was permitted to remain ungratified, even before it could be expressed. I fondly hoped that this would last for ever; but, alas! how cruelly was I doomed to be disappointed, and how great was the misery which was in store for me, and which was so soon about to descend upon my head with the most overwhelming violence.

"At length I thought that I noticed a difference in the behaviour of Clarissa towards me. It was less warm than it formerly was; she entered not so freely into conversation with me, as she had formerly done, and she frequently dissented from me in opinion upon subjects on which we had been once mutually agreed. She was at times testy and cross, even almost to insolence, and sometimes I would not see her at all for a day or two together.

"This strange alteration in her conduct was a source of great annoyance to me, and I was at a loss to account for it. I taxed my memory in vain to try to discover if I had said or done anything that should have given her cause for offence; but I could recollect nothing, and I became more bewildered and uneasy the longer I reflected on it; and now for the first time I began to fear that something was brooding to disturb my happiness. At length she seldom visited me at all, and I could no longer refrain from questioning Cecil upon the subject: the answers, however, that he gave me were evasive and unsatisfactory, and I could plainly see that my interrogatories were annoying to him, and this rendered me more uneasy and doubtful than ever. But I had soon much greater cause for anguish and anxiety of mind, and this was in a change also in the conduct of Cecil. He was less ardent and affectionate in the language he addressed towards me; nay, at times he was almost cold and repulsive, and seemed to take little or no pleasure in my society, though Heaven knows, I had abated nothing in my fond endearments towards him, and would willingly have laid down my life to serve him. You may imagine the agony of my feelings as I witnessed this unaccountable behaviour in the man whom I believed to be my husband, and to whom my heart was so fondly, so truly devoted, and yet I forbore to question him as to the

cause, for fear I should appear suspicious and dissatisfied. But when he absented himself from my presence for whole days together, and when he returned was sullen and reserved, you can guess what the torture, doubt, and suspense of my mind must have been, and the various conjectures that flashed upon my distracted brain. I could scarcely believe the evidence of my senses, so cruel, so sudden, and so unexpected was the change; but at length unable to bear it any longer, I implored him to give me an explanation, and thus at once to ease the agonising doubts and apprehensions that crowded upon my brain, and were almost too insupportable for endurance. He heard me impatiently, and when I had concluded, said—

"'You, are, it seems suspicious and dissatisfied, Amy, but I would advise you to conquer this restless disposition, and not to question me too closely upon a subject which it would not benefit you to be made acquainted with. I do not see that you have any just cause to complain of my conduct, since I believe that I have always done my duty towards you. Let that suffice you, and I must request that you will not annoy me by any future questions.'

"With these words, and without waiting for any reply from me, he abruptly quitted the room, and completely overwhelmed by the power of my emotions, I burst into a passionate flood of tears, and clasped my hands together in despair and dismay. Could this be the man who had made so many solemn and sacred vows to me of unalterable affection, and who had actually seemed almost to idolize me? Could this be he into whose hands I had so readily resigned my fate, and in whom I had placed the most implicit confidence? It appeared to be almost impossible; and a deadly chill fell upon my heart which was almost overpowering. The fearful truth seemed to be at once revealed to me; he could never surely have loved me with a pure and holy passion, or if he had done so, it was clear, too painfully clear that he loved me no longer. What nameless agony was there in that thought! I beat my breast, and for some time gave way to the most violent paroxysms of grief which it was impossible for me to control. And now the most dreadful ideas haunted my imagination. Should Cecil not prove to be what he had represented himself, and which his having employed such ruffians as those who had seized me in the first instance was sufficient to give me reason to suspect that he was not—and should he have deceived me, and I was not in reality

MRS. ASHTON RISING TO WELCOME THE PARKERS.

his wife—oh, God! how horrible would then be my fate! But the thought was too monstrous to be encouraged, and I endeavoured to banish it from my mind altogether. This, however, was a most difficult task to accomplish, and I succeeded but indifferently. My agony of mind was increased when I noticed that every day Cecil became more and more cold and distant towards me, and that he even absented himself from me more frequently, and for longer periods than he had pre-viously done. As for Clarissa, I now never saw her at all, for Cecil and myself always took our meals together, and I began to suspect that she had quitted the house altogether, and I was at a loss what to think of it. Cecil would now leave me at an early hour in the morning, and would sometimes not return till long after midnight, and during these periods I was left entirely to the solitude of my own thoughts. It was in vain that I tried to solve the mystery, for the longer I ruminated on it the more I became entangled in the mazes of fruitless conjecture. How wretched was the life I now led, and every day it became more sad and insupportable. How deeply did I now regret that I had ever yielded to the solicitations of Cecil, or that I had fallen into his power; and in vain did I rack my brain to imagine what would be the result of it. It was quite evident to me that Cecil had something particular upon his mind which he did not think proper to divulge to me, and what the nature of that most probably was I shuddered to think upon; but still I feared to question him again upon the subject, after what he had said to me on a former occasion, and thus was I left in a state of doubt and perplexity which it was quite agonising even to think upon.

"What also created my surprise was that I seldom saw any of the servants about the house, and those that I did always avoided having any communication with me, and had evidently received instructions to that effect. What could be the meaning of this? It was strange, most strange; but it was completely beyond my comprehension. Thus wore away several days, and still no change took place in my circumstances, and nothing whatever occurred to throw any light upon the subject. Being thus left to the solitude of my own dismal thoughts, I would frequently wander through the different apartments of the house in order to endeavour to amuse my mind that way; and thus I wore away many of the tedious hours that I was left alone. There was one room which had attracted my attention and excited my curiosity more than the rest; and here I often seated myself and gave free indulgence to the thoughts that continually occupied my mind. This apartment was situated in what appeared to be the most ancient part of the building, and certainly presented no very cheerful aspect; however, it was quite in accordance with my feelings, and I felt myself more at home there than anywhere else. It was a large room, with oaken wainscoting, and richly carved mouldings, and the furniture was all of the most ancient description, and in many instances had been suffered to fall into decay. Quaint-looking old tables and chairs there were, and several portraits and other pictures, upon which the dust of time had been suffered to gather, decorated the walls. One of these had always attracted my attention more than the rest, and one evening I took more particular notice of it than usual.

"It was the portrait of a knight in armour, of gigantic dimensions, for the picture reached nearly from the floor to the ceiling, and altogether it had a curious and rather imposing effect. I was examining this painting minutely the evening I have mentioned, when happening to put my hand near the frame, I was surprised to feel a strong current of air, which seemed to proceed from some opening, and this induced me to inspect it more narrowly. I applied my hands to a certain portion of the frame, which seemed to have a more particular appearance than the rest, and it immediately slid back with the greatest ease; and you may judge of my astonishment when I beheld a secret door concealed behind it, and which was partially open. My curiosity was immediately excited; and, as there was no one to observe me, I was determined to gratify it. I threw open the door, and then, as well as the darkness would permit, I perceived a small, low passage, leading to a flight of stairs. My curiosity was more excited than ever, for I could not help thinking that this might probably lead to some discovery relating to the mysterious behaviour of Cecil, and I returned to my own room in order to procure a lantern, and impatient to enter upon my examination. I soon returned, and having taken care to secure the door, so that it should not close upon me, I entered the place, and having traversed the passage, I commenced descending the stairs, which were narrow and winding, and seemed to lead to some secret underground place at the back of the building. A strange feeling came over me as I proceeded, and I could not divest my mind of the impression that this adventure would lead to the discovery of something of importance.

"At length I arrived at the bottom of the stairs, and then found myself upon the entrance of another narrow and winding passage, which seemed to wind entirely round that wing of the building in which it was placed. I proceeded on my way, cautiously, but without fear, though I frequently paused to listen whether I could hear any sound beyond; but nothing of the kind saluted my ears, and I continued to traverse the passage until I came to the end of it, when I perceived a low gothic archway, beyond which was a flight of broken stone steps, and which seemed to lead to some vaults or dungeons, much further underneath the building. I must confess that the gloomy aspect of this place somewhat daunted me, and I hesitated, for I knew not what danger there might be beyond; but as I had advanced so far, I resolved to gratify my curiosity to the fullest extent, and I therefore proceeded, and, with some difficulty, at last alighted at the foot of the steps, and found myself in a long arched avenue; but casting my eyes along it, I started at beholding a strange reflection of light, which seemed to proceed from some door, and at the same time the voices of several men engaged in conversation greeted my ears, and made me hesitate whether to recede or advance, for I knew not what danger might threaten; but still something urged me to proceed, and I could not resist the temptation, even let the consequences be whatever they might, for I could not help thinking that some important discovery was about to be made, in which I was immediately concerned and interested. I, therefore, closed my lantern, and advanced with silent and cautious steps towards the place from whence the light seemed to issue, and then perceived that it proceeded from an iron door which was standing partly open. I, however, paused, and listened attentively, for I heard the voices of several men in earnest conversation, and I was anxious to discover, if possible, who and what they were. I was not lonk kept in suspense, for at that moment the following words greeted my ears, spoken in the gruff voice of a man—

" ' Ay, we have managed our business well for some years, and there is not much fear of our being discovered now. Who would ever suspect what is daily and nightly going forward under the old Manor House, or that it forms the refuge for one of the most desperate and extensive gang of coiners that ever infested the country?'

" ' Coiners !' I gasped to myself—and the blood chilled in my veins. ' Oh, God! the fearful mystery is, then, at last unravelled, and I see the full extent of my misery! I am lost—ruined—betrayed! Oh, Cecil—villain!——'

" I paused, for suddenly the voice of another speaker greeted my ears, and the tones of which struck to my heart like a dagger.

" ' You say right, Crosby,' he remarked. ' No one could ever suppose that such are the transactions that take place within this old building, or that the gay and accomplished gallant, Charles Cecil, as he is called, is the head of the gang. But to business, or we shall never be able to complete the large order we have in hand, for our agents on the continent, by the time we have promised.'

" It was with difficulty that I could repress a scream, or save myself from sinking to the earth, as I made this fearful discovery; and you may judge of the horror of my feelings much better than it is possible I can describe them. I advanced, however, at last, cautiously towards the door, and ventured to peep in, and then a scene met my gaze which it is impossible that I can ever forget. In a large vault, in which was a furnace, and all the other implements for coining, a number of the most savage-looking men were engaged in their lawless avocation, and in one of whom, to my horror and amazement, I immediately recognised the man who had officiated as the clergyman at my pretended marriage ; and seated in the centre of the vault, and apparently watching and superintending the proceedings, was my brutal betrayer—the wretch from whom · I have to date all my misfortunes. How my blood chilled in my veins as I beheld him! But there was another object now attracted my attention, who excited equal surprise and disgust in my bosom : this was no other than the pretended sister of Cecil, and whom he had evidently used as the instrument to work my destruction. But how different was now her appearance to what it had been when she was assuming that character! She was meanly clad, her face and hands were dirty, from the smoke and charcoal, as though she took an active part in the unlawful proceedings of the coiners, and altogether her looks were coarse and vulgar. Here, then, was a plain proof of the shameful manner in which I had been betrayed, and of the utter ruin and disgrace into which I had been plunged. I wrung my hands in the agony and despair of my feelings, and still continued at the door, and anxiously watched all that passed; for I was so situated that none of the men could observe me, and I was fully determined, now that I had proceeded thus far, to fathom the truth to the bottom.

" ' Now, Mabel,' said Cecil, addressing himself to her whom I had hitherto known as Clarissa, ' you must bustle about, for there must be no skulkers here. You must remember that you are not now acting the lady, and doing the amiable, as you were a short time since.'

" ' I know it,' answered Mabel, ' and I have no wish to be. I am more in my native element as I am, though I think you must admit that I played my part to admiration.'

" ' Yes,' returned Cecil. ' Ha, ha, ha ! How completely we deceived the pretty innocent—eh?'

" ' We did,' coincided Mabel; ' but, now that you have obtained the gratification of your wishes, and have grown tired of her, how do you mean to dispose of her?—for she is only in the way while she remains here.'

" ' Why,' replied Cecil, ' that is a subject upon which I have not as yet exactly made up my mind. She is only in the way, as you say; but I have no doubt that I shall find some effectual means of getting rid of her before long.'

" I could endure no more; my brain swam round—the blood curdled in my veins—the blackest despair pressed upon my heart, and I gave utterance to a loud and piercing shriek, and was obliged to cling for support to the door-post, to prevent myself from falling. The cry immediately alarmed Cecil and the other coiners, and they made a simultaneous rush towards the spot where I was standing, and a fearful oath escaped the lips of Cecil when he recognised me; and seizing me fiercely by the arm, he dragged me into the centre of the place, as he exclaimed, in a hoarse and infuriated voice—

" ' Ha!—discovered! Rash fool! this curiosity shall cost you dear !'

" ' Oh, mercy—mercy, husband !' I cried, scarcely knowing what I uttered in the agitation and terror of my feelings.

" ' Husband !' he repeated, with a look of savage scorn : 'idiot ! you are no wife of mine. It was all a plot to deceive you, and to quiet your delicate scruples, and it succeeded far better than my most sanguine hopes could anticipate."

" This brutal acknowledgment of the guilty truth, and the confirmation of my disgrace and ruin, were too much for me to bear, and with another piercing cry, my senses left me."

CHAPTER XXXIX.

THE CRITICAL SITUATION OF AMY.—THE SLEEPING POTION.—THE BRUTAL CONDUCT OF CECIL.—HER DESERTION, AND SUBSEQUENT ADVENTURES.

" On my recovery," continued the unfortunate Amy, after a pause, " I found myself lying upon the floor in an ill-furnished and gloomy-looking room ; the windows of which were strongly barred, and showed me that I was a prisoner. By my side was a pitcher of water and some coarse bread, and everything indicated but too plainly what the fate was to which I was consigned.

" At first I had but a dreamy recollection of what had happened ; but it all quickly rushed upon my memory with overwhelming force, and starting to my feet, I groaned aloud in my despair. How

shall I now attempt to portray the anguish and distraction of my feelings? For a few minutes I was completely mad, and paced the room backwards and forwards in the most disordered manner. Then I tried the door, which I found to be fastened, and that convinced me, I if had wanted anything more to satisfy me, that I was a prisoner. And what was the fate which awaited me? Was it death ? Death by the hands of my betrayer? Alas ! what mattered it now that I discovered the cruel manner in which I had been deceived, and the wretched and degraded being that I now was?

" ' Death !' I ejaculated ; ' oh, that would be a mercy to me ; for now what have I to hope for in the world, since I have thus miserably fallen? What is there for a wretched outcast like me, but misery, scorn, and persecution? Oh, Cecil! Cecil! could I ever have believed this of thee? Cruel man, how base must be the heart which could prompt you to such a deed ! But it is clear that you are a villain, the votary of crime, insensible alike to all shame or feeling ! Oh, why was I so shamefully, so easily deceived? Ought not his clandestine seizure of me at once to have opened my eyes, and convinced me of the wretch I had to deal with ? Alas! I have been much to blame, and am now most terribly punished for it. I shall go mad! I shall go mad !'

" Again I beat my breast and tore my hair, in the agony of my despair, and the utter frenzy of my feelings ; and then I again traversed the gloomy room with the most disordered steps, and recalled to my mind all that I had seen and heard with emotions of the most unbounded horror. Then I called frantically upon the name of my betrayer, but the echoes of my own voice alone answered me, and the anguish of my mind increased every minute.

" In this tedious and torturing manner hour after hour passed away, and no one came to see me ; but at length I heard the door of the room in which I was confined unbolted and unlocked, and immediately afterwards my betrayer stood before me. How is it possible for me to describe my feelings as he entered the room? I gazed at him with mingled looks of fear, reproach, and supplication ; but his countenance was stern and determined, and his whole demeanour cold and immovable. He stood contemplating me for a few minutes with folded arms, and I was totally unable to give utterance to a syllable ; but at length he said—

" ' So, girl, mere idle curiosity has tempted you to penetrate my secrets ; what think you should be the reward for such boldness?'

"'Oh, Cecil,' I returned, in a voice half choked with sobs, 'if I may still call you by that name, have pity on me, I beseech you; are you not satisfied with that which you have already inflicted upon me, but that you must seek to add to my misery? Guilty man! view here the victim of your cold-hearted treachery and villany, and if such a thing as remorse can penetrate to your soul, oh, repent, ere it is too late.'

"'Pshaw!' cried Cecil, in accents of impatience, 'I came not here to listen to a lecture on morality, but rather to warn you of what you have incurred by penetrating into that which you had no right to do. You have discovered my secret, and should you be restored to liberty you might, from a feeling of revenge, immediately denounce me and my associates; but that must be prevented.'

"'Oh, Cecil,' I ejaculated, and at the same time gazing into his face with the most earnest looks of supplication and remonstrance, 'pause ere you proceed to any act of violence. What would you do?'

"'That will be a subject for after consideration,' he replied; 'but, at any rate, for the present you must remain a prisoner here, for it would not be safe to set you at liberty.'

"'Oh, Cecil,' I once more ventured to appeal to him, 'have you no spark of humanity left within your breast? Have you, indeed, forgotten all those vows of ardent affection that you once so solemnly professed towards me?'

"'Nay, Amy,' returned the heartless villain, 'it is useless to talk of that now, for it is all past. It was but a dream, a delusive dream, from which you have now awakened, and I do not see why I should trouble myself any further about the business. Had you not have been equally culpable with myself, you would not have been so ready to yield to my persuasions; and, therefore, you must put up with the consequences of your folly and imprudence.'

"'Cruel, cruel man,' I exclaimed, fixing upon him a look of the keenest reproach; 'and can you talk thus to the poor, innocent, friendless girl whom you have so inhumanly betrayed?—are you entirely callous to every feeling of compassion?—and——'

"'You might as well spare yourself the trouble of talking to me thus,' he replied, 'for there is nothing that you now can say which can make any impression on me.

It is enough for me that I have triumphed in my designs, and that I have not suffered a simple and obdurate girl to defeat me. But enough on that subject; here you must remain confined until I have come to some decision how to dispose of you.'

"'Oh, Cecil!' I cried, wringing my hands, 'again I implore you to beware what you do; for, although you may treat what I say at present with indifference and contempt, you may yet have ample cause to repent of your conduct towards me when it is too late. Cruelly—shamefully even though you have treated me, still would I show that mercy towards you which you are so tenacious of evincing towards me. I will never betray you— you have nothing whatever to fear from me.'

"'And think you I am to be so easily deluded?' he said: 'think you that I will allow a foolish, inexperienced female to deceive me? No, Amy; you have much mistaken my character if you judge thus erroneously of me. Here, I repeat, you must remain, until I have more maturely considered my plans, and see clearly what course it will be most prudent for me to adopt. At any rate, I must have some better security than your bare word before I part from you.'

"'What would you do with me?' I demanded, looking in his face with some expression of alarm. 'If it be my life you seek, take it at once; for after the monstrous injustice you have acted towards me—the ruin, disgrace, and desolation you have brought upon me, it is no longer valuable to me. Take it, I say, and end at once the miseries of that unfortunate and friendless being whom you have by your black-hearted treachery rendered an outcast upon society, but keep her not here, exposed to that horror of mind which is far worse than a thousand of the most torturing and lingering deaths that the utmost stretch of cruelty can inflict. Oh! man—man, how basely have you abused the fond and unsuspecting confidence that I reposed in you! Have you no feelings of compunction? Are you altogether destitute of that proper sense of honour which should constitute you as a man, one of the noblest works of God? Reflect— reflect, and hurry not your soul to perdition while there may yet be time to save it.'

"I could perceive that he was somewhat abashed and confounded by the energy of my manner, and he turned away his head for a few moments, to conceal, I suppose, the effect it had upon him; but he quickly recovered himself, and turning to me with a look of indifference, he said—

"'Again I tell you, woman, that this preaching is all lost upon me, and that you might as well spare your breath as to give utterance to it. It is enough for me to know that your prying curiosity has discovered my secret, and I place too little reliance upon your sex to place that in your power which probably would consign me to an ignominious death, goaded on, as I am convinced you would be, by a spirit of revenge.'

"'Cecil,' I said, 'you wrong me by such a supposition. You have wronged me—irretrievably wronged me—blasted a'l my fond hopes—taken the basest advantage of my innocence and inexperience of the world, but still my woman's heart would not suffer me to injure you in the slightest degree. No; I would rather have you live for repentance—to become, if possible, a better man, and to reflect maturely and seriously upon that hapless being whose heart you have rendered desolate for ever. Oh! think of what I was and what I am now—deceived by your too-eloquent and flattering tongue, and specious promises, and do not close your heart altogether to the wretched, helpless, friendless creature, that your treachery has made so.'

"'No more—no more!' he returned, impatiently. 'All these arguments are for the present entirely lost upon me. You know me now for what I am, and can, therefore, not expect much from me. You believed me to be a gentleman and a man of honour: so I was once, and until the injustice of the world beggared me in fortune and reputation, and left me no other means than to retaliate upon it. I am a man of crime—how made so it matters not; but it is too late to repent now, and the truth is, I do not feel the least inclination to do so. Among my present associates, I find that sincerity of friendship which I never experienced from the gaudy butterflies—or, rather, the locusts—who flattered me, and fawned and cringed to me while I had the golden food that their cupidity sought, and I do not seek for change. That golden food I now manufacture—at least the counterfeit of it—and reap a rich harvest by so doing, while at the same time I gratify my revenge against those who once made a victim of me, and laughed exultingly at their triumph. I have done so for years with impunity, and no one has had the slightest suspicion from what source my stores were derived. Think you, then, that I am going to throw this inexhaustible fortune,

my life, and those of my devoted associates, to the winds, by trusting to the bare word of one who, whatever may be her denial of the fact, I am convinced must feel a spirit of revenge against me? No; it were an absurdity—a gross outrage upon common sense to imagine so for an instant. You will, therefore, perceive, Amy, that you plead to me in vain, and that my mind is made up to protect myself and my faithful colleagues at the risk of all consequences.'

"'Oh, God!' I exclaimed, looking at him with an expression of the most indescribable horror, 'then you will not pity me?—you close your heart against me, and what am I to expect that my fate will be?'

"'That much—nay, altogether depends upon yourself,' he answered, 'and to offer any other arguments than those which I have already given utterance to would only be a waste of time.'

"'Must I, then, remain here in degradation,' I demanded, 'since you are not my husband? Were you, indeed, so, notwithstanding the lawless life you are leading, my sense of legal duty to you might learn me to submit, though my heart might break in the effort; but, as it is, better would it be for me to perish at once than to be subjected to such a fate as that.'

"'Your fate is now bound up with mine,' he returned, with an ironical and triumphant smile, 'although no priest has legally united us, and you must abide by the consequences. Had you never have discovered my secret, it would have made all the difference, and I might have suffered you to depart to where you thought proper, on the promise that you would never annoy me again, reveal to any person my real character, or the place of my retreat; but as it is——'

"'Cecil,' I interrupted, 'in spite of all that I have suffered from you, notwithstanding the irreparable—the brutal injuries you have inflicted upon me, all these conditions I promise faithfully to agree and adhere to, if you will permit me to leave here unmolested. I am totally ignorant of in what part of the country this house is situated; and, therefore, you have the power in your own hands of preventing me from betraying you, if you will convey me secretly from hence, and leave me to endeavour to find that dear native place from which you so heartlessly tore me. There, probably, I might again find a temporary shelter, though my heart is broken and it will not be long, I am convinced, that I shall require an earthly home.'

"He looked at me steadfastly for a few moments, when I had given utterance to these few pathetic words, and I saw that he was somewhat moved; but he quickly resumed his former demeanour and said—

"You require that which is extravagant and preposterous, Amy; you ask me to do that against which all reason and idea of self-protection are opposed. But I am not to be so easily deluded, believe me; I know full well that you must view me with feelings of malignity and detestation, and it must be my care to guard against the effects of those passions by every means in my power. Here, at any rate, you are secure, and no danger can result from the discovery you have made, but once at liberty, I am convinced that I should not be safe for a moment, and I must, therefore, be a fool if I did not act as prudence and necessity dictate. However, it is useless to prolong this interview. I must have time to reflect upon the course it will be most safe for me to pursue; and when we meet again I may be in a better condition to talk to you further upon this subject. Till then, farewell.'

"He moved towards the door as he thus spoke, but I followed him, and endeavoured to arrest him in his purpose, while I ejaculated—

"'Oh, Cecil, and can you indeed leave me thus, wretched, uncertain, and despairing? For the love of Heaven, take some compassion on me, and let me at least know the fate that you contemplate against me. Remember my former innocent condition, a condition which would never have been changed had it not been for the guilty artifices you devised for my destruction, and the too implicit confidence which my inexperience of the world led me to place in your honour, and at least have some pity for me. Think of the time when I believed you all that was amiable, and candidly acknowledged the fatal passion with which you had inspired me, for I thought you worthy of it, and——'

"'Bah!' he interrupted, with a cold and impatient look; 'this whining cant is intolerable, and I will no longer listen to it. I have already said enough, and having my own interest and safety to study, must act according. We shall meet again; till then be satisfied; and when you have brought reason to your aid, you will probably not be altogether disposed to deny that I have acted at least with forbearance, in not having sacrificed you at once, the moment I found that you had made yourself acquainted with my secret.'

"With these words, and without giving me time enough to recover myself to make any reply, he abruptly left the room, and I heard him lock and bolt the door after him; thus too fearfully convincing me that I was a prisoner, and likewise of the hopelessness of my situation. But it was not so much that as the brutal conduct he had evinced towards me; the base, the hypocritical part he had acted, and the real and guilty character I had discovered of him, that tortured me, and drove my brain almost to distraction. It seemed to be almost impossible that one who had appeared to be all that was good and amiable and honourable that could be combined in man, could prove to be such a villain, and to have acted with such consummate duplicity, especially towards one whose helplessness and unprotected state ought rather to have excited his warmest sympathy and compassion. Alas! under what a fearful delusion had I laboured, and how awfully had I now to reap the consequences.

"For a few minutes after he had left the room, I stood transfixed as a statue to the spot, with my hands pressed upon my burning temples, and my brain wandering without being able to fix itself upon one certain idea; but when I did at last arouse myself to a certain degree of recollection, to what a state of horror was I awakened. I beat my breast and tore my hair in a state of the wildest distraction, and had I had the means of self-destruction at hand, I am convinced that I should have, in the height of my despair and frenzy, rushed unbidden into the presence of my Maker. So perfectly horrible were all the circumstances of my fate, that it seemed to be almost incredible that they could have taken place, and I hesitated some minutes to arrive at the conclusion that they were founded in reality. But too soon the awful truth appeared to me in all its most apparent colours, and I rushed backwards and forwards in the miserable room where I was confined with all the air of a maniac, in fact, at that time, I was a maniac in every sense of the word.

"'Poor, lost, ruined wretch!' I at last groaned, as I threw myself in a chair, the only one that the room contained; 'what is now to become of you? where can you look for pity or consolation? Such are the fruits of your mad credulity, and you are justly punished. And yet, surely, after all, I am not so much to blame. How was I to protect myself against the artifices of one who was formed every way to captivate and allure? Oh, I have indeed been the victim of a most cruel fate, and certainly I am to be more pitied than condemned. But can this possibly be the same individual whom I once believed to be all that is good and virtuous, and whom, under that fatal impression, I loved so faithfully, so fondly? It seems to me to be impossible, and yet, nevertheless, it is too fearfully true. Oh, Cecil, Cecil! you have much to answer for for this monstrous act of iniquity. Would to Heaven that I had perished at the same time as my beloved parents; why, oh, why was I reserved for such a fate as this? And should he even restore me to liberty, whither could I direct my wretched footsteps, destitute, friendless, miserable, degraded outcast as I am? Who would look upon me, or extend the hand of friendship towards me? No one, for my degradation is stamped in legible characters upon my brow, and all must despise and loathe me. Oh, it were better that I were dead, and it would be a mercy to me were my betrayer to plunge a knife in my heart, and thus terminate an existence which his crime has rendered at once offensive and insupportable. Fool, fool that I was to suffer myself to labour under the delusion that I have done; but who could have doubted one who was so abundantly gifted with all the powers to deceive? And here in this gloomy place I must be left to all the solitude of my own dismal and torturing thoughts! Surely my brain can never withstand so severe a trial.'

"I rocked myself to and fro in my chair, in the intense agony of my feelings, and I scarcely knew what I was about, but at length a copious flood of tears came to my relief, and for a brief period afterwards I became somewhat more tranquil: but again the same agonising thoughts rushed upon my brain, and in this condition I continued throughout the day, and no one again came to visit me. Night came on, and I was left in total darkness, for I was neither supplied with a candle nor a lamp, and, consequently, my situation was rendered even more dismal and wretched than before. Surely to treat me in this manner was a stretch of refined cruelty that was entirely uncalled for under any of the circumstances, and showed at once the true baseness of heart which Cecil possessed. Was it not enough for his purpose that he should detain me as a prisoner, but that he must also seek to torture me thus? It seemed as though it were his wish to indirectly murder me, or drive me mad, and it was impossible that my reason could long retain her seat, if I was long subjected to such a horrible situation as this. Had I been guilty of the most hideous crime, had I inflicted upon him the greatest injury, he could not possibly have visited me more severely with his vengeance, and it showed at once the base and brutal heart that he possessed.

"You, my dear friends, may judge of my sufferings at this awful and unexpected change in my circumstances; I cannot find language sufficiently powerful to describe them as they deserve."

"Alas! my dear cousin," said our hero, "how deeply do I sympathise with you in your sufferings, and with what feelings of disgust and abhorrence do I view the conduct of the heartless wretch who could so cruelly deceive you, and then inflict upon you tortures that only the mind of a fiend could conceive."

"And yet," observed Amy, "you must blame me for so readily yielding to the persuasions of one who was almost an entire stranger to me, especially after the clandestine means he had adopted to get me in his power."

"Ah, no, Amy," replied Mary, "indeed you reproach yourself unjustly; to him alone is all the censure strictly due. What a heartless scoundrel must he have been to have taken so base an advantage of your innocence. But he took the readiest means of accomplishing his wicked designs by seizing you in the manner he did; how were you to help yourself, even if you had made ever so determined a resistance, when you were in his power?"

"Most true," returned Amy, "he was, indeed, a crafty villain; and after his numerous professions, and the plausibility of his manners, how could I suspect him? And then the urbanity of manner which that bad woman, his pretended sister, evinced towards me, tended still more to deceive me, and to lead me into the snare that was laid for me. Oh, surely never was unfortunate damsel the victim of a more cruel plot than myself."

"And may curses light upon the wretch who was the author of all," said Richard; "but Heaven will not suffer him to escape its just retribution. Amy, give not way to useless regret, for you have nothing to reproach yourself with; and every sensible and humane person who hears your history cannot but sympathise with you, and execrate the conduct of the villain who has been the cause of all your misery."

"But, alas!" sighed Amy, "is it possible that I can ever banish from my memory the dismal past? Ah! no—it would be a useless task for me to attempt to do so, and the more I think of it, the more poignant becomes my anguish. I can never know peace of mind again."

"Say not so," observed Mary; "time will ameliorate your grief, and restore you

AMY'S ANGUISH ON SHOWING THE PORTRAIT OF HER HUSBAND.

to tranquillity, if not to complete happiness. You must not give way to despair. Thank God that you have at last found a good and honourable protector in your present husband."

"Oh, yes," replied Amy, "most fervently do I respond to that prayer; for to my husband I owe a debt of gratitude which it is impossible that I can ever sufficiently repay. Believe me, I revere him—sincerely revere him, though I cannot love him."

"We do believe you, Amy," said our hero, "for we know your heart too well to entertain a different opinion of you. I am prepared to honour and respect Mr. Ashton for the kindness he has shown towards you, and for befriending you in the midst of all the troubles by which you were surrounded."

"True," coincided Amy. "Oh, what praise is due to him for the unparalleled generosity of his conduct! What would have become of me—poor, forlorn and deserted creature as I was—had it not been for him? I shudder to think of it. But let me resume my melancholy history, and bring it to a conclusion as quickly as possible; for I fear that I have already detained you too long, and that you will begin to think me tedious."

Richard and his wife returned no answer to this, and after pausing for a few minutes, in order to compose her feelings and collect her thoughts, Amy resumed her narrative in the following words:—

"Dreadful were my sufferings that night: I was, indeed, entirely bereft of reason, and unconscious of what I did. There was a straw mattress in one corner of the room, on the floor; but could I think of retiring to rest? Ah, no!—there was now no rest for me, and I continued to pace the room, wringing my hands, and giving utterance to the most melancholy lamentations. How I survived the night I know not. It's a wonder that my heart did not break. Daylight at length appeared, and that was some relief to me, though my mind, as you may imagine, continued in a state bordering on distraction; and I gave vent to the anguish of my feelings in the most melancholy lamentations, at the same time that I earnestly supplicated the Supreme to terminate my existence, since all the fond hopes and anticipations I had once encouraged were now so completely annihilated. I could expect no mercy or sympathy from Cecil, after his cruel conduct towards me; and even should his guilty soul be stung with remorse, what atonement could he make to me for the irreparable injuries he had done me? None—none whatever, and I could not even now think upon his name without a shudder of disgust and horror. And should he even suffer me to depart from the old Manor, whither could I go? Where could I seek a friend or a shelter? Alas! how deplorable, destitute, and helpless was my condition, and nothing but the most unutterable misery and despair met my eyes, in whatever direction I turned them. Most bitterly did I deplore the hour that I was born, or that which first introduced my detrayer to me. I had now no doubt but that the ruffians from whom he had rescued me in the first instance were connected with him, and that, from the first time that he had seen me, he had determined upon my destruction. The opportunities he afterwards had of being in my society must have convinced him of my utter inexperience in the world, and inspired him with confidence in the success of his nefarious designs, and the resolute course he subsequently adopted

placed me completely at his mercy, and rendered all resistance on my part entirely useless. Besides, how could I for a moment suspect one whose professions were so honourable, and who had made so powerful an impression upon my too-susceptible heart? It was impossible that I could do so: the deceiver saw at once the advantage he had obtained, and too well did he play his part. These and similar thoughts continued to torture me throughout the day, and it was in vain that I tried to gain the least degree of consolation. The day passed drearily and tediously away like the previous one, and Cecil did not visit me. Night again came on, and brought with it redoubled horrors. I continued to traverse the room in an agony of mind which I need not attempt to describe, and my misery and despair every moment increased instead of abating. But at length, quite worn out with thinking and bodily fatigue, I threw myself on the mattress, and endeavoured to compose myself to sleep; but it was some time ere I could do so, and then it brought me no relief, for the most frightful and torturing visions were presented to my disordered imagination, and I frequently started in terror, and gazed wildly around me, while large drops of perspiration, caused by the excitement of my feelings, stood upon my temples, and my whole frame was convulsed with emotion. But it would be impossible for me to give you anything like an adequate idea of my sufferings, and I must, therefore, leave it to your imagination. Another day dawned upon my misery, and again the door of the room in which I was confined was opened, and my betrayer stood before me. I started at his appearance, and fixed upon him a mingled look of reproach and supplication; but it seemed to make no favourable impression upon him, and he contemplated me for some time in sullen silence; but at length, advancing nearer to me, and looking steadfastly in my face, he said—

" 'Well, Amy, I trust that by this time you are brought to a due sense of the folly and imprudence of your conduct in having the curiosity to pry into my secrets, since you see the consequences it has brought upon you.'

" 'It was accident alone that revealed the fearful secret to me,' I replied. 'But oh! Cecil, have you the cruelty and hardness of heart to visit me thus with your vengeance? Have you no feelings of remorse for the terrible wrongs you have inflicted upon me? Alas—alas! how brutally have you deceived me, and what a wretched, degraded being have you made me!'

" 'Hold!' he said, impatiently, and looking sternly in my face. 'I came not here to listen to a lecture. That which is done cannot be recalled, and it is useless, therefore, to murmur at it. You know me now in my real character, and all connection between us is at an end. It is in my power to keep you here confined, and to subject you to the greatest misery; but on more mature consideration, I have no wish to do so, and would much rather release myself from your presence altogether, and, on certain conditions, I will restore you to liberty.'

" 'Oh! name them,' I eagerly exclaimed, 'and, though I am now a wretched outcast, know not where to go, and have not a friend in the world, I will comply with them, and leave my future fate in the hands of Providence, though I see nothing but the darkest despair before me.'

" 'You say you know not in what part of the country this house is situated?' he said.

" 'Oh no,' I answered—'I have not the least idea.'

" 'Enough,' he returned ; 'but you must swear never to reveal to any one who is likely to do me any injury what you have here seen, or what has happened. Do you agree?'

" 'I do,' replied I, in a faint voice. 'But, oh! Cecil, surely you must feel some degree of compassion for that poor girl whom you have so deeply wronged, and whose prospects you have for ever blighted?'

" 'Psha!' he returned, 'this is not to the purpose. I have no patience to listen to your whining observations. It must be enough for you that I restore you to liberty: as for your future fate. I have nothing whatever to do with it.'

" 'Oh, God!' I gasped forth, fixing upon the heartless man, whom I had once believed to be all that was good, a look of the utmost horror, 'and can this, indeed, be he who once professed so ardent an affection for me, and to whom I sacrificed my young heart? It seems to me impossible, and that my brain is labouring under some fearful delusion.'

" 'Cease this nonsense,' he replied, 'for it can have no other possible effect on me than to cause me to change my mind. But let us at once to business.'

" As he thus spoke, he drew a small phial, containing some dark liquid, from his pocket, and pouring the contents into a glass, which he had also brought with him, he presented it towards me, at the same time he added—

" 'If you would wish me to comply with your request, you must drink the contents of this glass.'

" A deadly feeling of horror came over me, and I stared at him aghast.

" 'Oh! Cecil,' I at length ejaculated, 'what fearful deed would you now do? Wretched, guilty, and misguided man, is it my life you seek?'

" 'No,' he answered, coldly, 'for if such were, indeed, my design, I could have no difficulty at all in immediately accomplishing it. I am no assassin, however great a villain I may be in other respects. This is merely an opiate to steep the senses in unconsciousness, and to enable me the better to execute my purpose with safety. Will you drink it? If you refuse, be the consequences on your own head. Come, my patience is nearly exhausted. Why do you hesitate?'

" 'Alas! alas !' I sighed with a shudder; 'how shall I act? What a horrible fate is mine! Oh, Cecil, Cecil, can you indeed be so totally insensible to every feeling of humanity? Oh, spare me, spare me! mercy! mercy!"

" 'Do you then refuse?' he demanded, in a stern voice. 'You seek liberty, and this is the only means by which you can obtain it !'

" I took the glass solemnly in my hand, and raising it towards my lips, I said—

" 'Why should I hesitate? Even though this be the draught of death, ought I not rather to welcome it, since I am now rendered so wretched and hopeless a being? All-merciful God! pardon me my sins, and forgive the guilty man who has been the cause of my destruction. Father of Mercy, into thine hands I commit my spirit!'

" With these words I fixed upon Cecil a look which was sufficient to penetrate to his very soul, and raising the glass to my lips, I drained the contents to the very dregs. I cannot describe the strange and powerful sensation which almost immediately came over me. The blood seemed to rush boiling hot through my veins, and my limbs quivered and tottered under me. My brain turned giddy; the form of Cecil gradually faded from my sight; a mist gathered before my eyes, and I remember no more.

" What had taken place during the time that I was in this state of insensibility, I know not, nor how long I had been in it; but when I again recovered, I found myself lying on a heap of straw in a kind of shed or out-house, and felt benumbed with cold, as if I had lain there for some time. It was night, and the moon was shining brightly in through a hole in the roof. I started to my feet as well as I could, and clasping my forehead, gazed around me with astonishment and eager curiosity. It was some time before I could recall my recollection, but then the whole truth flashed upon my memory, and I concluded that Cecil had administered the opiate to me in order the better to enable him to bear me secretly away from the Manor, and to prevent me from having the slightest idea as to what part of the country it was situated in. I proceeded hastily to the door of the shed, which I opened, and looked eagerly out upon the scene beyond. It was cold and cheerless enough, Heaven knows; it was a wild and extensive moor which met my gaze, and there was not the least signs of a human habitation as far as my eyes could penetrate. In what part of the country was I, and whither could I direct my footsteps? Oh, God! what an awful situation was mine. My heart was ready to burst, and my brain seemed to be on fire, so intense was the agony of my feelings. Without a farthing in the world, without a friend to whom I could apply, what was to become of me? Oh, why had I ever again awakened to a sense of my misery? Great God! what a cruel miscreant must Cecil be to serve me in the manner he had done!—I returned into the shed, and throwing myself again upon the heap of straw, I beat my breast in the utter despair of my feelings. My brain was distracted and bewildered, and I knew not what to do.

"'Oh, Cecil!' I ejaculated, 'surely a terrible retribution will overtake you for your monstrous conduct towards me. Wretched, wretched Amy, what have you ever done to merit such a dreadful fate as this? Oh, that I were dead, for what have I now to hope for in this world?'

"Sobs choked my further utterance, and I tossed myself backwards and forwards on my rude pallet of straw in a state bordering upon madness. How I passed that fearful night I cannot describe to you; but I was afraid to venture from the wretched place in which I was, for I knew not where to go in the solemn darkness of the night, and in a part of the country with which I was entirely unacquainted, and my limbs were too weak and exhausted to suffer me to travel. I tried to compose myself to sleep, but what a fruitless task was that; how was it possible that I could sleep placed in the dreadful situation in which I was? All the painful events of my past life passed in rapid succession before my eyes, and madness almost seized upon my brain. How bitter were the lamentations I uttered, and how bitter did I reproach the inhuman conduct of Cecil, and curse the hour that I ever beheld him.''

"Ah, Amy," observed our heroine, "yours was indeed a most awful fate, and I wonder how you ever found strength sufficient to bear up against such extraordinary and unparalleled trials."

"God only knows!" replied Amy, "and, as I now recall them to my memory, the blood freezes within my veins. It was a wonder that, in the frenzy of my despair, I did not lay violent hands upon myself. But at length I sank into a kind of torpor, and in that state I continued during the remainder of the night, and when the morning at length dawned, I started suddenly to my feet, and endeavoured to consider what was better to be done, under the fearful circumstances by which I was surrounded; but my mind was too much bewildered to suffer me to come to any satisfactory conclusion. It was some time since I had partaken of any food, and I felt faint and completely exhausted. But where could I seek for relief? Who was there who would take pity on the wretched wanderer? It was impossible that I could long survive in such a forlorn and destitute condition. Could I find my way to my native village, I might find those who would take compassion on me; but I shuddered at the thought of returning to that place, which I had quitted in so mysterious a manner, and especially after what had happened to me. How could I answer the questions which curiosity would be sure to put to me, and what explanation could I give of my conduct, without revealing the whole of the fearful truth? Alas! alas! I saw no way of relieving myself and despair fell upon my heart.

"'Great God of Heaven, look down with mercy upon me,' I exclaimed, clasping my hands together; 'for without thy interposition, what will, what can become of me? Oh, Cecil, cruel man, surely remorse will sooner or later fix itself upon your guilty soul, and render you miserable. It is impossible that offended Heaven will for ever permit you to escape that punishment which the crimes you have committed so justly merit.'

"Again I wrung my hands together, and for a few minutes I stood in a state of stupefaction, and gazing vacantly around me. But at length I aroused myself, and determined to wander forth as well as my trembling limbs would permit me, and endeavour to find some place where I might possibly move some humane person to take compassion on me, and to afford me temporary relief. I quitted the hovel, and with slow and trembling footsteps bent my way across the moor, in what direction I cared not, for all seemed alike to me, and I could form not the slightest conjecture in what part of the country I was, though I had no doubt that Cecil had taken good care to remove me far from the Manor House. Although the weather was fine and dry, the air was cold, and I, therefore, wrapped my cloak closer around my form, in order to shield me from its influence. How my trembling limbs supported me throughout this weary journey I know not; but I was frequently compelled to stop, in order to rest myself, and to try to consider what was best to be done. I hoped to meet some person who might inform me where I was, and probably direct me to some place where I might find some trifling assistance in my dreadful emergency, but not a soul did I encounter, and all seemed lonely and deserted. The wild moor seemed to be almost interminable, and my courage almost failed me; for the cruel fates seemed to have conspired against me, and to mock my sufferings. I was again compelled to pause, to rest myself, and then I wrung my hands together, and the bitterest sobs escaped my bosom.

"'How useless is this struggle,' I ejaculated; 'what prospect of relief is there fo, me? My weary limbs sink beneath me and it is impossible that I can proceed much further. Surely it would be better were I dead at once.'

"Still, however, and notwithstanding it was with the greatest difficulty, I proceeded slowly on my way, but without encountering a human being. In this manner, I suppose, a couple of hours had elapsed, when I at length arrived at the end of the moor, and found myself emerging upon a winding road, which I hoped might lead me to some town or village. I mustered all my strength, and again imploring the aid of the Supreme, I proceeded on my way, though it was with a sad heart that I did so; for what prospect was there before me? What assistance could I hope to find from strangers? and my heart revolted at the idea of being compelled to sue for charity. There was nothing whatever to sustain me in this dilemma, and I wonder that I did not sink at once under the fearful trial.

"I had proceeded some distance along this road, when my eyes were suddenly gladdened by the sight of a solitary cottage, and at the door of which I saw a female standing, who seemed to observe me at the same moment, and to watch me approach with some curiosity. I took my way towards the cottage with a trembling heart, and scarcely knowing how to address the woman; but when I had got within a few paces of it, my strength failed me, a sudden giddiness seized upon my brain, my limbs tottered beneath me, and I fainted. On recovering, I found myself in the parlour of the cottage, and supported by the female whom I had seen standing at the door, and who was attending upon me with much apparent kindness and solicitude.

"'Poor thing!' she said, in accents which bespoke the sympathy she felt for me, 'you seem very ill and exhausted. Have you travelled far?'

"'Alas! my good woman,' I replied, 'many a weary mile, and I know not whither to direct my course. I am a wretched outcast, without a friend in the world, though, could I reach my native village, I might probably meet with some assistance; still, I trust to God, it is little more that I shall require in this world, for I am now tired of my wretched existence.'

"Here convulsive sobs choked my further utterance, and the woman seemed to be much moved by my emotion.

"'Oh, my good girl,' she said, 'you must not give way to these dismal feelings, for Providence is good, and never fails to relieve those who place a firm and virtuous reliance on it. In what part of the country is your native village situated?'

"I informed her, and she shook her head, and said—

"'Ah! that is a long, long way from here, and if you are without money, I fear that you will find a difficulty in reaching it. I am sorry that, being so miserably poor myself, it is not in my power to assist you, or I would most willingly do so.'

"'I thank you, my good woman, for the kind feeling you evince towards me—a poor wandering stranger,' I replied; 'if you will allow me to rest myself for a short time, I shall probably be able to resume my journey.'

"'Oh, yes,' said the woman; 'you are welcome to do that, and likewise to partake of such humble refreshment as my cottage will afford. I am deeply sorry to see one so young exposed to such misfortunes as those you have evidently experienced, and to be placed in the painful situation that you are.'

"'Alas!' I sighed, 'I am, indeed, the victim of one of the most cruel fates that could possibly fall to the lot of mankind, and Heaven only knows what will be the result of it. But pray tell me in what part of the country I am?'

"'Not far from Penzance, in Cornwall,' she answered.

"'Ah!' I ejaculated, 'so far from my native village? What a misfortune is this! How shall I ever be enabled to reach it? Would that I had never again revived to consciousness!'

"'Nay, my good girl,' returned the kind-hearted woman, 'again I say that you must not give way to these melancholy thoughts, but endeavour to calm your feelings, and to be firm and confident. Something will yet occur to release you from your present difficulties when you least expect it. But come; I will bring you some refreshments, and they may serve to revive you, and to fill you with fresh hope and courage.'

"I could but return to her my warmest thanks for her kindness and attention, of which I stood so much in need in my present deplorable situation, and she quitted the room, and I was left to my own dismal meditations, which I need scarcely say were of the most overwhelming nature. When she was gone, a torrent of tears came to the relief of my overcharged heart, and I then sank upon my knees, and in the most fervent accents implored the protection of the Supreme. In this attitude the cottager found me on her return to the room, and she did not offer to interrupt me; but I quickly arose, and having placed the humble repast she had brought upon a small table, she requested me to be seated, and to partake of it freely.

"'I wish it was in my power to supply you with better fare,' she remarked; 'but, such as it is, you are heartily welcome, so do not stand upon any ceremony, but make yourself quite at home.'

"'Oh, how kind is this!' said I, gratefully; 'it is, indeed, many hours since I have partaken of any kind of food; I am faint and exhausted, and this is most welcome. I know not what would have become of me had not Providence fortunately guided my footsteps to your cottage. May Heaven bless you for your benevolence!'

"'Pray say no more about it,' she returned, 'for what little I am enabled to do I do with a free good will, and I only wish it was in my power to relieve you more. But you are in such an exhausted state that I am sure you are unable to travel further without rest, and I am happy to say that that accommodation I can afford you. My husband is at present from home, and I do not expect him to return till to-morrow, and till then you are welcome to remain here.'

"How grateful was I for this in the exhausted and deplorable situation in which I was placed, and I scarcely knew how to return my thanks; but the good woman would not hear them, and she again urged me to partake of the repast which she had brought me, with which request I complied, and ate much more heartily than I thought I should have been able to have done. Though the provisions were of the coarsest kind, and my mind was in such a melancholy and dejected state, never had I partaken of anything with a keener relish; and when I had done, I felt considerably refreshed, and again poured forth my feelings of sincere and fervent gratitude to my hospitable benefactress.

"'I have been the victim of the most atrocious villany,' I sighed; 'and Heaven only knows what will in future become of me. Basely deceived by one in whom I placed every confidence, I have been cruelly abandoned by him to misery and despair.'

"'Ah! my poor girl,' said the woman, 'I do, indeed, most sincerely pity you, and cannot but execrate the conduct of the individual of whom you complain. This is a wicked world that we live in, and there are too many that take a delight in working the misery of their fellow creatures.'

"'Alas!' I replied, 'that is most true, and bitterly, indeed, have I experienced it; it would have been better for me had I never been born.'

"'Say not so,' she remarked, 'for though you have so young experienced such severe troubles as those that you say you have, you may yet be restored to happiness and content.'

"'Ah, no,' I answered, with a deep sigh, 'that can never be; the blow is struck which entirely crushes all my prospects for the future. What have I now to hope, abandoned as I am, and without a friend in the world to whom I can look for sympathy or consolation?'

"'Your case is certainly a most deplorable and painful one,' she returned; 'but still you must not give way to despair; the Almighty will raise you up friends where you least expected to find them. But you are worn out with fatigue, and a few hours' rest, of which you stand so much in need, will serve to revive you. If you will attend me, I will conduct you to a chamber.'

"'I am, indeed, weary,' I observed, 'and I will, therefore, most gladly avail myself of your kind offer; but I am afraid that I shall put you to much inconvenience.'

"'Not at all,' she replied, 'so do not let that trouble you. I only wish that it were in my power to do more for you, for although you are an entire stranger to me, I cannot help feeling the deepest sympathy towards one placed in your unfortunate situation, especially one of my own sex. God grant that you may speedily meet with some permanent relief, that is the only harm that old Bridget wishes you.'

"Overwhelmed by the kindness and urbanity of the poor woman's manner, I fervently pressed her hand in token of my acknowledgment, but I could not return any answer that would be at all adequate to express my feelings. She then motioned me to follow her, which I did, and she led me towards a door which opened into a small back room, in which was a clean bed, and other humble articles of furniture.

"'Here you can repose yourself as long as you think proper,' she observed, 'for no one will offer to disturb you, and I trust that you will be able to compose your feelings, and to look forward to the future with hope. For the present farewell.'

"I could but again press the hand of the humane Bridget in silence, and she then retired from the room, and I was once more left to myself. My brain was so bewildered and distracted by the melancholy events that had taken place, and which had plunged me into such a painful dilemma, that for a few minutes after she was gone I could not collect my thoughts, and was in almost a state of unconsciousness; but the stern and fearful reality at length rushed upon me with the most overwhelming force, and I wrung my hands in the poignant anguish of my feelings, and the most convulsive sobs escaped my bosom, and for a few minutes prevented me from giving utterance to my feelings in words.

"'My God! my God!' I said at last, 'what a truly wretched being I am; what is now to become of me alone in this dreary world, and without one single individual to whom I can apply for assistance and consolation? Oh, Cecil, cruel, ungrateful Cecil, never could I have imagined that you could act towards me in the inhuman and heartless manner that you have done. How basely, how villanously have you deceived the poor girl who placed such implicit confidence in your honour. Surely you will yet have bitter cause to repent of your perfidious conduct; but it is now too late to recal the past; I am a wretched and degraded being, and I shudder to contemplate the fate to which I am consigned. It would have been a mercy to me had you deprived me of existence, since you have so brutally annihilated all my hopes.'

"Such were the torturing thoughts that continued to agitate my mind for some time, and I could not think of seeking that rest of which I stood so much in need. But at length, completely worn out with the fatigue I had undergone, I did throw myself upon the bed, and sleep at last descended upon my senses. But my slumbers were far from refreshing, for they were disturbed by painful dreams, and at length I awoke, and not feeling inclined to rest again, I arose, and having once more earnestly and devoutly supplicated the merciful interposition of the Almighty in my behalf, I returned to the room in which Bridget was seated.

"I found that she had prepared a comfortable tea, and she greeted me with as much cordiality and friendship of manner as if we had been acquainted for years.

"'You look very pale and haggard, my poor girl,' she remarked, feelingly. "I am afraid that you have rested but badly.'

"'Most true, my kind friend,' I replied, 'my mind is too much disturbed to suffer me to rest, and did you but know all that I have suffered, you would not wonder at it. Alas! I am indeed a truly wretched being, and the sooner that death may put a period to my sufferings the better.'

"'Oh, no,' returned Bridget, 'you must not think so, for you are yet young, and you know nor the happiness that may yet be in store for you.'

"'Happiness!' I repeated, with a sigh, and mournfully shaking my head; 'oh, no, that can never again be mine ; it would be madness for me to encourage such an idea. All my hopes are entirely annihilated, and I see nothing but the most abject misery before me. I shudder to think of the future, and see no means whatever of extricating myself from the difficulties by which I am on every side surrounded, and surely such accumulated miseries are more than human fortitude can find strength to support.'

"'Your situation, from all that you have said,' observed Bridget, 'is certainly a most deplorable one, but there is no knowing how soon Providence may interpose in your behalf, and restore you to that tranquillity of which it seems you have been so unjustly deprived.'

"'I would fain think as you have expressed yourself, my good woman,' I answered, 'but when I take into consideration all the circumstances by which I am surrounded, how is it possible that I can do so? Ah, no; there is no hope for me, and in whichever way I direct my eyes, I see nothing but misery before me. But why should I trouble you with my sorrows?'

"'You may believe me that I deeply sympathise with you in your misfortunes,' she said, 'and only wish that it was in my power to advise and assist you; but on this you may depend, namely, that you have my best wishes for your future welfare.'

"'I am certain of that,' I returned, 'and most grateful am I to you for the sympathy which you express towards me, an entire stranger to you.'

"'Oh, I require no thanks,' said Bridget, 'what it is in my humble power to perform towards any of my fellow-creatures in distress, I do with a free good will, and I only regret that I have not the means to act according to my wishes. But have you no friends, no relations living to whom you can apply in your difficulties?'

"'Alas! no,' I replied. 'I am a poor, friendless orphan, and that renders my situation the more utterly deplorable and hopeless.'

"'It is a sad job,' observed Bridget, 'and every humane person must commiserate with you in your misfortunes. The Almighty will raise you up those friends of whom you stand in need, I do most fervently hope.'

"I again expressed my heartfelt thanks to her for the interest which she seemed to take in my fate, and the kind and charitable wishes to which she had given utterance, and I then, at her urgent request, partook of the meal which she had prepared, and which so greatly refreshed me. I should become tedious were I to relate all the particulars of the conversation which passed between us during the evening, and my narrative has already greatly exceeded the limits to which I had originally prescribed myself; it may be sufficient to say that she seemed every minute to take a deeper interest in my fate, and I was completely overwhelmed by the expressions of sympathy to which she gave utterance, and was thankful to Providence that I had at least met with this temporary but seasonable relief. We retired to rest at an early hour, and I slept much more calmly than I had a right to expect under all the circumstances, and in the morning I arose much recruited in strength, though still labouring under the same melancholy agony of mind. And could it be wondered at, when the dismal prospect which was spread before me is taken into consideration? In another hour or two I must

again resume my weary journey; and whither was I to go, without a penny in the world, in a part of the country which was entirely unknown to me, and without a friend to whom I could apply in the midst of my difficulties? The thought was a dreadful one, and poor Bridget in vain tried to comfort me, and again and again she expressed her regret that she was unable to afford me any further assistance, or to accommodate me by remaining at her cottage until such time as I might be enabled to come to some arrangement as to the best course it would be most prudent for me to adopt.

"'But you see, my poor girl,' she added, 'that myself and my husband are so miserably poor, that we find it a difficult task to support ourselves, and this cottage is so small that we have scarcely room to accommodate ourselves, or else I am sure you should be most cordially welcome.'

"'Do not mention it, my kind friend, I replied; 'you have already done more than I had any right to expect towards an entire stranger, and whatever may be my future destiny, I must ever remember you with feelings of the most unbounded gratitude. God, I trust, will reward you; for too much reason have I to fear it will never be in my power to do so, even if we should ever meet again.'

"'Say no more about it,' she returned, 'for I am fully satisfied in the approval of my own conscience for that which I have done. I hope that, after all, your future prospects may not turn out so bad as you anticipate.'

"'Alas!' I sighed, 'I have but little cause to hope: my fate seems sealed, and I can but anticipate the worst. Would that I could reach my native village: I might then, perhaps, find those who would assist me and sympathise with me; but how can I reach it, so far away from it as I am, and in my present destitute condition?'

"'I know not what to advise you,' replied Bridget, 'for your situation is a most desperate one; but try to muster all the fortitude and perseverance that you can, and you may providentially yet be able to surmount the many difficulties by which you are at present surrounded.'

"I shook my head mournfully, for it was in vain that I endeavoured to think as she had expressed herself; and after I had partaken of breakfast, and some further conversation, I prepared myself to depart, but completely at a loss in what direction to proceed, and torturing myself with the painful thought as to what would become of me. How great was the anguish of

AMY RELATING HER STORY TO PARKER AND HIS WIFE,

my feelings, and how bitterly I reproached my heartless betrayer for the cruelty of his conduct, I need not attempt to describe; and my emotion was so great that I could not without difficulty control it within the bounds of reason; but at length, finding it was useless any longer to delay, I took my departure, old Bridget separating from me with the most fervent expressions of regret, and uttering the best wishes for my future welfare.

"I was now again a houseless wanderer, and as I proceeded on my lonely way, and revolved the terrors of my situation in my mind, the anguish of my feelings may be imagined. The day was fine, but it was extremely cold, and the wind blew piercingly around my delicate form, thus increasing my misery. In fact, sometimes my fevered brain was driven to a state bordering upon madness, and I was frequently obliged to pause, and to give vent to my feelings.

"'Oh, Cecil,' I ejaculated, 'cruel even

as you have proved yourself to be, did you but know the sufferings to which I am at present exposed, your heart must surely be stung with some feeling of remorse. But no, such a man as he must be entirely insensible to pity, or he never could have acted in the manner he has done. And this is he whom I thought so good and honourable, and on whom I had fixed my heart's fondest devotions; oh, how have I deceived myself; and I am now plunged into that misery and ruin from which it will be impossible for me to extricate myself. Fatal was the hour that I ever beheld him, for I might now have been happy, instead of the wretched outcast that I am. Who will now take pity on, or relieve the unfortunate Amy? Will they not rather, when they shall become acquainted with what has happened to me, despise me, and spurn me from them? Oh, yes, my conscience and my foreboding heart too thoroughly assure me that they will, and even the sufferings that I have already experienced I fear are far less terrible than those that are yet in store for me.'

"Tears and sobs prevented my further utterance, and it was some time ere I could regain anything like a degree of composure. I again proceeded on my way, which was dreary enough, and I met with few individuals on the road; in fact, I was anxious to avoid them, for I imagined that every one whom I met would look upon me with contempt and derision. I passed through several towns and villages on my way, but without meeting with any prospect of relief, and night at length set in dark and gloomy, and I knew not where I could find a shelter. It was impossible, I was well convinced, that I could continue to wander much longer in the condition in which I was, and the anguish and despair of my feelings increased every moment. My limbs were completely exhausted, and I could only proceed but slowly, and that not without the greatest difficulty, and to add to my misery, it was evident that a storm was gathering, and what then would become of me, exposed as I should be to its fury? I could not help shuddering at the thought, and most earnestly did I implore the mercy of the most High, for without His aid I must assuredly perish.

"The storm which I had anticipated at length commenced, and the rain came down in overwhelming torrents, so that I was at length completely drenched to the skin, and so worn out with fatigue that I could scarcely advance one limb before the other. In this wretched and pitiable manner I continued slowly to travel for about half an hour longer, and the intensity of my sufferings I need not attempt to describe to you.

"At length I entered a woody part of the country, and casting my eyes anxiously around me as far as they could penetrate through the darkness, I beheld several lights gleaming in the distance, which came upon me by surprise, the more so as they did not appear to proceed from any human dwellings, but rather to issue from the earth. I hesitated, and was for a few moments undecided how to act—whether to proceed towards them or to avoid them; for the idea of robbers occurred to my imagination, and in that case my situation would be worse than ever. However, I at last formed the resolution, and made towards them; and as I approached them nearer, I could perceive that they proceeded from two or three rude tents, and in which I could distinguish the forms of several individuals, of both sexes, moving about. I again paused, and considered what was best to be done; but at last I concluded that they were gipsies, and I determined, at all hazards, to appeal to their humanity; for it was impossible that I could proceed any further in my present exhausted condition, and in such a storm as that which was then raging. With trembling steps I advanced towards the tents, and then beheld more distinctly a number of men, women, and children, grouped around the different fires that were kindled on the earth, and the expressions of whose features, and their general appearance, convinced me that I was right in the conjecture I had formed that they were gipsies. I approached nearer with slow and faltering steps, and at length they seemed to behold me, for they started to their feet with an exclamation, and one of them, a man, hastily quitted the tent, and advanced towards me. He was a dark, savage-looking man, and I could not behold him without some feelings of terror; but it was now too late to retreat, and there was nothing left for me to do but to brave the worst.

"'Who are you?' he demanded in a coarse voice, 'and what brings you here at this hour of the night?'

"I trembled at the uncouth manners and appearance of the gipsy, and it was with difficulty that I faltered out—

"'I am a poor, unfortunate, wandering girl, without a friend, and entirely destitute; I am wet and weary, and would fain rest myself for awhile before the fire, if you would allow me.'

"The gipsy again scrutinised me for a minute or two, and then several of his companions, among whom were a couple of women, came from the tent, and also surveyed me narrowly. They then consulted with the man who had first spoken to me, and after a few moments one of the women, a black-eyed, handsome brunette, turned to me, and in rather gentle accents said—

"'The gipsy ever holds out the right hand of friendship and hospitality to those who are in distress; that, your appearance bespeaks you to be, so follow us, and such accommodation as our rude tent will afford, Zarah tells you you are welcome to.'

"I tried to thank her, but was too much overpowered by my feelings to do so, and inspired with confidence by the observations and the manners of the gipsy woman, I followed them into the tent, which was a large one, and in the centre of which a cheerful wood fire, kindled on the earth, was blazing, and cast a lurid glare upon the sunburnt features of the wandering tribe. These consisted of several men and women, who were seated round the fire drinking and smoking, and who eyed me with much curiosity when I entered; but the woman who had called herself Zarah having said a few words to them in under tones, they nodded assent, as I imagined, and made use of no observations. Zarah now removed my wet cloak, and placed her own on my shoulders, leading me at the same time to a seat by the fire, and then retired to another part of the tent, leaving me in the midst of the gipsies.

"As you may very well guess, I felt very much embarrassed at finding myself in such strange company, more especially as the man who had first spoken to me, the most ferocious looking of them all, and whose name I afterwards learnt was Martin, was standing opposite to me, and was eyeing me with looks that were anything but pleasant to me, and caused me to shudder involuntarily.

"'You are young,' he said, in rather more gentle accents than he had before addressed to me, 'and it is hard for you to be placed in such a situation as you appear before us. You say that you are destitute, that you have no home, no friends; is it so?'

"'Alas!' I sighed, in a faint voice, 'it is too true; I am, indeed, a wretched being.'

"'And what has brought you to this miserable state?' interrogated Martin. I shuddered at the question, and for a moment or two I hesitated what answer I should make but at length I replied—

"'Misfortunes, of that terrible and melancholy nature which I dare not explain.'

"'A-hem!' ejaculated the gipsy, with an expression of countenance which made me shudder more than before, 'I see, I see; the old story—man's deceit, and woman's weakness; ha! ha!'

"At this his companions exchanged significant glances together, and I became more embarrassed than ever; when Zarah returned, bringing with her some refreshments, which she placed before me, and also a tumbler of wine.

"'You are hungry, I dare say,' she observed, 'therefore, eat, drink, and welcome; you may find worse fare than in the gipsy tent.'

"The kindness of this woman's words inspired me with fresh confidence, and I thanked her warmly; she then took a seat by my side, and Martin and the other gipsies, at a sign from her, retired to another part of the tent, and I partook of the provisions she had brought me with a good appetite, while she continued to eye me with much apparent commiseration, but made use of no observation. Suddenly I was aroused from the strange thoughts that had crowded upon my brain, by hearing the gipsies sing the following chorus:—

"'In the forest, in the dell,
    We the gipsy wand'rers dwell,
    To every part we careless roam,
    Ev'ry spot we make our home.
    All we get we freely share,
    Never scanty is our fare;
    We laugh and joke, we sing and drink,
    And never let our spirits sink.
    Ever jovial, ever free,
    The merry wand'ring tribe are we.'

"This chorus was sung in a wild but not unmusical style, which rendered the effect peculiarly novel to my ears, and not at all unpleasing; and when it was concluded, the gipsies again betook themselves to their carousal, and seemed determined to enjoy themselves to the fullest extent, and after a short pause, during which time she seemed to eye me with much curiosity and interest, Zarah said—

"'You are unfortunate, and rude though the gipsy tribe are in manners and speech, they yet are not strangers to pity. You are welcome here, I repeat, to such shelter as our rude tent will afford, and methinks you will at least find the warmth of this fire, and our roof and walls of canvas, far preferable to wandering in the open air, exposed to all the inclemency of such a tempestuous night as this.'

" 'Oh, yes,' I answered, in fervent tones, encouraged by her words, 'and I cannot sufficiently express to you my acknowledgments for your kindness and hospitality.'

" 'No thanks, damsel,' returned Zarah, 'the gipsy needs them not; what they do in kindness they do with a right good will, though it is not often they meet with the same return. Whither are you going?'

" 'Alas!' I replied, 'I scarcely know, for I have now no settled home, though could I but reach my native village I might chance to find that assistance of which I stand so much in need.'

" 'And where is that village situated?' inquired Zarah. I informed her.

" 'It is a long distance,' she said, 'and without means you will find some difficulty in reaching there. But what has been the cause of your present distress?'

" 'The blackest treachery that ever was practised upon a poor, friendless, and unsuspecting girl,' I answered, and tears started to my eyes.

" 'Ah!' she ejaculated, 'I understand, and you need not explain to me any further. Poor girl, I pity you, for I, too, have experienced that of the base treachery of mankind, which makes me always sympathise with my unfortunate fellow-creatures. Time was when Zarah was far differently situated to what she is now; when she was honoured, courted, and admired, and Calumny dared not point its ruthless finger at her ; but no matter, it is past now, and the gipsy is happy in the lot in which Fate has cast her.'

" Her words affected me, for in the few observations she had made use of I read her whole history, which seemed to be similar to my own. A silence of a few minutes ensued, in which interval I succeeded in somewhat composing my feelings, and became considerably more confident in my singular situation.

" 'The world,' at length observed Zarah, 'as the common acceptation has it, can have no further charms for you, since you say that you have experienced so much of its injustice, and have no friends to whom you can appeal for sympathy or assistance. What think you of the gipsy's life? It is a wild and wandering one I admit, but it has its pleasures, and they are manifold. We are free and uncontrolled as the air we breathe ; we have no lordly masters to dictate to us; no tyrannical tax-gatherer to come and rob us of our stores; in every place we visit we find friends; the woodland shade or the flowery dell forms our home, the bright blue sky our canopy; we live on the daintiest fare that ever graced the board of the proud and wealthy; no cares ever beset our minds: then tell me, what life can ever surpass that of the wandering gipsy tribe?'

" 'You say true, Zarah,' remarked Martin, coming forward at that moment; 'the gipsy's life is indeed a life of pleasure and freedom, and the proudest and the wealthiest in the land might justly envy us our lot were they acquainted with it. This fair damsel has met with misfortunes that have rendered her friendless and destitute, and I think that she cannot do better than join our band, and I can only say, for my own part, that in me she shall ever find a friend and protector.'

" I shuddered at the boldness of the man's words, and the repulsive and sinister expression of his swarthy countenance as he gave utterance to them, and I turned away with a feeling of the most ineffable contempt and disgust. Zarah frowned upon him, and it was evident from her manners altogether that she possessed some authority among the gipsies. The man seemed somewhat abashed by her looks, and remained silent.

" 'No more, Martin,' said Zarah, authoritatively, 'it will be time enough for you to give your opinion when you are asked. Leave us; I would talk to this young woman alone.'

" 'Well,' observed Martin, suppressing his anger as well as he could, 'you need not be so cross, Zarah; I meant no harm by what I said, but you are always raising some objections to me. However, I have done; it is not worth arguing about.'

" With these words he once more retired to his companions, a circumstance which afforded me much relief ; for there was something in the appearance and behaviour of that man which made me shudder, and filled my mind with dread. and after a pause, Zarah again addressed me.

" 'You must not mind what Martin says,' she observed, 'for he dare not offer you any insult while you are under my protection, and that of the rest of the band. What I have said to you, I would, however, have you weigh well in your mind, and we will talk further upon the subject to-morrow. I feel interested in your fate, and would befriend you if I could. The gipsy's life you will find to be, if you remain among us, all that I have represented it to you ; and I can promise you that, if you will consent to conform to our rules, which are as binding as the laws of the country, that I can, by the influence I possess, get you admitted one of our tribe.'

"This extraordinary proposition took me so much by surprise that I scarcely knew how to answer, and Zarah watched my looks with much apparent anxiety, and seemed to await my reply with considerable impatience. At length I said—

"'I know not how to express myself for the kindness of your intentions, and the deep interest which you seem to take in the welfare of one who is an entire stranger to you. Alas! I have indeed experienced vicissitudes, troubles, and injustice sufficient to make the world hateful to me, especially as I am now cast friendless upon it, and know not how I can even exist; but I am afraid that you would find me but a sorry companion, and——'

"'Nay,' she interrupted, 'strange as this wandering life would at first, doubtless, appear to you, you would, I am certain, soon get used to it, and never once have cause to regret the course you have taken. Rude though we are in manners and speech, we possess warm hearts, and are like one family together. No discord ever enters within our circle, or if it should chance to do so, it is quickly suppressed by the wise laws we have adopted for the guidance of our conduct, and woe to them who should seek to act with treachery towards us. But I will not press the subject further to-night. I will leave you to reflect upon what I have said. You require rest, and here you may obtain it without fear of interruption. In yonder corner you will find a mattress, and should you require anything in the night, you will find me in the adjoining tent. Fear not, for Zarah assures you that no harm shall come to you.'

"'This kindness,' I observed, 'deserves, and has my warmest gratitude; I will weigh well your observations in my mind, which seem to spring from the best of motives, and give you my answer in the morning. Good-night.'

"'Good-night,' responded the gipsy, and then turning to her companions she said—

"'Come, the hour is late, and there is no more time for revelry. To rest, to rest; the stranger will remain here, and no one will venture to obtrude upon her privacy.'

"'Ay, to rest,' said the gipsies in a breath, and they then dispersed, and Zarah having pressed my hand with a warmth which showed the nature of her feelings also retired from the tent, and left me to myself, and in a state of mind which there is no occasion for me to attempt to describe.

"For some time after they were gone, I was so bewildered by the singularity of all that had taken place, and the extraordinary situation in which I found myself, that I found it impossible to arrange my thoughts, and for awhile I remained in almost a state of apathy. But the noise of the storm which still raged violently, at length aroused me, and I looked anxiously around the curious place in which I found myself, and could scarcely persuade myself that I was in my waking senses, for it had more the appearance of some remarkable dream, than reality. The tent, though rude, was yet well constructed to keep it secure from the rain, and the fire, which still blazed upon the earth, Zarah having added some more fuel to it previous to her departure, gave it even a cheerful aspect. I drew the canvas across the opening, and then proceeded to examine it more minutely. In the centre was a common deal table, and several small casks formed the only seats for the accommodation of the gipsy band. In the corner which Zarah had pointed out to me, was a mattress, the covering of which, although coarse, was clean; but my mind was too occupied for the present for me to retire to rest; and, notwithstanding all that Zarah had said to me, I could not help fearing to do so, especially when I recalled to my recollection the bold and repulsive looks and observations which Martin had addressed to me. I seated myself once more near the fire, and resigned myself to meditation.

"'For what am I reserved?' I said; 'what a remarkable change is this in my destiny; but still it seems that Providence has not yet entirely deserted me, or I should not have met with this temporary, but seasonable relief. Surely I must have perished, if I had been left exposed to all the horrors of the night; and I ought to feel grateful to Heaven that I was not.— But yet it would have been a happy release for me from the miseries to which it seems too evident I am destined. Cecil, the fate to which you have by your cruel treachery consigned me, is a dreadful one, and Heaven only knows how I shall ever find fortitude sufficient to support it. Will not your conscience most bitterly reproach you, some time or other, for the base and inhuman conduct you have pursued towards me?—Oh, yes, it must do so, unless you are insensible to every feeling of remorse and shame. And to discover you to be the man of crime that you are; how terrible is that thought. Never did villany surely before conceal itself under so fair a guise; who could for a moment have suspected the real character of the man who appeared to be the very soul of honour and virtue? No wonder that I was deceived by him, young and inexperienced in the guilty artifices of the world as I was. And yet I was much to blame, in yielding so easily to his persuasions; but still, how could I help myself when I was so completely in his power?—Alas! alas! I have indeed been the victim of a most cruel fate, and God only knows what will be the final result of it. Oh, my poor parents, had you but still been living this would never, I am certain, have happened, and I might now have been as happy and as free from care as I was in the earliest days of my childhood. Those were indeed days of bliss, and when I contrast them with the present, my heart shudders with horror.'

"I sobbed aloud as these melancholy thoughts occurred to me, and my heart was too full to suffer me to give expression to my feelings in words. I now reflected upon what Zarah had said to me, and it engaged my deepest attention. There was something about the gipsy woman which greatly interested me, and I was prepossessed in favour of her. She was, as I before said, young, and very handsome, and there was something altogether in her language and general conduct which convinced me that she had moved in the highest station of society, for even in the simplicity of her gipsy manners, and notwithstanding the rude associates with whom she mingled, she could not conceal the numerous accomplishment with which Nature had endowed her; and I felt certain that it must have been misfortunes of no common description that had reduced her to her present situation. Indeed, from the remarks that had fallen from her, I judged that it had been her lot to have to encounter a fate similar to my own, and from the sufferings that I had experienced, I naturally sympathised with her. But the proposition she had made to me—that engaged my principal attention, and required the most serious consideration. It was a most extraordinary one, and I was completely bewildered by it, and at a loss what conclusion to come to. To become the companion of such wild and uncultivated individuals as the gipsy tribe was most repugnant to my feelings, so different had been the nature of my life; and yet the character which Zarah had given me of them had not failed to make a deep impression on me, notwithstanding the rude behaviour and repulsive appearance of Martin, and for some time I hesitated how I should act. But, if I did not accept of this offer, what was to become of me? I had nowhere to go, no means of obtain-

ing a subsistence, for in my present destitute condition, it was not likely that I should find many friends who would sympathise with me, or render me any assistance, even if it should lie in their power. This was a most torturing thought, and the longer I encouraged it, the more bewildered and distracted I became. You, my dear friends, may judge of the nature of my feelings on such an occasion as this, and I need not trouble you by attempting to describe them.".

"Alas, Amy," observed our heroine, "your fate has been a most remarkable and painful one, and I can only rejoice that Providence gave you strength to support it with the patience and fortitude that you have done, and has at last placed you in the position that you are at present."

"Oh, yes," replied Amy, "I am most grateful for the mercy which has been shown me in the midst of all my misfortunes, but still happines can never again be mine. I feel that that is utterly impossible."

"You must not give way to despair, Amy," said Richard, "for you know not what is yet in store for you. Your narrative, I need not say, deeply interests me; pray proceed."

"I will," returned Amy, "for I fear that I have already detained you too long; but I have not much more to relate, and will come to the conclusion as soon as possible. I continued to ruminate in the manner I have described for some time longer, and could come to no satisfactory conclusion, though at times I was half resolved to accept the offer of Zarah, and in future to resign myself to the wandering life which she and her companions pursued; at any rate till something might happily occur to work a favourable change in my destiny, though there was certainly not the remotest prospect of that at present, and nothing could be more deplorable or hopeless than the situation in which I was now placed, and from which I saw no reasonable means of extricating myself. Oh, who would ever have thought that I should meet with such a fate as that which had so unfortunately befallen me? Could I have imagined that such would have been my lot, I must have died in the anticipation of it. If I did not accept of the offer of Zarah, I had nothing to do but to wander on my weary way, without a farthing in the world, and to endeavour to reach my native village, which, under the painful and peculiar circumstances in which I was placed, was a most desperate and almost hopeless task to accomplish. And even if I should succeed in reaching there, to whom could I apply? Who would pity or relieve me? I shuddered at the thought of again looking any one in the face who knew me, after what had happened; for would they not spurn me as something loathsome?

"'Oh, what a wretched, what a degraded being have I become,' I cried; 'I hate and despise myself, and cannot but think that all mankind must look upon me with reproach and suspicion. They will not believe but that I voluntarily abandoned myself to the guilty passions of my seducer, and that I required no persuasion to elope with him, and afterwards to yield to his wishes. And yet, surely it would be most cruel and uncharitable to condemn me thus, when Heaven knows how little I deserve it. I will endeavour to think differently, and to become firm.'

"Alas! how difficult, how almost useless were my efforts to do so; for there was nothing whatever to inspire me with the least hope. I arose from my seat in the same uneasy and dirordered state of mind, and for a few minutes I walked about the tent, and was almost unconscious as to where I was, or what had happened to me; but at length I walked to the entrance of the tent, and looked out upon the night. The storm had abated, but the wind still moaned in sullen gusts, and the rain descended slowly. I listened attentively, but no sounds from the other tents reached my ears, and I, therefore, concluded that the gipsies had retired to rest, and were wrapped in the arms of sleep, so I returned to my seat with an idea of security, for the present, at any rate. The same dismal thoughts in which I had previously indulged, again crowded upon my brain, and I felt, indeed, most truly wretched. But at length the heat of the fire made me feel drowsy, and I at last resolved to endeavour to gain a short respite from my cares and anxieties by a few hours' repose. Previous, however, to my seeking the rude pallet which was provided for me, I sank upon my knees, and supplicated the Supreme. After this, I felt more composed and resigned, and stretching my weary limbs on the mattress, I soon fell asleep. The most painful dreams were, however, presented to my imagination, and my slumbers were anything but undisturbed or refreshing. At any rate, I did not awake till the morning, and looking up, and at first having only a faint recollection of where I was, I beheld Zarah seated in the tent, and watching me anxiously. On seeing that I was awake, she arose from her seat, and advancing towards me, she extended

her hand, which I seized eagerly, and raised it respectfully to my lips.

"'How have you slept?' she inquired.

"'Oh, as well as I could expect,' I replied; 'and I cannot but repeat my thanks for the relief you have afforded me.'

"'I require them not,' she returned; 'but come, we will rejoin the band in one of the other tents, where our morning meal is prepared.'

"I would much rather have remained where I was, in preference to encountering the gaze of the gipsies; but I did not like to raise any objection, and, therefore, followed her, and she led the way to the largest tent, in which the whole of the gipsies were assembled, and I perceived a repast prepared with much more order than I could have expected, and spread upon the table. The gipsies rose on my entrance, and welcomed me in their simple manner, but with much more politeness than I could have expected, and I felt less embarrassed than I had hitherto done. Myself and Zarah took our seats at another table, and the meal passed over in comparative silence.

"'When it was concluded, Zarah desired me to follow her, as she had something to say to me in private, and guessing what she meant, I obeyed, and we returned to the tent in which I had been during the night, and being seated, after a pause she said—

"'I have consulted with my companions since we last met, on the subject we were conversing upon last night, and they are willing to receive you as a member of the tribe, if the same is agreeable to your feelings and inclination. What say you? Have you reflected upon my observations?'

"'I have,' I answered, 'and cannot but duly appreciate the friendly and humane feeling which made you make the offer; but still I have found it impossible to come to any decision at present.'

"'Why should you hesitate?' demanded Zarah; 'you will find that honour and fidelity are prized amongst us, and that no one will ever attempt to insult your feelings. You are friendless and destitute—we offer you friendship and plenty. If you reject it, where are you to go, if all is true that you have stated? What is to become of you?'

"'True,' I returned, 'my situation is, indeed, most hopeless and deplorable; but still the life you propose is so strange and so novel to me, that I cannot make up my mind to enter upon it.'

"'Nay,' you have nothing to fear,' remarked Zarah, 'for I am certain that every one of the band will strive to make you comfortable, and you will soon get used to our wandering course of life. It has constant change and unrestrained liberty to recommend it; and did they but know the pleasures that are attached to it, how many are there who would envy us our lot! I confess that I feel an interest in your joining us, as I wish for a companion who has met with a similar fate to my own, which I imagine, from what you have said, that you have, and believe me that you will find no one who will more sincerely sympathise with you than Zarah the gipsy.'

"'I do believe you,' I said, 'and thank you for it; but the man, Martin?'

"'Ah!' returned the gipsy, 'I see he has alarmed you by the abruptness and vulgarity of his manners; but if he is your only obstacle, you have nothing to fear from him; he would bring down upon his head the most terrible vengeance of the band should he attempt anything wrong. But he will not be bold enough to do that, I am convinced of it; come, do not hesitate longer, for there is nothing criminal in what I propose, and it is the only means you have at present of extricating yourself from your difficulties, therefore I consider that it should not be slightly rejected.'

"She was so urgent in her manner, and the arguments she made use of were so forcible and so plausible, that I hesitated for a few minutes, and knew not what answer to make her; but still there was something in the vagabond gipsy life which I could not at all reconcile with my feelings, and I could not make up my mind to comply with her request.

"'I must admit the force of all your arguments, my good friend,' I remarked, 'and I beg of you not for a moment to suppose that I entertain any suspicions to the disparagement of yourself and your associates; but still it is a subject of too much importance to decide hastily upon. If you will, therefore permit me to reside amongst you for a day or two, I will endeavour to make up my mind, and let you know the result of my delibertion.'

"'Be it so,' answered Zarah, 'and I have not the least doubt but that you will decide according to my wishes. In two or three days your mind will probably have become more calm, and you will see the necessity of your adopting some immediate and reasonable plan for the future. What you see of the behaviour of the band in that time, you may be sure will be the same in future, and that, although the gipsies' life is wild, yet care or trouble are ever strangers to their bosoms.'

"'Enough, Zarah,' I replied, 'you may rest assured, as I said before, that I will give this important business my most serious consideration.'

"She seemed pleased with my observations, and after some further conversation, she retired from the tent, promising to see me again before long, and left me to my own meditations, which you may be sure most busily occupied me. Her proposition was one that I could not but reflect upon deeply, and the earnestness with which she had urged it, and the kindness of her manner, could not fail to make a favourable impression upon me.

"Of the wandering race, which are more or less to be found in every quarter of the world, but in greater abundance where persecution is less high, I heard much; besides, I had been in the south, and along the south coast from Dover to Portsmouth, where they are to be found in large numbers, but from the placards posted on every eligible place announcing that gipsies would be prosecuted if found encamping there, I came to the conclusion that they must be regarded in a very dubious light in those localities; and farmers are suspicious of their honesty, for they assert that they lose more lambs and poultry during one month's residence of the gipsies in their locality, than during the rest of the year. But the gross ignorance and superstition of this part of the united kingdom is proverbial, from recent exhibitions of the predilection prevalent when any pretender to divine missions comes amongst them. No wonder, then, that they should ascribe all, or nearly all, their misfortunes to an inoffensive people, to whom they ascribe the possession of supernatural powers.

"It was also known to me that some who had studied the gipsy character had ascribed to it every virtue that a more refined society strive to take credit to themselves for; and it is also said that they rigorously punish every species of vice, and applaud every noble action in their dark-skinned family. By those who hold the character of this race in a favourable point of view, the members of the fraternity are described as getting honest livelihoods by following the occupation of braziers of tin, iron and brass articles, while others are employed in making and selling decoctions of various herbs for the cure of complaints, in which art they display a great knowledge of the vegetable world. The women, it is well known, employ a great portion of their

CECIL TAKING LEAVE OF AMY AT HER COTTAGE-DOOR.

time in pretending to divine the future fate of strangers who are credulous enough to come to them for that purpose.

"After mature consideration, I thought there could be no harm in associating with a set of harmless, honest people, whose virtues I could imitate, and whose vices, if they had any, I could shun.

"'And why should I hesitate?' I soliloquised; 'what prospect is there before me if I do not avail myself of the opportunity which is presented to me? What

hould I now care for the opinion of the world? and who is to know me in my ow character? If I can believe all that Zarah has said, and I cannot doubt her, I shall find here warmer hearts than I have long experienced.'

"As these thoughts occurred to me, my mind began to waver, and I was half resolved to agree at once to the proposition of Zarah, for otherwise I saw no other prospect but one of the most utter destitution before me. But still it was a subject

No. 65.

which required the most serious consideration, and I determined that I would not decide too hastily. The recollection of the bold looks and coarse manners of the gipsy, Martin, also caused me to hesitate, for notwithstanding all that Zarah had said to the contrary, I could not help looking upon him with a sensation of dread, for to me it seemed but too plain that I had sufficient cause to look upon his marked conduct towards me with apprehension and suspicion.

"The gipsies were wandering about in different parts of the country during the day, so that myself and Zarah were left to the free and uninterrupted indulgence of our own conversation, and we talked as familiarly and as friendly together as if we had been on the most intimate terms for years. Every sentiment she gave utterance to displayed the most refined taste and intelligence, and I every moment could not help becoming more and more impressed in favour of her, and was convinced that she was calculated to adorn a far different station in society to that into which Fate had cast her; but fearful of appearing impertinently curious, and that I might arouse some painful recollections in her breast that she would fain bury in oblivion, I abstained from questioning her as to the secret of her history, the hints she had thrown out being sufficient to convince me that she had been the victim of a similar fate to my own, and, therefore, from the woeful experience I myself had too fatally undergone, you may believe, I could not but view her with the deepest sympathy.

"Thus did that day pass away, and by the kind attentions and solicitude of Zarah, my feelings gradually became more calm and tranquil. But still the extraordinary situation in which I found myself could not but excite my utmost wonder and bewilder my brain, and bitterly did I mentally reproach my betrayer for the cruelty of his conduct. At night the gipsies again assembled in their tents, and caroused in the same manner as they had done on the night I was introduced to them. I would fain have avoided their company, for their boisterous mirth was in ill accordance with the nature of my feelings, but Zarah suggested to me that it would be much better for me to endeavour to conciliate their good opinion by joining their society for a short time, assuring me that no one would attempt for a moment to insult me, but that, on the contrary, I should find that they would treat me with the utmost respect, and I, therefore, reluctantly complied, and accompanied her to the tent

in which they were assembled, and they certainly welcomed me in the most cordial manner, though the rudeness and singularity of their appearance caused me to feel some uneasiness and embarrassment, in spite of my efforts to the contrary. Martin was present among them, but I averted my glances from him as much as possible, though whenever I did venture to raise my eyes towards him, I found that his gaze was fixed earnestly upon me, and with an expression that confused and agitated me, and made me involuntarily shudder.

"There was something about the appearance of that man which convinced me he was a villain at heart; and in spite of the assurances of Zarah, I could not help looking upon him with secret dread and suspicion, and to be anxious to be away from his presence. I remained in the tent with the gipsies for about an hour, during which time I paid but little attention to the conversation that passed among them, for it possessed but little interest for me, and my thoughts were too busily occupied other ways; but at length I pleaded indisposition as an excuse for retiring, and I was permitted to leave the tent, accompanied by Zarah.

"'I perceive plainly,' she remarked, 'that you feel yourself not at all easy in your present situation, which I own must be a novel and rather embarrassing one to you, especially under the peculiar circumstances in which you have been introduced to us; but I again assure you that you have nothing to fear, and that you may command every feeling of sympathy and respect from me. I have experienced too many troubles and vicissitudes myself, not to commiserate with the misfortunes of my fellow creatures.'

"'I believe the goodness of your heart, Zarah,' I answered, 'and cannot but feel most grateful to you for the kind interest you take in the fate of one who is an entire stranger to you. But the boldness and earnestness of the looks which Martin fixes upon me, I cannot but acknowledge make me feel a sensation of dread whenever I am in his presence, which I find it impossible to conquer.'

"I will keep a keen eye upon his actions,' observed Zarah, 'but I am satisfied that you need be under no apprehension of him, nor any other of the band, we never outrage the laws of hospitality and humanity. Martin, I confess, is not very prepossessing in his manners, but, still, I do not think that he possesses altogether the depraved heart which he might seem to have; and I am certain that he would not venture to attempt anything wrong against one whom we have undertaken to protect and to befriend to the full extent in our power. With that assurance rest satisfied, and endeavour to become confident.'

"'I will do so, Zarah,' I returned, pressing her hand; 'I will also well consider the proposition you have made to me, and probably be prepared to give you a decisive answer to-morrow.'

"'I hope that you will,' said Zarah, 'and that your answer will be in accordance with my wishes; for nothing could gratify me more than to have such a companion as yourself, for I cannot but flatter myself, from all that I have yet been able to see of you, and from the conversations we have had since we have been by accident introduced to each other, that our tastes are similar. Besides, you say that you have no friends nor no one to whom you can apply for assistance in your present unfortunate situation, and, therefore, if you reject my offer, what is to become of you?'

"'Alas! that is too true,' I returned. 'I am, indeed, now a poor wretched being, abandoned by one in whose honour and integrity I so firmly relied: cast entirely upon the wide and cheerless world, without one kind friend or relation to sympathise with me, or to offer me even the smallest degree of consolation, and it matters little, therefore, what may become of me. It would be a mercy to me were I dead.'

"'Oh, say not so,' she remonstrated in the kindest accents; 'you must not thus resign yourself entirely to despair, for you know not what may yet be in store for you. Among our band you may find more sincere and warmer friends than you can now imagine, although they wear a rough exterior; and for my own part, I can only again say that I will do all in my power to console you, and to make you happy and contented under the peculiar circumstances in which fate has placed you.'

"'I do believe you, Zarah,' I replied, 'and can only again repeat my thanks for your kind solicitude.'

"'Then endeavour to calm your feelings,' she observed, 'and to look forward to the future with a firmness and confidence, and all will yet turn out better than you now anticipate. One so young, and apparently so amiable, will not surely always be suffered to linger in misery. Come,' she added, with a smile, 'you know that it is the province of our tribe to penetrate the secrets of futurity, and I do not, there-

fore, hesitate to prognosticate for you future happiness and content.'

"'Happiness!' I sighed, shaking my head mournfully; 'alas! that can never more be mine; it would be little short of madness to encourage such a thought. That blow has been struck which must render me miserable for ever, and which has completely annihilated all my prospect. Oh, did you but know my melancholy history, you would then see what a truly wretched and hopeless individual I must be.'

"'I have no doubt that you have suffered great cruelty and injustice,' she returned; 'at some future period, should you remain among us, you will probably confide to me the particulars of your history, and I will make you acquainted with the troubles I have myself experienced, and which have placed me in the situation in which you find me; but at present I do not wish to harrow up your feelings by a recital of your wrongs. Good-night, and I hope when we meet again, you will have become more composed and tranquil.'

"I could but repeat my thanks to her for her kindness, and she then retired and left me to myself. The observations she had given utterance to had made a deep impression on me; but still I was unable to come to any determination, for there was something in the vagrant life of the wandering tribe, which was particularly repugnant to my feelings, and notwithstanding the desperate nature of my prospects, I hesitated to accept the offer which had been made to me, though from the manner in which Zarah had behaved to me during the short time I had been among them, I could not but entertain the highest opinion of her, and to believe that she was quite sincere in the professions she had made. But the thought of Martin troubled me more than all, and rendered me doubtful and suspicious, and it was, therefore, in vain that I tried to come to some satisfactory decision.

"'Oh, Cecil,' I soliloquised, 'how much have you to answer for in having brought me by your cruel treachery to the deplorable situation in which I am placed. Surely your soul must some time or other be stung with the most bitter feelings of remorse for the heavy wrongs you have inflicted upon that unsuspecting girl whose only fault was in loving you too fondly, and who placed every confidence in the honour and sincerity of the vows which you so frequently gave utterance to. Alas! what a poor deluded creature have I been, and who is there now that will pity me, or try to ameliorate the sorrows of my heart? Will they not rather point at me the finger of scorn and calumny, as though I were something loathsome? They will. Why, then, should I seek again to enter that world where there is now no hope for me? Why should I hesitate to yield to the request of Zarah, and thus endeavour to find those friends among the gipsy tribe which I may in vain look for elsewhere? I will at once decide, and trust to the protection of Providence for the future.'

"Such were the conflicting thoughts that continued to agitate my mind, and I did not feel inclined to retire to rest. All was now hushed in the other tents, and I had no doubt, therefore, that the gipsies had retired for the night, and as the hour was now getting late, and I was exhausted with thinking, I determined also to seek my pallet. First, however, I threw myself on my knees, and earnestly invoked the protection of Heaven, and then having secured the entrance to the tent in the best manner I could, I threw myself, dressed as I was, on the mattress, and soon fell asleep. How long I had been so I had no means of ascertaining, but I was suddenly aroused by a noise in the tent, and hastily raising my head and opening my eyes, I beheld by the light of the lamp which was burning by my side, the dark shadow of a human form retreating towards the entrance to the tent, which was open. Instantly I started to my feet, and rushed towards him. He turned hastily round as I advanced, I having caught hold of a portion of his dress, and I uttered a loud scream of terror when I beheld that it was the gipsy Martin.

"'Ah! villain!' I exclaimed, 'why this daring intrusion at this hour of the night? What infamous purpose brings you here? Speak, I command you.'

"'Silence!' he replied; 'you wrong me by these suspicions! I—I meant you no harm; I thought I heard you call for help, and feared that some danger might threaten you. It was that alone which brought me hither. Calm your agitation, and forget that this has ever happened; there is no one who would sooner resent any insult offered to you, than Martin.'

"'Liar!' exclaimed a stern and angry voice, and looking up I beheld Zarah standing in the tent with a pistol in her hand, which she levelled in a menacing manner at the head of Martin. 'Liar!' she repeated; 'are these your tricks, dog? Is this your conduct towards an innocent and defenceless woman, who has placed herself under our protection, and to whom

we have offered the right hand of friendship and hospitality? What guilty purpose brought you hither?'

"'Nay,' said the ruffian, in a conciliatory tone; 'be not so warm, good Zarah; I meant no harm; I have only made a mistake, which I supposed was caused by the strength of the extra wine I drank last night. I say again that I thought I heard her call for help, and merely came here to offer her assistance in case she might stand in need of it; but I hope the young woman will forgive me, and I am sorry that I have alarmed her.'

"'This is but an idle excuse,' replied Zarah, fixing upon him an angry and penetrating look; 'but begone, and see in what manner you will be able to answer for your conduct to the band tomorrow.'

"Martin muttered something between his teeth, and. he then retired from the tent, leaving me and Zarah together. I was in a state of the greatest alarm and agitation, as you may imagine, and Zarah seemed to be no less enraged and embarrassed at what had happened.

"'Oh, Zarah,' I at length ejaculated, 'how this adventure has frightened and disgusted me. It proves, beyond all doubt, that the apprehensions I entertained respecting that man, were not altogether groundless. I shudder to think of the wicked designs he is evidently contemplating against me; it would be madness, it would be preposterous to take any serious notice of the extravagant and ridiculous excuse he made for his intrusion here.'

"'The daring scoundrel,' returned Zarah, 'I cannot sufficiently express the indignation which his conduct has excited in my breast; but do not unnecessarily alarm yourself, for now that he has been discovered, he will not again attempt to insult you, or to intrude upon your privacy; and he will have to answer dearly to the band for the outrage which he has this night committed.'

"'Alas! Zarah,' I replied, 'how can I consider myself safe while I am near that daring man, who it is clear has some base design against my peace? I shudder at the thought, and it seems but too painfully clear that there is no future peace for me.'

"'Say not so, my poor girl,' said Zarah, in a soothing voice, 'but rather look forward to the best, and with the most sanguine expectations. I will pledge you my word that you shall be no more annoyed by this man, and that you shall receive the utmost care, attention, and respect from the rest of the band. But we will discuss this subject more fully to-morrow ; retire again to rest. You have nothing further now to fear, for I shall be upon the watch, and Martin will not again venture to intrude upon you, now that he has been once detected, for if he did, he would be sure to bring down upon his head the most summary vengeance of the band.'

"I returned no answer, for my mind was too bewildered and distracted to do so, and Zarah, having warmly pressed my hand, again quitted the tent. For a short time after she had departed, I was in such a state of agitation that I knew not how to collect my ideas ; but fear was the predominant feeling which reigned in my breast, and as to think of again retiring to rest, that was impossible.

"'It is too evident,' I ejaculated, 'in spite of all that Zarah has said to the contrary, it will not be safe for me to remain here, and exposed to the brutal designs of this man. Alas! alas! there is now no resting place for me! Providence has entirely deserted me, and I must again wander forth a wretched outcast, ignorant whither to direct my footsteps, or where to seek a friend. Yes, I must immediately begone, for I feel that I am surrounded by the most imminent peril while I remain here. Kind Zarah, I do not like to leave you thus, after the manner in which you have treated me, but I have no alternative. God of Heaven look down with mercy upon me, for without Your interposition, destitute as I am, what, oh, what will become of me?'

"I paused for a time, and the anguish of my mind may be imagined ; but still I was fully determined to fly from the place without a moment's delay, if I had the opportunity, for the idea of Martin caused me the greatest terror.

"I heard a distant clock strike the hour of two, and all was still around. I advanced towards the entrance to the tent, and looked out. There was no one to observe me, and I thought, therefore, that there was not a moment to be lost. I returned to the tent, and kneeling down I earnestly and devoutly besought the protection of the Almighty ; then wrapping my cloak more closely around me, I stole hastily forth into the open air, and with a throbbing heart, I passed by the other tents as quickly as possible, and never stopped or ventured even to look back until I had got to some considerable distance, when I paused, and tried to recover my breath, and to compose myself. This was, however, no easy task ; for I was in a most violent state of agitation, and

various and conflicting were the thoughts that agitated my brain. I almost repented the step I had been induced to take, and was half inclined to return to the tent. What an ungrateful being must Zarah, who had taken such an interest in my fate, think me, to abandon them without one word at parting! But still the danger to which I should be exposed from the ruffian Martin was uppermost in my thoughts, and in spite of all the misery which I might plunge myself into by so doing, I determined to proceed, and to leave my future fate in the hands of Heaven. The morning was gloomy and cold, and everything around me had the most gloomy aspect, though not a human being met my eyes. I committed myself once more to the care of the Supreme, and then with a sad heart I proceeded on my dreary way.

"I will not detain you by detailing all that I suffered during that day. I passed through several towns and villages, but I had not the courage to ask for any relief, and, indeed, I shrank from observation as though I were some guilty being. Night again set in, dark, cold, and cheerless, and I was ready to sink to the earth with the fatigue I had undergone, and from the want of food.

"What would become of me I knew not; where could I obtain a shelter for the night? and it was quite impossible, faint as I was, that I could travel much further. I shuddered at the dismal prospect before me, and clasped my hands together in agony; but I was perfectly at a loss what to do. However, it was no use remaining where I was, and I, therefore, proceeded as well as I was able, although Heaven only knows how I suffered in the arduous efforts I was obliged to make. In this deplorable manner I slowly moved on my way for more than an hour, and at length I beheld lights glimmering at some short distance, and which evidently proceeded from some human dwelling.

"I mustered all the remaining strength I could, and made towards it, determined at all hazards to ask for shelter, for it was quite impossible that my feeble and tottering limbs could support me much longer. I at length came near the place from whence the lights proceeded, and I could then perceive that it was a gentleman's mansion, and I hesitated what to do, for probably I should only get insulted, for making so bold as to disturb the inmates at such an hour of the night. I, however, had not much time for deliberation—my strength was completely exhausted—a deadly sickness came over me, and I had only just time to ring the bell, when I sank senseless upon the step of the door.

"When I recovered my senses, the scene which presented itself to my gaze was so different to that I had so shortly before experienced, that my brain was bewildered, and I knew not what to think. I was reclining on a bed, in a comfortable and handsomely furnished chamber, and a benevolent and motherly-looking woman was in attendance upon me, and seemed to regard me with the greatest interest and compassion, and on seeing me open my eyes, she kindly inquired how I found myself, and whether there was anything that she could do for me.

" 'Do for me?' I repeated, and I was so much confused and agitated that I scarcely knew what I said; 'ah, no; what right have I, a poor, wretched, friendless being to expect anything from a complete stranger? I fear I am already intruding by——'

" 'You are not intruding at all, my poor girl,' interrupted my attendant, 'and I am only happy to think that you were guided hither, for you are in a most deplorable condition, and must evidently have suffered much.'

" 'Suffered!' I repeated, in a melancholy voice; 'oh, yes, I have, indeed, and God only knows what is still in store for me. But where am I?'

" 'You are in the mansion of a gentleman named Ashton, who is regarded with the utmost esteem by all who know him, for the benevolence and urbanity of his disposition,' replied the woman. 'You were found by two of the servants lying senseless on the threshold of the door, and by his orders you were immediately taken into the house, and every attention paid to your recovery.'

" 'Oh, how kind was that,' I ejaculated; 'may the blessings of Heaven descend upon the head of this benevolent gentleman for his humanity towards one of the most unfortunate of human beings.'

" 'Rest your mind contented,' said the good woman 'for you are in the house of a friend who never yet refused to relieve his fellow creatures in distress. Drink this glass of wine, which may serve to revive you, and then try to compose yourself to sleep, for if I may judge from your appearance, you must stand in need of rest. In the morning I trust that you may be sufficiently recovered to be introduced to my master, Mr. Ashton, and if he can do anything to assist you, you may depend upon him.'

"I repeated my acknowledgments, and the woman having desired me to ring a small hand-bell, which she had placed on a table by the side of my bed, if I should require anything, retired from the room. I need not seek to describe to you my feelings when she was gone, and I could scarcely believe the evidence of my senses: but it was quite clear that Providence had not yet deserted me, and some small degree of hope began to revive in my breast. At length sleep came to my relief, and I did not awake till daylight, when I found the woman again in the chamber, and that she had in readiness a slight repast, which was suited to my condition. She anxiously inquired after my health, and I informed her that I felt considerably better, though I was yet extremely weak, and I again expressed to her my heartfelt thanks to her and her master for the great kindness with which I had been treated.

"I will not detain you much longer, as I have little more to relate than that with which I have already made you acquainted. That day I was introduced to Mr. Ashton, who received me with much kindness and solicitude, and the urbanity of his manner won my immediate esteem; indeed, so favourable was the impression he had made upon me, that I answered all the questions he put to me, as to the cause of my being reduced to such a painful condition as that I was placed in when I was introduced to him, without hesitation; and emboldened by the kindness of his remarks, he soon became acquainted with all the melancholy particulars of my history. He listened to me with the deepest interest, and when I had concluded, he expressed in the warmest terms the sympathy he felt for me, and his utmost abhorrence of the treacherous conduct of Cecil, and finally he desired that I should remain at his house, as long as I pleased, or, at any rate, till some arrangements could be made for the future, and he promised that to all he could do to promote the restoration of my happiness, I should be heartily welcome. I was completely overwhelmed with this unexampled generosity, and knew not how to express my acknowledgments in language sufficiently powerful; but he interrupted me impatiently, and I could plainly see that the interest which he took in my welfare was of the most powerful and generous description. Thus days and weeks passed away, and I began to feel myself quite at home in the house of my benefactor, and he seemed to be never so happy as when he was in my society. But I have now related everything; with what subsequently took place, I have already made you acquainted, and there is, therefore, no occasion for me to repeat it now. My mournful tale is at an end, and I think you will be ready to admit that I have drained the bitter draught of sorrow to the very dregs."

CHAPTER XL.

THE MEETING OF THE PARKERS AND MR. ASHTON.—THE ATTEMPTED BURGLARY.—THE MURDER.—THE ROBBER.—THE DISCOVERY.—RICHARD PARKER IS DETECTED AND APPREHENDED.

THUS did Amy conclude her interesting narrative, to which our hero and his wife had listened with the most breathless attention; and when she had arrived at the end, they again expressed their sympathy for the sufferings she had experienced, and their detestation for the cruel conduct of Cecil. The rest of the day was passed in conversation upon the future prospects of them all, and Amy tried to encourage them to hope that the time was not far distant when they would be restored to complete happiness. But in that expectation Richard could by no means join, notwithstanding that he had hitherto been enabled to escape all the difficulties and dangers by which he had been surrounded. In the evening Amy received a letter from her husband, informing her that she might expect him home on the following day, and Richard and his wife looked forward to the time with some degree of anxiety and impatience, for they were eager to know what kind of a reception they should meet with from him, though, after what Amy had told them, they could not but anticipate that it would be all that they could wish.

Towards the afternoon on the following day, Mr. Ashton returned home, and Amy saw him alone first, in order that she might apprise him of the unexpected guests that he had to receive. They were not long kept in suspense, however, for the door of the apartment in which they were seated was opened, and Mr. Ashton entered the room, and greeted them with all that hearty welcome which showed at once the goodness of his heart, and how deeply he sympathised with them in their misfortunes. An explanation followed, and they soon became as free and familar with each other as though they had been on the most intimate terms for years.

Mr. Ashton, as has been before observed, was a gentleman of the most insinuating manners, and the deformity of his person was forgotten in the pleasure of his conversation, for there was not a subject but he could discuss with the most masterly eloquence, and every word he uttered showed the extensive knowledge he possessed, and the vast accomplishments of his mind. The hours passed away in the most agreeable manner; but at length the time arrived to separate. Mr. Ashton, however, having some papers to arrange, and which it was necessary to attend to without delay, remained in the room for some time longer for that purpose, and Amy, our hero, and his wife sought their chambers. Richard and Mary continued to converse for some time, for they did not feel exactly disposed to retire to rest, and more than an hour and a half flew unconsciously by without their taking any notice of it. At length, however, they were startled from the conversation in which they had been engaged, by hearing a confused noise from the room below in which they had left Mr. Ashton, but which they at first imagined was only caused by that gentleman being in the act of retiring to rest; they were, however, soon convinced that such was not the case, for on their opening the chamber door, and going to the top of the stairs and listening they could hear a noise like that of struggling, and then a faint cry of "murder" and "help!"

"Good God !" cried the alarmed Mrs. Parker; "what can be the matter? There is some danger, that is certain. Did you not hear that cry, Richard?"

"Yes," replied the latter, "it was in the voice of Mr. Ashton, and seemed to proceed from the room whence we left him. There is something wrong, and my heart forebodes the worst. Hark! there again !"

They now distinctly heard two or three groans, and then all was again silent.

"Some one must have got into the house," said Richard; "it is no use to stand here. I will alarm the servants and endeavour to unravel this mystery. Ah ! fortunately, here is a pistol," he added, taking one down from above the mantelpiece; "remain you here, Mary, and I will see at once what is the matter."

"Oh, Richard," said his wife, "but you know not what danger may threaten, and it is necessary that you should act with the utmost precaution."

"Oh, I fear not," answered our hero. "Wait here, and I will soon return."

Mary, however, found it impossible to do so, her suspense and anxiety were so great, and she, therefore, slowly and cautiously followed her husband, and they had nearly got to the room in which they supposed Mr. Ashton to be, when they saw two or three of the male servants, who had also been alarmed by the noise in the apartment, ascending the stairs. Richard motioned them to silence, and they approached nearer to the door, from underneath which they were horrorstruck to behold a stream of blood flowing, and they were now satisfied that some dreadful crime had been committed, and they shuddered for the life of Mr. Ashton. There was not a moment to be lost, however, and Richard was the first to advance towards the door, which he noiselessly opened, and was followed clusely by the servants.

On entering the room what a scene of horror presented itself.! The unfortunate Mr. Ashton was stretched upon the floor, apparently quite dead, and weltering in his blood, and at that moment a strange man was just in the act of raising one of the windows, apparently with the intention of making his escape by it.

"Ah! villain! murderer!" cried our hero, rushing towards him, and grasping him by the collar; "what infernal crime have you been perpetrating?"

The man muttered a terrible curse, and struggled to release himself, at the same time making several thrusts at Richard with a sharp-pointed knife, and with which, no doubt, he had committed the horrible murder, and our hero, in self-defence, discharged the contents of the pistol at him, and the ruffian, with a dreadful curse, sunk bleeding to the floor. Amy, whom the noise and confusion had alarmed, rushed into the room, and she uttered a frantic scream at the horrible scene which presented itself. But no sooner did she behold the features of the murderer, than she exclaimed—

"Great God of Heaven!—oh, Richard Parker!—it is my betrayer, Cecil!"

"Ah!" gasped forth the murderer, "is it even so?—Amy! And he who is the cause of my death, to be no other than Richard Parker, he whose life is forfeited to the offended laws of his country."

There was now a loud knocking at the outer-door, which was opened, and two of the coast-guard made their appearance, they having been attracted thither by the report of the pistol. Amy having found that her husband was quite dead, he having been stabbed in various parts of the body, had fainted; and every one stood completely appalled at the dreadful tragedy which had been enacted.

"I have received my death-blow," gasped forth the guilty Cecil; "my career is at an end, and may eternal curses light upon the head of him to whom I owe my death; but revenge is still mine. Hark ye," he added, addressing himself to the officers, "seize this man; it is Richard Parker, the mutineer and the murderer of Captain Arlington; yon senseless woman, his own cousin, has just denounced him."

"Richard Parker!" said the men, with looks of astonishment, and advancing towards our hero.

"Ay," returned that unfortunate man; "it is too true that I am that much-wronged individual. It is useless to deny it now; all hope is at an end. I yield quietly to my fate. But oh, for the love of Heaven, be kind to my poor wife and child."

"Richard," shrieked his frantic wife, and clinging despairingly to him, "they shall not tear you from me, and drag you to an ignominious death; oh, mercy! mercy! spare my husband; do not consign him to that horrible fate which he so little deserves, but——"

"Madam," interrupted one of the men, with much civility, and apparent compassion, "we pity your situation, and that of your husband and child; but we have no alternative, as you must be aware; we must perform our duty. Mr. Parker, you must consider yourself our prisoner."

"I submit," replied our hero, calmly; "but, oh, my Mary, what will become of you, and you, my noble-hearted boy, when I am gone?"

Mary heard him not, for her senses had left her, and the hapless boy, William, clung to his father's knees, and looked imploringly up in his face, while his whole demeanour and the expression of his features were such as to excite the deepest sympathy in the breasts of all who beheld him.

"Wretch! murderer!" cried Richard, turning to the guilty Cecil, who was evidently fast dying; "what could urge you to betray me, stranger as I am to you?"

"I perish by your hands, do I not?" demanded Cecil, in a hoarse, hollow voice, "and think you that I will ever suffer myself to be robbed of my revenge? No, and even in death I triumph; curse, curse ye all!"

And with a frightful groan the assassin fell back, and immediately expired.

———

AMY'S ANGUISH ON FINDING HERSELF A PRISONER.

CHAPTER XLI.

THE LAST SCENE OF ALL.

WE must pass over the scene of this frightful tragedy as quickly as possible, for it is too horrible to dwell upon ; the painful denouement of an eventful story is fast approaching, and we must soon drop the curtain upon the principal actors in our drama. Would that we could do so amidst the sun shine of happiness and pros-
perity, instead of the gloom of misery and despair; but, alas ! the fearful truth must be told, as the melancholy and untimely fate of the hero of our tale must be patent to most of our readers. The close of his earthly career had now almost arrived, and he could have met death by any other means without a murmur had it not been for his wife and child; but to die by such a death as that to which he was doomed was too horrible to think of, and his manly heart revolted at the bare idea. Oh, that

he had fallen in the battle's heat, then would his memory have been honoured instead of a scandal and a reproach resting upon the heads of his innocent wife and child, who he thought it was impossible could survive the horror and ignominy of his death. Surely the Supreme had dealt too severely by him; but, no, he would not arraign, he would not presume to arraign His Almighty will.

Such were the agonising thoughts that passed with the rapidity of lightning through the brain of the unfortunate man, as he gazed upon the prostrate forms of his wife and child, who had become insensible. In spite of all his efforts to the contrary, manly tears started to his eyes, but he dashed them hastily away, and then turning to the officers, in a firmer voice than could have been expected, he said,—

"Do your duty, my good men, it is not my place to offer any resistance to you, for I know that your task must be a painful one to perform, if the feelings of humanity glow within your breasts. Delay not, for it will be better for me to depart while these beloved beings are in a state of unconsciousness; but, oh," he added, turning to the servants who were present, and who were moved to tears, "for the love of Heaven be kind to them, and endeavour to comfort them in this the most trying hour of their affliction. Farewell my Mary, faithful, most affectionate and devoted of wives; adieu, my sweet boy, and may the Great God of Heaven look down with mercy upon you both, and enable you to bear this awful blow with fortitude and resignation."

As he gave utterance to these words, he stooped down, and again and again he kissed his wife and child frantically, sobbing all the time in the most convulsive manner as though his heart would break. He then motioned to the officers, and they led the way from the house.

For some minutes after they were gone, the servants stood gazing at each other with expressions of the utmost consternation and grief; but at length they aroused themselves into action, and conveyed their mistress, and Mary, and her child, from this scene of bloodshed and horror, and having placed them each on a bed, they adopted every means for their recovery. But our heroine and her son were the first who showed any signs of returning animation, and that was not until the following morning, when Mary started up in her bed, and wildly inquired for her husband. Those who were in attendance upon her hesitated to reply, but the recollection of all the dreadful events seemed to flash upon her brain with electric force, and in accents that thrilled to the very souls of all who heard it, she exclaimed—

"Ah! it is useless to attempt to deceive me, for I remember all the dreadful truth now!—They have torn him from me! They have conveyed him to a dismal dungeon, and ere long they will drag him to an awful and ignominious death! Horror! horror! Oh, Richard, my beloved husband, and has it then indeed at last come to this? But they shall not separate him from me! I will share his prison with him; and we will at least die together! Richard, dear Richard, husband!—I come to join you!"

So violent were her struggles that it was with difficulty they could prevent her from rising from the bed; but at length she sunk back completely exhausted, and she once more became unconscious of all around her. In this state she remained the whole of the day; as for Amy, she was only partially revived to show that her senses were fled, and probably for ever.

Nothing could equal the excitement which this dreadful occurrence caused in the neighbourhood, and great was the sympathy which was expressed by every person for the unfortunate Amy, our heroine, and her son. The next day, however, all the exertions of those who were in attendance upon her could not prevent Mary from hastening from the house, and hurrying to the prison to which her husband had been taken, determined as she was, if possible, to have an interview with him, and to describe the nature of her feelings is a task which we feel ourselves totally inadequate to perform. On her arrival there, what was her agony and despair to find that he had been conveyed on board a vessel preparatory to his being despatched before the proper authorities. It was a wonder how the distracted woman could find strength sufficient to bear such an event with anything like a degree of fortitude; but she did so with more than the courage of a heroine, though her heart, at the same time, was ready to break. She returned to the house, but it was only with the determination to follow her husband as quickly as possible, if she had to pursue the whole of the weary journey penniless, and on foot. In the domestics of the late Mr. Ashton, she found friends to aid her in her terrible emergency; amongst themselves they humanely subscribed to supply her with the means of carrying her noble, though melancholy intentions into effect, and she started by the coach to the place of her destination.

In the meantime what were the feelings of our hero on the occasion of the dreadful situation in which he was placed? Imagination may pourtray them, but it is impossible that any language, however powerful or eloquent, could do so. After all the many escapes that he had had, and when his prospects had assumed a brighter aspect than they had ever done before, to be thus entrapped, was almost insupportable, and the state of agony and horror to which his wife and child would be reduced at the certainty of the ignominious fate which so soon awaited him, froze the very blood in his veins to reflect upon, and almost drove him to madness. That he could expect any mercy from the offended laws of his country he never for a moment flattered himself, and what would become of those so dear to him after he was gone, he shuddered even to think upon. Those in whose custody he was, seemed to sympathise with him sincerely, and they afforded him all the consolation in their power; but, alas! what consolation was it likely that he could receive under all the awful circumstances in which he was placed? He prayed earnestly to Heaven that he might die before the frightful doom which had been already awarded against him could be carried into effect, for that, at any rate, would save his wife and child the shame which would otherwise be attached to them.

* * * * * *

Poor Mary and her child quickly arrived at the place of their destination, and were allowed to have an interview with the unfortunate prisoner. The scene which followed was of the most heart-rending description, and we will not harrow up the feelings of the reader by dwelling upon it. Their faithful friend, Adams, did all he could to console them in this dreadful hour, but, alas! what consolation was there for the poor sufferers?

The capture of Richard Parker caused the greatest sensation, and deep was the sympathy felt for him by all those who had known him under far different and more prosperous circumstances; but, alas! there was no hope for him; he was already doomed, and his execution was fixed for an early day.

That fatal day arrived, and deep was the gloom which prevailed in the neighbourhood were the awful scene was to take place. Mary and her child, who had been suffered to remain with the unfortunate man on board the Sandwich, had, worn out with fatigue, gradually sunk under the influence of sleep, and with what feelings of indescribable agony did Parker

stand by and watch them, while nearer and nearer the fatal hour approached.

"Poor Mary," sighed the wretched man, "my poor heart-broken wife, and you, my dear and innocent boy—oh, if it were pleasing in the sight of Heaven, would that this sleep might wane into the last slumber. To Thy bounty and providence Almighty Father," he continued, kneeling and raising his eyes towards Heaven, "I do resign these, my best beloved; and, oh, ye gentle spirits that attend the suffering, minister to her widowed heart sweet hope and consolation; help and sustain her through the ills of earth, and when, tried by affliction, You deem her ripe for Heaven, may her death be gentle as her life was holy. My boy—my——there is the mother in his face—I cannot look upon it —bless you, my sweet one—bless you, Mary—ah! she wakes!"

At that moment our heroine started from the sea-chest on which she had been sleeping, and looking anxiously around her, she exclaimed—

"Parker!—oh, cruel, cruel mockery!"

"Mary," said her husband, "even now you smiled, and now——"

"'Twas in my dream," interrupted Mary. "I thought—oh, to awaken from such a vision to such a dreadful reality! —I thought we were in our little cottage by the river-side, beneath that humble, happy roof, where, with love to blunt the sting of poverty, we wore away about eight joyous months; there, as plain as e'er I saw it, was the room—there the honeysuckle clustering at the window— there was our little garden and the distant fields—I saw the sun rising through the trees, and heard the lark carolling in gladness to the sky: I wake, and see a dungeon—hear your fetters—my husband's fetters—I see, and hear all this, and yet I live!—I did not think my heart was so hard!"

"Mary," replied her husband, pointing to the boy, "look there. There is the golden link must hold you to the earth. If, tired of this weary world, you yearn for death, look in his innocent face, and learn sweet resignation."

"Yes, for his sake, I will consent to live," sighed the heart-broken woman. "But, oh, Parker, must we part? Is there no hope?"

"Since the period of our earliest love," replied her husband, "we have had but one soul between us. I will not sully the last hour we may spend together with falsehood. Nerve your woman's heart, my poor girl, for as certain as the hour arrives, is certain do I perish. If you love me, Mary, be firm, be worthy of your husband. Ah, Mary!" he added, as the report of a gun was heard.

"You see," she faltered out, sinking into his arms, "I am calm—calm!"

Adams now hastily entered, but seeing the situation of Mary, was again retiring, when Parker called upon him to stay, and Mary reviving, exclaimed—

"Are they come so soon?"

"Hush, hush, my love!" replied Richard, "'tis Adams, our friend."

"Is there no hope?" eagerly asked Mary, "is——"

"See, Mary," interrupted our hero, as the boy came forward, "you have awakened the child. My poor boy, you have slept but badly, I fear?"

"Oh, no, indeed, father," replied the boy; "but why are you up so early?"

"I—I am going a journey, William."

"Then I'm sure you'll take me with you," said the child; "and mother too—nay, I know she'll not stay behind."

"Poor boy!" said old Adams, in a broken voice. "I say, Richard, suppose I take him a turn upon the maindeck?"

"Do so," replied Richard; "oh, take him away, and remember, I leave to my king and country my child, my only child."

Adams pressed his hand, and then departed with the boy. Another report of a gun was heard, and Richard, turning to his wife, said,—

"Mary, the time draws near."

"And no hope?" she gasped forth. "Oh, heartless, savage men !"

"You judge them harshly, Mary; though they might have saved the mutineer, they must not, cannot save the murderer. I slew Arlington, I offered him up a sacrifice to my resentment, and I die the happier that I leave him not to breathe the same air with you. Mary, the moments fly; let us say that bitter word, for it must be uttered."

"I will not quit you!" she cried, frantically clinging to him; "husband, husband, we'll die together!"

Adams now returned with the boy, and Richard said,—

"Look there, Mary, our child, our child !"

"Ay, be proud of him," said Adams, "you know, Richard, you said you gave him to your king."

The hollow roll of the drum was now heard.

"I am prepared," ejaculated our hero. "Mary !"

"They are here," said Adams, aside to Parker.

"Farewell! farewell!" sobbed the latter.

The death-bell tolled—Mary stood for a few moments paralysed with horror; Parker kissed her and his son, and then stole gently off to meet his fate. Again a gun fired, Mary shrieked and became insensible, and she and William were borne away by poor old Adams.

*   *   *   *   *   *

Let us pass hastily over the last sad moments of the unfortunate Richard Parker. His manly firmness never for an instant forsook him. Turning to those assembled around him, he said—

"My shipmates, you have often seen me brave death in defence of my king and my native land; now behold me meet it on a scaffold. Farewell. Adam's, Heaven, bless you !"

"Bless you, Dick," sobbed the old man. "I can't look at you, but there's my hand."

"My shipmates," said our hero, in a firm voice, "hear the last words of Richard Parker. Here's health to my king, and God bless him! Confusion to his enemies, and salvation to my soul!"

*   *   *   *   *

About twenty years since, there resided in an humble dwelling in the neighbourhood of Strutton Ground, Westminster, an aged and lonely woman, who held no intercourse with any one, and who was always attired in mourning. This was the widow of the unfortunate Richard Parker!

www.ingramcontent.com/pod-product-compliance
Lightning Source LLC
Chambersburg PA
CBHW080943020726
47505CB00009B/2128